THE PORTRAIT OF A LADY

AN AUTHORITATIVE TEXT
HENRY JAMES AND THE NOVEL
REVIEWS AND CRITICISM

A NORTON CRITICAL EDITION

HENRY JAMES

THE PORTRAIT
OF A LADY

AN AUTHORITATIVE TEXT
HENRY JAMES AND THE NOVEL
REVIEWS AND CRITICISM

Edited by

ROBERT D. BAMBERG

KENT STATE UNIVERSITY

W · W · NORTON & COMPANY

New York · London

Copyright © 1975 by W. W. Norton & Company, Inc.

FIRST EDITION

Library of Congress Cataloging in Publication Data

James, Henry, 1843–1916
   The portrait of a lady.

   (A Norton critical edition)
   Bibliography: p.
   1. James, Henry, 1843–1916. The portrait of a lady.
I. Bamberg, Robert D., ed. II. Title.
PZ3.J234Po50 [PS2116]   813'.4   74–19457
ISBN 0–393–04385–1
ISBN 0–393–09259–3 (pbk.)

5   6   7   8   9   0

Contents

Preface

Although there is only one novel by Henry James called *The Portrait of a Lady*, we have what amounts to two separate "Portraits." The first appeared in 1880–81 and the other, with extensive retouching, was unveiled over a quarter century later in 1908. At first glance the two Portraits look pretty much alike despite James's more than five thousand substantive revisions ranging from single words to pages of text. James's view of his subject and deftness of touch was so sure that the changes did not substantially alter the outlines of the Portrait or its essential statement. But if the careful viewer is given the opportunity to inspect closely the myriads of brush strokes by which the Portrait was altered he will be startled by the differences and his vision of its statement strengthened. The first Portrait was drawn by a successful young author still in his thirties, pleased by the celebrity of "Daisy Miller," proud that *The Portrait of a Lady* would be his most important achievement to date, and triumphant in finding his subject and rendering it. By the time of the second Portrait, the Master, now in his sixties, had almost completed his artistic life's task and was in the process of collecting, revising, and prefacing his fiction for the "definitive" New York Edition, convinced that he could improve his writing in nearly every sentence and that nothing of his produced before 1890 "could come with any credit through the ordeal of a critical inspection."[1]

James conceived the outlines of the novel in 1878, according to Leon Edel, the author's foremost biographer.[2] In this year, he published "Daisy Miller;" he began his extensive critical study of Hawthorne; and his elder brother, the philosopher William James, was married. By the end of 1879, James was writing to the critical and somewhat domineering William, who had demanded greater "fatness and bigness" in Henry's stories: "I have determined that the novel I write this year shall be big."[3] Then, according to Edel, he seems to have set the "big" novel aside while he wrote *Washington Square*,[4] and when he travelled to Florence in 1880 he returned to writing it and took up the "old beginning, made long before"[5] and

1. Theodora Bosanquet, "The Revised Version," *The Little Review*, 5 (August, 1918), p. 57.
2. Henry James, *The Portrait of a Lady*, ed. Leon Edel (New York, 1956), p. xvi.
3. Ralph Barton Perry, *The Thought and Character of William James* (Boston, 1935) I, 380. Also, Virginia Harlow,

"Thomas Sergeant Perry and Henry James," *Boston Public Library Quarterly*, 1 (July, 1949) pp. 43–60.
4. Leon Edel, *Henry James, The Conquest of London: 1870–1881* (Philadelphia, 1962), p. 397.
5. *The Notebooks of Henry James*, ed. F. O Matthiessen and Kenneth B. Murdock (New York, 1947), p. 29.

worked intensely at it for over a year, even after he returned to London.[6] Before he was finished writing it, the novel began to appear in serial form in *Macmillan's Magazine* (October, 1880) and one month later in America in *The Atlantic Monthly*, the serialization running concurrently in the two countries until November and December, 1881. In November, 1881, it was published in book form on the two continents but in separate editions.[7]

This Norton Critical Edition reprints the text of the revised New York Edition, but it also provides Textual Notes, which allow easy comparison of the revisions since passages from the 1881 edition are printed alongside equivalent revisions from the 1908 edition. In both versions, however, one is struck by the sense of urgency hovering over the narrator's lightly ironic diction and leisurely syntax as he describes the inexorable resolution of Isabel's fate. In the background of this portrait of a young woman seeking both freedom and fulfillment James has sketched a social picture as immediate for our times as it was a century ago. Great social changes are taking place Mr. Touchett reminds his auditors on the grassy lawn at Gardencourt, and he advises them to find a good woman, for after all, "the ladies will save us." But neither the radical English lord nor the alienated intellectual nor the energetic American businessman is destined to marry the girl from Albany. Isabel Archer will affront her destiny by allying herself and her fortune with an expatriate dilettante who could never have anticipated this young American woman's ferocious reaction to his desiccated conventionality. The elements of Isabel Archer's characterization are as common today as they were valid yesterday: the relatively uneducated young woman of theoretic bent and high purpose, fearless but innocent; "a certain garden-like quality . . . which made her feel that introspection was, after all, an exercise in the open air, and that a visit to the recesses of one's spirit was harmless when one returned from it with a lapful of roses;" the ambivalence toward money; the need to confuse instinctive drives with high moral purpose; the relative inability to take advice or to learn from the past; the outer alertness and the emerging capacity for inner awareness; the ability to live with one's own mistakes and to reject the easy solutions; the stoic reaction to disappointed hope. Here, indeed, is a young woman becoming a lady under the greatest pressures.

A comparison of the two editions can offer the reader real guidance toward the elucidation of the author's meaning, and this Norton Critical Edition includes two articles on the revisions. F. O. Matthiessen's well-known study is separated by a whole generation

6. *Notebooks*, pp. 29–31; Oscar Cargill, *The Novels of Henry James* (New York, 1961), pp. 78–119 (contains much factual information about the novel).

7. Leon Edel and Dan Laurence, *A Bibliography of Henry James* (London, 1961), pp. 52–53.

from Anthony J. Mazzella's previously unpublished essay, but both are examples of the close textual scrutiny which James's style can sustain.

In addition, the section on "Henry James and the Novel" includes autobiographical information which has been excerpted from Henry James's own *Notebooks*, from his autobiographical writings, and from his travel books. All of this material is relevant to the subtle interrelationship which exists between the author and his works.

Finally, a work of literature need not stand independently of its audience or of the critical tradition surrounding it, and the Criticism section is intended to provide the reader with historical perspective. The four contemporary reviews which are reprinted, three of them from American magazines and one British, were all published in 1882 and give us some sense of the more perceptive responses to the first edition. The Essays in Criticism, on the other hand, were all written within the past thirty years and are all presumably based on readings of the 1908 edition. They are chosen to exhibit the characteristically broad variety of critical responses which began in the 1940's, with the resurgence of interest in James, and which have continued unabated until the present. The Selected Bibliography is intended to help the reader select his way through the enormous body of material which has been written about Henry James.

For their cheerful and diligent aid in helping to prepare this edition, I wish to express my deep gratitude to Candy Ryan, Diane Blumenthal, Jane McVeigh, Cathy Gable, Alexander Bartnicki, and Michael Warren. I also wish to thank John Benedict, Emily Garlin, and Mill Jonakait of W. W. Norton and Co., Inc., for their very careful editing and most useful suggestions.

ROBERT D. BAMBERG

The Text of
The Portrait of a Lady

Preface to the New York Edition

"The Portrait of a Lady" was, like "Roderick Hudson," begun in Florence, during three months spent there in the spring of 1879.[1] Like "Roderick" and like "The American," it had been designed for publication in "The Atlantic Monthly," where it began to appear in 1880. It differed from its two predecessors, however, in finding a course also open to it, from month to month, in "Macmillan's Magazine"; which was to be for me one of the last occasions of simultaneous "serialisation" in the two countries that the changing conditions of literary intercourse between England and the United States had up to then left unaltered. It is a long novel, and I was long in writing it; I remember being again much occupied with it, the following year, during a stay of several weeks made in Venice. I had rooms on Riva Schiavoni, at the top of a house near the passage leading off to San Zaccaria; the waterside life, the wondrous lagoon spread before me, and the ceaseless human chatter of Venice came in at my windows, to which I seem to myself to have been constantly driven, in the fruitless fidget of composition, as if to see whether, out in the blue channel, the ship of some right suggestion, of some better phrase, of the next happy twist of my subject, the next true touch for my canvas, mightn't come into sight. But I recall vividly enough that the response most elicited, in general, to these restless appeals was the rather grim admonition that romantic and historic sites, such as the land of Italy abounds in, offer the artist a questionable aid to concentration when they themselves are not to be the subject of it. They are too rich in their own life and too charged with their own meanings merely to help him out with a lame phrase; they draw him away from his small question to their own greater ones; so that, after a little, he feels, while thus yearning toward them in his difficulty, as if he were asking an army of glorious veterans to help him to arrest a peddler who has given him the wrong change.

There are pages of the book which, in the reading over, have seemed to make me see again the bristling curve of the wide Riva, the large colour-spots of the balconied houses and the repeated undulation of the little hunchbacked bridges, marked by the rise and drop again, with the wave, of foreshortened clicking pedestrians. The Venetian footfall and the Venetian cry—all talk there, wherever uttered, having the pitch of a call across the water—come

1. The visit was actually in 1880.

3

in once more at the window, renewing one's old impression of the delighted senses and the divided, frustrated mind. How can places that speak *in general* so to the imagination not give it, at the moment, the particular thing it wants? I recollect again and again, in beautiful places, dropping into that wonderment. The real truth is, I think, that they express, under this appeal, only too much— more than, in the given case, one has use for; so that one finds one's self working less congruously, after all, so far as the surrounding picture is concerned, than in presence of the moderate and the neutral, to which we may lend something of the light of our vision. Such a place as Venice is too proud for such charities; Venice doesn't borrow, she but all magnificently gives. We profit by that enormously, but to do so we must either be quite off duty or be on it in her service alone. Such, and so rueful, are these reminiscences; though on the whole, no doubt, one's book, and one's "literary effort" at large, were to be the better for them. Strangely fertilising, in the long run, does a wasted effort of attention often prove. It all depends on *how* the attention has been cheated, has been squandered. There are high-handed insolent frauds, and there are insidious sneaking ones. And there is, I fear, even on the most designing artist's part, always witless enough good faith, always anxious enough desire, to fail to guard him against their deceits.

Trying to recover here, for recognition, the germ of my idea, I see that it must have consisted not at all in any conceit of a "plot," nefarious name, in any flash, upon the fancy, of a set of relations, or in any one of those situations that, by a logic of their own, immediately fall, for the fabulist, into movement, into a march or a rush, a patter of quick steps; but altogether in the sense of a single character, the character and aspect of a particular engaging young woman, to which all the usual elements of a "subject," certainly of a setting, were to need to be super-added. Quite as interesting as the young woman herself, at her best, do I find, I must again repeat, this projection of memory upon the whole matter of the growth, in one's imagination, of some such apology for a motive. These are the fascinations of the fabulist's art, these lurking forces of expansion, these necessities of upspringing in the seed, these beautiful determinations, on the part of the idea entertained, to grow as tall as possible, to push into the light and the air and thickly flower there; and, quite as much, these fine possibilities of recovering, from some good standpoint on the ground gained, the intimate history of the business—of retracing and reconstructing its steps and stages. I have always fondly remembered a remark that I heard fall years ago from the lips of Ivan Turgenieff in regard to his own experience of the usual origin of the fictive picture. It began for him almost always with the vision of some person or persons, who hovered before him, soliciting him, as the active or passive figure, interesting him and appealing to him just as they were and by what they were. He saw them, in that fashion, as *disponibles*, saw them subject to the chances, the complications of existence, and saw them vividly, but then had to find for them the right relations, those that would most bring them out; to imagine, to invent and select and piece together the situations most useful and favourable to the sense of the creatures themselves, the complications they would be most likely to produce and to feel.

"To arrive at these things is to arrive at my 'story,' " he said, "and that's the way I look for it. The result is that I'm often accused of not having 'story' enough. I seem to myself to have as much as I need—to show my people, to exhibit their relations with each other; for that is all my measure. If I watch them long enough I see them come together, I see them *placed*, I see them engaged in this or that act and in this or that difficulty. How they look and move and speak and behave, always in the setting I have found for them, is my account of them—of which I dare say, alas, *que cela manque souvent d'architecture*. But I would rather, I think, have too little architecture than too much—when there's danger of its interfering with my measure of the truth. The French of course like more of it than I give—having by their own genius such a hand for it; and indeed one must give all one can. As for the origin of one's wind-blown germs themselves, who shall say, as you ask, where *they* come from? We have to go too far back, too far behind, to say. Isn't it all we can say that they come from every quarter of heaven, that they are *there* at almost any turn of the road? They accumulate, and we are always picking them over, selecting among them. They are the breath of life—by which I mean that life, in its own way, breathes them upon us. They are so, in a manner prescribed and imposed—floated into our minds by the current of life. That reduces to imbecility the vain critic's quarrel, so often, with one's subject, when he hasn't the wit to accept it. Will he point out then which other it should properly have been?—his office being, essentially *to* point out. *Il en serait bien embarrassé.* Ah, when he points out what I've done or failed to do with it, that's another matter: there he's on his ground. I give him up my 'architecture,' " my distinguished friend concluded, "as much as he will."

So this beautiful genius, and I recall with comfort the gratitude I drew from his reference to the intensity of suggestion that may reside in the stray figure, the unattached character, the image *en disponibilité*. It gave me higher warrant than I seemed then to have met for just that blest habit of one's own imagination, the trick of investing some conceived or encountered individual, some brace or group of individuals, with the germinal property and authority. I was myself so much more antecedently conscious of my figures than of their setting—a too preliminary, a preferential interest in which struck me as in general such a putting of the cart before the horse. I might envy, though I couldn't emulate, the imaginative writer so constituted as to see his fable first and to make out its agents afterwards: I could think so little of any fable that didn't need its agents positively to launch it; I could think so little of any situation that didn't depend for its interest on the nature of the persons situated, and thereby on their way of taking it. There are methods of so-called presentation, I believe—among novelists who have appeared to flourish—that offer the situation as indifferent to that support; but I have not lost the sense of the value for me, at the time, of the admirable Russian's testimony to my not needing, all superstitiously, to try and perform any such gymnastic. Other echoes from the same source linger with me, I confess, as unfadingly—if it be not all indeed one much-embracing echo. It was impossible after that not to read, for one's uses, high lucidity into the tormented and disfigured and bemuddled question of the objective value, and even quite into that of the critical appreciation, of "subject" in the novel.

One had had from an early time, for that matter, the instinct of the right estimate of such values and of its reducing to the inane the dull dispute over the "immoral" subject and the moral. Recognising so promptly the one measure of the worth of a given subject, the question about it that, rightly answered, disposes of all others—is it valid, in a word, is it genuine, is it sincere, the result of some direct impression or perception of life?—I had found small edification, mostly, in a critical pretension that had neglected from the first all delimitation of ground and all definition of terms. The air of my earlier time shows, to memory, as darkened, all round, with that vanity—unless the difference to-day be just in one's own final impatience, the lapse of one's attention. There is, I think, no more nutritive or suggestive truth in this connexion than that of the perfect dependence of the "moral" sense of a work of art on the amount of felt life concerned in producing it. The question comes back thus, obviously, to the kind and the degree of the artist's prime sensibility, which is the soil out of which his subject springs. The quality and capacity of that soil, its ability to "grow" with due freshness and straightness any vision of life, represents, strongly or weakly, the projected morality. That element is but another name for the more or less close connexion of the subject with some mark made on the intelligence, with some sincere experience. By which, at the same time, of course, one is far from contending that this enveloping air of the artist's humanity—which gives the last touch to the worth of the work—is not a widely and wondrously varying element; being on one occasion a rich and magnificent medium and on another a comparatively poor and ungenerous one. Here we get exactly the high price of the novel as a literary form—its power not only, while preserving that form with closeness, to range through all the differences of the individual relation to its general subject-matter, all the varieties of outlook on life, of disposition to reflect and project, created by conditions that are never the same from man to man (or, so far as that goes, from man to woman), but positively to appear more true to its character in proportion as it strains, or tends to burst, with a latent extravagnce, its mould.

The house of fiction has in short not one window, but a million —a number of possible windows not to be reckoned, rather; every one of which has been pierced, or is still pierceable, in its vast front, by the need of the individual vision and by the pressure of the individual will. These apertures, of dissimilar shape and size, hang so, all together, over the human scene that we might have expected of them a greater sameness of report than we find. They are but windows at the best, mere holes in a dead wall, disconnected, perched aloft; they are not hinged doors opening straight upon life. But they have this mark of their own that at each of them stands a figure with a pair of eyes, or at least with a field-glass, which forms, again and again, for observation, a unique instrument, insuring to the person making use of it an impression distinct from every other. He and his neighbours are watching the same show, but one seeing more where the other sees less, one seeing black where the other sees white, one seeing big where the other sees small, one seeing coarse where the other sees fine. And so on, and so on; there is fortunately no saying on what, for the particular pair of eyes, the window may *not* open; "fortunately" by reason, precisely, of this incalculability of range. The spreading field, the human scene, is the "choice of subject"; the pierced aperture, either broad or balconied or slit-like and low-browed, is the "literary form"; but they are, singly or together, as nothing without the posted presence of the watcher—without, in other words, the consciousness of the artist. Tell me what the artist is, and I will tell you of what he has *been* conscious. Thereby I shall express to you at once his boundless freedom and his "moral" reference.

All this is a long way round, however, for my word about my dim first move toward "The Portrait," which was exactly my grasp of a single character—an acquisition I had made, moreover, after a fashion not here to be retraced. Enough that I was, as seemed to me, in complete possession of it, that I had been so for a long time, that this had made it familiar and yet had not blurred its charm, and that, all urgently, all tormentingly, I saw it in motion and, so to speak, in transit. This amounts to saying that I saw it as bent upon its fate—some fate or other; *which,* among the possibilities, being precisely the question. Thus I had my vivid individual—vivid, so strangely, in spite of being still at large, not confined by the conditions, not engaged in the tangle, to which we look for much of the impress that constitutes an identity. If the apparition was still all to be placed how came it to be vivid?—since we puzzle such quantities out, mostly, just by the business of placing them. One could answer such a question beautifully, doubtless, if one could do so subtle, if not so monstrous, a thing as to write the history of the growth of one's imagination. One would describe then what, at a given time, had extraordinarily happened to it, and one would so, for instance, be in a position to tell, with an approach to clearness, how, under favour of occasion, it had been able to take over (take over straight from life) such and such a constituted, animated figure or form. The figure has to that extent, as you see, *been* placed—placed in the imagination that detains it, preserves, protects, enjoys it, conscious of its presence in the dusky, crowded, heterogeneous back-shop of the mind very much as a wary dealer in precious odds and ends, competent to make an "advance" on rare objects confided to him, is conscious of the rare little "piece" left in deposit by the reduced, mysterious lady of title or the speculative amateur, and which is already there to disclose its merit afresh as soon as a key shall have clicked in a cupboard-door.

That may be, I recognise, a somewhat superfine analogy for the particular "value" I here speak of, the image of the young feminine nature that I had had for so considerable a time all curiously at my disposal; but it appears to fond memory quite to fit the fact—with the recall, in addition, of my pious desire but to place my treasure right. I quite remind myself thus of the dealer resigned not to "realise," resigned to keeping the precious object locked up indefinitely rather than commit it, at no matter what price, to vulgar hands. For there *are* dealers in these forms and figures and treasures capable of that refinement. The point is, however, that this single small corner-stone, the conception of a certain young woman affronting her destiny, had begun with being all my outfit for the large building of "The Portrait of a Lady." It came to be a square and spacious house—or has at least seemed so to me in this going over it again; but, such as it is, it had to be put up round my young woman while she stood there in perfect isolation. That is to me, artistically speaking, the circumstance of interest; for I have lost myself once more, I confess, in the curiosity of analysing the structure. By what process of logical accretion was this slight "personality," the mere slim shade of an intelligent but presumptuous girl, to find itself endowed with the high attributes of a Subject? —and indeed by what thinness, at the best, would such a subject not be vitiated?

Millions of presumptuous girls, intelligent or not intelligent, daily affront their destiny, and what is it open to their destiny to *be*, at the most, that we should make an ado about it? The novel is of its very nature an "ado," an ado about something, and the larger the form it takes the greater of course the ado. Therefore, consciously, that was what one was in for—for positively organising an ado about Isabel Archer.

One looked it well in the face, I seem to remember, this extravagance; and with the effect precisely of recognising the charm of the problem. Challenge any such problem with any intelligence, and you immediately see how full it is of substance; the wonder being, all the while, as we look at the world, how absolutely, how inordinately, the Isabel Archers, and even much smaller female fry, insist on mattering. George Eliot has admirably noted it—"In these frail vessels is borne onward through the ages the treasure of human affection." In "Romeo and Juliet" Juliet has to be important, just as, in "Adam Bede" and "The Mill on the Floss" and "Middlemarch" and "Daniel Deronda," Hetty Sorrel and Maggie Tulliver and Rosamond Vincy and Gwendolen Harleth have to be; with that much of firm ground, that much of bracing air, at the disposal all the while of their feet and their lungs. They are typical, none the less, of a class difficult, in the individual case, to make a centre of interest; so difficult in fact that many an expert painter, as for instance Dickens and Walter Scott, as for instance even, in the main, so subtle a hand as that of R. L. Stevenson, has preferred to leave the task unattempted. There are in fact writers as to whom we make out that their refuge from this is to assume it to be not worth their attempting; by which pusillanimity in truth their honour is scantly saved. It is never an attestation of a value, or even of our imperfect sense of one, it is never a tribute to any truth at all, that we shall represent that value badly. It never makes up, artistically, for an artist's dim feeling about a thing that he shall "do" the thing as ill as possible. There are better ways than that, the best of all of which is to begin with less stupidity.

It may be answered meanwhile, in regard to Shakespeare's and to George Eliot's testimony, that their concession to the "importance" of their Juliets and Cleopatras and Portias (even with Portia as the very type and model of the young person intelligent and presumptuous) and to that of their Hettys and Maggies and Rosamonds and Gwendolens, suffers the abatement that these slimnesses are, when figuring as the main props of the theme, never suffered to be sole ministers of its appeal, but have their inadequacy eked out with comic relief and underplots, as the playwrights say, when not with murders and battles and the great mutations of the world. If they are shown as "mattering" as much as they could possibly pretend to, the proof of it is in a hundred other persons, made of much stouter stuff, and each involved moreover in a hundred relations which matter to *them* concomitantly with that one. Cleopatra matters, beyond bounds, to Antony, but his colleagues, his antagonists, the state of Rome and the impending battle also prodigiously matter; Portia matters to Antonio, and to Shylock, and to the Prince of Morocco, to the fifty aspiring princes, but for these gentry there are other lively concerns; for Antonio, notably, there are Shylock and Bassanio and his lost ventures and the extremity of his predicament. This extremity indeed, by the same token, matters to Portia—though its doing so becomes of interest all by the fact that Portia matters to *us*. That she does so, at any rate, and that almost everything comes round to it again, supports my contention as to this fine example of the value recognised in the mere young thing. (I say "mere" young thing because I guess that even Shakespeare, preoccupied mainly though he may have been with the passions of princes, would scarce have pretended to found the best of his appeal for her on her high social position.) It is an example exactly of the deep difficulty braved—the difficulty of making George Eliot's "frail vessel," if not the all-in-all for our attention, at least the clearest of the call.

Now to see deep difficulty braved is at any time, for the really addicted artist, to feel almost even as a pang the beautiful incentive, and to feel it verily in such sort as to wish the danger intensified. The difficulty most worth tackling can only be for him, in these conditions, the greatest the case permits of. So I remember feeling here (in presence, always, that is, of the particular uncertainty of my ground), that there would be one way better than another—oh, ever so much better than any other!—of making it fight out its battle. The frail vessel, that charged with George Eliot's "treasure," and thereby of such importance to those who curiously approach it, has likewise possibilities of importance to itself, possibilities which permit of treatment and in fact peculiarly require it from the moment they are considered at all. There is always the escape from any close account of the weak agent of such spells by using as a bridge for evasion, for retreat and flight, the view of her relation to those surrounding her. Make it predominantly a view of *their* relation and the trick is played: you give the general sense of her effect, and you give it, so far as the raising on it of a superstructure goes, with the maximum of ease. Well, I recall perfectly how little, in my now quite established connexion, the maximum of ease appealed to me, and how I seemed to get rid of it by an honest transposition of the weights in the two scales. "Place the centre of the subject in the young woman's own consciousness," I said to myself, "and you get as interesting and as beautiful a difficulty as you could wish. Stick to *that*—for the centre; put the heaviest weight into *that* scale, which will be so largely the scale of her relation to herself. Make her only interested enough, at the same time, in the things that are not herself, and this relation needn't fear to be too limited. Place meanwhile in the other scale the lighter weight (which is usually the one that tips the balance of interest): press least hard, in short, on the consciousness of your heroine's satellites, especially the male; make it an interest contributive only to the greater one. See, at all events, what can be done in this way. What better field could there be for a due ingenuity? The girl hovers, inextinguishable, as a charming creature, and the job will be to translate her into the highest terms of that formula, and as nearly as possible moreover into *all* of them. To depend upon her and her little concerns wholly to see you through will necessitate, remember, your really 'doing' her."

So far I reasoned, and it took nothing less than that technical rigour, I now easily see, to inspire me with the right confidence for erecting on such a plot of ground the neat and careful and proportioned pile of bricks that arches over it and that was thus to form, constructionally speaking, a literary monument. Such is the aspect that to-day "The Portrait" wears for me: a structure reared with an "architectural" competence, as Turgenieff would have said, that makes it, to the author's own sense, the most proportioned of his productions after "The Ambassadors"—which was to follow it so many years later and which has, no doubt, a superior roundness. On one thing I was determined; that, though I should clearly have to pile brick upon brick for the creation of an interest, I would leave no pretext for saying that anything is out of line, scale or perspective. I would build large—in fine embossed vaults and painted arches, as who should say, and yet never let it appear that the chequered pavement, the ground under the reader's feet, fails to stretch at every point to the base of the walls. That precautionary spirit, on re-perusal of the book, is the old note that most touches me: it testifies so, for my own ear, to the anxiety of my provision for the reader's amusement. I felt, in view of the possible limitations of my subject, that no such provision could be excessive, and the development of the latter was simply the general form of that earnest quest. And I find indeed that this is the only account I can give myself of the evolution of the fable: it is all under the head thus named that I conceive the needful accretion as having taken place, the right complications as having started. It was naturally of the essence that the young woman should be herself complex; that was rudimentary—or was at any rate the light in which Isabel Archer had originally dawned. It went, however, but a certain way, and other lights, contending, conflicting lights, and of as many different colours, if possible, as the rockets, the Roman candles and Cather-ine-wheels of a "pyrotechnic display," would be employable to attest that she was. I had, no doubt, a groping instinct for the right complications, since I am quite unable to track the footsteps of those that constitute, as the case stands, the general situation exhib-ited. They are there, for what they are worth, and as numerous as might be; but my memory, I confess, is a blank as to how and whence they came.

I seem to myself to have waked up one morning in possession of them—of Ralph Touchett and his parents, of Madame Merle, of Gilbert Osmond and his daughter and his sister, of Lord Warbur-ton, Caspar Goodwood and Miss Stackpole, the definite array of contributions to Isabel Archer's history. I recognised them, I knew them, they were the numbered pieces of my puzzle, the concrete terms of my "plot." It was as if they had simply, by an impulse of their own, floated into my ken, and all in response to my primary question: "Well, what will she *do?*" Their answer seemed to be that if I would trust them they would show me; on which, with an urgent appeal to them to make it at least as interesting as they could, I trusted them. They were like the group of attendants and entertainers who come down by train when people in the country give a party; they represented the contract for carrying the party on. That was an excellent relation with them—a possible one even with so broken a reed (from her slightness of cohesion) as Henrietta Stackpole. It is a familiar truth to the novelist, at the strenuous hour, that, as certain elements in any work are of the essence, so others are only of the form; that as this or that character, this or that disposition of the material, belongs to the subject directly, so to speak, so this or that other belongs to it but indirectly—belongs intimately to the treatment. This is a truth, however, of which he rarely gets the benefit—since it could be assured to him, really, but by criticism based upon perception, criticism which is too little of this world. He must not think of benefits, moreover, I freely recog-nise, for that way dishonour lies: he has, that is, but one to think of —the benefit, whatever it may be, involved in his having cast a spell upon the simpler, the very simplest, forms of attention. This is all he is entitled to; he is entitled to nothing, he is bound to admit, that can come to him, from the reader, as a result on the latter's part of any act of reflexion or discrimination. He may *enjoy* this finer tribute—that is another affair, but on condition only of taking it as a gratuity "thrown in," a mere miraculous windfall, the fruit of a tree he may not pretend to have shaken. Against reflexion, against discrimination, in his interest, all earth and air conspire; wherefore it is that, as I say, he must in many a case have schooled himself, from the first, to work but for a "living wage." The living wage is the reader's grant of the least possible quantity of attention required for consciousness of a "spell." The occasional charming "tip" is an act of his intelligence over and beyond this, a golden apple, for the writer's lap, straight from the wind-stirred tree. The artist may of course, in wanton moods, dream of some Paradise (for art) where the direct appeal to the intelligence might be legalised; for to such extravagances as these his yearning mind can scarce hope ever completely to close itself. The most he can do is to remember they *are* extravagances.

All of which is perhaps but a gracefully devious way of saying that Henrietta Stackpole was a good example, in "The Portrait," of the truth to which I just adverted—as good an example as I could name were it not that Maria Gostrey, in "The Ambassadors," then in the bosom of time, may be mentioned as a better. Each of these persons is but wheels to the coach; neither belongs to the body of that vehicle, or is for a moment accommodated with a seat inside. There the subject alone is ensconced, in the form of its "hero and heroine," and the privileged high officials, say, who ride with the king and queen. There are reasons why one would have liked this to be felt, as in general one would like almost anything to be felt, in one's work, that one has one's self contributively felt. We have seen, however, how idle is that pretension, which I should be sorry to make too much of. Maria Gostrey and Miss Stackpole then are cases, each, of the light *ficelle*, not of the true agent; they may run beside the coach "for all they are worth," they may cling to it till they are out of breath (as poor Miss Stackpole all so visibly does), but neither, all the while, so much as gets her foot on the step, neither ceases for a moment to tread the dusty road. Put it even that they are like the fishwives who helped to bring back to Paris from Versailles, on that most ominous day of the first half of the French Revolution, the carriage of the royal family. The only thing is that I may well be asked, I acknowledge, why then, in the present fiction, I have suffered Henrietta (of whom we have indubitably too much) so officiously, so strangely, so almost inexplicably, to pervade. I will presently say what I can for that anomaly—and in the most conciliatory fashion.

A point I wish still more to make is that if my relation of confidence with the actors in my drama, who *were*, unlike Miss Stackpole, true agents, was an excellent one to have arrived at, there still remained my relation with the reader, which was another affair altogether and as to which I felt no one to be trusted but myself. That solicitude was to be accordingly expressed in the artful patience with which, as I have said, I piled brick upon brick. The bricks, for the whole counting-over—putting for bricks little touches and inventions and enhancements by the way—affect me in truth as well-nigh innumerable and as ever so scrupulously fitted together and packed-in. It is an effect of detail, of the minutest; though, if one were in this connexion to say all, one would express the hope that the general, the ampler air of the modest monument still survives. I do at least seem to catch the key to a part of this abundance of small anxious, ingenious illustration as I recollect putting my finger, in my young woman's interest, on the most obvious of her predicates. "What will she 'do'? Why, the first thing she'll do will be to come to Europe; which in fact will form, and all inevitably, no small part of her principal adventure. Coming to Europe is even for the 'frail vessels,' in this wonderful age, a mild adventure; but what is truer than that on one side—the side of their independence of flood and field, of the moving accident, of battle and murder and sudden death—her adventures are to be mild? Without her sense of them, her sense *for* them, as one may say, they are next to nothing at all; but isn't the beauty and the difficulty just in showing their mystic conversion by that sense, conversion into the stuff of drama or, even more delightful word still, of 'story'?" It was all as clear, my contention, as a silver bell. Two very good instances, I think, of this effect of conversion, two cases of the rare chemistry, are the pages in which Isabel, coming into the drawing-room at Gardencourt, coming in from a wet walk or whatever, that rainy afternoon, finds Madame Merle in possession of the place, Madame Merle seated, all absorbed but all serene, at the piano, and deeply recognises, in the striking of such an hour, in the presence there, among the gathering shades, of this personage, of whom a moment before she had never so much as heard, a turning-point in her life. It is dreadful to have too much, for any artistic demonstration, to dot one's i's and insist on one's intentions, and I am not eager to do it now; but the question here was that of producing the maximum of intensity with the minimum of strain.

The interest was to be raised to its pitch and yet the elements to be kept in their key; so that, should the whole thing duly impress, I might show what an "exciting" inward life may do for the person leading it even while it remains perfectly normal. And I cannot think of a more consistent application of that ideal unless it be in the long statement, just beyond the middle of the book, of my young woman's extraordinary meditative vigil on the occasion that was to become for her such a landmark. Reduced to its essence, it is but the vigil of searching criticism; but it throws the action further forward than twenty "incidents" might have done. It was designed to have all the vivacity of incident and all the economy of picture. She sits up, by her dying fire, far into the night, under the spell of recognitions on which she finds the last sharpness suddenly wait. It is a representation simply of her motionlessly *seeing,* and an attempt withal to make the mere still lucidity of her act as "interesting" as the surprise of a caravan or the identification of a pirate. It represents, for that matter, one of the identifications dear to the novelist, and even indispensable to him; but it all goes on without her being approached by another person and without her leaving her chair. It is obviously the best thing in the book, but it is only a supreme illustration of the general plan. As to Henrietta, my apology for whom I just left incomplete, she exemplifies, I fear, in her superabundance, not an element of my plan, but only an excess of my zeal. So early was to begin my tendency to *overtreat*, rather than undertreat (when there was choice or danger) my subject. (Many members of my craft, I gather, are far from agreeing with me, but I have always held overtreating the minor disservice.) "Treating" that of "The Portrait" amounted to never forgetting, by any lapse, that the thing was under a special obligation to be amusing. There was the danger of the noted "thinness"—which was to be averted, tooth and nail, by cultivation of the lively. That is at least how I see it to-day. Henrietta must have been at that time a part of my wonderful notion of the lively. And then there was another matter. I had, within the few preceding years, come to live in London, and the "international" light lay, in those days, to my sense, thick and rich upon the scene. It was the light in which so much of the picture hung. But that *is* another matter. There is really too much to say.

HENRY JAMES.

The Portrait of a Lady

Volume I

I

Under certain circumstances there are few hours in life more agreeable than the hour dedicated to the ceremony known as afternoon tea. There are circumstances in which, whether you partake of the tea or not—some people of course never do,—the situation is in itself delightful. Those that I have in mind in beginning to unfold this simple history offered an admirable setting to an innocent pastime. The implements of the little feast had been disposed upon the lawn of an old English country-house, in what I should call the perfect middle of a splendid summer afternoon. Part of the afternoon had waned, but much of it was left, and what was left was of the finest and rarest quality. Real dusk would not arrive for many hours; but the flood of summer light had begun to ebb, the air had grown mellow, the shadows were long upon the smooth, dense turf. They lengthened slowly, however, and the scene expressed that sense of leisure still to come which is perhaps the chief source of one's enjoyment of such a scene at such an hour. From five o'clock to eight is on certain occasions a little eternity; but on such an occasion as this the interval could be only an eternity of pleasure. The persons concerned in it were taking their pleasure quietly, and they were not of the sex which is supposed to furnish the regular votaries of the ceremony I have mentioned. The shadows on the perfect lawn were straight and angular; they were the shadows of an old man sitting in a deep wicker-chair near the low table on which the tea had been served, and of two younger men strolling to and fro, in desultory talk, in front of him. The old man had his cup in his hand; it was an unusually large cup, of a different pattern from the rest of the set and painted in brilliant colours. He disposed of its contents with much circumspection, holding it for a long time close to his chin, with his face turned to the house. His companions had either finished their tea or were indifferent to their privilege; they smoked cigarettes as they continued to stroll. One of them, from time to time, as he passed, looked with a certain attention at the elder man, who, unconscious of observation, rested his eyes upon the rich red front of his dwelling. The house that rose beyond the lawn was a structure to repay such consideration and was the most characteristic object in the peculiarly English picture I have attempted to sketch.

It ·stood upon a low hill, above the river—the river being the Thames at some forty miles from London. A long gabled front of red brick, with the complexion of which time and the weather had played all sorts of pictorial tricks, only, however, to improve and refine it, presented to the lawn its patches of ivy, its clustered chimneys, its windows smothered in creepers. The house had a name and a history; the old gentleman taking his tea would have been delighted to tell you these things: how it had been built under Edward the Sixth, had offered a night's hospitality to the great Elizabeth (whose august person had extended itself upon a huge, magnificent and terribly angular bed which still formed the principal honour of the sleeping apartments), had been a good deal bruised and defaced in Cromwell's wars, and then, under the Restoration, repaired and much enlarged; and how, finally, after having been remodelled and disfigured in the eighteenth century, it had passed into the careful keeping of a shrewd American banker, who had bought it originally because (owing to circumstances too complicated to set forth) it was offered at a great bargain: bought it with much grumbling at its ugliness, its antiquity, its incommodity, and who now, at the end of twenty years, had become conscious of a real aesthetic passion for it, so that he knew all its points and would tell you just where to stand to see them in combination and just the hour when the shadows of its various protuberances—which fell so softly upon the warm, weary brickwork—were of the right measure. Besides this, as I have said, he could have counted off most of the successive owners and occupants, several of whom were known to general fame; doing so, however, with an undemonstrative conviction that the latest phase of its destiny was not the least honourable. The front of the house overlooking that portion of the lawn with which we are concerned was not the entrance-front; this was in quite another quarter. Privacy here reigned supreme, and the wide carpet of turf that covered the level hill-top seemed but the extension of a luxurious interior. The great still oaks and beeches flung down a shade as dense as that of velvet curtains; and the place was furnished, like a room, with cushioned seats, with rich-coloured rugs, with the books and papers that lay upon the grass. The river was at some distance; where the ground began to slope the lawn, properly speaking, ceased. But it was none the less a charming walk down to the water.

The old gentleman at the tea-table, who had come from America thirty years before, had brought with him, at the top of his baggage, his American physiognomy; and he had not only brought it with him, but he had kept it in the best order, so that, if necessary, he might have taken it back to his own country with perfect confidence. At present, obviously, nevertheless, he was not likely to displace himself; his journeys were over and he was taking the rest that precedes the great rest. He had a narrow, clean-shaven face, with features evenly distributed and an expression of placid acuteness. It was evidently a face in which the range of representation was not large, so that the air of contented shrewdness was all the more of a merit. It seemed to tell that he had been successful in life, yet it seemed to tell also that his success had not been exclusive and invidious, but had had much of the inoffensiveness of failure. He had certainly had a great experience of men, but there was an almost rustic simplicity in the faint smile that played upon his lean, spacious cheek and lighted up his humorous eye as he at last slowly and carefully deposited his big tea-cup upon the table. He was neatly dressed, in well-brushed black; but a shawl was folded upon his knees, and his feet were encased in thick, embroidered slippers. A beautiful collie dog lay upon the grass near his chair, watching the master's face almost as tenderly as the master took in the still more magisterial physiognomy of the house; and a little bristling, bustling terrier bestowed a desultory attendance upon the other gentlemen.

One of these was a remarkably well-made man of five-and-thirty, with a face as English as that of the old gentleman I have just sketched was something else; a noticeably handsome face, fresh-coloured, fair and frank, with firm, straight features, a lively grey eye and the rich adornment of a chestnut beard. This person had a certain fortunate, brilliant exceptional look—the air of a happy temperament fertilised by a high civilisation—which would have made almost any observer envy him at a venture. He was booted and spurred, as if he had dismounted from a long ride; he wore a white hat, which looked too large for him; he held his two hands behind him, and in one of them—a large white, well-shaped fist—was crumpled a pair of soiled dog-skin gloves.

His companion, measuring the length of the lawn beside him, was a person of quite a different pattern, who, although he might have excited grave curiosity, would not, like the other, have provoked you to wish yourself, almost blindly, in his place. Tall, lean, loosely and feebly put together, he had an ugly, sickly, witty, charming face, furnished, but by no means decorated, with a straggling moustache and whisker. He looked clever and ill—a combination by no means felicitous; and he wore a brown velvet jacket. He carried his hands in his pockets, and there was something in the way he did it that showed the habit was inveterate. His gait had a shambling, wandering quality; he was not very firm on his legs. As I have said, whenever he passed the old man in the chair he rested his eyes upon him; and at this moment, with their faces brought into relation, you would easily have seen they were father and son. The father caught his son's eye at last and gave him a mild, responsive smile.

"I'm getting on very well," he said.

"Have you drunk your tea?" asked the son.

"Yes, and enjoyed it."

"Shall I give you some more?"

The old man considered, placidly. "Well, I guess I'll wait and see." He had, in speaking, the American tone.

"Are you cold?" the son enquired.

The father slowly rubbed his legs. "Well, I don't know. I can't tell till I feel."

"Perhaps some one might feel for you," said the younger man, laughing.

"Oh, I hope some one will always feel for me! Don't you feel for me, Lord Warburton?"

"Oh, yes, immensely," said the gentleman addressed as Lord Warburton, promptly. "I'm bound to say you look wonderfully comfortable."

"Well, I suppose I am, in most respects." And the old man looked down at his green shawl and smoothed it over his knees. "The fact is I've been comfortable so many years that I suppose I've got so used to it I don't know it."

"Yes, that's the bore of comfort," said Lord Warburton. "We only know when we're uncomfortable."

"It strikes me we're rather particular," his companion remarked.

"Oh yes, there's no doubt we're particular," Lord Warburton murmured. And then the three men remained silent a while; the two younger ones standing looking down at the other, who presently asked for more tea. "I should think you would be very unhappy with that shawl," Lord Warburton resumed while his companion filled the old man's cup again.

"Oh no, he must have the shawl!" cried the gentleman in the velvet coat. "Don't put such ideas as that into his head."

"It belongs to my wife," said the old man simply.

"Oh, if it's for sentimental reasons—" And Lord Warburton made a gesture of apology.

"I suppose I must give it to her when she comes," the old man went on.

"You'll please to do nothing of the kind. You'll keep it to cover your poor old legs."

"Well, you mustn't abuse my legs," said the old man. "I guess they are as good as yours."

"Oh, you're perfectly free to abuse mine," his son replied, giving him his tea.

"Well, we're two lame ducks; I don't think there's much difference."

"I'm much obliged to you for calling me a duck. How's your tea?"

"Well, it's rather hot."

"That's intended to be a merit."

"Ah, there's a great deal of merit," murmured the old man kindly. "He's a very good nurse, Lord Warburton."

"Isn't he a bit clumsy?" asked his lordship.

"Oh no, he's not clumsy—considering that he's an invalid himself. He's a very good nurse—for a sick-nurse. I call him my sick-nurse because he's sick himself."

"Oh, come, daddy!" the ugly young man exclaimed.

"Well, you are; I wish you weren't. But I suppose you can't help it."

"I might try: that's an idea," said the young man.

"Were you ever sick, Lord Warburton?" his father asked.

Lord Warburton considered a moment. "Yes, sir, once, in the Persian Gulf."

"He's making light of you daddy," said the other young man. "That's a sort of joke."

"Well, there seem to be so many sorts now," daddy replied, serenely. "You don't look as if you had been sick, any way, Lord Warburton."

"He's sick of life; he was just telling me so; going on fearfully about it," said Lord Warburton's friend.

"Is that true, sir?" asked the old man gravely.

"If it is, your son gave me no consolation. He's a wretched fellow to talk to—a regular cynic. He doesn't seem to believe in anything."

"That's another sort of joke," said the person accused of cynicism.

"It's because his health is so poor," his father explained to Lord Warburton. "It affects his mind and colours his way of looking at things; he seems to feel as if he had never had a chance. But it's almost entirely theoretical, you know; it doesn't seem to affect his spirits. I've hardly ever seen him when he wasn't cheerful—about as he is at present. He often cheers me up."

The young man so described looked at Lord Warburton and laughed. "Is it a glowing eulogy or an accusation of levity? Should you like me to carry out my theories, daddy?"

"By Jove, we should see some queer things!" cried Lord Warburton.

"I hope you haven't taken up that sort of tone," said the old man.

"Warburton's tone is worse than mine; he pretends to be bored. I'm not in the least bored; I find life only too interesting."

"Ah, *too* interesting; you shouldn't allow it to be that, you know!"

"I'm never bored when I come here," said Lord Warburton. "One gets such uncommonly good talk."

"Is that another sort of joke?" asked the old man. "You've no excuse for being bored anywhere. When I was your age I had never heard of such a thing."

"You must have developed very late."

"No, I developed very quick; that was just the reason. When I was twenty years old I was very highly developed indeed. I was working tooth and nail. You wouldn't be bored if you had something to do; but all you young men are too idle. You think too much of your pleasure. You're too fastidious, and too indolent, and too rich."

"Oh, I say," cried Lord Warburton, "you're hardly the person to accuse a fellow-creature of being too rich!"

"Do you mean because I'm a banker?" asked the old man.

"Because of that, if you like; and because you have—haven't you?—such unlimited means."

"He isn't very rich," the other young man mercifully pleaded. "He has given away an immense deal of money."

"Well, I suppose it was his own," said Lord Warburton; "and in that case could there be a better proof of wealth? Let not a public benefactor talk of one's being too fond of pleasure."

"Daddy's very fond of pleasure—of other people's."

The old man shook his head. "I don't pretend to have contributed anything to the amusement of my contemporaries."

"My dear father, you're too modest!"

"That's a kind of joke, sir," said Lord Warburton.

"You young men have too many jokes. When there are no jokes you've nothing left."

"Fortunately there are always more jokes," the ugly young man remarked.

"I don't believe it—I believe things are getting more serious. You young men will find that out."

"The increasing seriousness of things, then—that's the great opportunity of jokes."

"They'll have to be grim jokes," said the old man. "I'm convinced there will be great changes; and not all for the better."

"I quite agree with you, sir," Lord Warburton declared. "I'm very sure there will be great changes, and that all sorts of queer things will happen. That's why I find so much difficulty in applying your advice; you know you told me the other day that I ought to 'take hold' of something. One hesitates to take hold of a thing that may the next moment be knocked sky-high."

"You ought to take hold of a pretty woman," said his companion. "He's trying hard to fall in love," he added, by way of explanation, to his father.

"The pretty women themselves may be sent flying!" Lord Warburton exclaimed.

"No, no, they'll be firm," the old man rejoined; "they'll not be affected by the social and political changes I just referred to."

"You mean they won't be abolished? Very well, then, I'll lay hands on one as soon as possible and tie her round my neck as a life-preserver."

"The ladies will save us," said the old man; "that is the best of them will—for I make a difference between them. Make up to a good one and marry her, and your life will become much more interesting."

A momentary silence marked perhaps on the part of his auditors a sense of the magnanimity of this speech, for it was a secret neither for his son nor for his visitor that his own experiment in matrimony had not been a happy one. As he said, however, he made a difference; and these words may have been intended as a confession of personal error; though of course it was not in place for either of his companions to remark that apparently the lady of his choice had not been one of the best.

"If I marry an interesting woman I shall be interested: is that what you say?" Lord Warburton asked. "I'm not at all keen about marrying—your son misrepresented me; but there's no knowing what an interesting woman might do with me."

"I should like to see your idea of an interesting woman," said his friend.

"My dear fellow, you can't see ideas—especially such highly ethereal ones as mine. If I could only see it myself—that would be a great step in advance."

"Well, you may fall in love with whomsoever you please; but you mustn't fall in love with my niece," said the old man.

His son broke into a laugh. "He'll think you mean that as a provocation! My dear father, you've lived with the English for thirty years, and you've picked up a good many of the things they say. But you've never learned the things they don't say!"

"I say what I please," the old man returned with all his serenity.

"I haven't the honour of knowing your niece," Lord Warburton said. "I think it's the first time I've heard of her."

"She's a niece of my wife's; Mrs. Touchett brings her to England."

Then young Mr. Touchett explained. "My mother, you know, has been spending the winter in America, and we're expecting her back. She writes that she has discovered a niece and that she has invited her to come out with her."

"I see—very kind of her," said Lord Warburton. "Is the young lady interesting?"

"We hardly know more about her than you; my mother has not gone into details. She chiefly communicates with us by means of telegrams, and her telegrams are rather inscrutable. They say women don't know how to write them, but my mother has thoroughly mastered the art of condensation. 'Tired America, hot weather awful, return England with niece, first steamer decent cabin.' That's the sort of message we get from her—that was the last that came. But there had been another before, which I think contained the first mention of the niece. 'Changed hotel, very bad, impudent clerk, address here. Taken sister's girl, died last year, go to Europe, two sisters, quite independent.' Over that my father and I have scarcely stopped puzzling; it seems to admit of so many interpretations."

"There's one thing very clear in it," said the old man; "she has given the hotel-clerk a dressing."

"I'm not sure even of that, since he has driven her from the field. We thought at first that the sister mentioned might be the sister of the clerk; but the subsequent mention of a niece seems to prove that the allusion is to one of my aunts. Then there was a question as to whose the two other sisters were; they are probably two of my late aunt's daughters. But who's 'quite independent,' and in what sense is the term used?—that point's not yet settled. Does the expression apply more particularly to the young lady my mother has adopted, or does it characterise her sisters equally?—and is it used in a moral or in a financial sense? Does it mean that they've been left well off, or that they wish to be under no obligations? or does it simply mean that they're fond of their own way?"

"Whatever else it means, it's pretty sure to mean that," Mr. Touchett remarked.

"You'll see for yourself," said Lord Warburton. "When does Mrs. Touchett arrive?"

"We're quite in the dark; as soon as she can find a decent cabin. She may be waiting for it yet; on the other hand she may already have disembarked in England."

"In that case she would probably have telegraphed to you."

"She never telegraphs when you would expect it—only when you don't," said the old man. "She likes to drop on me suddenly; she thinks she'll find me doing something wrong. She has never done so yet, but she's not discouraged."

"It's her share in the family trait, the independence she speaks of." Her son's appreciation of the matter was more favourable. "Whatever the high spirit of those young ladies may be, her own is a match for it. She likes to do everything for herself and has no belief in any one's power to help her. She thinks me of no more use than a postage-stamp without gum, and she would never forgive me if I should presume to go to Liverpool to meet her."

"Will you at least let me know when your cousin arrives?" Lord Warburton asked.

"Only on the condition I've mentioned—that you don't fall in love with her!" Mr. Touchett replied.

"That strikes me as hard. Don't you think me good enough?"

"I think you too good—because I shouldn't like her to marry you. She hasn't come here to look for a husband, I hope; so many young ladies are doing that, as if there were no good ones at home. Then she's probably engaged; American girls are usually engaged, I believe. Moreover I'm not sure, after all, that you'd be a remarkable husband."

"Very likely she's engaged; I've known a good many American girls, and they always were; but I could never see that it made any difference, upon my word! As for my being a good husband," Mr. Touchett's visitor pursued, "I'm not sure of that either. One can but try!"

"Try as much as you please, but don't try on my niece," smiled the old man, whose opposition to the idea was broadly humorous.

"Ah, well," said Lord Warburton with a humour broader still, "perhaps, after all, she's not worth trying on!"

II

While this exchange of pleasantries took place between the two Ralph Touchett wandered away a little, with his usual slouching gait, his hands in his pockets and his little rowdyish terrier at his heels. His face was turned toward the house, but his eyes were bent musingly on the lawn; so that he had been an object of observation to a person who had just made her appearance in the ample door-way for some moments before he perceived her. His attention was called to her by the conduct of his dog, who had suddenly darted forward with a little volley of shrill barks, in which the note of wel-come, however, was more sensible than that of defiance. The person in question was a young lady, who seemed immediately to interpret the greeting of the small beast. He advanced with great rapidity and stood at her feet, looking up and barking hard; whereupon, without hesitation, she stopped and caught him in her hands, holding him face to face while he continued his quick chatter. His master now had had time to follow and to see that Bunchie's new friend was a tall girl in a black dress, who at first sight looked pretty. She was bare-headed, as if she were staying in the house—a fact which con-veyed perplexity to the son of its master, conscious of that immun-ity from visitors which had for some time been rendered necessary by the latter's ill-health. Meantime the two other gentlemen had also taken note of the new-comer.

"Dear me, who's that strange woman?" Mr. Touchett had asked.

"Perhaps it's Mrs. Touchett's niece—the independent young lady," Lord Warburton suggested. "I think she must be, from the way she handles the dog."

The collie, too, had now allowed his attention to be diverted, and he trotted toward the young lady in the doorway, slowly setting his tail in motion as he went.

"But where's my wife then?" murmured the old man.

"I suppose the young lady has left her somewhere: that's a part of the independence."

The girl spoke to Ralph, smiling, while she still held up the terrier. "Is this your little dog, sir?"

"He was mine a moment ago; but you've suddenly acquired a remarkable air of property in him."

"Couldn't we share him?" asked the girl. "He's such a perfect little darling."

Ralph looked at her a moment, she was unexpectedly pretty. "You may have him altogether," he then replied.

The young lady seemed to have a great deal of confidence, both in herself and in others; but this abrupt generosity made her blush. "I ought to tell you that I'm probably your cousin," she brought out, putting down the dog. "And here's another!" she added quickly, as the collie came up.

"Probably?" the young man exclaimed, laughing. "I supposed it was quite settled! Have you arrived with my mother?"

"Yes, half an hour ago."

"And has she deposited you and departed again?"

"No, she went straight to her room, and she told me that, if I should see you, I was to say to you that you must come to her there at a quarter to seven."

The young man looked at his watch. "Thank you very much; I shall be punctual." And then he looked at his cousin. "You're very welcome here. I'm delighted to see you."

She was looking at everything, with an eye that denoted clear perception—at her companion, at the two dogs, at the two gentlemen under the trees, at the beautiful scene that surrounded her. "I've never seen anything so lovely as this place. I've been all over the house; it's too enchanting."

"I'm sorry you should have been here so long without our knowing it."

"Your mother told me that in England people arrived very quietly; so I thought it was all right. Is one of those gentlemen your father?"

"Yes, the elder one—the one sitting down," said Ralph.

The girl gave a laugh. "I don't suppose it's the other. Who's the other?"

"He a friend of ours—Lord Warburton."

"Oh, I hoped there would be a lord; it's just like a novel!" And then, "Oh you adorable creature!" she suddenly cried, stooping down and picking up the small dog again.

She remained standing where they had met, making no offer to advance or to speak to Mr. Touchett, and while she lingered so near the threshold, slim and charming, her interlocutor wondered if she expected the old man to come and pay her his respects. American girls were used to a great deal of deference, and it had been intimated that this one had a high spirit. Indeed Ralph could see that in her face.

"Won't you come and make acquaintance with my father?" he nevertheless ventured to ask. "He's old and infirm—he doesn't leave his chair."

"Ah, poor man, I'm very sorry!" the girl exclaimed, immediately moving forward. "I got the impression from your mother that he was rather—rather intensely active."

Ralph Touchett was silent a moment. "She hasn't seen him for a year."

"Well, he has a lovely place to sit. Come along, little hound."

"It's a dear old place," said the young man, looking sidewise at his neighbour.

"What's his name?" she asked, her attention having again reverted to the terrier.

"My father's name?"

"Yes," said the young lady with amusement; "but don't tell him I asked you."

They had come by this time to where old Mr. Touchett was sitting, and he slowly got up from his chair to introduce himself.

"My mother has arrived," said Ralph, "and this is Miss Archer."

The old man placed his two hands on her shoulders, looked at her a moment with extreme benevolence and then gallantly kissed her. "It's a great pleasure to me to see you here; but I wish you had given us a chance to receive you."

"Oh, we were received," said the girl. "There were about a dozen servants in the hall. And there was an old woman curtseying at the gate."

"We can do better than that—if we have notice!" And the old man stood there smiling, rubbing his hands and slowly shaking his head at her. "But Mrs. Touchett doesn't like receptions."

"She went straight to her room."

"Yes—and locked herself in. She always does that. Well, I suppose I shall see her next week." And Mrs. Touchett's husband slowly resumed his former posture.

"Before that," said Miss Archer. "She's coming down to dinner —at eight o'clock. Don't you forget a quarter to seven," she added, turning with a smile to Ralph.

"What's to happen at a quarter to seven?"

"I'm to see my mother," said Ralph.

"Ah, happy boy!" the old man commented. "You must sit down —you must have some tea," he observed to his wife's niece.

"They gave me some tea in my room the moment I got there," this young lady answered. "I'm sorry you're out of health," she added, resting her eyes upon her venerable host.

"Oh, I'm an old man, my dear; it's time for me to be old. But I shall be the better for having you here."

She had been looking all round her again—at the lawn, the great trees, the reedy, silvery Thames, the beautiful old house; and while engaged in this survey she had made room in it for her companions; a comprehensiveness of observation easily conceivable on the part of a young woman who was evidently both intelligent and excited. She had seated herself and had put away the little dog; her white hands, in her lap, were folded upon her black dress; her head was erect, her eye lighted, her flexible figure turned itself easily this way and that, in sympathy with the alertness with which she evidently caught impressions. Her impressions were numerous, and they were all reflected in a clear, still smile. "I've never seen anything so beautiful as this."

"It's looking very well," said Mr. Touchett. "I know the way it strikes you. I've been through all that. But you're very beautiful yourself," he added with a politeness by no means crudely jocular and with the happy consciousness that his advanced age gave him the privilege of saying such things—even to young persons who might possibly take alarm at them.

What degree of alarm this young person took need not be exactly measured; she instantly rose, however, with a blush which was not a refutation. "Oh yes, of course I'm lovely!" she returned with a quick laugh. "How old is your house? Is it Elizabethan?"

"It's early Tudor," said Ralph Touchett.

She turned toward him, watching his face. "Early Tudor? How very delightful! And I suppose there are a great many others."

"There are many much better ones."

"Don't say that, my son!" the old man protested. "There's nothing better than this."

"I've got a very good one; I think in some respects it's rather better," said Lord Warburton, who as yet had not spoken, but who had kept an attentive eye upon Miss Archer. He slightly inclined himself, smiling; he had an excellent manner with women. The girl appreciated it in an instant; she had not forgotten that this was Lord Warburton. "I should like very much to show it to you," he added.

"Don't believe him," cried the old man; "don't look at it! It's a wretched old barrack—not to be compared with this."

"I don't know—I can't judge," said the girl, smiling at Lord Warburton.

In this discussion Ralph Touchett took no interest whatever; he stood with his hands in his pockets, looking greatly as if he should like to renew his conversation with his new-found cousin. "Are you very fond of dogs?" he enquired by way of beginning. He seemed to recognise that it was an awkward beginning for a clever man.

"Very fond of them indeed."

"You must keep the terrier, you know," he went on, still awkwardly.

"I'll keep him while I'm here, with pleasure."

"That will be for a long time, I hope."

"You're very kind. I hardly know. My aunt must settle that."

"I'll settle it with her—at a quarter to seven." And Ralph looked at his watch again.

"I'm glad to be here at all," said the girl.

"I don't believe you allow things to be settled for you."

"Oh yes; if they're settled as I like them."

"I shall settle this as I like it," said Ralph. "It's most unaccountable that we should never have known you."

"I was there—you had only to come and see me."

"There? Where do you mean?"

"In the United States: in New York and Albany and other American places."

"I've been there—all over, but I never saw you. I can't make it out."

Miss Archer just hesitated. "It was because there had been some disagreement between your mother and my father, after my mother's death, which took place when I was a child. In consequence of it we never expected to see you."

"Ah, but I don't embrace all my mother's quarrels—heaven forbid!" the young man cried. "You've lately lost your father?" he went on more gravely.

"Yes; more than a year ago. After that my aunt was very kind to me; she came to see me and proposed that I should come with her to Europe."

"I see," said Ralph. "She has adopted you."

"Adopted me?" The girl stared, and her blush came back to her, together with a momentary look of pain which gave her interlocutor some alarm. He had underestimated the effect of his words. Lord Warburton, who appeared constantly desirous of a nearer view of Miss Archer, strolled toward the two cousins at the moment, and as he did so she rested her wider eyes on him. "Oh no; she has not adopted me. I'm not a candidate for adoption."

"I beg a thousand pardons," Ralph murmured. "I meant—I meant—" He hardly knew what he meant.

"You meant she has taken me up. Yes; she likes to take people up. She has been very kind to me; but," she added with a certain visible eagerness of desire to be explicit, "I'm very fond of my liberty."

"Are you talking about Mrs. Touchett?" the old man called out from his chair. "Come here, my dear, and tell me about her. I'm always thankful for information."

The girl hesitated again, smiling. "She's really very benevolent," she answered; after which she went over to her uncle, whose mirth was excited by her words.

Lord Warburton was left standing with Ralph Touchett, to whom in a moment he said: "You wished a while ago to see my idea of an interesting woman. There it is!"

III

Mrs. Touchett was certainly a person of many oddities, of which her behaviour on returning to her husband's house after many months was a noticeable specimen. She had her own way of doing all that she did, and this is the simplest description of a character which, although by no means without liberal motions, rarely succeeded in giving an impression of suavity. Mrs. Touchett might do a great deal of good, but she never pleased. This way of her own, of which she was so fond, was not intrinsically offensive—it was just unmistakeably distinguished from the ways of others. The edges of her conduct were so very clear-cut that for susceptible persons it sometimes had a knife-like effect. That hard fineness came out in her deportment during the first hours of her return from America, under circumstances in which it might have seemed that her first act would have been to exchange greetings with her husband and son. Mrs. Touchett, for reasons which she deemed excellent, always retired on such occasions into impenetrable seclusion, postponing the more sentimental ceremony until she had repaired the disorder of dress with a completeness which had the less reason to be of high importance as neither beauty nor vanity were concerned in it. She was a plain-faced old woman, without graces and without any great elegance, but with an extreme respect for her own motives. She was usually prepared to explain these—when the explanation was asked as a favour; and in such a case they proved totally different from those that had been attributed to her. She was virtually separated from her husband, but she appeared to perceive nothing irregular in the situation. It had become clear, at an early stage of their community, that they should never desire the same thing at the same moment, and this appearance had prompted her to rescue disagreement from the vulgar realm of accident. She did what she could to erect it into a law—a much more edifying aspect of it—by going to live in Florence, where she bought a house and established herself; and by leaving her husband to take care of the English branch of his bank. This arrangement greatly pleased her; it was so felicitously definite. It struck her husband in the same light, in a foggy square in London, where it was at times the most definite fact he discerned; but he would have preferred that such unnatural things should have a greater vagueness. To agree to disagree had cost him an effort; he was ready to agree to almost anything but that, and saw no reason why either assent or dissent should be so terribly consistent. Mrs. Touchett indulged in no regrets nor speculations, and usually came once a year to spend a month with her husband, a period during which she apparently took pains to convince him that she had adopted the right system. She was not fond of the English style of life, and had three or four reasons for it to which she currently alluded; they bore upon minor points of that ancient order, but for Mrs. Touchett they amply justified non-residence. She detested bread-sauce, which, as she said, looked like a poultice and tasted like soap; she objected to the consumption of beer by her maid-servants; and she affirmed that the British laundress (Mrs. Touchett was very particular about the appearance of her linen) was not a mistress of her art. At fixed intervals she paid a visit to her own country; but this last had been longer than any of its predecessors.

She had taken up her niece—there was little doubt of that. One wet afternoon, some four months earlier than the occurrence lately narrated, this young lady had been seated alone with a book. To say she was so occupied is to say that her solitude did not press upon her; for her love of knowledge had a fertilising quality and her imagination was strong. There was at this time, however, a want of fresh taste in her situation which the arrival of an unexpected visitor did much to correct. The visitor had not been announced; the girl heard her at last walking about the adjoining room. It was in an old house at Albany, a large, square, double house, with a notice of sale in the windows of one of the lower apartments. There were two entrances, one of which had long been out of use but had never been removed. They were exactly alike—large white doors, with an arched frame and wide side-lights, perched upon little "stoops" of red stone, which descended sidewise to the brick pavement of the street. The two houses together formed a single dwelling, the party-wall having been removed and the rooms placed in communition. These rooms, above-stairs, were extremely numerous, and were painted all over exactly alike, in a yellowish white which had grown sallow with time. On the third floor there was a sort of arched passage, connecting the two sides of the house, which Isabel and her sisters used in their childhood to call the tunnel and which, though it was short and well-lighted, always seemed to the girl to be strange and lonely, especially on winter afternoons. She had been in the house, at different periods, as a child; in those days her grandmother lived there. Then there had been an absence of ten years, followed by a return to Albany before her father's death. Her grandmother, old Mrs. Archer, had exercised, chiefly within the limits of the family, a large hospitality in the early period, and the little girls often spent weeks under her roof—weeks of which Isabel had the happiest memory. The manner of life was different from that of her own home—larger, more plentiful, practically more festal; the discipline of the nursery was delightfully vague and the opportunity of listening to the conversation of one's elders (which with Isabel was a highly-valued pleasure) almost unbounded. There was a constant coming and going; her grandmother's sons and daughters and their children appeared to be in the enjoyment of standing invitations to arrive and remain, so that the house offered to a certain extent the appearance of a bustling provincial inn kept by a gentle old landlady who sighed a great deal and never presented a bill. Isabel of course knew nothing about bills; but even as a child she thought her grandmother's home romantic. There was a covered piazza behind it, furnished with a wing which was a source of tremulous interest; and beyond this was a long garden, sloping down to the stable and containing peach-trees of barely credible familiarity. Isabel had stayed with her grandmother at various seasons, but somehow all her visits had a flavour of peaches. On the other side, across the street, was an old house that was called the Dutch House —a peculiar structure dating from the earliest colonial time, composed of bricks that had been painted yellow, crowned with a gable that was pointed out to strangers, defended by a rickety wooden paling and standing sidewise to the street. It was occupied by a primary school for children of both sexes, kept or rather let go, by a demonstrative lady of whom Isabel's chief recollection was that her hair was fastened with strange bedroomy combs at the temples and that she was the widow of some one of consequence. The little girl had been offered the opportunity of laying a foundation of knowledge in this establishment; but having spent a single day in it, she had protested against its laws and had been allowed to stay at home, where, in the September days, when the windows of the

Dutch House were open, she used to hear the hum of childish voices repeating the multiplication-table—an incident in which the elation of liberty and the pain of exclusion were indistinguishably mingled. The foundation of her knowledge was really laid in the idleness of her grandmother's house, where, as most of the other inmates were not reading people, she had uncontrolled use of a library full of books with frontispieces, which she used to climb upon a chair to take down. When she had found one to her taste —she was guided in the selection chiefly by the frontispiece—she carried it into a mysterious apartment which lay beyond the library and which was called, traditionally, no one knew why, the office. Whose office it had been and at what period it had flourished, she never learned; it was enough for her that it contained an echo and a pleasant musty smell and that it was a chamber of disgrace for old pieces of furniture whose infirmities were not always apparent (so that the disgrace seemed unmerited and rendered them victims of injustice) and with which, in the manner of children, she had established relations almost human, certainly dramatic. There was an old haircloth sofa in especial, to which she had confided a hundred childish sorrows. The place owed much of its mysterious melancholy to the fact that it was properly entered from the second door of the house, the door that had been condemned, and that it was secured by bolts which a particularly slender little girl found it impossible to slide. She knew that this silent, motionless portal opened into the street; if the sidelights had not been filled with green paper she might have looked out upon the little brown stoop and the well-worn brick pavement. But she had no wish to look out, for this would have interfered with her theory that there was a strange, unseen place on the other side—a place which became to the child's imagination, according to its different moods, a region of delight or of terror.

It was in the "office" still that Isabel was sitting on that melancholy afternoon of early spring which I have just mentioned. At this time she might have had the whole house to choose from, and the room she had selected was the most depressed of its scenes. She had never opened the bolted door nor removed the green paper (renewed by other hands) from its side-lights; she had never assured herself that the vulgar street lay beyond. A crude, cold rain fell heavily; the spring-time was indeed an appeal—and it seemed a cynical, insincere appeal—to patience. Isabel, however, gave as little heed as possible to cosmic treacheries; she kept her eyes on her book and tried to fix her mind. It had lately occurred to her that her mind was a good deal of a vagabond, and she had spent much ingenuity in training it to a military step and teaching it to advance, to halt, to retreat, to perform even more complicated man-

oeuvres, at the word of command. Just now she had given it marching orders and it had been trudging over the sandy plains of a history of German Thought. Suddenly she became aware of a step very
different from her own intellectual pace; she listened a little and perceived that some one was moving in the library, which communicated with the office. It struck her first as the step of a person from
whom she was looking for a visit, then almost immediately
announced itself as the tread of a woman and a stranger—her possible visitor being neither. It had an inquisitive, experimental quality
which suggested that it would not stop short of the threshold of the
office; and in fact the doorway of this apartment was presently occupied by a lady who paused there and looked very hard at our heroine. She was a plain, elderly woman, dressed in a comprehensive
waterproof mantle; she had a face with a good deal of rather violent
point.

"Oh," she began, "is that where you usually sit?" She looked
about at the heterogeneous chairs and tables.

"Not when I have visitors," said Isabel, getting up to receive the
intruder.

She directed their course back to the library while the visitor continued to look about her. "You seem to have plenty of other rooms;
they're in rather better condition. But everything's immensely
worn."

"Have you come to look at the house?" Isabel asked. "The servant will show it to you."

"Send her away; I don't want to buy it. She has probably gone to
look for you and is wandering about upstairs; she didn't seem at all
intelligent. You had better tell her it's no matter." And then, since
the girl stood there hesitating and wondering, this unexpected critic
said to her abruptly: "I suppose you're one of the daughters?"

Isabel thought she had very strange manners. "It depends upon
whose daughters you mean."

"The late Mr. Archer's—and my poor sister's."

"Ah," said Isabel slowly, "you must be our crazy Aunt Lydia!"

"Is that what your father told you to call me? I'm your Aunt
Lydia, but I'm not at all crazy: I haven't a delusion! And which of
the daughters are you?"

"I'm the youngest of the three, and my name's Isabel."

"Yes; the others are Lilian and Edith. And are you the prettiest?"

"I haven't the least idea," said the girl.

"I think you must be." And in this way the aunt and the niece
made friends. The aunt had quarrelled years before with her broth-
er-in-law, after the death of her sister, taking him to task for the
manner in which he brought up his three girls. Being a high-tem-

pered man he had requested her to mind her own business, and she
had taken him at his word. For many years she held no communication with him and after his death had addressed not a word to his
daughters, who had been bred in that disrespectful view of her
which we have just seen Isabel betray. Mrs. Touchett's behaviour
was, as usual, perfectly deliberate. She intended to go to America to
look after her investments (with which her husband, in spite of his
great financial position, had nothing to do) and would take advantage of this opportunity to enquire into the condition of her nieces.
There was no need of writing, for she should attach no importance
to any account of them she should elicit by letter; she believed,
always, in seeing for one's self. Isabel found, however, that she
knew a good deal about them, and knew about the marriage of the
two elder girls; knew that their poor father had left very little
money, but that the house in Albany, which had passed into his
hands, was to be sold for their benefit; knew, finally, that Edmund
Ludlow, Lilian's husband, had taken upon himself to attend to this
matter, in consideration of which the young couple, who had come
to Albany during Mr. Archer's illness, were remaining there for the
present and, as well as Isabel herself, occupying the old place.

"How much money do you expect for it?" Mrs. Touchett asked
of her companion, who had brought her to sit in the front parlour,
which she had inspected without enthusiasm.

"I haven't the least idea," said the girl.

"That's the second time you have said that to me," her aunt
rejoined. "And yet you don't look at all stupid."

"I'm not stupid; but I don't know anything about money."

"Yes, that's the way you were brought up—as if you were to
inherit a million. What have you in point of fact inherited?"

"I really can't tell you. You must ask Edmund and Lilian; they'll
be back in half an hour."

"In Florence we should call it a very bad house," said Mrs.
Touchett; "but here, I dare say, it will bring a high price. It ought
to make a considerable sum for each of you. In addition to that you
must have something else; it's most extraordinary your not knowing.
The position's of value, and they'll probably pull it down and make
a row of shops. I wonder you don't do that yourself; you might let
the shops to great advantage."

Isabel stared; the idea of letting shops was new to her. "I hope
they won't pull it down," she said; "I'm extremely fond of it."

"I don't see what makes you fond of it; your father died here."

"Yes; but I don't dislike it for that," the girl rather strangely
returned. "I like places in which things have happened—even if
they're sad things. A great many people have died here; the place
has been full of life."

"Is that what you call being full of life?"

"I mean full of experience—of people's feelings and sorrows. And not of their sorrows only, for I've been very happy here as a child."

"You should go to Florence if you like houses in which things have happened—especially deaths. I live in an old palace in which three people have been murdered; three tnat were known and I don't know how many more besides."

"In an old palace?" Isabel repeated.

"Yes, my dear; a very different affair from this. This is very bourgeois."

Isabel felt some emotion, for she had always thought highly of her grandmother's house. But the emotion was of a kind which led her to say: "I should like very much to go to Florence."

"Well, if you'll be very good, and do everything I tell you I'll take you there," Mrs. Touchett declared.

Our young woman's emotion deepened; she flushed a little and smiled at her aunt in silence. "Do everything you tell me? I don't think I can promise that."

"No, you don't look like a person of that sort. You're fond of your own way; but it's not for me to blame you."

"And yet, to go to Florence," the girl exclaimed in a moment, "I'd promise almost anything!"

Edmund and Lilian were slow to return, and Mrs. Touchett had an hour's uninterrupted talk with her niece, who found her a strange and interesting figure: a figure essentially—almost the first she had ever met. She was as eccentric as Isabel had always supposed; and hitherto, whenever the girl had heard people described as eccentric, she had thought of them as offensive or alarming. The term had always suggested to her something grotesque and even sinister. But her aunt made it a matter of high but easy irony, or comedy, and led her to ask herself if the common tone, which was all she had known, had ever been as interesting. No one certainly had on any occasion so held her as this little thin-lipped, bright-eyed, foreign-looking woman, who retrieved an insignificant appearance by a distinguished manner and, sitting there in a well-worn waterproof, talked with striking familiarity of the courts of Europe. There was nothing flighty about Mrs. Touchett, but she recognised no social superiors, and, judging the great ones of the earth in a way that spoke of this, enjoyed the consciousness of making an impression on a candid and susceptible mind. Isabel at first had answered a good many questions, and it was from her answers apparently that Mrs. Touchett derived a high opinion of her intelligence. But after this she had asked a good many, and her aunt's answers, whatever turn they took, struck her as food for deep reflexion. Mrs. Touchett waited for the return of her other niece as long as she thought rea-

sonable, but as at six o'clock Mrs. Ludlow had not come in she prepared to take her departure.

"Your sister must be a great gossip. Is she accustomed to staying
out so many hours?"

"You've been out almost as long as she," Isabel replied; "she can
have left the house but a short time before you came in."

Mrs. Touchett looked at the girl without resentment; she
appeared to enjoy a bold retort and to be disposed to be gracious.
"Perhaps she hasn't had so good an excuse as I. Tell her at any rate
that she must come and see me this evening at that horrid hotel.
She may bring her husband if she likes, but she needn't bring you. I
shall see plenty of you later."

IV

Mrs. Ludlow was the eldest of the three sisters, and was usually
thought the most sensible; the classification being in general that
Lilian was the practical one, Edith the beauty and Isabel the "intellectual" superior. Mrs. Keyes, the second of the group, was the wife
of an officer of the United States Engineers, and as our history is
not further concerned with her it will suffice that she was indeed very
pretty and that she formed the ornament of those various military
stations, chiefly in the unfashionable West, to which, to her deep
chagrin, her husband was successively relegated. Lilian had married
a New York lawyer, a young man with a loud voice and an enthusiasm for his profession; the match was not brilliant, any more than
Edith's, but Lilian had occasionally been spoken of as a young
woman who might be thankful to marry at all—she was so much
plainer than her sisters. She was, however, very happy, and now, as
the mother of two peremptory little boys and the mistress of a
wedge of brown stone violently driven into Fifty-third Street,
seemed to exult in her condition as in a bold escape. She was short
and solid, and her claim to figure was questioned, but she was conceded presence, though not majesty; she had moreover, as people
said, improved since her marriage, and the two things in life of
which she was most distinctly conscious were her husband's force in
argument and her sister Isabel's originality. "I've never kept up with
Isabel—it would have taken *all* my time," she had often remarked;
in spite of which, however, she held her rather wistfully in sight;
watching her as a motherly spaniel might watch a free greyhound.
"I want to see her safely married—that's what I want to see," she
frequently noted to her husband.

"Well, I must say I should have no particular desire to marry
her," Edmund Ludlow was accustomed to answer in an extremely
audible tone.

"I know you say that for argument; you always take the opposite ground. I don't see what you've against her except that she's so original."

"Well, I don't like originals; I like translations," Mr. Ludlow had more than once replied. "Isabel's written in a foreign tongue. I can't make her out. She ought to marry an Armenian or a Portuguese."

"That's just what I'm afraid she'll do!" cried Lilian, who thought Isabel capable of anything.

She listened with great interest to the girl's account of Mrs. Touchett's appearance and in the evening prepared to comply with their aunt's commands. Of what Isabel then said no report has remained, but her sister's words had doubtless prompted a word spoken to her husband as the two were making ready for their visit. "I do hope immensely she'll do something handsome for Isabel; she has evidently taken a great fancy to her."

"What is it you wish her to do?" Edmund Ludlow asked. "Make her a big present?"

"No indeed; nothing of the sort. But take an interest in her—sympathise with her. She's evidently just the sort of person to appreciate her. She has lived so much in foreign society; she told Isabel all about it. You know you've always thought Isabel rather foreign."

"You want her to give her a little foreign sympathy, eh? Don't you think she gets enough at home?"

"Well, she ought to go abroad," said Mrs. Ludlow. "She's just the person to go abroad."

"And you want the old lady to take her, is that it?"

"She has offered to take her—she's dying to have Isabel go. But what I want her to do when she gets her there is to give her all the advantages. I'm sure all we've got to do," said Mrs. Ludlow, "is to give her a chance."

"A chance for what?"

"A chance to develop."

"Oh Moses!" Edmund Ludlow exclaimed. "I hope she isn't going to develop any more!"

"If I were not sure you only said that for argument I should feel very badly," his wife replied. "But you know you love her."

"*Do* you know I love you?" the young man said, jocosely, to Isabel a little later, while he brushed his hat.

"I'm sure I don't care whether you do or not!" exclaimed the girl; whose voice and smile, however, were less haughty than her words.

"Oh, she feels so grand since Mrs. Touchett's visit," said her sister.

But Isabel challenged this assertion with a good deal of seriousness. "You must not say that, Lily. I don't feel grand at all."

"I'm sure there's no harm," said the conciliatory Lily.

"Ah, but there's nothing in Mrs. Touchett's visit to make one feel grand."

"Oh," exclaimed Ludlow, "she's grander than ever!"

"Whenever I feel grand," said the girl, "it will be for a better reason."

Whether she felt grand or no, she at any rate felt different, felt as if something had happened to her. Left to herself for the evening she sat a while under the lamp, her hands empty, her usual avocations unheeded. Then she rose and moved about the room, and from one room to another, preferring the places where the vague lamplight expired. She was restless and even agitated; at moments she trembled a little. The importance of what had happened was out of proportion to its appearance; there had really been a change in her life. What it would bring with it was as yet extremely indefinite; but Isabel was in a situation that gave a value to any change. She had a desire to leave the past behind her and, as she said to herself, to begin afresh. This desire indeed was not a birth of the present occasion; it was as familiar as the sound of the rain upon the window and it had led to her beginning afresh a great many times. She closed her eyes as she sat in one of the dusky corners of the quiet parlour; but it was not with a desire for dozing forgetfulness. It was on the contrary because she felt too wide-eyed and wished to check the sense of seeing too many things at once. Her imagination was by habit ridiculously active; when the door was not open it jumped out of the window. She was not accustomed indeed to keep it behind bolts; and at important moments, when she would have been thankful to make use of her judgement alone, she paid the penalty of having given undue encouragement to the faculty of seeing without judging. At present, with her sense that the note of change had been struck, came gradually a host of images of the things she was leaving behind her. The years and hours of her life came back to her, and for a long time, in a stillness broken only by the ticking of the big bronze clock, she passed them in review. It had been a very happy life and she had been a very fortunate person —this was the truth that seemed to emerge most vividly. She had had the best of everything, and in a world in which the circumstances of so many people made them unenviable it was an advantage never to have known anything particularly unpleasant. It appeared to Isabel that the unpleasant had been even too absent from her knowledge, for she had gathered from her acquaintance with literature that it was often a source of interest and even of instruction. Her father had kept it away from her—her handsome, much-loved father, who always had such an aversion to it. It was a great felicity to have been his daughter; Isabel rose even to pride in her parentage. Since his death she had seemed to see him as turning his braver side to his children and as not having managed to ignore the ugly quite so much in practice as in aspiration. But this only made her tenderness for him greater; it was scarcely even painful to have to suppose him too generous, too good-natured, too indifferent to sordid considerations. Many persons had held that he carried this indifference too far, especially the large number of those to whom he owed money. Of their opinions Isabel was never very definitely informed; but it may interest the reader to know that, while they had recognised in the late Mr. Archer a remarkably handsome head and a very taking manner (indeed, as one of them had said, he was always taking something), they had declared that he was making a very poor use of his life. He had squandered a substantial fortune, he had been deplorably convivial, he was known to have gambled freely. A few very harsh critics went so far as to say that he had not even brought up his daughters. They had had no regular education and no permanent home: they had been at once spoiled and neglected; they had lived with nursemaids and governesses (usually very bad ones) or had been sent to superficial schools, kept by the French, from which, at the end of a month, they had been removed in tears. This view of the matter would have excited Isabel's indignation, for to her own sense her opportunities had been large. Even when her father had left his daughters for three months at Neufchatel with a French *bonne*[1] who had eloped with a Russian nobleman staying at the same hotel—even in this irregular situation (an incident of the girl's eleventh year) she had been neither frightened nor ashamed, but had thought it a romantic episode in a liberal education. Her father had a large way of looking at life, of which his restlessness and even his occasional incoherency of conduct had been only a proof. He wished his daughters, even as children, to see as much of the world as possible; and it was for this purpose that, before Isabel was fourteen, he had transported them three times across the Atlantic, giving them on each occasion, however, but a few months' view of the subject proposed: a course which had whetted our heroine's curiosity without enabling her to satisfy it. She ought to have been a partisan of her father, for she was the member of his trio who most "made up" to him for the disagreeables he didn't mention. In his last days his general willingness to take leave of a world in which the difficulty of doing as one liked appeared to increase as one grew older had been sensibly modified by the pain of separation from his clever, his superior, his remarkable girl. Later, when the journeys to Europe ceased, he still had shown his children all sorts of indulgence, and if he had been troubled about money-matters nothing disturbed their irreflective consciousness of many possessions. Isabel, though she danced very well, had

1. A maidservant, nurse.

not the recollection of having been in New York a successful member of the choreographic circle; her sister Edith was, as every one said, so very much more fetching. Edith was so striking an example of success that Isabel could have no illusions as to what constituted this advantage, or as to the limits of her own power to frisk and jump and shriek—above all with rightness of effect. Nineteen persons out of twenty (including the younger sister herself) pronounced Edith infinitely the prettier of the two; but the twentieth, besides reversing this judgement, had the entertainment of thinking all the others aesthetic vulgarians. Isabel had in the depths of her nature an even more unquenchable desire to please than Edith; but the depths of this young lady's nature were a very out-of-the-way place, between which and the surface communication was interrupted by a dozen capricious forces. She saw the young men who came in large numbers to see her sister; but as a general thing they were afraid of her; they had a belief that some special preparation was required for talking with her. Her reputation of reading a great deal hung about her like the cloudy envelope of a goddess in an epic; it was supposed to engender difficult questions and to keep the conversation at a low temperature. The poor girl liked to be thought clever, but she hated to be thought bookish; she used to read in secret and, though her memory was excellent, to abstain from showy reference. She had a great desire for knowledge, but she really preferred almost any source of information to the printed page; she had an immense curiosity about life and was constantly staring and wondering. She carried within herself a great fund of life, and her deepest enjoyment was to feel the continuity between the movements of her own soul and the agitations of the world. For this reason she was fond of seeing great crowds and large stretches of country, of reading about revolutions and wars, of looking at historical pictures—a class of efforts as to which she had often committed the conscious solecism of forgiving them much bad painting for the sake of the subject. While the Civil War went on she was still a very young girl; but she passed months of this long period in a state of almost passionate excitement, in which she felt herself at times (to her extreme confusion) stirred almost indiscriminately by the valour of either army. Of course the circumspection of suspicious swains had never gone the length of making her a social proscript; for the number of those whose hearts, as they approached her, beat only just fast enough to remind them they had heads as well, had kept her unacquainted with the supreme disciplines of her sex and age. She had had everything a girl could have: kindness, admiration, bonbons, bouquets, the sense of exclusion from none of the privileges of the world she lived in, abundant opportunity for dancing, plenty of new dresses, the London *Specta-*

tor, the latest publications, the music of Gounod, the poetry of Browning, the prose of George Eliot.[2]

These things now, as memory played over them, resolved themselves into a multitude of scenes and figures. Forgotten things came back to her; many others, which she had lately thought of great moment, dropped out of sight. The result was kaleidoscopic, but the movement of the instrument was checked at last by the servant's coming in with the name of a gentleman. The name of the gentleman was Caspar Goodwood; he was a straight young man from Boston, who had known Miss Archer for the last twelve-month and who, thinking her the most beautiful young woman of her time, had pronounced the time, according to the rule I have hinted at, a foolish period of history. He sometimes wrote to her and had within a week or two written from New York. She had thought it very possible he would come in—had indeed all the rainy day been vaguely expecting him. Now that she learned he was there, nevertheless, she felt no eagerness to receive him. He was the finest young man she had ever seen, was indeed quite a splendid young man; he inspired her with a sentiment of high, of rare respect. She had never felt equally moved to it by any other person. He was supposed by the world in general to wish to marry her, but this of course was between themselves. It at least may be affirmed that he had travelled from New York to Albany expressly to see her; having learned in the former city, where he was spending a few days and where he had hoped to find her, that she was still at the State capital. Isabel delayed for some minutes to go to him; she moved about the room with a new sense of complications. But at last she presented herself and found him standing near the lamp. He was tall, strong and somewhat stiff; he was also lean and brown. He was not romantically, he was much rather obscurely, handsome; but his physiognomy had an air of requesting your attention, which it rewarded according to the charm you found in blue eyes of remarkable fixedness, the eyes of a complexion other than his own, and a jaw of the somewhat angular mould which is supposed to bespeak resolution. Isabel said to herself that it bespoke resolution to-night; in spite of which, in half an hour, Caspar Goodwood, who had arrived hopeful as well as resolute, took his way back to his lodging with the feeling of a man defeated. He was not, it may be added, a man weakly to accept defeat.

2. This particular *Spectator* (founded in 1828) was a weekly periodical of "educated radicalism." Charles Gounod (1818–1893) is best known for his sacred music and lyric operas. The years of Robert Browning's (1812–1889) marriage to Elizabeth Barrett were spent primarily in Florence, the scene of a number of his better-known poems. George Eliot's (1819–1880) *Middlemarch* began to appear in *Harper's Weekly* on December 16, 1871.

v

Ralph Touchett was a philosopher, but nevertheless he knocked at his mother's door (at a quarter to seven) with a good deal of eagerness. Even philosophers have their preferences, and it must be admitted that of his progenitors his father ministered most to his sense of the sweetness of filial dependence. His father, as he had often said to himself, was the more motherly; his mother, on the other hand, was paternal, and even, according to the slang of the day, gubernatorial. She was nevertheless very fond of her only child and had always insisted on his spending three months of the year with her. Ralph rendered perfect justice to her affection and knew that in her thoughts and her thoroughly arranged and servanted life his turn always came after the other nearest subjects of her solicitude, the various punctualities of performance of the workers of her will. He found her completely dressed for dinner, but she embraced her boy with her gloved hands and made him sit on the sofa beside her. She enquired scrupulously about her husband's health and about the young man's own, and, receiving no very brilliant account of either, remarked that she was more than ever convinced of her wisdom in not exposing herself to the English climate. In this case she also might have given way. Ralph smiled at the idea of his mother's giving way, but made no point of reminding her that his own infirmity was not the result of the English climate, from which he absented himself for a considerable part of each year.

He had been a very small boy when his father, Daniel Tracy Touchett, a native of Rutland, in the State of Vermont, came to England as subordinate partner in a banking-house where some ten years later he gained preponderant control. Daniel Touchett saw before him a life-long residence in his adopted country, of which, from the first, he took a simple, sane and accommodating view. But, as he said to himself, he had no intention of disamericanising, nor had he a desire to teach his only son any such subtle art. It had been for himself so very soluble a problem to live in England assimilated yet unconverted that it seemed to him equally simple his lawful heir should after his death carry on the grey old bank in the white American light. He was at pains to intensify this light, however, by sending the boy home for his education. Ralph spent several terms at an American school and took a degree at an American university, after which, as he struck his father on his return as even redundantly native, he was placed for some three years in residence at Oxford. Oxford swallowed up Harvard, and Ralph became at last English enough. His outward conformity to the manners that surrounded him was none the less the mask of a mind that greatly enjoyed its independence, on which nothing long imposed itself, and which, naturally inclined to adventure and irony, indulged in a boundless liberty of appreciation. He began with being a young man of promise; at Oxford he distinguished himself, to his father's ineffable satisfaction, and the people about him said it was a thousand pities so clever a fellow should be shut out from a career. He might have had a career by returning to his own country (though this point is shrouded in uncertainty) and even if Mr. Touchett had been willing to part with him (which was not the case) it would have gone hard with him to put a watery waste permanently between himself and the old man whom he regarded as his best friend. Ralph was not only fond of his father, he admired him—he enjoyed the opportunity of observing him. Daniel Touchett, to his perception, was a man of genius, and though he himself had no aptitude for the banking mystery he made a point of learning enough of it to measure the great figure his father had played. It was not this, however, he mainly relished; it was the fine ivory surface, polished as by the English air, that the old man had opposed to possibilities of penetration. Daniel Touchett had been neither at Harvard nor at Oxford, and it was his own fault if he had placed in his son's hands the key to modern criticism. Ralph, whose head was full of ideas which his father had never guessed, had a high esteem for the latter's originality. Americans, rightly or wrongly, are commended for the ease with which they adapt themselves to foreign conditions; but Mr. Touchett had made of the very limits of his pliancy half the ground of his general success. He had retained in their freshness most of his marks of primary pressure; his tone, as his son always noted with pleasure, was that of the more luxuriant part of New England. At the end of his life he had become, on his own ground, as mellow as he was rich; he combined consummate shrewdness with the disposition superficially to fraternise, and his "social position," on which he had never wasted a care, had the firm perfection of an unthumbed fruit. It was perhaps his want of imagination and of what is called the historic consciousness; but to many of the impressions usually made by English life upon the cultivated stranger his sense was completely closed. There were certain differences he had never perceived, certain habits he had never formed, certain obscurities he had never sounded. As regards these latter, on the day he *had* sounded them his son would have thought less well of him.

Ralph, on leaving Oxford, had spent a couple of years in travelling; after which he had found himself perched on a high stool in his father's bank. The responsibility and honour of such positions is not, I believe, measured by the height of the stool, which depends upon other considerations: Ralph, indeed, who had very long legs, was fond of standing, and even of walking about, at his work. To this exercise, however, he was obliged to devote but a limited period, for at the end of some eighteen months he had become aware of his being seriously out of health. He had caught a violent cold, which fixed itself on his lungs and threw them into dire confusion. He had to give up work and apply, to the letter, the sorry injunction to take care of himself. At first he slighted the task; it appeared to him it was not himself in the least he was taking care of, but an uninteresting and uninterested person with whom he had nothing in common. This person, however, improved on acquaintance, and Ralph grew at last to have a certain grudging tolerance, even an undemonstrative respect, for him. Misfortune makes strange bedfellows, and our young man, feeling that he had something at stake in the matter—it usually struck him as his reputation for ordinary wit —devoted to his graceless charge an amount of attention of which note was duly taken and which had at least the effect of keeping the poor fellow alive. One of his lungs began to heal, the other promised to follow its example, and he was assured he might outweather a dozen winters if he would betake himself to those climates in which consumptives chiefly congregate. As he had grown extremely fond of London, he cursed the flatness of exile: but at the same time that he cursed he conformed, and gradually, when he found his sensitive organ grateful even for grim favours, he conferred them with a lighter hand. He wintered abroad, as the phrase is; basked in the sun, stopped at home when the wind blew, went to bed when it rained, and once or twice, when it had snowed overnight, almost never got up again.

A secret hoard of indifference—like a thick cake a fond old nurse might have slipped into his first school outfit—came to his aid and helped to reconcile him to sacrifice; since at the best he was too ill for aught but that arduous game. As he said to himself, there was really nothing he had wanted very much to do, so that he had at least not renounced the field of valour. At present, however, the fragrance of forbidden fruit seemed occasionally to float past him and remind him that the finest of pleasures is the rush of action. Living as he now lived was like reading a good book in a poor translation—a meagre entertainment for a young man who felt that he might have been an excellent linguist. He had good winters and poor winters, and while the former lasted he was sometimes the sport of a vision of virtual recovery. But this vision was dispelled some three years before the occurrence of the incidents with which this history opens: he had on that occasion remained later than usual in England and had been overtaken by bad weather before reaching Algiers. He arrived more dead than alive and lay there for several weeks between life and death. His convalescence was a miracle, but the first use he made of it was to assure himself that such miracles happen but once. He said to himself that his hour was in sight and that it behoved him to keep his eyes upon it, yet that it was also open to him to spend the interval as agreeably as might be consistent with such a preoccupation. With the prospect of losing them the simple use of his faculties became an exquisite pleasure; it seemed to him the joys of contemplation had never been sounded. He was far from the time when he had found it hard that he should be obliged to give up the idea of distinguishing himself; an idea none the less importunate for being vague and none the less delightful for having had to struggle in the same breast with bursts of inspiring self-criticism. His friends at present judged him more cheerful, and attributed it to a theory, over which they shook their heads knowingly, that he would recover his health. His serenity was but the array of wild flowers niched in his ruin.

It was very probably this sweet-tasting property of the observed thing in itself that was mainly concerned in Ralph's quickly-stirred interest in the advent of a young lady who was evidently not insipid. If he was consideringly disposed, something told him, here was occupation enough for a succession of days. It may be added, in summary fashion, that the imagination of loving—as distinguished from that of being loved—had still a place in his reduced sketch. He had only forbidden himself the riot of expression. However, he shouldn't inspire his cousin with a passion, nor would she be able, even should she try, to help him to one. "And now tell me about the young lady," he said to his mother. "What do you mean to do with her?"

Mrs. Touchett was prompt. "I mean to ask your father to invite her to stay three or four weeks at Gardencourt."

"You needn't stand on any such ceremony as that," said Ralph. "My father will ask her as a matter of course."

"I don't know about that. She's my niece; she's not his."

"Good Lord, dear mother; what a sense of property! That's all the more reason for his asking her. But after that—I mean after three months (for it's absurd asking the poor girl to remain but for three or four paltry weeks)—what do you mean to do with her?"

"I mean to take her to Paris. I mean to get her clothing."

"Ah yes, that's of course. But independently of that?"

"I shall invite her to spend the autumn with me in Florence."

"You don't rise above detail, dear mother," said Ralph. "I should like to know what you mean to do with her in a general way."

"My duty!" Mrs. Touchett declared. "I suppose you pity her very much," she added.

"No, I don't think I pity her. She doesn't strike me as inviting compassion. I think I envy her. Before being sure, however, give me a hint of where you see your duty."

"In showing her four European countries—I shall leave her the choice of two of them—and in giving her the opportunity of perfecting herself in French, which she already knows very well."

Ralph frowned a little. "That sounds rather dry—even allowing her the choice of two of the countries."

"If it's dry," said his mother with a laugh, "you can leave Isabel alone to water it! She is as good as a summer rain, any day."

"Do you mean she's a gifted being?"

"I don't know whether she's a gifted being, but she's a clever girl —with a strong will and a high temper. She has no idea of being bored."

"I can imagine that," said Ralph; and then he added abruptly: "How do you two get on?"

"Do you mean by that that I'm a bore? I don't think she finds me one. Some girls might, I know; but Isabel's too clever for that. I think I greatly amuse her. We get on because I understand her; I know the sort of girl she is. She's very frank, and I'm very frank: we know just what to expect of each other."

"Ah, dear mother," Ralph exclaimed, "one always knows what to expect of *you*! You've never surprised me but once, and that's to-day—in presenting me with a pretty cousin whose existence I had never suspected."

"Do you think her so very pretty?"

"Very pretty indeed; but I don't insist upon that. It's her general air of being some one in particular that strikes me. Who is this rare creature, and what is she? Where did you find her, and how did you make her acquaintance?"

"I found her in an old house at Albany, sitting in a dreary room on a rainy day, reading a heavy book and boring herself to death. She didn't know she was bored, but when I left her no doubt of it she seemed very grateful for the service. You may say I shouldn't have enlightened her—I should have let her alone. There's a good deal in that, but I acted conscientiously; I thought she was meant for something better. It occurred to me that it would be a kindness to take her about and introduce her to the world. She thinks she knows a great deal of it—like most American girls; but like most American girls she's ridiculously mistaken. If you want to know, I thought she would do me credit. I like to be well thought of, and for a woman of my age there's no greater convenience, in some ways, than an attractive niece. You know I had seen nothing of my sister's children for years; I disapproved entirely of the father. But I always meant to do something for them when he should have gone to his reward. I ascertained where they were to be found and, without any preliminaries, went and introduced myself. There are two others of them, both of whom are married; but I saw only the elder, who has, by the way, a very uncivil husband. The wife, whose name

is Lily, jumped at the idea of my taking an interest in Isabel; she
said it was just what her sister needed—that some one should take
an interest in her. She spoke of her as you might speak of some
young person of genius—in want of encouragement and patronage.
It may be that Isabel's a genius; but in that case I've not yet
learned her special line. Mrs. Ludlow was especially keen about my
taking her to Europe; they all regard Europe over there as a land of
emigration, of rescue, a refuge for their superfluous population.
Isabel herself seemed very glad to come, and the thing was easily
arranged. There was a little difficulty about the money-question, as
she seemed averse to being under pecuniary obligations. But she
has a small income and she supposes herself to be travelling at her
own expense."

Ralph had listened attentively to this judicious report, by which
his interest in the subject of it was not impaired. "Ah, if she's a
genius," he said, "we must find out her special line. Is it by chance
for flirting?"

"I don't think so. You may suspect that at first, but you'll be
wrong. You won't, I think, in any way, be easily right about her."

"Warburton's wrong then!" Ralph rejoicingly exclaimed. "He flat-
ters himself he has made that discovery."

His mother shook her head. "Lord Warburton won't understand
her. He needn't try."

"He's very intelligent," said Ralph; "but it's right he should be
puzzled once in a while."

"Isabel will enjoy puzzling a lord," Mrs. Touchett remarked.

Her son frowned a little. "What does she know about lords?"

"Nothing at all: that will puzzle him all the more."

Ralph greeted these words with a laugh and looked out of the
window. Then, "Are you not going down to see my father?" he
asked.

"At a quarter to eight," said Mrs. Touchett.

Her son looked at his watch. "You've another quarter of an hour
then. Tell me some more about Isabel." After which, as Mrs.
Touchett declined his invitation, declaring that he must find out for
himself, "Well," he pursued, "she'll certainly do you credit. But
won't she also give you trouble?"

"I hope not; but if she does I shall not shrink from it. I never do
that."

"She strikes me as very natural," said Ralph.

"Natural people are not the most trouble."

"No," said Ralph; "you yourself are a proof of that. You're
extremely natural, and I'm sure you have never troubled any one. It
takes trouble to do that. But tell me this; it just occurs to me. Is
Isabel capable of making herself disagreeable?"

"Ah," cried his mother, "you ask too many questions! Find that out for yourself."

His questions, however, were not exhausted. "All this time," he said, "you've not told me what you intend to do with her."

"Do with her? You talk as if she were a yard of calico. I shall do absolutely nothing with her, and she herself will do everything she chooses. She gave me notice of that."

"What you meant then, in your telegram, was that her character's independent."

"I never know what I mean in my telegrams—especially those I send from America. Clearness is too expensive. Come down to your father."

"It's not yet a quarter to eight," said Ralph.

"I must allow for his impatience," Mrs. Touchett answered.

Ralph knew what to think of his father's impatience; but, making no rejoinder, he offered his mother his arm. This put it in his power, as they descended together, to stop her a moment on the middle landing of the staircase—the broad, low, wide-armed staircase of time-blackened oak which was one of the most striking features of Gardencourt. "You've no plan of marrying her?" he smiled.

"Marrying her? I should be sorry to play her such a trick! But apart from that, she's perfectly able to marry herself. She has every facility."

"Do you mean to say she has a husband picked out?"

"I don't know about a husband, but there's a young man in Boston—!"

Ralph went on; he had no desire to hear about the young man in Boston. "As my father says, they're always engaged!"

His mother had told him that he must satisfy his curiosity at the source, and it soon became evident he should not want for occasion. He had a good deal of talk with his young kinswoman when the two had been left together in the drawing-room. Lord Warburton, who had ridden over from his own house, some ten miles distant, remounted and took his departure before dinner; and an hour after this meal was ended Mr. and Mrs. Touchett, who appeared to have quite emptied the measure of their forms, withdrew, under the valid pretext of fatigue, to their respective apartments. The young man spent an hour with his cousin; though she had been travelling half the day she appeared in no degree spent. She was really tired; she knew it, and knew she should pay for it on the morrow; but it was her habit at this period to carry exhaustion to the furthest point and confess to it only when dissimulation broke down. A fine hypocrisy was for the present possible; she was interested; she was, as she said to herself, floated. She asked Ralph to show her the pictures; there were a great many in the house, most of them of his own choosing.

The best were arranged in an oaken gallery, of charming proportions, which had a sitting-room at either end of it and which in the
evening was usually lighted. The light was insufficient to show the
pictures to advantage, and the visit might have stood over to the
morrow. This suggestion Ralph had ventured to make; but Isabel
looked disappointed—smiling still, however—and said: "If you
please I should like to see them just a little." She was eager, she
knew she was eager and now seemed so; she couldn't help it. "She
doesn't take suggestions," Ralph said to himself; but he said it without irritation; her pressure amused and even pleased him. The
lamps were on brackets, at intervals, and if the light was imperfect
it was genial. It fell upon the vague squares of rich colour and on
the faded gilding of heavy frames; it made a sheen on the polished
floor of the gallery. Ralph took a candlestick and moved about,
pointing out the things he liked; Isabel, inclining to one picture
after another, indulged in little exclamations and murmurs. She
was evidently a judge; she had a natural taste; he was struck with
that. She took a candlestick herself and held it slowly here and
there; she lifted it high, and as she did so he found himself pausing
in the middle of the place and bending his eyes much less upon the
pictures than on her presence. He lost nothing, in truth, by these
wandering glances, for she was better worth looking at than most
works of art. She was undeniably spare, and ponderably light, and
proveably tall; when people had wished to distinguish her from the
other two Miss Archers they had always called her the willowy one.
Her hair, which was dark even to blackness, had been an object of
envy to many women; her light grey eyes, a little too firm perhaps
in her graver moments, had an enchanting range of concession.
They walked slowly up one side of the gallery and down the other,
and then she said: "Well, now I know more than I did when I
began!"

"You apparently have a great passion for knowledge," her cousin
returned.

"I think I have; most girls are horridly ignorant."

"You strike me as different from most girls."

"Ah, some of them *would*—but the way they're talked to!" murmured Isabel, who preferred not to dilate just yet on herself. Then
in a moment, to change the subject, "Please tell me—isn't there a
ghost?" she went on.

"A ghost?"

"A castle-spectre, a thing that appears. We call them ghosts in
America."

"So we do here, when we see them."

"You do see them then? You ought to, in this romantic old
house."

"It's not a romantic old house," said Ralph. "You'll be disappointed if you count on that. It's a dismally prosaic one; there's no romance here but what you may have brought with you."

"I've brought a great deal; but it seems to me I've brought it to the right place."

"To keep it out of harm, certainly; nothing will ever happen to it here, between my father and me."

Isabel looked at him a moment. "Is there never any one here but your father and you?"

"My mother, of course."

"Oh, I know your mother; she's not romantic. Haven't you other people?"

"Very few."

"I'm sorry for that; I like so much to see people," said Isabel.

"Oh, we'll invite all the county to amuse you," said Ralph.

"Now you're making fun of me," the girl answered rather gravely. "Who was the gentleman on the lawn when I arrived?"

"A county neighbour; he doesn't come very often."

"I'm sorry for that; I liked him," said Isabel.

"Why, it seemed to me that you barely spoke to him," Ralph objected.

"Never mind, I like him all the same. I like your father too, immensely."

"You can't do better than that. He's the dearest of the dear."

"I'm so sorry he is ill," said Isabel.

"You must help me to nurse him; you ought to be a good nurse."

"I don't think I am; I've been told I'm not; I'm said to have too many theories. But you haven't told me about the ghost," she added.

Ralph, however, gave no heed to this observation. "You like my father and you like Lord Warburton. I infer also that you like my mother."

"I like your mother very much, because—because—" And Isabel found herself attempting to assign a reason for her affection for Mrs. Touchett.

"Ah, we never know why!" said her companion, laughing.

"I always know why," the girl answered. "It's because she doesn't expect one to like her. She doesn't care whether one does or not."

"So you adore her—out of perversity? Well, I take greatly after my mother," said Ralph.

"I don't believe you do at all. You wish people to like you, and you try to make them do it."

"Good heavens, how you see through one!" he cried with a dismay that was not altogether jocular.

"But I like you all the same," his cousin went on. "The way to clinch the matter will be to show me the ghost."

Ralph shook his head sadly. "I might show it to you, but you'd never see it. The privilege isn't given to every one; it's not enviable. It has never been seen by a young, happy, innocent person like you. You must have suffered first, have suffered greatly, have gained some miserable knowledge. In that way your eyes are opened to it. I saw it long ago," said Ralph.

"I told you just now I'm very fond of knowledge," Isabel answered.

"Yes, of happy knowledge—of pleasant knowledge. But you haven't suffered, and you're not made to suffer. I hope you'll never see the ghost!"

She had listened to him attentively, with a smile on her lips, but with a certain gravity in her eyes. Charming as he found her, she had struck him as rather presumptuous—indeed it was a part of her charm; and he wondered what she would say. "I'm not afraid, you know," she said: which seemed quite presumptuous enough.

"You're not afraid of suffering?"

"Yes, I'm afraid of suffering. But I'm not afraid of ghosts. And I think people suffer too easily," she added.

"I don't believe *you* do," said Ralph, looking at her with his hands in his pockets.

"I don't think that's a fault," she answered. "It's not absolutely necessary to suffer; we were not made for that."

"You were not, certainly."

"I'm not speaking of myself." And she wandered off a little.

"No, it isn't a fault," said her cousin. "It's a merit to be strong."

"Only, if you don't suffer they call you hard," Isabel remarked.

They passed out of the smaller drawing-room, into which they had returned from the gallery, and paused in the hall, at the foot of the staircase. Here Ralph presented his companion with her bed-room candle, which he had taken from a niche. "Never mind what they call you. When you do suffer they call you an idiot. The great point's to be as happy as possible."

She looked at him a little; she had taken her candle and placed her foot on the oaken stair. "Well," she said, "that's what I came to Europe for, to be as happy as possible. Good-night."

"Good-night! I wish you all success, and shall be very glad to contribute to it!"

She turned away, and he watched her as she slowly ascended. Then, with his hands always in his pockets, he went back to the empty drawing-room.

VI

Isabel Archer was a young person of many theories; her imagination was remarkably active. It had been her fortune to possess a finer mind than most of the persons among whom her lot was cast; to have a larger perception of surrounding facts and to care for knowledge that was tinged with the unfamiliar. It is true that among her contemporaries she passed for a young woman of extraordinary profundity; for these excellent people never withheld their admiration from a reach of intellect of which they themselves were not conscious, and spoke of Isabel as a prodigy of learning, a creature reported to have read the classic authors—in translations. Her paternal aunt, Mrs. Varian, once spread the rumour that Isabel was writing a book—Mrs. Varian having a reverence for books, and averred that the girl would distinguish herself in print. Mrs. Varian thought highly of literature, for which she entertained that esteem that is connected with a sense of privation. Her own large house, remarkable for its assortment of mosaic tables and decorated ceilings, was unfurnished with a library, and in the way of printed volumes contained nothing but half a dozen novels in paper on a shelf in the apartment of one of the Miss Varians. Practically, Mrs. Varian's acquaintance with literature was confined to *The New York Interviewer*; as she very justly said, after you had read the *Interviewer* you had lost all faith in culture. Her tendency, with this, was rather to keep the *Interviewer* out of the way of her daughters; she was determined to bring them up properly, and they read nothing at all. Her impression with regard to Isabel's labours was quite illusory; the girl had never attempted to write a book and had no desire for the laurels of authorship. She had no talent for expression and too little of the consciousness of genius; she only had a general idea that people were right when they treated her as if she were rather superior. Whether or no she were superior, people were right in admiring her if they thought her so; for it seemed to her often that her mind moved more quickly than theirs, and this encouraged an impatience that might easily be confounded with superiority. It may be affirmed without delay that Isabel was probably very liable to the sin of self-esteem; she often surveyed with complacency the field of her own nature; she was in the habit of taking for granted, on scanty evidence, that she was right; she treated herself to occasions of homage. Meanwhile her errors and delusions were frequently such as a biographer interested in preserving the dignity of his subject must shrink from specifying. Her thoughts were a tangle of vague outlines which had never been corrected by the judgement of people speaking with authority. In matters of opinion she had had her own way, and it had led her into a thousand ridiculous zigzags. At moments she discovered she was grotesquely wrong, and then she treated herself to a week of passionate humility. After this she held her head higher than ever again; for it was of no use, she had an unquenchable desire to think well of herself. She had a theory that it was only under this provision life was worth living; that one should be one of the best, should be conscious of a fine organisation (she couldn't help knowing her organisation was fine), should move in a realm of light, of natural wisdom, of happy impulse, of inspiration gracefully chronic. It was almost as unnecessary to cultivate doubt of one's self as to cultivate doubt of one's best friend: one should try to be one's own best friend and to give one's self, in this manner, distinguished company. The girl had a certain nobleness of imagination which rendered her a good many services and played her a great many tricks. She spent half her time in thinking of beauty and bravery and magnanimity; she had a fixed determination to regard the world as a place of brightness, of free expansion, of irresistible action: she held it must be detestable to be afraid or ashamed. She had an infinite hope that she should never do anything wrong. She had resented so strongly, after discovering them, her mere errors of feeling (the discovery always made her tremble as if she had escaped from a trap which might have caught her and smothered her) that the chance of inflicting a sensible injury upon another person, presented only as a contingency, caused her at moments to hold her breath. That always struck her as the worst thing that could happen to her. On the whole, reflectively, she was in no uncertainty about the things that were wrong. She had no love of their look, but when she fixed them hard she recognised them. It was wrong to be mean, to be jealous, to be false, to be cruel; she had seen very little of the evil of the world, but she had seen women who lied and who tried to hurt each other. Seeing such things had quickened her high spirit; it seemed indecent not to scorn them. Of course the danger of a high spirit was the danger of inconsistency—the danger of keeping up the flag after the place has surrendered; a sort of behaviour so crooked as to be almost a dishonour to the flag. But Isabel, who knew little of the sorts of artillery to which young women are exposed, flattered herself that such contradictions would never be noted in her own conduct. Her life should always be in harmony with the most pleasing impression she should produce; she would be what she appeared, and she would appear what she was. Sometimes she went so far as to wish that she might find herself some day in a difficult position, so that she should have the pleasure of being as heroic as the occasion demanded. Altogether, with her meagre knowledge, her inflated ideals, her confidence at once innocent and dogmatic, her temper at once exacting and indulgent, her mixture of curiosity and fastidiousness, of vivacity and indifference, her desire to look very well and to be if possible even better, her determination to see, to try, to know, her combination of the delicate, desultory, flame-like spirit and the eager and personal creature of conditions: she would be an easy victim of scientific criticism if she were not intended to awaken on the reader's part an impulse more tender and more purely expectant.

It was one of her theories that Isabel Archer was very fortunate in being independent, and that she ought to make some very enlightened use of that state. She never called it the state of solitude, much less of singleness; she thought such descriptions weak, and, besides, her sister Lily constantly urged her to come and abide. She had a friend whose acquaintance she had made shortly before her father's death, who offered so high an example of useful activity that Isabel always thought of her as a model. Henrietta Stackpole had the advantage of an admired ability; she was thoroughly launched in journalism, and her letters to the *Interviewer*, from Washington, Newport, the White Mountains and other places, were universally quoted. Isabel pronounced them with confidence "ephemeral," but she esteemed the courage, energy and good-humour of the writer, who, without parents and without property, had adopted three of the children of an infirm and widowed sister and was paying their school-bills out of the proceeds of her literary labour. Henrietta was in the van of progress and had clear-cut views on most subjects; her cherished desire had long been to come to Europe and write a series of letters to the *Interviewer* from the radical point of view—an enterprise the less difficult as she knew perfectly in advance what her opinions would be and to how many objections most European institutions lay open. When she heard that Isabel was coming she wished to start at once; thinking, naturally, that it would be delightful the two should travel together. She had been obliged, however, to postpone this enterprise. She thought Isabel a glorious creature, and had spoken of her covertly in some of her letters, though she never mentioned the fact to her friend, who would not have taken pleasure in it and was not a regular student of the *Interviewer*. Henrietta, for Isabel, was chiefly a proof that a woman might suffice to herself and be happy. Her resources were of the obvious kind; but even if one had not the journalistic talent and a genius for guessing, as Henrietta said, what the public was going to want, one was not therefore to conclude that one had no vocation, no beneficent aptitude of any sort, and resign one's self to being frivolous and hollow. Isabel was stoutly determined not to be hollow. If one should wait with the right patience one would find some happy work to one's hand. Of course, among her theories, this young lady was not without a collection of views on the subject of marriage. The first on the list was a conviction of the vulgarity of thinking too much of it. From lapsing into eagerness on this point she earnestly prayed she might be delivered; she held that a woman ought to be able to live to herself, in the absence of exceptional flimsiness, and that it was perfectly possible to be happy without the society of a more or less coarse-minded person of another sex. The girl's prayer was very sufficiently answered; something pure and proud that there was in her—something cold and dry an unappreciated suitor with a taste for analysis might have called it—had hitherto kept her from any great vanity of conjecture on the article of possible husbands. Few of the men she saw seemed worth a ruinous expenditure, and it made her smile to think that one of them should present himself as an incentive to hope and a reward of patience. Deep in her soul—it was the deepest thing there—lay a belief that if a certain light should dawn she could give herself completely; but this image, on the whole, was too formidable to be attractive. Isabel's thoughts hovered about it, but they seldom rested on it long; after a little it ended in alarms. It often seemed to her that she thought too much about herself; you could have made her colour, any day in the year, by calling her a rank egoist. She was always planning out her development, desiring her perfection, observing her progress. Her nature had, in her conceit, a certain garden-like quality, a suggestion of perfume and murmuring boughs, of shady bowers and lengthening vistas, which made her feel that introspection was, after all, an exercise in the open air, and that a visit to the recesses of one's spirit was harmless when one returned from it with a lapful of roses. But she was often reminded that there were other gardens in the world than those of her remarkable soul, and that there were moreover a great many places which were not gardens at all— only dusky pestiferous tracts, planted thick with ugliness and misery. In the current of that repaid curiosity on which she had lately been floating, which had conveyed her to this beautiful old England and might carry her much further still, she often checked herself with the thought of the thousands of people who were less happy than herself—a thought which for the moment made her fine, full consciousness appear a kind of immodesty. What should one do with the misery of the world in a scheme of the agreeable for one's self? It must be confessed that this question never held her long. She was too young, too impatient to live, too unacquainted with pain. She always returned to her theory that a young woman whom after all every one thought clever should begin by getting a general impression of life. This impression was necessary to prevent mistakes, and after it should be secured she might make the unfortunate condition of others a subject of special attention.

England was a revelation to her, and she found herself as diverted as a child at a pantomime. In her infantine excursions to Europe she had seen only the Continent, and seen it from the nursery window; Paris, not London, was her father's Mecca, and into many of his interests there his children had naturally not entered. The images of that time moreover had grown faint and remote, and the old-world quality in everything that she now saw had all the charm of strangeness. Her uncle's house seemed a picture made real;

no refinement of the agreeable was lost upon Isabel; the rich perfection of Gardencourt at once revealed a world and gratified a need.
The large, low rooms, with brown ceilings and dusky corners, the
deep embrasures and curious casements, the quiet light on dark,
polished panels, the deep greenness outside, that seemed always
peeping in, the sense of well-ordered privacy in the centre of a
"property"—a place where sounds were felicitously accidental,
where the tread was muffled by the earth itself and in the thick
mild air all friction dropped out of contact and all shrillness out of
talk—these things were much to the taste of our young lady, whose
taste played a considerable part in her emotions. She formed a fast
friendship with her uncle, and often sat by his chair when he had
had it moved out to the lawn. He passed hours in the open air, sitting with folded hands like a placid, homely household god, a god
of service, who had done his work and received his wages and was
trying to grow used to weeks and months made up only of off-days.
Isabel amused him more than she suspected—the effect she produced upon people was often different from what she supposed—
and he frequently gave himself the pleasure of making her chatter.
It was by this term that he qualified her conversation, which had
much of the "point" observable in that of the young ladies of her
country, to whom the ear of the world is more directly presented
than to their sisters in other lands. Like the mass of American girls
Isabel had been encouraged to express herself; her remarks had been
attended to; she had been expected to have emotions and opinions.
Many of her opinions had doubtless but a slender value, many of
her emotions passed away in the utterance; but they had left a trace
in giving her the habit of seeming at least to feel and think, and in
imparting moreover to her words when she was really moved that
prompt vividness which so many people had regarded as a sign of
superiority. Mr. Touchett used to think that she reminded him of
his wife when his wife was in her teens. It was because she was fresh
and natural and quick to understand, to speak—so many characteristics of her niece—that he had fallen in love with Mrs. Touchett.
He never expressed this analogy to the girl herself, however; for if
Mrs. Touchett had once been like Isabel, Isabel was not at all like
Mrs. Touchett. The old man was full of kindness for her; it was a
long time, as he said, since they had had any young life in the
house; and our rustling, quickly-moving, clear-voiced heroine was as
agreeable to his sense as the sound of flowing water. He wanted to
do something for her and wished she would ask it of him. She
would ask nothing but questions; it is true that of these she asked a
quantity. Her uncle had a great fund of answers, though her pressure sometimes came in forms that puzzled him. She questioned
him immensely about England, about the British constitution, the

English character, the state of politics, the manners and customs of the royal family, the peculiarities of the aristocracy, the way of living and thinking of his neighbours; and in begging to be enlightened on these points she usually enquired whether they corresponded with the descriptions in the books. The old man always looked at her a little with his fine dry smile while he smoothed down the shawl spread across his legs.

"The books?" he once said: "well, I don't know much about the books. You must ask Ralph about that. I've always ascertained for myself—got my information in the natural form. I never asked many questions even; I just kept quiet and took notice. Of course I've had very good opportunities—better than what a young lady would naturally have. I'm of an inquisitive disposition, though you mightn't think it if you were to watch me: however much you might watch me I should be watching you more. I've been watching these people for upwards of thirty-five years, and I don't hesitate to say that I've acquired considerable information. It's a very fine country on the whole—finer perhaps than what we give it credit for on the other side. There are several improvements I should like to see introduced; but the necessity of them doesn't seem to be generally felt as yet. When the necessity of a thing is generally felt they usually manage to accomplish it; but they seem to feel pretty comfortable about waiting till then. I certainly feel more at home among them than I expected to when I first came over; I suppose it's because I've had a considerable degree of success. When you're successful you naturally feel more at home."

"Do you suppose that if I'm successful I shall feel at home?" Isabel asked.

"I should think it very probable, and you certainly will be successful. They like American young ladies very much over here; they show them a great deal of kindness. But you mustn't feel too much at home, you know."

"Oh, I'm by no means sure it will *satisfy* me," Isabel judicially emphasised. "I like the place very much, but I'm not sure I shall like the people."

"The people are very good people; especially if you like them."

"I've no doubt they're good," Isabel rejoined; "but are they pleasant in society? They won't rob me nor beat me; but will they make themselves agreeable to me? That's what I like people to do. I don't hesitate to say so, because I always appreciate it. I don't believe they're very nice to girls; they're not nice to them in the novels."

"I don't know about the novels." said Mr. Touchett. "I believe the novels have a great deal of ability, but I don't suppose they're very accurate. We once had a lady who wrote novels staying here; she was a friend of Ralph's and he asked her down. She was very positive, quite up to everything; but she was not the sort of person you could depend on for evidence. Too free a fancy—I suppose that was it. She afterwards published a work of fiction in which she was understood to have given a representation—something in the nature of a caricature, as you might say—of my unworthy self. I didn't read it, but Ralph just handed me the book with the principal passages marked. It was understood to be a description of my conversation; American peculiarities, nasal twang, Yankee notions, stars and stripes. Well, it was not at all accurate; she couldn't have listened very attentively. I had no objection to her giving a report of my conversation, if she liked; but I didn't like the idea that she hadn't taken the trouble to listen to it. Of course I talk like an American —I can't talk like a Hottentot. However I talk, I've made them understand me pretty well over here. But I don't talk like the old gentleman in that lady's novel. He wasn't an American; we wouldn't have him over there at any price. I just mention that fact to show you that they're not always accurate. Of course, as I've no daughters, and as Mrs. Touchett resides in Florence, I haven't had much chance to notice about the young ladies. It sometimes appears as if the young women in the lower class were not very well treated; but I guess their position is better in the upper and even to some extent in the middle."

"Gracious," Isabel exclaimed; "how many classes have they? About fifty, I suppose."

"Well, I don't know that I ever counted them. I never took much notice of the classes. That's the advantage of being an American here; you don't belong to any class."

"I hope so," said Isabel. "Imagine one's belonging to an English class!"

"Well, I guess some of them are pretty comfortable—especially towards the top. But for me there are only two classes: the people I trust and the people I don't. Of those two, my dear Isabel, you belong to the first."

"I'm much obliged to you," said the girl quickly. Her way of taking compliments seemed sometimes rather dry; she got rid of them as rapidly as possible. But as regards this she was sometimes misjudged; she was thought insensible to them, whereas in fact she was simply unwilling to show how infinitely they pleased her. To show that was to show too much. "I'm sure the English are very conventional," she added.

"They've got everything pretty well fixed," Mr. Touchett admitted. "It's all settled beforehand—they don't leave it to the last moment."

"I don't like to have everything settled before-hand," said the girl. "I like more unexpectedness."

Her uncle seemed amused at her distinctness of preference. "Well, it's settled beforehand that you'll have great success," he rejoined. "I suppose you'll like that."

"I shall not have success if they're too stupidly conventional. I'm not in the least stupidly conventional. I'm just the contrary. That's what they won't like."

"No, no you're all wrong," said the old man. "You can't tell what they'll like. They're very inconsistent; that's their principal interest."

"Ah well," said Isabel, standing before her uncle with her hands clasped about the belt of her black dress and looking up and down the lawn—"that will suit me perfectly!"

VII

The two amused themselves, time and again, with talking of the attitude of the British public as if the young lady had been in a position to appeal to it; but in fact the British public remained for the present profoundly indifferent to Miss Isabel Archer, whose fortune had dropped her, as her cousin said, into the dullest house in England. Her gouty uncle received very little company, and Mrs. Touchett, not having cultivated relations with her husband's neighbours, was not warranted in expecting visits from them. She had, however, a peculiar taste; she liked to receive cards. For what is usually called social intercourse she had very little relish; but nothing pleased her more than to find her hall-table whitened with oblong morsels of symbolic pasteboard. She flattered herself that she was a very just woman, and had mastered the sovereign truth that nothing in this world is got for nothing. She had played no social part as mistress of Gardencourt, and it was not to be supposed that, in the surrounding country, a minute account should be kept of her comings and goings. But it is by no means certain that she did not feel it to be wrong that so little notice was taken of them and that her failure (really very gratuitous) to make herself important in the neighbourhood had not much to do with the acrimony of her allusions to her husband's adopted country. Isabel presently found herself in the singular situation of defending the British constitution against her aunt; Mrs. Touchett having formed the habit of sticking pins into this venerable instrument. Isabel always felt an impulse to pull out the pins; not that she imagined they inflicted any damage on the tough old parchment, but because it seemed to her her aunt might make better use of her sharpness. She was very critical herself—it was incidental to her age, her sex and her nationality; but she was very sentimental as well, and there was something in Mrs. Touchett's dryness that set her own moral fountains flowing.

"Now what's your point of view?" she asked of her aunt. "When you criticise everything here you should have a point of view. Yours doesn't seem to be American—you thought everything over there so disagreeable. When I criticise I have mine; it's thoroughly American!"

"My dear young lady," said Mrs. Touchett, "there are as many points of view in the world as there are people of sense to take them. You may say that doesn't make them very numerous! American? Never in the world; that's shockingly narrow. My point of view, thank God, is personal!"

Isabel thought this a better answer than she admitted; it was a tolerable description of her own manner of judging, but it would not have sounded well for her to say so. On the lips of a person less advanced in life and less enlightened by experience than Mrs. Touchett such a declaration would savour of immodesty, even of arrogance. She risked it nevertheless in talking with Ralph, with whom she talked a great deal and with whom her conversation was of a sort that gave a large licence to extravagance. Her cousin used, as the phrase is, to chaff her; he very soon established with her a reputation for treating everything as a joke, and he was not a man to neglect the privileges such a reputation conferred. She accused him of an odious want of seriousness, of laughing at all things, beginning with himself. Such slender faculty of reverence as he possessed centred wholly upon his father; for the rest, he exercised his wit indifferently upon his father's son, this gentleman's weak lungs, his useless life, his fantastic mother, his friends (Lord Warburton in especial), his adopted, and his native country, his charming new-found cousin. "I keep a band of music in my ante-room," he said once to her. "It has orders to play without stopping; it renders me two excellent services. It keeps the sounds of the world from reaching the private apartments, and it makes the world think that dancing's going on within." It was dance-music indeed that you usually heard when you came withing ear-shot of Ralph's band; the liveliest waltzes seemed to float upon the air. Isabel often found herself irritated by this perpetual fiddling; she would have liked to pass through the ante-room, as her cousin called it, and enter the private apartments. It mattered little that he had assured her they were a very dismal place; she would have been glad to undertake to sweep them and set them in order. It was but half-hospitality to let her remain outside; to punish him for which Isabel administered innumerable taps with the ferule of her straight young wit. It must be said that her wit was exercised to a large extent in self-defence, for her cousin amused himself with calling her "Columbia" and accusing her of a patriotism so heated that it scorched. He drew a caricature of her in which she was represented as a very pretty young woman dressed, on the lines of the prevailing fashion, in the folds of the national banner. Isabel's chief dread in life at this period of her development was that she should appear narrow-minded; what she feared next afterwards was that she should really be so. But she nevertheless made no scruple of abounding in her cousin's sense and pretending to sigh for the charms of her native land. She would be as American as it pleased him to regard her, and if he chose to laugh at her she would give him plenty of occupation. She defended England against his mother, but when Ralph sang its praises on purpose, as she said, to work her up, she found herself able to differ from him on a variety of points. In fact, the quality of this small ripe country seemed as sweet to her as the taste of an October pear; and her satisfaction was at the root of the good spirits which enabled her to take her cousin's chaff and return it in kind. If her good-humour flagged at moments it was not because she thought herself ill-used, but because she suddenly felt sorry for Ralph. It seemed to her he was talking as a blind and had little heart in what he said.

"I don't know what's the matter with you," she observed to him once; "but I suspect you're a great humbug."

"That's your privilege," Ralph answered, who had not been used to being so crudely addressed.

"I don't know what you care for; I don't think you care for anything. You don't really care for England when you praise it; you don't care for America even when you pretend to abuse it."

"I care for nothing but you, dear cousin," said Ralph.

"If I could believe even that, I should be very glad."

"Ah well, I should hope so!" the young man exclaimed.

Isabel might have believed it and not have been far from the truth. He thought a great deal about her; she was constantly present to his mind. At a time when his thoughts had been a good deal of a burden to him her sudden arrival, which promised nothing and was an open-handed gift of fate, had refreshed and quickened them, given them wings and something to fly for. Poor Ralph had been for many weeks steeped in melancholy; his outlook, habitually sombre, lay under the shadow of a deeper cloud. He had grown anxious about his father, whose gout, hitherto confined to his legs, had begun to ascend into regions more vital. The old man had been gravely ill in the spring, and the doctors had whispered to Ralph that another attack would be less easy to deal with. Just now he appeared disburdened of pain, but Ralph could not rid himself of a suspicion that this was a subterfuge of the enemy, who was waiting to take him off his guard. If the manoeuvre should succeed there would be little hope of any great resistance. Ralph had always taken for granted that his father would survive him—that his own name would be the first grimly called. The father and son had been close companions, and the idea of being left alone with the remnant of a tasteless life on his hands was not gratifying to the young man, who had always and tacitly counted upon his elder's help in making the best of a poor business. At the prospect of losing his great motive Ralph lost indeed his one inspiration. If they might die at the same time it would be all very well; but without the encouragement of his father's society he should barely have patience to await his own turn. He had not the incentive of feeling that he was indispensable to his mother; it was a rule with his mother to have no regrets. He bethought himself of course that it had been a small kindness to his father to wish that, of the two, the active rather than the passive party should know the felt wound; he remembered that the old man had always treated his own forecast of an early end as a clever fallacy, which he should be delighted to discredit so far as he might by dying first. But of the two triumphs, that of refuting a sophistical son and that of holding on a while longer to a state of being which, with all abatements, he enjoyed, Ralph deemed it no sin to hope the latter might be vouchsafed to Mr. Touchett.

These were nice questions, but Isabel's arrival put a stop to his puzzling over them. It even suggested there might be a compensation for the intolerable ennui of surviving his genial sire. He wondered whether he were harbouring "love" for this spontaneous young woman from Albany; but he judged that on the whole he was not. After he had known her for a week he quite made up his mind to this, and every day he felt a little more sure. Lord Warburton had been right about her; she was a really interesting little figure. Ralph wondered how their neighbour had found it out so soon; and then he said it was only another proof of his friend's high abilities, which he had always greatly admired. If his cousin were to be nothing more than an entertainment to him, Ralph was conscious she was an entertainment of a high order. "A character like that," he said to himself—"a real little passionate force to see at play is the finest thing in nature. It's finer than the finest work of art—than a Greek bas-relief, than a great Titian,[1] than a Gothic cathedral. It's very pleasant to be so well treated where one had least looked for it. I had never been more blue, more bored, than for a week before she came; I had never expected less that anything pleasant would happen. Suddenly I receive a Titian, by the post, to hang on my wall—a Greek bas-relief to stick over my chimney-piece. The key of a beautiful edifice is thrust into my hand, and I'm told to walk in and admire. My poor boy, you've been sadly ungrateful, and now you had better keep very quiet and never grumble again." The sentiment of these reflexions was very just; but it was not exactly true that Ralph Touchett had had a key put into his hand. His cousin was a very brilliant girl, who would take, as he

1. Tiziano Vecelli (Titian) (1477–1576), Venetian painter.

said, a good deal of knowing; but she needed the knowing, and his attitude with regard to her, though it was comtemplative and critical, was not judicial. He surveyed the edifice from the outside and admired it greatly; he looked in at the windows and received an impression of proportions equally fair. But he felt that he saw it only by glimpses and that he had not yet stood under the roof. The door was fastened, and though he had keys in his pocket he had a conviction that none of them would fit. She was intelligent and generous; it was a fine free nature; but what was she going to do with herself? This question was irregular, for with most women one had no occasion to ask it. Most women did with themselves nothing at all; they waited, in attitudes more or less gracefully passive, for a man to come that way and furnish them with a destiny. Isabel's originality was that she gave one an impression of having intentions of her own. "Whenever she executes them," said Ralph "may I be there to see!"

It devolved upon him of course to do the honours of the place. Mr. Touchett was confined to his chair, and his wife's position was that of rather a grim visitor; so that in the line of conduct that opened itself to Ralph duty and inclination were harmoniously mixed. He was not a great walker, but he strolled about the grounds with his cousin—a pastime for which the weather remained favourable with a persistency not allowed for in Isabel's somewhat lugubrious prevision of the climate; and in the long afternoons, of which the length was but the measure of her gratified eagerness, they took a boat on the river, the dear little river, as Isabel called it, where the opposite shore seemed still a part of the foreground of the landscape; or drove over the country in a phaeton—a low, capacious, thick-wheeled phaeton formerly much used by Mr. Touchett, but which he had now ceased to enjoy. Isabel enjoyed it largely and, handling the reins in a manner which approved itself to the groom as "knowing," was never weary of driving her uncle's capital horses through winding lanes and byways full of the rural incidents she had confidently expected to find; past cottages thatched and timbered, past ale-houses latticed and sanded, past patches of ancient common and glimpses of empty parks, between hedgerows made thick by midsummer. When they reached home they usually found tea had been served on the lawn and that Mrs. Touchett had not shrunk from the extremity of handing her husband his cup. But the two for the most part sat silent; the old man with his head back and his eyes closed, his wife occupied with her knitting and wearing that appearance of rare profundity with which some ladies consider the movement of their needles.

One day, however, a visitor had arrived. The two young persons, after spending an hour on the river, strolled back to the house and perceived Lord Warburton sitting under the trees and engaged in

conversation, of which even at a distance the desultory character
was appreciable, with Mrs. Touchett. He had driven over from his
own place with a portmanteau and had asked, as the father and son
often invited him to do, for a dinner and a lodging. Isabel, seeing
him for half an hour on the day of her arrival, had discovered in
this brief space that she liked him; he had indeed rather sharply registered himself on her fine sense and she had thought of him several
times. She had hoped she should see him again—hoped too that
she should see a few others. Gardencourt was not dull; the place
itself was sovereign, her uncle was more and more a sort of golden
grandfather, and Ralph was unlike any cousin she had ever encountered—her idea of cousins having tended to gloom. Then her
impressions were still so fresh and so quickly renewed that there was
as yet hardly a hint of vacancy in the view. But Isabel had need to
remind herself that she was interested in human nature and that
her foremost hope in coming abroad had been that she should see a
great many people. When Ralph said to her, as he had done several
times, "I wonder you find this endurable; you ought to see some of
the neighbours and some of our friends, because we have really got
a few, though you would never suppose it"—when he offered to
invite what he called a "lot of people" and make her acquainted
with English society, she encouraged the hospitable impulse and
promised in advance to hurl herself into the fray. Little, however,
for the present, had come of his offers, and it may be confided to
the reader that if the young man delayed to carry them out it was
because he found the labour of providing for his companion by no
means so severe as to require extraneous help. Isabel had spoken to
him very often about "specimens;" it was a word that played a considerable part in her vocabulary; she had given him to understand
that she wished to see English society illustrated by eminent cases.

"Well now, there's a specimen," he said to her as they walked up
from the riverside and he recognised Lord Warburton.

"A specimen of what?" asked the girl.

"A specimen of an English gentleman."

"Do you mean they're all like him?"

"Oh no; they're not all like him."

"He's a favourable specimen then," said Isabel; "because I'm
sure he's nice."

"Yes, he's very nice. And he's very fortunate."

The fortunate Lord Warburton exchanged a handshake with our
heroine and hoped she was very well. "But I needn't ask that," he
said, "since you've been handling the oars."

"I've been rowing a little," Isabel answered; "but how should you
know it?"

"Oh, I know *he* doesn't row; he's too lazy," said his lordship,
indicating Ralph Touchett with a laugh.

"He has a good excuse for his laziness," Isabel rejoined, lowering her voice a little.

"Ah, he has a good excuse for everything!" cried Lord Warburton, still with his sonorous mirth.

"My excuse for not rowing is that my cousin rows so well," said Ralph. "She does everything well. She touches nothing that she doesn't adorn!"

"It makes one want to be touched, Miss Archer," Lord Warburton declared.

"Be touched in the right sense and you'll never look the worse for it," said Isabel, who, if it pleased her to hear it said that her accomplishments were numerous, was happily able to reflect that such complacency was not the indication of a feeble mind, inasmuch as there were several things in which she excelled. Her desire to think well of herself had at least the element of humility that it always needed to be supported by proof.

Lord Warburton not only spent the night at Gardencourt, but he was persuaded to remain over the second day; and when the second day was ended he determined to postpone his departure till the morrow. During this period he addressed many of his remarks to Isabel, who accepted this evidence of his esteem with a very good grace. She found herself liking him extremely; the first impression he had made on her had had weight, but at the end of an evening spent in his society she scarce fell short of seeing him—though quite without luridity—as a hero of romance. She retired to rest with a sense of good fortune, with a quickened consciousness of possible felicities. "It's very nice to know two such charming people as those," she said, meaning by "those" her cousin and her cousin's friend. It must be added moreover that an incident had occurred which might have seemed to put her good-humour to the test. Mr. Touchett went to bed at half-past nine o'clock, but his wife remained in the drawing-room with the other members of the party. She prolonged her vigil for something less than an hour, and then, rising, observed to Isabel that it was time they should bid the gentlemen good-night. Isabel had as yet no desire to go to bed; the occasion wore, to her sense, a festive character, and feasts were not in the habit of terminating so early. So, without further thought, she replied, very simply—

"Need I go, dear aunt? I'll come up in half an hour."

"It's impossible I should wait for you," Mrs. Touchett answered.

"Ah, you needn't wait! Ralph will light my candle," Isabel gaily engaged.

"I'll light your candle; do let me light your candle, Miss Archer!" Lord Warburton exclaimed. "Only I beg it shall not be before midnight."

Mrs. Touchett fixed her bright little eyes upon him a moment and transferred them coldly to her niece. "You can't stay alone with the gentlemen. You're not—you're not at your blest Albany, my dear."

Isabel rose, blushing. "I wish I were," she said.

"Oh, I say, mother!" Ralph broke out.

"My dear Mrs. Touchett!" Lord Warburton murmured.

"I didn't make your country, my lord," Mrs. Touchett said majestically. "I must take it as I find it."

"Can't I stay with my own cousin?" Isabel enquired.

"I'm not aware that Lord Warburton is your cousin."

"Perhaps *I* had better go to bed!" the visitor suggested. "That will arrange it."

Mrs. Touchett gave a little look of despair and sat down again. "Oh, if it's necessary I'll stay up till midnight."

Ralph meanwhile handed Isabel her candlestick. He had been watching her; it had seemed to him her temper was involved—an accident that might be interesting. But if he had expected anything of a flare he was disappointed, for the girl simply laughed a little, nodded good-night and withdrew accompanied by her aunt. For himself he was annoyed at his mother, though he thought she was right. Above-stairs the two ladies separated at Mrs. Touchett's door. Isabel had said nothing on her way up.

"Of course you're vexed at my interfering with you," said Mrs. Touchett.

Isabel considered. "I'm not vexed, but I'm surprised—and a good deal mystified. Wasn't it proper I should remain in the drawing-room?"

"Not in the least. Young girls here—in decent houses—don't sit alone with the gentlemen late at night."

"You were very right to tell me then," said Isabel. "I don't understand it, but I'm very glad to know it."

"I shall always tell you," her aunt answered, "whenever I see you taking what seems to me too much liberty."

"Pray do; but I don't say I shall always think your remonstrance just."

"Very likely not. You're too fond of your own ways."

"Yes, I think I'm very fond of them. But I always want to know the things one shouldn't do."

"So as to do them?" asked her aunt.

"So as to choose," said Isabel.

VIII

As she was devoted to romantic effects Lord Warburton ventured to express a hope that she would come some day and see his house, a very curious old place. He extracted from Mrs. Touchett a promise that she would bring her niece to Lockleigh, and Ralph signified his willingness to attend the ladies if his father should be able to spare him. Lord Warburton assured our heroine that in the mean time his sisters would come and see her. She knew something about his sisters, having sounded him, during the hours they spent together while he was at Gardencourt, on many points connected with his family. When Isabel was interested she asked a great many questions, and as her companion was a copious talker she urged him on this occasion by no means in vain. He told her he had four sisters and two brothers and had lost both his parents. The brothers and sisters were very good people—"not particularly clever, you know," he said, "but very decent and pleasant;" and he was so good as to hope Miss Archer might know them well. One of the brothers was in the Church, settled in the family living, that of Lockleigh, which was a heavy, sprawling parish, and was an excellent fellow in spite of his thinking differently from himself on every conceivable topic. And then Lord Warburton mentioned some of the opinions held by his brother, which were opinions Isabel had often heard expressed and that she supposed to be entertained by a considerable portion of the human family. Many of them indeed she supposed she had held herself, till he assured her she was quite mistaken, that it was really impossible, that she had doubtless imagined she entertained them, but that she might depend that, if she thought them over a little, she would find there was nothing in them. When she answered that she had already thought several of the questions involved over very attentively he declared that she was only another example of what he had often been struck with—the fact that, of all the people in the world, the Americans were the most grossly superstitious. They were rank Tories and bigots, every one of them; there were no conservatives like American conservatives. Her uncle and her cousin were there to prove it; nothing could be more mediæval than many of their wives; they had ideas that people in England nowadays were ashamed to confess to; and they had the impudence moreover, said his lordship, laughing, to pretend they knew more about the needs and dangers of this poor stupid old England than he who was born in it and owned a considerable slice of it—the more shame to him! From all of which Isabel gathered that Lord Warburton was a nobleman of the newest pattern, a reformer, a radical, a contemner of ancient ways. His other brother, who was in the army in India, was rather wild and pig-headed and had not been of much use as yet but to make debts for Warburton to pay—one of the most precious privileges of an elder brother. "I don't think I shall pay any more," said her friend; "he lives a monstrous deal better than I do, enjoys unheard-of luxuries and thinks himself a much finer gentleman than I. As I'm a consistent radical I go in only for equality; I don't go in for the superiority of the younger brothers." Two of his four sisters, the second and fourth, were married, one of them having done very well, as they said, the other only so-so. The husband of the elder, Lord Haycock, was a very good fellow, but unfortunately a horrid Tory; and his wife, like all good English wives, was worse than her husband. The other had espoused a smallish squire in Norfolk and, though married but the other day, had already five children. This information and much more Lord Warburton imparted to his young American listener, taking pains to make many things clear and to lay bare to her apprehension the peculiarities of English life. Isabel was often amused at his explicitness and at the small allowance he seemed to make either for her own experience or for her imagination. "He thinks I'm a barbarian," she said, "and that I've never seen forks and spoons;" and she used to ask him artless questions for the pleasure of hearing him answer seriously. Then when he had fallen into the trap, "It's a pity you can't see me in my war-paint and feathers," she remarked; "if I had known how kind you are to the poor savages I would have brought over my native costume!" Lord Warburton had travelled through the United States and knew much more about them than Isabel; he was so good as to say that America was the most charming country in the world, but his recollections of it appeared to encourage the idea that Americans in England would need to have a great many things explained to them. "If I had only had you to explain things to me in America!" he said. "I was rather puzzled in your country; in fact I was quite bewildered, and the trouble was that the explanations only puzzled me more. You know I think they often gave me the wrong ones on purpose; they're rather clever about that over there. But when I explain you can trust me; about what I tell you there's no mistake." There was no mistake at least about his being very intelligent and cultivated and knowing almost everything in the world. Although he gave the most interesting and thrilling glimpses Isabel felt he never did it to exhibit himself, and though he had had rare chances and had tumbled in, as she put it, for high prizes, he was as far as possible from making a merit of it. He had enjoyed the best things of life, but they had not spoiled his sense of proportion. His quality was a mixture of the effect of rich experience—oh, so easily come by!—with a modesty at times almost boyish; the sweet and wholesome savour of which—it was as agreeable as something tasted—lost nothing from the addition of a tone of responsible kindness.

"I like your specimen English gentleman very much," Isabel said to Ralph after Lord Warburton had gone.

"I like him too—I love him well," Ralph returned. "But I pity him more."

Isabel looked at him askance. "Why, that seems to me his only fault—that one can't pity him a little. He appears to have every-thing, to know everything, to *be* everything."

"Oh, he's in a bad way!" Ralph insisted.

"I suppose you don't mean in health?"

"No, as to that he's detestably sound. What I mean is that he's a man with a great position who's playing all sorts of tricks with it. He doesn't take himself seriously."

"Does he regard himself as a joke?"

"Much worse; he regards himself as an imposition—as an abuse."

"Well, perhaps he is," said Isabel.

"Perhaps he is—though on the whole I don't think so. But in that case what's more pitiable than a sentient, self-conscious abuse planted by other hands, deeply rooted but aching with a sense of its injustice? For me, in his place, I could be as solemn as a statue of Buddha. He occupies a position that appeals to my imagination. Great responsibilities, great opportunities, great consideration, great wealth, great power, a natural share in the public affairs of a great country. But he's all in a muddle about himself, his position, his power, and indeed about everything in the world. He's the victim of a critical age; he has ceased to believe in himself and he doesn't know what to believe in. When I attempt to tell him (because if I were he I know very well what I should believe in) he calls me a pampered bigot. I believe he seriously thinks me an awful Philis-tine; he says I don't understand my time. I understand it certainly better than he, who can neither abolish himself as a nuisance nor maintain himself as an institution."

"He doesn't look very wretched," Isabel observed.

"Possibly not; though, being a man of a good deal of charming taste, I think he often has uncomfortable hours. But what is it to say of a being of his opportunities that he's not miserable? Besides, I believe he is."

"I don't," said Isabel.

"Well," her cousin rejoined, "if he isn't he ought to be!"

In the afternoon she spent an hour with her uncle on the lawn, where the old man sat, as usual, with his shawl over his legs and his large cup of diluted tea in his hands. In the course of conversation he asked her what she thought of their late visitor.

Isabel was prompt. "I think he's charming."

"He's a nice person," said Mr. Touchett, "but I don't recom-mend you to fall in love with him."

"I shall not do it then; I shall never fall in love but on your rec-ommendation. Moreover," Isabel added, "my cousin gives me rather a sad account of Lord Warburton."

"Oh, indeed? I don't know what there may be to say, but you must remember that Ralph *must* talk."

"He thinks your friend's too subversive—or not subversive enough! I don't quite understand which," said Isabel.

The old man shook his head slowly, smiled and put down his cup. "I don't know which either. He goes very far, but it's quite possible he doesn't go far enough. He seems to want to do away with a good many things, but he seems to want to remain himself. I suppose that's natural, but it's rather inconsistent."

"Oh, I hope he'll remain himself," said Isabel. "If he were to be done away with his friends would miss him sadly."

"Well, said the old man, "I guess he'll stay and amuse his friends. I should certainly miss him very much here at Gardencourt. He always amuses me when he comes over, and I think he amuses himself as well. There's a considerable number like him, round in society; they're very fashionable just now. I don't know what they're trying to do—whether they're trying to get up a revolution. I hope at any rate they'll put it off till after I'm gone. You see they want to disestablish[1] everything; but I'm a pretty big landowner here, and I don't want to be disestablished. I wouldn't have come over if I had thought they were going to behave like that," Mr. Touchett went on with expanding hilarity. "I came over because I thought England was a safe country. I call it a regular fraud if they are going to introduce any considerable changes; there'll be a large number disappointed in that case."

"Oh, I do hope they'll make a revolution!" Isabel exclaimed. "I should delight in seeing a revolution."

"Let me see," said her uncle, with a humorous intention; "I forget whether you're on the side of the old or on the side of the new. I've heard you take such opposite views."

"I'm on the side of both. I guess I'm a little on the side of everything. In a revolution—after it was well begun—I think I should be a high, proud loyalist. One sympathises more with them, and they've a chance to behave so exquisitely. I mean so picturesquely."

"I don't know that I understand what you mean by behaving picturesquely, but it seems to me that you do that always, my dear."

"Oh, you lovely man, if I could believe that!" the girl interrupted.

"I'm afraid, after all, you won't have the pleasure of going gracefully to the guillotine here just now," Mr. Touchett went on. "If you want to see a big outbreak you must pay us a long visit. You see, when you come to the point it wouldn't suit them to be taken at their word."

"Of whom are you speaking?"

"Well, I mean Lord Warburton and his friends—the radicals of

---

1. To alter the status of something established by authority or general acceptance. Often, it meant depriving the church of official government support.

the upper class. Of course I only know the way it strikes me. They talk about the changes, but I don't think they quite realise. You and I, you know, we know what it is to have lived under democratic institutions: I always thought them very comfortable, but I was used to them from the first. And then I ain't a lord; you're a lady, my dear, but I ain't a lord. Now over here I don't think it quite comes home to them. It's a matter of every day and every hour, and I don't think many of them would find it as pleasant as what they've got. Of course if they want to try, it's their own business; but I expect they won't try very hard."

"Don't you think they're sincere?" Isabel asked.

"Well, they want to *feel* earnest," Mr. Touchett allowed; "but it seems as if they took it out in theories mostly. Their radical views are a kind of amusement; they've got to have some amusement, and they might have coarser tastes than that. You see they're very luxurious, and these progressive ideas are about their biggest luxury. They make them feel moral and yet don't damage their position. They think a great deal of their position; don't let one of them ever persuade you he doesn't, for if you were to proceed on that basis you'd be pulled up very short."

Isabel followed her uncle's argument, which he unfolded with his quaint distinctness, most attentively, and though she was unacquainted with the British aristocracy she found it in harmony with her general impressions of human nature. But she felt moved to put in a protest on Lord Warburton's behalf. "I don't believe Lord Warburton's a humbug; I don't care what the others are. I should like to see Lord Warburton put to the test."

"Heaven deliver me from my friends!" Mr. Touchett answered. "Lord Warburton's a very amiable young man—a very fine young man. He has a hundred thousand a year. He owns fifty thousand acres of the soil of this little island and ever so many other things besides. He has half a dozen houses to live in. He has a seat in Parliament as I have one at my own dinner-table. He has elegant tastes—cares for literature, for art, for science, for charming young ladies. The most elegant is his taste for the new views. It affords him a great deal of pleasure—more perhaps than anything else, except the young ladies. His old house over there—what does he call it, Lockleigh?—is very attractive; but I don't think it's as pleasant as this. That doesn't matter, however—he has so many others. His views don't hurt any one as far as I can see; they certainly don't hurt himself. And if there were to be a revolution he would come off very easily. They wouldn't touch him, they'd leave him as he is: he's too much liked."

"Ah, he couldn't be a martyr even if he wished!" Isabel sighed. "That's a very poor position."

"He'll never be a martyr unless you make him one," said the old man.

Isabel shook her head; there might have been something laughable in the fact that she did it with a touch of melancholy. "I shall never make any one a martyr."

"You'll never be one, I hope."

"I hope not. But you don't pity Lord Warburton then as Ralph does?"

Her uncle looked at her a while with genial acuteness. "Yes, I do, after all!"

IX

The two Misses Molyneux, this nobleman's sisters, came presently to call upon her, and Isabel took a fancy to the young ladies, who appeared to her to show a most original stamp. It is true that when she described them to her cousin by that term he declared that no epithet could be less applicable than this to the two Misses Molyneux, since there were fifty thousand young women in England who exactly resembled them. Deprived of this advantage, however, Isabel's visitors retained that of an extreme sweetness and shyness of demeanour, and of having, as she thought, eyes like the balanced basins, the circles of "ornamental water," set, in parterres,[1] among the geraniums.

"They're not morbid, at any rate, whatever they are," our heroine said to herself; and she deemed this a great charm, for two or three of the friends of her girlhood had been regrettably open to the charge (they would have been so nice without it), to say nothing of Isabel's having occasionally suspected it as a tendency of her own. The Misses Molyneux were not in their first youth, but they had bright, fresh complexions and something of the smile of childhood. Yes, their eyes, which Isabel admired, were round, quiet and contented, and their figures, also of a generous roundness, were encased in sealskin jackets. Their friendliness was great, so great that they were almost embarrassed to show it; they seemed somewhat afraid of the young lady from the other side of the world and rather looked than spoke their good wishes. But they made it clear to her that they hoped she would come to luncheon at Lockleigh, where they lived with their brother, and then they might see her very, very often. They wondered if she wouldn't come over some day and sleep: they were expecting some people on the twenty-ninth, so perhaps she would come while the people were there.

"I'm afraid it isn't any one very remarkable," said the elder sister; "but I dare say you'll take us as you find us."

1. Areas and paths devoted to ornamental flower beds.

"I shall find you delightful; I think you're enchanting just as you are,"replied Isabel, who often praised profusely.

Her visitors flushed, and her cousin told her, after they were gone, that if she said such things to those poor girls they would think she was in some wild, free manner practising on them: he was sure it was the first time they had been called enchanting.

"I can't help it," Isabel answered. "I think it's lovely to be so quiet and reasonable and satisfied. I should like to be like that."

"Heaven forbid!" cried Ralph with ardour.

"I mean to try and imitate them," said Isabel. "I want very much to see them at home."

She had this pleasure a few days later, when, with Ralph and his mother, she drove over to Lockleigh. She found the Misses Molyneux sitting in a vast drawing-room (she perceived afterwards it was one of several) in a wilderness of faded chintz; they were dressed on this occasion in black velveteen. Isabel liked them even better at home than she had done at Gardencourt, and was more than ever struck with the fact that they were not morbid. It had seemed to her before that if they had a fault it was a want of play of mind; but she presently saw they were capable of deep emotion. Before luncheon she was alone with them for some time, on one side of the room, while Lord Warburton, at a distance, talked to Mrs. Touchett.

"Is it true your brother's such a great radical?" Isabel asked. She knew it was true, but we have seen that her interest in human nature was keen, and she had a desire to draw the Misses Molyneux out.

"Oh dear, yes; he's immensely advanced," said Mildred, the younger sister.

"At the same time Warburton's very reasonable," Miss Molyneux observed.

Isabel watched him a moment at the other side of the room; he was clearly trying hard to make himself agreeable to Mrs. Touchett. Ralph had met the frank advances of one of the dogs before the fire that the temperature of an English August, in the ancient expanses, had not made an impertinence. "Do you suppose your brother's sincere?" Isabel enquired with a smile.

"Oh, he must be, you know!" Mildred exclaimed quickly, while the elder sister gazed at our heroine in silence.

"Do you think he would stand the test?"

"The test?"

"I mean for instance having to give up all this."

"Having to give up Lockleigh?" said Miss Molyneux, finding her voice.

"Yes, and the other places; what are they called?"

The two sisters exchanged an almost frightened glance. "Do you mean—do you mean on account of the expense?" the younger one asked.

"I dare say he might let one or two of his houses," said the other.

"Let them for nothing?" Isabel demanded.

"I can't fancy his giving up his property," said Miss Molyneux.

"Ah, I'm afraid he is an impostor!" Isabel returned. "Don't you think it's a false position?"

Her companions, evidently, had lost themselves. "My brother's position?" Miss Molyneux enquired.

"It's thought a very good position," said the younger sister. "It's the first position in this part of the county."

"I dare say you think me very irreverent," Isabel took occasion to remark. "I suppose you revere your brother and are rather afraid of him."

"Of course one looks up to one's brother," said Miss Molyneux simply.

"If you do that he must be very good—because you, evidently, are beautifully good."

"He's most kind. It will never be known, the good he does."

"His ability is known," Mildred added; "every one thinks it's immense."

"Oh, I can see that," said Isabel. "But if I were he I should wish to fight to the death: I mean for the heritage of the past. I should hold it tight."

"I think one ought to be liberal," Mildred argued gently. "We've always been so, even from the earliest times."

"Ah well," said Isabel, "you've made a great success of it; I don't wonder you like it. I see you're very fond of crewels."

When Lord Warburton showed her the house, after luncheon, it seemed to her a matter of course that it should be a noble picture. Within, it had been a good deal modernised—some of its best points had lost their purity; but as they saw it from the gardens, a stout grey pile, of the softest, deepest, most weather-fretted hue, rising from a broad, still moat, it affected the young visitor as a castle in a legend. The day was cool and rather lustreless; the first note of autumn had been struck, and the watery sunshine rested on the walls in blurred and desultory gleams, washing them, as it were, in places tenderly chosen, where the ache of antiquity was keenest. Her host's brother, the Vicar, had come to luncheon, and Isabel had had five minutes' talk with him—time enough to institute a search for a rich ecclesiasticism and give it up as vain. The marks of the Vicar of Lockleigh were a big, athletic figure, a candid, natural countenance, a capacious appetite and a tendency to indiscriminate laughter. Isabel learned afterwards from her cousin that before taking orders he had been a mighty wrestler and that he was still, on occasion—in the privacy of the family circle as it were—quite capable of flooring his man. Isabel liked him—she was in the mood for liking everything; but her imagination was a good deal taxed to think of him as a source of spiritual aid. The whole party, on leaving lunch, went to walk in the grounds; but Lord Warburton exercised some ingenuity in engaging his least familiar guest in a stroll apart from the others.

"I wish you to see the place properly, seriously," he said. "You can't do so if your attention is distracted by irrelevant gossip." His own conversation (though he told Isabel a good deal about the house, which had a very curious history) was not purely archæological; he reverted at intervals to matters more personal—matters personal to the young lady as well as to himself. But at last, after a pause of some duration, returning for a moment to their ostensible theme, "Ah, well," he said, "I'm very glad indeed you like the old barrack. I wish you could see more of it—that you could stay here a while. My sisters have taken an immense fancy to you—if that would be any inducement."

"There's no want to inducements," Isabel answered; "but I'm afraid I can't make engagements. I'm quite in my aunt's hands."

"Ah, pardon me if I say I don't exactly believe that. I'm pretty sure you can do whatever you want."

"I'm sorry if I make that impression on you; I don't think it's a nice impression to make."

"It has the merit of permitting me to hope." And Lord Warburton paused a moment.

"To hope what?"

"That in future I may see you often."

"Ah," said Isabel, "to enjoy that pleasure I needn't be so terribly emancipated."

"Doubtless not; and yet, at the same time, I don't think your uncle likes me."

"You're very much mistaken. I've heard him speak very highly of you."

"I'm glad you have talked about me," said Lord Warburton. "But, I nevertheless don't think he'd like me to keep coming to Gardencourt."

"I can't answer for my uncle's tastes," the girl rejoined, "though I ought as far as possible to take them into account. But for myself I shall be very glad to see you."

"Now that's what I like to hear you say. I'm charmed when you say that."

"You're easily charmed, my lord," said Isabel.

"No, I'm not easily charmed!" And then he stopped a moment. "But you've charmed me, Miss Archer."

These words were uttered with an indefinable sound which startled the girl; it struck her as the prelude to something grave: she had heard the sound before and she recognised it. She had no wish, however, that for the moment such a prelude should have a sequel, and she said as gaily as possible and as quickly as an appreciable degree of agitation would allow her: "I'm afraid there's no prospect of my being able to come here again."

"Never?" said Lord Warburton.

"I won't say 'never'; I should feel very melodramatic."

"May I come and see you then some day next week?"

"Most assuredly. What is there to prevent it?"

"Nothing tangible. But with you I never feel safe. I've a sort of sense that you're always summing people up."

"You don't of necessity lose by that."

"It's very kind of you to say so; but, even if I gain, stern justice is not what I most love. Is Mrs. Touchett going to take you abroad?"

"I hope so."

"Is England not good enough for you?"

"That's a very Machiavellian speech; it doesn't deserve an answer. I want to see as many countries as I can."

"Then you'll go on judging, I suppose."

"Enjoying, I hope, too."

"Yes, that's what you enjoy most; I can't make out what you're up to," said Lord Warburton. "You strike me as having mysterious purposes—vast designs."

"You're so good as to have a theory about me which I don't at all fill out. Is there anything mysterious in a purpose entertained and executed every year, in the most public manner, by fifty thousand of my fellow-countrymen—the purpose of improving one's mind by foreign travel?"

"You can't improve your mind, Miss Archer," her companion declared. "It's already a most formidable instrument. It looks down on us all; it despises us."

"Despises you? You're making fun of me," said Isabel seriously.

"Well, you think us 'quaint'—that's the same thing. I won't be thought 'quaint,' to begin with; I'm not so in the least. I protest."

"That protest is one of the quaintest things I've ever heard," Isabel answered with a smile.

Lord Warburton was briefly silent. "You judge only from the outside—you don't care," he said presently. "You only care to amuse yourself." The note she had heard in his voice a moment before reappeared, and mixed with it now was an audible strain of bitterness—a bitterness so abrupt and inconsequent that the girl was afraid she had hurt him. She had often heard that the English are a highly eccentric people, and she had even read in some ingenious author that they are at bottom the most romantic of races.

Was Lord Warburton suddenly turning romantic—was he going to make her a scene, in his own house, only the third time they had met? She was reassured quickly enough by her sense of his great good manners, which was not impaired by the fact that he had already touched the furthest limit of good taste in expressing his admiration of a young lady who had confided in his hospitality. She was right in trusting to his good manners, for he presently went on, laughing a little and without a trace of the accent that had discomposed her: "I don't mean of course that you amuse yourself with trifles. You select great materials; the foibles, the afflictions of human nature, the peculiarities of nations!"

"As regards that," said Isabel, "I should find in my own nation entertainment for a lifetime. But we've a long drive, and my aunt will soon wish to start." She turned back toward the others and Lord Warburton walked beside her in silence. But before they reached the others, "I shall come and see you next week," he said.

She had received an appreciable shock, but as it died away she felt that she couldn't pretend to herself that it was altogether a painful one. Nevertheless she made answer to his declaration, coldly enough, "Just as you please." And her coldness was not the calculation of her effect—a game she played in a much smaller degree than would have seemed probable to many critics. It came from a certain fear.

go to Pg 90 x

The day after her visit to Lockleigh she received a note from her friend Miss Stackpole—a note of which the envelope, exhibiting in conjunction the postmark of Liverpool and the neat calligraphy of the quick-fingered Henrietta, caused her some liveliness of emotion. "Here I am, my lovely friend," Miss Stackpole wrote; "I managed to get off at last. I decided only the night before I left New York—the *Interviewer* having come round to my figure. I put a few things into a bag, like a veteran journalist, and came down to the steamer in a street-car. Where are you and where can we meet? I suppose you're visiting at some castle or other and have already acquired the correct accent. Perhaps even you have married a lord; I almost hope you have, for I want some introductions to the first people and shall count on you for a few. The *Interviewer* wants some light on the nobility. My first impressions (of the people at large) are not rose-coloured; but I wish to talk them over with you, and you know that, whatever I am, at least I'm not superficial. I've also something very particular to tell you. Do appoint a meeting as quickly as you can; come to London (I should like so much to visit the sights with you) or else let me come to you, *wherever you are.* I will do so with pleasure; for you know everything interests me and I wish to see as much as possible of the inner life."

Isabel judged best not to show this letter to her uncle; but she acquainted him with its purport, and, as she expected, he begged her instantly to assure Miss Stackpole, in his name, that he should be delighted to receive her at Gardencourt. "Though she's a literary lady," he said, "I suppose that, being an American, she won't show me up, as that other one did. She has seen others like me."

"She has seen no other so delightful!" Isabel answered; but she was not altogether at ease about Henrietta's reproductive instincts, which belonged to that side of her friend's character which she regarded with least complacency. She wrote to Miss Stackpole, however, that she would be very welcome under Mr. Touchett's roof; and this alert young woman lost no time in announcing her prompt approach. She had gone up to London, and it was from that centre that she took the train for the station nearest to Gardencourt, where Isabel and Ralph were in waiting to receive her.

"Shall I love her or shall I hate her?" Ralph asked while they moved along the platform.

"Whichever you do will matter very little to her," said Isabel. "She doesn't care a straw what men think of her."

"As a man I'm bound to dislike her then. She must be a kind of monster. Is she very ugly?"

"No, she's decidedly pretty."

"A female interviewer—a reporter in petticoats? I'm very curious to see her," Ralph conceded.

"It's very easy to laugh at her but it is not easy to be as brave as she."

"I should think not; crimes of violence and attacks on the person require more or less pluck. Do you suppose she'll interview *me*?"

"Never in the world. She'll not think you of enough importance."

"You'll see," said Ralph. "She'll send a description of us all, including Bunchie, to her newspaper."

"I shall ask her not to," Isabel answered.

"You think she's capable of it then?"

"Perfectly."

"And yet you've made her your bosom-friend?"

"I've not made her my bosom-friend; but I like her in spite of her faults."

"Ah well," said Ralph, "I'm afraid I shall dislike her in spite of her merits."

"You'll probably fall in love with her at the end of three days."

"And have my love-letters published in the *Interviewer*? Never!" cried the young man.

The train presently arrived, and Miss Stackpole, promptly descending, proved, as Isabel had promised, quite delicately, even though rather provincially, fair. She was a neat, plump person, of medium stature, with a round face, a small mouth, a delicate complexion, a bunch of light brown ringlets at the back of her head and a peculiarly open, surprised-looking eye. The most striking point in her appearance was the remarkable fixedness of this organ, which rested without impudence or defiance, but as if in conscientious exercise of a natural right, upon every object it happened to encounter. It rested in this manner upon Ralph himself, a little arrested by Miss Stackpole's gracious and comfortable aspect, which hinted that it wouldn't be so easy as he had assumed to disapprove of her. She rustled, she shimmered, in fresh, dove-coloured draperies, and Ralph saw at a glance that she was as crisp and new and comprehensive as a first issue before the folding. From top to toe she had probably no misprint. She spoke in a clear, high voice—a voice not rich but loud; yet after she had taken her place with her companions in Mr. Touchett's carriage she struck him as not all in the large type, the type of horrid "headings," that he had expected. She answered the enquiries made to her by Isabel, however, and in which the young man ventured to join, with copious lucidity; and later, in the library at Gardencourt, when she had made the acquaintance of Mr. Touchett (his wife not having thought it necessary to appear) did more to give the measure of her confidence in her powers.

"Well, I should like to know whether you consider yourselves American or English," she broke out. "If once I knew I could talk to you accordingly."

"Talk to us anyhow and we shall be thankful," Ralph liberally answered.

She fixed her eyes on him, and there was something in their character that reminded him of large polished buttons—buttons that might have fixed the elastic loops of some tense receptacle: he seemed to see the reflection of surrounding objects on the pupil. The expression of a button is not usually deemed human, but there was something in Miss Stackpole's gaze that made him, as a very modest man, feel vaguely embarrassed—less inviolate, more dishonoured, than he liked. This sensation, it must be added, after he had spent a day or two in her company, sensibly diminished, though it never wholly lapsed. "I don't suppose that you're going to undertake to persuade me that *you're* an American," she said.

"To please you I'll be an Englishman, I'll be a Turk!"

"Well, if you can change about that way you're very welcome," Miss Stackpole returned.

"I'm sure you undertand everything and that differences of nationality are no barrier to you," Ralph went on.

Miss Stackpole gazed at him still. "Do you mean the foreign languages?"

"The languages are nothing. I mean the spirit—the genius."

"I'm not sure that I understand you," said the correspondent of the *Interviewer*; "but I expect I shall before I leave."

"He's what's called a cosmopolite," Isabel suggested.

"That means he's a little of everything and not much of any. I must say I think patriotism is like charity—it begins at home."

"Ah, but where does home begin, Miss Stackpole?" Ralph enquired.

"I don't know where it begins, but I know where it ends. It ended a long time before I got here."

"Don't you like it over here?" asked Mr. Touchett with his aged, innocent voice.

"Well, sir, I haven't quite made up my mind what ground I shall take. I feel a good deal cramped. I felt it on the journey from Liverpool to London."

"Perhaps you were in a crowded carriage," Ralph suggested.

"Yes, but it was crowded with friends—a party of Americans whose acquaintance I had made upon the steamer; a lovely group from Little Rock, Arkansas. In spite of that I felt cramped—I felt something pressing upon me; I couldn't tell what it was. I felt at the very commencement as if I were not going to accord with the atmosphere. But I suppose I shall make my own atmosphere. That's the true way—then you can breathe. Your surroundings seem very attractive."

"Ah, we too are a lovely group!" said Ralph. "Wait a little and you'll see."

Miss Stackpole showed every disposition to wait and evidently was prepared to make a considerable stay at Gardencourt. She occupied herself in the mornings with literary labour; but in spite of this Isabel spent many hours with her friend, who, once her daily task performed, deprecated, in fact defied, isolation. Isabel speedily found occasion to desire her to desist from celebrating the charms of their common sojourn in print, having discovered, on the second morning of Miss Stackpole's visit, that she was engaged on a letter to the *Interviewer*, of which the title, in her exquisitely neat and legible hand (exactly that of the copybooks which our heroine remembered at school) was "Americans and Tudors—Glimpses of Gardencourt." Miss Stackpole, with the best conscience in the world, offered to read her letter to Isabel, who immediately put in her protest.

"I don't think you ought to do that. I don't think you ought to describe the place."

Henrietta gazed at her as usual. "Why, it's just what the people want, and it's a lovely place."

"It's too lovely to be put in the newspapers, and it's not what my uncle wants."

"Don't you believe that!" cried Henrietta. "They're always delighted afterwards."

"My uncle won't be delighted—nor my cousin either. They'll consider it a breach of hospitality."

Miss Stackpole showed no sense of confusion; she simply wiped her pen, very neatly, upon an elegant little implement which she kept for the purpose, and put away her manuscript. "Of course if you don't approve I won't do it; but I sacrifice a beautiful subject."

"There are plenty of other subjects, there are subjects all round you. We'll take some drives; I'll show you some charming scenery."

"Scenery's not my department; I always need a human interest. You know I'm deeply human, Isabel; I always was," Miss Stackpole rejoined. "I was going to bring in your cousin—the alienated American. There's a great demand just now for the alienated American, and your cousin's a beautiful specimen. I should have handled him severely."

"He would have died of it!" Isabel exclaimed. "Not of the severity, but of the publicity."

"Well, I should have liked to kill him a little. And I should have delighted to do your uncle, who seems to me a much nobler type—the American faithful still. He's a grand old man; I don't see how he can object to my paying him honour."

Isabel looked at her companion in much wonderment; it struck her as strange that a nature in which she found so much to esteem should break down so in spots. "My poor Henrietta," she said, "you've no sense of privacy."

Henrietta coloured deeply, and for a moment her brilliant eyes were suffused, while Isabel found her more than ever inconsequent. "You do me great injustice," said Miss Stackpole with dignity. "I've never written a word about myself!"

"I'm very sure of that; but it seems to me one should be modest for others also!"

"Ah, that's very good!" cried Henrietta, seizing her pen again. "Just let me make a note of it and I'll put it in somewhere." She was a thoroughly good-natured woman, and half an hour later she was in as cheerful a mood as should have been looked for in a newspaper-lady in want of matter. "I've promised to do the social side," she said to Isabel; "and how can I do it unless I get ideas? If I can't describe this place don't you know some place I *can* describe?" Isabel promised she would bethink herself, and the next day, in conversation with her friend, she happened to mention her visit to Lord Warburton's ancient house. "Ah, you must take me there—that's just the place for me!" Miss Stackpole cried. "I must get a glimpse of the nobility."

"I can't take you," said Isabel; "but Lord Warburton's coming here, and you'll have a chance to see him and observe him. Only if you intend to repeat his conversation I shall certainly give him warning."

"Don't do that," her companion pleaded; "I want him to be natural."

"An Englishman's never so natural as when he's holding his tongue," Isabel declared.

It was not apparent, at the end of three days, that her cousin had, according to her prophecy, lost his heart to their visitor, though he had spent a good deal of time in her society. They strolled about the park together and sat under the trees, and in the afternoon, when it was delightful to float along the Thames, Miss Stackpole occupied a place in the boat in which hitherto Ralph had had but a single companion. Her presence proved somehow less irreducible to soft particles than Ralph had expected in the natural perturbation of his sense of the perfect solubility of that of his cousin; for the correspondent of the *Interviewer* prompted mirth in him, and he had long since decided that the *crescendo* of mirth should be the flower of his declining days. Henrietta, on her side, failed a little to justify Isabel's declaration with regard to her indifference to masculine opinion; for poor Ralph appeared to have presented himself to her as an irritating problem, which it would be almost immoral not to work out.

"What does he do for a living?" she asked of Isabel the evening of her arrival. "Does he go round all day with his hands in his pockets?"

"He does nothing," smiled Isabel; "he's a gentleman of large leisure."

"Well, I call that a shame—when I have to work like a car-conductor," Miss Stackpole replied. "I should like to show him up."

"He's in wretched health; he's quite unfit for work," Isabel urged.

"Pshaw! don't you believe it. I work when I'm sick," cried her friend. Later, when she stepped into the boat on joining the water-party, she remarked to Ralph that she supposed he hated her and would like to drown her.

"Ah no," said Ralph, "I keep my victims for a slower torture. And you'd be such an interesting one!"

"Well, you do torture me; I may say that. But I shock all your prejudices; that's one comfort."

"My prejudices? I haven't a prejudice to bless myself with. There's intellectual poverty for you."

"The more shame to you; I've some delicious ones. Of course I spoil your flirtation, or whatever it is you call it, with your cousin, but I don't care for that, as I render her the service of drawing you out. She'll see how thin you are."

"Ah, do draw me out!" Ralph exclaimed. "So few people will take the trouble."

Miss Stackpole, in this undertaking, appeared to shrink from no effort; resorting largely, whenever the opportunity offered, to the natural expedient of interrogation. On the following day the weather was bad, and in the afternoon the young man, by way of providing indoor amusement, offered to show her the pictures. Henrietta strolled through the long gallery in his society, while he pointed out its principal ornaments and mentioned the painters and subjects. Miss Stackpole looked at the pictures in perfect silence, committing herself to no opinion, and Ralph was gratified by the fact that she delivered herself of none of the little ready-made ejaculations of delight of which the visitors to Gardencourt were so frequently lavish. This young lady indeed, to do her justice, was but little addicted to the use of conventional terms; there was something earnest and inventive in her tone, which at times, in its strained deliberation, suggested a person of high culture speaking a foreign language. Ralph Touchett subsequently learned that she had at one time officiated as art-critic to a journal of the other world; but she appeared, in spite of this fact, to carry in her pocket none of the small change of admiration. Suddenly, just after he had called her attention to a charming Constable,[1] she turned and looked at him as if he himself had been a picture.

"Do you always spend your time like this?" she demanded.

"I seldom spend it so agreeably."

"Well, you know what I mean—without any regular occupation."

"Ah," said Ralph, "I'm the idlest man living."

Miss Stackpole directed her gaze to the Constable again, and Ralph bespoke her attention for a small Lancret[2] hanging near it, which represented a gentleman in a pink doublet and hose and a ruff, leaning against the pedestal of the statue of a nymph in a garden and playing the guitar to two ladies seated on the grass. "That's my ideal of a regular occupation," he said.

Miss Stackpole turned to him again, and, though her eyes had rested upon the picture, he saw she had missed the subject. She was thinking of something much more serious. "I don't see how you can reconcile it to your conscience."

"My dear lady, I *have* no conscience!"

"Well, I advise you to cultivate one. You'll need it the next time you go to America."

"I shall probably never go again."

"Are you ashamed to show yourself?"

1. John Constable (1776–1837), English painter known for landscapes and pastoral scenes.
2. Nicholas Lancret (1690–1743), French painter, whom James thought inferior to his more elegant contemporary, Watteau (*The Painter's Eye* [London, 1956], p. 76). [1st ed.: "Watteau."]

Ralph meditated with a mild smile. "I suppose that if one has no conscience one has no shame."

"Well, you've got plenty of assurance," Henrietta declared. "Do you consider it right to give up your country?"

"Ah, one doesn't give up one's country any more than one gives up one's grandmother. They're both antecedent to choice—elements of one's composition that are not to be eliminated."

"I suppose that means that you've tried and been worsted. What do they think of you over here?"

"They delight in me."

"That's because you truckle to them."

"Ah, set it down a little to my natural charm!" Ralph sighed.

"I don't know anything about your natural charm. If you've got any charm it's quite unnatural. It's wholly acquired—or at least you've tried hard to acquire it, living over here. I don't say you've succeeded. It's a charm that I don't appreciate, anyway. Make yourself useful in some way, and then we'll talk about it."

"Well, now, tell me what I shall do," said Ralph.

"Go right home, to begin with."

"Yes, I see. And then?"

"Take right hold of something."

"Well, now, what sort of thing?"

"Anything you please, so long as you take hold. Some new idea, some big work."

"Is it very difficult to take hold?" Ralph enquired.

"Not if you put your heart into it."

"Ah, my heart," said Ralph. "If it depends upon my heart—!"

"Haven't you got a heart?"

"I had one a few days ago, but I've lost it since."

"You're not serious," Miss Stackpole remarked; "that's what's the matter with you." But for all this, in a day or two, she again permitted him to fix her attention and on the later occasion assigned a different cause to her mysterious perversity. "I know what's the matter with you, Mr. Touchett," she said. "You think you're too good to get married."

"I thought so till I knew you, Miss Stackpole." Ralph answered; "and then I suddenly changed my mind."

"Oh pshaw!" Henrietta groaned.

"Then it seemed to me," said Ralph, "that I was not good enough."

"It would improve you. Besides, it's your duty."

"Ah," cried the young man, "one has so many duties! Is that a duty too?"

"Of course it is—did you never know that before? It's every one's duty to get married."

Ralph meditated a moment; he was disappointed. There was

something in Miss Stackpole he had begun to like; it seemed to him that if she was not a charming woman she was at least a very good "sort." She was wanting in distinction, but, as Isabel had said, she was brave: she went into cages, she flourished lashes, like a spangled lion-tamer. He had not supposed her to be capable of vulgar arts, but these last words struck him as a false note. When a marriageable young woman urges matrimony on an unencumbered young man the most obvious explanation of her conduct is not the altruistic impulse.

"Ah, well now, there's a good deal to be said about that," Ralph rejoined.

"There may be, but that's the principal thing. I must say I think it looks very exclusive, going round all alone, as if you thought no woman was good enough for you. Do you think you're better than any one else in the world? In America it's usual for people to marry."

"If it's my duty," Ralph asked, "is it not, by analogy, yours as well?"

Miss Stackpole's ocular surfaces unwinkingly caught the sun. "Have you the fond hope of finding a flaw in my reasoning? Of course I've as good a right to marry as any one else."

"Well then," said Ralph, "I won't say it vexes me to see you single. It delights me rather."

"You're not serious yet. You never will be."

"Shall you not believe me to be so on the day I tell you I desire to give up the practice of going round alone?"

Miss Stackpole looked at him for a moment in a manner which seemed to announce a reply that might technically be called encouraging. But to his great surprise this expression suddenly resolved itself into an appearance of alarm and even of resentment. "No, not even then," she answered dryly. After which she walked away.

"I've not conceived a passion for your friend," Ralph said that evening to Isabel. "though we talked some time this morning about it."

"And you said something she didn't like," the girl replied.

Ralph stared. "Has she complained of me?"

"She told me she thinks there's something very low in the tone of Europeans towards women."

"Does she call me a European?"

"One of the worst. She told me you had said to her something that an American never would have said. But she didn't repeat it."

Ralph treated himself to a luxury of laughter. "She's an extraordinary combination. Did she think I was making love to her?"

"No; I believe even Americans do that. But she apparently thought you mistook the intention of something she had said, and put an unkind construction on it."

"I thought she was proposing marriage to me and I accepted her. Was that unkind?"

Isabel smiled. "It was unkind to *me*. I don't want you to marry."

"My dear cousin, what's one to do among you all?" Ralph demanded. "Miss Stackpole tells me it's my bounden duty, and that it's hers, in general, to see I do mine!"

"She has a great sense of duty," said Isabel gravely. "She has indeed, and it's the motive of everything she says. That's what I like her for. She thinks it's unworthy of you to keep so many things to yourself. That's what she wanted to express. If you thought she was trying to—to attract you, you were very wrong."

"It's true it was an odd way, but I did think she was trying to attract me. Forgive my depravity."

"You're very conceited. She had no interested views, and never supposed you would think she had."

"One must be very modest then to talk with such women," Ralph said humbly. "But it's a very strange type. She's too personal —considering that she expects other people not to be. She walks in without knocking at the door."

"Yes," Isabel admitted, "she doesn't sufficiently recognize the existence of knockers; and indeed I'm not sure that she doesn't think them rather a pretentious ornament. She thinks one's door should stand ajar. But I persist in liking her."

"I persist in thinking her too familiar," Ralph rejoined, naturally somewhat uncomfortable under the sense of having been doubly deceived in Miss Stackpole.

"Well," said Isabel, smiling, "I'm afraid it's because she's rather vulgar that I like her."

"She would be flattered by your reason!"

"If I should tell her I wouldn't express it in that way. I should say it's because there's something of the 'people' in her."

"What do you know about the people? and what does she, for that matter?"

"She knows a great deal, and I know enough to feel that she's a kind of emanation of the great democracy—of the continent, the country, the nation. I don't say that she sums it all up, that would be too much to ask of her. But she suggests it; she vividly figures it."

"You like her then for patriotic reasons. I'm afraid it is on those very grounds I object to her."

"Ah," said Isabel with a kind of joyous sigh, "I like so many things! If a thing strikes me with a certain intensity I accept it. I don't want to swagger, but I suppose I'm rather versatile. I like people to be totally different from Henrietta—in the style of Lord Warburton's sisters for instance. So long as I look at the Misses Molyneux they seem to me to answer a kind of ideal. Then Henrietta presents herself, and I'm straightway convinced by *her*; not so much in respect to herself as in respect to what masses behind her."

"Ah, you mean the back view of her," Ralph suggested.

"What she says is true," his cousin answered; "you'll never be serious. I like the great country stretching away beyond the rivers and across the prairies, blooming and smiling and spreading till it stops at the green Pacific! A strong, sweet, fresh odour seems to rise from it, and Henrietta—pardon my simile—has something of that odour in her garments."

Isabel blushed a little as she concluded this speech, and the blush, together with the momentary ardour she had thrown into it, was so becoming to her that Ralph stood smiling at her for a moment after she had ceased speaking. "I'm not sure the Pacific's so green as that," he said; "but you're a young woman of imagination. Henrietta, however, does smell of the Future—it almost knocks one down!"

XI

He took a resolve after this not to misinterpret her words even when Miss Stackpole appeared to strike the personal note most strongly. He bethought himself that persons, in her view, were simple and homogeneous organisms, and that he, for his own part, was too perverted a representative of the nature of man to have a right to deal with her in strict reciprocity. He carried out his resolve with a great deal of tact, and the young lady found in renewed contact with him no obstacle to the exercise of her genius for unshrinking enquiry, the general application of her confidence. Her situation at Gardencourt therefore, appreciated as we have seen her to be by Isabel and full of appreciation herself of that free play of intelligence which, to her sense, rendered Isabel's character a sister-spirit, and of the easy venerableness of Mr. Touchett, whose noble tone, as she said, met with her full approval—her situation at Gardencourt would have been perfectly comfortable had she not conceived an irresistible mistrust of the little lady for whom she had at first supposed herself obliged to "allow" as mistress of the house. She presently discovered, in truth, that this obligation was of the lightest and that Mrs. Touchett cared very little how Miss Stackpole behaved. Mrs. Touchett had defined her to Isabel as both an adventuress and a bore—adventuresses usually giving one more of a thrill; she had expressed some surprise at her niece's having selected such a friend, yet had immediately added that she knew Isabel's friends were her own affair and that she had never undertaken to like them all or to restrict the girl to those she liked.

"If you could see none but the people I like, my dear, you'd have a very small society," Mrs. Touchett frankly admitted; "and I don't think I like any man or woman well enough to recommend them to you. When it comes to recommending it's a serious affair. I don't like Miss Stackpole—everything about her displeases me; she talks so much too loud and looks at one as if one wanted to look at *her* —which one doesn't. I'm sure she has lived all her life in a board-ing-house, and I detest the manners and the liberties of such places. If you ask me if I prefer my own manners, which you doubtless think very bad, I'll tell you that I prefer them immensely. Miss Stackpole knows I detest boarding-house civilisation, and she detests me for detesting it, because she thinks it the highest in the world. She'd like Gardencourt a great deal better if it were a boarding-house. For me, I find it almost too much of one! We shall never get on together therefore, and there's no use trying."

Mrs. Touchett was right in guessing that Henrietta disapproved of her, but she had not quite put her finger on the reason. A day or two after Miss Stackpole's arrival she had made some invidious reflexions on American hotels, which excited a vein of counter-argu-ment on the part of the correspondent of the *Interviewer*, who in the exercise of her profession had acquainted herself, in the western world, with every form of caravansary. Henrietta expressed the opin-ion that American hotels were the best in the world, and Mrs. Touchett, fresh from a renewed struggle with them, recorded a con-viction that they were the worst. Ralph, with his experimental geni-ality, suggested, by way of healing the breach, that the truth lay between the two extremes and that the establishments in question ought to be described as fair middling. This contribution to the dis-cussion, however, Miss Stackpole rejected with scorn. Middling indeed! If they were not the best in the world they were the worst, but there was nothing middling about an American hotel.

"We judge from different points of view, evidently," said Mrs. Touchett. "I like to be treated as an individual; you like to be treated as a 'party.'"

"I don't know what you mean," Henrietta replied. "I like to be treated as an American lady."

"Poor American ladies!" cried Mrs. Touchett with a laugh. "They're the slaves of slaves."

"They're the companions of freemen," Henrietta retorted.

"They're the companions of their servants—the Irish chamber-maid and the negro waiter. They share their work."

"Do you call the domestics in an American household 'slaves'?" Miss Stackpole enquired. "If that's the way you desire to treat them, no wonder you don't like America."

"If you've not good servants you're miserable," Mrs. Touchett serenely said. "They're very bad in America, but I've five perfect ones in Florence."

"I don't see what you want with five," Henrietta couldn't help observing. "I don't think I should like to see five persons surrounding me in that menial position."

"I like them in that position better than in some others," proclaimed Mrs. Touchett with much meaning.

"Should you like me better if I were your butler, dear?" her husband asked.

"I don't think I should: you wouldn't at all have the *tenue*."[1]

"The companions of freemen—I like that, Miss Stackpole," said Ralph. "It's a beautiful description."

"When I said freemen I didn't mean you, sir!"

And this was the only reward that Ralph got for his compliment. Miss Stackpole was baffled; she evidently thought there was something treasonable in Mrs. Touchett's appreciation of a class which she privately judged to be a mysterious survival of feudalism. It was perhaps because her mind was oppressed with this image that she suffered some days to elapse before she took occasion to say to Isabel: "My dear friend, I wonder if you're growing faithless."

"Faithless? Faithless to you, Henrietta?"

"No, that would be a great pain; but it's not that."

"Faithless to my country then?"

"Ah, that I hope will never be. When I wrote to you from Liverpool I said I had something particular to tell you. You've never asked me what it is. Is it because you've suspected?"

"Suspected what? As a rule I don't think I suspect," said Isabel. "I remember now that phrase in your letter, but I confess I had forgotten it. What have you to tell me?"

Henrietta looked disappointed, and her steady gaze betrayed it. "You don't ask that right—as if you thought it important. You're changed—you're thinking of other things."

"Tell me what you mean, and I'll think of that."

"Will you really think of it? That's what I wish to be sure of."

"I've not much control of my thoughts, but I'll do my best," said Isabel. Henrietta gazed at her, in silence, for a period which tried Isabel's patience, so that our heroine added at last: "Do you mean that you're going to be married?"

"Not till I've seen Europe!" said Miss Stackpole. "What are you laughing at?" she went on. "What I mean is that Mr. Goodwood came out in the steamer with me."

"Ah!" Isabel responded.

"You say *that* right. I had a good deal of talk with him; he has come after you."

"Did he tell you so?"

"No, he told me nothing; that's how I knew it," said Henrietta

1. Proper manner, deportment.

cleverly. "He said very little about you, but I spoke of you a good deal."

Isabel waited. At the mention of Mr. Goodwood's name she had turned a little pale. "I'm very sorry you did that," she observed at last.

"It was a pleasure to me, and I liked the way he listened. I could have talked a long time to such a listener; he was so quiet, so intense; he drank it all in."

"What did you say about me?" Isabel asked.

"I said you were on the whole the finest creature I know."

"I'm very sorry for that. He thinks too well of me already; he oughtn't to be encouraged."

"He's dying for a little encouragement. I see his face now, and his earnest absorbed look while I talked. I never saw an ugly man look so handsome."

"He's very simple-minded," said Isabel. "And he's not so ugly."

"There's nothing so simplifying as a grand passion."

"It's not a grand passion; I'm very sure it's not that."

"You don't say that as if you were sure."

Isabel gave rather a cold smile. "I shall say it better to Mr. Goodwood himself."

"He'll soon give you a chance," said Henrietta. Isabel offered no answer to this assertion, which her companion made with an air of great confidence. "He'll find you changed," the latter pursued. "You've been affected by your new surroundings."

"Very likely. I'm affected by everything."

"By everything but Mr. Goodwood!" Miss Stackpole exclaimed with a slightly harsh hilarity.

Isabel failed even to smile back and in a moment she said: "Did he ask you to speak to me?"

"Not in so many words. But his eyes asked it—and his hand-shake, when he bade me good-bye."

"Thank you for doing so." And Isabel turned away.

"Yes, you're changed; you've got new ideas over here," her friend continued.

"I hope so," said Isabel; "one should get as many new ideas as possible."

"Yes; but they shouldn't interfere with the old ones when the old ones have been the right ones."

Isabel turned about again. "If you mean that I had any idea with regard to Mr. Goodwood—!" But she faltered before her friend's implacable glitter.

"My dear child, you certainly encouraged him."

Isabel made for the moment as if to deny this charge; instead of which, however, she presently answered: "It's very true. I did encourage him." And then she asked if her companion had learned from Mr. Goodwood what he intended to do. It was a concession to her curiosity, for she disliked discussing the subject and found Henrietta wanting in delicacy.

"I asked him, and he said he meant to do nothing," Miss Stackpole answered. "But I don't believe that; he's not a man to do nothing. He is a man of high, bold action. Whatever happens to him he'll always do something, and whatever he does will always be right."

"I quite believe that." Henrietta might be wanting in delicacy, but it touched the girl, all the same, to hear this declaration.

"Ah, you *do* care for him!" her visitor rang out.

"Whatever he does will always be right," Isabel repeated. "When a man's of that infallible mould what does it matter to him what one feels?"

"It may not matter to him, but it matters to one's self."

"Ah, what it matters to me—that's not what we're discussing," said Isabel with a cold smile.

This time her companion was grave. "Well, I don't care; you *have* changed. You're not the girl you were a few short weeks ago, and Mr. Goodwood will see it. I expect him here any day."

"I hope he'll hate me then," said Isabel.

"I believe you hope it about as much as I believe him capable of it."

To this observation our heroine made no return; she was absorbed in the alarm given her by Henrietta's intimation that Caspar Goodwood would present himself at Gardencourt. She pretended to herself, however, that she thought the event impossible, and, later, she communicated her disbelief to her friend. For the next forty-eight hours, nevertheless, she stood prepared to hear the young man's name announced. The feeling pressed upon her; it made the air sultry, as if there were to be a change of weather; and the weather, socially speaking, had been so agreeable during Isabel's stay at Gardencourt that any change would be for the worse. Her suspense indeed was dissipated the second day. She had walked into the park in company with the sociable Bunchie, and after strolling about for some time, in a manner at once listless and restless, had seated herself on a garden-bench, within sight of the house, beneath a spreading beech, where, in a white dress ornamented with black ribbons, she formed among the flickering shadows a graceful and harmonious image. She entertained herself for some moments with talking to the little terrier, as to whom the proposal of an ownership divided with her cousin had been applied as impartially as possible —as impartially as Bunchie's own somewhat fickle and inconstant sympathies would allow. But she was notified for the first time, on this occasion, of the finite character of Bunchie's intellect; hitherto she had been mainly struck with its extent. It seemed to her at last that she would do well to take a book; formerly, when heavy-hearted, she had been able, with the help of some well-chosen volume, to transfer the seat of consciousness to the organ of pure reason. Of late, it was not to be denied, literature had seemed a fading light, and even after she had reminded herself that her uncle's library was provided with a complete set of those authors which no gentleman's collection should be without, she sat motionless and empty-handed, her eyes bent on the cool green turf of the lawn. Her meditations were presently interrupted by the arrival of a servant who handed her a letter. The letter bore the London postmark and was addressed in a hand she knew—that came into her vision, already so held by him, with the vividness of the writer's voice or his face. This document proved short and may be given entire.

My DEAR MISS ARCHER—I don't know whether you will have heard of my coming to England, but even if you have not it will scarcely be a surprise to you. You will remember that when you gave me my dismissal at Albany, three months ago, I did not accept it. I protested against it. You in fact appeared to accept my protest and to admit that I had the right on my side. I had come to see you with the hope that you would let me bring you over to my conviction; my reasons for entertaining this hope had been of the best. But you disappointed it; I found you changed, and you were able to give me no reason for the change. You admitted that you were unreasonable, and it was the only concession you would make; but it was a very cheap one, because that's not your character. No, you are not, and you never will be, arbitrary or capricious. Therefore it is that I believe you will let me see you again. You told me that I'm not disagreeable to you, and I believe it; for I don't see why that should be. I shall always think of you; I shall never think of any one else. I came to England simply because you are here; I couldn't stay at home after you had gone: I hated the country because you were not in it. If I like this country at present it is only because it holds you. I have been to England before, but have never enjoyed it much. May I not come and see you for half an hour? This at present is the dearest wish of yours faithfully

CASPAR GOODWOOD.

Isabel read this missive with such deep attention that she had not perceived an approaching tread on the soft grass. Looking up, however, as she mechanically folded it she saw Lord Warburton standing before her.

XII

She put the letter into her pocket and offered her visitor a smile of welcome, exhibiting no trace of discomposure and half surprised at her coolness.

"They told me you were out here," said Lord Warburton; "and as there was no one in the drawing-room and it's really you that I wish to see, I came out with no more ado."

Isabel had got up; she felt a wish, for the moment, that he should not sit down beside her. "I was just going indoors."

"Please don't do that; it's much jollier here; I've ridden over from Lockleigh; it's a lovely day." His smile was peculiarly friendly and pleasing, and his whole person seemed to emit that radiance of good-feeling and good fare which had formed the charm of the girl's first impression of him. It surrounded him like a zone of fine June weather.

"We'll walk about a little then," said Isabel, who could not divest herself of the sense of an intention on the part of her visitor and who wished both to elude the intention and to satisfy her curiosity about it. It had flashed upon her vision once before, and it had given her on that occasion, as we know, a certain alarm. This alarm was composed of several elements, not all of which were disagreeable; she had indeed spent some days in analysing them and had succeeded in separating the pleasant part of the idea of Lord Warburton's "making up" to her from the painful. It may appear to some readers that the young lady was both precipitate and unduly fastidious; but the latter of these facts, if the charge be true, may serve to exonerate her from the discredit of the former. She was not eager to convince herself that a territorial magnate, as she had heard Lord Warburton called, was smitten with her charms; the fact of a declaration from such a source carrying with it really more questions than it would answer. She had received a strong impression of his being a "personage," and she had occupied herself in examining the image so conveyed. At the risk of adding to the evidence of her self-sufficiency it must be said that there had been moments when this possibility of admiration by a personage represented to her an aggression almost to the degree of an affront, quite to the degree of an inconvenience. She had never yet known a personage; there had been no personages, in this sense, in her life; there were probably none such at all in her native land. When she had thought of individual eminence she had thought of it on the basis of character and wit—of what one might like in a gentleman's mind and in his talk. She herself was a character—she couldn't help being aware of that; and hitherto her visions of a completed consciousness had concerned themselves largely with moral images—

things as to which the question would be whether they pleased her sublime soul. Lord Warburton loomed up before her, largely and brightly, as a collection of attributes and powers which were not to be measured by this simple rule, but which demanded a different sort of appreciation—an appreciation that the girl, with her habit of judging quickly and freely, felt she lacked patience to bestow. He appeared to demand of her something that no one else, as it were, had presumed to do. What she felt was that a territorial, a political, a social magnate had conceived the design of drawing her into the system in which he rather invidiously lived and moved. A certain instinct, not imperious, but persuasive, told her to resist—murmured to her that virtually she had a system and an orbit of her own. It told her other things besides—things which both contradicted and confirmed each other; that a girl might do much worse than trust herself to such a man and that it would be very interesting to see something of his system from his own point of view; that on the other hand, however, there was evidently a great deal of it which she should regard only as a complication of every hour, and that even in the whole there was something stiff and stupid which would make it a burden. Furthermore there was a young man lately come from America who had no system at all, but who had a character of which it was useless for her to try to persuade herself that the impression on her mind had been light. The letter she carried in her pocket all sufficiently reminded her of the contrary. Smile not, however, I venture to repeat, at this simple young woman from Albany who debated whether she should accept an English peer before he had offered himself and who was disposed to believe that on the whole she could do better. She was a person of great good faith, and if there was a great deal of folly in her wisdom those who judge her severely may have the satisfaction of finding that, later, she became consistently wise only at the cost of an amount of folly which will constitute almost a direct appeal to charity.

Lord Warburton seemed quite ready to walk, to sit or to do anything that Isabel should propose, and he gave her this assurance with his usual air of being particularly pleased to exercise a social virtue. But he was, nevertheless, not in command of his emotions, and as he strolled beside her for a moment, in silence, looking at her without letting her know it, there was something embarrassed in his glance and his misdirected laughter. Yes, assuredly—as we have touched on the point, we may return to it for a moment again—the English are the most romantic people in the world and Lord Warburton was about to give an example of it. He was about to take a step which would astonish all his friends and displease a great many of them, and which had superficially nothing to recommend it. The young lady who trod the turf beside him had come from a queer

country across the sea which he knew a good deal about; her antecedents, her associations were very vague to his mind except in so
far as they were generic, and in this sense they showed as distinct
and unimportant. Miss Archer had neither a fortune nor the sort of
beauty that justifies a man to the multitude, and he calculated that
he had spent about twenty-six hours in her company. He had
summed up all this—the perversity of the impulse, which had
declined to avail itself of the most liberal opportunities to subside,
and the judgement of mankind, as exemplified particularly in the
more quickly-judging half of it: he had looked these things well in
the face and then had dismissed them from his thoughts. He cared
no more for them than for the rosebud in his buttonhole. It is the
good fortune of a man who for the greater part of a lifetime has
abstained without effort from making himself disagreeable to his
friends, that when the need comes for such a course it is not dis-
credited by irritating associations.

"I hope you had a pleasant ride," said Isabel, who observed her
companion's hesitancy.

"It would have been pleasant if for nothing else than that it
brought me here."

"Are you so fond of Gardencourt?" the girl asked, more and
more sure that he meant to make some appeal to her; wishing not
to challenge him if he hesitated, and yet to keep all the quietness of
her reason if he proceeded. It suddenly came upon her that her situation was one which a few weeks ago she would have deemed
deeply romantic: the park of an old English country-house, with the
foreground embellished by a "great" (as she supposed) nobleman
in the act of making love to a young lady who, on careful inspection, should be found to present remarkable analogies with herself.
But if she was now the heroine of the situation she succeeded
scarcely the less in looking at it from the outside.

"I care nothing for Gardencourt," said her companion. "I care
only for you."

"You've known me too short a time to have a right to say that,
and I can't believe you're serious."

These words of Isabel's were not perfectly sincere, for she had no
doubt whatever that he himself was. They were simply a tribute to
the fact, of which she was perfectly aware, that those he had just
uttered would have excited surprise on the part of a vulgar world.
And, moreover, if anything beside the sense she had already
acquired that Lord Warburton was not a loose thinker had been
needed to convince her, the tone in which he replied would quite
have served the purpose.

"One's right in such a matter is not measured by the time, Miss
Archer; it's measured by the feeling itself. If I were to wait three

months it would make no difference; I shall not be more sure of
what I mean than I am to-day. Of course I've seen you very little,
but my impression dates from the very first hour we met. I lost no
time, I fell in love with you then. It was at first sight, as the novels
say; I know now that's not a fancy-phrase, and I shall think better
of novels for evermore. Those two days I spent here settled it; I
don't know whether you suspected I was doing so, but I paid—
mentally speaking I mean—the greatest possible attention to you.
Nothing you said, nothing you did, was lost upon me. When you
came to Lockleigh the other day—or rather when you went away—
I was perfectly sure. Nevertheless I made up my mind to think it
over and to question myself narrowly. I've done so; all these days
I've done nothing else. I don't make mistakes about such things;
I'm a very judicious animal. I don't go off easily, but when I'm
touched, it's for life. It's for life, Miss Archer, it's for life." Lord
Warburton repeated in the kindest, tenderest, pleasantest voice
Isabel had ever heard, and looking at her with eyes charged with
the light of a passion that had sifted itself clear of the baser parts of
emotion—the heat, the violence, the unreason—and that burned as
steadily as a lamp in a windless place.

By tacit consent, as he talked, they had walked more and more
slowly, and at last they stopped and he took her hand. "Ah, Lord
Warburton, how little you know me!" Isabel said very gently.
Gently too she drew her hand away.

"Don't taunt me with that; that I don't know you better makes
me unhappy enough already; it's all my loss. But that's what I
want, and it seems to me I'm taking the best way. If you'll be my
wife, then I shall know you, and when I tell you all the good I
think of you you'll not be able to say it's from ignorance."

"If you know me little I know you even less," said Isabel.

"You mean that, unlike yourself, I may not improve on acquaintance? Ah, of course that's very possible. But think, to speak to you
as I do, how determined I must be to try and give satisfaction! You
do like me rather, don't you?"

"I like you very much, Lord Warburton," she answered; and at
this moment she liked him immensely.

"I thank you for saying that; it shows you don't regard me as a
stranger. I really believe I've filled all the other relations of life very
creditably, and I don't see why I shouldn't fill this one—in which I
offer myself to you—seeing that I care so much more about it. Ask
the people who know me well; I've friends who'll speak for me."

"I don't need the recommendation of your friends," said Isabel.

"Ah now, that's delightful of you. You believe in me yourself."

"Completely," Isabel declared. She quite glowed there, inwardly,
with the pleasure of feeling she did.

The light in her companion's eyes turned into a smile, and he gave a long exhalation of joy. "If you're mistaken, Miss Archer, let me lose all I possess!"

She wondered whether he meant this for a reminder that he was rich, and, on the instant, felt sure that he didn't. He was sinking that, as he would have said himself; and indeed he might safely leave it to the memory of any interlocutor, especially of one to whom he was offering his hand. Isabel had prayed that she might not be agitated, and her mind was tranquil enough, even while she listened and asked herself what it was best she should say, to indulge in this incidental criticism. What she should say, had she asked herself? Her foremost wish was to say something if possible not less kind than what he had said to her. His words had carried perfect conviction with them; she felt she did, all so mysteriously, matter to him. "I thank you more than I can say for your offer," she returned at last. "It does me great honour."

"Ah, don't say that!" he broke out. "I was afraid you'd say something like that. I don't see what you've to do with that sort of thing. I don't see why you should thank me—it's I who ought to thank you for listening to me: a man you know so little coming down on you with such a thumper! Of course it's a great question; I must tell you that I'd rather ask it than have it to answer myself. But the way you've listened—or at least your having listened at all —gives me some hope."

"Don't hope too much," Isabel said.

"Oh Miss Archer!" her companion murmured, smiling again, in his seriousness, as if such a warning might perhaps be taken but as the play of high spirits, the exuberance of elation.

"Should you be greatly surprised if I were to beg you not to hope at all?" Isabel asked.

"Surprised? I don't know what you mean by surprise. It wouldn't be that; it would be a feeling very much worse."

Isabel walked on again; she was silent for some minutes. "I'm very sure that, highly as I already think of you, my opinion of you, if I should know you well, would only rise. But I'm by no means sure that you wouldn't be disappointed. And I say that not in the least out of conventional modesty; it's perfectly sincere."

"I'm willing to risk it, Miss Archer," her companion replied.

"It's a great question, as you say. It's a very difficult question."

"I don't expect you of course to answer it outright. Think it over as long as may be necessary. If I can gain by waiting I'll gladly wait a long time. Only remember that in the end my dearest happiness depends on your answer."

"I should be very sorry to keep you in suspense," said Isabel.

"Oh, don't mind. I'd much rather have a good answer six months hence than a bad one to-day."

"But it's very probable that even six months hence I shouldn't be able to give you one that you'd think good."

"Why not, since you really like me?"

"Ah, you must never doubt that," said Isabel.

"Well then, I don't see what more you ask!"

"It's not what I ask; it's what I can give. I don't think I should suit you; I really don't think I should."

"You needn't worry about that. That's my affair. You needn't be a better royalist than the king."

"It's not only that," said Isabel; "but I'm not sure I wish to marry any one."

"Very likely you don't. I've no doubt a great many women begin that way," said his lordship, who, be it averred, did not in the least believe in the axiom he thus beguiled his anxiety by uttering. "But they're frequently persuaded."

"Ah, that's because they want to be!" And Isabel lightly laughed.

Her suitor's countenance fell, and he looked at her for a while in silence. "I'm afraid it's my being an Englishman that makes you hesitate," he said presently. "I know your uncle thinks you ought to marry in your own country."

Isabel listened to this assertion with some interest; it had never occurred to her that Mr. Touchett was likely to discuss her matrimonial prospects with Lord Warburton. "Has he told you that?"

"I remember his making the remark. He spoke perhaps of Americans generally."

"He appears himself to have found it very pleasant to live in England." Isabel spoke in a manner that might have seemed a little perverse, but which expressed both her constant perception of her uncle's outward felicity and her general disposition to elude any obligation to take a restricted view.

It gave her companion hope, and he immediately cried with warmth: "Ah, my dear Miss Archer, old England's a very good sort of country, you know! And it will be still better when we've furbished it up a little"

"Oh, don't furbish it, Lord Warburton; leave it alone. I like it this way."

"Well then, if you like it, I'm more and more unable to see your objection to what I propose."

"I'm afraid I can't make you understand."

"You ought at least to try. I've a fair intelligence. Are you afraid—afraid of the climate? We can easily live elsewhere, you know. You can pick out your climate, the whole world over."

These words were uttered with a breadth of candour that was like the embrace of strong arms—that was like the fragrance straight in her face, and by his clean, breathing lips, of she knew not what strange gardens, what charged airs. She would have given her little finger at that moment to feel strongly and simply the impulse to answer: "Lord Warburton, it's impossible for me to do better in this wonderful world, I think, than commit myself, very gratefully, to your loyalty." But though she was lost in admiration of her opportunity she managed to move back into the deepest shade of it, even as some wild, caught creature in a vast cage. The "splendid" security so offered her was *not* the greatest she could conceive. What she finally bethought herself of saying was something very different—something that deferred the need of really facing her crisis. "Don't think me unkind if I ask you to say no more about this to-day."

"Certainly, certainly!" her companion cried. "I wouldn't bore you for the world."

"You've given me a great deal to think about, and I promise you to do it justice."

"That's all I ask of you, of course—and that you'll remember how absolutely my happiness is in your hands."

Isabel listened with extreme respect to this admonition, but she said after a minute: "I must tell you that what I shall think about is some way of letting you know that what you ask is impossible—letting you know it without making you miserable."

"There's no way to do that, Miss Archer. I won't say that if you refuse me you'll kill me; I shall not die of it. But I shall do worse; I shall live to no purpose."

"You'll live to marry a better woman than I."

"Don't say that, please," said Lord Warburton very gravely. "That's fair to neither one of us."

"To marry a worse one then."

"If there are better women than you I prefer the bad ones. That's all I can say," he went on with the same earnestness. "There's no accounting for tastes."

His gravity made her feel equally grave, and she showed it by again requesting him to drop the subject for the present. "I'll speak to you myself—very soon. Perhaps I shall write to you."

"At your convenience, yes," he replied. "Whatever time you take, it must seem to me long, and I suppose I must make the best of that."

"I shall not keep you in suspense; I only want to collect my mind a little."

He gave a melancholy sigh and stood looking at her a moment, with his hands behind him, giving short nervous shakes to his hunting-crop. "Do you know I'm very much afraid of it—of that remarkable mind of yours?"

Our heroine's biographer can scarcely tell why, but the question made her start and brought a conscious blush to her cheek. She returned his look a moment, and then with a note in her voice that might almost have appealed to his compassion, "So am I, my lord!" she oddly exclaimed.

His compassion was not stirred, however; all he possessed of the faculty of pity was needed at home. "Ah! be merciful, be merciful," he murmured.

"I think you had better go," said Isabel. "I'll write to you."

"Very good; but whatever you write I'll come and see you, you know." And then he stood reflecting, his eyes fixed on the observant countenance of Bunchie, who had the air of having understood all that had been said and of pretending to carry off the indiscretion by a simulated fit of curiosity as to the roots of an ancient oak. "There's one thing more," he went on. "You know, if you don't like Lockleigh—if you think it's damp or anything of that sort—you need never go within fifty miles of it. It's not damp, by the way; I've had the house thoroughly examined; it's perfectly safe and right. But if you shouldn't fancy it you needn't dream of living in it. There's no difficulty whatever about that; there are plenty of houses. I thought I'd just mention it; some people don't like a moat, you know. Good-bye."

"I adore a moat," said Isabel. "Good-bye."

He held out his hand, and she gave him hers a moment—a moment long enough for him to bend his handsome bared head and kiss it. Then, still agitating, in his mastered emotion, his implement of the chase, he walked rapidly away. He was evidently much upset.

Isabel herself was upset, but she had not been affected as she would have imagined. What she felt was not a great responsibility, a great difficulty of choice; it appeared to her there had been no choice in the question. She couldn't marry Lord Warburton; the idea failed to support any enlightened prejudice in favour of the free exploration of life that she had hitherto entertained or was now capable of entertaining. She must write this to him, she must convince him, and that duty was comparatively simple. But what disturbed her, in the sense that it struck her with wonderment, was this very fact that it cost her so little to refuse a magnificent "chance." With whatever qualifications one would, Lord Warburton had offered her a great opportunity; the situation might have discomforts, might contain oppressive, might contain narrowing elements, might prove really but a stupefying anodyne; but she did her sex no injustice in believing that nineteen women out of twenty would have accommodated themselves to it without a pang. Why then upon her also should it not irresistibly impose itself? Who was she, what was she, that she should hold herself superior? What view of life, what design upon fate, what conception of happiness, had she that pretended to be larger than these large, these fabulous occasions? If she wouldn't do such a thing as that then she must do great things, she must do something greater. Poor Isabel found ground to remind herself from time to time that she must not be too proud, and nothing could be more sincere than her prayer to be delivered from such a danger: the isolation and loneliness of pride had for her mind the horror of a desert place. If it had been pride that interfered with her accepting Lord Warburton such a *bêtise*[1] was singularly misplaced; and she was so conscious of liking him that she ventured to assure herself it was the very softness, and the fine intelligence, of sympathy. She liked him too much to marry him, that was the truth; something assured her there was a fallacy somewhere in the glowing logic of the proposition—as *he* saw it— even though she mightn't put her very finest finger-point on it; and to inflict upon a man who offered so much a wife with a tendency to criticise would be a peculiarly discreditable act. She had promised him she would consider his question, and when, after he had left her, she wandered back to the bench where he had found her and lost herself in meditation, it might have seemed that she was keeping her vow. But this was not the case; she was wondering if she were not a cold, hard, priggish person, and, on her at last getting up and going rather quickly back to the house, felt, as she had said to her friend, really frightened at herself.

XIII

It was this feeling and not the wish to ask advice—she had no desire whatever for that—that led her to speak to her uncle of what had taken place. She wished to speak to some one; she should feel more natural, more human, and her uncle, for this purpose, presented himself in a more attractive light than either her aunt or her friend Henrietta. Her cousin of course was a possible confidant; but she would have had to do herself violence to air this special secret to Ralph. So the next day, after breakfast, she sought her occasion. Her uncle never left his apartment till the afternoon, but he received his cronies, as he said, in his dressing-room. Isabel had quite taken her place in the class so designated, which, for the rest, included the old man's son, his physician, his personal servant, and even Miss Stackpole. Mrs. Touchett did not figure in the list, and this was an obstacle the less to Isabel's finding her host alone. He sat in a complicated mechanical chair, at the open window of his

1. Folly, lack of tact.

room, looking westward over the park and the river, with his newspapers and letters piled up beside him, his toilet freshly and min-
utely made, and his smooth, speculative face composed to benevolent expectation.

She approached her point directly. "I think I ought to let you
know that Lord Warburton has asked me to marry him. I suppose I
ought to tell my aunt; but it seems best to tell you first."

The old man expressed no surprise, but thanked her for the confidence she showed him. "Do you mind telling me whether you
accepted him?" he then enquired.

"I've not answered him definitely yet; I've taken a little time to
think of it, because that seems more respectful. But I shall not
accept him."

Mr. Touchett made no comment upon this; he had the air of
thinking that, whatever interest he might take in the matter from
the point of view of sociability, he had no active voice in it. "Well,
I told you you'd be a success over here. Americans are highly appreciated."

"Very highly indeed," said Isabel. "But at the cost of seeming
both tasteless and ungrateful, I don't think I can marry Lord Warburton."

"Well," her uncle went on, "of course an old man can't judge for
a young lady. I'm glad you didn't ask me before you made up your
mind. I suppose I ought to tell you," he added slowly, but as if it
were not of much consequence, "that I've known all about it these
three days."

"About Lord Warburton's state of mind?"

"About his intentions, as they say here. He wrote me a very
pleasant letter, telling me all about them. Should you like to see his
letter?" the old man obligingly asked.

"Thank you; I don't think I care about that. But I'm glad he
wrote to you; it was right that he should, and he would be certain
to do what was right."

"Ah well, I guess you do like him!" Mr. Touchett declared. "You
needn't pretend you don't."

"I like him extremely; I'm very free to admit that. But I don't
wish to marry any one just now."

"You think some one may come along whom you may like better.
Well, that's very likely," said Mr. Touchett, who appeared to wish
to show his kindness to the girl by easing off her decision, as it
were, and finding cheerful reasons for it.

"I don't care if I don't meet any one else. I like Lord Warburton
quite well enough." She fell into that appearance of a sudden
change of point of view with which she sometimes startled and even
displeased her interlocutors.

Her uncle, however, seemed proof against either of these impressions. "He's a very fine man," he resumed in a tone which might have passed for that of encouragement. "His letter was one of the pleasantest I've received for some weeks. I suppose one of the reasons I liked it was that it was all about you; that is all except the part that was about himself. I suppose he told you all that."

"He would have told me everything I wished to ask him," Isabel said.

"But you didn't feel curious?"

"My curiosity would have been idle—once I had determined to decline his offer."

"You didn't find it sufficiently attractive?" Mr. Touchett enquired.

She was silent a little. "I suppose it was that," she presently admitted. "But I don't know why."

"Fortunately ladies are not obliged to give reasons," said her uncle. "There's a great deal that's attractive about such an idea; but I don't see why the English should want to entice us away from our native land. I know that we try to attract them over there, but that's because our population is insufficient. Here, you know, they're rather crowded. However, I presume there's room for charming young ladies everywhere."

"There seems to have been room here for you," said Isabel, whose eyes had been wandering over the large pleasure-spaces of the park.

Mr. Touchett gave a shrewd, conscious smile. "There's room everywhere, my dear, if you'll pay for it. I sometimes think I've paid too much for this. Perhaps you also might have to pay too much."

"Perhaps I might," the girl replied.

That suggestion gave her something more definite to rest on than she had found in her own thoughts, and the fact of this association of her uncle's mild acuteness with her dilemma seemed to prove that she was concerned with the natural and reasonable emotions of life and not altogether a victim to intellectual eagerness and vague ambitions—ambitions reaching beyond Lord Warburton's beautiful appeal, reaching to something indefinable and possibly not commendable. In so far as the indefinable had an influence upon Isabel's behaviour at this juncture, it was not the conception, even unformulated, of a union with Caspar Goodwood; for however she might have resisted conquest at her English suitor's large quiet hands she was at least as far removed from the disposition to let the young man from Boston take positive possession of her. The sentiment in which she sought refuge after reading his letter was a critical view of his having come abroad; for it was part of the influence he had upon her that he seemed to deprive her of the sense of freedom. There was a disagreeably strong push, a kind of hardness of presence, in his way of rising before her. She had been haunted at moments by the image, by the danger, of his disapproval and had wondered—a consideration she had never paid in equal degree to any one else—whether he would like what she did. The difficulty was that more than any man she had ever known, more than poor Lord Warburton (she had begun now to give his lordship the benefit of this epithet), Caspar Goodwood expressed for her an energy —and she had already felt it as a power—that was of his very nature. It was in no degree a matter of his "advantages"—it was a matter of the spirit that sat in his clear-burning eyes like some tireless watcher at a window. She might like it or not, but he insisted, ever, with his whole weight and force: even in one's usual contact with him one had to reckon with that. The idea of a diminished liberty was particularly disagreeable to her at present, since she had just given a sort of personal accent to her independence by looking so straight at Lord Warburton's big bribe and yet turning away from it. Sometimes Caspar Goodwood had seemed to range himself on the side of her destiny, to be the stubbornest fact she knew; she said to herself at such moments that she might evade him for a time, but that she must make terms with him at last—terms which would be certain to be favourable to himself. Her impulse had been to avail herself of the things that helped her to resist such an obligation; and this impulse had been much concerned in her eager acceptance of her aunt's invitation, which had come to her at an hour when she expected from day to day to see Mr. Goodwood and when she was glad to have an answer ready for something she was sure he would say to her. When she had told him at Albany, on the evening of Mrs. Touchett's visit, that she couldn't then discuss difficult questions, dazzled as she was by the great immediate opening of her aunt's offer of "Europe," he declared that this was no answer at all; and it was now to obtain a better one that he was following her across the sea. To say to herself that he was a kind of grim fate was well enough for a fanciful young woman who was able to take much for granted in him; but the reader has a right to a nearer and a clearer view.

He was the son of a proprietor of well-known cotton-mills in Massachusetts—a gentleman who had accumulated a considerable fortune in the exercise of this industry. Caspar at present managed the works, and with a judgement and a temper which, in spite of keen competition and languid years, had kept their prosperity from dwindling. He had received the better part of his education at Harvard College, where, however, he had gained renown rather as a gymnast and an oarsman than as a gleaner of more dispersed knowledge. Later on he had learned that the finer intelligence too could vault and pull and strain—might even, breaking the record, treat itself to rare exploits. He had thus discovered in himself a sharp eye for the mystery of mechanics, and had invented an improvement in the cotton-spinning process which was now largely used and was known by his name. You might have seen it in the newspapers in connection with this fruitful contrivance; assurance of which he had given to Isabel by showing her in the columns of the New York *Interviewer* an exhaustive article on the Goodwood patent—an article not prepared by Miss Stackpole, friendly as she had proved herself to his more sentimental interests. There were intricate, bristling things he rejoiced in; he liked to organise, to contend, to administer; he could make people work his will, believe in him, march before him and justify him. This was the art, as they said, of managing men—which rested, in him, further, on a bold though brooding ambition. It struck those who knew him well that he might do greater things than carry on a cotton-factory; there was nothing cottony about Caspar Goodwood, and his friends took for granted that he would somehow and somewhere write himself in bigger letters. But it was as if something large and confused, something dark and ugly, would have to call upon him: he was not after all in harmony with mere smug peace and greed and gain, an order of things of which the vital breath was ubiquitous advertisement. It pleased Isabel to believe that he might have ridden, on a plunging steed, the whirlwind of a great war—a war like the Civil strife that had overdarkened her conscious childhood and his ripening youth.

She liked at any rate this idea of his being by character and in fact a mover of men—liked it much better than some other points in his nature and aspect. She cared nothing for his cotton-mill—the Goodwood patent left her imagination absolutely cold. She wished him no ounce less of his manhood, but she sometimes thought he would be rather nicer if he looked, for instance, a little differently. His jaw was too square and set and his figure too straight and stiff: these things suggested a want of easy consonance with the deeper rhythms of life. Then she viewed with reserve a habit he had of dressing always in the same manner; it was not apparently that he wore the same clothes continually, for, on the contrary, his garments had a way of looking rather too new. But they all seemed of the same piece; the figure, the stuff, was so drearily usual. She had reminded herself more than once that this was a frivolous objection to a person of his importance; and then she had amended the rebuke by saying that it would be a frivolous objection only if she were in love with him. She was not in love with him and therefore might criticise his small defects as well as his great—which latter consisted in the collective reproach of his being too serious, or, rather, not of his being so, since one could never be, but certainly of his seeming so. He showed his appetites and designs too simply and artlessly; when one was alone with him he talked too much about the same subject, and when other people were present he talked too little about anything. And yet he was of supremely strong, clean make—which was so much: she saw the different fitted parts of him as she had seen, in museums and portraits, the different fitted parts of armoured warriors—in plates of steel handsomely inlaid with gold. It was very strange: where, ever, was any tangible link between her impression and her act? Caspar Goodwood had never corresponded to her idea of a delightful person, and she supposed that this was why he left her so harshly critical. When, however, Lord Warburton, who not only did correspond with it, but gave an extension to the term, appealed to her approval, she found herself still unsatisfied. It was certainly strange.

The sense of her incoherence was not a help to answering Mr. Goodwood's letter, and Isabel determined to leave it a while unhonoured. If he had determined to persecute her he must take the consequences; foremost among which was his being left to perceive how little it charmed her that he should come down to Gardencourt. She was already liable to the incursions of one suitor at this place, and though it might be pleasant to be appreciated in opposite quarters there was a kind of grossness in entertaining two such passionate pleaders at once, even in a case where the entertainment should consist of dismissing them. She made no reply to Mr. Goodwood; but at the end of three days she wrote to Lord Warburton, and the letter belongs to our history.

Dear Lord Warburton—A great deal of earnest thought has not led me to change my mind about the suggestion you were so kind as to make me the other day. I am not, I am really and truly not, able to regard you in the light of a companion for life; or to think of your home—your various homes—as the settled seat of my existence. These things cannot be reasoned about, and I very earnestly entreat you not to return to the subject we discussed so exhaustively. We see our lives from our own point of view; that is the privilege of the weakest and humblest of us; and I shall never be able to see mine in the manner you proposed. Kindly let this suffice you, and do me the justice to believe that I have given your proposal the deeply respectful consideration it deserves. It is with this very great regard that I remain sincerely yours,

Isabel Archer.

While the author of this missive was making up her mind to despatch it Henrietta Stackpole formed a resolve which was accompanied by no demur. She invited Ralph Touchett to take a walk with her in the garden, and when he had assented with that alacrity which seemed constantly to testify to his high expectations, she informed him that she had a favour to ask of him. It may be admitted that at this information the young man flinched; for we know that Miss Stackpole had struck him as apt to push an advantage. The alarm was unreasoned, however; for he was clear about the area of her indiscretion as little as advised of its vertical depth, and he made a very civil profession of the desire to serve her. He was afraid of her and presently told her so. "When you look at me in a certain way my knees knock together, my faculties desert me; I'm filled with trepidation and I ask only for strength to execute your commands. You've an address that I've never encountered in any woman."

"Well," Henrietta replied good-humouredly, "if I had not known before that you were trying somehow to abash me I should know it now. Of course I'm easy game—I was brought up with such different customs and ideas. I'm not used to your arbitrary standards, and I've never been spoken to in America as you have spoken to me. If a gentleman conversing with me over there were to speak to me like that I shouldn't know what to make of it. We take everything more naturally over there, and, after all, we're a great deal more simple. I admit that; I'm very simple myself. Of course if you choose to laugh at me for it you're very welcome; but I think on the whole I would rather be myself than you. I'm quite content to be myself; I don't want to change. There are plenty of people that appreciate me just as I am. It's true they're nice fresh free-born Americans!" Henrietta had lately taken up the tone of helpless innocence and large concession. "I want you to assist me a little," she went on. "I don't care in the least whether I amuse you while you do so; or, rather, I'm perfectly willing your amusement should be your reward. I want you to help me about Isabel."

"Has she injured you?" Ralph asked.

"If she had I shouldn't mind, and I should never tell you. What I'm afraid of is that she'll injure herself."

"I think that's very possible," said Ralph.

His companion stopped in the garden-walk, fixing on him perhaps the very gaze that unnerved him. "That too would amuse you, I suppose. The way you do say things! I never heard any one so indifferent."

"To Isabel? Ah, not that!"

"Well, you're not in love with her, I hope."

"How can that be, when I'm in love with Another?"

"You're in love with yourself, that's the Other!" Miss Stackpole declared. "Much good may it do you! But if you wish to be serious once in your life here's a chance; and if you really care for your cousin here's an opportunity to prove it. I don't expect you to understand her; that's too much to ask. But you needn't do that to grant my favour. I'll supply the necessary intelligence."

"I shall enjoy that immensely!" Ralph exclaimed. "I'll be Caliban and you shall be Ariel."[1]

"You're not at all like Caliban, because you're sophisticated, and Caliban was not. But I'm not talking about imaginary characters; I'm talking about Isabel. Isabel's intensely real. What I wish to tell you is that I find her fearfully changed."

"Since you came, do you mean?"

"Since I came and before I came. She's not the same as she once so beautifully was."

"As she was in America?"

"Yes, in America. I suppose you know she comes from there. She can't help it, but she does."

"Do you want to change her back again?"

"Of course I do, and I want you to help me."

"Ah," said Ralph, "I'm only Caliban; I'm not Prospero."

"You were Prospero enough to make her what she has become. You've acted on Isabel Archer since she came here, Mr. Touchett."

"I, my dear Miss Stackpole? Never in the world. Isabel Archer has acted on me—yes; she acts on every one. But I've been absolutely passive."

"You're too passive then. You had better stir yourself and be careful. Isabel's changing every day; she's drifting away—right out to sea. I've watched her and I can see it. She's not the bright American girl she was. She's taking different views, a different colour, and turning away from her old ideals. I want to save those ideals, Mr. Touchett, and that's where you come in."

"Not surely as an ideal?"

"Well, I hope not," Henrietta replied promptly. "I've got a fear in my heart that she's going to marry one of these fell Europeans, and I want to prevent it."

"Ah, I see," cried Ralph; "and to prevent it you want me to step in and marry her?"

"Not quite; that remedy would be as bad as the disease, for you're the typical, the fell European from whom I wish to rescue her. No; I wish you to take an interest in another person—a young man to whom she once gave great encouragement and whom she now doesn't seem to think good enough. He's a thoroughly grand man and a very dear friend of mine, and I wish very much you would invite him to pay a visit here."

Ralph was much puzzled by this appeal, and it is perhaps not to the credit of his purity of mind that he failed to look at it at first in

1. Caliban, Ariel, and Prospero are all in Shakespeare's *The Tempest*.

the simplest light. It wore, to his eyes, a tortuous air, and his fault was that he was not quite sure that anything in the world could really be as candid as this request of Miss Stackpole's appeared. That a young woman should demand that a gentleman whom she described as her very dear friend should be furnished with an opportunity to make himself agreeable to another young woman, a young woman whose attention had wandered and whose charms were greater—this was an anomaly which for the moment challenged all his ingenuity of interpretation. To read between the lines was easier than to follow the text, and to suppose that Miss Stackpole wished the gentleman invited to Gardencourt on her own account was the sign not so much of a vulgar as of an embarrassed mind. Even from this venial act of vulgarity, however, Ralph was saved, and saved by a force that I can only speak of as inspiration. With no more outward light on the subject than he already possessed he suddenly acquired the conviction that it would be a sovereign injustice to the correspondent of the *Interviewer* to assign a dishonourable motive to any act of hers. This conviction passed into his mind with extreme rapidity; it was perhaps kindled by the pure radiance of the young lady's imperturbable gaze. He returned this challenge a moment, consciously, resisting an inclination to frown as one frowns in the presence of larger luminaries. "Who's the gentleman you speak of?"

"Mr. Caspar Goodwood—of Boston. He has been extremely attentive to Isabel—just as devoted to her as he can live. He has followed her out here and he's at present in London. I don't know his address, but I guess I can obtain it."

"I've never heard of him," said Ralph.

"Well, I suppose you haven't heard of every one. I don't believe he has ever heard of you; but that's no reason why Isabel shouldn't marry him."

Ralph gave a mild ambiguous laugh. "What a rage you have for marrying people! Do you remember how you wanted to marry *me* the other day?"

"I've got over that. You don't know how to take such ideas. Mr. Goodwood does, however; and that's what I like about him. He's a splendid man and a perfect gentleman, and Isabel knows it."

"Is she very fond of him?"

"If she isn't she ought to be. He's simply wrapped up in her."

"And you wish me to ask him here," said Ralph reflectively.

"It would be an act of true hospitality."

"Caspar Goodwood," Ralph continued—"it's rather a striking name."

"I don't care anything about his name. It might be Ezekiel Jenkins, and I should say the same. He's the only man I have ever seen whom I think worthy of Isabel."

"You're a very devoted friend," said Ralph.

"Of course I am. If you say that to pour scorn on me I don't care."

"I don't say it to pour scorn on you; I'm very much struck with it."

"You're more satiric than ever, but I advise you not to laugh at Mr. Goodwood."

"I assure you I'm very serious; you ought to understand that," said Ralph.

In a moment his companion understood it. "I believe you are; now you're too serious."

"You're difficult to please."

"Oh, you're very serious indeed. You won't invite Mr. Goodwood."

"I don't know," said Ralph. "I'm capable of strange things. Tell me a little about Mr. Goodwood. What's he like?"

"He's just the opposite of you. He's at the head of a cotton-factory; a very fine one."

"Has he pleasant manners?" asked Ralph.

"Splendid manners—in the American style."

"Would he be an agreeable member of our little circle?"

"I don't think he'd care much about our little circle. He'd concentrate on Isabel."

"And how would my cousin like that?"

"Very possibly not at all. But it will be good for her. It will call back her thoughts."

"Call them back—from where?"

"From foreign parts and other unnatural places. Three months ago she gave Mr. Goodwood every reason to suppose he was acceptable to her, and it's not worthy of Isabel to go back on a real friend simply because she has changed the scene. I've changed the scene too, and the effect of it has been to make me care more for my old associations than ever. It's my belief that the sooner Isabel changes it back again the better. I know her well enough to know that she would never be truly happy over here, and I wish her to form some strong American tie that will act as a preservative."

"Aren't you perhaps a little too much in a hurry?" Ralph enquired. "Don't you think you ought to give her more of a chance in poor old England?"

"A chance to ruin her bright young life? One's never too much in a hurry to save a precious human creature from drowning."

"As I understand it then," said Ralph, "you wish me to push Mr. Goodwood overboard after her. Do you know," he added, "that I've never heard her mention his name?"

Henrietta gave a brilliant smile. "I'm delighted to hear that; it proves how much she thinks of him."

Ralph appeared to allow that there was a good deal in this, and he surrendered to thought while his companion watched him askance. "If I should invite Mr. Goodwood," he finally said, "it would be to quarrel with him."

"Don't do that; he'd prove the better man."

"You certainly are doing your best to make me hate him! I really don't think I can ask him. I should be afraid of being rude to him."

"It's just as you please," Henrietta returned. "I had no idea you were in love with her yourself."

"Do you really believe that?" the young man asked with lifted eyebrows.

"That's the most natural speech I've ever heard you make! Of course I believe it," Miss Stackpole ingeniously said.

"Well," Ralph concluded, "to prove to you that you're wrong I'll invite him. It must be of course as a friend of yours."

"It will not be as a friend of mine that he'll come; and it will not be to prove to me that I'm wrong that you'll ask him—but to prove it to yourself!"

These last words of Miss Stackpole's (on which the two presently separated) contained an amount of truth which Ralph Touchett was obliged to recognise; but it so far took the edge from too sharp a recognition that, in spite of his suspecting it would be rather more indiscreet to keep than to break his promise, he wrote Mr. Goodwood a note of six lines, expressing the pleasure it would give Mr. Touchett the elder that he should join a little party at Gardencourt, of which Miss Stackpole was a valued member. Having sent his letter (to the care of a banker whom Henrietta suggested) he waited in some suspense. He had heard this fresh formidable figure named for the first time; for when his mother had mentioned on her arrival that there was a story about the girl's having an "admirer" at home, the idea had seemed deficient in reality and he had taken no pains to ask questions the answers to which would involve only the vague or the disagreeable. Now, however, the native admiration of which his cousin was the object had become more concrete; it took the form of a young man who had followed her to London, who was interested in a cotton-mill and had manners in the most splendid of the American styles. Ralph had two theories about this intervener. Either his passion was a sentimental fiction of Miss Stackpole's (there was always a sort of tacit understanding among women, born of the solidarity of the sex, that they should discover or invent lovers for each other), in which case he was not to be feared and would probably not accept the invitation; or else he would accept the invitation and in this event prove himself a creature too irrational to demand further consideration. The latter clause of Ralph's argument might have seemed incoherent; but it embodied his conviction that if Mr. Goodwood were interested in Isabel in the serious manner described by Miss Stackpole he would not care to present himself at Gardencourt on a summons from the latter lady. "On this supposition," said Ralph, "he must regard her as a thorn on the stem of his rose; as an intercessor he must find her wanting in tact."

Two days after he had sent his invitation he received a very short note from Caspar Goodwood, thanking him for it, regretting that other engagements made a visit to Gardencourt impossible and presenting many compliments to Miss Stackpole. Ralph handed the note to Henrietta, who, when she had read it, exclaimed: "Well, I never have heard of anything so stiff!"

"I'm afraid he doesn't care so much about my cousin as you suppose," Ralph observed.

"No, it's not that; it's some subtler motive. His nature's very deep. But I'm determined to fathom it, and I shall write to him to know what he means."

His refusal of Ralph's overtures was vaguely disconcerting; from the moment he declined to come to Gardencourt our friend began to think him of importance. He asked himself what it signified to him whether Isabel's admirers should be desperadoes or laggards; they were not rivals of his and were perfectly welcome to act out their genius. Nevertheless he felt much curiosity as to the result of Miss Stackpole's promised enquiry into the causes of Mr. Goodwood's stiffness—a curiosity for the present ungratified, inasmuch as when he asked her three days later if she had written to London she was obliged to confess she had written in vain. Mr. Goodwood had not replied.

"I suppose he's thinking it over," she said; "he thinks everything over; he's not *really* at all impetuous. But I'm accustomed to having my letters answered the same day." She presently proposed to Isabel, at all events, that they should make an excursion to London together. "If I must tell the truth," she observed, "I'm not seeing much at this place, and I shouldn't think you were either. I've not even seen that aristocrat—what's his name?—Lord Washburton. He seems to let you severely alone."

"Lord Warburton's coming to-morrow, I happen to know," replied her friend, who had received a note from the master of Lockleigh in answer to her own letter. "You'll have every opportunity of turning him inside out."

"Well, he may do for one letter, but what's one letter when you want to write fifty? I've described all the scenery in this vicinity and raved about all the old women and donkeys. You may say what you please, scenery doesn't make a vital letter. I must go back to London and get some impressions of real life. I was there but three days before I came away, and that's hardly time to get in touch."

As Isabel, on her journey from New York to Gardencourt, had

seen even less of the British capital than this, it appeared a happy suggestion of Henrietta's that the two should go thither on a visit of pleasure. The idea struck Isabel as charming; she was curious of the thick detail of London, which had always loomed large and rich to her. They turned over their schemes together and indulged in visions of romantic hours. They would stay at some picturesque old inn—one of the inns described by Dickens[2] —and drive over the town in those delightful hansoms. Henrietta was a literary woman, and the great advantage of being a literary woman was that you could go everywhere and do everything. They would dine at a coffee-house and go afterwards to the play; they would frequent the Abbey and the British Museum and find out where Doctor Johnson had lived, and Goldsmith and Addison. Isabel grew eager and presently unveiled the bright vision to Ralph, who burst into a fit of laughter which scarce expressed the sympathy she had desired.

"It's a delightful plan," he said. "I advise you to go to the Duke's Head in Covent Garden,[3] an easy, informal, old-fashioned place, and I'll have you put down at my club."

"Do you mean it's improper?" Isabel asked. "Dear me, isn't anything proper here? With Henrietta surely I may go anywhere; she isn't hampered in that way. She has travelled over the whole American continent and can at least find her way about this minute island."

"Ah then," said Ralph, "let me take advantage of her protection to go up to town as well. I may never have a chance to travel so safely!"

XIV

Miss Stackpole would have prepared to start immediately; but Isabel, as we have seen, had been notified that Lord Warburton would come again to Gardencourt, and she believed it her duty to remain there and see him. For four or five days he had made no response to her letter; then he had written, very briefly, to say he would come to luncheon two days later. There was something in these delays and postponements that touched the girl and renewed her sense of his desire to be considerate and patient, not to appear to urge her too grossly; a consideration the more studied that she was so sure he "really liked" her. Isabel told her uncle she had written to him, mentioning also his intention of coming; and the old man, in consequence, left his room earlier than usual and made his appearance at the two o'clock repast. This was by no means an act of vigilance on his part, but the fruit of a benevolent belief that his

2. There are numerous studies of London as it was described in Dickens's fiction, among them B. W. Matz, *Dickensian Inns and Taverns* (London, 1922).

3. Covent Garden hotels were not considered suitable for young ladies. [1st ed.: "Tavistock Hotel," which was for men only.]

being of the company might help to cover any conjoined straying away in case Isabel should give their noble visitor another hearing. That personage drove over from Lockleigh and brought the elder of his sisters with him, a measure presumably dictated by reflexions of the same order as Mr. Touchett's. The two visitors were introduced to Miss Stackpole, who, at luncheon, occupied a seat adjoining Lord Warburton's. Isabel, who was nervous and had no relish for the prospect of again arguing the question he had so prematurely opened, could not help admiring his good-humoured self-possession, which quite disguised the symptoms of that preoccupation with her presence it was natural she should suppose him to feel. He neither looked at her nor spoke to her, and the only sign of his emotion was that he avoided meeting her eyes. He had plenty of talk for the others, however, and he appeared to eat his luncheon with discrimination and appetite. Miss Molyneux, who had a smooth, nun-like forehead and wore a large silver cross suspended from her neck, was evidently preoccupied with Henrietta Stackpole, upon whom her eyes constantly rested in a manner suggesting a conflict between deep alienation and yearning wonder. Of the two ladies from Lockleigh she was the one Isabel had liked best; there was such a world of hereditary quiet in her. Isabel was sure moreover that her mild forehead and silver cross referred to some weird Anglican mystery —some delightful reinstitution perhaps of the quaint office of the canoness. She wondered what Miss Molyneux would think of her if she knew Miss Archer had refused her brother; and then she felt sure that Miss Molyneux would never know—that Lord Warburton never told her such things. He was fond of her and kind to her, but on the whole he told her little. Such, at least, was Isabel's theory; when, at table, she was not occupied in conversation she was usually occupied in forming theories about her neighbours. According to Isabel, if Miss Molyneux should ever learn what had passed between Miss Archer and Lord Warburton she would probably be shocked at such a girl's failure to rise; or no, rather (this was our heroine's last position) she would impute to the young American but a due consciousness of inequality.

Whatever Isabel might have made of her opportunities, at all events, Henrietta Stackpole was by no means disposed to neglect those in which she now found herself immersed. "Do you know you're the first lord I've ever seen?" she said very promptly to her neighbour. "I suppose you think I'm awfully benighted."

"You've escaped seeing some very ugly men," Lord Warburton answered, looking a trifle absently about the table.

"Are they very ugly? They try to make us believe in America that they're all handsome and magnificent and that they wear wonderful robes and crowns."

"Ah, the robes and crowns are gone out of fashion," said Lord Warburton, "like your tomahawks and revolvers."

"I'm sorry for that; I think an aristocracy ought to be splendid," Henrietta declared. "If it's not that, what is it?"

"Oh, you know, it isn't much, at the best," her neighbour allowed. "Won't you have a potato?"

"I don't care much for these European potatoes. I shouldn't know you from an ordinary American gentleman."

"Do talk to me as if I *were* one," said Lord Warburton. "I don't see how you manage to get on without potatoes; you must find so few things to eat over here."

Henrietta was silent a little; there was a chance he was not sincere. "I've had hardly any appetite since I've been here," she went on at last; "so it doesn't much matter. I don't approve of *you*, you know; I feel as if I ought to tell you that."

"Don't approve of me?"

"Yes; I don't suppose any one ever said such a thing to you before, did they? I don't approve of lords as an institution. I think the world has got beyond them—far beyond."

"Oh, so do I. I don't approve of myself in the least. Sometimes it comes over me—how I should object to myself if I were not myself, don't you know? But that's rather good, by the way—not to be vainglorious."

"Why don't you give it up then?" Miss Stackpole enquired.

"Give up—a—?" asked Lord Warburton, meeting her harsh inflexion with a very mellow one.

"Give up being a lord."

"Oh, I'm so little of one! One would really forget all about it if you wretched Americans were not constantly reminding one. However, I do think of giving it up, the little there is left of it, one of these days."

"I should like to see you do it!" Henrietta exclaimed rather grimly.

"I'll invite you to the ceremony; we'll have a supper and a dance."

"Well," said Miss Stackpole, "I like to see all sides. I don't approve of a privileged class, but I like to hear what they have to say for themselves."

"Mighty little, as you see!"

"I should like to draw you out a little more," Henrietta continued. "But you're always looking away. You're afraid of meeting my eye. I see you want to escape me."

"No, I'm only looking for those despised potatoes."

"Please explain about that young lady—your sister—then. I don't understand about her. Is she a Lady?"

"She's a capital good girl."

"I don't like the way you say that—as if you wanted to change the subject. Is her position inferior to yours?"

"We neither of us have any position to speak of; but she's better off than I, because she has none of the bother."

"Yes, she doesn't look as if she had much bother. I wish I had as little bother as that. You do produce quiet people over here, whatever else you may do."

"Ah, you see one takes life easily, on the whole," said Lord Warburton. "And then you know we're very dull. Ah, we can be dull when we try!"

"I should advise you to try something else. I shouldn't know what to talk to your sister about; she looks so different. Is that silver cross a badge?"

"A badge?"

"A sign of rank."

Lord Warburton's glance had wandered a good deal, but at this it met the gaze of his neighbour. "Oh yes," he answered in a moment; "the women go in for those things. The silver cross is worn by the eldest daughters of Viscounts." Which was his harmless revenge for having occasionally had his credulity too easily engaged in America. After luncheon he proposed to Isabel to come into the gallery and look at the pictures; and though she knew he had seen the pictures twenty times she complied without criticising this pretext. Her conscience now was very easy; ever since she sent him her letter she had felt particularly light of spirit. He walked slowly to the end of the gallery, staring at its contents and saying nothing; and then he suddenly broke out: "I hoped you wouldn't write to me that way."

"It was the only way, Lord Warburton," said the girl. "Do try and believe that."

"If I could believe it of course I should let you alone. But we can't believe by willing it; and I confess I don't understand. I could understand your disliking me; that I could understand well. But that you should admit you do—"

"What have I admitted?" Isabel interrupted, turning slightly pale.

"That you think me a good fellow; isn't that it?" She said nothing, and he went on: "You don't seem to have any reason, and that gives me a sense of injustice."

"I have a reason, Lord Warburton." She said it in a tone that made his heart contract.

"I should like very much to know it."

"I'll tell you some day when there's more to show for it."

"Excuse my saying that in the mean time I must doubt of it."

"You make me very unhappy," said Isabel.

"I'm not sorry for that; it may help you to know how I feel. Will you kindly answer me a question?" Isabel made no audible assent, but he apparently saw in her eyes something that gave him courage to go on: "Do you prefer some one else?"

"That's a question I'd rather not answer."

"Ah, you *do* then!" her suitor murmured with bitterness.

The bitterness touched her, and she cried out: "You're mistaken! I don't."

He sat down on a bench, unceremoniously, doggedly, like a man in trouble; leaning his elbows on his knees and staring at the floor. "I can't even be glad of that," he said at last, throwing himself back against the wall; "for that would be an excuse."

She raised her eyebrows in surprise. "An excuse? Must I excuse myself?"

He paid, however, no answer to the question. Another idea had come into his head. "Is it my political opinions? Do you think I go too far?"

"I can't object to your political opinions, because I don't understand them."

"You don't care what I think!" he cried, getting up. "It's all the same to you."

Isabel walked to the other side of the gallery and stood there showing him her charming back, her light slim figure, the length of her white neck as she bent her head, and the density of her dark braids. She stopped in front of a small picture as if for the purpose of examining it; and there was something so young and free in her movement that her very pliancy seemed to mock at him. Her eyes, however, saw nothing; they had suddenly been suffused with tears. In a moment he followed her, and by this time she had brushed her tears away; but when she turned round her face was pale and the expression of her eyes strange. "That reason that I wouldn't tell you —I'll tell it you after all. It's that I can't escape my fate."

"Your fate?"

"I should try to escape it if I were to marry you."

"I don't understand. Why should not *that* be your fate as well as anything else?"

"Because it's not," said Isabel femininely. "I know it's not. It's not my fate to give up—I know it can't be."

Poor Lord Warburton stared, an interrogative point in either eye. "Do you call marrying *me* giving up?"

"Not in the usual sense. It's getting—getting—getting a great deal. But it's giving up other chances."

"Other chances for what?"

"I don't mean chances to marry," said Isabel, her colour quickly coming back to her. And then she stopped, looking down with a deep frown, as if it were hopeless to attempt to make her meaning clear.

"I don't think it presumptuous in me to suggest that you'll gain more than you'll lose," her companion observed.

"I can't escape unhappiness," said Isabel. "In marrying you I shall be trying to."

"I don't know whether you'd try to, but you certainly would: that I must in candour admit!" he exclaimed with an anxious laugh.

"I mustn't—I can't!" cried the girl.

"Well, if you're bent on being miserable I don't see why you should make *me* so. Whatever charms a life of misery may have for you, it has none for me."

"I'm not bent on a life of misery," said Isabel. "I've always been intensely determined to be happy, and I've often believed I should be. I've told people that; you can ask them. But it comes over me every now and then that I can never be happy in any extraordinary way; not by turning away, by separating myself."

"By separating yourself from what?"

"From life. From the usual chances and dangers, from what most people know and suffer."

Lord Warburton broke into a smile that almost denoted hope. "Why, my dear Miss Archer," he began to explain with the most considerate eagerness, "I don't offer you any exoneration from life or from any chances or dangers whatever. I wish I could; depend upon it I would! For what do you take me, pray? Heaven help me, I'm not the Emperor of China! All I offer you is the chance of taking the common lot in a comfortable sort of way. The common lot? Why, I'm devoted to the common lot! Strike an alliance with me, and I promise you that you shall have plenty of it. You shall separate from nothing whatever—not even from your friend Miss Stackpole."

"She'd never approve of it," said Isabel, trying to smile and take advantage of this side-issue; despising herself too, not a little, for doing so.

"Are we speaking of Miss Stackpole?" his lordship asked impatiently. "I never saw a person judge things on such theoretic grounds."

"Now I suppose you're speaking of me," said Isabel with humility; and she turned away again, for she saw Miss Molyneux enter the gallery, accompanied by Henrietta and by Ralph.

Lord Warburton's sister addressed him with a certain timidity and reminded him she ought to return home in time for tea, as she was expecting company to partake of it. He made no answer—apparently not having heard her; he was preoccupied, and with good reason. Miss Molyneux—as if he had been Royalty—stood like a lady-in-waiting.

"Well, I never, Miss Molyneux!" said Henrietta Stackpole. "If I wanted to go he'd have to go. If I wanted my brother to do a thing he'd have to do it."

"Oh, Warburton does everything one wants," Miss Molyneux answered with a quick, shy laugh. "How very many pictures you have!" she went on, turning to Ralph.

"They look a good many, because they're all put together," said Ralph. "But it's really a bad way."

"Oh, I think it's so nice. I wish we had a gallery at Lockleigh. I'm so very fond of pictures," Miss Molyneux went on, persistently, to Ralph, as if she were afraid Miss Stackpole would address her again. Henrietta appeared at once to fascinate and to frighten her.

"Ah yes, pictures are very convenient," said Ralph, who appeared to know better what style of reflexion was acceptable to her.

"They're so very pleasant when it rains," the young lady continued. "It has rained of late so very often."

I'm sorry you're going away, Lord Warburton," said Henrietta. "I wanted to get a great deal more out of you."

"I'm not going away," Lord Warburton answered.

"Your sister says you must. In America the gentlemen obey the ladies."

"I'm afraid we have some people to tea," said Miss Molyneux, looking at her brother.

"Very good, my dear. We'll go."

"I hoped you would resist!" Henrietta exclaimed. "I wanted to see what Miss Molyneux would do."

"I never do anything," said this young lady.

"I suppose in your position it's sufficient for you to exist!" Miss Stackpole returned. "I should like very much to see you at home."

"You must come to Lockleigh again," said Miss Molyneux, very sweetly, to Isabel, ignoring this remark of Isabel's friend.

Isabel looked into her quiet eyes a moment, and for that moment seemed to see in their grey depths the reflexion of everything she had rejected in rejecting Lord Warburton—the peace, the kindness, the honour, the possessions, a deep security and a great exclusion. She kissed Miss Molyneux and then she said: "I'm afraid I can never come again."

"Never again?"

"I'm afraid I'm going away."

"Oh, I'm so very sorry," said Miss Molyneux. "I think that's so very wrong of you."

Lord Warburton watched this little passage; then he turned away and stared at a picture. Ralph, leaning against the rail before the picture with his hands in his pockets, had for the moment been watching him.

"I should like to see you at home," said Henrietta, whom Lord Warburton found beside him. "I should like an hour's talk with you; there are a great many questions I wish to ask you."

"I shall be delighted to see you," the proprietor of Lockleigh answered; "but I'm certain not to be able to answer many of your questions. When will you come?"

"Whenever Miss Archer will take me. We're thinking of going to London, but we'll go and see you first. I'm determined to get some satisfaction out of you."

"If it depends upon Miss Archer I'm afraid you won't get much. She won't come to Lockleigh; she doesn't like the place."

"She told me it was lovely!" said Henrietta.

Lord Warburton hesitated. "She won't come, all the same. You had better come alone," he added.

Henrietta straightened herself, and her large eyes expanded. "Would you make that remark to an English lady?" she enquired with soft asperity.

Lord Warburton stared. "Yes, if I liked her enough."

"You'd be careful not to like her enough. If Miss Archer won't visit your place again it's because she doesn't want to take me. I know what she thinks of me, and I suppose you think the same—that I oughtn't to bring in individuals." Lord Warburton was at a loss; he had not been made acquainted with Miss Stackpole's professional character and failed to catch her allusion. "Miss Archer has been warning you!" she therefore went on.

"Warning me?"

"Isn't that why she came off alone with you here—to put you on your guard?"

"Oh dear, no," said Lord Warburton brazenly; "our talk had no such solemn character as that."

"Well, you've been on your guard—intensely. I suppose it's natural to you; that's just what I wanted to observe. And so, too, Miss Molyneux—she wouldn't commit herself. *You* have been warned, anyway," Henrietta continued, addressing this young lady; "but for you it wasn't necessary."

"I hope not," said Miss Molyneux vaguely.

"Miss Stackpole takes notes," Ralph soothingly explained. "She's a great satirist; she sees through us all and she works us up."

"Well, I must say I never have had such a collection of bad material!" Henrietta declared, looking from Isabel to Lord Warburton and from this nobleman to his sister and to Ralph. "There's something the matter with you all; you're as dismal as if you had got a bad cable."

"You do see through us, Miss Stackpole," said Ralph in a low tone, giving her a little intelligent nod as he led the party out of the gallery. "There's something the matter with us all."

Isabel came behind these two; Miss Molyneux, who decidedly liked her immensely, had taken her arm, to walk beside her over the polished floor. Lord Warburton strolled on the other side with his hands behind him and his eyes lowered. For some moments he said nothing; and then, "Is it true you're going to London?" he asked.

"I believe it has been arranged."

"And when shall you come back?"

"In a few days; but probably for a very short time. I'm going to Paris with my aunt."

"When, then, shall I see you again?"

"Not for a good while," said Isabel. "But some day or other, I hope."

"Do you really hope it?"

"Very much."

He went a few steps in silence; then he stopped and put out his hand. "Good-bye."

"Good-bye," said Isabel.

Miss Molyneux kissed her again, and she let the two depart. After it, without rejoining Henrietta and Ralph, she retreated to her own room; in which apartment, before dinner, she was found by Mrs. Touchett, who had stopped on her way to the saloon. "I may as well tell you," said that lady, "that your uncle has informed me of your relations with Lord Warburton."

Isabel considered. "Relations? They're hardly relations. That's the strange part of it: he has seen me but three or four times."

"Why did you tell your uncle rather than me?" Mrs. Touchett dispassionately asked.

Again the girl hesitated. "Because he knows Lord Warburton better."

"Yes, but I know you better."

"I'm not sure of that," said Isabel, smiling.

"Neither am I, after all; especially when you give me that rather conceited look. One would think you were awfully pleased with yourself and had carried off a prize! I suppose that when you refuse an offer like Lord Warburton's it's because you expect to do something better."

"Ah, my uncle didn't say that!" cried Isabel, smiling still.

xv

It had been arranged that the two young ladies should proceed to London under Ralph's escort, though Mrs. Touchett looked with little favour on the plan. It was just the sort of plan, she said, that

Miss Stackpole would be sure to suggest, and she enquired if the correspondent of the *Interviewer* was to take the party to stay at her favourite boarding-house.

"I don't care where she takes us to stay, so long as there's local colour," said Isabel. "That's what we're going to London for."

"I suppose that after a girl has refused an English lord she may do anything," her aunt rejoined. "After that one needn't stand on trifles."

"Should you have liked me to marry Lord Warburton?" Isabel enquired.

"Of course I should."

"I thought you disliked the English so much."

"So I do; but it's all the greater reason for making use of them."

"Is that your idea of marriage?" And Isabel ventured to add that her aunt appeared to her to have made very little use of Mr. Touchett.

"Your uncle's not an English nobleman," said Mrs. Touchett, "though even if he had been I should still probably have taken up my residence in Florence."

"Do you think Lord Warburton could make me any better than I am?" the girl asked with some animation. "I don't mean I'm too good to improve. I mean—I mean that I don't love Lord Warburton enough to marry him."

"You did right to refuse him then," said Mrs. Touchett in her smallest, sparest voice. "Only, the next great offer you get, I hope you'll manage to come up to your standard."

"We had better wait till the offer comes before we talk about it. I hope very much I may have no more offers for the present. They upset me completely."

"You probably won't be troubled with them if you adopt permanently the Bohemian manner of life. However, I've promised Ralph not to criticise."

"I'll do whatever Ralph says is right," Isabel returned. "I've unbounded confidence in Ralph."

"His mother's much obliged to you!" this lady dryly laughed.

"It seems to me indeed she ought to feel it!" Isabel irrepressibly answered.

Ralph had assured her that there would be no violation of decency in their paying a visit—the little party of three—to the sights of the metropolis; but Mrs. Touchett took a different view. Like many ladies of her country who had lived a long time in Europe, she had completely lost her native tact on such points, and in her reaction, not in itself deplorable, against the liberty allowed to young persons beyond the seas, had fallen into gratuitous and exaggerated scruples. Ralph accompanied their visitors to town and

go to 131

established them at a quiet inn in a street that ran at right angles to
Piccadilly. His first idea had been to take them to his father's house
in Winchester Square, a large, dull mansion which at this period of
the year was shrouded in silence and brown holland; but he
bethought himself that, the cook being at Gardencourt, there was
no one in the house to get them their meals, and Pratt's Hotel[1]
accordingly became their resting-place. Ralph, on his side, found
quarters in Winchester Square, having a "den" there of which he
was very fond and being familiar with deeper fears than that of a
cold kitchen. He availed himself largely indeed of the resources of
Pratt's Hotel, beginning his day with an early visit to his fellow
travellers, who had Mr. Pratt in person, in a large bulging white
waistcoat, to remove their dish-covers. Ralph turned up, as he said,
after breakfast, and the little party made out a scheme of entertainment for the day. As London wears in the month of September a
face blank but for its smears of prior service, the young man, who
occasionally took an apologetic tone, was obliged to remind his
companion, to Miss Stackpole's high derision, that there wasn't a
creature in town.

"I suppose you mean the artistocracy are absent," Henrietta
answered; "but I don't think you could have a better proof that if
they were absent altogether they wouldn't be missed. It seems to
me the place is about as full as it can be. There's no one here, of
course, but three or four millions of people. What is it you call
them—the lower-middle class? They're only the population of
London, and that's of no consequence."

Ralph declared that for him the aristocracy left no void that Miss
Stackpole herself didn't fill, and that a more contented man was
nowhere at that moment to be found. In this he spoke the truth,
for the stale September days, in the huge half-empty town, had a
charm wrapped in them as a coloured gem might be wrapped in a
dusty cloth. When he went home at night to the empty house in
Winchester Square, after a chain of hours with his comparatively
ardent friends, he wandered into the big dusky dining-room, where
the candle he took from the hall-table, after letting himself in, constituted the only illumination. The square was still, the house was
still; when he raised one of the windows of the dining-room to let
in the air he heard the slow creak of the boots of a lone constable.
His own step, in the empty place, seemed loud and sonorous; some
of the carpets had been raised, and whenever he moved he roused a
melancholy echo. He sat down in one of the armchairs; the big dark
dining table twinkled here and there in the small candle-light; the
pictures on the wall, all of them very brown, looked vague and
incoherent. There was a ghostly presence as of dinners long since di-

1. A "family" hotel, mentioned in the *Notebooks*, p. 18.

gested, of table-talk that had lost its actuality. This hint of the supernatural perhaps had something to do with the fact that his imagin-
tion took a flight and that he remained in his chair a long time
beyond the hour at which he should have been in bed; doing nothing, not even reading the evening paper. I say he did nothing, and I
maintain the phrase in the face of the fact that he thought at these
moments of Isabel. To think of Isabel could only be for him an idle
pursuit, leading to nothing and profiting little to any one. His
cousin had not yet seemed to him so charming as during these days
spent in sounding, tourist-fashion, the deeps and shallows of the met-
ropolitan element. Isabel was full of premises, conclusions, emotions;
if she had come in search of local colour she found it everywhere.
She asked more questions than he could answer, and launched brave
theories, as to historic cause and social effect, that he was equally
unable to accept or to refute. The party went more than once to
the British Museum and to that brighter palace of art² which
reclaims for antique variety so large an area of a monotonous
suburb; they spent a morning in the Abbey and went on a penny-
steamer to the Tower; they looked at pictures both in public and
private collections and sat on various occasions beneath the great
trees in Kensington Gardens. Henrietta proved an indestructible
sight-seer and a more lenient judge than Ralph had ventured to
hope. She had indeed many disappointments, and London at large
suffered from her vivid remembrance of the strong points of the
American civic idea: but she made the best of its dingy dignities
and only heaved an occasional sigh and uttered a desultory "Well!"
which led no further and lost itself in retrospect. The truth was
that, as she said herself, she was not in her element. "I've not a
sympathy with inanimate objects," she remarked to Isabel at the
National Gallery;³ and she continued to suffer from the meagreness
of the glimpse that had as yet been vouchsafed to her of the inner
life. Landscapes by Turner⁴ and Assyrian bulls were a poor substitute for the literary dinner-parties at which she had hoped to meet
the genius and renown of Great Britain.

"Where are your public men, where are your men and women of
intellect?" she enquired of Ralph, standing in the middle of Trafalgar Square as if she had supposed this to be a place where she
would naturally meet a few. "That's one of them on the top of the
column, you say—Lord Nelson? Was he a lord too? Wasn't he
high enough, that they had to stick him a hundred feet in the air?
That's the past—I don't care about the past; I want to see some of

2. Probably the South Kensington Museum, opened in 1857, and now called
the Victoria and Albert Museum.
3. On Trafalgar Square, the Gallery was
described by James in an essay in 1877

(*The Painter's Eye*, p. 122).
4. J. M. W. Turner (1775–1851), English
landscape painter, chiefly a water-color-
ist.

the leading minds of the present. I won't say of the future, because I don't believe much in your future." Poor Ralph had few leading minds among his acquaintance and rarely enjoyed the pleasure of button-holing a celebrity; a state of things which appeared to Miss Stackpole to indicate a deplorable want of enterprise. "If I were on the other side I should call," she said, "and tell the gentleman, whoever he might be, that I had heard a great deal about him and had come to see for myself. But I gather from what you say that this is not the custom here. You seem to have plenty of meaningless customs, but none of those that would help along. We *are* in advance, certainly. I suppose I shall have to give up the social side altogether;" and Henrietta, though she went about with her guide-book and pencil and wrote a letter to the *Interviewer* about the Tower (in which she described the execution of Lady Jane Grey),[5] had a sad sense of falling below her mission.

The incident that had preceded Isabel's departure from Garden-court left a painful trace in our young woman's mind: when she felt again in her face, as from a recurrent wave, the cold breath of her last suitor's surprise, she could only muffle her head till the air cleared. She could not have done less than what she did; this was certainly true. But her necessity, all the same, had been as graceless as some physical act in a strained attitude, and she felt no desire to take credit for her conduct. Mixed with this imperfect pride, never-theless, was a feeling of freedom which in itself was sweet and which, as she wandered through the great city with her ill-matched companions, occasionally throbbed into odd demonstrations. When she walked in Kensington Gardens she stopped the children (mainly of the poorer sort) whom she saw playing on the grass; she asked them their names and gave them sixpence and, when they were pretty, kissed them. Ralph noticed these quaint charities; he noticed everything she did. One afternoon, that his companions might pass the time, he invited them to tea in Winchester Square, and he had the house set in order as much as possible for their visit. There was another guest to meet them, an amiable bachelor, an old friend of Ralph's who happened to be in town and for whom prompt commerce with Miss Stackpole appeared to have neither difficulty nor dread. Mr. Bantling, a stout, sleek, smiling man of forty, wonderfully dressed, universally informed and incoherently amused, laughed immoderately at everything Henrietta said, gave her several cups of tea, examined in her society the *bric-à-brac*, of which Ralph had a considerable collection, and afterwards, when the host proposed they should go out into the square and pretend it

---

5. Executed in 1554 in the Tower of London, with her husband. She had been proclaimed queen after the death of Ed- ward VI in a short-lived attempt to ex- clude Mary, a Catholic, from the throne.

was a *fête-champêtre*,[6] walked round the limited enclosure several times with her and, at a dozen turns of their talk, bounded responsive—as with a positive passion for argument—to her remarks upon the inner life.

"Oh, I see; I dare say you found it very quiet at Gardencourt. Naturally there's not much going on there when there's such a lot of illness about. Touchett's very bad, you know; the doctors have forbidden his being in England at all, and he has only come back to take care of his father. The old man, I believe, has half a dozen things the matter with him. They call it gout, but to my certain knowledge he has organic disease so developed that you may depend upon it he'll go, some day soon, quite quickly. Of course that sort of thing makes a dreadfully dull house; I wonder they have people when they can do so little for them. Then I believe Mr. Touchett's always squabbling with his wife; she lives away from her husband, you know, in that extraordinary American way of yours. If you want a house where there's always something going on, I recommend you to go down and stay with my sister, Lady Pensil, in Bedfordshire. I'll write her to-morrow and I'm sure she'll be delighted to ask you. I know just what you want—you want a house where they go in for theatricals and picnics and that sort of thing. My sister's just that sort of woman; she's always getting up something or other and she's always glad to have the sort of people who help her. I'm sure she'll ask you down by return of post: she's tremendously fond of distinguished people and writers. She writes herself, you know; but I haven't read everything she has written. It's usually poetry, and I don't go in much for poetry—unless it's Byron. I suppose you think a great deal of Byron in America," Mr. Bantling continued, expanding in the stimulating air of Miss Stackpole's attention, bringing up his sequences promptly and changing his topic with an easy turn of hand. Yet he none the less gracefully kept in sight of the idea, dazzling to Henrietta, of her going to stay with Lady Pensil in Bedforshire. "I understand what you want; you want to see some genuine English sport. The Touchetts aren't English at all, you know; they have their own habits, their own language, their own food—some odd religion even, I believe, of their own. The old man thinks it's wicked to hunt, I'm told. You must get down to my sister's in time for the theatricals, and I'm sure she'll be glad to give you a part. I'm sure you act well; I know you're very clever. My sister's forty years old and has seven children, but she's going to play the principal part. Plain as she is she makes up awfully well—I *will* say for her. Of course you needn't act if you don't want to."

In this manner Mr. Bantling delivered himself while they strolled over the grass in Winchester Square, which, although it had been

6. A village feast.

peppered by the London soot, invited the tread to linger. Henrietta thought her blooming, easy-voiced bachelor, with his impressibility to feminine merit and his splendid range of suggestion, a very agreeable man, and she valued the opportunity he offered her. "I don't know but I *would* go, if your sister should ask me. I think it would be my duty. What do you call her name?"

"Pensil. It's an odd name, but it isn't a bad one."

"I think one name's as good as another. But what's her rank?"

"Oh, she's a baron's wife; a convenient sort of rank. You're fine enough and you're not too fine."

"I don't know but what she'd be too fine for me. What do you call the place she lives in—Bedfordshire?"

"She lives away in the northern corner of it. It's a tiresome country, but I dare say you won't mind it. I'll try and run down while you're there."

All this was very pleasant to Miss Stackpole, and she was sorry to be obliged to separate from Lady Pensil's obliging brother. But it happened that she had met the day before, in Piccadilly, some friends whom she had not seen for a year: the Miss Climbers, two ladies from Wilmington, Delaware, who had been travelling on the Continent and were now preparing to re-embark. Henrietta had had a long interview with them on the Piccadilly pavement, and though the three ladies all talked at once they had not exhausted their store. It had been agreed therefore that Henrietta should come and dine with them in their lodgings in Jermyn Street at six o'clock on the morrow, and she now bethought herself of this engagement. She prepared to start for Jermyn Street, taking leave first of Ralph Touchett and Isabel, who, seated on garden chairs in another part of the enclosure, were occupied—if the term may be used—with an exchange of amenities less pointed than the practical colloquy of Miss Stackpole and Mr. Bantling. When it had been settled between Isabel and her friend that they should be reunited at some reputable hour at Pratt's Hotel, Ralph remarked that the latter must have a cab. She couldn't walk all the way to Jermyn Street.

"I suppose you mean it's improper for me to walk alone!" Henrietta exclaimed. "Merciful powers, have I come to this?"

"There's not the slightest need of your walking alone," Mr. Bantling gaily interposed. "I should be greatly pleased to go with you."

"I simply meant that you'd be late for dinner," Ralph returned. "Those poor ladies may easily believe that we refuse, at the last, to spare you."

"You had better have a hansom, Henrietta," said Isabel.

"I'll get you a hansom if you'll trust me," Mr. Bantling went on. "We might walk a little till we meet one."

"I don't see why I shouldn't trust him, do *you*?" Henrietta enquired of Isabel.

"I don't see what Mr. Bantling could do to you," Isabel obligingly answered; "but, if you like, we'll walk with you till you find your cab."

"Never mind; we'll go alone. Come on, Mr. Bantling, and take care you get me a good one."

Mr. Bantling promised to do his best, and the two took their departure, leaving the girl and her cousin together in the square, over which a clear September twilight had now begun to gather. It was perfectly still; the wide quadrangle of dusky houses showed lights in none of the windows, where the shutters and blinds were closed; the pavements were a vacant expanse, and, putting aside two small children from a neighbouring slum, who, attracted by symptoms of abnormal animation in the interior, poked their faces between the rusty rails of the enclosure, the most vivid object within sight was the big red pillar-post on the southeast corner.

"Henrietta will ask him to get into the cab and go with her to Jermyn Street," Ralph observed. He always spoke of Miss Stackpole as Henrietta.

"Very possibly," said his companion.

"Or rather, no, she won't," he went on. "But Bantling will ask leave to get in."

"Very likely again. I'm very glad they're such good friends."

"She has made a conquest. He thinks her a brilliant woman. It may go far," said Ralph.

Isabel was briefly silent. "I call Henrietta a very brilliant woman, but I don't think it will go far. They would never really know each other. He has not the least idea what she really is, and she has no just comprehension of Mr. Bantling."

"There's no more usual basis of union than a mutual misunderstanding. But it ought not to be so difficult to understand Bob Bantling," Ralph added. "He is a very simple organism."

"Yes, but Henrietta's a simpler one still. And, pray, what am I to do?" Isabel asked, looking about her through the fading light, in which the limited land-scape-gardening of the square took on a large and effective appearance. "I don't imagine that you'll propose that you and I, for our amusement, shall drive about London in a hansom."

"There's no reason we shouldn't stay here—if you don't dislike it. It's very warm; there will be half an hour yet before dark; and if you permit it I'll light a cigarette."

"You may do what you please," said Isabel, "if you'll amuse me till seven o'clock. I propose at that hour to go back and partake of a simple and solitary repast—two poached eggs and a muffin—at Pratt's Hotel."

"Mayn't I dine with you?" Ralph asked.

"No, you'll dine at your club."

They had wandered back to their chairs in the centre of the square again, and Ralph had lighted his cigarette. It would have given him extreme pleasure to be present in person at the modest little feast she had sketched; but in default of this he liked even being forbidden. For the moment, however, he liked immensely being alone with her, in the thickening dusk, in the centre of the multitudinous town; it made her seem to depend upon him and to be in his power. This power he could exert but vaguely; the best exercise of it was to accept her decisions submissively—which indeed there was already an emotion in doing. "Why won't you let me dine with you?" he demanded after a pause.

"Because I don't care for it."

"I suppose you're tired of me."

"I shall be an hour hence. You see I have the gift of foreknowledge."

"Oh, I shall be delightful meanwhile," said Ralph. But he said nothing more, and as she made no rejoinder they sat some time in a stillness which seemed to contradict his promise of entertainment. It seemed to him she was preoccupied, and he wondered what she was thinking about; there were two or three very possible subjects. At last he spoke again. "Is your objection to my society this evening caused by your expectation of another visitor?"

She turned her head with a glance of her clear, fair eyes. "Another visitor? What visitor should I have?"

He had none to suggest; which made his question seem to himself silly as well as brutal. "You've a great many friends that I don't know. You've a whole past from which I was perversely excluded."

"You were reserved for my future. You must remember that my past is over there across the water. There's none of it here in London."

"Very good, then, since your future is seated beside you. Capital thing to have your future so handy." And Ralph lighted another cigarette and reflected that Isabel probably meant she had received news that Mr. Caspar Goodwood had crossed to Paris. After he had lighted his cigarette he puffed it a while, and then he resumed. "I promised just now to be very amusing; but you see I don't come up to the mark, and the fact is there's a good deal of temerity in one's undertaking to amuse a person like you. What do you care for my feeble attempts? You've grand ideas—you've a high standard in such matters. I ought at least to bring in a band of music or a company of mountebanks."

"One mountebank's enough, and you do very well. Pray go on, and in another ten minutes I shall begin to laugh."

"I assure you I'm very serious," said Ralph. "You do really ask a great deal."

"I don't know what you mean. I ask nothing!"

"You accept nothing," said Ralph. She coloured, and now suddenly it seemed to her that she guessed his meaning. But why should he speak to her of such things? He hesitated a little and then he continued: "There's something I should like very much to say to you. It's a question I wish to ask. It seems to me I've a right to ask it, because I've a kind of interest in the answer."

"Ask what you will," Isabel replied gently, "and I'll try to satisfy you."

"Well then, I hope you won't mind my saying that Warburton has told me of something that has passed between you."

Isabel suppressed a start; she sat looking at her open fan. "Very good; I suppose it was natural he should tell you."

"I have his leave to let you know he has done so. He has some hope still," said Ralph.

"Still?"

"He had it a few days ago."

"I don't believe he has any now," said the girl.

"I'm very sorry for him then; he's such an honest man."

"Pray, did he ask you to talk to me?"

"No, not that. But he told me because he couldn't help it. We're old friends, and he was greatly disappointed. He sent me a line asking me to come and see him, and I drove over to Lockleigh the day before he and his sister lunched with us. He was very heavy-hearted; he had just got a letter from you."

"Did he show you the letter?" asked Isabel with momentary loftiness.

"By no means. But he told me it was a neat refusal. I was very sorry for him," Ralph repeated.

For some moments Isabel said nothing; then at last, "Do you know how often he had seen me?" she enquired. "Five or six times."

"That's to your glory."

"It's not for that I say it."

"What then do you say it for? Not to prove that poor Warburton's state of mind's superficial, because I'm pretty sure you don't think that."

Isabel certainly was unable to say she thought it; but presently she said something else. "If you've not been requested by Lord Warburton to argue with me, then you're doing it disinterestedly— or for the love of argument."

"I've no wish to argue with you at all. I only wish to leave you alone. I'm simply greatly interested in your own sentiments."

"I'm greatly obliged to you!" cried Isabel with a slightly nervous laugh.

"Of course you mean that I'm meddling in what doesn't concern me. But why shouldn't I speak to you of this matter without annoying you or embarrassing myself? What's the use of being your cousin if I can't have a few privileges? What's the use of adoring you without hope of a reward if I can't have a few compensations? What's the use of being ill and disabled and restricted to mere spectatorship at the game of life if I really can't see the show when I've paid so much for my ticket? Tell me this," Ralph went on while she listened to him with quickened attention. "What had you in mind when you refused Lord Warburton?"

"What had I in mind?"

"What was the logic—the view of your situation—that dictated so remarkable an act?"

"I didn't wish to marry him—if that's logic."

"No, that's not logic—and I knew that before. It's really nothing, you know. What was it you *said* to yourself? You certainly said more than that."

Isabel reflected a moment, then answered with a question of her own. "Why do you call it a remarkable act? That's what your mother thinks too."

"Warburton's such a thorough good sort; as a man, I consider he has hardly a fault. And then he's what they call here no end of a swell. He has immense possessions, and his wife would be thought a superior being. He unites the intrinsic and the extrinsic advantages."

Isabel watched her cousin to see how far he would go. "I refused him because he was too perfect then. I'm not perfect myself, and he's too good for me. Besides, his perfection would irritate me."

"That's ingenious rather than candid," said Ralph. "As a fact you think nothing in the world too perfect for you."

"Do you think I'm so good?"

"No, but you're exacting, all the same, without the excuse of thinking yourself good. Nineteen women out of twenty, however, even of the most exacting sort, would have managed to do with Warburton. Perhaps you don't know how he has been stalked."

"I don't wish to know. But it seems to me," said Isabel, "that one day when we talked of him you mentioned odd things in him."

Ralph smokingly considered. "I hope that what I said then had no weight with you; for they were not faults, the things I spoke of: they were simply peculiarities of his position. If I had known he wished to marry you I'd never have alluded to them. I think I said that as regards that position he was rather a sceptic. It would have been in your power to make him a believer."

"I think not. I don't understand the matter, and I'm not conscious of any mission of that sort. You're evidently disappointed," Isabel added, looking at her cousin with rueful gentleness. "You'd have liked me to make such a marriage."

"Not in the least. I'm absolutely without a wish on the subject. I don't pretend to advise you, and I content myself with watching you—with the deepest interest."

She gave rather a conscious sigh. "I wish I could be as interesting to myself as I am to you!"

"There you're not candid again; you're extremely interesting to yourself. Do you know, however," said Ralph, "that if you've really given Warburton his final answer I'm rather glad it has been what it was. I don't mean I'm glad for you, and still less of course for him. I'm glad for myself."

"Are *you* thinking of proposing to me?"

"By no means. From the point of view I speak of that would be fatal; I should kill the goose that supplies me with the material of my inimitable omelettes. I use that animal as the symbol of my insane illusions. What I mean is that I shall have the thrill of seeing what a young lady does who won't marry Lord Warburton."

"That's what your mother counts upon too," said Isabel.

"Ah, there will be plenty of spectators! We shall hang on the rest of your career. I shall not see all of it, but I shall probably see the most interesting years. Of course if you were to marry our friend you'd still have a career—a very decent, in fact a very brilliant one. But relatively speaking it would be a little prosaic. It would be definitely marked out in advance; it would be wanting in the unexpected. You know I'm extremely fond of the unexpected, and now that you've kept the game in your hands I depend on your giving us some grand example of it."

"I don't understand you very well," said Isabel, "but I do so well enough to be able to say that if you look for grand examples of anything from me I shall disappoint you."

"You'll do so only by disappointing yourself—and that will go hard with you!"

To this she made no direct reply; there was an amount of truth in it that would bear consideration. At last she said abruptly: "I don't see what harm there is in my wishing not to tie myself. I don't want to begin life by marrying. There are other things a woman can do."

"There's nothing she can do so well. But you're of course so many-sided."

"If one's two-sided it's enough," said Isabel.

"You're the most charming of polygons!" her companion broke out. At a glance from his companion, however, he became grave, and to prove it went on: "You want to see life—you'll be hanged if you don't, as the young men say."

"I don't think I want to see it as the young men want to see it. But I do want to look about me."

"You want to drain the cup of experience."

"No, I don't wish to touch the cup of experience. It's a poisoned drink! I only want to see for myself."

"You want to see, but not to feel," Ralph remarked.

"I don't think that if one's a sentient being one can make the distinction. I'm a good deal like Henrietta. The other day when I asked her if she wished to marry she said: 'Not till I've seen Europe!' I too don't wish to marry till I've seen Europe."

"You evidently expect a crowned head will be struck with you."

"No, that would be worse than marrying Lord Warburton. But it's getting very dark," Isabel continued, "and I must go home." She rose from her place, but Ralph only sat still and looked at her. As he remained there she stopped, and they exchanged a gaze that was full on either side, but especially on Ralph's, of utterances too vague for words.

"You've answered my question," he said at last. "You've told me what I wanted. I'm greatly obliged to you."

"It seems to me I've told you very little."

"You've told me the great thing: that the world interests you and that you want to throw yourself into it."

Her silvery eyes shone a moment in the dusk. "I never said that."

"I think you meant it. Don't repudiate it. It's so fine!"

"I don't know what you're trying to fasten upon me, for I'm not in the least an adventurous spirit. Women are not like men."

Ralph slowly rose from his seat and they walked together to the gate of the square. "No," he said; "women rarely boast of their courage. Men do so with a certain frequency."

"Men have it to boast of!"

"Women have it too. You've a great deal."

"Enough to go home in a cab to Pratt's Hotel, but not more."

Ralph unlocked the gate, and after they had passed out he fastened it. "We'll find your cab," he said; and as they turned toward a neighbouring street in which this quest might avail he asked her again if he mightn't see her safely to the inn.

"By no means," she answered; "you're very tired; you must go home and go to bed."

The cab was found, and he helped her into it, standing a moment at the door. "When people forget I'm a poor creature I'm often incommoded," he said. "But it's worse when they remember it!"

XVI

She had had no hidden motive in wishing him not to take her

home; it simply struck her that for some days past she had consumed an inordinate quantity of his time, and the independent spirit of the American girl whom extravagance of aid places in an attitude that she ends by finding "affected" had made her decide that for these few hours she must suffice to herself. She had moreover a great fondness for intervals of solitude, which since her arrival in England had been but meagrely met. It was a luxury she could always command at home and she had wittingly missed it. That evening, however, an incident occurred which—had there been a critic to note it—would have taken all colour from the theory that the wish to be quite by herself had caused her to dispense with her cousin's attendance. Seated toward nine o'clock in the dim illumination of Pratt's Hotel and trying with the aid of two tall candles to lose herself in a volume she had brought from Gardencourt, she succeeded only to the extent of reading other words than those printed on the page—words that Ralph had spoken to her that afternoon. Suddenly the well-muffled knuckle of the waiter was applied to the door, which presently gave way to his exhibition, even as a glorious trophy, of the card of a visitor. When this memento had offered to her fixed sight the name of Mr. Caspar Goodwood she let the man stand before her without signifying her wishes.

"Shall I show the gentleman up, ma'am?" he asked with a slightly encouraging inflexion.

Isabel hesitated still and while she hesitated glanced at the mirror. "He may come in," she said at last; and waited for him not so much smoothing her hair as girding her spirit.

Caspar Goodwood was accordingly the next moment shaking hands with her, but saying nothing till the servant had left the room. "Why didn't you answer my letter?" he then asked in a quick, full, slightly peremptory tone—the tone of a man whose questions were habitually pointed and who was capable of much insistence.

She answered by a ready question, "How did you know I was here?"

"Miss Stackpole let me know," said Caspar Goodwood. "She told me you would probably be at home alone this evening and would be willing to see me."

"Where did she see you—to tell you that?"

"She didn't see me; she wrote to me."

Isabel was silent; neither had sat down; they stood there with an air of defiance, or at least of contention. "Henrietta never told me she was writing to you," she said at last. "This is not kind of her."

"Is it so disagreeable to you to see me?" asked the young man.

"I didn't expect it. I don't like such surprises."

"But you knew I was in town; it was natural we should meet."

"Do you call this meeting? I hoped I shouldn't see you. In so big a place as London it seemed very possible."

"It was apparently repugnant to you even to write to me," her visitor went on.

Isabel made no reply; the sense of Henrietta Stackpole's treachery, as she momentarily qualified it, was strong within her. "Henrietta's certainly not a model of all the delicacies!" she exclaimed with bitterness. "It was a great liberty to take."

"I suppose I'm not a model either—of those virtues or of any others. The fault's mine as much as hers."

As Isabel looked at him it seemed to her that his jaw had never been more square. This might have displeased her, but she took a different turn. "No, it's not your fault so much as hers. What you've done was inevitable, I suppose, for *you*."

"It was indeed!" cried Caspar Goodwood with a voluntary laugh. "And now that I've come, at any rate, mayn't I stay?"

"You may sit down, certainly."

She went back to her chair again, while her visitor took the first place that offered, in the manner of a man accustomed to pay little thought to that sort of furtherance. "I've been hoping every day for an answer to my letter. You might have written me a few lines."

"It wasn't the trouble of writing that prevented me; I could as easily have written you four pages as one. But my silence was an intention," Isabel said. "I thought it the best thing."

He sat with eyes fixed on hers while she spoke; then he lowered them and attached them to a spot in the carpet as if he were making a strong effort to say nothing but what he ought. He was a strong man in the wrong, and he was acute enough to see that an uncompromising exhibition of his strength would only throw the falsity of his position into relief. Isabel was not incapable of tasting any advantage of position over a person of this quality, and though little desirous to flaunt it in his face she could enjoy being able to say "You know you oughtn't to have written to me yourself!" and to say it with an air of triumph.

Caspar Goodwood raised his eyes to her own again; they seemed to shine through a vizard of a helmet. He had a strong sense of justice and was ready any day in the year—over and above this—to argue the question of his rights. "You said you hoped never to hear from me again; I know that. But I never accepted any such rule as my own. I warned you that you should hear very soon."

"I didn't say I hoped *never* to hear from you," said Isabel.

"Not for five years then; for ten years; twenty years. It's the same thing."

"Do you find it so? It seems to me there's a great difference. I can imagine that at the end of ten years we might have a very pleasant correspondence. I shall have matured my epistolary style."

She looked away while she spoke these words, knowing them of so much less earnest a cast than the countenance of her listener. Her eyes, however, at last came back to him, just as he said very irrelevantly: "Are you enjoying your visit to your uncle?"

"Very much indeed." She dropped, but then she broke out. "What good do you expect to get by insisting?"

"The good of not losing you."

"You've no right to talk of losing what's not yours. And even from your own point of view," Isabel added, "You ought to know when to let one alone."

"I disgust you very much," said Caspar Goodwood gloomily; not as if to provoke her to compassion for a man conscious of this blighting fact, but as if to set it well before himself, so that he might endeavour to act with his eyes on it.

"Yes, you don't at all delight me, you don't fit in, not in any way, just now, and the worst is that your putting it to the proof in this manner is quite unnecessary." It wasn't certainly as if his nature had been soft, so that pin-pricks would draw blood from it; and from the first of her acquaintance with him, and of her having to defend herself against a certain air that he had of knowing better what was good for her than she knew herself, she had recognised the fact that perfect frankness was her best weapon. To attempt to spare his sensibility or to escape from him edgewise, as one might do from a man who had barred the way less sturdily—this, in dealing with Caspar Goodwood, who would grasp at everything of every sort that one might give him, was wasted agility. It was not that he had not susceptibilities, but his passive surface, as well as his active, was large and hard, and he might always be trusted to dress his wounds, so far as they required it, himself. She came back, even for her measure of possible pangs and aches in him, to her old sense that he was naturally plated and steeled, armed essentially for aggression.

"I can't reconcile myself to that," he simply said. There was a dangerous liberality about it; for she felt how open it was to him to make the point that he had not always disgusted her.

"I can't reconcile myself to it either, and it's not the state of things that ought to exist between us. If you'd only try to banish me from your mind for a few months we should be on good terms again."

"I see. If I should cease to think of you at all for a prescribed time, I should find I could keep it up indefinitely."

"Indefinitely is more than I ask. It's more even than I should like."

"You know that what you ask is impossible," said the young man, taking his adjective for granted in a manner she found irritating.

"Aren't you capable of making a calculated effort?" she demanded. "You're strong for everything else; why shouldn't you be strong for that?"

"An effort calculated for what?" And then as she hung fire, "I'm capable of nothing with regard to you," he went on, "but just of being infernally in love with you. If one's strong one loves only the more strongly."

"There's a good deal in that;" and indeed our young lady felt the force of it—felt it thrown off, into the vast of truth and poetry, as practically a bait to her imagination. But she promptly came round. "Think of me or not, as you find most possible; only leave me alone."

"Until when?"

"Well, for a year or two."

"Which do you mean? Between one year and two there's all the difference in the world."

"Call it two then," said Isabel with a studied effect of eagerness.

"And what shall I gain by that?" her friend asked with no sign of wincing.

"You'll have obliged me greatly."

"And what will be my reward?"

"Do you need a reward for an act of generosity?"

"Yes, when it involves a great sacrifice."

"There's no generosity without some sacrifice. Men don't understand such things. If you make the sacrifice you'll have all my admiration."

"I don't care a cent for your admiration—not one straw, with nothing to show for it. When will you marry me? That's the only question."

"Never—if you go on making me feel only as I feel at present."

"What do I gain then by not trying to make you feel otherwise?"

"You'll gain quite as much as by worrying me to death!" Caspar Goodwood bent his eyes again and gazed a while into the crown of his hat. A deep flush overspread his face; she could see her sharpness had at last penetrated. This immediately had a value—classic, romantic, redeeming, what did she know?—for her; "the strong man in pain" was one of the categories of the human appeal, little charm as he might exert in the given case. "Why do you make me say such things to you?" she cried in a trembling voice. "I only want to be gentle—to be thoroughly kind. It's not delightful to me to feel people care for me and yet to have to try and reason them out of it. I think others also ought to be considerate; we have each to judge for ourselves. I know you're considerate, as much as you can be; you've good reasons for what you do. But I really don't want to marry, or to talk about it at all now. I shall probably never do it—no, never. I've a perfect right to feel that way, and it's no kindness to a woman to press her so hard, to urge her against her will. If I give you pain I can only say I'm very sorry. It's not my fault; I can't marry you simply to please you. I won't say that I shall always remain your friend, because when women say that, in these situations, it passes, I believe, for a sort of mockery. But try me some day."

Caspar Goodwood, during this speech, had kept his eyes fixed upon the name of his hatter, and it was not until some time after she had ceased speaking that he raised them. When he did so the sight of a rosy, lovely eagerness in Isabel's face threw some confusion into his attempt to analyse her words. "I'll go home—I'll go to-morrow—I'll leave you alone," he brought out at last. "Only," he heavily said, "I hate to lose sight of you!"

"Never fear. I shall do no harm."

"You'll marry some one else, as sure as I sit here," Caspar Goodwood declared.

"Do you think that a generous charge?"

"Why not? Plenty of men will try to make you."

"I told you just now that I don't wish to marry and that I almost certainly never shall."

"I know you did, and I like your 'almost certainly'! I put no faith in what you say."

"Thank you very much. Do you accuse me of lying to shake you off? You say very delicate things."

"Why should I not say that? You've given me no pledge of anything at all."

"No, that's all that would be wanting!"

"You may perhaps even believe you're safe—from wishing to be. But you're not," the young man went on as if preparing himself for the worst.

"Very well then. We'll put it that I'm not safe. Have it as you please."

"I don't know, however," said Caspar Goodwood, "that my keeping you in sight would prevent it."

"Don't you indeed? I'm after all very much afraid of you. Do you think I'm so very easily pleased?" she asked suddenly, changing her tone.

"No—I don't; I shall try to console myself with that. But there are a certain number of very dazzling men in the world, no doubt;

and if there were only one it would be enough. The most dazzling of all will make straight for you. You'll be sure to take no one who isn't dazzling."

"If you mean by dazzling brilliantly clever," Isabel said—"and I can't imagine what else you mean—I don't need the aid of a clever man to teach me how to live. I can find it out for myself."

"Find out how to live alone? I wish that, when you have, you'd teach *me!*"

She looked at him a moment; then with a quick smile, "Oh, *you* ought to marry!" she said.

He might be pardoned if for an instant this exclamation seemed to him to sound the infernal note, and it is not on record that her motive for discharging such a shaft had been of the clearest. He oughtn't to stride about lean and hungry, however—she certainly felt *that* for him. "God forgive you!" he murmured between his teeth as he turned away.

Her accent had put her slightly in the wrong, and after a moment she felt the need to right herself. The easiest way to do it was to place him where she had been. "You do me great injustice —you say what you don't know!" she broke out. "I shouldn't be an easy victim—I've proved it."

"Oh, to me, perfectly."

"I've proved it to others as well." And she paused a moment. "I refused a proposal of marriage last week; what they call—no doubt —a dazzling one."

"I'm very glad to hear it," said the young man gravely.

"It was a proposal many girls would have accepted; it had everything to recommend it." Isabel had not proposed to herself to tell this story, but, now she had begun, the satisfaction of speaking it out and doing herself justice took possession of her. "I was offered a great position and a great fortune—by a person whom I like extremely."

Caspar watched her with intense interest. "Is he an Englishman?"

"He's an English nobleman," said Isabel.

Her visitor received this announcement at first in silence, but at last said: "I'm glad he's disappointed."

"Well then, as you have companions in misfortune, make the best of it."

"I don't call him a companion," said Caspar grimly.

"Why not—since I declined his offer absolutely?"

"That doesn't make him my companion. Besides, he's an Englishman."

"And pray isn't an Englishman a human being?" Isabel asked.

"Oh, those people? They're not of *my* humanity, and I don't care what becomes of them."

"You're very angry," said the girl. "We've discussed this matter quite enough."

"Oh yes, I'm very angry. I plead guilty to that!"

She turned away from him, walked to the open window and stood a moment looking into the dusky void of the street, where a turbid gaslight alone represented social animation. For some time neither of these young persons spoke; Caspar lingered near the chimney-piece with eyes gloomily attached. She had virtually requested him to go—he knew that; but at the risk of making himself odious he kept his ground. She was too nursed a need to be easily renounced, and he had crossed the sea all to wring from her some scrap of a vow. Presently she left the window and stood again before him. "You do me very little justice—after my telling you what I told you just now. I'm sorry I told you—since it matters so little to you."

"Ah," cried the young man, "if you were thinking of *me* when you did it!" And then he paused with the fear that she might contradict so happy a thought.

"I was thinking of you a little," said Isabel.

"A little? I don't understand. If the knowledge of what I feel for you had any weight with you at all, calling it a 'little' is a poor account of it."

Isabel shook her head as if to carry off a blunder. "I've refused a most kind, noble gentleman. Make the most of that."

"I thank you then," said Caspar Goodwood gravely. "I thank you immensely."

"And now you had better go home."

"May I not see you again?" he asked.

"I think it's better not. You'll be sure to talk of this, and you see it leads to nothing."

"I promise you not to say a word that will annoy you."

Isabel reflected and then answered: "I return in a day or two to my uncle's, and I can't propose to you to come there. It would be too inconsistent."

Caspar Goodwood, on his side, considered. "You must do me justice too. I received an invitation to your uncle's more than a week ago, and I declined it."

She betrayed surprise. "From whom was your invitation?"

"From Mr. Ralph Touchett, whom I suppose to be your cousin. I declined it because I had not your authorisation to accept it. The suggestion that Mr. Touchett should invite me appeared to have come from Miss Stackpole."

"It certainly never did from me. Henrietta really goes very far," Isabel added.

"Don't be too hard on her—that touches *me*."

"No; if you declined you did quite right, and I thank you for it." And she gave a little shudder of dismay at the thought that Lord Warburton and Mr. Goodwood might have met at Gardencourt: it would have been so awkward for Lord Warburton.

"When you leave your uncle where do you go?" her companion asked.

"I go abroad with my aunt—to Florence and other places."

The serenity of this announcement struck a chill to the young man's heart; he seemed to see her whirled away into circles from which he was inexorably excluded. Nevertheless he went on quickly with his questions. "And when shall you come back to America?"

"Perhaps not for a long time. I'm very happy here."

"Do you mean to give up your country?"

"Don't be an infant!"

"Well, you'll be out of my sight indeed!" said Caspar Goodwood.

"I don't know," she answered rather grandly. "The world—with all these places so arranged and so touching each other—comes to strike one as rather small."

It's a sight too big for *me!*" Caspar exclaimed with a simplicity our young lady might have found touching if her face had not been set against concessions.

This attitude was part of a system, a theory, that she had lately embraced, and to be thorough she said after a moment: "Don't think me unkind if I say it's just *that*—being out of your sight— that I like. If you were in the same place I should feel you were watching me, and I don't like that—I like my liberty too much. If there's a thing in the world I'm fond of," she went on with a slight recurrence of grandeur, "it's my personal independence."

But whatever there might be of the too superior in this speech moved Caspar Goodwood's admiration; there was nothing he winced at in the large air of it. He had never supposed she hadn't wings and the need of beautiful free movements—he wasn't, with his own long arms and strides, afraid of any force in her. Isabel's words, if they had been meant to shock him, failed of the mark and only made him smile with the sense that here was common ground. "Who would wish less to curtail your liberty than I? What can give me greater pleasure than to see you perfectly independent—doing whatever you like? It's to make you independent that I want to marry you."

"That's a beautiful sophism," said the girl with a smile more beautiful still.

"An unmarried woman—a girl of your age—isn't independent. There are all sorts of things she can't do. She's hampered at every step."

"That's as she looks at the question," Isabel answered with much spirit. "I'm not in my first youth—I can do what I choose—I belong quite to the independent class. I've neither father nor mother; I'm poor and of a serious disposition; I'm not pretty. I therefore am not bound to be timid and conventional; indeed I can't afford such luxuries. Besides, I try to judge things for myself; to judge wrong, I think, is more honourable than not to judge at all. I don't wish to be a mere sheep in the flock; I wish to choose my fate and know something of human affairs beyond what other people think it compatible with propriety to tell me." She paused a moment, but not long enough for her companion to reply. He was apparently on the point of doing so when she went on: "Let me say this to you, Mr. Goodwood. You're so kind as to speak of being afraid of my marrying. If you should hear a rumour that I'm on the point of doing so—girls are liable to have such things said about them—remember what I have told you about my love of liberty and venture to doubt it."

There was something passionately positive in the tone in which she gave him this advice, and he saw a shining candour in her eyes that helped him to believe her. On the whole he felt reassured, and you might have perceived it by the manner in which he said, quite eagerly: "You want simply to travel for two years? I'm quite willing to wait two years, and you may do what you like in the interval. If that's all you want, pray say so. I don't want you to be conventional; do I strike you as conventional myself? Do you want to improve your mind? Your mind's quite good enough for me; but if it interests you to wander about a while and see different countries I shall be delighted to help you in any way in my power."

"You're very generous; that's nothing new to me. The best way to help me will be to put as many hundred miles of sea between us as possible."

"One would think you were going to commit some atrocity!" said Caspar Goodwood.

"Perhaps I am. I wish to be free even to do that if the fancy takes me."

"Well then," he said slowly, "I'll go home." And he put out his hand, trying to look contented and confident.

Isabel's confidence in him, however, was greater than any he could feel in her. Not that he thought her capable of committing an atrocity; but, turn it over as he would, there was something ominous in the way she reserved her option. As she took his hand she felt a great respect for him; she knew how much he cared for her and she thought him magnanimous. They stood so for a moment, looking at each other, united by a hand-clasp which was not merely passive on her side. "That's right," she said very kindly, almost tenderly. "You'll lose nothing by being a reasonable man."

"But I'll come back, wherever you are, two years hence," he returned with characteristic grimness.

We have seen that our young lady was inconsequent, and at this she suddenly changed her note. "Ah, remember, I promise nothing —absolutely nothing!" Then more softly, as if to help him to leave her: "And remember too that I shall not be an easy victim!"

"You'll get very sick of your independence."

"Perhaps I shall; it's even very probable. When that day comes I shall be very glad to see you."

She had laid her hand on the knob of the door that led into her room, and she waited a moment to see whether her visitor would not take his departure. But he appeared unable to move; there was still an immense unwillingness in his attitude and a sore remonstrance in his eyes. "I must leave you now," said Isabel; and she opened the door and passed into the other room.

The apartment was dark, but the darkness was tempered by a vague radiance sent up through the window from the court of the hotel, and Isabel could make out the masses of the furniture, the dim shining of the mirror and the looming of the big four-posted bed. She stood still a moment, listening, and at last she heard Caspar Goodwood walk out of the sitting-room and close the door behind him. She stood still a little longer, and then, by an irresistible impulse, dropped on her knees before her bed and hid her face in her arms.

XVII

She was not praying; she was trembling—trembling all over. Vibration was easy to her, was in fact too constant with her, and she found herself now humming like a smitten harp. She only asked, however, to put on the cover, to case herself again in brown holland, but she wished to resist her excitement, and the attitude of devotion, which she kept for some time, seemed to help her to be still. She intensely rejoiced that Caspar Goodwood was gone; there was something in having thus got rid of him that was like the payment, for a stamped receipt, of some debt too long on her mind. As she felt the glad relief she bowed her head a little lower; the sense was there, throbbing in her heart; it was part of her emotion, but it was a thing to be ashamed of—it was profane and out of place. It was not for some ten minutes that she rose from her knees, and even when she came back to the sitting-room her tremor had not quite subsided. It had had, verily, two causes: part of it was to be accounted for by her long discussion with Mr. Goodwood, but it might be feared that the rest was simply the enjoyment she found in the exercise of her power. She sat down in the same chair again and took up her book, but without going through the form of opening the volume. She leaned back, with that low, soft, aspiring murmur with which she often uttered her response to accidents of which the brighter side was not superficially obvious, and yielded to the satisfaction of having refused two ardent suitors in a fortnight. That love of liberty of which she had given Caspar Goodwood so bold a sketch was as yet almost exclusively theoretic; she had not been able to indulge it on a large scale. But it appeared to her she had done something; she had tasted of the delight, if not of battle, at least of victory; she had done what was truest to her plan. In the glow of this consciousness the image of Mr. Goodwood taking his sad walk homeward through the dingy town presented itself with a certain reproachful force; so that, as at the same moment the door of the room was opened, she rose with an apprehension that he had come back. But it was only Henrietta Stackpole returning from her dinner.

Miss Stackpole immediately saw that our young lady had been "through" something, and indeed the discovery demanded no great penetration. She went straight up to her friend, who received her without a greeting. Isabel's elation in having sent Caspar Goodwood back to America presupposed her being in a manner glad he had come to see her; but at the same time she perfectly remembered Henrietta had had no right to set a trap for her. "Has he been here, dear?" the latter yearningly asked.

Isabel turned away and for some moments answered nothing. "You acted very wrongly," she declared at last.

"I acted for the best. I only hope you acted as well."

"You're not the judge. I can't trust you," said Isabel.

This declaration was unflattering, but Henrietta was much too unselfish to heed the charge it conveyed; she cared only for what it intimated with regard to her friend. "Isabel Archer," she observed with equal abruptness and solemnity, "if you marry one of these people I'll never speak to you again!"

"Before making so terrible a threat you had better wait till I'm asked," Isabel replied. Never having said a word to Miss Stackpole about Lord Warburton's overtures, she had now no impulse whatever to justify herself to Henrietta by telling her that she had refused that nobleman.

"Oh, you'll be asked quick enough, once you get off on the Continent. Annie Climber was asked three times in Italy—poor plain little Annie."

"Well, if Annie Climber wasn't captured why should I be?"

"I don't believe Annie was pressed; but you'll be."

"That's a flattering conviction," said Isabel without alarm.

"I don't flatter you, Isabel, I tell you the truth!" cried her friend. "I hope you don't mean to tell me that you didn't give Mr. Goodwood some hope."

"I don't see why I should tell you anything; as I said to you just now, I can't trust you. But since you're so much interested in Mr. Goodwood I won't conceal from you that he returns immediately to America."

"You don't mean to say you've sent him off?" Henrietta almost shrieked.

"I asked him to leave me alone; and I ask you the same, Henrietta." Miss Stackpole glittered for an instant with dismay, and then passed to the mirror over the chimney-piece and took off her bonnet. "I hope you've enjoyed your dinner," Isabel went on.

But her companion was not to be diverted by frivolous propositions. "Do you know where you're going, Isabel Archer?"

"Just now I'm going to bed," said Isabel with persistent frivolity.

"Do you know where you're drifting?" Henrietta pursued, holding out her bonnet delicately.

"No, I haven't the least idea, and I find it very pleasant not to know. A swift carriage, of a dark night, rattling with four horses over roads that one can't see—that's my idea of happiness."

"Mr. Goodwood certainly didn't teach you to say such things as that—like the heroine of an immoral novel," said Miss Stackpole. "You're drifting to some great mistake."

Isabel was irritated by her friend's interference, yet she still tried to think what truth this declaration could represent. She could think of nothing that diverted her from saying: "You must be very fond of me, Henrietta, to be willing to be so aggressive."

"I love you intensely, Isabel," said Miss Stackpole with feeling.

"Well, if you love me intensely let me as intensely alone. I asked that of Mr. Goodwood, and I must also ask it of you."

"Take care you're not let alone too much."

"That's what Mr. Goodwood said to me. I told him I must take the risks."

"You're a creature of risks—you make me shudder!" cried Henrietta. "When does Mr. Goodwood return to America?"

"I don't know—he didn't tell me."

"Perhaps you didn't enquire," said Henrietta with the note of righteous irony.

"I gave him too little satisfaction to have the right to ask questions of him."

This assertion seemed to Miss Stackpole for a moment to bid

defiance to comment; but at last she exclaimed: "Well, Isabel, if I didn't know you I might think you were heartless!"

"Take care," said Isabel; "you're spoiling me."

"I'm afraid I've done that already. I hope, at least," Miss Stackpole added, "that he may cross with Annie Climber!"

Isabel learned from her the next morning that she had determined not to return to Gardencourt (where old Mr. Touchett had promised her a renewed welcome), but to await in London the arrival of the invitation that Mr. Bantling had promised her from his sister Lady Pensil. Miss Stackpole related very freely her conversation with Ralph Touchett's sociable friend and declared to Isabel that she really believed she had now got hold of something that would lead to something. On the receipt of Lady Pensil's letter—Mr. Bantling had virtually guaranteed the arrival of this document—she would immediately depart for Bedfordshire, and if Isabel cared to look out for her impressions in the *Interviewer* she would certainly find them. Henrietta was evidently going to see something of the inner life this time.

"Do you know where you're drifting, Henrietta Stackpole?" Isabel asked, imitating the tone in which her friend had spoken the night before.

"I'm drifting to a big position—that of the Queen of American Journalism. If my next letter isn't copied all over the West I'll swallow my penwiper!"

She had arranged with her friend Miss Annie Climber, the young lady of the continental offers, that they should go together to make those purchases which were to constitute Miss Climber's farewell to a hemisphere in which she at least had been appreciated; and she presently repaired to Jermyn Street to pick up her companion. Shortly after her departure Ralph Touchett was announced, and as soon as he came in Isabel saw he had something on his mind. He very soon took his cousin into his confidence. He had received from his mother a telegram to the effect that his father had had a sharp attack of his old malady, that she was much alarmed and that she begged he would instantly return to Gardencourt. On this occasion at least Mrs. Touchett's devotion to the electric wire was not open to criticism.

"I've judged it best to see the great doctor, Sir Matthew Hope, first," Ralph said; "by great good luck he's in town. He's to see me at half-past twelve, and I shall make sure of his coming down to Gardencourt—which he will do the more readily as he has already seen my father several times, both there and in London. There's an express at two-forty-five, which I shall take; and you'll come back with me or remain here a few days longer, exactly as you prefer."

"I shall certainly go with you," Isabel returned. "I don't suppose

I can be of any use to my uncle, but if he's ill I shall like to be near him."

"I think you're fond of him," said Ralph with a certain shy pleasure in his face. "You appreciate him, which all the world hasn't done. The quality's too fine."

"I quite adore him," Isabel after a moment said.

"That's very well. After his son he's your greatest admirer."

She welcomed this assurance, but she gave secretly a small sigh of relief at the thought that Mr. Touchett was one of those admirers who couldn't propose to marry her. This, however, was not what she spoke; she went on to inform Ralph that there were other reasons for her not remaining in London. She was tired of it and wished to leave it; and then Henrietta was going away—going to stay in Bedfordshire.

"In Bedfordshire?"

"With Lady Pensil, the sister of Mr. Bantling, who has answered for an invitation."

Ralph was feeling anxious, but at this he broke into a laugh. Suddenly, none the less, his gravity returned. "Bantling's a man of courage. But if the invitation should get lost on the way?"

"I thought the British post-office was impeccable."

"The good Homer sometimes nods,"[1] said Ralph. "However," he went on more brightly, "the good Bantling never does, and, whatever happens, he'll take care of Henrietta."

Ralph went to keep his appointment with Sir Mathew Hope, and Isabel made her arrangements for quitting Pratt's Hotel. Her uncle's danger touched her nearly, and while she stood before her open trunk, looking about her vaguely for what she should put into it, the tears suddenly rose to her eyes. It was perhaps for this reason that when Ralph came back at two o'clock to take her to the station she was not yet ready. He found Miss Stackpole, however, in the sitting-room, where she had just risen from her luncheon, and this lady immediately expressed her regret at his father's illness.

"He's a grand old man," she said; "he's faithful to the last. If it's really to be the last—pardon my alluding to it, but you must often have thought of the possibility—I'm sorry that I shall not be at Gardencourt."

"You'll amuse yourself much more in Bedfordshire."

"I shall be sorry to amuse myself at such a time," said Henrietta with much propriety. But she immediately added: "I should like so to commemorate the closing scene."

"My father may live a long time," said Ralph simply. Then, adverting to topics more cheerful, he interrogated Miss Stackpole as to her own future.

1. The original of this common phrase,   is in Horace's *Ars Poetica* (1.359).
meaning "even the best make mistakes,"

Now that Ralph was in trouble she addressed him in a tone of larger allowance and told him that she was much indebted to him for having made her acquainted with Mr. Bantling. "He has told me just the things I want to know," she said; "all the society-items and all about the royal family. I can't make out that what he tells me about the royal family is much to their credit; but he says that's only my peculiar way of looking at it. Well, all I want is that he should give me the facts; I can put them together quick enough, once I've got them." And she added that Mr. Bantling had been so good as to promise to come and take her out that afternoon.

"To take you where?" Ralph ventured to enquire.

"To Buckingham Palace. He's going to show me over it, so that I may get some idea how they live."

"Ah," said Ralph, "we leave you in good hands. The first thing we shall hear is that you're invited to Windsor Castle."

"If they ask me, I shall certainly go. Once I get started I'm not afraid. But for all that," Henrietta added in a moment, "I'm not satisfied; I'm not at peace about Isabel."

"What is her last misdemeanour?"

"Well, I've told you before, and I suppose there's no harm in my going on. I always finish a subject that I take up. Mr. Goodwood was here last night."

Ralph opened his eyes; he even blushed a little—his blush being the sign of an emotion somewhat acute. He remembered that Isabel, in separating from him in Winchester Square, had repudiated his suggestion that her motive in doing so was the expectation of a visitor at Pratt's Hotel, and it was a new pang to him to have to suspect her of duplicity. On the other hand, he quickly said to himself, what concern was it of his that she should have made an appointment with a lover? Had it not been thought graceful in every age that young ladies should make a mystery of such appointments? Ralph gave Miss Stackpole a diplomatic answer. "I should have thought that, with the views you expressed to me the other day, this would satisfy you perfectly."

"That he should come to see her? That was very well, as far as it went. It was a little plot of mine; I let him know that we were in London, and when it had been arranged that I should spend the evening out I sent him a word—the word we just utter to the 'wise.' I hoped he would find her alone; I won't pretend I didn't hope that you'd be out of the way. He came to see her, but he might as well have stayed away."

"Isabel was cruel?"—and Ralph's face lighted with the relief of his cousin's not having shown duplicity.

"I don't exactly know what passed between them. But she gave him no satisfaction—she sent him back to America."

"Poor Mr. Goodwood!" Ralph sighed.

"Her only idea seems to be to get rid of him," Henrietta went on.

"Poor Mr. Goodwood!" Ralph repeated. The exclamation, it must be confessed, was automatic; it failed exactly to express his thoughts, which were taking another line.

"You don't say that as if you felt it. I don't believe you care."

"Ah," said Ralph, "you must remember that I don't know this interesting young man—that I've never seen him."

"Well, I shall see him, and I shall tell him not to give up. If I didn't believe Isabel would come round," Miss Stackpole added— "well, I'd give up myself. I mean I'd give *her* up!"

XVIII

It had occurred to Ralph that, in the conditions, Isabel's parting with her friend might be of a slightly embarrassed nature, and he went down to the door of the hotel in advance of his cousin, who, after a slight delay, followed with the traces of an unaccepted remonstrance, as he thought, in her eyes. The two made the journey to Gardencourt in almost unbroken silence, and the servant who met them at the station had no better news to give them of Mr. Touchett—a fact which caused Ralph to congratulate himself afresh on Sir Matthew Hope's having promised to come down in the five o'clock train and spend the night. Mrs. Touchett, he learned, on reaching home, had been constantly with the old man and was with him at that moment; and this fact made Ralph say to himself that, after all, what his mother wanted was just easy occasion. The finer natures were those that shone at the larger times. Isabel went to her own room, noting throughout the house that perceptible hush which precedes a crisis. At the end of an hour, however, she came downstairs in search of her aunt, whom she wished to ask about Mr. Touchett. She went into the library, but Mrs. Touchett was not there, and as the weather, which had been damp and chill, was now altogether spoiled, it was not probable she had gone for her usual walk in the grounds. Isabel was on the point of ringing to send a question to her room, when this purpose quickly yielded to an unexpected sound—the sound of low music proceeding apparently from the saloon. She knew her aunt never touched the piano, and the musician was therefore probably Ralph, who played for his own amusement. That he should have resorted to this recreation at the present time indicated apparently that his anxiety about his father had been relieved; so that the girl took her way, almost with restored cheer, toward the source of the harmony. The drawing-room at Gardencourt was an apartment of great distances, and, as the piano was placed at the end of it furthest removed from the door at which she entered, her arrival was not noticed by the person seated before the instrument. This person was neither Ralph nor his mother; it was a lady whom Isabel immediately saw to be a stranger to herself, though her back was presented to the door. This back—an ample and well-dressed one—Isabel viewed for some moments with surprise. The lady was of course a visitor who had arrived during her absence and who had not been mentioned by either of the servants—one of them her aunt's maid—of whom she had had speech since her return. Isabel had already learned, however, with what treasures of reserve the function of receiving orders may be accompanied, and she was particularly conscious of having been treated with dryness by her aunt's maid, through whose hands she had slipped perhaps a little too mistrustfully and with an effect of plumage but the more lustrous. The advent of a guest was in itself far from disconcerting; she had not yet divested herself of a young faith that each new aquaintance would exert some momentous influence on her life. By the time she had made these reflexions she became aware that the lady at the piano played remarkably well. She was playing something of Schubert's—Isabel knew not what, but recognised Schubert[1]—and she touched the piano with a discretion of her own. It showed skill, it showed feeling; Isabel sat down noiselessly on the nearest chair and waited till the end of the piece. When it was finished she felt a strong desire to thank the player, and rose from her seat to do so, while at the same time the stranger turned quickly round, as if but just aware of her presence.

"That's very beautiful, and your playing makes it more beautiful still," said Isabel with all the young radiance with which she usually uttered a truthful rapture.

"You don't think I disturbed Mr. Touchett then?" the musician answered as sweetly as this compliment deserved. "The house is so large and his room so far away that I thought I might venture, especially as I played just—just *du bout des doigts*."[2]

"She's a Frenchwoman," Isabel said to herself; "she says that as if she were French." And this supposition made the visitor more interesting to our speculative heroine. "I hope my uncle's doing well," Isabel added. "I should think that to hear such lovely music as that would really make him feel better."

The lady smiled and discriminated. "I'm afraid there are moments in life when even Schubert has nothing to say to us. We must admit, however, that they are our worst."

"I'm not in that state now then," said Isabel. "On the contrary I should be so glad if you would play something more."

"If it will give you pleasure—delighted." And this obliging person took her place again and struck a few chords, while Isabel sat down nearer the instrument. Suddenly the new-comer stopped

1. [1st ed.: "Beethoven."]   2. At the tip of my fingers.

with her hands on the keys, half-turning and looking over her shoulder. She was forty years old and not pretty, though her expression charmed. "Pardon me," she said; "but are you the niece—the young American?"

"I'm my aunt's niece," Isabel replied with simplicity.

The lady at the piano sat still a moment longer, casting her air of interest over her shoulder. "That's very well; we're compatriots." And then she began to play.

"Ah then she's not French," Isabel murmured; and as the opposite supposition had made her romantic it might have seemed that this revelation would have marked a drop. But such was not the fact; rarer even than to be French seemed it to be American on such interesting terms.

The lady played in the same manner as before, softly and solemnly, and while she played the shadows deepened in the room. The autumn twilight gathered in, and from her place Isabel could see the rain, which had now begun in earnest, washing the cold-looking lawn and the wind shaking the great trees. At last, when the music had ceased, her companion got up and, coming nearer with a smile, before Isabel had time to thank her again, said: "I'm very glad you've come back; I've heard a great deal about you."

Isabel thought her a very attractive person, but nevertheless spoke with a certain abruptness in reply to this speech. "From whom have you heard about me?"

The stranger hesitated a single moment and then, "From your uncle," she answered. "I've been here three days, and the first day he let me come and pay him a visit in his room. Then he talked constantly of you."

"As you didn't know me that must rather have bored you."

"It made me want to know you. All the more that since then—your aunt being so much with Mr. Touchett—I've been quite alone and have got rather tired of my own society. I've not chosen a good moment for my visit."

A servant had come in with lamps and was presently followed by another bearing the tea-tray. On the appearance of this repast Mrs. Touchett had apparently been notified, for she now arrived and addressed herself to the tea-pot. Her greeting to her niece did not differ materially from her manner of raising the lid of this receptacle in order to glance at the contents: in neither act was it becoming to make a show of avidity. Questioned about her husband she was unable to say he was better; but the local doctor was with him, and much light was expected from this gentleman's consultation with Sir Matthew Hope.

"I suppose you two ladies have made acquaintance," she pursued. "If you haven't I recommend you to do so; for so long as we continue—Ralph and I—to cluster about Mr. Touchett's bed you're not likely to have much society but each other."

"I know nothing about you but that you're a great musician," Isabel said to the visitor.

"There's a good deal more than that to know," Mrs. Touchett affirmed in her little dry tone.

"A very little of it, I am sure, will content Miss Archer!" the lady exclaimed with a light laugh. "I'm an old friend of your aunt's. I've lived much in Florence. I'm Madame Merle." She made this last announcement as if she were referring to a person of tolerably distinct identity. For Isabel, however, it represented little; she could only continue to feel that Madame Merle had as charming a manner as any she had ever encountered.

"She's not a foreigner in spite of her name," said Mrs. Touchett. "She was born—I always forget where you were born."

"It's hardly worth while then I should tell you."

"On the contrary," said Mrs. Touchett, who rarely missed a logical point; "if I remembered your telling me would be quite superfluous."

Madame Merle glanced at Isabel with a sort of world-wide smile, a thing that over-reached frontiers. "I was born under the shadow of the national banner."

"She's too fond of mystery," said Mrs. Touchett; "that's her great fault."

"Ah," exclaimed Madame Merle, "I've great faults, but I don't think that's one of them; it certainly isn't the greatest. I came into the world in the Brooklyn navy-yard. My father was a high officer in the United States Navy, and had a post—a post of responsibility— in that establishment at the time. I suppose I ought to love the sea, but I hate it. That's why I don't return to America. I love the land; the great thing is to love something."

Isabel, as a dispassionate witness, had not been struck with the force of Mrs. Touchett's characterisation of her visitor, who had an expressive, communicative, responsive face, by no means of the sort which, to Isabel's mind, suggested a secretive disposition. It was a face that told of an amplitude of nature and of quick and free motions and, though it had no regular beauty, was in the highest degree engaging and attaching. Madame Merle was a tall, fair, smooth woman; everything in her person was round and replete, though without those accumulations which suggest heaviness. Her features were thick but in perfect proportion and harmony, and her complexion had a healthy clearness. Her grey eyes were small but full of light and incapable of stupidity—incapable, according to some people, even of tears; she had a liberal, full-rimmed mouth which when she smiled drew itself upward to the left side in a manner that most people thought very odd, some very affected and a few very graceful. Isabel inclined to range herself in the last category. Madame Merle had thick, fair hair, arranged somehow "classically" and as if she were a Bust, Isabel judged—a Juno or a Niobe;[3] and large white hands, of a perfect shape, a shape so perfect that their possessor, preferring to leave them unadorned, wore no jewelled rings. Isabel had taken her at first, as we have seen, for a Frenchwoman; but extended observation might have ranked her as a German—a German of high degree, perhaps an Austrian, a baroness, a countess, a princess. It would never have been supposed she had come into the world in Brooklyn—though one could doubtless not have carried through any argument that the air of distinction marking her in so eminent a degree was inconsistent with such a birth. It was true that the national banner had floated immediately over her cradle, and the breezy freedom of the stars and stripes might have shed an influence upon the attitude she there took towards life. And yet she had evidently nothing of the fluttered, flapping quality of a morsel of bunting in the wind; her manner expressed the repose and confidence which come from a large experience. Experience, however, had not quenched her youth; it had simply made her sympathetic and supple. She was in a word a woman of strong impulses kept in admirable order. This commended itself to Isabel as an ideal combination.

The girl made these reflexions while the three ladies sat at their tea, but that ceremony was interrupted before long by the arrival of the great doctor from London, who had been immediately ushered into the drawing-room. Mrs. Touchett took him off to the library for a private talk; and then Madame Merle and Isabel parted, to meet again at dinner. The idea of seeing more of this interesting woman did much to mitigate Isabel's sense of the sadness now settling on Gardencourt.

When she came into the drawing-room before dinner she found the place empty; but in the course of a moment Ralph arrived. His anxiety about his father had been lightened; Sir Matthew Hope's view of his condition was less depressed than his own had been. The doctor recommended that the nurse alone should remain with the old man for the next three or four hours; so that Ralph, his mother and the great physician himself were free to dine at table. Mrs. Touchett and Sir Matthew appeared; Madame Merle was the last.

Before she came Isabel spoke of her to Ralph, who was standing before the fireplace. "Pray who is this Madame Merle?"

"The cleverest woman I know, not excepting yourself," said Ralph.

3. Niobe wept for her dead children from which her tears continued to flow. until she turned into a stone column

"I thought she seemed very pleasant."

"I was sure you'd think her very pleasant."

"Is that why you invited her?"

"I didn't invite her, and when we came back from London I didn't know she was here. No one invited her. She's a friend of my mother's, and just after you and I went to town my mother got a note from her. She had arrived in England (she usually lives abroad, though she has first and last spent a good deal of time here), and asked leave to come down for a few days. She's a woman who can make such proposals with perfect confidence; she's so welcome wherever she goes. And with my mother there could be no question of hesitating; she's the one person in the world whom my mother very much admires. If she were not herself (which she after all much prefers), she would like to be Madame Merle. It would indeed be a great change."

"Well, she's very charming," said Isabel. "And she plays beautifully."

"She does everything beautifully. She's complete."

Isabel looked at her cousin a moment. "You don't like her."

"On the contrary, I was once in love with her."

"And she didn't care for you, and that's why you don't like her."

"How can we have discussed such things? Monsieur Merle was then living."

"Is he dead now?"

"So she says."

"Don't you believe her?"

"Yes, because the statement agrees with the probabilities. The husband of Madame Merle would be likely to pass away."

Isabel gazed at her cousin again. "I don't know what you mean. You mean something—that you don't mean. What was Monsieur Merle?"

"The husband of Madame."

"You're very odious. Has she any children?"

"Not the least little child—fortunately."

"Fortunately?"

"I mean fortunately for the child. She'd be sure to spoil it."

Isabel was apparently on the point of assuring her cousin for the third time that he was odious; but the discussion was interrupted by the arrival of the lady who was the topic of it. She came rustling in quickly, apologising for being late, fastening a bracelet, dressed in dark blue satin, which exposed a white bosom that was ineffectually covered by a curious silver necklace. Ralph offered her his arm with the exaggerated alertness of a man who was no longer a lover.

Even if this had still been his condition, however, Ralph had other things to think about. The great doctor spent the night at Gardencourt and, returning to London on the morrow, after another consultation with Mr. Touchett's own medical adviser, concurred in Ralph's desire that he should see the patient again on the day following. On the day following Sir Matthew Hope reappeared at Gardencourt, and now took a less encouraging view of the old man, who had grown worse in the twenty-four hours. His feebleness was extreme, and to his son, who constantly sat by his bedside, it often seemed that his end must be at hand. The local doctor, a very sagacious man, in whom Ralph had secretly more confidence than in his distinguished colleague, was constantly in attendance, and Sir Matthew Hope came back several times. Mr. Touchett was much of the time unconscious; he slept a great deal; he rarely spoke. Isabel had a great desire to be useful to him and was allowed to watch with him at hours when his other attendants (of whom Mrs. Touchett was not the least regular) went to take rest. He never seemed to know her, and she always said to herself "Suppose he should die while I'm sitting here;" an idea which excited her and kept her awake. Once he opened his eyes for a while and fixed them upon her intelligently, but when she went to him, hoping he would recognise her, he closed them and relapsed into stupor. The day after this, however, he revived for a longer time; but on this occasion Ralph only was with him. The old man began to talk, much to his son's satisfaction, who assured him that they should presently have him sitting up.

"No, my boy," said Mr. Touchett, "not unless you bury me in a sitting posture, as some of the ancients—was it the ancients?—used to do."

"Ah, daddy, don't talk about that," Ralph murmured. "You mustn't deny that you're getting better."

"There will be no need of my denying it if you don't say it," the old man answered. "Why should we prevaricate just at the last? We never prevaricated before. I've got to die some time, and it's better to die when one's sick than when one's well. I'm very sick—as sick as I shall ever be. I hope you don't want to prove that I shall ever be worse than this? That would be too bad. You don't? Well then."

Having made this excellent point he became quiet; but the next time that Ralph was with him he again addressed himself to conversation. The nurse had gone to her supper and Ralph was alone in charge, having just relieved Mrs. Touchett, who had been on guard since dinner. The room was lighted only by the flickering fire, which of late had become necessary, and Ralph's tall shadow was projected over wall and ceiling with an outline constantly varying but always grotesque.

"Who's that with me—is it my son?" the old man asked.

"Yes, it's your son, daddy."

"And is there no one else?"

"No one else."

Mr. Touchett said nothing for a while; and then, "I want to talk a little," he went on.

"Won't it tire you?" Ralph demurred.

"It won't matter if it does. I shall have a long rest. I want to talk about *you*."

Ralph had drawn nearer to the bed; he sat leaning forward with his hand on his father's. "You had better select a brighter topic."

"You were always bright; I used to be proud of your brightness. I should like so much to think you'd do something."

"If you leave us," said Ralph, "I shall do nothing but miss you."

"That's just what I don't want; it's what I want to talk about. You must get a new interest."

"I don't want a new interest, daddy. I have more old ones than I know what to do with."

The old man lay there looking at his son; his face was the face of the dying, but his eyes were the eyes of Daniel Touchett. He seemed to be reckoning over Ralph's interests. "Of course you have your mother," he said at last. "You'll take care of her."

"My mother will always take care of herself," Ralph returned.

"Well," said his father, "perhaps as she grows older she'll need a little help."

"I shall not see that. She'll outlive me."

"Very likely she will; but that's no reason—!" Mr. Touchett let his phrase die away in a helpless but not quite querulous sigh and remained silent again.

"Don't trouble yourself about us," said his son. "My mother and I get on very well together, you know."

"You get on by always being apart; that's not natural."

"If you leave us we shall probably see more of each other."

"Well," the old man observed with wandering irrelevance, "it can't be said that my death will make much difference in your mother's life."

"It will probably make more than you think."

"Well, she'll have more money," said Mr. Touchett. "I've left her a good wife's portion, just as if she had been a good wife."

"She has been one, daddy, according to her own theory. She has never troubled you."

"Ah, some troubles are pleasant," Mr. Touchett murmured. "Those you've given me for instance. But your mother has been less —less—what shall I call it? less out of the way since I've been ill. I presume she knows I've noticed it."

"I shall certainly tell her so; I'm glad you mention it."

"It won't make any difference to her; she doesn't do it to please me. She does it to please—to please—" And he lay a while trying to think why she did it. "She does it because it suits her. But that's not what I want to talk about," he added. "It's about *you*. You'll be very well off."

"Yes," said Ralph, "I know that. But I hope you've not forgotten the talk we had a year ago—when I told you exactly what money I should need and begged you to make some good use of the rest."

"Yes, yes, I remember. I made a new will—in a few days. I suppose it was the first time such a thing had happened—a young man trying to get a will made against him."

"It is not against me," said Ralph. "It would be against me to have a large property to take care of. It's impossible for a man in my state of health to spend much money, and enough is as good as a feast."

"Well, you'll have enough—and something over. There will be more than enough for one—there will be enough for two."

"That's too much," said Ralph.

"Ah, don't say that. The best thing you can do, when I'm gone, will be to marry."

Ralph had foreseen what his father was coming to, and this suggestion was by no means fresh. It had long been Mr. Touchett's most ingenious way of taking the cheerful view of his son's possible duration. Ralph had usually treated it facetiously; but present circumstances proscribed the facetious. He simply fell back in his chair and returned his father's appealing gaze.

"If I, with a wife who hasn't been very fond of me, have had a very happy life," said the old man, carrying his ingenuity further still, "what a life mightn't you have if you should marry a person different from Mrs. Touchett. There are more different from her than there are like her." Ralph still said nothing; and after a pause his father resumed softly: "What do you think of your cousin?"

At this Ralph started, meeting the question with a strained smile. "Do I understand you to propose that I should marry Isabel?"

"Well, that's what it comes to in the end. Don't you like Isabel?"

"Yes, very much." And Ralph got up from his chair and wandered over to the fire. He stood before it an instant and then he stooped and stirred it mechanically. "I like Isabel very much," he repeated.

"Well," said his father, "I know she likes you. She has told me how much she likes you."

"Did she remark that she would like to marry me?"

"No, but she can't have anything against you. And she's the most charming young lady I've ever seen. And she would be good to you. I have thought a great deal about it."

"So have I," said Ralph, coming back to the bedside again. "I don't mind telling you that."

"You *are* in love with her, then? I should think you would be. It's as if she came over on purpose."

"No, I'm not in love with her; but I should be if—if certain things were different."

"Ah, things are always different from what they might be," said the old man. "If you wait for them to change you'll never do anything. I don't know whether you know," he went on; "but I suppose there's no harm in my alluding to it at such an hour as this: there was some one wanted to marry Isabel the other day, and she wouldn't have him."

"I know she refused Warburton: he told me himself."

"Well, that proves there's a chance for somebody else."

"Somebody else took his chance the other day in London—and got nothing by it."

"Was it you?" Mr. Touchett eagerly asked.

"No, it was an older friend; a poor gentleman who came over from America to see about it."

"Well, I'm sorry for him, whoever he was. But it only proves what I say—that the way's open to you."

"If it is, dear father, it's all the greater pity that I'm unable to tread it. I haven't many convictions; but I have three or four that I hold strongly. One is that people, on the whole, had better not marry their cousins. Another is that people in an advanced stage of pulmonary disorder had better not marry at all."

The old man raised his weak hand and moved it to and fro before his face. "What do you mean by that? You look at things in a way that would make everything wrong. What sort of cousin is a cousin that you had never seen for more than twenty years of her life? We're all each other's cousins, and if we stopped at that the human race would die out. It's just the same with your bad lung. You're a great deal better than you used to be. All you want is to lead a natural life. It is a great deal more natural to marry a pretty young lady that you're in love with than it is to remain single on false principles."

"I'm not in love with Isabel," said Ralph.

"You said just now that you would be if you didn't think it wrong. I want to prove to you that it isn't wrong."

"It will only tire you, dear daddy," said Ralph, who marvelled at his father's tenacity and at his finding strength to insist. "Then where shall we all be?"

"Where shall you be if I don't provide for you? You won't have anything to do with the bank, and you won't have me to take care of. You say you've so many interests; but I can't make them out."

Ralph leaned back in his chair with folded arms; his eyes were fixed for some time in meditation. At last, with the air of a man fairly mustering courage, "I take a great interest in my cousin," he said, "but not the sort of interest you desire. I shall not live many years; but I hope I shall live long enough to see what she does with herself. She's entirely independent of me; I can exercise very little influence upon her life. But I should like to do something for her."

"What should you like to do?"

"I should like to put a little wind in her sails."

"What do you mean by that?"

"I should like to put it into her power to do some of the things she wants. She wants to see the world for instance. I should like to put money in her purse."

"Ah, I'm glad you've thought of that," said the old man. "But I've thought of it too. I've left her a legacy—five thousand pounds."

"That's capital; it's very kind of you. But I should like to do a little more."

Something of that veiled acuteness with which it had been on Daniel Touchett's part the habit of a lifetime to listen to a financial proposition still lingered in the face in which the invalid had not obliterated the man of business. "I shall be happy to consider it," he said softly.

"Isabel's poor then. My mother tells me that she has but a few hundred dollars a year. I should like to make her rich."

"What do you mean by rich?"

"I call people rich when they're able to meet the requirements of their imagination. Isabel has a great deal of imagination."

"So have you, my son," said Mr. Touchett, listening very attentively but a little confusedly.

"You tell me I shall have money enough for two. What I want is that you should kindly relieve me of my superfluity and make it over to Isabel. Divide my inheritance into two equal halves and give her the second."

"To do what she likes with?"

"Absolutely what she likes."

"And without an equivalent?"

"What equivalent could there be?"

"The one I've already mentioned."

"Her marrying—some one or other? It's just to do away with anything of that sort that I make my suggestion. If she has an easy income she'll never have to marry for a support. That's what I want cannily to prevent. She wishes to be free, and your bequest will make her free."

"Well, you seem to have thought it out," said Mr. Touchett.

"But I don't see why you appeal to me. The money will be yours, and you can easily give it to her yourself."

Ralph openly stared. "Ah, dear father, *I* can't offer Isabel money!"

The old man gave a groan. "Don't tell me you're not in love with her! Do you want *me* to have the credit of it?"

"Entirely. I should like it simply to be a clause in your will, without the slightest reference to me."

"Do you want me to make a new will then?"

"A few words will do it; you can attend to it the next time you feel a little lively."

"You must telegraph to Mr. Hilary then. I'll do nothing without my solicitor."

"You shall see Mr. Hilary to-morrow."

"He'll think we've quarrelled, you and I," said the old man.

"Very probably; I shall like him to think it," said Ralph, smiling; "and, to carry out the idea, I give you notice that I shall be very sharp, quite horrid and strange, with you."

The humour of this appeared to touch his father, who lay a little while taking it in. "I'll do anything you like," Mr. Touchett said at last; "but I'm not sure it's right. You say you want to put wind in her sails; but aren't you afraid of putting too much?"

"I should like to see her going before the breeze!" Ralph answered.

"You speak as if it were for your mere amusement."

"So it is, a good deal."

"Well, I don't think I understand," said Mr. Touchett with a sigh. "Young men are very different from what I was. When I cared for a girl—when I was young—I wanted to do more than look at her. You've scruples that I shouldn't have had, and you've ideas that I shouldn't have had either. You say Isabel wants to be free, and that her being rich will keep her from marrying for money. Do you think that she's a girl to do that?"

"By no means. But she has less money than she has ever had before. Her father then gave her everything, because he used to spend his capital. She has nothing but the crumbs of that feast to live on, and she doesn't really know how meagre they are—she has yet to learn it. My mother has told me all about it. Isabel will learn it when she's really thrown upon the world, and it would be very painful to me to think of her coming to the consciousness of a lot of wants she should be unable to satisfy."

"I've left her five thousand pounds. She can satisfy a good many wants with that."

"She can indeed. But she would probably spend it in two or three years."

"You think she'd be extravagant then?"

"Most certainly," said Ralph, smiling serenely.

Poor Mr. Touchett's acuteness was rapidly giving place to pure confusion. "It would merely be a question of time then, her spending the larger sum?"

"No—though at first I think she'd plunge into that pretty freely: she'd probably make over a part of it to each of her sisters. But after that she'd come to her senses, remember she has still a lifetime before her, and live within her means."

"Well, you *have* worked it out," said the old man helplessly. "You do take an interest in her, certainly."

"You can't consistently say I go too far. You wished me to go further."

"Well, I don't know," Mr. Touchett answered. "I don't think I enter into your spirit. It seems to me immoral."

"Immoral, dear daddy?"

"Well, I don't know that it's right to make everything so easy for a person."

"It surely depends upon the person. When the person's good, your making things easy is all to the credit of virtue. To facilitate the execution of good impulses, what can be a nobler act?"

This was a little difficult to follow, and Mr. Touchett considered it for awhile. At last he said: "Isabel's a sweet young thing; but do you think she's so good as that?"

"She's as good as her best opportunities," Ralph returned.

"Well," Mr. Touchett declared, "she ought to get a great many opportunities for sixty thousand pounds."

"I've no doubt she will."

"Of course I'll do what you want," said the old man. "I only want to understand it a little."

"Well, dear daddy, don't you understand it now?" his son caressingly asked. "If you don't we won't take any more trouble about it. We'll leave it alone."

Mr. Touchett lay a long time still. Ralph supposed he had given up the attempt to follow. But at last, quite lucidly, he began again. "Tell me this first. Doesn't it occur to you that a young lady with sixty thousand pounds may fall a victim to the fortune-hunters?"

"She'll hardly fall a victim to more than one."

"Well, one's too many."

"Decidedly. That's a risk, and it has entered into my calculation. I think it's appreciable, but I think it's small, and I'm prepared to take it."

Poor Mr Touchett's acuteness had passed into perplexity, and his perplexity now passed into admiration. "Well, you *have* gone into it!" he repeated. "But I don't see what good you're to get of it."

Ralph leaned over his father's pillows and gently smoothed them; he was aware their talk had been unduly prolonged. "I shall get just the good I said a few moments ago I wished to put into Isabel's reach—that of having met the requirements of my imagination. But it's scandalous, the way I've taken advantage of you!"

XIX

As Mrs. Touchett had foretold, Isabel and Madame Merle were thrown much together during the illness of their host, so that if they had not become intimate it would have been almost a breach of good manners. Their manners were of the best, but in addition to this they happened to please each other. It is perhaps too much to say that they swore an eternal friendship, but tacitly at least they called the future to witness. Isabel did so with a perfectly good conscience, though she would have hesitated to admit she was intimate with her new friend in the high sense she privately attached to this term. She often wondered indeed if she ever had been, or ever could be, intimate with any one. She had an ideal of friendship as well as of several other sentiments, which it failed to seem to her in this case—it had not seemed to her in other cases—that the actual completely expressed. But she often reminded herself that there were essential reasons why one's ideal could never become concrete. It was a thing to believe in, not to see—a matter of faith, not of experience. Experience, however, might supply us with very creditable imitations of it, and the part of wisdom was to make the best of these. Certainly, on the whole, Isabel had never encountered a more agreeable and interesting figure than Madame Merle; she had never met a person having less of that fault which is the principal obstacle to friendship—the air of reproducing the more tiresome, the stale, the too-familiar parts of one's own character. The gates of the girl's confidence were opened wider than they had ever been; she said things to this amiable auditress that she had not yet said to any one. Sometimes she took alarm at her candour: it was as if she had given to a comparative stranger the key to her cabinet of jewels. These spiritual gems were the only ones of any magnitude that Isabel possessed, but there was all the greater reason for their being carefully guarded. Afterwards, however, she always remembered that one should never regret a generous error and that if Madame Merle had not the merits she attributed to her, so much the worse for Madame Merle. There was no doubt she had great merits—she was charming, sympathetic, intelligent, cultivated. More than this (for it had not been Isabel's ill-fortune to go through life without meeting in her own sex several persons of whom no less could fairly be said), she was rare, superior and preëminent. There are many amiable people in the world, and Madame Merle was far from being vulgarly good-natured and restlessly witty. She knew how to think—an accomplishment rare in women; and she had thought to very good purpose. Of course, too, she knew how to feel; Isabel couldn't have spent a week with her without being sure of that. This was indeed Madame Merle's great talent, her most perfect gift. Life had told upon her; she had felt it strongly, and it was part of the satisfaction to be taken in her society that when the girl talked of what she was pleased to call serious matters this lady understood her so easily and quickly. Emotion, it is true, had become with her rather historic; she made no secret of the fact that the fount of passion, thanks to having been rather violently tapped at one period, didn't flow quite so freely as of yore. She proposed moreover, as well as expected, to cease feeling; she freely admitted that of old she had been a little mad, and now she pretended to be perfectly sane.

"I judge more than I used to," she said to Isabel, "but it seems to me one has earned the right. One can't judge till one's forty; before that we're too eager, too hard, too cruel, and in addition much too ignorant. I'm sorry for you; it will be a long time before you're forty. But every gain's a loss of some kind; I often think that after forty one *can't* really feel. The freshness, the quickness have certainly gone. You'll keep them longer than most people; it will be a great satisfaction to me to see you some years hence. I want to see what life makes of you. One thing's certain—it can't spoil you. It may pull you about horribly, but I defy it to break you up."

Isabel received this assurance as a young soldier, still panting from a slight skirmish in which he has come off with honour, might receive a pat on the shoulder from his colonel. Like such a recognition of merit it seemed to come with authority. How could the lightest word do less on the part of a person who was prepared to say, of almost everything Isabel told her, "Oh, I've been in that, my dear; it passes, like everything else." On many of her interlocutors Madame Merle might have produced an irritating effect; it was disconcertingly difficult to surprise her. But Isabel, though by no means incapable of desiring to be effective, had not at present this impulse. She was too sincere, too interested in her judicious companion. And then moreover Madame Merle never said such things in the tone of triumph or of boastfulness; they dropped from her like cold confessions.

A period of bad weather had settled upon Gardencourt; the days grew shorter and there was an end to the pretty tea-parties on the lawn. But our young woman had long indoor conversations with her fellow visitor, and in spite of the rain the two ladies often sallied forth for a walk, equipped with the defensive apparatus which the English climate and the English genius have between them brought to such perfection. Madame Merle liked almost everything, includ-

stopped here

ing the English rain. "There's always a little of it and never too much at once," she said; "and it never wets you and it always smells good." She declared that in England the pleasures of smell were great—that in this inimitable island there was a certain mixture of fog and beer and soot which, however odd it might sound, was the national aroma, and was most agreeable to the nostril; and she used to lift the sleeve of her British overcoat and bury her nose in it, inhaling the clear, fine scent of the wool. Poor Ralph Touchett, as soon as the autumn had begun to define itself, became almost a prisoner; in bad weather he was unable to step out of the house, and he used sometimes to stand at one of the windows with his hands in his pockets and, from a countenance half-rueful, half-critical, watch Isabel and Madame Merle as they walked down the avenue under a pair of umbrellas. The roads about Gardencourt were so firm, even in the worst weather, that the two ladies always came back with a healthy glow in their cheeks, looking at the soles of their neat, stout boots and declaring that their walk had done them inexpressible good. Before luncheon, always, Madame Merle was engaged; Isabel admired and envied her rigid possession of her morning. Our heroine had always passed for a person of resources and had taken a certain pride in being one; but she wandered, as by the wrong side of the wall of a private garden, round the enclosed talents, accomplishments, aptitudes of Madame Merle. She found herself desiring to emulate them, and in twenty such ways this lady presented herself as a model. "I should like awfully to be *so!*" Isabel secretly exclaimed, more than once, as one after another of her friend's fine aspects caught the light, and before long she knew that she had learned a lesson from a high authority. It took no great time indeed for her to feel herself, as the phrase is, under an influence. "What's the harm," she wondered, "so long as it's a good one? The more one's under a good influence the better. The only thing is to see our steps as we take them—to understand them as we go. That, no doubt, I shall always do. I needn't be afraid of becoming too pliable; isn't it my fault that I'm not pliable enough?" It is said that imitation is the sincerest flattery; and if Isabel was sometimes moved to gape at her friend aspiringly and despairingly it was not so much because she desired herself to shine as because she wished to hold up the lamp for Madame Merle. She liked her extremely, but was even more dazzled than attracted. She sometimes asked herself what Henrietta Stackpole would say to her thinking so much of this perverted product of their common soil, and had a conviction that it would be severely judged. Henrietta would not at all subscribe to Madame Merle; for reasons she could not have defined this truth came home to the girl. On the other hand she was equally sure that, should the occasion offer, her new friend would strike off some happy view of her old: Madame Merle was too humorous, too observant, not to do justice to Henrietta, and on becoming acquainted with her would probably give the measure of a tact which Miss Stackpole couldn't hope to emulate. She appeared to have in her experience a touchstone for everything, and somewhere in the capacious pocket of her genial memory she would find the key to Henrietta's value. "That's the great thing," Isabel solemnly pondered; "that's the supreme good fortune: to be in a better position for appreciating people than they are for appreciating you." And she added that such, when one considered it, was simply the essence of the aristocratic situation. In this light, if in none other, one should aim at the aristocratic situation.

I may not count over all the links in the chain which led Isabel to think of Madame Merle's situation as aristocratic—a view of it never expressed in any reference made to it by that lady herself. She had known great things and great people, but she had never played a great part. She was one of the small ones of the earth; she had not been born to honours; she knew the world too well to nourish fatuous illusions on the article of her own place in it. She had encountered many of the fortunate few and was perfectly aware of those points at which their fortune differed from hers. But if by her informed measure she was no figure for a high scene, she had yet to Isabel's imagination a sort of greatness. To be so cultivated and civilised, so wise and so easy, and still make so light of it—that was really to be a great lady, especially when one so carried and presented one's self. It was as if somehow she had all society under contribution, and all the arts and graces it practised—or was the effect rather that of charming uses found *for* her, even from a distance, subtle service rendered by her to a clamorous world wherever she might be? After breakfast she wrote a succession of letters, as those arriving for her appeared innumerable: her correspondence was a source of surprise to Isabel when they sometimes walked together to the village post-office to deposit Madame Merle's offering to the mail. She knew more people, as she told Isabel, than she knew what to do with, and something was always turning up to be written about. Of painting she was devotedly fond, and made no more of brushing in a sketch than of pulling off her gloves. At Gardencourt she was perpetually taking advantage of an hour's sunshine to go out with a camp-stool and a box of water-colours. That she was a brave musician we have already perceived, and it was evidence of the fact that when she seated herself at the piano, as she always did in the evening, her listeners resigned themselves without a murmur to losing the grace of her talk. Isabel, since she had known her, felt ashamed of her own facility, which she now looked upon as basely inferior; and indeed, though she had been thought rather a prodigy at home, the loss to society when, in taking her place upon the music-stool, she turned her back to the room, was usually deemed greater than the gain. When Madame Merle was neither writing, nor painting, nor touching the piano, she was usually employed upon wonderful tasks of rich embroidery, cushions, curtains, decorations for the chimney-piece; an art in which her bold, free invention was as noted as the agility of her needle. She was never idle, for when engaged in none of the ways I have mentioned she was either reading (she appeared to Isabel to read "everything important"), or walking out, or playing patience with the cards, or talking with her fellow inmates. And with all this she had always the social quality, was never rudely absent and yet never too seated. She laid down her pastimes as easily as she took them up; she worked and talked at the same time, and appeared to impute scant worth to anything she did. She gave away her sketches and tapestries; she rose from the piano or remained there, according to the convenience of her auditors, which she always unerringly divined. She was in short the most comfortable, profitable, amenable person to live with. If for Isabel she had a fault it was that she was not natural; by which the girl meant, not that she was either affected or pretentious, since from these vulgar vices no woman could have been more exempt, but that her nature had been too much overlaid by custom and her angles too much rubbed away. She had become too flexible, too useful, was too ripe and too final. She was in a word too perfectly the social animal that man and woman are supposed to have been intended to be; and she had rid herself of every remnant of that tonic wildness which we may assume to have belonged even to the most amiable persons in the ages before country-house life was the fashion. Isabel found it difficult to think of her in any detachment or privacy, she existed only in her relations, direct or indirect, with her fellow mortals. One might wonder what commerce she could possibly hold with her own spirit. One always ended, however, by feeling that a charming surface doesn't necessarily prove one superficial; this was an illusion in which, in one's youth, one had but just escaped being nourished. Madame Merle was not superficial—not she. She was deep, and her nature spoke none the less in her behaviour because it spoke a conventional tongue. "What's language at all but a convention?" said Isabel. "She has the good taste not to pretend, like some people I've met, to express herself by original signs."

"I'm afraid you've suffered much," she once found occasion to say to her friend in response to some allusion that had appeared to reach far.

"What makes you think that?" Madame Merle asked with the amused smile of a person seated at a game of guesses. "I hope I haven't too much the droop of the misunderstood."

"No; but you sometimes say things that I think people who have always been happy wouldn't have found out."

"I haven't always been happy," said Madame Merle, smiling still, but with a mock gravity, as if she were telling a child a secret. "Such a wonderful thing!"

But Isabel rose to the irony. "A great many people give me the impression of never having for a moment felt anything."

"It's very true; there are many more iron pots certainly than porcelain. But you may depend on it that every one bears some mark; even the hardest iron pots have a little bruise, a little hole somewhere. I flatter myself that I'm rather stout, but if I must tell you the truth I've been shockingly chipped and cracked. I do very well for service yet, because I've been cleverly mended; and I try to remain in the cupboard—the quiet, dusky cupboard where there's an odour of stale spices—as much as I can. But when I've to come out and into a strong light—then, my dear, I'm a horror!"

I know not whether it was on this occasion or on some other that when the conversation had taken the turn I have just indicated she said to Isabel that she would some day a tale unfold.[1] Isabel assured her she should delight to listen to one, and reminded her more than once of this engagement. Madame Merle, however, begged repeatedly for a respite, and at last frankly told her young companion that they must wait till they knew each other better. This would be sure to happen; a long friendship so visibly lay before them. Isabel assented, but at the same time enquired if she mightn't be trusted —if she appeared capable of a betrayal of confidence.

"It's not that I'm afraid of your repeating what I say," her fellow visitor answered; "I'm afraid, on the contrary, of your taking it too much to yourself. You'd judge me too harshly; you're of the cruel age." She preferred for the present to talk to Isabel of Isabel, and exhibited the greatest interest in our heroine's history, sentiments, opinions, prospects. She made her chatter and listened to her chatter with infinite good nature. This flattered and quickened the girl, who was struck with all the distinguished people her friend had known and with her having lived, as Mrs. Touchett said, in the best company in Europe. Isabel thought the better of herself for enjoying the favour of a person who had so large a field of comparison; and it was perhaps partly to gratify the sense of profiting by comparison that she often appealed to these stores of reminiscence. Madame Merle had been a dweller in many lands and had social

1. "I could a tale unfold whose lightest word/Would harrow up thy soul" (*Hamlet*, I.v).

ties in a dozen different countries. "I don't pretend to be educated," she would say, "but I think I know my Europe;" and she spoke one day of going to Sweden to stay with an old friend, and another of proceeding to Malta to follow up a new acquaintance. With England, where she had often dwelt, she was thoroughly familiar, and for Isabel's benefit threw a great deal of light upon the customs of the country and the character of the people, who "after all," as she was fond of saying, were the most convenient in the world to live with.

"You mustn't think it strange her remaining here at such a time as this, when Mr. Touchett's passing away," that gentleman's wife remarked to her niece. "She is incapable of a mistake; she's the most tactful woman I know. It's a favour to me that she stays; she's putting off a lot of visits at great houses," said Mrs. Touchett, who never forgot that when she herself was in England her social value sank two or three degrees in the scale. "She has her pick of places; she's not in want of a shelter. But I've asked her to put in this time because I wish you to know her. I think it will be a good thing for you. Serena Merle hasn't a fault."

"If I didn't already like her very much that description might alarm me," Isabel returned.

"She's never the least little bit 'off.' I've brought you out here and I wish to do the best for you. Your sister Lily told me she hoped I would give you plenty of opportunities. I give you one in putting you in relation with Madame Merle. She's one of the most brilliant women in Europe."

"I like her better than I like your description of her," Isabel persisted in saying.

"Do you flatter yourself that you'll ever feel her open to criticism? I hope you'll let me know when you do."

"That will be cruel—to you," said Isabel.

"You needn't mind me. You won't discover a fault in her."

"Perhaps not. But I dare say I shan't miss it."

"She knows absolutely everything on earth there is to know," said Mrs. Touchett.

Isabel after this observed to their companion that she hoped she knew Mrs. Touchett considered she hadn't a speck on her perfection. On which "I'm obliged to you," Madame Merle replied, "but I'm afraid your aunt imagines, or at least alludes to, no aberrations that the clock-face doesn't register."

"So that you mean you've a wild side that's unknown to her?"

"Ah no, I fear my darkest sides are my tamest. I mean that having no faults, for your aunt, means that one's never late for dinner—that is for *her* dinner. I was not late, by the way, the other day, when you came back from London; the clock was just at eight when I came into the drawing-room: it was the rest of you that were before the time. It means that one answers a letter the day one gets it and that when one comes to stay with her one doesn't bring too much luggage and is careful not to be taken ill. For Mrs. Touchett those things constitute virtue; it's a blessing to be able to reduce it to its elements."

Madame Merle's own conversation, it will be perceived, was enriched with bold, free touches of criticism, which, even when they had a restrictive effect, never struck Isabel as ill-natured. It couldn't occur to the girl for instance that Mrs. Touchett's accomplished guest was abusing her; and this for very good reasons. In the first place Isabel rose eagerly to the sense of her shades; in the second Madame Merle implied that there was a great deal more to say; and it was clear in the third that for a person to speak to one without ceremony of one's near relations was an agreeable sign of that person's intimacy with one's self. These signs of deep communion multiplied as the days elapsed, and there was none of which Isabel was more sensible than of her companion's preference for making Miss Archer herself a topic. Though she referred frequently to the incidents of her own career she never lingered upon them; she was as little of a gross egotist as she was of a flat gossip.

"I'm old and stale and faded," she said more than once; "I'm of no more interest than last week's newspaper. You're young and fresh and of to-day; you've the great thing—you've actuality. I once had it—we all have it for an hour. You, however, will have it for longer. Let us talk about you then; you can say nothing I shall not care to hear. It's a sign that I'm growing old—that I like to talk with younger people. I think it's a very pretty compensation. If we can't have youth within us we can have it outside, and I really think we see it and feel it better that way. Of course we must be in sympathy with it—that I shall always be. I don't know that I shall ever be ill-natured with old people—I hope not; there are certainly some old people I adore. But I shall never be anything but abject with the young; they touch me and appeal to me too much. I give you *carte blanche*[2] then; you can even be impertinent if you like; I shall let it pass and horribly spoil you. I speak as if I were a hundred years old, you say? Well, I am, if you please; I was born before the French Revolution. Ah, my dear, *je viens de loin*;[3] I belong to the old, old world. But it's not of that I want to talk; I want to talk about the new. You must tell me more about America; you never tell me enough. Here I've been since I was brought here as a helpless child, and it's ridiculous, or rather it's scandalous, how little I know about that splendid, dreadful, funny country—surely

2. A free hand.
3. I come from far back; I'm an old-timer.

the greatest and drollest of them all. There are a great many of us like that in these parts, and I must say I think we're a wretched set of people. You should live in your own land; whatever it may be you have your natural place there. If we're not good Americans we're certainly poor Europeans; we've no natural place here. We're mere parasites, crawling over the surface; we haven't our feet in the soil. At least one can know it and not have illusions. A woman perhaps can get on; a woman, it seems to me, has no natural place anywhere; wherever she finds herself she has to remain on the surface and, more or less, to crawl. You protest, my dear? you're horrified? you declare you'll never crawl? It's very true that I don't see you crawling; you stand more upright than a good many poor creatures. Very good; on the whole, I don't think you'll crawl. But the men, the Americans; *je vous demande un peu,*[4] what do they make of it over here? I don't envy them trying to arrange themselves. Look at poor Ralph Touchett; what sort of a figure do you call that? Fortunately he has a consumption; I say fortunately, because it gives him something to do. His consumption's his *carrière;*[5] it's a kind of position. You can say: 'Oh, Mr. Touchett, he takes care of his lungs, he knows a great deal about climates.' But without that who would he be, what would he represent? 'Mr. Ralph Touchett: an American who lives in Europe.' That signifies absolutely nothing—it's impossible anything should signify less. 'He's very cultivated,' they say: 'he has a very pretty collection of old snuff-boxes.' The collection is all that's wanted to make it pitiful. I'm tired of the sound of the word; I think it's grotesque. With the poor old father it's different; he has his identity, and it's rather a massive one. He represents a great financial house, and that, in our day, is as good as anything else. For an American, at any rate, that will do very well. But I persist in thinking your cousin very lucky to have a chronic malady so long as he doesn't die of it. It's much better than the snuff-boxes. If he weren't ill, you say, he'd do something?—he'd take his father's place in the house. My poor child, I doubt it; I don't think he's at all fond of the house. However, you know him better than I, though I used to know him rather well, and he may have the benefit of the doubt. The worst case, I think, is a friend of mine, a countryman of ours, who lives in Italy (where he also was brought before he knew better), and who is one of the most delightful men I know. Some day you must know him. I'll bring you together and then you'll see what I mean. He's Gilbert Osmond—he lives in Italy; that's all one can say about him or make of him. He's exceedingly clever, a man made to be distinguished; but, as I tell you, you exhaust the description when you say he's Mr. Osmond who lives

4. I only ask you.   5. Career.

tout bêtement[6] in Italy. No career, no name, no position, no fortune, no past, no future, no anything. Oh yes, he paints, if you please—paints in water-colours; like me, only better than I. His painting's pretty bad; on the whole I'm rather glad of that. Fortunately he's very indolent, so indolent that it amounts to a sort of position. He can say, 'Oh, I do nothing; I'm too deadly lazy. You can do nothing to-day unless you get up at five o'clock in the morning.' In that way he becomes a sort of exception; you feel he might do something if he'd only rise early. He never speaks of his painting —to people at large; he's too clever for that. But he has a little girl —a dear little girl; he does speak of *her*. He's devoted to her, and if it were a career to be an excellent father he'd be very distinguished. But I'm afraid that's no better than the snuff-boxes; perhaps not even so good. Tell me what they do in America," pursued Madame Merle, who, it must be observed parenthetically, did not deliver herself all at once of these reflexions, which are presented in a cluster for the convenience of the reader. She talked of Florence, where Mr. Osmond lived and where Mrs. Touchett occupied a mediæval palace; she talked of Rome, where she herself had a little *pied-à-terre*[7] with some rather good old damask. She talked of places, of people and even, as the phrase is, of "subjects"; and from time to time she talked of their kind old host and of the prospect of his recovery. From the first she had thought this prospect small, and Isabel had been struck with the positive, discriminating, competent way in which she took the measure of his remainder of life. One evening she announced definitely that he wouldn't live.

"Sir Matthew Hope told me so as plainly as was proper," she said; "standing there, near the fire, before dinner. He makes himself very agreeable, the great doctor. I don't mean his saying that has anything to do with it. But he says such things with great tact. I had told him I felt ill at my ease, staying here at such a time; it seemed to me so indiscreet—it wasn't as if I could nurse. 'You must remain, you must remain,' he answered; 'your office will come later.' Wasn't that a very delicate way of saying both that poor Mr. Touchett would go and that I might be of some use as a consoler? In fact, however, I shall not be of the slightest use. You aunt will console herself; she, and she alone, knows just how much consolation she'll require. It would be a very delicate matter for another person to undertake to administer the dose. With your cousin it will be different; he'll miss his father immensely. But I should never presume to condole with Mr. Ralph; we're not on those terms." Madame Merle had alluded more than once to some undefined incongruity in her relations with Ralph Touchett; so Isabel took this occasion of asking her if they were not good friends.

6. Quite foolishly.
7. A small apartment or occasional lodging.

"Perfectly, but he doesn't like me."

"What have you done to him?"

"Nothing whatever. But one has no need of a reason for that."

"For not liking you? I think one has need of a very good reason."

"You're very kind. Be sure you have one ready for the day you begin."

"Begin to dislike you? I shall never begin."

"I hope not; because if you do you'll never end. That's the way with your cousin; he doesn't get over it. It's an antipathy of nature—if I can call it that when it's all on his side. I've nothing whatever against him and don't bear him the least little grudge for not doing me justice. Justice is all I want. However, one feels that he's a gentleman and would never say anything underhand about one. *Cartes sur table,*"[8] Madame Merle subjoined in a moment, "I'm not afraid of him."

"I hope not indeed," said Isabel, who added something about his being the kindest creature living. She remembered, however, that on her first asking him about Madame Merle he had answered her in a manner which this lady might have thought injurious without being explicit. There was something between them, Isabel said to herself, but she said nothing more than this. If it were something of importance it should inspire respect; if it were not it was not worth her curiosity. With all her love of knowledge she had a natural shrinking from raising curtains and looking into unlighted corners. The love of knowledge coexisted in her mind with the finest capacity for ignorance.

But Madame Merle sometimes said things that startled her, made her raise her clear eyebrows at the time and think of the words afterwards. "I'd give a great deal to be your age again," she broke out once with a bitterness which, though diluted in her customary amplitude of ease, was imperfectly disguised by it. "If I could only begin again—if I could have my life before me!"

"Your life's before you yet," Isabel answered gently, for she was vaguely awe-struck.

"No; the best part's gone, and gone for nothing."

"Surely not for nothing," said Isabel.

"Why not—what have I got? Neither husband, nor child, nor fortune, nor position, nor the traces of a beauty that I never had."

"You have many friends, dear lady."

"I'm not so sure!" cried Madame Merle.

"Ah, you're wrong. You have memories, graces, talents—"

But Madame Merle interrupted her. "What have my talents brought me? Nothing but the need of using them still, to get through the hours, the years, to cheat myself with some pretence of movement, of unconsciousness. As for my graces and memories the

8. Open and aboveboard; to put one's cards on the table.

less said about them the better. You'll be my friend till you find a better use for your friendship."

"It will be for you to see that I don't then," said Isabel.

"Yes; I would make an effort to keep you." And her companion looked at her gravely. "When I say I should like to be your age I mean with your qualities—frank, generous, sincere like you. In that case I should have made something better of my life."

"What should you have liked to do that you've not done?"

Madame Merle took a sheet of music—she was seated at the piano and had abruptly wheeled about on the stool when she first spoke—and mechanically turned the leaves. "I'm very ambitious!" she at last replied.

"And your ambitions have not been satisfied? They must have been great."

"They *were* great. I should make myself ridiculous by talking of them."

Isabel wondered what they could have been—whether Madame Merle had aspired to wear a crown. "I don't know what your idea of success may be, but you seem to me to have been successful. To me indeed you're a vivid image of success."

Madame Merle tossed away the music with a smile. "What's *your* idea of success?"

"You evidently think it must be a very tame one. It's to see some dream of one's youth come true."

"Ah," Madame Merle exclaimed, "that I've never seen! But my dreams were so great—so preposterous. Heaven forgive me, I'm dreaming now!" And she turned back to the piano and began grandly to play. On the morrow she said to Isabel that her definition of success had been very pretty, yet frightfully sad. Measured in that way, who had ever succeeded? The dreams of one's youth, why they were enchanting, they were divine! Who had ever seen such things come to pass?

"I myself—a few of them," Isabel ventured to answer.

"Already? They must have been dreams of yesterday."

"I began to dream very young," Isabel smiled.

"Ah, if you mean the aspirations of your childhood—that of having a pink sash and a doll that could close her eyes."

"No, I don't mean that."

"Or a young man with a fine moustache going down on his knees to you."

"No, nor that either," Isabel declared with still more emphasis.

Madame Merle appeared to note this eagerness. "I suspect that's what you do mean. We've all had the young man with the moustache. He's the inevitable young man; he doesn't count."

Isabel was silent a little but then spoke with extreme and characteristic inconsequence. "Why shouldn't he count? There are young men and young men."

"And yours was a paragon—is that what you mean?" asked her friend with a laugh. "If you've had the identical young man you dreamed of, then that was success, and I congratulate you with all my heart. Only in that case why didn't you fly with him to his castle in the Apennines?"

"He has no castle in the Apennines."

"What has he? An ugly brick house in Fortieth Street? Don't tell me that; I refuse to recognise that as an ideal."

"I don't care anything about his house," said Isabel.

"That's very crude of you. When you've lived as long as I you'll see that every human being has his shell and that you must take the shell into account. By the shell I mean the whole envelope of circumstances. There's no such thing as an isolated man or woman; we're each of us made up of some cluster of appurtenances. What shall we call our 'self'? Where does it begin? where does it end? It overflows into everything that belongs to us—and then it flows back again. I know a large part of myself is in the clothes I choose to wear. I've a great respect for *things!* One's self—for other people— is one's expression of one's self; and one's house, one's furniture, one's garments, the books one reads, the company one keeps—these things are all expressive."

This was very metaphysical; not more so, however, than several observations Madame Merle had already made. Isabel was fond of metaphysics, but was unable to accompany her friend into this bold analysis of the human personality. "I don't agree with you. I think just the other way. I don't know whether I succeed in expressing myself, but I know that nothing else expresses me. Nothing that belongs to me is any measure of me; everything's on the contrary a limit, a barrier, and a perfectly arbitrary one. Certainly the clothes which, as you say, I choose to wear, don't express me; and heaven forbid they should!"

"You dress very well," Madame Merle lightly interposed.

"Possibly; but I don't care to be judged by that. My clothes may express the dressmaker, but they don't express me. To begin with it's not my own choice that I wear them; they're imposed upon me by society."

"Should you prefer to go without them?" Madame Merle enquired in a tone which virtually terminated the discussion.

I am bound to confess, though it may cast some discredit on the sketch I have given of the youthful loyalty practised by our heroine toward this accomplished woman, that Isabel had said nothing whatever to her about Lord Warburton and had been equally reticent on the subject of Caspar Goodwood. She had not, however, concealed the fact that she had had opportunities of marrying and had even let her friend know of how advantageous a kind they had been. Lord Warburton had left Lockleigh and was gone to Scotland, taking his sisters with him; and though he had written to Ralph more than once to ask about Mr. Touchett's health the girl was not liable to the embarrassment of such enquiries as, had he still been in the neighbourhood, he would probably have felt bound to make in person. He had excellent ways, but she felt sure that if he had come to Gardencourt he would have seen Madame Merle, and that if he had seen her he would have liked her and betrayed to her that he was in love with her young friend. It so happened that during this lady's previous visits to Gardencourt—each of them much shorter than the present—he had either not been at Lockleigh or had not called at Mr. Touchett's. Therefore, though she knew him by name as the great man of that county, she had no cause to suspect him as a suitor of Mrs. Touchett's freshly-imported niece.

"You've plenty of time," she had said to Isabel in return for the mutilated confidences which our young woman made her and which didn't pretend to be perfect, though we have seen that at moments the girl had compunctions at having said so much. "I'm glad you've done nothing yet—that you have it still to do. It's a very good thing for a girl to have refused a few good offers—so long of course as they are not the best she's likely to have. Pardon me if my tone seems horribly corrupt; one must take the worldly view sometimes. Only don't keep on refusing for the sake of refusing. It's a pleasant exercise of power; but accepting's after all an exercise of power as well. There's always the danger of refusing once too often. It was not the one I fell into— I didn't refuse often enough. You're an exquisite creature, and I should like to see you married to a prime minister. But speaking strictly, you know, you're not what is technically called a *parti*.[9] You're extremely good-looking and extremely clever; in yourself you're quite exceptional. You appear to have the vaguest ideas about your earthly possessions; but from what I can make out you're not embarrassed with an income. I wish you had a little money."

"I wish I had!" said Isabel, simply, apparently forgetting for the moment that her poverty had been a venial fault for two gallant gentlemen.

In spite of Sir Matthew Hope's benevolent recommendation Madame Merle did not remain to the end, as the issue of poor Mr. Touchett's malady had now come frankly to be designated. She was under pledges to other people which had at last to be redeemed,

9. Marriageable; a good match.

and she left Gardencourt with the understanding that she should in any event see Mrs. Touchett there again, or else in town, before quitting England. Her parting with Isabel was even more like the beginning of a friendship than their meeting had been. "I'm going to six places in succession, but I shall see no one I like so well as you. They'll all be old friends, however; one doesn't make new friends at my age. I've made a great exception for you. You must remember that and must think as well of me as possible. You must reward me by believing in me."

By way of answer Isabel kissed her, and, though some women kiss with facility, there are kisses and kisses, and this embrace was satisfactory to Madame Merle. Our young lady, after this, was much alone; she saw her aunt and cousin only at meals, and discovered that of the hours during which Mrs. Touchett was invisible only a minor portion was now devoted to nursing her husband. She spent the rest in her own apartments, to which access was not allowed even to her niece, apparently occupied there with mysterious and inscrutable exercises. At table she was grave and silent; but her solemnity was not an attitude—Isabel could see it was a conviction. She wondered if her aunt repented of having taken her own way so much; but there was no visible evidence of this—no tears, no sighs, no exaggeration of a zeal always to its own sense adequate. Mrs. Touchett seemed simply to feel the need of thinking things over and summing them up; she had a little moral account-book—with columns unerringly ruled and a sharp steel clasp—which she kept with exemplary neatness. Uttered reflection had with her ever, at any rate, a practical ring. "If I had foreseen this I'd not have proposed your coming abroad now," she said to Isabel after Madame Merle had left the house. "I'd have waited and sent for you next year."

"So that perhaps I should never have known my uncle? It's a great happiness to me to have come now."

"That's very well. But it was not that you might know your uncle that I brought you to Europe." A perfectly veracious speech; but, as Isabel thought, not as perfectly timed. She had leisure to think of this and other matters. She took a solitary walk every day and spent vague hours in turning over books in the library. Among the subjects that engaged her attention were the adventures of her friend Miss Stackpole, with whom she was in regular correspondence. Isabel liked her friend's private epistolary style better than her public; that is she felt her public letters would have been excellent if they had not been printed. Henrietta's career, however, was not so successful as might have been wished even in the interest of her private felicity; that view of the inner life of Great Britain which she was so eager to take appeared to dance before her like an *ignis fatuus*.[1] The invitation from Lady Pensil, for mysterious reasons, had never arrived; and poor Mr. Bantling himself, with all his friendly ingenuity, had been unable to explain so grave a dereliction on the part of a missive that had obviously been sent. He had evidently taken Henrietta's affairs much to heart, and believed that he owed her a set-off to this illusory visit to Bedfordshire. "He says he should think I would go to the Continent," Henrietta wrote; "and as he thinks of going there himself I suppose his advice is sincere. He wants to know why I don't take a view of French life; and it's a fact that I want very much to see the new Republic. Mr. Bantling doesn't care much about the Republic, but he thinks of going over to Paris anyway. I must say he's quite as attentive as I could wish, and at least I shall have seen one polite Englishman. I keep telling Mr. Bantling that he ought to have been an American, and you should see how that pleases him. Whenever I say so he always breaks out with the same exclamation—'Ah, but really, come now!' " A few days later she wrote that she had decided to go to Paris at the end of the week and that Mr. Bantling had promised to see her off—perhaps even would go as far as Dover with her. She would wait in Paris till Isabel should arrive, Henrietta added; speaking quite as if Isabel were to start on her continental journey alone and making no allusion to Mrs. Touchett. Bearing in mind his interest in their late companion, our heroine communicated several passages from this correspondence to Ralph, who followed with an emotion akin to suspense the career of the representative of the *Interviewer*.

"It seems to me she's doing very well," he said, "going over to Paris with an ex-Lancer! If she wants something to write about she has only to describe that episode."

"It's not conventional, certainly," Isabel answered; "but if you mean that—as far as Henrietta is concerned—it's not perfectly innocent, you're very much mistaken. You'll never understand Henrietta."

"Pardon me, I understand her perfectly. I didn't at all at first, but now I've the point of view. I'm afraid, however, that Bantling hasn't; he may have some surprises. Oh, I understand Henrietta as well as if I had made her!"

Isabel was by no means sure of this, but she abstained from expressing further doubt, for she was disposed in these days to extend a great charity to her cousin. One afternoon less than a week after Madame Merle's departure she was seated in the library with a volume to which her attention was not fastened. She had placed herself in a deep window-bench, from which she looked out into the

1. Will o' the wisp; a modern construction meaning "foolish fire."

dull, damp park; and as the library stood at right angles to the entrance-front of the house she could see the doctor's brougham, which had been waiting for the last two hours before the door. She was struck with his remaining so long, but at last she saw him appear in the portico, stand a moment slowly drawing on his gloves and looking at the knees of his horse, and then get into the vehicle and roll away. Isabel kept her place for half an hour; there was a great stillness in the house. It was so great that when she at last heard a soft, slow step on the deep carpet of the room she was almost startled by the sound. She turned quickly away from the window and saw Ralph Touchett standing there with his hands still in his pockets, but with a face absolutely void of its usual latent smile. She got up and her movement and glance were a question.

"It's all over," said Ralph.

"Do you mean that my uncle——?" And Isabel stopped.

"My dear father died an hour ago."

"Ah, my poor Ralph!" she gently wailed, putting out her two hands to him.

xx

Some fortnight after this Madame Merle drove up in a hansom cab to the house in Winchester Square. As she descended from her vehicle she observed, suspended between the dining-room windows, a large, neat, wooden tablet, on whose fresh black ground were inscribed in white paint the words—"This noble freehold mansion to be sold"; with the name of the agent to whom application should be made. "They certainly lose no time," said the visitor as, after sounding the big brass knocker, she waited to be admitted; "it's a practical country!" And within the house, as she ascended to the drawing-room, she perceived numerous signs of abdication; pictures removed from the walls and placed upon sofas, windows undraped and floors laid bare. Mrs. Touchett presently received her and intimated in a few words that condolences might be taken for granted.

"I know what you're going to say—he was a very good man. But I know it better than any one, because I gave him more chance to show it. In that I think I was a good wife." Mrs. Touchett added that at the end her husband apparently recognised this fact. "He has treated me most liberally," she said; "I won't say more liberally than I expected, because I didn't expect. You know that as a general thing I don't expect. But he chose, I presume, to recognise the fact that though I lived much abroad and mingled—you may say freely—in foreign life, I never exhibited the smallest preference for any one else."

"For any one but yourself," Madame Merle mentally observed; but the reflexion was perfectly inaudible.

"I never sacrificed my husband to another," Mrs. Touchett continued with her stout curtness.

"Oh no," thought Madame Merle; "you never did anything for another!"

There was a certain cynicism in these mute comments which demands an explanation; the more so as they are not in accord either with the view—somewhat superficial perhaps—that we have hitherto enjoyed of Madame Merle's character or with the literal facts of Mrs. Touchett's history; the more so, too, as Madame Merle had a well-founded conviction that her friend's last remark was not in the least to be construed as a side-thrust at herself. The truth is that the moment she had crossed the threshold she received an impression that Mr. Touchett's death had had subtle consequences and that these consequences had been profitable to a little circle of persons among whom she was not numbered. Of course it was an event which would naturally have consequences; her imagination had more than once rested upon this fact during her stay at Gardencourt. But it had been one thing to foresee such a matter mentally and another to stand among its massive records. The idea of a distribution of property—she would almost have said of spoils —just now pressed upon her senses and irritated her with a sense of exclusion. I am far from wishing to picture her as one of the hungry mouths or envious hearts of the general herd, but we have already learned of her having desires that had never been satisfied. If she had been questioned, she would of course have admitted—with a fine proud smile—that she had not the faintest claim to a share in Mr. Touchett's relics. "There was never anything in the world between us," she would have said. "There was never that, poor man!"—with a fillip of her thumb and her third finger. I hasten to add, moreover, that if she couldn't at the present moment keep from quite perversely yearning she was careful not to betray herself. She had after all as much sympathy for Mrs. Touchett's gains as for her losses.

"He has left me this house," the newly-made widow said; "but of course I shall not live in it; I've a much better one in Florence. The will was opened only three days since, but I've already offered the house for sale. I've also a share in the bank; but I don't yet understand if I'm obliged to leave it there. If not I shall certainly take it out. Ralph, of course, has Gardencourt; but I'm not sure that he'll have means to keep up the place. He's naturally left very well off, but his father has given away an immense deal of money; there are bequests to a string of third cousins in Vermont. Ralph, however, is very fond of Gardencourt and would be quite capable of living there—in summer—with a maid-of-all-work and a gardener's boy. There's one remarkable clause in my husband's will," Mrs. Touchett added. "He has left my niece a fortune."

"A fortune!" Madame Merle softly repeated.

"Isabel steps into something like seventy thousand pounds."

Madame Merle's hands were clasped in her lap; at this she raised them, still clasped, and held them a moment against her bosom while her eyes, a little dilated, fixed themselves on those of her friend. "Ah," she cried, "the clever creature!"

Mrs. Touchett gave her a quick look. "What do you mean by that?"

For an instant Madame Merle's colour rose and she dropped her eyes. "It certainly is clever to achieve such results—without an effort!"

"There assuredly was no effort. Don't call it an achievement."

Madame Merle was seldom guilty of the awkwardness of retracting what she had said; her wisdom was shown rather in maintaining it and placing it in a favourable light. "My dear friend, Isabel would certainly not have had seventy thousand pounds left her if she had not been the most charming girl in the world. Her charm includes great cleverness."

"She never dreamed, I'm sure, of my husband's doing anything for her; and I never dreamed of it either, for he never spoke to me of his intention," Mrs. Touchett said. "She had no claim upon him whatever; it was no great recommendation to him that she was my niece. Whatever she achieved she achieved unconsciously."

"Ah," rejoined Madame Merle, "those are the greatest strokes!"

Mrs. Touchett reserved her opinion. "The girl's fortunate; I don't deny that. But for the present she's simply stupefied."

"Do you mean that she doesn't know what to do with the money?"

"That, I think, she has hardly considered. She doesn't know what to think about the matter at all. It has been as if a big gun were suddenly fired off behind her; she's feeling herself to see if she be hurt. It's but three days since she received a visit from the principal executor, who came in person, very gallantly, to notify her. He told me afterwards that when he had made his little speech she suddenly burst into tears. The money's to remain in the affairs of the bank, and she's to draw the interest."

Madame Merle shook her head with a wise and now quite benignant smile. "How very delicious! After she has done that two or three times she'll get used to it." Then after a silence, "What does your son think of it?" she abruptly asked.

"He left England before the will was read—used up by his fatigue and anxiety and hurrying off to the south. He's on his way to the Riviera and I've not yet heard from him. But it's not likely he'll ever object to anything done by his father."

"Didn't you say his own share had been cut down?"

"Only at his wish. I know that he urged his father to do something for the people in America. He's not in the least addicted to looking after number one."

"It depends upon whom he regards as number one!" said Madame Merle. And she remained thoughtful a moment, her eyes bent on the floor. "Am I not to see your happy niece?" she asked at last as she raised them.

"You may see her; but you'll not be struck with her being happy. She has looked as solemn, these three days, as a Cimabue Madonna!"[1] And Mrs. Touchett rang for a servant.

Isabel came in shortly after the footman had been sent to call her; and Madame Merle thought, as she appeared, that Mrs. Touchett's comparison had its force. The girl was pale and grave—an effect not mitigated by her deeper mourning; but the smile of her brightest moments came into her face as she saw Madame Merle, who went forward, laid her hand on our heroine's shoulder and, after looking at her a moment, kissed her as if she were returning the kiss she had received from her at Gardencourt. This was the only allusion the visitor, in her great good taste, made for the present to her young friend's inheritance.

Mrs. Touchett had no purpose of awaiting in London the sale of her house. After selecting from among its furniture the objects she wished to transport to her other abode, she left the rest of its contents to be disposed of by the auctioneer and took her departure for the Continent. She was of course accompanied on this journey by her niece, who now had plenty of leisure to measure and weigh and otherwise handle the windfall on which Madame Merle had covertly congratulated her. Isabel thought very often of the fact of her accession of means, looking at it in a dozen different lights; but we shall not now attempt to follow her train of thought or to explain exactly why her new consciousness was at first oppressive. This failure to rise to immediate joy was indeed but brief; the girl presently made up her mind that to be rich was a virtue because it was to be able to *do*, and that to do could only be sweet. It was the graceful contrary of the stupid side of weakness—especially the feminine variety. To be weak was, for a delicate young person, rather graceful, but, after all, as Isabel said to herself, there was a larger grace than that. Just now, it is true, there was not much to do—once she had sent off a cheque to Lily and another to poor Edith; but she was thankful for the quiet months which her mourning robes and her aunt's fresh widowhood compelled them to spend together. The acquisition of power made her serious; she scrutinised her power with a kind of tender ferocity, but was not eager to exercise it. She began to do so during a stay of some weeks which she eventually made with her aunt in Paris, though in ways that will inevitably

---

1. Giovanni Cimabue (ca. 1240–ca. 1302), Florentine painter and mosaicist.

present themselves as trivial. They were the ways most naturally imposed in a city in which the shops are the admiration of the world, and that were prescribed unreservedly by the guidance of Mrs. Touchett, who took a rigidly practical view of the transformation of her niece from a poor girl to a rich one. "Now that you're a young woman of fortune you must know how to play the part—I mean to play it well," she said to Isabel once for all; and she added that the girl's first duty was to have everything handsome. "You don't know how to take care of your things, but you must learn," she went on; this was Isabel's second duty. Isabel submitted, but for the present her imagination was not kindled; she longed for opportunities, but these were not the opportunities she meant.

Mrs. Touchett rarely changed her plans, and, having intended before her husband's death to spend a part of the winter in Paris, saw no reason to deprive herself—still less to deprive her companion—of this advantage. Though they would live in great retirement she might still present her niece, informally, to the little circle of her fellow countrymen dwelling upon the skirts of the Champs Elysées. With many of these amiable colonists Mrs. Touchett was intimate; she shared their expatriation, their convictions, their pastimes, their ennui. Isabel saw them arrive with a good deal of assiduity at her aunt's hotel, and pronounced on them with a trenchancy doubtless to be accounted for by the temporary exaltation of her sense of human duty. She made up her mind that their lives were, though luxurious, inane, and incurred some disfavour by expressing this view on bright Sunday afternoons, when the American absentees were engaged in calling on each other. Though her listeners passed for people kept exemplarily genial by their cooks and dressmakers, two or three of them thought her cleverness, which was generally admitted, inferior to that of the new theatrical pieces. "You all live here this way, but what does it lead to?" she was pleased to ask. "It doesn't seem to lead to anything, and I should think you'd get very tired of it."

Mrs. Touchett thought the question worthy of Henrietta Stackpole. The two ladies had found Henrietta in Paris, and Isabel constantly saw her; so that Mrs. Touchett had some reason for saying to herself that if her niece were not clever enough to originate almost anything, she might be suspected of having borrowed that style of remark from her journalistic friend. The first occasion on which Isabel had spoken was that of a visit paid by the two ladies to Mrs. Luce, an old friend of Mrs. Touchett's and the only person in Paris she now went to see. Mrs. Luce had been living in Paris since the days of Louis Philippe;[2] she used to say jocosely that she

2. Louis Philippe, a constitutional monarch, reigned from the Revolution of 1830 until the Revolution of 1848 and the establishment of the Second Republic.

was one of the generation of 1830—a joke of which the point was not always taken. When it failed Mrs. Luce used to explain—"Oh yes, I'm one of the romantics;" her French had never become quite perfect. She was always at home on Sunday afternoons and surrounded by sympathetic compatriots, usually the same. In fact she was at home at all times, and reproduced with wondrous truth in her well-cushioned little corner of the brilliant city, the domestic tone of her native Baltimore. This reduced Mr. Luce, her worthy husband, a tall, lean, grizzled, well-brushed gentleman who wore a gold eye-glass and carried his hat a little too much on the back of his head, to mere platonic praise of the "distractions" of Paris— they were his great word—since you would never have guessed from what cares he escaped to them. One of them was that he went every day to the American banker's, where he found a post-office that was almost as sociable and colloquial an institution as in an American country town. He passed an hour (in fine weather) in a chair in Champs Elysées, and he dined uncommonly well at his own table, seated above a waxed floor which it was Mrs. Luce's happiness to believe had a finer polish than any other in the French capital. Occasionally he dined with a friend or two at the Café Anglais,[3] where his talent for ordering a dinner was a source of felicity to his companions and an object of admiration even to the headwaiter of the establishment. These were his only known pastimes, but they had beguiled his hours for upwards of half a century, and they doubtless justified his frequent declaration that there was no place like Paris. In no other place, on these terms, could Mr. Luce flatter himself that he was enjoying life. There was nothing like Paris, but it must be confessed that Mr. Luce thought less highly of this scene of his dissipations than in earlier days. In the list of his resources his political reflections should not be omitted, for they were doubtless the animating principle of many hours that superficially seemed vacant. Like many of his fellow colonists Mr. Luce was a high—or rather a deep—conservative, and gave no countenance to the government lately established in France. He had no faith in its duration and would assure you from year to year that its end was close at hand. "They want to be kept down, sir, to be kept down; nothing but the strong hand—the iron heel—will do for them," he would frequently say of the French people; and his ideal of a fine showy clever rule was that of the superseded Empire. "Paris is much less attractive than in the days of the Emperor; *he* knew how to make a city pleasant," Mr. Luce had often remarked to Mrs. Touchett, who was quite of his own way of thinking and wished to know what one had crossed that odious Atlantic for but to get away from republics.

3. One of the best restaurants in Paris.

"Why, madam, sitting in the Champs Elysées, opposite to the Palace of Industry, I've seen the court-carriages from the Tuileries pass up and down as many as seven times a day. I remember one occasion when they went as high as nine. What do you see now? It's no use talking, the style's all gone. Napoleon knew what the French people want, and there'll be a dark cloud over Paris, *our* Paris, till they get the Empire back again."

Among Mrs. Luce's visitors on Sunday afternoons was a young man with whom Isabel had had a good deal of conversation and whom she found full of valuable knowledge. Mr. Edward Rosier—Ned Rosier as he was called—was native to New York and had been brought up in Paris, living there under the eye of his father who, as it happened, had been an early and intimate friend of the late Mr. Archer. Edward Rosier remembered Isabel as a little girl; it had been his father who came to the rescue of the small Archers at the inn at Neufchâtel (he was travelling that way with the boy and had stopped at the hotel by chance), after their *bonne* had gone off with the Russian prince and when Mr. Archer's whereabouts remained for some days a mystery. Isabel remembered perfectly the neat little male child whose hair smelt of a delicious cosmetic and who had a *bonne* all his own, warranted to lose sight of him under no provocation. Isabel took a walk with the pair beside the lake and thought little Edward as pretty as an angel—a comparison by no means conventional in her mind, for she had a very definite conception of a type of features which she supposed to be angelic and which her new friend perfectly illustrated. A small pink face surmounted by a blue velvet bonnet and set off by a stiff embroidered collar had become the countenance of her childish dreams; and she had firmly believed for some time afterwards that the heavenly hosts conversed among themselves in a queer little dialect of French-English, expressing the properest sentiments, as when Edward told her that he was "defended"[4] by his *bonne* to go near the edge of the lake, and that one must always obey to one's *bonne*. Ned Rosier's English had improved; at least it exhibited in a less degree the French variation. His father was dead and his *bonne* dismissed, but the young man still conformed to the spirit of their teaching—he never went to the edge of the lake. There was still something agreeable to the nostrils about him and something not offensive to nobler organs. He was a very gentle and gracious youth, with what are called cultivated tastes—an acquaintance with old china, with good wine, with the bindings of books, with the *Almanach de Gotha*,[5] with the best shops, the best hotels, the hours of railway-trains. He could order a dinner almost as well as Mr. Luce, and it was proba-

---

4. The governess was using the French word *defense* to keep him from going near the water.

5. A periodical record giving data concerning the royal, princely, and noble families of Europe.

ble that as his experience accumulated he would be a worthy succes-
sor to that gentleman, whose rather grim politics he also advocated
in a soft and innocent voice. He had some charming rooms in Paris,
decorated with old Spanish altar-lace, the envy of his female friends,
who declared that his chimney-piece was better draped than the
high shoulders of many a duchess. He usually, however, spent a
part of every winter at Pau,[6] and had once passed a couple of months
in the United States.

He took a great interest in Isabel and remembered perfectly the
walk at Neufchâtel, when she would persist in going so near the
edge. He seemed to recognise this same tendency in the subversive
enquiry that I quoted a moment ago, and set himself to answer our
heroine's question with greater urbanity than it perhaps deserved.
"What does it lead to, Miss Archer? Why Paris leads everywhere.
You can't go anywhere unless you come here first. Every one that
comes to Europe has got to pass through. You don't mean it in that
sense so much? You mean what good it does you? Well, how can
you penetrate futurity? How can you tell what lies ahead? If it's a
pleasant road I don't care where it leads. I like the road, Miss
Archer; I like the dear old asphalte. You can't get tired of it—you
can't if you try. You think you would, but you wouldn't; there's
always something new and fresh. Take the Hôtel Drouot,[7] now;
they sometimes have three and four sales a week. Where can you
get such things as you can here? In spite of all they say I maintain
they're cheaper too, if you know the right places. I know plenty of
places, but I keep them to myself. I'll tell you, if you like, as a particular favour; only you mustn't tell any one else. Don't you go anywhere without asking me first; I want you to promise me that. As a
general thing avoid the Boulevards; there's very little to be done on
the Boulevards. Speaking conscientiously—*sans blague*[8]—I don't believe any one knows Paris better than I. You and Mrs. Touchett must
come and breakfast with me some day, and I'll show you my things;
je ne vous dis que ça![9] There has been a great deal of talk about London of late; it's the fashion to cry up London. But there's nothing in
it—you can't do anything in London. No Louis Quinze—nothing of
the First Empire; nothing but their eternal Queen Anne.[1] It's good
for one's bed-room, Queen Anne—for one's washing-room; but it
isn't proper for a *salon*.[2] Do I spend my life at the auctioneer's?"
Mr. Rosier pursued in answer to another question of Isabel's. "Oh
no; I haven't the means. I wish I had. You think I'm a mere trifler;

6. Tourist center in southwest France.
7. Also known as the Hôtel des Ventes
Mobilières, it was noted for its extensive
auctions of works of art.
8. Without fooling; no kidding.
9. That's all I'm saying.

1. Styles of French and English decorative arts and crafts identified with the
reigns of Louis XV (1715–1774), Queen
Anne (1702–1714), and Napoleon
(1804–1815).
2. Drawing room.

I can tell by the expression of your face—you've got a wonderfully expressive face. I hope you don't mind my saying that; I mean it as a kind of warning. You think I ought to do something, and so do I, so long as you leave it vague. But when you come to the point you see you have to stop. I can't go home and be a shopkeeper. You think I'm very well fitted? Ah, Miss Archer, you overrate me. I can buy very well, but I can't sell; you should see when I sometimes try to get rid of my things. It takes much more ability to make other people buy than to buy yourself. When I think how clever they must be, the people who make *me* buy! Ah no; I couldn't be a shopkeeper. I can't be a doctor; it's a repulsive business. I can't be a clergyman; I haven't got convictions. And then I can't pronounce the names right in the Bible. They're very difficult, in the Old Testament particularly. I can't be a lawyer; I don't understand—how do you call it?—the American *procédure*. Is there anything else? There's nothing for a gentleman in America. I should like to be a diplomatist; but American diplomacy—that's not for gentlemen either. I'm sure if you had seen the last min—"

Henrietta Stackpole, who was often with her friend when Mr. Rosier, coming to pay his compliments late in the afternoon, expressed himself after the fashion I have sketched, usually interrupted the young man at this point and read him a lecture on the duties of the American citizen. She thought him most unnatural; he was worse than poor Ralph Touchett. Henrietta, however, was at this time more than ever addicted to fine criticism, for her conscience had been freshly alarmed as regards Isabel. She had not congratulated this young lady on her augmentations and begged to be excused from doing so.

"If Mr. Touchett had consulted me about leaving you the money," she frankly asserted, "I'd have said to him 'Never!' "

"I see," Isabel had answered. "You think it will prove a curse in disguise. Perhaps it will."

"Leave it to some one you care less for—that's what I should have said."

"To yourself for instance?" Isabel suggested jocosely. And then, "Do you really believe it will ruin me?" she asked in quite another tone.

"I hope it won't ruin you; but it will certainly confirm your dangerous tendencies."

"Do you mean the love of luxury—of extravagance?"

"No, no," said Henrietta; "I mean your exposure on the moral side. I approve of luxury; I think we ought to be as elegant as possible. Look at the luxury of our western cities; I've seen nothing over here to compare with it. I hope you'll never become grossly sensual;

but I'm not afraid of that. The peril for you is that you live too much in the world of your own dreams. You're not enough in contact with reality—with the toiling, striving, suffering, I may even say sinning, world that surrounds you. You're too fastidious; you've too many graceful illusions. Your newly-acquired thousands will shut you up more and more to the society of a few selfish and heartless people who will be interested in keeping them up."

Isabel's eyes expanded as she gazed at this lurid scene. "What are my illusions?" she asked. "I try so hard not to have any."

"Well," said Henrietta, "you think you can lead a romantic life, that you can live by pleasing yourself and pleasing others. You'll find you're mistaken. Whatever life you lead you must put your soul in it—to make any sort of success of it; and from the moment you do that it ceases to be romance, I assure you: it becomes grim reality! And you can't always please yourself; you must sometimes please other people. That, I admit, you're very ready to do; but there's another thing that's still more important—you must often *dis*please others. You must always be ready for that—you must never shrink from it. That doesn't suit you at all—you're too fond of admiration, you like to be thought well of. You think we can escape disagreeable duties by taking romantic views—that's your great illusion, my dear. But we can't. You must be prepared on many occasions in life to please no one at all—not even yourself."

Isabel shook her head sadly; she looked troubled and frightened. "This, for you, Henrietta," she said, "must be one of those occasions!"

It was certainly true that Miss Stackpole, during her visit to Paris, which had been professionally more remunerative than her English sojourn, had not been living in the world of dreams. Mr. Bantling, who had now returned to England, was her companion for the first four weeks of her stay; and about Mr. Bantling there was nothing dreamy. Isabel learned from her friend that the two had led a life of great personal intimacy and that this had been a peculiar advantage to Henrietta, owing to the gentleman's remarkable knowledge of Paris. He had explained everything, shown her everything, been her constant guide and interpreter. They had breakfasted together, dined together, gone to the theatre together, supped together, really in a manner quite lived together. He was a true friend, Henrietta more than once assured our heroine; and she had never supposed that she could like any Englishman so well. Isabel could not have told you why, but she found something that ministered to mirth in the alliance the correspondent of the *Interviewer* had struck with Lady Pensil's brother; her amusement moreover subsisted in face of the fact that she thought it a credit to each of them. Isabel couldn't rid herself of a suspicion that they were playing somehow at cross-purposes—that the simplicity of each had been entrapped. But this simplicity was on either side none the less honourable. It was as graceful on Henrietta's part to believe that Mr. Bantling took an interest in the diffusion of lively journalism and in consolidating the position of lady-correspondents as it was on the part of his companion to suppose that the cause of the *Interviewer* —a periodical of which he never formed a very definite conception—was, if subtly analysed (a task to which Mr. Bantling felt himself quite equal), but the cause of Miss Stackpole's need of demonstrative affection. Each of these groping celibates supplied at any rate a want of which the other was impatiently conscious. Mr. Bantling, who was of rather a slow and a discursive habit, relished a prompt, keen, positive woman, who charmed him by the influence of a shining, challenging eye and a kind of bandbox freshness, and who kindled a perception of raciness in a mind to which the usual fare of life seemed unsalted. Henrietta, on the other hand, enjoyed the society of a gentleman who appeared somehow, in his way, made, by expensive, roundabout, almost "quaint" processes, for her use, and whose leisured state, though generally indefensible, was a decided boon to a breathless mate, and who was furnished with an easy, traditional, though by no means exhaustive, answer to almost any social or practical question that could come up. She often found Mr. Bantling's answers very convenient, and in the press of catching the American post would largely and showily address them to publicity. It was to be feared that she was indeed drifting toward those abysses of sophistication as to which Isabel, wishing for a good-humoured retort, had warned her. There might be danger in store for Isabel; but it was scarcely to be hoped that Miss Stackpole, on her side, would find permanent rest in any adoption of the views of a class pledged to all the old abuses. Isabel continued to warn her good-humouredly; Lady Pensil's obliging brother was sometimes, on our heroine's lips, an object of irreverent and facetious allusion. Nothing, however, could exceed Henrietta's amiability on this point; she used to abound in the sense of Isabel's irony and to enumerate with elation the hours she had spent with this perfect man of the world—a term that had ceased to make with her, as previously, for opprobrium. Then, a few moments later, she would forget that they had been talking jocosely and would mention with impulsive earnestness some expedition she had enjoyed in his company. She would say: "Oh, I know all about Versailles; I went there with Mr. Bantling. I was bound to see it thoroughly—I warned him when we went out there that I was thorough: so we spent three days at the hotel and wandered all over the place. It was lovely weather—a kind of Indian summer, only not so good. We just lived in that park. Oh yes; you can't tell me anything about Versailles."

Henrietta appeared to have made arrangements to meet her gallant friend during the spring in Italy.

XXI

Mrs. Touchett, before arriving in Paris, had fixed the day for her departure and by the middle of February had begun to travel southward. She interrupted her journey to pay a visit to her son, who at San Remo, on the Italian shore of the Mediterranean, had been spending a dull, bright winter beneath a slow-moving white umbrella. Isabel went with her aunt as a matter of course, though Mrs. Touchett, with homely, customary logic, had laid before her a pair of alternatives.

"Now, of course, you're completely your own mistress and are as free as the bird on the bough. I don't mean you were not so before, but you're at present on a different footing—property erects a kind of barrier. You can do a great many things if you're rich which would be severely criticised if you were poor. You can go and come, you can travel alone, you can have your own establishment: I mean of course if you'll take a companion—some decayed gentlewoman, with a darned cashmere and dyed hair, who paints on velvet. You don't think you'd like that? Of course you can do as you please; I only want you to understand how much you're at liberty. You might take Miss Stackpole as your *dame de compagnie*;[1] she'd keep people off very well. I think, however, that it's a great deal better you should remain with me, in spite of there being no obligation. It's better for several reasons, quite apart from your liking it. I shouldn't think you'd like it, but I recommend you to make the sacrifice. Of course whatever novelty there may have been at first in my society has quite passed away, and you see me as I am—a dull, obstinate, narrow-minded old woman."

"I don't think you're at all dull," Isabel had replied to this.

"But you do think I'm obstinate and narrow-minded? I told you so!" said Mrs. Touchett with much elation at being justified.

Isabel remained for the present with her aunt, because, in spite of eccentric impulses, she had a great regard for what was usually deemed decent, and a young gentlewoman without visible relations had always struck her as a flower without foliage. It was true that Mrs. Touchett's conversation had never again appeared so brilliant as that first afternoon in Albany, when she sat in her damp waterproof and sketched the opportunities that Europe would offer to a young person of taste. This, however, was in a great measure the girl's own fault; she had got a glimpse of her aunt's experience, and her imagination constantly anticipated the judgements and emotions of a woman who had very little of the same faculty. Apart from this, Mrs. Touchett had a great merit; she was as honest as a

1. Lady companion.

pair of compasses. There was a comfort in her stiffness and firmness; you knew exactly where to find her and were never liable to chance encounters and concussions. On her own ground she was perfectly present, but was never over-inquisitive as regards the territory of her neighbour. Isabel came at last to have a kind of undemonstrable pity for her; there seemed something so dreary in the condition of a person whose nature had, as it were, so little surface—offered so limited a face to the accretions of human contact. Nothing tender, nothing sympathetic, had ever had a chance to fasten upon it—no wind-sown blossom, no familiar softening moss. Her offered, her passive extent, in other words, was about that of a knife-edge. Isabel had reason to believe none the less that as she advanced in life she made more of those concessions to the sense of something obscurely distinct from convenience—more of them than she independently exacted. She was learning to sacrifice consistency to considerations of that inferior order for which the excuse must be found in the particular case. It was not to the credit of her absolute rectitude that she should have gone the longest way round to Florence in order to spend a few weeks with her invalid son; since in former years it had been one of her most definite convictions that when Ralph wished to see her he was at liberty to remember that Palazzo Crescentini contained a large apartment known as the quarter of the signorino.

"I want to ask you something," Isabel said to this young man the day after her arrival at San Remo—"something I've thought more than once of asking you by letter, but that I've hesitated on the whole to write about. Face to face, nevertheless, my question seems easy enough. Did you know your father intended to leave me so much money?"

Ralph stretched his legs a little further than usual and gazed a little more fixedly at the Mediterranean. "What does it matter, my dear Isabel, whether I knew? My father was very obstinate."

"So," said the girl, "you did know."

"Yes; he told me. We even talked it over a little."

"What did he do it for?" asked Isabel abruptly.

"Why, as a kind of compliment."

"A compliment on what?"

"On your so beautifully existing."

"He liked me too much," she presently declared.

"That's a way we all have."

"If I believed that I should be very unhappy. Fortunately I don't believe it. I want to be treated with justice; I want nothing but that."

"Very good. But you must remember that justice to a lovely being is after all a florid sort of sentiment."

"I'm not a lovely being. How can you say that, at the very

moment when I'm asking such odious questions? I must seem to you delicate!"

"You seem to me troubled," said Ralph.

"I am troubled."

"About what?"

For a moment she answered nothing; then she broke out: "Do you think it good for me suddenly to be made so rich? Henrietta doesn't."

"Oh, hang Henrietta!" said Ralph coarsely. "If you ask *me* I'm delighted at it."

"Is that why your father did it—for your amusement?"

"I differ with Miss Stackpole," Ralph went on more gravely. "I think it very good for you to have means."

Isabel looked at him with serious eyes. "I wonder whether you know what's good for me—or whether you care."

"If I know depend upon it I care. Shall I tell you what it is? Not to torment yourself."

"Not to torment you, I suppose you mean."

"You can't do that; I'm proof. Take things more easily. Don't ask yourself so much whether this or that is good for you. Don't question your conscience so much—it will get out of tune like a strummed piano. Keep it for great occasions. Don't try so much to form your character—it's like trying to pull open a tight, tender young rose. Live as you like best, and your character will take care of itself. Most things are good for you; the exceptions are very rare, and a comfortable income's not one of them." Ralph paused, smiling; Isabel had listened quickly. "You've too much power of thought—above all too much conscience," Ralph added. "It's out of all reason, the number of things you think wrong. Put back your watch. Diet your fever. Spread your wings; rise above the ground. It's never wrong to do that."

She had listened eagerly, as I say; and it was her nature to understand quickly. "I wonder if you appreciate what you say. If you do, you take a great responsibility."

"You frighten me a little, but I think I'm right," said Ralph, persisting in cheer.

"All the same what you say is very true," Isabel pursued. "You could say nothing more true. I'm absorbed in myself—I look at life too much as a doctor's prescription. Why indeed should we perpetually be thinking whether things are good for us, as if we were patients lying in a hospital? Why should I be so afraid of not doing right? As if it mattered to the world whether I do right or wrong!"

"You're a capital person to advise," said Ralph; "you take the wind out of *my* sails!"

She looked at him as if she had not heard him—though she was following out the train of reflexion which he himself had kindled. "I try to care more about the world than about myself—but I always come back to myself. It's because I'm afraid." She stopped; her voice had trembled a little. "Yes, I'm afraid; I can't tell you. A large fortune means freedom, and I'm afraid of that. It's such a fine thing, and one should make such a good use of it. If one shouldn't one would be ashamed. And one must keep thinking; it's a constant effort. I'm not sure it's not a greater happiness to be powerless."

"For weak people I've no doubt it's a greater happiness. For weak people the effort not to be contemptible must be great."

"And how do you know I'm not weak?" Isabel asked.

"Ah," Ralph answered with a flush that the girl noticed, "if you are I'm awfully sold!"

The charm of the Mediterranean coast only deepened for our heroine on acquaintance, for it was the threshold of Italy, the gate of admirations. Italy, as yet imperfectly seen and felt, stretched before her as a land of promise, a land in which a love of the beautiful might be comforted by endless knowledge. Whenever she strolled upon the shore with her cousin—and she was the companion of his daily walk—she looked across the sea, with longing eyes, to where she knew that Genoa lay. She was glad to pause, however, on the edge of this larger adventure; there was such a thrill even in the preliminary hovering. It affected her moreover as a peaceful interlude, as a hush of the drum and fife in a career which she had little warrant as yet for regarding as agitated, but which nevertheless she was constantly picturing to herself by the light of her hopes, her fears, her fancies, her ambitions, her predilections, and which reflected these subjective accidents in a manner sufficiently dramatic. Madame Merle had predicted to Mrs. Touchett that after their young friend had put her hand into her pocket half a dozen times she would be reconciled to the idea that it had been filled by a munificent uncle; and the event justified, as it had so often justified before, that lady's perspicacity. Ralph Touchett had praised his cousin for being morally inflammable, that is for being quick to take a hint that was meant as good advice. His advice had perhaps helped the matter; she had at any rate before leaving San Remo grown used to feeling rich. The consciousness in question found a proper place in rather a dense little group of ideas that she had about herself, and often it was by no means the least agreeable. It took perpetually for granted a thousand good intentions. She lost herself in a maze of visions; the fine things to be done by a rich, independent, generous girl who took a large human view of occasions and obligations were sublime in the mass. Her fortune therefore became to her mind a part of her better self; it gave her importance, gave her even, to her own imagination, a certain ideal beauty.

What it did for her in the imagination of others is another affair, and on this point we must also touch in time. The visions I have just spoken of were mixed with other debates. Isabel liked better to think of the future than of the past; but at times, as she listened to the murmur of the Mediterranean waves, her glance took a backward flight. It rested upon two figures which, in spite of increasing distance, were still sufficiently salient; they were recognisable without difficulty as those of Caspar Goodwood and Lord Warburton. It was strange how quickly these images of energy had fallen into the background of our young lady's life. It was in her disposition at all times to lose faith in the reality of absent things; she could summon back her faith, in case of need, with an effort, but the effort was often painful even when the reality had been pleasant. The past was apt to look dead and its revival rather to show the livid light of a judgement-day. The girl moreover was not prone to take for granted that she herself lived in the mind of others—she had not the fatuity to believe she left indelible traces. She was capable of being wounded by the discovery that she had been forgotten; but of all liberties the one she herself found sweetest was the liberty to forget. She had not given her last shilling, sentimentally speaking, either to Caspar Goodwood or to Lord Warburton, and yet couldn't but feel them appreciably in debt to her. She had of course reminded herself that she was to hear from Mr. Goodwood again; but this was not to be for another year and a half, and in that time a great many things might happen. She had indeed failed to say to herself that her American suitor might find some other girl more comfortable to woo; because, though it was certain many other girls would prove so, she had not the smallest belief that this merit would attract him. But she reflected that she herself might know the humiliation of change, might really, for that matter, come to the end of the things that were not Caspar (even though there appeared so many of them), and find rest in those very elements of his presence which struck her now as impediments to the finer respiration. It was conceivable that these impediments should some day prove a sort of blessing in disguise—a clear and quiet harbour enclosed by a brave granite breakwater. But that day could only come in its order, and she couldn't wait for it with folded hands. That Lord Warburton should continue to cherish her image seemed to her more than a noble humility or an enlightened pride ought to wish to reckon with. She had so definitely undertaken to preserve no record of what had passed between them that a corresponding effort on his own part would be eminently just. This was not, as it may seem, merely a theory tinged with sarcasm. Isabel candidly believed that his lordship would, in the usual phrase, get over his disappointment. He had been deeply affected—this she believed, and she was still capable of deriving pleasure from the belief; but it was absurd that a man both so intelligent and so honourably dealt with should cultivate a scar out of proportion to any wound. Englishmen liked moreover to be comfortable, said Isabel, and there could be little comfort for Lord Warburton, in the long run, in brooding over a self-sufficient American girl who had been but a casual acquaintance. She flattered herself that, should she hear from one day to another that he had married some young woman of his own country who had done more to deserve him, she should receive the news without a pang even of surprise. It would have proved that he believed she was firm—which was what she wished to seem to him. That alone was grateful to her pride.

XXII

On one of the first days of May, some six months after old Mr. Touchett's death, a small group that might have been described by a painter as composing well was gathered in one of the many rooms of an ancient villa crowning an olive-muffled hill outside of the Roman gate of Florence. The villa was a long, rather blank-looking structure, with the far-projecting roof which Tuscany loves and which, on the hills that encircle Florence, when considered from a distance, makes so harmonious a rectangle with the straight, dark, definite cypresses that usually rise in groups of three or four beside it. The house had a front upon a little grassy, empty, rural piazza which occupied a part of the hill-top; and this front, pierced with a few windows in irregular relations and furnished with a stone bench lengthily adjusted to the base of the structure and useful as a lounging-place to one or two persons wearing more or less of that air of undervalued merit which in Italy, for some reason or other, always gracefully invests any one who confidently assumes a perfectly passive attitude—this antique, solid, weather-worn, yet imposing front had a somewhat incommunicative character. It was the mask, not the face of the house. It had heavy lids, but no eyes; the house in reality looked another way—looked off behind, into splendid openness and the range of the afternoon light. In that quarter the villa overhung the slope of its hill and the long valley of the Arno, hazy with Italian colour. It had a narrow garden, in the manner of a terrace, productive chiefly of tangles of wild roses and other old stone benches, mossy and sun-warmed. The parapet of the terrace was just the height to lean upon, and beneath it the ground declined into the vagueness of olive-crops and vineyards. It is not, however, with the outside of the place that we are concerned; on this bright morning of ripened spring its tenants had reason to prefer the shady side of the wall. The windows of the ground-floor, as you saw them from the piazza, were, in their noble proportions, extremely architectural;

but their function seemed less to offer communication with the
world than to defy the world to look in. They were massively cross-
barred, and placed at such a height that curiosity, even on tiptoe,
expired before it reached them. In an apartment lighted by a row of
three of these jealous apertures—one of the several distinct apartments into which the villa was divided and which were mainly occupied by foreigners of random race long resident in Florence—a gentleman was seated in company with a young girl and two good sisters from a religious house. The room was, however, less sombre
than our indications may have represented, for it had a wide, high
door, which now stood open into the tangled garden behind; and
the tall iron lattices admitted on occasion more than enough of the
Italian sunshine. It was moreover a seat of ease, indeed of luxury,
telling of arrangements subtly studied and refinements frankly proclaimed, and containing a variety of those faded hangings of damask
and tapestry, those chests and cabinets of carved and time-polished
oak, those angular specimens of pictorial art in frames as pedantically primitive, those perverse-looking relics of mediæval brass and
pottery, of which Italy has long been the not quite exhausted store-
house. These things kept terms with articles of modern furniture in
which large allowance had been made for a lounging generation; it
was to be noticed that all the chairs were deep and well padded and
that much space was occupied by a writing-table of which the ingenious perfection bore the stamp of London and the nineteenth century. There were books in profusion and magazines and newspapers,
and a few small, odd, elaborate pictures, chiefly in water-colour.
One of these productions stood on a drawing-room easel before
which, at the moment we begin to be concerned with her, the
young girl I have mentioned had placed herself. She was looking at
the picture in silence.

Silence—absolute silence—had not fallen upon her companions;
but their talk had an appearance of embarrassed continuity. The
two good sisters had not settled themselves in their respective
chairs; their attitude expressed a final reserve and their faces showed
the glaze of prudence. They were plain, ample, mild-featured
women, with a kind of business-like modesty to which the impersonal aspect of their stiffened linen and of the serge that draped
them as if nailed on frames gave an advantage. One of them, a
person of a certain age, in spectacles, with a fresh complexion and a
full cheek, had a more discriminating manner than her colleague, as
well as the responsibility of their errand, which apparently related
to the young girl. This object of interest wore her hat—an ornament of extreme simplicity and not at variance with her plain
muslin gown, too short for her years, though it must already have

been "let out." The gentleman who might have been supposed to be entertaining the two nuns was perhaps conscious of the difficulties of his function, it being in its way as arduous to converse with the very meek as with the very mighty. At the same time he was clearly much occupied with their quiet charge, and while she turned her back to him his eyes rested gravely on her slim, small figure. He was a man of forty, with a high but well-shaped head, on which the hair, still dense, but prematurely grizzled, had been cropped close. He had a fine, narrow, extremely modelled and composed face, of which the only fault was just this effect of its running a trifle too much to points; an appearance to which the shape of the beard contributed not a little. This beard, cut in the manner of the portraits of the sixteenth century and surmounted by a fair moustache, of which the ends had a romantic upward flourish, gave its wearer a foreign, traditionary look and suggested that he was a gentleman who studied style. His conscious, curious eyes, however, eyes at once vague and penetrating, intelligent and hard, expressive of the observer as well as of the dreamer, would have assured you that he studied it only within well-chosen limits, and that in so far as he sought it he found it. You would have been much at a loss to determine his original clime and country; he had none of the superficial signs that usually render the answer to this question an insipidly easy one. If he had English blood in his veins it had probably received some French or Italian commixture; but he suggested, fine gold coin as he was, no stamp nor emblem of the common mintage that provides for general circulation; he was the elegant complicated medal struck off for a special occasion. He had a light, lean, rather languid-looking figure, and was apparently neither tall nor short. He was dressed as a man dresses who takes little other trouble about it than to have no vulgar things.

"Well, my dear, what do you think of it?" he asked of the young girl. He used the Italian tongue, and used it with perfect ease; but this would not have convinced you he was Italian.

The child turned her head earnestly to one side and the other. "It's very pretty, papa. Did you make it yourself?"

"Certainly I made it. Don't you think I'm clever?"

"Yes, papa, very clever; I also have learned to make pictures." And she turned round and showed a small, fair face painted with a fixed and intensely sweet smile.

"You should have brought me a specimen of your powers."

"I've brought a great many; they're in my trunk."

"She draws very—very carefully," the elder of the nuns remarked, speaking in French.

"I'm glad to hear it. Is it you who have instructed her?"

"Happily no," said the good sister, blushing a little. "*Ce n'est pas ma partie.*[1] I teach nothing. I leave that to those who are wiser. We've an excellent drawing-master, Mr.—Mr.—what is his name?" she asked of her companion.

Her companion looked about at the carpet. "It's a German name," she said in Italian, as if it needed to be translated.

"Yes," the other went on, "he's a German, and we've had him many years."

The young girl, who was not heeding the conversation, had wandered away to the open door of the large room and stood looking into the garden. "And you, my sister, are French," said the gentleman.

"Yes, sir," the visitor gently replied. "I speak to the pupils in my own tongue. I know no other. But we have sisters of other countries—English, German, Irish. They all speak their proper language."

The gentleman gave a smile. "Has my daughter been under the care of one of the Irish ladies?" And then, as he saw that his visitors suspected a joke, though failing to understand it, "You're very complete," he instantly added.

"Oh, yes, we're complete. We've everything, and everything's of the best."

"We have gymnastics," the Italian sister ventured to remark. "But not dangerous."

"I hope not. Is that *your* branch?" A question which provoked much candid hilarity on the part of the two ladies; on the subsidence of which their entertainer, glancing at his daughter, remarked that she had grown.

"Yes, but I think she has finished. She'll remain—not big," said the French sister.

"I'm not sorry. I prefer women like books—very good and not too long. But I know," the gentleman said, "no particular reason why my child should be short."

The nun gave a temperate shrug, as if to intimate that such things might be beyond our knowledge. "She's in very good health; that's the best thing."

"Yes, she looks sound." And the young girl's father watched her a moment. "What do you see in the garden?" he asked in French.

"I see many flowers," she replied in a sweet, small voice and with an accent as good as his own.

"Yes, but not many good ones. However, such as they are, go out and gather some for *ces dames.*"

The child turned to him with her smile heightened by pleasure. "May I, truly?"

"Ah, when I tell you," said her father.

1. That's not in my line; that's not what I do.

The girl glanced at the elder of the nuns. "May I, truly, *ma mère?*"

"Obey monsieur your father, my child," said the sister, blushing again.

The child, satisfied with this authorisation, descended from the threshold and was presently lost to sight. "You don't spoil them," said her father gaily.

"For everything they must ask leave. That's our system. Leave is freely granted, but they must ask it."

"Oh, I don't quarrel with your system; I've no doubt it's excellent. I sent you my daughter to see what you'd make of her. I had faith."

"One must have faith," the sister blandly rejoined, gazing through her spectacles.

"Well, has my faith been rewarded? What have you made of her?"

The sister dropped her eyes a moment. "A good Christian, monsieur."

Her host dropped his eyes as well; but it was probable that the movement had in each case a different spring. "Yes, and what else?"

He watched the lady from the convent, probably thinking she would say that a good Christian was everything; but for all her simplicity she was not so crude as that. "A charming young lady—a real little woman—a daughter in whom you will have nothing but contentment."

"She seems to me very *gentille*,"[2] said the father. "She's really pretty."

"She's perfect. She has no faults."

"She never had any as a child, and I'm glad you have given her none."

"We love her too much," said the spectacled sister with dignity. "And as for faults, how can we give what we have not? *Le couvent n'est pas comme le monde, monsieur.*[3] She's our daughter, as you may say. We've had her since she was so small."

"Of all those we shall lose this year she's the one we shall miss most," the younger woman murmured deferentially.

"Ah, yes, we shall talk long of her," said the other. "We shall hold her up to the new ones." And at this the good sister appeared to find her spectacles dim; while her companion, after fumbling a moment, presently drew forth a pocket-handkerchief of durable texture.

"It's not certain you'll lose her; nothing's settled yet," their host

2. Nice.
3. The convent is not like any other place, sir. (Literally, "not like the world.")

rejoined quickly; not as if to anticipate their tears, but in the tone of a man saying what was most agreeable to himself.

"We should be very happy to believe that. Fifteen is very young to leave us."

"Oh," exclaimed the gentleman with more vivacity than he had yet used, "it is not I who wish to take her away. I wish you could keep her always!"

"Ah, monsieur," said the elder sister, smiling and getting up, "good as she is, she's made for the world. *Le monde y gagnera.*"[4]

"If all the good people were hidden away in convents how would the world get on?" her companion softly enquired, rising also.

This was a question of a wider bearing than the good woman apparently supposed; and the lady in spectacles took a harmonising view by saying comfortably: "Fortunately there are good people everywhere."

"If you're going there will be two less here," her host remarked gallantly.

For this extravagant sally his simple visitors had no answer, and they simply looked at each other in decent deprecation; but their confusion was speedily covered by the return of the young girl with two large bunches of roses—one of them all white, the other red.

"I give you your choice, mamman Catherine," said the child. "It's only the colour that's different, mamman Justine; there are just as many roses in one bunch as in the other."

The two sisters turned to each other, smiling and hesitating, with "Which will you take?" and "No, it's for you to choose."

"I'll take the red, thank you," said mother Catherine in the spectacles. "I'm so red myself. They'll comfort us on our way back to Rome."

"Ah, they won't last," cried the young girl. "I wish I could give you something that would last!"

"You've given us a good memory of yourself, my daughter. That will last!"

"I wish nuns could wear pretty things. I would give you my blue beads," the child went on.

"And do you go back to Rome to-night?" her father enquired.

"Yes, we take the train again. We've so much to do *là-bas.*"[5]

"Are you not tired?"

"We are never tired."

"Ah, my sister, sometimes," murmured the junior votaress.

"Not to-day, at any rate. We have rested too well here. *Que Dieu vous garde, ma fille.*"[6]

Their host, while they exchanged kisses with his daughter, went

4. The world will be the better for it.
5. There.

6. God protect you, my child.

forward to open the door through which they were to pass; but as
he did so he gave a slight exclamation, and stood looking beyond.
The door opened into a vaulted ante-chamber, as high as a chapel
and paved with red tiles; and into this ante-chamber a lady had just
been admitted by a servant, a lad in shabby livery, who was now
ushering her toward the apartment in which our friends were
grouped. The gentleman at the door, after dropping his exclamation, remained silent; in silence too the lady advanced. He gave her
no further audible greeting and offered her no hand, but stood aside
to let her pass into the saloon. At the threshold she hesitated. "Is
there any one?" she asked.

"Some one you may see."

She went in and found herself confronted with the two nuns and
their pupil, who was coming forward, between them, with a hand in
the arm of each. At the sight of the new visitor they all paused, and
the lady, who had also stopped, stood looking at them. The young
girl gave a little soft cry: "Ah, Madame Merle!"

The visitor had been slightly startled, but her manner the next
instant was none the less gracious. "Yes, it's Madame Merle, come
to welcome you home." And she held out two hands to the girl,
who immediately came up to her, presenting her forehead to be
kissed. Madame Merle saluted this portion of her charming little
person and then stood smiling at the two nuns. They acknowledged
her smile with a decent obeisance, but permitted themselves no
direct scrutiny of this imposing, brilliant woman, who seemed to
bring in with her something of the radiance of the outer world.

"These ladies have brought my daughter home, and now they
return to the convent," the gentleman explained.

"Ah, you go back to Rome? I've lately come from there. It's very
lovely now," said Madame Merle.

The good sisters, standing with their hands folded into their
sleeves, accepted this statement uncritically; and the master of the
house asked his new visitor how long it was since she had left
Rome. "She came to see me at the convent," said the young girl
before the lady addressed had time to reply.

"I've been more than once, Pansy," Madame Merle declared.
"Am I not your great friend in Rome?"

"I remember the last time best," said Pansy, "because you told
me I should come away."

"Did you tell her that?" the child's father asked.

"I hardly remember. I told her what I thought would please her.
I've been in Florence a week. I hoped you would come to see me."

"I should have done so if I had known you were there. One
doesn't know such things by inspiration—though I suppose one
ought. You had better sit down."

These two speeches were made in a particular tone of voice—a tone half-lowered and carefully quiet, but as from habit rather than from any definite need. Madame Merle looked about her, choosing her seat. "You're going to the door with these women? Let me of course not interrupt the ceremony. *Je vous salue, mesdames,*"[7] she added, in French, to the nuns, as if to dismiss them.

"This lady's a great friend of ours; you will have seen her at the convent," said their entertainer. "We've much faith in her judgement, and she'll help me to decide whether my daughter shall return to you at the end of the holidays."

"I hope you'll decide in our favour, madame," the sister in spectacles ventured to remark.

"That's Mr. Osmond's pleasantry; I decide nothing," said Madame Merle, but also as in pleasantry. "I believe you've a very good school, but Miss Osmond's friends must remember that she's very naturally meant for the world."

"That's what I've told monsieur," sister Catherine answered. "It's precisely to fit her for the world," she murmured, glancing at Pansy, who stood, at a little distance, attentive to Madame Merle's elegant apparel.

"Do you hear that, Pansy? You're very naturally meant for the world," said Pansy's father.

The child fixed him an instant with her pure young eyes. "Am I not meant for you, papa?"

Papa gave a quick, light laugh. "That doesn't prevent it! I'm of the world, Pansy."

"Kindly permit us to retire," said sister Catherine. "Be good and wise and happy in any case, my daughter."

"I shall certainly come back and see you," Pansy returned, recommencing her embraces, which were presently interrupted by Madame Merle.

"Stay with me, dear child," she said, "while your father takes the good ladies to the door."

Pansy stared, disappointed, yet not protesting. She was evidently impregnated with the idea of submission, which was due to any one who took the tone of authority; and she was a passive spectator of the operation of her fate. "May I not see mamman Catherine get into the carriage?" she nevertheless asked very gently.

"It would please me better if you'd remain with me," said Madame Merle, while Mr. Osmond and his companions, who had bowed low again to the other visitor, passed into the ante-chamber.

"Oh yes, I'll stay," Pansy answered; and she stood near Madame Merle, surrendering her little hand, which this lady took. She stared out of the window; her eyes had filled with tears.

7. I greet you, ladies. This is a word play on: *"Je vous salue, Marie"*—"Hail, Mary."

"I'm glad they've taught you to obey," said Madame Merle. "That's what good little girls should do."

"Oh yes, I obey very well," cried Pansy with soft eagerness, almost with boastfulness, as if she had been speaking of her piano-playing. And then she gave a faint, just audible sigh.

Madame Merle, holding her hand, drew it across her own fine palm and looked at it. The gaze was critical, but it found nothing to deprecate; the child's small hand was delicate and fair. "I hope they always see that you wear gloves," she said in a moment. "Little girls usually dislike them."

"I used to dislike them, but I like them now," the child made answer.

"Very good, I'll make you a present of a dozen."

"I thank you very much. What colours will they be?" Pansy demanded with interest.

Madame Merle meditated. "Useful colours."

"But very pretty?"

"Are you very fond of pretty things?"

"Yes; but—but not too fond," said Pansy with a trace of asceticism.

"Well, they won't be too pretty," Madame Merle returned with a laugh. She took the child's other hand and drew her nearer; after which, looking at her a moment, "Shall you miss mother Catherine?" she went on.

"Yes—when I think of her."

"Try then not to think of her. Perhaps some day," added Madame Merle, "you'll have another mother."

"I don't think that's necessary," Pansy said, repeating her little soft conciliatory sigh. "I had more than thirty mothers at the convent."

Her father's step sounded again in the ante-chamber, and Madame Merle got up, releasing the child. Mr. Osmond came in and closed the door; then, without looking at Madame Merle, he pushed one or two chairs back into their places. His visitor waited a moment for him to speak, watching him as he moved about. Then at last she said: "I hoped you'd have come to Rome. I thought it possible you'd have wished yourself to fetch Pansy away."

"That was a natural supposition; but I'm afraid it's not the first time I've acted in defiance of your calculations."

"Yes," said Madame Merle, "I think you very perverse."

Mr. Osmond busied himself for a moment in the room—there was plenty of space in it to move about—in the fashion of a man mechanically seeking pretexts for not giving an attention which may be embarrassing. Presently, however, he had exhausted his pretexts; there was nothing left for him—unless he took up a book—but to stand with his hands behind him looking at Pansy. "Why didn't you come and see the last of mamman Catherine?" he asked of her abruptly in French.

Pansy hesitated a moment, glancing at Madame Merle. "I asked her to stay with me," said this lady, who had seated herself again in another place.

"Ah, that was better," Osmond conceded. With which he dropped into a chair and sat looking at Madame Merle; bent forward a little, his elbows on the edge of the arms and his hands interlocked.

"She's going to give me some gloves," said Pansy.

"You needn't tell that to every one, my dear," Madame Merle observed.

"You're very kind to her," said Osmond. "She's supposed to have everything she needs."

"I should think she had had enough of the nuns."

"If we're going to discuss that matter she had better go out of the room."

"Let her stay," said Madame Merle. "We'll talk of something else."

"If you like I won't listen," Pansy suggested with an appearance of candour which imposed conviction.

"You may listen, charming child, because you won't understand," her father replied. The child sat down, deferentially, near the open door, within sight of the garden, into which she directed her innocent, wistful eyes; and Mr. Osmond went on irrelevantly, addressing himself to his other companion. "You're looking particularly well."

"I think I always look the same," said Madame Merle.

"You always *are* the same. You don't vary. You're a wonderful woman."

"Yes, I think I am."

"You sometimes change your mind, however. You told me on your return from England that you wouldn't leave Rome again for the present."

"I'm pleased that you remember so well what I say. That was my intention. But I've come to Florence to meet some friends who have lately arrived and as to whose movements I was at that time uncertain."

"That reason's characteristic. You're always doing something for your friends."

Madame Merle smiled straight at her host. "It's less characteristic than your comment upon it—which is perfectly insincere. I don't, however, make a crime of that," she added, "because if you don't believe what you say there's no reason *why* you should. I don't ruin myself for my friends; I don't deserve your praise. I care greatly for myself."

"Exactly; but yourself includes so many other selves—so much of every one else and of everything. I never knew a person whose life touched so many other lives."

"What do you call one's life?" asked Madame Merle. "One's appearance, one's movements, one's engagements, one's society?"

"I call *your* life your ambitions," said Osmond.

Madame Merle looked a moment at Pansy. "I wonder if she understands that," she murmured.

"You see she can't stay with us!" And Pansy's father gave rather a joyless smile. "Go into the garden, *mignonne*,[8] and pluck a flower or two for Madame Merle," he went on in French.

"That's just what I wanted to do," Pansy exclaimed, rising with promptness and noiselessly departing. Her father followed her to the open door, stood a moment watching her, and then came back, but remained standing, or rather strolling to and fro, as if to cultivate a sense of freedom which in another attitude might be wanting.

"My ambitions are principally for you," said Madame Merle, looking up at him with a certain courage.

"That comes back to what I say. I'm part of your life—I and a thousand others. You're not selfish—I can't admit that. If you were selfish, what should I be? What epithet would properly describe me?"

"You're indolent. For me that's your worst fault."

"I'm afraid it's really my best."

"You don't care," said Madame Merle gravely.

"No; I don't think I care much. What sort of a fault do you call that? My indolence, at any rate, was one of the reasons I didn't go to Rome. But it was only one of them."

"It's not of importance—to me at least—that you didn't go; though I should have been glad to see you. I'm glad you're not in Rome now—which you might be, would probably be, if you had gone there a month ago. There's something I should like you to do at present in Florence."

"Please remember my indolence," said Osmond.

"I do remember it; but I beg you to forget it. In that way you'll have both the virtue and the reward. This is not a great labour, and it may prove a real interest. How long is it since you made a new acquaintance?"

"I don't think I've made any since I made yours."

"It's time then you should make another. There's a friend of mine I want you to know."

Mr. Osmond, in his walk, had gone back to the open door again and was looking at his daughter as she moved about in the intense

8. Dear.

sunshine. "What good will it do me?" he asked with a sort of genial crudity.

Madame Merle waited. "It will amuse you." There was nothing crude in this rejoinder; it had been thoroughly well considered.

"If you say that, you know, I believe it," said Osmond, coming toward her. "There are some points in which my confidence in you is complete. I'm perfectly aware, for instance, that you know good society from bad."

"Society is all bad."

"Pardon me. That isn't—the knowledge I impute to you—a common sort of wisdom. You've gained it in the right way—experimentally; you've compared an immense number of more or less impossible people with each other."

"Well, I invite you to profit by my knowledge."

"To profit? Are you very sure that I shall?"

"It's what I hope. It will depend on yourself. If I could only induce you to make an effort!"

"Ah, there you are! I knew something tiresome was coming. What in the world—that's likely to turn up here—is worth an effort."

Madame Merle flushed as with a wounded intention. "Don't be foolish, Osmond. No one knows better than you what *is* worth an effort. Haven't *I* seen you in old days?"

"I recognise some things. But they're none of them probable in this poor life."

"It's the effort that makes them probable," said Madame Merle.

"There's something in that. Who then is your friend?"

"The person I came to Florence to see. She's a niece of Mrs. Touchett, whom you'll not have forgotten."

"A niece? The word niece suggests youth and ignorance. I see what you're coming to."

"Yes, she's young—twenty-three years old. She's a great friend of mine. I met her for the first time in England, several months ago, and we struck up a grand alliance. I like her immensely, and I do what I don't do every day—I admire her. You'll do the same."

"Not if I can help it."

"Precisely. But you won't be able to help it."

"Is she beautiful, clever, rich, splendid, universally intelligent and unprecedentedly virtuous? It's only on those conditions that I care to make her acquaintance. You know I asked you some time ago never to speak to me of a creature who shouldn't correspond to that description. I know plenty of dingy people; I don't want to know any more."

"Miss Archer isn't dingy; she's as bright as the morning. She corresponds to your description; it's for that I wish you to know her. She fills all your requirements."

"More or less, of course."

"No; quite literally. She's beautiful, accomplished, generous and, for an American, well-born. She's also very clever and very amiable, and she has a handsome fortune."

Mr. Osmond listened to this in silence, appearing to turn it over in his mind with his eyes on his informant. "What do you want to do with her?" he asked at last.

"What you see. Put her in your way."

"Isn't she meant for something better than that?"

"I don't pretend to know what people are meant for," said Madame Merle. "I only know what I can do with them."

"I'm sorry for Miss Archer!" Osmond declared.

Madame Merle got up. "If that's a beginning of interest in her I take note of it."

The two stood there face to face; she settled her mantilla, looking down at it as she did so. "You're looking very well," Osmond repeated still less relevantly than before. "You have some idea. You're never so well as when you've got an idea; they're always becoming to you."

In the manner and tone of these two persons, on first meeting at any juncture, and especially when they met in the presence of others, was something indirect and circumspect, as if they had approached each other obliquely and addressed each other by implication. The effect of each appeared to be to intensify to an appreciable degree the self-consciousness of the other. Madame Merle of course carried off any embarrassment better than her friend; but even Madame Merle had not on this occasion the form she would have liked to have—the perfect self-possession she would have wished to wear for her host. The point to be made is, however, that at a certain moment the element between them, whatever it was, always levelled itself and left them more closely face to face than either ever was with any one else. This was what had happened now. They stood there knowing each other well and each on the whole willing to accept the satisfaction of knowing as a compensation for the inconvenience—whatever it might be—of being known. "I wish very much you were not so heartless," Madame Merle quietly said. "It has always been against you, and it will be against you now."

"I'm not so heartless as you think. Every now and then something touches me—as for instance your saying just now that your ambitions are for me. I don't understand it; I don't see how or why they should be. But it touches me, all the same."

"You'll probably understand it even less as time goes on. There are some things you'll never understand. There's no particular need you should."

"You, after all, are the most remarkable of women," said Osmond. "You have more in you than almost any one. I don't see why you think Mrs. Touchett's niece should matter very much to me, when—when—" But he paused a moment.

"When I myself have mattered so little?"

"That of course is not what I meant to say. When I've known and appreciated such a woman as you."

"Isabel Archer's better than I," said Madame Merle.

Her companion gave a laugh. "How little you must think of her to say that!"

"Do you suppose I'm capable of jealousy? Please answer me that."

"With regard to me? No; on the whole I don't."

"Come and see me then, two days hence. I'm staying at Mrs. Touchett's—Palazzo Crescentini—and the girl will be there."

"Why didn't you ask me that at first simply, without speaking of the girl?" said Osmond. "You could have had her there at any rate."

Madame Merle looked at him in the manner of a woman whom no question he could ever put would find unprepared. "Do you wish to know why? Because I've spoken of you to her."

Osmond frowned and turned away. "I'd rather not know that." Then in a moment he pointed out the easel supporting the little water-colour drawing. "Have you seen what's there—my last?"

Madame Merle drew near and considered. "Is it the Venetian Alps—one of your last year's sketches?"

"Yes—but how you guess everything!"

She looked a moment longer, then turned away. "You know I don't care for your drawings."

"I know it, yet I'm always surprised at it. They're really so much better than most people's."

"That may very well be. But as the only thing you do—well, it's so little. I should have liked you to do so many other things: those were my ambitions."

"Yes; you've told me many times—things that were impossible."

"Things that were impossible," said Madame Merle. And then in quite a different tone: "In itself your little picture's very good." She looked about the room—at the old cabinets, pictures, tapestries, surfaces of faded silk. "Your rooms at least are perfect. I'm struck with that afresh whenever I come back; I know none better anywhere. You understand this sort of thing as nobody anywhere does. You've such adorable taste."

"I'm sick of my adorable taste," said Gilbert Osmond.

"You must nevertheless let Miss Archer come and see it. I've told her about it."

"I don't object to showing my things—when people are not idiots."

"You do it delightfully. As cicerone[9] of your museum you appear to particular advantage."

Mr. Osmond, in return for this compliment, simply looked at once colder and more attentive. "Did you say she was rich?"

"She has seventy thousand pounds."

"*En écus bien comptés?*"[1]

"There's no doubt whatever about her fortune. I've seen it, as I may say."

"Satisfactory woman!—I mean *you*. And if I go to see her shall I see the mother?"

"The mother? She has none—nor father either."

"The aunt then—whom did you say?—Mrs. Touchett."

"I can easily keep her out of the way."

"I don't object to her," said Osmond; "I rather like Mrs. Touchett. She has a sort of old-fashioned character that's passing away—a vivid identity. But that long jackanapes the son—is he about the place?"

"He's there, but he won't trouble you."

"He's a good deal of a donkey."

"I think you're mistaken. He's a very clever man. But he's not fond of being about when I'm there, because he doesn't like me."

"What could be more asinine than that? Did you say she has looks?" Osmond went on.

"Yes; but I won't say it again, lest you should be disappointed in them. Come and make a beginning; that's all I ask of you."

"A beginning of what?"

Madame Merle was silent a little. "I want you of course to marry her."

"The beginning of the end? Well, I'll see for myself. Have you told her that?"

"For what do you take me? She's not so coarse a piece of machinery—nor am I."

"Really," said Osmond after some meditation, "I don't understand your ambitions."

"I think you'll understand this one after you've seen Miss Archer. Suspend your judgement." Madam Merle, as she spoke, had drawn near the open door of the garden, where she stood a moment looking out. "Pansy has really grown pretty," she presently added.

"So it seemed to me."

"But she has had enough of the convent."

9. A guide who explains antiquities to tourists.
1. In carefully counted money?

"I don't know," said Osmond. "I like what they've made of her. It's very charming."

"That's not the convent. It's the child's nature."

"It's the combination, I think. She's as pure as a pearl."

"Why doesn't she come back with my flowers then?" Madame Merle asked. "She's not in a hurry."

"We'll go and get them."

"She doesn't like me," the visitor murmured as she raised her parasol and they passed into the garden.

XXIII

Madame Merle, who had come to Florence on Mrs. Touchett's arrival at the invitation of this lady—Mrs. Touchett offering her for a month the hospitality of Palazzo Crescentini—the judicious Madame Merle spoke to Isabel afresh about Gilbert Osmond and expressed the hope she might know him; making, however, no such point of the matter as we have seen her do in recommending the girl herself to Mr. Osmond's attention. The reason of this was perhaps that Isabel offered no resistance whatever to Madame Merle's proposal. In Italy, as in England, the lady had a multitude of friends, both among the natives of the country and its heterogeneous visitors. She had mentioned to Isabel most of the people the girl would find it well to "meet"—of course, she said, Isabel could know whomever in the wide world she would—and had placed Mr. Osmond near the top of the list. He was an old friend of her own; she had known him these dozen years; he was one of the cleverest and most agreeable men—well, in Europe simply. He was altogether above the respectable average; quite another affair. He wasn't a professional charmer—far from it, and the effect he produced depended a good deal on the state of his nerves and his spirits. When not in the right mood he could fall as low as any one, saved only by his looking at such hours rather like a demoralised prince in exile. But if he cared or was interested or rightly challenged—just exactly rightly it had to be—then one felt his cleverness and his distinction. Those qualities didn't depend, in him, as in so many people, on his not committing or exposing himself. He had his perversities—which indeed Isabel would find to be the case with all the men really worth knowing—and didn't cause his light to shine equally for all persons. Madame Merle, however, thought she could undertake that for Isabel he would be brilliant. He was easily bored, too easily, and dull people always put him out; but a quick and cultivated girl like Isabel would give him a stimulus which was too absent from his life. At any rate he was a person not to miss. One shouldn't attempt to live in Italy without making a friend of Gilbert Osmond, who knew more about the country than any one except two or three German professors. And if they had more knowledge than he it was he who had most perception and taste— being artistic through and through. Isabel remembered that her friend had spoken of him during their plunge, at Gardencourt, into the deeps of talk, and wondered a little what was the nature of the tie binding these superior spirits. She felt that Madame Merle's ties always somehow had histories, and such an impression was part of the interest created by this inordinate woman. As regards her relations with Mr. Osmond, however, she hinted at nothing but a long-established calm friendship. Isabel said she should be happy to know a person who had enjoyed so high a confidence for so many years. "You ought to see a great many men," Madame Merle remarked; "you ought to see as many as possible, so as to get used to them."

"Used to them?" Isabel repeated with that solemn stare which sometimes seemed to proclaim her deficient in the sense of comedy. "Why, I'm not afraid of them—I'm as used to them as the cook to the butcher-boys."

"Used to them, I mean, so as to despise them. That's what one comes to with most of them. You'll pick out, for your society, the few whom you don't despise."

This was a note of cynicism that Madame Merle didn't often allow herself to sound; but Isabel was not alarmed, for she had never supposed that as one saw more of the world the sentiment of respect became the most active of one's emotions. It was excited, none the less, by the beautiful city of Florence, which pleased her not less than Madame Merle had promised; and if her unassisted perception had not been able to gauge its charms she had clever companions as priests to the mystery. She was in no want indeed of aesthetic illumination, for Ralph found it a joy that renewed his own early passion to act as cicerone to his eager young kinswoman. Madame Merle remained at home; she had seen the treasures of Florence again and again and had always something else to do. But she talked of all things with remarkable vividness of memory —she recalled the right-hand corner of the large Perugino and the position of the hands of the Saint Elizabeth in the picture next to it.[1] She had her opinions as to the character of many famous works of art, differing often from Ralph with great sharpness and defending her interpretations with as much ingenuity as good-humour. Isabel listened to the discussions taking place between the two with a sense that she might derive much benefit from them and that they were among the advantages she couldn't have enjoyed for instance

1. Pietro Perugino (ca. 1450–1523), Italian painter. There was a Madonna of Perugino's in the Uffizi Gallery in which St. Sebastian's feet figure prominently in the lower right-hand corner. The reference to St. Elizabeth's hands might be to Albertinelli's *The Visitation of St. Elizabeth*, also in the Uffizi.

in Albany. In the clear May mornings before the formal breakfast
—this repast at Mrs. Touchett's was served at twelve o'clock—she
wandered with her cousin through the narrow and sombre Florentine streets, resting a while in the thicker dusk of some historic
church or the vaulted chambers of some dispeopled convent. She
went to the galleries and palaces; she looked at the pictures and
statues that had hitherto been great names to her, and exchanged
for a knowledge which was sometimes a limitation a presentiment
which proved usually to have been a blank. She performed all those
acts of mental prostration in which, on a first visit to Italy, youth
and enthusiasm so freely indulge; she felt her heart beat in the presence of immortal genius and knew the sweetness of rising tears in
eyes to which faded fresco and darkened marble grew dim. But the
return, every day, was even pleasanter than the going forth; the
return into the wide, monumental court of the great house in which
Mrs. Touchett, many years before, had established herself, and into
the high, cool rooms where the carven rafters and pompous frescoes
of the sixteenth century looked down on the familiar commodities
of the age of advertisement. Mrs. Touchett inhabited an historic
building in a narrow street whose very name recalled the strife of
mediæval factions; and found compensation for the darkness of
her frontage in the modicity of her rent and the brightness of a
garden where nature itself looked as archaic as the rugged architecture of the palace and which cleared and scented the rooms in regular use. To live in such a place was, for Isabel, to hold to her ear all
day a shell of the sea of the past. This vague eternal rumour kept
her imagination awake.

Gilbert Osmond came to see Madame Merle, who presented him
to the young lady lurking at the other side of the room. Isabel took
on this occasion little part in the talk; she scarcely even smiled
when the others turned to her invitingly; she sat there as if she had
been at the play and had paid even a large sum for her place. Mrs.
Touchett was not present, and these two had it, for the effect of
brilliancy, all their own way. They talked of the Florentine, the
Roman, the cosmopolite world, and might have been distinguished
performers figuring for a charity. It all had the rich readiness that
would have come from rehearsal. Madame Merle appealed to her as
if she had been on the stage, but she could ignore any learnt cue
without spoiling the scene—though of course she thus put dreadfully in the wrong the friend who had told Mr. Osmond she could
be depended on. This was no matter for once; even if more had
been involved she could have made no attempt to shine. There was
something in the visitor that checked her and held her in suspense
—made it more important she should get an impression of him
than that she should produce one herself. Besides, she had little

skill in producing an impression which she knew to be expected: nothing could be happier, in general, than to seem dazzling, but she had a perverse unwillingness to glitter by arrangement. Mr. Osmond, to do him justice, had a well-bred air of expecting nothing, a quiet ease that covered everything, even the first show of his own wit. This was the more grateful as his face, his head, was sensitive; he was not handsome, but he was fine, as fine as one of the drawings in the long gallery² above the bridge of the Uffizi. And his very voice was fine—the more strangely that, with its clearness, it yet somehow wasn't sweet. This had had really to do with making her abstain from interference. His utterance was the vibration of glass, and if she had put out her finger she might have changed the pitch and spoiled the concert. Yet before he went she had to speak.

"Madame Merle," he said, "consents to come up to my hill-top some day next week and drink tea in my garden. It would give me much pleasure if you would come with her. It's thought rather pretty—there's what they call a general view. My daughter too would be so glad—or rather, for she's too young to have strong emotions, *I* should be so glad—so very glad." And Mr. Osmond paused with a slight air of embarrassment, leaving his sentence unfinished. "I should be so happy if you could know my daughter," he went on a moment afterwards.

Isabel replied that she should be delighted to see Miss Osmond and that if Madame Merle would show her the way to the hill-top she should be very grateful. Upon this assurance the visitor took his leave; after which Isabel fully expected her friend would scold her for having been so stupid. But to her surprise that lady, who indeed never fell into the mere matter-of-course, said to her in a few moments: "You were charming, my dear; you were just as one would have wished you. You're never disappointing."

A rebuke might possibly have been irritating, though it is much more probable that Isabel would have taken it in good part; but, strange to say, the words that Madame Merle actually used caused her the first feeling of displeasure she had known this ally to excite. "That's more than I intended," she answered coldly. "I'm under no obligation that I know of to charm Mr. Osmond."

Madame Merle perceptibly flushed, but we know it was not her habit to retract. "My dear child, I didn't speak for him, poor man; I spoke for yourself. It's not of course a question as to his liking you; it matters little whether he likes you or not! But I thought you liked *him*."

"I did," said Isabel honestly. "But I don't see what that matters either."

2. A gallery of art on the upper story of the Uffizi which at that time contained the richest and most varied collection of art in the world.

"Everything that concerns you matters to me," Madame Merle returned with her weary nobleness; "especially when at the same time another old friend's concerned."

Whatever Isabel's obligations may have been to Mr. Osmond, it must be admitted that she found them sufficient to lead her to put to Ralph sundry questions about him. She thought Ralph's judgements distorted by his trials, but she flattered herself she had learned to make allowance for that.

"Do I know him?" said her cousin. "Oh, yes, I 'know' him; not well, but on the whole enough. I've never cultivated his society, and he apparently has never found mine indispensable to his happiness. Who is he, what is he? He's a vague, unexplained American who has been living these thirty years, or less, in Italy. Why do I call him unexplained? Only as a cover for my ignorance; I don't know his antecedents, his family, his origin. For all I do know he may be a prince in disguise; he rather looks like one, by the way—like a prince who has abdicated in a fit of fastidiousness and has been in a state of disgust ever since. He used to live in Rome; but of late years he has taken up his abode here; I remember hearing him say that Rome has grown vulgar. He has a great dread of vulgarity; that's his special line; he hasn't any other that I know of. He lives on his income, which I suspect of not being vulgarly large. He's a poor but honest gentleman—that's what he calls himself. He married young and lost his wife, and I believe he has a daughter. He also has a sister, who's married to some small Count or other, of these parts; I remember meeting her of old. She's nicer than he, I should think, but rather impossible. I remember there used to be some stories about her. I don't think I recommend you to know her. But why don't you ask Madame Merle about these people? She knows them all much better than I."

"I ask you because I want your opinion as well as hers," said Isabel.

"A fig for my opinion! If you fall in love with Mr. Osmond what will you care for that?"

"Not much, probably. But meanwhile it has a certain importance. The more information one has about one's dangers the better."

"I don't agree to that—it may make them dangers. We know too much about people in these days; we hear too much. Our ears, our minds, our mouths, are stuffed with personalities. Don't mind anything any one tells you about any one else. Judge every one and everything for yourself."

"That's what I try to do," said Isabel; "but when you do that people call you conceited."

"You're not to mind them—that's precisely my argument; not to mind what they say about yourself any more than what they say about your friend or your enemy."

Isabel considered. "I think you're right; but there are some things I can't help minding: for instance when my friend's attacked or when I myself am praised."

"Of course you're always at liberty to judge the critic. Judge people as critics, however," Ralph added, "and you'll condemn them all!"

"I shall see Mr. Osmond for myself," said Isabel. "I've promised to pay him a visit."

"To pay him a visit?"

"To go and see his view, his pictures, his daughter—I don't know exactly what. Madame Merle's to take me; she tells me a great many ladies call on him."

"Ah, with Madame Merle you may go anywhere, *de confiance*,"[3] said Ralph. "She knows none but the best people."

Isabel said no more about Mr. Osmond, but she presently remarked to her cousin that she was not satisfied with his tone about Madame Merle. "It seems to me you insinuate things about her. I don't know what you mean, but if you've any grounds for disliking her I think you should either mention them frankly or else say nothing at all."

Ralph, however, resented this charge with more apparent earnestness than he commonly used. "I speak of Madame Merle exactly as I speak *to* her: with an even exaggerated respect."

"Exaggerated, precisely. That's what I complain of."

"I do so because Madame Merle's merits are exaggerated."

"By whom, pray? By me? If so I do her a poor service."

"No, no; by herself."

"Ah, I protest!" Isabel earnestly cried. "If ever there was a woman who made small claims—!"

"You put your finger on it," Ralph interrupted. "Her modesty's exaggerated. She has no business with small claims—she has a perfect right to make large ones."

"Her merits are large then. You contradict yourself."

"Her merits are immense," said Ralph. "She's indescribably blameless; a pathless desert of virtue; the only woman I know who never gives one a chance."

"A chance for what?"

"Well, say to call her a fool! She's the only woman I know who has but that one little fault."

Isabel turned away with impatience. "I don't understand you; you're too paradoxical for my plain mind."

"Let me explain. When I say she exaggerates I don't mean it in

3. With confidence.

the vulgar sense—that she boasts, overstates, gives too fine an account of herself. I mean literally that she pushes the search for perfection too far—that her merits are in themselves overstrained. She's too good, too kind, too clever, too learned, too accomplished, too everything. She's too complete, in a word. I confess to you that she acts on my nerves and that I feel about her a good deal as the intensely human Athenian felt about Aristides the Just."[4]

Isabel looked hard at her cousin; but the mocking spirit, if it lurked in his words, failed on this occasion to peep from his face. "Do you wish Madame Merle to be banished?"

"By no means. She's much too good company. I delight in Madame Merle," said Ralph Touchett simply.

"You're very odious, sir!" Isabel exclaimed. And then she asked him if he knew anything that was not to the honour of her brilliant friend.

"Nothing whatever. Don't you see that's just what I mean? On the character of every one else you may find some little black speck; if I were to take half an hour to it, some day, I've no doubt I should be able to find one on yours. For my own, of course, I'm spotted like a leopard. But on Madame Merle's nothing, nothing, nothing!"

"That's just what I think!" said Isabel with a toss of her head. "That is why I like her so much."

"She's a capital person for you to know. Since you wish to see the world you couldn't have a better guide."

"I suppose you mean by that that she's worldly?"

"Worldly? No," said Ralph, "she's the great round world itself!"

It had certainly not, as Isabel for the moment took it into her head to believe, been a refinement of malice in him to say that he delighted in Madame Merle. Ralph Touchett took his refreshment wherever he could find it, and he would not have forgiven himself if he had been left wholly unbeguiled by such a mistress of the social art. There are deep-lying sympathies and antipathies, and it may have been that, in spite of the administered justice she enjoyed at his hands, her absence from his mother's house would not have made life barren to him. But Ralph Touchett had learned more or less inscrutably to attend, and there could have been nothing so "sustained" to attend to as the general performance of Madame Merle. He tasted her in sips, he let her stand, with an opportuneness she herself could not have surpassed. There were moments when he felt almost sorry for her; and these, oddly enough, were the moments when his kindness was least demonstrative. He was sure she had been yearningly ambitious and that what she had visibly accom-

4. Aristides (ca. 530–468 B.C.), Athenian statesman and general famed for his probity in public life. At least one citizen voted to ostracize Aristides because he was tired of hearing everyone call him "the Just."

plished was far below her secret measure. She had got herself into perfect training, but had won none of the prizes. She was always plain Madame Merle, the widow of a Swiss *négociant*,[5] with a small income and a large acquaintance, who stayed with people a great deal and was almost as universally "liked" as some new volume of smooth twaddle. The contrast between this position and any one of some half-dozen others that he supposed to have at various moments engaged her hope had an element of the tragical. His mother thought he got on beautifully with their genial guest; to Mrs. Touchett's sense two persons who dealt so largely in too-ingenious theories of conduct—that is of their own—would have much in common. He had given due consideration to Isabel's intimacy with her eminent friend, having long since made up his mind that he could not, without opposition, keep his cousin to himself; and he made the best of it, as he had done of worse things. He believed it would take care of itself; it wouldn't last forever. Neither of these two superior persons knew the other as well as she supposed, and when each had made an important discovery or two there would be, if not a rupture, at least a relaxation. Meanwhile he was quite willing to admit that the conversation of the elder lady was an advantage to the younger, who had a great deal to learn and would doubtless learn it better from Madame Merle than from some other instructors of the young. It was not probable that Isabel would be injured.

XXIV

It would certainly have been hard to see what injury could arise to her from the visit she presently paid to Mr. Osmond's hill-top. Nothing could have been more charming than this occasion—a soft afternoon in the full maturity of the Tuscan spring. The companions drove out of the Roman Gate, beneath the enormous blank superstructure which crowns the fine clear arch of that portal and makes it nakedly impressive, and wound between high-walled lanes into which the wealth of blossoming orchards overdrooped and flung a fragrance, until they reached the small superurban piazza, of crooked shape, where the long brown wall of the villa occupied in part by Mr. Osmond formed a principal, or at least a very imposing, object. Isabel went with her friend through a wide, high court, where a clear shadow rested below and a pair of light-arched galleries, facing each other above, caught the upper sunshine upon their slim columns and the flowering plants in which they were dressed. There was something grave and strong in the place; it looked somehow as if, once you were in, you would need an act of energy to get out. For Isabel, however, there was of course as yet no thought of

5. Merchant, trader.

getting out, but only of advancing. Mr. Osmond met her in the cold ante-chamber—it was cold even in the month of May—and ushered her, with her conductress, into the apartment to which we have already been introduced. Madame Merle was in front, and while Isabel lingered a little, talking with him, she went forward familiarly and greeted two persons who were seated in the saloon. One of these was little Pansy, on whom she bestowed a kiss; the other was a lady whom Mr. Osmond indicated to Isabel as his sister, the Countess Gemini. "And that's my little girl," he said, "who has just come out of her convent."

Pansy had on a scant white dress, and her fair hair was neatly arranged in a net; she wore her small shoes tied sandal-fashion about her ankles. She made Isabel a little conventional curtsey and then came to be kissed. The Countess Gemini simply nodded without getting up: Isabel could see she was a woman of high fashion. She was thin and dark and not at all pretty, having features that suggested some tropical bird—a long beak-like nose, small, quickly-moving eyes and a mouth and chin that receded extremely. Her expression, however, thanks to various intensities of emphasis and wonder, of horror and joy, was not inhuman, and, as regards her appearance, it was plain she understood herself and made the most of her points. Her attire, voluminous and delicate, bristling with elegance, had the look of shimmering plumage, and her attitudes were as light and sudden as those of a creature who perched upon twigs. She had a great deal of manner; Isabel, who had never known any one with so much manner, immediately classed her as the most affected of women. She remembered that Ralph had not recommended her as an acquaintance; but she was ready to acknowledge that to a casual view the Countess Gemini revealed no depths. Her demonstrations suggested the violent waving of some flag of general truce—white silk with fluttering streamers.

"You'll believe I'm glad to see you when I tell you it's only because I knew you were to be here that I came myself. I don't come and see my brother—I make him come and see me. This hill of his is impossible—I don't see what possesses him. Really, Osmond, you'll be the ruin of my horses some day, and if it hurts them you'll have to give me another pair. I heard them wheezing to-day; I assure you I did. It's very disagreeable to hear one's horses wheezing when one's sitting in the carriage; it sounds too as if they weren't what they should be. But I've always had good horses; whatever else I may have lacked I've always managed that. My husband doesn't know much, but I think he knows a horse. In general Italians don't, but my husband goes in, according to his poor light, for everything English. My horses are English—so it's all the greater pity they should be ruined. I must tell you," she went on, directly addressing Isabel, "that Osmond doesn't often invite me; I don't think he likes to have me. It was quite my own idea, coming to-day. I like to see new people, and I'm sure you're very new. But don't sit there; that chair's not what it looks. There are some very good seats here, but there are also some horrors."

These remarks were delivered with a series of little jerks and pecks, of roulades of shrillness, and in an accent that was as some fond recall of good English, or rather of good American, in adversity.

"I don't like to have you, my dear?" said her brother. "I'm sure you're invaluable."

"I don't see any horrors anywhere," Isabel returned, looking about her. "Everything seems to me beautiful and precious."

"I've a few good things," Mr. Osmond allowed; "indeed I've nothing very bad. But I've not what I should have liked."

He stood there a little awkwardly, smiling and glancing about; his manner was an odd mixture of the detached and the involved. He seemed to hint that nothing but the right "values" was of any consequence. Isabel made a rapid induction: perfect simplicity was not the badge of his family. Even the little girl from the convent, who, in her prim white dress, with her small submissive face and her hands locked before her, stood there as if she were about to partake of her first communion, even Mr. Osmond's diminutive daughter had a kind of finish that was not entirely artless.

"You'd have liked a few things from the Uffizi and the Pitti— that's what you'd have liked," said Madame Merle.

"Poor Osmond, with his old curtains and crucifixes!" the Countess Gemini exclaimed; she appeared to call her brother only by his family-name. Her ejaculation had no particular object; she smiled at Isabel as she made it and looked at her from head to foot.

Her brother had not heard her; he seemed to be thinking what he could say to Isabel. "Won't you have some tea?—you must be very tired," he at last bethought himself of remarking.

"No indeed, I'm not tired; what have I done to tire me?" Isabel felt a certain need of being very direct, of pretending to nothing; there was something in the air, in her general impression of things —she could hardly have said what it was—that deprived her of all disposition to put herself forward. The place, the occasion, the combination of people, signified more than lay on the surface; she would try to understand—she would not simply utter graceful platitudes. Poor Isabel was doubtless not aware that many women would have uttered graceful platitudes to cover the working of their observation. It must be confessed that her pride was a trifle alarmed. A man she had heard spoken of in terms that excited interest and who was evidently capable of distinguishing himself, had invited her, a young lady not lavish of her favours, to come to his house. Now that she had done so the burden of the entertainment rested naturally on his wit. Isabel was not rendered less observant, and for the moment, we judge, she was not rendered more indulgent, by perceiving that Mr. Osmond carried his burden less complacently than might have been expected. "What a fool I was to have let myself so needlessly in—!" she could fancy his exclaiming to himself.

"You'll be tired when you go home, if he shows you all his bibelots and gives you a lecture on each," said the Countess Gemini.

"I'm not afraid of that; but if I'm tired I shall at least have learned something."

"Very little, I suspect. But my sister's dreadfully afraid of learning anything," said Mr. Osmond.

"Oh, I confess to that; I don't want to know anything more—I know too much already. The more you know the more unhappy you are."

"You should not undervalue knowledge before Pansy, who has not finished her education," Madame Merle interposed with a smile.

"Pansy will never know any harm," said the child's father. "Pansy's a little convent-flower."

"Oh, the convents, the convents!" cried the Countess with a flutter of her ruffles. "Speak to me of the convents! You may learn anything there; I'm a convent-flower myself. I don't pretend to be good, but the nuns do. Don't you see what I mean?" she went on, appealing to Isabel.

Isabel was not sure she saw, and she answered that she was very bad at following arguments. The Countess then declared that she herself detested arguments, but that this was her brother's taste—he would always discuss. "For me," she said, "one should like a thing or one shouldn't; one can't like everything, of course. But one shouldn't attempt to reason it out—you never know where it may lead you. There are some very good feelings that may have bad reasons, don't you know? And then there are very bad feelings, sometimes, that have good reasons. Don't you see what I mean? I don't care anything about reasons, but I know what I like."

"Ah, that's the great thing," said Isabel, smiling and suspecting that her acquaintance with this lightly-flitting personage would not lead to intellectual repose. If the Countess objected to argument Isabel at this moment had as little taste for it, and she put out her hand to Pansy with a pleasant sense that such a gesture committed her to nothing that would admit of a divergence of views. Gilbert Osmond apparently took a rather hopeless view of his sister's tone; he turned the conversation to another topic. He presently sat down on the other side of his daughter, who had shyly brushed Isabel's fingers with her own, but he ended by drawing her out of her chair

and making her stand between his knees, leaning against him while
he passed his arm round her slimness. The child fixed her eyes on
Isabel with a still, disinterested gaze which seemed void of an intention, yet conscious of an attraction. Mr. Osmond talked of many
things; Madame Merle had said he could be agreeable when he
chose, and to-day, after a little, he appeared not only to have chosen
but to have determined. Madame Merle and the Countess Gemini
sat a little apart, conversing in the effortless manner of persons who
knew each other well enough to take their ease; but every now and
then Isabel heard the Countess, at something said by her companion, plunge into the latter's lucidity as a poodle splashes after a
thrown stick. It was as if Madame Merle were seeing how far she
would go. Mr. Osmond talked of Florence, of Italy, of the pleasure
of living in that country and of the abatements to the pleasure.
There were both satisfactions and drawbacks; the drawbacks were
numerous; strangers were too apt to see such a world as all romantic.
It met the case soothingly for the human, for the social failure—by
which he meant the people who couldn't "realise," as they said, on
their sensibility: they could keep it about them there, in their poverty, without ridicule, as you might keep an heirloom or an inconvenient entailed place that brought you in nothing. Thus there were
advantages in living in the country which contained the greatest
sum of beauty. Certain impressions you could get only there.
Others, favourable to life, you never got, and you got some that
were very bad. But from time to time you got one of a quality that
made up for everything. Italy, all the same, had spoiled a great
many people; he was even fatuous enough to believe at times that
he himself might have been a better man if he had spent less of his
life there. It made one idle and dilettantish and second-rate; it had
no discipline for the character, didn't cultivate in you, otherwise
expressed, the successful social and other "cheek" that flourished in
Paris and London. "We're sweetly provincial," said Mr. Osmond,
"and I'm perfectly aware that I myself am as rusty as a key that has
no lock to fit it. It polishes me up a little to talk with you—not
that I venture to pretend I can turn that very complicated lock I
suspect your intellect of being! But you'll be going away before I've
seen you three times, and I shall perhaps never see you after that.
That's what it is to live in a country that people come to. When
they're disagreeable here it's bad enough; when they're agreeable it's
still worse. As soon as you like them they're off again! I've been
deceived too often; I've ceased to form attachments, to permit
myself to feel attractions. You mean to stay—to settle? That would
be really comfortable. Ah yes, your aunt's a sort of guarantee; I
believe she may be depended on. Oh, she's an old Florentine; I
mean literally an old one; not a modern outsider. She's a contempo-

rary of the Medici;[1] she must have been present at the burning of Savonarola,[2] and I'm not sure she didn't throw a handful of chips into the flame. Her face is very much like some faces in the early pictures; little, dry, definite faces that must have had a good deal of expression, but almost always the same one. Indeed I can show you her portrait in a fresco of Ghirlandaio's.[3] I hope you don't object to my speaking that way of your aunt, eh? I've an idea you don't. Perhaps you think that's even worse. I assure you there's no want of respect in it, to either of you. You know I'm a particular admirer of Mrs. Touchett."

While Isabel's host exerted himself to entertain her in this somewhat confidential fashion she looked occasionally at Madame Merle, who met her eyes with an inattentive smile in which, on this occasion, there was no infelicitous intimation that our heroine appeared to advantage. Madame Merle eventually proposed to the Countess Gemini that they should go into the garden, and the Countess, rising and shaking out her feathers, began to rustle toward the door. "Poor Miss Archer!" she exclaimed, surveying the other group with expressive compassion. "She has been brought quite into the family."

"Miss Archer can certainly have nothing but sympathy for a family to which you belong," Mr. Osmond answered, with a laugh which, though it had something of a mocking ring, had also a finer patience.

"I don't know what you mean by that! I'm sure she'll see no harm in me but what you tell her. I'm better than he says, Miss Archer," the Countess went on. "I'm only rather an idiot and a bore. Is that all he has said? Ah then, you keep him in good-humour. Has he opened on one of his favourite subjects? I give you notice that there are two or three that he treats *à fond*.[4] In that case you had better take off your bonnet."

"I don't think I know what Mr. Osmond's favourite subjects are," said Isabel, who had risen to her feet.

The Countess assumed for an instant an attitude of intense meditation, pressing one of her hands, with the finger-tips gathered together, to her forehead. "I'll tell you in a moment. One's Machiavelli; the other's Vittoria Colonna; the next is Metastasio."[5]

1. A powerful, talented family which directed the fortunes of Florence from the fifteenth to the eighteenth centuries. Their patronage of the arts led Florence to become the greatest depository of European culture since Athens.
2. Girolamo Savonarola (1452–1498), Italian religious reformer who became the spiritual ruler of Florence when the Medici were temporarily exiled in 1494.
3. Domenico Ghirlandaio (1449–1494), Florentine painter. There were numerous frescoes of his in Florence.

4. Thoroughly, exhaustively.
5. Niccolò Machiavelli (1469–1527), Florentine author and statesman, whose book *The Prince* is a guide for gaining and holding political power. Vittoria Colonna (1492–1547), of a noble Roman family, a poetess who was held in high esteem by Michelangelo, her friend. Pietro Metastasio (1698–1782), poet and dramatist, known in particular for operatic melodramas, some of which were set to music by Handel and Mozart.

"Ah, with me," said Madame Merle, passing her arm into the Countess Gemini's as if to guide her course to the garden, "Mr. Osmond's never so historical."

"Oh you," the Countess answered as they moved away, "you yourself are Machiavelli—you yourself are Vittoria Colonna!"

"We shall hear next that poor Madame Merle is Metastasio!" Gilbert Osmond resignedly sighed.

Isabel had got up on the assumption that they too were to go into the garden; but her host stood there with no apparent inclination to leave the room, his hands in the pockets of his jacket and his daughter, who had now locked her arm into one of his own, clinging to him and looking up while her eyes moved from his own face to Isabel's. Isabel waited, with a certain unuttered contentedness, to have her movements directed; she liked Mr. Osmond's talk, his company: she had what always gave her a very private thrill, the consciousness of a new relation. Through the open doors of the great room she saw Madame Merle and the Countess stroll across the fine grass of the garden; then she turned, and her eyes wandered over the things scattered about her. The understanding had been that Mr. Osmond should show her his treasures; his pictures and cabinets all looked like treasures. Isabel after a moment went toward one of the pictures to see it better; but just as she had done so he said to her abruptly: "Miss Archer, what do you think of my sister?"

She faced him with some surprise. "Ah, don't ask me that—I've seen your sister too little."

"Yes, you've seen her very little; but you must have observed that there is not a great deal of her to see. What do you think of our family tone?" he went on with his cool smile. "I should like to know how it strikes a fresh, unprejudiced mind. I know what you're going to say—you've had almost no observation of it. Of course this is only a glimpse. But just take notice, in future, if you have a chance. I sometimes think we've got into a rather bad way, living off here among things and people not our own, without responsibilities or attachments, with nothing to hold us together or keep us up; marrying foreigners, forming artificial tastes, playing tricks with our natural mission. Let me add, though, that I say that much more for myself than for my sister. She's a very honest lady—more so than she seems. She's rather unhappy, and as she's not of a serious turn she doesn't tend to show it tragically: she shows it comically instead. She has got a horrid husband, though I'm not sure she makes the best of him. Of course, however, a horrid husband's an awkward thing. Madame Merle gives her excellent advice, but it's a good deal like giving a child a dictionary to learn a language with. He can look out the words, but he can't put them together. My sister needs a grammar, but unfortunately she's not grammatical. Pardon my troubling you with these details; my sister was very right in saying you've been taken into the family. Let me take down that picture; you want more light."

He took down the picture, carried it toward the window, related some curious facts about it. She looked at the other works of art, and he gave her such further information as might appear most acceptable to a young lady making a call on a summer afternoon. His pictures, his medallions and tapestries were interesting; but after a while Isabel felt the owner much more so, and independently of them, thickly as they seemed to overhang him. He resembled no one she had ever seen; most of the people she knew might be divided into groups of half a dozen specimens. There were one or two exceptions to this; she could think for instance of no group that would contain her aunt Lydia. There were other people who were, relatively speaking, original—original, as one might say, by courtesy —such as Mr. Goodwood, as her cousin Ralph, as Henrietta Stackpole, as Lord Warburton, as Madame Merle. But in essentials, when one came to look at them, these individuals belonged to types already present to her mind. Her mind contained no class offering a natural place to Mr. Osmond—he was a specimen apart. It was not that she recognised all these truths at the hour, but they were falling into order before her. For the moment she only said to herself that this "new relation" would perhaps prove her very most distinguished. Madame Merle had had that note of rarity, but what quite other power it immediately gained when sounded by a man! It was not so much what he said and did, but rather what he withheld, that marked him for her as by one of those signs of the highly curious that he was showing her on the underside of old plates and in the corner of sixteenth-century drawings: he indulged in no striking deflections from common usage, he was an original without being an eccentric. She had never met a person of so fine a grain. The peculiarity was physical, to begin with, and it extended to impalpabilities. His dense, delicate hair, his overdrawn, retouched features, his clear complexion, ripe without being coarse, the very evenness of the growth of his beard, and that light, smooth slenderness of structure which made the movement of a single one of his fingers produce the effect of an expressive gesture—these personal points struck our sensitive young woman as signs of quality, of intensity, somehow as promises of interest. He was certainly fastidious and critical; he was probably irritable. His sensibility had governed him—possibly governed him too much; it had made him impatient of vulgar troubles and had led him to live by himself, in a sorted, sifted, arranged world, thinking about art and beauty and history. He had consulted his taste in everything—his taste alone perhaps, as a sick man consciously incurable consults at last only his lawyer: that was what made him so different from every one else. Ralph had something of this same quality, this appearance of thinking that life was a matter of connoisseurship; but in Ralph it was an anomaly, a kind of humorous excrescence, whereas in Mr. Osmond it was the keynote, and everything was in harmony with it. She was certainly far from understanding him completely; his meaning was not at all times obvious. It was hard to see what he meant for instance by speaking of his provincial side—which was exactly the side she would have taken him most to lack. Was it a harmless paradox, intended to puzzle her? or was it the last refinement of high culture? She trusted she should learn in time; it would be very interesting to learn. If it was provincial to have that harmony, what then was the finish of the capital? And she could put this question in spite of so feeling her host a shy personage; since such shyness as his —the shyness of ticklish nerves and fine perceptions—was perfectly consistent with the best breeding. Indeed it was almost a proof of standards and touchstones other than the vulgar: he must be so sure the vulgar would be first on the ground. He wasn't a man of easy assurance, who chatted and gossiped with the fluency of a superficial nature; he was critical of himself as well as of others, and, exacting a good deal of others, to think them agreeable, probably took a rather ironical view of what he himself offered: a proof into the bargain that he was not grossly conceited. If he had not been shy he wouldn't have effected that gradual, subtle, successful conversion of it to which she owed both what pleased her in him and what mystified her. If he had suddenly asked her what she thought of the Countess Gemini, that was doubtless a proof that he was interested in her; it could scarely be as a help to knowledge of his own sister. That he should be so interested showed an enquiring mind; but it was a little singular he should sacrifice his fraternal feeling to his curiosity. This was the most eccentric thing he had done.

There were two other rooms, beyond the one in which she had been received, equally full of romantic objects, and in these apartments Isabel spent a quarter of an hour. Everything was in the last degree curious and precious, and Mr. Osmond continued to be the kindest of ciceroni as he led her from one fine piece to another and still held his little girl by the hand. His kindness almost surprised our young friend, who wondered why he should take so much trouble for her; and she was oppressed at last with the accumulation of beauty and knowledge to which she found herse.. introduced. There was enough for the present; she had ceased to attend to what he said; she listened to him with attentive eyes, but was not thinking of what he told her. He probably thought her quicker, cleverer in every way, more prepared, than she was. Madame Merle would have pleasantly exaggerated; which was a pity, because in the end he would be sure to find out, and then perhaps even her real intelligence wouldn't reconcile him to his mistake. A part of Isabel's fatigue came from the effort to appear as intelligent as she believed Madame Merle had described her, and from the fear (very unusual with her) of exposing—not her ignorance; for that she cared comparatively little—but her possible grossness of perception. It would have annoyed her to express a liking for something he, in his superior enlightenment, would think she oughtn't to like; or to pass by something at which the truly initiated mind would arrest itself. She had no wish to fall into that grotesqueness—in which she had seen women (and it was a warning) serenely, yet ignobly, flounder. She was very careful therefore as to what she said, as to what she noticed or failed to notice; more careful than she had ever been before.

They came back into the first of the rooms, where the tea had been served; but as the two other ladies were still on the terrace, and as Isabel had not yet been made acquainted with the view, the paramount distinction of the place, Mr. Osmond directed her steps into the garden without more delay. Madame Merle and the Countess had had chairs brought out, and as the afternoon was lovely the Countess proposed they should take their tea in the open air. Pansy therefore was sent to bid the servant bring out the preparations. The sun had got low, the golden light took a deeper tone, and on the mountains and the plain that stretched beneath them the masses of purple shadow glowed as richly as the places that were still exposed. The scene had an extraordinary charm. The air was almost solemnly still, and the large expanse of the landscape, with its gardenlike culture and nobleness of outline, its teeming valley and delicately-fretted hills, its peculiarly human-looking touches of habitation, lay there in splendid harmony and classic grace. "You seem so well pleased that I think you can be trusted to come back," Osmond said as he led his companion to one of the angles of the terrace.

"I shall certainly come back," she returned, "in spite of what you say about its being bad to live in Italy. What was that you said about one's natural mission? I wonder if I should forsake my natural mission if I were to settle in Florence."

"A woman's natural mission is to be where she's most appreciated."

"The point's to find out where that is."

"Very true—she often wastes a great deal of time in the enquiry. People ought to make it very plain to her."

"Such a matter would have to be made very plain to me," smiled Isabel.

"I'm glad, at any rate, to hear you talk of settling. Madame Merle had given me an idea that you were of a rather roving disposition. I thought she spoke of your having some plan of going round the world."

"I'm rather ashamed of my plans; I make a new one every day."

"I don't see why you should be ashamed; it's the greatest of pleasures."

"It seems frivolous, I think," said Isabel. "One ought to choose something very deliberately, and be faithful to that."

"By that rule then, I've not been frivolous."

"Have you never made plans?"

"Yes, I made one years ago, and I'm acting on it to-day."

"It must have been a very pleasant one," Isabel permitted herself to observe.

"It was very simple. It was to be as quiet as possible."

"As quiet?" the girl repeated.

"Not to worry—not to strive nor struggle. To resign myself. To be content with little." He spoke these sentences slowly, with short pauses between, and his intelligent regard was fixed on his visitor's with the conscious air of a man who has brought himself to confess something.

"Do you call that simple?" she asked with mild irony.

"Yes, because it's negative."

"Has your life been negative?"

"Call it affirmative if you like. Only it has affirmed my indifference. Mind you, not my natural indifference—I *had* none. But my studied, my wilful renunciation."

She scarcely understood him; it seemed a question whether he were joking or not. Why should a man who struck her as having a great fund of reserve suddenly bring himself to be so confidential? This was his affair, however, and his confidences were interesting. "I don't see why you should have renounced," she said in a moment.

"Because I could do nothing. I had no prospects, I was poor, and I was not a man of genius. I had no talents even; I took my measure early in life. I was simply the most fastidious young gentleman living. There were two or three people in the world I envied—the Emperor of Russia, for instance, and the Sultan of Turkey! There were even moments when I envied the Pope of Rome—for the consideration he enjoys. I should have been delighted to be considered to that extent; but since that couldn't be I didn't care for anything less, and I made up my mind not to go in for honours. The leanest gentleman can always consider himself, and fortunately I *was*, though lean, a gentleman. I could do nothing in Italy—I couldn't even be an Italian patriot. To do that I should have had to get out of the country; and I was too fond of it to leave it, to say nothing of my being too well satisfied with it, on the whole, as it then was, to wish it altered. So I've passed a great many years here on that quiet plan I spoke of. I've not been at all unhappy. I don't mean to say I've cared for nothing; but the things I've cared for have been definite—limited. The events of my life have been absolutely unperceived by any one save myself; getting an old silver crucifix at a bargain (I've never bought anything dear, of course), or discovering, as I once did, a sketch by Correggio[6] on a panel daubed over by some inspired idiot."

This would have been rather a dry account of Mr. Osmond's career if Isabel had fully believed it; but her imagination supplied the human element which she was sure had not been wanting. His life had been mingled with other lives more than he admitted; naturally she couldn't expect him to enter into this. For the present she abstained from provoking further revelations; to intimate that he had not told her everything would be more familiar and less considerate than she now desired to be—would in fact be uproariously vulgar. He had certainly told her quite enough. It was her present inclination, however, to express a measured sympathy for the success with which he had preserved his independence. "That's a very pleasant life," she said, "to renounce everything but Correggio!"

"Oh, I've made in my way a good thing of it. Don't imagine I'm whining about it. It's one's own fault if one isn't happy."

This was large; she kept down to something smaller. "Have you lived here always?"

"No, not always. I lived a long time at Naples, and many years in Rome. But I've been here a good while. Perhaps I shall have to change, however; to do something else. I've no longer myself to think of. My daughter's growing up and may very possibly not care so much for the Correggios and crucifixes as I. I shall have to do what's best for Pansy."

"Yes, do that," said Isabel. "She's such a dear little girl."

"Ah," cried Gilbert Osmond beautifully, "she's a little saint of heaven! She is my great happiness!"

XXV

While this sufficiently intimate colloquy (prolonged for some time after we cease to follow it) went forward Madame Merle and her companion, breaking a silence of some duration, had begun to exchange remarks. They were sitting in an attitude of unexpressed expectancy; an attitude especially marked on the part of the Countess Gemini, who, being of a more nervous temperament than her friend, practised with less success the art of disguising impatience.

6. Antonio Allegri da Correggio (ca. 1494–1534). Since he often decorated chapels, he would present sketches for approval. James, in 1874, praised his "naturalness of manner" (*The Painter's Eye*, p. 81).

What these ladies were waiting for would not have been apparent and was perhaps not very definite to their own minds. Madame Merle waited for Osmond to release their young friend from her *tête-à-tête*, and the Countess waited because Madame Merle did. The Countess, moreover, by waiting, found the time ripe for one of her pretty perversities. She might have desired for some minutes to place it. Her brother wandered with Isabel to the end of the garden, to which point her eyes followed them.

"My dear," she then observed to her companion, "you'll excuse me if I don't congratulate you!"

"Very willingly, for I don't in the least know why you should."

"Haven't you a little plan that you think rather well of?" And the Countess nodded at the sequestered couple.

Madame Merle's eyes took the same direction; then she looked serenely at her neighbour. "You know I never understand you very well," she smiled.

"No one can understand better than you when you wish. I see that just now you *don't* wish."

"You say things to me that no one else does," said Madame Merle gravely, yet without bitterness.

"You mean things you don't like? Doesn't Osmond sometimes say such things?"

"What your brother says has a point."

"Yes, a poisoned one sometimes. If you mean that I'm not so clever as he you mustn't think I shall suffer from your sense of our difference. But it will be much better that you should understand me."

"Why so?" asked Madame Merle. "To what will it conduce?"

"If I don't approve of your plan you ought to know it in order to appreciate the danger of my interfering with it."

Madame Merle looked as if she were ready to admit that there might be something in this; but in a moment she said quietly: "You think me more calculating than I am."

"It's not your calculating I think ill of; it's your calculating wrong. You've done so in this case."

"You must have made extensive calculations yourself to discover that."

"No, I've not had time. I've seen the girl but this once," said the Countess, "and the conviction has suddenly come to me. I like her very much."

"So do I," Madame Merle mentioned.

"You've a strange way of showing it."

"Surely I've given her the advantage of making your acquaintance."

"That indeed," piped the Countess, "is perhaps the best thing that could happen to her!"

Madame Merle said nothing for some time. The Countess's manner was odious, was really low; but it was an old story, and with her eyes upon the violet slope of Monte Morello she gave herself up to reflection. "My dear lady," she finally resumed, "I advise you not to agitate yourself. The matter you allude to concerns three persons much stronger of purpose than yourself."

"Three persons? You and Osmond of course. But is Miss Archer also very strong of purpose?"

"Quite as much so as we."

"Ah then," said the Countess radiantly, "if I convince her it's her interest to resist you she'll do so successfully!"

"Resist us? Why do you express yourself so coarsely? She's not exposed to compulsion or deception."

"I'm not sure of that. You're capable of anything, you and Osmond. I don't mean Osmond by himself, and I don't mean you by yourself. But together you're dangerous—like some chemical combination."

"You had better leave us alone then," smiled Madame Merle.

"I don't mean to touch you—but I shall talk to that girl."

"My poor Amy," Madame Merle murmured, "I don't see what has got into your head."

"I take an interest in her—that's what has got into my head. I like her."

Madame Merle hesitated a moment. "I don't think she likes you."

The Countess's bright little eyes expanded and her face was set in a grimace. "Ah, you *are* dangerous—even by yourself!"

"If you want her to like you don't abuse your brother to her," said Madame Merle.

"I don't suppose you pretend she has fallen in love with him in two interviews."

Madame Merle looked a moment at Isabel and at the master of the house. He was leaning against the parapet, facing her, his arms folded; and she at present was evidently not lost in the mere impersonal view, persistently as she gazed at it. As Madame Merle watched her she lowered her eyes; she was listening, possibly with a certain embarrassment, while she pressed the point of her parasol into the path. Madame Merle rose from her chair. "Yes, I think so!" she pronounced.

The shabby footboy, summoned by Pansy—he might, tarnished as to livery and quaint as to type, have issued from some stray sketch of old-time manners, been "put in" by the brush of a Longhi or a Goya[1]—had come out with a small table and placed it on the

1. Pietro Longhi (1702–1805), Venetian painter, and Francisco José de Goya (1746–1828), Spanish painter and en- graver. Both were penetrating observers and interpreters of their respective social worlds.

grass, and then had gone back and fetched the tea-tray; after which he had again disappeared, to return with a couple of chairs. Pansy had watched these proceedings with the deepest interest, standing with her small hands folded together upon the front of her scanty frock; but she had not presumed to offer assistance. When the tea-table had been arranged, however, she gently approached her aunt.

"Do you think papa would object to my making the tea?"

The Countess looked at her with a deliberately critical gaze and without answering her question, "My poor niece," she said, "is that your best frock?"

"Ah no," Pansy answered, "it's just a little *toilette*[2] for common occasions."

"Do you call it a common occasion when I come to see you?—to say nothing of Madame Merle and the pretty lady yonder."

Pansy reflected a moment, turning gravely from one of the persons mentioned to the other. Then her face broke into its perfect smile. "I have a pretty dress, but even that one's very simple. Why should I expose it beside your beautiful things?"

"Because it's the prettiest you have; for me you must always wear the prettiest. Please put it on the next time. It seems to me they don't dress you so well as they might."

The child sparingly stroked down her antiquated skirt. "It's a good little dress to make tea—don't you think? Don't you believe papa would allow me?"

"Impossible for me to say, my child," said the Countess. "For me, your father's ideas are unfathomable. Madame Merle understands them better. Ask *her*."

Madame Merle smiled with her usual grace. "It's a weighty question—let me think. It seems to me it would please your father to see a careful little daughter making his tea. It's the proper duty of the daughter of the house—when she grows up."

"So it seems to me, Madame Merle!" Pansy cried. "You shall see how well I'll make it. A spoonful for each." And she began to busy herself at the table.

"Two spoonfuls for me," said the Countess, who, with Madame Merle, remained for some moments watching her. "Listen to me, Pansy," the Countess resumed at last. "I should like to know what you think of your visitor."

"Ah, she's not mine—she's papa's," Pansy objected.

"Miss Archer came to see you as well," said Madame Merle.

"I'm very happy to hear that. She has been very polite to me."

"Do you like her then?" the Countess asked.

"She's charming—charming," Pansy repeated in her little neat conversational tone. "She pleases me thoroughly."

2. Dress.

"And how do you think she pleases your father?"

"Ah really, Countess!" murmured Madame Merle dissuasively. "Go and call them to tea," she went on to the child.

"You'll see if they don't like it!" Pansy declared; and departed to summon the others, who had still lingered at the end of the terrace.

"If Miss Archer's to become her mother it's surely interesting to know if the child likes her," said the Countess.

"If your brother marries again it won't be for Pansy's sake," Madame Merle replied. "She'll soon be sixteen, and after that she'll begin to need a husband rather than a stepmother."

"And will you provide the husband as well?"

"I shall certainly take an interest in her marrying fortunately. I imagine you'll do the same."

"Indeed I shan't!" cried the Countess. "Why should I, of all women, set such a price on a husband?"

"You didn't marry fortunately; that's what I'm speaking of. When I say a husband I mean a good one."

"There are no good ones. Osmond won't be a good one."

Madame Merle closed her eyes a moment. "You're irritated just now; I don't know why," she presently said. "I don't think you'll really object either to your brother's or to your niece's marrying, when the time comes for them to do so; and as regards Pansy I'm confident that we shall some day have the pleasure of looking for a husband for her together. Your large acquaintance will be a great help."

"Yes, I'm irritated," the Countess answered. "You often irritate me. Your own coolness is fabulous. You're a strange woman."

"It's much better that we should always act together," Madame Merle went on.

"Do you mean that as a threat?" asked the Countess rising.

Madame Merle shook her head as for quiet amusement. "No indeed, you've not my coolness!"

Isabel and Mr. Osmond were now slowly coming toward them and Isabel had taken Pansy by the hand. "Do you pretend to believe he'd make her happy?" the Countess demanded.

"If he should marry Miss Archer I suppose he'd behave like a gentleman."

The Countess jerked herself into a succession of attitudes. "Do you mean as most gentlemen behave? That would be much to be thankful for! Of course Osmond's a gentleman; his own sister needn't be reminded of that. But does he think he can marry any girl he happens to pick out? Osmond's a gentleman, of course; but I must say I've *never*, no, no, never, seen any one of Osmond's pretensions! What they're all founded on is more than I can say. I'm his own sister; I might be supposed to know. Who is he, if you

please? What has he ever done? If there had been anything particularly grand in his origin—if he were made of some superior clay—I
presume I should have got some inkling of it. If there had been any
great honours or splendours in the family I should certainly have
made the most of them: they would have been quite in my line.
But there's nothing, nothing, nothing. One's parents were charming
people of course; but so were yours, I've no doubt. Every one's a
charming person now-a-days. Even I'm a charming person; don't
laugh, it has literally been said. As for Osmond, he has always
appeared to believe that he's descended from the gods."

"You may say what you please," said Madame Merle, who had
listened to this quick outbreak none the less attentively, we may
believe, because her eye wandered away from the speaker and her
hands busied themselves with adjusting the knots of ribbon on her
dress. "You Osmonds are a fine race—your blood must flow from
some very pure source. Your brother, like an intelligent man, has
had the conviction of it if he has not had the proofs. You're modest
about it, but you yourself are extremely distinguished. What do you
say about your niece? The child's a little princess. Nevertheless,"
Madame Merle added, "it won't be an easy matter for Osmond to
marry Miss Archer. Yet he can try."

"I hope she'll refuse him. It will take him down a little."

"We mustn't forget that he is one of the cleverest of men."

"I've heard you say that before, but I haven't yet discovered what
he has done."

"What he has done? He has done nothing that has had to be
undone. And he has known how to wait."

"To wait for Miss Archer's money? How much of it is there?"

"That's not what I mean," said Madame Merle. "Miss Archer
has seventy thousand pounds."

"Well, it's a pity she's so charming," the Countess declared. "To
be sacrificed, any girl would do. She needn't be superior."

"If she weren't superior your brother would never look at her. He
must have the best."

"Yes," returned the Countess as they went forward a little to
meet the others, "he's very hard to satisfy. That makes me tremble
for her happiness!"

XXVI

Gilbert Osmond came to see Isabel again; that is he came to Palazzo Crescentini. He had other friends there as well, and to Mrs.
Touchett and Madame Merle he was always impartially civil; but
the former of these ladies noted the fact that in the course of a fortnight he called five times, and compared it with another fact that
she found no difficulty in remembering. Two visits a year had hith-

erto constituted his regular tribute to Mrs. Touchett's worth, and she had never observed him select for such visits those moments, of almost periodical recurrence, when Madame Merle was under her roof. It was not for Madame Merle that he came; these two were old friends and he never put himself out for her. He was not fond of Ralph—Ralph had told her so—and it was not supposable that Mr. Osmond had suddenly taken a fancy to her son. Ralph was imperturbable—Ralph had a kind of loose-fitting urbanity that wrapped him about like an ill-made overcoat, but of which he never divested himself; he thought Mr. Osmond very good company and was willing at any time to look at him in the light of hospitality. But he didn't flatter himself that the desire to repair a past injustice was the motive of their visitor's calls; he read the situation more clearly. Isabel was the attraction, and in all conscience a sufficient one. Osmond was a critic, a student of the exquisite, and it was natural he should be curious of so rare an apparition. So when his mother observed to him that it was plain what Mr. Osmond was thinking of, Ralph replied that he was quite of her opinion. Mrs. Touchett had from far back found a place on her scant list for this gentleman, though wondering dimly by what art and what process —so negative and so wise as they were—he had everywhere effectively imposed himself. As he had never been an importunate visitor he had had no chance to be offensive, and he was recommended to her by his appearance of being as well able to do without her as she was to do without him—a quality that always, oddly enough, affected her as providing ground for a relation with her. It gave her no satisfaction, however, to think that he had taken it into his head to marry her niece. Such an alliance, on Isabel's part, would have an air of almost morbid perversity. Mrs. Touchett easily remembered that the girl had refused an English peer; and that a young lady with whom Lord Warburton had not successfully wrestled should content herself with an obscure American dilettante, a middle-aged widower with an uncanny child and an ambiguous income, this answered to nothing in Mrs. Touchett's conception of success. She took, it will be observed, not the sentimental, but the political, view of matrimony—a view which has always had much to recommend it. "I trust she won't have the folly to listen to him," she said to her son; to which Ralph replied that Isabel's listening was one thing and Isabel's answering quite another. He knew she had listened to several parties, as his father would have said, but had made them listen in return; and he found much entertainment in the idea that in these few months of his knowing her he should observe a fresh suitor at her gate. She had wanted to see life, and fortune was serving her to her taste; a succession of fine gentlemen going down on their knees to her would do as well as anything else. Ralph looked forward to a fourth, a fifth, a tenth besieger; he had no conviction she would stop at a third. She would keep the gate ajar and open a parley; she would certainly not allow number three to come in. He expressed this view, somewhat after this fashion, to his mother, who looked at him as if he had been dancing a jig. He had such a fanciful, pictorial way of saying things that he might as well address her in the deaf-mute's alphabet.

"I don't think I know what you mean," she said; "you use too many figures of speech; I could never understand allegories. The two words in the language I most respect are Yes and No. If Isabel wants to marry Mr. Osmond she'll do so in spite of all your comparisons. Let her alone to find a fine one herself for anything she undertakes. I know very little about the young man in America; I don't think she spends much of her time in thinking of him, and I suspect he has got tired of waiting for her. There's nothing in life to prevent her marrying Mr. Osmond if she only looks at him in a certain way. That's all very well; no one approves more than I of one's pleasing one's self. But she takes her pleasure in such odd things; she's capable of marrying Mr. Osmond for the beauty of his opinions or for his autograph of Michael Angelo. She wants to be disinterested: as if she were the only person who's in danger of not being so! Will *he* be so disinterested when he has the spending of her money? That was her idea before your father's death, and it has acquired new charms for her since. She ought to marry some one of whose disinterestedness she shall herself be sure; and there would be no such proof of that as his having a fortune of his own."

"My dear mother, I'm not afraid," Ralph answered. "She's making fools of us all. She'll please herself, of course; but she'll do so by studying human nature at close quarters and yet retaining her liberty. She has started on an exploring expedition, and I don't think she'll change her course, at the outset, at a signal from Gilbert Osmond. She may have slackened speed for an hour, but before we know it she'll be steaming away again. Excuse another metaphor."

Mrs. Touchett excused it perhaps, but was not so much reassured as to withhold from Madame Merle the expression of her fears. "You who know everything," she said, "you must know this: whether that curious creature's really making love to my niece."

"Gilbert Osmond?" Madame Merle widened her clear eyes and, with a full intelligence, "Heaven help us," she exclaimed, "that's an idea!"

"Hadn't it occurred to you?"

"You make me feel an idiot, but I confess it hadn't. I wonder," she added, "if it has occurred to Isabel."

"Oh, I shall now ask her," said Mrs. Touchett.

Madame Merle reflected. "Don't put it into her head. The thing would be to ask Mr. Osmond."

"I can't do that," said Mrs. Touchett. "I won't have him enquire of me—as he perfectly may with that air of his, given Isabel's situation—what business it is of mine."

"I'll ask him myself," Madame Merle bravely declared.

"But what business—for *him*—is it of yours?"

"It's being none whatever is just why I can afford to speak. It's so much less my business than any one's else that he can put me off with anything he chooses. But it will be by the way he does this that I shall know."

"Pray let me hear then," said Mrs. Touchett, "of the fruits of your penetration. If I can't speak to him, however, at least I can speak to Isabel."

Her companion sounded at this the note of warning. "Don't be too quick with her. Don't inflame her imagination."

"I never did anything in life to any one's imagination. But I'm always sure of her doing something—well, not of *my* kind."

"No, you wouldn't like this," Madame Merle observed without the point of interrogation.

"Why in the world should I, pray? Mr. Osmond has nothing the least solid to offer."

Again Madame Merle was silent while her thoughtful smile drew up her mouth even more charmingly than usual toward the left corner. "Let us distinguish. Gilbert Osmond's certainly not the first comer. He's a man who in favourable conditions might very well make a great impression. He has made a great impression, to my knowledge, more than once."

"Don't tell me about his probably quite cold-blooded love-affairs; they're nothing to me!" Mrs. Touchett cried. "What you say's precisely why I wish he would cease his visits. He has nothing in the world that I know of but a dozen or two of early masters and a more or less pert little daughter."

"The early masters are now worth a good deal of money," said Madame Merle, "and the daughter's a very young and very innocent and very harmless person."

"In other words she's an insipid little chit. Is that what you mean? Having no fortune she can't hope to marry as they marry here; so that Isabel will have to furnish her either with a maintenance or with a dowry."

"Isabel probably wouldn't object to being kind to her. I think she likes the poor child."

"Another reason then for Mr. Osmond's stopping at home! Otherwise, a week hence, we shall have my niece arriving at the conviction that her mission in life's to prove that a stepmother may sacrifice herself—and that, to prove it, she must first become one."

"She would make a charming stepmother," smiled Madame Merle; "but I quite agree with you that she had better not decide upon her mission too hastily. Changing the form of one's mission's almost as difficult as changing the shape of one's nose: there they are, each, in the middle of one's face and one's character—one has to begin too far back. But I'll investigate and report to you."

All this went on quite over Isabel's head; she had no suspicions that her relations with Mr. Osmond were being discussed. Madame Merle had said nothing to put her on her guard; she alluded no more pointedly to him than to the other gentlemen of Florence, native and foreign, who now arrived in considerable numbers to pay their respects to Miss Archer's aunt. Isabel thought him interesting —she came back to that; she liked so to think of him. She had carried away an image from her visit to his hill-top which her subsequent knowledge of him did nothing to efface and which put on for her a particular harmony with other supposed and divined things, histories within histories: the image of a quiet, clever, sensitive, distinguished man, strolling on a moss-grown terrace above the sweet Val d'Arno[1] and holding by the hand a little girl whose bell-like clearness gave a new grace to childhood. The picture had no flourishes, but she liked its lowness of tone and the atmosphere of summer twilight that pervaded it. It spoke of the kind of personal issue that touched her most nearly; of the choice between objects, subjects, contacts—what might she call them?—of a thin and those of a rich association; of a lonely, studious life in a lovely land; of an old sorrow that sometimes ached to-day; of a feeling of pride that was perhaps exaggerated, but that had an element of nobleness; of a care for beauty and perfection so natural and so cultivated together that the career appeared to stretch beneath it in the disposed vistas and with the ranges of steps and terraces and fountains of a formal Italian garden—allowing only for arid places freshened by the natural dews of a quaint half-anxious, half-helpless fatherhood. At Palazzo Crescentini Mr. Osmond's manner remained the same; diffident at first—oh self-conscious beyond doubt! and full of the effort (visible only to a sympathetic eye) to overcome this disadvantage; an effort which usually resulted in a great deal of easy, lively, very positive, rather aggressive, always suggestive talk. Mr. Osmond's talk was not injured by the indication of an eagerness to shine; Isabel found no difficulty in believing that a person was sincere who had so many of the signs of strong conviction—as for instance an explicit and graceful appreciation of anything that might be said on his own side of the question, said perhaps by Miss Archer in especial. What continued to please this young woman was that while he talked so for amusement he didn't talk, as she

1. The scenic valley of the River Arno.

had heard people, for "effect." He uttered his ideas as if, odd as they often appeared, he were used to them and had lived with them; old polished knobs and heads and handles, of precious substance, that could be fitted if necessary to new walking-sticks—not switches plucked in destitution from the common tree and then too elegantly waved about. One day he brought his small daughter with him, and she rejoiced to renew acquaintance with the child, who, as she presented her forehead to be kissed by every member of the circle, reminded her vividly of an *ingénue*[2] in a French play. Isabel had never seen a little person of this pattern; American girls were very different—different too were the maidens of England. Pansy was so formed and finished for her tiny place in the world, and yet in imagination, as one could see, so innocent and infantine. She sat on the sofa by Isabel; she wore a small grenadine mantle and a pair of the useful gloves that Madame Merle had given her—little grey gloves with a single button. She was like a sheet of blank paper— the ideal *jeune fille*[3] of foreign fiction. Isabel hoped that so fair and smooth a page would be covered with an edifying text.

The Countess Gemini also came to call upon her, but the Countess was quite another affair. She was by no means a blank sheet; she had been written over in a variety of hands, and Mrs. Touchett, who felt by no means honoured by her visit, pronounced that a number of unmistakeable blots were to be seen upon her surface. The Countess gave rise indeed to some discussion between the mistress of the house and the visitor from Rome, in which Madame Merle (who was not such a fool as to irritate people by always agreeing with them) availed herself felicitously enough of that large license of dissent which her hostess permitted as freely as she practised it. Mrs. Touchett had declared it a piece of audacity that this highly compromised character should have presented herself at such a time of day at the door of a house in which she was esteemed so little as she must long have known herself to be at Palazzo Crescentini. Isabel had been made acquainted with the estimate prevailing under that roof: it represented Mr. Osmond's sister as a lady who had so mismanaged her improprieties that they had ceased to hang together at all—which was at the least what one asked of such matters—and had become the mere floating fragments of a wrecked renown, incommoding social circulation. She had been married by her mother—a more administrative person, with an appreciation of foreign titles which the daughter, to do her justice, had probably by this time thrown off—to an Italian nobleman who had perhaps given her some excuse for attempting to quench the consciousness of outrage. The Countess, however, had consoled herself outrageously, and the list of her excuses had now lost itself in

2. Innocent, ingenuous person.   3. Girl, maiden.

the labyrinth of her adventures. Mrs. Touchett had never consented to receive her, though the Countess had made overtures of old. Florence was not an austere city; but, as Mrs. Touchett said, she had to draw the line somewhere.

Madame Merle defended the luckless lady with a great deal of zeal and wit. She couldn't see why Mrs. Touchett should make a scapegoat of a woman who had really done no harm, who had only done good in the wrong way. One must certainly draw the line, but while one was about it one should draw it straight: it was a very crooked chalk-mark that would exclude the Countess Gemini. In that case Mrs. Touchett had better shut up her house; this perhaps would be the best course so long as she remained in Florence. One must be fair and not make arbitrary differences: the Countess had doubtless been imprudent, she had not been so clever as other women. She was a good creature, not clever at all; but since when had that been a ground of exclusion from the best society? For ever so long now one had heard nothing about her, and there could be no better proof of her having renounced the error of her ways than her desire to become a member of Mrs. Touchett's circle. Isabel could contribute nothing to this interesting dispute, not even a patient attention; she contented herself with having given a friendly welcome to the unfortunate lady, who, whatever her defects, had at least the merit of being Mr. Osmond's sister. As she liked the brother Isabel thought it proper to try and like the sister: in spite of the growing complexity of things she was still capable of these primitive sequences. She had not received the happiest impression of the Countess on meeting her at the villa, but was thankful for an opportunity to repair the accident. Had not Mr. Osmond remarked that she was a respectable person? To have proceeded from Gilbert Osmond this was a crude proposition, but Madame Merle bestowed upon it a certain improving polish. She told Isabel more about the poor Countess than Mr. Osmond had done, and related the history of her marriage and its consequences. The Count was a member of an ancient Tuscan family, but of such small estate that he had been glad to accept Amy Osmond, in spite of the questionable beauty which had yet not hampered her career, with the modest dowry her mother was able to offer—a sum about equivalent to that which had already formed her brother's share of their patrimony. Count Gemini since then, however, had inherited money, and now they were well enough off, as Italians went, though Amy was horribly extravagant. The Count was a low-lived brute; he had given his wife every pretext. She had no children; she had lost three within a year of their birth. Her mother, who had bristled with pretensions to elegant learning and published descriptive poems and corresponded on Italian subjects with the English weekly journals, her mother had died three years after the Countess's marriage, the father, lost in the grey American dawn of the situation, but reputed originally rich and wild, having died much earlier. One could see this in Gilbert Osmond, Madame Merle held—see that he had been brought up by a woman; though, to do him justice, one would suppose it had been by a more sensible woman than the American Corinne,[4] as Mrs. Osmond had liked to be called. She had brought her children to Italy after her husband's death, and Mrs. Touchett remembered her during the year that followed her arrival. She thought her a horrible snob; but this was an irregularity of judgment on Mrs. Touchett's part, for she, like Mrs. Osmond, approved of political marriages. The Countess was very good company and not really the featherhead she seemed; all one had to do with her was to observe the simple condition of not believing a word she said. Madame Merle had always made the best of her for her brother's sake; he appreciated any kindness shown to Amy, because (if it had to be confessed for him) he rather felt she let down their common name. Naturally he couldn't like her style, her shrillness, her egotism, her violations of taste and above all of truth: she acted badly on his nerves, she was not *his* sort of woman. What was his sort of woman? Oh, the very opposite of the Countess, a woman to whom the truth should be habitually sacred. Isabel was unable to estimate the number of times her visitor had, in half an hour, profaned it: the Countess indeed had given her an impression of rather silly sincerity. She had talked almost exclusively about herself; how much she should like to know Miss Archer; how thankful she should be for a real friend; how base the people in Florence were; how tired she was of the place; how much she should like to live somewhere else—in Paris, in London, in Washington; how impossible it was to get anything nice to wear in Italy except a little old lace; how dear the world was growing everywhere; what a life of suffering and privation she had led. Madame Merle listened with interest to Isabel's account of this passage, but she had not needed it to feel exempt from anxiety. On the whole she was not afraid of the Countess, and she could afford to do what was altogether best —not to appear so.

Isabel had meanwhile another visitor, whom it was not, even behind her back, so easy a matter to patronise. Henrietta Stackpole, who had left Paris after Mrs. Touchett's departure for San Remo and had worked her way down, as she said, through the cities of North Italy, reached the banks of the Arno about the middle of May. Madame Merle surveyed her with a single glance, took her in from head to foot, and after a pang of despair determined to endure her. She determined indeed to delight in her. She mightn't be

4. Corinna (6th century, B.C.), a lyric poetess of Boeotia, who wrote in a sim- ple style and, it is said, instructed Pindar.

inhaled as a rose, but she might be grasped as a nettle. Madame Merle genially squeezed her into insignificance, and Isabel felt that in foreseeing this liberality she had done justice to her friend's intelligence. Henrietta's arrival had been announced by Mr. Bantling, who, coming down from Nice while she was at Venice, and expecting to find her in Florence, which she had not yet reached, called at Palazzo Crescentini to express his disappointment. Henrietta's own advent occurred two days later and produced in Mr. Bantling an emotion amply accounted for by the fact that he had not seen her since the termination of the episode at Versailles. The humorous view of his situation was generally taken, but it was uttered only by Ralph Touchett, who, in the privacy of his own apartment, when Bantling smoked a cigar there, indulged in goodness knew what strong comedy on the subject of the all-judging one and her British backer. This gentleman took the joke in perfectly good part and candidly confessed that he regarded the affair as a positive intellectual adventure. He liked Miss Stackpole extremely; he thought she had a wonderful head on her shoulders, and found great comfort in the society of a woman who was not perpetually thinking about what would be said and how what she did, how what *they* did—and they had done things!—would look. Miss Stackpole never cared how anything looked, and, if she didn't care, pray why should he? But his curiosity had been roused; he wanted awfully to see if she ever *would* care. He was prepared to go as far as she—he didn't see why he should break down first.

Henrietta showed no signs of breaking down. Her prospects had brightened on her leaving England, and she was now in the full enjoyment of her copious resources. She had indeed been obliged to sacrifice her hopes with regard to the inner life; the social question, on the Continent, bristled with difficulties even more numerous than those she had encountered in England. But on the Continent there was the outer life, which was palpable and visible at every turn, and more easily convertible to literary uses than the customs of those opaque islanders. Out of doors in foreign lands, as she ingeniously remarked, one seemed to see the right side of the tapestry; out of doors in England one seemed to see the wrong side, which gave one no notion of the figure. The admission costs her historian a pang, but Henrietta, despairing of more occult things, was now paying much attention to the outer life. She had been studying it for two months at Venice, from which city she sent to the *Interviewer* a conscientious account of the gondolas, the Piazza, the Bridge of Sighs, the pigeons and the young boatman who chanted Tasso.[5] The *Interviewer* was perhaps disappointed, but Henrietta was at least seeing Europe. Her present purpose was to get down to

5. Torquato Tasso (1544–1595), author of *Jerusalem Delivered*, also wrote lyric poetry.

Rome before the malaria should come on—she apparently supposed that it began on a fixed day; and with this design she was to spend at present but few days in Florence. Mr. Bantling was to go with her to Rome, and she pointed out to Isabel that as he had been there before, as he was a military man and as he had had a classical education—he had been bred at Eton, where they study nothing but Latin and Whyte-Melville,[6] said Miss Stackpole—he would be a most useful companion in the city of the Cæsars. At this juncture Ralph had the happy idea of proposing to Isabel that she also, under his own escort, should make a pilgrimage to Rome. She expected to pass a portion of the next winter there—that was very well; but meantime there was no harm in surveying the field. There were ten days left of the beautiful month of May—the most precious month of all to the true Rome-lover. Isabel would become a Rome-lover; that was a foregone conclusion. She was provided with a trusty companion of her own sex, whose society, thanks to the fact of other calls on this lady's attention, would probably not be oppressive. Madame Merle would remain with Mrs. Touchett; she had left Rome for the summer and wouldn't care to return. She professed herself delighted to be left at peace in Florence; she had locked up her apartment and sent her cook home to Palestrina.[7] She urged Isabel, however, to assent to Ralph's proposal, and assured her that a good introduction to Rome was not a thing to be despised. Isabel in truth needed no urging, and the party of four arranged its little journey. Mrs. Touchett, on this occasion, had resigned herself to the absence of a duenna;[8] we have seen that she now inclined to the belief that her niece should stand alone. One of Isabel's preparations consisted of her seeing Gilbert Osmond before she started and mentioning her intention to him.

"I should like to be in Rome with you," he commented. "I should like to see you on that wonderful ground."

She scarcely faltered. "You might come then."

"But you'll have a lot of people with you."

"Ah," Isabel admitted, "of course I shall not be alone."

For a moment he said nothing more. "You'll like it," he went on at last. "They've spoiled it, but you'll rave about it."

"Ought I to dislike it because, poor old dear—the Niobe of Nations, you know—it has been spoiled?" she asked.

"No, I think not. It has been spoiled so often," he smiled. "If I were to go, what should I do with my little girl?"

"Can't you leave her at the villa?"

6. George John Whyte-Melville (1821–1878), novelist who wrote primarily about hunting, was educated at Eton and served in Crimea.
7. A town near Rome.
8. A chaperon.

"I don't know that I like that—though there's a very good old woman who looks after her. I can't afford a governess."

"Bring her with you then," said Isabel promptly.

Mr. Osmond looked grave. "She has been in Rome all winter, at her convent; and she's too young to make journeys of pleasure."

"You don't like bringing her forward?" Isabel enquired.

"No, I think young girls should be kept out of the world."

"I was brought up on a different system."

"You? Oh, with you it succeeded, because you—you were exceptional."

"I don't see why," said Isabel, who, however, was not sure there was not some truth in the speech.

Mr. Osmond didn't explain; he simply went on: "If I thought it would make her resemble you to join a social group in Rome I'd take her there to-morrow."

"Don't make her resemble me," said Isabel. "Keep her like herself."

"I might send her to my sister," Mr. Osmond observed. He had almost the air of asking advice; he seemed to like to talk over his domestic matters with Miss Archer.

"Yes," she concurred; "I think that wouldn't do much towards making her resemble me!"

After she had left Florence Gilbert Osmond met Madame Merle at the Countess Gemini's. There were other people present; the Countess's drawing-room was usually well filled, and the talk had been general, but after a while Osmond left his place and came and sat on an ottoman half-behind, half-beside Madame Merle's chair. "She wants me to go to Rome with her," he remarked in a low voice.

"To go with her?"

"To be there while she's there. She proposed it."

"I suppose you mean that you proposed it and she assented."

"Of course I gave her a chance. But she's encouraging—she's very encouraging."

"I rejoice to hear it—but don't cry victory too soon. Of course you'll go to Rome."

"Ah," said Osmond, "it makes one work, this idea of yours!"

"Don't pretend you don't enjoy it—you're very ungrateful. You've not been so well occupied these many years."

"The way you take it's beautiful," said Osmond. "I ought to be grateful for that."

"Not too much so, however," Madame Merle answered. She talked with her usual smile, leaning back in her chair and looking round the room. "You've made a very good impression, and I've seen for myself that you've received one. You've not come to Mrs. Touchett's seven times to oblige me."

"The girl's not disagreeable," Osmond quietly conceded.

Madame Merle dropped her eye on him a moment, during which her lips closed with a certain firmness. "Is that all you can find to say about that fine creature?"

"All? Isn't it enough? Of how many people have you heard me say more?"

She made no answer to this, but still presented her talkative grace to the room. "You're unfathomable," she murmured at last. "I'm frightened at the abyss into which I shall have cast her."

He took it almost gaily. "You can't draw back—you've gone too far."

"Very good; but you must do the rest yourself."

"I shall do it," said Gilbert Osmond.

Madame Merle remained silent and he changed his place again; but when she rose to go he also took leave. Mrs. Touchett's victoria was awaiting her guest in the court, and after he had helped his friend into it he stood there detaining her. "You're very indiscreet," she said rather wearily; "you shouldn't have moved when I did."

He had taken off his hat; he passed his hand over his forehead. "I always forget; I'm out of the habit."

"You're quite unfathomable," she repeated, glancing up at the windows of the house, a modern structure in the new part of the town.

He paid no heed to this remark, but spoke in his own sense. "She's really very charming. I've scarcely known any one more graceful."

"It does me good to hear you say that. The better you like her the better for me."

"I like her very much. She's all you described her, and into the bargain capable, I feel, of great devotion. She has only one fault."

"What's that?"

"Too many ideas."

"I warned you she was clever."

"Fortunately they're very bad ones," said Osmond.

"Why is that fortunate?"

"*Dame*,[9] if they must be sacrificed!"

Madame Merle leaned back, looking straight before her; then she spoke to the coachman. But her friend again detained her. "If I go to Rome what shall I do with Pansy?"

"I'll go and see her," said Madame Merle.

XXVII

I may not attempt to report in its fulness our young woman's

9. Indeed, well (an interjection).

response to the deep appeal of Rome, to analyse her feelings as she trod the pavement of the Forum or to number her pulsations as she crossed the threshold of Saint Peter's. It is enough to say that her impression was such as might have been expected of a person of her freshness and her eagerness. She had always been fond of history, and here was history in the stones of the street and the atoms of the sunshine. She had an imagination that kindled at the mention of great deeds, and wherever she turned some great deed had been acted. These things strongly moved her, but moved her all inwardly. It seemed to her companions that she talked less than usual, and Ralph Touchett, when he appeared to be looking listlessly and awkwardly over her head, was really dropping on her an intensity of observation. By her own measure she was very happy; she would even have been willing to take these hours for the happiest she was ever to know. The sense of the terrible human past was heavy to her, but that of something altogether contemporary would suddenly give it wings that it could wave in the blue. Her consciousness was so mixed that she scarcely knew where the different parts of it would lead her, and she went about in a repressed ecstasy of contemplation, seeing often in the things she looked at a great deal more than was there, and yet not seeing many of the items enumerated in her Murray.[1] Rome, as Ralph said, confessed to the psychological moment. The herd of reëchoing tourists had departed and most of the solemn places had relapsed into solemnity. The sky was a blaze of blue, and the plash of the fountains in their mossy niches had lost its chill and doubled its music. On the corners of the warm, bright streets one stumbled on bundles of flowers. Our friends had gone one afternoon—it was the third of their stay—to look at the latest excavations in the Forum, these labours having been for some time previous largely extended. They had descended from the modern street to the level of the Sacred Way, along which they wandered with a reverence of step which was not the same on the part of each. Henrietta Stackpole was struck with the fact that ancient Rome had been paved a good deal like New York, and even found an analogy between the deep chariot-ruts traceable in the antique street and the overjangled iron grooves which express the intensity of American life. The sun had begun to sink, the air was a golden haze, and the long shadows of broken column and vague pedestal leaned across the field of ruin. Henrietta wandered away with Mr. Bantling, whom it was apparently delightful to her to hear speak of Julius Caesar as a "cheeky old boy," and Ralph addressed such elucidations as he was prepared to offer to the attentive ear of our heroine. One of the humble archæologists who hover about the place had put himself at the disposal of the two, and repeated his

1. John Murray, a London publishing house, produced a series of respected "Handbooks" for travelers.

lesson with a fluency which the decline of the season had done nothing to impair. A process of digging was on view in a remote corner of the Forum, and he presently remarked that if it should please the *signori* to go and watch it a little they might see something of interest. The proposal commended itself more to Ralph than to Isabel, weary with much wandering; so that she admonished her companion to satisfy his curiosity while she patiently awaited his return. The hour and the place were much to her taste—she should enjoy being briefly alone. Ralph accordingly went off with the cicerone while Isabel sat down on a prostrate column near the foundations of the Capitol. She wanted a short solitude, but she was not long to enjoy it. Keen as was her interest in the rugged relics of the Roman past that lay scattered about her and in which the corrosion of centuries had still left so much of individual life, her thoughts, after resting a while on these things, had wandered, by a concatenation of stages it might require some subtlety to trace, to regions and objects charged with a more active appeal. From the Roman past to Isabel Archer's future was a long stride, but her imagination had taken it in a single flight and now hovered in slow circles over the nearer and richer field. She was so absorbed in her thoughts, as she bent her eyes upon a row of cracked but not dislocated slabs covering the ground at her feet, that she had not heard the sound of approaching footsteps before a shadow was thrown across the line of her vision. She looked up and saw a gentleman—a gentleman who was not Ralph come back to say that the excavations were a bore. This personage was startled as she was startled; he stood there baring his head to her perceptibly pale surprise.

"Lord Warburton!" Isabel exclaimed as she rose.

"I had no idea it was you. I turned that corner and came upon you."

She looked about her to explain. "I'm alone, but my companions have just left me. My cousin's gone to look at the work over there."

"Ah yes; I see." And Lord Warburton's eyes wandered vaguely in the direction she had indicated. He stood firmly before her now; he had recovered his balance and seemed to wish to show it, though very kindly. "Don't let me disturb you," he went on, looking at her dejected pillar. "I'm afraid you're tired."

"Yes, I'm rather tired." She hesitated a moment, but sat down again. "Don't let me interrupt *you*," she added.

"Oh dear, I'm quite alone, I've nothing on earth to do. I had no idea you were in Rome. I've just come from the East. I'm only passing through."

"You've been making a long journey," said Isabel, who had learned from Ralph that Lord Warburton was absent from England.

"Yes, I came abroad for six months—soon after I saw you last.

I've been in Turkey and Asia Minor; I came the other day from Athens." He managed not to be awkward, but he wasn't easy, and after a longer look at the girl he came down to nature. "Do you wish me to leave you, or will you let me stay a little?"

She took it all humanely. "I don't wish you to leave me, Lord Warburton: I'm very glad to see you."

"Thank you for saying that. May I sit down?"

The fluted shaft on which she had taken her seat would have afforded a resting-place to several persons, and there was plenty of room even for a highly-developed Englishman. This fine specimen of that great class seated himself near our young lady, and in the course of five minutes he had asked her several questions, taken rather at random and to which, as he put some of them twice over, he apparently somewhat missed catching the answer; had given her too some information about himself which was not wasted upon her calmer feminine sense. He repeated more than once that he had not expected to meet her, and it was evident that the encounter touched him in a way that would have made preparation advisable. He began abruptly to pass from the impunity of things to their solemnity, and from their being delightful to their being impossible. He was splendidly sunburnt; even his multitudinous beard had been burnished by the fire of Asia. He was dressed in the loose-fitting, heterogeneous garments in which the English traveller in foreign lands is wont to consult his comfort and affirm his nationality; and with his pleasant steady eyes, his bronzed complexion, fresh beneath its seasoning, his manly figure, his minimising manner and his general air of being a gentleman and an explorer, he was such a representative of the British race as need not in any clime have been disavowed by those who have a kindness for it. Isabel noted these things and was glad she had always liked him. He had kept, evidently in spite of shocks, every one of his merits—properties these partaking of the essence of great decent houses, as one might put it; resembling their innermost fixtures and ornaments, not subject to vulgar shifting and removable only by some whole break-up. They talked of the matters naturally in order; her uncle's death, Ralph's state of health, the way she had passed her winter, her visit to Rome, her return to Florence, her plans for the summer, the hotel she was staying at; and then of Lord Warburton's own adventures, movements, intentions, impressions and present domicile. At last there was a silence, and it said so much more than either had said that it scarce needed his final words. "I've written to you several times."

"Written to me? I've never had your letters."

"I never sent them. I burned them up."

"Ah," laughed Isabel, "it was better that you should do that than I!"

"I thought you wouldn't care for them," he went on with a simplicity that touched her. "It seemed to me that after all I had no right to trouble you with letters."

"I should have been very glad to have news of you. You know how I hoped that—that—" But she stopped; there would be such a flatness in the utterance of her thought.

"I know what you're going to say. You hoped we should always remain good friends." This formula, as Lord Warburton uttered it, was certainly flat enough; but then he was interested in making it appear so.

She found herself reduced simply to "Please don't talk of all that"; a speech which hardly struck her as improvement on the other.

"It's a small consolation to allow me!" her companion exclaimed with force.

"I can't pretend to console you," said the girl, who, all still as she sat there, threw herself back with a sort of inward triumph on the answer that had satisfied him so little six months before. He was pleasant, he was powerful, he was gallant; there was no better man than he. But her answer remained.

"It's very well you don't try to console me; it wouldn't be in your power," she heard him say through the medium of her strange elation.

"I hoped we should meet again, because I had no fear you would attempt to make me feel I had wronged you. But when you do that—the pain's greater than the pleasure." And she got up with a small conscious majesty, looking for her companions.

"I don't want to make you feel that; of course I can't say that. I only just want you to know one or two things—in fairness to myself, as it were. I won't return to the subject again. I felt very strongly what I expressed to you last year; I couldn't think of anything else. I tried to forget—energetically, systematically. I tried to take an interest in somebody else. I tell you this because I want you to know I did my duty. I didn't succeed. It was for the same purpose I went abroad—as far away as possible. They say travelling distracts the mind, but it didn't distract mine. I've thought of you perpetually, ever since I last saw you. I'm exactly the same. I love you just as much, and everything I said to you then is just as true. This instant at which I speak to you shows me again exactly how, to my great misfortune, you just insuperably *charm* me. There—I can't say less. I don't mean, however, to insist; it's only for a moment. I may add that when I came upon you a few minutes since, without the smallest idea of seeing you, I was, upon my honour, in the very act of wishing I knew where you were." He had recovered his self-control, and while he spoke it became complete. He might have been addressing a small committee—making all quietly and clearly a statement of importance; aided by an occasional look at a paper of notes concealed in his hat, which he had not again put on. And the committee, assuredly, would have felt the point proved.

"I've often thought of you, Lord Warburton," Isabel answered. "You may be sure I shall always do that." And she added in a tone of which she tried to keep up the kindness and keep down the meaning: "There's no harm in that on either side."

They walked along together, and she was prompt to ask about his sisters and request him to let them know she had done so. He made for the moment no further reference to their great question, but dipped again into shallower and safer waters. But he wished to know when she was to leave Rome, and on her mentioning the limit of her stay declared he was glad it was still so distant.

"Why do you say that if you yourself are only passing through?" she enquired with some anxiety.

"Ah, when I said I was passing through I didn't mean that one would treat Rome as if it were Clapham Junction.[2] To pass through Rome is to stop a week or two."

"Say frankly that you mean to stay as long as I do!"

His flushed smile, for a little, seemed to sound her. "You won't like that. You're afraid you'll see too much of me."

"It doesn't matter what I like. I certainly can't expect you to leave this delightful place on my account. But I confess I'm afraid of you."

"Afraid I'll begin again? I promise to be very careful."

They had gradually stopped and they stood a moment face to face. "Poor Lord Warburton!" she said with a compassion intended to be good for both of them.

"Poor Lord Warburton indeed! But I'll be careful."

"You may be unhappy, but you shall not make *me* so. That I can't allow."

"If I believed I could make you unhappy I think I should try it.' At this she walked in advance and he also proceeded. "I'll never say a word to displease you."

"Very good. If you do, our friendship's at an end."

"Perhaps some day—after a while—you'll give me leave."

"Give you leave to make me unhappy?"

He hesitated. "To tell you again—" But he checked himself. "I'll keep it down. I'll keep it down always."

Ralph Touchett had been joined in his visit to the excavation by Miss Stackpole and her attendant, and these three now emerged from among the mounds of earth and stone collected round the aperture and came into sight of Isabel and her companion. Poor Ralph hailed his friend with joy qualified by wonder, and Henrietta

2. A small, suburban railway station near London.

exclaimed in a high voice, "Gracious, there's that lord!" Ralph and his English neighbour greeted with the austerity with which, after long separations, English neighbours greet, and Miss Stackpole rested her large intellectual gaze upon the sunburnt traveller. But she soon established her relation to the crisis. "I don't suppose you remember me, sir."

"Indeed I do remember you," said Lord Warburton. "I asked you to come and see me, and you never came."

"I don't go everywhere I'm asked," Miss Stackpole answered coldly.

"Ah well, I won't ask you again," laughed the master of Lockleigh.

"If you do I'll go; so be sure!"

Lord Warburton, for all his hilarity, seemed sure enough. Mr. Bantling had stood by without claiming a recognition, but he now took occasion to nod to his lordship, who answered him with a friendly "Oh, you here, Bantling?" and a hand-shake.

"Well," said Henrietta, "I didn't know you knew him!"

"I guess you don't know every one I know," Mr. Bantling rejoined facetiously.

"I thought that when an Englishman knew a lord he always told you."

"Ah, I'm afraid Bantling was ashamed of me," Lord Warburton laughed again. Isabel took pleasure in that note; she gave a small sigh of relief as they kept their course homeward.

The next day was Sunday; she spent her morning over two long letters—one to her sister Lily, the other to Madame Merle; but in neither of these epistles did she mention the fact that a rejected suitor had threatened her with another appeal. Of a Sunday afternoon all good Romans (and the best Romans are often the northern barbarians) follow the custom of going to vespers[3] at Saint Peter's; and it had been agreed among our friends that they would drive together to the great church. After lunch, an hour before the carriage came, Lord Warburton presented himself at the Hôtel de Paris and paid a visit to the two ladies, Ralph Touchett and Mr. Bantling having gone out together. The visitor seemed to have wished to give Isabel a proof of his intention to keep the promise made her the evening before; he was both discreet and frank—not even dumbly importunate or remotely intense. He thus left her to judge what a mere good friend he could be. He talked about his travels, about Persia, about Turkey, and when Miss Stackpole asked him whether it would "pay" for her to visit those countries assured her they offered a great field to female enterprise. Isabel did him justice, but she wondered what his purpose was and what he

3. Evening office; the Roman rite includes prayers, psalms, and the *Magnificat*.

expected to gain even by proving the superior strain of his sincerity. If he expected to melt her by showing what a good fellow he was, he might spare himself the trouble. She knew the superior strain of everything about him, and nothing he could now do was required to light the view. Moreover his being in Rome at all affected her as a complication of the wrong sort—she liked so complications of the right. Nevertheless, when, on bringing his call to a close, he said he too should be at Saint Peter's and should look out for her and her friends, she was obliged to reply that he must follow his convenience.

In the church, as she strolled over its tesselated acres, he was the first person she encountered. She had not been one of the superior tourists who are "disappointed" in Saint Peter's and find it smaller than its fame; the first time she passed beneath the huge leathern curtain that strains and bangs at the entrance, the first time she found herself beneath the far-arching dome and saw the light drizzle down through the air thickened with incense and with the reflections of marble and gilt, of mosaic and bronze, her conception of greatness rose and dizzily rose. After this it never lacked space to soar. She gazed and wondered like a child or a peasant, she paid her silent tribute to the seated sublime. Lord Warburton walked beside her and talked of Saint Sophia of Constantinople; she feared for instance that he would end by calling attention to his exemplary conduct. The service had not yet begun, but at Saint Peter's there is much to observe, and as there is something almost profane in the vastness of the place, which seems meant as much for physical as for spiritual exercise, the different figures and groups, the mingled worshippers and spectators, may follow their various intentions without conflict or scandal. In that splendid immensity individual indiscretion carries but a short distance. Isabel and her companions, however, were guilty of none; for though Henrietta was obliged in candour to declare that Michael Angelo's dome suffered by comparison with that of the Capitol at Washington, she addressed her protest chiefly to Mr. Bantling's ear and reserved it in its more accentuated form for the columns of the *Interviewer*. Isabel made the circuit of the church with his lordship, and as they drew near the choir on the left of the entrance the voices of the Pope's singers were borne to them over the heads of the large number of persons clustered outside the doors. They paused a while on the skirts of this crowd, composed in equal measure of Roman cockneys and inquisitive strangers, and while they stood there the sacred concert went forward. Ralph, with Henrietta and Mr. Bantling, was apparently within, where Isabel, looking beyond the dense group in front of her, saw the afternoon light, silvered by clouds of incense that seemed to mingle with the splendid chant, slope through the embossed recesses of high windows. After a while the singing stopped and then Lord Warburton seemed disposed to move off with her. Isabel could only accompany him; whereupon she found herself confronted with Gilbert Osmond, who appeared to have been standing at a short distance behind her. He now approached with all the forms—he appeared to have multiplied them on this occasion to suit the place.

"So you decided to come?" she said as she put out her hand.

"Yes, I came last night and called this afternoon at your hotel. They told me you had come here, and I looked about for you."

"The others are inside," she decided to say.

"I didn't come for the others," he promptly returned.

She looked away; Lord Warburton was watching them; perhaps he had heard this. Suddenly she remembered it to be just what he had said to her the morning he came to Gardencourt to ask her to marry him. Mr. Osmond's words had brought the colour to her cheek, and this reminiscence had not the effect of dispelling it. She repaired any betrayal by mentioning to each companion the name of the other, and fortunately at this moment Mr. Bantling emerged from the choir, cleaving the crowd with British valour and followed by Miss Stackpole and Ralph Touchett. I say fortunately, but this is perhaps a superficial view of the matter; since on perceiving the gentleman from Florence Ralph Touchett appeared to take the case as not committing him to joy. He didn't hang back, however, from civility, and presently observed to Isabel, with due benevolence, that she would soon have all her friends about her. Miss Stackpole had met Mr. Osmond in Florence, but she had already found occasion to say to Isabel that she liked him no better than her other admirers —than Mr. Touchett and Lord Warburton, and even than little Mr. Rosier in Paris. "I don't know what it's in you," she had been pleased to remark, "but for a nice girl you do attract the most unnatural people. Mr. Goodwood's the only one I've any respect for, and he's just the one you don't appreciate.".

"What's your opinion of Saint Peter's?" Mr. Osmond was meanwhile enquiring of our young lady.

"It's very large and very bright," she contented herself with replying.

"It's too large; it makes one feel like an atom."

"Isn't that the right way to feel in the greatest of human temples?" she asked with rather a liking for her phrase.

"I suppose it's the right way to feel everywhere, when one *is* nobody. But I like it in a church as little as anywhere else."

"You ought indeed to be a Pope!" Isabel exclaimed, remembering something he had referred to in Florence.

"Ah, I should have enjoyed that!" said Gilbert Osmond.

Lord Warburton meanwhile had joined Ralph Touchett, and the two strolled away together. "Who's the fellow speaking to Miss Archer?" his lordship demanded.

"His name's Gilbert Osmond—he lives in Florence," Ralph said.

"What is he besides?"

"Nothing at all. Oh yes, he's an American; but one forgets that —he's so little of one."

"Has he known Miss Archer long?"

"Three or four weeks."

"Does she like him?"

"She's trying to find out."

"And will she?"

"Find out—?" Ralph asked.

"Will she like him?"

"Do you mean will she accept him?"

"Yes," said Lord Warburton after an instant; "I suppose that's what I horribly mean."

"Perhaps not if one does nothing to prevent it," Ralph replied.

His lordship stared a moment, but apprehended. "Then we must be perfectly quiet?"

"As quiet as the grave. And only on the chance!" Ralph added.

"The chance she may?"

"The chance she may not?"

Lord Warburton took this at first in silence, but he spoke again. "Is he awfully clever?"

"Awfully," said Ralph.

His companion thought. "And what else?"

"What more do you want?" Ralph groaned.

"Do you mean what more does *she?*"

Ralph took him by the arm to turn him: they had to rejoin the others. "She wants nothing that *we* can give her."

"Ah well, if she won't have You—!" said his lordship handsomely as they went.

Volume II

XXVIII

On the morrow, in the evening, Lord Warburton went again to see his friends at their hotel, and at this establishment he learned that they had gone to the opera. He drove to the opera with the idea of paying them a visit in their box after the easy Italian fashion; and when he had obtained his admittance—it was one of the secondary theatres—looked about the large, bare, ill-lighted house. An act had just terminated and he was at liberty to pursue his quest. After scanning two or three tiers of boxes he perceived in one of the largest of these receptacles a lady whom he easily recognised. Miss Archer was seated facing the stage and partly screened by the curtain of the box; and beside her, leaning back in his chair, was Mr. Gilbert Osmond. They appeared to have the place to themselves, and Warburton supposed their companions had taken advantage of the recess to enjoy the relative coolness of the lobby. He stood a while with his eyes on the interesting pair; he asked himself if he should go up and interrupt the harmony. At last he judged that Isabel had seen him, and this accident determined him. There should be no marked holding off. He took his way to the upper regions and on the staircase met Ralph Touchett slowly descending, his hat at the inclination of ennui and his hands where they usually were.

"I saw you below a moment since and was going down to you. I feel lonely and want company," was Ralph's greeting.

"You've some that's very good which you've yet deserted."

"Do you mean my cousin? Oh, she has a visitor and doesn't want me. Then Miss Stackpole and Bantling have gone out to a café to eat an ice—Miss Stackpole delights in an ice. I didn't think *they* wanted me either. The opera's very bad; the women look like laundresses and sing like peacocks. I feel very low."

"You had better go home," Lord Warburton said without affectation.

"And leave my young lady in this sad place? Ah no, I must watch over her."

"She seems to have plenty of friends."

"Yes, that's why I must watch," said Ralph with the same large mock-melancholy.

"If she doesn't want you it's probable she doesn't want me."

"No, you're different. Go to the box and stay there while I walk about."

Lord Warburton went to the box, where Isabel's welcome was as to a friend so honourably old that he vaguely asked himself what queer temporal province she was annexing. He exchanged greetings with Mr. Osmond, to whom he had been introduced the day before and who, after he came in, sat blandly apart and silent, as if repudiating competence in the subjects of allusion now probable. It struck her second visitor that Miss Archer had, in operatic conditions, a radiance, even a slight exaltation; as she was, however, at all times a keenly-glancing, quickly-moving, completely animated young woman, he may have been mistaken on this point. Her talk with him moreover pointed to presence of mind; it expressed a kindness so ingenious and deliberate as to indicate that she was in undisturbed possession of her faculties. Poor Lord Warburton had moments of bewilderment. She had discouraged him, formally, as much as a woman could; what business had she then with such arts and such felicities, above all with such tones of reparation—preparation? Her voice had tricks of sweetness, but why play them on *him*? The others came back; the bare, familiar, trivial opera began again. The box was large, and there was room for him to remain if he would sit a little behind and in the dark. He did so for half an hour, while Mr. Osmond remained in front, leaning forward, his elbows on his knees, just behind Isabel. Lord Warburton heard nothing, and from his gloomy corner saw nothing but the clear profile of this young lady defined against the dim illumination of the house. When there was another interval no one moved. Mr. Osmond talked to Isabel, and Lord Warburton kept his corner. He did so but for a short time, however; after which he got up and bade good-night to the ladies. Isabel said nothing to detain him, but it didn't prevent his being puzzled again. Why should she mark so one of his values—quite the wrong one—when she would have nothing to do with another, which was quite the right? He was angry with himself for being puzzled, and then angry for being angry. Verdi's music did little to comfort him, and he left the theatre and walked homeward, without knowing his way, through the tortuous, tragic streets of Rome, where heavier sorrows than his had been carried under the stars.

"What's the character of that gentleman?" Osmond asked of Isabel after he had retired.

"Irreproachable—don't you see it?"

"He owns about half England; that's his character," Henrietta remarked. "That's what they call a free country!"

"Ah, he's a great proprietor? Happy man!" said Gilbert Osmond.

"Do you call that happiness—the ownership of wretched human beings?" cried Miss Stackpole. "He owns his tenants and has thousands of them. It's pleasant to own something, but inanimate objects are enough for me. I don't insist on flesh and blood and minds and consciences."

"It seems to me you own a human being or two," Mr. Bantling suggested jocosely. "I wonder if Warburton orders his tenants about as you do me."

"Lord Warburton's a great radical," Isabel said. "He has very advanced opinions."

"He has very advanced stone walls. His park's enclosed by a gigantic iron fence, some thirty miles round," Henrietta announced for the information of Mr. Osmond. "I should like him to converse with a few of our Boston radicals."

"Don't they approve of iron fences?" asked Mr. Bantling.

"Only to shut up wicked conservatives. I always feel as if I were talking to *you* over something with a neat top-finish of broken glass."

"Do you know him well, this unreformed reformer?" Osmond went on, questioning Isabel.

"Well enough for all the use I have for him."

"And how much of a use is that?"

"Well, I like to like him."

" 'Liking to like'—why, it makes a passion!" said Osmond.

"No"—she considered—"keep that for liking to *dis*like."

"Do you wish to provoke me then," Osmond laughed, "to a passion for *him?*"

She said nothing for a moment, but then met the light question with a disproportionate gravity. "No, Mr. Osmond; I don't think I should ever dare to provoke you. Lord Warburton, at any rate," she more easily added, "is a very nice man."

"Of great ability?" her friend enquired.

"Of excellent ability, and as good as he looks."

"As good as he's good-looking do you mean? He's very good-looking. How detestably fortunate!—to be a great English magnate, to be clever and handsome into the bargain, and, by way of finishing off, to enjoy your high favour! That's a man I could envy."

Isabel considered him with interest. "You seem to me to be always envying some one. Yesterday it was the Pope; to-day it's poor Lord Warburton."

"My envy's not dangerous; it wouldn't hurt a mouse. I don't want to destroy the people—I only want to *be* them. You see it would destroy only myself."

"You'd like to be the Pope?" said Isabel.

"I should love it—but I should have gone in for it earlier. But why"—Osmond reverted—"do you speak of your friend as poor?"

"Women—when they are very, very good—sometimes pity men after they've hurt them; that's their great way of showing kindness," said Ralph, joining in the conversation for the first time and with a cynicism so transparently ingenious as to be virtually innocent.

"Pray, have I hurt Lord Warburton?" Isabel asked, raising her eyebrows as if the idea were perfectly fresh.

"It serves him right if you have," said Henrietta while the curtain rose for the ballet.

Isabel saw no more of her attributive victim for the next twenty-four hours, but on the second day after the visit to the opera she encountered him in the gallery of the Capitol,[1] where he stood before the lion of the collection, the statue of the Dying

1. The most important hill in ancient Rome, and site of the Capitoline Museum.

Gladiator.[2] She had come in with her companions, among whom, on this occasion again, Gilbert Osmond had his place, and the party, having ascended the staircase, entered the first and finest of the rooms. Lord Warburton addressed her alertly enough, but said in a moment that he was leaving the gallery. "And I'm leaving Rome," he added. "I must bid you good-bye." Isabel, inconsequently enough, was now sorry to hear it. This was perhaps because she had ceased to be afraid of his renewing his suit; she was thinking of something else. She was on the point of naming her regret, but she checked herself and simply wished him a happy journey; which made him look at her rather unlightedly. "I'm afraid you'll think me very 'volatile.' I told you the other day I wanted so much to stop."

"Oh no; you could easily change your mind."

"That's what I have done."

"*Bon voyage* then."

"You're in a great hurry to get rid of me," said his lordship quite dismally.

"Not in the least. But I hate partings."

"You don't care what I do," he went on pitifully.

Isabel looked at him a moment. "Ah," she said, "you're not keeping your promise!"

He coloured like a boy of fifteen. "If I'm not, then it's because I can't; and that's why I'm going."

"Good-bye then."

"Good-bye." He lingered still, however. "When shall I see you again?"

Isabel hesitated, but soon, as if she had had a happy inspiration: "Some day after you're married."

"That will never be. It will be after you are."

"That will do as well," she smiled.

"Yes, quite as well. Good-bye."

They shook hands, and he left her alone in the glorious room, among the shining antique marbles. She sat down in the centre of the circle of these presences, regarding them vaguely, resting her eyes on their beautiful blank faces; listening, as it were, to their eternal silence. It is impossible, in Rome at least, to look long at a great company of Greek sculptures without feeling the effect of their noble quietude; which, as with a high door closed for the ceremony, slowly drops on the spirit the large white mantle of peace. I say in Rome especially, because the Roman air is an exquisite medium for such impressions. The golden sunshine mingles with

2. *The Dying Gladiator*, known also as *The Dying Gaul*, probably by Epigonos (ca. 250 B.C.) of Pergamon (a center of Hellenistic culture). Hawthorne de-scribed the statue as "noble and most pathetic" (*The Marble Faun* [Columbus, Ohio, 1968], p. 5).

them, the deep stillness of the past, so vivid yet, though it is nothing but a void full of names, seems to throw a solemn spell upon them. The blinds were partly closed in the windows of the Capitol, and a clear, warm shadow rested on the figures and made them more mildly human. Isabel sat there a long time, under the charm of their motionless grace, wondering to what, of their experience, their absent eyes were open, and how, to our ears, their alien lips would sound. The dark red walls of the room threw them into relief: the polished marble floor reflected their beauty. She had seen them all before, but her enjoyment repeated itself, and it was all the greater because she was glad again, for the time, to be alone. At last, however, her attention lapsed, drawn off by a deeper tide of life. An occasional tourist came in, stopped and stared a moment at the Dying Gladiator, and then passed out of the other door, creaking over the smooth pavement. At the end of half an hour Gilbert Osmond reappeared, apparently in advance of his companions. He strolled toward her slowly, with his hands behind him and his usual enquiring, yet not quite appealing smile. "I'm surprised to find you alone, I thought you had company."

"So I have—the best." And she glanced at the Antinous and the Faun.[3]

"Do you call them better company than an English peer?"

"Ah, my English peer left me some time ago." She got up, speaking with intention a little dryly.

Mr. Osmond noted her dryness, which contributed for him to the interest of his question. "I'm afraid that what I heard the other evening is true: you're rather cruel to that nobleman."

Isabel looked a moment at the vanquished Gladiator. "It's not true. I'm scrupulously kind."

"That's exactly what I mean!" Gilbert Osmond returned, and with such happy hilarity that his joke needs to be explained. We know that he was fond of originals, of rarities, of the superior and the exquisite; and now that he had seen Lord Warburton, whom he thought a very fine example of his race and order, he perceived a new attraction in the idea of taking to himself a young lady who had qualified herself to figure in his collection of choice objects by declining so noble a hand. Gilbert Osmond had a high appreciation of this particular patriciate; not so much for its distinction, which he thought easily surpassable, as for its solid actuality. He had never forgiven his star for not appointing him to an English dukedom, and he could measure the unexpectedness of such conduct as Isabel's. It would be proper that the woman he might marry should have done something of that sort.

3. Among the other sculptures encircling *The Dying Gladiator* were *The Antinous of the Capitol* and *The Faun of Praxiteles*. Part of Hawthorne's description of the Faun reads: "An amiable and sensual creature, easy, mirthful, apt for jollity" (*The Marble Faun*, p. 9).

XXIX

Ralph Touchett, in talk with his excellent friend, had rather markedly qualified, as we know, his recognition of Gilbert Osmond's personal merits; but he might really have felt himself illiberal in the light of that gentleman's conduct during the rest of the visit to Rome. Osmond spent a portion of each day with Isabel and her companions, and ended by affecting them as the easiest of men to live with. Who wouldn't have seen that he could command, as it were, both tact and gaiety?—which perhaps was exactly why Ralph had made his old-time look of superficial sociability a reproach to him. Even Isabel's invidious kinsman was obliged to admit that he was just now a delightful associate. His good-humour was imperturbable, his knowledge of the right fact, his production of the right word, as convenient as the friendly flicker of a match for your cigarette. Clearly he was amused—as amused as a man could be who was so little ever surprised, and that made him almost applausive. It was not that his spirits were visibly high—he would never, in the concert of pleasure, touch the big drum by so much as a knuckle: he had a mortal dislike to the high, ragged note, to what he called random ravings. He thought Miss Archer sometimes of too precipitate a readiness. It was pity she had that fault, because if she had not had it she would really have had none; she would have been as smooth to his general need of her as handled ivory to the palm. If he was not personally loud, however, he was deep, and during these closing days of the Roman May he knew a complacency that matched with slow irregular walks under the pines of the Villa Borghese,[1] among the small sweet meadow-flowers and the mossy marbles. He was pleased with everything; he had never before been pleased with so many things at once. Old impressions, old enjoyments, renewed themselves; one evening, going home to his room at the inn, he wrote down a little sonnet to which he prefixed the title of "Rome Revisited." A day or two later he showed this piece of correct and ingenious verse to Isabel, explaining to her that it was an Italian fashion to commemorate the occasions of life by a tribute to the muse.

He took his pleasures in general singly; he was too often—he would have admitted that—too sorely aware of something wrong, something ugly; the fertilising dew of a conceivable felicity too seldom descended on his spirit. But at present he was happy—happier than he had perhaps ever been in his life, and the feeling had a large foundation. This was simply the sense of success—the most agreeable emotion of the human heart. Osmond had never had too much of it; in this respect he had the irritation of satiety, as he knew perfectly well and often reminded himself. "Ah no, I've not

1. A summer palace and grounds in Rome.

been spoiled; certainly I've not been spoiled," he used inwardly to repeat. "If I do succeed before I die I shall thoroughly have earned it." He was too apt to reason as if "earning" this boon consisted above all of covertly aching for it and might be confined to that exercise. Absolutely void of it, also, his career had not been; he might indeed have suggested to a spectator here and there that he was resting on vague laurels. But his triumphs were, some of them, now too old; others had been too easy. The present one had been less arduous than might have been expected, but had been easy—that is had been rapid—only because he had made an altogether exceptional effort, a greater effort than he had believed it in him to make. The desire to have something or other to show for his "parts"—to show somehow or other—had been the dream of his youth; but as the years went on the conditions attached to any marked proof of rarity had affected him more and more as gross and detestable; like the swallowing of mugs of beer to advertise what one could "stand." If an anonymous drawing on a museum wall had been conscious and watchful it might have known this peculiar pleasure of being at last and all of a sudden identified—as from the hand of a great master—by the so high and so unnoticed fact of style. His "style" was what the girl had discovered with a little help; and now, beside herself enjoying it, she should publish it to the world without his having any of the trouble. She should do the thing *for* him, and he would not have waited in vain.

Shortly before the time fixed in advance for her departure this young lady received from Mrs. Touchett a telegram running as follows: "Leave Florence 4th June for Bellaggio,[2] and take you if you have not other views. But can't wait if you dawdle in Rome."

The dawdling in Rome was very pleasant, but Isabel had different views, and she let her aunt know she would immediately join her. She told Gilbert Osmond that she had done so, and he replied that, spending many of his summers as well as his winters in Italy, he himself would loiter a little longer in the cool shadow of Saint Peter's. He would not return to Florence for ten days more, and in that time she would have started for Bellaggio. It might be months in this case before he should see her again. This exchange took place in the large decorated sitting-room occupied by our friends at the hotel; it was late in the evening, and Ralph Touchett was to take his cousin back to Florence on the morrow. Osmond had found the girl alone; Miss Stackpole had contracted a friendship with a delightful American family on the fourth floor and had mounted the interminable staircase to pay them a visit. Henrietta contracted friendships, in travelling, with great freedom, and had formed in railway-carriages several that were among her most valued ties. Ralph was making arrangements for the morrow's journey, and

2. A popular resort near Lake Como.

Isabel sat alone in a wilderness of yellow upholstery. The chairs and sofas were orange; the walls and windows were draped in purple and gilt. The mirrors, the pictures, had great flamboyant frames; the ceiling was deeply vaulted and painted over with naked muses and cherubs. For Osmond the place was ugly to distress; the false colours, the sham splendour were like vulgar, bragging, lying talk. Isabel had taken in hand a volume of Ampère,[3] presented. on their arrival in Rome, by Ralph; but though she held it in her lap with her finger vaguely kept in the place she was not impatient to pursue her study. A lamp covered with a drooping veil of pink tissue-paper burned on the table beside her and diffused a strange pale rosiness over the scene.

"You say you'll come back; but who knows?" Gilbert Osmond said. "I think you're much more likely to start on your voyage round the world. You're under no obligation to come back; you can do exactly what you choose; you can roam through space."

"Well, Italy's a part of space," Isabel answered. "I can take it on the way."

"On the way round the world? No, don't do that. Don't put us in a parenthesis—give us a chapter to ourselves. I don't want to see you on your travels. I'd rather see you when they're over. I should like to see you when you're tired and satiated," Osmond added in a moment. "I shall prefer you in that state."

Isabel, with her eyes bent, fingered the pages of M. Ampère. "You turn things into ridicule without seeming to do it, though not, I think, without intending it. You've no respect for my travels —you think them ridiculous."

"Where do you find that?"

She went on in the same tone, fretting the edge of her book with the paper-knife. "You see my ignorance, my blunders, the way I wander about as if the world belonged to me, simply because—because it has been put into my power to do so. You don't think a woman ought to do that. You think it bold and ungraceful."

"I think it beautiful," said Osmond. "You know my opinions— I've treated you to enough of them. Don't you remember my telling you that one ought to make one's life a work of art? You looked rather shocked at first; but then I told you that it was exactly what you seemed to me to be trying to do with your own."

She looked up from her book. "What you despise most in the world is bad, is stupid art."

"Possibly. But yours seem to me very clear and very good."

"If I were to go to Japan next winter you would laugh at me," she went on.

Osmond gave a smile—a keen one, but not a laugh, for the tone

3. Jean Jacques Ampère (1800–1864), French critic, scholar, and traveler; author of a history of Rome.

of their conversation was not jocose. Isabel had in fact her solemnity; he had seen it before. "You have an imagination that startles one!"

"That's exactly what I say. You think such an idea absurd."

"I would give my little finger to go to Japan; it's one of the countries I want most to see. Can't you believe that, with my taste for old lacquer?"

"I haven't a taste for old lacquer to excuse me," said Isabel.

"You've a better excuse—the means of going. You're quite wrong in your theory that I laugh at you. I don't know what has put it into your head."

"It wouldn't be remarkable if you did think it ridiculous that I should have the means to travel when you've not; for you know everything, and I know nothing."

"The more reason why you should travel and learn," smiled Osmond. "Besides," he added as if it were a point to be made, "I don't know everything."

Isabel was not struck with the oddity of his saying this gravely; she was thinking that the pleasantest incident of her life—so it pleased her to qualify these too few days in Rome, which she might musingly have likened to the figure of some small princess of one of the ages of dress overmuffled in a mantle of state and dragging a train that it took pages or historians to hold up—that this felicity was coming to an end. That most of the interest of the time had been owing to Mr. Osmond was a reflexion she was not just now at pains to make; she had already done the point abundant justice. But she said to herself that if there were a danger they should never meet again, perhaps after all it would be as well. Happy things don't repeat themselves, and her adventure wore already the changed, the seaward face of some romantic island from which, after feasting on purple grapes, she was putting off while the breeze rose. She might come back to Italy and find him different—this strange man who pleased her just as he was; and it would be better not to come than run the risk of that. But if she was not to come the greater the pity that the chapter was closed; she felt for a moment a pang that touched the source of tears. The sensation kept her silent, and Gilbert Osmond was silent too; he was looking at her. "Go everywhere," he said at last, in a low, kind voice; "do everything; get everything out of life. Be happy—be triumphant."

"What do you mean by being triumphant?"

"Well, doing what you like."

"To triumph, then, it seems to me, is to fail! Doing all the vain things one likes is often very tiresome."

"Exactly," said Osmond with his quiet quickness. "As I intimated just now, you'll be tired some day." He paused a moment and then he went on: "I don't know whether I had better not wait till then for something I want to say to you."

"Ah, I can't advise you without knowing what it is. But I'm horrid when I'm tired," Isabel added with due inconsequence.

"I don't believe that. You're angry, sometimes—that I can believe, though I've never seen it. But I'm sure you're never 'cross.' "

"Not even when I lose my temper?"

"You don't lose it—you find it, and that must be beautiful." Osmond spoke with a noble earnestness. "They must be great moments to see."

"If I could only find it now!" Isabel nervously cried.

"I'm not afraid; I should fold my arms and admire you. I'm speaking very seriously." He leaned forward, a hand on each knee; for some moments he bent his eyes on the floor. "What I wish to say to you," he went on at last, looking up, "is that I find I'm in love with you."

She instantly rose. "Ah, keep that till I *am* tired!"

"Tired of hearing it from others?" He sat there raising his eyes to her. "No, you may heed it now or never, as you please. But after all I must say it now." She had turned away, but in the movement she had stopped herself and dropped her gaze upon him. The two remained a while in this situation, exchanging a long look—the large, conscious look of the critical hours of life. Then he got up and came near her, deeply respectful, as if he were afraid he had been too familiar. "I'm absolutely in love with you."

He had repeated the announcement in a tone of almost impersonal discretion, like a man who expected very little from it but who spoke for his own needed relief. The tears came into her eyes: this time they obeyed the sharpness of the pang that suggested to her somehow the slipping of a fine bolt—backward, forward, she couldn't have said which. The words he had uttered made him, as he stood there, beautiful and generous, invested him as with the golden air of early autumn; but, morally speaking, she retreated before them—facing him still—as she had retreated in the other cases before a like encounter. "Oh don't say that, please," she answered with an intensity that expressed the dread of having, in this case too, to choose and decide. What made her dread great was precisely the force which, as it would seem, ought to have banished all dread—the sense of something within herself, deep down, that she supposed to be inspired and trustful passion. It was there like a large sum stored in a bank—which there was a terror in having to begin to spend. If she touched it, it would all come out.

"I haven't the idea that it will matter much to you," said Osmond. "I've too little to offer you. What I have—it's enough for me; but it's not enough for you. I've neither fortune, nor fame, nor extrinsic advantages of any kind. So I offer nothing. I only tell you because I think it can't offend you, and some day or other it may give you pleasure. It gives me pleasure, I assure you," he went on, standing there before her, considerately inclined to her, turning his hat, which he had taken up, slowly round with a movement which had all the decent tremor of awkwardness and none of its oddity, and presenting to her his firm, refined, slightly ravaged face. "It gives me no pain, because it's perfectly simple. For me you'll always be the most important woman in the world."

Isabel looked at herself in this character—looked intently, thinking she filled it with a certain grace. But what she said was not an expression of any such complacency. "You don't offend me; but you ought to remember that, without being offended, one may be incommoded, troubled." "Incommoded:" she heard herself saying that, and it struck her as a ridiculous word. But it was what stupidly came to her.

"I remember perfectly. Of course you're surprised and startled. But if it's nothing but that, it will pass away. And it will perhaps leave something that I may not be ashamed of."

"I don't know what it may leave. You see at all events that I'm not overwhelmed," said Isabel with rather a pale smile. "I'm not too troubled to think. And I think that I'm glad we're separating—that I leave Rome to-morrow."

"Of course I don't agree with you there."

"I don't at all *know* you," she added abruptly; and then she coloured as she heard herself saying what she had said almost a year before to Lord Warburton.

"If you were not going away you'd know me better."

"I shall do that some other time."

"I hope so. I'm very easy to know."

"No, no," she emphatically answered—"there you're not sincere. You're not easy to know; no one could be less so."

"Well," he laughed, "I said that because I know myself. It may be a boast, but I do."

"Very likely; but you're very wise."

"So are you, Miss Archer!" Osmond exclaimed.

"I don't feel so just now. Still, I'm wise enough to think you had better go. Good-night."

"God bless you!" said Gilbert Osmond, taking the hand which she failed to surrender. After which he added: "If we meet again you'll find me as you leave me. If we don't I shall be so all the same."

"Thank you very much. Good-bye."

There was something quietly firm about Isabel's visitor; he might go of his own movement, but wouldn't be dismissed. "There's one thing more. I haven't asked anything of you—not even a thought in the future; you must do me that justice. But there's a little service I should like to ask. I shall not return home for several days; Rome's delightful, and it's a good place for a man in my state of mind. Oh, I know you're sorry to leave it; but you're right to do what your aunt wishes."

"She doesn't even wish it!" Isabel broke out strangely.

Osmond was apparently on the point of saying something that would match these words, but he changed his mind and rejoined simply: "Ah well, it's proper you should go with her, very proper. Do everything that's proper; I go in for that. Excuse my being so patronising. You say you don't know me, but when you do you'll discover what a worship I have for propriety."

"You're not conventional?" Isabel gravely asked.

"I like the way you utter that word! No, I'm not conventional: I'm convention itself. You don't understand that?" And he paused a moment, smiling. "I should like to explain it." Then with a sudden, quick, bright naturalness, "Do come back again," he pleaded. "There are so many things we might talk about."

She stood there with lowered eyes. "What service did you speak of just now?"

"Go and see my little daughter before you leave Florence. She's alone at the villa; I decided not to send her to my sister, who hasn't at all my ideas. Tell her she must love her poor father very much," said Gilbert Osmond gently.

"It will be a great pleasure to me to go," Isabel answered. "I'll tell her what you say. Once more good-bye."

On this he took a rapid, respectful leave. When he had gone she stood a moment looking about her and seated herself slowly and with an air of deliberation. She sat there till her companions came back, with folded hands, gazing at the ugly carpet. Her agitation— for it had not diminished—was very still, very deep. What had happened was something that for a week past her imagination had been going forward to meet; but here, when it came, she stopped—that sublime principle somehow broke down. The working of this young lady's spirit was strange, and I can only give it to you as I see it, not hoping to make it seem altogether natural. Her imagination, as I say, now hung back: there was a last vague space it couldn't cross —a dusky, uncertain tract which looked ambiguous and even slightly treacherous, like a moorland seen in the winter twilight. But she was to cross it yet.

xxx

She returned on the morrow to Florence, under her cousin's

escort, and Ralph Touchett, though usually restive under railway discipline, thought very well of the successive hours passed in the train that hurried his companion away from the city now distinguished by Gilbert Osmond's preference—hours that were to form the first stage in a larger scheme of travel. Miss Stackpole had remained behind; she was planning a little trip to Naples, to be carried out with Mr. Bantling's aid. Isabel was to have three days in Florence before the 4th of June, the date of Mrs. Touchett's departure, and she determined to devote the last of these to her promise to call on Pansy Osmond. Her plan, however, seemed for a moment likely to modify itself in deference to an idea of Madame Merle's. This lady was still at Casa Touchett; but she too was on the point of leaving Florence, her next station being an ancient castle in the mountains of Tuscany, the residence of a noble family of that country, whose acquaintance (she had known them, as she said, "forever") seemed to Isabel, in the light of certain photographs of their immense crenellated dwelling which her friend was able to show her, a precious privilege. She mentioned to this fortunate woman that Mr. Osmond had asked her to take a look at his daughter, but didn't mention that he had also made her a declaration of love.

"*Ah, comme cela se trouve!*"[1] Madame Merle exclaimed. "I myself have been thinking it would be a kindness to pay the child a little visit before I go off."

"We can go together then," Isabel reasonably said: "reasonably" because the proposal was not uttered in the spirit of enthusiasm. She had prefigured her small pilgrimage as made in solitude; she should like it better so. She was nevertheless prepared to sacrifice this mystic sentiment to her great consideration for her friend.

That personage finely meditated. "After all, why should we both go; having, each of us, so much to do during these last hours?"

"Very good; I can easily go alone."

"I don't know about your going alone—to the house of a handsome bachelor. He has been married—but so long ago!"

Isabel stared. "When Mr. Osmond's away what does it matter?"

"They don't know he's away, you see."

"They? Whom do you mean?"

"Every one. But perhaps it doesn't signify."

"If you were going why shouldn't I?" Isabel asked.

"Because I'm an old frump and you're a beautiful young woman."

"Granting all that, you've not promised."

"How much you think of your promises!" said the elder woman in mild mockery.

---

1. Ah, so that's how it is!

"I think a great deal of my promises. Does that surprise you?"

"You're right," Madame Merle audibly reflected. "I really think you wish to be kind to the child."

"I wish very much to be kind to her."

"Go and see her then; no one will be the wiser. And tell her I'd have come if you hadn't. Or rather," Madame Merle added, "*don't* tell her. She won't care."

As Isabel drove, in the publicity of an open vehicle, along the winding way which led to Mr. Osmond's hill-top, she wondered what her friend had meant by no one's being the wiser. Once in while, at large intervals, this lady, whose voyaging discretion, as a general thing, was rather of the open sea than of the risky channel, dropped a remark of ambiguous quality, struck a note that sounded false. What cared Isabel Archer for the vulgar judgements of obscure people? and did Madame Merle suppose that she was capable of doing a thing at all if it had to be sneakingly done? Of course not: she must have meant something else—something which in the press of the hours that preceded her departure she had not had time to explain. Isabel would return to this some day; there were sorts of things as to which she liked to be clear. She heard Pansy strumming at the piano in another place as she herself was ushered into Mr. Osmond's drawing-room; the little girl was "practising," and Isabel was pleased to think she performed this duty with rigour. She immediately came in, smoothing down her frock, and did the honours of her father's house with a wide-eyed earnestness of courtesy. Isabel sat there half an hour, and Pansy rose to the occasion as the small, winged fairy in the pantomime soars by the aid of the dissimulated wire—not chattering, but conversing, and showing the same respectful interest in Isabel's affairs that Isabel was so good as to take in hers. Isabel wondered at her; she had never had so directly presented to her nose the white flower of cultivated sweetness. How well the child had been taught, said our admiring young woman; how prettily she had been directed and fashioned; and yet how simple, how natural, how innocent she had been kept! Isabel was fond, ever, of the question of character and quality, of sounding, as who should say, the deep personal mystery, and it had pleased her, up to this time, to be in doubt as to whether this tender slip were not really all-knowing. Was the extremity of her candour but the perfection of self-consciousness? Was it put on to please her father's visitor, or was it the direct expression of an unspotted nature? The hour that Isabel spent in Mr. Osmond's beautiful empty, dusky rooms—the windows had been half-darkened, to keep out the heat, and here and there, through an easy crevice, the splendid summer day peeped in, lighting a gleam of faded colour or tarnished gilt in the rich gloom—her interview with the daughter of the house, I say, effectually settled this question. Pansy was really a blank page, a pure white surface, successfully kept so; she had neither art, nor guile, nor temper, nor talent—only two or three small exquisite instincts: for knowing a friend, for avoiding a mistake, for taking care of an old toy or a new frock. Yet to be so tender was to be touching withal, and she could be felt as an easy victim of fate. She would have no will, no power to resist, no sense of her own importance; she would easily be mystified, easily crushed: her force would be all in knowing when and where to cling. She moved about the place with her visitor, who had asked leave to walk through the other rooms again, where Pansy gave her judgement on several works of art. She spoke of her prospects, her occupations, her father's intentions; she was not egotistical, but felt the propriety of supplying the information so distingushed a guest would naturally expect.

"Please tell me," she said, "did papa, in Rome, go to see Madame Catherine? He told me he would if he had time. Perhaps he had not time. Papa likes a great deal of time. He wished to speak about my education; it isn't finished yet, you know. I don't know what they can do with me more; but it appears it's far from finished. Papa told me one day he thought he would finish it himself; for the last year or two, at the convent, the masters that teach the tall girls are so very dear. Papa's not rich, and I should be very sorry if he were to pay much money for me, because I don't think I'm worth it. I don't learn quickly enough, and I have no memory. For what I'm told, yes—especially when it's pleasant; but not for what I learn in a book. There was a young girl who was my best friend, and they took her away from the convent, when she was fourteen, to make—how do you say it in English?—to make a *dot*.[2] You don't say it in English? I hope it isn't wrong; I only mean they wished to keep the money to marry her. I don't know whether it is for that that papa wishes to keep the money—to marry *me*. It costs so much to marry!" Pansy went on with a sigh; "I think papa might make that economy. At any rate I'm too young to think about it yet, and I don't care for any gentleman; I mean for any but him. If he were not my papa I should like to marry him; I would rather be his daughter than the wife of—of some strange person. I miss him very much, but not so much as you might think, for I've been so much away from him. Papa has always been principally for holidays. I miss Madame Catherine almost more; but you must not tell him that. You shall not see him again? I'm very sorry, and he'll be sorry too. Of every one who comes here I like you the best. That's not a great compliment, for there are not many people. It was very kind

2. Dowry.

of you to come to-day—so far from your house; for I'm really as yet only a child. Oh, yes, I've only the occupations of a child. When did *you* give them up, the occupations of a child? I should like to know how old you are, but I don't know whether it's right to ask. At the convent they told us that we must never ask the age. I don't like to do anything that's not expected; it looks as if one had not been properly taught. I myself—I should never like to be taken by surprise. Papa left directions for everything. I go to bed very early. When the sun goes off that side I go into the garden. Papa left strict orders that I was not to get scorched. I always enjoy the view; the mountains are so graceful. In Rome, from the convent, we saw nothing but roofs and bell-towers. I practise three hours. I don't play very well. You play yourself? I wish very much you'd play something for me; papa has the idea that I should hear good music. Madame Merle has played for me several times; that's what I like best about Madame Merle; she has great facility. I shall never have facility. And I've no voice—just a small sound like the squeak of a slate-pencil making flourishes."

Isabel gratified this respectful wish, drew off her gloves and sat down to the piano, while Pansy, standing beside her, watched her white hands move quickly over the keys. When she stopped she kissed the child good-bye, held her close, looked at her long. "Be very good," she said; "give pleasure to your father."

"I think that's what I live for," Pansy answered. "He has not much pleasure; he's rather a sad man."

Isabel listened to this assertion with an interest which she felt it almost a torment to be obliged to conceal. It was her pride that obliged her, and a certain sense of decency; there were still other things in her head which she felt a strong impulse, instantly checked, to say to Pansy about her father; there were things it would have given her pleasure to hear the child, to make the child, say. But she no sooner became conscious of these things than her imagination was hushed with horror at the idea of taking advantage of the little girl—it was of this she would have accused herself— and of exhaling into that air where he might still have a subtle sense for it any breath of her charmed state. She had come—she had come; but she had stayed only an hour. She rose quickly from the music-stool; even then, however, she lingered a moment, still holding her small companion, drawing the child's sweet slimness closer and looking down at her almost in envy. She was obliged to confess it to herself—she would have taken a passionate pleasure in talking of Gilbert Osmond to this innocent, diminutive creature who was so near him. But she said no other word; she only kissed Pansy once again. They went together through the vestibule, to the door that opened on the court; and there her young hostess stopped, looking rather wistfully beyond. "I may go no further. I've promised papa not to pass this door."

"You're right to obey him; he'll never ask you anything unreasonable."

"I shall always obey him. But when will you come again?"

"Not for a long time, I'm afraid."

"As soon as you can, I hope. I'm only a little girl," said Pansy, "but I shall always expect you." And the small figure stood in the high, dark doorway, watching Isabel cross the clear, grey court and disappear into the brightness beyond the big *portone*,[3] which gave a wider dazzle as it opened.

XXXI

Isabel came back to Florence, but only after several months; an interval sufficiently replete with incident. It is not, however, during this interval that we are closely concerned with her; our attention is engaged again on a certain day in the late spring-time, shortly after her return to Palazzo Crescentini and a year from the date of the incidents just narrated. She was alone on this occasion, in one of the smaller of the numerous rooms devoted by Mrs. Touchett to social uses, and there was that in her expression and attitude which would have suggested that she was expecting a visitor. The tall window was open, and though its green shutters were partly drawn the bright air of the garden had come in through a broad interstice and filled the room with warmth and perfume. Our young woman stood near it for some time, her hands clasped behind her; she gazed abroad with the vagueness of unrest. Too troubled for attention she moved in a vain circle. Yet it could not be in her thought to catch a glimpse of her visitor before he should pass into the house, since the entrance to the palace was not through the garden, in which stillness and privacy always reigned. She wished rather to forestall his arrival by a process of conjecture, and to judge by the expression of her face this attempt gave her plenty to do. Grave she found herself, and positively more weighted, as by the experience of the lapse of the year she had spent in seeing the world. She had ranged, she would have said, through space and surveyed much of mankind, and was therefore now, in her own eyes, a very different person from the frivolous young woman from Albany who had begun to take the measure of Europe on the lawn at Gardencourt a couple of years before. She flattered herself she had harvested wisdom and learned a great deal more of life than this light-minded creature had even suspected. If her thoughts just now had inclined themselves to retrospect, instead of fluttering their wings nervously about the present,

3. Main entrance.

they would have evoked a multitude of interesting pictures. These pictures would have been both landscapes and figure-pieces; the latter, however, would have been the more numerous. With several of the images that might have been projected on such a field we are already acquainted. There would be for instance the conciliatory Lily, our heroine's sister and Edmund Ludlow's wife, who had come out from New York to spend five months with her relative. She had left her husband behind her, but had brought her children, to whom Isabel now played with equal munificence and tenderness the part of maiden-aunt. Mr. Ludlow, toward the last, had been able to snatch a few weeks from his forensic triumphs and, crossing the ocean with extreme rapidity, had spent a month with the two ladies in Paris before taking his wife home. The little Ludlows had not yet, even from the American point of view, reached the proper tourist-age; so that while her sister was with her Isabel had confined her movements to a narrow circle. Lily and the babies had joined her in Switzerland in the month of July, and they had spent a summer of fine weather in an Alpine valley where the flowers were thick in the meadows and the shade of great chestnuts made a resting-place for such upward wanderings as might be undertaken by ladies and children on warm afternoons. They had afterwards reached the French capital, which was worshipped, and with costly ceremonies, by Lily, but thought of as noisily vacant by Isabel, who in these days made use of her memory of Rome as she might have done, in a hot and crowded room, of a phial of something pungent hidden in her handkerchief.

Mrs. Ludlow sacrificed, as I say, to Paris, yet had doubts and wonderments not allayed at that altar; and after her husband had joined her found further chagrin in his failure to throw himself into these speculations. They all had Isabel for subject; but Edmund Ludlow, as he had always done before, declined to be surprised, or distressed, or mystified, or elated, at anything his sister-in-law might have done or have failed to do. Mrs. Ludlow's mental motions were sufficiently various. At one moment she thought it would be so natural for that young woman to come home and take a house in New York—the Rossiters', for instance, which had an elegant conservatory and was just round the corner from her own; at another she couldn't conceal her surprise at the girl's not marrying some member of one of the great aristocracies. On the whole, as I have said, she had fallen from high communion with the probabilities. She had taken more satisfaction in Isabel's accession of fortune than if the money had been left to herself; it had seemed to her to offer just the proper setting for her sister's slightly meagre, but scarce the less eminent figure. Isabel had developed less, however, than Lily had thought likely—development, to Lily's understanding, being somehow mysteriously connected with morning-calls and evening-parties. Intellectually, doubtless, she had made immense strides; but she appeared to have achieved few of those social conquests of which Mrs. Ludlow had expected to admire the trophies. Lily's conception of such achievements was extremely vague; but this was exactly what she had expected of Isabel—to give it form and body. Isabel could have done as well as she had done in New York; and Mrs. Ludlow appealed to her husband to know whether there was any privilege she enjoyed in Europe which the society of that city might not offer her. We know ourselves that Isabel had made conquests—whether inferior or not to those she might have effected in her native land it would be a delicate matter to decide; and it is not altogether with a feeling of complacency that I again mention that she had not rendered these honourable victories public. She had not told her sister the history of Lord Warburton, nor had she given her a hint of Mr. Osmond's state of mind; and she had had no better reason for her silence than that she didn't wish to speak. It was more romantic to say nothing, and, drinking deep, in secret, of romance, she was as little disposed to ask poor Lily's advice as she would have been to close that rare volume forever. But Lily knew nothing of these discriminations, and could only pronounce her sister's career a strange anti-climax—an impression confirmed by the fact that Isabel's silence about Mr. Osmond, for instance, was in direct proportion to the frequency with which he occupied her thoughts. As this happened very often it sometimes appeared to Mrs. Ludlow that she had lost her courage. So uncanny a result of so exhilarating an incident as inheriting a fortune was of course perplexing to the cheerful Lily; it added to her general sense that Isabel was not at all like other people.

Our young lady's courage, however, might have been taken as reaching its height after her relations had gone home. She could imagine braver things than spending the winter in Paris—Paris had sides by which it so resembled New York, Paris was like smart, neat prose—and her close correspondence with Madame Merle did much to stimulate such flights. She had never had a keener sense of freedom, of the absolute boldness and wantonness of liberty, than when she turned away from the platform at the Euston Station[1] on one of the last days of November, after the departure of the train that was to convey poor Lily, her husband and her children to their ship at Liverpool. It had been good for her to regale; she was very conscious of that; she was very observant, as we know, of what was good for her, and her effort was constantly to find something that was good enough. To profit by the present advantage till the latest

1. London terminus of the London and North Western Railway.

moment she had made the journey from Paris with the unenvied travellers. She would have accompanied them to Liverpool as well, only Edmund Ludlow had asked her, as a favour, not to do so; it made Lily so fidgety and she asked such impossible questions. Isabel watched the train move away; she kissed her hand to the elder of her small nephews, a demonstrative child who leaned dangerously far out of the window of the carriage and made separation an occasion of violent hilarity, and then she walked back into the foggy London street. The world lay before her—she could do whatever she chose. There was a deep thrill in it all, but for the present her choice was tolerably discreet; she chose simply to walk back from Euston Square to her hotel. The early dusk of a November afternoon had already closed in; the street-lamps, in the thick, brown air, looked weak and red; our heroine was unattended and Euston Square was a long way from Piccadilly. But Isabel performed the journey with a positive enjoyment of its dangers and lost her way almost on purpose, in order to get more sensations, so that she was disappointed when an obliging policeman easily set her right again. She was so fond of the spectacle of human life that she enjoyed even the aspect of gathering dusk in the London streets—the moving crowds, the hurrying cabs, the lighted shops, the flaring stalls, the dark, shining dampness of everything. That evening, at her hotel, she wrote to Madame Merle that she should start in a day or two for Rome. She made her way down to Rome without touching at Florence—having gone first to Venice and then proceeded southward by Ancona.[2] She accomplished this journey without other assistance than that of her servant, for her natural protectors were not now on the ground. Ralph Touchett was spending the winter at Corfu,[3] and Miss Stackpole, in the September previous, had been recalled to America by a telegram from the *Interviewer*. This journal offered its brilliant correspondent a fresher field for her genius than the mouldering cities of Europe, and Henrietta was cheered on her way by a promise from Mr. Bantling that he would soon come over to see her. Isabel wrote to Mrs. Touchett to apologise for not presenting herself just yet in Florence, and her aunt replied characteristically enough. Apologies, Mrs. Touchett intimated, were of no more use to her than bubbles, and she herself never dealt in such articles. One either did the thing or one didn't, and what one "would" have done belonged to the sphere of the irrelevant, like the idea of a future life or of the origin of things. Her letter was frank, but (a rare case with Mrs. Touchett) not so frank as it pretended. She easily forgave her niece for not stopping at Florence, because she took it for a sign that Gilbert Osmond was

2. **Seaport on the Adriatic.**   3. **One of the Ionian Isles, in Greece.**

less in question there than formerly. She watched of course to see if he would now find a pretext for going to Rome, and derived some comfort from learning that he had not been guilty of an absence.

Isabel, on her side, had not been a fortnight in Rome before she proposed to Madame Merle that they should make a little pilgrimage to the East. Madame Merle remarked that her friend was restless, but she added that she herself had always been consumed with the desire to visit Athens and Constantinople. The two ladies accordingly embarked on this expedition, and spent three months in Greece, in Turkey, in Egypt. Isabel found much to interest her in these countries, though Madame Merle continued to remark that even among the most classic sites, the scenes most calculated to suggest repose and reflexion, a certain incoherence prevailed in her. Isabel travelled rapidly and recklessly; she was like a thirsty person draining cup after cup. Madame Merle meanwhile, as lady-in-waiting to a princess circulating *incognita*, panted a little in her rear. It was on Isabel's invitation she had come, and she imparted all due dignity to the girl's uncountenanced state. She played her part with the tact that might have been expected of her, effacing herself and accepting the position of a companion whose expenses were profusely paid. The situation, however, had no hardships, and people who met this reserved though striking pair on their travels would not have been able to tell you which was patroness and which client. To say that Madame Merle improved on acquaintance states meagrely the impression she made on her friend, who had found her from the first so ample and so easy. At the end of an intimacy of three months Isabel felt she knew her better; her character had revealed itself, and the admirable woman had also at last redeemed her promise of relating her history from her own point of view—a consummation the more desirable as Isabel had already heard it related from the point of view of others. This history was so sad a one (in so far as it concerned the late M. Merle, a positive adventurer, she might say, though originally so plausible, who had taken advantage, years before, of her youth and of an inexperience in which doubtless those who knew her only now would find it difficult to believe); it abounded so in startling and lamentable incidents that her companion wondered a person so *éprouvée*[4] could have kept so much of her freshness, her interest in life. Into this freshness of Madame Merle's she obtained a considerable insight; she seemed to see it as professional, as slightly mechanical, carried about in its case like the fiddle of the virtuoso, or blanketed and bridled like the "favourite" of the jockey. She liked her as much as ever, but there was a corner of the curtain that never was lifted; it was as if she had remained after all something of a public per-

4. Tested, tried.

former, condemned to emerge only in character and in costume. She had once said that she came from a distance, that she belonged to the "old, old" world, and Isabel never lost the impression that she was the product of a different moral or social clime from her own, that she had grown up under other stars.

She believed then that at bottom she had a different morality. Of course the morality of civilised persons has always much in common; but our young woman had a sense in her of values gone wrong or, as they said at the shops, marked down. She considered, with the presumption of youth, that a morality differing from her own must be inferior to it; and this conviction was an aid to detecting an occasional flash of cruelty, an occasional lapse from candour, in the conversation of a person who had raised delicate kindness to an art and whose pride was too high for the narrow ways of deception. Her conception of human motives might, in certain lights, have been acquired at the court of some kingdom in decadence, and there were several in her list of which our heroine had not even heard. She had not heard of everything, that was very plain; and there were evidently things in the world of which it was not advantageous to hear. She had once or twice had a positive scare; since it so affected her to have to exclaim, of her friend, "Heaven forgive her, she doesn't understand me!" Absurd as it may seem this discovery operated as a shock, left her with a vague dismay in which there was even an element of foreboding. The dismay of course subsided, in the light of some sudden proof of Madame Merle's remarkable intelligence; but it stood for a high-water-mark in the ebb and flow of confidence. Madame Merle had once declared her belief that when a friendship ceases to grow it immediately begins to decline —there being no point of equilibrium between liking more and liking less. A stationary affection, in other words, was impossible—it must move one way or the other. However that might be, the girl had in these days a thousand uses for her sense of the romantic, which was more active than it had ever been. I do not allude to the impulse it received as she gazed at the Pyramids in the course of an excursion from Cairo, or as she stood among the broken columns of the Acropolis and fixed her eyes upon the point designated to her as the Strait of Salamis; deep and memorable as these emotions had remained. She came back by the last of March from Egypt and Greece and made another stay in Rome. A few days after her arrival Gilbert Osmond descended from Florence and remained three weeks, during which the fact of her being with his old friend Madame Merle, in whose house she had gone to lodge, made it virtually inevitable that he should see her every day. When the last of April came she wrote to Mrs. Touchett that she should now rejoice to accept an invitation given long before, and went to pay a visit to

Palazzo Crescentini, Madame Merle on this occasion remaining in Rome. She found her aunt alone; her cousin was still at Corfu. Ralph, however, was expected in Florence from day to day, and Isabel, who had not seen him for upwards of a year, was prepared to give him the most affectionate welcome.

XXXII

It was not of him, nevertheless, that she was thinking while she stood at the window near which we found her a while ago, and it was not of any of the matters I have rapidly sketched. She was not turned to the past, but to the immediate, impending hour. She had reason to expect a scene, and she was not fond of scenes. She was not asking herself what she should say to her visitor; this question had already been answered. What he would say to her—that was the interesting issue. It could be nothing in the least soothing—she had warrant for this, and the conviction doubtless showed in the cloud on her brow. For the rest, however, all clearness reigned in her; she had put away her mourning and she walked in no small shimmering splendour. She only felt older—ever so much, and as if she were "worth more" for it, like some curious piece in an antiquary's collection. She was not at any rate left indefinitely to her apprehensions, for a servant at last stood before her with a card on his tray. "Let the gentleman come in," she said, and continued to gaze out of the window after the footman had retired. It was only when she had heard the door close behind the person who presently entered that she looked round.

Caspar Goodwood stood there—stood and received a moment, from head to foot, the bright, dry gaze with which she rather withheld than offered a greeting. Whether his sense of maturity had kept pace with Isabel's we shall perhaps presently ascertain; let me say meanwhile that to her critical glance he showed nothing of the injury of time. Straight, strong and hard, there was nothing in his appearance that spoke positively either of youth or of age; if he had neither innocence nor weakness, so he had no practical philosophy. His jaw showed the same voluntary cast as in earlier days; but a crisis like the present had in it of course something grim. He had the air of a man who had travelled hard; he said nothing at first, as if he had been out of breath. This gave Isabel time to make a reflexion: "Poor fellow, what great things he's capable of, and what a pity he should waste so dreadfully his splendid force! What a pity too that one can't satisfy everybody!" It gave her time to do more —to say at the end of a minute: "I can't tell you how I hoped you wouldn't come!"

"I've no doubt of that." And he looked about him for a seat. Not only had he come, but he meant to settle.

"You must be very tired," said Isabel, seating herself, and generously, as she thought, to give him his opportunity.

"No, I'm not at all tired. Did you ever know me to be tired?"

"Never; I wish I had! When did you arrive?"

"Last night, very late; in a kind of snail-train they call the express. These Italian trains go at about the rate of an American funeral."

"That's in keeping—you must have felt as if you were coming to bury me!" And she forced a smile of encouragement to an easy view of their situation. She had reasoned the matter well out, making it perfectly clear that she broke no faith and falsified no contract; but for all this she was afraid of her visitor. She was ashamed of her fear; but she was devoutly thankful there was nothing else to be ashamed of. He looked at her with his stiff insistence, an insistence in which there was such a want of tact; especially when the dull dark beam in his eye rested on her as a physical weight.

"No, I didn't feel that; I couldn't think of you as dead. I wish I could!" he candidly declared.

"I thank you immensely."

"I'd rather think of you as dead than as married to another man."

"That's very selfish of you!" she returned with the ardour of a real conviction. "If you're not happy yourself others have yet a right to be."

"Very likely it's selfish; but I don't in the least mind your saying so. I don't mind anything you can say now—I don't feel it. The cruellest things you could think of would be mere pin-pricks. After what you've done I shall never feel anything—I mean anything but that. That I shall feel all my life."

Mr. Goodwood made these detached assertions with dry deliberateness, in his hard, slow American tone, which flung no atmospheric colour over propositions intrinsically crude. The tone made Isabel angry rather than touched her; but her anger perhaps was fortunate, inasmuch as it gave her a further reason for controlling herself. It was under the pressure of this control that she became, after a little, irrelevant. "When did you leave New York?"

He threw up his head as if calculating. "Seventeen days ago."

"You must have travelled fast in spite of your slow trains."

"I came as fast as I could. I'd have come five days ago if I had been able."

"It wouldn't have made any difference, Mr. Goodwood," she coldly smiled.

"Not to you—no. But to me."

"You gain nothing that I see."

"That's for me to judge!"

"Of course. To me it seems that you only torment yourself." And then, to change the subject, she asked him if he had seen Henrietta Stackpole. He looked as if he had not come from Boston to Florence to talk of Henrietta Stackpole; but he answered, distinctly enough, that this young lady had been with him just before he left America. "She came to see you?" Isabel then demanded.

"Yes, she was in Boston, and she called at my office. It was the day I had got your letter."

"Did you tell her?" Isabel asked with a certain anxiety.

"Oh, no," said Caspar Goodwood simply; "I didn't want to do that. She'll hear it quick enough; she hears everything."

"I shall write to her, and then she'll write to me and scold me," Isabel declared, trying to smile again.

Caspar, however, remained sternly grave. "I guess she'll come right out," he said.

"On purpose to scold me?"

"I don't know. She seemed to think she had not seen Europe thoroughly."

"I'm glad you tell me that," Isabel said. "I must prepare for her."

Mr. Goodwood fixed his eyes for a moment on the floor; then at last, raising them, "Does she know Mr. Osmond?" he enquired.

"A little. And she doesn't like him. But of course I don't marry to please Henrietta," she added. It would have been better for poor Caspar if she had tried a little more to gratify Miss Stackpole; but he didn't say so; he only asked, presently, when her marriage would take place. To which she made answer that she didn't know yet. "I can only say it will be soon. I've told no one but yourself and one other person—an old friend of Mr. Osmond's."

"Is it a marriage your friends won't like?" he demanded.

"I really haven't an idea. As I say, I don't marry for my friends."

He went on, making no exclamation, no comment, only asking questions, doing it quite without delicacy. "Who and what then is Mr. Gilbert Osmond?"

"Who and what? Nobody and nothing but a very good and very honourable man. He's not in business," said Isabel. "He's not rich; he's not known for anything in particular."

She disliked Mr. Goodwood's questions, but she said to herself that she owed it to him to satisfy him as far as possible. The satisfaction poor Caspar exhibited was, however, small; he sat very upright, gazing at her. "Where does he come from? Where does he belong?"

She had never been so little pleased with the way he said "belawng." "He comes from nowhere. He has spent most of his life in Italy."

"You said in your letter he was American. Hasn't he a native place?"

"Yes, but he has forgotten it. He left it as a small boy."

"Has he never gone back?"

"Why should he go back?" Isabel asked, flushing all defensively. "He has no profession."

"He might have gone back for his pleasure. Doesn't he like the United States?"

"He doesn't know them. Then he's very quiet and very simple— he contents himself with Italy."

"With Italy and with you," said Mr. Goodwood with gloomy plainness and no appearance of trying to make an epigram. "What has he ever done?" he added abruptly.

"That I should marry him? Nothing at all," Isabel replied while her patience helped itself by turning a little to hardness. "If he had done great things would you forgive me any better? Give me up, Mr. Goodwood; I'm marrying a perfect nonentity. Don't try to take an interest in him. You can't."

"I can't appreciate him; that's what you mean. And you don't mean in the least that he's a perfect nonentity. You think he's grand, you think he's great, though no one else thinks so."

Isabel's colour deepened; she felt this really acute of her companion, and it was certainly a proof of the aid that passion might render perceptions she had never taken for fine. "Why do you always come back to what others think? I can't discuss Mr. Osmond with you."

"Of course not," said Caspar reasonably. And he sat there with his air of stiff helplessness, as if not only this were true, but there were nothing else that they might discuss.

"You see how little you gain," she accordingly broke out—"how little comfort or satisfaction I can give you."

"I didn't expect you to give me much."

"I don't understand then why you came."

"I came because I wanted to see you once more—even just as you are."

"I appreciate that; but if you had waited a while, sooner or later we should have been sure to meet, and our meeting would have been pleasanter for each of us than this."

"Waited till after you're married? That's just what I didn't want to do. You'll be different then."

"Not very. I shall still be a great friend of yours. You'll see."

"That will make it all the worse," said Mr. Goodwood grimly.

"Ah, you're unaccommodating! I can't promise to dislike you in order to help you to resign yourself."

"I shouldn't care if you did!"

Isabel got up with a movement of repressed impatience and walked to the window, where she remained a moment looking out. When she turned round her visitor was still motionless in his place. She came toward him again and stopped, resting her hand on the back of the chair she had just quitted. "Do you mean you came simply to look at me? That's better for you perhaps than for me."

"I wished to hear the sound of your voice," he said.

"You've heard it, and you see it says nothing very sweet."

"It gives me pleasure, all the same." And with this he got up.

She had felt pain and displeasure on receiving early that day the news he was in Florence and by her leave would come within an hour to see her. She had been vexed and distressed, though she had sent back word by his messenger that he might come when he would. She had not been better pleased when she saw him; his being there at all was so full of heavy implications. It implied things she could never assent to—rights, reproaches, remonstrance, rebuke, the expectation of making her change her purpose. These things, however, if implied, had not been expressed; and now our young lady, strangely enough, began to resent her visitor's remarkable self-control. There was a dumb misery about him that irritated her; there was a manly staying of his hand that made her heart beat faster. She felt her agitation rising, and she said to herself that she was angry in the way a woman is angry when she has been in the wrong. She was not in the wrong; she had fortunately not that bitterness to swallow; but, all the same, she wished he would denounce her a little. She had wished his visit would be short; it had no purpose, no propriety; yet now that he seemed to be turning away she felt a sudden horror of his leaving her without uttering a word that would give her an opportunity to defend herself more than she had done in writing to him a month before, in a few carefully chosen words, to announce her engagement. If she were not in the wrong, however, why should she desire to defend herself? It was an excess of generosity on Isabel's part to desire that Mr. Goodwood should be angry. And if he had not meanwhile held himself hard it might have made him so to hear the tone in which she suddenly exclaimed, as if she were accusing him of having accused her: "I've not deceived you! I was perfectly free!"

"Yes, I know that," said Caspar.

"I gave you full warning that I'd do as I chose."

"You said you'd probably never marry, and you said it with such a manner that I pretty well believed it."

She considered this an instant. "No one can be more surprised than myself at my present intention."

"You told me that if I heard you were engaged I was not to

believe it," Caspar went on. "I heard it twenty days ago from your-self, but I remembered what you had said. I thought there might be some mistake, and that's partly why I came."

"If you wish me to repeat it by word of mouth, that's soon done. There's no mistake whatever."

"I saw that as soon as I came into the room."

"What good would it do you that I shouldn't marry?" she asked with a certain fierceness.

"I should like it better than this."

"You're very selfish, as I said before."

"I know that. I'm selfish as iron."

"Even iron sometimes melts! If you'll be reasonable I'll see you again."

"Don't you call me reasonable now?"

"I don't know what to say to you," she answered with sudden humility.

"I shan't trouble you for a long time," the young man went on. He made a step towards the door, but he stopped. "Another reason why I came was that I wanted to hear what you would say in explanation of your having changed your mind."

Her humbleness as suddenly deserted her. "In explanation? Do you think I'm bound to explain?"

He gave her one of his long dumb looks. "You were very positive. I did believe it."

"So did I. Do you think I could explain if I would?"

"No, I suppose not. Well," he added, "I've done what I wished. I've seen you."

"How little you make of these terrible journeys," she felt the poverty of her presently replying.

"If you're afraid I'm knocked up—in any such way as that—you may be at your ease about it." He turned away, this time in earnest, and no hand-shake, no sign of parting, was exchanged between them. At the door he stopped with his hand on the knob. "I shall leave Florence to-morrow," he said without a quaver.

"I'm delighted to hear it!" she answered passionately. Five min-utes after he had gone out she burst into tears.

XXXIII

Her fit of weeping, however, was soon smothered, and the signs of it had vanished when, an hour later, she broke the news to her aunt. I use this expression because she had been sure Mrs. Touchett would not be pleased; Isabel had only waited to tell her till she had seen Mr. Goodwood. She had an odd impression that it would not be honourable to make the fact public before she should have heard what Mr. Goodwood would say about it. He had said rather less than she expected, and she now had a somewhat angry sense of having lost time. But she would lose no more; she waited till Mrs. Touchett came into the drawing-room before the mid-day breakfast, and then she began. "Aunt Lydia, I've something to tell you."

Mrs. Touchett gave a little jump and looked at her almost fiercely. "You needn't tell me; I know what it is."

"I don't know how you know."

"The same way that I know when the window's open—by feeling a draught. You're going to marry that man."

"What man do you mean?" Isabel enquired with great dignity.

"Madame Merle's friend—Mr. Osmond."

"I don't know why you call him Madame Merle's friend. Is that the principal thing he's known by?"

"If he's not her friend he ought to be—after what she has done for him!" cried Mrs. Touchett. "I shouldn't have expected it of her; I'm disappointed."

"If you mean that Madame Merle has had anything to do with my engagement you're greatly mistaken," Isabel declared with a sort of ardent coldness.

"You mean that your attractions were sufficient, without the gentleman's having had to be lashed up? You're quite right. They're immense, your attractions, and he would never have presumed to think of you if she hadn't put him up to it. He has a very good opinion of himself, but he was not a man to take trouble. Madame Merle took the trouble *for* him."

"He has taken a great deal for himself!" cried Isabel with a voluntary laugh.

Mrs. Touchett gave a sharp nod. "I think he must, after all, to have made you like him so much."

"I thought he even pleased *you*."

"He did, at one time; and that's why I'm angry with him."

"Be angry with me, not with him," said the girl.

"Oh, I'm always angry with you; that's no satisfaction! Was it for this that you refused Lord Warburton?"

"Please don't go back to that. Why shouldn't I like Mr. Osmond, since others have done so?"

"Others, at their wildest moments, never wanted to marry him. There's nothing *of* him," Mrs. Touchett explained.

"Then he can't hurt me," said Isabel.

"Do you think you're going to be happy? No one's happy, in such doings, you should know."

"I shall set the fashion then. What does one marry for?"

"What *you* will marry for, heaven only knows. People usually marry as they go into partnership—to set up a house. But in your partnership you'll bring everything."

"Is it that Mr. Osmond isn't rich? Is that what you're talking about?" Isabel asked.

"He has no money; he has no name; he has no importance. I value such things and I have the courage to say it; I think they're very precious. Many other people think the same, and they show it. But they give some other reason."

Isabel hesitated a little. "I think I value everything that's valuable. I care very much for money, and that's why I wish Mr. Osmond to have a little."

"Give it to him then; but marry some one else."

"His name's good enough for me," the girl went on. "It's a very pretty name. Have I such a fine one myself?"

"All the more reason you should improve on it. There are only a dozen American names. Do you marry him out of charity?"

"It was my duty to tell you, Aunt Lydia, but I don't think it's my duty to explain to you. Even if it were I shouldn't be able. So please don't remonstrate; in talking about it you have me at a disadvantage. I can't talk about it."

"I don't remonstrate, I simply answer you: I must give some sign of intelligence. I saw it coming, and I said nothing. I never meddle."

"You never do, and I'm greatly obliged to you. You've been very considerate."

"It was not considerate—it was convenient," said Mrs. Touchett. "But I shall talk to Madame Merle."

"I don't see why you keep bringing her in. She has been a very good friend to me."

"Possibly; but she has been a poor one to me."

"What has she done to you?"

"She has deceived me. She had as good as promised me to prevent your engagement."

"She couldn't have prevented it."

"She can do anything; that's what I've always liked her for. I knew she could play any part; but I understood that she played them one by one. I didn't understand that she would play two at the same time."

"I don't know what part she may have played to you," Isabel said; "that's between yourselves. To me she has been honest and kind and devoted."

"Devoted, of course; she wished you to marry her candidate. She told me she was watching you only in order to interpose."

"She said that to please you," the girl answered; conscious, however, of the inadequacy of the explanation.

"To please me by deceiving me? She knows me better. Am I pleased to-day?"

"I don't think you're ever much pleased," Isabel was obliged to reply. "If Madame Merle knew you would learn the truth what had she to gain by insincerity?"

"She gained time, as you see. While I waited for her to interfere you were marching away, and she was really beating the drum."

"That's very well. But by your own admission you saw I was marching, and even if she had given the alarm you wouldn't have tried to stop me."

"No, but some one else would."

"Whom do you mean?" Isabel asked, looking very hard at her aunt.

Mrs. Touchett's little bright eyes, active as they usually were, sustained her gaze rather than returned it. "Would you have listened to Ralph?"

"Not if he had abused Mr. Osmond."

"Ralph doesn't abuse people; you know that perfectly. He cares very much for you."

"I know he does," said Isabel; "and I shall feel the value of it now, for he knows that whatever I do I do with reason."

"He never believed you would do this. I told him you were capable of it, and he argued the other way."

"He did it for the sake of argument," the girl smiled. "You don't accuse him of having deceived you; why should you accuse Madame Merle?"

"He never pretended he'd prevent it."

"I'm glad of that!" cried Isabel gaily. "I wish very much," she presently added, "that when he comes you'd tell him first of my engagement."

"Of course I'll mention it," said Mrs. Touchett. "I shall say nothing more to you about it, but I give you notice I shall talk to others."

"That's as you please. I only meant that it's rather better the announcement should come from you than from me."

"I quite agree with you; it's much more proper!" And on this the aunt and the niece went to breakfast, where Mrs. Touchett, as good as her word, made no allusion to Gilbert Osmond. After an interval of silence, however, she asked her companion from whom she had received a visit an hour before.

"From an old friend—an American gentleman," Isabel said with a colour in her cheek.

"An American gentleman of course. It's only an American gentleman who calls at ten o'clock in the morning."

"It was half-past ten; he was in a great hurry; he goes away this evening."

"Couldn't he have come yesterday, at the usual time?"

"He only arrived last night."

"He spends but twenty-four hours in Florence?" Mrs. Touchett cried. "He's an American gentleman truly."

"He is indeed," said Isabel, thinking with perverse admiration of what Caspar Goodwood had done for her.

Two days afterward Ralph arrived; but though Isabel was sure that Mrs. Touchett had lost no time in imparting to him the great fact, he showed at first no open knowledge of it. Their prompted talk was naturally of his health; Isabel had many questions to ask about Corfu. She had been shocked by his appearance when he came into the room; she had forgotten how ill he looked. In spite of Corfu he looked very ill to-day, and she wondered if he were really worse or if she were simply disaccustomed to living with an invalid. Poor Ralph made no nearer approach to conventional beauty as he advanced in life, and the now apparently complete loss of his health had done little to mitigate the natural oddity of his person. Blighted and battered, but still responsive and still ironic, his face was like a lighted lantern patched with paper and unsteadily held; his thin whisker languished upon a lean cheek; the exorbitant curve of his nose defined itself more sharply. Lean he was altogether, lean and long and loose-jointed; an accidental cohesion of relaxed angles. His brown velvet jacket had become perennial; his hands had fixed themselves in his pockets; he shambled and stumbled and shuffled in a manner that denoted great physical helplessness. It was perhaps this whimsical gait that helped to mark his character more than ever as that of the humorous invalid—the invalid for whom even his own disabilities are part of the general joke. They might well indeed with Ralph have been the chief cause of the want of seriousness marking his view of a world in which the reason for his own continued presence was past finding out. Isabel had grown fond of his ugliness; his awkwardness had become dear to her. They had been sweetened by association; they struck her as the very terms on which it had been given him to be charming. He was so charming that her sense of his being ill had hitherto had a sort of comfort in it; the state of his health had seemed not a limitation, but a kind of intellectual advantage; it absolved him from all professional and official emotions and left him the luxury of being exclusively personal. The personality so resulting was delightful; he had remained proof against the staleness of disease; he had had to consent to be deplorably ill, yet had somehow escaped being formally sick. Such had been the girl's impression of her cousin; and when she had pitied him it was only on reflection. As she reflected a good deal she had allowed him a certain amount of compassion; but she always had a dread of wasting that essence—a precious article, worth more to the giver than to any one else. Now, however, it took no great sensibility to feel that poor Ralph's tenure of life was less elastic than it should be. He was a bright, free, generous spirit, he had all the illumination of wisdom and none of its pedantry, and yet he was distressfully dying.

Isabel noted afresh that life was certainly hard for some people, and she felt a delicate glow of shame as she thought how easy it now promised to become for herself. She was prepared to learn that Ralph was not pleased with her engagement; but she was not prepared, in spite of her affection for him, to let this fact spoil the situation. She was not even prepared, or so she thought, to resent his want of sympathy; for it would be his privilege—it would be indeed his natural line—to find fault with any step she might take toward marriage. One's cousin always pretended to hate one's husband; that was traditional, classical; it was part of one's cousin's always pretending to adore one. Ralph was nothing if not critical; and though she would certainly, other things being equal, have been as glad to marry to please him as to please any one, it would be absurd to regard as important that her choice should square with his views. What were his views after all? He had pretended to believe she had better have married Lord Warburton; but this was only because she had refused that excellent man. If she had accepted him Ralph would certainly have taken another tone; he always took the opposite. You could criticise any marriage; it was the essence of a marriage to be open to criticism. How well she herself, should she only give her mind to it, might criticise this union of her own! She had other employment, however, and Ralph was welcome to relieve her of the care. Isabel was prepared to be most patient and most indulgent. He must have seen that, and this made it the more odd he should say nothing. After three days had elapsed without his speaking our young woman wearied of waiting; dislike it as he would, he might at least go through the form. We, who know more about poor Ralph than his cousin, may easily believe that during the hours that followed his arrival at Palazzo Crescentini he had privately gone through many forms. His mother had literally greeted him with the great news, which had been even more sensibly chilling than Mrs. Touchett's maternal kiss. Ralph was shocked and humiliated; his calculations had been false and the person in the world in whom he was most interested was lost. He drifted about the house like a rudderless vessel in a rocky stream, or sat in the garden of the palace on a great cane chair, his long legs extended, his head thrown back and his hat pulled over his eyes. He felt cold about the heart; he had never liked anything less. What could he do, what could he say? If the girl were irreclaimable could he pretend to like it? To attempt to reclaim her was permissible only if the attempt should succeed. To try to persuade her of anything sordid or sinister in the man to whose deep art she had succumbed would be decently discreet only in the event of her being persuaded. Otherwise he should simply have damned himself. It cost him an equal effort to speak his thought and to dissemble; he could neither assent with sincerity not protest with hope. Meanwhile he knew— or rather he supposed—that the affianced pair were daily renewing their mutual vows. Osmond at this moment showed himself little at Palazzo Crescentini; but Isabel met him every day elsewhere, as she was free to do after their engagement had been made public. She had taken a carriage by the month, so as not to be indebted to her aunt for the means of pursuing a course of which Mrs. Touchett disapproved, and she drove in the morning to the Cascine.[1] This suburban wilderness, during the early hours, was void of all intruders, and our young lady, joined by her lover in its quietest part, strolled with him a while through the grey Italian shade and listened to the nightingales.

XXXIV

One morning, on her return from her drive, some half-hour before luncheon, she quitted her vehicle in the court of the palace and, instead of ascending the great staircase, crossed the court, passed beneath another archway and entered the garden. A sweeter spot at this moment could not have been imagined. The stillness of noontide hung over it, and the warm shade, enclosed and still, made bowers like spacious caves. Ralph was sitting there in the clear gloom, at the base of a statue of Terpsichore[1]—a dancing nymph with taper fingers and inflated draperies in the manner of Bernini;[2] the extreme relaxation of his attitude suggested at first to Isabel that he was asleep. Her light footstep on the grass had not roused him, and before turning away she stood for a moment looking at him. During this instant he opened his eyes; upon which she sat down on a rustic chair that matched with his own. Though in her irritation she had accused him of indifference she was not blind to the fact that he had visibly had something to brood over. But she had explained his air of absence partly by the languor of his increased weakness, partly by worries connected with the property inherited from his father—the fruit of eccentric arrangements of which Mrs. Touchett disapproved and which, as she had told Isabel, now encountered opposition from the other partners in the bank. He ought to have gone to England, his mother said, instead of coming to Florence; he had not been there for months, and took no more interest in the bank than in the state of Patagonia.[3]

1. A large park outside Florence. *Murray's Handbook for Travellers in Northern Italy*, which Isabel is probably reading, calls it "rather unjustly depreciated by travellers" (p. 548).

1. The muse of the dance and patroness of lyric poetry.
2. Giovanni Bernini (1598-1680), architect and sculptor of the Baroque period.
3. The desolate, southernmost region of Argentina.

"I'm sorry I waked you," Isabel said; "you look too tired."

"I feel too tired. But I was not asleep. I was thinking of you."

"Are you tired of that?"

"Very much so. It leads to nothing. The road's long and I never arrive."

"What do you wish to arrive at?" she put to him, closing her parasol.

"At the point of expressing to myself properly what I think of your engagement."

"Don't think too much of it," she lightly returned.

"Do you mean that it's none of my business?"

"Beyond a certain point, yes."

"That's the point I want to fix. I had an idea you may have found me wanting in good manners. I've never congratulated you."

"Of course I've noticed that. I wondered why you were silent."

"There have been a good many reasons. I'll tell you now," Ralph said. He pulled off his hat and laid it on the ground; then he sat looking at her. He leaned back under the protection of Bernini, his head against his marble pedestal, his arms dropped on either side of him, his hands laid upon the rests of his wide chair. He looked awkward, uncomfortable; he hesitated long. Isabel said nothing; when people were embarrassed she was usually sorry for them, but she was determined not to help Ralph to utter a word that should not be to the honour of her high decision. "I think I've hardly got over my surprise," he went on at last. "You were the last person I expected to see caught."

"I don't know why you call it caught."

"Because you're going to be put into a cage."

"If I like my cage, that needn't trouble you," she answered.

"That's what I wonder at; that's what I've been thinking of."

"If you've been thinking you may imagine how I've thought! I'm satisfied that I'm doing well."

"You must have changed immensely. A year ago you valued your liberty beyond everything. You wanted only to see life."

"I've seen it," said Isabel. "It doesn't look to me now, I admit, such an inviting expanse."

"I don't pretend it is; only I had an idea that you took a genial view of it and wanted to survey the whole field."

"I've seen that one can't do anything so general. One must choose a corner and cultivate that."

"That's what I think. And one must choose as good a corner as possible. I had no idea, all winter, while I read your delightful letters, that you were choosing. You said nothing about it, and your silence put me off my guard."

"It was not a matter I was likely to write to you about. Besides, I knew nothing of the future. It has all come lately. If you had been on your guard, however," Isabel asked, "what would you have done?"

"I should have said 'Wait a little longer.' "

"Wait for what?"

"Well, for a little more light," said Ralph with rather an absurd smile, while his hands found their way into his pockets.

"Where should my light have come from? From you?"

"I might have struck a spark or two."

Isabel had drawn off her gloves; she smoothed them out as they lay upon her knee. The mildness of this movement was accidental, for her expression was not conciliatory. "You're beating about the bush, Ralph. You wish to say you don't like Mr. Osmond, and yet you're afraid."

" 'Willing to wound and yet afraid to strike'?[4] I'm willing to wound *him*, yes—but not to wound you. I'm afraid of you, not of him. If you marry him it won't be a fortunate way for me to have spoken."

"*If* I marry him! Have you had any expectation of dissuading me?"

"Of course that seems to you too fatuous."

"No," said Isabel after a little; "it seems to me too touching."

"That's the same thing. It makes me so ridiculous that you pity me."

She stroked out her long gloves again. "I know you've a great affection for me. I can't get rid of that."

"For heaven's sake don't try. Keep that well in sight. It will convince you how intensely I want you to do well."

"And how little you trust me!"

There was a moment's silence; the warm noon-tide seemed to listen. "I trust you, but I don't trust him," said Ralph.

She raised her eyes and gave him a wide, deep look. "You've said it now, and I'm glad you've made it so clear. But you'll suffer by it."

"Not if you're just."

"I'm very just," said Isabel. "What better proof of it can there be than that I'm not angry with you? I don't know what's the matter with me, but I'm not. I was when you began, but it has passed away. Perhaps I ought to be angry, but Mr. Osmond wouldn't think so. He wants me to know everything; that's what I like him for. You've nothing to gain, I know that. I've never been so nice to you, as a girl, that you should have much reason for wishing me to remain one. You give very good advice; you've often done so. No, I'm very quiet; I've always believed in your wisdom," she

4. Alexander Pope, *Epistle to Dr. Arbuthnot*, 1.203.

went on, boasting of her quietness, yet speaking with a kind of contained exaltation. It was her passionate desire to be just; it touched Ralph to the heart, affected him like a caress from a creature he had injured. He wished to interrupt, to reassure her; for a moment he was absurdly inconsistent; he would have retracted what he had said. But she gave him no chance; she went on, having caught a glimpse, as she thought, of the heroic line and desiring to advance in that direction. "I see you've some special idea; I should like very much to hear it. I'm sure it's disinterested; I feel that. It seems a strange thing to argue about, and of course I ought to tell you definitely that if you expect to dissuade me you may give it up. You'll not move me an inch; it's too late. As you say, I'm caught. Certainly it won't be pleasant for you to remember this, but your pain will be in your own thoughts. I shall never reproach you."

"I don't think you ever will," said Ralph. "It's not in the least the sort of marriage I thought you'd make."

"What sort of marriage was that, pray?"

"Well, I can hardly say. I hadn't exactly a positive view of it, but I had a negative. I didn't think you'd decide for—well, for *that* type."

"What's the matter with Mr. Osmond's type, if it be one? His being so independent, so individual, is what I most see in him," the girl declared. "What do you know against him? You know him scarcely at all."

"Yes," Ralph said, "I know him very little, and I confess I haven't facts and items to prove him a villain. But all the same I can't help feeling that you're running a grave risk."

"Marriage is always a grave risk, and his risk's as grave as mine."

"That's his affair! If he's afraid, let him back out. I wish to God he would."

Isabel reclined in her chair, folding her arms and gazing a while at her cousin. "I don't think I understand you," she said at last coldly. "I don't know what you're talking about."

"I believed you'd marry a man of more importance."

Cold, I say, her tone had been, but at this a colour like a flame leaped into her face. "Of more importance to whom? It seems to me enough that one's husband should be of importance to one's self!"

Ralph blushed as well; his attitude embarrassed him. Physically speaking he proceeded to change it; he straightened himself, then leaned forward, resting a hand on each knee. He fixed his eyes on the ground; he had an air of the most respectful deliberation. "I'll tell you in a moment what I mean," he presently said. He felt agitated, intensely eager; now that he had opened the discussion he wished to discharge his mind. But he wished also to be superlatively gentle.

Isabel waited a little—then she went on with majesty. "In everything that makes one care for people Mr. Osmond is pre-eminent. There may be nobler natures, but I've never had the pleasure of meeting one. Mr. Osmond's is the finest I know; he's good enough for me, and interesting enough, and clever enough. I'm far more struck with what he has and what he represents than with what he may lack."

"I had treated myself to a charming vision of your future," Ralph observed without answering this; "I had amused myself with planning out a high destiny for you. There was to be nothing of this sort in it. You were not to come down so easily or so soon."

"Come down, you say?"

"Well, that renders my sense of what has happened to you. You seemed to me to be soaring far up in the blue—to be sailing in the bright light, over the heads of men. Suddenly some one tosses up a faded rosebud—a missile that should never have reached you—and straight you drop to the ground. It hurts me," said Ralph audaciously, "hurts me as if I had fallen myself!"

The look of pain and bewilderment deepened in his companion's face. "I don't understand you in the least," she repeated. "You say you amused yourself with a project for my career—I don't understand that. Don't amuse yourself too much, or I shall think you're doing it at my expense."

Ralph shook his head. "I'm not afraid of your not believing that I've had great ideas for you."

"What do you mean by my soaring and sailing?" she pursued. "I've never moved on a higher plane than I'm moving on now. There's nothing higher for a girl than to marry a—a person she likes," said poor Isabel, wandering into the didactic.

"It's your liking the person we speak of that I venture to criticise, my dear cousin. I should have said that the man for you would have been a more active, larger, freer sort of nature." Ralph hesitated, then added: "I can't get over the sense that Osmond is somehow—well, small." He had uttered the last word with no great assurance; he was afraid she would flash out again. But to his surprise she was quiet; she had the air of considering.

"Small?" She made it sound immense.

"I think he's narrow, selfish. He takes himself so seriously!"

"He has a great respect for himself; I don't blame him for that," said Isabel. "It makes one more sure to respect others."

Ralph for a moment felt almost reassured by her reasonable tone. "Yes, but everything is relative; one ought to feel one's relation to things—to others. I don't think Mr. Osmond does that."

"I've chiefly to do with his relation to me. In that he's excellent."

"He's the incarnation of taste," Ralph went on, thinking hard how he could best express Gilbert Osmond's sinister attributes without putting himself in the wrong by seeming to describe him coarsely. He wished to describe him impersonally, scientifically. "He judges and measures, approves and condemns, altogether by that."

"It's a happy thing then that his taste should be exquisite."

"It's exquisite, indeed, since it has led him to select you as his bride. But have you ever seen such a taste—a really exquisite one—ruffled?"

"I hope it may never be my fortune to fail to gratify my husband's."

At these words a sudden passion leaped to Ralph's lips. "Ah, that's wilful, that's unworthy of you! You were not meant to be measured in that way—you were meant for something better than to keep guard over the sensibilities of a sterile dilettante!"

Isabel rose quickly and he did the same, so that they stood for a moment looking at each other as if he had flung down a defiance or an insult. But "You go too far," she simply breathed.

"I've said what I had on my mind—and I've said it because I love you!"

Isabel turned pale: was he too on that tiresome list? She had a sudden wish to strike him off. "Ah then, you're not disinterested!"

"I love you, but I love without hope," said Ralph quickly, forcing a smile and feeling that in that last declaration he had expressed more than he intended.

Isabel moved away and stood looking into the sunny stillness of the garden; but after a little she turned back to him. "I'm afraid your talk then is the wildness of despair! I don't understand it—but it doesn't matter. I'm not arguing with you; it's impossible I should; I've only tried to listen to you. I'm much obliged to you for attempting to explain," she said gently, as if the anger with which she had just sprung up had already subsided. "It's very good of you to try to warn me, if you're really alarmed; but I won't promise to think of what you've said: I shall forget it as soon as possible. Try and forget it yourself; you've done your duty, and no man can do more. I can't explain to you what I feel, what I believe, and I wouldn't if I could." She paused a moment and then went on with an inconsequence that Ralph observed even in the midst of his eagerness to discover some symptom of concession. "I can't enter into your idea of Mr. Osmond; I can't do it justice, because I see him in quite another way. He's not important—no, he's not important; he's a man to whom importance is supremely indifferent. If that's what you mean when you call him 'small,' then he's as small as you please. I call that large—it's the largest thing I know. I won't pretend to argue with you about a person I'm going to marry," Isabel repeated. "I'm not in the least concerned to defend

Mr. Osmond; he's not so weak as to need my defence. I should think it would seem strange even to yourself that I should talk of him so quietly and coldly, as if he were any one else. I wouldn't talk of him at all to any one but you; and you, after what you've said—I may just answer you once for all. Pray, would you wish me to make a mercenary marriage—what they call a marriage of ambition? I've only one ambition—to be free to follow out a good feeling. I had others once, but they've passed away. Do you complain of Mr. Osmond because he's not rich? That's just what I like him for. I've fortunately money enough; I've never felt so thankful for it as to-day. There have been moments when I should like to go and kneel down by your father's grave: he did perhaps a better thing than he knew when he put it into my power to marry a poor man—a man who has borne his poverty with such dignity, with such indifference. Mr. Osmond has never scrambled nor struggled—he has cared for no worldly prize. If that's to be narrow, if that's to be selfish, then it's very well. I'm not frightened by such words, I'm not even displeased; I'm only sorry that you should make a mistake. Others might have done so, but I'm surprised that *you* should. You might know a gentleman when you see one—you might know a fine mind. Mr. Osmond makes no mistakes! He knows everything, he understands everything, he has the kindest, gentlest, highest spirit. You've got hold of some false idea. It's a pity, but I can't help it; it regards you more than me." Isabel paused a moment, looking at her cousin with an eye illumined by a sentiment which contradicted the careful calmness of her manner—a mingled sentiment, to which the angry pain excited by his words and the wounded pride of having needed to justify a choice of which she felt only the nobleness and purity, equally contributed. Though she paused Ralph said nothing; he saw she had more to say. She was grand, but she was highly solicitous; she was indifferent, but she was all in a passion. "What sort of a person should you have liked me to marry?" she asked suddenly. "You talk about one's soaring and sailing, but if one marries at all one touches the earth. One has human feelings and needs, one has a heart in one's bosom, and one must marry a particular individual. Your mother has never forgiven me for not having come to a better understanding with Lord Warburton, and she's horrified at my contenting myself with a person who has none of his great advantages—no property, no title, no honours, no houses, nor lands, nor position, nor reputation, nor brilliant belongings of any sort. It's the total absence of all these things that pleases me. Mr. Osmond's simply a very lonely, a very cultivated and a very honest man—he's not a prodigious proprietor."

Ralph had listened with great attention, as if everything she said merited deep consideration; but in truth he was only half thinking of the things she said, he was for the rest simply accommodating himself to the weight of his total impression—the impression of her ardent good faith. She was wrong, but she believed; she was deluded, but she was dismally consistent. It was wonderfully characteristic of her that, having invented a fine theory about Gilbert Osmond, she loved him not for what he really possessed, but for his very poverties dressed out as honours. Ralph remembered what he had said to his father about wishing to put it into her power to meet the requirements of her imagination. He had done so, and the girl had taken full advantage of the luxury. Poor Ralph felt sick; he felt ashamed. Isabel had uttered her last words with a low solemnity of conviction which virtually terminated the discussion, and she closed it formally by turning away and walking back to the house. Ralph walked beside her, and they passed into the court together and reached the big staircase. Here he stopped and Isabel paused, turning on him a face of elation—absolutely and perversely of gratitude. His opposition had made her own conception of her conduct clearer to her. "Shall you not come up to breakfast?" she asked.

"No; I want no breakfast; I'm not hungry."

"You ought to eat," said the girl; "you live on air."

"I do, very much, and I shall go back into the garden and take another mouthful. I came thus far simply to say this. I told you last year that if you were to get into trouble I should feel terribly sold. That's how I feel to-day."

"Do you think I'm in trouble?"

"One's in trouble when one's in error."

"Very well," said Isabel; "I shall never complain of my trouble to you!" And she moved up the staircase.

Ralph, standing there with his hands in his pockets, followed her with his eyes; then the lurking chill of the high-walled court struck him and made him shiver, so that he returned to the garden to breakfast on the Florentine sunshine.

XXXV

Isabel, when she strolled in the Cascine with her lover, felt no impulse to tell him how little he was approved at Palazzo Crescentini. The discreet opposition offered to her marriage by her aunt and her cousin made on the whole no great impression upon her; the moral of it was simply that they disliked Gilbert Osmond. This dislike was not alarming to Isabel; she scarcely even regretted it; for it served mainly to throw into higher relief the fact, in every way so honourable, that she married to please herself. One did other things to please other people; one did this for a more personal satisfaction; and Isabel's satisfaction was confirmed by her lover's admirable good conduct. Gilbert Osmond was in love, and he had never deserved less than during these still, bright days, each of them numbered, which preceded the fulfilment of his hopes, the harsh criticism passed upon him by Ralph Touchett. The chief impression produced on Isabel's spirit by this criticism was that the passion of love separated its victim terribly from every one but the loved object. She felt herself disjoined from every one she had ever known before—from her two sisters, who wrote to express a dutiful hope that she would be happy, and a surprise, somewhat more vague, at her not having chosen a consort who was the hero of a richer accumulation of anecdote; from Henrietta, who, she was sure, would come out, too late, on purpose to remonstrate; from Lord Warburton, who would certainly console himself, and from Caspar Goodwood, who perhaps would not; from her aunt, who had cold, shallow ideas about marriage, for which she was not sorry to display her contempt; and from Ralph, whose talk about having great views for her was surely but a whimsical cover for a personal disappointment. Ralph apparently wished her not to marry at all—that was what it really meant—because he was amused with the spectacle of her adventure as a single woman. His disappointment made him say angry things about the man she had preferred even to him: Isabel flattered herself that she believed Ralph had been angry. It was the more easy for her to believe this because, as I say, she had now little free or unemployed emotion for minor needs, and accepted as an incident, in fact quite as an ornament, of her lot the idea that to prefer Gilbert Osmond as she preferred him was perforce to break all other ties. She tasted of the sweets of this preference, and they made her conscious, almost with awe, of the invidious and remorseless tide of the charmed and possessed condition, great as was the traditional honour and imputed virtue of being in love. It was the tragic part of happiness; one's right was always made of the wrong of some one else.

The elation of success, which surely now flamed high in Osmond, emitted meanwhile very little smoke for so brilliant a blaze. Contentment, on his part, took no vulgar form; excitement, in the most self-conscious of men, was a kind of ecstasy of self-control. This disposition, however, made him an admirable lover; it gave him a constant view of the smitten and dedicated state. He never forgot himself, as I say; and so he never forgot to be graceful and tender, to wear the appearance—which presented indeed no difficulty—of stirred senses and deep intentions. He was immensely pleased with his young lady; Madame Merle had made him a present of incalculable value. What could be a finer thing to live with than a high spirit attuned to softness? For would not the softness be all for one's self, and the strenuousness for society, which admired the air of superiority? What could be a happier gift in a companion than a quick, fanciful mind which saved one repetitions and reflected one's thought on a polished, elegant surface? Osmond hated to see his thought reproduced literally—that made it look stale and stupid; he preferred it to be freshened in the reproduction even as "words" by music. His egotism had never taken the crude form of desiring a dull wife; this lady's intelligence was to be a silver plate, not an earthen one—a plate that he might heap up with ripe fruits, to which it would give a decorative value, so that talk might become for him a sort of served dessert. He found the silver quality in this perfection in Isabel; he could tap her imagination with his knuckle and make it ring. He knew perfectly, though he had not been told, that their union enjoyed little favour with the girl's relations; but he had always treated her so completely as an independent person that it hardly seemed necessary to express regret for the attitude of her family. Nevertheless, one morning, he made an abrupt allusion to it. "It's the difference in our fortune they don't like," he said. "They think I'm in love with your money."

"Are you speaking of my aunt—of my cousin?" Isabel asked. "How do you know what they think?"

"You've not told me they're pleased, and when I wrote to Mrs. Touchett the other day she never answered my note. If they had been delighted I should have had some sign of it, and the fact of my being poor and you rich is the most obvious explanation of their reserve. But of course when a poor man marries a rich girl he must be prepared for imputations. I don't mind them; I only care for one thing—for your not having the shadow of a doubt. I don't care what people of whom I ask nothing think—I'm not even capable perhaps of wanting to know. I've never so concerned myself, God forgive me, and why should I begin to-day, when I have taken to myself a compensation for everything? I won't pretend I'm sorry you're rich; I'm delighted. I delight in everything that's yours—whether it be money or virtue. Money's a horrid thing to follow, but a charming thing to meet. It seems to me, however, that I've sufficiently proved the limits of my itch for it: I never in my life tried to earn a penny, and I ought to be less subject to suspicion than most of the people one sees grubbing and grabbing. I suppose it's their business to suspect—that of your family; it's proper on the whole they should. They'll like me better some day; so will you, for that matter. Meanwhile my business is not to make myself bad blood, but simply to be thankful for life and love." "It has made me better, loving you," he said on another occasion; "it has made me wiser and easier and—I won't pretend to deny—brighter and nicer and even stronger. I used to want a great many things before and to be angry I didn't have them. Theoretically I was satisfied, as I once told you. I flattered myself I had limited my wants. But I was subject to irritation; I used to have morbid, sterile, hateful fits of hunger, of desire. Now I'm really satisfied, because I can't think of anything better. It's just as when one has been trying to spell out a book in the twilight and suddenly the lamp comes in. I had been putting out my eyes over the book of life and finding nothing to reward me for my pains; but now that I can read it properly I see it's a delightful story. My dear girl, I can't tell you how life seems to stretch there before us—what a long summer afternoon awaits us. It's the latter half of an Italian day—with a golden haze, and the shadows just lengthening, and that divine delicacy in the light, the air, the landscape, which I have loved all my life and which you love to-day. Upon my honour, I don't see why we shouldn't get on. We've got what we like—to say nothing of having each other. We've the faculty of admiration and several capital convictions. We're not stupid, we're not mean, we're not under bonds to any kind of ignorance or dreariness. You're remarkably fresh, and I'm remarkably well-seasoned. We've my poor child to amuse us; we'll try and make up some little life for her. It's all soft and mellow—it has the Italian colouring."

They made a good many plans, but they left themselves also a good deal of latitude; it was a matter of course, however, that they should live for the present in Italy. It was in Italy that they had met, Italy had been a party to their first impressions of each other, and Italy should be a party to their happiness. Osmond had the attachment of old acquaintance and Isabel the stimulus of new, which seemed to assure her a future at a high level of consciousness of the beautiful. The desire for unlimited expansion had been succeeded in her soul by the sense that life was vacant without some private duty that might gather one's energies to a point. She had told Ralph she had "seen life" in a year or two and that she was already tired, not of the act of living, but of that of observing. What had become of all her ardours, her aspirations, her theories, her high estimate of her independence and her incipient conviction that she should never marry? These things had been absorbed in a more primitive need—a need the answer to which brushed away numberless questions, yet gratified infinite desires. It simplified the situation at a stroke, it came down from above like the light of the stars, and it needed no explanation. There was explanation enough in the fact that he was her lover, her own, and that she should be able to be of use to him. She could surrender to him with a kind of humility, she could marry him with a kind of pride; she was not only taking, she was giving.

He brought Pansy with him two or three times to the Cascine— Pansy who was very little taller than a year before, and not much older. That she would always be a child was the conviction expressed by her father, who held her by the hand when she was in her sixteenth year and told her to go and play while he sat down a little with the pretty lady. Pansy wore a short dress and a long coat; her hat always seemed too big for her. She found pleasure in walking off, with quick, short steps, to the end of the alley, and then in walking back with a smile that seemed an appeal for approbation. Isabel approved in abundance, and the abundance had the personal touch that the child's affectionate nature craved. She watched her indications as if for herself also much depended on them—Pansy already so represented part of the service she could render, part of the responsibility she could face. Her father took so the childish view of her that he had not yet explained to her the new relation in which he stood to the elegant Miss Archer. "She doesn't know," he said to Isabel; "she doesn't guess; she thinks it perfectly natural that you and I should come and walk here together simply as good friends. There seems to me something enchantingly innocent in that; it's the way I like her to be. No, I'm not a failure, as I used to think; I've succeeded in two things. I'm to marry the woman I adore, and I've brought up my child, as I wished, in the old way."

He was very fond, in all things, of the "old way"; that had struck Isabel as one of his fine, quiet, sincere notes. "It occurs to me that you'll not know whether you've succeeded until you've told her," she said. "You must see how she takes your news. She may be horrified—she may be jealous."

"I'm not afraid of that; she's too fond of you on her own account. I should like to leave her in the dark a little longer—to see if it will come into her head that if we're not engaged we ought to be."

Isabel was impressed by Osmond's artistic, the plastic view, as it somehow appeared, of Pansy's innocence—her own appreciation of it being more anxiously moral. She was perhaps not the less pleased when he told her a few days later that he had communicated the fact to his daughter, who had made such a pretty little speech—"Oh, then I shall have a beautiful sister!" She was neither surprised nor alarmed; she had not cried, as he expected.

"Perhaps she had guessed it," said Isabel.

"Don't say that; I should be disgusted if I believed that. I thought it would be just a little shock; but the way she took it proves that her good manners are paramount. That's also what I wished. You shall see for yourself; to-morrow she shall make you her congratulations in person."

The meeting, on the morrow, took place at the Countess Gemini's, whither Pansy had been conducted by her father, who knew that Isabel was to come in the afternoon to return a visit made her by the Countess on learning that they were to become sisters-in-law.

Calling at Casa Touchett the visitor had not found Isabel at home; but after our young woman had been ushered into the Countess's drawing-room Pansy arrived to say that her aunt would presently appear. Pansy was spending the day with that lady, who thought her of an age to begin to learn how to carry herself in company. It was Isabel's view that the little girl might have given lessons in deportment to her relative, and nothing could have justified this conviction more than the manner in which Pansy acquitted herself while they waited together for the Countess. Her father's decision, the year before, had finally been to send her back to the convent to receive the last graces, and Madame Catherine had evidently carried out her theory that Pansy was to be fitted for the great world.

"Papa has told me that you've kindly consented to marry him," said this excellent woman's pupil. "It's very delightful; I think you'll suit very well."

"You think I shall suit *you?*"

"You'll suit me beautifully; but what I mean is that you and papa will suit each other. You're both so quiet and so serious. You're not so quiet as he—or even as Madame Merle; but you're more quiet than many others. He should not for instance have a wife like my aunt. She's always in motion, in agitation—to-day especially; you'll see when she comes in. They told us at the convent it was wrong to judge our elders, but I suppose there's no harm if we judge them favourably. You'll be a delightful companion for papa."

"For you too, I hope," Isabel said.

"I speak first of him on purpose. I've told you already what I myself think of you; I liked you from the first. I admire you so much that I think it will be a good fortune to have you always before me. You'll be my model; I shall try to imitate you though I'm afraid it will be very feeble. I'm very glad for papa—he needed something more than me. Without you I don't see how he could have got it. You'll be my stepmother, but we mustn't use that word. They're always said to be cruel; but I don't think you'll ever so much as pinch or even push me. I'm not afraid at all."

"My good little Pansy," said Isabel gently, "I shall be ever so kind to you." A vague, inconsequent vision of her coming in some odd way to need it had intervened with the effect of a chill.

"Very well then, I've nothing to fear," the child returned with her note of prepared promptitude. What teaching she had had, it seemed to suggest—or what penalties for non-performance she dreaded!

Her description of her aunt had not been incorrect; the Countess Gemini was further than ever from having folded her wings. She entered the room with a flutter through the air and kissed Isabel first on the forehead and then on each cheek as if according to some ancient prescribed rite. She drew the visitor to a sofa and, looking at her with a variety of turns of the head, began to talk very much as if, seated brush in hand before an easel, she were applying a series of considered touches to a composition of figures already sketched in. "If you expect me to congratulate you I must beg you to excuse me. I don't suppose you care if I do or not; I believe you're supposed not to care—through being so clever—for all sorts of ordinary things. But I care myself if I tell fibs; I never tell them unless there's something rather good to be gained. I don't see what's to be gained with you—especially as you wouldn't believe me. I don't make professions any more than I make paper flowers or flouncey lampshades—I don't know how. My lampshades would be sure to take fire, my roses and my fibs to be larger than life. I'm very glad for my own sake that you're to marry Osmond; but I won't pretend I'm glad for yours. You're very brilliant—you know that's the way you're always spoken of; you're an heiress and very good-looking and original, not *banal*; so it's a good thing to have you in the family. Our family's very good, you know; Osmond will have told you that; and my mother was rather distinguished—she was called the American Corinne. But we're dreadfully fallen, I think, and perhaps you'll pick us up. I've great confidence in you; there are ever so many things I want to talk to you about. I never congratulate any girl on marrying; I think they ought to make it somehow not quite so awful a steel trap. I suppose Pansy oughtn't to hear all this; but that's what she has come to me for—to acquire the tone of society. There's no harm in her knowing what horrors she may be in for. When first I got an idea that my brother had designs on you I thought of writing to you, to recommend you, in the strongest terms, not to listen to him. Then I thought it would be disloyal, and I hate anything of that kind. Besides, as I say, I was enchanted for myself; and after all I'm very selfish. By the way, you won't respect me, not one little mite, and we shall never be intimate. I should like it, but you won't. Some day, all the same, we shall be better friends than you will believe at first. My husband will come and see you, though, as you probably know, he's on no sort of terms with Osmond. He's very fond of going to see pretty women, but I'm not afraid of you. In the first place I don't care what he does. In the second, you won't care a straw for him; he won't be a bit, at any time, your affair, and, stupid as he is, he'll see you're not his. Some day, if you can stand it, I'll tell you all about him. Do you think my niece ought to go out of the room? Pansy, go and practise a little in my boudoir."

"Let her stay, please," said Isabel. "I would rather hear nothing that Pansy may not!"

XXXVI

One afternoon of the autumn of 1876, toward dusk, a young man of pleasing appearance rang at the door of a small apartment on the third floor of an old Roman house. On its being opened he enquired for Madame Merle; whereupon the servant, a neat, plain woman, with a French face and a lady's maid's manner, ushered him into a diminutive drawing-room and requested the favour of his name. "Mr. Edward Rosier," said the young man, who sat down to wait till his hostess should appear.

The reader will perhaps not have forgotten that Mr. Rosier was an ornament of the American circle in Paris, but it may also be remembered that he sometimes vanished from its horizon. He had spent a portion of several winters at Pau, and as he was a gentleman of constituted habits he might have continued for years to pay his annual visit to this charming resort. In the summer of 1876, however, an incident befell him which changed the current not only of his thoughts, but of his customary sequences. He passed a month in the Upper Engadine[1] and encountered at Saint Moritz a charming young girl. To this little person he began to pay, on the spot, particular attention: she struck him as exactly the household angel he had long been looking for. He was never precipitate, he was nothing if not discreet, so he forbore for the present to declare his passion; but it seemed to him when they parted—the young lady to go down into Italy and her admirer to proceed to Geneva, where he was under bonds to join other friends—that he should be romantically wretched if he were not to see her again. The simplest way to do so was to go in the autumn to Rome, where Miss Osmond was domiciled with her family. Mr. Rosier started on his pilgrimage to the Italian capital and reached it on the first of November. It was a pleasant thing to do, but for the young man there was a strain of the heroic in the enterprise. He might expose himself, unseasoned, to the poison of the Roman air, which in November lay, notoriously, much in wait. Fortune, however, favours the brave; and this adventurer, who took three grains of quinine a day, had at the end of a month no cause to deplore his temerity. He had made to a certain extent good use of his time; he had devoted it in vain to finding a flaw in Pansy Osmond's composition. She was admirably finished; she had had the last touch; she was really a consummate piece. He thought of her in amorous meditation a good deal as he might have thought of a Dresden-china shepherdess. Miss Osmond, indeed, in the bloom of her juvenility, had a hint of the rococo which Rosier, whose taste was predominantly for that manner, could not fail to appreciate. That he esteemed the productions of comparatively frivolous periods would have been apparent from the

1. Swiss valley noted for its resorts.

attention he bestowed upon Madame Merle's drawing-room, which, although furnished with specimens of every style, was especially rich in articles of the last two centuries. He had immediately put a glass into one eye and looked round; and then "By Jove, she has some jolly good things!" he had yearningly murmured. The room was small and densely filled with furniture; it gave an impression of faded silk and little statuettes which might totter if one moved. Rosier got up and wandered about with his careful tread, bending over the tables charged with knick-knacks and the cushions embossed with princely arms. When Madame Merle came in she found him standing before the fireplace with his nose very close to the great lace flounce attached to the damask cover of the mantel. He had lifted it delicately, as if he were smelling it.

"It's old Venetian," she said; "it's rather good."

"It's too good for this; you ought to wear it."

"They tell me you have some better in Paris, in the same situation."

"Ah, but I can't wear mine," smiled the visitor.

"I don't see why you shouldn't! I've better lace than that to wear."

His eyes wandered, lingeringly, round the room again. "You've some very good things."

"Yes, but I hate them."

"Do you want to get rid of them?" the young man quickly asked.

"No, it's good to have something to hate: one works it off!"

"I love my things," said Mr. Rosier as he sat there flushed with all his recognitions. "But it's not about them, nor about yours, that I came to talk to you." He paused a moment and then, with greater softness: "I care more for Miss Osmond than for all the *bibelots*[2] in Europe!"

Madame Merle opened wide eyes. "Did you come to tell me that?"

"I came to ask your advice."

She looked at him with a friendly frown, stroking her chin with her large white hand. "A man in love, you know, doesn't ask advice."

"Why not, if he's in a difficult position? That's often the case with a man in love. I've been in love before, and I know. But never so much as this time—really never so much. I should like particularly to know what you think of my prospects. I'm afraid that for Mr. Osmond I'm not—well, a real collector's piece."

"Do you wish me to intercede?" Madame Merle asked with her fine arms folded and her handsome mouth drawn up to the left.

"If you could say a good word for me I should be greatly obliged.

2. Curios, odds and ends.

There will be no use in my troubling Miss Osmond unless I have good reason to believe her father will consent."

"You're very considerate; that's in your favour. But you assume in rather an off-hand way that *I* think you a prize."

"You've been very kind to me," said the young man. "That's why I came."

"I'm always kind to people who have good Louis Quatorze.[3] It's very rare now, and there's no telling what one may get by it." With which the left-hand corner of Madame Merle's mouth gave expression to the joke.

But he looked, in spite of it, literally apprehensive and consistently strenuous. "Ah, I thought you liked me for myself!"

"I like you very much; but, if you please, we won't analyse. Pardon me if I seem patronising, but I think you a perfect little gentleman. I must tell you, however, that I've not the marrying of Pansy Osmond."

"I didn't suppose that. But you've seemed to me intimate with her family, and I thought you might have influence."

Madame Merle considered. "Whom do you call her family?"

"Why, her father; and—how do you say it in English?—her *belle-mère*."[4]

"Mr. Osmond's her father, certainly; but his wife can scarcely be termed a member of her family. Mrs. Osmond has nothing to do with marrying her."

"I'm sorry for that," said Rosier with an amiable sigh of good faith. "I think Mrs. Osmond would favour me."

"Very likely—if her husband doesn't."

He raised his eyebrows. "Does she take the opposite line from him?"

"In everything. They think quite differently."

"Well," said Rosier, "I'm sorry for that; but it's none of my business. She's very fond of Pansy."

"Yes, she's very fond of Pansy."

"And Pansy has a great affection for her. She has told me how she loves her as if she were her own mother."

"You must, after all, have had some very intimate talk with the poor child," said Madame Merle. "Have you declared your sentiments?"

"Never!" cried Rosier, lifting his neatly-gloved hand. "Never till I've assured myself of those of the parents."

"You always wait for that? You've excellent principles; you observe the proprieties."

"I think you're laughing at me," the young man murmured,

3. A style of arts and crafts identified with the reign of Louis XIV (1634–1715).
4. Stepmother.

dropping back in his chair and feeling his small moustache. "I didn't expect that of you, Madame Merle."

She shook her head calmly, like a person who saw things as she saw them. "You don't do me justice. I think your conduct in excellent taste and the best you could adopt. Yes, that's what I think."

"I wouldn't agitate her—only to agitate her; I love her too much for that," said Ned Rosier.

"I'm glad, after all, that you've told me," Madame Merle went on. "Leave it to me a little; I think I can help you."

"I said you were the person to come to!" her visitor cried with prompt elation.

"You were very clever," Madame Merle returned more dryly. "When I say I can help you I mean once assuming your cause to be good. Let us think a little if it is."

"I'm awfully decent, you know," said Rosier earnestly. "I won't say I've no faults, but I'll say I've no vices."

"All that's negative, and it always depends, also, on what people call vices. What's the positive side? What's the virtuous? What have you got besides your Spanish lace and your Dresden teacups?"

"I've a comfortable little fortune—about forty thousand francs a year. With the talent I have for arranging, we can live beautifully on such an income."

"Beautifully, no. Sufficiently, yes. Even that depends on where you live."

"Well, in Paris. I would undertake it in Paris."

Madame Merle's mouth rose to the left. "It wouldn't be famous; you'd have to make use of the teacups, and they'd get broken."

"We don't want to be famous. If Miss Osmond should have everything pretty it would be enough. When one's as pretty as she one can afford—well, quite cheap *faience*.[5] She ought never to wear anything but muslin—without the sprig," said Rosier reflectively.

"Wouldn't you even allow her the sprig? She'd be much obliged to you at any rate for that theory."

"It's the correct one, I assure you; and I'm sure she'd enter into it. She understands all that; that's why I love her."

"She's a very good little girl, and most tidy—also extremely graceful. But her father, to the best of my belief, can give her nothing."

Rosier scarce demurred. "I don't in the least desire that he should. But I may remark, all the same, that he lives like a rich man."

"The money's his wife's; she brought him a large fortune."

"Mrs. Osmond then is very fond of her stepdaughter; she may do something."

---

5. Glazed earthenware, but the word *faience* became synonymous for pottery, china, and crockery.

"For a love-sick swain you have your eyes about you!" Madame Merle exclaimed with a laugh.

"I esteem a *dot* very much. I can do without it, but I esteem it."

"Mrs. Osmond," Madame Merle went on, "will probably prefer to keep her money for her own children."

"Her own children? Surely she has none."

"She may have yet. She had a poor little boy, who died two years ago, six months after his birth. Others therefore may come."

"I hope they will, if it will make her happy. She's a splendid woman."

Madame Merle failed to burst into speech. "Ah, about her there's much to be said. Splendid as you like! We've not exactly made out that you're a *parti*. The absence of vices is hardly a source of income."

"Pardon me, I think it may be," said Rosier quite lucidly.

"You'll be a touching couple, living on your innocence!"

"I think you underrate me."

"You're not so innocent as that? Seriously," said Madame Merle, "of course forty thousand francs a year and a nice character are a combination to be considered. I don't say it's to be jumped at, but there might be a worse offer. Mr. Osmond, however, will probably incline to believe he can do better."

"*He* can do so perhaps; but what can his daughter do? She can't do better than marry the man she loves. For she does, you know," Rosier added eagerly.

"She does—I know it."

"Ah," cried the young man, "I said you were the person to come to."

"But I don't know how *you* know it, if you haven't asked her," Madame Merle went on.

"In such a case there's no need of asking and telling; as you say, we're an innocent couple. How did *you* know it?"

"I who am not innocent? By being very crafty. Leave it to me; I'll find out for you."

Rosier got up and stood smoothing his hat. "You say that rather coldly. Don't simply find out how it is, but try to make it as it should be."

"I'll do my best. I'll try to make the most of your advantages."

"Thank you so very much. Meanwhile then I'll say a word to Mrs. Osmond."

"*Gardez-vous-en bien!*"[6] And Madame Merle was on her feet. "Don't set her going, or you'll spoil everything."

Rosier gazed into his hat; he wondered whether his hostess *had* been after all the right person to come to. "I don't think I under-

6. Take good care not to!

stand you. I'm an old friend of Mrs. Osmond, and I think she would like me to succeed."

"Be an old friend as much as you like; the more old friends she has the better, for she doesn't get on very well with some of her new. But don't for the present try to make her take up the cudgels for you. Her husband may have other views, and, as a person who wishes her well, I advise you not to multiply points of difference between them."

Poor Rosier's face assumed an expression of alarm; a suit for the hand of Pansy Osmond was even a more complicated business than his taste for proper transitions had allowed. But the extreme good sense which he concealed under a surface suggesting that of a careful owner's "best set" came to his assistance. "I don't see that I'm bound to consider Mr. Osmond so very much!" he exclaimed.

"No, but you should consider *her*. You say you're an old friend. Would you make her suffer?"

"Not for the world."

"Then be very careful, and let the matter alone till I've taken a few soundings."

"Let the matter alone, dear Madame Merle? Remember that I'm in love."

"Oh, you won't burn up! Why did you come to me, if you're not to heed what I say?"

"You're very kind; I'll be very good," the young man promised. "But I'm afraid Mr. Osmond's pretty hard," he added in his mild voice as he went to the door.

Madame Merle gave a short laugh. "It has been said before. But his wife isn't easy either."

"Ah, she's a splendid woman!" Ned Rosier repeated, for departure.

He resolved that his conduct should be worthy of an aspirant who was already a model of discretion; but he saw nothing in any pledge he had given Madame Merle that made it improper he should keep himself in spirits by an occasional visit to Miss Osmond's home. He reflected constantly on what his adviser had said to him, and turned over in his mind the impression of her rather circumspect tone. He had gone to her *de confiance*, as they put it in Paris; but it was possible he had been precipitate. He found difficulty in thinking of himself as rash—he had incurred this reproach so rarely; but it certainly was true that he had known Madame Merle only for the last month, and that his thinking her a delightful woman was not, when one came to look into it, a reason for assuming that she would be eager to push Pansy Osmond into his arms, gracefully arranged as these members might be to receive her. She had indeed shown him benevolence, and she was a person of consideration among the girl's people, where she had a rather striking appearance (Rosier had more than once wondered how she managed it) of being intimate without being familiar. But possibly he had exaggerated these advantages. There was no particular reason why she should take trouble for him; a charming woman was charming to every one, and Rosier felt rather a fool when he thought of his having appealed to her on the ground that she had distinguished him. Very likely—though she had appeared to say it in joke—she was really only thinking of his *bibelots*. Had it come into her head that he might offer her two or three of the gems of his collection? If she would only help him to marry Miss Osmond he would present her with his whole museum. He could hardly say so to her outright; it would seem too gross a bribe. But he should like her to believe it.

It was with these thoughts that he went again to Mrs. Osmond's, Mrs. Osmond having an "evening"—she had taken the Thursday of each week—when his presence could be accounted for on general principles of civility. The object of Mr. Rosier's well-regulated affection dwelt in a high house in the very heart of Rome; a dark and massive structure overlooking a sunny *piazzetta*[7] in the neighbourhood of the Farnese Palace.[8] In a palace, too, little Pansy lived—a palace by Roman measure, but a dungeon to poor Rosier's apprehensive mind. It seemed to him of evil omen that the young lady he wished to marry, and whose fastidious father he doubted of his ability to conciliate, should be immured in a kind of domestic fortress, a pile which bore a stern old Roman name, which smelt of historic deeds, of crime and craft and violence, which was mentioned in "Murray" and visited by tourists who looked, on a vague survey, disappointed and depressed, and which had frescoes by Caravaggio[9] in the *piano nobile*[1] and a row of mutilated statues and dusty urns in the wide, nobly-arched loggia[2] overhanging the damp court where a fountain gushed out of a mossy niche. In a less preoccupied frame of mind he could have done justice to the Palazzo Roccanera;[3] he could have entered into the sentiment of Mrs. Osmond, who had once told him that on settling themselves in Rome she and her husband had chosen this habitation for the love of local colour. It had local colour enough, and though he knew less about architecture than about Limoges[4] enamels he could see that the proportions of the windows and even the details of the

7. A small public square.
8. A magnificent sixteenth-century Roman palace.
9. Michelangelo de Caravaggio (1573–1610) spent about a decade painting in Rome.
1. The main floor of the house, in which the reception rooms are situated.
2. An arched, open gallery.

3. The name of the Osmonds' mansion implies a fortress.
4. Painted enamels were produced in Limoges, France, for over six centuries. At first they were religious in nature, but by the eighteenth century they were primarily pretty snuffboxes and elegant umbrella handles.

cornice had quite the grand air. But Rosier was haunted by the conviction that at picturesque periods young girls had been shut up there to keep them from their true loves, and then, under the threat of being thrown into convents, had been forced into unholy marriages. There was one point, however, to which he always did justice when once he found himself in Mrs. Osmond's warm, rich-looking reception-rooms, which were on the second floor. He acknowledged that these people were very strong in "good things." It was a taste of Osmond's own—not at all of hers; this she had told him the first time he came to the house, when, after asking himself for a quarter of an hour whether they had even better "French" than he in Paris, he was obliged on the spot to admit that they had, very much, and vanquished his envy, as a gentleman should, to the point of expressing to his hostess his pure admiration of her treasures. He learned from Mrs. Osmond that her husband had made a large collection before their marriage and that, though he had annexed a number of fine pieces within the last three years, he had achieved his greatest finds at a time when he had not the advantage of her advice. Rosier interpreted this information according to principles of his own. For "advice" read "cash," he said to himself; and the fact that Gilbert Osmond had landed his highest prizes during his impecunious season confirmed his most cherished doctrine—the doctrine that a collector may freely be poor if he be only patient. In general, when Rosier presented himself on a Thursday evening, his first recognition was for the walls of the saloon; there were three or four objects his eyes really yearned for. But after his talk with Madame Merle he felt the extreme seriousness of his position; and now, when he came in, he looked about for the daughter of the house with such eagerness as might be permitted a gentleman whose smile, as he crossed a threshold, always took everything comfortable for granted.

XXXVII

Pansy was not in the first of the rooms, a large apartment with a concave ceiling and walls covered with old red damask; it was here Mrs. Osmond usually sat—though she was not in her most customary place to-night—and that a circle of more especial intimates gathered about the fire. The room was flushed with subdued, diffused brightness; it contained the larger things and—almost always—an odour of flowers. Pansy on this occasion was presumably in the next of the series, the resort of younger visitors, where tea was served. Osmond stood before the chimney, leaning back with his hands behind him; he had one foot up and was warming the sole. Half a dozen persons, scattered near him, were talking together; but he was not in the conversation; his eyes had an expression, frequent with them, that seemed to represent them as engaged with objects more worth their while than the appearances actually thrust upon them. Rosier, coming in unannounced, failed to attract his attention; but the young man, who was very punctilious, though he was even exceptionally conscious that it was the wife, not the husband, he had come to see, went up to shake hands with him. Osmond put out his left hand, without changing his attitude.

"How d' ye do? My wife's somewhere about."

"Never fear; I shall find her," said Rosier cheerfully.

Osmond, however, took him in; he had never in his life felt himself so efficiently looked at. "Madame Merle has told him, and he doesn't like it," he privately reasoned. He had hoped Madame Merle would be there, but she was not in sight; perhaps she was in one of the other rooms or would come later. He had never especially delighted in Gilbert Osmond, having a fancy he gave himself airs. But Rosier was not quickly resentful, and where politeness was concerned had ever a strong need of being quite in the right. He looked round him and smiled, all without help, and then in a moment, "I saw a jolly good piece of Capo di Monte[1] to-day," he said.

Osmond answered nothing at first; but presently, while he warmed his boot-sole, "I don't care a fig for Capo di Monte!" he returned.

"I hope you're not losing your interest?"

"In old pots and plates? Yes, I'm losing my interest."

Rosier for an instant forgot the delicacy of his position. "You're not thinking of parting with a—a piece or two?"

"No, I'm not thinking of parting with anything at all, Mr. Rosier," said Osmond, with his eyes still on the eyes of his visitor.

"Ah, you want to keep, but not to add," Rosier remarked brightly.

"Exactly. I've nothing I wish to match."

Poor Rosier was aware he had blushed; he was distressed at his want of assurance. "Ah, well, I have!" was all he could murmur; and he knew his murmur was partly lost as he turned away. He took his course to the adjoining room and met Mrs. Osmond coming out of the deep doorway. She was dressed in black velvet; she looked high and splendid, as he had said, and yet oh so radiantly gentle! We know what Mr. Rosier thought of her and the terms in which, to Madame Merle, he had expressed his admiration. Like his appreciation of her dear little stepdaughter it was based partly on his eye for decorative character, his instinct for authenticity; but also on a sense for uncatalogued values, for that secret of a "lustre" beyond any recorded losing or rediscovering, which his devotion to brittle

---

1. Capodimonte, near Naples, produced hard porcelain in rococo style in the eighteenth century. In the next century it was imitated in large quantities by French manufacturers.

wares had still not disqualified him to recognise. Mrs. Osmond, at present, might well have gratified such tastes. The years had touched her only to enrich her; the flower of her youth had not faded, it only hung more quietly on its stem. She had lost something of that quick eagerness to which her husband had privately taken exception—she had more the air of being able to wait. Now, at all events, framed in the gilded doorway, she struck our young man as the picture of a gracious lady. "You see I'm very regular," he said. "But who should be if I'm not?"

"Yes, I've known you longer than any one here. But we mustn't indulge in tender reminiscences. I want to introduce you to a young lady."

"Ah, please, what young lady?" Rosier was immensely obliging; but this was not what he had come for.

"She sits there by the fire in pink and has no one to speak to."

Rosier hesitated a moment. "Can't Mr. Osmond speak to her? He's within six feet of her."

Mrs. Osmond also hesitated. "She's not very lively, and he doesn't like dull people."

"But she's good enough for me? Ah now, that's hard!"

"I only mean that you've ideas for two. And then you're so obliging."

"So is your husband."

"No, he's not—to me." And Mrs. Osmond vaguely smiled.

"That's a sign he should be doubly so to other women."

"So I tell him," she said, still smiling.

"You see I want some tea," Rosier went on, looking wistfully beyond.

"That's perfect. Go and give some to my young lady."

"Very good; but after that I'll abandon her to her fate. The simple truth is I'm dying to have a little talk with Miss Osmond."

"Ah," said Isabel, turning away, "I can't help you there!"

Five minutes later, while he handed a tea-cup to the damsel in pink, whom he had conducted into the other room, he wondered whether, in making to Mrs. Osmond the profession I have just quoted, he had broken the spirit of his promise to Madame Merle. Such a question was capable of occupying this young man's mind for a considerable time. At last, however, he became—comparatively speaking—reckless; he cared little what promises he might break. The fate to which he had threatened to abandon the damsel in pink proved to be none so terrible; for Pansy Osmond, who had given him the tea for his companion—Pansy was as fond as ever of making tea—presently came and talked to her. Into this mild colloquy Edward Rosier entered little; he sat by moodily, watching his small sweetheart. If we look at her now through his eyes we shall at first not see much to remind us of the obedient little girl who, at Florence, three years before, was sent to walk short distances in the Cascine while her father and Miss Archer talked together of matters sacred to elder people. But after a moment we shall perceive that if at nineteen Pansy has become a young lady she doesn't really fill out the part; that if she has grown very pretty she lacks in a deplorable degree the quality known and esteemed in the appearance of females as style; and that if she is dressed with great freshness she wears her smart attire with an undisguised appearance of saving it —very much as if it were lent her for the occasion. Edward Rosier, it would seem, would have been just the man to note these defects; and in point of fact there was not a quality of this young lady, of any sort, that he had not noted. Only he called her qualities by names of his own—some of which indeed were happy enough. "No, she's unique—she's absolutely unique," he used to say to himself; and you may be sure that not for an instant would he have admitted to you that she was wanting in style. Style? Why, she had the style of a little princess; if you couldn't see it you had no eye. It was not modern, it was not conscious, it would produce no impression in Broadway; the small, serious damsel, in her stiff little dress, only looked like an Infanta of Velasquez.[2] This was enough for Edward Rosier, who thought her delightfully old-fashioned. Her anxious eyes, her charming lips, her slip of a figure, were as touching as a childish prayer. He had now an acute desire to know just to what point she liked him—a desire which made him fidget as he sat in his chair. It made him feel hot, so that he had to pat his forehead with his handkerchief; he had never been so uncomfortable. She was such a perfect *jeune fille*, and one couldn't make of a *jeune fille* the enquiry requisite for throwing light on such a point. A *jeune fille* was what Rosier had always dreamed of—a *jeune fille* who should yet not be French, for he had felt that this nationality would complicate the question. He was sure Pansy had never looked at a newspaper and that, in the way of novels, if she had read Sir Walter Scott it was the very most. An American *jeune fille*—what could be better than that? She would be frank and gay, and yet would not have walked alone, nor have received letters from men, nor have been taken to the theatre to see the comedy of manners. Rosier could not deny that, as the matter stood, it would be a breach of hospitality to appeal directly to this unsophisticated creature; but he was now in imminent danger of asking himself if hospitality were the most sacred thing in the world. Was not the sentiment that he entertained for Miss Osmond of infinitely greater

2. Diego de Velásquez (1599–1660), Spanish painter who painted a number of portraits of the *Infanta* ("Princess")   Margarita Teresa, daughter of Philip IV of Spain.

importance? Of greater importance to him—yes; but not probably to the master of the house. There was one comfort; even if this gentleman had been placed on his guard by Madame Merle he would not have extended the warning to Pansy; it would not have been part of his policy to let her know that a prepossessing young man was in love with her. But he *was* in love with her, the prepossessing young man; and all these restrictions of circumstance had ended by irritating him. What had Gilbert Osmond meant by giving him two fingers of his left hand? If Osmond was rude, surely he himself might be bold. He felt extremely bold after the dull girl in so vain a disguise of rose-colour had responded to the call of her mother, who came in to say, with a significant simper at Rosier, that she must carry her off to other triumphs. The mother and daughter departed together, and now it depended only upon him that he should be virtually alone with Pansy. He had never been alone with her before; he had never been alone with a *jeune fille*. It was a great moment; poor Rosier began to pat his forehead again. There was another room beyond the one in which they stood—a small room that had been thrown open and lighted, but that, the company not being numerous, had remained empty all the evening. It was empty yet; it was upholstered in pale yellow; there were several lamps; through the open door it looked the very temple of authorised love. Rosier gazed a moment through this aperture; he was afraid that Pansy would run away, and felt almost capable of stretching out a hand to detain her. But she lingered where the other maiden had left them, making no motion to join a knot of visitors on the far side of the room. For a little it occurred to him that she was frightened—too frightened perhaps to move; but a second glance assured him she was not, and he then reflected that she was too innocent indeed for that. After a supreme hesitation he asked her if he might go and look at the yellow room, which seemed so attractive yet so virginal. He had been there already with Osmond, to inspect the furniture, which was of the First French Empire,[3] and especially to admire the clock (which he didn't really admire), an immense classic structure of that period. He therefore felt that he had now begun to manœuvre.

"Certainly, you may go," said Pansy; "and if you like I'll show you." She was not in the least frightened.

"That's just what I hoped you'd say; you're so very kind," Rosier murmured.

They went in together; Rosier really thought the room very ugly, and it seemed cold. The same idea appeared to have struck Pansy. "It's not for winter evenings; it's more for summer," she said. "It's papa's taste; he has so much."

3. A neo-classic style of arts and crafts identified with the Napoleonic First Empire (1804–1815); the furniture was massive and sumptuous.

He had a good deal, Rosier thought; but some of it was very bad. He looked about him; he hardly knew what to say in such a situation. "Doesn't Mrs. Osmond care how her rooms are done? Has she no taste?" he asked.

"Oh yes, a great deal; but it's more for literature," said Pansy—"and for conversation. But papa cares also for those things. I think he knows everything."

Rosier was silent a little. "There's one thing I'm sure he knows!" he broke out presently. "He knows that when I come here it's, with all respect to him, with all respect to Mrs. Osmond, who's so charming—it's really," said the young man, "to see you!"

"To see me?" And Pansy raised her vaguely-troubled eyes.

"To see you; that's what I come for," Rosier repeated, feeling the intoxication of a rupture with authority.

Pansy stood looking at him, simply, intently, openly; a blush was not needed to make her face more modest. "I thought it was for that."

"And it was not disagreeable to you?"

"I couldn't tell; I didn't know. You never told me," said Pansy.

"I was afraid of offending you."

"You don't offend me," the young girl murmured, smiling as if an angel had kissed her.

"You like me then, Pansy?" Rosier asked very gently, feeling very happy.

"Yes—I like you."

They had walked to the chimney-piece where the big cold Empire clock was perched; they were well within the room and beyond observation from without. The tone in which she had said these four words seemed to him the very breath of nature, and his only answer could be to take her hand and hold it a moment. Then he raised it to his lips. She submitted, still with her pure, trusting smile, in which there was something ineffably passive. She liked him —she had liked him all the while; now anything might happen! She was ready—she had been ready always, waiting for him to speak. If he had not spoken she would have waited for ever; but when the word came she dropped like the peach from the shaken tree. Rosier felt that if he should draw her toward him and hold her to his heart she would submit without a murmur, would rest there without a question. It was true that this would be a rash experiment in a yellow Empire *salottino*.[4] She had known it was for her he came, and yet like what a perfect little lady she had carried it off!

"You're very dear to me," he murmured, trying to believe that there was after all such a thing as hospitality.

She looked a moment at her hand, where he had kissed it. "Did you say papa knows?"

4. A study or small room.

"You told me just now he knows everything."

"I think you must make sure," said Pansy.

"Ah, my dear, when once I'm sure of *you!*" Rosier murmured in her ear; whereupon she turned back to the other rooms with a little air of consistency which seemed to imply that their appeal should be immediate.

The other rooms meanwhile had become conscious of the arrival of Madame Merle, who, wherever she went, produced an impression when she entered. How she did it the most attentive spectator could not have told you, for she neither spoke loud, nor laughed profusely, nor moved rapidly, nor dressed with splendour, nor appealed in any appreciable manner to the audience. Large, fair, smiling, serene, there was something in her very tranquillity that diffused itself, and when people looked round it was because of a sudden quiet. On this occasion she had done the quietest thing she could do; after embracing Mrs. Osmond, which was more striking, she had sat down on a small sofa to commune with the master of the house. There was a brief exchange of commonplaces between these two—they always paid, in public, a certain formal tribute to the commonplace—and then Madame Merle, whose eyes had been wandering, asked if little Mr. Rosier had come this evening.

"He came nearly an hour ago—but he has disappeared," Osmond said.

"And where's Pansy?"

"In the other room. There are several people there."

"He's probably among them," said Madame Merle.

"Do you wish to see him?" Osmond asked in a provokingly pointless tone.

Madame Merle looked at him a moment; she knew each of his tones to the eighth of a note. "Yes, I should like to say to him that I've told you what he wants, and that it interests you but feebly."

"Don't tell him that. He'll try to interest me more—which is exactly what I don't want. Tell him I hate his proposal."

"But you don't hate it."

"It doesn't signify; I don't love it. I let him see that, myself, this evening; I was rude to him on purpose. That sort of thing's a great bore. There's no hurry."

"I'll tell him that you'll take time and think it over."

"No, don't do that. He'll hang on."

"If I discourage him he'll do the same."

"Yes, but in the one case he'll try to talk and explain—which would be exceedingly tiresome. In the other he'll probably hold his tongue and go in for some deeper game. That will leave me quiet. I hate talking with a donkey."

"Is that what you call poor Mr. Rosier?"

"Oh, he's a nuisance—with his eternal majolica."[5]

Madame Merle dropped her eyes; she had a faint smile. "He's a gentleman, he has a charming temper; and, after all, an income of forty thousand francs!"

"It's misery—'genteel' misery," Osmond broke in. "It's not what I've dreamed of for Pansy."

"Very good then. He has promised me not to speak to her."

"Do you believe him?" Osmond asked absent-mindedly.

"Perfectly. Pansy has thought a great deal about him; but I don't suppose you consider that that matters."

"I don't consider it matters at all; but neither do I believe she has thought of him."

"That opinion's more convenient," said Madame Merle quietly.

"Has she told you she's in love with him?"

"For what do you take her? And for what do you take me?" Madame Merle added in a moment.

Osmond had raised his foot and was resting his slim ankle on the other knee; he clasped his ankle in his hand familiarly—his long, fine forefinger and thumb could make a ring for it—and gazed a while before him. "This kind of thing doesn't find me unprepared. It's what I educated her for. It was all for this—that when such a case should come up she should do what I prefer."

"I'm not afraid that she'll not do it."

"Well then, where's the hitch?"

"I don't see any. But, all the same, I recommend you not to get rid of Mr. Rosier. Keep him on hand; he may be useful."

"I can't keep him. Keep him yourself."

"Very good; I'll put him into a corner and allow him so much a day." Madame Merle had, for the most part, while they talked, been glancing about her; it was her habit in this situation, just as it was her habit to interpose a good many blank-looking pauses. A long drop followed the last words I have quoted; and before it had ended she saw Pansy come out of the adjoining room, followed by Edward Rosier. The girl advanced a few steps and then stopped and stood looking at Madame Merle and at her father.

"He has spoken to her," Madame Merle went on to Osmond.

Her companion never turned his head. "So much for your belief in his promises. He ought to be horse-whipped."

"He intends to confess, poor little man!"

Osmond got up; he had now taken a sharp look at his daughter. "It doesn't matter," he murmured, turning away.

Pansy after a moment came up to Madame Merle with her little manner of unfamiliar politeness. This lady's reception of her was not more intimate; she simply, as she rose from the sofa, gave her a

5. Tin-glaze earthware painted in bright ("Majorca") colors.

friendly smile.

"You're very late," the young creature gently said.

"My dear child, I'm never later than I intend to be."

Madame Merle had not got up to be gracious to Pansy; she moved toward Edward Rosier. He came to meet her and, very quickly, as if to get it off his mind, "I've spoken to her!" he whispered.

"I know it, Mr. Rosier."

"Did she tell you?"

"Yes, she told me. Behave properly for the rest of the evening, and come and see me to-morrow at a quarter past five." She was severe, and in the manner in which she turned her back to him there was a degree of contempt which caused him to mutter a decent imprecation.

He had no intention of speaking to Osmond; it was neither the time nor the place. But he instinctively wandered toward Isabel, who sat talking with an old lady. He sat down on the other side of her; the old lady was Italian, and Rosier took for granted she understood no English. "You said just now you wouldn't help me," he began to Mrs. Osmond. "Perhaps you'll feel differently when you know—when you know—!"

Isabel met his hesitation. "When I know what?"

"That she's all right."

"What do you mean by that?"

"Well, that we've come to an understanding."

"She's all wrong," said Isabel. "It won't do."

Poor Rosier gazed at her half-pleadingly, half-angrily; a sudden flush testified to his sense of injury. "I've never been treated so," he said. "What is there against me, after all? That's not the way I'm usually considered. I could have married twenty times."

"It's a pity you didn't. I don't mean twenty times, but once, comfortably," Isabel added, smiling kindly. "You're not rich enough for Pansy."

"She doesn't care a straw for one's money."

"No, but her father does."

"Ah yes, he has proved that!" cried the young man.

Isabel got up, turning away from him, leaving her old lady without ceremony; and he occupied himself for the next ten minutes in pretending to look at Gilbert Osmond's collection of miniatures, which were neatly arranged on a series of small velvet screens. But he looked without seeing; his cheek burned; he was too full of his sense of injury. It was certain that he had never been treated that way before; he was not used to being thought not good enough. He knew how good he was, and if such a fallacy had not been so pernicious he could have laughed at it. He searched again for Pansy, but she had disappeared, and his main desire was now to get out of the house. Before doing so he spoke once more to Isabel; it was not agreeable to him to reflect that he had just said a rude thing to her —the only point that would now justify a low view of him.

"I referred to Mr. Osmond as I shouldn't have done, a while ago," he began. "But you must remember my situation."

"I don't remember what you said," she answered coldly.

"Ah, you're offended, and now you'll never help me."

She was silent an instant, and then with a change of tone: "It's not that I won't; I simply can't!" Her manner was almost passionate.

"If you *could*, just a little, I'd never again speak of your husband save as an angel."

"The inducement's great," said Isabel gravely—inscrutably, as he afterwards, to himself, called it; and she gave him, straight in the eyes, a look which was also inscrutable. It made him remember somehow that he had known her as a child; and yet it was keener than he liked, and he took himself off.

XXXVIII

He went to see Madame Merle on the morrow, and to his surprise she let him off rather easily. But she made him promise that he would stop there till something should have been decided. Mr. Osmond had had higher expectations; it was very true that as he had no intention of giving his daughter a portion such expectations were open to criticism or even, if one would, to ridicule. But she would advise Mr. Rosier not to take that tone; if he would possess his soul in patience he might arrive at his felicity. Mr. Osmond was not favourable to his suit, but it wouldn't be a miracle if he should gradually come round. Pansy would never defy her father, he might depend on that; so nothing was to be gained by precipitation. Mr. Osmond needed to accustom his mind to an offer of a sort that he had not hitherto entertained, and this result must come of itself —it was useless to try to force it. Rosier remarked that his own situation would be in the meanwhile the most uncomfortable in the world, and Madame Merle assured him that she felt for him. But, as she justly declared, one couldn't have everything one wanted; she had learned that lesson for herself. There would be no use in his writing to Gilbert Osmond, who had charged her to tell him as much. He wished the matter dropped for a few weeks and would himself write when he should have anything to communicate that it might please Mr. Rosier to hear.

"He doesn't like your having spoken to Pansy. Ah, he doesn't like it at all," said Madame Merle.

"I'm perfectly willing to give him a chance to tell me so!"

"If you do that he'll tell you more than you care to hear. Go to the house, for the next month, as little as possible, and leave the rest to me."

"As little as possible? Who's to measure the possibility?"

"Let me measure it. Go on Thursday evenings with the rest of the world, but don't go at all at odd times, and don't fret about Pansy. I'll see that she understands everything. She's a calm little nature; she'll take it quietly."

Edward Rosier fretted about Pansy a good deal, but he did as he was advised, and awaited another Thursday evening before returning to Palazzo Roccanera. There had been a party at dinner, so that though he went early the company was already tolerably numerous. Osmond, as usual, was in the first room, near the fire, staring straight at the door, so that, not to be distinctly uncivil, Rosier had to go and speak to him.

"I'm glad that you can take a hint," Pansy's father said, slightly closing his keen, conscious eyes.

"I take no hints. But I took a message, as I supposed it to be."

"You took it? Where did you take it?"

It seemed to poor Rosier he was being insulted, and he waited a moment, asking himself how much a true lover ought to submit to. "Madame Merle gave me, as I understood it, a message from you—to the effect that you declined to give me the opportunity I desire, the opportunity to explain my wishes to you." And he flattered himself he spoke rather sternly.

"I don't see what Madame Merle has to do with it. Why did you apply to Madame Merle?"

"I asked her for an opinion—for nothing more. I did so because she had seemed to me to know you very well."

"She doesn't know me so well as she thinks," said Osmond.

"I'm sorry for that, because she has given me some little ground for hope."

Osmond stared into the fire a moment. "I set a great price on my daughter."

"You can't set a higher one than I do. Don't I prove it by wishing to marry her?"

"I wish to marry her very well," Osmond went on with a dry impertinence which, in another mood, poor Rosier would have admired.

"Of course I pretend she'd marry well in marrying me. She couldn't marry a man who loves her more—or whom, I may venture to add, she loves more."

"I'm not bound to accept your theories as to whom my daughter loves"—Osmond looked up with a quick, cold smile.

"I'm not theorising. Your daughter has spoken."

"Not to me," Osmond continued, now bending forward a little and dropping his eyes to his boot-toes.

"I have her promise, sir!" cried Rosier with the sharpness of exasperation.

As their voices had been pitched very low before, such a note attracted some attention from the company. Osmond waited till this little movement had subsided; then he said, all undisturbed: "I think she has no recollection of having given it."

They had been standing with their faces to the fire, and after he had uttered these last words the master of the house turned round again to the room. Before Rosier had time to reply he perceived that a gentleman—a stranger—had just come in, unannounced, according to the Roman custom, and was about to present himself to his host. The latter smiled blandly, but somehow blankly; the visitor had a handsome face and a large, fair beard, and was evidently an Englishman.

"You apparently don't recognise me," he said with a smile that expressed more than Osmond's.

"Ah yes, now I do. I expected so little to see you."

Rosier departed and went in direct pursuit of Pansy. He sought her, as usual, in the neighbouring room, but he again encountered Mrs. Osmond in his path. He gave his hostess no greeting—he was too righteously indignant, but said to her crudely: "Your husband's awfully cold-blooded."

She gave the same mystical smile he had noticed before. "You can't expect every one to be as hot as yourself."

"I don't pretend to be cold, but I'm cool. What has he been doing to his daughter?"

"I've no idea."

"Don't you take any interest?" Rosier demanded with his sense that she too was irritating.

For a moment she answered nothing; then, "No!" she said abruptly and with a quickened light in her eyes which directly contradicted the word.

"Pardon me if I don't believe that. Where's Miss Osmond?"

"In the corner, making tea. Please leave her there."

Rosier instantly discovered his friend, who had been hidden by intervening groups. He watched her, but her own attention was entirely given to her occupation. "What on earth has he done to her?" he asked again imploringly. "He declares to me she has given me up."

"She has not given you up," Isabel said in a low tone and without looking at him.

"Ah, thank you for that! Now I'll leave her alone as long as you think proper!"

He had hardly spoken when he saw her change colour, and became aware that Osmond was coming toward her accompanied by the gentleman who had just entered. He judged the latter, in spite of the advantage of good looks and evident social experience, a little embarrassed. "Isabel," said her husband, "I bring you an old friend."

Mrs. Osmond's face, though it wore a smile, was, like her old friend's, not perfectly confident. "I'm very happy to see Lord Warburton," she said. Rosier turned away and, now that his talk with her had been interrupted, felt absolved from the little pledge he had just taken. He had a quick impression that Mrs. Osmond wouldn't notice what he did.

Isabel in fact, to do him justice, for some time quite ceased to observe him. She had been startled; she hardly knew if she felt a pleasure or a pain. Lord Warburton, however, now that he was face to face with her, was plainly quite sure of his own sense of the matter; though his grey eyes had still their fine original property of keeping recognition and attestation strictly sincere. He was "heavier" than of yore and looked older; he stood there very solidly and sensibly.

"I suppose you didn't expect to see me," he said; "I've but just arrived. Literally, I only got here this evening. You see I've lost no time in coming to pay you my respects. I knew you were at home on Thursdays."

"You see the fame of your Thursdays has spread to England," Osmond remarked to his wife.

"It's very kind of Lord Warburton to come so soon; we're greatly flattered," Isabel said.

"Ah well, it's better than stopping in one of those horrible inns," Osmond went on.

"The hotel seems very good; I think it's the same at which I saw you four years since. You know it was here in Rome that we first met; it's a long time ago. Do you remember where I bade you good-bye?" his lordship asked of his hostess. "It was in the Capitol, in the first room."

"I remember that myself," said Osmond. "I was there at the time."

"Yes, I remember you there. I was very sorry to leave Rome—so sorry that, somehow or other, it became almost a dismal memory, and I've never cared to come back till to-day. But I knew you were living here," her old friend went on to Isabel, "and I assure you I've often thought of you. It must be a charming place to live in," he added with a look, round him, at her established home, in which she might have caught the dim ghost of his old ruefulness.

"We should have been glad to see you at any time," Osmond observed with propriety.

"Thank you very much. I haven't been out of England since then. Till a month ago I really supposed my travels over."

"I've heard of you from time to time," said Isabel, who had already, with her rare capacity for such inward feats, taken the measure of what meeting him again meant for her.

"I hope you've heard no harm. My life has been a remarkably complete blank."

"Like the good reigns in history," Osmond suggested. He appeared to think his duties as a host now terminated—he had performed them so conscientiously. Nothing could have been more adequate, more nicely measured, than his courtesy to his wife's old friend. It was punctilious, it was explicit, it was everything but natural—a deficiency which Lord Warburton, who, himself, had on the whole a good deal of nature, may be supposed to have perceived. "I'll leave you and Mrs. Osmond together," he added. "You have reminiscences into which I don't enter."

"I'm afraid you lose a good deal!" Lord Warburton called after him, as he moved away, in a tone which perhaps betrayed overmuch an appreciation of his generosity. Then the visitor turned on Isabel the deeper, the deepest, consciousness of his look, which gradually became more serious. "I'm really very glad to see you."

"It's very pleasant. You're very kind."

"Do you know that you're changed—a little?"

She just hesitated. "Yes—a good deal."

"I don't mean for the worse, of course; and yet how can I say for the better?"

"I think I shall have no scruple in saying that to *you*," she bravely returned.

"Ah well, for me—it's a long time. It would be a pity there shouldn't be something to show for it." They sat down and she asked him about his sisters, with other enquiries of a somewhat perfunctory kind. He answered her questions as if they interested him, and in a few moments she saw—or believed she saw—that he would press with less of his whole weight than of yore. Time had breathed upon his heart and, without chilling it, given it a relieved sense of having taken the air. Isabel felt her usual esteem for Time rise at a bound. Her friend's manner was certainly that of a contented man, one who would rather like people, or like her at least, to know him for such. "There's something I must tell you without more delay," he resumed. "I've brought Ralph Touchett with me."

"Brought him with you?" Isabel's surprise was great.

"He's at the hotel; he was too tired to come out and has gone to bed."

"I'll go to see him," she immediately said.

"That's exactly what I hoped you'd do. I had an idea you hadn't seen much of him since your marriage, that in fact your relations were a—a little more formal. That's why I hesitated—like an awkward Briton."

"I'm as fond of Ralph as ever," Isabel answered. "But why has he come to Rome?" The declaration was very gentle, the question a little sharp.

"Because he's very far gone, Mrs. Osmond."

"Rome then is no place for him. I heard from him that he had determined to give up his custom of wintering abroad and to remain in England, indoors, in what he called an artificial climate."

"Poor fellow, he doesn't succeed with the artificial! I went to see him three weeks ago, at Gardencourt, and found him thoroughly ill. He has been getting worse every year, and now he has no strength left. He smokes no more cigarettes! He had got up an artificial climate indeed; the house was as hot as Calcutta. Nevertheless he had suddenly taken it into his head to start for Sicily. I didn't believe in it—neither did the doctors, nor any of his friends. His mother, as I suppose you know, is in America, so there was no one to prevent him. He stuck to his idea that it would be the saving of him to spend the winter at Catania.[1] He said he could take servants and furniture, could make himself comfortable, but in point of fact he hasn't brought anything. I wanted him at least to go by sea, to save fatigue; but he said he hated the sea and wished to stop at Rome. After that, though I thought it all rubbish, I made up my mind to come with him. I'm acting as—what do you call it in America?—as a kind of moderator. Poor Ralph's very moderate now. We left England a fortnight ago, and he has been very bad on the way. He can't keep warm, and the further south we come the more he feels the cold. He has got rather a good man, but I'm afraid he's beyond human help. I wanted him to take with him some clever fellow—I mean some sharp young doctor; but he wouldn't hear of it. If you don't mind my saying so, I think it was a most extraordinary time for Mrs. Touchett to decide on going to America."

Isabel had listened eagerly; her face was full of pain and wonder. "My aunt does that at fixed periods and lets nothing turn her aside. When the date comes round she starts; I think she'd have started if Ralph had been dying."

"I sometimes think he *is* dying," Lord Warburton said.

Isabel sprang up. "I'll go to him then now."

He checked her; he was a little disconcerted at the quick effect of his words. "I don't mean I thought so to-night. On the contrary, to-day, in the train, he seemed particularly well; the idea of our reaching Rome—he's very fond of Rome, you know—gave him strength. An hour ago, when I bade him good-night, he told me he was very tired, but very happy. Go to him in the morning; that's all

1. A Sicilian port and winter resort.

I mean. I didn't tell him I was coming here; I didn't decide to till after we had separated. Then I remembered he had told me you had an evening, and that it was this very Thursday. It occurred to me to come in and tell you he's here, and let you know you had perhaps better not wait for him to call. I think he said he hadn't written to you." There was no need of Isabel's declaring that she would act upon Lord Warburton's information; she looked, as she sat there, like a winged creature held back. "Let alone that I wanted to see you for myself," her visitor gallantly added.

"I don't understand Ralph's plan; it seems to me very wild," she said. "I was glad to think of him between those thick walls at Gardencourt."

"He was completely alone there; the thick walls were his only company."

"You went to see him; you've been extremely kind."

"Oh dear, I had nothing to do," said Lord Warburton.

"We hear, on the contrary, that you're doing great things. Every one speaks of you as a great statesman, and I'm perpetually seeing your name in the *Times*, which, by the way, doesn't appear to hold it in reverence. You're apparently as wild a radical as ever."

"I don't feel nearly so wild; you know the world has come round to me. Touchett and I have kept up a sort of parliamentary debate all the way from London. I tell him he's the last of the Tories, and he calls me the King of the Goths[2]—says I have, down to the details of my personal appearance, every sign of the brute. So you see there's life in him yet."

Isabel had many questions to ask about Ralph, but she abstained from asking them all. She would see for herself on the morrow. She perceived that after a little Lord Warburton would tire of that subject—he had a conception of other possible topics. She was more and more able to say to herself that he had recovered, and, what is more to the point, she was able to say it without bitterness. He had been for her, of old, such an image of urgency, of insistence, of something to be resisted and reasoned with, that his reappearance at first menaced her with a new trouble. But she was now reassured; she could see he only wished to live with her on good terms, that she was to understand he had forgiven her and was incapable of the bad taste of making pointed allusions. This was not a form of revenge, of course; she had no suspicion of his wishing to punish her by an exhibition of disillusionment; she did him the justice to believe it had simply occurred to him that she would now take a good-natured interest in knowing he was resigned. It was the resig-

2. Theodoric the Great (ca. 454–526), king of the Ostrogoths, who invaded and conquered Italy in 488. His rule was long and beneficent but long remembered as the invasion of Europe by the barbarians. [1st ed.: "the head of the Communists."]

nation of a healthy, manly nature, in which sentimental wounds could never fester. British politics had cured him; she had known they would. She gave an envious thought to the happier lot of men, who are always free to plunge into the healing waters of action. Lord Warburton of course spoke of the past, but he spoke of it without implications; he even went so far as to allude to their former meeting in Rome as a very jolly time. And he told her he had been immensely interested in hearing of her marriage and that it was a great pleasure for him to make Mr. Osmond's acquaintance—since he could hardly be said to have made it on the other occasion. He had not written to her at the time of that passage in her history, but he didn't apologise to her for this. The only thing he implied was that they were old friends, intimate friends. It was very much as an intimate friend that he said to her, suddenly, after a short pause which he had occupied in smiling, as he looked about him, like a person amused, at a provincial entertainment, by some innocent game of guesses—

"Well now, I suppose you're very happy and all that sort of thing?"

Isabel answered with a quick laugh; the tone of his remark struck her almost as the accent of comedy. "Do you suppose if I were not I'd tell you?"

"Well, I don't know. I don't see why not."

"I do then. Fortunately, however, I'm very happy."

"You've got an awfully good house."

"Yes, it's very pleasant. But that's not my merit—it's my husband's."

"You mean he has arranged it?"

"Yes, it was nothing when we came."

"He must be very clever."

"He has a genius for upholstery," said Isabel.

"There's a great rage for that sort of thing now. But you must have a taste of your own."

"I enjoy things when they're done, but I've no ideas. I can never propose anything."

"Do you mean you accept what others propose?"

"Very willingly, for the most part."

"That's a good thing to know. I shall propose to you something."

"It will be very kind. I must say, however, that I've in a few small ways a certain initiative. I should like for instance to introduce you to some of these people."

"Oh, please don't; I prefer sitting here. Unless it be to that young lady in the blue dress. She has a charming face."

"The one talking to the rosy young man? That's my husband's daughter."

"Lucky man, your husband. What a dear little maid!"

"You must make her acquaintance."

"In a moment—with pleasure. I like looking at her from here." He ceased to look at her, however, very soon; his eyes constantly reverted to Mrs. Osmond. "Do you know I was wrong just now in saying you had changed?" he presently went on. "You seem to me, after all, very much the same."

"And yet I find it a great change to be married," said Isabel with mild gaiety.

"It affects most people more than it has affected you. You see I haven't gone in for that."

"It rather surprises me."

"You ought to understand it, Mrs. Osmond. But I do want to marry," he added more simply.

"It ought to be very easy," Isabel said, rising—after which she reflected, with a pang perhaps too visible, that she was hardly the person to say this. It was perhaps because Lord Warburton divined the pang that he generously forbore to call her attention to her not having contributed then to the facility.

Edward Rosier had meanwhile seated himself on an ottoman beside Pansy's tea-table. He pretended at first to talk to her about trifles, and she asked him who was the new gentleman conversing with her stepmother.

"He's an English lord," said Rosier. "I don't know more."

"I wonder if he'll have some tea. The English are so fond of tea."

"Never mind that; I've something particular to say to you."

"Don't speak so loud—every one will hear," said Pansy.

"They won't hear if you continue to look that way; as if your only thought in life was the wish the kettle would boil."

"It has just been filled; the servants never know!"—and she sighed with the weight of her responsibility.

"Do you know what your father said to me just now? That you didn't mean what you said a week ago."

"I don't mean everything I say. How can a young girl do that? But I mean what I say to *you*."

"He told me you had forgotten me."

"Ah no, I don't forget," said Pansy, showing her pretty teeth in a fixed smile.

"Then everything's just the very same?"

"Ah no, not the very same. Papa has been terribly severe."

"What has he done to you?"

"He asked me what *you* had done to me, and I told him everything. Then he forbade me to marry you."

"You needn't mind that."

"Oh yes, I must indeed. I can't disobey papa."

"Not for one who loves you as I do, and whom you pretend to love?"

She raised the lid of the tea-pot, gazing into this vessel for a moment; then she dropped six words into its aromatic depths. "I love you just as much."

"What good will that do me?"

"Ah," said Pansy, raising her sweet, vague eyes, "I don't know that."

"You disappoint me," groaned poor Rosier.

She was silent a little; she handed a tea-cup to a servant. "Please don't talk any more."

"Is this to be all my satisfaction?"

"Papa said I was not to talk with you."

"Do you sacrifice me like that? Ah, it's too much!"

"I wish you'd wait a little," said the girl in a voice just distinct enough to betray a quaver.

"Of course I'll wait if you'll give me hope. But you take my life away."

"I'll not give you up—oh no!" Pansy went on.

"He'll try and make you marry some one else."

"I'll never do that."

"What then are we to wait for?"

She hesitated again. "I'll speak to Mrs. Osmond and she'll help us." It was in this manner that she for the most part designated her stepmother.

"She won't help us much. She's afraid."

"Afraid of what?"

"Of your father, I suppose."

Pansy shook her little head. "She's not afraid of any one. We must have patience."

"Ah, that's an awful word," Rosier groaned; he was deeply disconcerted. Oblivious of the customs of good society, he dropped his head into his hands and, supporting it with a melancholy grace, sat staring at the carpet. Presently he became aware of a good deal of movement about him and, as he looked up, saw Pansy making a curtsey—it was still her little curtsey of the convent—to the English lord whom Mrs. Osmond had introduced.

XXXIX

It will probably not surprise the reflective reader that Ralph Touchett should have seen less of his cousin since her marriage than he had done before that event—an event of which he took such a view as could hardly prove a confirmation of intimacy. He had uttered his thought, as we know, and after this had held his peace, Isabel not having invited him to resume a discussion which marked an era in their relations. That discussion had made a difference—the difference he feared rather than the one he hoped. It had not chilled the girl's zeal in carrying out her engagement, but it had come dangerously near to spoiling a friendship. No reference was ever again made between them to Ralph's opinion of Gilbert Osmond, and by surrounding this topic with a sacred silence they managed to preserve a semblance of reciprocal frankness. But there was a difference, as Ralph often said to himself—there was a difference. She had not forgiven him, she never would forgive him: that was all he had gained. She thought she had forgiven him; she believed she didn't care; and as she was both very generous and very proud these convictions represented a certain reality. But whether or no the event should justify him he would virtually have done her a wrong, and the wrong was of the sort that women remember best. As Osmond's wife she could never again be his friend. If in this character she should enjoy the felicity she expected, she would have nothing but contempt for the man who had attempted, in advance, to undermine a blessing so dear; and if on the other hand his warning should be justified the vow she had taken that he should never know it would lay upon her spirit such a burden as to make her hate him. So dismal had been, during the year that followed his cousin's marriage, Ralph's prevision of the future; and if his meditations appear morbid we must remember he was not in the bloom of health. He consoled himself as he might by behaving (as he deemed) beautifully, and was present at the ceremony by which Isabel was united to Mr. Osmond, and which was performed in Florence in the month of June. He learned from his mother that Isabel at first had thought of celebrating her nuptials in her native land, but that as simplicity was what she chiefly desired to secure she had finally decided, in spite of Osmond's professed willingness to make a journey of any length, that this characteristic would be best embodied in their being married by the nearest clergyman in the shortest time. The thing was done therefore at the little American chapel, on a very hot day, in the presence only of Mrs. Touchett and her son, of Pansy Osmond and the Countess Gemini. That severity in the proceedings of which I just spoke was in part the result of the absence of two persons who might have been looked for on the occasion and who would have lent it a certain richness. Madame Merle had been invited, but Madame Merle, who was unable to leave Rome, had written a gracious letter of excuses. Henrietta Stackpole had not been invited, as her departure from America, announced to Isabel by Mr. Goodwood, was in fact frustrated by the duties of her profession; but she had sent a letter, less gracious than Madame Merle's, intimating that, had she been able to cross the Atlantic, she would have been present not only as a witness but as a critic. Her return to Europe had taken place somewhat later, and she had effected a meeting with Isabel in the autumn, in Paris, when she had indulged—perhaps a trifle too freely—her critical genius. Poor Osmond, who was chiefly the subject of it, had protested so sharply that Henrietta was obliged to declare to Isabel that she had taken a step which put a barrier between them. "It isn't in the least that you've married—it is that you have married *him*," she had deemed it her duty to remark; agreeing, it will be seen, much more with Ralph Touchett than she suspected, though she had few of his hesitations and compunctions. Henrietta's second visit to Europe, however, was not apparently to have been made in vain; for just at the moment when Osmond had declared to Isabel that he really must object to that newspaper-woman, and Isabel had answered that it seemed to her he took Henrietta too hard, the good Mr. Bantling had appeared upon the scene and proposed that they should take a run down to Spain. Henrietta's letters from Spain had proved the most acceptable she had yet published, and there had been one in especial, dated from the Alhambra[1] and entitled 'Moors and Moonlight,' which generally passed for her masterpiece. Isabel had been secretly disappointed at her husband's not seeing his way simply to take the poor girl for funny. She even wondered if his sense of fun, or of the funny—which would be his sense of humour, wouldn't it?—were by chance defective. Of course she herself looked at the matter as a person whose present happiness had nothing to grudge to Henrietta's violated conscience. Osmond had thought their alliance a kind of monstrosity; he couldn't imagine what they had in common. For him, Mr. Bantling's fellow tourist was simply the most vulgar of women, and he had also pronounced her the most abandoned. Against this latter clause of the verdict Isabel had appealed with an ardour that had made him wonder afresh at the oddity of some of his wife's tastes. Isabel could explain it only by saying that she liked to know people who were as different as possible from herself. "Why then don't you make the acquaintance of your washerwoman?" Osmond had enquired; to which Isabel had answered that she was afraid her washerwoman wouldn't care for her. Now Henrietta cared so much.

Ralph had seen nothing of her for the greater part of the two years that had followed her marriage; the winter that formed the beginning of her residence in Rome he had spent again at San Remo, where he had been joined in the spring by his mother, who afterwards had gone with him to England, to see what they were doing at the bank—an operation she couldn't induce him to perform. Ralph had taken a lease of his house at San Remo, a small villa which he had occupied still another winter; but late in the

1. Moorish palace in Granada, Spain.

month of April of this second year he had come down to Rome. It was the first time since her marriage that he had stood face to face with Isabel; his desire to see her again was then of the keenest. She had written to him from time to time, but her letters told him nothing he wanted to know. He had asked his mother what she was making of her life, and his mother had simply answered that she supposed she was making the best of it. Mrs. Touchett had not the imagination that communes with the unseen, and she now pretended to no intimacy with her niece, whom she rarely encountered. This young woman appeared to be living in a sufficiently honourable way, but Mrs. Touchett still remained of the opinion that her marriage had been a shabby affair. It had given her no pleasure to think of Isabel's establishment, which she was sure was a very lame business. From time to time, in Florence, she rubbed against the Countess Gemini, doing her best always to minimise the contact; and the Countess reminded her of Osmond, who make her think of Isabel. The Countess was less talked of in these days; but Mrs. Touchett augured no good of that: it only proved how she had been talked of before. There was a more direct suggestion of Isabel in the person of Madame Merle; but Madame Merle's relations with Mrs. Touchett had undergone a perceptible change. Isabel's aunt had told her, without circumlocution, that she had played too ingenious a part; and Madame Merle, who never quarrelled with any one, who appeared to think no one worth it, and who had performed the miracle of living, more or less, for several years with Mrs. Touchett and showing no symptom of irritation—Madame Merle now took a very high tone and declared that this was an accusation from which she couldn't stoop to defend herself. She added, however (without stooping), that her behaviour had been only too simple, that she had believed only what she saw, that she saw Isabel was not eager to marry and Osmond not eager to please (his repeated visits had been nothing; he was boring himself to death on his hill-top and he came merely for amusement). Isabel had kept her sentiments to herself, and her journey to Greece and Egypt had effectually thrown dust in her companion's eyes. Madame Merle accepted the event—she was unprepared to think of it as a scandal; but that she had played any part in it, double or single, was an imputation against which she proudly protested. It was doubtless in consequence of Mrs. Touchett's attitude, and of the injury it offered to habits consecrated by many charming seasons, that Madame Merle had, after this, chosen to pass many months in England, where her credit was quite unimpaired. Mrs. Touchett had done her a wrong; there are some things that can't be forgiven. But Madame Merle suffered in silence; there was always something exquisite in her dignity.

Ralph, as I say, had wished to see for himself; but while engaged in this pursuit he had yet felt afresh what a fool he had been to put the girl on her guard. He had played the wrong card, and now he had lost the game. He should see nothing, he should learn nothing; for him she would always wear a mask. His true line would have been to profess delight in her union, so that later, when, as Ralph phrased it, the bottom should fall out of it, she might have the pleasure of saying to him that he had been a goose. He would gladly have consented to pass for a goose in order to know Isabel's real situation. At present, however, she neither taunted him with his fallacies nor pretended that her own confidence was justified; if she wore a mask it completely covered her face. There was something fixed and mechanical in the serenity painted on it; this was not an expression, Ralph said—it was a representation, it was even an advertisement. She had lost her child; that was a sorrow, but it was a sorrow she scarcely spoke of; there was more to say about it than she could say to Ralph. It belonged to the past, moreover; it had occurred six months before and she had already laid aside the tokens of mourning. She appeared to be leading the life of the world; Ralph heard her spoken of as having a "charming position." He observed that she produced the impression of being peculiarly enviable, that it was supposed, among many people, to be a privilege even to know her. Her house was not open to every one, and she had an evening in the week to which people were not invited as a matter of course. She lived with a certain magnificence, but you needed to be a member of her circle to perceive it; for there was nothing to gape at, nothing to criticise, nothing even to admire, in the daily proceedings of Mr. and Mrs. Osmond. Ralph, in all this, recognised the hand of the master; for he knew that Isabel had no faculty for producing studied impressions. She struck him as having a great love of movement, of gaiety, of late hours, of long rides, of fatigue; an eagerness to be entertained, to be interested, even to be bored, to make acquaintances, to see people who were talked about, to explore the neighbourhood of Rome, to enter into relation with certain of the mustiest relics of its old society. In all this there was much less discrimination than in that desire for comprehensiveness of development on which he had been used to exercise his wit. There was a kind of violence in some of her impulses, of crudity in some of her experiments, which took him by surprise: it seemed to him that she even spoke faster, moved faster, breathed faster, than before her marriage. Certainly she had fallen into exaggerations— she who used to care so much for the pure truth; and whereas of old she had a great delight in good-humoured argument, in intellectual play (she never looked so charming as when in the genial heat of discussion she received a crushing blow full in the face and brushed it away as a feather), she appeared now to think there was nothing worth people's either differing about or agreeing upon. Of old she had been curious, and now she was indifferent, and yet in spite of her indifference her activity was greater than ever. Slender still, but lovelier than before, she had gained no great maturity of aspect; yet there was an amplitude and a brilliancy in her personal arrangements that gave a touch of insolence to her beauty. Poor human-hearted Isabel, what perversity had bitten her? Her light step drew a mass of drapery behind it; her intelligent head sustained a majesty of ornament. The free, keen girl had become quite another person; what he saw was the fine lady who was supposed to represent something. What did Isabel represent? Ralph asked himself; and he could only answer by saying that she represented Gilbert Osmond. "Good heavens, what a function," he then woefully exclaimed. He was lost in wonder at the mystery of things.

He recognised Osmond, as I say; he recognised him at every turn. He saw how he kept all things within limits; how he adjusted, regulated, animated their manner of life. Osmond was in his element; at last he had material to work with. He always had an eye to effect, and his effects were deeply calculated. They were produced by no vulgar means, but the motive was as vulgar as the art was great. To surround his interior with a sort of invidious sanctity, to tantalise society with a sense of exclusion, to make people believe his house was different from every other, to impart to the face that he presented to the world a cold originality—this was the ingenious effort of the personage to whom Isabel had attributed a superior morality. "He works with superior material," Ralph said to himself; "it's rich abundance compared with his former resources." Ralph was a clever man; but Ralph had never—to his own sense—been so clever as when he observed, *in petto*,[2] that under the guise of caring only for intrinsic values Osmond lived exclusively for the world. Far from being its master as he pretended to be, he was its very humble servant, and the degree of its attention was his only measure of success. He lived with his eye on it from morning till night, and the world was so stupid it never suspected the trick. Everything he did was *pose*—*pose* so subtly considered that if one were not on the lookout one mistook it for impulse. Ralph had never met a man who lived so much in the land of consideration. His tastes, his studies, his accomplishments, his collections, were all for a purpose. His life on his hill-top at Florence had been the conscious attitude of years. His solitude, his ennui, his love for his daughter, his good manners, his bad manners, were so many features of a mental image constantly present to him as a model of impertinence and mystification. His ambition was not to please the world, but to please himself by exciting the world's curiosity and then declining to satisfy it. It had made him feel great, ever, to play the world a trick. The thing he had done in his life most directly to please himself was his marrying

2. To himself.

Miss Archer; though in this case indeed the gullible world was in a manner embodied in poor Isabel, who had been mystified to the top of her bent. Ralph of course found a fitness in being consistent; he had embraced a creed, and as he had suffered for it he could not in honour forsake it. I give this little sketch of its articles for what they may at the time have been worth. It was certain that he was very skilful in fitting the facts to his theory—even the fact that during the month he spent in Rome at this period the husband of the woman he loved appeared to regard him not in the least as an enemy.

For Gilbert Osmond Ralph had not now that importance. It was not that he had the importance of a friend; it was rather that he had none at all. He was Isabel's cousin and he was rather unpleasantly ill—it was on this basis that Osmond treated with him. He made the proper enquiries, asked about his health, about Mrs. Touchett, about his opinion of winter climates, whether he were comfortable at his hotel. He addressed him, on the few occasions of their meeting, not a word that was not necessary; but his manner had always the urbanity proper to conscious success in the presence of conscious failure. For all this, Ralph had had, toward the end, a sharp inward vision of Osmond's making it of small ease to his wife that she should continue to receive Mr. Touchett. He was not jealous—he had not that excuse; no one could be jealous of Ralph. But he made Isabel pay for her old-time kindness, of which so much was still left; and as Ralph had no idea of her paying too much, so when his suspicion had become sharp, he had taken himself off. In doing so he had deprived Isabel of a very interesting occupation: she had been constantly wondering what fine principle was keeping him alive. She had decided that it was his love of conversation; his conversation had been better than ever. He had given up walking; he was no longer a humorous stroller. He sat all day in a chair—almost any chair would serve, and was so dependent on what you would do for him that, had not his talk been highly contemplative, you might have thought he was blind. The reader already knows more about him than Isabel was ever to know, and the reader may therefore be given the key to the mystery. What kept Ralph alive was simply the fact that he had not yet seen enough of the person in the world in whom he was most interested: he was not yet satisfied. There was more to come; he couldn't make up his mind to lose that. He wanted to see what she would make of her husband —or what her husband would make of her. This was only the first act of the drama, and he was determined to sit out the performance. His determination had held good; it had kept him going some eighteen months more, till the time of his return to Rome with Lord Warburton. It had given him indeed such an air of intending to live indefinitely that Mrs. Touchett, though more accessible to

confusions of thought in the matter of this strange, unremunerative
—and unremunerated—son of hers than she had ever been before,
had, as we have learned, not scrupled to embark for a distant land.
If Ralph had been kept alive by suspense it was with a good deal of
the same emotion—the excitement of wondering in what state she
should find him—that Isabel mounted to his apartment the day
after Lord Warburton had notified her of his arrival in Rome.

She spent an hour with him; it was the first of several visits. Gilbert Osmond called on him punctually, and on their sending their
carriage for him Ralph came more than once to Palazzo Roccanera.
A fortnight elapsed, at the end of which Ralph announced to Lord
Warburton that he thought after all he wouldn't go to Sicily. The
two men had been dining together after a day spent by the latter in
ranging about the Campagna.[3] They had left the table, and Warburton, before the chimney, was lighting a cigar, which he instantly
removed from his lips.

"Won't go to Sicily? Where then will you go?"

"Well, I guess I won't go anywhere," said Ralph, from the sofa,
all shamelessly.

"Do you mean you'll return to England?"

"Oh dear no; I'll stay in Rome."

"Rome won't do for you. Rome's not warm enough."

"It will have to do. I'll make it do. See how well I've been."

Lord Warburton looked at him a while, puffing a cigar and as if
trying to see it. "You've been better than you were on the journey,
certainly. I wonder how you lived through that. But I don't understand your condition. I recommend you to try Sicily."

"I can't try," said poor Ralph. "I've done trying. I can't move
further. I can't face that journey. Fancy me between Scylla and
Charybdis![4] I don't want to die on the Sicilian plains—to be
snatched away, like Proserpine[5] in the same locality, to the Plu-
tonian shades."

"What the deuce then did you come for?" his lordship enquired.

"Because the idea took me. I see it won't do. It really doesn't
matter where I am now. I've exhausted all remedies, I've swallowed
all climates. As I'm here I'll stay. I haven't a single cousin in Sicily
—much less a married one."

"Your cousin's certainly an inducement. But what does the
doctor say?"

"I haven't asked him, and I don't care a fig. If I die here Mrs.
Osmond will bury me. But I shall not die here."

"I hope not." Lord Warburton continued to smoke reflectively.

3. Undulating lowlands near Rome, rich
with villas and ruins, aqueducts and
tombs.
4. Odysseus had to sail between the sea
monster, Scylla, and the whirlpool, Charybdis, popularly believed to be the straits
of Messina, separating Sicily from the
mainland.
5. The Roman name for Persephone,
who was seized by Hades as she was
gathering flowers. She was especially
worshipped in Sicily.

"Well, I must say," he resumed, "for myself I'm very glad you don't insist on Sicily. I had a horror of that journey."

"Ah, but for you it needn't have mattered. I had no idea of dragging you in my train."

"I certainly didn't mean to let you go alone."

"My dear Warburton, I never expected you to come further than this," Ralph cried.

"I should have gone with you and seen you settled," said Lord Warburton.

"You're a very good Christian. You're a very kind man."

"Then I should have come back here."

"And then you'd have gone to England."

"No, no; I should have stayed."

"Well," said Ralph, "if that's what we are both up to, I don't see where Sicily comes in!"

His companion was silent; he sat staring at the fire. At last, looking up, "I say, tell me this," he broke out; "did you really mean to go to Sicily when we started?"

"Ah, *vous m'en demandez trop!*[6] Let me put a question first. Did you come with me quite—platonically?"

"I don't know what you mean by that. I wanted to come abroad."

"I suspect we've each been playing our little game."

"Speak for yourself. I made no secret whatever of my desiring to be here a while."

"Yes, I remember you said you wished to see the Minister of Foreign Affairs."

"I've seen him three times. He's very amusing."

"I think you've forgotten what you came for," said Ralph.

"Perhaps I have," his companion answered rather gravely.

These two were gentlemen of a race which is not distinguished by the absence of reserve, and they had travelled together from London to Rome without an allusion to matters that were uppermost in the mind of each. There was an old subject they had once discussed, but it had lost its recognised place in their attention, and even after their arrival in Rome, where many things led back to it, they had kept the same half-diffident, half-confident silence.

"I recommend you to get the doctor's consent, all the same," Lord Warburton went on, abruptly, after an interval.

"The doctor's consent will spoil it. I never have it when I can help it."

"What then does Mrs. Osmond think?" Ralph's friend demanded.

"I've not told her. She'll probably say that Rome's too cold and even offer to go with me to Catania. She's capable of that."

"In your place I should like it."

6. You ask me more than I can answer!

"Her husband won't like it."

"Ah well, I can fancy that; though it seems to me you're not bound to mind his likings. They're his affair."

"I don't want to make any more trouble between them," said Ralph.

"Is there so much already?"

"There's complete preparation for it. Her going off with me would make the explosion. Osmond isn't fond of his wife's cousin."

"Then of course he'd make a row. But won't he make a row if you stop here?"

"That's what I want to see. He made one the last time I was in Rome, and then I thought it my duty to disappear. Now I think it's my duty to stop and defend her."

"My dear Touchett, your defensive powers—!" Lord Warburton began with a smile. But he saw something in his companion's face that checked him. "Your duty, in these premises, seems to me rather a nice question," he observed instead.

Ralph for a short time answered nothing. "It's true that my defensive powers are small," he returned at last; "but as my aggressive ones are still smaller Osmond may after all not think me worth his gunpowder. At any rate," he added, "there are things I'm curious to see."

"You're sacrificing your health to your curiosity then?"

"I'm not much interested in my health, and I'm deeply interested in Mrs. Osmond."

"So am I. But not as I once was," Lord Warburton added quickly. This was one of the allusions he had not hitherto found occasion to make.

"Does she strike you as very happy?" Ralph enquired, emboldened by this confidence.

"Well, I don't know; I've hardly thought. She told me the other night she was happy."

"Ah, she told *you*, of course," Ralph exclaimed, smiling.

"I don't know that. It seems to me I was rather the sort of person she might have complained to."

"Complained? She'll never complain. She has done it—what she *has* done—and she knows it. She'll complain to you least of all. She's very careful."

"She needn't be. I don't mean to make love to her again."

"I'm delighted to hear it. There can be no doubt at least of *your* duty."

"Ah no," said Lord Warburton gravely; "none!"

"Permit me to ask," Ralph went on, "whether it's to bring out the fact that you don't mean to make love to her that you're so very civil to the little girl?"

Lord Warburton gave a slight start; he got up and stood before the fire, looking at it hard. "Does that strike you as very ridiculous?"

"Ridiculous? Not in the least, if you really like her."

"I think her a delightful little person. I don't know when a girl of that age has pleased me more."

"She's a charming creature. Ah, she at least is genuine."

"Of course there's the difference in our ages—more than twenty years."

"My dear Warburton," said Ralph, "are you serious?"

"Perfectly serious—as far as I've got."

"I'm very glad. And, heaven help us," cried Ralph, "how cheered-up old Osmond will be!"

His companion frowned. "I say, don't spoil it. I shouldn't propose for his daughter to please *him*."

"He'll have the perversity to be pleased all the same."

"He's not so fond of me as that," said his lordship.

"As that? My dear Warburton, the drawback of your position is that people needn't be fond of you at all to wish to be connected with you. Now, with me in such a case, I should have the happy confidence that they loved me."

Lord Warburton seemed scarcely in the mood for doing justice to general axioms—he was thinking of a special case. "Do you judge she'll be pleased?"

"The girl herself? Delighted, surely."

"No, no; I mean Mrs. Osmond."

Ralph looked at him a moment. "My dear fellow, what has she to do with it?"

"Whatever she chooses. She's very fond of Pansy."

"Very true—very true." And Ralph slowly got up. "It's an interesting question—how far her fondness for Pansy will carry her." He stood there a moment with his hands in his pockets and rather a clouded brow. "I hope, you know, that you're very—very sure. The deuce!" he broke off. "I don't know how to say it."

"Yes, you do; you know how to say everything."

"Well, it's awkward. I hope you're sure that among Miss Osmond's merits her being—a—so near her stepmother isn't a leading one?"

"Good heavens, Touchett!" cried Lord Warburton angrily, "for what do you take me?"

XL

Isabel had not seen much of Madame Merle since her marriage, this lady having indulged in frequent absences from Rome. At one time she had spent six months in England; at another she had passed a portion of a winter in Paris. She had made numerous visits to distant friends and gave countenance to the idea that for the future she should be a less inveterate Roman than in the past. As she had been inveterate in the past only in the sense of constantly having an apartment in one of the sunniest niches of the Pincian[1] —an apartment which often stood empty—this suggested a prospect of almost constant absence; a danger which Isabel at one period had been much inclined to deplore. Familiarity had modified in some degree her first impression of Madame Merle, but it had not essentially altered it; there was still much wonder of admiration in it. That personage was armed at all points; it was a pleasure to see a character so completely equipped for the social battle. She carried her flag discreetly, but her weapons were polished steel, and she used them with a skill which struck Isabel as more and more that of a veteran. She was never weary, never overcome with disgust; she never appeared to need rest or consolation. She had her own ideas; she had of old exposed a great many of them to Isabel, who knew also that under an appearance of extreme self-control her highly-cultivated friend concealed a rich sensibility. But her will was mistress of her life; there was something gallant in the way she kept going. It was as if she had learned the secret of it—as if the art of life were some clever trick she had guessed. Isabel, as she herself grew older, became acquainted with revulsions, with disgusts; there were days when the world looked black and she asked herself with some sharpness what it was that she was pretending to live for. Her old habit had been to live by enthusiasm, to fall in love with suddenly-perceived possibilities, with the idea of some new adventure. As a younger person she had been used to proceed from one little exaltation to the other: there were scarcely any dull places between. But Madame Merle had suppressed enthusiasm; she fell in love now-a-days with nothing; she lived entirely by reason and by wisdom. There were hours when Isabel would have given anything for lessons in this art; if her brilliant friend had been near she would have made an appeal to her. She had become aware more than before of the advantage of being like that—of having made one's self a firm surface, a sort of corselet of silver.

But, as I say, it was not till the winter during which we lately renewed acquaintance with our heroine that the personage in question made again a continuous stay in Rome. Isabel now saw more of her than she had done since her marriage; but by this time Isabel's needs and inclinations had considerably changed. It was not at present to Madame Merle that she would have applied for instruction; she had lost the desire to know this lady's clever trick. If she had troubles she must keep them to herself, and if life was difficult it

1. "The Pincian Hill is the favorite promenade of the Roman aristocracy"—Hawthorne.

would not make it easier to confess herself beaten. Madame Merle was doubtless of great use to herself and an ornament to any circle; but was she—would she be—of use to others in periods of refined embarrassment? The best way to profit by her friend—this indeed Isabel had always thought—was to imitate her, to be as firm and bright as she. She recognised no embarrassments, and Isabel, considering this fact, determined for the fiftieth time to brush aside her own. It seemed to her too, on the renewal of an intercourse which had virtually been interrupted, that her old ally was different, was almost detached—pushing to the extreme a certain rather artifical fear of being indiscreet. Ralph Touchett, we know, had been of the opinion that she was prone to exaggeration, to forcing the note—was apt, in the vulgar phrase, to overdo it. Isabel had never admitted this charge—had never indeed quite understood it; Madame Merle's conduct, to her perception, always bore the stamp of good taste, was always "quiet." But in this matter of not wishing to intrude upon the inner life of the Osmond family it at last occurred to our young woman that she overdid a little. That of course was not the best taste; that was rather violent. She remembered too much that Isabel was married; that she had now other interests; that though she, Madame Merle, had known Gilbert Osmond and his little Pansy very well, better almost than any one, she was not after all of the inner circle. She was on her guard; she never spoke of their affairs till she was asked, even pressed—as when her opinion was wanted; she had a dread of seeming to meddle. Madame Merle was as candid as we know, and one day she candidly expressed this dread to Isabel.

"I *must* be on my guard," she said; "I might so easily, without suspecting it, offend you. You would be right to be offended, even if my intention should have been of the purest. I must not forget that I knew your husband long before you did; I must not let that betray me. If you were a silly woman you might be jealous. You're not a silly woman; I know that perfectly. But neither am I; therefore I'm determined not to get into trouble. A little harm's very soon done; a mistake's made before one knows it. Of course if I had wished to make love to your husband I had ten years to do it in, and nothing to prevent; so it isn't likely I shall begin to-day, when I'm so much less attractive than I' was. But if I were to annoy you by seeming to take a place that doesn't belong to me, you wouldn't make that reflection, you'd simply say I was forgetting certain differences. I'm determined not to forget them. Certainly a good friend isn't always thinking of that; one doesn't suspect one's friends of injustice. I don't suspect you, my dear, in the least; but I suspect human nature. Don't think I make myself uncomfortable; I'm not always watching myself. I think I sufficiently prove it in talking to you as I do now.

All I wish to say is, however, that if you were to be jealous—that's the form it would take—I should be sure to think it was a little my fault. It certainly wouldn't be your husband's."

Isabel had had three years to think over Mrs. Touchett's theory that Madame Merle had made Gilbert Osmond's marriage. We know how she had at first received it. Madame Merle might have made Gilbert Osmond's marriage, but she certainly had not made Isabel Archer's. That was the work of—Isabel scarcely knew what: of nature, providence, fortune, of the eternal mystery of things. It was true her aunt's complaint had been not so much of Madame Merle's activity as of her duplicity: she had brought about the strange event and then she had denied her guilt. Such a guilt would not have been great, to Isabel's mind; she couldn't make a crime of Madame Merle's having been the producing cause of the most important friendship she had ever formed. This had occurred to her just before her marriage, after her little discussion with her aunt and at a time when she was still capable of that large inward reference, the tone almost of the philosophic historian, to her scant young annals. If Madame Merle had desired her change of state she could only say it had been a very happy thought. With her, moreover, she had been perfectly straightforward; she had never concealed her high opinion of Gilbert Osmond. After their union Isabel discovered that her husband took a less convenient view of the matter; he seldom consented to finger, in talk, this roundest and smoothest bead of their social rosary.

"Don't you like Madame Merle?" Isabel had once said to him. "She thinks a great deal of you."

"I'll tell you once for all," Osmond had answered. "I liked her once better than I do to-day. I'm tired of her, and I'm rather ashamed of it. She's so almost unnaturally good! I'm glad she's not in Italy; it makes for relaxation—for a sort of moral *détente*.[2] Don't talk of her too much; it seems to bring her back. She'll come back in plenty of time."

Madame Merle, in fact, had come back before it was too late—too late, I mean, to recover whatever advantage she might have lost. But meantime, if, as I have said, she was sensibly different, Isabel's feelings were also not quite the same. Her consciousness of the situation was as acute as of old, but it was much less satisfying. A dissatisfied mind, whatever else it may miss, is rarely in want of reasons; they bloom as thick as buttercups in June. The fact of Madame Merle's having had a hand in Gilbert Osmond's marriage ceased to be one of her titles to consideration; it might have been written, after all, that there was not so much to thank her for. As time went on there was less and less, and Isabel once said to herself

2. Easing off, slackening.

that perhaps without her these things would not have been. That reflection indeed was instantly stifled; she knew an immediate horror at having made it. "Whatever happens to me let me not be unjust," she said; "let me bear my burdens myself and not shift them upon others!" This disposition was tested, eventually, by that ingenious apology for her present conduct which Madame Merle saw fit to make and of which I have given a sketch; for there was something irritating—there was almost an air of mockery—in her neat discriminations and clear convictions. In Isabel's mind to-day there was nothing clear; there was a confusion of regrets, a complication of fears. She felt helpless as she turned away from her friend, who had just made the statements I have quoted: Madame Merle knew so little what she was thinking of! She was herself moreover so unable to explain. Jealous of her—jealous of her with Gilbert? The idea just then suggested no near reality. She almost wished jealousy had been possible; it would have made in a manner for refreshment. Wasn't it in a manner one of the symptoms of happiness? Madame Merle, however, was wise, so wise that she might have been pretending to know Isabel better than Isabel knew herself. This young woman had always been fertile in resolutions—many of them of an elevated character; but at no period had they flourished (in the privacy of her heart) more richly than to-day. It is true that they all had a family likeness; they might have been summed up in the determination that if she was to be unhappy it should not be by a fault of her own. Her poor winged spirit had always had a great desire to do its best, and it had not as yet been seriously discouraged. It wished, therefore, to hold fast to justice—not to pay itself by petty revenges. To associate Madame Merle with its disappointment would be a petty revenge—especially as the pleasure to be derived from that would be perfectly insincere. It might feed her sense of bitterness, but it would not loosen her bonds. It was impossible to pretend that she had not acted with her eyes open; if ever a girl was a free agent she had been. A girl in love was doubtless not a free agent; but the sole source of her mistake had been within herself. There had been no plot, no snare; she had looked and considered and chosen. When a woman had made such a mistake, there was only one way to repair it—just immensly (oh, with the highest grandeur!) to accept it. One folly was enough, especially when it was to last for ever; a second one would not much set it off. In this vow of reticence there was a certain nobleness which kept Isabel going; but Madame Merle had been right, for all that, in taking her precautions.

One day about a month after Ralph Touchett's arrival in Rome Isabel came back from a walk with Pansy. It was not only a part of her general determination to be just that she was at present very thankful for Pansy—it was also a part of her tenderness for things that were pure and weak. Pansy was dear to her, and there was nothing else in her life that had the rightness of the young creature's attachment or the sweetness of her own clearness about it. It was like a soft presence—like a small hand in her own; on Pansy's part it was more than an affection—it was a kind of ardent coercive faith. On her own side her sense of the girl's dependence was more than a pleasure; it operated as a definite reason when motives threatened to fail her. She had said to herself that we must take our duty where we find it, and that we must look for it as much as possible. Pansy's sympathy was a direct admonition; it seemed to say that here was an opportunity, not eminent perhaps, but unmistakeable. Yet an opportunity for what Isabel could hardly have said; in general, to be more for the child than the child was able to be for herself. Isabel could have smiled, in these days, to remember that her little companion had once been ambiguous, for she now perceived that Pansy's ambiguities were simply her own grossness of vision. She had been unable to believe any one could care so much —so extraordinarily much—to please. But since then she had seen this delicate faculty in operation, and now she knew what to think of it. It was the whole creature—it was a sort of genius. Pansy had no pride to interfere with it, and though she was constantly extending her conquests she took no credit for them. The two were constantly together; Mrs. Osmond was rarely seen without her stepdaughter. Isabel liked her company; it had the effect of one's carrying a nosegay composed all of the same flower. And then not to neglect Pansy, not under any provocation to neglect her—this she had made an article of religion. The young girl had every appearance of being happier in Isabel's society than in that of any one save her father, whom she admired with an intensity justified by the fact that, as paternity was an exquisite pleasure to Gilbert Osmond, he had always been luxuriously mild. Isabel knew how Pansy liked to be with her and how she studied the means of pleasing her. She had decided that the best way of pleasing her was negative, and consisted in not giving her trouble—a conviction which certainly could have had no reference to trouble already existing. She was therefore ingeniously passive and almost imaginatively docile; she was careful even to moderate the eagerness with which she assented to Isabel's propositions and which might have implied that she could have thought otherwise. She never interrupted, never asked social questions, and though she delighted in approbation, to the point of turning pale when it came to her, never held out her hand for it. She only looked toward it wistfully—an attitude which, as she grew older, made her eyes the prettiest in the world. When during the second winter at Palazzo Roccanera she began to go to parties, to dances, she always, at a reasonable hour, lest Mrs. Osmond should be tired, was the first to propose departure. Isabel appreciated the sacrifice of the late dances, for she knew her little companion had a passionate pleasure in this exercise, taking her steps to the music like a conscientious fairy. Society, moreover, had no drawbacks for her; she liked even the tiresome parts—the heat of ball-rooms, the dulness of dinners, the crush at the door, the awkward waiting for the carriage. During the day, in this vehicle, beside her stepmother, she sat in a small fixed, appreciative posture, bending forward and faintly smiling, as if she had been taken to drive for the first time.

On the day I speak of they had been driven out of one of the gates of the city and at the end of half an hour had left the carriage to await them by the roadside while they walked away over the short grass of the Campagna, which even in the winter months is sprinkled with delicate flowers. This was almost a daily habit with Isabel, who was fond of a walk and had a swift length of step, though not so swift a one as on her first coming to Europe. It was not the form of exercise that Pansy loved best, but she liked it, because she liked everything; and she moved with a shorter undulation beside her father's wife, who afterwards, on their return to Rome, paid a tribute to her preferences by making the circuit of the Pincian or the Villa Borghese. She had gathered a handful of flowers in a sunny hollow, far from the walls of Rome, and on reaching Palazzo Roccanera she went straight to her room, to put them into water. Isabel passed into the drawing-room, the one she herself usually occupied, the second in order from the large antechamber which was entered from the staircase and in which even Gilbert Osmond's rich devices had not been able to correct a look of rather grand nudity. Just beyond the threshold of the drawing-room she stopped short, the reason for her doing so being that she had received an impression. The impression had, in strictness, nothing unprecedented; but she felt it as something new, and the soundlessness of her step gave her time to take in the scene before she interrupted it. Madame Merle was there in her bonnet, and Gilbert Osmond was talking to her; for a minute they were unaware she had come in. Isabel had often seen that before, certainly; but what she had not seen, or at least had not noticed, was that their colloquy had for the moment converted itself into a sort of familiar silence, from which she instantly perceived that her entrance would startle them. Madame Merle was standing on the rug, a little way from the fire; Osmond was in a deep chair, leaning back and looking at her. Her head was erect, as usual, but her eyes were bent on his. What struck Isabel first was that he was sitting while Madame Merle stood; there was an anomaly in this that arrested her. Then she perceived that they had arrived at a desultory pause in their exchange of ideas and were musing, face to face, with the freedom of old friends who sometimes exchange ideas without uttering them. There was nothing to shock in this; they were old friends in fact. But the thing made an image, lasting only a moment, like a sudden flicker of light. Their relative positions, their absorbed mutual gaze, struck her as something detected. But it was all over by the time she had fairly seen it. Madame Merle had seen her and had welcomed her without moving; her husband, on the other hand, had instantly jumped up. He presently murmured something about wanting a walk and, after having asked their visitor to excuse him, left the room.

"I came to see you, thinking you would have come in; and as you hadn't I waited for you," Madame Merle said.

"Didn't he ask you to sit down?" Isabel asked with a smile.

Madame Merle looked about her. "Ah, it's very true; I was going away."

"You must stay now."

"Certainly. I came for a reason; I've something on my mind."

"I've told you that before," Isabel said—"that it takes something extraordinary to bring you to this house."

"And you know what I've told *you*; that whether I come or whether I stay away, I've always the same motive—the affection I bear you."

"Yes, you've told me that."

"You look just now as if you didn't believe it," said Madame Merle.

"Ah," Isabel answered, "the profundity of your motives, that's the last thing I doubt!"

"You doubt sooner of the sincerity of my words."

Isabel shook her head gravely. "I know you've always been kind to me."

"As often as you would let me. You don't always take it; then one has to let you alone. It's not to do you a kindness, however, that I've come to-day; it's quite another affair. I've come to get rid of a trouble of my own—to make it over to you. I've been talking to your husband about it."

"I'm surprised at that; he doesn't like troubles."

"Especially other people's; I know very well. But neither do you, I suppose. At any rate, whether you do or not, you must help me. It's about poor Mr. Rosier."

"Ah," said Isabel reflectively, "it's his trouble then, not yours."

"He has succeeded in saddling me with it. He comes to see me ten times a week, to talk about Pansy."

"Yes, he wants to marry her. I know all about it."

Madame Merle hesitated. "I gathered from your husband that perhaps you didn't."

"How should he know what I know? He has never spoken to me of the matter."

"It's probably because he doesn't know how to speak of it."

"It's nevertheless the sort of question in which he's rarely at fault."

"Yes, because as a general thing he knows perfectly well what to think. To-day he doesn't."

"Haven't you been telling him?" Isabel asked.

Madame Merle gave a bright, voluntary smile. "Do you know you're a little dry?"

"Yes; I can't help it. Mr. Rosier has also talked to me."

"In that there's some reason. You're so near the child."

"Ah," said Isabel, "for all the comfort I've given him! If you think me dry, I wonder what *he* thinks."

"I believe he thinks you can do more than you have done."

"I can do nothing."

"You can do more at least than I. I don't know what mysterious connection he may have discovered between me and Pansy; but he came to me from the first, as if I held his fortune in my hand. Now he keeps coming back, to spur me up, to know what hope there is, to pour out his feelings."

"He's very much in love," said Isabel.

"Very much—for him."

"Very much for Pansy, you might say as well."

Madame Merle dropped her eyes a moment. "Don't you think she's attractive?"

"The dearest little person possible—but very limited."

"She ought to be all the easier for Mr. Rosier to love. Mr. Rosier's not unlimited."

"No," said Isabel, "he has about the extent of one's pocket-handkerchief—the small ones with lace borders." Her humour had lately turned a good deal to sarcasm, but in a moment she was ashamed of exercising it on so innocent an object as Pansy's suitor. "He's very kind, very honest," she presently added; "and he's not such a fool as he seems."

"He assures me that she delights in him," said Madame Merle.

"I don't know; I've not asked her."

"You've never sounded her a little?"

"It's not my place; it's her father's."

"Ah, you're too literal!" said Madame Merle.

"I must judge for myself."

Madame Merle gave her smile again. "It isn't easy to help you."

"To help me?" said Isabel very seriously. "What do you mean?"

"It's easy to displease you. Don't you see how wise I am to be careful? I notify you, at any rate, as I notified Osmond, that I wash my hands of the love-affairs of Miss Pansy and Mr. Edward Rosier. *Je n'y peux rien, moi!*[3] I can't talk to Pansy about him. Especially," added Madame Merle, "as I don't think him a paragon of husbands."

Isabel reflected a little; after which, with a smile, "You don't wash your hands then!" she said. After which again she added in another tone: "You can't—you're too much interested."

Madame Merle slowly rose; she had given Isabel a look as rapid as the intimation that had gleamed before our heroine a few moments before. Only this time the latter saw nothing. "Ask him the next time, and you'll see."

"I can't ask him; he has ceased to come to the house. Gilbert has let him know that he's not welcome."

"Ah yes," said Madame Merle, "I forgot that—though it's the burden of his lamentation. He says Osmond has insulted him. All the same," she went on, "Osmond doesn't dislike him so much as he thinks." She had got up as if to close the conversation, but she lingered, looking about her, and had evidently more to say. Isabel perceived this and even saw the point she had in view; but Isabel also had her own reasons for not opening the way.

"That must have pleased him, if you've told him," she answered, smiling.

"Certainly I've told him; as far as that goes I've encouraged him. I've preached patience, have said that his case isn't desperate if he'll only hold his tongue and be quiet. Unfortunately he has taken it into his head to be jealous."

"Jealous?"

"Jealous of Lord Warburton, who, he says, is always here."

Isabel, who was tired, had remained sitting; but at this she also rose. "Ah!" she exclaimed simply, moving slowly to the fireplace. Madame Merle observed her as she passed and while she stood a moment before the mantel-glass and pushed into its place a wandering tress of hair.

"Poor Mr. Rosier keeps saying there's nothing impossible in Lord Warburton's falling in love with Pansy," Madame Merle went on.

Isabel was silent a little; she turned away from the glass. "It's true—there's nothing impossible," she returned at last, gravely and more gently.

"So I've had to admit to Mr. Rosier. So, too, your husband thinks."

"That I don't know."

---

3. There's nothing I can do about it, personally.

"Ask him and you'll see."

"I shall not ask him," said Isabel.

"Pardon me; I forgot you had pointed that out. Of course," Madame Merle added, "you've had infinitely more observation of Lord Warburton's behaviour than I."

"I see no reason why I shouldn't tell you that he likes my step-daughter very much."

Madame Merle gave one of her quick looks again. "Likes her, you mean—as Mr. Rosier means?"

"I don't know how Mr. Rosier means; but Lord Warburton has let me know that he's charmed with Pansy."

"And you've never told Osmond?" This observation was immediate, precipitate; it almost burst from Madame Merle's lips.

Isabel's eyes rested on her. "I suppose he'll know in time; Lord Warburton has a tongue and knows how to express himself."

Madame Merle instantly became conscious that she had spoken more quickly than usual, and the reflection brought the colour to her cheek. She gave the treacherous impulse time to subside and then said as if she had been thinking it over a little: "That would be better than marrying poor Mr. Rosier."

"Much better, I think."

"It would be very delightful; it would be a great marriage. It's really very kind of him."

"Very kind of him?"

"To drop his eyes on a simple little girl."

"I don't see that."

"It's very good of you. But after all, Pansy Osmond—"

"After all, Pansy Osmond's the most attractive person he has ever known!" Isabel exclaimed.

Madame Merle stared, and indeed she was justly bewildered. "Ah, a moment ago I thought you seemed rather to disparage her."

"I said she was limited. And so she is. And so's Lord Warburton."

"So are we all, if you come to that. If it's no more than Pansy deserves, all the better. But if she fixes her affections on Mr. Rosier I won't admit that she deserves it. That will be too perverse."

"Mr. Rosier's a nuisance!" Isabel cried abruptly.

"I quite agree with you, and I'm delighted to know that I'm not expected to feed his flame. For the future, when he calls on me, my door shall be closed to him." And gathering her mantle together Madame Merle prepared to depart. She was checked, however, on her progress to the door, by an inconsequent request from Isabel.

"All the same, you know, be kind to him."

She lifted her shoulders and eyebrows and stood looking at her friend. "I don't understand your contradictions! Decidedly I shan't be kind to him, for it will be a false kindness. I want to see her married to Lord Warburton."

"You had better wait till he asks her."

"If what you say's true, he'll ask her. Especially," said Madame Merle in a moment, "if you make him."

"If I make him?"

"It's quite in your power. You've great influence with him."

Isabel frowned a little. "Where did you learn that?"

"Mrs. Touchett told me. Not you—never!" said Madame Merle, smiling.

"I certainly never told you anything of the sort."

"You *might* have done so—so far as opportunity went—when we were by way of being confidential with each other. But you really told me very little; I've often thought so since."

Isabel had thought so too, and sometimes with a certain satisfaction. But she didn't admit it now—perhaps because she wished not to appear to exult in it. "You seem to have had an excellent informant in my aunt," she simply returned.

"She let me know you had declined an offer of marriage from Lord Warburton, because she was greatly vexed and was full of the subject. Of course I think you've done better in doing as you did. But if you wouldn't marry Lord Warburton yourself, make him the reparation of helping him to marry some one else."

Isabel listened to this with a face that persisted in not reflecting the bright expressiveness of Madame Merle's. But in a moment she said, reasonably and gently enough: "I should be very glad indeed if, as regards Pansy, it could be arranged." Upon which her companion, who seemed to regard this as a speech of good omen, embraced her more tenderly than might have been expected and triumphantly withdrew.

XLI

Osmond touched on this matter that evening for the first time; coming very late into the drawing-room, where she was sitting alone. They had spent the evening at home, and Pansy had gone to bed; he himself had been sitting since dinner in a small apartment in which he had arranged his books and which he called his study. At ten o'clock Lord Warburton had come in, as he always did when he knew from Isabel that she was to be at home; he was going somewhere else and he sat for half an hour. Isabel, after asking him for news of Ralph, said very little to him, on purpose; she wished him to talk with her stepdaughter. She pretended to read; she even went after a little to the piano; she asked herself if she mightn't leave the room. She had come little by little to think well of the idea of Pansy's becoming the wife of the master of beautiful Lockleigh, though at first it had not presented itself in a manner to excite her enthusiasm. Madame Merle, that afternoon, had applied the match to an accumulation of inflammable material. When Isabel was unhappy she always looked about her—partly from impulse and partly by theory—for some form of positive exertion. She could never rid herself of the sense that unhappiness was a state of disease—of suffering as opposed to doing. To "do"—it hardly mattered what—would therefore be an escape, perhaps in some degree a remedy. Besides, she wished to convince herself that she had done everything possible to content her husband; she was determined not to be haunted by visions of his wife's limpness under appeal. It would please him greatly to see Pansy married to an English nobleman, and justly please him, since this nobleman was so sound a character. It seemed to Isabel that if she could make it her duty to bring about such an event she should play the part of a good wife. She wanted to be that; she wanted to be able to believe sincerely, and with proof of it, that she had been that. Then such an undertaking had other recommendations. It would occupy her, and she desired occupation. It would even amuse her, and if she could really amuse herself she perhaps might be saved. Lastly, it would be a service to Lord Warburton, who evidently pleased himself greatly with the charming girl. It was a little "weird" he should —being what he was; but there was no accounting for such impressions. Pansy might captivate any one—any one at least but Lord Warburton. Isabel would have thought her too small, too slight, perhaps even too artificial for that. There was always a little of the doll about her, and that was not what he had been looking for. Still who could say what men ever were looking for? They looked for what they found; they knew what pleased them only when they saw it. No theory was valid in such matters, and nothing was more unaccountable or more natural than anything else. If he had cared for *her* it might seem odd he should care for Pansy, who was so different; but he had not cared for her so much as he had supposed. Or if he had, he had completely got over it, and it was natural that, as that affair had failed, he should think something of quite another sort might succeed. Enthusiasm, as I say, had not come at first to Isabel, but it came to-day and made her feel almost happy. It was astonishing what happiness she could still find in the idea of procuring a pleasure for her husband. It was a pity, however, that Edward Rosier had crossed their path!

At this reflection the light that had suddenly gleamed upon that path lost something of its brightness. Isabel was unfortunately as sure that Pansy thought Mr. Rosier the nicest of all the young men —as sure as if she had held an interview with her on the subject. It was very tiresome she should be so sure, when she had carefully abstained from informing herself; almost as tiresome as that poor Mr. Rosier should have taken it into his own head. He was certainly very inferior to Lord Warburton. It was not the difference in fortune so much as the difference in the men; the young American was really so light a weight. He was much more of the type of the useless fine gentleman than the English nobleman. It was true that there was no particular reason why Pansy should marry a statesman; still, if a statesman admired her, that was his affair, and she would make a perfect little pearl of a peeress.

It may seem to the reader that Mrs. Osmond had grown of a sudden strangely cynical, for she ended by saying to herself that this difficulty could probably be arranged. An impediment that was embodied in poor Rosier could not anyhow present itself as a dangerous one; there were always means of levelling secondary obstacles. Isabel was perfectly aware that she had not taken the measure of Pansy's tenacity, which might prove to be inconveniently great; but she inclined to see her as rather letting go, under suggestion, than as clutching under deprecation—since she had certainly the faculty of assent developed in a very much higher degree than that of protest. She would cling, yes, she would cling; but it really mattered to her very little what she clung to. Lord Warburton would do as well as Mr. Rosier—especially as she seemed quite to like him; she had expressed this sentiment to Isabel without a single reservation; she had said she thought his conversation most interesting—he had told her all about India. His manner to Pansy had been of the rightest and easiest—Isabel noticed that for herself, as she also observed that he talked to her not in the least in a patronising way, reminding himself of her youth and simplicity, but quite as if she understood his subjects with that sufficiency with which she followed those of the fashionable operas. This went far enough for attention to the music and the barytone. He was careful only to be kind—he was as kind as he had been to another fluttered young chit at Gardencourt. A girl might well be touched by that; she remembered how she herself had been touched, and said to herself that if she had been as simple as Pansy the impression would have been deeper still. She had not been simple when she refused him; that operation had been as complicated as, later, her acceptance of Osmond had been. Pansy, however, in spite of *her* simplicity, really did understand, and was glad that Lord Warburton should talk to her, not about her partners and bouquets, but about the state of Italy, the condition of the peasantry, the famous grist-tax,[1] the *pellagra*,[2] his impressions of Roman society. She looked at him, as she

1. A tax on the grinding of food grains, introduced in Italy in 1868 and known as the "tax on the food of the poor."

2. A disease caused by nutritional deficiency, from the Italian "polle agra" (rough skin).

drew her needle through her tapestry, with sweet submissive eyes, and when she lowered them she gave little quiet oblique glances at his person, his hands, his feet, his clothes, as if she were considering him. Even his person, Isabel might have reminded her, was better than Mr. Rosier's. But Isabel contented herself at such moments with wondering where this gentleman was; he came no more at all to Palazzo Roccanera. It was surprising, as I say, the hold it had taken of her—the idea of assisting her husband to be pleased.

It was surprising for a variety of reasons which I shall presently touch upon. On the evening I speak of, while Lord Warburton sat there, she had been on the point of taking the great step of going out of the room and leaving her companions alone. I say the great step, because it was in this light that Gilbert Osmond would have regarded it, and Isabel was trying as much as possible to take her husband's view. She succeeded after a fashion, but she fell short of the point I mention. After all she couldn't rise to it; something held her and made this impossible. It was not exactly that it would be base or insidious; for women as a general thing practise such manœuvres with a perfectly good conscience, and Isabel was instinctively much more true than false to the common genius of her sex. There was a vague doubt that interposed—a sense that she was not quite sure. So she remained in the drawing-room, and after a while Lord Warburton went on to his party, of which he promised to give Pansy a full account on the morrow. After he had gone she wondered if she had prevented something which would have happened if she had absented herself for a quarter of an hour; and then she pronounced—always mentally—that when their distinguished visitor should wish her to go away he would easily find means to let her know it. Pansy said nothing whatever about him after he had gone, and Isabel studiously said nothing, as she had taken a vow of reserve until after he should have declared himself. He was a little longer in coming to this than might seem to accord with the description he had given Isabel of his feelings. Pansy went to bed, and Isabel had to admit that she could not now guess what her stepdaughter was thinking of. Her transparent little companion was for the moment not to be seen through.

She remained alone, looking at the fire, until, at the end of half an hour, her husband came in. He moved about a while in silence and then sat down; he looked at the fire like herself. But she now had transferred her eyes from the flickering flame in the chimney to Osmond's face, and she watched him while he kept his silence. Covert observation had become a habit with her; an instinct, of which it is not an exaggeration to say that it was allied to that of self-defence, had made it habitual. She wished as much as possible to know his thoughts, to know what he would say, beforehand, so that she might prepare her answer. Preparing answers had not been her strong point of old; she had rarely in this respect got further than thinking afterwards of clever things she might have said. But she had learned caution—learned it in a measure from her husband's very countenance. It was the same face she had looked into with eyes equally earnest perhaps, but less penetrating, on the terrace of a Florentine villa; except that Osmond had grown slightly stouter since his marriage. He still, however, might strike one as very distinguished.

"Has Lord Warburton been here?" he presently asked.

"Yes, he stayed half an hour."

"Did he see Pansy?"

"Yes; he sat on the sofa beside her."

"Did he talk with her much?"

"He talked almost only to her."

"It seems to me he's attentive. Isn't that what you call it?"

"I don't call it anything," said Isabel; "I've waited for you to give it a name."

"That's a consideration you don't always show," Osmond answered after a moment.

"I've determined, this time, to try and act as you'd like. I've so often failed of that."

Osmond turned his head slowly, looking at her. "Are you trying to quarrel with me?"

"No, I'm trying to live at peace."

"Nothing's more easy; you know I don't quarrel myself."

"What do you call it when you try to make me angry?" Isabel asked.

"I don't try; if I've done so it has been the most natural thing in the world. Moreover I'm not in the least trying now."

Isabel smiled. "It doesn't matter. I've determined never to be angry again."

"That's an excellent resolve. Your temper isn't good."

"No—it's not good." She pushed away the book she had been reading and took up the band of tapestry Pansy had left on the table.

"That's partly why I've not spoken to you about this business of my daughter's," Osmond said, designating Pansy in the manner that was most frequent with him. "I was afraid I should encounter opposition—that you too would have views on the subject. I've sent little Rosier about his business."

"You were afraid I'd plead for Mr. Rosier? Haven't you noticed that I've never spoken to you of him?"

"I've never given you a chance. We've so little conversation in these days. I know he was an old friend of yours."

"Yes; he's an old friend of mine." Isabel cared little more for him than for the tapestry that she held in her hand; but it was true that he was an old friend and that with her husband she felt a desire not to extenuate such ties. He had a way of expressing contempt for them which fortified her loyalty to them, even when, as in the present case, they were in themselves insignificant. She sometimes felt a sort of passion of tenderness for memories which had no other merit than that they belonged to her unmarried life. "But as regards Pansy," she added in a moment, "I've given him no encouragement."

"That's fortunate," Osmond observed.

"Fortunate for me, I suppose you mean. For him it matters little."

"There's no use talking of him," Osmond said. "As I tell you, I've turned him out."

"Yes; but a lover outside's always a lover. He's sometimes even more of one. Mr. Rosier still has hope."

"He's welcome to the comfort of it! My daughter has only to sit perfectly quiet to become Lady Warburton."

"Should you like that?" Isabel asked with a simplicity which was not so affected as it may appear. She was resolved to assume nothing, for Osmond had a way of unexpectedly turning her assumptions against her. The intensity with which he would like his daughter to become Lady Warburton had been the very basis of her own recent reflections. But that was for herself; she would recognise nothing until Osmond should have put it into words; she would not take for granted with him that he thought Lord Warburton a prize worth an amount of effort that was unusual among the Osmonds. It was Gilbert's constant intimation that for him nothing in life was a prize; that he treated as from equal to equal with the most distinguished people in the world, and that his daughter had only to look about her to pick out a prince. It cost him therefore a lapse from consistency to say explicitly that he yearned for Lord Warburton and that if this nobleman should escape his equivalent might not be found; with which moreover it was another of his customary implications that he was never inconsistent. He would have liked his wife to glide over the point. But strangely enough, now that she was face to face with him and although an hour before she had almost invented a scheme for pleasing him, Isabel was not accommodating, would not glide. And yet she knew exactly the effect on his mind of her question: it would operate as an humiliation. Never mind; he was terribly capable of humiliating *her*—all the more so that he was also capable of waiting for great opportunities and of showing sometimes an almost unaccountable indifference to small ones. Isabel perhaps took a small opportunity because she would not have availed herself of a great one.

Osmond at present acquitted himself very honourably. "I should like it extremely; it would be a great marriage. And then Lord Warburton has another advantage: he's an old friend of yours. It would be pleasant for him to come into the family. It's very odd Pansy's admirers should all be your old friends."

"It's natural that they should come to see me. In coming to see me they see Pansy. Seeing her it's natural they should fall in love with her."

"So I think. But you're not bound to do so."

"If she should marry Lord Warburton I should be very glad," Isabel went on frankly. "He's an excellent man. You say, however, that she has only to sit perfectly still. Perhaps she won't sit perfectly still. If she loses Mr. Rosier she may jump up!"

Osmond appeared to give no heed to this; he sat gazing at the fire. "Pansy would like to be a great lady," he remarked in a moment with a certain tenderness of tone. "She wishes above all to please," he added.

"To please Mr. Rosier, perhaps."

"No, to please me."

"Me too a little, I think," said Isabel.

"Yes, she has a great opinion of you. But she'll do what I like."

"If you're sure of that, it's very well," she went on.

"Meantime," said Osmond, "I should like our distinguished visitor to speak."

"He has spoken—to me. He has told me it would be a great pleasure to him to believe she could care for him."

Osmond turned his head quickly, but at first he said nothing. Then, "Why didn't you tell me that?" he asked sharply.

"There was no opportunity. You know how we live. I've taken the first chance that has offered."

"Did you speak to him of Rosier?"

"Oh yes, a little."

"That was hardly necessary."

"I thought it best he should know, so that, so that—" And Isabel paused.

"So that what?"

"So that he might act accordingly."

"So that he might back out, do you mean?"

"No, so that he might advance while there's yet time."

"That's not the effect it seems to have had."

"You should have patience," said Isabel. "You know Englishmen are shy."

"This one's not. He was not when he made love to *you*."

She had been afraid Osmond would speak of that; it was disagreeable to her. "I beg your pardon; he was extremely so," she returned.

He answered nothing for some time; he took up a book and

fingered the pages while she sat silent and occupied herself with Pansy's tapestry. "You must have a great deal of influence with him," Osmond went on at last. "The moment you really wish it you can bring him to the point."

This was more offensive still; but she felt the great naturalness of his saying it, and it was after all extremely like what she had said to herself. "Why should I have influence?" she asked. "What have I ever done to put him under an obligation to me?"

"You refused to marry him," said Osmond with his eyes on his book.

"I must not presume too much on that," she replied.

He threw down the book presently and got up, standing before the fire with his hands behind him. "Well, I hold that it lies in your hands. I shall leave it there. With a little good-will you may manage it. Think that over and remember how much I count on you." He waited a little, to give her time to answer; but she answered nothing, and he presently strolled out of the room.

XLII

She had answered nothing because his words had put the situation before her and she was absorbed in looking at it. There was something in them that suddenly made vibrations deep, so that she had been afraid to trust herself to speak. After he had gone she leaned back in her chair and closed her eyes; and for a long time, far into the night and still further, she sat in the still drawing-room, given up to her meditation. A servant came in to attend to the fire, and she bade him bring fresh candles and then go to bed. Osmond had told her to think of what he had said; and she did so indeed, and of many other things. The suggestion from another that she had a definite influence on Lord Warburton—this had given her the start that accompanies unexpected recognition. Was it true that there was something still between them that might be a handle to make him declare himself to Pansy—a susceptibility, on his part, to approval, a desire to do what would please her? Isabel had hitherto not asked herself the question, because she had not been forced; but now that it was directly presented to her she saw the answer, and the answer frightened her. Yes, there was something—something on Lord Warburton's part. When he had first come to Rome she believed the link that united them to be completely snapped; but little by little she had been reminded that it had yet a palpable existence. It was as thin as a hair, but there were moments when she seemed to hear it vibrate. For herself nothing was changed; what she once thought of him she always thought; it was needless this feeling should change; it seemed to her in fact a better feeling than ever. But he? had he still the idea that she might be more to him than other women? Had he the wish to profit by the memory of the few moments of intimacy through which they had once passed? Isabel knew she had read some of the signs of such a disposition. But what were his hopes, his pretensions, and in what strange way were they mingled with his evidently very sincere appreciation of poor Pansy? Was he in love with Gilbert Osmond's wife, and if so what comfort did he expect to derive from it? If he was in love with Pansy he was not in love with her stepmother, and if he was in love with her stepmother he was not in love with Pansy. Was she to cultivate the advantage she possessed in order to make him commit himself to Pansy, knowing he would do so for her sake and not for the small creature's own—was this the service her husband had asked of her? This at any rate was the duty with which she found herself confronted—from the moment she admitted to herself that her old friend had still an uneradicated predilection for her society. It was not an agreeable task; it was in fact a repulsive one. She asked herself with dismay whether Lord Warburton were pretending to be in love with Pansy in order to cultivate another satisfaction and what might be called other chances. Of this refinement of duplicity she presently acquitted him; she preferred to believe him in perfect good faith. But if his admiration for Pansy were a delusion this was scarcely better than its being an affectation. Isabel wandered among these ugly possibilities until she had completely lost her way; some of them, as she suddenly encountered them, seemed ugly enough. Then she broke out of the labyrinth, rubbing her eyes, and declared that her imagination surely did her little honour and that her husband's did him even less. Lord Warburton was as disinterested as he need be, and she was no more to him than she need wish. She would rest upon this till the contrary should be proved; proved more effectually than by a cynical intimation of Osmond's.

Such a resolution, however, brought her this evening but little peace, for her soul was haunted with terrors which crowded to the foreground of thought as quickly as a place was made for them. What had suddenly set them into livelier motion she hardly knew, unless it were the strange impression she had received in the afternoon of her husband's being in more direct communication with Madame Merle than she suspected. That impression came back to her from time to time, and now she wondered it had never come before. Besides this, her short interview with Osmond half an hour ago was a striking example of his faculty for making everything wither that he touched, spoiling everything for her that he looked at. It was very well to undertake to give him a proof of loyalty; the real fact was that the knowledge of his expecting a thing raised a presumption against it. It was as if he had had the evil eye; as if his presence were a blight and his favour a misfortune. Was the fault in himself, or only in the deep mistrust she had conceived for him? This mistrust was now the clearest result of their short married life; a gulf had opened between them over which they looked at each other with eyes that were on either side a declaration of the deception suffered. It was a strange opposition, of the like of which she had never dreamed—an opposition in which the vital principle of the one was a thing of contempt to the other. It was not her fault —she had practised no deception; she had only admired and believed. She had taken all the first steps in the purest confidence, and then she had suddenly found the infinite vista of a multiplied life to be a dark, narrow alley with a dead wall at the end. Instead of leading to the high places of happiness, from which the world would seem to lie below one, so that one could look down with a sense of exaltation and advantage, and judge and choose and pity, it led rather downward and earthward, into realms of restriction and depression where the sound of other lives, easier and freer, was heard as from above, and where it served to deepen the feeling of failure. It was her deep distrust of her husband—this was what darkened the world. That is a sentiment easily indicated, but not so easily explained, and so composite in its character that much time and still more suffering had been needed to bring it to its actual perfection. Suffering, with Isabel, was an active condition; it was not a chill, a stupor, a despair; it was a passion of thought, of speculation, of response to every pressure. She flattered herself that she had kept her failing faith to herself, however—that no one suspected it but Osmond. Oh, he knew it, and there were times when she thought he enjoyed it. It had come gradually—it was not till the first year of their life together, so admirably intimate at first, had closed that she had taken the alarm. Then the shadows had begun to gather; it was as if Osmond deliberately, almost malignantly, had put the lights out one by one. The dusk at first was vague and thin, and she could still see her way in it. But it steadily deepened, and if now and again it had occasionally lifted there were certain corners of her prospect that were impenetrably black. These shadows were not an emanation from her own mind: she was very sure of that; she had done her best to be just and temperate, to see only the truth. They were a part, they were a kind of creation and consequence, of her husband's very presence. They were not his misdeeds, his turpitudes; she accused him of nothing—that is but of one thing, which was *not* a crime. She knew of no wrong he had done; he was not violent, he was not cruel: she simply believed he hated her. That was all she accused him of, and the miserable part of it was precisely that it was not a crime, for against a crime she might have found redress. He had discovered that she was so different, that she was not what he had believed she would prove to be. He had thought at first he could change her, and she had done her best to be what he would like. But she was, after all, herself—she couldn't help that; and now there was no use pretending, wearing a mask or a dress, for he knew her and had made up his mind. She was not afraid of him; she had no apprehension he would hurt her; for the ill-will he bore her was not of that sort. He would if possible never give her a pretext, never put himself in the wrong. Isabel, scanning the future with dry, fixed eyes, saw that he would have the better of her there. She would give him many pretexts, she would often put herself in the wrong. There were times when she almost pitied him; for if she had not deceived him in intention she understood how completely she must have done so in fact. She had effaced herself when he first knew her; she had made herself small, pretending there was less of her than there really was. It was because she had been under the extraordinary charm that he, on his side, had taken pains to put forth. He was not changed; he had not disguised himself, during the year of his courtship, any more than she. But she had seen only half his nature then, as one saw the disk of the moon when it was partly masked by the shadow of the earth. She saw the full moon now—she saw the whole man. She had kept still, as it were, so that he should have a free field, and yet in spite of this she had mistaken a part for the whole.

Ah, she had been immensely under the charm! It had not passed away; it was there still: she still knew perfectly what it was that made Osmond delightful when he chose to be. He had wished to be when he made love to her, and as she had wished to be charmed it was not wonderful he had succeeded. He had succeeded because he had been sincere; it never occurred to her now to deny him that. He admired her—he had told her why: because she was the most imaginative woman he had known. It might very well have been true; for during those months she had imagined a world of things that had no substance. She had had a more wondrous vision of him, fed through charmed senses and oh such a stirred fancy!— she had not read him right. A certain combination of features had touched her, and in them she had seen the most striking of figures. That he was poor and lonely and yet that somehow he was noble— that was what had interested her and seemed to give her her opportunity. There had been an indefinable beauty about him—in his situation, in his mind, in his face. She had felt at the same time that he was helpless and ineffectual, but the feeling had taken the form of a tenderness which was the very flower of respect. He was like a sceptical voyager strolling on the beach while he waited for the tide, looking seaward yet not putting to sea. It was in all this she had found her occasion. She would launch his boat for him; she would be his providence; it would be a good thing to love him. And she had loved him, she had so anxiously and yet so ardently given herself—a good deal for what she found in him, but a good deal also for what she brought him and what might enrich the gift. As she looked back at the passion of those full weeks she perceived in it a kind of maternal strain—the happiness of a woman who felt that she was a contributor, that she came with charged hands. But for her money, as she saw to-day, she would never have done it. And then her mind wandered off to poor Mr. Touchett, sleeping under English turf, the beneficent author of infinite woe! For this was the fantastic fact. At bottom her money had been a burden, had been on her mind, which was filled with the desire to transfer the weight of it to some other conscience, to some more prepared receptacle. What would lighten her own conscience more effectually than to make it over to the man with the best taste in the world? Unless she should have given it to a hospital there would have been nothing better she could do with it; and there was no charitable institution in which she had been as much interested as in Gilbert Osmond. He would use her fortune in a way that would make her think better of it and rub off a certain grossness attaching to the good luck of an unexpected inheritance. There had been nothing very delicate in inheriting seventy thousand pounds; the delicacy had been all in Mr. Touchett's leaving them to her. But to marry Gilbert Osmond and bring him such a portion—in that there would be delicacy for her as well. There would be less for him—that was true; but that was his affair, and if he loved her he wouldn't object to her being rich. Had he not had the courage to say he was glad she was rich?

Isabel's cheek burned when she asked herself if she had really married on a factitious theory, in order to do something finely appreciable with her money. But she was able to answer quickly enough that this was only half the story. It was because a certain ardour took possession of her—a sense of the earnestness of his affection and a delight in his personal qualities. He was better than any one else. This supreme conviction had filled her life for months, and enough of it still remained to prove to her that she could not have done otherwise. The finest—in the sense of being the subtlest—manly organism she had ever known had become her property, and the recognition of her having but to put out her hands and take it had been originally a sort of act of devotion. She had not been mistaken about the beauty of his mind; she knew that organ perfectly now. She had lived with it, she had lived *in* it almost—it appeared to have become her habitation. If she had been captured it had taken a firm hand to seize her; that reflection perhaps had some worth. A mind more ingenious, more pliant, more cultivated, more trained to admirable exercises, she had not encountered; and it was this exquisite instrument she had now to reckon with. She lost herself in infinite dismay when she thought of the magnitude of *his* deception. It was a wonder, perhaps, in view of this, that he didn't hate her more. She remembered perfectly the first sign he had given of it—it had been like the bell that was to ring up the curtain upon the real drama of their life. He said to her one day that she had too many ideas and that she must get rid of them. He had told her that already, before their marriage; but then she had not noticed it: it had come back to her only afterwards. This time she might well have noticed it, because he had really meant it. The words had been nothing superficially; but when in the light of deepening experience she had looked into them they had then appeared portentous. He had really meant it—he would have liked her to have nothing of her own but her pretty appearance. She had known she had too many ideas; she had more even than he had supposed, many more than she had expressed to him when he had asked her to marry him. Yes, she *had* been hypocritical; she had liked him so much. She had too many ideas for herself; but that was just what one married for, to share them with some one else. One couldn't pluck them up by the roots, though of course one might suppress them, be careful not to utter them. It had not been this, however, his objecting to her opinions; this had been nothing. She had no opinions—none that she would not have been eager to sacrifice in the satisfaction of feeling herself loved for it. What he had meant had been the whole thing —her character, the way she felt, the way she judged. This was what she had kept in reserve; this was what he had not known until he had found himself—with the door closed behind, as it were—set down face to face with it. She had a certain way of looking at life which he took as a personal offence. Heaven knew that now at least it was a very humble, accommodating way! The strange thing was that she should not have suspected from the first that his own had been so different. She had thought it so large, so enlightened, so perfectly that of an honest man and a gentleman. Hadn't he assured her that he had no superstitions, no dull limitations, no prejudices that had lost their freshness? Hadn't he all the appearance of a man living in the open air of the world, indifferent to small considerations, caring only for truth and knowledge and believing that two intelligent people ought to look for them together and, whether they found them or not, find at least some happiness in the search? He had told her he loved the conventional, but there was a sense in which this seemed a noble declaration. In that sense, that of the love of harmony and order and decency and of all the stately offices of life, she went with him freely, and his warning had contained nothing ominous. But when, as the months had elapsed, she had followed him further and he had led her into the mansion of his own habitation, then, *then* she had seen where she really was.

She could live it over again, the incredulous terror with which she had taken the measure of her dwelling. Between those four walls she had lived ever since; they were to surround her for the rest of her life. It was the house of darkness, the house of dumbness, the house of suffocation. Osmond's beautiful mind gave it neither light nor air; Osmond's beautiful mind indeed seemed to peep down from a small high window and mock at her. Of course it had not been physical suffering; for physical suffering there might have been a remedy. She could come and go; she had her liberty; her husband was perfectly polite. He took himself so seriously; it was something appalling. Under all his culture, his cleverness, his amenity, under his good-nature, his facility, his knowledge of life, his egotism lay hidden like a serpent in a bank of flowers. She had taken him seriously, but she had not taken him so seriously as that. How could she —especially when she had known him better? She was to think of him as he thought of himself—as the first gentleman in Europe. So it was that she had thought of him at first, and that indeed was the reason she had married him. But when she began to see what it implied she drew back; there was more in the bond than she had meant to put her name to. It implied a sovereign contempt for every one but some three or four very exalted people whom he envied, and for everything in the world but half a dozen ideas of his own. That was very well; she would have gone with him even there a long distance; for he pointed out to her so much of the baseness and shabbiness of life, opened her eyes so wide to the stupidity, the depravity, the ignorance of mankind, that she had been properly impressed with the infinite vulgarity of things and of the virtue of keeping one's self unspotted by it. But this base, ignoble world, it appeared, was after all what one was to live for; one was to keep it for ever in one's eye, in order not to enlighten or convert or redeem it, but to extract from it some recognition of one's own superiority. On the one hand it was despicable, but on the other it afforded a standard. Osmond had talked to Isabel about his renunciation, his indifference, the ease with which he dispensed with the usual aids to success; and all this had seemed to her admirable. She had thought it a grand indifference, an exquisite independence. But indifference was really the last of his qualities; she had never seen any one who thought so much of others. For herself, avowedly, the world had always interested her and the study of her fellow creatures been her constant passion. She would have been willing, however, to renounce all her curiosities and sympathies for the sake of a personal life, if the person concerned had only been able to make her believe it was a gain! This at least was her present conviction; and the thing certainly would have been easier than to care for society as Osmond cared for it.

He was unable to live without it, and she saw that he had never really done so; he had looked at it out of his window even when he appeared to be most detached from it. He had his ideal, just as she had tried to have hers; only it was strange that people should seek for justice in such different quarters. His ideal was a conception of high prosperity and propriety, of the aristocratic life, which she now saw that he deemed himself always, in essence at least, to have led. He had never lapsed from it for an hour; he would never have recovered from the shame of doing so. That again was very well; here too she would have agreed; but they attached such different ideas, such different associations and desires, to the same formulas. Her notion of the aristocratic life was simply the union of great knowledge with great liberty; the knowledge would give one a sense of duty and the liberty a sense of enjoyment. But for Osmond it was altogether a thing of forms, a conscious, calculated attitude. He was fond of the old, the consecrated, the transmitted; so was she, but she pretended to do what she chose with it. He had an immense esteem for tradition; he had told her once that the best thing in the world was to have it, but that if one was so unfortunate as not to have it one must immediately proceed to make it. She knew that he meant by this that she hadn't it, but that he was better off; though from what source he had derived his traditions she never learned. He had a very large collection of them, however; that was very certain, and after a little she began to see. The great thing was to act in accordance with them; the great thing not only for him but for her. Isabel had an undefined conviction that to serve for another person than their proprietor traditions must be of a thoroughly superior kind; but she nevertheless assented to this intimation that she too must march to the stately music that floated down from unknown periods in her husband's past; she who of old had been so free of step, so desultory, so devious, so much the reverse of processional. There were certain things they must do, a certain posture they must take, certain people they must know and not know. When she saw this rigid system close about her, draped though it was in pictured tapestries, that sense of darkness and suffocation of which I have spoken took possession of her; she seemed shut up with an odour of mould and decay. She had resisted of course; at first very humorously, ironically, tenderly; then, as the situation grew more serious, eagerly, passionately, pleadingly. She had pleaded the cause of freedom, of doing as they chose, of not caring for the aspect and denomination of their life—the cause of other instincts and longings, of quite another ideal.

Then it was that her husband's personality, touched as it never had been, stepped forth and stood erect. The things she had said were answered only by his scorn, and she could see he was ineffably ashamed of her. What did he think of her—that she was base, vulgar, ignoble? He at least knew now that she had no traditions! It had not been in his prevision of things that she should reveal such flatness; her sentiments were worthy of a radical newspaper or a Unitarian preacher. The real offence, as she ultimately perceived, was her having a mind of her own at all. Her mind was to be his— attached to his own like a small garden-plot to a deer-park. He would rake the soil gently and water the flowers; he would weed the beds and gather an occasional nosegay. It would be a pretty piece of property for a proprietor already far-reaching. He didn't wish her to be stupid. On the contrary, it was because she was clever that she had pleased him. But he expected her intelligence to operate altogether in his favour, and so far from desiring her mind to be a blank he had flattered himself that it would be richly receptive. He had expected his wife to feel with him and for him, to enter into his opinions, his ambitions, his preferences; and Isabel was obliged to confess that this was no great insolence on the part of a man so accomplished and a husband originally at least so tender. But there were certain things she could never take in. To begin with, they were hideously unclean. She was not a daughter of the Puritans, but for all that she believed in such a thing as chastity and even as decency. It would appear that Osmond was far from doing anything of the sort; some of his traditions made her push back her skirts. Did all women have lovers? Did they all lie and even the best have their price? Were there only three or four that didn't deceive their husbands? When Isabel heard such things she felt a greater scorn for them than for the gossip of a village parlour—a scorn that kept its freshness in a very tainted air. There was the taint of her sister-in-law: did her husband judge only by the Countess Gemini? This lady very often lied, and she practised deceptions that were not simply verbal. It was enough to find these facts assumed among Osmond's traditions—it was enough without giving them such a general extension. It was her scorn of his assumptions, it was this that made him draw himself up. He had plenty of contempt, and it was proper his wife should be as well furnished; but that she should turn the hot light of her disdain upon his own conception of things —this was a danger he had not allowed for. He believed he should have regulated her emotions before she came to it; and Isabel could easily imagine how his ears had scorched on his discovering he had been too confident. When one had a wife who gave one that sensation there was nothing left but to hate her.

She was morally certain now that this feeling of hatred, which at first had been a refuge and a refreshment, had become the occupation and comfort of his life. The feeling was deep, because it was sincere; he had had the revelation that she could after all dispense with him. If to herself the idea was startling, if it presented itself at first as a kind of infidelity, a capacity for pollution, what infinite effect might it not be expected to have had upon *him?* It was very simple; he despised her; she had no traditions and the moral horizon of a Unitarian minister. Poor Isabel, who had never been able to understand Unitarianism! This was the certitude she had been living with now for a time that she had ceased to measure. What was coming—what was before them? That was her constant question. What would he do—what ought *she* to do? When a man hated his wife what did it lead to? She didn't hate him, that she was sure of, for every little while she felt a passionate wish to give him a pleasant surprise. Very often, however, she felt afraid, and it used to come over her, as I have intimated, that she had deceived him at the very first. They were strangely married, at all events, and it was a horrible life. Until that morning he had scarcely spoken to her for a week; his manner was as dry as a burned-out fire. She knew there was a special reason; he was displeased at Ralph Touchett's staying on in Rome. He thought she saw too much of her cousin—he had told her a week before it was indecent she should go to him at his hotel. He would have said more than this if Ralph's invalid state had not appeared to make it brutal to denounce him; but having had to contain himself had only deepened his disgust. Isabel read all this as she would have read the hour on the clock-face; she was as perfectly aware that the sight of her interest in her cousin stirred her husband's rage as if Osmond had locked her into her room—which she was sure was what he wanted to do. It was her honest belief that on the whole she was not defiant, but she certainly couldn't pretend to be indifferent to Ralph. She believed he was dying at last and that she should never see him again, and this gave her a tenderness for him that she had never known before. Nothing was a pleasure to her now; how could anything be a pleasure to a woman who knew that she had thrown away her life? There was an everlasting weight on her heart—there was a livid light on everything. But Ralph's little visit was a lamp in the darkness; for the hour that she sat with him her ache for herself became somehow her ache for *him*. She felt to-day as if he had been her brother. She had never had a brother, but if she had and she were in trouble and he were dying, he would be dear to her as Ralph was. Ah yes, if Gilbert was jealous of her there was perhaps some reason; it didn't make Gilbert look better to sit for half an hour with Ralph. It was not that they talked of him—it was not that she complained. His name was never uttered between them. It was simply that Ralph was generous and that her husband was not. There was something in Ralph's talk, in his smile, in the mere fact of his being in Rome, that made the blasted circle round which she walked more spacious. He made her feel the good of the world; he made her feel what might have been. He was after all as intelligent as Osmond—quite apart from his being better. And thus it seemed to her an act of devotion to conceal her misery from him. She concealed it elaborately; she was perpetually, in their talk, hanging out curtains and arranging screens. It lived before her again—it had never had time to die—that morning in the garden at Florence when he had warned her against Osmond. She had only to close her eyes to see the place, to hear his voice, to feel the warm, sweet air. How could he have known? What a mystery, what a wonder of wisdom! As intelligent as Gilbert? He was much more intelligent— to arrive at such a judgement as that. Gilbert had never been so deep, so just. She had told him then that from her at least he should never know if he was right; and this was what she was taking care of now. It gave her plenty to do; there was passion, exaltation, religion in it. Women find their religion sometimes in strange exercises, and Isabel at present, in playing a part before her cousin, had an idea that she was doing him a kindness. It would have been a kindness perhaps if he had been for a single instant a dupe. As it was, the kindness consisted mainly in trying to make him believe that he had once wounded her greatly and that the event had put him to shame, but that, as she was very generous and he was so ill, she bore him no grudge and even considerately forbore to flaunt her happiness in his face. Ralph smiled to himself, as he lay on his sofa, at this extraordinary form of consideration; but he forgave her for having forgiven him. She didn't wish him to have the pain of knowing she was unhappy: that was the great thing, and it didn't matter that such knowledge would rather have righted him.

For herself, she lingered in the soundless saloon long after the fire had gone out. There was no danger of her feeling the cold; she was in a fever. She heard the small hours strike, and then the great ones, but her vigil took no heed of time. Her mind, assailed by visions, was in a state of extraordinary activity, and her visions might as well come to her there, where she sat up to meet them, as on her pillow, to make a mockery of rest. As I have said, she believed she was not defiant, and what could be a better proof of it than that she should linger there half the night, trying to persuade herself that there was no reason why Pansy shouldn't be married as you would put a letter in the post-office? When the clock struck four she got up; she was going to bed at last, for the lamp had long since gone out and the candles burned down to their sockets. But even then she stopped again in the middle of the room and stood there gazing at a remembered vision—that of her husband and Madame Merle unconsciously and familiarly associated.

XLIII

Three nights after this she took Pansy to a great party, to which Osmond, who never went to dances, did not accompany them. Pansy was as ready for a dance as ever; she was not of a generalising turn and had not extended to other pleasures the interdict she had seen placed on those of love. If she was biding her time or hoping to circumvent her father she must have had a prevision of success. Isabel thought this unlikely; it was much more likely that Pansy had simply determined to be a good girl. She had never had such a chance, and she had a proper esteem for chances. She carried herself no less attentively than usual and kept no less anxious an eye upon her vaporous skirts; she held her bouquet very tight and counted over the flowers for the twentieth time. She made Isabel feel old; it seemed so long since she had been in a flutter about a ball. Pansy, who was greatly admired, was never in want of partners, and very soon after their arrival she gave Isabel, who was not dancing, her bouquet to hold. Isabel had rendered her this service for some minutes when she became aware of the near presence of Edward Rosier. He stood before her; he had lost his affable smile and wore a look of almost military resolution. The change in his appearance would have made Isabel smile if she had not felt his case to be at bottom a hard one: he had always smelt so much more of heliotrope than of gunpowder. He looked at her a moment somewhat fiercely, as if to notify her he was dangerous, and then dropped his eyes on her bouquet. After he had inspected it his glance softened and he said quickly: "It's all pansies; it must be hers!"

Isabel smiled kindly. "Yes, it's hers; she gave it to me to hold."

"May I hold it a little, Mrs. Osmond?" the poor young man asked.

"No, I can't trust you; I'm afraid you wouldn't give it back."

"I'm not sure that I should; I should leave the house with it instantly. But may I not at least have a single flower?"

Isabel hesitated a moment, and then, smiling still, held out the bouquet. "Choose one yourself. It's frightful what I'm doing for you."

"Ah, if you do no more than this, Mrs. Osmond!" Rosier exclaimed with his glass in one eye, carefully choosing his flower.

"Don't put it into your button-hole," she said. "Don't for the world!"

"I should like her to see it. She has refused to dance with me, but I wish to show her that I believe in her still."

"It's very well to show it to her, but it's out of place to show it to others. Her father has told her not to dance with you."

"And is that all *you* can do for me? I expected more from you,

Mrs. Osmond," said the young man in a tone of fine general reference. "You know our acquaintance goes back very far—quite into
the days of our innocent childhood."

"Don't make me out too old," Isabel patiently answered. "You
come back to that very often, and I've never denied it. But I must
tell you that, old friends as we are, if you had done me the honour
to ask me to marry you I should have refused you on the spot."

"Ah, you don't esteem me then. Say at once that you think me a
mere Parisian trifler!"

"I esteem you very much, but I'm not in love with you. What I
mean by that, of course, is that I'm not in love with you for
Pansy."

"Very good; I see. You pity me—that's all." And Edward Rosier
looked all round, inconsequently, with his single glass. It was a revelation to him that people shouldn't be more pleased; but he was at
least too proud to show that the deficiency struck him as general.

Isabel for a moment said nothing. His manner and appearance
had not the dignity of the deepest tragedy; his little glass, among
other things, was against that. But she suddenly felt touched; her
own unhappiness, after all, had something in common with his, and
it came over her, more than before, that here, in recognisable, if not
in romantic form, was the most affecting thing in the world—young
love struggling with adversity. "Would you really be very kind to
her?" she finally asked in a low tone.

He dropped his eyes devoutly and raised the little flower that he
held in his fingers to his lips. Then he looked at her. "You pity me;
but don't you pity *her* a little?"

"I don't know; I'm not sure. She'll always enjoy life."

"It will depend on what you call life!" Mr. Rosier effectively said.
"She won't enjoy being tortured."

"There'll be nothing of that."

"I'm glad to hear it. She knows what she's about. You'll see."

"I think she does, and she'll never disobey her father. But she's
coming back to me," Isabel added, "and I must beg you to go
away."

Rosier lingered a moment till Pansy came in sight on the arm of
her cavalier; he stood just long enough to look her in the face. Then
he walked away, holding up his head; and the manner in which he
achieved this sacrifice to expediency convinced Isabel he was very
much in love.

Pansy, who seldom got disarranged in dancing, looking perfectly
fresh and cool after this exercise, waited a moment and then took
back her bouquet. Isabel watched her and saw she was counting the
flowers; whereupon she said to herself that decidedly there were
deeper forces at play than she had recognised. Pansy had seen
Rosier turn away, but she said nothing to Isabel about him; she

talked only of her partner, after he had made his bow and retired; of the music, the floor, the rare misfortune of having already torn her dress. Isabel was sure, however, she had discovered her lover to have abstracted a flower; though this knowledge was not needed to account for the dutiful grace with which she responded to the appeal of her next partner. That perfect amenity under acute constraint was part of a larger system. She was again led forth by a flushed young man, this time carrying her bouquet; and she had not been absent many minutes when Isabel saw Lord Warburton advancing through the crowd. He presently drew near and bade her good-evening; she had not seen him since the day before. He looked about him, and then "Where's the little maid?" he asked. It was in this manner that he had formed the harmless habit of alluding to Miss Osmond.

"She's dancing," said Isabel. "You'll see her somewhere."

He looked among the dancers and at last caught Pansy's eye. "She sees me, but she won't notice me," he then remarked. "Are you not dancing?"

"As you see, I'm a wall-flower."

"Won't you dance with me?"

"Thank you; I'd rather you should dance with the little maid."

"One needn't prevent the other—especially as she's engaged."

"She's not engaged for everything, and you can reserve yourself. She dances very hard, and you'll be the fresher."

"She dances beautifully," said Lord Warburton, following her with his eyes. "Ah, at last," he added, "she has given me a smile." He stood there with his handsome, easy, important physiognomy; and as Isabel observed him it came over her, as it had done before, that it was strange a man of his mettle should take an interest in a little maid. It struck her as a great incongruity; neither Pansy's small fascinations, nor his own kindness, his good-nature, not even his need for amusement, which was extreme and constant, were sufficient to account for it. "I should like to dance with you," he went on in a moment, turning back to Isabel; "but I think I like even better to talk with you."

"Yes, it's better, and it's more worthy of your dignity. Great statesmen oughtn't to waltz."

"Don't be cruel. Why did you recommend me then to dance with Miss Osmond?"

"Ah, that's different. If you danced with her it would look simply like a piece of kindness—as if you were doing it for her amusement. If you dance with me you'll look as if you were doing it for your own."

"And pray haven't I a right to amuse myself?"

"No, not with the affairs of the British Empire on your hands."

"The British Empire be hanged! You're always laughing at it."

"Amuse yourself with talking to me," said Isabel.

"I'm not sure it's really a recreation. You're too pointed; I've always to be defending myself. And you strike me as more than usually dangerous to-night. Will you absolutely not dance?"

"I can't leave my place. Pansy must find me here."

He was silent a little. "You're wonderfully good to her," he said suddenly.

Isabel stared a little and smiled. "Can you imagine one's not being?"

"No indeed. I know how one is charmed with her. But you must have done a great deal for her."

"I've taken her out with me," said Isabel, smiling still. "And I've seen that she has proper clothes."

"Your society must have been a great benefit to her. You've talked to her, advised her, helped her to develop."

"Ah yes, if she isn't the rose she has lived near it."

She laughed, and her companion did as much; but there was a certain visible preoccupation in his face which interfered with complete hilarity. "We all try to live as near it as we can," he said after a moment's hesitation.

Isabel turned away; Pansy was about to be restored to her, and she welcomed the diversion. We know how much she liked Lord Warburton; she thought him pleasanter even than the sum of his merits warranted; there was something in his friendship that appeared a kind of resource in case of indefinite need; it was like having a large balance at the bank. She felt happier when he was in the room; there was something reassuring in his approach; the sound of his voice reminded her of the beneficence of nature. Yet for all that it didn't suit her that he should be too near her, that he should take too much of her good-will for granted. She was afraid of that; she averted herself from it; she wished he wouldn't. She felt that if he should come too near, as it were, it might be in her to flash out and bid him keep his distance. Pansy came back to Isabel with another rent in her skirt, which was the inevitable consequence of the first and which she displayed to Isabel with serious eyes. There were too many gentlemen in uniform; they wore those dreadful spurs, which were fatal to the dresses of little maids. It hereupon became apparent that the resources of women are innumerable. Isabel devoted herself to Pansy's desecrated drapery; she fumbled for a pin and repaired the injury; she smiled and listened to her account of her adventures. Her attention, her sympathy were immediate and active; and they were in direct proportion to a sentiment with which they were in no way connected—a lively conjecture as to whether Lord Warburton might be trying to make love to her. It was not simply his words just then; it was others as well; it was the reference and the continuity. This was what she thought about while she pinned up Pansy's dress. If it were so, as she feared, he was of course unwitting; he himself had not taken account of his intention. But this made it none the more auspicious, made the situation none the less impossible. The sooner he should get back into right relations with things the better. He immediately began to talk to Pansy—on whom it was certainly mystifying to see that he dropped a smile of chastened devotion. Pansy replied, as usual, with a little air of conscientious aspiration; he had to bend toward her a good deal in conversation, and her eyes, as usual, wandered up and down his robust person as if he had offered it to her for exhibition. She always seemed a little frightened; yet her fright was not of the painful character that suggests dislike; on the contrary, she looked as if she knew that he knew she liked him. Isabel left them together a little and wandered toward a friend whom she saw near and with whom she talked till the music of the following dance began, for which she knew Pansy to be also engaged. The girl joined her presently, with a little fluttered flush, and Isabel, who scrupulously took Osmond's view of his daughter's complete dependence, consigned her, as a precious and momentary loan, to her appointed partner. About all this matter she had her own imaginations, her own reserves; there were moments when Pansy's extreme adhesiveness made each of them, to her sense, look foolish. But Osmond had given her a sort of tableau[1] of her position as his daughter's duenna, which consisted of gracious alternations of concession and contraction; and there were directions of his which she liked to think she obeyed to the letter. Perhaps, as regards some of them, it was because her doing so appeared to reduce them to the absurd.

After Pansy had been led away, she found Lord Warburton drawing near her again. She rested her eyes on him steadily; she wished she could sound his thoughts. But he had no appearance of confusion. "She has promised to dance with me later," he said.

"I'm glad of that. I suppose you've engaged her for the cotillion."[2]

At this he looked a little awkward. "No, I didn't ask her for that. It's a quadrille."[3]

"Ah, you're not clever!" said Isabel almost angrily. "I told her to keep the cotillion in case you should ask for it."

"Poor little maid, fancy that!" And Lord Warburton laughed frankly. "Of course I will if you like."

"If I like? Oh, if you dance with her only because I like it—!"

"I'm afraid I bore her. She seems to have a lot of young fellows on her book."

Isabel dropped her eyes, reflecting rapidly; Lord Warburton stood there looking at her and she felt his eyes on her face. She felt much

1. List, schedule.
2. A series of elaborate and varied dances.
3. A square dance of French origin for four or more couples.

inclined to ask him to remove them. She didn't do so, however; she only said to him, after a minute, with her own raised: "Please let me understand."

"Understand what?"

"You told me ten days ago that you'd like to marry my step-daughter. You've not forgotten it!"

"Forgotten it? I wrote to Mr. Osmond about it this morning."

"Ah," said Isabel, "he didn't mention to me that he had heard from you."

Lord Warburton stammered a little. "I—I didn't send my letter."

"Perhaps you forgot *that*."

"No, I wasn't satisfied with it. It's an awkward sort of letter to write, you know. But I shall send it to-night."

"At three o'clock in the morning?"

"I mean later, in the course of the day."

"Very good. You still wish then to marry her?"

"Very much indeed."

"Aren't you afraid that you'll bore her?" And as her companion stared at this enquiry Isabel added: "If she can't dance with you for half an hour how will she be able to dance with you for life?"

"Ah," said Lord Warburton readily, "I'll let her dance with other people! About the cotillion, the fact is I thought that you—that you—"

"That I would do it with you? I told you I'd do nothing."

"Exactly; so that while it's going on I might find some quiet corner where we may sit down and talk."

"Oh," said Isabel gravely, "you're much too considerate of me."

When the cotillion came Pansy was found to have engaged herself, thinking, in perfect humility, that Lord Warburton had no intentions. Isabel recommended him to seek another partner, but he assured her that he would dance with no one but herself. As, however, she had, in spite of the remonstrances of her hostess, declined other invitations on the ground that she was not dancing at all, it was not possible for her to make an exception in Lord Warburton's favour.

"After all I don't care to dance," he said; "it's a barbarous amusement: I'd much rather talk." And he intimated that he had discovered exactly the corner he had been looking for—a quiet nook in one of the smaller rooms, where the music would come to them faintly and not interfere with conversation. Isabel had decided to let him carry out his idea; she wished to be satisfied. She wandered away from the ball-room with him, though she knew her husband desired she should not lose sight of his daughter. It was with his daughter's *prétendant*,[4] however; that would make it right for

4. Suitor, wooer.

Osmond. On her way out of the ball-room she came upon Edward Rosier, who was standing in a doorway, with folded arms, looking at the dance in the attitude of a young man without illusions. She stopped a moment and asked him if he were not dancing.

"Certainly not, if I can't dance with *her!*" he answered.

"You had better go away then," said Isabel with the manner of good counsel.

"I shall not go till she does!" And he let Lord Warburton pass without giving him a look.

This nobleman, however, had noticed the melancholy youth, and he asked Isabel who her dismal friend was, remarking that he had seen him somewhere before.

"It's the young man I've told you about, who's in love with Pansy."

"Ah yes, I remember. He looks rather bad."

"He has reason. My husband won't listen to him."

"What's the matter with him?" Lord Warburton enquired. "He seems very harmless."

"He hasn't money enough, and he isn't very clever."

Lord Warburton listened with interest; he seemed struck with this account of Edward Rosier. "Dear me; he looked a well-set-up young fellow."

"So he is, but my husband's very particular."

"Oh, I see." And Lord Warburton paused a moment. "How much money has he got?" he then ventured to ask.

"Some forty thousand francs a year."

"Sixteen hundred pounds? Ah, but that's very good, you know."

"So I think. My husband, however, has larger ideas."

"Yes; I've noticed that your husband has very large ideas. Is he really an idiot, the young man?"

"An idiot? Not in the least; he's charming. When he was twelve years old I myself was in love with him."

"He doesn't look much more than twelve to-day," Lord Warburton rejoined vaguely, looking about him. Then with more point, "Don't you think we might sit here?" he asked.

"Wherever you please." The room was a sort of boudoir, pervaded by a subdued, rose-coloured light; a lady and gentleman moved out of it as our friends came in. "It's very kind of you to take such an interest in Mr. Rosier," Isabel said.

"He seems to me rather ill-treated. He had a face a yard long. I wondered what ailed him."

"You're a just man," said Isabel. "You've a kind thought even for a rival."

Lord Warburton suddenly turned with a stare. "A rival! Do you call him my rival?"

"Surely—if you both wish to marry the same person."

"Yes—but since he has no chance!"

"I like you, however that may be, for putting yourself in his place. It shows imagination."

"You like me for it?" And Lord Warburton looked at her with an uncertain eye. "I think you mean you're laughing at me for it."

"Yes, I'm laughing at you a little. But I like you as somebody to laugh at."

"Ah well, then, let me enter into his situation a little more. What do you suppose one could do for him?"

"Since I have been praising your imagination I'll leave you to imagine that yourself," Isabel said. "Pansy too would like you for that."

"Miss Osmond? Ah, she, I flatter myself, likes me already."

"Very much, I think."

He waited a little; he was still questioning her face. "Well then, I don't understand you. You don't mean that she cares for him?"

"Surely I've told you I thought she did."

A quick blush sprang to his brow. "You told me she would have no wish apart from her father's, and as I've gathered that he would favour me—!" He paused a little and then suggested "Don't you see?" through his blush.

"Yes, I told you she has an immense wish to please her father, and that it would probably take her very far."

"That seems to me a very proper feeling," said Lord Warburton.

"Certainly; it's a very proper feeling." Isabel remained silent for some moments; the room continued empty; the sound of the music reached them with its richness softened by the interposing apartments. Then at last she said: "But it hardly strikes me as the sort of feeling to which a man would wish to be indebted for a wife."

"I don't know; if the wife's a good one and he thinks she does well!"

"Yes, of course you must think that."

"I do; I can't help it. You call that very British, of course."

"No, I don't. I think Pansy would do wonderfully well to marry you, and I don't know who should know it better than you. But you're not in love."

"Ah, yes I am, Mrs. Osmond!"

Isabel shook her head. "You like to think you are while you sit here with me. But that's not how you strike me."

"I'm not like the young man in the doorway. I admit that. But what makes it so unnatural? Could any one in the world be more loveable than Miss Osmond?"

"No one, possibly. But love has nothing to do with good reasons."

"I don't agree with you. I'm delighted to have good reasons."

"Of course you are. If you were really in love you wouldn't care a straw for them."

"Ah, really in love—really in love!" Lord Warburton exclaimed, folding his arms, leaning back his head and stretching himself a little. "You must remember that I'm forty-two years old. I won't pretend I'm as I once was."

"Well, if you're sure," said Isabel, "it's all right."

He answered nothing; he sat there, with his head back, looking before him. Abruptly, however, he changed his position; he turned quickly to his friend. "Why are you so unwilling, so sceptical?"

She met his eyes, and for a moment they looked straight at each other. If she wished to be satisfied she saw something that satisfied her; she saw in his expression the gleam of an idea that she was uneasy on her own account—that she was perhaps even in fear. It showed a suspicion, not a hope, but such as it was it told her what she wanted to know. Not for an instant should he suspect her of detecting in his proposal of marrying her step-daughter an implication of increased nearness to herself, or of thinking it, on such a betrayal, ominous. In that brief, extremely personal gaze, however, deeper meanings passed between them than they were conscious of at the moment.

"My dear Lord Warburton," she said, smiling, "you may do, so far as I'm concerned, whatever comes into your head."

And with this she got up and wandered into the adjoining room, where, within her companion's view, she was immediately addressed by a pair of gentlemen, high personages in the Roman world, who met her as if they had been looking for her. While she talked with them she found herself regretting she had moved; it looked a little like running away—all the more as Lord Warburton didn't follow her. She was glad of this, however, and at any rate she was satisfied. She was so well satisfied that when, in passing back into the ballroom, she found Edward Rosier still planted in the doorway, she stopped and spoke to him again. "You did right not to go away. I've some comfort for you."

"I need it," the young man softly wailed, "when I see you so awfully thick with *him!*"

"Don't speak of him; I'll do what I can for you. I'm afraid it won't be much, but what I can I'll do."

He looked at her with gloomy obliqueness. "What has suddenly brought you round?"

"The sense that you are an inconvenience in doorways!" she answered, smiling as she passed him. Half an hour later she took leave, with Pansy, and at the foot of the staircase the two ladies, with many other departing guests, waited a while for their carriage. Just as it approached Lord Warburton came out of the house and assisted them to reach their vehicle. He stood a moment at the door, asking Pansy if she had amused herself; and she, having answered him, fell back with a little air of fatigue. Then Isabel, at the window, detaining him by a movement of her finger, murmured gently: "Don't forget to send your letter to her father!"

XLIV

The Countess Gemini was often extremely bored—bored, in her own phrase, to extinction. She had not been extinguished, however, and she struggled bravely enough with her destiny, which had been to marry an unaccommodating Florentine who insisted upon living in his native town, where he enjoyed such consideration as might attach to a gentleman whose talent for losing at cards had not the merit of being incidental to an obliging disposition. The Count Gemini was not liked even by those who won from him; and he bore a name which, having a measurable value in Florence,[1] was, like the local coin of the old Italian states, without currency in other parts of the peninsula. In Rome he was simply a very dull Florentine, and it is not remarkable that he should not have cared to pay frequent visits to a place where, to carry it off, his dulness needed more explanation than was convenient. The Countess lived with her eyes upon Rome, and it was the constant grievance of her life that she had not an habitation there. She was ashamed to say how seldom she had been allowed to visit that city; it scarcely made the matter better that there were other members of the Florentine nobility who never had been there at all. She went whenever she could; that was all she could say. Or rather not all, but all she said she could say. In fact she had much more to say about it, and had often set forth the reasons why she hated Florence and wished to end her days in the shadow of Saint Peter's. They are reasons, however, that do not closely concern us, and were usually summed up in the declaration that Rome, in short, was the Eternal City and that Florence was simply a pretty little place like any other. The Countess apparently needed to connect the idea of eternity with her amusements. She was convinced that society was infinitely more interesting in Rome, where you met celebrities all winter at evening parties. At Florence there were no celebrities; none at least that one had heard of. Since her brother's marriage her impatience had greatly increased; she was so sure his wife had a more brilliant life than herself. She was not so intellectual as Isabel, but she was intellectual enough to do justice to Rome—not to the ruins and the catacombs, not even perhaps to the monuments and museums, the

---

1. By 1865–1870, when it was the provincial capital of Italy, Florence had become the hospitable residence of exiles, political refugees, artists, and writers. When the capital moved to Rome, Florence was left somewhat impoverished and disordered.

church ceremonies and the scenery; but certainly to all the rest. She heard a great deal about her sister-in-law and knew perfectly that Isabel was having a beautiful time. She had indeed seen it for herself on the only occasion on which she had enjoyed the hospitality of Palazzo Roccanera. She had spent a week there during the first winter of her brother's marriage, but she had not been encouraged to renew this satisfaction. Osmond didn't want her—that she was perfectly aware of; but she would have gone all the same, for after all she didn't care two straws about Osmond. It was her husband who wouldn't let her, and the money question was always a trouble. Isabel had been very nice; the Countess, who had liked her sister-in-law from the first, had not been blinded by envy to Isabel's personal merits. She had always observed that she got on better with clever women than with silly ones like herself; the silly ones could never understand her wisdom, whereas the clever ones—the really clever ones—always understood her silliness. It appeared to her that, different as they were in appearance and general style, Isabel and she had somewhere a patch of common ground that they would set their feet upon at last. It was not very large, but it was firm, and they should both know it when once they had really touched it. And then she lived, with Mrs. Osmond, under the influence of a pleasant surprise; she was constantly expecting that Isabel would "look down" on her, and she as constantly saw this operation postponed. She asked herself when it would begin, like fire-works, or Lent, or the opera season; not that she cared much, but she wondered what kept it in abeyance. Her sister-in-law regarded her with none but level glances and expressed for the poor Countess as little contempt as admiration. In reality Isabel would as soon have thought of despising her as of passing a moral judgement on a grasshopper. She was not indifferent to her husband's sister, however; she was rather a little afraid of her. She wondered at her; she thought her very extraordinary. The Countess seemed to her to have no soul; she was like a bright rare shell, with a polished surface and a remarkably pink lip, in which something would rattle when you shook it. This rattle was apparently the Countess's spiritual principle, a little loose nut that tumbled about inside of her. She was too odd for disdain, too anomalous for comparisons. Isabel would have invited her again (there was no question of inviting the Count); but Osmond, after his marriage, had not scrupled to say frankly that Amy was a fool of the worst species—a fool whose folly had the irrepressibility of genius. He said at another time that she had no heart; and he added in a moment that she had given it all away—in small pieces, like a frosted wedding-cake. The fact of not having been asked was of course another obstacle to the Countess's going again to Rome; but at the period with which this history has now to deal she was in receipt of an invitation to spend several weeks at Palazzo Roccanera. The proposal had come from Osmond himself, who wrote to his sister that she must be prepared to be very quiet. Whether or no she found in this phrase all the meaning he had put into it I am unable to say; but she accepted the invitation on any terms. She was curious, moreover; for one of the impressions of her former visit had been that her brother had found his match. Before the marriage she had been sorry for Isabel, so sorry as to have had serious thoughts—if any of the Countess's thoughts were serious—of putting her on her guard. But she had let that pass, and after a little she was reassured. Osmond was as lofty as ever, but his wife would not be an easy victim. The Countess was not very exact at measurements, but it seemed to her that if Isabel should draw herself up she would be the taller spirit of the two. What she wanted to learn now was whether Isabel had drawn herself up; it would give her immense pleasure to see Osmond overtopped.

Several days before she was to start for Rome a servant brought her the card of a visitor—a card with the simple superscription "Henrietta C. Stackpole." The Countess pressed her finger-tips to her forehead; she didn't remember to have known any such Henrietta as that. The servant then remarked that the lady had requested him to say that if the Countess should not recognize her name she would know her well enough on seeing her. By the time she appeared before her visitor she had in fact reminded herself that there was once a literary lady at Mrs. Touchett's; the only woman of letters she had ever encountered—that is the only modern one, since she was the daughter of a defunct poetess. She recognised Miss Stackpole immediately, the more so that Miss Stackpole seemed perfectly unchanged; and the Countess, who was thoroughly good-natured, thought it rather fine to be called on by a person of that sort of distinction. She wondered if Miss Stackpole had come on account of her mother—whether she had heard of the American Corinne. Her mother was not at all like Isabel's friend; the Countess could see at a glance that this lady was much more contemporary; and she received an impression of the improvements that were taking place—chiefly in distant countries—in the character (the professional character) of literary ladies. Her mother had been used to wear a Roman scarf thrown over a pair of shoulders timorously bared of their tight black velvet (oh the old clothes!) and a gold laurel-wreath set upon a multitude of glossy ringlets. She had spoken softly and vaguely, with the accent of her "Creole" ancestors, as she always confessed; she sighed a great deal and was not at all enterprising. But Henrietta, the Countess could see, was always closely buttoned and compactly braided; there was something brisk and business-like in her appearance; her manner was almost conscientiously familiar. It was as impossible to imagine her ever vaguely sighing as to imagine a letter posted without its address. The Countess could not but feel that the correspondent of the *Interviewer* was much more in the movement than the American Corinne. She explained that she had called on the Countess because she was the only person she knew in Florence, and that when she visited a foreign city she liked to see something more than superficial travellers. She knew Mrs. Touchett, but Mrs. Touchett was in America, and even if she had been in Florence Henrietta would not have put herself out for her, since Mrs. Touchett was not one of her admirations.

"Do you mean by that that I am?" the Countess graciously asked.

"Well, I like you better than I do her," said Miss Stackpole. "I seem to remember that when I saw you before you were very interesting. I don't know whether it was an accident or whether it's your usual style. At any rate I was a good deal struck with what you said. I made use of it afterwards in print."

"Dear me!" cried the Countess, staring and half-alarmed; "I had no idea I ever said anything remarkable! I wish I had known it at the time."

"It was about the position of woman in this city," Miss Stackpole remarked. "You threw a good deal of light upon it."

"The position of woman's very uncomfortable. Is that what you mean? And you wrote it down and published it?" the Countess went on. "Ah, do let me see it!"

"I'll write to them to send you the paper if you like," Henrietta said. "I didn't mention your name; I only said a lady of high rank. And then I quoted your views."

The Countess threw herself hastily backward, tossing up her clasped hands. "Do you know I'm rather sorry you didn't mention my name? I should have rather liked to see my name in the papers. I forget what my views were; I have so many! But I'm not ashamed of them. I'm not at all like my brother—I suppose you know my brother? He thinks it a kind of scandal to be put in the papers; if you were to quote him he'd never forgive you."

"He needn't be afraid; I shall never refer to him," said Miss Stackpole with bland dryness. "That's another reason," she added, "why I wanted to come to see you. You know Mr. Osmond married my dearest friend."

"Ah, yes; you were a friend of Isabel's. I was trying to think what I knew about you."

"I'm quite willing to be known by that," Henrietta declared. "But that isn't what your brother likes to know me by. He has tried to break up my relations with Isabel."

"Don't permit it," said the Countess.

"That's what I want to talk about. I'm going to Rome."

"So am I!" the Countess cried. "We'll go together."

"With great pleasure. And when I write about my journey I'll mention you by name as my companion."

The Countess sprang from her chair and came and sat on the sofa beside her visitor. "Ah, you must send me the paper! My husband won't like it, but he need never see it. Besides, he doesn't know how to read."

Henrietta's large eyes became immense. "Doesn't know how to read? May I put that into my letter?"

"Into your letter?"

"In the *Interviewer*. That's my paper."

"Oh yes, if you like; with his name. Are you going to stay with Isabel?"

Henrietta held up her head, gazing a little in silence at her hostess. "She has not asked me. I wrote to her I was coming, and she answered that she would engage a room for me at a *pension*.[2] She gave no reason."

The Countess listened with extreme interest. "The reason's Osmond," she pregnantly remarked.

"Isabel ought to make a stand," said Miss Stackpole. "I'm afraid she has changed a great deal. I told her she would."

"I'm sorry to hear it; I hoped she would have her own way. Why doesn't my brother like you?" the Countess ingenuously added.

"I don't know and I don't care. He's perfectly welcome not to like me; I don't want every one to like me; I should think less of myself if some people did. A journalist can't hope to do much good unless he gets a good deal hated; that's the way he knows how his work goes on. And it's just the same for a lady. But I didn't expect it of Isabel."

"Do you mean that she hates you?" the Countess enquired.

"I don't know; I want to see. That's what I'm going to Rome for."

"Dear me, what a tiresome errand!" the Countess exclaimed.

"She doesn't write to me in the same way; it's easy to see there's a difference. If you know anything," Miss Stackpole went on, "I should like to hear it beforehand, so as to decide on the line I shall take."

The Countess thrust out her under lip and gave a gradual shrug. "I know very little; I see and hear very little of Osmond. He doesn't like me any better than he appears to like you."

"Yet you're not a lady correspondent," said Henrietta pensively.

"Oh, he has plenty of reasons. Nevertheless they've invited me— I'm to stay in the house!" And the Countess smiled almost fiercely;

2. Boarding house or small residential hotel.

her exultation, for the moment, took little account of Miss Stack-pole's disappointment.

This lady, however, regarded it very placidly. "I shouldn't have gone if she *had* asked me. That is I think I shouldn't; and I'm glad I hadn't to make up my mind. It would have been a very difficult question. I shouldn't have liked to turn away from her, and yet I shouldn't have been happy under her roof. A *pension* will suit me very well. But that's not all."

"Rome's very good just now," said the Countess; "there are all sorts of brilliant people. Did you ever hear of Lord Warburton?"

"Hear of him? I know him very well. Do you consider him very brilliant?" Henrietta enquired.

"I don't know him, but I'm told he's extremely *grand seigneur*.[3] He's making love to Isabel."

"Making love to her?"

"So I'm told; I don't know the details," said the Countess lightly. "But Isabel's pretty safe."

Henrietta gazed earnestly at her companion; for a moment she said nothing. "When do you go to Rome?" she enquired abruptly.

"Not for a week, I'm afraid."

"I shall go to-morrow," Henrietta said. "I think I had better not wait."

"Dear me, I'm sorry; I'm having some dresses made. I'm told Isabel receives immensely. But I shall see you there; I shall call on you at your *pension*." Henrietta sat still—she was lost in thought; and suddenly the Countess cried: "Ah, but if you don't go with me you can't describe our journey!"

Miss Stackpole seemed unmoved by this consideration; she was thinking of something else and presently expressed it. "I'm not sure that I understand you about Lord Warburton."

"Understand me? I mean he's very nice, that's all."

"Do you consider it nice to make love to married women?" Henrietta enquired with unprecedented distinctness.

The Countess stared, and then with a little violent laugh: "It's certain all the nice men do it. Get married and you'll see!" she added.

"That idea would be enough to prevent me," said Miss Stack-pole. "I should want my own husband; I shouldn't want any one else's. Do you mean that Isabel's guilty—guilty—?" And she paused a little, choosing her expression.

"Do I mean she's guilty? Oh dear no, not yet, I hope. I only mean that Osmond's very tiresome and that Lord Warburton, as I hear, is a great deal at the house. I'm afraid you're scandalised."

"No, I'm just anxious," Henrietta said.

3. Lordly.

"Ah, you're not very complimentary to Isabel! You should have more confidence. I'll tell you," the Countess added quickly: "if it will be a comfort to you I engage to draw him off."

Miss Stackpole answered at first only with the deeper solemnity of her gaze. "You don't understand me," she said after a while. "I haven't the idea you seem to suppose. I'm not afraid for Isabel—in that way. I'm only afraid she's unhappy—that's what I want to get at."

The Countess gave a dozen turns of the head; she looked impatient and sarcastic. "That may very well be; for my part I should like to know whether Osmond is." Miss Stackpole had begun a little to bore her.

"If she's really changed that must be at the bottom of it," Henrietta went on.

"You'll see; she'll tell you," said the Countess.

"Ah, she may *not* tell me—that's what I'm afraid of!"

"Well, if Osmond isn't amusing himself—in his own old way—I flatter myself I shall discover it," the Countess rejoined.

"I don't care for that," said Henrietta.

"I do immensely! If Isabel's unhappy I'm very sorry for her, but I can't help it. I might tell her something that would make her worse, but I can't tell her anything that would console her. What did she go and marry him for? If she had listened to me she'd have got rid of him. I'll forgive her, however, if I find she has made things hot for him! If she has simply allowed him to trample upon her I don't know that I shall even pity her. But I don't think that's very likely. I count upon finding that if she's miserable she has at least made *him* so."

Henrietta got up; these seemed to her, naturally, very dreadful expectations. She honestly believed she had no desire to see Mr. Osmond unhappy; and indeed he could not be for her the subject of a flight of fancy. She was on the whole rather disappointed in the Countess, whose mind moved in a narrower circle than she had imagined, though with a capacity for coarseness even there. "It will be better if they love each other," she said for edification.

"They can't. He can't love any one."

"I presumed that was the case. But it only aggravates my fear for Isabel. I shall positively start to-morrow."

"Isabel certainly has devotees," said the Countess, smiling very vividly. "I declare I don't pity her."

"It may be I can't assist her," Miss Stackpole pursued, as if it were well not to have illusions.

"You can have wanted to, at any rate; that's something. I believe that's what you came from America for," the Countess suddenly added.

"Yes, I wanted to look after her," Henrietta said serenely.

Her hostess stood there smiling at her with small bright eyes and an eager-looking nose; with cheeks into each of which a flush had come. "Ah, that's very pretty—*c'est bien gentil!*[4] Isn't it what they call friendship?"

"I don't know what they call it. I thought I had better come."

"She's very happy—she's very fortunate," the Countess went on. "She has others besides." And then she broke out passionately. "She's more fortunate than I! I'm as unhappy as she—I've a very bad husband; he's a great deal worse than Osmond. And I've no friends. I thought I had, but they're gone. No one, man or woman, would do for me what you've done for her."

Henrietta was touched; there was nature in this bitter effusion. She gazed at her companion a moment, and then: "Look here, Countess, I'll do anything for you that you like. I'll wait over and travel with you."

"Never mind," the Countess answered with a quick change of tone: "only describe me in the newspaper!"

Henrietta, before leaving her, however, was obliged to make her understand that she could give no fictitious representation of her journey to Rome. Miss Stackpole was a strictly veracious reporter. On quitting her she took the way to the Lung' Arno, the sunny quay beside the yellow river where the bright-faced inns familiar to tourists stand all in a row. She had learned her way before this through the streets of Florence (she was very quick in such matters), and was therefore able to turn with great decision of step out of the little square which forms the approach to the bridge of the Holy Trinity.[5] She proceeded to the left, toward the Ponte Vecchio,[6] and stopped in front of one of the hotels which overlook that delightful structure. Here she drew forth a small pocket-book, took from it a card and a pencil and, after meditating a moment, wrote a few words. It is our privilege to look over her shoulder, and if we exercise it we may read the brief query: "Could I see you this evening for a few moments on a very important matter?" Henrietta added that she should start on the morrow for Rome. Armed with this little document she approached the porter, who now had taken up his station in the doorway, and asked if Mr. Goodwood were at home. The porter replied, as porters always reply, that he had gone out about twenty minutes before; whereupon Henrietta presented her card and begged it might be handed him on his return. She left the inn and pursued her course along the quay to the severe portico of the Uffizi, through which she presently reached the entrance of the famous gallery of paintings. Making her way in, she ascended the high staircase which leads to the upper chambers. The long corri-

4. It's really nice.
5. One of the four bridges which crossed the Arno in the nineteenth century, and a favorite evening walk.
6. This ancient bridge was also a street of jeweller's and goldsmith's shops, with a gallery running above the shops.

dor, glazed on one side and decorated with antique busts, which gives admission to these apartments, presented an empty vista in which the bright winter light twinkled upon the marble floor. The gallery is very cold and during the midwinter weeks but scantily visited. Miss Stackpole may appear more ardent in her quest of artistic beauty than she has hitherto struck us as being, but she had after all her preferences and admirations. One of the latter was the little Correggio of the Tribune[7]—the Virgin kneeling down before the sacred infant, who lies in a litter of straw, and clapping her hands to him while he delightedly laughs and crows. Henrietta had a special devotion to this intimate scene—she thought it the most beautiful picture in the world. On her way, at present, from New York to Rome, she was spending but three days in Florence, and yet reminded herself that they must not elapse without her paying another visit to her favourite work of art. She had a great sense of beauty in all ways, and it involved a good many intellectual obligations. She was about to turn into the Tribune[8] when a gentleman came out of it; whereupon she gave a little exclamation and stood before Caspar Goodwood.

"I've just been at your hotel," she said. "I left a card for you."

"I'm very much honoured," Caspar Goodwood answered as if he really meant it.

"It was not to honour you I did it; I've called on you before and I know you don't like it. It was to talk to you a little about something."

He looked for a moment at the buckle in her hat. "I shall be very glad to hear what you wish to say."

"You don't like to talk with me," said Henrietta. "But I don't care for that; I don't talk for your amusement. I wrote a word to ask you to come and see me; but since I've met you here this will do as well."

"I was just going away," Goodwood stated; "but of course I'll stop." He was civil, but not enthusiastic.

Henrietta, however, never looked for great professions, and she was so much in earnest that she was thankful he would listen to her on any terms. She asked him first, none the less, if he had seen all the pictures.

"All I want to. I've been here an hour."

"I wonder if you've seen my Correggio," said Henrietta. "I came up on purpose to have a look at it." She went into the Tribune and he slowly accompanied her.

"I suppose I've seen it, but I didn't know it was yours. I don't remember pictures—especially that sort." She had pointed out her

7. This painting, sometimes called *The Adoration of the Child*, is often considered charming but somewhat contrived and affected.

8. In the Uffizi, a sumptuous room which contained the Venus de Medici.

favourite work, and he asked her if it was about Correggio she wished to talk with him.

"No," said Henrietta, "it's about something less harmonious!" They had the small, brilliant room, a splendid cabinet of treasures, to themselves; there was only a custode hovering about the Medicean Venus. "I want you to do me a favour," Miss Stackpole went on.

Caspar Goodwood frowned a little, but he expressed no embarrassment at the sense of not looking eager. His face was that of a much older man than our earlier friend. "I'm sure it's something I shan't like," he said rather loudly.

"No, I don't think you'll like it. If you did it would be no favour."

"Well, let's hear it," he went on in the tone of a man quite conscious of his patience.

"You may say there's no particular reason why you should do me a favour. Indeed I only know of one: the fact that if you'd let me I'd gladly do *you* one." Her soft, exact tone, in which there was no attempt at effect, had an extreme sincerity; and her companion, though he presented rather a hard surface, couldn't help being touched by it. When he was touched he rarely showed it, however, by the usual signs; he neither blushed, nor looked away, nor looked conscious. He only fixed his attention more directly; he seemed to consider with added firmness. Henrietta continued therefore disinterestedly, without the sense of an advantage. "I may say now, indeed—it seems a good time—that if I've ever annoyed you (and I think sometimes I have) it's because I knew I was willing to suffer annoyance for you. I've troubled you—doubtless. But I'd *take* trouble for you."

Goodwood hesitated. "You're taking trouble now."

"Yes, I am—some. I want you to consider whether it's better on the whole that you should go to Rome."

"I thought you were going to say that!" he answered rather artlessly.

"You *have* considered it then?"

"Of course I have, very carefully. I've looked all round it. Otherwise I shouldn't have come so far as this. That's what I stayed in Paris two months for. I was thinking it over."

"I'm afraid you decided as you liked. You decided it was best because you were so much attracted."

"Best for whom, do you mean?" Goodwood demanded.

"Well, for yourself first. For Mrs. Osmond next."

"Oh, it won't do *her* any good! I don't flatter myself that."

"Won't it do her some harm?—that's the question."

"I don't see what it will matter to her. I'm nothing to Mrs. Osmond. But if you want to know, I do want to see her myself."

"Yes, and that's why you go."

"Of course it is. Could there be a better reason?"

"How will it help you?—that's what I want to know," said Miss Stackpole.

"That's just what I can't tell you. It's just what I was thinking about in Paris."

"It will make you more discontented."

"Why do you say 'more' so?" Goodwood asked rather sternly. "How do you know I'm discontented?"

"Well," said Henrietta, hesitating a little, "you seem never to have cared for another."

"How do you know what I care for?" he cried with a big blush. "Just now I care to go to Rome."

Henrietta looked at him in silence, with a sad yet luminous expression. "Well," she observed at last, "I only wanted to tell you what I think; I had it on my mind. Of course you think it's none of my business. But nothing is any one's business, on that principle."

"It's very kind of you; I'm greatly obliged to you for your interest," said Caspar Goodwood. "I shall go to Rome and I shan't hurt Mrs. Osmond."

"You won't hurt her, perhaps. But will you help her?—that's the real issue."

"Is she in need of help?" he asked slowly, with a penetrating look.

"Most women always are," said Henrietta, with conscientious evasiveness and generalising less hopefully than usual. "If you go to Rome," she added, "I hope you'll be a true friend—not a selfish one!" And she turned off and began to look at the pictures.

Caspar Goodwood let her go and stood watching her while she wandered round the room; but after a moment he rejoined her. "You've heard something about her here," he then resumed. "I should like to know what you've heard."

Henrietta had never prevaricated in her life, and, though on this occasion there might have been a fitness in doing so, she decided, after thinking some minutes, to make no superficial exception. "Yes, I've heard," she answered; "but as I don't want you to go to Rome I won't tell you."

"Just as you please. I shall see for myself," he said. Then inconsistently, for him, "You've heard she's unhappy!" he added.

"Oh, you won't see that!" Henrietta exclaimed.

"I hope not. When do you start?"

"To-morrow, by the evening train. And you?"

Goodwood hung back; he had no desire to make his journey to Rome in Miss Stackpole's company. His indifference to this advantage was not of the same character as Gilbert Osmond's, but it had at this moment an equal distinctness. It was rather a tribute to Miss

Stackpole's virtues than a reference to her faults. He thought her very remarkable, very brilliant, and he had, in theory, no objection to the class to which she belonged. Lady correspondents appeared to him a part of the natural scheme of things in a progressive country, and though he never read their letters he supposed that they ministered somehow to social prosperity. But it was this very eminence of their position that made him wish Miss Stackpole didn't take so much for granted. She took for granted that he was always ready for some allusion to Mrs. Osmond; she had done so when they met in Paris, six weeks after his arrival in Europe, and she had repeated the assumption with every successive opportunity. He had no wish whatever to allude to Mrs. Osmond; he was *not* always thinking of her; he was perfectly sure of that. He was the most reserved, the least colloquial of men, and this enquiring authoress was constantly flashing her lantern into the quiet darkness of his soul. He wished she didn't care so much; he even wished, though it might seem rather brutal of him, that she would leave him alone. In spite of this, however, he just now made other reflections—which show how widely different, in effect, his ill-humour was from Gilbert Osmond's. He desired to go immediately to Rome; he would have liked to go alone, in the night-train. He hated the European railway-carriages, in which one sat for hours in a vise, knee to knee and nose to nose with a foreigner to whom one presently found one's self objecting with all the added vehemence of one's wish to have the window open; and if they were worse at night even than by day, at least at night one could sleep and dream of an American saloon-car. But he couldn't take a night-train when Miss Stackpole was starting in the morning; it struck him that this would be an insult to an unprotected woman. Nor could he wait until after she had gone unless he should wait longer than he had patience for. It wouldn't do to start the next day. She worried him; she oppressed him; the idea of spending the day in a European railway-carriage with her offered a complication of irritations. Still, she was a lady travelling alone; it was his duty to put himself out for her. There could be no two questions about that; it was a perfectly clear necessity. He looked extremely grave for some moments and then said, wholly without the flourish of gallantry but in a tone of extreme distinctness, "Of course if you're going to-morrow I'll go too, as I may be of assistance to you."

"Well, Mr. Goodwood, I should hope so!" Henrietta returned imperturbably.

XLV

I have already had reason to say that Isabel knew her husband to be displeased by the continuance of Ralph's visit to Rome. That knowledge was very present to her as she went to her cousin's hotel the day after she had invited Lord Warburton to give a tangible proof of his sincerity; and at this moment, as at others, she had a sufficient perception of the sources of Osmond's opposition. He wished her to have no freedom of mind, and he knew perfectly well that Ralph was an apostle of freedom. It was just because he was this, Isabel said to herself, that it was a refreshment to go and see him. It will be perceived that she partook of this refreshment in spite of her husband's aversion to it, that is partook of it, as she flattered herself, discreetly. She had not as yet undertaken to act in direct opposition to his wishes; he was her appointed and inscribed master; she gazed at moments with a sort of incredulous blankness at this fact. It weighed upon her imagination, however; constantly present to her mind were all the traditionary decencies and sanctities of marriage. The idea of violating them filled her with shame as well as with dread, for on giving herself away she had lost sight of this contingency in the perfect belief that her husband's intentions were as generous as her own. She seemed to see, none the less, the rapid approach of the day when she should have to take back something she had solemnly bestown. Such a ceremony would be odious and monstrous; she tried to shut her eyes to it meanwhile. Osmond would do nothing to help it by beginning first; he would put that burden upon her to the end. He had not yet formally forbidden her to call upon Ralph; but she felt sure that unless Ralph should very soon depart this prohibition would come. How could poor Ralph depart? The weather as yet made it impossible. She could perfectly understand her husband's wish for the event; she didn't, to be just, see how he *could* like her to be with her cousin. Ralph never said a word against him, but Osmond's sore, mute protest was none the less founded. If he should positively interpose, if he should put forth his authority, she would have to decide, and that wouldn't be easy. The prospect made her heart beat and her cheeks burn, as I say, in advance; there were moments when, in her wish to avoid an open rupture, she found herself wishing Ralph would start even at a risk. And it was of no use that, when catching herself in this state of mind, she called herself a feeble spirit, a coward. It was not that she loved Ralph less, but that almost anything seemed preferable to repudiating the most serious act—the single sacred act—of her life. That appeared to make the whole future hideous. To break with Osmond once would be to break for ever; any open acknowledgement of irreconcilable needs would be an admission that their whole attempt had proved a failure. For them there could be no condonement, no compromise, no easy forgetfulness, no formal readjustment. They had attempted only one thing, but that one thing was to have been exquisite. Once they missed it nothing else would do; there was no conceivable substitute for that success. For the moment, Isabel went to the Hôtel de Paris as often as she thought well; the measure of propriety was in the canon of taste, and there couldn't have been a better proof that morality was, so to speak, a matter of earnest appreciation. Isabel's application of that measure had been particularly free to-day, for in addition to the general truth that she couldn't leave Ralph to die alone she had something important to ask of him. This indeed was Gilbert's business as well as her own.

She came very soon to what she wished to speak of. "I want you to answer me a question. It's about Lord Warburton."

"I think I guess your question," Ralph answered from his armchair, out of which his thin legs protruded at greater length than ever.

"Very possibly you guess it. Please then answer it."

"Oh, I don't say I can do that."

"You're intimate with him," she said; "you've a great deal of observation of him."

"Very true. But think how he must dissimulate!"

"Why should he dissimulate? That's not his nature."

"Ah, you must remember that the circumstances are peculiar," said Ralph with an air of private amusement.

"To a certain extent—yes. But is he really in love?"

"Very much, I think. I can make that out."

"Ah!" said Isabel with a certain dryness.

Ralph looked at her as if his mild hilarity had been touched with mystification. "You say that as if you were disappointed."

Isabel got up, slowly smoothing her gloves and eyeing them thoughtfully. "It's after all no business of mine."

"You're very philosophic," said her cousin. And then in a moment: "May I enquire what you're talking about?"

Isabel stared. "I thought you knew. Lord Warburton tells me he wants, of all things in the world, to marry Pansy. I've told you that before, without eliciting a comment from you. You might risk one this morning, I think. Is it your belief that he really cares for her?"

"Ah, for Pansy, no!" cried Ralph very positively.

"But you said just now he did."

Ralph waited a moment. "That he cared for you, Mrs. Osmond."

Isabel shook her head gravely. "That's nonsense, you know."

"Of course it is. But the nonsense is Warburton's, not mine."

"That would be very tiresome." She spoke, as she flattered herself, with much subtlety.

"I ought to tell you indeed," Ralph went on, "that to me he has denied it."

"It's very good of you to talk about it together! Has he also told you that he's in love with Pansy?"

"He has spoken very well of her—very properly. He has let me know, of course, that he thinks she would do very well at Lockleigh."

"Does he really think it?"

"Ah, what Warburton really thinks—!" said Ralph.

Isabel fell to smoothing her gloves again; they were long, loose gloves on which she could freely expend herself. Soon, however, she looked up, and then, "Ah, Ralph, you give me no help!" she cried abruptly and passionately.

It was the first time she had alluded to the need for help, and the words shook her cousin with their violence. He gave a long murmur of relief, of pity, of tenderness; it seemed to him that at last the gulf between them had been bridged. It was this that made him exclaim in a moment: "How unhappy you must be!"

He had no sooner spoken than she recovered her self-possession, and the first use she made of it was to pretend she had not heard him. "When I talk of your helping me I talk great nonsense," she said with a quick smile. "The idea of my troubling you with my domestic embarrassments! The matter's very simple; Lord Warburton must get on by himself. I can't undertake to see him through."

"He ought to succeed easily," said Ralph.

Isabel debated. "Yes—but he has not always succeeded."

"Very true. You know, however, how that always surprised me. Is Miss Osmond capable of giving us a surprise?"

"It will come from him, rather. I seem to see that after all he'll let the matter drop."

"He'll do nothing dishonourable," said Ralph.

"I'm very sure of that. Nothing can be more honourable than for him to leave the poor child alone. She cares for another person, and it's cruel to attempt to bribe her by magnificent offers to give him up."

"Cruel to the other person perhaps—the one she cares for. But Warburton isn't obliged to mind that."

"No, cruel to her," said Isabel. "She would be very unhappy if she were to allow herself to be persuaded to desert poor Mr. Rosier. That idea seems to amuse you; of course you're not in love with him. He has the merit—for Pansy—of being in love with Pansy. She can see at a glance that Lord Warburton isn't."

"He'd be very good to her," said Ralph.

"He has been good to her already. Fortunately, however, he has not said a word to disturb her. He could come and bid her good-bye to-morrow with perfect propriety."

"How would your husband like that?"

"Not at all; and he may be right in not liking it. Only he must obtain satisfaction himself."

"Has he commissioned you to obtain it?" Ralph ventured to ask.

"It was natural that as an old friend of Lord Warburton's—an older friend, that is, than Gilbert—I should take an interest in his intentions."

"Take an interest in his renouncing them, you mean?"

Isabel hesitated, frowning a little. "Let me understand. Are you pleading his cause?"

"Not in the least. I'm very glad he shouldn't become your step-daughter's husband. It makes such a very queer relation to you!" said Ralph, smiling. "But I'm rather nervous lest your husband should think you haven't pushed him enough."

Isabel found herself able to smile as well as he. "He knows me well enough not to have expected me to push. He himself has no intention of pushing, I presume. I'm not afraid I shall not be able to justify myself!" she said lightly.

Her mask had dropped for an instant, but she had put it on again, to Ralph's infinite disappointment. He had caught a glimpse of her natural face and he wished immensely to look into it. He had an almost savage desire to hear her complain of her husband—hear her say that she should be held accountable for Lord Warburton's defection. Ralph was certain that this was her situation; he knew by instinct, in advance, the form that in such an event Osmond's displeasure would take. It could only take the meanest and cruellest. He would have liked to warn Isabel of it—to let her see at least how he judged for her and how he knew. It little mattered that Isabel would know much better; it was for his own satisfaction more than for hers that he longed to show her he was not deceived. He tried and tried again to make her betray Osmond; he felt cold-blooded, cruel, dishonourable almost, in doing so. But it scarcely mattered, for he only failed. What had she come for then, and why did she seem almost to offer him a chance to violate their tacit convention? Why did she ask him his advice if she gave him no liberty to answer her? How could they talk of her domestic embarrassments, as it pleased her humorously to designate them, if the principal factor was not to be mentioned? These contradictions were themselves but an indication of her trouble, and her cry for help, just before, was the only thing he was bound to consider. "You'll be decidedly at variance, all the same," he said in a moment. And as she answered nothing, looking as if she scarce understood, "You'll find yourselves thinking very differently," he continued.

"That may easily happen, among the most united couples!" She took up her parasol; he saw she was nervous, afraid of what he might say. "It's a matter we can hardly quarrel about, however," she added; "for almost all the interest is on his side. That's very natural. Pansy's after all his daughter—not mine." And she put out her hand to wish him good-bye.

Ralph took an inward resolution that she shouldn't leave him without his letting her know that he knew everything: it seemed too great an opportunity to lose. "Do you know what his interest will make him say?" he asked as he took her hand. She shook her head, rather dryly—not discouragingly—and he went on. "It will make him say that your want of zeal is owing to jealousy." He stopped a moment; her face made him afraid.

"To jealousy?"

"To jealousy of his daughter."

She blushed red and threw back her head. "You're not kind," she said in a voice that he had never heard on her lips.

"Be frank with me and you'll see," he answered.

But she made no reply; she only pulled her hand out of his own, which he tried still to hold, and rapidly withdrew from the room. She made up her mind to speak to Pansy, and she took an occasion on the same day, going to the girl's room before dinner. Pansy was already dressed; she was always in advance of the time: it seemed to illustrate her pretty patience and the graceful stillness with which she could sit and wait. At present she was seated, in her fresh array, before the bed-room fire; she had blown out her candles on the completion of her toilet, in accordance with the economical habits in which she had been brought up and which she was now more careful than ever to observe; so that the room was lighted only by a couple of logs. The rooms in Palazzo Roccanera were as spacious as they were numerous, and Pansy's virginal bower was an immense chamber with a dark, heavily-timbered ceiling. Its diminutive mistress, in the midst of it, appeared but a speck of humanity, and as she got up, with quick deference, to welcome Isabel, the latter was more than ever struck with her shy sincerity. Isabel had a difficult task—the only thing was to perform it as simply as possible. She felt bitter and angry, but she warned herself against betraying this heat. She was afraid even of looking too grave, or at least too stern; she was afraid of causing alarm. But Pansy seemed to have guessed she had come more or less as a confessor; for after she had moved the chair in which she had been sitting a little nearer to the fire and Isabel had taken her place in it, she kneeled down on a cushion in front of her, looking up and resting her clasped hands on her step-mother's knees. What Isabel wished to do was to hear from her own lips that her mind was not occupied with Lord Warburton; but if she desired the assurance she felt herself by no means at liberty to provoke it. The girl's father would have qualified this as rank treachery; and indeed Isabel knew that if Pansy should display the smallest germ of a disposition to encourage Lord Warburton her own duty was to hold her tongue. It was difficult to interrogate without appearing to suggest; Pansy's supreme simplicity, an innocence even more complete than Isabel had yet judged it, gave to the most tentative enquiry something of the effect of an admonition. As she knelt there in the vague firelight, with her pretty dress dimly shining, her hands folded half in appeal and half in submission, her soft eyes, raised and fixed, full of the seriousness of the situation, she looked to Isabel like a childish martyr decked out for sacrifice and scarcely presuming even to hope to avert it. When Isabel said to her that she had never yet spoken to her of what might have been going on in relation to her getting married, but that her silence had not been indifference or ignorance, had only been the desire to leave her at liberty, Pansy bent forward, raised her face nearer and nearer, and with a little murmur which evidently expressed a deep longing, answered that she had greatly wished her to speak and that she begged her to advise her now.

"It's difficult for me to advise you," Isabel returned. "I don't know how I can undertake that. That's for your father; you must get his advice and, above all, you must act on it."

At this Pansy dropped her eyes; for a moment she said nothing. "I think I should like your advice better than papa's," she presently remarked.

"That's not as it should be," said Isabel coldly. "I love you very much, but your father loves you better."

"It isn't because you love me—it's because you're a lady," Pansy answered with the air of saying something very reasonable. "A lady can advise a young girl better than a man."

"I advise you then to pay the greatest respect to your father's wishes."

"Ah yes," said the child eagerly, "I must do that."

"But if I speak to you now about your getting married it's not for your own sake, it's for mine," Isabel went on. "If I try to learn from you what you expect, what you desire, it's only that I may act accordingly."

Pansy stared, and then very quickly, "Will you do everything I want?" she asked.

"Before I say yes I must know what such things are."

Pansy presently told her that the only thing she wanted in life was to marry Mr. Rosier. He had asked her and she had told him she would do so if her papa would allow it. Now her papa wouldn't allow it.

"Very well then, it's impossible," Isabel pronounced.

"Yes, it's impossible," said Pansy without a sigh and with the same extreme attention in her clear little face.

"You must think of something else then," Isabel went on; but Pansy, sighing at this, told her that she had attempted that feat without the least success.

"You think of those who think of you," she said with a faint smile. "I know Mr. Rosier thinks of me."

"He ought not to," said Isabel loftily. "Your father has expressly requested he shouldn't."

"He can't help it, because he knows I think of *him*."

"You shouldn't think of him. There's some excuse for him, perhaps; but there's none for you."

"I wish you would try to find one," the girl exclaimed as if she were praying to the Madonna.

"I should be very sorry to attempt it," said the Madonna with unusual frigidity. "If you knew some one else was thinking of you, would you think of him?"

"No one can think of me as Mr. Rosier does; no one has the right."

"Ah, but I don't admit Mr. Rosier's right!" Isabel hypocritically cried.

Pansy only gazed at her, evidently much puzzled; and Isabel, taking advantage of it, began to represent to her the wretched consequences of disobeying her father. At this Pansy stopped her with the assurance that she would never disobey him, would never marry without his consent. And she announced, in the serenest, simplest tone, that, though she might never marry Mr. Rosier, she would never cease to think of him. She appeared to have accepted the idea of eternal singleness; but Isabel of course was free to reflect that she had no conception of its meaning. She was perfectly sincere; she was prepared to give up her lover. This might seem an important step toward taking another, but for Pansy, evidently, it failed to lead in that direction. She felt no bitterness toward her father; there was no bitterness in her heart; there was only the sweetness of fidelity to Edward Rosier, and a strange, exquisite intimation that she could prove it better by remaining single than even by marrying him.

"Your father would like you to make a better marriage," said Isabel. "Mr. Rosier's fortune is not at all large."

"How do you mean better—if that would be good enough? And I have myself so little money; why should I look for a fortune?"

"Your having so little is a reason for looking for more." With which Isabel was grateful for the dimness of the room; she felt as if her face were hideously insincere. It was what she was doing for

Osmond; it was what one had to do for Osmond! Pansy's solemn eyes, fixed on her own, almost embarrassed her; she was ashamed to think she had made so light of the girl's preference.

"What should you like me to do?" her companion softly demanded.

The question was a terrible one, and Isabel took refuge in timorous vagueness. "To remember all the pleasure it's in your power to give your father."

"To marry some one else, you mean—if he should ask me?"

For a moment Isabel's answer caused itself to be waited for; then she heard herself utter it in the stillness that Pansy's attention seemed to make. "Yes—to marry some one else."

The child's eyes grew more penetrating; Isabel believed she was doubting her sincerity, and the impression took force from her slowly getting up from her cushion. She stood there a moment with her small hands unclasped and then quavered out: "Well, I hope no one will ask me!"

"There has been a question of that. Some one else would have been ready to ask you."

"I don't think he can have been ready," said Pansy.

"It would appear so—if he had been sure he'd succeed."

"If he had been sure? Then he wasn't ready!"

Isabel thought this rather sharp; she also got up and stood a moment looking into the fire. "Lord Warburton has shown you great attention," she resumed; "of course you know it's of him I speak." She found herself, against her expectation, almost placed in the position of justifying herself; which led her to introduce this nobleman more crudely than she had intended.

"He has been very kind to me, and I like him very much. But if you mean that he'll propose for me I think you're mistaken."

"Perhaps I am. But your father would like it extremely."

Pansy shook her head with a little wise smile. "Lord Warburton won't propose simply to please papa."

"Your father would like you to encourage him," Isabel went on mechanically.

"How can I encourage him?"

"I don't know. Your father must tell you that."

Pansy said nothing for a moment; she only continued to smile as if she were in possession of a bright assurance. "There's no danger —no danger!" she declared at last.

There was a conviction in the way she said this, and a felicity in her believing it, which conduced to Isabel's awkwardness. She felt accused of dishonesty, and the idea was disgusting. To repair her self-respect she was on the point of saying that Lord Warburton had let her know that there *was* a danger. But she didn't; she only said—in her embarrassment rather wide of the mark—that he surely had been most kind, most friendly.

"Yes, he has been very kind," Pansy answered. "That's what I like him for."

"Why then is the difficulty so great?"

"I've always felt sure of his knowing that I don't want—what did you say I should do?—to encourage him. He knows I don't want to marry, and he wants me to know that he therefore won't trouble me. That's the meaning of his kindness. It's as if he said to me: 'I like you very much, but if it doesn't please you I'll never say it again.' I think that's very kind, very noble," Pansy went on with deepening positiveness. "That is all we've said to each other. And he doesn't care for me either. Ah no, there's no danger."

Isabel was touched with wonder at the depths of perception of which this submissive little person was capable; she felt afraid of Pansy's wisdom—began almost to retreat before it. "You must tell your father that," she remarked reservedly.

"I think I'd rather not," Pansy unreservedly answered.

"You oughtn't to let him have false hopes."

"Perhaps not; but it will be good for me that he should. So long as he believes that Lord Warburton intends anything of the kind you say, papa won't propose any one else. And that will be an advantage for me," said the child very lucidly.

There was something brilliant in her lucidity, and it made her companion draw a long breath. It relieved this friend of a heavy responsibility. Pansy had a sufficient illumination of her own, and Isabel felt that she herself just now had no light to spare from her small stock. Nevertheless it still clung to her that she must be loyal to Osmond, that she was on her honour in dealing with his daughter. Under the influence of this sentiment she threw out another suggestion before she retired—a suggestion with which it seemed to her that she should have done her utmost. "Your father takes for granted at least that you would like to marry a nobleman."

Pansy stood in the open doorway; she had drawn back the curtain for Isabel to pass. "I think Mr. Rosier looks like one!" she remarked very gravely.

XLVI

Lord Warburton was not seen in Mrs. Osmond's drawing-room for several days, and Isabel couldn't fail to observe that her husband said nothing to her about having received a letter from him. She couldn't fail to observe, either, that Osmond was in a state of expectancy and that, though it was not agreeable to him to betray it, he thought their distinguished friend kept him waiting quite too long. At the end of four days he alluded to his absence.

"What has become of Warburton? What does he mean by treating one like a tradesman with a bill?'

"I know nothing about him," Isabel said. "I saw him last Friday at the German ball. He told me then that he meant to write to you."

"He has never written to me."

"So I supposed, from your not having told me."

"He's an odd fish," said Osmond comprehensively. And on Isabel's making no rejoinder he went on to enquire whether it took his lordship five days to indite a letter. "Does he form his words with such difficulty?"

"I don't know," Isabel was reduced to replying. "I've never had a letter from him."

"Never had a letter? I had an idea that you were at one time in intimate correspondence."

She answered that this had not been the case, and let the conversation drop. On the morrow, however, coming into the drawing-room late in the afternoon, her husband took it up again.

"When Lord Warburton told you of his intention of writing what did you say to him?" he asked.

She just faltered. "I think I told him not to forget it."

"Did you believe there was a danger of that?"

"As you say, he's an odd fish."

"Apparently he has forgotten it," said Osmond. "Be so good as to remind him."

"Should you like me to write to him?" she demanded.

"I've no objection whatever."

"You expect too much of me."

"Ah yes, I expect a great deal of you."

"I'm afraid I shall disappoint you," said Isabel.

"My expectations have survived a good deal of disappointment."

"Of course I know that. Think how I must have disappointed myself! If you really wish hands laid on Lord Warburton you must lay them yourself."

For a couple of minutes Osmond answered nothing; then he said: "That won't be easy, with you working against me."

Isabel started; she felt herself beginning to tremble. He had a way of looking at her through half-closed eyelids, as if he were thinking of her but scarcely saw her, which seemed to her to have a wonderfully cruel intention. It appeared to recognise her as a disagreeable necessity of thought, but to ignore her for the time as a presence. That effect had never been so marked as now. "I think you accuse me of something very base," she returned.

"I accuse you of not being trustworthy. If he doesn't after all come forward it will be because you've kept him off. I don't know that it's base: it is the kind of thing a woman always thinks she may do. I've no doubt you've the finest ideas about it."

"I told you I would do what I could," she went on.

"Yes, that gained you time."

It came over her, after he had said this, that she had once thought him beautiful. "How much you must want to make sure of him!" she exclaimed in a moment.

She had no sooner spoken than she perceived the full reach of her words, of which she had not been conscious in uttering them. They made a comparison between Osmond and herself, recalled the fact that she had once held this coveted treasure in her hand and felt herself rich enough to let it fall. A momentary exultation took possession of her—a horrible delight in having wounded him; for his face instantly told her that none of the force of her exclamation was lost. He expressed nothing otherwise, however; he only said quickly: "Yes, I want it immensely."

At this moment a servant came in to usher a visitor, and he was followed the next by Lord Warburton, who received a visible check on seeing Osmond. He looked rapidly from the master of the house to the mistress; a movement that seemed to denote a reluctance to interrupt or even a perception of ominous conditions. Then he advanced, with his English address, in which a vague shyness seemed to offer itself as an element of good-breeding; in which the only defect was a difficulty in achieving transitions. Osmond was embarrassed; he found nothing to say; but Isabel remarked, promptly enough, that they had been in the act of talking about their visitor. Upon this her husband added that they hadn't known what was become of him—they had been afraid he had gone away. "No," he explained, smiling and looking at Osmond; "I'm only on the point of going." And then he mentioned that he found himself suddenly recalled to England: he should start on the morrow or the day after. "I'm awfully sorry to leave poor Touchett!" he ended by exclaiming.

For a moment neither of his companions spoke; Osmond only leaned back in his chair, listening. Isabel didn't look at him; she could only fancy how he looked. Her eyes were on their visitor's face, where they were the more free to rest that those of his lordship carefully avoided them. Yet Isabel was sure that had she met his glance she would have found it expressive. "You had better take poor Touchett with you," she heard her husband say, lightly enough, in a moment.

"He had better wait for warmer weather," Lord Warburton answered. "I shouldn't advise him to travel just now."

He sat there a quarter of an hour, talking as if he might not soon see them again—unless indeed they should come to England, a course he strongly recommended. Why shouldn't they come to England in the autumn?—that struck him as a very happy thought. It would give him such pleasure to do what he could for them—to have them come and spend a month with him. Osmond, by his own admission, had been to England but once; which was an absurd state of things for a man of his leisure and intelligence. It was just the country for him—he would be sure to get on well there. Then Lord Warburton asked Isabel if she remembered what a good time she had had there and if she didn't want to try it again. Didn't she want to see Gardencourt once more? Gardencourt was really very good. Touchett didn't take proper care of it, but it was the sort of place you could hardly spoil by letting it alone. Why didn't they come and pay Touchett a visit? He surely must have asked them. Hadn't asked them? What an ill-mannered wretch!—and Lord Warburton promised to give the master of Gardencourt a piece of his mind. Of course it was a mere accident; he would be delighted to have them. Spending a month with Touchett and a month with himself, and seeing all the rest of the people they must know there, they really wouldn't find it half bad. Lord Warburton added that it would amuse Miss Osmond as well, who had told him that she had never been to England and whom he had assured it was a country she deserved to see. Of course she didn't need to go to England to be admired—that was her fate everywhere; but she would be an immense success there, she certainly would, if that was any inducement. He asked if she were not at home: couldn't he say good-bye? Not that he liked good-byes—he always funked them. When he left England the other day he hadn't said good-bye to a two-legged creature. He had had half a mind to leave Rome without troubling Mrs. Osmond for a final interview. What could be more dreary than final interviews? One never said the things one wanted—one remembered them all an hour afterwards. On the other hand one usually said a lot of things one shouldn't, simply from a sense that one had to say something. Such a sense was upsetting; it muddled one's wits. He had it at present, and that was the effect it produced on him. If Mrs. Osmond didn't think he spoke as he ought she must set it down to agitation; it was no light thing to part with Mrs. Osmond. He was really very sorry to be going. He had thought of writing to her instead of calling—but he would write to her at any rate, to tell her a lot of things that would be sure to occur to him as soon as he had left the house. They must think seriously about coming to Lockleigh.

If there was anything awkward in the conditions of his visit or in the announcement of his departure it failed to come to the surface. Lord Warburton talked about his agitation; but he showed it in no other manner, and Isabel saw that since he had determined on a retreat he was capable of executing it gallantly. She was very glad for him; she liked him quite well enough to wish him to appear to carry a thing off. He would do that on any occasion—not from impudence but simply from the habit of success; and Isabel felt it out of her husband's power to frustrate this faculty. A complex operation, as she sat there, went on in her mind. On one side she listened to their visitor; said what was proper to him; read, more or less, between the lines of what he said himself; and wondered how he would have spoken if he had found her alone. On the other she had a perfect consciousness of Osmond's emotion. She felt almost sorry for him; he was condemned to the sharp pain of loss without the relief of cursing. He had had a great hope, and now, as he saw it vanish into smoke, he was obliged to sit and smile and twirl his thumbs. Not that he troubled himself to smile very brightly; he treated their friend on the whole to as vacant a countenance as so clever a man could very well wear. It was indeed a part of Osmond's cleverness that he could look consummately uncompromised. His present appearance, however, was not a confession of disappoint-ment; it was simply a part of Osmond's habitual system, which was to be inexpressive exactly in proportion as he was really intent. He had been intent on this prize from the first; but he had never allowed his eagerness to irradiate his refined face. He had treated his possible son-in-law as he treated every one—with an air of being interested in him only for his own advantage, not for any profit to a person already so generally, so perfectly provided as Gilbert Osmond. He would give no sign now of an inward rage which was the result of a vanished prospect of gain—not the faintest nor sub-tlest. Isabel could be sure of that, if it was any satisfaction to her. Strangely, very strangely, it was a satisfaction; she wished Lord Warburton to triumph before her husband, and at the same time she wished her husband to be very superior before Lord Warburton. Osmond, in his way, was admirable; he had, like their visitor, the advantage of an acquired habit. It was not that of succeeding, but it was something almost as good—that of not attempting. As he leaned back in his place, listening but vaguely to the other's friendly offers and suppressed explanations—as if it were only proper to assume that they were addressed essentially to his wife—he had at least (since so little else was left him) the comfort of thinking how well he personally had kept out of it, and how the air of indiffer-ence, which he was now able to wear, had the added beauty of con-sistency. It was something to be able to look as if the leave-taker's movements had no relation to his own mind. The latter did well, certainly; but Osmond's performance was in its very nature more finished. Lord Warburton's position was after all an easy one; there was no reason in the world why he shouldn't leave Rome. He had

had beneficent inclinations but they had stopped short of fruition; he had never committed himself, and his honour was safe. Osmond appeared to take but a moderate interest in the proposal that they should go and stay with him and in his allusion to the success Pansy might extract from their visit. He murmured a recognition, but left Isabel to say that it was a matter requiring grave consideration. Isabel, even while she made this remark, could see the great vista which had suddenly opened out in her husband's mind, with Pansy's little figure marching up the middle of it.

Lord Warburton had asked leave to bid good-bye to Pansy, but neither Isabel nor Osmond had made any motion to send for her. He had the air of giving out that his visit must be short; he sat on a small chair, as if it were only for a moment, keeping his hat in his hand. But he stayed and stayed; Isabel wondered what he was waiting for. She believed it was not to see Pansy; she had an impression that on the whole he would rather not see Pansy. It was of course to see herself alone—he had something to say to her. Isabel had no great wish to hear it, for she was afraid it would be an explanation, and she could perfectly dispense with explanations. Osmond, however, presently got up, like a man of good taste to whom it had occurred that so inveterate a visitor might wish to say just the last word of all to the ladies. "I've a letter to write before dinner," he said; "you must excuse me. I'll see if my daughter's disengaged, and if she is she shall know you're here. Of course when you come to Rome you'll always look us up. Mrs. Osmond will talk to you about the English expedition: she decides all those things."

The nod with which, instead of a hand-shake, he wound up this little speech was perhaps rather a meagre form of salutation; but on the whole it was all the occasion demanded. Isabel reflected that after he left the room Lord Warburton would have no pretext for saying, "Your husband's very angry"; which would have been extremely disagreeable to her. Nevertheless, if he had done so, she would have said: "Oh, don't be anxious. He doesn't hate *you*: it's me that he hates!"

It was only when they had been left alone together that her friend showed a certain vague awkwardness—sitting down in another chair, handling two or three of the objects that were near him. "I hope he'll make Miss Osmond come," he presently remarked. "I want very much to see her."

"I'm glad it's the last time," said Isabel.

"So am I. She doesn't care for me."

"No, she doesn't care for you."

"I don't wonder at it," he returned. Then he added with inconsequence: "You'll come to England, won't you?"

"I think we had better not."

"Ah, you owe me a visit. Don't you remember that you were to have come to Lockleigh once, and you never did?"

"Everything's changed since then," said Isabel.

"Not changed for the worse, surely—as far as we're concerned. To see you under my roof"—and he hung fire but an instant—"would be a great satisfaction."

She had feared an explanation; but that was the only one that occurred. They talked a little of Ralph, and in another moment Pansy came in, already dressed for dinner and with a little red spot in either cheek. She shook hands with Lord Warburton and stood looking up into his face with a fixed smile—a smile that Isabel knew, though his lordship probably never suspected it, to be near akin to a burst of tears.

"I'm going away," he said. "I want to bid you good-bye."

"Good-bye, Lord Warburton." Her voice perceptibly trembled.

"And I want to tell you how much I wish you may be very happy."

"Thank you, Lord Warburton," Pansy answered.

He lingered a moment and gave a glance at Isabel. "You ought to be very happy—you've got a guardian angel."

"I'm sure I shall be happy," said Pansy in the tone of a person whose certainties were always cheerful.

"Such a conviction as that will take you a great way. But if it should ever fail you, remember—remember—" And her interlocutor stammered a little. "Think of me sometimes, you know!" he said with a vague laugh. Then he shook hands with Isabel in silence, and presently he was gone.

When he had left the room she expected an effusion of tears from her stepdaughter; but Pansy in fact treated her to something very different.

"I think you *are* my guardian angel!" she exclaimed very sweetly.

Isabel shook her head. "I'm not an angel of any kind. I'm at the most your good friend."

"You're a very good friend then—to have asked papa to be gentle with me."

"I've asked your father nothing," said Isabel, wondering.

"He told me just now to come to the drawing-room, and then he gave me a very kind kiss."

"Ah," said Isabel, "that was quite his own idea!"

She recognised the idea perfectly; it was very characteristic, and she was to see a great deal more of it. Even with Pansy he couldn't put himself the least in the wrong. They were dining out that day, and after their dinner they went to another entertainment; so that it was not till late in the evening that Isabel saw him alone. When Pansy kissed him before going to bed he returned her embrace with even more than his usual munificence, and Isabel wondered if he meant it as a hint that his daughter had been injured by the mach-inations of her stepmother. It was a partial expression, at any rate, of what he continued to expect of his wife. She was about to follow Pansy, but he remarked that he wished she would remain; he had something to say to her. Then he walked about the drawing-room a little, while she stood waiting in her cloak.

"I don't understand what you wish to do," he said in a moment. "I should like to know—so that I may know how to act."

"Just now I wish to go to bed. I'm very tired."

"Sit down and rest; I shall not keep you long. Not there—take a comfortable place." And he arranged a multitude of cushions that were scattered in picturesque disorder upon a vast divan. This was not, however, where she seated herself; she dropped into the nearest chair. The fire had gone out; the lights in the great room were few. She drew her cloak about her; she felt mortally cold. "I think you're trying to humiliate me," Osmond went on. "It's a most absurd undertaking."

"I haven't the least idea what you mean," she returned.

"You've played a very deep game; you've managed it beautifully."

"What is it that I've managed?"

"You've not quite settled it, however; we shall see him again." And he stopped in front of her, with his hands in his pockets, look-ing down at her thoughtfully, in his usual way, which seemed meant to let her know that she was not an object, but only a rather disagreeable incident, of thought.

"If you mean that Lord Warburton's under an obligation to come back you're wrong," Isabel said. "He's under none whatever."

"That's just what I complain of. But when I say he'll come back I don't mean he'll come from a sense of duty."

"There's nothing else to make him. I think he has quite exhausted Rome."

"Ah no, that's a shallow judgement. Rome's inexhaustible." And Osmond began to walk about again. "However, about that perhaps there's no hurry," he added. "It's rather a good idea of his that we should go to England. If it were not for the fear of finding your cousin there I think I should try to persuade you."

"It may be that you'll not find my cousin," said Isabel.

"I should like to be sure of it. However, I shall be as sure as pos-sible. At the same time I should like to see his house, that you told me so much about at one time: what do you call it?—Gardencourt. It must be a charming thing. And then, you know, I've a devotion to the memory of your uncle: you made me take a great fancy to him. I should like to see where he lived and died. That indeed is a detail. Your friend was right. Pansy ought to see England."

"I've no doubt she would enjoy it," said Isabel.

"But that's a long time hence; next autumn's far off," Osmond continued; "and meantime there are things that more nearly interest us. Do you think me so very proud?" he suddenly asked.

"I think you very strange."

"You don't understand me."

"No, not even when you insult me."

"I don't insult you; I'm incapable of it. I merely speak of certain facts, and if the allusion's an injury to you the fault's not mine. It's surely a fact that you have kept all this matter quite in your own hands."

"Are you going back to Lord Warburton?" Isabel asked. "I'm very tired of his name."

"You shall hear it again before we've done with it."

She had spoken of his insulting her, but it suddenly seemed to her that this ceased to be a pain. He was going down—down; the vision of such a fall made her almost giddy: that was the only pain. He was too strange, too different; he didn't touch her. Still, the working of his morbid passion was extraordinary, and she felt a rising curiosity to know in what light he saw himself justified. "I might say to you that I judge you've nothing to say to me that's worth hearing," she returned in a moment. "But I should perhaps be wrong. There's a thing that would be worth my hearing—to know in the plainest words of what it is you accuse me."

"Of having prevented Pansy's marriage to Warburton. Are those words plain enough?"

"On the contrary, I took a great interest in it. I told you so; and when you told me that you counted on me—that I think was what you said—I accepted the obligation. I was a fool to do so, but I did it."

"You pretended to do it, and you even pretended reluctance to make me more willing to trust you. Then you began to use your ingenuity to get him out of the way."

"I think I see what you mean," said Isabel.

"Where's the letter you told me he had written me?" her husband demanded.

"I haven't the least idea; I haven't asked him."

"You stopped it on the way," said Osmond.

Isabel slowly got up; standing there in her white cloak, which covered her to her feet, she might have represented the angel of disdain, first cousin to that of pity. "Oh, Gilbert, for a man who was so fine—!" she exclaimed in a long murmur.

"I was never so fine as you. You've done everything you wanted. You've got him out of the way without appearing to do so, and you've placed me in the position in which you wished to see me—

that of a man who has tried to marry his daughter to a lord, but has grotesquely failed."

"Pansy doesn't care for him. She's very glad he's gone," Isabel said.

"That has nothing to do with the matter."

"And he doesn't care for Pansy."

"That won't do; you told me he did. I don't know why you wanted this particular satisfaction," Osmond continued; "you might have taken some other. It doesn't seem to me that I've been presumptuous—that I have taken too much for granted. I've been very modest about it, very quiet. The idea didn't originate with me. He began to show that he liked her before I ever thought of it. I left it all to you."

"Yes, you were very glad to leave it to me. After this you must attend to such things yourself."

He looked at her a moment; then he turned away. "I thought you were very fond of my daughter."

"I've never been more so than to-day."

"Your affection is attended with immense limitations. However, that perhaps is natural."

"Is this all you wished to say to me?" Isabel asked, taking a candle that stood on one of the tables.

"Are you satisfied? Am I sufficiently disappointed?"

"I don't think that on the whole you're disappointed. You've had another opportunity to try to stupefy me."

"It's not that. It's proved that Pansy can aim high."

"Poor little Pansy!" said Isabel as she turned away with her candle.

XLVII

It was from Henrietta Stackpole that she learned how Caspar Goodwood had come to Rome; an event that took place three days after Lord Warburton's departure. This latter fact had been preceded by an incident of some importance to Isabel—the temporary absence, once again, of Madame Merle, who had gone to Naples to stay with a friend, the happy possessor of a villa at Posilippo.[1] Madame Merle had ceased to minister to Isabel's happiness, who found herself wondering whether the most discreet of women might not also by chance be the most dangerous. Sometimes, at night, she had strange visions; she seemed to see her husband and her friend —his friend—in dim, indistinguishable combination. It seemed to her that she had not done with her; this lady had something in reserve. Isabel's imagination applied itself actively to this elusive point, but every now and then it was checked by a nameless dread,

1. A suburb of Naples.

so that when the charming woman was away from Rome she had almost a consciousness of respite. She had already learned from Miss Stackpole that Caspar Goodwood was in Europe, Henrietta having written to make it known to her immediately after meeting him in Paris. He himself never wrote to Isabel, and though he was in Europe she thought it very possible he might not desire to see her. Their last interview, before her marriage, had had quite the character of a complete rupture; if she remembered rightly he had said he wished to take his last look at her. Since then he had been the most discordant survival of her earlier time—the only one in fact with which a permanent pain was associated. He had left her that morning with a sense of the most superfluous of shocks: it was like a collision between vessels in broad daylight. There had been no mist, no hidden current to excuse it, and she herself had only wished to steer wide. He had bumped against her prow, however, while her hand was on the tiller, and—to complete the metaphor —had given the lighter vessel a strain which still occasionally betrayed itself in a faint creaking. It had been horrid to see him, because he represented the only serious harm that (to her belief) she had ever done in the world: he was the only person with an unsatisfied claim on her. She had made him unhappy, she couldn't help it; and his unhappiness was a grim reality. She had cried with rage, after he had left her, at—she hardly knew what: she tried to think it had been at his want of consideration. He had come to her with his unhappiness when her own bliss was so perfect; he had done his best to darken the brightness of those pure rays. He had not been violent, and yet there had been a violence in the impression. There had been a violence at any rate in something somewhere; perhaps it was only in her own fit of weeping and in that after-sense of the same which had lasted three or four days.

The effect of his final appeal had in short faded away, and all the first year of her marriage he had dropped out of her books. He was a thankless subject of reference; it was disagreeable to have to think of a person who was sore and sombre about you and whom you could yet do nothing to relieve. It would have been different if she had been able to doubt, even a little, of his unreconciled state, as she doubted of Lord Warburton's; unfortunately it was beyond question, and this aggressive, uncompromising look of it was just what made it unattractive. She could never say to herself that here was a sufferer who had compensations, as she was able to say in the case of her English suitor. She had no faith in Mr. Goodwood's compensations and no esteem for them. A cotton-factory was not a compensation for anything—least of all for having failed to marry Isabel Archer. And yet, beyond that, she hardly knew what he had

—save of course his intrinsic qualities. Oh, he was intrinsic enough; she never thought of his even looking for artificial aids. If he extended his business—that, to the best of her belief, was the only form exertion could take with him—it would be because it was an enterprising thing, or good for the business; not in the least because he might hope it would overlay the past. This gave his figure a kind of bareness and bleakness which made the accident of meeting it in memory or in apprehension a peculiar concussion; it was deficient in the social drapery commonly muffling, in an overcivilized age, the sharpness of human contacts. His perfect silence, moreover, the fact that she never heard from him and very seldom heard any mention of him, deepened this impression of his loneliness. She asked Lily for news of him, from time to time; but Lily knew nothing of Boston—her imagination was all bounded on the east by Madison Avenue. As time went on Isabel had thought of him oftener, and with fewer restrictions; she had had more than once the idea of writing to him. She had never told her husband about him—never let Osmond know of his visits to her in Florence; a reserve not dictated in the early period by a want of confidence in Osmond, but simply by the consideration that the young man's disappointment was not her secret but his own. It would be wrong of her, she had believed, to convey it to another, and Mr. Goodwood's affairs could have, after all, little interest for Gilbert. When it had come to the point she had never written to him; it seemed to her that, considering his grievance, the least she could do was to let him alone. Nevertheless she would have been glad to be in some way nearer to him. It was not that it ever occurred to her that she might have married him; even after the consequences of her actual union had grown vivid to her that particular reflection, though she indulged in so many, had not had the assurance to present itself. But on finding herself in trouble he had become a member of that circle of things with which she wished to set herself right. I have mentioned how passionately she needed to feel that her unhappiness should not have come to her through her own fault. She had no near prospect of dying, and yet she wished to make her peace with the world—to put her spiritual affairs in order. It came back to her from time to time that there was an account still to be settled with Caspar, and she saw herself disposed or able to settle it to-day on terms easier for him than ever before. Still, when she learned he was coming to Rome she felt all afraid; it would be more disagreeable for him than for any one else to make out—since he *would* make it out, as over a falsified balance-sheet or something of that sort—the intimate disarray of her affairs. Deep in her breast she believed that he had invested his all in her happiness, while the others had invested only a part. He was one more person from whom she should have to conceal her stress. She was reassured, however, after he arrived in Rome, for he spent several days without coming to see her.

Henrietta Stackpole, it may well be imagined, was much more punctual, and Isabel was largely favoured with the society of her friend. She threw herself into it, for now that she had made such a point of keeping her conscience clear, that was one way of proving she had not been superficial—the more so as the years, in their flight, had rather enriched than blighted those peculiarities which had been humorously criticised by persons less interested than Isabel, and which were still marked enough to give loyalty a spice of heroism. Henrietta was as keen and quick and fresh as ever, and as neat and bright and fair. Her remarkably open eyes, lighted like great glazed railway-stations, had put up no shutters; her attire had lost none of its crispness, her opinions none of their national reference. She was by no means quite unchanged, however; it struck Isabel she had grown vague. Of old she had never been vague; though undertaking many enquiries at once, she had managed to be entire and pointed about each. She had a reason for everything she did; she fairly bristled with motives. Formerly, when she came to Europe it was because she wished to see it, but now, having already seen it, she had no such excuse. She didn't for a moment pretend that the desire to examine decaying civilisations had anything to do with her present enterprise; her journey was rather an expression of her independence of the old world than of a sense of further obligations to it. "It's nothing to come to Europe," she said to Isabel; "it doesn't seem to me one needs so many reasons for that. It is something to stay at home; this is much more important." It was not therefore with a sense of doing anything very important that she treated herself to another pilgrimage to Rome; she had seen the place before and carefully inspected it; her present act was simply a sign of familiarity, of her knowing all about it, of her having as good a right as any one else to be there. This was all very well, and Henrietta was restless; she had a perfect right to be restless too, if one came to that. But she had after all a better reason for coming to Rome than that she cared for it so little. Her friend easily recognised it, and with it the worth of the other's fidelity. She had crossed the stormy ocean in midwinter because she had guessed that Isabel was sad. Henrietta guessed a great deal, but she had never guessed so happily as that. Isabel's satisfactions just now were few, but even if they had been more numerous there would still have been something of individual joy in her sense of being justified in having always thought highly of Henrietta. She had made large concessions with regard to her, and had yet insisted that, with all abatements, she was very valuable. It was not her own triumph, however, that

she found good; it was simply the relief of confessing to this confidant, the first person to whom she had owned it, that she was not
in the least at her ease. Henrietta had herself approached this point
with the smallest possible delay, and had accused her to her face of
being wretched. She was a woman, she was a sister, she was not
Ralph, nor Lord Warburton, nor Caspar Goodwood, and Isabel
could speak.

"Yes, I'm wretched," she said very mildly. She hated to hear herself say it; she tried to say it as judicially as possible.

"What does he do to you?" Henrietta asked, frowning as if she
were enquiring into the operations of a quack doctor.

"He does nothing. But he doesn't like me."

"He's very hard to please!" cried Miss Stackpole. "Why don't
you leave him?"

"I can't change that way," Isabel said.

"Why not, I should like to know? You won't confess that you've
made a mistake. You're too proud."

"I don't know whether I'm too proud. But I can't publish my
mistake. I don't think that's decent. I'd much rather die."

"You won't think so always," said Henrietta.

"I don't know what great unhappiness might bring me to; but it
seems to me I shall always be ashamed. One must accept one's
deeds. I married him before all the world; I was perfectly free; it
was impossible to do anything more deliberate. One can't change
that way," Isabel repeated.

"You *have* changed, in spite of the impossibility. I hope you
don't mean to say you like him."

Isabel debated. "No, I don't like him. I can tell you, because I'm
weary of my secret. But that's enough; I can't announce it on the
housetops."

Henrietta gave a laugh. "Don't you think you're rather too considerate?"

"It's not of him that I'm considerate—it's of myself!" Isabel
answered.

It was not surprising Gilbert Osmond should not have taken
comfort in Miss Stackpole; his instinct had naturally set him in
opposition to a young lady capable of advising his wife to withdraw
from the conjugal roof. When she arrived in Rome he had said to
Isabel that he hoped she would leave her friend the interviewer
alone; and Isabel had answered that he at least had nothing to fear
from her. She said to Henrietta that as Osmond didn't like her she
couldn't invite her to dine, but they could easily see each other in
other ways. Isabel received Miss Stackpole freely in her own sitting-
room, and took her repeatedly to drive, face to face with Pansy,
who, bending a little forward, on the opposite seat of the carriage,

gazed at the celebrated authoress with a respectful attention which Henrietta occasionally found irritating. She complained to Isabel that Miss Osmond had a little look as if she should remember everything one said. "I don't want to be remembered that way," Miss Stackpole declared; "I consider that my conversation refers only to the moment, like the morning papers. Your stepdaughter, as she sits there, looks as if she kept all the back numbers and would bring them out some day against me." She could not teach herself to think favourably of Pansy, whose absence of initiative, of conversation, of personal claims, seemed to her, in a girl of twenty, unnatural and even uncanny. Isabel presently saw that Osmond would have liked her to urge a little the cause of her friend, insist a little upon his receiving her, so that he might appear to suffer for good manners' sake. Her immediate acceptance of his objections put him too much in the wrong—it being in effect one of the disadvantages of expressing contempt that you cannot enjoy at the same time the credit of expressing sympathy. Osmond held to his credit, and yet he held to his objections—all of which were elements difficult to reconcile. The right thing would have been that Miss Stackpole should come to dine at Palazzo Roccanera once or twice, so that (in spite of his superficial civility, always so great) she might judge for herself how little pleasure it gave him. From the moment, however, that both the ladies were so unaccommodating, there was nothing for Osmond but to wish the lady from New York would take herself off. It was surprising how little satisfaction he got from his wife's friends; he took occasion to call Isabel's attention to it.

"You're certainly not fortunate in your intimates; I wish you might make a new collection," he said to her one morning in reference to nothing visible at the moment, but in a tone of ripe reflection which deprived the remark of all brutal abruptness. "It's as if you had taken the trouble to pick out the people in the world that I have least in common with. Your cousin I have always thought a conceited ass—besides his being the most ill-favoured animal I know. Then it's insufferably tiresome that one can't tell him so; one must spare him on account of his health. His health seems to me the best part of him; it gives him privileges enjoyed by no one else. If he's so desperately ill there's only one way to prove it; but he seems to have no mind for that. I can't say much more for the great Warburton. When one really thinks of it, the cool insolence of that performance was something rare! He comes and looks at one's daughter as if she were a suite of apartments; he tries the door-handles and looks out of the windows, raps on the walls and almost thinks he'll take the place. Will you be so good as to draw up a lease? Then, on the whole, he decides that the rooms are too small; he doesn't think he could live on a third floor; he must look out for a *piano nobile*. And he goes away after having got a month's lodging in the poor little apartment for nothing. Miss Stackpole, however, is your most wonderful invention. She strikes me as a kind of monster. One hasn't a nerve in one's body that she doesn't set quivering. You know I never have admitted that she's a woman. Do you know what she reminds me of? Of a new steel pen—the most odious thing in nature. She talks as a steel pen writes; aren't her letters, by the way, on ruled paper? She thinks and moves and walks and looks exactly as she talks. You may say that she doesn't hurt me, inasmuch as I don't see her. I don't see her, but I hear her; I hear her all day long. Her voice is in my ears; I can't get rid of it. I know exactly what she says, and every inflexion of the tone in which she says it. She says charming things about me, and they give you great comfort. I don't like at all to think she talks about me—I feel as I should feel if I knew the footman were wearing my hat."

Henrietta talked about Gilbert Osmond, as his wife assured him, rather less than he suspected. She had plenty of other subjects, in two of which the reader may be supposed to be especially interested. She let her friend know that Caspar Goodwood had discovered for himself that she was unhappy, though indeed her ingenuity was unable to suggest what comfort he hoped to give her by coming to Rome and yet not calling on her. They met him twice in the street, but he had no appearance of seeing them; they were driving, and he had a habit of looking straight in from of him, as if he proposed to take in but one object at a time. Isabel could have fancied she had seen him the day before; it must have been with just that face and step that he had walked out of Mrs. Touchett's door at the close of their last interview. He was dressed just as he had been dressed on that day, Isabel remembered the colour of his cravat; and yet in spite of this familiar look there was a strangeness in his figure too, something that made her feel it afresh to be rather terrible he should have come to Rome. He looked bigger and more overtopping than of old, and in those days he certainly reached high enough. She noticed that the people whom he passed looked back after him; but he went straight forward, lifting above them a face like a February sky.

Miss Stackpole's other topic was very different; she gave Isabel the latest news about Mr. Bantling. He had been out in the United States the year before, and she was happy to say she had been able to show him considerable attention. She didn't know how much he had enjoyed it, but she would undertake to say it had done him good; he wasn't the same man when he left as he had been when he came. It had opened his eyes and shown him that England wasn't everything. He had been very much liked in most places, and thought extremely simple—more simple than the English were commonly supposed to be. There were people who had thought him affected; she didn't know whether they meant that his simplicity was an affectation. Some of his questions were too discouraging; he thought all the chambermaids were farmers' daughters—or all the farmers' daughters were chambermaids—she couldn't exactly remember which. He hadn't seemed able to grasp the great school system; it had been really too much for him. On the whole he had behaved as if there were too much of everything—as if he could only take in a small part. The part he had chosen was the hotel system and the river navigation. He had seemed really fascinated with the hotels; he had a photograph of every one he had visited. But the river steamers were his principal interest; he wanted to do nothing but sail on the big boats. They had travelled together from New York to Milwaukee, stopping at the most interesting cities on the route; and whenever they started afresh he had wanted to know if they could go by the steamer. He seemed to have no idea of geography—had an impression that Baltimore was a Western city and was perpetually expecting to arrive at the Mississippi. He appeared never to have heard of any river in America but the Mississippi and was unprepared to recognise the existence of the Hudson, though obliged to confess at last that it was fully equal to the Rhine. They had spent some pleasant hours in the palace-cars; he was always ordering ice-cream from the coloured man. He could never get used to that idea—that you could get ice-cream in the cars. Of course you couldn't, nor fans, nor candy, nor anything in the English cars! He found the heat quite overwhelming, and she had told him she indeed expected it was the biggest he had ever experienced. He was now in England, hunting—"hunting round" Henrietta called it. These amusements were those of the American red men; we had left that behind long ago, the pleasures of the chase. It seemed to be generally believed in England that we wore tomahawks and feathers; but such a costume was more in keeping with English habits. Mr. Bantling would not have time to join her in Italy, but when she should go to Paris again he expected to come over. He wanted very much to see Versailles again; he was very fond of the ancient *régime*.[2] They didn't agree about that, but that was what she liked Versailles for, that you could see the ancient *régime* had been swept away. There were no dukes and marquises there now; she remembered on the contrary one day when there were five American families, walking all round. Mr. Bantling was very anxious that she should take up the subject of England again, and he thought she might get on better with it now; England had changed a good deal within two or three years. He was determined that if she went there

2. *Ancien régime* describes the order of things in France prior to the social changes of the French Revolution (1789).

he should go to see his sister, Lady Pensil, and that this time the invitation should come to her straight. The mystery about that other one had never been explained.

Caspar Goodwood came at last to Palazzo Roccanera; he had written Isabel a note beforehand, to ask leave. This was promptly granted; she would be at home at six o'clock that afternoon. She spent the day wondering what he was coming for—what good he expected to get of it. He had presented himself hitherto as a person destitute of the faculty of compromise, who would take what he had asked for or take nothing. Isabel's hospitality, however, raised no questions, and she found no great difficulty in appearing happy enough to deceive him. It was her conviction at least that she deceived him, made him say to himself that he had been misinformed. But she also saw, so she believed, that he was not disappointed, as some other men, she was sure, would have been; he had not come to Rome to look for an opportunity. She never found out what he had come for; he offered her no explanation; there could be none but the very simple one that he wanted to see her. In other words he had come for his amusement. Isabel followed up this induction with a good deal of eagerness, and was delighted to have found a formula that would lay the ghost of this gentleman's ancient grievance. If he had come to Rome for his amusement this was exactly what she wanted, for if he cared for amusement he had got over his heartache. If he had got over his heartache everything was as it should be and her responsibilities were at an end. It was true that he took his recreation a little stiffly, but he had never been loose and easy and she had every reason to believe he was satisfied with what he saw. Henrietta was not in his confidence, though he was in hers, and Isabel consequently received no side-light upon his state of mind. He was open to little conversation on general topics; it came back to her that she had said of him once, years before, "Mr. Goodwood speaks a good deal, but he doesn't talk." He spoke a good deal now, but he talked perhaps as little as ever; considering, that is, how much there was in Rome to talk about. His arrival was not calculated to simplify her relations with her husband, for if Mr. Osmond didn't like her friends Mr. Goodwood had no claim upon his attention save as having been one of the first of them. There was nothing for her to say of him but that he was the very oldest; this rather meagre synthesis exhausted the facts. She had been obliged to introduce him to Gilbert; it was impossible she should not ask him to dinner, to her Thursday evenings, of which she had grown very weary, but to which her husband still held for the sake not so much of inviting people as of not inviting them.

To the Thursdays Mr. Goodwood came regularly, solemnly, rather early; he appeared to regard them with a good deal of gravity.

Isabel every now and then had a moment of anger; there was something so literal about him; she thought he might know that she didn't know what to do with him. But she couldn't call him stupid; he was not that in the least; he was only extraordinarily honest. To be as honest as that made a man very different from most people; one had to be almost equally honest with *him*. She made this latter reflection at the very time she was flattering herself she had persuaded him that she was the most light-hearted of women. He never threw any doubt on this point, never asked her any personal questions. He got on much better with Osmond than had seemed probable. Osmond had a great dislike to being counted on; in such a case he had an irresistible need of disappointing you. It was in virtue of this principle that he gave himself the entertainment of taking a fancy to a perpendicular Bostonian whom he had been depended upon to treat with coldness. He asked Isabel if Mr. Goodwood also had wanted to marry her, and expressed surprise at her not having accepted him. It would have been an excellent thing, like living under some tall belfry which would strike all the hours and make a queer vibration in the upper air. He declared he liked to talk with the great Goodwood; it wasn't easy at first, you had to climb up an interminable steep staircase, up to the top of the tower; but when you got there you had a big view and felt a little fresh breeze. Osmond, as we know, had delightful qualities, and he gave Caspar Goodwood the benefit of them all. Isabel could see that Mr. Goodwood thought better of her husband than he had ever wished to; he had given her the impression that morning in Florence of being inaccessible to a good impression. Gilbert asked him repeatedly to dinner, and Mr. Goodwood smoked a cigar with him afterwards and even desired to be shown his collections. Gilbert said to Isabel that he was very original; he was as strong and of as good a style as an English portmanteau,—he had plenty of straps and buckles which would never wear out, and a capital patent lock. Caspar Goodwood took to riding on the Campagna and devoted much time to this exercise; it was therefore mainly in the evening that Isabel saw him. She bethought herself of saying to him one day that if he were willing he could render her a service. And then she added smiling:

"I don't know, however, what right I have to ask a service of you."

"You're the person in the world who has most right," he answered. "I've given you assurances that I've never given any one else."

The service was that he should go and see her cousin Ralph, who was ill at the Hôtel de Paris, alone, and be as kind to him as possible. Mr. Goodwood had never seen him, but he would know who the poor fellow was; if she was not mistaken Ralph had once invited him to Gardencourt. Caspar remembered the invitation perfectly,

and, though he was not supposed to be a man of imagination, had
enough to put himself in the place of a poor gentleman who lay
dying at a Roman inn. He called at the Hôtel de Paris and, on being
shown into the presence of the master of Gardencourt, found Miss
Stackpole sitting beside his sofa. A singular change had in fact
occurred in this lady's relations with Ralph Touchett. She had not
been asked by Isabel to go and see him, but on hearing that he was
too ill to come out had immediately gone of her own motion. After
this she had paid him a daily visit—always under the conviction
that they were great enemies. "Oh yes, we're intimate enemies,"
Ralph used to say; and he accused her freely—as freely as the
humour of it would allow—of coming to worry him to death. In
reality they became excellent friends, Henrietta much wondering
that she should never have liked him before. Ralph liked her exactly
as much as he had always done; he had never doubted for a
moment that she was an excellent fellow. They talked about everything and always differed; about everything, that is, but Isabel—a
topic as to which Ralph always had a thin forefinger on his lips.
Mr. Bantling on the other hand proved a great resource; Ralph was
capable of discussing Mr. Bantling with Henrietta for hours. Discussion was stimulated of course by their inevitable difference of view
—Ralph having amused himself with taking the ground that the
genial ex-guardsman was a regular Machiavelli. Caspar Goodwood
could contribute nothing to such a debate; but after he had been left
alone with his host he found there were various other matters they
could take up. It must be admitted that the lady who had just gone
out was not one of these; Caspar granted all Miss Stackpole's merits
in advance, but had no further remark to make about her. Neither,
after the first allusions, did the two men expatiate upon Mrs.
Osmond—a theme in which Goodwood perceived as many dangers
as Ralph. He felt very sorry for that unclassable personage; he
couldn't bear to see a pleasant man, so pleasant for all his queerness, so beyond anything to be done. There was always something
to be done, for Goodwood, and he did it in this case by repeating
several times his visit to the Hôtel de Paris. It seemed to Isabel that
she had been very clever; she had artfully disposed of the superfluous Caspar. She had given him an occupation; she had converted
him into a caretaker of Ralph. She had a plan of making him travel
northward with her cousin as soon as the first mild weather should
allow it. Lord Warburton had brought Ralph to Rome and Mr.
Goodwood should take him away. There seemed a happy symmetry
in this, and she was now intensely eager that Ralph should depart.
She had a constant fear he would die there before her eyes and a
horror of the occurrence of this event at an inn, by her door, which
he had so rarely entered. Ralph must sink to his last rest in his own
dear house, in one of those deep, dim chambers of Gardencourt

where the dark ivy would cluster round the edges of the glimmering window. There seemed to Isabel in these days something sacred in Gardencourt; no chapter of the past was more perfectly irrecoverable. When she thought of the months she had spent there the tears rose to her eyes. She flattered herself, as I say, upon her ingenuity, but she had need of all she could muster; for several events occurred which seemed to confront and defy her. The Countess Gemini arrived from Florence—arrived with her trunks, her dresses, her chatter, her falsehoods, her frivolity, the strange, the unholy legend of the number of her lovers. Edward Rosier, who had been away somewhere,—no one, not even Pansy, knew where,—reappeared in Rome and began to write her long letters, which she never answered. Madame Merle returned from Naples and said to her with a strange smile: "What on earth did you do with Lord Warburton?" As if it were any business of hers!

XLVIII

One day, toward the end of February, Ralph Touchett made up his mind to return to England. He had his own reasons for his decision, which he was not bound to communicate; but Henrietta Stackpole, to whom he mentioned his intention, flattered herself that she guessed them. She forbore to express them, however; she only said, after a moment, as she sat by his sofa: "I suppose you know you can't go alone?"

"I've no idea of doing that," Ralph answered. "I shall have people with me."

"What do you mean by 'people'? Servants whom you pay?"

"Ah," said Ralph jocosely, "after all, they're human beings."

"Are there any women among them?" Miss Stackpole desired to know.

"You speak as if I had a dozen! No, I confess I haven't a soubrette[1] in my employment."

"Well," said Henrietta calmly, "you can't go to England that way. You must have a woman's care."

"I've had so much of yours for the past fortnight that it will last me a good while."

"You've not had enough of it yet. I guess I'll go with you," said Henrietta.

"Go with me?" Ralph slowly raised himself from his sofa.

"Yes, I know you don't like me, but I'll go with you all the same. It would be better for your health to lie down again."

Ralph looked at her a little; then he slowly relapsed. "I like you very much," he said in a moment.

Miss Stackpole gave one of her infrequent laughs. "You needn't

1. A waiting maid.

think that by saying that you can buy me off. I'll go with you, and what is more I'll take care of you."

"You're a very good woman," said Ralph.

"Wait till I get you safely home before you say that. It won't be easy. But you had better go, all the same."

Before she left him, Ralph said to her: "Do you really mean to take care of me?"

"Well, I mean to try."

"I notify you then that I submit. Oh, I submit!" And it was perhaps a sign of submission that a few minutes after she had left him alone he burst into a loud fit of laughter. It seemed to him so inconsequent, such a conclusive proof of his having abdicated all functions and renounced all exercise, that he should start on a journey across Europe under the supervision of Miss Stackpole. And the great oddity was that the prospect pleased him; he was gratefully, luxuriously passive. He felt even impatient to start; and indeed he had an immense longing to see his own house again. The end of everything was at hand; it seemed to him he could stretch out his arm and touch the goal. But he wanted to die at home; it was the only wish he had left—to extend himself in the large quiet room where he had last seen his father lie, and close his eyes upon the summer dawn.

That same day Caspar Goodwood came to see him, and he informed his visitor that Miss Stackpole had taken him up and was to conduct him back to England. "Ah then," said Caspar, "I'm afraid I shall be a fifth wheel to the coach. Mrs. Osmond has made *me* promise to go with you."

"Good heavens—it's the golden age! You're all too kind."

"The kindness on my part is to her; it's hardly to you."

"Granting that, *she's* kind," smiled Ralph.

"To get people to go with you? Yes, that's a sort of kindness," Goodwood answered without lending himself to the joke. "For myself, however," he added, "I'll go so far as to say that I would much rather travel with you and Miss Stackpole than with Miss Stackpole alone."

"And you'd rather stay here than do either," said Ralph. "There's really no need of your coming. Henrietta's extraordinarily efficient."

"I'm sure of that. But I've promised Mrs. Osmond."

"You can easily get her to let you off."

"She wouldn't let me off for the world. She wants me to look after you, but that isn't the principal thing. The principal thing is that she wants me to leave Rome."

"Ah, you see too much in it," Ralph suggested.

"I bore her," Goodwood went on; "she has nothing to say to me, so she invented that."

"Oh then, if it's a convenience to her I certainly will take you with me. Though I don't see why it should be a convenience," Ralph added in a moment.

"Well," said Caspar Goodwood simply, "she thinks I'm watching her."

"Watching her?"

"Trying to make out if she's happy."

"That's easy to make out," said Ralph. "She's the most visibly happy woman I know."

"Exactly so; I'm satisfied," Goodwood answered dryly. For all his dryness, however, he had more to say. "I've been watching her; I was an old friend and it seemed to me I had the right. She pretends to be happy; that was what she undertook to be; and I thought I should like to see for myself what it amounts to. I've seen," he continued with a harsh ring in his voice, "and I don't want to see any more. I'm now quite ready to go."

"Do you know it strikes me as about time you should?" Ralph rejoined. And this was the only conversation these gentlemen had about Isabel Osmond.

Henrietta made her preparations for departure, and among them she found it proper to say a few words to the Countess Gemini, who returned at Miss Stackpole's *pension* the visit which this lady had paid her in Florence.

"You were very wrong about Lord Warburton," she remarked to the Countess. "I think it right you should know that."

"About his making love to Isabel? My poor lady, he was at her house three times a day. He has left traces of his passage!" the Countess cried.

"He wished to marry your niece; that's why he came to the house."

The Countess stared, and then with an inconsiderate laugh: "Is that the story that Isabel tells? It isn't bad, as such things go. If he wishes to marry my niece, pray why doesn't he do it? Perhaps he has gone to buy the wedding-ring and will come back with it next month, after I'm gone."

"No, he'll not come back. Miss Osmond doesn't wish to marry him."

"She's very accommodating! I knew she was fond of Isabel, but I didn't know she carried it so far."

"I don't understand you," said Henrietta coldly, and reflecting that the Countess was unpleasantly perverse. "I really must stick to my point—that Isabel never encouraged the attentions of Lord Warburton."

"My dear friend, what do you and I know about it? All we know is that my brother's capable of everything."

"I don't know what your brother's capable of," said Henrietta with dignity.

"It's not her encouraging Warburton that I complain of; it's her sending him away. I want particularly to see him. Do you suppose she thought I would make him faithless?" the Countess continued with audacious insistence. "However, she's only keeping him, one can feel that. The house is full of him there; he's quite in the air. Oh yes, he has left traces; I'm sure I shall see him yet."

"Well," said Henrietta after a little, with one of those inspirations which had made the fortune of her letters to the *Interviewer*, "perhaps he'll be more successful with you than with Isabel!"

When she told her friend of the offer she had made Ralph Isabel replied that she could have done nothing that would have pleased her more. It had always been her faith that at bottom Ralph and this young woman were made to understand each other. "I don't care whether he understands me or not," Henrietta declared. "The great thing is that he shouldn't die in the cars."

"He won't do that," Isabel said, shaking her head with an extension of faith.

"He won't if I can help it. I see you want us all to go. I don't know what you want to do."

"I want to be alone," said Isabel.

"You won't be that so long as you've so much company at home."

"Ah, they're part of the comedy. You others are spectators."

"Do you call it a comedy, Isabel Archer?" Henrietta rather grimly asked.

"The tragedy then if you like. You're all looking at me; it makes me uncomfortable."

Henrietta engaged in this act for a while. "You're like the stricken deer, seeking the innermost shade. Oh, you do give me such a sense of helplessness!" she broke out.

"I'm not at all helpless. There are many things I mean to do."

"It's not you I'm speaking of; it's myself. It's too much, having come on purpose, to leave you just as I find you."

"You don't do that; you leave me much refreshed," Isabel said.

"Very mild refreshment—sour lemonade! I want you to promise me something."

"I can't do that. I shall never make another promise. I made such a solemn one four years ago, and I've succeeded so ill in keeping it."

"You've had no encouragement. In this case I should give you the greatest. Leave your husband before the worst comes; that's what I want you to promise."

"The worst? What do you call the worst?"

"Before your character gets spoiled."

"Do you mean my disposition? It won't get spoiled," Isabel answered, smiling. "I'm taking very good care of it. I'm extremely struck," she added, turning away, "with the off-hand way in which you speak of a woman's leaving her husband. It's easy to see you've never had one!"

"Well," said Henrietta as if she were beginning an argument, "nothing is more common in our Western cities, and it's to them, after all, that we must look in the future." Her argument, however, does not concern this history, which has too many other threads to unwind. She announced to Ralph Touchett that she was ready to leave Rome by any train he might designate, and Ralph immediately pulled himself together for departure. Isabel went to see him at the last, and he made the same remark that Henrietta had made. It struck him that Isabel was uncommonly glad to get rid of them all.

For all answer to this she gently laid her hand on his, and said in a low tone, with a quick smile: "My dear Ralph—!"

It was answer enough, and he was quite contented. But he went on in the same way, jocosely, ingenuously: "I've seen less of you than I might, but it's better than nothing. And then I've heard a great deal about you."

"I don't know from whom, leading the life you've done."

"From the voices of the air! Oh, from no one else; I never let other people speak of you. They always say you're 'charming,' and that's so flat."

"I might have seen more of you certainly," Isabel said. "But when one's married one has so much occupation."

"Fortunately I'm not married. When you come to see me in England I shall be able to entertain you with all the freedom of a bachelor." He continued to talk as if they should certainly meet again, and succeeded in making the assumption appear almost just. He made no allusion to his term being near, to the probability that he should not outlast the summer. If he preferred it so, Isabel was willing enough; the reality was sufficiently distinct without their erecting finger-posts in conversation. That had been well enough for the earlier time, though about this, as about his other affairs, Ralph had never been egotistic. Isabel spoke of his journey, of the stages into which he should divide it, of the precautions he should take. "Henrietta's my greatest precaution," he went on. "The conscience of that woman's sublime."

"Certainly she'll be very conscientious."

"Will be? She has been! It's only because she thinks it's her duty that she goes with me. There's a conception of duty for you."

"Yes, it's a generous one," said Isabel, "and it makes me deeply ashamed. I ought to go with you, you know."

"Your husband wouldn't like that."

"No, he wouldn't like it. But I might go, all the same."

"I'm startled by the boldness of your imagination. Fancy my being a cause of disagreement between a lady and her husband!"

"That's why I don't go," said Isabel simply—yet not very lucidly.

Ralph understood well enough, however. "I should think so, with all those occupations you speak of."

"It isn't that. I'm afraid," said Isabel. After a pause she repeated, as if to make herself, rather than him, hear the words: "I'm afraid."

Ralph could hardly tell what her tone meant; it was so strangely deliberate—apparently so void of emotion. Did she wish to do public penance for a fault of which she had not been convicted? or were her words simply an attempt at enlightened self-analysis? However this might be, Ralph could not resist so easy an opportunity. "Afraid of your husband?"

"Afraid of myself!" she said, getting up. She stood there a moment and then added: "If I were afraid of my husband that would be simply my duty. That's what women are expected to be."

"Ah yes," laughed Ralph; "but to make up for it there's always some man awfully afraid of some woman!"

She gave no heed to this pleasantry, but suddenly took a different turn. "With Henrietta at the head of your little band," she exclaimed abruptly, "there will be nothing left for Mr. Goodwood!"

"Ah, my dear Isabel," Ralph answered, "he's used to that. There *is* nothing left for Mr. Goodwood."

She coloured and then observed, quickly, that she must leave him. They stood together a moment; both her hands were in both of his. "You've been my best friend," she said.

"It was for you that I wanted—that I wanted to live. But I'm of no use to you."

Then it came over her more poignantly that she should not see him again. She could not accept that; she could not part with him that way. "If you should send for me I'd come," she said at last.

"Your husband won't consent to that."

"Oh yes, I can arrange it."

"I shall keep that for my last pleasure!" said Ralph.

In answer to which she simply kissed him. It was a Thursday, and that evening Caspar Goodwood came to Palazzo Roccanera. He was among the first to arrive, and he spent some time in conversation with Gilbert Osmond, who almost always was present when his wife received. They sat down together, and Osmond, talkative, communicative, expansive, seemed possessed with a kind of intellectual gaiety. He leaned back with his legs crossed, lounging and chatting, while Goodwood, more restless, but not at all lively, shifted his position, played with his hat, made the little sofa creak beneath him. Osmond's face wore a sharp, aggressive smile; he was as a man whose perceptions have been quickened by good news. He remarked to Goodwood that he was sorry they were to lose him; he himself should particularly miss him. He saw so few intelligent men—they were surprisingly scarce in Rome. He must be sure to come back; there was something very refreshing, to an inveterate Italian like himself, in talking with a genuine outsider.

"I'm very fond of Rome, you know," Osmond said; "but there's nothing I like better than to meet people who haven't that superstition. The modern world's after all very fine. Now you're thoroughly modern and yet are not at all common. So many of the moderns we see are such very poor stuff. If they're the children of the future we're willing to die young. Of course the ancients too are often very tiresome. My wife and I like everything that's really new—not the mere pretence of it. There's nothing new, unfortunately, in ignorance and stupidity. We see plenty of that in forms that offer themselves as a revelation of progress, of light. A revelation of vulgarity! There's a certain kind of vulgarity which I believe is really new; I don't think there ever was anything like it before. Indeed I don't find vulgarity, at all, before the present century. You see a faint menace of it here and there in the last, but to-day the air has grown so dense that delicate things are literally not recognised. Now, we've *liked you*—!" With which he hesitated a moment, laying his hand gently on Goodwood's knee and smiling with a mixture of assurance and embarrassment. "I'm going to say something extremely offensive and patronising, but you must let me have the satisfaction of it. We've liked you because—because you've reconciled us a little to the future. If there are to be a certain number of people like you—*à la bonne heure!*[2] I'm talking for my wife as well as for myself, you see. She speaks for me, my wife; why shouldn't I speak for her? We're as united, you know, as the candlestick and the snuffers. Am I assuming too much when I say that I think I've understood from you that your occupations have been—a—commercial? There's a danger in that, you know; but it's the way you have escaped that strikes us. Excuse me if my little compliment seems in execrable taste; fortunately my wife doesn't hear me. What I mean is that you *might have been*—a—what I was mentioning just now. The whole American world was in a conspiracy to make you so. But you resisted, you've something about you that saved you. And yet you're so modern, so modern; the most modern man we know! We shall always be delighted to see you again."

I have said that Osmond was in good humour, and these remarks will give ample evidence of the fact. They were infinitely more personal than he usually cared to be, and if Caspar Goodwood had attended to them more closely he might have thought that the de-

2. That's capital, grand.

fence of delicacy was in rather odd hands. We may believe, however, that Osmond knew very well what he was about, and that if he chose to use the tone of patronage with a grossness not in his habits he had an excellent reason for the escapade. Goodwood had only a vague sense that he was laying it on somehow; he scarcely knew where the mixture was applied. Indeed he scarcely knew what Osmond was talking about; he wanted to be alone with Isabel, and that idea spoke louder to him than her husband's perfectly-pitched voice. He watched her talking with other people and wondered when she would be at liberty and whether he might ask her to go into one of the other rooms. His humour was not, like Osmond's, of the best; there was an element of dull rage in his consciousness of things. Up to this time he had not disliked Osmond personally; he had only thought him very well-informed and obliging and more than he had supposed like the person whom Isabel Archer would naturally marry. His host had won in the open field a great advantage over him, and Goodwood had too strong a sense of fair play to have been moved to underrate him on that account. He had not tried positively to think well of him; this was a flight of sentimental benevolence of which, even in the days when he came nearest to reconciling himself to what had happened, Goodwood was quite incapable. He accepted him as rather a brilliant personage of the amateurish kind, afflicted with a redundancy of leisure which it amused him to work off in little refinements of conversation. But he only half trusted him; he could never make out why the deuce Osmond should lavish refinements of any sort upon *him*. It made him suspect that he found some private entertainment in it, and it ministered to a general impression that his triumphant rival had in his composition a streak of perversity. He knew indeed that Osmond could have no reason to wish him evil; he had nothing to fear from him. He had carried off a supreme advantage and could afford to be kind to a man who had lost everything. It was true that Goodwood had at times grimly wished he were dead and would have liked to kill him; but Osmond had no means of knowing this, for practice had made the younger man perfect in the art of appearing inaccessible to-day to any violent emotion. He cultivated this art in order to deceive himself, but it was others that he deceived first. He cultivated it, moreover, with very limited success; of which there could be no better proof than the deep, dumb irritation that reigned in his soul when he heard Osmond speak of his wife's feelings as if he were commissioned to answer for them.

That was all he had had an ear for in what his host said to him this evening; he had been conscious that Osmond made more of a point even than usual of referring to the conjugal harmony prevailing at Palazzo Roccanera. He had been more careful than ever to speak as if he and his wife had all things in sweet community and it were as natural to each of them to say "we" as to say "I." In all this there was an air of intention that had puzzled and angered our poor Bostonian, who could only reflect for his comfort that Mrs. Osmond's relations with her husband were none of his business. He had no proof whatever that her husband misrepresented her, and if he judged her by the surface of things was bound to believe that she liked her life. She had never given him the faintest sign of discontent. Miss Stackpole had told him that she had lost her illusions, but writing for the papers had made Miss Stackpole sensational. She was too fond of early news. Moreover, since her arrival in Rome she had been much on her guard; she had pretty well ceased to flash her lantern at him. This indeed, it may be said for her, would have been quite against her conscience. She had now seen the reality of Isabel's situation, and it had inspired her with a just reserve. Whatever could be done to improve it the most useful form of assistance would not be to inflame her former lovers with a sense of her wrongs. Miss Stackpole continued to take a deep interest in the state of Mr. Goodwood's feelings, but she showed it at present only by sending him choice extracts, humorous and other, from the American journals, of which she received several by every post and which she always perused with a pair of scissors in her hand. The articles she cut out she placed in an envelope addressed to Mr. Goodwood, which she left with her own hand at his hotel. He never asked her a question about Isabel: hadn't he come five thousand miles to see for himself? He was thus not in the least authorised to think Mrs. Osmond unhappy; but the very absence of authorisation operated as an irritant, ministered to the harshness with which, in spite of his theory that he had ceased to care, he now recognised that, so far as she was concerned, the future had nothing more for him. He had not even the satisfaction of knowing the truth; apparently he could not even be trusted to respect her if she *were* unhappy. He was hopeless, helpless, useless. To this last character she had called his attention by her ingenious plan for making him leave Rome. He had no objection whatever to doing what he could for her cousin, but it made him grind his teeth to think that of all the services she might have asked of him this was the one she had been eager to select. There had been no danger of her choosing one that would have kept him in Rome.

To-night what he was chiefly thinking of was that he was to leave her to-morrow and that he had gained nothing by coming but the knowledge that he was as little wanted as ever. About herself he had gained no knowledge; she was imperturbable, inscrutable, impenetrable. He felt the old bitterness, which he had tried so hard to swallow, rise again in his throat, and he knew there are disap-

pointments that last as long as life. Osmond went on talking; Goodwood was vaguely aware that he was touching again upon his perfect intimacy with his wife. It seemed to him for a moment that
the man had a kind of demonic imagination; it was impossible that
without malice he should have selected so unusual a topic. But
what did it matter, after all, whether he were demonic or not, and
whether she loved him or hated him? She might hate him to the
death without one's gaining a straw one's self. "You travel, by the
by, with Ralph Touchett," Osmond said. "I suppose that means
you'll move slowly?"

"I don't know. I shall do just as he likes."

"You're very accommodating. We're immensely obliged to you;
you must really let me say it. My wife has probably expressed to you
what we feel. Touchett has been on our minds all winter; it had
looked more than once as if he would never leave Rome. He ought
never to have come; it's worse than an imprudence for people in
that state to travel; it's a kind of indelicacy. I wouldn't for the
world be under such an obligation to Touchett as he has been to—
to my wife and me. Other people inevitably have to look after him,
and every one isn't so generous as you."

"I've nothing else to do," Caspar said dryly.

Osmond looked at him a moment askance. "You ought to marry,
and then you'd have plenty to do. It's true that in that case you
wouldn't be quite so available for deeds of mercy."

"Do you find that as a married man you're so much occupied?"
the young man mechanically asked.

"Ah, you see, being married's in itself an occupation. It isn't
always active; it's often passive; but that takes even more attention.
Then my wife and I do so many things together. We read, we
study, we make music, we walk, we drive—we talk even, as when
we first knew each other. I delight, to this hour, in my wife's conversation. If you're ever bored take my advice and get married.
Your wife indeed may bore you, in that case; but you'll never bore
yourself. You'll always have something to say to yourself—always
have a subject of reflection."

"I'm not bored," said Goodwood. "I've plenty to think about
and to say to myself."

"More than to say to others!" Osmond exclaimed with a light
laugh. "Where shall you go next? I mean after you've consigned
Touchett to his natural caretakers—I believe his mother's at last
coming back to look after him. That little lady's superb; she
neglects her duties with a finish—! Perhaps you'll spend the
summer in England?"

"I don't know. I've no plans."

"Happy man! That's a little bleak, but it's very free."

"Oh yes, I'm very free."

"Free to come back to Rome I hope," said Osmond as he saw a group of new visitors enter the room. "Remember that when you do come we count on you!"

Goodwood had meant to go away early, but the evening elapsed without his having a chance to speak to Isabel otherwise than as one of several associated interlocutors. There was something perverse in the inveteracy with which she avoided him; his unquenchable rancour discovered an intention where there was certainly no appearance of one. There was absolutely no appearance of one. She met his eyes with her clear hospitable smile, which seemed almost to ask that he would come and help her to entertain some of her visitors. To such suggestions, however, he opposed but a stiff impatience. He wandered about and waited; he talked to the few people he knew, who found him for the first time rather self-contradictory. This was indeed rare with Caspar Goodwood, though he often contradicted others. There was often music at Palazzo Roccanera, and it was usually very good. Under cover of the music he managed to contain himself; but toward the end, when he saw the people beginning to go, he drew near to Isabel and asked her in a low tone if he might not speak to her in one of the other rooms, which he had just assured himself was empty. She smiled as if she wished to oblige him but found herself absolutely prevented. "I'm afraid it's impossible. People are saying good-night, and I must be where they can see me."

"I shall wait till they are all gone then."

She hesitated a moment. "Ah, that will be delightful!" she exclaimed.

And he waited, though it took a long time yet. There were several people, at the end, who seemed tethered to the carpet. The Countess Gemini, who was never herself till midnight, as she said, displayed no consciousness that the entertainment was over; she had still a little circle of gentlemen in front of the fire, who every now and then broke into a united laugh. Osmond had disappeared—he never bade good-bye to people; and as the Countess was extending her range, according to her custom at this period of the evening, Isabel had sent Pansy to bed. Isabel sat a little apart; she too appeared to wish her sister-in-law would sound a lower note and let the last loiterers depart in peace.

"May I not say a word to you now?" Goodwood presently asked her.

She got up immediately, smiling. "Certainly, we'll go somewhere else if you like." They went together, leaving the Countess with her little circle, and for a moment after they had crossed the threshold neither of them spoke. Isabel would not sit down; she stood in the middle of the room slowly fanning herself; she had for him the same familiar grace. She seemed to wait for him to speak. Now that he was alone with her all the passion he had never stifled surged into his senses; it hummed in his eyes and made things swim round him. The bright, empty room grew dim and blurred, and through the heaving veil he felt her hover before him with gleaming eyes and parted lips. If he had seen more distinctly he would have perceived her smile was fixed and a trifle forced—that she was frightened at what she saw in his own face. "I suppose you wish to bid me good-bye?" she said.

"Yes—but I don't like it. I don't want to leave Rome," he answered with almost plaintive honesty.

"I can well imagine. It's wonderfully good of you. I can't tell you how kind I think you."

For a moment more he said nothing. "With a few words like that you make me go."

"You must come back some day," she brightly returned.

"Some day? You mean as long a time hence as possible."

"Oh no; I don't mean all that."

"What *do* you mean? I don't understand! But I said I'd go, and I'll go," Goodwood added.

"Come back whenever you like," said Isabel with attempted lightness.

"I don't care a straw for your cousin!" Caspar broke out.

"Is that what you wished to tell me?"

"No, no; I didn't want to tell you anything; I wanted to ask you —" he paused a moment, and then—"what have you really made of your life?" he said, in a low, quick tone. He paused again, as if for an answer; but she said nothing, and he went on: "I can't understand, I can't penetrate you! What am I to believe—what do you want me to think?" Still she said nothing; she only stood looking at him, now quite without pretending to ease. "I'm told you're unhappy, and if you are I should like to know it. That would be something for me. But you yourself say you're happy, and you're somehow so still, so smooth, so hard. You're completely changed. You conceal everything; I haven't really come near you."

"You come very near," Isabel said gently, but in a tone of warning.

"And yet I don't touch you! I want to know the truth. Have you done well?"

"You ask a great deal."

"Yes—I've always asked a great deal. Of course you won't tell me. I shall never know if you can help it. And then it's none of my business." He had spoken with a visible effort to control himself, to give a considerate form to an inconsiderate state of mind. But the sense that it was his last chance, that he loved her and had lost her, that she would think him a fool whatever he should say, suddenly gave him a lash and added a deep vibration to his low voice. "You're perfectly inscrutable, and that's what makes me think you've something to hide. I tell you I don't care a straw for your cousin, but I don't mean that I don't like him. I mean that it isn't because I like him that I go away with him. I'd go if he were an idiot and you should have asked me. If you should ask me I'd go to Siberia to-morrow. Why do you want me to leave the place? You must have some reason for that; if you were as contented as you pretend you are you wouldn't care. I'd rather know the truth about you, even if it's damnable, than have come here for nothing. That isn't what I came for. I thought I shouldn't care. I came because I wanted to assure myself that I needn't think of you any more. I haven't thought of anything else, and you're quite right to wish me to go away. But if I must go, there's no harm in my letting myself out for a single moment, is there? If you're really hurt—if *he* hurts you—nothing *I* say will hurt you. When I tell you I love you it's simply what I came for. I thought it was for something else; but it was for that. I shouldn't say it if I didn't believe I should never see you again. It's the last time—let me pluck a single flower! I've no right to say that, I know; and you've no right to listen. But you don't listen; you never listen, you're always thinking of something else. After this I must go, of course; so I shall at least have a reason. Your asking me is no reason, not a real one. I can't judge by your husband," he went on irrelevantly, almost incoherently; "I don't understand him; he tells me you adore each other. Why does he tell me that? What business is it of mine? When I say that to you, you look strange. But you always look strange. Yes, you've something to hide. It's none of my business—very true. But I love you," said Caspar Goodwood.

As he said, she looked strange. She turned her eyes to the door by which they had entered and raised her fan as if in warning. "You've behaved so well; don't spoil it," she uttered softly.

"No one hears me. It's wonderful what you tried to put me off with. I love you as I've never loved you."

"I know it. I knew it as soon as you consented to go."

"You can't help it—of course not. You would if you could, but you can't, unfortunately. Unfortunately for me, I mean. I ask nothing—nothing, that is, I shouldn't. But I do ask one sole satisfaction:—that you tell me—that you tell me—!"

"That I tell you what?"

"Whether I may pity you."

"Should you like that?" Isabel asked, trying to smile again.

"To pity you? Most assuredly! That at least would be doing something. I'd give my life to it."

She raised her fan to her face, which it covered all except her eyes. They rested a moment on his. "Don't give your life to it; but give a thought to it every now and then." And with that she went back to the Countess Gemini.

XLIX

Madame Merle had not made her appearance at Palazzo Roccanera on the evening of that Thursday of which I have narrated some of the incidents, and Isabel, though she observed her absence, was not surprised by it. Things had passed between them which added no stimulus to sociability, and to appreciate which we must glance a little backward. It has been mentioned that Madame Merle returned from Naples shortly after Lord Warburton had left Rome, and that on her first meeting with Isabel (whom, to do her justice, she came immediately to see) her first utterance had been an enquiry as to the whereabouts of this nobleman, for whom she appeared to hold her dear friend accountable.

"Please don't talk of him," said Isabel for answer; "we've heard so much of him of late."

Madame Merle bent her head on one side a little, protestingly, and smiled at the left corner of her mouth. 'You've heard, yes. But you must remember that I've not, in Naples. I hoped to find him here and to be able to congratulate Pansy."

"You may congratulate Pansy still; but not on marrying Lord Warburton."

"How you say that! Don't you know I had set my heart on it?" Madame Merle asked with a great deal of spirit, but still with the intonation of good-humour.

Isabel was discomposed, but she was determined to be good-humoured too. "You shouldn't have gone to Naples then. You should have stayed here to watch the affair."

"I had too much confidence in you. But do you think it's too late?"

"You had better ask Pansy," said Isabel.

"I shall ask her what you've said to her."

These words seemed to justify the impulse of self-defence aroused on Isabel's part by her perceiving that her visitor's attitude was a critical one. Madame Merle, as we know, had been very discreet hitherto; she had never criticised; she had been markedly afraid of intermeddling. But apparently she had only reserved herself for this occasion, since she now had a dangerous quickness in her eye and an air of irritation which even her admirable ease was not able to transmute. She had suffered a disappointment which excited Isabel's surprise—our heroine having no knowledge of her zealous interest in Pansy's marriage; and she betrayed it in a manner which quickened Mrs. Osmond's alarm. More clearly than ever before Isabel heard a cold, mocking voice proceed from she knew not where, in the dim void that surrounded her, and declare that this bright, strong, definite, worldly woman, this incarnation of the practical, the personal, the immediate, was a powerful agent in her destiny. She was nearer to her than Isabel had yet discovered, and her nearness was not the charming accident she had so long supposed. The sense of accident indeed had died within her that day when she happened to be struck with the manner in which the wonderful lady and her own husband sat together in private. No definite suspicion had as yet taken its place; but it was enough to make her view this friend with a different eye, to have been led to reflect that there was more intention in her past behaviour than she had allowed for at the time. Ah yes, there had been intention, there had been intention, Isabel said to herself; and she seemed to wake from a long pernicious dream. What was it that brought home to her that Madame Merle's intention had not been good? Nothing but the mistrust which had lately taken body and which married itself now to the fruitful wonder produced by her visitor's challenge on behalf of poor Pansy. There was something in this challenge which had at the very outset excited an answering defiance; a nameless vitality which she could see to have been absent from her friend's professions of delicacy and caution. Madame Merle had been unwilling to interfere, certainly, but only so long as there was nothing to interfere with. It will perhaps seem to the reader that Isabel went fast in casting doubt, on mere suspicion, on a sincerity proved by several years of good offices. She moved quickly indeed, and with reason, for a strange truth was filtering into her soul. Madame Merle's interest was identical with Osmond's: that was enough. "I think Pansy will tell you nothing that will make you more angry," she said in answer to her companion's last remark.

"I'm not in the least angry. I've only a great desire to retrieve the situation. Do you consider that Warburton has left us for ever?"

"I can't tell you; I don't understand you. It's all over; please let it rest. Osmond has talked to me a great deal about it, and I've nothing more to say or to hear. I've no doubt," Isabel added, "that he'll be very happy to discuss the subject with you."

"I know what he thinks; he came to see me last evening."

"As soon as you had arrived? Then you know all about it and you needn't apply to me for information."

"It isn't information I want. At bottom it's sympathy. I had set my heart on that marriage; the idea did what so few things do—it satisfied the imagination."

"Your imagination, yes. But not that of the persons concerned."

"You mean by that of course that I'm not concerned. Of course not directly. But when one's such an old friend one can't help having something at stake. You forget how long I've known Pansy. You mean, of course," Madame Merle added, "that *you* are one of the persons concerned."

"No; that's the last thing I mean. I'm very weary of it all."

Madame Merle hesitated a little. "Ah yes, your work's done."

"Take care what you say," said Isabel very gravely.

"Oh, I take care; never perhaps more than when it appears least. Your husband judges you severely."

Isabel made for a moment no answer to this; she felt choked with bitterness. It was not the insolence of Madame Merle's informing her that Osmond had been taking her into his confidence as against his wife that struck her most; for she was not quick to believe that this was meant for insolence. Madame Merle was very rarely insolent, and only when it was exactly right. It was not right now, or at least it was not right yet. What touched Isabel like a drop of corrosive acid upon an open wound was the knowledge that Osmond dishonoured her in his words as well as in his thoughts. "Should you like to know how I judge *him?*" she asked at last.

"No, because you'd never tell me. And it would be painful for me to know."

There was a pause, and for the first time since she had known her Isabel thought Madame Merle disagreeable. She wished she would leave her. "Remember how attractive Pansy is, and don't despair," she said abruptly, with a desire that this should close their interview.

But Madame Merle's expansive presence underwent no contraction. She only gathered her mantle about her and, with the movement, scattered upon the air a faint, agreeable fragrance. "I don't despair; I feel encouraged. And I didn't come to scold you; I came if possible to learn the truth. I know you'll tell it if I ask you. It's an immense blessing with you that one can count upon that. No, you won't believe what a comfort I take in it."

"What truth do you speak of?" Isabel asked, wondering.

"Just this: whether Lord Warburton changed his mind quite of his own movement or because you recommended it. To please himself I mean, or to please you. Think of the confidence I must still have in you, in spite of having lost a little of it," Madame Merle continued with a smile, "to ask such a question as that!" She sat looking at her friend, to judge the effect of her words, and then went on: "Now don't be heroic, don't be unreasonable, don't take offence. It seems to me I do you an honour in speaking so. I don't know another woman to whom I would do it. I haven't the least idea that any other woman would tell me the truth. And don't you see how well it is that your husband should know it? It's true that he doesn't appear to have had any tact whatever in trying to extract it; he has indulged in gratuitous suppositions. But that doesn't alter the fact that it would make a difference in his view of his daughter's prospects to know distinctly what really occurred. If Lord Warburton simply got tired of the poor child, that's one thing, and it's a pity. If he gave her up to please you it's another. That's a pity too, but in a different way. Then, in the latter case, you'd perhaps resign yourself to not being pleased—to simply seeing your stepdaughter married. Let him off—let us have him!"

Madame Merle had proceeded very deliberately, watching her companion and apparently thinking she could proceed safely. As she went on Isabel grew pale; she clasped her hands more tightly in her lap. It was not that her visitor had at last thought it the right time to be insolent; for this was not what was most apparent. It was a worse horror than that. "Who are you—what are you?" Isabel murmured. "What have you to do with my husband?" It was strange that for the moment she drew as near to him as if she had loved him.

"Ah then, you take it heroically! I'm very sorry. Don't think, however, that I shall do so."

"What have you to do with me?" Isabel went on.

Madame Merle slowly got up, stroking her muff, but not removing her eyes from Isabel's face. "Everything!" she answered.

Isabel sat there looking up at her, without rising; her face was almost a prayer to be enlightened. But the light of this woman's eyes seemed only a darkness. "Oh misery!" she murmured at last; and she fell back, covering her face with her hands. It had come over her like a high-surging wave that Mrs. Touchett was right. Madame Merle had married her. Before she uncovered her face again that lady had left the room.

Isabel took a drive alone that afternoon; she wished to be far away, under the sky, where she could descend from her carriage and tread upon the daisies. She had long before this taken old Rome into her confidence, for in a world of ruins the ruin of her happiness seemed a less unnatural catastrophe. She rested her weariness upon things that had crumbled for centuries and yet still were upright; she dropped her secret sadness into the silence of lonely places, where its very modern quality detached itself and grew objective, so that as she sat in a sun-warmed angle on a winter's day, or stood in a mouldy church to which no one came, she could almost smile at it and think of its smallness. Small it was, in the large Roman record, and her haunting sense of the continuity of the human lot easily carried her from the less to the greater. She had become deeply, tenderly acquainted with Rome; it interfused and moderated her passion. But she had grown to think of it chiefly as the place where people had suffered. This was what came to her in the starved churches, where the marble columns, transferred from pagan ruins, seemed to offer her a companionship in endurance and the musty incense to be a compound of long-unanswered prayers. There was no gentler nor less consistent heretic than Isabel; the firmest of worshippers, gazing at dark altar-pictures or clustered candles, could not have felt more intimately the suggestiveness of these objects nor have been more liable at such moments to a spiritual visitation. Pansy, as we know, was almost always her companion, and of late the Countess Gemini, balancing a pink parasol, had lent brilliancy to their equipage; but she still occasionally found herself alone when it suited her mood and where it suited the place. On such occasions she had several resorts; the most accessible of which perhaps was a seat on the low parapet which edges the wide grassy space before the high, cold front of Saint John Lateran, whence you look across the Campagna at the far-trailing outline of the Alban Mount and at that mighty plain, between, which is still so full of all that has passed from it. After the departure of her cousin and his companions she roamed more than usual; she carried her sombre spirit from one familiar shrine to the other. Even when Pansy and the Countess were with her she felt the touch of a vanished world. The carriage, leaving the walls of Rome behind, rolled through narrow lanes where the wild honeysuckle had begun to tangle itself in the hedges, or waited for her in quiet places where the fields lay near, while she strolled further and further over the flower-freckled turf, or sat on a stone that had once had a use and gazed through the veil of her personal sadness at the splendid sadness of the scene —at the dense, warm light, the far gradations and soft confusions of colour, the motionless shepherds in lonely attitudes, the hills where the cloud-shadows had the lightness of a blush.

On the afternoon I began with speaking of, she had taken a resolution not to think of Madame Merle; but the resolution proved vain, and this lady's image hovered constantly before her. She asked herself, with an almost childlike horror of the supposition, whether to this intimate friend of several years the great historical epithet of *wicked* were to be applied. She knew the idea only by the Bible and other literary works; to the best of her belief she had had no personal acquaintance with wickedness. She had desired a large acquaintance with human life, and in spite of her having flattered herself that she cultivated it with some success this elementary privilege had been denied her. Perhaps it was not wicked—in the historic sense—to be even deeply false; for that was what Madame Merle had been—deeply, deeply, deeply. Isabel's Aunt Lydia had made this discovery long before, and had mentioned it to her niece; but Isabel had flattered herself at this time that she had a much richer view of things, especially of the spontaneity of her own career and the nobleness of her own interpretations, than poor stiffly-reasoning Mrs. Touchett. Madame Merle had done what she wanted; she had brought about the union of her two friends; a reflection which could not fail to make it a matter of wonder that she should so much have desired such an event. There were people who had the match-making passion, like the votaries of art for art; but Madame Merle, great artist as she was, was scarcely one of these. She thought too ill of marriage, too ill even of life; she had desired that particular marriage but had not desired others. She had therefore had a conception of gain, and Isabel asked herself where she had found her profit. It took her naturally a long time to discover, and even then her discovery was imperfect. It came back to her that Madame Merle, though she had seemed to like her from their first meeting at Gardencourt, had been doubly affectionate after Mr. Touchett's death and after learning that her young friend had been subject to the good old man's charity. She had found her profit not in the gross device of borrowing money, but in the more refined idea of introducing one of her intimates to the young woman's fresh and ingenuous fortune. She had naturally chosen her closest intimate, and it was already vivid enough to Isabel that Gilbert occupied this position. She found herself confronted in this manner with the conviction that the man in the world whom she had supposed to be the least sordid had married her, like a vulgar adventurer, for her money. Strange to say, it had never before occurred to her; if she had thought a good deal of harm of Osmond she had not done him this particular injury. This was the worst she could think of, and she had been saying to herself that the worst was still to come. A man might marry a woman for her money perfectly well; the thing was often done. But at least he should let her know. She wondered whether, since he had wanted her money, her money would now satisfy him. Would he take her money and let her go? Ah, if Mr. Touchett's great charity would but help her to-day it would be blessed indeed! It was not slow to occur to her that if Madame Merle had wished to do Gilbert a service his recognition to her of the boon must have lost its warmth. What must be his feelings to-day in regard to his too zealous benefactress, and what expression must they have found on the part of such a master of irony? It is a singular, but a characteristic, fact that before Isabel returned from her silent drive she had broken its silence by the soft exclamation: "Poor, poor Madame Merle!"

Her compassion would perhaps have been justified if on this same afternoon she had been concealed behind one of the valuable curtains of time-softened damask which dressed the interesting little *salon* of the lady to whom it referred; the carefully-arranged apartment to which we once paid a visit in company with the discreet

Mr. Rosier. In that apartment, towards six o'clock, Gilbert Osmond was seated, and his hostess stood before him as Isabel had seen her stand on an occasion commemorated in this history with an emphasis appropriate not so much to its apparent as to its real importance.

"I don't believe you're unhappy; I believe you like it," said Madame Merle.

"Did I say I was unhappy?" Osmond asked with a face grave enough to suggest that he might have been.

"No, but you don't say the contrary, as you ought in common gratitude."

"Don't talk about gratitude," he returned dryly. "And don't aggravate me," he added in a moment.

Madame Merle slowly seated herself, with her arms folded and her white hands arranged as a support to one of them and an ornament, as it were, to the other. She looked exquisitely calm but impressively sad. "On your side, don't try to frighten me. I wonder if you guess some of my thoughts."

"I trouble about them no more than I can help. I've quite enough of my own."

"That's because they're so delightful."

Osmond rested his head against the back of his chair and looked at his companion with a cynical directness which seemed also partly an expression of fatigue. "You do aggravate me," he remarked in a moment. "I'm very tired."

"*Eh moi donc!*"[1] cried Madame Merle.

"With you it's because you fatigue yourself. With me it's not my own fault."

"When I fatigue myself it's for you. I've given you an interest. That's a great gift."

"Do you call it an interest?" Osmond enquired with detachment.

"Certainly, since it helps you to pass your time."

"The time has never seemed longer to me than this winter."

"You've never looked better; you've never been so agreeable, so brilliant."

"Damn my brilliancy!" he thoughtfully murmured. "How little, after all, you know me!"

"If I don't know you I know nothing," smiled Madame Merle. "You've the feeling of complete success."

"No, I shall not have that till I've made you stop judging me."

"I did that long ago. I speak from old knowledge. But you express yourself more too."

Osmond just hung fire. "I wish you'd express yourself less!"

"You wish to condemn me to silence? Remember that I've never been a chatterbox. At any rate there are three or four things I

1. And what about me!

should like to say to you first. Your wife doesn't know what to do with herself," she went on with a change of tone.

"Pardon me; she knows perfectly. She has a line sharply drawn. She means to carry out her ideas."

"Her ideas to-day must be remarkable."

"Certainly they are. She has more of them than ever."

"She was unable to show me any this morning," said Madame Merle. "She seemed in a very simple, almost in a stupid, state of mind. She was completely bewildered."

"You had better say at once that she was pathetic."

"Ah no, I don't want to encourage you too much."

He still had his head against the cushion behind him; the ankle of one foot rested on the other knee. So he sat for a while. "I should like to know what's the matter with you," he said at last.

"The matter—the matter—!" And here Madame Merle stopped. Then she went on with a sudden outbreak of passion, a burst of summer thunder in a clear sky: "The matter is that I would give my right hand to be able to weep, and that I can't!"

"What good would it do you to weep?"

"It would make me feel as I felt before I knew you."

"If I've dried your tears, that's something. But I've seen you shed them."

"Oh, I believe you'll make me cry still. I mean make me howl like a wolf. I've a great hope, I've a great need, of that. I was vile this morning; I was horrid," she said.

"If Isabel was in the stupid state of mind you mention she probably didn't perceive it," Osmond answered.

"It was precisely my deviltry that stupefied her. I couldn't help it; I was full of something bad. Perhaps it was something good; I don't know. You've not only dried up my tears; you've dried up my soul."

"It's not I then that am responsible for my wife's condition," Osmond said. "It's pleasant to think that I shall get the benefit of your influence upon her. Don't you know the soul is an immortal principle? How can it suffer alteration?"

"I don't believe at all that it's an immortal principle. I believe it can perfectly be destroyed. That's what has happened to mine, which was a very good one to start with; and it's you I have to thank for it. You're *very* bad," she added with gravity in her emphasis.

"Is this the way we're to end?" Osmond asked with the same studied coldness.

"I don't know how we're to end. I wish I did! How do bad people end?—especially as to their *common* crimes. You have made me as bad as yourself."

"I don't understand you. You seem to me quite good enough,"

said Osmond, his conscious indifference giving an extreme effect to the words.

Madame Merle's self-possession tended on the contrary to diminish, and she was nearer losing it than on any occasion on which we have had the pleasure of meeting her. The glow of her eye turned sombre; her smile betrayed a painful effort. "Good enough for anything that I've done with myself? I suppose that's what you mean."

"Good enough to be always charming!" Osmond exclaimed, smiling too.

"Oh God!" his companion murmured; and, sitting there in her ripe freshness, she had recourse to the same gesture she had provoked on Isabel's part in the morning: she bent her face and covered it with her hands.

"Are you going to weep after all?" Osmond asked; and on her remaining motionless he went on: "Have I ever complained to you?"

She dropped her hands quickly. "No, you've taken your revenge otherwise—you have taken it on *her*."

Osmond threw back his head further; he looked a while at the ceiling and might have been supposed to be appealing, in an informal way, to the heavenly powers. "Oh, the imagination of women! It's always vulgar, at bottom. You talk of revenge like a third-rate novelist."

"Of course you haven't complained. You've enjoyed your triumph too much."

"I'm rather curious to know what you call my triumph."

"You've made your wife afraid of you."

Osmond changed his position; he leaned forward, resting his elbows on his knees and looking a while at a beautiful old Persian rug, at his feet. He had an air of refusing to accept any one's valuation of anything, even of time, and of preferring to abide by his own; a peculiarity which made him at moments an irritating person to converse with. "Isabel's not afraid of me, and it's not what I wish," he said at last. "To what do you want to provoke me when you say such things as that?"

"I've thought over all the harm you can do me," Madame Merle answered. "Your wife was afraid of me this morning, but in me it was really you she feared."

"You may have said things that were in very bad taste; I'm not responsible for that. I didn't see the use of your going to see her at all: you're capable of acting without her. I've not made *you* afraid of me that I can see," he went on; "how then should I have made her? You're at least as brave. I can't think where you've picked up such rubbish; one might suppose you knew me by this time." He got up as he spoke and walked to the chimney, where he stood a moment bending his eye, as if he had seen them for the first time, on the delicate specimens of rare porcelain with which it was covered. He took up a small cup and held it in his hand; then, still holding it and leaning his arm on the mantel, he pursued: "You always see too much in everything; you overdo it; you lose sight of the real. I'm much simpler than you think."

"I think you're very simple." And Madame Merle kept her eye on her cup. "I've come to that with time. I judged you, as I say, of old; but it's only since your marriage that I've understood you. I've seen better what you have been to your wife than I ever saw what you were for me. Please be very careful of that precious object."

"It already has a wee bit of a tiny crack," said Osmond dryly as he put it down. "If you didn't understand me before I married it was cruelly rash of you to put me into such a box. However, I took a fancy to my box myself; I thought it would be a comfortable fit. I asked very little; I only asked that she should like me."

"That she should like you so much!"

"So much, of course; in such a case one asks the maximum. That she should adore me, if you will. Oh yes, I wanted that."

"I never adored you," said Madame Merle.

"Ah, but you pretended to!"

"It's true that you never accused me of being a comfortable fit," Madame Merle went on.

"My wife has declined—declined to do anything of the sort," said Osmond. "If you're determined to make a tragedy of that, the tragedy's hardly for her."

"The tragedy's for me!" Madame Merle exclaimed, rising with a long low sigh but having a glance at the same time for the contents of her mantel-shelf. "It appears that I'm to be severely taught the disadvantages of a false position."

"You express yourself like a sentence in a copy-book. We must look for our comfort where we can find it. If my wife doesn't like me, at least my child does. I shall look for compensations in Pansy. Fortunately I haven't a fault to find with her."

"Ah," she said softly, "if I had a child—!"

Osmond waited, and then, with a little formal air, "The children of others may be a great interest!" he announced.

"You're more like a copy-book than I. There's something after all that holds us together."

"Is it the idea of the harm I may do you?" Osmond asked.

"No; it's the idea of the good I may do for you. It's that," Madame Merle pursued, "that made me so jealous of Isabel. I want it to be *my* work," she added, with her face, which had grown hard and bitter, relaxing to its habit of smoothness.

Her friend took up his hat and his umbrella, and after giving the former article two or three strokes with his coat-cuff, "On the whole, I think," he said, "you had better leave it to me."

After he had left her she went, the first thing, and lifted from the mantel-shelf the attenuated coffee-cup in which he had mentioned the existence of a crack; but she looked at it rather abstractedly. "Have I been so vile all for nothing?" she vaguely wailed.

L

As the Countess Gemini was not acquainted with the ancient monuments Isabel occasionally offered to introduce her to these interesting relics and to give their afternoon drive an antiquarian aim. The Countess, who professed to think her sister-in-law a prodigy of learning, never made an objection, and gazed at masses of Roman brickwork as patiently as if they had been mounds of modern drapery. She had not the historic sense, though she had in some directions the anecdotic, and as regards herself the apologetic, but she was so delighted to be in Rome that she only desired to float with the current. She would gladly have passed an hour every day in the damp darkness of the Baths of Titus[1] if it had been a condition of her remaining at Palazzo Roccanera. Isabel, however, was not a severe cicerone; she used to visit the ruins chiefly because they offered an excuse for talking about other matters than the love-affairs of the ladies of Florence, as to which her companion was never weary of offering information. It must be added that during these visits the Countess forbade herself every form of active research; her preference was to sit in the carriage and exclaim that everything was most interesting. It was in this manner that she had hitherto examined the Coliseum, to the infinite regret of her niece, who— with all the respect that she owed her—could not see why she should not descend from the vehicle and enter the building. Pansy had so little chance to ramble that her view of the case was not wholly disinterested; it may be divined that she had a secret hope that, once inside, her parents' guest might be induced to climb to the upper tiers. There came a day when the Countess announced her willingness to undertake this feat—a mild afternoon in March when the windy month expressed itself in occasional puffs of spring. The three ladies went into the Coliseum together, but Isabel left her companions to wander over the place. She had often ascended to those desolate ledges from which the Roman crowd used to bellow applause and where now the wild flowers (when they are allowed) bloom in the deep crevices; and to-day she felt weary and disposed to sit in the despoiled arena. It made an intermission too, for the Countess often asked more from one's attention than she gave in return; and Isabel

---

1. In the 1870's this most interesting of ruins on the Esquiline Hill was exhibited by one cicerone carrying a dim torch (A. J. C. Hare, *Walks in Rome* [London, 1871], p. 363).

believed that when she was alone with her niece she let the dust
gather for a moment on the ancient scandals of the Arnide.[2] She so
remained below therefore, while Pansy guided her undiscriminating
aunt to the steep brick staircase at the foot of which the custodian
unlocks the tall wooden gate. The great enclosure was half in
shadow; the western sun brought out the pale red tone of the great
blocks of travertine—the latent colour that is the only living element in the immense ruin. Here and there wandered a peasant or a
tourist, looking up at the far sky-line where, in the clear stillness, a
multitude of swallows kept circling and plunging. Isabel presently
became aware that one of the other visitors, planted in the middle
of the arena, had turned his attention to her own person and was
looking at her with a certain little poise of the head which she had
some weeks before perceived to be characteristic of baffled but
indestructible purpose. Such an attitude, to-day, could belong only
to Mr. Edward Rosier; and this gentleman proved in fact to have
been considering the question of speaking to her. When he had
assured himself that she was unaccompanied he drew near, remarking that though she would not answer his letters she would perhaps
not wholly close her ears to his spoken eloquence. She replied that
her stepdaughter was close at hand and that she could only give
him five minutes; whereupon he took out his watch and sat down
upon a broken block.

"It's very soon told," said Edward Rosier. "I've sold all my bibelots!" Isabel gave instinctively an exclamation of horror; it was if he
had told her he had had all his teeth drawn. "I've sold them by auction at the Hôtel Drouot," he went on. "The sale took place three
days ago, and they've telegraphed me the result. It's magnificent."

"I'm glad to hear it; but I wish you had kept your pretty things."

"I have the money instead—fifty thousand dollars. Will Mr.
Osmond think me rich enough now?"

"Is it for that you did it?" Isabel asked gently.

"For what else in the world could it be? That's the only thing I
think of. I went to Paris and made my arrangements. I couldn't
stop for the sale; I couldn't have seen them going off; I think it
would have killed me. But I put them into good hands, and they
brought high prices. I should tell you I have kept my enamels. Now
I have the money in my pocket, and he can't say I'm poor!" the
young man exclaimed defiantly.

"He'll say now that you're not wise," said Isabel, as if Gilbert
Osmond had never said this before.

Rosier gave her a sharp look. "Do you mean that without my
bibelots I'm nothing? Do you mean they were the best thing about

me? That's what they told me in Paris; oh they were very frank about it. But they hadn't seen *her!*"

"My dear friend, you deserve to succeed," said Isabel very kindly.

"You say that so sadly that it's the same as if you said I shouldn't." And he questioned her eyes with the clear trepidation of his own. He had the air of a man who knows he has been the talk of Paris for a week and is full half a head taller in consequence, but who also has a painful suspicion that in spite of this increase of stature one or two persons still have the perversity to think him diminutive. "I know what happened here while I was away," he went on. "What does Mr. Osmond expect after she has refused Lord Warburton?"

Isabel debated. "That she'll marry another nobleman."

"What other nobleman?"

"One that he'll pick out."

Rosier slowly got up, putting his watch into his waistcoat-pocket. "You're laughing at some one, but this time I don't think it's at me."

"I didn't mean to laugh," said Isabel. "I laugh very seldom. Now you had better go away."

"I feel very safe!" Rosier declared without moving. This might be; but it evidently made him feel more so to make the announcement in rather a loud voice, balancing himself a little complacently on his toes and looking all round the Coliseum as if it were filled with an audience. Suddenly Isabel saw him change colour; there was more of an audience than he had suspected. She turned and perceived that her two companions had returned from their excursion. "You must really go away," she said quickly.

"Ah, my dear lady, pity me!" Edward Rosier murmured in a voice strangely at variance with the announcement I have just quoted. And then he added eagerly, like a man who in the midst of his misery is seized by a happy thought: "Is that lady the Countess Gemini? I've a great desire to be presented to her."

Isabel looked at him a moment. "She has no influence with her brother."

"Ah, what a monster you make him out!" And Rosier faced the Countess, who advanced, in front of Pansy, with an animation partly due perhaps to the fact that she perceived her sister-in-law to be engaged in conversation with a very pretty young man.

"I'm glad you've kept your enamels!" Isabel called as she left him. She went straight to Pansy, who, on seeing Edward Rosier, had stopped short, with lowered eyes. "We'll go back to the carriage," she said gently.

"Yes, it's getting late," Pansy returned more gently still. And she went on without a murmur, without faltering or glancing back.

Isabel, however, allowing herself this last liberty, saw that a meeting had immediately taken place between the Countess and Mr. Rosier. He had removed his hat and was bowing and smiling; he had evidently introduced himself, while the Countess's expressive back displayed to Isabel's eye a gracious inclination. These facts, none the less, were presently lost to sight, for Isabel and Pansy took their places again in the carriage. Pansy, who faced her stepmother, at first kept her eyes fixed on her lap; then she raised them and rested them on Isabel's. There shone out of each of them a little melancholy ray—a spark of timid passion which touched Isabel to the heart. At the same time a wave of envy passed over her soul, as she compared the tremulous longing, the definite ideal of the child with her own dry despair. "Poor little Pansy!" she affectionately said.

"Oh never mind!" Pansy answered in the tone of eager apology.

And then there was a silence; the Countess was a long time coming. "Did you show your aunt everything, and did she enjoy it?" Isabel asked at last.

"Yes, I showed her everything. I think she was very much pleased."

"And you're not tired, I hope."

"Oh no, thank you, I'm not tired."

The Countess still remained behind, so that Isabel requested the footman to go into the Coliseum and tell her they were waiting. He presently returned with the announcement that the Signora Contessa begged them not to wait—she would come home in a cab!

About a week after this lady's quick sympathies had enlisted themselves with Mr. Rosier, Isabel, going rather late to dress for dinner, found Pansy sitting in her room. The girl seemed to have been awaiting her; she got up from her low chair. "Pardon my taking the liberty," she said in a small voice. "It will be the last—for some time."

Her voice was strange, and her eyes, widely opened, had an excited, frightened look. "You're not going away!" Isabel exclaimed.

"I'm going to the convent."

"To the convent?"

Pansy drew nearer, till she was near enough to put her arms round Isabel and rest her head on her shoulder. She stood this way a moment, perfectly still; but her companion could feel her tremble. The quiver of her little body expressed everything she was unable to say. Isabel nevertheless pressed her. "Why are you going to the convent?"

"Because papa thinks it best. He says a young girl's better, every now and then, for making a little retreat. He says the world, always the world, is very bad for a young girl. This is just a chance for a little seclusion—a little reflexion." Pansy spoke in short detached sentences, as if she could scarce trust herself; and then she added with a triumph of self-control: "I think papa's right; I've been so much in the world this winter."

Her announcement had a strange effect on Isabel; it seemed to carry a larger meaning than the girl herself knew. "When was this decided?" she asked. "I've heard nothing of it."

"Papa told me half an hour ago; he thought it better it shouldn't be too much talked about in advance. Madame Catherine's to come for me at a quarter past seven, and I'm only to take two frocks. It's only for a few weeks; I'm sure it will be very good. I shall find all those ladies who used to be so kind to me, and I shall see the little girls who are being educated. I'm very fond of little girls," said Pansy with an effect of diminutive grandeur. "And I'm also very fond of Mother Catherine. I shall be very quiet and think a great deal."

Isabel listened to her, holding her breath; she was almost awe-struck. "Think of *me* sometimes."

"Ah, come and see me soon!" cried Pansy; and the cry was very different from the heroic remarks of which she had just delivered herself.

Isabel could say nothing more; she understood nothing; she only felt how little she yet knew her husband. Her answer to his daughter was a long, tender kiss.

Half an hour later she learned from her maid that Madame Catherine had arrived in a cab and had departed again with the signorina. On going to the drawing-room before dinner she found the Countess Gemini alone, and this lady characterised the incident by exclaiming, with a wonderful toss of the head, *"En voilà, ma chère, une pose!"*[3] But if it was an affectation she was at a loss to see what her husband affected. She could only dimly perceive that he had more traditions than she supposed. It had become her habit to be so careful as to what she said to him that, strange as it may appear, she hesitated, for several minutes after he had come in, to allude to his daughter's sudden departure: she spoke of it only after they were seated at table. But she had forbidden herself ever to ask Osmond a question. All she could do was to make a declaration, and there was one that came very naturally. "I shall miss Pansy very much."

He looked a while, with his head inclined a little, at the basket of flowers in the middle of the table. "Ah yes," he said at last, "I had thought of that. You must go and see her, you know; but not too often. I dare say you wonder why I sent her to the good sisters; but I doubt if I can make you understand. It doesn't matter; don't trou-

3. There you are, my dear, what a pose.

ble yourself about it. That's why I had not spoken of it. I didn't believe you would enter into it. But I've always had the idea; I've always thought it a part of the education of one's daughter. One's daughter should be fresh and fair; she should be innocent and gentle. With the manners of the present time she is liable to become so dusty and crumpled. Pansy's a little dusty, a little dishevelled; she has knocked about too much. This bustling, pushing rabble that calls itself society—one should take her out of it occasionally. Convents are very quiet, very convenient, very salutary. I like to think of her there, in the old garden, under the arcade, among those tranquil virtuous women. Many of them are gentlewomen born; several of them are noble. She will have her books and her drawing, she will have her piano. I've made the most liberal arrangements. There is to be nothing ascetic; there's just to be a certain little sense of sequestration. She'll have time to think, and there's something I want her to think about." Osmond spoke deliberately, reasonably, still with his head on one side, as if he were looking at the basket of flowers. His tone, however, was that of a man not so much offering an explanation as putting a thing into words—almost into pictures—to see, himself, how it would look. He considered a while the picture he had evoked and seemed greatly pleased with it. And then he went on: "The Catholics are very wise after all. The convent is a great institution; we can't do without it; it corresponds to an essential need in families, in society. It's a school of good manners; it's a school of repose. Oh, I don't want to detach my daughter from the world," he added; "I don't want to make her fix her thoughts on any other. This one's very well, as *she* should take it, and she may think of it as much as she likes. Only she must think of it in the right way."

Isabel gave an extreme attention to this little sketch; she found it indeed intensely interesting. It seemed to show her how far her husband's desire to be effective was capable of going—to the point of playing theoretic tricks on the delicate organism of his daughter. She could not understand his purpose, no—not wholly; but she understood it better than he supposed or desired, inasmuch as she was convinced that the whole proceeding was an elaborate mystification, addressed to herself and destined to act upon her imagination. He had wanted to do something sudden and arbitrary, something unexpected and refined; to mark the difference between his sympathies and her own, and show that if he regarded his daughter as a precious work of art it was natural he should be more and more careful about the finishing touches. If he wished to be effective he had succeeded; the incident struck a chill into Isabel's heart. Pansy had known the convent in her childhood and had found a happy home there; she was fond of the good sisters, who were very fond of her, and there was therefore for the moment no definite hardship in her lot. But all the same the girl had taken fright; the impression her father desired to make would evidently be sharp enough. The old Protestant tradition had never faded from Isabel's imagination, and as her thoughts attached themselves to this striking example of her husband's genius—she sat looking, like him, at the basket of flowers—poor little Pansy became the heroine of a tragedy. Osmond wished it to be known that he shrank from nothing, and his wife found it hard to pretend to eat her dinner. There was a certain relief presently, in hearing the high, strained voice of her sister-in-law. The Countess too, apparently, had been thinking the thing out, but had arrived at a different conclusion from Isabel.

"It's very absurd, my dear Osmond," she said, "to invent so many pretty reasons for poor Pansy's banishment. Why don't you say at once that you want to get her out of my way? Haven't you discovered that I think very well of Mr. Rosier? I do indeed; he seems to me *simpaticissimo*.[4] He has made me believe in true love; I never did before! Of course you've made up your mind that with those convictions I'm dreadful company for Pansy."

Osmond took a sip of a glass of wine; he looked perfectly good-humoured. "My dear Amy," he answered, smiling as if he were uttering a piece of gallantry, "I don't know anything about your convictions, but if I suspected that they interfere with mine it would be much simpler to banish *you*."

LI

The Countess was not banished, but she felt the insecurity of her tenure of her brother's hospitality. A week after this incident Isabel received a telegram from England, dated from Gardencourt and bearing the stamp of Mrs. Touchett's authorship. "Ralph cannot last many days," it ran, "and if convenient would like to see you. Wishes me to say that you must come only if you've not other duties. Say, for myself, that you used to talk a good deal about your duty and to wonder what it was; shall be curious to see whether you've found it out. Ralph is really dying, and there's no other company." Isabel was prepared for this news, having received from Henrietta Stackpole a detailed account of her journey to England with her appreciative patient. Ralph had arrived more dead than alive, but she had managed to convey him to Gardencourt, where he had taken to his bed, which, as Miss Stackpole wrote, he evidently would never leave again. She added that she had really had two patients on her hands instead of one, inasmuch as Mr. Goodwood, who had been of no earthly use, was quite as ailing, in a different way, as Mr. Touchett. Afterwards she wrote that she had been

4. Especially nice or genial. [1st ed.: "delightful."]

obliged to surrender the field to Mrs. Touchett, who had just returned from America and had promptly given her to understand that she didn't wish any interviewing at Gardencourt. Isabel had written to her aunt shortly after Ralph came to Rome, letting her know of his critical condition and suggesting that she should lose no time in returning to Europe. Mrs. Touchett had telegraphed an acknowledgement of this admonition, and the only further news Isabel received from her was the second telegram I have just quoted.

Isabel stood a moment looking at the latter missive; then, thrusting it into her pocket, she went straight to the door of her husband's study. Here she again paused an instant, after which she opened the door and went in. Osmond was seated at the table near the window with a folio volume before him, propped against a pile of books. This volume was open at a page of small coloured plates, and Isabel presently saw that he had been copying from it the drawing of an antique coin. A box of water-colours and fine brushes lay before him, and he had already transferred to a sheet of immaculate paper the delicate, finely-tinted disk. His back was turned toward the door, but he recognised his wife without looking round.

"Excuse me for disturbing you," she said.

"When I come to your room I always knock," he answered, going on with his work.

"I forgot; I had something else to think of. My cousin's dying."

"Ah, I don't believe that," said Osmond, looking at his drawing through a magnifying glass. "He was dying when we married; he'll outlive us all."

Isabel gave herself no time, no thought, to appreciate the careful cynicism of this declaration; she simply went on quickly, full of her intention: "My aunt has telegraphed for me; I must go to Gardencourt."

"Why must you go to Gardencourt?" Osmond asked in the tone of impartial curiosity.

"To see Ralph before he dies."

To this, for some time, he made no rejoinder; he continued to give his chief attention to his work, which was of a sort that would brook no negligence. "I don't see the need of it," he said at last. "He came to see you here. I didn't like that; I thought his being in Rome a great mistake. But I tolerated it because it was to be the last time you should see him. Now you tell me it's not to have been the last. Ah, you're not grateful!"

"What am I to be grateful for?"

Gilbert Osmond laid down his little implements, blew a speck of dust from his drawing, slowly got up, and for the first time looked at his wife. "For my not having interfered while he was here."

"Oh yes, I am. I remember perfectly how distinctly you let me know you didn't like it. I was very glad when he went away."

"Leave him alone then. Don't run after him."

Isabel turned her eyes away from him; they rested upon his little drawing. "I must go to England," she said, with a full consciousness that her tone might strike an irritable man of taste as stupidly obstinate.

"I shall not like it if you do," Osmond remarked.

"Why should I mind that? You won't like it if I don't. You like nothing I do or don't do. You pretend to think I lie."

Osmond turned slightly pale; he gave a cold smile. "That's why you must go then? Not to see your cousin, but to take a revenge on me."

"I know nothing about revenge."

"I do," said Osmond. "Don't give me an occasion."

"You're only too eager to take one. You wish immensely that I would commit some folly."

"I should be gratified in that case if you disobeyed me."

"If I disobeyed you?" said Isabel in a low tone which had the effect of mildness.

"Let it be clear. If you leave Rome to-day it will be a piece of the most deliberate, the most calculated, opposition."

"How can you call it calculated? I received my aunt's telegram but three minutes ago."

"You calculate rapidly; it's a great accomplishment. I don't see why we should prolong our discussion; you know my wish." And he stood there as if he expected to see her withdraw.

But she never moved; she couldn't move, strange as it may seem; she still wished to justify herself; he had the power, in an extraordinary degree, of making her feel this need. There was something in her imagination he could always appeal to against her judgement. "You've no reason for such a wish," said Isabel, "and I've every reason for going. I can't tell you how unjust you seem to me. But I think you know. It's your own opposition that's calculated. It's malignant."

She had never uttered her worst thought to her husband before, and the sensation of hearing it was evidently new to Osmond. But he showed no surprise, and his coolness was apparently a proof that he had believed his wife would in fact be unable to resist for ever his ingenious endeavour to draw her out. "It's all the more intense then," he answered. And he added almost as if he were giving her a friendly counsel: "This is a very important matter." She recognised that; she was fully conscious of the weight of the occasion; she knew that between them they had arrived at a crisis. Its gravity made her careful; she said nothing, and he went on. "You say I've no reason? I have the very best. I dislike, from the bottom of my soul, what you intend to do. It's dishonourable; it's indelicate; it's indecent. Your cousin is nothing whatever to me, and I'm under no obligation to make concessions to him. I've already made the very handsomest. Your relations with him, while he was here, kept me on pins and needles; but I let that pass, because from week to week I expected him to go. I've never liked him and he has never liked me. That's why you like him—because he hates me," said Osmond with a quick, barely audible tremor in his voice. "I've an ideal of what my wife should do and should not do. She should not travel across Europe alone, in defiance of my deepest desire, to sit at the bed-side of other men. Your cousin's nothing to you; he's nothing to us. You smile most expressively when I talk about *us*, but I assure you that *we, we,* Mrs. Osmond, is all I know. I take our marriage seriously; you appear to have found a way of not doing so. I'm not aware that we're divorced or separated; for me we're indissolubly united. You are nearer to me than any human creature, and I'm nearer to you. It may be a disagreeable proximity; it's one, at any rate, of our own deliberate making. You don't like to be reminded of that, I know; but I'm perfectly willing, because—because—" And he paused a moment, looking as if he had something to say which would be very much to the point. "Because I think we should accept the consequences of our actions, and what I value most in life is the honour of a thing!"

He spoke gravely and almost gently; the accent of sarcasm had dropped out of his tone. It had a gravity which checked his wife's quick emotion; the resolution with which she had entered the room found itself caught in a mesh of fine threads. His last words were not a command, they constituted a kind of appeal; and, though she felt that any expression of respect on his part could only be a refinement of egotism, they represented something transcendent and absolute, like the sign of the cross or the flag of one's country. He spoke in the name of something sacred and precious—the observance of a magnificent form. They were as perfectly apart in feeling as two disillusioned lovers had ever been; but they had never yet separated in act. Isabel had not changed; her old passion for justice still abode within her; and now, in the very thick of her sense of her husband's blasphemous sophistry, it began to throb to a tune which for a moment promised him the victory. It came over her that in his wish to preserve appearances he was after all sincere, and that this, as far as it went, was a merit. Ten minutes before she had felt all the joy of irreflective action—a joy to which she had so long been a stranger; but action had been suddenly changed to slow renunciation, transformed by the blight of Osmond's touch. If she must renounce, however, she would let him know she was a victim rather than a dupe. "I know you're a master of the art of mockery," she said. "How can you speak of an indissoluble union—how can you speak of your being contented? Where's our union when you accuse me of falsity? Where's your contentment when you have nothing but hideous suspicion in your heart?"

"It is in our living decently together, in spite of such drawbacks."

"We don't live decently together!" cried Isabel.

"Indeed we don't if you go to England."

"That's very little; that's nothing. I might do much more."

He raised his eyebrows and even his shoulders a little: he had lived long enough in Italy to catch this trick. "Ah, if you've come to threaten me I prefer my drawing." And he walked back to his table, where he took up the sheet of paper on which he had been working and stood studying it.

"I suppose that if I go you'll not expect me to come back," said Isabel.

He turned quickly round, and she could see this movement at least was not designed. He looked at her a little, and then, "Are you out of your mind?" he enquired.

"How can it be anything but a rupture?" she went on; "especially if all you say is true?" She was unable to see how it could be anything but a rupture; she sincerely wished to know what else it might be.

He sat down before his table."I really can't argue with you on the hypothesis of your defying me," he said. And he took up one of his little brushes again.

She lingered but a moment longer; long enough to embrace with her eye his whole deliberately indifferent yet most expressive figure; after which she quickly left the room. Her faculties, her energy, her passion, were all dispersed again; she felt as if a cold, dark mist had suddenly encompassed her. Osmond possessed in a supreme degree the art of eliciting any weakness. On her way back to her room she found the Countess Gemini standing in the open doorway of a little parlour in which a small collection of heterogeneous books had been arranged. The Countess had an open volume in her hand; she appeared to have been glancing down a page which failed to strike her as interesting. At the sound of Isabel's step she raised her head.

"Ah my dear," she said, "you, who are so literary, do tell me some amusing book to read! Everything here's of a dreariness—! Do you think this would do me any good?"

Isabel glanced at the title of the volume she held out, but without reading or understanding it. "I'm afraid I can't advise you. I've had bad news. My cousin, Ralph Touchett, is dying."

The Countess threw down her book. "Ah, he was so simpatico. I'm awfully sorry for you."

"You would be sorrier still if you knew."

"What is there to know? You look very badly," the Countess added. "You must have been with Osmond."

Half an hour before Isabel would have listened very coldly to an intimation that she should ever feel a desire for the sympathy of her sister-in-law, and there can be no better proof of her present embarrassment than the fact that she almost clutched at this lady's fluttering attention. "I've been with Osmond," she said, while the Countess's bright eyes glittered at her.

"I'm sure then he has been odious!" the Countess cried. "Did he say he was glad poor Mr. Touchett's dying?"

"He said it's impossible I should go to England."

The Countess's mind, when her interests were concerned, was agile; she already foresaw the extinction of any further brightness in her visit to Rome. Ralph Touchett would die, Isabel would go into mourning, and then there would be no more dinner-parties. Such a prospect produced for a moment in her countenance an expressive grimace; but this rapid, picturesque play of feature was her only tribute to disappointment. After all, she reflected, the game was almost played out; she had already overstayed her invitation. And then she cared enough for Isabel's trouble to forget her own, and she saw that Isabel's trouble was deep. It seemed deeper than the mere death of a cousin, and the Countess had no hesitation in connecting her exasperating brother with the expression of her sister-in-law's eyes. Her heart beat with an almost joyous expectation, for if she had wished to see Osmond overtopped the conditions looked favourable now. Of course if Isabel should go to England she herself would immediately leave Palazzo Roccanera; nothing would induce her to remain there with Osmond. Nevertheless she felt an immense desire to hear that Isabel would go to England. "Nothing's impossible for you, my dear," she said caressingly. "Why else are you rich and clever and good?"

"Why indeed? I feel stupidly weak."

"Why does Osmond say it's impossible?" the Countess asked in a tone which sufficiently declared that she couldn't imagine.

From the moment she thus began to question her, however, Isabel drew back; she disengaged her hand, which the Countess had affectionately taken. But she answered this enquiry with frank bitterness. "Because we're so happy together that we can't separate even for a fortnight."

"Ah," cried the Countess while Isabel turned away, "when I want to make a journey my husband simply tells me I can have no money!"

Isabel went to her room, where she walked up and down for an hour. It may appear to some readers that she gave herself much trouble, and it is certain that for a woman of a high spirit she had allowed herself easily to be arrested. It seemed to her that only now she fully measured the great undertaking of matrimony. Marriage meant that in such a case as this, when one had to choose, one chose as a matter of course for one's husband. "I'm afraid—yes, I'm afraid," she said to herself more than once, stopping short in her walk. But what she was afraid of was not her husband—his displeasure, his hatred, his revenge; it was not even her own later judgement of her conduct—a consideration which had often held her in check; it was simply the violence there would be in going when Osmond wished her to remain. A gulf of difference had opened between them, but nevertheless it was his desire that she should stay, it was a horror to him that she should go. She knew the nervous fineness with which he could feel an objection. What he thought of her she knew, what he was capable of saying to her she had felt; yet they were married, for all that, and marriage meant that a woman should cleave to the man with whom, uttering tremendous vows, she had stood at the altar. She sank down on her sofa at last and buried her head in a pile of cushions.

When she raised her head again the Countess Gemini hovered before her. She had come in all unperceived; she had a strange smile on her thin lips and her whole face had grown in an hour a shining intimation. She lived assuredly, it might be said, at the window of her spirit, but now she was leaning far out. "I knocked," she began, "but you didn't answer me. So I ventured in. I've been looking at you for the last five minutes. You're very unhappy."

"Yes; but I don't think you can comfort me."

"Will you give me leave to try?" And the Countess sat down on the sofa beside her. She continued to smile, and there was something communicative and exultant in her expression. She appeared to have a deal to say, and it occurred to Isabel for the first time that her sister-in-law might say something really human. She made play with her glittering eyes, in which there was an unpleasant fascination. "After all," she soon resumed, "I must tell you, to begin with, that I don't understand your state of mind. You seem to have so many scruples, so many reasons, so many ties. When I discovered, ten years ago, that my husband's dearest wish was to make me miserable—of late he has simply let me alone—ah, it was a wonderful simplification! My poor Isabel, you're not simple enough."

"No, I'm not simple enough," said Isabel.

"There's something I want you to know," the Countess declared —"because I think you ought to know it. Perhaps you do; perhaps you've guessed it. But if you have, all I can say is that I understand still less why you shouldn't do as you like."

"What do you wish me to know?" Isabel felt a foreboding that made her heart beat faster. The Countess was about to justify herself, and this alone was portentous.

But she was nevertheless disposed to play a little with her subject.

"In your place I should have guessed it ages ago. Have you never really suspected?"

"I've guessed nothing. What should I have suspected? I don't know what you mean."

"That's because you've such a beastly pure mind. I never saw a woman with such a pure mind!" cried the Countess.

Isabel slowly got up. "You're going to tell me something horrible."

"You can call it by whatever name you will!" And the Countess rose also, while her gathered perversity grew vivid and dreadful. She stood a moment in a sort of glare of intention and, as seemed to Isabel even then, of ugliness; after which she said: "My first sister-in-law had no children."

Isabel stared back at her; the announcement was an anticlimax. "Your first sister-in-law?"

"I suppose you know at least, if one may mention it, that Osmond has been married before! I've never spoken to you of his wife; I thought it mightn't be decent or respectful. But others, less particular, must have done so. The poor little woman lived hardly three years and died childless. It wasn't till after her death that Pansy arrived."

Isabel's brow had contracted to a frown; her lips were parted in pale, vague wonder. She was trying to follow; there seemed so much more to follow than she could see. "Pansy's not my husband's child then?"

"Your husband's—in perfection! But no one else's husband's. Some one else's wife's. Ah, my good Isabel," cried the Countess, "with you one must dot one's i's!"

"I don't understand. Whose wife's?" Isabel asked.

"The wife of a horrid little Swiss who died—how long?—a dozen, more than fifteen, years ago. He never recognised Miss Pansy, nor, knowing what he was about, would have anything to say to her; and there was no reason why he should. Osmond did, and that was better; though he had to fit on afterwards the whole rigmarole of his own wife's having died in childbirth, and of his having, in grief and horror, banished the little girl from his sight for as long as possible before taking her home from nurse. His wife had really died, you know, of quite another matter and in quite another place: in the Piedmontese mountains, where they had gone, one August, because her health appeared to require the air, but where she was suddenly taken worse—fatally ill. The story passed, sufficiently; it was covered by the appearances so long as nobody heeded, as nobody cared to look into it. But of course *I* knew—without researches," the Countess lucidly proceeded; "as also, you'll understand, without a word said between us—I mean between

Osmond and me. Don't you see him looking at me, in silence, that way, to settle it?—that is to settle *me* if I should say anything. I said nothing, right or left—never a word to a creature, if you can believe that of me: on my honour, my dear, I speak of the thing to you now, after all this time, as I've never, never spoken. It was to be enough for me, from the first, that the child was my niece—from the moment she was my brother's daughter. As for her veritable mother—!" But with this Pansy's wonderful aunt dropped—as, involuntarily, from the impression of her sister-in-law's face, out of which more eyes might have seemed to look at her than she had ever had to meet.

She had spoken no name, yet Isabel could but check, on her own lips, an echo of the unspoken. She sank to her seat again, hanging her head. "Why have you told me this?" she asked in a voice the Countess hardly recognised.

"Because I've been so bored with your not knowing. I've been bored, frankly, my dear, with not having told you; as if, stupidly, all this time I couldn't have managed! *Ça me dépasse,*[1] if you don't mind my saying so, the things, all round you, that you've appeared to succeed in not knowing. It's a sort of assistance—aid to innocent ignorance—that I've always been a bad hand at rendering; and in this connexion, that of keeping quiet for my brother, my virtue has at any rate finally found itself exhausted. It's not a black lie, moreover, you know," the Countess inimitably added. "The facts are exactly what I tell you."

"I had no idea," said Isabel presently; and looked up at her in a manner that doubtless matched the apparent witlessness of this confession.

"So I believed—though it was hard to believe. Had it never occurred to you that he was for six or seven years her lover?"

"I don't know. Things *have* occurred to me, and perhaps that was what they all meant."

"She has been wonderfully clever, she has been magnificent, about Pansy!" the Countess, before all this view of it, cried.

"Oh, no idea, for me," Isabel went on, "ever *definitely* took that form." She appeared to be making out to herself what had been and what hadn't. "And as it is—I don't understand."

She spoke as one troubled and puzzled, yet the poor Countess seemed to have seen her revelation fall below its possibilities of effect. She had expected to kindle some responsive blaze, but had barely extracted a spark. Isabel showed as scarce more impressed than she might have been, as a young woman of approved imagination, with some fine sinister passage of public history. "Don't you recognise how the child could never pass for *her* husband's?—that is

1. It's beyond me.

with M. Merle himself," her companion resumed. "They had been separated too long for that, and he had gone to some far country—I think to South America. If she had ever had children—which I'm not sure of—she had lost them. The conditions happened to make it workable, under stress (I mean at so awkward a pinch), that Osmond should acknowledge the little girl. His wife was dead—very true; but she had not been dead too long to put a certain accommodation of dates out of the question—from the moment, I mean, that suspicion wasn't started; which was what they had to take care of. What was more natural than that poor Mrs. Osmond, at a distance and for a world not troubling about trifles, should have left behind her, *poverina*,[2] the pledge of her brief happiness that had cost her her life? With the aid of a change of residence—Osmond had been living with her at Naples at the time of their stay in the Alps, and he in due course left it for ever—the whole history was successfully set going. My poor sister-in-law, in her grave, couldn't help herself, and the real mother, to save *her* skin, renounced all visible property in the child."

"Ah, poor, poor woman!" cried Isabel, who herewith burst into tears. It was a long time since she had shed any; she had suffered a high reaction from weeping. But now they flowed with an abundance in which the Countess Gemini found only another discomfiture.

"It's very kind of you to pity her!" she discordantly laughed. "Yes indeed, you have a way of your own—!"

"He must have been false to his wife—and so very soon!" said Isabel with a sudden check.

"That's all that's wanting—that you should take up *her* cause!" the Countess went on. "I quite agree with you, however, that it was much too soon."

"But to me, to me—?" And Isabel hesitated as if she had not heard; as if her question—though it was sufficiently there in her eyes—were all for herself.

"To you he has been faithful? Well, it depends, my dear, on what you call faithful. When he married you he was no longer the lover of another woman—*such* a lover as he had been, *cara mia*,[3] between their risks and their precautions, while the thing lasted! That state of affairs had passed away; the lady had repented, or at all events, for reasons of her own, drawn back: she had always had, too, a worship of appearances so intense that even Osmond himself had got bored with it. You may therefore imagine what it was—when he couldn't patch it on conveniently to *any* of those he goes in for! But the whole past was between them."

"Yes," Isabel mechanically echoed, "the whole past is between them."

2. **Poor little one.**   3. **My dear girl.**

"Ah, this later past is nothing. But for six or seven years, as I say, they had kept it up."

She was silent a little. "Why then did she want him to marry me?"

"Ah my dear, that's her superiority! Because you had money; and because she believed you would be good to Pansy."

"Poor woman—and Pansy who doesn't like her!" cried Isabel.

"That's the reason she wanted some one whom Pansy would like. She knows it; she knows everything."

"Will she know that you've told me this?"

"That will depend upon whether you tell her. She's prepared for it, and do you know what she counts upon for her defence? On your believing that I lie. Perhaps you do; don't make yourself uncomfortable to hide it. Only, as it happens this time, I don't. I've told plenty of little idiotic fibs, but they've never hurt any one but myself."

Isabel sat staring at her companion's story as at a bale of fantastic wares some strolling gypsy might have unpacked on the carpet at her feet. "Why did Osmond never marry her?" she finally asked.

"Because she had no money." The Countess had an answer for everything, and if she lied she lied well. "No one knows, no one has ever known, what she lives on, or how she has got all those beautiful things. I don't believe Osmond himself knows. Besides, she wouldn't have married him."

"How can she have loved him then?"

"She doesn't love him in that way. She did at first, and then, I suppose, she would have married him; but at that time her husband was living. By the time M. Merle had rejoined—I won't say his ancestors, because he never had any—her relations with Osmond had changed, and she had grown more ambitious. Besides, she has never had, about him," the Countess went on, leaving Isabel to wince for it so tragically afterwards—"she *had* never had, what you might call any illusions of *intelligence*. She hoped she might marry a great man; that has always been her idea. She has waited and watched and plotted and prayed; but she has never succeeded. I don't call Madame Merle a success, you know. I don't know what she may accomplish yet, but at present she has very little to show. The only tangible result she has ever achieved—except, of course, getting to know every one and staying with them free of expense— has been her bringing you and Osmond together. Oh, she did that, my dear; you needn't look as if you doubted it. I've watched them for years; I know everything—everything. I'm thought a great scatterbrain, but I've had enough application of mind to follow up those two. She hates me, and her way of showing it is to pretend to be for ever defending me. When people say I've had fifteen lovers she looks horrified and declares that quite half of them were never proved. She has been afraid of me for years, and she has taken great comfort in the vile, false things people have said about me. She has been afraid I'd expose her, and she threatened me one day when Osmond began to pay his court to you. It was at his house in Florence; do you remember that afternoon when she brought you there and we had tea in the garden? She let me know then that if I should tell tales two could play at that game. She pretends there's a good deal more to tell about me than about her. It would be an interesting comparison! I don't care a fig what she may say, simply because I know *you* don't care a fig. You can't trouble your head about me less than you do already. So she may take her revenge as she chooses; I don't think she'll frighten you very much. Her great idea has been to be tremendously irreproachable—a kind of full-blown lily— the incarnation of propriety. She has always worshipped that god. There should be no scandal about Cæsar's wife, you know; and, as I say, she has always hoped to marry Cæsar. That was one reason she wouldn't marry Osmond; the fear that on seeing her with Pansy people would put things together—would even see a resemblance. She has had a terror lest the mother should betray herself. She has been awfully careful; the mother has never done so."

"Yes, yes, the mother has done so," said Isabel, who had listened to all this with a face more and more wan. "She betrayed herself to me the other day, though I didn't recognise her. There appeared to have been a chance of Pansy's making a great marriage, and in her disappointment at its not coming off she almost dropped the mask."

"Ah, that's where she'd dish herself!" cried the Countess. "She has failed so dreadfully that she's determined her daughter shall make it up."

Isabel started at the words "her daughter," which her guest threw off so familiarly. "It seems very wonderful," she murmured; and in this bewildering impression she had almost lost her sense of being personally touched by the story.

"Now don't go and turn against the poor innocent child!" the Countess went on. "She's very nice, in spite of her deplorable origin. I myself have liked Pansy; not, naturally, because she was *hers*, but because she had become yours."

"Yes, she has become mine. And how the poor woman must have suffered at seeing me—!" Isabel exclaimed while she flushed at the thought.

"I don't believe she has suffered; on the contrary, she has enjoyed. Osmond's marriage has given his daughter a great little lift. Before that she lived in a hole. And do you know what the mother thought? That you might take such a fancy to the child that you'd do something for her. Osmond of course could never give her a portion. Osmond was really extremely poor; but of course you know all about that. Ah, my dear," cried the Countess, "why did you ever inherit money?" She stopped a moment as if she saw something singular in Isabel's face. "Don't tell me now that you'll give her a *dot*. You're capable of that, but I would refuse to believe it. Don't try to be too good. Be a little easy and natural and nasty; feel a little wicked, for the comfort of it, once in your life!"

"It's very strange. I suppose I ought to know, but I'm sorry," Isabel said."I'm much obliged to you."

"Yes, you seem to be!" cried the Countess with a mocking laugh. "Perhaps you are—perhaps you're not. You don't take it as I should have thought."

"How should I take it?" Isabel asked.

"Well, I should say as a woman who has been made use of." Isabel made no answer to this; she only listened, and the Countess went on. "They've always been bound to each other; they remained so even after she broke off—or *he* did. But he has always been more for her than she has been for him. When their little carnival was over they made a bargain that each should give the other complete liberty, but that each should also do everything possible to help the other on. You may ask me how I know such a thing as that. I know it by the way they've behaved. Now see how much better women are than men! She has found a wife for Osmond, but Osmond has never lifted a little finger for *her*. She was worked for him, plotted for him, suffered for him; she has even more than once found money for him; and the end of it is that he's tired of her. She's an old habit; there are moments when he needs her, but on the whole he wouldn't miss her if she were removed. And, what's more, to-day she knows it. So you needn't be jealous!" the Countess added humorously.

Isabel rose from her sofa again; she felt bruised and scant of breath; her head was humming with new knowledge. "I'm much obliged to you," she repeated. And then she added abruptly, in quite a different tone: "How do you know all this?"

This enquiry appeared to ruffle the Countess more than Isabel's expression of gratitude pleased her. She gave her companion a bold stare, with which, "Let us assume that I've invented it!" she cried. She too, however, suddenly changed her tone and, laying her hand on Isabel's arm, said with the penetration of her sharp bright smile: "Now will you give up your journey?"

Isabel started a little; she turned away. But she felt weak and in a moment had to lay her arm upon the mantel-shelf for support. She stood a minute so, and then upon her arm she dropped her dizzy head, with closed eyes and pale lips.

"I've done wrong to speak—I've made you ill!" the Countess cried.

"Ah, I must see Ralph!" Isabel wailed; not in resentment, not in the quick passion her companion had looked for; but in a tone of far-reaching, infinite sadness.

LII

There was a train for Turin and Paris that evening; and after the Countess had left her Isabel had a rapid and decisive conference with her maid, who was discreet, devoted and active. After this she thought (except of her journey) only of one thing. She must go and see Pansy; from her she couldn't turn away. She had not seen her yet, as Osmond had given her to understand that it was too soon to begin. She drove at five o'clock to a high door in a narrow street in the quarter of the Piazza Navona,¹ and was admitted by the portress of the convent, a genial and obsequious person. Isabel had been at this institution before; she had come with Pansy to see the sisters. She knew they were good women, and she saw that the large rooms were clean and cheerful and that the well-used garden had sun for winter and shade for spring. But she disliked the place, which affronted and almost frightened her; not for the world would she have spent a night there. It produced to-day more than before the impression of a well-appointed prison; for it was not possible to pretend Pansy was free to leave it. This innocent creature had been presented to her in a new and violent light, but the secondary effect of the revelation was to make her reach out a hand.

The portress left her to wait in the parlour of the convent while she went to make it known that there was a visitor for the dear young lady. The parlour was a vast, cold apartment, with new-looking furniture; a large clean stove of white porcelain, unlighted, a collection of wax flowers under glass, and a series of engravings from religious pictures on the walls. On the other occasion Isabel had thought it less like Rome than like Philadelphia, but to-day she made no reflexions; the apartment only seemed to her very empty and very soundless. The portress returned at the end of some five minutes, ushering in another person. Isabel got up, expecting to see one of the ladies of the sisterhood, but to her extreme surprise found herself confronted with Madame Merle. The effect was strange, for Madame Merle was already so present to her vision that her appearance in the flesh was like suddenly, and rather awfully, seeing a painted picture move. Isabel had been thinking all day of her falsity, her audacity, her ability, her probable suffering; and these dark things seemed to flash with a sudden light as she entered the room. Her being there at all had the character of ugly evidence, of handwritings, of profaned relics, of grim things produced in court. It made Isabel feel faint; if it had been necessary to speak on the spot she would have been quite unable. But no such necessity

1. A vast square near the Pantheon.

was distinct to her; it seemed to her indeed that she had absolutely
nothing to say to Madame Merle. In one's relations with this lady,
however, there were never any absolute necessities; she had a
manner which carried off not only her own deficiencies but those of
other people. But she was different from usual; she came in slowly,
behind the portress, and Isabel instantly perceived that she was not
likely to depend upon her habitual resources. For her too the occasion was exceptional, and she had undertaken to treat it by the light
of the moment. This gave her a peculiar gravity; she pretended not
even to smile, and though Isabel saw that she was more than ever
playing a part it seemed to her that on the whole the wonderful
woman had never been so natural. She looked at her young friend
from head to foot, but not harshly nor defiantly; with a cold gentleness rather, and an absence of any air of allusion to their last meeting. It was as if she had wished to mark a distinction. She had been
irritated then, she was reconciled now.

"You can leave us alone," she said to the portress; "in five minutes this lady will ring for you." And then she turned to Isabel,
who, after noting what has just been mentioned, had ceased to
notice and had let her eyes wander as far as the limits of the room
would allow. She wished never to look at Madame Merle again.
"You're surprised to find me here, and I'm afraid you're not
pleased," this lady went on. "You don't see why I should have
come; it's as if I had anticipated you. I confess I've been rather
indiscreet—I ought to have asked your permission." There was
none of the oblique movement of irony in this; it was said simply
and mildly; but Isabel, far afloat on a sea of wonder and pain, could
not have told herself with what intention it was uttered. "But I've
not been sitting long," Madame Merle continued; "that is I've not
been long with Pansy. I came to see her because it occurred to me
this afternoon that she must be rather lonely and perhaps even a
little miserable. It may be good for a small girl; I know so little
about small girls; I can't tell. At any rate it's a little dismal. Therefore I came—on the chance. I knew of course that you'd come, and
her father as well; still, I had not been told other visitors were forbidden. The good woman—what's her name? Madame Catherine
—made no objection whatever. I stayed twenty minutes with
Pansy; she has a charming little room, not in the least conventual,
with a piano and flowers. She has arranged it delightfully; she has so
much taste. Of course it's all none of my business, but I feel happier since I've seen her. She may even have a maid if she likes; but
of course she has no occasion to dress. She wears a little black frock;
she looks so charming. I went afterwards to see Mother Catherine,
who has a very good room too; I assure you I don't find the poor
sisters at all monastic. Mother Catherine has a most coquettish

little toilet-table, with something that looked uncommonly like a bottle of eau-de-Cologne. She speaks delightfully of Pansy; says it's a great happiness for them to have her. She's a little saint of heaven and a model to the oldest of them. Just as I was leaving Madame Catherine the portress came to say to her that there was a lady for the signorina. Of course I knew it must be you, and I asked her to let me go and receive you in her place. She demurred greatly—I must tell you that—and said it was her duty to notify the Mother Superior; it was of such high importance that you should be treated with respect. I requested her to let the Mother Superior alone and asked her how she supposed I would treat you!"

So Madame Merle went on, with much of the brilliancy of a woman who had long been a mistress of the art of conversation. But there were phases and gradations in her speech, not one of which was lost upon Isabel's ear, though her eyes were absent from her companion's face. She had not proceeded far before Isabel noted a sudden break in her voice, a lapse in her continuity, which was in itself a complete drama. This subtle modulation marked a momentous discovery—the perception of an entirely new attitude on the part of her listener. Madame Merle had guessed in the space of an instant that everything was at end between them, and in the space of another instant she had guessed the reason why. The person who stood there was not the same one she had seen hitherto, but was a very different person—a person who knew her secret. This discovery was tremendous, and from the moment she made it the most accomplished of women faltered and lost her courage. But only for that moment. Then the conscious stream of her perfect manner gathered itself again and flowed on as smoothly as might be to the end. But it was only because she had the end in view that she was able to proceed. She had been touched with a point that made her quiver, and she needed all the alertness of her will to repress her agitation. Her only safety was in her not betraying herself. She resisted this, but the startled quality of her voice refused to improve—she couldn't help it—while she heard herself say she hardly knew what. The tide of her confidence ebbed, and she was able only just to glide into port, faintly grazing the bottom.

Isabel saw it all as distinctly as if it had been reflected in a large clear glass. It might have been a great moment for her, for it might have been a moment of triumph. That Madame Merle had lost her pluck and saw before her the phantom of exposure—this in itself was a revenge, this in itself was almost the promise of a brighter day. And for a moment during which she stood apparently looking out of the window, with her back half-turned, Isabel enjoyed that knowledge. On the other side of the window lay the garden of the convent; but this is not what she saw; she saw nothing of the budding plants and the glowing afternoon. She saw, in the crude light of that revelation which had already become a part of experience and to which the very frailty of the vessel in which it had been offered her only gave an intrinsic price, the dry staring fact that she had been an applied handled hung-up tool, as senseless and convenient as mere shaped wood and iron. All the bitterness of this knowledge surged into her soul again; it was as if she felt on her lips the taste of dishonour. There was a moment during which, if she had turned and spoken, she would have said something that would hiss like a lash. But she closed her eyes, and then the hideous vision dropped. What remained was the cleverest woman in the world standing there within a few feet of her and knowing as little what to think as the meanest. Isabel's only revenge was to be silent still —to leave Madame Merle in this unprecedented situation. She left her there for a period that must have seemed long to this lady, who at last seated herself with a movement which was in itself a confession of helplessness. Then Isabel turned slow eyes, looking down at her. Madame Merle was very pale; her own eyes covered Isabel's face. She might see what she would, but her danger was over. Isabel would never accuse her, never reproach her; perhaps because she never would give her the opportunity to defend herself.

"I'm come to bid Pansy good-bye," our young woman said at last. "I go to England to-night."

"Go to England to-night!" Madame Merle repeated sitting there and looking up at her.

"I'm going to Gardencourt. Ralph Touchett's dying."

"Ah, you'll feel that." Madame Merle recovered herself; she had a chance to express sympathy. "Do you go alone?"

"Yes; without my husband."

Madame Merle gave a low vague murmur; a sort of recognition of the general sadness of things. "Mr. Touchett never liked me, but I'm sorry he's dying. Shall you see his mother?"

"Yes; she has returned from America."

"She used to be very kind to me; but she has changed. Others too have changed," said Madame Merle with a quiet noble pathos. She paused a moment, then added: "And you'll see dear old Gardencourt again!"

"I shall not enjoy it much," Isabel answered.

"Naturally—in your grief. But it's on the whole, of all the houses I know, and I know many, the one I should have liked best to live in. I don't venture to send a message to the people," Madame Merle added; "but I should like to give my love to the place."

Isabel turned away. "I had better go to Pansy. I've not much time."

While she looked about her for the proper egress, the door

opened and admitted one of the ladies of the house, who advanced
with a discreet smile, gently rubbing, under her long loose sleeves, a
pair of plump white hands. Isabel recognised Madame Catherine,
whose acquaintance she had already made, and begged that she
would immediately let her see Miss Osmond. Madame Catherine
looked doubly discreet, but smiled very blandly and said: "It will be
good for her to see you. I'll take you to her myself." Then she
directed her pleased guarded vision to Madame Merle.

"Will you let me remain a little?" this lady asked. "It's so good
to be here."

"You may remain always if you like!" And the good sister gave a
knowing laugh.

She led Isabel out of the room, through several corridors, and up
a long staircase. All these departments were solid and bare, light
and clean; so, thought Isabel, are the great penal establishments.
Madame Catherine gently pushed open the door of Pansy's room
and ushered in the visitor; then stood smiling with folded hands
while the two others met and embraced.

"She's glad to see you," she repeated; "it will do her good." And
she placed the best chair carefully for Isabel. But she made no
movement to seat herself; she seemed ready to retire. "How does
this dear child look?" she asked of Isabel, lingering a moment.

"She looks pale," Isabel answered.

"That's the pleasure of seeing you. She's very happy. *Elle éclaire
la maison*,"[2] said the good sister.

Pansy wore, as Madame Merle had said, a little black dress; it
was perhaps this that made her look pale. "They're very good to me
—they think of everything!" she exclaimed with all her customary
eagerness to accommodate.

"We think of you always—you're a precious charge," Madame
Catherine remarked in the tone of a woman with whom benevolence was a habit and whose conception of duty was the acceptance
of every care. It fell with a leaden weight on Isabel's ears; it seemed
to represent the surrender of a personality, the authority of the
Church.

When Madame Catherine had left them together Pansy kneeled
down and hid her head in her stepmother's lap. So she remained
some moments, while Isabel gently stroked her hair. Then she got
up, averting her face and looking about the room. "Don't you think
I've arranged it well? I've everything I have at home."

"It's very pretty; you're very comfortable." Isabel scarcely knew
what she could say to her. On the one hand she couldn't let her
think she had come to pity her, and on the other it would be a dull
mockery to pretend to rejoice with her. So she simply added after a
moment: "I've come to bid you good-bye. I'm going to England."

2. She brightens the place.

Pansy's white little face turned red. "To England! Not to come back?"

"I don't know when I shall come back."

"Ah, I'm sorry," Pansy breathed with faintness. She spoke as if she had no right to criticise; but her tone expressed a depth of disappointment.

"My cousin, Mr. Touchett, is very ill; he'll probably die. I wish to see him," Isabel said.

"Ah yes; you told me he would die. Of course you must go. And will papa go?"

"No; I shall go alone."

For a moment the girl said nothing. Isabel had often wondered what she thought of the apparent relations of her father with his wife; but never by a glance, by an intimation, had she let it be seen that she deemed them deficient in an air of intimacy. She made her reflexions, Isabel was sure; and she must have had a conviction that there were husbands and wives who were more intimate than that. But Pansy was not indiscreet even in thought; she would as little have ventured to judge her gentle stepmother as to criticise her magnificent father. Her heart may have stood almost as still as it would have done had she seen two of the saints in the great picture in the convent-chapel turn their painted heads and shake them at each other. But as in this latter case she would (for very solemnity's sake) never have mentioned the awful phenomenon, so she put away all knowledge of the secrets of larger lives than her own. "You'll be very far away," she presently went on.

"Yes; I shall be far away. But it will scarcely matter," Isabel explained; "since so long as you're here I can't be called near you."

"Yes, but you can come and see me; though you've not come very often."

"I've not come because your father forbade it. To-day I bring nothing with me. I can't amuse you."

"I'm not to be amused. That's not what papa wishes."

"Then it hardly matters whether I'm in Rome or in England."

"You're not happy, Mrs. Osmond," said Pansy.

"Not very. But it doesn't matter."

"That's what I say to myself. What does it matter? But I should like to come out."

"I wish indeed you might."

"Don't leave me here," Pansy went on gently.

Isabel said nothing for a minute; her heart beat fast. "Will you come away with me now?" she asked.

Pansy looked at her pleadingly. "Did papa tell you to bring me?"

"No; it's my own proposal."

"I think I had better wait then. Did papa send me no message?"

"I don't think he knew I was coming."

"He thinks I've not had enough," said Pansy. "But I have. The ladies are very kind to me and the little girls come to see me. There are some very little ones—such charming children. Then my room —you can see for yourself. All that's very delightful. But I've had enough. Papa wished me to think a little—and I've thought a great deal."

"What have you thought?"

"Well, that I must never displease papa."

"You knew that before."

"Yes; but I know it better. I'll do anything—I'll do anything," said Pansy. Then, as she heard her own words, a deep, pure blush came into her face. Isabel read the meaning of it; she saw the poor girl had been vanquished. It was well that Mr. Edward Rosier had kept his enamels! Isabel looked into her eyes and saw there mainly a prayer to be treated easily. She laid her hand on Pansy's as if to let her know that her look conveyed no diminution of esteem; for the collapse of the girl's momentary resistance (mute and modest though it had been) seemed only her tribute to the truth of things. She didn't presume to judge others, but she had judged herself; she had seen the reality. She had no vocation for struggling with combinations; in the solemnity of sequestration there was something that overwhelmed her. She bowed her pretty head to authority and only asked of authority to be merciful. Yes; it was very well that Edward Rosier had reserved a few articles!

Isabel got up; her time was rapidly shortening. "Good-bye then. I leave Rome to-night."

Pansy took hold of her dress; there was a sudden change in the child's face. "You look strange; you frighten me."

"Oh, I'm very harmless," said Isabel.

"Perhaps you won't come back?"

"Perhaps not. I can't tell."

"Ah, Mrs. Osmond, you won't leave me!"

Isabel now saw she had guessed everything. "My dear child, what can I do for you?" she asked.

"I don't know—but I'm happier when I think of you."

"You can always think of me."

"Not when you're so far. I'm a little afraid," said Pansy.

"What are you afraid of?"

"Of papa—a little. And of Madame Merle. She has just been to see me."

"You must not say that," Isabel observed.

"Oh, I'll do everything they want. Only if you're here I shall do it more easily."

Isabel considered. "I won't desert you," she said at last. "Good-bye, my child."

Then they held each other a moment in a silent embrace, like two sisters; and afterwards Pansy walked along the corridor with her visitor to the top of the staircase. "Madame Merle has been here," she remarked as they went; and as Isabel answered nothing she added abruptly: "I don't like Madame Merle!"

Isabel hesitated, then stopped. "You must never say that—that you don't like Madame Merle."

Pansy looked at her in wonder; but wonder with Pansy had never been a reason for non-compliance. "I never will again," she said with exquisite gentleness. At the top of the staircase they had to separate, as it appeared to be part of the mild but very definite discipline under which Pansy lived that she should not go down. Isabel descended, and when she reached the bottom the girl was standing above. "You'll come back?" she called out in a voice that Isabel remembered afterwards.

"Yes—I'll come back."

Madame Catherine met Mrs. Osmond below and conducted her to the door of the parlour, outside of which the two stood talking a minute. "I won't go in," said the good sister. "Madame Merle's waiting for you."

At this announcement Isabel stiffened; she was on the point of asking if there were no other egress from the convent. But a moment's reflexion assured her that she would do well not to betray to the worthy nun her desire to avoid Pansy's other friend. Her companion grasped her arm very gently and, fixing her a moment with wise, benevolent eyes, said in French and almost familiarly: "*Eh bien, chère Madame, qu'en pensez-vous?*"[3]

"About my step-daughter? Oh, it would take long to tell you."

"We think it's enough," Madame Catherine distinctly observed. And she pushed open the door of the parlour.

Madame Merle was sitting just as Isabel had left her, like a woman so absorbed in thought that she had not moved a little finger. As Madame Catherine closed the door she got up, and Isabel saw that she had been thinking to some purpose. She had recovered her balance; she was in full possession of her resources. "I found I wished to wait for you," she said urbanely. "But it's not to talk about Pansy."

Isabel wondered what it could be to talk about, and in spite of Madame Merle's declaration she answered after a moment: "Madame Catherine says it's enough."

"Yes; it also seems to me enough. I wanted to ask you another word about poor Mr. Touchett," Madame Merle added. "Have you reason to believe that he's really at his last?"

"I've no information but a telegram. Unfortunately it only confirms a probability."

"I'm going to ask you a strange question," said Madame Merle.

3. Well, my dear madam, what do you think of it?

"Are you very fond of your cousin?" And she gave a smile as strange as her utterance.

"Yes, I'm very fond of him. But I don't understand you."

She just hung fire. "It's rather hard to explain. Something has occurred to me which may not have occurred to you, and I give you the benefit of my idea. Your cousin did you once a great service. Have you never guessed it?"

"He has done me many services."

"Yes; but one was much above the rest. He made you a rich woman."

"*He* made me—?"

Madame Merle appearing to see herself successful, she went on more triumphantly: "He imparted to you that extra lustre which was required to make you a brilliant match. At bottom it's him you've to thank." She stopped; there was something in Isabel's eyes.

"I don't understand you. It was my uncle's money."

"Yes; it was your uncle's money, but it was your cousin's idea. He brought his father over to it. Ah, my dear, the sum was large!"

Isabel stood staring; she seemed to-day to live in a world illumined by lurid flashes. "I don't know why you say such things. I don't know what you know."

"I know nothing but what I've guessed. But I've guessed that."

Isabel went to the door and, when she had opened it, stood a moment with her hand on the latch. Then she said—it was her only revenge: "I believed it was you I had to thank!"

Madame Merle dropped her eyes; she stood there in a kind of proud penance. "You're very unhappy, I know. But I'm more so."

"Yes; I can believe that. I think I should like never to see you again."

Madame Merle raised her eyes. "I shall go to America," she quietly remarked while Isabel passed out.

LIII

It was not with surprise, it was with a feeling which in other circumstances would have had much of the effect of joy, that as Isabel descended from the Paris Mail at Charing Cross[1] she stepped into the arms, as it were—or at any rate into the hands—of Henrietta Stackpole. She had telegraphed to her friend from Turin, and though she had not definitely said to herself that Henrietta would meet her, she had felt her telegram would produce some helpful result. On her long journey from Rome her mind had been given up to vagueness; she was unable to question the future. She performed this journey with sightless eyes and took little pleasure in the countries she traversed, decked out though they were in the richest fresh-

1. Close to Trafalgar Square and the terminus of the South Eastern Railway.

ness of spring. Her thoughts followed their course through other countries—strange-looking, dimly-lighted, pathless lands, in which there was no change of seasons, but only, as it seemed, a perpetual dreariness of winter. She had plenty to think about; but it was neither reflexion nor conscious purpose that filled her mind. Disconnected visions passed through it, and sudden dull gleams of memory, of expectation. The past and the future came and went at their will, but she saw them only in fitful images, which rose and fell by a logic of their own. It was extraordinary the things she remembered. Now that she was in the secret, now that she knew something that so much concerned her and the eclipse of which had made life resemble an attempt to play whist with an imperfect pack of cards, the truth of things, their mutual relations, their meaning, and for the most part their horror, rose before her with a kind of architectural vastness. She remembered a thousand trifles; they started to life with the spontaneity of a shiver. She had thought them trifles at the time; now she saw that they had been weighted with lead. Yet even now they were trifles after all, for of what use was it to her to understand them? Nothing seemed of use to her to-day. All purpose, all intention, was suspended; all desire too save the single desire to reach her much-embracing refuge. Gardencourt had been her starting-point, and to those muffled chambers it was at least a temporary solution to return. She had gone forth in her strength; she would come back in her weakness, and if the place had been a rest to her before, it would be a sanctuary now. She envied Ralph his dying, for if one were thinking of rest that was the most perfect of all. To cease utterly, to give it all up and not know anything more—this idea was as sweet as the vision of a cool bath in a marble tank, in a darkened chamber, in a hot land.

She had moments indeed in her journey from Rome which were almost as good as being dead. She sat in her corner, so motionless, so passive, simply with the sense of being carried, so detached from hope and regret, that she recalled to herself one of those Etruscan figures couched upon the receptacle of their ashes. There was nothing to regret now—that was all over. Not only the time of her folly, but the time of her repentance was far. The only thing to regret was that Madame Merle had been so—well, so unimaginable. Just here her intelligence dropped, from literal inability to say what it was that Madame Merle had been. Whatever it was it was for Madame Merle herself to regret it; and doubtless she would do so in America, where she had announced she was going. It concerned Isabel no more; she only had an impression that she should never again see Madame Merle. This impression carried her into the future, of which from time to time she had a mutilated glimpse. She saw herself, in the distant years, still in the attitude of a woman who had her life to live, and these intimations contradicted the spirit of the present hour. It might be desirable to get quite away, really away, further away than little grey-green England, but this privilege was evidently to be denied her. Deep in her soul—deeper than any appetite for renunciation—was the sense that life would be her business for a long time to come. And at moments there was something inspiring, almost enlivening, in the conviction. It was a proof of strength—it was a proof she should some day be happy again. It couldn't be she was to live only to suffer; she was still young, after all, and a great many things might happen to her yet. To live only to suffer—only to feel the injury of life repeated and enlarged—it seemed to her she was too valuable, too capable, for that. Then she wondered if it were vain and stupid to think so well of herself. When had it ever been a guarantee to be valuable? Wasn't all history full of the destruction of precious things? Wasn't it much more probable that if one were fine one would suffer? It involved then perhaps an admission that one had a certain grossness; but Isabel recognised, as it passed before her eyes, the quick vague shadow of a long future. She should never escape; she should last to the end. Then the middle years wrapped her about again and the grey curtain of her indifference closed her in.

Henrietta kissed her, as Henrietta usually kissed, as if she were afraid she should be caught doing it; and then Isabel stood there in the crowd, looking about her, looking for her servant. She asked nothing; she wished to wait. She had a sudden perception that she should be helped. She rejoiced Henrietta had come; there was something terrible in an arrival in London. The dusky, smoky, far-arching vault of the station, the strange, livid light, the dense, dark, pushing crowd, filled her with a nervous fear and made her put her arm into her friend's. She remembered she had once liked these things; they seemed part of a mighty spectacle in which there was something that touched her. She remembered how she walked away from Euston, in the winter dusk, in the crowded streets, five years before. She could not have done that to-day, and the incident came before her as the deed of another person.

"It's too beautiful that you should have come," said Henrietta, looking at her as if she thought Isabel might be prepared to challenge the proposition. "If you hadn't—if you hadn't; well, I don't know," remarked Miss Stackpole, hinting ominously at her powers of disapproval.

Isabel looked about without seeing her maid. Her eyes rested on another figure, however, which she felt she had seen before; and in a moment she recognised the genial countenance of Mr. Bantling. He stood a little apart, and it was not in the power of the multitude that pressed about him to make him yield an inch of the ground he had taken—that of abstracting himself discreetly while the two ladies performed their embraces.

"There's Mr. Bantling," said Isabel, gently, irrelevantly, scarcely caring much now whether she should find her maid or not.

"Oh yes, he goes everywhere with me. Come here, Mr. Bantling!" Henrietta exclaimed. Whereupon the gallant bachelor advanced with a smile—a smile tempered, however, by the gravity of the occasion. "Isn't it lovely she has come?" Henrietta asked. "He knows all about it," she added; "we had quite a discussion. He said you wouldn't, I said you would."

"I thought you always agreed," Isabel smiled in return. She felt she could smile now; she had seen in an instant, in Mr. Bantling's brave eyes, that he had good news for her. They seemed to say he wished her to remember he was an old friend of her cousin—that he understood, that it was all right. Isabel gave him her hand; she thought of him, extravagantly, as a beautiful blameless knight.

"Oh, I always agree," said Mr. Bantling. "But she doesn't, you know."

"Didn't I tell you that a maid was a nuisance?" Henrietta enquired. "Your young lady has probably remained at Calais."

"I don't care," said Isabel, looking at Mr. Bantling, whom she had never found so interesting.

"Stay with her while I go and see," Henrietta commanded, leaving the two for a moment together.

They stood there at first in silence, and then Mr. Bantling asked Isabel how it had been on the Channel.

"Very fine. No, I believe it was very rough," she said, to her companion's obvious surprise. After which she added: "You've been to Gardencourt, I know."

"Now how do you know that?"

"I can't tell you—except that you look like a person who has been to Gardencourt."

"Do you think I look awfully sad? It's awfully sad there, you know."

"I don't believe you ever look awfully sad. You look awfully kind," said Isabel with a breadth that cost her no effort. It seemed to her she should never again feel a superficial embarrassment.

Poor Mr. Bantling, however, was still in this inferior stage. He blushed a good deal and laughed, he assured her that he was often very blue, and that when he was blue he was awfully fierce. "You can ask Miss Stackpole, you know. I was at Gardencourt two days ago."

"Did you see my cousin?"

"Only for a little. But he had been seeing people; Warburton had been there the day before. Ralph was just the same as usual, except that he was in bed and that he looks tremendously ill and that he can't speak," Mr. Bantling pursued. "He was awfully jolly and funny all the same. He was just as clever as ever. It's awfully wretched."

Even in the crowded, noisy station this simple picture was vivid. "Was that late in the day?"

"Yes; I went on purpose. We thought you'd like to know."

"I'm greatly obliged to you. Can I go down to-night?"

"Ah, I don't think *she'll* let you go," said Mr. Bantling. "She wants you to stop with her. I made Touchett's man promise to telegraph me to-day, and I found the telegram an hour ago at my club. 'Quiet and easy,' that's what it says, and it's dated two o'clock. So you see you can wait till to-morrow. You must be awfully tired."

"Yes, I'm awfully tired. And I thank you again."

"Oh," said Mr. Bantling, "we were certain you would like the last news." On which Isabel vaguely noted that he and Henrietta seemed after all to agree. Miss Stackpole came back with Isabel's maid, whom she had caught in the act of proving her utility. This excellent person, instead of losing herself in the crowd, had simply attended to her mistress's luggage, so that the latter was now at liberty to leave the station. "You know you're not to think of going to the country to-night," Henrietta remarked to her. "It doesn't matter whether there's a train or not. You're to come straight to me in Wimpole Street. There isn't a corner to be had in London, but I've got you one all the same. It isn't a Roman palace, but it will do for a night."

"I'll do whatever you wish," Isabel said.

"You'll come and answer a few questions; that's what I wish."

"She doesn't say anything about dinner, does she, Mrs. Osmond?" Mr. Bantling enquired jocosely.

Henrietta fixed him a moment with her speculative gaze. "I see you're in a great hurry to get your own. You'll be at the Paddington Station[2] to-morrow morning at ten."

"Don't come for my sake, Mr. Bantling," said Isabel.

"He'll come for mine," Henrietta declared as she ushered her friend into a cab. And later, in a large dusky parlour in Wimpole Street—to do her justice there had been dinner enough—she asked those questions to which she had alluded at the station. "Did your husband make you a scene about your coming?" That was Miss Stackpole's first enquiry.

"No; I can't say he made a scene."

"He didn't object then?"

"Yes, he objected very much. But it was not what you'd call a scene."

---

2. **Terminus of the Great Western Railway for the west and southwest of England.**

"What was it then?"

"It was a very quiet conversation."

Henrietta for a moment regarded her guest. "It must have been hellish," she then remarked. And Isabel didn't deny that it had been hellish. But she confined herself to answering Henrietta's questions, which was easy, as they were tolerably definite. For the present she offered her no new information. "Well," said Miss Stackpole at last, "I've only one criticism to make. I don't see why you promised little Miss Osmond to go back."

"I'm not sure I myself see now," Isabel replied. "But I did then."

"If you've forgotten your reason perhaps you won't return."

Isabel waited a moment. "Perhaps I shall find another."

"You'll certainly never find a good one."

"In default of a better my having promised will do," Isabel suggested.

"Yes; that's why I hate it."

"Don't speak of it now. I've a little time. Coming away was a complication, but what will going back be?"

"You must remember, after all, that he won't make you a scene!" said Henrietta with much intention.

"He will, though," Isabel answered gravely. "It won't be the scene of a moment; it will be a scene of the rest of my life."

For some minutes the two women sat and considered this remainder, and then Miss Stackpole, to change the subject, as Isabel had requested, announced abruptly: "I've been to stay with Lady Pensil!"

"Ah, the invitation came at last!"

"Yes; it took five years. But this time she wanted to see me."

"Naturally enough."

"It was more natural than I think you know," said Henrietta, who fixed her eyes on a distant point. And then she added, turning suddenly: "Isabel Archer, I beg your pardon. You don't know why? Because I criticised you, and yet I've gone further than you. Mr. Osmond, at least, was born on the other side!"

It was a moment before Isabel grasped her meaning; this sense was so modestly, or at least so ingeniously, veiled. Isabel's mind was not possessed at present with the comicality of things; but she greeted with a quick laugh the image that her companion had raised. She immediately recovered herself, however, and with the right excess of intensity, "Henrietta Stackpole," she asked, "are you going to give up your country?"

"Yes, my poor Isabel, I am. I won't pretend to deny it; I look the fact in the face. I'm going to marry Mr. Bantling and locate right here in London."

"It seems very strange," said Isabel, smiling now.

"Well yes, I suppose it does. I've come to it little by little. I think I know what I'm doing; but I don't know as I can explain."

"One can't explain one's marriage," Isabel answered. "And yours doesn't need to be explained. Mr. Bantling isn't a riddle."

"No, he isn't a bad pun—or even a high flight of American humour. He has a beautiful nature," Henrietta went on. "I've studied him for many years and I see right through him. He's as clear as the style of a good prospectus. He's not intellectual, but he appreciates intellect. On the other hand he doesn't exaggerate its claims. I sometimes think we do in the United States."

"Ah," said Isabel, "you're changed indeed! It's the first time I've ever heard you say anything against your native land."

"I only say that we're too infatuated with mere brain-power; that, after all, isn't a vulgar fault. But I *am* changed; a woman has to change a good deal to marry."

"I hope you'll be very happy. You will at last—over here—see something of the inner life."

Henrietta gave a little significant sigh. "That's the key to the mystery, I believe. I couldn't endure to be kept off. Now I've as good a right as any one!" she added with artless elation.

Isabel was duly diverted, but there was a certain melancholy in her view. Henrietta, after all, had confessed herself human and feminine, Henrietta whom she had hitherto regarded as a light keen flame, a disembodied voice. It was a disappointment to find she had personal susceptibilities, that she was subject to common passions, and that her intimacy with Mr. Bantling had not been completely original. There was a want of originality in her marrying him— there was even a kind of stupidity; and for a moment, to Isabel's sense, the dreariness of the world took on a deeper tinge. A little later indeed she reflected that Mr. Bantling himself at least was original. But she didn't see how Henrietta could give up her country. She herself had relaxed her hold of it, but it had never been her country as it had been Henrietta's. She presently asked her if she had enjoyed her visit to Lady Pensil.

"Oh yes," said Henrietta, "she didn't know what to make of me."

"And was that very enjoyable?"

"Very much so, because she's supposed to be a master mind. She thinks she knows everything; but she doesn't understand a woman of my modern type. It would be so much easier for her if I were only a little better or a little worse. She's so puzzled; I believe she thinks it's my duty to go and do something immoral. She thinks it's immoral that I should marry her brother; but, after all, that isn't immoral enough. And she'll never understand my mixture—never!"

"She's not so intelligent as her brother then," said Isabel. "He appears to have understood."

"Oh no, he hasn't!" cried Miss Stackpole with decision. "I really believe that's what he wants to marry me for—just to find out the mystery and the proportions of it. That's a fixed idea—a kind of fascination."

"It's very good in you to humour it."

"Oh well," said Henrietta, "I've something to find out too!" And Isabel saw that she had not renounced an allegiance, but planned an attack. She was at last about to grapple in earnest with England.

Isabel also perceived, however, on the morrow, at the Paddington Station, where she found herself, at ten o'clock, in the company both of Miss Stackpole and Mr. Bantling, that the gentleman bore his perplexities lightly. If he had not found out everything he had found out at least the great point—that Miss Stackpole would not be wanting in initiative. It was evident that in the selection of a wife he had been on his guard against this deficiency.

"Henrietta has told me, and I'm very glad," Isabel said as she gave him her hand.

"I dare say you think it awfully odd," Mr. Bantling replied, resting on his neat umbrella.

"Yes, I think it awfully odd."

"You can't think it so awfully odd as I do. But I've always rather liked striking out a line," said Mr. Bantling serenely.

LIV

Isabel's arrival at Gardencourt on this second occasion was even quieter than it had been on the first. Ralph Touchett kept but a small household, and to the new servants Mrs. Osmond was a stranger; so that instead of being conducted to her own apartment she was coldly shown into the drawing-room and left to wait while her name was carried up to her aunt. She waited a long time; Mrs. Touchett appeared in no hurry to come to her. She grew impatient at last; she grew nervous and scared—as scared as if the objects about her had begun to show for conscious things, watching her trouble with grotesque grimaces. The day was dark and cold; the dusk was thick in the corners of the wide brown rooms. The house was perfectly still—with a stillness that Isabel remembered; it had filled all the place for days before the death of her uncle. She left the drawing-room and wandered about—strolled into the library and along the gallery of pictures, where, in the deep silence, her footstep made an echo. Nothing was changed; she recognised everything she had seen years before; it might have been only yesterday she had stood there. She envied the security of valuable "pieces" which change by no hair's breadth, only grow in value, while their owners lose inch by inch youth, happiness, beauty; and she became aware that she was walking about as her aunt had done on the day she had come to see her in Albany. She was changed enough since then—that had been the beginning. It suddenly struck her that if her Aunt Lydia had not come that day in just that way and found her alone, everything might have been different. She might have had another life and she might have been a woman more blest. She stopped in the gallery in front of a small picture—a charming and precious Bonington[1]—upon which her eyes rested a long time. But she was not looking at the picture; she was wondering whether if her aunt had not come that day in Albany she would have married Caspar Goodwood.

Mrs. Touchett appeared at last, just after Isabel had returned to the big uninhabited drawing-room. She looked a good deal older, but her eye was as bright as ever and her head as erect; her thin lips seemed a repository of latent meanings. She wore a little grey dress of the most undecorated fashion, and Isabel wondered, as she had wondered the first time, if her remarkable kinswoman resembled more a queen-regent or the matron of a gaol. Her lips felt very thin indeed on Isabel's hot cheek.

"I've kept you waiting because I've been sitting with Ralph," Mrs. Touchett said. "The nurse had gone to luncheon and I had taken her place. He has a man who's supposed to look after him, but the man's good for nothing; he's always looking out of the window—as if there were anything to see! I didn't wish to move, because Ralph seemed to be sleeping and I was afraid the sound would disturb him. I waited till the nurse came back; I remembered you knew the house."

"I find I know it better even than I thought; I've been walking everywhere," Isabel answered. And then she asked if Ralph slept much.

"He lies with his eyes closed; he doesn't move. But I'm not sure that it's always sleep."

"Will he see me? Can he speak to me?"

Mrs. Touchett declined the office of saying. "You can try him," was the limit of her extravagance. And then she offered to conduct Isabel to her room. "I thought they had taken you there; but it's not my house, it's Ralph's; and I don't know what they do. They must at least have taken your luggage; I don't suppose you've brought much. Not that I care, however. I believe they're given you the same room you had before; when Ralph heard you were coming he said you must have that one."

"Did he say anything else?"

"Ah, my dear, he doesn't chatter as he used!" cried Mrs. Touchett as she preceded her niece up the staircase.

It was the same room, and something told Isabel it had not been

1. Richard Parkes Bonington (1801–1828), English landscape and genre painter.

slept in since she occupied it. Her luggage was there and was not voluminous; Mrs. Touchett sat down a moment with her eyes upon it. "Is there really no hope?" our young woman asked as she stood before her.

"None whatever. There never has been. It has not been a successful life."

"No—it has only been a beautiful one." Isabel found herself already contradicting her aunt; she was irritated by her dryness.

"I don't know what you mean by that; there's no beauty without health. That is a very odd dress to travel in."

Isabel glanced at her garment. "I left Rome at an hour's notice; I took the first that came."

"Your sisters, in America, wished to know how you dress. That seemed to be their principal interest. I wasn't able to tell them— but they seemed to have the right idea: that you never wear anything less than black brocade."

"They think I'm more brilliant than I am; I'm afraid to tell them the truth," said Isabel. "Lily wrote me you had dined with her."

"She invited me four times, and I went once. After the second time she should have let me alone. The dinner was very good; it must have been expensive. Her husband has a very bad manner. Did I enjoy my visit to America? Why should I have enjoyed it? I didn't go for my pleasure."

These were interesting items, but Mrs. Touchett soon left her niece, whom she was to meet in half an hour at the midday meal. For this repast the two ladies faced each other at an abbreviated table in the melancholy dining-room. Here, after a little, Isabel saw her aunt not to be so dry as she appeared, and her old pity for the poor woman's inexpressiveness, her want of regret, of disappointment, came back to her. Unmistakeably she would have found it a blessing to-day to be able to feel a defeat, a mistake, even a shame or two. She wondered if she were not even missing those enrichments of consciousness and privately trying—reaching out for some aftertaste of life, dregs of the banquet; the testimony of pain or the cold recreation of remorse. On the other hand perhaps she was afraid; if she should begin to know remorse at all it might take her too far. Isabel could perceive, however, how it had come over her dimly that she had failed of something, that she saw herself in the future as an old woman without memories. Her little sharp face looked tragical. She told her niece that Ralph had as yet not moved, but that he probably would be able to see her before dinner. And then in a moment she added that he had seen Lord Warburton the day before; an announcement which startled Isabel a little, as it seemed an intimation that this personage was in the neighbourhood and that an accident might bring them together. Such an accident would not be happy; she had not come to England to struggle again with Lord Warburton. She none the less presently said to her aunt that he had been very kind to Ralph; she had seen something of that in Rome.

"He has something else to think of now," Mrs. Touchett returned. And she paused with a gaze like a gimlet.

Isabel saw she meant something, and instantly guessed what she meant. But her reply concealed her guess; her heart beat faster and she wished to gain a moment. "Ah yes—the House of Lords and all that."

"He's not thinking of the Lords; he's thinking of the ladies. At least he's thinking of one of them; he told Ralph he's engaged to be married."

"Ah, to be married!" Isabel mildly exclaimed.

"Unless he breaks it off. He seemed to think Ralph would like to know. Poor Ralph can't go to the wedding, though I believe it's to take place very soon."

"And who's the young lady?"

"A member of the aristocracy; Lady Flora, Lady Felicia—something of that sort."

"I'm very glad," Isabel said. "It must be a sudden decision."

"Sudden enough, I believe; a courtship of three weeks. It has only just been made public."

"I'm very glad," Isabel repeated with a larger emphasis. She knew her aunt was watching her—looking for the signs of some imputed soreness, and the desire to prevent her companion from seeing anything of this kind enabled her to speak in the tone of quick satisfaction, the tone almost of relief. Mrs. Touchett of course followed the tradition that ladies, even married ones, regard the marriage of their old lovers as an offence to themselves. Isabel's first care therefore was to show that however that might be in general she was not offended now. But meanwhile, as I say, her heart beat faster; and if she sat for some moments thoughtful—she presently forgot Mrs. Touchett's observation—it was not because she had lost an admirer. Her imagination had traversed half Europe; it halted, panting, and even trembling a little, in the city of Rome. She figured herself announcing to her husband that Lord Warburton was to lead a bride to the altar, and she was of course not aware how extremely wan she must have looked while she made this intellectual effort. But at last she collected herself and said to her aunt: "He was sure to do it some time or other."

Mrs. Touchett was silent; then she gave a sharp little shake of the head. "Ah, my dear, you're beyond me!" she cried suddenly. They went on with their luncheon in silence; Isabel felt as if she had heard of Lord Warburton's death. She had known him only as a suitor, and now that was all over. He was dead for poor Pansy; by

Pansy he might have lived. A servant had been hovering about; at last Mrs. Touchett requested him to leave them alone. She had finished her meal; she sat with her hands folded on the edge of the table. "I should like to ask you three questions," she observed when the servant had gone.

"Three are a great many."

"I can't do with less; I've been thinking. They're all very good ones."

"That's what I'm afraid of. The best questions are the worst," Isabel answered. Mrs. Touchett had pushed back her chair, and as her niece left the table and walked, rather consciously, to one of the deep windows, she felt herself followed by her eyes.

"Have you ever been sorry you didn't marry Lord Warburton?" Mrs. Touchett enquired.

Isabel shook her head slowly, but not heavily. "No, dear aunt."

"Good. I ought to tell you that I propose to believe what you say."

"Your believing me's an immense temptation," she declared, smiling still.

"A temptation to lie? I don't recommend you to do that, for when I'm misinformed I'm as dangerous as a poisoned rat. I don't mean to crow over you."

"It's my husband who doesn't get on with me," said Isabel.

"I could have told him he wouldn't. I don't call that crowing over *you*," Mrs. Touchett. "Do you still like Serena Merle?" she went on.

"Not as I once did. But it doesn't matter, for she's going to America."

"To America? She must have done something very bad."

"Yes—very bad."

"May I ask what it is?"

"She made a convenience of me."

"Ah," cried Mrs. Touchett, "so she did of me! She does of every one."

"She'll make a convenience of America," said Isabel, smiling again and glad that her aunt's questions were over.

It was not till the evening that she was able to see Ralph. He had been dozing all day; at least he had been lying unconscious. The doctor was there, but after a while went away—the local doctor, who had attended his father and whom Ralph liked. He came three or four times a day; he was deeply interested in his patient. Ralph had had Sir Matthew Hope, but he had got tired of this celebrated man, to whom he had asked his mother to send word he was now dead and was therefore without further need of medical advice. Mrs. Touchett had simply written to Sir Matthew that her son disliked him. On the day of Isabel's arrival Ralph gave no sign, as I have related, for many hours; but toward evening he raised himself and said he knew that she had come. How he knew was not apparent, inasmuch as for fear of exciting him no one had offered the information. Isabel came in and sat by his bed in the dim light; there was only a shaded candle in a corner of the room. She told the nurse she might go—she herself would sit with him for the rest of the evening. He had opened his eyes and recognised her, and had moved his hand, which lay helpless beside him, so that she might take it. But he was unable to speak; he closed his eyes again and remained perfectly still, only keeping her hand in his own. She sat with him a long time—till the nurse came back; but he gave no further sign. He might have passed away while she looked at him; he was already the figure and pattern of death. She had thought him far gone in Rome, and this was worse; there was but one change possible now. There was a strange tranquillity in his face; it was as still as the lid of a box. With this he was a mere lattice of bones; when he opened his eyes to greet her it was as if she were looking into immeasurable space. It was not till midnight that the nurse came back; but the hours, to Isabel, had not seemed long; it was exactly what she had come for. If she had come simply to wait she found ample occasion, for he lay three days in a kind of grateful silence. He recognised her and at moments seemed to wish to speak; but he found no voice. Then he closed his eyes again, as if he too were waiting for something—for something that certainly would come. He was so absolutely quiet that it seemed to her what was coming had already arrived; and yet she never lost the sense that they were still together. But they were not always together; there were other hours that she passed in wandering through the empty house and listening for a voice that was not poor Ralph's. She had a constant fear; she thought it possible her husband would write to her. But he remained silent, and she only got a letter from Florence and from the Countess Gemini. Ralph, however, spoke at last—on the evening of the third day.

"I feel better to-night," he murmured, abruptly, in the soundless dimness of her vigil; "I think I can say something." She sank upon her knees beside his pillow; took his thin hand in her own; begged him not to make an effort—not to tire himself. His face was of necessity serious—it was incapable of the muscular play of a smile; but its owner apparently had not lost a perception of incongruities. "What does it matter if I'm tired when I've all eternity to rest? There's no harm in making an effort when it's the very last of all. Don't people always feel better just before the end? I've often heard of that; it's what I was waiting for. Ever since you've been here I thought it would come. I tried two or three times; I was afraid you'd get tired of sitting there." He spoke slowly, with painful breaks and long pauses; his voice seemed to come from a distance.

When he ceased he lay with his face turned to Isabel and his large unwinking eyes open into her own. "It was very good of you to come," he went on. "I thought you would; but I wasn't sure."

"I was not sure either till I came," said Isabel.

"You've been like an angel beside my bed. You know they talk about the angel of death. It's the most beautiful of all. You've been like that; as if you were waiting for me."

"I was not waiting for your death; I was waiting for—for this. This is not death, dear Ralph."

"Not for you—no. There's nothing makes us feel so much alive as to see others die. That's the sensation of life—the sense that we remain. I've had it—even I. But now I'm of no use but to give it to others. With me it's all over." And then he paused. Isabel bowed her head further, till it rested on the two hands that were clasped upon his own. She couldn't see him now; but his far-away voice was close to her ear. "Isabel," he went on suddenly, "I wish it were over for you." She answered nothing; she had burst into sobs; she remained so, with her buried face. He lay silent, listening to her sobs; at last he gave a long groan. "Ah, what is it you have done for me?"

"What is it you did for me?" she cried, her now extreme agitation half smothered by her attitude. She had lost all her shame, all wish to hide things. Now he must know; she wished him to know, for it brought them supremely together, and he was beyond the reach of pain. "You did something once—you know it. O Ralph, you've been everything! What have I done for you—what can I do to-day? I would die if you could live. But I don't wish you to live; I would die myself, not to lose you." Her voice was as broken as his own and full of tears and anguish.

"You won't lose me—you'll keep me. Keep me in your heart; I shall be nearer to you than I've ever been. Dear Isabel, life is better; for in life there's love. Death is good—but there's no love."

"I never thanked you—I never spoke—I never was what I should be!" Isabel went on. She felt a passionate need to cry out and accuse herself, to let her sorrow possess her. All her troubles, for the moment, became single and melted together into this present pain. "What must you have thought of me? Yet how could I know? I never knew, and I only know to-day because there are people less stupid than I."

"Don't mind people," said Ralph. "I think I'm glad to leave people."

She raised her head and her clasped hands; she seemed for a moment to pray to him. "Is it true—is it true?" she asked.

"True that you've been stupid? Oh no," said Ralph with a sensible intention of wit.

"That you made me rich—that all I have is yours?"

He turned away his head, and for some time said nothing. Then at last: "Ah, don't speak of that—that was not happy." Slowly he moved his face toward her again, and they once more saw each other. "But for that—but for that—!" And he paused. "I believe I ruined you," he wailed.

She was full of the sense that he was beyond the reach of pain; he seemed already so little of this world. But even if she had not had it she would still have spoken, for nothing mattered now but the only knowledge that was not pure anguish—the knowledge that they were looking at the truth together. "He married me for the money," she said. She wished to say everything; she was afraid he might die before she had done so.

He gazed at her a little, and for the first time his fixed eyes lowered their lids. But he raised them in a moment, and then, "He was greatly in love with you," he answered.

"Yes, he was in love with me. But he wouldn't have married me if I had been poor. I don't hurt you in saying that. How can I? I only want you to understand. I always tried to keep you from understanding; but that's all over."

"I always understood," said Ralph.

"I thought you did, and I didn't like it. But now I like it."

"You don't hurt me—you make me very happy." And as Ralph said this there was an extraordinary gladness in his voice. She bent her head again, and pressed her lips to the back of his hand. "I always understood," he continued, "though it was so strange—so pitiful. You wanted to look at life for yourself—but you were not allowed; you were punished for your wish. You were ground in the very mill of the conventional!"

"Oh yes, I've been punished," Isabel sobbed.

He listened to her a little, and then continued: "Was he very bad about your coming?"

"He made it very hard for me. But I don't care."

"It is all over then between you?"

"Oh no; I don't think anything's over."

"Are you going back to him?" Ralph gasped.

"I don't know—I can't tell. I shall stay here as long as I may. I don't want to think—I needn't think. I don't care for anything but you, and that's enough for the present. It will last a little yet. Here on my knees, with you dying in my arms, I'm happier than I have been for a long time. And I want you to be happy—not to think of anything sad; only to feel that I'm near you and I love you. Why should there be pain? In such hours as this what have we to do with pain? That's not the deepest thing; there's something deeper."

Ralph evidently found from moment to moment greater difficulty in speaking; he had to wait longer to collect himself. At first he appeared to make no response to these last words; he let a long time elapse. Then he murmured simply: "You must stay here."

"I should like to stay—as long as seems right."

"As seems right—as seems right?" He repeated her words. "Yes, you think a great deal about that."

"Of course one must. You're very tired," said Isabel.

"I'm very tired. You said just now that pain's not the deepest thing. No—no. But it's very deep. If I could stay—"

"For me you'll always be here," she softly interrupted. It was easy to interrupt him.

But he went on, after a moment: "It passes, after all; it's passing now. But love remains. I don't know why we should suffer so much. Perhaps I shall find out. There are many things in life. You're very young."

"I feel very old," said Isabel.

"You'll grow young again. That's how I see you. I don't believe —I don't believe—" But he stopped again; his strength failed him.

She begged him to be quiet now. "We needn't speak to understand each other," she said.

"I don't believe that such a generous mistake as yours can hurt you for more than a little."

"Oh Ralph, I'm very happy now," she cried through her tears.

"And remember this," he continued, "that if you've been hated you've also been loved. Ah but, Isabel—*adored!*" he just audibly and lingeringly breathed.

"Oh my brother!" she cried with a movement of still deeper prostration.

LV

He had told her, the first evening she ever spent at Gardencourt, that if she should live to suffer enough she might some day see the ghost with which the old house was duly provided. She apparently had fulfilled the necessary condition; for the next morning, in the cold, faint dawn, she knew that a spirit was standing by her bed. She had lain down without undressing, it being her belief that Ralph would not outlast the night. She had no inclination to sleep; she was waiting, and such waiting was wakeful. But she closed her eyes; she believed that as the night wore on she should hear a knock at her door. She heard no knock, but at the time the darkness began vaguely to grow grey she started up from her pillow as abruptly as if she had received a summons. It seemed to her for an instant that he was standing there—a vague, hovering figure in the vagueness of the room. She stared a moment; she saw his white face—his kind eyes; then she saw there was nothing. She was not afraid; she was only sure. She quitted the place and in her certainty passed through dark corridors and down a flight of oaken steps that shone in the vague light of a hall-window. Outside Ralph's door she stopped a moment, listening, but she seemed to hear only the hush that filled it. She opened the door with a hand as gentle as if she were lifting a veil from the face of the dead, and saw Mrs. Touchett sitting motionless and upright beside the couch of her son, with one of his hands in her own. The doctor was on the other side, with poor Ralph's further wrist resting in his professional fingers. The two nurses were at the foot between them. Mrs. Touchett took no notice of Isabel, but the doctor looked at her very hard; then he gently placed Ralph's hand in a proper position, close beside him. The nurse looked at her very hard too, and no one said a word; but Isabel only looked at what she had come to see. It was fairer than Ralph had ever been in life, and there was a strange resemblance to the face of his father, which, six years before, she had seen lying on the same pillow. She went to her aunt and put her arm around her; and Mrs. Touchett, who as a general thing neither invited nor enjoyed caresses, submitted for a moment to this one, rising, as might be, to take it. But she was stiff and dry-eyed; her acute white face was terrible.

"Dear Aunt Lydia," Isabel murmured.

"Go and thank God you've no child," said Mrs. Touchett, disengaging herself.

Three days after this a considerable number of people found time, at the height of the London "season," to take a morning train down to a quiet station in Berkshire and spend half an hour in a small grey church which stood within an easy walk. It was in the green burial-place of this edifice that Mrs. Touchett consigned her son to earth. She stood herself at the edge of the grave, and Isabel stood beside her; the sexton himself had not a more practical interest in the scene than Mrs. Touchett. It was a solemn occasion, but neither a harsh nor a heavy one; there was a certain geniality in the appearance of things. The weather had changed to fair; the day, one of the last of the treacherous May-time, was warm and windless, and the air had the brightness of the hawthorn and the blackbird. If it was sad to think of poor Touchett, it was not too sad, since death, for him, had had no violence. He had been dying so long; he was so ready; everything had been so expected and prepared. There were tears in Isabel's eyes, but they were not tears that blinded. She looked through them at the beauty of the day, the splendour of nature, the sweetness of the old English churchyard, the bowed heads of good friends. Lord Warburton was there, and a group of gentlemen all unknown to her, several of whom, as she afterwards learned, were connected with the bank; and there were others whom she knew. Miss Stackpole was among the first, with honest Mr.

Bantling beside her; and Caspar Goodwood, lifting his head higher than the rest—bowing it rather less. During much of the time Isabel was conscious of Mr. Goodwood's gaze; he looked at her somewhat harder than he usually looked in public, while the others had fixed their eyes upon the churchyard turf. But she never let him see that she saw him; she thought of him only to wonder that he was still in England. She found she had taken for granted that after accompanying Ralph to Gardencourt he had gone away; she remembered how little it was a country that pleased him. He was there, however, very distinctly there; and something in his attitude seemed to say that he was there with a complex intention. She wouldn't meet his eyes, though there was doubtless sympathy in them; he made her rather uneasy. With the dispersal of the little group he disappeared, and the only person who came to speak to her—though several spoke to Mrs. Touchett—was Henrietta Stackpole. Henrietta had been crying.

Ralph had said to Isabel that he hoped she would remain at Gardencourt, and she made no immediate motion to leave the place. She said to herself that it was but common charity to stay a little with her aunt. It was fortunate she had so good a formula; otherwise she might have been greatly in want of one. Her errand was over; she had done what she had left her husband to do. She had a husband in a foreign city, counting the hours of her absence; in such a case one needed an excellent motive. He was not one of the best husbands, but that didn't alter the case. Certain obligations were involved in the very fact of marriage, and were quite independent of the quantity of enjoyment extracted from it. Isabel thought of her husband as little as might be; but now that she was at a distance, beyond its spell, she thought with a kind of spiritual shudder of Rome. There was a penetrating chill in the image, and she drew back into the deepest shade of Gardencourt. She lived from day to day, postponing, closing her eyes, trying not to think. She knew she must decide, but she decided nothing; her coming itself had not been a decision. On that occasion she had simply started. Osmond gave no sound and now evidently would give none; he would leave it all to her. From Pansy she heard nothing, but that was very simple: her father had told her not to write.

Mrs. Touchett accepted Isabel's company, but offered her no assistance; she appeared to be absorbed in considering, without enthusiasm but with perfect lucidity, the new conveniences of her own situation. Mrs. Touchett was not an optimist, but even from painful occurrences she managed to extract a certain utility. This consisted in the reflexion that, after all, such things happened to other people and not to herself. Death was disagreeable, but in this case it was her son's death, not her own; she had never flattered herself that her own would be disagreeable to any one but Mrs. Touch-ett. She was better off than poor Ralph, who had left all the com-modities of life behind him, and indeed all the security; since the worst of dying was, to Mrs. Touchett's mind, that it exposed one to be taken advantage of. For herself she was on the spot; there was nothing so good as that. She made known to Isabel very punctually —it was the evening her son was buried—several of Ralph's testa-mentary arrangements. He had told her everything, had consulted her about everything. He left her no money; of course she had no need of money. He left her the furniture of Gardencourt, exclusive of the pictures and books and the use of the place for a year; after which it was to be sold. The money produced by the sale was to constitute an endowment for a hospital for poor persons suffering from the malady of which he died; and of this portion of the will Lord Warburton was appointed executor. The rest of his property, which was to be withdrawn from the bank, was disposed of in var-ious bequests, several of them to those cousins in Vermont to whom his father had already been so bountiful. Then there were a number of small legacies.

"Some of them are extremely peculiar," said Mrs. Touchett; "he has left considerable sums to persons I never heard of. He gave me a list, and I asked then who some of them were, and he told me they were people who at various times had seemed to like him. Apparently he thought you didn't like him, for he hasn't left you a penny. It was his opinion that you had been handsomely treated by his father, which I'm bound to say I think you were—though I don't mean that I ever heard him complain of it. The pictures are to be dispersed; he has distributed them about, one by one, as little keepsakes. The most valuable of the collection goes to Lord War-burton. And what do you think he has done with his library? It sounds like a practical joke. He has left it to your friend Miss Stack-pole—'in recognition of her services to literature.' Does he mean her following him up from Rome? Was that a service to literature? It contains a great many rare and valuable books, and as she can't carry it about the world in her trunk he recommends her to sell it at auction. She will sell it of course at Christie's, and with the pro-ceeds she'll set up a newspaper. Will that be a service to litera-ture?"

This question Isabel forbore to answer, as it exceeded the little interrogatory to which she had deemed it necessary to submit on her arrival. Besides, she had never been less interested in literature than to-day, as she found when she occasionally took down from the shelf one of the rare and valuable volumes of which Mrs. Touchett had spoken. She was quite unable to read; her attention had never been so little at her command. One afternoon, in the library, about a week after the ceremony in the churchyard, she was trying to fix it for an hour; but her eyes often wandered from the book in her hand to the open window, which looked down the long avenue. It was in this way that she saw a modest vehicle approach the door and perceived Lord Warburton sitting, in rather an uncomfortable attitude, in a corner of it. He had always had a high standard of courtesy, and it was therefore not remarkable, under the circumstances, that he should have taken the trouble to come down from London to call on Mrs. Touchett. It was of course Mrs. Touchett he had come to see, and not Mrs. Osmond; and to prove to herself the validity of this thesis Isabel presently stepped out of the house and wandered away into the park. Since her arrival at Gardencourt she had been but little out of doors, the weather being unfavourable for visiting the grounds. This evening, however, was fine, and at first it struck her as a happy thought to have come out. The theory I have just mentioned was plausible enough, but it brought her little rest, and if you had seen her pacing about you would have said she had a bad conscience. She was not pacified when at the end of a quarter of an hour, finding herself in view of the house, she saw Mrs. Touchett emerge from the portico accompanied by her visitor. Her aunt had evidently proposed to Lord Warburton that they should come in search of her. She was in no humour for visitors and, if she had had a chance, would have drawn back behind one of the great trees. But she saw she had been seen and that nothing was left her but to advance. As the lawn at Gardencourt was a vast expanse this took some time; during which she observed that, as he walked beside his hostess, Lord Warburton kept his hands rather stiffly behind him and his eyes upon the ground. Both persons apparently were silent; but Mrs. Touchett's thin little glance, as she directed it toward Isabel, had even at a distance an expression. It seemed to say with cutting sharpness: "Here's the eminently amenable nobleman you might have married!" When Lord Warburton lifted his own eyes, however, that was not what they said. They only said "This is rather awkward, you know, and I depend upon you to help me." He was very grave, very proper and, for the first time since Isabel had known him, greeted her without a smile. Even in his days of distress he had always begun with a smile. He looked extremely self-conscious.

"Lord Warburton has been so good as to come out to see me," said Mrs. Touchett. "He tells me he didn't know you were still here. I know he's an old friend of yours, and as I was told you were not in the house I brought him out to see for himself."

"Oh, I saw there was a good train at 6:40, that would get me back in time for dinner," Mrs. Touchett's companion rather irrelevantly explained. "I'm so glad to find you've not gone."

"I'm not here for long, you know," Isabel said with a certain eagerness.

"I suppose not; but I hope it's for some weeks. You came to England sooner than—a—than you thought?"

"Yes, I came very suddenly."

Mrs. Touchett turned away as if she were looking at the condition of the grounds, which indeed was not what it should be, while Lord Warburton hesitated a little. Isabel fancied he had been on the point of asking about her husband—rather confusedly—and then had checked himself. He continued immitigably grave, either because he thought it becoming in a place over which death had just passed, or for more personal reasons. If he was conscious of personal reasons it was very fortunate that he had the cover of the former motive; he could make the most of that. Isabel thought of all this. It was not that his face was sad, for that was another matter; but it was strangely inexpressive.

"My sisters would have been so glad to come if they had known you were still here—if they had thought you would see them," Lord Warburton went on. "Do kindly let them see you before you leave England."

"It would give me great pleasure; I have such a friendly recollection of them."

"I don't know whether you would come to Lockleigh for a day or two? You know there's always that old promise." And his lordship coloured a little as he made this suggestion, which gave his face a somewhat more familiar air. "Perhaps I'm not right in saying that just now; of course you're not thinking of visiting. But I meant what would hardly be a visit. My sisters are to be at Lockleigh at Whitsuntide for five days; and if you could come then—as you say you're not to be very long in England—I would see that there should be literally no one else."

Isabel wondered if not even the young lady he was to marry would be there with her mamma; but she did not express this idea. "Thank you extremely," she contented herself with saying; "I'm afraid I hardly know about Whitsuntide."

"But I have your promise—haven't I?—for some other time."

There was an interrogation in this; but Isabel let it pass. She looked at her interlocutor a moment, and the result of her observation was that—as had happened before—she felt sorry for him. "Take care you don't miss your train," she said. And then she added: "I wish you every happiness."

He blushed again, more than before, and he looked at his watch. "Ah yes, 6.40; I haven't much time, but I've a fly at the door.

Thank you very much." It was not apparent whether the thanks applied to her having reminded him of his train or to the more sentimental remark. "Good-bye, Mrs. Osmond; good-bye." He shook hands with her, without meeting her eyes, and then he turned to Mrs. Touchett, who had wandered back to them. With her his parting was equally brief; and in a moment the two ladies saw him move with long steps across the lawn.

"Are you very sure he's to be married?" Isabel asked of her aunt.

"I can't be surer than he; but he seems sure. I congratulated him, and he accepted it."

"Ah," said Isabel, "I give it up!"—while her aunt returned to the house and to those avocations which the visitor had interrupted.

She gave it up, but she still thought of it—thought of it while she strolled again under the great oaks whose shadows were long upon the acres of turf. At the end of a few minutes she found herself near a rustic bench, which, a moment after she had looked at it, struck her as an object recognised. It was not simply that she had seen it before, nor even that she had sat upon it; it was that on this spot something important had happened to her—that the place had an air of association. Then she remembered that she had been sitting there, six years before, when a servant brought her from the house the letter in which Caspar Goodwood informed her that he had followed her to Europe; and that when she had read the letter she looked up to hear Lord Warburton announcing that he should like to marry her. It was indeed an historical, an interesting, bench; she stood and looked at it as if it might have something to say to her. She wouldn't sit down on it now—she felt rather afraid of it. She only stood before it, and while she stood the past came back to her in one of those rushing waves of emotion by which persons of sensibility are visited at odd hours. The effect of this agitation was a sudden sense of being very tired, under the influence of which she overcame her scruples and sank into the rustic seat. I have said that she was restless and unable to occupy herself; and whether or no, if you had seen her there, you would have admired the justice of the former epithet, you would at least have allowed that at this moment she was the image of a victim of idleness. Her attitude had a singular absence of purpose; her hands, hanging at her sides, lost themselves in the folds of her black dress; her eyes gazed vaguely before her. There was nothing to recall her to the house; the two ladies, in their seclusion, dined early and had tea at an indefinite hour. How long she had sat in this position she could not have told you; but the twilight had grown thick when she became aware that she was not alone. She quickly straightened herself, glancing about, and then saw what had become of her solitude. She was sharing it with Caspar Goodwood, who stood looking at her, a few yards off, and whose footfall on the unresonant turf, as he came near, she had not heard. It occurred to her in the midst of this that it was just so Lord Warburton had surprised her of old.

She instantly rose, and as soon as Goodwood saw he was seen he started forward. She had had time only to rise when, with a motion that looked like violence, but felt like—she knew not what, he grasped her by the wrist and made her sink again into the seat. She closed her eyes; he had not hurt her; it was only a touch, which she had obeyed. But there was something in his face that she wished not to see. That was the way he had looked at her the other day in the churchyard; only at present it was worse. He said nothing at first; she only felt him close to her—beside her on the bench and pressingly turned to her. It almost seemed to her that no one had ever been so close to her as that. All this, however, took but an instant, at the end of which she had disengaged her wrist, turning her eyes upon her visitant. "You've frightened me," she said.

"I didn't mean to," he answered, "but if I did a little, no matter. I came from London a while ago by the train, but I couldn't come here directly. There was a man at the station who got ahead of me. He took a fly that was there, and I heard him give the order to drive here. I don't know who he was, but I didn't want to come with him; I wanted to see you alone. So I've been waiting and walking about. I've walked all over, and I was just coming to the house when I saw you here. There was a keeper, or some one, who met me; but that was all right, because I had made his acquaintance when I came here with your cousin. Is that gentleman gone? Are you really alone? I want to speak to you." Goodwood spoke very fast; he was as excited as when they had parted in Rome. Isabel had hoped that condition would subside; and she shrank into herself as she perceived that, on the contrary, he had only let out sail. She had a new sensation; he had never produced it before; it was a feeling of danger. There was indeed something really formidable in his resolution. She gazed straight before her; he, with a hand on each knee, leaned forward, looking deeply into her face. The twilight seemed to darken round them. "I want to speak to you," he repeated; "I've something particular to say. I don't want to trouble you—as I did the other day in Rome. That was of no use; it only distressed you. I couldn't help it; I knew I was wrong. But I'm not wrong now; please don't think I am," he went on with his hard, deep voice melting a moment into entreaty. "I came here to-day for a purpose. It's very different. It was vain for me to speak to you then; but now I can help you."

She couldn't have told you whether it was because she was afraid, or because such a voice in the darkness seemed of necessity a boon; but she listened to him as she had never listened before; his words dropped deep into her soul. They produced a sort of stillness in all her being; and it was with an effort, in a moment, that she answered him. "How can you help me?" she asked in a low tone, as if she were taking what he had said seriously enough to make the enquiry in confidence.

"By inducing you to trust me. Now I know—to-day I know. Do you remember what I asked you in Rome? Then I was quite in the dark. But to-day I know on good authority; everything's clear to me to-day. It was a good thing when you made me come away with your cousin. He was a good man, a fine man, one of the best; he told me how the case stands for you. He explained everything; he guessed my sentiments. He was a member of your family and he left you—so long as you should be in England—to my care," said Goodwood as if he were making a great point. "Do you know what he said to me the last time I saw him—as he lay there where he died? He said: 'Do everything you can for her; do everything she'll let you.'"

Isabel suddenly got up. "You had no business to talk about me!"

"Why not—why not, when we talked in that way?" he demanded, following her fast. "And he was dying—when a man's dying it's different." She checked the movement she had made to leave him; she was listening more than ever; it was true that he was not the same as that last time. That had been aimless, fruitless passion, but at present he had an idea, which she scented in all her being. "But it doesn't matter!" he exclaimed, pressing her still harder, though now without touching a hem of her garment. "If Touchett had never opened his mouth I should have known all the same. I had only to look at you at your cousin's funeral to see what's the matter with you. You can't deceive me any more; for God's sake be honest with a man who's so honest with you. You're the most unhappy of women, and your husband's the deadliest of fiends."

She turned on him as if he had struck her. "Are you mad?" she cried.

"I've never been so sane; I see the whole thing. Don't think it's necessary to defend him. But I won't say another word against him; I'll speak only of you," Goodwood added quickly. "How can you pretend you're not heart-broken? You don't know what to do—you don't know where to turn. It's too late to play a part; didn't you leave all that behind you in Rome? Touchett knew all about it, and I knew it too—what it would cost you to come here. It will have cost you your life? Say it will"—and he flared almost into anger: "give me one word of truth! When I know such a horror as that, how can I keep myself from wishing to save you? What would you think of me if I should stand still and see you go back to your reward? 'It's awful, what she'll have to pay for it!'—that's what Touchett said to me. I may tell you that, mayn't I? He was such a near relation!" cried Goodwood, making his queer grim point again. "I'd sooner have been shot than let another man say those things to me; but he was different; he seemed to me to have the right. It was after he got home—when he saw he was dying, and when I saw it too. I understand all about it: you're afraid to go back. You're perfectly alone; you don't know where to turn. You can't turn anywhere; you know that perfectly. Now it is therefore that I want you to think of *me*."

"To think of 'you'?" Isabel said, standing before him in the dusk. The idea of which she had caught a glimpse a few moments before now loomed large. She threw back her head a little; she stared at it as if it had been a comet in the sky.

"You don't know where to turn. Turn straight to *me*. I want to persuade you to trust me," Goodwood repeated. And then he paused with his shining eyes. "Why should you go back—why should you go through that ghastly form?"

"To get away from *you!*" she answered. But this expressed only a little of what she felt. The rest was that she had never been loved before. She had believed it, but this was different; this was the hot wind of the desert, at the approach of which the others dropped dead, like mere sweet airs of the garden. It wrapped her about; it lifted her off her feet, while the very taste of it, as of something potent, acrid and strange, forced open her set teeth.

At first, in rejoinder to what she had said, it seemed to her that he would break out into greater violence. But after an instant he was perfectly quiet; he wished to prove he was sane, that he had reasoned it all out. "I want to prevent that, and I think I may, if you'll only for once listen to me. It's too monstrous of you to think of sinking back into that misery, of going to open your mouth to that poisoned air. It's you that are out of your mind. Trust me as if I had the care of you. Why shouldn't we be happy—when it's here before us, when it's so easy? I'm yours for ever—for ever and ever. Here I stand; I'm as firm as a rock. What have you to care about? You've no children; that perhaps would be an obstacle. As it is you've nothing to consider. You must save what you can of your life; you mustn't lose it all simply because you've lost a part. It would be an insult to you to assume that you care for the look of the thing, for what people will say, for the bottomless idiocy of the world. We've nothing to do with all that; we're quite out of it; we look at things as they are. You took the great step in coming away; the next is nothing; it's the natural one. I swear, as I stand here, that a woman deliberately made to suffer is justified in anything in life—in going down into the streets if that will help her! I know how you suffer, and that's why I'm here. We can do absolutely as we please; to whom under the sun do we owe anything? What is it that holds us, what is it that has the smallest right to interfere in such a question as this? Such a question is between ourselves—and to say that is to settle it! Were we born to rot in our misery—were we born to be afraid? I never knew *you* afraid! If you'll only trust me, how little you will be disappointed! The world's all before us—and the world's very big. I know something about that."

Isabel gave a long murmur, like a creature in pain; it was as if he were pressing something that hurt her. "The world's very small," she said at random; she had an immense desire to appear to resist. She said it at random, to hear herself say something; but it was not what she meant. The world, in truth, had never seemed so large; it seemed to open out, all round her, to take the form of a mighty sea, where she floated in fathomless waters. She had wanted help, and here was help; it had come in a rushing torrent. I know not whether she believed everything he said; but she believed just then that to let him take her in his arms would be the next best thing to her dying. This belief, for a moment, was a kind of rapture, in which she felt herself sink and sink. In the movement she seemed to beat with her feet, in order to catch herself, to feel something to rest on.

"Ah, be mine as I'm yours!" she heard her companion cry. He had suddenly given up argument, and his voice seemed to come, harsh and terrible, through a confusion of vaguer sounds.

This however, of course, was but a subjective fact, as the meta-physicians say; the confusion, the noise of waters, all the rest of it, were in her own swimming head. In an instant she became aware of this. "Do me the greatest kindness of all," she panted. "I beseech you to go away!"

"Ah, don't say that. Don't kill me!" he cried.

She clasped her hands; her eyes were streaming with tears. "As you love me, as you pity me, leave me alone!"

He glared at her a moment through the dusk, and the next instant she felt his arms about her and his lips on her own lips. His kiss was like white lightning, a flash that spread, and spread again, and stayed; and it was extraordinarily as if, while she took it, she felt each thing in his hard manhood that had least pleased her, each aggressive fact of his face, his figure, his presence, justified of its intense identity and made one with this act of possession. So had she heard of those wrecked and under water following a train of images before they sink. But when darkness returned she was free. She never looked about her; she only darted from the spot. There were lights in the windows of the house; they shone far across the lawn. In an extraordinarily short time—for the distance was considerable —she had moved through the darkness (for she saw nothing) and reached the door. Here only she paused. She looked all about her; she listened a little; then she put her hand on the latch. She had not known where to turn; but she knew now. There was a very straight path.

Two days afterwards Caspar Goodwood knocked at the door of the house in Wimpole Street in which Henrietta Stackpole occupied furnished lodgings. He hardly removed his hand from the knocker when the door was opened and Miss Stackpole herself stood before him. She had on her hat and jacket; she was on the point of going out. "Oh, good-morning," he said, "I was in hopes I should find Mrs. Osmond."

Henrietta kept him waiting a moment for her reply; but there was a good deal of expression about Miss Stackpole even when she was silent. "Pray what led you to suppose she was here?"

"I went down to Gardencourt this morning, and the servant told me she had come to London. He believed she was to come to you."

Again Miss Stackpole held him—with an intention of perfect kindness—in suspense. "She came here yesterday, and spent the night. But this morning she started for Rome."

Caspar Goodwood was not looking at her; his eyes were fastened on the doorstep. "Oh, she started—?" he stammered. And without finishing his phrase or looking up he stiffly averted himself. But he couldn't otherwise move.

Henrietta had come out, closing the door behind her, and now she put out her hand and grasped his arm. "Look here, Mr. Goodwood," she said; "just you wait!"

On which he looked up at her—but only to guess, from her face, with a revulsion, that she simply meant he was young. She stood shining at him with that cheap comfort, and it added, on the spot, thirty years to his life. She walked him away with her, however, as if she had given him now the key to patience.

Textual Appendix

This edition reproduces the text of the New York Edition of 1908.[1] The list which follows is not a complete collation of that text with the First Edition of 1881, in that it compares all the substantial changes but not the changes in "accidentals": primarily the hundreds of commas which were deleted from the earlier text and the apostrophes added to the later edition primarily to indicate omissions (e.g., "I've" instead of "I have"). Although James seldom changed the wording in dialogue, he dropped numerous clumsy instances of "that" when used as a conjunction or relative pronoun, and achieved greater informality in dialogue by repeatedly using contractions in the New York Edition: "You would simply say" (1881) almost invariably became, in 1908, "you'd simply say."[2]

Since this edition focuses on the many changes between the two editions, we have not collated the few changes made between the first edition and the earlier periodical versions which appeared in England (*Macmillan's Magazine*, October, 1880, to November, 1881) and America (*Atlantic Monthly*, November, 1880, to December, 1881). Besides an occasional change of name (from "Geraldine" to "Serena" Merle) or place (a winter spent by Ralph Touchett at Algiers rather than Corfu), the periodical versions are fundamentally similar to the First Edition.[3] The First Edition was published in November, 1881, in England and America, although the American edition bears the date "1882" on the title page.[4]

For the New York Edition, James believed that he had not only "revised" the novel but had literally rewritten it. "To revise is to see, or to look over," he wrote in a passage on revision, "which means in the case of a written thing neither more nor less than to re-read it."[5] As James re-read his novels in preparing them for the New York Edition he felt that he was "re-seeing" them again, not merely polishing them up, as one might incorrectly assume from skimming over the thousands of changes which range from the substitution of single words to sentences and paragraphs of addi-

---

1. A very few typographical errors in that edition have been silently corrected (e.g., "glad very," I, 205, "none less," II, 213).

2. For a complete collation of the two editions, including James's own revised copy now at the Houghton Library and a listing of all comma variants, see Anthony J. Mazzella, "The Revised *Portrait of a Lady*, Text and Commentary" (Ph.D. dissertation, Columbia University, 1970).

3. For the best review of these changes see Sydney J. Krause, "James's Revisions of the Style of *The Portrait of a Lady*," *American Literature*, 30 (March,

1958), 67–88. (Krause tells us that there are somewhat fewer than two hundred passages of revisions between the serial publication and the first edition, no single revision exceeding two sentences.)

4. Leon Edel and Dan H. Laurence, *A Bibliography of Henry James* (London, 1961), pp. 52–54; Simon Nowell-Smith, "Texts of *The Portrait of a Lady* 1881–1882: The Bibliographical Evidence," *Papers of the Bibliographical Society of America*, 63 (1969), pp. 304–10.

5. Henry James, "Preface" to *The Golden Bowl* (1909; reprinted in *The Art of the Novel*, ed. R. P. Blackmur [New York, 1934], p. 338).

tions and deletions.[6] The manuscript notes in the Houghton Library at Harvard indicate, according to Edel, that James "worked over the novel . . . as if it were a first draft."[7]

The popular and critical reception of this definitive and selective (and quite expensive) edition was lukewarm, even though James wrote eighteen Prefaces for it which R. P. Blackmur has called the most sustained, eloquent, and original piece of literary criticism in existence.[8] The author's popularity had declined and the revisions were questioned by admirers of his earlier works who were subsequently "baffled" by his later style and who wondered "whether an author's published work does not belong to the public."[9] Others complained about the addition of foreign phrases, the piling-up of adverbs, and the "over-elaborated" figures of speech while expressing relief that he had not really laid violent hands on his portrait of the lady.[10] James's last secretary, Theodora Bosanquet, felt impelled to defend the revisions in 1918, two years after his death, and she reminded her readers of James's conviction that he was "paternally responsible for two distinct families" of literature and that he felt constrained to improve the appearance of his literary progeny prior to 1890 before he considered them fit for appearance in the company of his later ones.[11] Miss Bosanquet denied that substitution or rearrangement was the real business of revision; rather, "it was the demonstration of values implicit in his early works, the retrieval of countless lost opportunities for adequately rendering.' "[12] Even though more recent critics have acknowledged the revisions to be an improvement,[13] and numerous editors have tacitly concurred by reprinting the later version,[14] dissenting voices have been raised. Malcolm Cowley responded to the sympathetic analysis of the revisions by F. O. Matthiessen by stressing that the characteristics of James's later style—the syntactical complications, elegant variations, and verbal inversion, and the famous density ("little more than verbosity")—are symbolic of James's separation from the public and that they "violate the spirit of the language as shaped by the living and dead millions."[15]

Two views of the revising process complete the Textual Appendix. F. O. Matthiessen's "The Painter's Sponge and Varnish Bottle" originally appeared in the *American Bookman* in 1944, and a slightly altered version, reprinted here, was published as an appendix to his well-known *Henry*

6. Theodora Bosanquet, *Henry James at Work* (London, 1924), pp. 12–13; F. O. Matthiessen, "The Painter's Sponge and Varnish Bottle," in *Henry James: The Major Phase* (New York, 1944), pp. 152–86; Jörg Häsler, *Switzerland in the Life and Work of Henry James* (Basel, 1966), p. 159; and Krause.

7. Leon Edel, *Henry James*, Vol. 5, *The Master: 1901–1916* (Philadelphia, 1972), pp. 324–33; Henry James, *The Portrait of a Lady*, ed. Leon Edel (New York, 1956), p. xviii.

8. *The Art of the Novel*, p. viii.

9. "Why Mr. James Revised," *Literary Digest*, 39 (August 21, 1909), 275–276.

10. Clara F. McIntyre, "The Late Manner of Mr. Henry James," *PMLA*, 27 (1912), 354–71.

11. Theodora Bosanquet, "The Revised Version," *The Little Review*, 5 (August, 1918), 56.

12. *Ibid.*, 58.

13. Matthiessen; Krause. Few critics have used the revisions to any extent, but see William Bysshe Stein, "*The Portrait of a Lady*: Vis Inertiae," *Western Humanities Review*, 13 (Spring, 1959), 177–90.

14. One important exception is Oscar Cargill's Signet Classic edition, which is reprinted from the first edition: Henry James, *The Portrait of a Lady* (New York: New American Library, 1964).

15. Malcolm Cowley, "The Two Henry Jameses," *The New Republic*, February 5, 1945, pp. 177–78.

James: The Major Phase (1944). Anthony J. Mazzella's previously unpublished "The New Isabel" is based on evidence which he gathered while preparing his collation of the two editions for a Columbia University doctoral dissertation, "The Revised *Portrait of a Lady,* Text and Commentary" (1970).

The following list juxtaposes all the substantive variants (i.e., differences in wording) between the first American edition of 1881 and the New York Edition. The words in boldface, preceded by page and line numbers from this Norton Critical Edition, give the passage of the New York Edition text. Differences in punctuation, paragraphing, and spelling have not been listed except when they accompany a change in wording.

TEXTUAL VARIANTS

18.6 pictorial tricks, picturesque tricks,
18.7 presented to the lawn its patches of ivy, presented itself to the lawn, with its patches of ivy,
19.2 At present, But at present,
19.2 obviously, nevertheless, obviously,
19.5 features evenly distributed evenly distributed features,
19.6 representation expression
19.8 yet but
19.18 took in contemplated
19.35 quite a different pattern, quite another pattern,
20.2 seen seen that
20.11 the son his son
20.27 strikes me we're strikes me that we are
20.27 his companion remarked. said his companion.
20.32 Lord Warburton resumed said Lord Warburton,
22.18–19 you have—haven't you?—such unlimited means." you are so ridiculously wealthy."
22.20 the other young man mercifully pleaded. said the other young man, indicating his father.
22.36 things, then—that's things—that is
23.29–30 such highly ethereal ones such ethereal ones
23.30 could only see could see
23.38 returned declared,
23.45 come out come
24.42–43 "It's her share in the family trait, the independence she speaks of." Her son's appreciation of the matter was more favourable. "Whatever the high spirit "It's her independence," her son explained, more favourably. "Whatever that
25.7 replied. declared.
25.13–14 You'd be a remarkable husband." you would be a good husband."
25.17–18 husband," Mr. Touchett's visitor pursued, husband,
25.18 either. One either; one
25.20 smiled said

25.28 toward towards
25.29 on upon
25.30–31 ample doorway doorway
25.36 small beast. little terrier.
25.39 quick chatter. joyous demonstration.
26.17–18 perfect little darling." little darling."
26.20 then replied. said.
26.23–24 brought out, murmured,
26.27 arrived come
26.35 here. I'm here," he went on. "I am
26.36 clear perception— quick perception
27.2 girl young girl
27.7 small dog little terrier
27.9–10 so near the threshold, in the doorway,
27.10 if whether
27.20 intensely active." strong."
27.23 he has he has got
27.23 hound." dogs."
27.26–27 having again reverted to the terrier. having reverted to the terrier again.
27.29 with amusement; humorously;
28.8 commented. murmured.
28.9 observed to went on, addressing
28.10 got there," arrived,"
28.17 made room in it for her companions; also narrowly scrutinized her companions;
28.22 lighted, brilliant,
28.22 easily lightly
28.26 this." this," she declared.
28.31 persons girls,
28.33 person girl
28.35–36 returned with a quick laugh. exclaimed quickly, with a little laugh.
28.38 watching his face. watching his face a little.
28.45–29.1 slightly inclined himself, bent towards her a little,
29.12–13 He seemed to recognize that it was an awkward beginning and it was an awkward beginning
29.29–30 American places." places."

29.33 just hesitated. hesitated a moment.
29.37 heaven Heaven
29.41 come with her come
30.4 wider eyes startled eyes
30.5 me. me," she said.
30.15 again, a moment,
30.16 after which and then
30.26 although although it was
30.26 liberal motions, benevolence,
30.27 suavity. softness.
30.29–30 just unmistakeably simply very sharply
30.32 knife-like wounding
30.32–33 That hard fineness came out in her deportment This purity of outline was visible in her deportment
30.38–39 she had repaired the disorder of dress with a completeness She had achieved a toilet
30.41 graces coquetry
31.3 clear, apparent,
31.3 community, relations,
31.5 appearance fact
31.9–10 and by leaving her husband to take care of the English branch of his bank. leaving her husband in England to take care of his bank.
31.10–11 felicitously definite. extremely definite.
31.13 such unnatural things discomfort
31.20–21 the English style of life, England,
31.22 that ancient order, British civilization,
31.29 this last had been this last one had been
31.33–34 To say she was so occupied To say that she had a book
31.37 fresh taste lightness
31.38 correct. dispel.
31.41 one of the lower apartments. the parlour.
32.17 practically more festal; more sociable;
32.23 arrive and remain, stay with her,
32.27 home romantic. dwelling picturesque.
32.30 containing peach-trees of barely credible familiarity. containing certain capital peach-trees.
32.32–33 side, across side, opposite, across
32.38 kept or rather let go, kept in an ameteurish manner
32.40 fastened with strange bedroomy combs puffed out very much
32.44 protested against its laws expressed great disgust
33.18 certainly or
33.22–23 was secured was fastened
33.35 was the most depressed of its scenes. was the most joyless chamber it contained.
33.38 beyond. beyond it.
33.39 fell was falling
33.39–40 the spring-time was indeed an appeal—and it seemed a cynical, insincere appeal—to patience. the spring-time presented itself as a questionable improvement.
33.41 heed attention

33.41 cosmic treacheries; the incongruities of the season;
34.5 moving in walking about
34.7 was looking for a visit, had reason to expect a visit;
34.14–15 she had a face with a good deal of rather violent point. she had a sharp, but not an unpleasant face.
34.16 began, said,
34.16 She And she
34.20 while and
34.28 since while
34.36 I'm not at all crazy: I haven't a delusion! I am not crazy.
35.3 had she
35.11 them she them that she
35.20 old place. mansion.
35.21 expect for it?" expect to get for it?"
35.22 her companion, the girl,
35.29 What have you in point of fact inherited?" In point of fact, what have you inherited?"
35.33 dare say, suspect,
35.42–43 the girl rather strangely returned. said the girl, rather strangely.
36.9 bourgeois." *bourgeois."*
36.13 "I should "I should
36.15 declared. rejoined.
36.16 Our young woman's The girl's
36.19 person young lady
36.25–26 interesting figure: a figure essentially—almost the first she had ever met. interesting person.
36.28–29 offensive or alarming. The term disagreeable. To her imagination the term
36.29–30 even sinister. inharmonious.
36.30–33 But her aunt made it a matter of high but easy irony, or comedy, and led her to ask herself if the common tone, which was all she had known, had ever been as interesting. No one certainly had on any occasion so held her as this little thin-lipped, But her aunt infused a new vividness into the idea, and gave her so many fresh impressions that it seemed to her she had over-estimated the charms of conformity. She had never met any one so entertaining as this little thin-lipped,
36.36 the courts of Europe. European courts.
36.37–39 recognized no social superiors, and, judging the great ones of the earth in a way that spoke of this, enjoyed was fond of social grandeur, and she enjoyed
36.43–44 whatever turn they took, whatever they were,
36.44 food for deep reflexion. deeply interesting.
37.3 gossip. gossip," she said.
37.4 so many hours?" for hours?"
37.5 replied; answered;
37.8 gracious. gracious to her niece.
37.17 superior. one.
37.17 second of the group, second sister,
37.18 of in
37.19 suffice be enough to say
37.25 Edith's, Edith's had been,

37.28–30 the mistress of a wedge of brown stone violently driven into Fifty-third Street, seemed to exult in her condition as in a bold escape. the mistress of a house which presented a narrowness of new brown stone to Fifty-third Street, she had quite justified her claim to matrimony.

37.31–32 solid, and her claim to figure was questioned, but she was conceded presence, though not majesty; she had moreover, plump,

37.33 improved since her marriage, and the had improved since her marriage; the

37.35–38 "I've never kept up with Isabel—it would have taken *all* my time," she had often remarked; in spite of which, however, she held her rather wistfully in sight; watching her as a motherly spaniel might watch a free greyhound. "I have never felt like Isabel's sister, and I am sure I never shall," she had said to an intimate friend: a declaration which made it all the more creditable that she had been prolific in sisterly offices.

37.40 noted remarked

38.10 appearance visit,

38.11 their aunt's her

38.11 Isabel then said Isabel said to her

38.12–13 her sister's words had doubtless prompted a word spoken to her husband as the two were making ready for their visit. her sister's words must have prompted a remark that she made to her husband in the conjugal chamber as the two were getting ready to go to the hotel.

38.20 her. Isabel.

38.27 it?" it?" her husband asked.

38.34 Moses!" Jupiter!"

38.38 *Do* you Do *you*

38.41–42 less haughty than her words. sweeter than the words she uttered.

39.7–8 felt different, felt as if something had happened to her. felt busy; busy, I mean, with her thoughts.

39.9–10 her hands empty, her usual avocations unheeded. with empty hands, heedless of her usual avocations.

39.12 agitated; excited;

39.13–14 The importance of what had happened was out of proportion She felt that something had happened to her of which the importance was out of proportion

39.16 that which

39.22–23 a desire for dozing forgetfulness. It was on the contrary a desire to take a nap. On the contrary, it was

39.23 wide-eyed, wide-awake,

39.25–26 when the door was not open it jumped out of the window. if the door were not opened to it, it jumped out of the window.

39.35 person— girl—

39.39 unpleasant. disagreeable.

39.40 unpleasant disagreeable

39.45 felicity good fortune

39.45–40.2 Isabel rose even to pride in her parentage. Since his death she had seemed to see him as turning his braver side to his children and as not having managed to ignore the ugly Isabel was even proud of her parentage. Since his death she had gathered a vague impression that he turned his brighter side to his children, and that he had not eluded discomfort

40.4 suppose him think that he was

40.5 had held thought

40.9–10 had recognized in the late Mr. Archer a remarkably handsome head admitted that the late Mr. Archer had a remarkably handsome head

40.11–12 was making had made

40.18 superficial schools, strange schools,

40.19 the French, foreigners,

40.22 large. abundant.

40.23 who had eloped who eloped

40.26 romantic picturesque

40.33 the subject proposed: foreign lands;

40.35–37 she was the member of his trio who most "made up" to him for the disagreeables he didn't mention. In among his three daughters she was quite his favorite, and in

40.39 had been was

41.3 fetching. popular.

41.5–6 the limits of her own power to frisk and jump and shriek—above all with rightness of effect. the moderate character of her own triumphs.

41.10 aesthetic vulgarians. a parcel of fools.

41.23 showy reference. quotation.

41.28 soul heart

41.31 as to which to which

41.32 committed the conscious solecism of forgiving them gone so far as to forgive

41.38 suspicious swains the local youth

41.39 number proportion

41.40–42 to remind them they had heads as well, had kept her unacquainted with the supreme disciplines of her sex and age. to make it a sensible pleasure, was sufficient to redeem her maidenly career from failure.

41.43 bonbons, flattery,

41.44–42.2 abundant opportunity for dancing, plenty of new dresses, the London *Spectator,* the latest publications, the music of Gounod, the poetry of Browning, the prose of George Eliot. abundant opportunity for dancing, the latest publications, plenty of new dresses, the London *Spectator,* and a glimpse of contemporary aesthetics.

42.13–14 He sometimes wrote to her and had within a week or two written from New York. He sometimes wrote to Isabel, and he had lately written to her from New York.

42.16–17 Now that she learned he was there, nevertheless, Nevertheless, now that she learned he was there,

42.18 splendid magnificent

42.19–20 he inspired her with a sentiment of high, of rare respect. She had never felt equally moved to it by any other person. he filled her with a certain feeling of respect which she had never entertained for any one else.

42.25–26 State capital. capital.

42.27 new sense of complications. certain feeling of embarrassment.

42.29–30 He was not romantically, he was much rather obscurely, handsome; He was not especially good-looking,

42.32 rewarded rewarded or not,

42.32 blue eyes of remarkable fixedness, the eyes of a complexion other than his own, a blue eye of remarkable fixedness

42.36 in spite of which, in half an hour, but, nevertheless, an hour later

42.38–39 He was not, it may be added, a man weakly to accept defeat. He was not, however, a man to be discouraged by a defeat.

43.11–14 in her thoughts and her thoroughly arranged servanted life his turn always came after the other nearest subjects of her solicitude, the various punctualities of performance of the workers of her will. in her thoughts his turn always came after the care of her house and her conservatory (she was extremely fond of flowers).

43.18 remarked she remarked

43.20 given way. broken down.

43.21 giving way, breaking down,

43.22 infirmity enfeebled condition

43.25 a native of Rutland, who was a native of Rutland,

43.26 where in which

43.27 gained preponderant control. acquired a preponderant interest.

43.29 sane and accommodating view. cheerful, and eminently practical view.

43.30–31 no intention of disamericanizing, nor had he a desire to teach his only son any such subtle art. no intention of turning Englishman, nor had he any desire to convert his only son to the same sturdy faith.

43.32–33 to live in England assimilated yet unconverted to live in England, and yet not be of it,

43.33–35 equally simple his lawful heir should after his death carry on the grey old bank in the white American light. He was at pains to intensify this light, simple that after his death, his lawful heir should carry on the bank in a pure American spirit. He took pains to cultivate this spirit,

43.37 at in

43.37 university, college,

43.39 native, national,

44.2 adventure jocosity

44.10 a watery waste the ocean (which he detested)

44.12 he but he

44.14–15 no aptitude for the banking mystery no great fancy for the banking business,

44.17–19 the fine ivory surface, polished as by the English air, that the old man had opposed to possibilities of penetration. the old man's effective simplicity.

44.20 placed in put into

44.25–27 Mr. Touchett had made of the very limits of his pliancy half the ground of his general success. He had retained in their freshness most of his marks of primary pressure; Mr. Touchett had given evidence of this talent only up to a certain point. He had made himself thoroughly comfortable in England, but he had never attempted to pitch his thoughts in the English key. He had retained many characteristics of Rutland, Vermont;

44.29–33 he had become, on his own ground, as mellow as he was rich; he combined consummate shrewdness with the disposition superficially to fraternise, and his "social position," on which he had never wasted a care, had the firm perfection of an unthumbed fruit. especially, he was a gentle, refined, fastidious old man, who combined consummate shrewdness with a sort of fraternizing good-humour, and whose feeling about his own position in the world was quite of the democratic sort.

44.37 he had never he never

44.38 he had never he never

44.38 obscurities he had never sounded. mysteries he never understood.

44.39 the day he *had* sounded them the day that he had understood them

44.41 had spent spent

44.42 had found found

44.42 perched mounted

45.3–4 had become aware of his being became conscious that he was

45.5 on upon

45.5 dire confusion. extreme embarrassment.

45.6–7 apply, to the letter, the sorry injunction to take care of himself. embrace the sorry occupation known as taking care of one's self.

45.7 he slighted the task; it appeared to him he was greatly disgusted; it appeared to him that

45.8 least he least that he

45.11–12 even an undemonstrative respect, and even undemonstrative respect,

45.14 it usually struck him as his reputation for ordinary wit— it usually seemed to him to be his reputation for common sense—

45.15 his graceless charge his unattractive *protégé*

45.18 assured he assured that he

45.19 to those to one of those

45.20 As he had He had

45.21 he cursed the flatness of exile: and cursed this immitigable necessity;

45.23 found his sensitive organ grateful

even for grim favours, found that his sensitive organ was really grateful for such grim favours,

45.24 lighter hand. better grace.

45.26–27 it had snowed overnight, it snowed,

45.28–29 A secret hoard of indifference —like a thick cake a fond old nurse might have slipped into his first school outfit— A certain fund of indolence that he possessed

45.30 sacrifice; since doing nothing; for

45.31 aught but that arduous game. anything but a passive life.

45.32–33 at least not renounced the field of valour. given up nothing.

45.34 fragrance perfume

45.35 and to

45.35 of pleasures is the rush of action. pleasures of life are to be found in the world of action.

45.42 that this

45.44 arrived reached it

46.3 yet but

46.7 the joys of contemplation had never been sounded. that the delights of observation had never been suspected.

46.11 having had to having to

46.11–12 in the same breast with bursts of inspiring self-criticism. with a good deal of native indifference.

46.12 judged him more found him much more

46.14–15 His serenity was but the array of wild flowers niched in his ruin. The truth was that he had simply accepted the situation.

46.16–17 It was very probably this sweet-tasting property of the observed thing in itself It was very probably this sweet-tasting property of observation to which I allude (for he found himself in these last years much more inclined to notice the pleasant things of the world than the others)

46.18 advent arrival

46.19 If he was consideringly disposed, if he were observantly disposed,

46.20–22 It may be added, in summary fashion, that the imagination of loving —as distinguished from that of being loved—had still a place in his reduced sketch. He had only forbidden himself the riot of expression. However, he shouldn't inspire his cousin with a passion, nor would she be able, even should she try, to help him to one. It may be added, somewhat crudely, that the liberty of falling in love had a place in Ralph Touchett's programme. This was of course a liberty to be very temperately used; for though the safest form of any sentiment is that which is conditioned upon silence, it is not always the most comfortable, and Ralph had forbidden himself the arts of demonstration. But conscious observation of a lovely woman had struck him as the finest entertainment that the world now had to offer him, and if the inter-

est should become poignant, he flattered himself that he could carry it off quietly, as he had carried other discomforts. He speedily acquired a conviction, however, that he was not destined to fall in love with his cousin.

46.28 was prompt. hesitated a little.

46.37 take her to Paris. I mean to get her clothing." take her to Paris, to get her some clothes."

46.44–45 inviting compassion. a girl that suggests compassion.

46.46 where you see your duty." what your duty will direct you to do."

47.1 In showing It will direct me to show

47.2 in giving to give

47.4 allowing giving

47.14 she Isabel

47.15 Isabel's this one is

47.16 I greatly amuse her. I amuse her a good deal.

47.16 get on get on very well,

47.20 *you!* you!

47.23 so very pretty?" very pretty?"

47.30 left her no doubt of it told her,

47.31 service. hint.

47.32 enlightened told

47.37 she's ridiculously mistaken. she is very much mistaken.

47.39–40 greater convenience, in some ways, more becoming ornament

47.45 others of them, other sisters,

48.7 a land a sort of land

48.8 emigration, of rescue, emigration,

48.14 report, account of his pretty cousin,

48.15 the subject of it her

48.19 You won't, I think, in any way, be easily right about her." *(Omitted.)*

48.20 rejoicingly exclaimed. exclaimed.

48.29–30 looked out of the window. looked out of the window a little.

48.34 After which, as But

48.36 he pursued, said Ralph,

48.43–44 It *takes* trouble to do that. *(Omitted.)*

49.6 she that she

49.8 character's character was

49.10 in by

49.16 in into

49.19 time-blackened time-stained

49.19 features ornaments

49.20 smiled. said, smiling.

49.21 "Marrying her? "Marry her?

49.28 says, they're says," he exclaimed, "they are

49.29–30 satisfy his curiosity at the source, extract his information about his cousin from the girl herself,

49.30 evident evident to him that

49.30 occasion. opportunity.

49.31 He had a good deal of talk with his young kinswoman He had, for instance, a good deal of talk with her that same evening,

49.32 left left alone

49.35 ended concluded,

49.36 quite emptied the measure of their

forms, exhausted each other's conversation,

49.39 in no degree spent. to have no sense of weariness.

49.40 knew knew that

49.41 exhaustion fatigue

49.42 broke down. had become impossible.

49.42–43 A fine hypocrisy was for the present possible; For the present it was perfectly possible;

49.43–44 interested; she was, as she said to herself, floated. interested and excited.

49.45 many many of them

50.1 best best of them

50.4–5 stood over to the morrow. been deferred till the morrow.

50.8 knew knew that

50.8 now that she

50.8 she couldn't but she could not

50.10 pressure eagerness

50.13 sheen shining

50.15 inclining to bending toward

50.20 place gallery

50.21 presence. figure.

50.23 undeniably spare, and ponderably light, and proveably tall; thin, and light, and middling tall;

50.25 had always always

50.25 willowy thin

50.27 eyes, eye,

50.27 firm keen

50.28 range of concession. softness when she smiled.

50.33 returned. answered, laughing.

50.34 are horridly ignorant." seem to me so ignorant," said Isabel.

50.36 some of them *would*—**but the way they're talked to!"** some girls are so nice,"

50.37 to dilate just yet on herself. to talk about herself.

50.38 subject, subject, she went on,

50.41 "A castle-spectre, a thing that appears. We spectre, a phantom; we

50.46 romantic old house," romantic house,"

51.1 a dismally prosaic one; dismally prosaic;

51.16 gentleman on the lawn gentleman that was on the lawn

51.23 that. He's the dearest of the dear." that; he is a dear old man."

51.26–27 to have too many theories. to be too theoretic.

51.42 he cried cried Ralph,

52.5 said Ralph. said Ralph, smiling.

52.6 I'm I was

52.6 Isabel the girl

52.11 She Isabel

52.14–15 not afraid, you know," not afraid,"

52.24 wandered off turned away

53.6 creature reported young lady reputed

53.9 the girl Isabel

53.18 had lost all faith in culture. had no time for anything else.

53.18 tendency, with this, tendency, however,

53.20 properly, seriously,

53.22 girl had never girl never

53.23 for the laurels of authorship. to be an authoress.

53.24 too little had none

53.33–34 she treated herself to occasions of homage. impulsively, she often admired herself.

53.36 subject heroine

53.38 speaking who seemed to her to speak

53.40 At moments she discovered she was grotesquely wrong, Every now and then she found out she was wrong,

53.44 under this provision on this condition that

54.11 she held it must she thought it would

54.18 struck her as seemed to her

54.19 to her. to one.

54.21 no love of their look, but when she fixed them hard no taste for thinking of them, but whenever she looked at them fixedly

54.25 indecent not to right to

54.26 was is

54.28 crooked anomalous

54.30 women ladies

54.31 noted observed

54.35 might should

54.36 should might

54.43 creature of conditions: young girl;

55.3–4 that state. She never called it the state of solitude, much less of singleness; she thought such descriptions weak, her independence. She never called it loneliness; she thought that weak;

55.5 abide. stay with her.

55.7 high laudable

55.9 an admired ability; remarkable talent;

55.12 quoted. admired.

55.12–13 pronounced them with confidence "ephemeral," did not accept them unrestrictedly,

55.14 the writer, her friend,

55.17 Henrietta was in the van of progress Henrietta was a great radical,

55.28 student reader

55.35 frivolous and hollow. Isabel was stoutly determined not to be hollow. trivial and superficial. Isabel was resolutely determined not to be superficial.

55.36 with the right patience expectantly and trustfully

55.38 views on the subject of marriage. opinions on the question of marriage.

55.39–40 of the vulgarity of thinking too much of it. that it was very vulgar to think too much about it.

55.40 into eagerness into a state of eagerness

55.41 prayed she prayed that she

55.41–43 a woman ought to be able to live to herself, in the absence of exceptional flimsiness, a woman ought to be able to make up her life in singleness,

55.46 dry stiff
56.2 article subject
56.3–4 a ruinous expenditure, an expenditure of imagination,
56.10 ended in alarms. ended by frightening her.
56.12 colour, blush,
56.12 calling her a rank egoist. telling her that she was selfish.
56.13 her development, her own development,
56.13 her perfection, her own perfection,
56.14 her progress. her own progress.
56.14 in her conceit, for her own imagination
56.18 spirit mind
56.20–21 remarkable soul, virginal soul,
56.21 which that
56.23 repaid curiosity easy eagerness
56.28 fine, full consciousness absorbing happiness
56.34 This impression was This was
56.36 a subject an object
56.39 diverted entertained
56.41–42 Mecca, and into many of his interests there his children had naturally not entered. Mecca.
56.43 images impressions
56.43 grown become
57.9–10 all friction dropped out of contact and all shrillness out of talk— all shrillness dropped out of conversation—
57.13–15 sitting with folded hands like a placid, homely household god, a god of service, sitting placidly with folded hands, like a good old man
57.21 "point" vivacity
57.23 mass majority
57.30 prompt artless
57.40 wanted wished
57.41 and he
57.41 ask it ask something
57.41–42 She would ask But Isabel asked
57.42–43 a quantity. a great many.
57.43–44 her pressure interrogation
58.3 begging asking
58.4 corresponded correspond
58.7 shawl spread shawl that was spread
58.19 improvements I improvements that I
58.33–34 sure it will *satisfy* me," Isabel judicially emphasised. sure I shall like it," said Isabel, somewhat judicially.
59.1 quite up to everything; very positive;
59.1–2 person you person that you
59.2 evidence. Too free a fancy— testimony. Too much imagination—
59.16 there at any price. there!
59.21–22 upper and even to some extent in the middle." upper class."
59.23 "Gracious," "Dear me!"
59.34 the girl the young girl,
60.4 they're too stupidly conventional. they are conventional.
60.5 least stupidly conventional. least conventional.

60.38–39 seemed to her seemed to her that
61.5–6 sense to take them. sense.
61.16 extravagance. violent statements.
61.23 indifferently indiscriminately
61.24 his fantastic mother his anomalous mother,
61.35 assured her assured her that
61.42 heated fervid
61.44 on the lines in the height
62.2 really be so. be so.
62.8 work her up, torment her,
62.15 her her that
62.17 observed said
62.32–33 Ralph had been for many weeks Ralph for many weeks had been
62.39 disburdened of pain, tolerably comfortable,
62.44 first grimly called. first called.
63.4 Ralph lost indeed his one inspiration. Ralph was indeed mightily disgusted.
63.11 felt wound; pain of loss;
63.12 early end uncompleted career
63.17 hope hope that
63.19 suggested suggested that
63.21 harbouring "love" for falling in love with
63.22 judged decided
63.25–26 really interesting little figure. a thoroughly interesting woman.
63.26 their neighbour Lord Warburton
63.30 conscious conscious that
63.30–32 "A character like that," he said to himself—"a real little passionate force to see at play is the finest thing in nature. "A character like that," he said to himself, "is the finest thing in nature.
63.36–37 anything pleasant something agreeable
64.19 rather a a rather
64.21 mixed mingled
64.37 found found that
64.38 on upon
64.38–39 shrunk from the extremity of absolved herself from the obligation of
64.42 rare profundity extraordinary meditation
64.42 consider contemplate
64.44 persons, people,
64.45 on upon
65.6–7 he had indeed rather sharply registered himself on her fine sense he had made indeed a tolerably vivid impression on her mind,
65.8 hoped she hoped that she
65.10 sovereign, so delightful,
65.10–11 was more and more a sort of golden grandfather, was such a perfection of an uncle,
65.11 was unlike was so unlike
65.12 her idea of cousins having tended to gloom. her view of cousins being rather monotonous.
65.14 hint sense
65.14 view. prospect.
65.21 her the young girl
65.23 hurl herself into the fray. be delighted.

65.24 his Ralph's
65.26 providing for his companion entertaining his cousin
65.30 eminent cases. figures.
65.38 nice." good."
65.39 nice. good.
66.4 sonorous mirth. deep, agreeable laugh.
66.14–16 Her desire to think well of herself had at least the element of humility that it always needed to be supported by proof. Her desire to think well of herself always needed to be supported by proof; though it is possible that this fact is not the sign of a milder egotism.
66.20 many of his remarks much of his conversation
66.23 on upon
66.23 had had weight, was pleasant,
66.24–25 she scarce fell short of seeing him—though quite without luridity—as a hero of romance. she thought him quite one of the most delectable persons she had met.
66.26–27 possible felicities. the pleasantness of life.
66.34 observed she said
65.41–42 Isabel gaily engaged. said Isabel, smiling.
67.1 a moment for a moment,
67.2 them coldly them
67.3 your blest Albany, Albany,
67.12 I I
67.12 suggested. exclaimed.
67.15 midnight." midnight," she said.
67.17 him her him that her
67.17 involved— stirred—
67.18–19 anything of a flare an exhibition of temper,
67.24 you're vexed you are displeased
67.26 considered. reflected a moment.
67.26 vexed, displeased,
67.27 mystified. Wasn't it puzzled. Was it not
67.29 here—in decent houses—don't here don't
67.34 me be
67.37 you own ways." your liberty."
67.38 them. it.
67.44 devoted to romantic effects much interested in the picturesque,
67.45–68.1 house, a house, which was a
68.3 attend attend upon
68.6 sounded interrogated
68.9 urged asked
68.10 her her that
68.13 very decent and pleasant;" simple and respectable and trustworthy;"
68.14 Miss Archer might that Miss Archer should
68.15–16 family living, that of Lockleigh, which was a heavy, sprawling parish, parsonage at Lockleigh, which was rather a largish parish,
68.19 Isabel that Isabel
68.22 she that she
68.26–27 the questions involved them
68.36 knew know
68.37 slice part

68.44 shall will
68.44 her friend; Warburton;
69.7–8 though married but the other day, though she was married only the other day,
69.19 native national
69.33 gave said
69.33 thrilling glimpses Isabel felt entertaining things, Isabel perceived that
69.34 did it said them
69.34–35 had rare chances and had tumbled in, as she put it, for high prizes, had a great good fortune,
69.37–39 His quality was a mixture of the effect of rich experience—oh, so easily come by!— with a modesty at times almost boyish; His composition was a mixture of good-humoured manly force and a modesty that at times was almost boyish;
69.41 a tone of responsible kindness. a tone of kindness which was not boyish, inasmuch as there was a good deal of reflection and of conscience in it.
69.44 Ralph returned. said Ralph.
70.2 be be
70.5 sound. robust.
70.14–15 For me, in his place, I could be as solemn as a statue of Buddha. He For me, I could take the poor fellow very seriously; he
70.19 and indeed about everything in the world. and everything else.
70.23 a pampered bigot. an old-fashioned and narrow-minded person.
70.28–29 a good deal of charming taste, imagination,
70.30 being man
70.38 Isabel was prompt. "I think he's charming." charming," Isabel answered.
70.39 nice person," fine fellow,"
70.42–43 rather a a rather
70.45 must talk." is rather fanciful."
71.1 your friend's too subversive—or not subversive Lord Warburton is too radical—or not radical
71.27–28 you're on the side of the old or on the side of the new. you are a liberal or a conservative.
71.29 "I'm on the side of both. "I am both.
71.29–30 I guess I'm a little on the side of everything. I think I am a little of everything.
71.31 high, proud loyalist. conservative.
71.32 behave so exquisitely. I mean so picturesquely." behave so picturesquely."
71.37–38 going gracefully to the guillotine seeing a revolution
71.39 a big outbreak one,
72.5 And But
72.12 they want to feel earnest," they are very conscientious,"
72.17 yet don't damage yet they don't affect
72.22 quaint distinctness, mild, reflective, optimistic accent,
72.26 humbug; humbug," she said;

72.31–32 island and ever so many other things besides. island.
72.33 elegant very cultivated
72.35 elegant cultivated
72.36 pleasure— entertainment—
72.39 has so has got so
72.44 sighed. exclaimed.
73.4 melancholy. sadness.
73.14 show a most have a very
73.15 described spoke of
73.15 by that term as original,
73.17 since for that
73.20–22 having, as she thought, eyes like the balanced basins, the circles of "ornamental water," set, in parterres, among the geraniums. having, as she thought, the kindest eyes in the world.
73.27 suspected it as a tendency suspected that it might become a fault
73.30 Yes, their eyes, Their eyes,
73.30 admired, were round, quiet admired so much, were quiet
73.31 figures, also figures,
73.36 luncheon lunch
73.38 if whether
73.40 so and
74.3 flushed, blushed,
74.5 she was in some wild, free manner practising on them: she was quizzing them;
74.19 play of mind; vivacity;
74.20 they that they
74.21 luncheon lunch
74.24 your that your
74.33 clearly evidently
74.34 had met the frank advances was playing with
74.35 that which
74.35 expanses, spacious room,
75.5 demanded. inquired.
75.7 returned. exclaimed.
75.9 had lost themselves. were rapidly getting bewildered.
75.12 this part of the county." the county."
75.13 dare say suspect
75.14 remark. observe.
75.19 beautifully very
75.24–25 to fight to the death: I mean for the heritage of the past. I should hold it tight." to be a conservative. I should wish to keep everything."
75.30 luncheon, lunch,
75.35–36 affected the young visitor as a castle in a legend. seemed to Isabel a castle in a fairy-tale.
75.40 luncheon, lunch,
75.42 a rich ecclesiasticism theological characteristics
75.42 marks characteristics
75.44 indiscriminate abundant
76.7 least familiar guest youngest visitor
76.8 apart somewhat apart
76.16 barrack. house.
76.22 pardon excuse
76.37 "But, I nevertheless don't "But, all the same, I don't
77.13 summing people up." judging people."
77.20 I want to see as many countries as

I can." I want very much to see foreign lands as well."
77.35 'quaint' picturesque—
77.36 'quaint,' picturesque,
77.37 quaintest most picturesque
77.39 briefly silent. silent a moment.
77.45 are were
77.46 are were,
78.2 make her a scene, make a scene,
78.19 his this
78.20–21 not the calculation of her effect—a game she played not coquetry —a quality that she possessed
79.1 judged best not to show did not show
79.5–6 show me up, reproduce me,
79.12 alert enterprising
79.12–13 announcing her prompt approach. signifying her intention of arriving.
79.13 that centre the metropolis
79.15 her. the visitor.
79.16 Ralph asked asked Ralph
79.17 moved along the platform. stood on the platform, before the advent of the train.
79.24 conceded. declared.
79.27–28 crimes of violence and attacks on the person require more or less pluck. interviewing requires bravery.
79.28 me?" me?"
79.45–46 proved, as Isabel had promised, quite delicately, even though rather provincially, fair. proved to be, as Isabel had said, decidedly pretty.
79.46 neat, fair,
80.7 a little arrested who was somewhat disconcerted
80.8 hinted seemed to indicate
80.9–10 rustled, she shimmered, was very well dressed,
80.11–12 as crisp and new and comprehensive as a first issue before the folding. scrupulously, fastidiously neat.
80.12–13 had probably no misprint. carried not an ink-stain.
80.14 loud; yet loud, though
80.15–16 struck him as not all in the large type, the type of horrid "headings," that he had expected. struck him rather to his surprise, as not an abundant talker.
80.18 copious lucidity; a great deal of precision and distinctness;
80.21 confidence in her powers. conversational powers.
80.23 broke out. said.
80.25–26 liberally answered. answered, liberally.
80.27 on upon
80.28–29 buttons—buttons that might have fixed the elastic loops of some tense receptacle: buttons;
80.30 on upon
80.32 as as he was
80.33–34 less inviolate, more dishonoured, than he liked. and uncomfortable.
80.36 lapsed. disappeared.

80.40 returned. rejoined.

81.3 cosmopolite," cosmopolitan,"

81.10–11 his aged, innocent voice. his mild, wise, aged, innocent voice.

81.17 a lovely group a most lovely group

81.20 accord sympathize

81.21–22 That's the true way—then you can breathe. (*Omitted.*)

81.30 deprecated, in fact defied, isolation. was of an eminently social tendency.

81.31 desire request

81.33 on upon

82.10 drives; drives, and

82.23–24 struck her as strange appeared to her so strange

82.25 break down so in spots. exhibit such extraordinary disparities.

82.28 found her more than ever inconsequent. marvelled more than ever at her inconsistency.

82.34 put it in somewhere." put it in a letter."

82.36–37 newspaper-lady newspaper-correspondent

82.37 matter. material.

82.43 cried. exclaimed.

83.4 pleaded; begged;

83.7 declared. rejoined.

83.8–9 her cousin had, according to her prophecy, lost his heart to their visitor. his [sic] cousin had fallen in love with their visitor,

83.14–15 Her presence proved somehow less irreducible to soft particles Her society had a less insoluble quality

83.16 solubility adequacy

83.17 prompted mirth in him, made him laugh a good deal,

83.18–19 the *crescendo* of mirth should be the flower of his declining days. abundant laughter should be the embellishment of the remainder of his days.

83.19 failed a little to did not quite

83.22–23 almost immoral not to work out. superficial on her part not to solve.

83.27 smiled Isabel; said Isabel, smiling;

83.27–28 of large leisure." of leisure."

83.29 car-conductor," cotton-mill,"

83.42 ones. prejudices.

83.44 as I render her for I render your cousin

84.4 effort; trouble;

84.15 terms; phrases;

84.17 strained brilliant

84.19 journal of the other world; transatlantic journal;

84.25 agreeably." agreeably," said Ralph.

84.29 directed turned

84.30 Lancret Watteau

84.36 missed not apprehended

84.38 conscience." conscience," she said.

84.39 *have* have

85.1 mild gentle

85.6–7 They're both antecedent to choice—elements of one's composition that are not to be eliminated." It's antecedent to choice."

85.8 You've tried and been worsted. you would give it up if you could?

85.12 sighed. urged.

85.28 a heart?" any?"

85.32 the later this

85.38 groaned. exclaimed impatiently.

86.3 "sort." fellow.

86.4–5 she went into cages, she flourished lashes, like a spangled lion-tamer. there is always something fine about that.

86.19 ocular surfaces unwinkingly caught the sun. brilliant eyes expanded still further.

86.21 I've as I have got as

86.25 day day that

86.32 conceived a passion for fallen in love with

86.42 luxury of laughter. burst of resounding laughter.

87.3 *me*. me.

87.6 hers, in general, to hers to

87.9–10 unworthy of you to keep so many things to yourself. That's very frivolous for you to be single; that's

87.10 wanted to express. meant to express to you.

87.13 Forgive my depravity." Excuse my superficiality."

87.37–38 vividly figures it." she reminds me of it."

87.40 I that I

87.42 with a certain intensity I accept it. in a certain way, I like it.

87.43 swagger, boast,

88.1–2 straightway convinced by *her;* not so much in respect to herself as in respect to what masses behind her." immensely struck with her; not so much for herself as what stands behind her."

88.7 green Pacific! blue Pacific!

88.8 pardon excuse

88.14 so green as that," blue,"

88.14 a young woman a woman

88.15–16 Henrietta, however, does smell of the Future—it almost knocks one down!" Henrietta, however, is fragrant—Henrietta is decidedly fragrant!"

88.22 the nature of man human nature

88.24–25 renewed contact her relations

88.25–26 her genius for unshrinking enquiry, the general application of her confidence. that somewhat aggressive frankness which was the social expression of her nature.

88.28–29 free play of intelligence fine freedom of composition

88.31 noble general

88.33 for to

88.34 "allow" pay a certain deference

88.35 in truth, however,

88.37 defined spoken of

88.37–39 both an adventuress and a bore —adventuresses usually giving one more of a thrill; she had "a newspaper-woman," and

88.40 yet but she
88.41 had never undertaken never undertook
89.2–5 I don't like Miss Stackpole—everything about her displeases me; she talks so much too loud and looks at one as if one wanted to look at her—which one doesn't. I don't like Miss Stackpole—I don't like her tone. She talks too loud, and she looks at me too hard.
89.6 the manners and the liberties of such places. the style of manners that such a way of living produces.
89.9 knows knows that
89.19–20 acquainted herself, in the western world, with every form of caravansary. had acquired a large familiarity with the technical hospitality of her country.
89.21–22 Mrs. Touchett, fresh from a renewed struggle with them, recorded Mrs. Touchett recorded
89.37 retorted. rejoined.
89.44 serenely said. said, serenely.
90.4–5 proclaimed cried
90.5 with much meaning. with a laugh.
90.8 you wouldn't at all have the tenue.'' you would make a very poor butler.''
90.15 judged to be suspected of being
90.17 took occasion to say said
90.18 Isabel: Isabel in the morning, while they were alone together,
90.18 if whether
90.34 period which period of time which
90.35 added at last: said at last—
90.40 responded. exclaimed, quickly.
90.41 that that
91.3 waited. was silent a moment.
91.4 turned a little pale. coloured a little, and now her blush was slowly fading.
91.17 nothing so simplifying as a grand passion.'' nothing so simple as a great passion.''
91.18 grand passion; great passion;
91.28 slightly harsh hilarity. laugh.
91.29 smile back smile in reply;
91.38–39 old ones when the old ones have been the right ones.'' old ones.''
91.41–42 But she faltered before her friend's implacable glitter. And then she paused; Henrietta's bright eyes seemed to her to grow enormous.
91.43 him,'' him,'' said Miss Stackpole.
91.44 made appeared
91.44 as if to deny this charge; instead of which, however, to be on the point of denying this charge, but instead of this
92.1 asked if inquired whether
92.2 It This inquiry
92.3 her curiosity, curiosity,
92.3–4 she disliked discussing the subject and found Henrietta wanting in delicacy. she did not enjoy discussing the gentleman with Henrietta Stackpole, and she thought that in her treat-

ment of the subject this faithful friend lacked delicacy.
92.7 high, bold action. action.
92.8 will always be will be
92.10 that.'' that,'' said Isabel.
92.11 to hear this declaration. to hear this rich assertion made.
92.12 her visitor rang out. Henrietta murmured.
92.13 will always be will be
92.14 infallible supernatural
92.14–15 what one feels?'' whether one cares for him?''
92.18 with a cold smile. smiling a little.
92.20 have changed. have changed,'' she replied.
92.23 believe believe that
92.23 believe him believe that he is
92.25 return; rejoinder;
92.26 the alarm the feeling of alarm
92.27 Gardencourt. Gardencourt. Alarm is perhaps a violent term to apply to the uneasiness with which she regarded this contingency; but her uneasiness was keen, and there were various good reasons for it.
92.28 herself, however, that herself that
92.29 For but for
92.31 pressed upon her; was oppressive;
92.35 indeed however,
92.35 the on the
92.40 a graceful a very graceful
93.3–4 when heavy-hearted, when she felt heavy-hearted,
93.6 Of late, it Of late, however, it
93.10 her eyes bent with her eyes fixed
93.13 hand hand that
93.14–15 that came into her vision, already so held by him, with the vividness of the writer's voice or his face. that she seemed to know all the better, indeed, as the writer had been present to her mind when the letter was delivered.
93.15–16 proved short and may be given entire. proved to be short, and I may give it entire.
93.28 that's not your character. you are not unreasonable.
93.29 be, arbitrary or capricious. be.
93.35–36 it holds you. you are here.
93.36 but have but I have
93.40 This missive Mr. Goodwood's letter
93.40 deep profound
93.42 it the paper,
94.3 coolness. self-possession.
94.8 indoors.'' in-doors,'' she said.
94.9 jollier pleasanter
94.18 about it. regarding it.
94.22 the idea this idea
94.23 "making up" making love
94.28–29 the fact of because
94.29–30 carrying with it really more questions would point to more questions
94.31 his Lord Warburton's
94.31 a "personage," a personage,
94.32 image so conveyed. idea.

94.32–41 At the risk of adding to the evidence of her self-sufficiency it must be said that there had been moments when this possibility of admiration by a personage represented to her an aggression almost to the degree of an affront, quite to the degree of an inconvenience. She had never yet known a personage; there had been no personages, in this sense, in her life; there were probably none such at all in her native land. When she had thought of individual eminence she had thought of it on the basis of character and wit—of what one might like in a gentleman's mind and in his talk. At the risk of making the reader smile, it must be said that there had been moments when the intimation that she was admired by a "personage" struck her as an aggression which she would rather have been spared. She had never known a personage before; there were no personages in her native land. When she had thought of such matters as this, she had done so on the basis of character—of what one likes in a gentleman's mind and in his talk.

94.42–43 consciousness life
95.2 sublime soul. soul.
95.5 that which
95.6 felt she lacked patience felt that she lacked the patience
95.6–8 He appeared to demand of her something that no one else, as it were, had presumed to do. Of course, there would be a short cut to it, and as Lord Warburton was evidently a very fine fellow, it would probably also be a safe cut. Isabel was able to say all this to herself, but she was unable to feel the force of it.
95.10 he rather invidiously lived he lived
95.11–12 murmured it murmured
95.15 such a man such a man as Lord Warburton,
95.18 a complication of every hour, an incumbrance,
95.19 stiff and stupid heavy and rigid
95.20 a burden. unacceptable.
95.24 all sufficiently sufficiently
95.25 woman lady
95.44 had superficially superficially, had
96.3–4 showed as distinct and unimportant. revealed themselves with a certain vividness.
96.11 then then he
96.20 here," here,'' Lord Warburton answered.
96.22 appeal to her; demand of her;
96.27 "great" (as she supposed) nobleman local nobleman
96.30 was were
96.32 her companion. Lord Warburton;
96.37 he himself was. he was serious.
96.38 he had he himself had
96.39 a vulgar world. the public at large.
96.41 loose thinker frivolous person

96.42 replied replied to her
97.10 Lockleigh Gardencourt [sic]
97.13 done nothing else. thought of nothing else.
97.14 animal. fellow.
97.17 charged that shone
97.19 that which
97.23 gently. Gently gently; gently
97.35 she the girl
97.44–45 declared. She quite glowed there, inwardly, with the pleasure of feeling she did. declared; and it was the truth.
98.12–13 if possible not less kind than what he had said to her. as nearly as possible as kind as what he had said to her.
98.14–15 she did, all so mysteriously, matter to him. that he loved her.
98.16 returned rejoined
98.17 he Lord Warburton
98.20 a man you know a man whom you know
98.28 exuberance coquetry
98.38 replied. answered.
98.43 on upon
99.4 doubt that," doubt of that,''
99.8 that. That's that; that's
99.26 remark. He remark; he
99.29 Isabel spoke said Isabel,
99.31 outward felicity pictorial circumstances
99.33–34 cried with warmth: exclaimed warmly—
99.37 alone. I alone; I
99.42 try. I've a try; I have got a
99.45–100.2 a breadth of candour that was like the embrace of strong arms—that was like the fragrance straight in her face, and by his clean, breathing lips, of she knew not what strange gardens, what charged airs. She a tender eagerness which went to Isabel's heart, and she
100.4 me a woman
100.5 wonderful world, I thank, than commit myself very gratefully, world than to commit herself
100.6–10 she was lost in admiration of her opportunity she managed to move back into the deepest shade of it, even as some wild, caught creature in a vast cage. The "splendid" security so offered her was *not* the greatest she could conceive. she could conceive the impulse, she could not let it operate; her imagination was charmed, but it was not led captive.
100.11–12 that deferred the need of really facing her crisis. which altogether deferred the need of answering.
100.14 her companion cried. cried Lord Warburton.
100.16–17 promise you to promise you I will
100.19 how absolutely that
100.23 impossible—letting you know it without impossible, without
100.31 you I you, then I
100.31–32 ones. That's ones; that's
100.32 earnestness. gravity.

100.36 very soon. very soon," she said.
100.37 replied. answered.
100.44 hunting-crop. hunting-whip.
100.45 remarkable mind mind
101.5 oddly exclaimed. exclaimed.
101.6 all all that
101.10–11 see you, you know." see you."
101.11 reflecting, his reflecting, with his
101.15 oak. beech.
101.15 he went on. said Lord Warburton.
101.19 safe and right. sanitary.
101.23 adore delight in
101.25 handsome bared head head
101.26–27 still agitating, in his mastered emotion, his implement of the chase, shaking his hunting-whip with little quick strokes,
101.28 much upset. very nervous.
101.29 upset, nervous,
101.29 had not been was not
101.31–32 it appeared to her there had been no choice for it appeared to her that there was no choice
101.33–34 failed to support any enlightened prejudice in favor of the free exploration of life failed to correspond to any vision of happiness
101.36 that this
101.38–39 magnificent "chance." great opportunity.
101.41–43 might contain oppressive, might contain narrowing elements, might prove really but a stupefying anodyne; might contain elements that would displease her,
101.44–45 would have accommodated themselves to it without a pang. would accommodate themselves to it with extreme zeal.
101.45–102.1 irresistibly impose impose
102.4 these large, these fabulous occasions? this large occasion?
102.5 such a thing as that this,
102.6 ground occasion
102.9 danger: the danger; for the
102.10 had been were
102.11 such a *bétise* it
102.13–14 it was the very softness, and the fine intelligence, of sympathy. it was not.
102.15 the truth; the point;
102.15–17 something assured her there was a fallacy somewhere in the glowing logic of the proposition—as he saw it—even though she mightn't put her very finest finger-point on it; something told her that she should not be satisfied,
102.20 him she him that she
102.20 question, proposal,
102.23 vow. word.
102.24 if whether
102.24 priggish person, girl;
102.25–27 on her at last getting up and going rather quickly back to the house, felt, as she had said to her friend, really frightened at herself. when at last she got up and rather quickly went back to the house, it was

because, as she had said to Lord Warburton, she was really frightened at herself.
102.30–31 what had taken place. what Lord Warburton had said to her.
102.35 she would have had to do herself violence to air this special secret it would have been disagreeable to her to confide this particular matter
102.42 host uncle
103.5 She Isabel
103.5 directly. very directly.
103.10 then enquired. added.
103.20 both tasteless and ungrateful, ungrateful,
103.29–30 his letter?" it?"
103.30 obligingly asked. asked, obligingly.
103.42 one else. I one else; I
103.43 enough." She fell into that appearance enough," said Isabel with that appearance
104.1–2 impressions. sensations.
104.4 pleasantest I've pleasantest letters I have
104.6 that which
104.14 She The girl
104.14 a little. a moment.
104.21 presume suppose
104.30 That This
104.30 on upon
104.31–32 this association of her uncle's mild acuteness her uncle's genial shrewdness being associated
104.32–33 prove that prove to her that
104.35–36 beautiful appeal, reaching handsome offer
104.38 even however
104.39–41 however she might have resisted conquest at her English suitor's large quiet hands however little she might have felt warranted in lending a receptive ear to her English suitor,
104.42 positive complete
104.43 sought refuge ultimately took refuge,
104.45 deprive her of take from her
105.1–2 There was a disagreeably strong push, a kind of hardness of presence, in his way of rising before her. There was something too forcible, something oppressive and restrictive, in the manner in which he presented himself.
105.3 image, by the charge, of image of
105.3 and had and she had
105.4 equal degree one equal degree
105.8–12 expressed for her an energy— and she had already felt it as a power —that was of his very nature. It was in no degree a matter of his "advantages"—it was a matter of the spirit that sat in his clear-burning eyes like some tireless watcher at a window. gave her an impression of energy.
105.12–13 he insisted, ever, with his whole weight and force: at any rate, there was something very strong about him;
105.14 that. it.
105.15 her Isabel

105.15 since because it seemed to her that

105.16–18 by looking so straight at Lord Warburton's big bribe and yet turning away from it. making up her mind to refuse Lord Warburton.

105.25–26 an hour time

105.29 couldn't then could not now

105.30–31 dazzled as she was by the great immediate opening of her aunt's offer of "Europe," because she was preoccupied with the idea of going to Europe with her aunt,

105.32 was now to was to

105.32 was following followed

105.33 sea. seas.

105.33 of grim fate of fate

105.35–36 a nearer and a clearer view. demand a description less metaphysical.

105.37 of well-known of certain, well-known

105.39 at present now

105.40 works, and establishment,

105.40 a temper a brilliancy

105.41 their its

105.42 College, University,

105.43 renown rather more renown

105.44–45 gleaner of more dispersed knowledge. votary of culture.

105.45–106.2 Later on he had learned that the finer intelligence too could vault and pull and strain—might even, breaking the record, treat itself to rare exploits. Later he had become reconciled to culture, and though he was still fond of sport, he was capable of showing an excellent understanding of other matters.

106.2–3 He had thus discovered in himself a sharp eye for the mystery of mechanics, He had a remarkable aptitude for mechanics,

106.5 seen it in the newspapers seen his name in the papers

106.10–15 There were intricate, bristling things he rejoiced in; he liked to organise, to contend, to administer; he could make people work his will, believe in him, march before him and justify him. This was the art, as they said, of managing men—which rested, in him, further, on a bold though brooding ambition. It struck those who knew him well He had great talent for business, for administration, and for making people execute his purpose and carry out his views—for managing men, as the phrase was; and to give its complete value to this faculty, he had an insatiable, an almost fierce, ambition. It always struck people who knew him

106.18 he would somehow and somewhere write himself in bigger letters. he would not always content himself with that.

106.19–22 But it was as if something large and confused, something dark and ugly, would have to call upon him: he was not after all in harmony with mere smug peace and greed and gain, an order of things of which the vital breath was ubiquitous advertisement. It pleased Isabel to believe that he might have ridden, on a plunging steed, the whirlwind of a great war—a war like the Civil strife that had over-darkened her conscious childhood and his ripening youth. He had once said to Isabel that, if the United States were only not such a confoundedly peaceful nation, he would find his proper place in the army. He keenly regretted that the Civil War should have terminated just as he had grown old enough to wear shoulder-straps, and was sure that if something of the same kind would only occur again, he would make a display of striking military talent. It pleased Isabel to believe that he had the qualities of a famous captain, and she answered that, if it would help him on, she shouldn't object to a war—a speech which ranked among the three or four most encouraging ones he had elicited from her, and of which the value was not diminished by her subsequent regret at having said anything so heartless, inasmuch as she never communicated this regret to him.

106.26–27 by character and in fact a mover of men— potentially a commander of men—

106.28 nature and aspect. character and appearance.

106.28 for about

106.28 —the and the

106.30 no ounce less of his manhood, not an inch less a man than he was;

106.32 set grim,

106.33–34 consonance with the deeper rhythms of life. adaptability to some of the occasions of life.

106.34 viewed with reserve regarded with disfavor

106.37–38 they all seemed of the same piece; the figure, the stuff, was so drearily usual. they all seemed to be made of the same piece; the pattern, the cut, was in every case identical.

106.40 person of his importance; man of Mr. Goodwood's importance;

106.41 only if if

106.43 might she might

106.43 great— great ones—

106.45 being so, since being too serious for

106.45 be, be that,

106.45 but certainly but

107.1 appetites and designs seriousness

107.4–8 he was of supremely strong, clean make—which was so much: she saw the different fitted parts of him as she had seen, in museums and portraits, the different fitted parts of armoured warriors—in plates of steel handsomely inlaid with gold. he was the strongest man she had ever known, and she believed that at bottom he was the cleverest.

107.8–9 where, ever, was any tangible link between her impression and her act? she was far from understanding the contradictions among her own impressions.

107.11 he left her so harshly critical. he was so unsatisfactory.

107.15 The sense of her incoherence was not Such incongruities were not

107.16–17 unhonoured. unanswered.

107.18–19 how little it charmed her that he should come down that she did not approve of his coming

107.22–23 there was a kind of grossness in entertaining two such passionate pleaders Isabel had a personal shrinking from entertaining two lovers

107.24 made no reply sent no answer

107.26 history. history. It ran as follows.

107.27 earnest thought careful reflection

107.29–30 I am not, I am really and truly not, I do not find myself

107.30 a companion for life; a husband

107.31 think of regard

107.31–32 as the settled seat of my existence. in the light of my own.

107.39 very great regard feeling of respect

107.39 sincerely very truly

107.42 resolve resolution

107.43 demur. hesitation.

108.3–4 admitted confided to the reader

108.5 apt to push an advantage. indiscreet.

108.6–7 alarm was unreasoned, however; for he was clear about the area of her indiscretion as little as advised of its vertical depth, movement was unreasonable, however; for he had measured the limits of her discretion as little as he had explored its extent;

108.10 way my knees way," he said, "my knees

108.12 You've an address that I've You have a look which I have

108.15 somehow to abash me to turn me into ridicule

108.23 it that

108.26 nice fresh free-born Americans!" only Americans!"

108.30 willing willing that

108.36–37 perhaps the very gaze that unnerved him. a gaze which may perhaps have contained the quality that caused his knees to knock together.

108.40 Ah, not that!" Never in the world."

108.42 Another?" another?"

108.43 Other!" other!"

109.11–12 she once so beautifully was." she was."

109.14 know know that

109.27 views, a different colour, and views, and

109.32 fell Europeans, Europeans,

109.37 the fell European European

109.40–41 thoroughly grand man noble fellow,

110.6–7 woman, a young woman whose woman, whose

110.14 only speak of as inspiration. scarcely call anything less than inspiration.

110.20 challenge gaze

110.32 mild ambiguous laugh. small laugh.

110.33 me me

111.2 pour scorn on laugh at

111.4 pour scorn on laugh at

111.6 more satiric than ever, laughing worse than ever;

111.29 suppose he suppose that he

111.30 go back on turn her back upon

111.37 "Aren't you perhaps a little "Are you not a little

111.45 Henrietta Henrietta Stackpole

112.1 allow admit

112.2 surrendered to thought surrendered himself to meditation,

112.3 he finally said, he said,

112.8 Henrietta returned. said Henrietta.

112.13 ingeniously said. answered, ingeniously.

112.14 Ralph concluded, said Ralph,

112.22 suspecting it suspecting that it

112.23 than to break his promise, his promise than it would be to break it,

112.28–29 He had heard this fresh formidable figure named for the first time; He had heard of Mr. Caspar Goodwood by name for the first time;

112.29 mother had mentioned mother mentioned to him

112.31 had seemed seemed

112.31–32 he had taken Ralph took

112.33 involve suggest

112.37 most splendid of the American styles. American style.

112.38 intervener. young man.

112.43 prove would prove

113.14 subtler deeper

113.15 shall will

113.17 was vaguely disconcerting; made this young man vaguely uncomfortable;

113.18 our friend Ralph

113.25 if whether

113.26 confess she confess that she

113.27 replied. answered her.

113.29 not really at all impetuous. not at all impulsive.

113.30–31 She presently proposed to Isabel, at all events, Whether it was to pursue her investigations, or whether it was in compliance with still larger interests, is a point which remains somewhat uncertain; at all events, she presently proposed to Isabel

113.32 observed, said,

113.37 her friend, Isabel,

113.39 turning him inside out." examining him."

113.43 doesn't make a vital letter. makes a thin letter.

113.45 in touch." started."

114.1 British capital metropolis

114.3–5 she was curious of the thick detail of London, which had always loomed large and rich to her. she had a great desire to see something of London, which had always been the city of her imagination.
114.5 schemes scheme
114.6 romantic aesthetic
114.14 unveiled the bright vision mentioned these bright intentions
114.15 scarce expressed did not express
114.16–17 Duke's Head Tavistock Hotel
114.22–23 can at least find her way about this minute island." she can surely find her way about this simple little island."
114.28 start immediately; start for London immediately;
114.32 response answer
114.33 luncheon lunch
114.36 consideration the more studied discretion the more striking
114.37 "really liked" really liked
114.38 mentioning also his and let Mr. Touchett know of Lord Warburton's
114.40 two o'clock repast. lunch-table.
115.1–2 any conjoined straying away the visitor's temporary absence,
115.2 should give their noble visitor should find it needful to give Lord Warburton
115.3 That This
115.4 reflexions considerations
115.7 for of
115.8 prematurely precipitately
115.10–11 preoccupation with her presence admiration
115.13 eyes. eye.
115.18–19 suggesting a conflict between deep alienation and yearning wonder. which seemed to denote a conflict between attention and alienation.
115.20 Isabel that Isabel
115.22–24 referred to some weird Anglican mystery—some delightful reinstitution perhaps of the quaint office of the canoness. had a romantic meaning— that she was a member of a High Church sisterhood, had taken some picturesque vows.
115.33 such a girl's failure to rise; the young lady's indifference to such an opportunity;
115.34 position) impression)
115.35 but a due consciousness of inequality. a high sense of general fitness.
115.36–37 opportunities, at all events, opportunities,
115.42 a trifle absently vaguely
115.42 table. table, and laughing a little.
116.5–6 her neighbor allowed. Lord Warburton answered.
116.9 were were
116.12 little; moment;
116.12 chance chance that
116.19 beyond them— beyond that
116.37 have to have got to
117.7–8 whatever else you whatever you

117.20 which This
117.22 luncheon lunch
117.23 he that he
117.27 its contents the paintings
117.35 admit you admit what you
117.36–37 turning slightly pale. blushing a little.
117.41 Warburton." She said Warburton," said the girl; and she said
118.4 saw in her eyes something that saw something in her eyes which
118.14 She Isabel
118.14 in surprise. with a certain eagerness.
118.19 opinions, because opinions, Lord Warburton," said the girl, "because
118.23 walked walked away,
118.27–28 so young and free in her movement that her very pliancy seemed to mock at him. young and flexible in her movement, which her companion noticed.
118.28 Her Isabel's
118.32 strange. was strange.
118.35 were to marry should marry
118.36 that that
118.40 an with an
118.41 me me
118.44 chances for what?" chances?" Lord Warburton repeated, more and more puzzled.
118.45 quickly rapidly
119.4 it it is
119.4 suggest that you'll say that I think you will
119.5 her companion Lord Warburton
119.9 he Lord Warburton
119.12 me me
119.12 a life of misery unhappiness
119.14 a life of misery." being miserable,"
119.36 his lordship Lord Warburton
119.44 expecting company to partake of it. expecting some company.
119.45 preoccupied, and preoccupied— with
120.1–2 —as if he had been Royalty— stood like a lady-in-waiting. looked ladylike and patient, and awaited his pleasure.
120.13 afraid afraid that
120.15 "Ah "Oh
120.15 convenient," indispensable,"
120.18 has rained of late rains
120.24 have have got
120.31 returned. rejoined.
121.13 won't will not
121.15 hesitated. hesitated a moment.
121.26 failed to did not
121.27 she therefore went on. she went on.
121.31 brazenly; blushing;
121.39 soothingly explained. explained, humorously.
121.45 cable." telegram."
122.8 true true that
122.22 it, which,
122.23 room; in which room. In this
122.24 saloon. drawing-room.

122.25 that lady, her Aunt,
122.27 considered. hesitated an instant.
122.30 dispassionately asked. inquired, dryly, but dispassionately.
122.31 the girl Isabel
122.35–36 give me that rather conceited look. smile that way.
122.36–37 you were awfully pleased with yourself and had you had
122.44 on upon
123.2–3 her favourite a
123.13 greater more
123.21 I'm that I am
123.25 smallest, sparest voice. little, spare voice.
123.28 I that I
123.29 upset me completely." bother me fearfully."
123.32 criticise." criticise the affair."
123.33 returned. said.
123.35 this lady dryly laughed. cried this lady, with a laugh.
123.36 indeed she ought to feel it!" she ought to be,"
123.36–37 irrepressibly answered. rejoined, smiling.
123.41 had have
123.45 their visitors the two young ladies
124.9–10 being familiar with deeper fears than that of a cold kitchen. not being dependent on the local *cuisine.*
124.10 the resources that
124.15–16 As London wears in the month of September a face blank but for its smears of prior service, As London does not wear in the month of September its most brilliant face,
124.18 derision, irritation,
124.20 mean mean that
124.24 but except
124.30–32 had a charm wrapped in them as a coloured gem might be wrapped in a dusty cloth. borrowed a charm from his circumstances.
124.33–34 chain of hours with his comparatively ardent friends, a day spent with his inquisitive countrywomen,
124.38 lone constable. solitary policeman.
124.39 place, room,
124.44 presence as presence in the room, as
125.2 his Ralph's
125.7 him Ralph
125.11 full of premises, conclusions, emotions; constantly interested and often excited;
125.13–14 brave theories, as to historic cause and social effect, that little theories, that
125.21 Henrietta proved an indestructible Henrietta Stackpole proved to be an indefatigable
125.22 lenient judge good-natured critic
125.24–25 the strong points of the American civic idea; many of the cities of her native land;
125.25 dignities peculiarities
126.10 but and

126.10 would help along. one really wants.
126.15 sad drepressing
126.15 mission. own standard.
126.16 that which
126.17–20 our young woman's mind: when she felt again in her face, as from a recurrent wave, the cold breath of her last suitor's surprise, she could only muffle her head till the air cleared. the girl's mind; she took no pleasure in recalling Lord Warburton's magnanimous disappointment.
126.21–22 as graceless as some physical act in a strained attitude, a distasteful one,
126.23–24 Mixed with this imperfect pride, nevertheless, Nevertheless, mingled with this absence of an intellectual relish of it,
126.26 odd demonstrations. joyous excitement.
126.30 kissed she kissed
126.30 these quaint charities; such incidents;
126.31 she did. that Isabel did.
126.31–32 that his companions might pass the time, by way of amusing his companions,
126.33 for to do honour to
126.34 guest to meet them, guest, also, to meet the ladies,
126.35–37 for whom prompt commerce with Miss Stackpole appeared to have neither difficulty nor dread. who got on uncommonly well with Miss Stackpole.
126.37–39 Mr. Bantling, a stout, sleek, smiling man of forty, wonderfully dressed, universally informed and incoherently amused, Mr. Bantling, a stout, fair, smiling man of forty, who was extraordinarily well dressed, and whose contributions to the conversation were characterized by vivacity rather than continuity,
127.2–3 and, at a dozen turns of their talk, bounded responsive—as with a positive passion for argument— and listened with candid interest
127.5 "Oh, I see; "Oh, I see," said Mr. Bantling;
127.8 forbidden forbid
127.11 has organic disease so developed that you is dropsical as well, though he doesn't look it. You
127.12 he'll go, some day soon, quite quickly. he has got a lot of water somewhere.
127.13–14 a dreadfully dull house; I wonder they have people when they can do so little for them. it awfully slow for people in the house; I wonder they have them under such circumstances.
127.23 who that
127.30–32 and changing his topic with an easy turn of hand. Yet he none the less gracefully kept in sight of the idea, dazzling to Henrietta, of her going and at last changing his topic, with a nat-

ural eagerness to provide suitable conversation for so remarkable a woman.
He returned, however, ultimately to the
idea of Henrietta's going

127.33 want; you want," he repeated;
"you

**127.35–36 have their own habits, their
own language, their own food—some
odd religion even, I believe, of their
own.** live on a kind of foreign system;
they have got some awfully queer
ideas.

127.40 and has and she has

**127.41–42 Plain as she is she makes
up awfully well—I** *will* **say for her.**
(Omitted.)

128.3 splendid range of suggestion, suggestiveness of allusion,

128.5 *would* would

128.5 me. me," she said.

128.21 had had had

128.24 store. accumulated topics.

128.37–38 Mr. Bantling gaily interposed.
said Mr. Bantling, in an off-hand tone
expressive of gallantry.

128.39 returned. answered.

**128.40–41 "Those poor ladies can easily
believe that we refuse, at the last, to
spare you."** "Think of those poor ladies, in their impatience, waiting for
you."

128.45 you you

129.2 obligingly answered; answered,
smiling;

129.7 the girl Isabel

129.7 together standing

129.13 poked their faces were squeezing
their necks

129.14 rails railings

129.22 glad very [sic] very glad

129.25 briefly silent. silent a moment.

129.26 far. far," she rejoined at last.

129.29 union matrimony

129.31 organism." fellow."

129.32 a simpler one still. simpler still.

**130.9–10 submissively—which indeed there
was already an emotion in doing.** submissively. There was almost an emotion
in doing so.

130.11 demanded asked,

130.17 she Isabel

130.17–18 a stillness silence

130.19 him him that

130.27 know. know," he said, laughing
a little awkwardly.

130.35 resumed. went on.

130.36 just now a while ago

130.37 one's my

130.44 you you that

131.8 replied answered

131.10 Warburton Lord Warburton

131.12 suppressed a start; started a little;

131.19 an honest man." a fine fellow."

131.23 drove rode

131.31 me?" she enquired. Me?"

131.38 say say that

131.44–45 slightly nervous laugh. laugh.

132.9 she Isabel

132.10 mind your mind

132.11 mind?" my mind?"

132.15–16 It's really nothing, you know.
(Omitted.)

132.16 said said

132.18 moment, then answered moment
and then she answered this inquiry

132.21 thorough good sort; fine fellow;

132.21 consider think

132.22–23 no end of a swell. swell.

132.26 as while he spoke, as if

132.35 managed to do contented themselves

132.36 how he has been stalked." he
has been run after."

**132.38 one day when we talked of him
you mentioned odd things in him."**
you told me of several faults that he
has, one day when I spoke of him to
you.

132.39 smokingly considered. looked
grave.

133.1 sort. You're sort—You are

**133.2 looking at her cousin with rueful
gentleness.** looking gently but earnestly at her cousin.

133.3 make such a marriage." marry
Lord Warburton."

133.7 She gave rather a Isabel gave a
rather

133.14 you you

**133.16–17 the material of my inimitable
omelettes.** golden eggs.

133.18 thrill entertainment

133.21 hang on contemplate

133.24 decent, in fact a very honourable
and

133.29 grand magnificent

133.31 grand magnificent

133.31–32 anything from me anything

133.35 she Isabel

133.36 that which

**133.40–41 of course so many-
sided."** many-sided."

133.43 her companion Ralph

**133.45–46 life — you'll be hanged if
you don't,** life,

134.6 Ralph remarked. said Ralph.

134.8 distinction. distinction," Isabel returned.

134.10 till until

134.11 expect expect that

134.14 only sat still and looked at her.
sat still a moment, looking at her.

134.15 remained there did not follow
her,

**134.15–16 they exchanged a gaze that
was full** they remained awhile exchanging a gaze, full

134.18 he said said Ralph

134.23 Her Isabel's

134.23 dusk. darkness.

**134.35 in which this quest might
avail** in which it seemed that this
quest would be fruitful,

**134.40–41 "When people forget I'm a
poor creature I'm often incommoded,"**
"When people forget I am a sick man
I am often annoyed,"

134.45 She Isabel

134.45 him her cousin

135.1 struck her seemed to her

135.3–4 the American girl whom extravagance of aid places in an attitude that she ends by finding "affected" the American girl who ends by regarding perpetual assistance as a sort of derogation to her sanity

135.6 which and

135.7 had it had

135.7 meagrely met. scantily gratified.

135.8 wittingly missed it. missed it.

135.11 wish to be quite by herself love of solitude

135.11–12 her cousin's Ralph's

135.12 Seated toward She was sitting, towards

135.13 Hotel and trying Hotel, trying

135.14–15 she succeeded but succeeding

135.15–16 other words than those printed on the page—words other words on the page than those that were printed there—words.

135.18–19 gave way to his exhibition, even as a glorious trophy, of the card admitted him, bearing the card

135.19–20 When this memento had offered to her fixed sight This card, duly considered, offered to Isabel's startled vision

135.21 Goodwood she Goodwood. She

135.21 man servant

135.21 her without her inquiringly for some instants, without

135.23 asked with asked at last, with

135.25 glanced she glanced

135.26–27 not so much smoothing her hair as girding her spirit. with some emotion.

135.28–29 was accordingly the next moment shaking hands with her, but saying came in and shook hands with her. He said

135.30 room. "Why room again, then he said—"Why

135.30 then asked spoke

135.32 habitually usually

135.34 She answered by a ready question, Isabel answered him by a question.

135.41 neither had sat down; neither of them had seated themselves;

135.41–42 an air a certain air

135.42 me me that

135.43 she Isabel

136.2 big large

136.4 "It was apparently repugnant "Apparently it was disagreeable

136.4–5 her visitor went on. said Mr. Goodwood.

136.6 reply; answer to this;

136.7–8 "Henrietta's certainly not a model of all the delicacies!" "Henrietta's not delicate!"

136.9 with bitterness. with a certain bitterness.

136.10–11 not a model either—of those virtues or of any others. not delicate either.

136.13–14 her, but she took a different

turn. her; nevertheless she rejoined inconsequently—

136.14–15 What you've done was inevitable, I suppose, for *you."* What you have done is very natural."

136.16 was is

136.19 She Isabel

136.21 that sort of furtherance. the sort of chair he sat in.

136.22 letter. You letter," he said. "You

136.24–25 an intention," Isabel said. "I deliberate; I

136.25 the best thing." best."

136.26 spoke; said this;

136.28 ought. ought to say.

136.31–32 tasting any advantage finding it agreeable to have an advantage

136.33 little desirous to flaunt it she was not a girl to flaunt her advantage

136.33 she could enjoy she was woman enough to enjoy

136.35 an air a certain air

136.36 her own hers

136.36–37 they seemed to shine through the vizard of a helmet. they wore an expression of ardent remonstrance.

136.38 and was and he was

136.40–41 never accepted any such rule as my own. I warned never accepted the prohibition. I promised

136.42 *never* never

136.43 for ten years; twenty years. for ten years.

137.3–4 knowing them of so much less she knew they were of a much less

137.7 She dropped, but She hesitated, and

137.7 broke out. broke out with even greater irrelevance.

137.10 of about

137.13 disgust displease

137.16 on upon

137.17–18 you don't at all delight me, you don't fit in, not in any way, just now, you displease me very much,

137.18–20 your putting it to the proof in this manner is quite unnecessary." It wasn't certainly as if his nature had been soft, so that it is needless." Isabel knew that his was not a soft nature, from which

137.20 blood from it; blood;

137.27 grasp at take

137.30 hard firm,

137.31 wounds, so far as they required it, wounds

137.31–34 She came back, even for her measure of possible pangs and aches in him, to her old sense that he was naturally plated and steeled, armed essentially for aggression. In measuring the effect of his suffering, one might always reflect that he had a sound constitution.

137.35 simply said. said

137.36 it; this;

137.36 she felt how open it was Isabel felt that it was quite open

137.37 **make the point** say
137.37 **disgusted** displeased
137.42-43 **think of you at all for a pre-scribed time,** think of you for a few months
138.2 **she** that Isabel
138.4 **Aren't you capable** Are you not capable
138.4 **a calculated effort?"** an effort?"
138.7-9 **"An effort calculated for what?" and then as she hung fire, "I'm cap-able of nothing with regard to you,"** **he went on, "but just of being in-fernally in love with you.** "Because I am in love with you," said Caspar Goodwood simply.
138.11-13 **felt the force of it—felt it thrown off, into the vast of truth and poetry, as practically a bait to her imagination. But she promptly came round.** felt the force of it.
138.18-19 **there's all the difference in the world."** there is a great differ-ence."
138.20 **with a studied effect of eager-ness** wondering whether a little cyn-icism might not be effective.
138.21 **her friend asked with no sign** Mr. Goodwood asked giving no sign
138.27 **some sacrifice.** sacrifice.
138.28-29 **the sacrifice you'll have all my admiration."** this sacrifice I shall admire you greatly."
138.30-31 **"I don't care a cent for your admiration—not one straw, with noth-ing to show for it. When will you** "I don't care a straw for your ad-miration. Will you
138.31-32 **only question."** question."
138.33 **"Never—if you go on making me feel only as I feel at present."** "As-suredly not, if I feel as I feel at present."
138.34 **"What do I gain then by not trying to make you feel otherwise?"** "Then I ask again, what I shall gain."
138.36 **gazed a while** gazed for a while
138.37-38 **she could see her sharpness had at last penetrated.** and Isabel could perceive that this dart at last had struck home.
138.38-41 **This immediately had a value —classic, romantic, redeeming, what did she know?—for her; "the strong man in pain" was one of the cate-gories of the human appeal, little charm as he might exert in the given case.** To see a strong man in pain had something terrible for her, and she immediately felt very sorry for her visitor.
138.43 **thoroughly kind.** kind.
138.44 **people** that people
139.3-4 **I really don't want to marry, or to talk about it at all now.** I don't want to marry.
139.4-5 **never do it—no, never.** never marry.
139.6 **press her so hard, to urge** urge

her—to persuade
139.10 **situations, it passes,** circum-stances, it is supposed,
139.10 **for** to be
139.15 **a rosy,** a certain rosy,
139.16 **her words.** what she had said.
139.17 **brought out** murmured
139.18 **heavily said,** added in a louder tone—
139.19 **shall** will
139.20-21 **as sure as I sit here," Caspar Goodwood declared.** said Caspar Goodwood.
139.22 **that a** that is a
139.23 **try to make you."** ask you."
139.24-25 **almost certainly never shall."** shall probably never do so."
139.26-27 **did, and I like your 'almost certainly'! I put no faith in what you say."** did; but I don't believe it."
139.28-29 **Do you accuse me of lying to shake you off?** You appear to think I am attempting to deceive you;
139.30-31 **no pledge of anything at all."** no promise that you will not marry."
139.32 **wanting!"** wanting!" cried Isabel, with a bitter laugh.
139.33-34 **"You may perhaps even be-lieve you're safe—from wishing to be. But you're not," the young man** "You think you won't, but you will," her visitor
139.34 **as if preparing** as if he were preparing
139.36 **well then. We'll put it that I'm not safe.** well, I will then.
139.43 **to** and
139.44 **dazzling men** clever men
139.44-140.1 **world, no doubt; and if** world; if
140.1-2 **The most dazzling of all will make straight for you.** *(Omitted.)*
140.3 **isn't dazzling."** is not."
140.4-5 **"If you mean by dazzling bril-liantly clever," Isabel said—"and I can't imagine what else you mean—I don't** "I don't
140.6 **live. I** live," said Isabel. "I
140.7-8 **"Find out how to live alone? I wish that, when you have, you'd teach me!"** "To live alone, do you mean? I wish that when you have found that out, you would teach me."
140.9 **She looked** Isabel glanced
140.11 **He might** Poor Caspar may
140.12-15 **to sound the infernal note, and it is not on record that her motive for discharging such a shaft had been of the clearest. He oughtn't to stride about lean and hungry, however—she certainly felt *that* for him.** to have the infernal note, and I cannot take upon myself to say that Isabel uttered it in obedience to an impulse strictly celestial. It was a fact, however, that it had always seemed to her that Cas-par Goodwood, of all men, ought to enjoy the whole devotion of some tender woman.

140.16 teeth as he turned away. teeth, turning away.

140.17 Her accent Her exclamation

140.19 place him where she had been. put her suitor in the wrong.

140.24 —no doubt—a dazzling one." a brilliant one."

140.27 proposal proposal that

140.28 not proposed to herself hesitated

140.33 watched gazed at

140.33 intense great

140.36 Her visitor Mr. Goodwood

140.36–37 at first in silence, but at last said: in silence; then, at last, he said—

140.44 asked. inquired.

141.1–2 "Oh, those people? They're not of *my* humanity, and I don't care what becomes of them." "Oh, no; he's superhuman."

141.3 very angry," angry,"

141.5 very angry. angry.

141.6 She Isabel

141.7 void vacancy

141.10 with eyes with his eyes

141.10 attached. fixed upon our heroine.

141.11 go— withdraw—

141.12 odious odious to her

141.12–14 She was too nursed a need to be easily renounced, and he had crossed the sea all to wring from her some scrap of a vow. She was far too dear to him to be easily forfeited, and he had sailed across the Atlantic to extract some pledge from her.

141.14–15 again before him. before him again.

141.15 justice—after justice," she said, "—after

141.22–23 of what I feel for you that I love you

41.23–24 calling it a 'little' is a poor account of it." it must have had a good deal."

141.25 shook her head as shook her head impatiently, as

141.25 a blunder. a blush.

141.25–26 a most kind, noble gentleman. a noble gentleman.

141.34 reflected and then answered: reflected a little, and then she said—

141.35 there. It would be too there; it would be very

141.37 considered. debated within himself.

141.40 She betrayed surprise. *(Omitted.)*

141.40 invitation?" invitation?" Isabel asked, surprised.

142.1 never did from me. did not come from me

142.1 really certainly

142.3 me." me."

142.4 declined you did quite right, declined, that was very proper of you,

142.5 she Isabel

142.8 where do you go?" where are you going?"

142.8 her companion Caspar

142.10 I go I shall go

142.20–22 world—with all these places so arranged and so touching each other—comes to strike one as rather small." world strikes me as small."

142.23 a sight too big for *me!"* too large for me!"

142.23 simplicity simplicity which

142.28 *that—* that

142.29 place I place as I, I

142.30 that—I that. I

142.31 world world that

142.31 she Isabel

142.32 of grandeur, of the grandeur that had shown itself a moment before—

142.33 might be was

142.33 the too superior grandeur

142.34–47 there was nothing he winced at in the large air of it. He had never supposed she hadn't wings and the need of beautiful free movements—he wasn't, with his own long arms and strides, afraid of any force in her. there was nothing that displeased him in the sort of feeling it expressed. This feeling not only did no violence to his way of looking at the girl he wished to make his wife, but seemed a grace the more in so ardent a spirit. To his mind she had always had wings, and this was but the flutter of those stainless pinions. He was not afraid of having a wife with a certain largeness of movement; he was a man of long steps himself.

142.40 I? What I?" he asked. "What

143.7 poor and of a serious disposition; I'm poor; I am of a serious disposition, and

143.21 passionately almost passionately

143.22 she Isabel

143.23 that which

143.35 some atrocity!" a crime!"

143.42–43 an atrocity; a crime;

143.44 she Isabel

144.10 her: her, she added—

144.17 attitude and a sore remonstrance attitude—a deep remonstrance

144.26 little moment

144.31–34 Vibration was easy to her, was in fact too constant with her, and she found herself now humming like a smitten harp. She only asked, however, to put on the cover, to case herself again in brown holland, She was an excitable creature, and now she was much excited;

144.35 devotion, prayer,

144.36 intensely rejoiced that was extremely glad

144.37–38 something in having thus got rid of him that was like the payment, for a stamped receipt, of some debt too long on her mind. something exhilarating in having got rid of him.

144.38–39 As she felt the glad relief As Isabel became conscious of this feeling

144.39 sense feeling

144.40 part a part

144.42–43 and even when and when

144.43–44 her tremor had not quite subsided. she was still trembling a little.
144.44 It had had, verily, Her agitation had
145.6 often uttered her response to often expressed her gladness in
145.7 yielded to gave herself up to
145.8 in within
145.11 appeared seemed
145.13 she had done what was truest to her plan. she had done what she preferred.
145.14 the glow of this consciousness the midst of this agreeable sensation
145.17 rose with rose quickly with
145.20–21 our young lady had been "through" something, something had happened to Isabel,
145.22 She Henrietta
145.24 in a manner glad glad that
145.26 Henrietta that Henrietta
145.27 the latter yearningly asked. Miss Stackpole inquired, softly.
145.29 declared said
145.30 best. best, dear.
145.34 observed declared,
146.2 without alarm. with a laugh.
146.10–11 almost shrieked. broke out in dismay.
146.13 Miss Stackpole glittered for an instant with dismay, Miss Stackpole stood there with expanded eyes,
146.14 passed she went
146.15 went on. remarked, lightly, as she did so.
146.16 her companion Miss Stackpole
146.16–17 propositions. propositions, nor bribed by the offer of autobiographic opportunities.
146.19 pursued, went on,
146.27 yet she still tried but even in the midst of her irritation she tried
146.30 aggressive." disagreeable to me."
146.31 love you intensely, love you,
146.32 if you love me intensely let me as intensely alone. if you love me, let me alone.
147.22 the Queen of American Journalism. queen of American journalism.
147.31 saw saw that
147.32–33 received from his mother a telegram to the effect received a telegram from his mother, telling him
147.35 he Ralph
147.36–37 was not open to criticism. had nothing incongruous.
147.45 shall certainly will
147.45 returned. exclaimed.
148.1 shall should
148.3 "you're fond of him," you like him,"
148.4 face. eye.
148.6 "I quite adore him," Isabel after a moment said. "I think I love him," said Isabel, simply.
148.8 She Isabel
148.8 small sigh little sigh
148.11 spoke; said;

148.11–12 reasons for her not remaining reasons why she should not remain
148.15 Bedfordshire? Bedfordshire?" Ralph exclaimed, with surprise.
148.19 none the less, his gravity returned. however, he looked grave again.
148.29 rose to her eyes. rushed into her eyes.
148.32 her luncheon, the lunch-table,
148.35 pardon excuse
149.10 that afternoon. in the afternoon.
149.18 at peace satisfied
149.27 new pang novel sensation
149.32 gave made
149.34 this that
149.38 I sent him a word—the word we just utter to the 'wise.' I just sent him a word—a word to the wise.
149.42–43—and Ralph's face lighted with the relief of his cousin's not having shown duplicity. Ralph inquired, smiling, and relieved at learning that his cousin had not deceived him.
149.46 sighed. exclaimed.
150.3 Ralph repeated. repeated Ralph.
150.4 automatic; it somewhat mechanical. It
150.10 Miss Stackpole added— said Miss Stackpole,
150.11 give up myself. I mean I'd give her up!" said Miss Stackpole, give her up myself!"
150.14 in the conditions, under the circumstances,
150.15 her friend Miss Stackpole
150.18 eyes. eye.
150.26–27 just easy occasion. simply opportunity.
150.27 finer finest
150.27 at the larger times. on large occasions.
150.33 probable probable that
150.35 a question an inquiry
150.35 this purpose quickly yielded to her attention was taken by
150.37 saloon. drawing-room.
150.37 knew knew that
150.41 the girl Isabel
150.42 almost with restored cheer, toward the source of the harmony. to the drawing-room with much alertness.
150.45 she Isabel
151.3 though although
151.4 viewed contemplated
151.5 with in
151.9–10 with what treasures of reserve the function of receiving orders may be accompanied, that the British domestic is not effusive,
151.11–13 through whose hands she had slipped perhaps a little too mistrustfully and with an effect of plumage but the more lustrous. The advent of a guest was in itself far from disconcerting; whose offered assistance the young lady from Albany—versed, as young ladies are in Albany, in the very metaphysics of the toilet—had perhaps made too light of. The arrival of a visitor was far from disagreeable to Isabel;

151.15 young faith youthful impression
151.16 on upon
151.18 Schubert's— Beethoven's—
151.19 but recognized Schubert—and she touched the piano with a discretion of her own. It showed skill, it showed feeling; but she recognized Beethoven —and she touched the piano softly and discreetly, but with evident skill. Her touch was that of an artist;
151.24 stranger lady at the piano
151.24 but just aware she had become aware
151.33 visitor stranger
151.37 smiled and discriminated. gave a discriminating smile.
151.38 Schubert Beethoven
151.39 our worst." our worst moments."
151.40 now then," now,"
151.42 delighted." most willingly."
151.44 new-comer stranger
152.1–2 looking over her shoulder. looking over her shoulder at the girl.
152.2–3 and not pretty, though her expression charmed. and she was not pretty; but she had a delightful expression.
152.3 "Pardon me "Excuse me
152.5 Isabel replied with simplicity. said Isabel, with *naïveté*.
152.6–7 casting her air of interest over her shoulder. looking over her shoulder with her charming smile.
152.7 well; we're well," she said, "we are
152.10 romantic interesting,
152.11 marked a drop. diminished her effectiveness.
152.12–13 rarer even than to be French seemed it to be American on such interesting terms. for Isabel, as she listened to the music, found much stimulus to conjecture in the fact that an American should so strongly resemble a foreign woman.
152.14 The lady Her companion
152.19 her companion the lady
152.19–20 nearer with a smile, to her auditor, smiling,
152.22 but nevertheless spoke but she nevertheless said,
152.23 in reply in answer
152.29 must rather must
152.41 say he say that he
152.44 pursued. said.
153.11 little; but little;
153.12–13 as charming a manner as any she had ever encountered. a charming manner.
153.16 then I should tell you." I should tell you then."
153.20–21 sort of world-wide smile, a thing that over-reached frontiers. fine, frank smile.
154.36 an amplitude of nature a rich nature
153.36–37 free motions liberal impulses,
153.38 engaging and attaching. agreeable to contemplate.
153.39 smooth plump

153.40 suggest heaviness. minister to indolence.
153.41 in perfect proportion and harmony, there was a graceful harmony among them,
153.42–43 Her grey eyes were small but full of light and incapable of stupidity —incapable, She had a small grey eye with a great deal of light in it—an eye incapable of dullness, and
153.44 even of tears; she had a liberal, full-rimmed mouth incapable of tears; and a wide, firm mouth,
154.3–4 arranged somehow "classically" and as if she were a Bust, Isabel judged—a Juno or a Niobe; which was arranged with picturesque simplicity,
154.5 and large white hands, and a large white hand,
154.6 their possessor, its owner,
154.6 them it
154.6–7 jewelled rings. rings.
154.8–9 ranked her as a German—a German of high degree, perhaps an Austrian, a baroness, led her to say to herself that Madame Merle might be a German—a German of rank,
154.10–11 It would never have been supposed she had come into the world Isabel would never have supposed that she had been born
154.11 one she
154.12 carried through any argument justified her assumption
154.12–13 distinction marking her distinction, possessed by Madame Merle
154.15 her cradle, the spot of the lady's nativity,
154.16 attitude she there took attitude which she then and there took
154.17 she Madame Merle
154.18 manner deportment
154.22 strong ardent
154.22–23 This commended itself to Isabel as an ideal combination. What an ideal combination! thought Isabel.
154.24 The girl She
154.25 that this
154.28 for a private talk; to confer with him in private;
154.30–31 Isabel's sense of the sadness now settling on Gardencourt. Isabel's perception of the melancholy that now hung over Gardencourt.
154.35 depressed sombre
154.35 his own Ralph's
154.39 appeared; came in;
154.40 last. last to appear.
154.42 is this Madame Merle?" is Madame Merle?"
155.2 very pleasant." pleasant," said Ralph.
155.9 She's a Madame Merle is a
155.22 Monsieur Merle M. Merle
155.28 Monsieur Merle M. Merle
156.4 now on this occasion
156.7 must be was
156.7 doctor, a doctor, who was a
156.8 man, in whom man, and in whom

156.10 came back several times. returned several times to Gardencourt.
156.13 at hours several times
156.19 stupor. unconsciousness.
156.21 only was with him. was with him alone.
156.29 say it," say so,"
156.38–39 in charge, with him,
156.42 over upon the
157.5 demurred. inquired.
157.5 you." you."
157.9 topic." topic," he said.
157.11 think you'd think that you would
157.19 have have got
157.21 returned. answered.
157.26 quite exactly
158.2 because it suits her. to please herself.
158.3 you. you.
158.21 fresh. novel.
158.22–23 taking the cheerful view of his son's possible duration. expressing the optimistic view of his son's health.
158.23 facetiously; humorously;
158.24 proscribed the facetious. made the humorous tone impossible.
158.25 gaze. gaze in silence.
158.31 resumed softly: asked softly—
158.32 a strained smile a rather fixed smile.
158.35 Isabel?" her?"
158.40–41 has told me how much she likes you." told me so."
159.13 refused Warburton: refused Lord Warburton;
159.14 there's that there is
159.17 eagerly asked. asked, eagerly.
159.20 him, whoever he was. him.
159.26 pulmonary disorder pulmonary weakness
159.27 weak feeble
159.27 to and fro to and fro a little
159.30 had have
159.32 bad lung. weak lungs.
159.38–39 think it wrong. think it was wrong.
159.45 you've so many you have got so many
160.26–27 to meet the requirements of to gratify
160.31–32 make it over to give it to
160.32–33 give her the second." give the second half to her."
160.41–42 That's what I want cannily to prevent." *(Omitted.)*
161.3 openly stared. started a little.
161.5 me me
161.17 sharp, quite horrid and strange, sharp
161.19 Mr. Touchett he
161.24 mere amusement." entertainment."
161.30 say Isabel say that Isabel
161.34 before. Her father then before; but her father
161.40 wants she wants that she
162.6 "No—though at first "No, at first
162.8 she has that she had
162.10 helplessly. with a sigh.
162.14 Mr. Touchett the old man

162.23 young thing; young girl;
162.24 so good as good
162.25 Ralph returned. said Ralph.
162.31–32 caressingly asked. asked, caressingly.
162.32–33 it. We'll it; we will
162.34 lay a long time still. lay silent a long time.
162.34 he had that he had
162.35 follow. understand it.
162.35 quite lucidly, he he
162.45 repeated. exclaimed.
163.2 aware their talk had been unduly prolonged. aware that their conversation had been prolonged to a dangerous point.
163.3 the good I said a few moments ago the good that I said just now
163.4 met the requirements of my imagination. gratified my imagination.
163.8 so that and
163.14 though although
163.14 admit she admit that she
163.15 high sense sense which
163.16 if whether
163.18 which it failed to seem and it did not seem
163.20 expressed. expressed it.
163.21 never not
163.26 figure woman
163.27 person having woman who had
163.28–29 the stale, the too-familiar parts of one's own character. parts of one's own personality.
163.31 this amiable auditress Madame Merle
163.35 there that
163.35 for their being why they should be
163.36 she the girl
163.36 remembered said to herself
163.39–40 was charming was a charming,
163.40 cultivated. cultivated woman.
163.42 in her own sex several persons several persons of her own sex,
163.43 superior and preëminent. she was superior, she was pre-eminent.
163.43 are many are a great many
164.6–7 satisfaction to be taken satisfaction that Isabel found
164.8 this lady her companion
164.10 fount of passion, fountain of sentiment,
164.12–13 She proposed moreover, as well as expected, to cease feeling; Her pleasure was now to judge rather than to feel;
164.13–14 a little mad, rather foolish,
164.14 perfectly sane wise.
164.16 one has earned that I have earned
164.18 much too too
164.20 can't can't
164.29 less on the part less,
164.31 On Upon
164.32–33 disconcertingly difficult so difficult
164.35 impulse. motive.

164.38 cold confessions. grave confessions.

164.39 settled settled down

164.41 our young woman Isabel

164.41 indoor in-door

164.45 Madame Merle liked Madame Merle was very appreciative; she liked

165.8 inhaling to inhale

165.8 scent odour

165.12 from with

165.18–20 Before luncheon, always, Madame Merle was engaged; Isabel admired and envied her rigid possession of her morning. Before lunch Madame Merle was always engaged; Isabel admired the inveteracy with which she occupied herself.

165.21–23 wandered, as by the wrong side of the wall of a private garden, round the enclosed talents, accomplishments, aptitudes she envied the talents, the accomplishments, the aptitudes,

165.24 twenty such ways this lady this and other ways Madame Merle

165.25 "I should like awfully to be so!" "I should like to be like that!"

165.26 one after another one

165.27 fine aspects numerous facets suddenly

165.28 a high authority. this exemplary woman.

165.28–29 great time indeed for her to feel herself, very long time, indeed, for Isabel to feel that she was,

165.30 wondered, asked herself

165.33 no doubt, I think

165.34 isn't it my fault it is my fault

165.35 enough?" enough."

165.36–37 sometimes moved to gape at her friend aspiringly and despairingly tempted to reproduce in her deportment some of the most graceful features of that of her friend,

165.39 but was even more dazzled than attracted. but she admired her even more than she liked her.

165.40 asked herself wondered

165.41 perverted product of their common soil, brilliant fugitive from Brooklyn;

165.42 it would be severely judged. Henrietta would not at all subscribe to Henrietta would not approve of it. Henrietta would not like

165.43 reasons she reasons that she

165.44 the girl. Isabel.

166.1 strike off some happy view of her old: accommodate herself perfectly to her old;

166.7 value. virtues.

166.8 solemnly pondered; reflected;

166.10 such, this,

166.13 may not count over can not enumerate

166.18 nourish be guilty of any

166.19 article subject

166.19–20 encountered many known a good many

166.21–22 her informed measure she was no figure for a high scene, her own measure she was nothing of a personage,

166.23–30 To be so cultivated and civilised, so wise and so easy, and still make so light of it—that was really to be a great lady, especially when one so carried and presented one's self. It was as if somehow she had all society under contribution, and all the arts and graces it practised—or was the effect rather that of charming uses found for her, even from a distance, subtle service rendered by her to a clamorous world wherever she might be? To be so graceful, so gracious, so wise, so good, and to make so light of it all— that was really to be a great lady; especially when one looked so much like one. If Madame Merle, however, made light of her advantages as regards the world, it was not because she had not, for her own entertainment, taken them, as I have intimated, as seriously as possible. Her natural talents, for instance; these she had zealously cultivated.

166.30–31 she wrote a succession of letters, as those arriving for her appeared innumerable: she wrote a succession of letters;

166.33–34 offering to the mail. contribution to the mail.

166.34–35 more people, as she told Isabel than she knew what to do with, and a multitude of people, and, as she told Isabel, something

166.37 brushing in a sketch taking a sketch

166.40 brave musician brilliant musician

166.43 grace of her talk. entertainment of her talk.

166.44 her, Madame Merle,

166.44 facility, playing,

167.1 basely inferior; meager and artless;

167.1–2 had been thought rather a prodigy at home, had been thought to play very well,

167.6 tasks of rich embroidery, morsels of picturesque embroidery,

167.7 an art a sort of work

167.8 noted remarkable

167.9 when engaged when she was engaged

167.10–11 "everything important"), everything important),

167.13 quality; was never rudely absent and yet never too seated. quality; she never was preoccupied, she never pressed too hard.

167.15–16 and appeared to impute scant worth and she appeared to attach no importance

167.19 the most a most

167.19 amenable agreeable

167.21 was either was

167.22 since for

167.24 rubbed away. smoothed.

167.25 too useful, was too ripe and too final. too supple; she was too finished, too civilized.

167.30–31 to think of her in any detachment or privacy, to think of Madame Merle as an isolated figure;

167.31–32 relations, direct or indirect, relations

167.32–33 One might wonder what commerce she could possibly hold with her own spirit. One Isabel often wondered what her relations might be with her own soul. She

167.34 that a that having a

167.35 prove one prove that one

167.35 one's her

167.36 one had but just escaped she had only just sufficiently escaped

167.39 tongue. language.

167.42 she Isabel

167.43 to her friend in response to her, in response

167.43–44 allusion that had appeared to reach far. allusion that she had dropped.

168.1–2 the amused smile of a person seated at a game of guesses. a picturesque smile.

168.3 haven't too much the droop of the misunderstood." have not the pose of a martyr."

168.8 "Such "What

168.9 But Isabel rose to the irony. (Omitted.)

168.10 for a moment felt anything." felt anything very much," Isabel answered.

168.11–12 many more iron pots certainly than porcelain. more iron pots, I think, than porcelain ones.

168.12 on upon

168.12 bears some mark; has something;

168.14 stout, stout porcelain;

168.15 shockingly chipped chipped

168.20 or on some other or some other,

168.22 that she would some day a tale unfold. that some day she would relate her history.

168.23 one, it,

168.24–25 begged repeatedly for a respite, appeared to desire a postponement,

168.25 her young companion the young girl

168.26 they she

168.26–27 be sure to happen; certainly happen;

168.27 so visibly lay lay

168.28–29 enquired if she mightn't be trusted—if she appeared capable of a betrayal asked Madame Merle if she could not trust her—if she feared a betrayal

168.30–31 her fellow visitor the elder lady

168.33 of about

168.34 sentiments, her sentiments,

168.36–38 infinite good nature. This flattered and quickened the girl, who was struck with all the distinguished people her friend had known and with

her having lived, inexhaustible sympathy and good nature. In all this there was something flattering to the girl, who knew that Madame Merle knew a great many distinguished people, and had lived,

168.41 the sense this sense

168.42 appealed to these stores of reminiscence. begged her friend to tell her about the people she knew.

169.1 educated," learned,"

169.4 proceeding to Malta going to Wallachia

169.5 dwelt, stayed,

169.8–9 most convenient in the world to live with. finest people in the world.

169.10 remaining here staying in the house

169.11–12 that gentleman's wife remarked to her niece. Mrs. Touchett remarked to Isabel.

169.12 incapable of a mistake; incapable of doing anything indiscreet;

169.12–13 most tactful woman best-bred woman

169.17 to put in this time to stay

169.19 hasn't a fault." has no faults."

169.21 returned. said.

169.22 "She's never the least bit 'off.' "She never does anything wrong."

169.23 me she me that she

169.25 putting you in relation with Madame Merle. securing Madame Merle.

169.29 you'll ever feel her open to criticism? you will find a fault in her?

169.32 You won't discover a fault in her." You never will find one."

169.33 "Perhaps not. But I dare say I shan't miss it." "Perhaps not; but I think I shall not miss it."

169.34 "She knows absolutely everything on earth there is to know," "She is always up to the mark!"

169.36 observed to their companion said to Madame Merle

169.37 considered she hadn't a speck on her perfection. believed she had not a fault.

169.38 On which "I'm ¶"I am

169.38 you," Madame Merle replied, "but you, but

169.39–40 your aunt imagines, or at least alludes to, no aberrations that the clock-face doesn't register." your aunt has no perception of spiritual things," Madame Merle answered.

169.41 "So that you mean you've a wild side that's unknown to her?" "Do you mean by that that you have spiritual faults?"

169.42 I fear my darkest sides are my tamest. I mean nothing so flat!

170.7 own conversation, conversation,

170.10 couldn't occur never occurred

170.12 rose eagerly to the sense of her shades; agreed with her;

170.14 it was clear in the third that for a person to speak in the third, to speak

170.15–16 sign of that person's intimacy with one's self. sign of intimacy.
170.16 deep communion intimacy
170.19 referred alluded
170.20 career life,
170.21 a gross egotist an egotist
170.21 a flat gossip. a gossip.
170.26 nothing I shall nothing that I shall
170.29 outside, outside of us,
170.33 people I adore. people that I adore.
170.33 anything but abject ill-natured
170.34 and appeal to me too much. too much.
170.36 and horribly spoil you. I speak I talk
170.39 old, old world. old world.
170.39 want wish
170.40 want wish
170.43–171.1 that splendid, dreadful, funny country—surely the greatest and drollest of them all. the land of my birth.
171.2 in these parts, over here,
171.3 land; country;
171.17 he has he has got
171.18 carriére; career;
171.22–23 impossible anything impossible that anything
171.24 has a has got a
171.30 cousin cousin is
171.41 him or make of him. him.
171.42 I tell you, I say, say that he is
171.43 say he's say that he is
171.43–172.1 lives *tout bêtement* in Italy lives in Italy
172.8 feel he feel that he
172.11 her. her.
172.25 in which she took the measure which she took of the measure
172.29 mean his mean that his
172.31 told him said to him that
172.34 way of saying both that way both of saying that
172.40 immensely. sadly.
173.5 day you day when you
173.15 creature fellow
173.23 she Isabel
173.25–26 the finest capacity for ignorance. a still tender love of ignorance.
173.31 amplitude of ease, was imperfectly disguised smile, was by no means disguised
173.38 that I never had which I never had
173.39 many friends, friends,
173.41 memories, graces, memories,
173.42 But Madame Madame
173.45 movement, of unconsciousness. action.
173.45 graces and memories memories,
174.4–5 you." And her companion looked you," Madame Merle rejoined, looking
174.5 age I age," she went on, "I
174.11 leaves. "I'm leaves. At last she said—"I'm

174.12 she at last replied. (*Omitted.*)
174.15 were were
174.20 a vivid image an image
174.23 a very tame one. It's very tame," said Isabel. "It is
174.28 grandly to play. to play with energy.
174.29 yet but
174.30 had ever succeeded? had succeeded?
174.35 Isabel smiled. said Isabel, smiling.
174.39 fine moustache moustache
174.41 with still more emphasis. blushing.
174.42 appeared to note this eagerness. gave a glance at her blush which caused it to deepen.
174.45 silent a little but then spoke silent for a moment, and then,
175.1 inconsequence. inconsequence—
175.3 asked cried
175.5–6 congratulate you with all my heart. congratulate you.
175.16 some cluster a cluster
175.16–17 What shall we call our 'self'? What do you call one's self?
175.19 know a know that a
175.19 clothes dresses
175.21–22 one's furniture, one's garments, the books one reads, clothes, the books one reads,
175.26 was she was
175.30–31 everything's on the contrary a limit, on the contrary, it's a limit,
175.34 Madame Merle lightly interposed. interposed Madame Merle, skilfully
175.41 on upon
175.42–43 loyalty practised by our heroine toward loyalty which our heroine practised towards
175.45–176.1 She had not, however, concealed the fact Isabel had not concealed from her, however,
176.2–3 let her friend know of how advantageous a kind they had been. let her know that they were of a highly advantageous kind.
176.8 excellent ways, admirable self-control,
176.12 this lady's Madame Merle's
176.13 the present— the present one—
176.16 as a suitor of being a suitor
176.19 our young woman Isabel
176.24 Pardon Excuse
176.25 corrupt; worldly;
176.25 the wordly view that view
177.2 or else or
177.5 succession, but succession," she said, "but
177.8 and must think as well of me as possible. and you must think well of me.
177.12 Our young lady, Isabel,
177.14 hours during which hours that
177.17 apparently occupied there with in
177.19 see it see that it
177.20 if whether

177.22 **always to its own sense adequate.** which had always deemed itself sufficient.

177.26–27 **Uttered reflection had with her ever, at any rate, a practical ring.** *(Omitted.)*

177.29–30 **next year."** next year." Her remarks had usually a practical ring.

177.37 **vague hours** much time

177.37 **books** the books

177.41 **felt** thought

178.5 **He** Mr. Bantling, however,

178.14 **at least** at any rate

178.16 **should see how that** ought to see how it

178.20 **even would** even he would

178.25 **this correspondence** Miss Stackpole's letters

178.26 **representative** correspondent

178.28 **me she's** me that she is

178.29 **ex-Lancer!** ex-Guardsman!

178.35 **"Pardon** "Excuse

178.36 **I've the** I have got the

179.2 **brougham,** dog-cart,

179.4 **his** the doctor's

179.7 **roll** drive

179.16 **dear father** father

179.17 **she gently wailed,** the girl murmured,

179.17–18 **two hands** hand

179.20 **this** this incident

179.38 **most liberally,"** liberally,"

180.13 **an impression** a subtle impression

180.13–14 **subtle consequences** consequences

180.18 **such a matter** it

180.19 **and another to stand among its massive records.** and it was another to behold it actually.

180.22–23 **to picture her as one of the hungry mouths or envious hearts of the general herd,** to say that Madame Merle was one of the hungry ones of the world;

180.24 **learned of her having desires that** perceived that she had desires which

180.26 **fine proud smile—** most becoming smile—

180.30–31 **she couldn't at the present moment keep from quite perversely yearning** her private attitude at the present moment was somewhat incongruously invidious,

180.31 **was careful** was very careful

180.38 **if I'm** whether I am

180.40 **He's naturally** He is of course

181.1 **softly repeated.** repeated, softly.

181.12 **assuredly** certainly

181.12 **effort. Don't** effort; don't

181.13 **seldom** rarely

181.25 **reserved her opinion** gave a shrug.

181.35 **affairs of the bank,** the bank,

181.38 **"How very delicious! After** "After

181.41 **before the will was read—** just before it came out—

182.4 **her eyes bent on** with her eyes bent upon

182.5–6 **as she raised them.** looking up.

182.17 **kiss** kiss that

182.17 **her** Isabel

182.18 **the visitor,** that Madame Merle,

182.20–21 **had no purpose of awaiting in London the sale of her house.** did not remain in London until she had sold her house.

182.21 **the objects she** those objects which she

182.22 **other abode,** Florentine residence,

182.25–26 **to measure and weigh and otherwise handle** to comtemplate

182.27–28 **thought very often of the fact of her accession of means, looking at it** thought of it very often and looked at it

182.29 **now** at present

182.29 **follow her train of thought** enter into her meditations

182.29–32 **to explain exactly why her new consciousness was at first oppressive. This failure to rise to immediate joy was indeed but brief; the girl presently made up her mind** why it was that some of them were of a rather pessimistic cast. The pessimism of this young lady was transient; she ultimately made up her mind

182.33 **and that to do could only be sweet.** and to do was sweet.

182.33–35 **graceful contrary of the stupid side of weakness—especially the feminine variety.** contrary of weakness.

182.35 **delicate young person,** young lady,

182.40 **them to spend together.** the two ladies to spend.

182.43 **to do so during** to do so indeed during

182.43 **eventually** presently

182.44 **though** but

182.44–183.1 **inevitably present themselves as trivial.** probably be thought rather vulgar.

183.1–2 **ways most naturally imposed** ways that most naturally presented themselves

183.3 **and that were prescribed unreservedly by the guidance** especially under the guidance

183.15 **saw** she saw

183.21 **arrive** come

183.22 **at** to

183.22 **pronounced on** judged

183.22–23 **trenchancy doubtless** trenchancy which is doubtless

183.24–25 **lives were, though luxurious, inane,** manner of life was superficial,

183.27 **on** upon

183.28–29 **passed for people kept exemplarily genial by their cooks and dressmakers,** were the most good-natured people in the world,

183.30–31 **inferior to that of the new**

theatrical pieces. only a dangerous variation of impertinence.

183.31 it lead it all lead

184.2 used to used always to

184.3 quite very

184.6 and reproduced with wondrous truth and led

184.7–9 the domestic tone of her native Baltimore. This reduced Mr. Luce, her worthy husband, a tall, as quiet and domestic a life as she might have led in her native Baltimore. The existence of Mr. Luce, her worthy husband, was somewhat more inscrutable. Superficially indeed, there was no mystery about it; the mystery lay deeper, and resided in the wonder of his supporting existence at all. He was the most unoccupied man in Europe, for he not only had no duties, but he had no pleasures. Habits certainly he had, but they were few in number, and had been worn threadbare by forty years of use. Mr. Luce was a tall,

184.11–13 head, to mere platonic praise of the "distractions" of Paris—they were his great word—since you would never have guessed from what cares he escaped to them. One of them was that he went head. He went

184.14 he found a post-office that there was a post office which

184.15 as in as that of

184.19–20 the French capital. Paris.

184.23 pastimes, avocations,

184.29 this scene of his dissipations the French capital

184.30 resources occupations

184.30 reflections reveries

184.34 lately recently

184.39 showy clever rule government

184.39 superseded Empire. lately-abolished Empire.

184.40 *he* he

185.4 nine. nine times.

185.6–7 a dark cloud over Paris, *our* Paris, a cloud over Paris,

185.11 was native to New York was a native of New York,

185.13 early old

185.15 small little

185.16–17 had stopped stopped

185.21 all his of his

185.28 had become became

185.28–29 she had firmly she firmly

185.35 dismissed, was dismissed,

185.38 nostrils nostril

186.5–6 the high shoulders of many a duchess. many a duchess.

187.16 gentleman in gentleman to do in

187.24 poor Ralph Touchett Mr. Ralph Touchett

187.27 augmentations accession of fortune,

187.30 asserted, said,

187.41–42 exposure on the moral side. moral tendencies.

187.44 grossly sensual; sensual;

188.7 keeping them up." keeping up those illusions."

188.8 gazed at this lurid scene gazed upon this vivid but dusky picture of her future.

188.10 think think that

188.13 in it— into it—

188.14–15 grim reality! reality!

188.33 personal intimacy intimacy,

188.43 her and her

188.43–44 moreover subsisted in face of subsisted in the face of

189.1 each each of them

189.2–3 on either side none the less honourable. none the less honourable on either side;

189.6 his her

189.9–10 need of demonstrative affection. coquetry.

189.10 groping celibates harmless confederates

189.11 impatiently somewhat eagerly

189.12 rather a slow and a discursive habit, a rather slow and discursive habit,

189.13–14 by the influence of a shining, challenging eye with the spectacle of a brilliant eye

189.14 freshness, neatness,

189.17–19 a gentleman who appeared somehow, in his way, made, by expensive, roundabout, almost "quaint" processes, for her use, and whose a fresh-looking, professionless gentleman, whose

189.20 boon to a breathless mate, advantage to Miss Stackpole,

189.24–25 largely and showily address them to publicity. make use of them in her correspondence.

189.26 abysses of sophistication mysterious shallows

189.29–30 rest in any adoption of the views of a class pledged to all the old abuses. safety in the adoption of second-hand views.

189.35–37 this perfect man of the world —a term that had ceased to make with her, as previously, for opprobrium. the good Mr. Bantling.

189.39 enjoyed in his company. made in the company of the gallant ex-guardsman.

190.1–2 her gallant friend during the spring Mr. Bantling in the spring,

190.5 February had February she had

190.6 She interrupted She did not go directly to Florence, but interrupted

190.8-9 beneath a slow-moving white umbrella. under a white umbrella.

190.10 with homely, customary logic, with her usual homely logic,

190.12–13 your own mistress and are as free as the bird on the bough. I don't mean you your own mistress," she said. "Excuse me; I don't mean that you

190.14 at present on on

190.21 how much you're that you are

191.3 encounters and concussions. encounters with her.

191.3–4 perfectly present, but was always to be found; but she was

191.10 softening moss. moss.

191.10–11 Her offered, her passive Her passive

191.12 believe none the less believe, however,

191.12–15 she made more of those concessions to the sense of something obscurely distinct from convenience—more of them than she independently exacted. She was learning to sacrifice she grew more disposed to confer those sentimental favours which she was still unable to accept—to sacrifice

191.19 since for

191.21 that Palazzo that the Palazzo

191.22 large apartment known spacious apartment which was known

191.22 quarter room

191.25 "something I've "—something that I have

191.28 know your know that your

191.36 compliment." souvenir."

191.37–38 "A compliment on what?" ¶"On your so beautifully existing." *(Omitted.)*

191.39 she presently declared. said Isabel.

192.9 me me

192.12 went on said

192.13 it it's

192.14 looked at him with looked at him a moment with

192.23–24 tight, tender young rose. rosebud.

192.24–25 take care of itself. form itself.

192.27–28 power of thought—above all too much conscience." too much conscience,"

192.29–30 Put back your watch. Diet your fever. *(Omitted.)*

192.36 persisting in cheer. continuing to smile.

192.37 pursued. went on.

193.7 keep thinking; always be thinking—

193.8 not sure it's not sure that it's

193.12 flush that blush which

193.20 looked across looked a while across

193.22–24 adventure; there was such a thrill even in the preliminary hovering. It affected her moreover as a peaceful interlude, as a hush of the drum and fife knowledge; the stillness of these soft weeks seemed good to her. They were a peaceful interlude

193.30 their young friend Isabel

193.33 that lady's perspicacity. Madame Merle's perspicacity.

193.36 she had at any rate before leaving at any rate before she left

193.37 grown she had grown

193.37–38 in question found a proper place found a place

193.39 about herself, about her herself,

193.40 took perpetually for granted a thousand good intentions. was a perpetual implication of good intentions.

193.41 fine things to be done by fine things

193.42 occasions her opportunities

193.43 were sublime in the mass. might do, were really innumerable.

194.3 mixed intermingled

194.3 debates. reveries.

194.9 images of energy gentlemen

194.14–15 rather to show the livid light of a judgement-day. The girl to wear the supernatural aspect of a resurrection. Isabel

194.17 believe she believe that she

194.19 but and yet,

194.21–22 yet couldn't but feel them appreciably in debt to her. yet she did not regard them as appreciably in her debt.

194.25 She had indeed failed to say Isabel did not say

194.27 certain certain that

194.29–34 might know the humiliation of change, might really, for that matter, come to the end of the things that were not Caspar (even though there appeared so many of them), and find rest in those very elements of his presence which struck her now as impediments to the finer respiration. might change her humour—might weary of those things that were not Caspar (and there were so many things that were not Caspar!), and might find satisfaction in the very qualities which struck her to-day as his limitations.

194.34 these impediments his limitations

194.36 brave fine

194.39–40 more than a noble humility or an enlightened pride ought to wish to reckon with. more than modesty should not only expect, but even desire.

194.40–41 undertaken to preserve no record of what had passed between them undertaken to forget him, as a lover,

194.42 just. proper.

194.43 candidly believed really believed

194.44 get over his disappointment. get over it.

194.45 affected— smitten—

195.1–3 absurd that a man both so intelligent and so honourably dealt with should cultivate a scar out of proportion to any wound. absurd that a man so completely absolved from fidelity should stiffen himself in an attitude it would be more graceful to discontinue.

195.3–4 liked moreover to be liked to be

195.5 brooding over thinking of

195.7 She Isabel

195.8 woman lady

195.10 a pang even of surprise. an impulse of jealousy.

195.11–12 him. That alone was him; and this was

195.15–16 a small group that might have been described by a painter as composing well a picturesque little group

195.17 crowning which stood on the summit of

195.20 considered looked at

195.26 lengthily adjusted which ran along

195.26 useful as usually afforded

195.30 antique, ancient,

195.31–32 the mask, not the face of the house. the mask of the house; it was not its face.

195.37 other old old

196.1 seemed less seemed to be less

196.5 jealous obstructive

196.7 random race conflicting nationality

196.9 less sombre than our much less gloomy than my

196.13–15 It was moreover a seat of ease, indeed of luxury, telling of arrangements subtly studied and refinements frankly proclaimed, and containing a variety The place, moreover, was almost luxuriously comfortable; it told of habitation being practiced as a fine art. It contained a new variety

196.17 angular primitive

196.17–18 as pedantically primitive, pedantically rusty,

196.20 kept terms were intermingled

196.21 large allowance liberal concession

196.21 for a lounging generation; to cultivated sensibilities;

196.26 odd, elaborate pictures, modern pictures,

196.28 we when we

196.32 talk conversation

196.34–35 their attitude expressed a final reserve and their faces showed the glaze of prudence. their attitude was noticeably provisional, and they evidently wished to emphasize the transitory character of their presence.

196.35–36 ample, mild-featured women, comfortable, mild-faced women,

196.37–38 of the serge that draped them as if nailed on frames inexpressive serge

196.40–41 as well as and had evidently

196.42 This object of interest This young lady

196.42 ornament coiffure

196.43 simplicity and not simplicity, which was not

196.43 her a

196.44 too short for her years, too short for the wearer,

197.3–4 it being on its way as arduous to converse with the very meek as with the very mighty. to entertain a nun is, in fact, a sufficiently delicate operation.

197.5 clearly much occupied with their quiet charge, plainly much interested in his youthful companion,

197.6 on upon

197.7 high but well-shaped head, on well-shaped head, upon

197.9 fine, narrow, extremely modelled and composed face, thin, delicate, sharply-cut face,

197.10–11 just this effect of its running a trifle too much to points; that it looked too pointed;

197.11 the beard his beard

197.14 romantic picturesque

197.14–15 a foreign, a somewhat foreign,

197.16–18 style. His conscious, curious eyes, however, eyes at once vague and penetrating, intelligent and hard, expressive of the observer effect. His luminous intelligent eye, an eye which expressed both softness and keenness —the nature of the observer

197.18 you that, you, however, that

197.21 original clime and country; nationality;

197.24–27 but he suggested, fine gold coin as he was, no stamp nor emblem of the common mintage that provides for general circulation; he was the elegant complicated medal struck off for a special occasion. he was one of those persons who, in the matter of race, may, as the phrase is, pass for anything.

197.27–28 rather languid-looking lazy-looking

197.29–30 other trouble about it than to have no vulgar things. trouble about it.

197.33 you he was Italian. you that he was an Italian.

197.34 child girl

197.34 earnestly a little

197.36 "Certainly "Yes, my child;

197.38–39 painted with a fixed and intensely sweet smile. of which the natural and usual expression seemed to be a smile of perfect sweetness.

197.41 trunk." trunk," said the child.

198.13 visitor gently replied. woman replied, gently.

198.14 tongue. language.

198.15 proper language." own tongue."

198.18 though failing but failed

198.19 instantly added. said, instantly.

198.24 your your

198.28 —not big," little,"

198.30–31 I prefer women like books— very good and not too long. I like little women," the gentleman declared, frankly.

198.31 know," the gentleman said, "no know no

198.36 looks sound." looks well."

198.39 an accent a French accent

198.42 her smile heightened her smile brightened

198.43 truly?" truly?" she asked.

199.7 gaily. smiling.

199.10 it's excellent. it is a very good one.

199.20–21 **"Yes, and what else?"** "Yes," he said in a moment, "and what else?"
199.22 **thinking she** thinking that she
199.23 **everything; but** everything. ¶But
199.27 **gentille,"** nice,"
199.27–28 **really pretty."** very pretty."
199.34 **daughter,** child,
199.43 **certain you'll** certain that you will
200.24 **as in the other."** as another."
200.27 **red, thank you,"** red,"
200.36 **enquired.** asked.
201.10 **saloon.** drawing-room.
201.16 **also stopped,** stopped, too,
201.33 **asked his new visitor** asked Madame Merle
201.35 **the lady addressed** her father's visitor
201.36 **declared.** answered.
201.39 **come away."** leave the place."
201.42 **come to see** come and see
201.43 **there.** here.
202.1 **particular tone** peculiar tone
202.8 **their entertainer.** the host.
202.13–14 **said Madame Merle, but also as in pleasantry.** said Madame Merle, smiling still.
202.16 **very naturally meant** meant
202.19 **attentive to** looking at
202.21 **very naturally meant** meant
202.23 **fixed him** gazed at him
202.24 **papa?"** papa?" she asked.
202.27–28 **"Be good and wise and happy** "Be good,
202.29 **returned,** declared,
202.32 **dear child,"** my child,"
202.34 **yet** but
202.38 **she nevertheless asked** she asked
203.2 **good little girls** little girls
203.3 **cried** said
203.11–12 **made answer.** answered.
203.16 **meditated.** meditated a moment.
203.17 **"But very pretty?"** "But, will they be pretty?"
203.18 **very fond** fond
203.21 **won't** will not
203.21 **returned** answered,
203.22–23 **after which,** and then,
203.24 **Catherine?" she went on.** Catherine?"
203.37 **have wished yourself** have come
203.40 **"I think you very** "I think you are very
204.7 **Osmond conceded. With which** said Osmond. Then, at last,
204.8–9 **bent forward** leaning forward
204.9 **his** with his
204.41 **smiled** looked
204.41 **her host.** her interlocutor, smiling.
204.44 *why* why
205.1–2 **so much of every one else and** so much
205.6 *your* **life your** your life—your
205.10 **mignonne,** *ma bonne,*
205.19 **courage.** nobleness of expression.
205.31 **glad** glad that
205.36 **do remember** will remember
205.38 **real interest.** great pleasure.

206.3 **waited.** reflected a moment.
206.5 **that, you know,** that,
206.10–11 **"Pardon me. That isn't—the knowledge I impute to you—a common** "Excuse me. That isn't a common
206.12–13 **of more or less impossible people** of people
206.16 **on** upon
206.21 **flushed as with a wounded intention.** flushed a little, and her eye betrayed vexation.
206.22 **No one** There is no one
206.22 **what** *is* **worth** that there are many things worth
206.23 **Haven't** *I* **seen you in old days?"** (*Omitted.*)
206.24 **"I recognise some things.** "Many things, I admit.
206.24–25 **probable in this poor life."** probable things."
206.27 **Who then** Who
206.30 **youth and ignorance.** youth.
206.32 **twenty-three years old.** twenty-two years old.
206.34 **we struck up a grand alliance.** we took a great fancy to each other.
206.41 **a creature** any one
207.19 **less relevantly** more irrelevantly
207.19 **have some** have got some
207.20 **so well** as well
207.22 **manner and tone** manner
207.22–23 **at any juncture,** on any occasion,
207.24 **was** there was
207.24 **circumspect,** circumspect, which showed itself in glance and tone.
207.24–25 **as if they had approached** They approached
207.25 **obliquely and addressed** obliquely, as it were, and they addressed
207.26-27 **appreciable degree** embarrassing degree
207.28 **any embarrassment** such embarrassments
207.29 **form** manner
207.31 **wear for** exhibit to
207.31 **point to be made** point I wish to make
207.32 **element between them,** obstruction,
207.34 **either** either of them
207.35 **each** each of them
207.38–39 **Madame Merle quietly said.** said Madame Merle, quietly.
208.4 **most remarkable of women,"** most remarkable woman,"
208.7 **But he** and he
208.18 **Palazzo** the Palazzo
208.23 **no question he could ever put** no question that he could ask
208.27 **seen what's there—** seen that—
208.28 **considered.** looked at it a moment.
208.31 **She looked a moment longer, then turned** Madame Merle looked for a moment longer then she turned
208.35 **do—well,** do, it's

208.41 pictures, tapestries, surfaces the pictures, the tapestries, the surfaces

208.42 perfect. I'm perfect," she went on. "I am

208.44–45 nobody anywhere does. You've such adorable taste." no one else does."

208.46 "I'm sick of my adorable taste," said Gilbert Osmond. "I am very sick of it," said Osmond.

209.1 must nevertheless let must let

209.1 see it. see all this.

209.5 As cicerone of your museum As a *cicerone* in your own museum

209.7–8 looked at once colder and more attentive. turned upon his companion an eye expressive of perfect clairvoyance.

209.8 rich?" rich?" he asked in a moment.

209.13 you. you.

209.23 "He's a good deal of a donkey." "He's an awful ass."

209.26–27 say she has looks?" say that she was pretty?"

209.28–29 disappointed in them. disappointed.

209.31 a little. a moment.

209.35–36 She's not so coarse a piece of machinery—nor am I." She is a very delicate piece of machinery."

209.40 judgement." judgement till then."

209.42 really grown pretty," grown pretty,"

210.8 the visitor murmured murmured Madame Merle,

210.13 of Palazzo of the Palazzo

210.15 the hope she might the wish that she should

210.15 making, however, but made

210.22 "meet"— know—

210.23 whomever in the wide world whomever

210.23 and had and she had

210.25 dozen years; ten years;

210.26 most agreeable men—well, in Europe simply. most agreeable men it was possible to meet.

210.27–28 He wasn't a professional charmer— He was not perfect—

210.28 it, and the it; the

210.30–35 When not in the right mood he could fall as low as any one, saved only by his looking at such hours rather like a demoralised prince in exile. But if he cared or was interested or rightly challenged—just exactly rightly it had to be—then one felt his cleverness and his distinction. Those qualities didn't depend, in him, as in so many people, on his not committing or exposing himself. If he were not in the right mood he could be very unsatisfactory—like most people, after all; but when he chose to exert himself no man could do it to better purpose.

210.35–36 perversities peculiarities—

210.37 and didn't and he did not

210.42 person not to miss. person to know.

211.2–3 it was he who had most perception and taste—being artistic through and through. he had infinitely more taste; he had a taste which was quite by itself.

211.4–5 plunge, at Gardencourt, into the deeps of talk, multifarious colloquies at Gardencourt,

211.6 the tie binding these superior spirits, she felt the tie that united them. She was inclined to imagine

211.7 always somehow had histories, and such an impression was part were peculiar, and such a possibility was a part

211.8 inordinate suggestive

211.9 she Madame Merle

211.10 calm and tranquil

211.10 she that she

211.11 so high a confidence her friend's confidence

211.15 solemn stare exceedingly serious gaze

211.16 proclaim her proclaim that she was

211.16 the sense of comedy. a sense of humour—an intimation which at other moments she effectively refuted.

211.17–18 "Why, I'm not afraid of them —I'm as used to them as the cook to the butcher-boys." "I am not afraid of them."

211.22 This was a note of cynicism that This remark had a bitterness which

211.23 to sound; to betray;

211.23 alarmed, alarmed by it,

211.25 It This sentiment

211.26 none the less, however,

211.29 as priests to the mystery. to call attention to latent merits.

211.30 joy that pleasure which

211.31 early passion earlier sensations,

211.33 again and again so often,

211.33 something else to do. something to do.

211.35 recalled remembered

211.35 corner of angle in

211.36–37 it. She had it; and had

211.37 opinions own opinions

211.40 taking place which took place

211.42 advantages she couldn't have enjoyed for instance advantages which —for instance—she could not have enjoyed

212.2–3 she wandered Isabel wandered about

212.7 that which

212.17 the carven carven

212.18 on upon

212.19 the age of advertisement. the nineteenth.

212.23 where in which

212.24–27 cleared and scented the rooms in regular use. To live in such a place was, for Isabel, to hold to her ear all day a shell of the sea of the past. This vague eternal rumour kept her imagination awake. illumined the rooms that were in regular use. Isabel found that to live in such a place might be a source of happiness—almost of excitement. At first it had struck her as a sort of prison; but very soon its prison-like quality became a merit, for she discovered that it contained other prisoners than the members of her aunt's household. The spirit of the past was shut up there, like a refugee from the outer world; it lurked in lonely corners, and, at night, haunted even the rooms in which Mrs. Touchett diffused her matter-of-fact influence. Isabel used to hear vague echoes and strange reverberations; she had a sense of the hovering of unseen figures, of the flitting of ghosts. Often she paused, listening, half-startled, half-disappointed, on the great cold stone staircase.

212.29 lurking seated almost out of sight

212.29–30 Isabel took on this occasion little part in the talk; Isabel, on this occasion, took little share in the conversation;

212.31–32 invitingly; she sat there as if she had been at the play and had paid even a large sum for her place. appealingly; but sat there as an impartial auditor of their brilliant discourse.

212.33–41 had it, for the effect of brilliancy, all their own way. They talked of the Florentine, the Roman, the cosmopolite world, and might have been distinguished performers figuring for a charity. It all had the rich readiness that would have come from rehearsal. Madame Merle appealed to her as if she had been on the stage, but she could ignore any learnt cue without spoiling the scene—though of course she thus put dreadfully in the wrong the friend who had told Mr. Osmond she could be depended on. This was They talked extremely well; it struck Isabel almost as a dramatic entertainment, rehearsed in advance. Madame Merle referred everything to her, but the girl answered nothing, though she knew that this attitude would make Mr. Osmond think she was one of those dull people who bored him. It was the worse, too, that Madame Merle would have told him she was almost as much above the merely respectable average as he himself, and that she was putting her friend dreadfully in the wrong. But this was

212.41–42 if more had been involved she could have made no attempt if more had depended on it, Isabel could not have made an attempt

212.43 the visitor that checked her Mr. Osmond that arrested her

212.44 it more it seem more

212.44 she that she

212.45 she Isabel

213.2 happier, more charming,

213.3 glitter perform

213.5–6 a quiet ease that covered everything, even the first show of his own wit. This was the more grateful as his face, he was a quiet gentleman, with a colourless manner, who said elaborate things with a great deal of simplicity. Isabel, however, privately perceived that if he did not expect, he observed; she was very sure he was sensitive. His face

213.8 of at

213.8–12 And his very voice was fine—the more strangely that, with its clearness, it yet somehow wasn't sweet. This had had really to do with making her abstain from interference. His utterance was the vibration of glass, Mr. Osmond was very delicate; the tone of his voice alone would have proved it. It was the visitor's delicacy that made her abstain from interference. His talk was like the tinkling of glass,

213.13 Yet before he went she had to speak Before he went he made an appeal to her.

213.14 Merle," he said, "consents to Merle says she will

213.19 paused paused a moment,

213.23 replied answered

213.26 expected expected that

213.27 that lady, Madame Merle,

213.28 mere matter-of-course, matter-of-course,

213.34 ally lady

213.37 perceptibly flushed, coloured a moment;

213.41 him." him

214.2 her weary nobleness; a sort of noble gentleness,

214.5–6 put to Ralph ask Ralph

214.7 distorted by his trials, cynical,

214.7 herself she herself that she

214.9 'know' know

214.12 a vague, unexplained American a mysterious American,

214.13 thirty years, or less, twenty years, or more,

214.14 unexplained? mysterious?

214.15 I do know I know

214.17 fastidiousness magnanimity,

214.19 here; in Florence;

214.23 poor but honest poor

214.25 small little

214.27 impossible. wicked.

214.36 one's dangers a person

214.38 that—it may make them dangers. that.

214.40 anything anything that

215.3 Isabel considered. Isabel was silent a moment.

215.14 on upon

215.19 seems to me you seems to me that you

215.25 to to

215.30 earnestly cried. cried with fervour.

215.36–40 "She's indescribably blameless; a pathless desert of virtue; the only woman I know who never gives one a chance."¶"A chance for what?" ¶"Well, say to call her a fool!" She's She is perfect; she is

216.6 she acts on she acts a little on

216.9 face. eye.

216.10 banished?" banished?" she inquired.

216.16 On Upon

216.27 the great round world the world

216.30 refreshment entertainment

216.31–33 if he had been left wholly unbeguiled by such a mistress of the social art. if he had not been able to find a great deal in the society of a woman in whom the social virtues existed in polished perfection.

216.34–35 the administered justice she enjoyed at his hands, the intellectual justice he rendered her,

216.35–36 made life barren to him, made life seem barren.

216.36–39 had learned more or less inscrutably to attend, and there could have been nothing so "sustained" to attend to as the general performance of Madame Merle. He tasted her in sips, he let her stand, had learned to appreciate, and there could be no better field for such a talent than the table-talk of Madame Merle. He talked with her largely, treated her with conspicuous civility, occupied himself with her and let her alone,

216.39 opportuneness opportuneness which

216.42 she that she

216.43 yearningly richly

217.1 secret measure. ambition.

217.2 but had but she had

217.5–6 almost as universally "liked" as some new volume of smooth twaddle. universally liked.

217.7–8 others that he supposed to have at various moments engaged her hope others which he vividly imagined her to have had her eyes upon at various moments

217.9 genial pliable

217.10 persons people

217.10–11 too-ingenious theories of conduct—that is of their own— factitious theories of conduct

217.12 due consideration a great deal of consideration

217.13 her eminent friend, Madame Merle—

217.14–15 he made the best of it, as he had done of worse things. he regarded it on the whole with philosophic tolerance.

217.18 each had made an important discovery or two each of them had made certain discoveries,

217.28–29 a soft afternoon a soft afternoon in May,

217.29–30 Tuscan Spring. The companions Italian spring. The two ladies

217.34 fragrance, perfume,

217.35 where of which

217.36 a the

217.36–37 a very imposing, object. the most imposing, side.

217.41 something grave and strong in the place; something rather severe about the place;

217.42–43 you would need an act of energy to get out. it would not be easy to get out.

218.3 conductress, companion,

218.5 him, Mr. Osmond,

218.6 saloon. drawing-room.

218.8 indicated presented

218.10 her convent." a convent."

218.11 scant scanty

218.12 her small shoes a pair of slippers.

218.15 high fashion. fashion.

218.17 nose, small nose, a small

218.18 eyes eye,

218.18–20 Her expression, however, thanks to various intensities of emphasis and wonder, of horror and joy, was not inhuman, her face, however, thanks to a very human and feminine expression, was by no means disagreeable,

218.21 plain evident that

218.22–23 Her attire, voluminous and delicate, bristling with elegance, The soft brilliancy of her toilet

218.24 as light and sudden as those light and sudden, like those

218.24 who that

218.26 classed her classified the Countess Gemini

218.29 to on

218.29–31 the Countess Gemini revealed no depths. Her demonstrations suggested the violent waving of some flag of general truce—white silk with fluttering streamers. the Countess presented no appearance of wickedness. Nothing could have been kinder or more innocent than her greeting to Isabel.

218.32 believe believe that

218.32 it's that it is

218.36–37 it hurts them they receive an injury

218.37 wheezing panting

218.39 wheezing panting

218.42 knows does know

218.42 Italians the Italians

219.6–9 series of little jerks and pecks, or roulades of shrillness, and in an accent that was as some fond recall of good English, or rather of good American, in adversity. variety of little jerks and glances, in a tone which, although it expressed a high degree of good-nature, was rather shrill than sweet.

219.12 returned, declared,

219.13 beautiful and precious." very beautiful."

219.14 "I've a few "I have got a few
219.14 allowed; murmured;
219.17 the detached and the involved. the indifferent and the expressive
219.18 to hint to intimate
219.18 nothing but the right "values" was of any nothing was of much
219.24 that which
219.41 doubtless perhaps
219.43–44 A man A man whom
220.3 on his wit. upon himself.
220.4 we judge, I am afraid,
220.6–7 let myself so needlessly in—!" invited these women here!"
220.23 flutter of her ruffles. sharp laugh.
220.27 sure she sure that she
220.37 and but
220.43–44 tone; he tone, and he
220.45–46 shyly brushed Isabel's fingers with her own; taken Isabel's hand for a moment;
221.2 slimness. little waist.
221.4 yet but
221.9 but every every
221.10–13 Isabel heard the Countess, at something said by her companion, plunge into the latter's lucidity as a poodle splashes after a thrown stick. It was as if Madame Merle were seeing how far she would go. Isabel heard the Countess say something extravagant.
221.13 the pleasure. such pleasure.
221.15–16 were numerous; were pretty numerous;
221.16–21 apt to see such a world as all romantic. It met the case soothingly for the human, for the social failure—by which he meant the people who couldn't "realise," as they said, on their sensibility: they could keep it about them there, in their poverty, without ridicule, as you might keep an heirloom or an inconvenient entailed place that brought you in nothing. Thus there were apt to see Italy in rose-colour. On the whole it was better than other countries, if one was content to lead a quiet life and take things as they came. It was very dull sometimes, but there were
221.22–24 the greatest sum of beauty. Certain impressions you could get only there. Others, favourable to life, you never got, and you the most beauty. There were certain impressions that one could get only in Italy. There were others that one never got there, and one
221.25–26 you got one of a quality that made up one got a delightful one, which made up
221.26 Italy, all the same, had spoiled He was inclined to think that Italy had spoiled
221.29 made one made people
221.29–32 it had no discipline for the character, didn't cultivate in you, oth- erwise expressed, the successful social and other "cheek" that flourished in Paris and London. "We're sweetly provincial," there was nothing tonic in an Italian life. One was out of the current; one was not *dans le mouvement*, as the French said; one was too far from Paris and London. "We are gloriously provincial, I assure you,"
221.39 disagreeable here disagreeable
221.40 as you like as you find you like
221.44 on. upon.
222.17 feathers, soft plumage,
222.22–23 had also a finer patience. was not ill-natured.
222.26–27 rather an idiot and a bore. rather light.
222.35 moment. moment," she answered.
223.7 resignedly sighed. murmured, with a little melancholy smile.
223.9 her host Mr. Osmond
223.10 his hands with his hands
223.15–16 she had what always gave her a very private thrill, the consciousness of a new relation. she felt that she was being entertained.
223.18 fine grass deep grass
223.19 things scattered things that were scattered
223.20 Mr. Osmond her host
223.23 he Mr. Osmond
223.25 She faced him with some surprise. Isabel turned, with a good deal of surprise.
223.29 he went on with his cool smile. Osmond went on, smiling.
223.31 almost no observation too little observation
223.38–39 honest lady—more so than she seems. good woman—better than she seems.
223.39–40 of a serious turn of a very serious disposition,
223.41 horrid husband, nasty husband,
223.42 a horrid husband's a nasty husband is
224.2 Pardon Excuse
224.3 in saying you've in saying that you have
224.7 appear appear to be
224.9 medallions carvings
224.10–11 Isabel felt the owner much more so, and independently of them, thickly as they seemed to overhang him. Isabel became conscious that the owner was more interesting still.
224.19–20 types already types which were already
224.20 offering which offered
224.21–23 It was not that she recognized all these truths at the hour, but they were falling into order before her. Isabel did not say all these things to herself at the time; but she felt them, and afterwards they became distinct.
224.23–26 said to herself that this "new relation" would perhaps prove her very most distinguished. Madame

Merle had had that note of rarity, but what quite other power it immediately gained when sounded by a man! said to herself that Mr. Osmond had the interest of rareness.

224.28–30 **marked him for her as by one of those signs of the highly curious that he was showing her on the underside of old plates and in the corner of sixteenth-century drawings:** distinguished him;

224.32 **She** Isabel

224.34 **impalpabilities.** his immaterial part.

224.39–40 **struck our sensitive young woman as signs of quality, of intensity, somehow as promises of interest.** struck our observant young lady as the signs of an unusual sensibility.

224.44 **a sorted, sifted, arranged world,** a serene, impersonal way,

225.1–2 **perhaps, as a sick man consciously incurable consults at last only his lawyer:** perhaps;

225.6 **She** Isabel

225.9–10 **by speaking of his provincial side—which was exactly the side she would have taken him most to lack.** by saying that he was gloriously provincial—which was so exactly the opposite of what she had supposed.

225.12 **She trusted she** Isabel trusted that she

225.13–15 **If it was provincial to have that harmony, what then was the finish of the capital? And she could put this question in spite of so feeling her host a shy personage; since** If Mr. Osmond were provincial, pray what were the characteristics of the capital? Isabel could ask herself this question, in spite of having perceived that her host was a shy personage; for

225.17–19 **a proof of standards and touchstones other than the vulgar: he must be so sure the vulgar would be first on the ground. He** a proof of superior qualities. Mr. Osmond

225.22 **to think them agreeable, probably** (to think them agreeable), he probably

225.25 **effected** made

225.25–27 **successful conversion of it to which she owed both what pleased her in him and what mystified her. If he had suddenly** successful effort to overcome his shyness, to which Isabel felt that she owed both what pleased and what puzzled her in his conversation to-day. His suddenly

225.28 **Countess Gemini,** Countess of Gemini—

225.28–29 **interested in her;** interested in her feelings;

225.31 **he** that he

225.34 **romantic objects,** picturesque objects,

225.35–36 **in the last degree curious and precious,** very curious and valuable,

225.38 **and still held** still holding

225.39 **friend,** lady,

225.43 **but** but she

225.44–45 **thought her quicker, cleverer in every way, more prepared, than she was.** thought she was cleverer than she was;

226.1 **pleasantly exaggerated; told him so;**

226.2 **intelligence** cleverness

226.8 **something he,** something which her host,

226.10–12 **She had no wish to fall into that grotesqueness—in which she had seen women (and it was a warning) serenely, yet ignobly, flounder.** *(Omitted.)*

226.19 **the paramount distinction** which constituted the paramount distinction

226.23 **preparations.** tray.

226.26 **glowed** seemed to glow

226.33 **Osmond** Mr. Osmond

226.35 **she returned,** Isabel answered,

226.42 **she** a woman

226.45 **smiled Isabel.** said Isabel, smiling.

227.13–14 **Isabel permitted herself to observe.** said Isabel.

227.18 **little.”** a little.”

227.18 **spoke** uttered

227.18–19 **short pauses** little pauses

227.19 **regard was fixed on his visitor's** eyes were fixed upon Isabel's

227.20 **air of a man** look of a man

227.22 **she asked with mild irony.** Isabel asked, with a gentle laugh.

227.28 **She** Isabel

227.41–42 **The leanest gentleman** A gentleman

227.42–43 **I was, though lean, a gentleman.** I was a gentleman.

227.44 **get out** go out

227.45–228.2 **leave it, to say nothing of my being too well satisfied with it, on the whole, as it then was, to wish it altered.** leave it.

228.13 **naturally** of course

228.17–18 **desired to be—would in fact be uproariously vulgar.** desired to be.

228.19 **a measured sympathy** considerable sympathy

228.22–23 **“Oh, I've made in my way a good thing of it. Don't imagine I'm whining about it.** “Oh, I have been very happy; don't imagine me to suggest for a moment that I have not.

228.24 **This was large; she kept down to something smaller.** *(Omitted.)*

228.29 **and may very possibly not care** and it is very possible she may not care

228.31 **for Pansy.”** for her.”

228.33 **beautifully,** with feeling,

228.37 **went forward** was going on,

228.41–42 **her friend,** Madame Merle,

229.5–6 **one of her pretty perversities. She might have desired for some minutes to place it.** saying something discordant; a necessity of which she had been conscious for the last twenty minutes.

229.8 to which point her eyes followed them. and she followed the pair for a while with her eyes.

229.9 her companion, Madame Merle,

229.13 at the sequestered couple. towards the retreating couple.

229.16 smiled. answered, smiling.

229.18 don't wish." don't wish to."

229.20 yet but

229.24 a poisoned one a very sharp one

229.25–26 your sense of our difference. your saying it.

229.28 "To what will it conduce?" "what difference will it make?"

229.34 I think that I think

229.36–37 discover that." discover it."

229.38 not had time. not had time for that.

229.41 mentioned. declared.

229.43 "Surely I've "Surely—I have

229.45 piped the Countess, cried the Countess, with a laugh,

230.2 manner was odious, was really low; but it was an old story, manner was impertinent, but she did not suffer this to discompose her;

230.4 finally resumed, said at last,

230.12–13 She's not exposed to compulsion or deception." She is not to be subjected to force."

230.18 smiled Madame Merle. said Madame Merle, smiling.

230.27 dangerous—even dangerous," she cried, "even

230.30 with him in with him—in

230.33–35 facing her, his arms folded; and she at present was evidently not lost in the mere impersonal view, persistently as she gazed at it. facing her, with his arms folded; and she, at present, though she had her face turned to the opposite prospect, was evidently not scrutinizing it.

230.39 pronounced. said.

230.40–43 summoned by Pansy—he might, tarnished as to livery and quaint as to type, have issued from some stray sketch of old-time manners, been "put in" by the brush of a Longhi or a Goya—had summoned by Pansy, had

230.43–231.1 small table and placed it on the grass, small table, which he placed upon the grass,

231.2 had again disappeared, again disappeared,

231.5 assistance. assistance to the servant.

231.11 toilette toilet

231.15 turning looking

231.22 sparingly stroked down her antiquated skirt. stroked down her antiquated skirt, sparingly.

231.23 Don't you Do you not

231.27 better. Ask her." better; ask her."

231.28 grace. geniality.

231.39 Pansy objected. said Pansy.

231.40 said Madame Merle. Madame Merle remarked.

231.43 Pansy repeated said Pansy,

231.44 thoroughly." exceedingly."

232.1 "And how do you think "And you think

232.4 departed went off

232.5 had still lingered were still lingering

232.7 if whether

232.12 marrying fortunately. marrying well.

232.16 marry fortunately; marry well;

232.20 she presently said. she said, presently.

232.21 brother's brother,

232.27 fabulous. You're fabulous; you are

232.31 shook her head as for quiet amusement. shook her head, with a smile of sadness.

232.33 slowly coming coming

232.43 never, no, never,

232.44 founded on based upon

233.3 presume suppose

233.19 princess. duchess.

233.21 Yet But

233.31 charming," nice,"

233.35 returned rejoined

233.36 satisfy. please.

233.36 tremble fear

234.1 Mrs. Touchett's worth, Mrs. Touchett's charms,

234.2 observed him select observed that he selected

234.11 was willing would have been willing

234.11 to look at him in the light of hospitality. to take the hospitable view of his idiosyncracies.

234.16 he should be curious of so rare an apparition. he should admire an admirable person.

234.17 observed said

234.17 plain very plain

234.18–22 Mrs. Touchett had from far back found a place on her scant list for this gentleman, though wondering dimly by what art and what process—so negative and so wise as they were—he had everywhere effectively imposed himself. Mrs. Touchett had always liked Mr. Osmond; she thought him so much of a gentleman.

234.24 her Mrs. Touchett

234.25–26 always, oddly enough, affected her as providing ground for a relation with her. always excited her esteem.

234.31 with whom for whom

234.31 had not successfully wrestled had not been up to the mark

234.33 uncanny child and an ambiguous income, overgrown daughter and an income of nothing—

234.38 Isabel's her

234.39 knew knew that

234.39–40 listened to several parties, as

his father would have said, listened to others,

234.40–41 but had made them listen but that she had made them listen to her

234.42 few months of his knowing her few months that he had known her,

234.42–43 observe a fresh suitor see a third suitor

234.44 fine gentlemen gentlemen

234.45 would do as well as anything else. was by itself a respectable chapter of experience.

235.1 a fourth, a fifth, a tenth besieger; a fourth and a fifth *soupirant;*

235.1–2 conviction she conviction that she

235.9 figures of speech; metaphors;

235.11 comparisons. similes.

235.12 a fine one herself a favourable comparison

235.19–20 for the beauty of his opinions or for his autograph of Michael Angelo. for his opinions.

235.22 *he* he

235.25 she shall herself be sure; she should be sure, herself;

235.29 studying human nature at close quarters and yet studying human nature and

235.35 but was but she was

235.38 that curious creature's really that man is

235.39–40 "Gilbert Osmond?" Madame Merle widened her clear eyes and, with a full intelligence, Madame Merle opened her expressive eyes, and with a brilliant smile—

235.42 "Hadn't it occurred "Has it never occurred

235.43 feel an idiot, feel like a fool—

235.43 hadn't hasn't

235.44 she added, "if added Madame Merle, "whether

235.44 to Isabel." to her."

235.44 "Oh, I shall now ask her," "I think I will ask her,"

236.1 reflected. reflected a moment.

236.3–5 Mrs. Touchett. "I won't have him enquire of me—as he perfectly may with that air of his, given Isabel's situation—what business it is of mine." Mrs. Touchett; "it's none of my business."

236.6–8 bravely declared. ¶"But what business—for *him*—is it of yours?" ¶"It's being none whatever is just why I can afford to speak. It's declared, bravely. ¶"It's none of yours either." ¶"That's precisely why I can afford to ask him; it is

236.9–11 that he can put me off with anything he chooses. But it will be by the way he does this that I shall know." that in me the question will not seem to him embarrassing."

236.12–13 let me hear then," said Mrs. Touchett, "of the fruits of your

penetration.** let me know on the first day, then," said Mrs. Touchett.

236.13 him, however, him,

236.14 to Isabel." to her."

236.15 Her companion sounded at this the note of warning. *(Omitted.)*

236.16 her. Don't her; don't

236.17 anything in life anything

236.18 sure of her doing something—well, not of *my* kind." sure she will do something I don't like."

236.19 "No, you "You

236.21 "Why in the world "Why

236.21–22 nothing the least solid nothing

236.24 even more charmingly than usual more than usual

236.26 in favourable conditions under favourable circumstances

236.27 a great impression. an impression.

236.27 a great impression, an impression,

236.29 his probably quite cold-blooded love-affairs; his love-affairs;

236.33 more or less pert little daughter." grown-up daughter."

236.34 are now worth are worth

236.35 young and very innocent young

236.37 little chit. school-girl.

236.42 poor child." child."

236.43 reason then reason

236.44 my niece Isabel

237.1–2 smiled Madame Merle; said Madame Merle, smiling;

237.3–6 Changing the form of one's mission's almost as difficult as changing the shape of one's nose: there they are, each, in the middle of one's face and one's character—one has to begin too far back. But I'll Changing one's mission is often awkward! I will

237.7 suspicions suspicion

237.10 him Mr. Osmond

237.11 who now arrived who came

237.12–13 thought him interesting—she came back to that; thought him very pleasant;

237.13 liked so liked

237.15–17 which put on for her a particular harmony with other supposed and divined things, histories within histories: which happened to take her fancy particularly—

237.19–20 bell-like clearness sympathetic docility

237.20 grace aspect

237.20–21 had no flourishes, was not brilliant,

237.22–25 It spoke of the kind of personal issue that touched her most nearly; of the choice between objects, subjects, contacts—what might she call them?—of a thin and those of a rich association; It seemed to tell a story —a story of the sort that touched her most easily; to speak of a serious choice, a choice between things of a shallow, and things of a deep, interest;

237.26 of a feeling a feeling
237.27–28 of a care a care
237.29–32 that the career appeared to stretch beneath it in the disposed vistas and with the ranges of steps and terraces and fountains of a formal Italian garden—allowing only for arid places freshened by the natural dews that it had been the main occupation of a lifetime of which the arid places were watered with the sweet sense
237.32 Palazzo the Palazzo
237.34 diffident at first—oh self-conscious beyond doubt! shy at first,
237.37 always suggestive talk. and always effective talk.
237.42 own side of the question, own side,
237.43 in especial. in particular.
237.43–238.6 woman was that while he talked so for amusement he didn't talk, as she had heard people, for "effect." He uttered his ideas as if, odd as they often appeared, he were used to them and had lived with them; old polished knobs and heads and handles, of precious substance, that could be fitted if necessary to new walking-sticks—not switches plucked in destitution from the common tree and then too elegantly waved about. lady was his extraordinary subtlety. There was such a fine intellectual intention in what he said, and the movement of his wit was like that of a quick-flashing blade.
238.6 small daughter little daughter
238.7 she rejoiced Isabel was delighted
238.10 little person young girl
238.11 maidens of England. daughters of England.
238.11–13 Pansy was so formed and finished for her tiny place in the world, and yet in imagination, This young lady was so neat, so complete in her manner; and yet in character,
238.22 pronounced declared
238.24 The Countess gave rise indeed to some discussion The Countess Gemini was indeed the occasion of a slight discussion
238.27 felicitously enough humorously
238.29 declared pronounced
238.30 this highly compromised character the Countess Gemini
238.31 at such a time at this time
238.32–33 at Palazzo Crescentini at the Palazzo Crescentini
238.33–34 estimate prevailing under that roof: estimate which prevailed under this roof;
238.34–38 a lady who had so mismanaged her improprieties that they had ceased to hang together at all—which was at the least what one asked of such matters—and had become the mere floating fragments of a wrecked renown, incommoding social circulation. a kind of flighty reprobate.

238.39 a more administrative person, a heartless feather-head like herself,
238.43 outrage. neglect.
238.43–239.1 consoled herself outrageously, and the list of her excuses had now lost itself in the labyrinth of her adventures. consoled herself too well, and it was notorious in Florence that she had consoled others also.
239.5 luckless lady unhappy lady
239.7 a woman that poor countess,
239.16–17 For ever so long now one had heard nothing It was a long time since one had heard anything
239.22 unfortunate lady, Countess Gemini,
239.25 complexity perplexity
239.25–26 still capable of these primitive sequences. still perfectly capable of these rather primitive sequences of feeling.
239.27 but was but she was
239.28 the accident. this accident.
239.28 remarked declared
239.29 respectable person? good woman?
239.30 a crude proposition, rather a rough statement;
239.34 of such small estate so poor
239.35–36 in spite of the questionable beauty which had yet not hampered her career, in spite of her being no beauty,
239.42 pretext. excuse.
239.43–44 had bristled with pretensions to elegant learning and published descriptive poems had pretensions to "culture," wrote descriptive poems,
239.45 journals, journals—
240.1–3 the father, lost in the grey American dawn of the situation, but reputed originally rich and wild, having died much earlier. the father having died long before.
240.4 held— thought—
240.7 had liked liked
240.9 year years
240.13–14 not really the featherhead she seemed; all one had to do with her was to observe the simple condition of not such a fool as she seemed; one got on with her perfectly if one observed a single simple condition—that of
240.16 appreciated always appreciated
240.17–18 he rather felt she let down their common name. he was rather ashamed of her.
240.19–20 her shrillness, her egotism, her violations of taste and above all of truth: her loudness, her want of repose. She displeased him;
240.20 acted badly acted
240.22 to whom the truth should be habitually sacred. who should always speak the truth.
240.23–24 times her visitor had, in half an hour, profaned it: fibs her visitor had told her;
240.27 how base how nasty

240.29 Washington; or St. Petersburg;
240.33 account of this passage, account of her conversation with this plaintive butterfly;
240.37 had meanwhile had
240.41 reached the banks of the Arno arrived in Florence
240.42–44 took her in from head to foot, and after a pang of despair determined to endure her. comprehended her, and, after a moment's concentrated reflection, determined to like her.
240.44–241.2 She mightn't be inhaled as a rose, but she might be grasped as a nettle. Madame Merle genially squeezed her into insignificance, To like her was impossible; but the intenser sentiment might be managed. Madame Merle managed it beautifully,
241.3 liberality event
241.3–4 intelligence. breadth of mind.
241.6 called at came to the
241.11 uttered openly expressed
241.13–14 goodness knew what strong comedy Heaven knows what genial pleasantries
241.14 the all-judging the incisive Miss Stackpole
241.14–15 British backer. British ally.
241.16 candidly artlessly
241.16–17 a positive intellectual adventure. an intellectual flirtation.
241.20–21 how what she did, how what *they* did—and they had done things!— would look. how it would look.
241.22 anything it
241.23 if whether
241.24 *would* would
241.25 break down first. stop first.
241.26 breaking down. stopping at all.
241.26 had as we know, had
241.27 on upon
241.34 she Miss Stackpole
241.37–38 The admission costs her historian a pang, It is mortifying to be obliged to confess it,
242.6 had been bred was brought up
242.7 Latin and Whyte-Melville, Latin,
242.16 trusty companion well-tested companion
242.17 of other calls on this lady's attention, that she had other calls upon her sympathy,
242.19 She This lady
242.27–28 One of Isabel's preparations consisted of her seeing Isabel saw
242.29 mentioning mentioned
242.30 commented. said;
242.31 on that wonderful ground." there."
242.32 She scarcely faltered. She hesitated a moment.
242.36 rave about it." like it."
242.37–38 because, poor old dear—the Niobe of Nations, you know—it has been spoiled?" because it's spoiled?"
242.39 often," he smiled often.
243.3 said Isabel promptly. said Isabel, smiling.

243.6 enquired. suggested.
243.18 observed. suggested.
243.20 Miss Archer. Isabel.
243.21 she concurred; said the girl;
243.28 remarked announced,
243.32 and and that
243.35 rejoice am glad
244.3 conceded. remarked.
244.9 talkative grace conversational smile
244.11 cast her." dropped her!"
244.12 He took it almost gaily. Osmond gave a laugh.
244.15 Gilbert Osmond. Osmond.
244.18 her guest her
244.18–19 his friend Madame Merle
244.26 spoke in his own sense. said to Madame Merle, with a considerable appearance of earnestness—
244.29 "It does me good "I like
244.31 described her, said,
244.32 capable, I feel, she is capable
244.34 "Too many ideas." "She has too many ideas."
244.40 her friend Osmond
244.44–245.1 I may not attempt to report in its fulness our young woman's response to the deep appeal of Rome, I shall not undertake to give an account of Isabel's impressions of Rome,
245.2 the pavement the ancient pavement
245.3–4 her impression her perception of the endless interest of the place
245.4–5 expected of a person of her freshness and her eagerness. expected in a young woman of her intelligence and culture.
245.9 strongly moved her, but moved her all inwardly. excited her, but she was quietly excited.
245.10 talked spoke
245.12–13 dropping on her an intensity of observation. By her own measure dropping an eye of observation upon her. To her own knowledge
245.14–15 to take these hours for the happiest she was ever to know. to believe that these were to be on the whole the happiest hours of her life.
245.15 terrible mighty
245.15–19 to her, but that of something altogether contemporary would suddenly give it wings that it could wave in the blue. Her consciousness was so mixed that she scarcely knew where the different parts of it would lead her, upon her, but it was interfused in the strangest, suddenest, most capricious way, with the fresh, cool breath of the future. Her feelings were so mingled that she scarcely knew whither any of them would lead her,
245.19 a repressed ecstasy a kind of repressed ecstasy
245.22 her Murray. in "Murray."
245.22–23 confessed to the psychological moment. was in capital condition.
245.27 on upon

245.30 descended gone down
245.35 traceable which are traceable
245.36–37 overjangled iron grooves which express the intensity of American life. iron grooves which mark the course of the American horse-car.
245.38–39 vague pedestal leaned formless pedestal were thrown
245.40–41 whom it was apparently delightful to her to hear speak of Julius Caesar as a "cheeky old boy," in whose Latin reminiscences she was apparently much engrossed,
246.2 was on view was going on
246.5 of interest. interesting.
246.6 weary who was weary
246.6 admonished charged
246.8 taste—she taste, and she
246.9 briefly alone. alone.
246.11 wanted a short solitude, desired a quarter of an hour's solitude,
246.13 about around
246.17 charged with a more active appeal. more contemporaneous.
246.27 baring his head to her perceptibly pale surprise. smiling a little, blushing a good deal, and raising his hat.
246.28 as she rose. getting up.
246.29 you. I turned you," he said. "I turned
246.31 She Isabel
246.31 her to explain. her.
246.32 work digging
246.34 she Isabel
246.34–36 her now; he had recovered his balance and seemed to wish to show it, though very kindly. her; he had stopped smiling; he folded his arms with a kind of deliberation.
246.38 but sat and then she sat
246.39 "Don't "But don't
246.39 you," you,"
247.2–3 He managed not to be awkward, but he wasn't easy, and after a longer look at the girl he came down to nature. He spoke with visible embarrassment; this unexpected meeting caused him an emotion he was unable to conceal. He looked at Isabel a moment, and then he said, abruptly—
247.5 She took it all humanely. She looked up at him, gently.
247.8 she Isabel
247.13 to which, of which,
247.13 put asked
247.14 somewhat missed catching the answer; did not always heed the answer;
247.16 He repeated Lord Warburton, though he tried hard to seem easy, was agitated; he repeated
247.19–20 He began abruptly to pass from the impunity of things to their solemnity, and from their being delightful to their being impossible. He had abrupt alternations of gaiety and gravity; he appeared at one moment to seek his neighbor's eye and at the next to avoid it.
247.21 had been seemed to have been

247.25 pleasant steady eyes, clear grey eye,
247.26 seasoning, brownness,
247.26 minimising manner modest manner,
247.30–35 him. He had kept, evidently in spite of shocks, every one of his merits—properties these partaking of the essence of great decent houses, as one might put it; resembling their innermost fixtures and ornaments, not subject to vulgar shifting and removable only by some whole break-up. They talked of the matters naturally Lord Warburton. He was evidently as likeable as before, and the tone of his voice, which she had formerly thought delightful, was as good as an assurance that he would never change for the worse. They talked about the matters that were naturally
247.38 then of then
247.40–41 and it said so much more than either had said that it scarce needed his final words. and she knew what he was thinking of. His eyes were fixed on the ground; but at last he raised them and said gravely—
247.42 I've never had I have never got
247.44 laughed Isabel, said Isabel with a laugh,
247.46 for them," about them,"
248.1 that touched that might have touched
248.3–4 You know how You know that
248.4 But she Isabel
248.4–5 there would be such a flatness it seemed to her there would be a certain flatness
248.10 She Isabel
248.10 to to saying—
248.10–11 hardly struck her as improvement hardly seemed to her an improvement
248.13 her companion Lord Warburton
248.15 all still as as
248.16–17 threw herself back with a sort of inward triumph on the answer found it good to think that she had given him the answer
248.21 strange elation. quickened reflections.
248.25–26 she got up with a small conscious majesty, Isabel got up,
248.32 somebody else. some one else.
248.37–40 This instant at which I speak to you shows me again exactly how, to my great misfortune, you just insuperably charm me. There—I can't say less. (Omitted.)
248.40 I don't mean, however, to insist; However, I don't mean to trouble you now;
248.41 a few minutes a moment
248.42 was, upon my honour, was
248.43–44 self-control, and self-control, as I say, and
248.44–249.3 He might have been addressing a small committee—making all quietly and clearly a statement of

importance; aided by an occasional look at a paper of notes concealed in his hat, which he had not again put on. And the committee, assuredly, would have felt the point proved. He spoke plainly and simply, in a low tone of voice, in a matter-of-fact way. There might have been something impressive, even to a woman of less imagination than the one he addressed, in hearing this brilliant, brave-looking gentleman express himself so modestly and reasonably.

249.5–7 she added in a tone of which she tried to keep up the kindness and keep down the meaning: then she added, with a smile—

249.8 she was prompt to ask she asked kindly

249.9 request requested

249.9–12 He made for the moment no further reference to their great question, but dipped again into shallower and safer waters. But he wished to know when He said nothing more about his own feelings, but returned to those more objective topics they had already touched upon. Presently he asked her when

249.20 His flushed smile, for a little, seemed to sound her. Lord Warburton looked at her a moment, with an uncomfortable smile.

249.27–28 she said with a compassion intended to be good for both of them. said Isabel, with a melancholy smile.

249.30 *me* me

249.34 you." you" he promised, very gently.

249.36 leave." leave," he suggested.

249.37 leave to leave—to

249.38–39 "I'll keep it down. I'll keep it down always." "I will be silent," he said; "silent always."

249.43–44 Poor Ralph hailed his friend with joy qualified by wonder, Ralph Touchett gave signs of greeting to Lord Warburton,

250.1–3 Ralph and his English neighbor greeted with the austerity with which, after long separations, English neighbours greet, Ralph and his friend met each other with undemonstrative cordiality.

250.4–5 But she soon established her relation to the crisis. *(Omitted.)*

250.6 sir." sir," she soon remarked.

250.11 laughed the master of Lockleigh. said the master of Lockleigh, good-humouredly.

250.13 hilarity, good-humour,

250.22–23 Lord Warburton laughed again. said Lord Warburton, laughing.

250.23 took pleasure in that note; was glad to hear him laugh;

250.23–24 small sigh little sigh

250.24 kept their course took their way

250.25–26 over two long letters writing two long letters—

250.30 to vespers to hear vespers

250.36 a proof an example

250.37–38 frank—not even dumbly importunate or remotely intense. He thus left her frank; he made not even a tacit appeal, but left it for her

250.42 her they her that they

251.1 by proving the superior strain of his sincerity. by behaving heroically.

251.3–5 knew the superior strain of everything about him, and nothing he could now do was required to light the view. knew already he was a good fellow, and nothing he could do would add to this conviction.

251.5–7 affected her as a complication of the wrong sort—she liked so complications of the right. made her vaguely uneasy.

251.7 said said that

251.8 her Isabel

251.9 he must follow his convenience. it would be a pleasure to see him again.

251.19 rose and dizzily rose. received an extension.

251.20 she paid and paid

251.21 the seated sublime. the visible grandeur.

251.22–23 she feared for instance she was afraid

251.29 conflict or scandal. mutual scandal.

251.31–32 obliged in candour obliged

251.36 with his lordship, with Lord Warburton,

251.38 to them towards them

251.43 looking beyond the dense group above the heads of the dense group

251.45 slope sloping

252.2–3 move off with her. turn away again.

252.3 could only accompany him; for a moment did the same;

252.6–7 all the forms—he appeared to have multiplied them on this occasion to suit the place. a formal salutation.

252.8 as she put out her hand. putting out her hand.

252.11 she decided to say. said Isabel.

252.12 he promptly returned. Gilbert Osmond murmured, smiling.

252.13 looked away; turned away;

252.13 watching looking at

252.14 remembered it to be remembered that it was

252.17–18 She repaired any betrayal by mentioning to each companion Isabel sought refuge from her slight agitation in mentioning to each gentleman

252.19–20 emerged from made his way out of

252.22 since for

252.23–25 appeared to take the case as not committing him to joy. He didn't hang back, however, from civility, and presently observed to Isabel, with due benevolence, that exhibited symptoms of surprise which might not perhaps have seemed flattering to Mr. Osmond. It must be added, however, that these manifestations were momentary, and Ralph was presently able to say to his cousin, with due jocularity, that

252.26 her. Miss Stackpole her. His greeting to Mr. Osmond was apparently frank; that is, the two men shook hands and looked at each other. Miss Stackpole

252.27 Mr. Osmond the new-comer

252.29 and even than little and little

252.32 unnatural people. unpleasant people.

252.34–35 was meanwhile enquiring of our young lady. asked of Isabel.

252.36–37 she contented herself with replying. said that girl.

252.39–40 to feel in the greatest of human temples?" she asked with rather a liking for her phrase. to feel —in a church?" Isabel asked, with a faint but interested smile.

252.44 had referred to had said to her

253.2 fellow gentleman

253.3 demanded. inquired.

253.9–33
"Three or four weeks."
"Does she like him?"
"She's trying to find out."
"And will she?"
"Find out—?" Ralph asked.
"Will she like him?"
"Do you mean will she accept him?"
"Yes," said Lord Warburton after an instant; "I suppose that's what I horribly mean."
"Perhaps not if one does nothing to prevent it," Ralph replied.
His lordship stared a moment, but apprehended. "Then we must be perfectly quiet?"
"As quiet as the grave. And only on the chance!" Ralph added.
"The chance she may?"
"The chance she may not?"
Lord Warburton took this at first in silence, but he spoke again. "Is he awfully clever?"
"Awfully, " said Ralph.
His companion thought. "And what else?"
"What more do you want?" Ralph groaned.
"Do you mean what more does she?"
Ralph took him by the arm to turn him: they had to rejoin the others. "She wants nothing that we can give her."
"Ah well, if she won't have You—!" said his lordship handsomely as they went.
"No, about a fortnight."
"Does she like him?"
"Yes, I think she does."
"Is he a good fellow?"
Ralph hesitated a moment. "No, he's not," he said, at last.
"Why then does she like him?" pur-

sued Lord Warburton, with noble *naiveté*.
"Because she's a woman."
Lord Warburton was silent a moment. "There are other men who *are* good fellows," he presently said, "and them—and them—"
"And them she likes also!" Ralph interrupted, smiling.
"Oh, if you mean she likes him in that way!" And Lord Warburton turned round again. As far as he was concerned, however, the party was broken up. Isabel remained in conversation with the gentleman from Florence till they left the church, and her English lover consoled himself by lending such attention as he might to the strains which continued to proceed from the choir.

253.39 after the easy Italian fashion; in accordance with the time-honoured Italian custom;

253.40 when after

254.5 their that their

254.6 recess *entr'acte*

254.7 with his eyes on the interesting pair; he asked himself if watching the interesting pair in the box, and asking himself whether

254.8 the harmony. their harmonious colloquy.

254.8 he judged it became apparent

254.9–10 There should be no marked holding off. (Omitted.)

254.11 met he met

254.12 his hat at the inclination of ennui with his hat in the attitude of *ennui*

254.15 was Ralph's greeting. Ralph remarked.

254.16 which you've yet deserted." that you have deserted."

254.17 has a has got a

254.19 they they

254.27–28 large mock-melancholy. low-voiced mock-melancholy.

254.32–34 where Isabel's welcome was as to a friend so honourably old that he vaguely asked himself what queer temporal province she was annexing. where he received a very gracious welcome from the more attractive of its occupants.

254.36–39 sat blandly apart and silent, as if repudiating competence in the subjects of allusion now probable. It struck her second visitor that Miss Archer had, in operatic conditions, a radiance, even a slight exaltation; sat very quietly, scarcely mingling in the somewhat disjointed talk in which Lord Warburton engaged with Isabel. It seemed to the latter gentleman that Miss Archer looked very pretty; he even thought she looked excited;

254.41–42 Her talk with him moreover pointed to presence of mind; Her talk with him betrayed little agitation.

255.2–4 **what business had she then with such arts and such felicities, above all with such tones of reparation—preparation? Her voice had tricks of sweetness, but why play them on *him*?** what business had she then to have such soft, reassuring tones in her voice?
255.6 **him** Lord Warburton
255.7 **behind and** behind,
255.8 **remained** sat
255.8–9 **his elbows** with his elbows
255.13 **kept his corner.** remained in his corner.
255.16–18 **but it didn't prevent his being puzzled again. Why should she mark so one of his values—quite the wrong one—when she would have nothing to do with another, which was quite the right?** and then he was puzzled again. Why had she so sweet a voice—such a friendly accent?
255.22 **tragic** tragical
255.25 **he had retired.** the visitor had gone.
255.30–31 **wretched human beings?"** human beings?"
255.31 **has** he has
256.2–3 **talking to *you* over something with a neat top-finish of broken glass."** talking to you over a fence!"
256.6–17 **"Well enough for all the use I have for him."**
"And how much of a use is that?"
"Well, I like to like him."
"'Liking to like'—why, it makes a passion!" said Osmond.
"No"—she considered—"keep that for liking to *dis*like."
"Do you wish to provoke me then," Osmond laughed, "to a passion for *him*?"
She said nothing for a moment, but then met the light question with a disproportionate gravity. "No, Mr. Osmond; I don't think I should ever dare to provoke you. Lord Warburton, at any rate," she more easily added, "is a very nice man."
"Of great ability?" her friend enquired.
"Well enough."
"Do you like him?"
"Very much."
"Is he a man of ability?"
256.22 **high favour!** favour.
256.23 **Isabel considered him with interest.** Isabel gave a serious smile.
256.26–32 **it wouldn't hurt a mouse. I don't want to destroy the people—I only want to *be* them. You see it would destroy only myself."**
"You'd like to be the Pope?" said Isabel.
"I should love it—but I should have gone in for it earlier. But why"—Osmond reverted—"do you speak of your friend as poor?"
"Women—when they are very, very good—sometimes** it is very platonic.

Why do you call him poor?"
"Women usually
256.34 **and with** with
256.37 **fresh.** novel.
256.42 **stood** was standing
257.2 **had his place,** was numbered,
257.4 **addressed her alertly enough,** spoke to her with all his usual geniality,
257.6 **must bid** should bid
257.6–7 **Isabel, inconsequently enough, was now sorry** I shall not undertake to explain why, but Isabel was sorry
257.7 **This** It
257.9 **naming her regret,** saying she was sorry,
257.10–11 **journey; which made him look at her rather unlightedly.** journey. He looked at her with a somewhat heavy eye.
257.11–12 **you'll think me very 'volatile.'** you think me rather inconsistent," he said.
257.13 **to stop."** to stay a while."
257.17–18 **quite dismally.** rather dismally.
257.21 **a moment.** for a moment.
257.28 **but soon,** and then,
257.31 **she smiled.** said Isabel smiling.
257.33 **glorious room,** beautiful room,
257.34–35 **centre of the circle of these presences, regarding them** middle of the circle of statues, looking at them
257.39–40 **quietude; which, as with a high door closed for the ceremony, slowly drops on the spirit the large white mantle of peace.** quietude. It soothes and moderates the spirit, it purifies the imagination.
258.1 **deep stillness** great stillness
258.5 **mildly human.** perfectly human.
258.6–8 **wondering to what, of their experience, their absent eyes were open, and how, to our ears, their alien lips would sound.** seeing life between their gazing eyelids and purpose in their marble lips.
258.11 **glad again,** glad,
258.11–13 **At last, however, her attention lapsed, drawn off by a deeper tide of life.** At the last her thoughts wandered away from them, solicited by images of a vitality more complete.
258.13 **came in,** came into the room,
258.17 **toward** towards
258.17 **and** and with
258.18 **enquiring,** bright, inquiring,
258.18 **quite appealing** appealing
258.19 **alone,** alone," he said,
258.20 **she** Isabel
258.20–21 **Antinous and the Faun** circle of sculpture.
258.22 **them** this
258.23–24 **ago." She got up, speaking with intention** ago," said Isabel, getting up. She spoke, with intention,
258.25–26 **which contributed for him to the interest of his question.** but it did not prevent him from giving a laugh.

**258.30–31 Gilbert Osmond returned, and
with such happy hilarity** Gilbert Osmond exclaimed, so humourously

258.32 know knew

**258.36–37 by declining so noble a
hand.** by rejecting the splendid offer
of a British aristocrat.

**258.38–39 this particular patriciate; not
so much for its distinction, which he
thought easily surpassable, as for its
solid actuality. He** the British aristocracy—he

258.40 his star Providence

**258.40–41 appointing him to an English
dukedom, and he could** making him
an English duke—and could

258.41–42 such conduct as Isabel's this
conduct.

258.42 might marry should marry

**259.1–4 Ralph Touchett, in talk with his
excellent friend, had rather markedly
qualified, as we know, his recognition
of Gilbert Osmond's personal merits;
but he might really have felt himself
illiberal in the light of that gentleman's conduct** Ralph Touchett, for
reasons best known to himself, had
seen fit to say that Gilbert Osmond
was not a good fellow; but this assertion was not borne out by the gentleman's conduct.

259.5 Osmond He

**259.6–10 and ended by affecting them
as the easiest of men to live with.
Who wouldn't have seen that he could
command, as it were, both tact and
gaiety?—which perhaps was exactly
why Ralph had made his old-time look
of superficial sociability a reproach to
him. Even Isabel's invidious kinsman**
and gave every indication of being an
easy man to live with. It was impossible not to feel that he had excellent
points, and indeed this is perhaps why
Ralph Touchett made his want of
good-fellowship a reproach to him.
Even Ralph

259.11 associate. companion.

**259.12–19 his knowledge of the right
fact, his production of the right word,
as convenient as the friendly flicker of
a match for your cigarette. Clearly he
was amused—as amused as a man
could be who was so little ever surprised, and that made him almost applausive. It was not that his spirits
were visibly high—he would never, in
the concert of pleasure, touch the big
drum by so much as a knuckle: he
had a mortal dislike to the high, ragged note, to what he called random
ravings.** his knowledge universal, his
manners were the gentlest in the
world. His spirits were not visibly
high; it was difficult to think of Gilbert Osmond as boisterous; he had a
mortal dislike to loudness or eagerness.

259.19–20 sometimes of too precipitate

a readiness. sometimes too eager, too
pronounced.

**259.21–22 as smooth to his general need
of her as handled ivory to the
palm.** as bright and soft as an April
cloud.

259.23 he was not personally loud,
Osmond was not loud,

259.24 he knew a complacency he had
a gaiety

259.33 the occasions the pleasant occasions

**259.35–38 He took his pleasures in gen-
eral singly; he was too often—he
would have admitted that—too sorely
aware of something wrong, something
ugly; the fertilising dew of a conceivable felicity too seldom descended on
his spirit.** In general Osmond took his
pleasures singly; he was usually disgusted with something that seemed to
him ugly or offensive; his mind was
rarely visited with moods of comprehensive satisfaction.

259.42 he had the irritation of satiety,
he had never been spoiled;

260.1–2 he used inwardly to repeat. he
used to repeat to himself.

**260.2–5 thoroughly have earned it." He
was too apt to reason as if "earning"
his boon consisted above all of covertly aching for it and might be confined to that exercise.** have earned it
well."

260.5 void of it, also, void of success

**260.5–7 he might indeed have suggested
to a spectator here and there that he
was resting on vague laurels.** a very
moderate amount of reflection would
have assured him of this.

260.9 arduous difficult

260.9 but had but it had

260.10 that is had that is, it had

260.11 it in him it was in him

**260.12–13 to have something or other to
show for his "parts"—to show somehow or other—** to succeed greatly in
something or other—

**260.14–24 conditions attached to any
marked proof of rarity had affected
him more and more as gross and detestable; like the swallowing of mugs
of beer to advertise what one could
"stand." If an anonymous drawing on
a museum wall had been conscious
and watchful it might have known this
peculiar pleasure of being at last and
all of a sudden identified—as from the
hand of a great master—by the so high
and so unnoticed fact of style. His
"style" was what the girl had discovered with a little help; and now, beside herself enjoying it, she should
publish it to the world without his
having any of the trouble. She should
do the thing for him, and he would
not have waited in vain.** conditions
attached to success became so various
and repulsive that the idea of making
an effort gradually lost its charm. It

was not dead, however; it only slept; it revived after he had made the acquaintance of Isabel Archer. Osmond had felt that any enterprise in which the chance of failure was at all considerable would never have an attraction for him; to fail would have been unspeakably odious, would have left an ineffaceable stain upon his life. Success was to seem in advance definitely certain—certain, that is, on this one condition, that the effort should be an agreeable one to make. That of exciting an interest on the part of Isabel Archer corresponded to this description, for the girl had pleased him from the first of his seeing her. We have seen that she thought him "fine"; and Gilbert Osmond returned the compliment. We have also seen (or heard) that he had a great dread of vulgarity, and on this score his mind was at rest with regard to our young lady. He was not afraid that she would disgust him or irritate him; he had no fear that she would even, in the more special sense of the word, displease him. If she was too eager, she could be taught to be less so; that was a fault which diminished with growing knowledge. She might defy him, she might anger him; this was another matter from displeasing him, and on the whole a less serious one. If a woman were ungraceful and common, her whole quality was vitiated, and one could take no precautions against that; one's own delicacy would avail little. If, however, she were only wilful and high-tempered, the defect might be managed with comparative ease; for had one not a will of one's own that one had been keeping for years in the best condition—as pure and keen as a sword protected by its sheath?

Though I have tried to speak with extreme discretion, the reader may have gathered a suspicion that Gilbert Osmond was not untainted by selfishness. This is rather a coarse imputation to put upon a man of his refinement; and it behoves us at all times to remember the familiar proverb about those who live in glass houses. If Mr. Osmond was more selfish than most of his fellows, the fact will still establish itself. Lest it should fail to do so, I must decline to commit myself to an accusation so gross; the more especially as several of the items of our story would seen to point the other way. It is well known that there are few indications of selfishness more conclusive (on the part of a gentleman at least) than the preference for a single life. Gilbert Osmond, after having tasted of matrimony, had spent a succession of years in the full enjoyment of recovered singleness. He was familiar with the simplicity of purpose, the

lonely liberties, of bachelorhood. He had reached that period of life when it is supposed to be doubly difficult to renounce these liberties, endeared as they are by long association; and yet he was prepared to make the generous sacrifice. It would seem that this might fairly be set down to the credit of the noblest of our qualities—the faculty of self-devotion. Certain it is that Osmond's desire to marry had been deep and distinct. It had not been notorious; he had not gone about asking people whether they knew a nice little girl with a little money. Money was an object; but this was not his manner of proceeding, and no one knew—or even greatly cared—whether he wished to marry or not. Madame Merle knew—that we have already perceived. It was not that he had told her; on the whole he would not have cared to tell her. But there were things of which she had no need to be told—things as to which she had a sort of creative intuition. She had recognised a truth that was none the less pertinent for being very subtle: the truth that there was something very imperfect in Osmond's situation as it stood. He was a failure, of course; that was an old story; to Madame Merle's perception he would always be a failure. But there were degrees of ineffectiveness, and there was no need of taking one of the highest. Success, for Gilbert Osmond, would be to make himself felt; that was the only success to which he could now pretend. It is not a kind of distinction that is officially recognised—unless indeed the operation be performed upon multitudes of men. Osmond's line would be to impress himself not largely but deeply; a distinction of the most private sort. A single character might offer the whole measure of it; the clear and sensitive nature of a generous girl would make space for the record. The record of course would be complete if the young lady should have a fortune, and Madame Merle would have taken no pains to make Mr. Osmond acquainted with Mrs. Touchett's niece if Isabel had been as scantily dowered as when first she met her. He had waited all these years because he wanted only the best, and a portionless bride naturally would not have been the best. He had waited so long in vain that he finally almost lost his interest in the subject—not having kept it up by venturesome experiments. It had become improbable that the best was now to be had, and if he wished to make himself felt, there was soft and supple little Pansy, who would evidently respond to the slightest pressure. When at last the best did present itself Osmond recognised it like a gentleman. There was therefore no incongruity in his wishing to marry —it was his own idea of success, as well as that which Madame Merle, with her old-time interest in his affairs, entertained for him. Let it not, however, be supposed that he was guilty of the error of believing that Isabel's character was of that passive sort which offers a free field for domination. He was sure that she would constantly act—act in the sense of enthusiastic concession.

260.25 time fixed time which had been fixed

260.25 departure return to Florence,

260.26–27 running as follows: which ran as follows:

260.27 June for Bellaggio, June, Bellaggio,

260.29–30 different views, no other views,

260.30 let her aunt know wrote to her aunt that

260.33–34 in the cool shadow of Saint Peter's. among the Seven Hills.

260.34 would should

260.35 It might be months It might be long,

260.36 exchange conversation

260.37 occupied by our friends which our friends occupied

260.42 Henrietta Miss Stackpole

260.44 formed in railway-carriages several that formed several in railway carriages, which

261.5 For Osmond To Osmond

261.5 ugly to distress; painfully ugly;

261.6 were like vulgar, bragging, lying talk. made him suffer.

261.9–10 to pursue her study. to go on with her reading.

261.20 in into

261.24 bent, bent down,

261.24 Ampère. Ampère a little.

261.26 it. You've it," she said at last. "You have

261.29 She Isabel

261.38 your own." your own life."

261.39 She Isabel

261.40 is bad, is stupid art." is bad art."

261.41 very clear and very good." very good."

261.43 she went on. Isabel continued.

262.1–2 jocose. Isabel had in fact her solemnity; he had seen it jocular. Isabel was almost tremulously serious; he had seen her so

262.10 what has put it what put it

262.15–16 smiled Osmond. said Osmond, smiling.

262.16 as if it were a point to be made, more gravely,

262.20–24 to qualify these too few days in Rome, which she might musingly have likened to the figure of some small princess of one of the ages of dress overmuffled in a mantle of state and dragging a train that it took pages or historians to hold up—that this fe- licity was coming to an end. to qualify her little visit to Rome—was coming to an end.

262.24 of the time of this episode

262.25 was a reflexion this reflection

262.27–28 danger they should never meet again, danger that they should not meet again,

262.29–31 and her adventure wore already the changed, the seaward face of some romantic island from which, after feasting on purple grapes, she was putting off while the breeze rose. and these few days had been interfused with the element of success.

262.34–36 greater the pity that the chapter was closed; she felt for a moment a pang that touched the source of tears. greater was the pity that this happy week was over; for a moment she felt her heart throb with a kind of delicious pain.

262.41 "Well, doing "Doing

262.42–43 Doing all the vain things one likes Doing what we like

262.44 his quiet quickness. his quick responsiveness.

263.2 I want I wish

263.7 'cross.' " disagreeable."

263.10–11 Osmond spoke with a noble earnestness. "They must be great moments to see." Osmond spoke very simply—almost solemnly. "There must be something very noble about that."

263.12 Isabel nervously cried. the girl exclaimed, laughing, yet frowning.

263.14 leaned forward, a hand was leaning forward, with a hand

263.18 She instantly rose. Isabel instantly rose from her chair.

263.18 am am

263.19–20 He sat there raising his eyes to her. And Osmond sat there, looking up at her.

263.23 a while a moment

263.26 "I'm absolutely in love "I am thoroughly in love

263.29 who spoke for his own needed relief. spoke for his own relief.

263.29–34 her eyes: this time they obeyed the sharpness of the pang that suggested to her somehow the slipping of a fine bolt—backward, forward, she couldn't have said which. The words he had uttered made him, as he stood there, beautiful and generous, invested him as with the golden air of early autumn; Isabel's eyes—they were caused by an intenser throb of that pleasant pain I spoke of a moment ago. There was an immense sweetness in the words he had uttered;

263.35–36 as she had retreated in the other cases before a like encounter. as she had retreated in two or three cases that we know of in which the same words had been spoken.

263.36–37 she answered with an intensity that expressed the dread she an-

swered at last, in a tone of entreaty which had nothing of conventional modesty, but which expressed the dread

263.40–43 the sense of something within herself, deep down, that she supposed to be inspired and trustful passion. It was there like a large sum stored in a bank—which there was a terror in having to begin to spend. If she touched it, it would all come out. the consciousness of what was in her own heart. It was terrible to have to surrender herself to that.

264.5 considerately inclined to her, bending forward a little,

264.8 his firm, refined, slightly ravaged face. his keen, expressive, emphatic face.

264.11 thinking and thought that

264.13 any such complacency. this complacency.

264.16 and it struck her as and thought it

264.16–17 what stupidly came to her. the word that came to her.

264.26 "I don't at all *know* you," she added "I don't know you," said Isabel

264.32 she emphatically answered— said the girl, with a flash of bright eagerness;

264.34 he laughed, Osmond answered, with a laugh,

264.34 It That

264.41 surrender. After which he added: surrender to him. And then in a moment he added,

265.1 but wouldn't but he would not

265.2 more. more," he said.

265.9 Osmond was Osmond for a moment was

265.11 very proper. all the same.

265.15 Isabel gravely asked. said Isabel, very gravely.

265.17 he Osmond

265.20 pleaded. cried.

265.21 She Isabel

265.24–25 hasn't at all hasn't

265.30 and seated and then she seated

265.30 slowly and slowly,

265.33 What had happened That which had happened

265.35–36 —that sublime principle somehow broke down. —her imagination halted.

265.38–39 Her imagination, as I say, now hung back: Her imagination stopped, as I say;

265.44–266.1 She returned on the morrow to Florence, under her cousin's escort, Under her cousin's escort, Isabel returned on the morrow to Florence,

266.1–2 usually restive under railway discipline, usually he was not fond of railway journeys,

266.3 that which

266.5 a larger a still larger

266.6–7 carried out executed

266.7 aid. assistance.

266.7 three days but three days

266.10 call on go and see

266.11 an idea a plan

266.16 "forever" "for ever"

266.18–19 this fortunate woman Madame Merle

266.19 take a look at call upon

266.20 but didn't mention she did not mention to her

266.22 Madame Merle the elder lady

266.23–24 to pay the child a little visit before I go off." to take a look at the child before I go into the country."

266.25 Isabel reasonably said: "reasonably" said Isabel, reasonably. I say "reasonably,"

266.27 small pilgrimage visit

266.28–29 She was nevertheless prepared to sacrifice this mystic sentiment to her great consideration for her friend. Nevertheless, to her great consideration for Madame Merle she was prepared to sacrifice this mystic sentiment.

266.30 That personage finely meditated. "After all, why" Her friend meditated, with her usual suggestive smile. "After all," she presently said, "why

266.38 it doesn't signify." it doesn't matter."

266.43–44 said the elder woman in mild mockery. said Madame Merle, with a smile of genial mockery.

267.2 audibly reflected. reflected audibly.

267.6 "*don't* don't

267.8–9 the winding way the charming winding way

267.10 her friend Madame Merle

267.10 no one's being no one being

267.11–12 this lady, whose voyaging discretion, as a general thing, was rather of the open sea than of the risky channel, this lady, in whose discretion, as a general thing, there was something almost brilliant,

267.16 of doing a thing at all if it had to be sneakingly done? of doing a deed in secret?

267.19–20 sorts of things certain things

267.21 place apartment,

267.23 think she think that she

267.23–24 with rigour. She immediately faithfully. Presently Pansy

267.25 a wide-eyed earnestness of courtesy. the wide-eyed conscientiousness of a sensitive child,

267.26 half an hour, for half-an-hour,

267.26–28 Pansy rose to the occasion as the small, winged fairy in the pantomime soars by the aid of the dissimulated wire— Pansy entertained her like a little lady—

267.29 respectful courteous

267.30–31 she had never had so directly presented to her nose the white flower of cultivated sweetness. as I have said before, she had never seen a child like that.

267.32 the child she

267.32 admiring young woman; keen young lady,

267.34–36 Isabel was fond, ever, of the question of character and quality, of sounding, as who should say, the deep personal mystery, Isabel was fond of psychological problems,

267.37–38 whether this tender slip were not really all-knowing. whether Miss Pansy were not all-knowing.

267.38 the extremity of her candour her infantine serenity

267.40 an unspotted nature? a little neat, orderly character?

267.45 rich gloom—her interview rich-looking gloom—Isabel's interview

268.2–6 a pure white surface, successfully kept so; she had neither art, nor guile, nor temper, nor talent—only two or three small exquisite instincts: for knowing a friend, for avoiding a mistake, for taking care of an old toy or a new frock. Yet to be so tender was to be touching withal, and she could be felt as an easy victim of fate. a pure white surface; she was not clever enough for precocious co-quetries. She was not clever; Isabel could see that; she only had nice feelings. There was something touching about her; Isabel had felt it before; she would be an easy victim of fate.

268.7–9 her own importance; she would easily be mystified, easily crushed: her force would be all in knowing when and where to cling. her own importance; only an exquisite taste, and an appreciation, equally exquisite, of such affection as might be bestowed upon her. She would easily be mystified, easily crushed: her force would be solely in her power to cling.

268.10 her visitor, Isabel,

268.12 She spoke of She talked about

268.13 but felt but she felt

268.14 supplying the information so distinguished a guest giving Isabel the information that so observant a visitor

268.25 have no have got no

268.32 —to marry me. to marry me.

268.41–42 sorry, and he'll be sorry too. sorry for that.

269.1 I'm really I am

269.3 you you

269.13 much much that

269.14 has the idea wishes very much

269.17–18 just a small sound like the squeak of a slate-pencil making flourishes." just a little thread."

269.22–23 held her close, looked at her long. "Be very good," and held her a moment, looking at her.

"Be a good child."

269.26–27 she felt it almost a torment to be obliged to conceal. she felt it to be almost a torment that she was obliged to conceal from the child.

269.35–36 of exhaling into that air where he might still have a subtle sense for it any breath of her charmed state. of leaving an audible trace of her emotion behind.

269.39 the child's sweet slimness the child's little tender person

269.40 looking down at her almost in envy. looking down at her.

269.42 of about

269.43 so near him. near to him.

269.43 no other not another

269.44 once again. once more.

270.1 that opened on the court; which opened into the court;

270.1 her young hostess Pansy

270.2 no further. no further," she said.

270.3 pass this door." go out of this door."

270.12 dazzle gleam

270.18 to Palazzo to the Palazzo

270.19 incidents just narrated. incidents I have just narrated.

270.25–26 woman stood near it for some time, her hands lady stood for some time at the window, with her hands

270.26–29 she gazed abroad with the vagueness of unrest. Too troubled for attention she moved in a vain circle. Yet it could not be in her thought to catch a glimpse gazing into the brilliant aperture in the manner of a person relapsing into reverie. She was preoccupied; she was too restless to sit down, to work, to read. It was evidently not her design, however, to catch a glimpse

270.29 since for

270.31–32 She wished rather to forestall his arrival She was endeavouring rather to anticipate his arrival

270.33–37 Grave she found herself, and positively more weighted, as by the experience of the lapse of the year she had spent in seeing the world. She had ranged, she would have said, through space and surveyed much of mankind, and was therefore now, in her own eyes, a very different person She was extremely grave; not sad exactly, but deeply serious. The lapse of a year may doubtless account for a considerable increase of gravity; though this will depend a good deal upon the manner in which the year has been spent. Isabel had spent hers in seeing the world; she had moved about; she had travelled; she had exerted herself with an almost passionate activity. She was now, to her own sense, a very different person

270.38–39 take the measure of Europe on see Europe upon

270.40–41 she had harvested wisdom and learned a great deal more that she had gathered a rich experience, that she knew a great deal more

271.4 the images that might have been projected on such a field the figures concerned in these combinations

271.6 had come came
271.7–8 her relative. She had left Isabel. She left
271.8 had brought she brought
271.10 toward towards
271.12 had spent spent
271.15 had confined confined
271.19 for in
271.21–30 They had afterwards reached the French capital, which was worshipped, and with costly ceremonies, by Lily, but thought of as noisily vacant by Isabel, who in these days made use of her memory of Rome as she might have done, in a hot and crowded room, of a phial of something pungent hidden in her handkerchief.
Mrs. Ludlow sacrificed, as I say, to Paris, yet had doubts and wonderments not allayed at that altar; and after her husband had joined her found further chagrin in his failure to throw himself into these speculations. Afterwards they had come to Paris, a city beloved by Lily, but less appreciated by Isabel, who in those days was constantly thinking of Rome. Mrs. Ludlow enjoyed Paris, but she was nevertheless somewhat disappointed and puzzled; and after her husband had joined her she was in addition a good deal depressed at not being able to induce him to enter into these somewhat subtle and complex emotions.
271.30 subject; their object;
271.33–34 Mrs. Ludlow's mental motions were sufficiently various. Mrs. Ludlow's feelings were various.
271.35 that young woman Isabel
271.38–39 some member of one of the great aristocracies. some gentleman of rank in one of the foreign countries.
271.40 she had fallen from high communion with the probabilities. she was rather disappointed.
271.43–44 slightly meagre, but scarce the less eminent slender but eminent
272.9 she enjoyed that she enjoyed
272.14 rendered made
272.17 she had had she had
272.18–21 It was more romantic to say nothing, and, drinking deep, in secret, of romance, she was as little disposed to ask poor Lily's advice as she would have been to close that rare volume forever. It entertained her more to say nothing, and she had no idea of asking poor Lily's advice.
272.21–22 discriminations, and could only pronounce her sister's career a strange anti-climax— rich mysteries, and it is no wonder, therefore, that she pronounced her sister's career in Europe rather dull—
272.26 she had lost her courage. her sister was really losing her gaiety.
272.26 uncanny very strange
272.30–31 Our young lady's courage, however, might have been taken as reaching its height after her relations

had gone home. Isabel's gaiety, however—superficially speaking, at least—exhibited itself rather more after her sister had gone home.
272.32 braver things something more poetic
272.32–33 Paris—Paris had sides by which it so resembled New York, Paris—
272.34 close correspondence frequent correspondence
272.35 flights. fancies.
272.38 last days latter days
272.38 that which
272.40 to regale; to have them with her;
273.10 There was a deep thrill in it all, There was something exciting in the feeling,
273.14 our heroine our young lady
273.31–32 her genius her talents
273.34 to see and see
273.35 not presenting herself just yet in Florence, not coming just then to Florence,
273.37 no more use to her than bubbles, no more use than soap-bubbles,
273.39 "would" would
273.42 pretended. seemed.
273.43–274.1 she took it for a sign that Gilbert Osmond was less in question there than formerly. she thought it was a sign that there was nothing going on with Gilbert Osmond.
274.1–2 if he would now find a pretext for going to Rome, whether Mr. Osmond would now go to Rome,
274.2 derived took
274.3 from in
274.3 he had not been he was not
274.13 a cerain incoherence prevailed in her. her restlessness prevailed.
274.14 rapidly and recklessly; rapidly, eagerly, audaciously;
274.15–16 Madame Merle meanwhile, as lady-in-waiting to a princess circulating *incognita*, panted a little in her rear. Madame Merle, for the present, was a most efficient duenna.
274.17–18 all due dignity all necessary dignity
274.18 state. condition.
274.19 tact sagacity
274.19–20 her, effacing herself and accepting the position her; she effaced herself, she accepted the position
274.22 reserved though striking graceful
274.23 patroness the patroness
274.24 client. the client.
274.24–25 states meagerly the impression she made on her friend, would misrepresent the impression she made upon Isabel,
274.25 found thought
274.26 so ample and so easy. a perfectly enlightened woman.
274.27 she that she
274.28 the admirable woman Madame Merle

274.32–33 a positive adventurer, she might say, though originally so plausible, an adventurer of the lowest class,

274.37 her companion Isabel

274.37–38 a person so *éprouvée* could have kept the poor lady had kept

274.40–42 she seemed to see it as professional, as slightly mechanical, carried about in its case like the fiddle of the virtuoso, or blanketed and bridled like the "favourite" of the jockey. she saw that it was, after all, a tolerably artificial bloom.

274.42 She Isabel

274.43 a corner a certain corner

274.44 she Madame Merle

274.44–275.1 something of a public performer, condemned to emerge only in character and in costume. a foreigner.

275.3 "old, old" world, old world,

275.4 different moral or social clime different clime

275.6 She believed then that Isabel believed that

275.8–9 our young woman had a sense in her of values gone wrong or, as they said at the shops, marked down. Isabel suspected that her friend had esoteric views.

275.9 considered, believed,

275.10 differing which differed

275.13 person woman

275.14 whose pride was too high whose nature was too large

275.15–16 Her conception of human motives might, in certain lights, have been acquired at the court of some kingdom in decadence, Her conception of human motives was different from Isabel's,

275.20–21 She had once or twice had a positive scare; since it so affected her to have to exclaim, of her friend, Once or twice Isabel had a sort of fright, but the reader will be amused at the cause of it. Madame Merle, as we know, comprehended, responded, sympathised, with wonderful readiness; yet it had nevertheless happened that her young friend mentally exclaimed—

275.23 shock, left her with a vague dismay shock; it left Isabel with a vague horror

275.24 dismay horror

275.26–27 stood for a high-water-mark in the ˑebb and flow of confidence. left a sort of high-water mark in the development of this delightful intimacy.

275.27 declared her belief that said that, in her belief,

275.28 ceases ceased

275.28 begins ˑbegan

275.29 there being no point there was no point

275.29–30 liking more and liking less. liking a person more and liking him less.

275.31–33 However that might be, the girl had in these days a thousand uses for her sense of the romantic, which was more active than it had ever been. Without estimating the value of this doctrine, I may say that if Isabel's imagination, which had hitherto been so actively engaged on her friend's behalf, began at last to languish, she enjoyed her society not a particle less than before. If their friendship had declined, it had declined to a very comfortable level. The truth is that in these days the girl had other uses for her imagination, which was better occupied than it had ever been.

275.38 remained. been.

275.40 descended came down

275.44 rejoice be very happy

276.1 Palazzo the Palazzo

276.2 She Isabel

276.8 near which where

276.9 matters I have rapidly sketched. matters that I have just rapidly sketched.

276.9–10 not turned to the past, but to the immediate, not thinking of the past, but of the future; of the immediate,

276.14 issue. speculation.

276.14–16 nothing in the least soothing —she had warrant for this, and the conviction doubtless showed in the cloud on her brow. nothing agreeable; Isabel was convinced of this, and the conviction had something to do with her being rather paler than usual.

276.16–20 all clearness reigned in her; she had put away her mourning and she walked in no small shimmering splendour. She only felt older—ever so much, and as if she were "worth more" for it, like some curious piece in an antiquary's collection. she wore her natural brightness of aspect; even deep grief, with this vivid young lady, would have had a certain soft effulgence. She had laid aside her mourning, but she was still very simply dressed, and as she felt a good deal older than she had done a year before, it is probable that to a certain extent she looked so.

276.20 was not at any rate left was not left

276.21 a servant the servant

276.21–22 stood before her with a card on his tray. "Let came in and presented her a card. ¶"Let

276.22 she said, and continued said Isabel, who continued

276.28–29 Whether his sense of maturity had kept pace with Isabel's Whether on his side Mr. Goodwood felt himself older than on the first occasion of our meeting him is a point which

276.30 her Isabel's

276.31 strong and hard, strong, and fresh,

276.32–35 if he had neither innocence nor weakness, so he had no practical philosophy. His jaw showed the same voluntary cast as in earlier days; but a crisis like the present had in it of course something grim. he looked too deliberate, too serious to be young; and too eager, too active to be old. Old he would never be, and this would serve as a compensation for his never having known the age of chubbiness. Isabel perceived that his jaw had quite the same voluntary look that it had worn in earlier days; but she was prepared to admit that such a moment as the present was not a time for relaxation.

276.38 "Poor fellow, "Poor fellow," she mentally murmured,

276.39 a pity he should waste so dreadfully a pity that he should waste

276.41 hoped hoped that

276.43 he Caspar Goodwood

276.44 settle. stay a little.

277.1–2 and generously, generously,

277.4 arrive?" arrive here?"

277.8–9 coming to bury me!" And she forced a smile of encouragement to an easy view coming to a funeral," Isabel said, forcing a smile, in order to offer such encouragement as she might to an easy treatment

277.10 reasoned the matter well out, making it reasoned out the matter elaborately; she had made it

277.11 and falsified that she falsified

277.12 her visitor. him.

277.14 his stiff insistence, an insistence his stiff persistency—a persistency

277.15 such almost

277.15–16 when the dull dark as there was a dull dark

277.16 rested which rested

277.16 as almost like

277.17 I couldn't because I couldn't

277.18 he candidly declared. said Caspar Goodwood, plainly.

277.22 she returned Isabel cried,

277.23 have yet have

277.30–31 with dry deliberateness, with a sort of dry deliberateness,

277.35–36 she became, after a little, irrelevant. she said, after a little, irrelevantly, by way of answer to Mr. Goodwood's speech—

277.37 threw up his head as if calculating. threw up his head a moment, as if he were calculating.

277.41–42 she coldly smiled. said Isabel, smiling.

278.2 she Isabel

278.4 talk of talk about

278.5 been with him come to see him

278.6 you," Isabel then demanded. you?"

278.10–11 didn't want to do that. didn't want to.

278.11 quick enough; soon enough;

278.14–15 come right out," come out,"

278.22 enquired. asked.

278.24 she Isabel

278.27 To which she made answer that she didn't know yet. "I "I don't know yet. I

278.30 he demanded. Caspar Goodwood asked.

278.32–33 asking questions, doing it quite without delicacy. asking questions.

278.33–36 "Who and what then is Mr. Gilbert Osmond?"
"Who and what? Nobody and nothing but a very good and very honourable man.
"What is Mr. Osmond?"
"What is he? Nothing at all but a very good man.

278.40 was, however, small; was certainly small;

278.41–44 from? Where does he belong?"
She had never been so little pleased with the way he said "belawng." "He comes from nowhere.
from?" he went on.
"From nowhere.

279.1 he that he

279.5 flushing all defensively. flushing a little, and defensively.

279.9 very quiet and very simple— very simple—

279.14–15 replied while her patience helped itself by turning a little to hardness. replied, with a smile that had gradually become a trifle defiant.

279.17 a perfect nonentity. a nonentity.

279.20–21 a perfect nonentity. You think he's grand, you think he's great, a nonentity. You think he is a great man,

279.22 she felt this really acute she thought this very clever

279.23–24 a proof of the aid that passion might render perceptions she had never taken for fine. a proof of the clairvoyance of such a feeling as his.

279.30 she accordingly broke out— Isabel broke out—

279.34–35 even just as you are." as you are."

280.4 toward towards

280.7 he said. said Caspar.

280.10–11 on receiving early that day the news he was in Florence and by her leave would come when she received that morning the note in which he told her that he was in Florence, and, with her permission, would come

280.15 full of heavy implications. full of implication.

280.20 that which

280.21 that which

280.23 angry in the way a woman is angry when she has been in the wrong. as angry as a woman who had been in the wrong.

280.34 And if he had not meanwhile If he had not

280.40–41 with such a manner so positively

280.42 She considered this an instant. Isabel was silent an instant.

281.5 no mistake whatever." no mistake at all."

281.7 she Isabel

281.23 He Caspar

281.28–29 she felt the poverty of her presently replying. Isabel murmured.

281.30 afraid I'm knocked up—in any such way as that— afraid I am tired,

281.31 it." that."

281.34 he said without a quaver. he said.

281.35 she answered passionately. she answered, passionately. And he went out.

281.36 gone out gone

281.38 soon smothered, of brief duration,

282.5 she began. she said to her—

282.6 her the girl

282.21–22 without the gentleman's having had to be lashed up? without the gentleman being urged?

282.26 for for

282.30 like him so much." like him."

282.31 "I thought he even pleased you." "I thought you liked him yourself."

282.32 "He did, at one time; "I did,

282.37 since others have done so?" since you did?"

282.38 "Others, at their wildest moments, never wanted "I never wanted

282.39 of of

282.41–42 No one's happy, in such doings, you should know." No one is happy."

282.44 you you

283.9 to have a little." to have some."

283.41 told me told me that

284.21 the girl smiled. said Isabel, smiling.

284.25 Isabel the girl

284.28 shall say will say

284.29 shall talk will talk

284.33–34 the aunt and the niece the two ladies

284.34–35 as good as her word, was as good as her word, and

284.40 American gentleman American

284.40–41 American gentleman who American that

285.2 American gentleman American

285.6–8 in imparting to him the great fact, he showed at first no open knowledge of it. Their prompted talk in telling him the news, he betrayed at first no knowledge of the great fact. Their first talk

285.8 on about

285.11 she wondered if Isabel wondered whether

285.12 if she were whether she was

285.13 made no nearer approach to conventional beauty grew no handsomer

285.16–17 Blighted and battered, but still responsive and still ironic, his face was like a lighted lantern patched with paper and unsteadily held; His face wore its pleasant perpetual smile, which perhaps suggested wit rather than achieved it;

285.28 marking his view of a world with which he appeared to regard a world

285.29 continued presence presence

285.31 They had been sweetened These things were endeared

285.32 the very terms on which it had been given him to be charming. He conditions of his being so charming. Ralph

285.37 exclusively personal. The personality so resulting simply personal. This personality of Ralph's

285.37–40 he had remained proof against the staleness of disease; he had had to consent to be deplorably ill, yet had somehow escaped being formally sick. it had none of the staleness of disease; it was always easy and fresh and genial.

285.42 had allowed him had given him

285.43 she Isabel

285.43 that essence— compassion—

285.45 no great sensibility to feel no great ingenuity to discover

286.1 a bright, free, generous spirit, a dear, bright, generous fellow;

286.3 distressfully dying. dying.

286.4 noted afresh said to herself

286.8 him, her cousin,

286.16 him Ralph

286.17 to regard as to think it

286.18–19 to believe she had better have married to think she had better marry

286.21 opposite. opposite one.

286.23 should she if she would

286.26 most patient and most indulgent. wonderfully good-humoured

286.27 odd he odd that he

286.29 our young woman wearied of waiting; Isabel became impatient;

286.32 Palazzo the Palazzo

286.34 had been was

286.36–37 the person in the world in whom he was most interested was lost. his cousin was lost.

286.39 on on

286.39 his long legs with his long legs

286.42 the girl Isabel

286.44–45 to persuade her of anything sordid or sinister in the man to whose deep art she had succumbed to persuade her that the man to whom she had pledged her faith was a humbug

287.7 Palazzo the Palazzo

287.14 through in

287.22–23 and the warm shade, enclosed and still, made bowers like spacious caves. the warm shade was motionless, and the hot light made it pleasant.

287.32 he had visibly had something to brood over. he was visibly preoccupied.

287.32–33 **she had explained his air of absence partly by** she had attributed his long reveries partly to

287.34 **partly by worries connected with the property** partly to his being troubled about certain arrangements he had made as to the property

287.35 **the fruit of eccentric arrangements** arrangements

287.39 **took** he took

288.1 **too tired."** tired."

288.2 **too tired.** tired.

288.6 **she put to him,** Isabel said,

288.10 **she lightly returned.** said Isabel, lightly.

288.13 **want** wish

288.13 **idea you may have** idea that you have

288.16–17 **Ralph said.** said Ralph.

288.18–19 **leaned back under the protection of Bernini, his head against his marble pedestal,** leaned back, with his head against the marble pedestal of Terpsichore,

288.20 **rests** sides

288.21 **long.** for a long time.

288.24 **high decision.** ingenious purpose.

288.25 **he went on** he said

288.29 **she answered.** said Isabel.

288.35–36 **"It doesn't look to me now, I admit, such an inviting expanse."** "It doesn't seem to me so charming."

288.39 **can't do anything so general.** can't do that.

288.41–42 **as good a corner as possible.** a good corner.

289.6–7 **with rather an absurd smile,** with a rather absurd smile,

289.11 **mildness** gentleness

289.15–16 **" 'Willing to wound and yet afraid to strike'? I'm willing to wound *him*, yes—but not to wound you.** *(Omitted.)*

289.17–18 **it won't be a fortunate way for me to have spoken."** it won't be a nice thing to have said."

289.22 **too touching."** touching."

289.25 **She** Isabel

289.33–34 **and I'm glad you've made it so clear. But you'll suffer by it."** you will suffer for it."

289.44 **she** Isabel

290.8 **you've some special idea;** you have got some idea;

290.12 **move me an inch;** move me at all;

290.19–23 **I didn't think you'd decide for—well, for *that* type."** "What's the matter with Mr. Osmond's type, if it be one? His being so independent, so individual, is what *I* most see in him," the girl declared. I didn't think you would marry a man like Mr. Osmond."

290.25–26 **I confess I haven't facts and items to prove him a villain.** I know nothing against him.

290.27 **grave risk."** risk."

290.28 **grave risk,** risk,

290.28 **as grave** as great

290.29 **back out. I wish to God** recede; I wish

290.31 **reclined** leaned back

290.31 **folding her arms and gazing** folded her arms, and gazed

290.34 **believed** thought

291.1 **little—then** little, and then

291.4–7 **Mr. Osmond's is the finest I know; he's good enough for me, and interesting enough, and clever enough. I'm far more struck with what he has and what he represents than with what he may lack."** Mr. Osmond is the best I know; he is important enough for me."

291.8 **"I had treated myself to a charming vision** "I had a sort of vision

291.9 **observed** said,

291.9 **had amused** amused

291.10 **high destiny** kind of destiny

291.11–13 **or so soon."** "Come down, you say?" "Well, that renders my sense of what has happened to you. so soon." "To come down? What strange expressions you use! Is that your description of my marriage?" "It expresses my idea of it.

291.17 **straight you drop** down you drop

291.18 **"hurts me as if** "as if

291.21 **a project for my career—** planning out my future—

291.26 **she pursued.** the girl asked.

291.27 **plane** line

291.31 **cousin.** Isabel!

291.32–33 **hesitated, then added:** hesitated a moment, then he added,

291.33–34 **sense that Osmond is somehow—well, small."** belief that there's something small in Osmond."

291.34 **the last word with no great assurance;** these last words with a tremor of the voice;

291.35 **afraid** afraid that

291.37 **"Small?" She made it sound immense.** "Something small?" she said reflectively.

291.40 **"It makes one more sure to respect others."** "It's the proper way to respect others."

291.42–43 **one's relation to things—to others.** one's relations.

291.44 **his relation to me.** the relation in which he stands to me.

292.7 **bride.** wife.

292.7 **such a taste—a really exquisite one—** an exquisite taste

292.12 **of you! of** you!" he cried.

292.15 **he** Ralph

292.17 **But "You** "You

292.17 **simply breathed.** murmured.

292.18 **impossible I** impossible that I

292.36 **then went on** then she went on,

293.19 *you* you

293.25 **illumined** illuminated

293.30 **grand,** superb,

293.30–31 **highly solicitous;** eager;

293.31 **all in a passion.** secretly trembling.

293.38 his Lord Warburton's
293.42–43 a very lonely, a very culti-vated and a very honest man—he's not a prodigious proprietor." a man—he is not a proprietor!"
293.45 truth reality
294.3 ardent passionate
294.4 dismally consistent. consistent.
294.5 having invented she had invented
294.6 she loved and loved
294.8 her Isabel's
294.8–9 to meet the requirements of her imagination. to gratify her imagination.
294.10 luxury. privilege.
294.15 he Ralph
294.16–17 a face of elation—absolutely and perversely of gratitude. His oppo-sition had made a face full of a deep elation at his opposition having made
294.18 clearer more clear
294.22 mouthful. mouthful of it.
294.22 told you said to you
294.35 to tell him how little he was ap-proved at Palazzo to tell him that he was not thought well of at the Palazzo
294.37 no great impression little impres-sion
295.4 on Isabel's spirit upon Isabel's mind
295.14 to display to manifest
295.22–23 she had now little free or un-employed emotion for minor needs, she thought on the whole but little about it,
295.14 incident, in fact quite as an ornament, incident
295.26–29 they made her conscious, al-most with awe, of the invidious and remorseless tide of the charmed and possessed condition, great as was the traditional honour and imputed virtue of being in love. they made her feel that there was after all something very invidious in being in love; much as the sentiment was theoretically approved of.
295.30 tragic part; tragical side;
295.32–33 The elation of success, which surely now flamed high in Osmond, emitted meanwhile Gilbert Osmond was not demonstrative; the conscious-ness of success, which must now have flamed high within him, emitted
295.34 took no vulgar form; never took a vulgar form;
295.37 smitten and dedicated state. amorous character.
295.39–40 appearance—which presented indeed no difficulty—of stirred senses and deep intentions. the appearance of devoted intention.
296.2 on a polished, elegant surface? upon a scintillating surface?
296.2 hated disliked
296.4–5 freshened in the reproduction even as "words" by music. His egotism brightened in the reproduction. His egotism, if egotism it was,
296.5 desiring wishing for

296.8–9 talk might become for him a sort of served dessert. conversation might become a sort of perpetual des-sert.
296.9 silver silvery
296.9–10 this perfection perfection
296.12 their union enjoyed the union found
296.12 with among
296.22 had some sign of it, learnt it,
296.24 reserve. want of delight.
296.26 for your not having the shadow of a doubt. your thinking it's all right.
296.27–29 what people of whom I ask nothing think—I'm not even capable perhaps of wanting to know. I've never so concerned myself, God forgive me, what others think. I have never cared much,
296.3 pretend pretend that
296.32–33 Money's a horrid thing to fol-low, but a charming thing to meet. Money is a great advantage.
296.34 proved the limits of my itch for it: proved that I can get on without it;
296.36 than most of the people one sees grubbing and grabbing. than most people.
296.37 your family; your own family;
296.39–40 my business is not to make myself bad blood, my business is not to bother,
296.40 love." "It love. It
296.42–43 and—I won't pretend to deny —brighter and nicer and even stronger. and brighter.
296.44 angry angry that
296.45 flattered myself flattered myself that
297.6 see see that
297.12 Upon my honour, Upon my word,
297.14 capital convictions. excellent be-liefs.
297.15 not mean, not heavy,
297.15–16 any kind of ignorance and dreariness. any dull limitations.
297.16 remarkably fresh, very fresh,
297.16–17 remarkably well-seasoned. We've my poor child well-seasoned. We have got my poor child
297.26–27 at a high level of conscious-ness of the beautiful. of beautiful hours.
297.28 soul mind
297.29 that might gather which gathered
297.29–30 had told told
297.30 she that she
297.31 the act of living, but of that of observing. life, but of observation.
297.34–36 a more primitive need—a need the answer to which brushed away numberless questions, yet grati-fied infinite desires. a more primitive sentiment—a sentiment which answered all questions, satisfied all needs, solved all difficulties.
297.37 situation future
297.39–40 should be able was able

297.40–41 She could surrender to him with a kind of humility, she She

297.42 she was giving. but giving.

298.2–3 sat down a little sat down a while

298.4–5 She found pleasure in walking off, She amused herself with walking off,

298.5–6 then in walking then walking

298.7 approved gave her approbation

298.7–8 the abundance had the personal touch that it was of that demonstrative personal kind which

298.8–12 She watched her indications as if for herself also much depended on them—Pansy already so represented part of the service she could render, part of the responsibility she could face. Her father took so the childish view of her that he She watched her development with a kind of amused suspense; Pansy had already become a little daughter. She was treated so completely as a child that Osmond

298.14 guess; suspect;

298.21 one of his fine, quiet, sincere notes. "It occurs to me that an element in the refinement of his character. ¶"It seems to me

298.29–30 Osmond's artistic, the plastic view, as it somehow appeared, Osmond's aesthetic relish

298.31 more anxiously moral. more moral.

298.32–33 communicated the fact broken the news

298.34 beautiful sister!" sister!"

299.2 woman lady

299.3 arrived came in

299.4 that lady, her aunt,

299.4–5 thought her of an age to thought she was of an age when she should

299.7 her relative, the elder lady,

299.14 this excellent woman's the good woman's

299.16 you?" you?"

299.21 in motion, in agitation— moving;

299.29 a good fortune a great good fortune

299.33 word. word. You don't look at all like the word; it is somehow so ugly,

299.34–35 I don't think you'll ever so much as pinch or even push me. I think you will never be cruel.

299.35 not afraid at all." not afraid."

299.36–38 ever so kind to you." A vague, inconsequent vision of her coming in some odd way to need it had intervened with the effect of a chill. very kind to you."

299.39–42 the child returned with her note of prepared promptitude. What teaching she had had, it seemed to suggest—or what penalties for non-performance she dreaded! the child declared lightly.

299.44 further than ever from having folded her wings. less than ever in a state of repose.

299.45 with a flutter through the air with a great deal of expression,

300.1 on the forehead on her lips,

300.1–2 as if according to some ancient prescribed rite. She drew the visitor to a sofa in the short, quick manner of a bird drinking. She made Isabel sit down on the sofa beside her,

300.3 her our heroine

300.3–6 began to talk very much as if, seated brush in hand before an easel, she were applying a series of considered touches to a composition of figures already sketched in. delivered herself of a hundred remarks from which I offer the reader but a brief selection.

300.7 if whether

300.8–9 you're supposed not to care—through being so clever—for all sorts of ordinary things. you are very proud.

300.9 if I tell fibs; whether I tell fibs or not;

300.10 something rather good something

300.11 what's what there is

300.12–14 make professions any more than I make paper flowers or flouncey lampshades—I don't know how. My lampshades would be sure to take fire, my roses and my fibs to be larger than life. make phrases—I never made a phrase in my life. My fibs are always very crude.

300.15 you're to marry you are going to marry

300.16 brilliant— remarkable—

300.17 the way you're always spoken of; what people call you;

300.18 and original, not *banal;* and clever, very original;

300.21 we're dreadfully fallen, we are rather fallen,

300.24–25 they ought to make it somehow not quite so awful a steel trap. it's the worst thing she can do.

300.27–28 what horrors she may be in for. that it isn't such a blessing to get married.

300.29 on upon

300.33 won't respect me, not one little mite, and won't respect me, and

300.39–41 he won't be a bit, at any time, your affair, and, stupid as he is, he'll see you're not his. Some day, if you can stand it, I'll you will take his measure at a glance. Some day, I will

301.2 One afternoon of the autumn of 1876, toward dusk, One afternoon, towards dusk, in the autumn of 1876,

301.14 constituted habits tolerably inveterate habits

301.17 customary sequences. proceedings.

301.19–20 To this little person he began to pay, on the spot, particular attention: she struck him as exactly the household angel For this young lady he conceived a peculiar admiration; she was exactly the household angel

301.25 other friends— some friends
301.25–26 romantically wretched very unhappy
301.28 Mr. Rosier Rosier
301.31–33 He might expose himself, unseasoned, to the poison of the Roman air, which in November lay, notoriously, much in wait. He was nervous about the fever, and November, after all, was rather early in the season.
301.33–34 this adventurer, Mr. Rosier,
301.34 a day, every day,
301.36–37 he had devoted it in vain to finding a flaw in Pansy Osmond's composition. that is, he had perceived that Miss Pansy Osmond had not a flaw in her composition.
301.38 she had had the last touch; she was really a consummate piece. —she was in excellent style.
301.41 hint touch
302.5 yearningly murmured. murmured to himself.
302.18 smiled the visitor. said Rosier, smiling.
302.21 His eyes Rosier's eyes
302.24 quickly asked. asked quickly.
302.26 Mr. Rosier Rosier,
302.26–27 flushed with all his recognitions. smiling.
302.31 opened wide eyes. started a little.
302.34–35 friendly frown, stroking her chin with her large white hand. little frown stroking her chin.
302.40–41 I'm afraid that for Mr. Osmond I'm not—well, a real collector's piece." I'm afraid Mr. Osmond doesn't think me a phoenix."
302.43 handsome mouth mouth
303.4 *I* I
303.7–8 good Louis Quatorze. It's very rare now, and good *bibelots;*
303.8–9 With which And
303.11–12 But he looked, in spite of it, literally apprehensive and consistently strenuous. ¶Edward Rosier stared and blushed; his correct features were suffused with disappointment.
303.14 Pardon Excuse
303.19 Madame Merle considered. Madame Merle was silent a moment.
303.25 sigh of good faith. sigh.
303.28 He Edward Rosier
303.30 quite very
303.34–35 how she loves that she loves
303.39–40 till I've until I have
303.41–42 you observe the proprieties." your conduct is most estimable."
303.43 the young man poor Rosier
304.3–4 who saw things as she saw them. who saw things clearly.
304.4 in is in
304.10–11 her visitor cried with prompt elation. cried the young man, with an ingenuous radiance in his face.

304.13–14 assuming your cause to be good assuming that your cause is good.
304.14 if whether
304.15 "I'm awfully decent, you know," "I'm a dear little fellow,"
304.17–18 "All that's negative, and it always depends, also, on what people call vices. "All that is negative.
304.18 What's the virtuous? *(Omitted.)*
304.20 I've a I have got
304.21 I that I
304.26 famous; splendid;
304.28 famous. splendid.
304.29–30 one can afford—well, quite cheap *faïence.* one can afford to be simple.
304.31 muslin—without the sprig? muslin,"
304.32 "Wouldn't you even allow her the sprig? *(Omitted.)*
304.33 you at any rate for you for
304.36–37 and most tidy—also extremely graceful. and extremely graceful.
304.38 scarce demurred. hesitated a moment.
304.41 large fortune." fortune."
305.11 failed to burst into speech. was silent a moment.
305.15 "Pardon "Excuse
305.15 quite lucidly. with his persuasive smile.
305.21 Osmond, however, Osmond
305.23 *He* He
305.29 *you* you
305.39 Meanwhile then I'll Meanwhile, I will
305.41 Madame Merle was on her feet. Madame Merle rose, rapidly.
305.43 had had
306.12–13 suggesting that of a careful owner's "best set" suggesting sprigged porcelain,
306.14 very much!" much!"
306.15 her. her.
306.18 till I've until I have
306.25 Mr. Osmond's pretty hard," Mr. Osmond is rather difficult,
306.27 short laugh. light laugh.
306.29–30 for departure. passing out.
306.31 an aspirant a young man
306.35 his adviser, Madame Merle
306.37 rather circumspect tone. somewhat peculiar manner.
306.38 put it said
306.38 he that he
306.45 She had indeed shown him benevolence, Beyond this, Madame Merle had been very gracious to him,
397.6 rather a fool rather like a fool
307.7 having appealed to her appealing to Madame Merle
307.22 by Roman measure, in Roman parlance,
307.26 a pile which which
307.28–29 looked, on a vague survey, looked
307.36 had chosen chose
307.38 enamels enamel,
308.3 and then, and

308.8 **"good things." bibelots.**
308.11 **even better "French" than he in Paris,** better things than he,
308.12 **obliged on the spot** obliged
308.16 **annexed** obtained
308.17–18 **achieved his greatest finds** got his best things
308.20 **"cash," "money,"**
308.21 **highest prizes** great prizes
308.24–25 **recognition was for** glance was bestowed upon
308.25 **saloon;** room;
308.26 **his eyes** that his eyes
308.29–30 **a gentleman whose smile, as he crossed a threshold, always took everything comfortable for granted.** to a gentleman who always crossed a threshold with an optimistic smile.
308.34 **Mrs. Osmond** that Mrs. Osmond
308.34–35 **most customary** usually customary
308.36–37 **flushed with subdued, diffused brightness;** warm, with a sort of subdued brightness;
308.39 **next of the series,** chamber beyond,
308.43–309.2 **his eyes had an expression, frequent with them, that seemed to represent them as engaged with objects more worth their while than the appearances actually thrust upon them.** his eyes were fixed, abstractedly.
309.9 **Osmond, however, took him in;** Osmond stood looking at him;
309.9–10 **never in his life felt himself so efficiently looked at.** never before felt the keenness of this gentleman's eyes.
309.11 **he privately reasoned.** Rosier said to himself.
309.12 **in sight;** within sight;
309.14 **having a fancy** he had a fancy that
309.16 **had ever a strong need of being quite in the right.** he had an inveterate wish to be in the right.
309.17–18 **and smiled, all without help, and then in a moment,** smiling, and then, in a moment, he said:
309.18–19 **to-day," he said.** to-day."
309.25 **an instant** a moment
300.31 **I wish** that I wish
309.32 **aware** aware that
309.32 **blushed; he** blushed, and he
309.33 *I* I
309.33 **all he** all that he
309.34 **knew** knew that
309.37 **high and splendid, as he had said, and yet oh so radiantly gentle!** brilliant and noble.
309.40–310.1 **his eye for decorative character, his instinct for authenticity; but also on a sense for uncatalogued values, for that secret of a "lustre" beyond any recorded losing or rediscovering, which his devotion to brittle wares had still not disqualified him to recognize.** his fine sense of the plastic; but also on a relish for a more impalpable sort of merit—that merit of

a bright spirit which Rosier's devotion to brittle wares had not made him cease to regard as a quality.
310.24 **vaguely smiled.** smiled vaguely.
310.26 **she said,** said Mrs. Osmond,
310.31 **is** is that
310.33 **damsel** young lady
310.39 **he cared** and cared
310.40 **damsel** young lady
311.29 **enquiry requisite** inquiry necessary
311.32 **Pansy** that Pansy
311.34–35 **what could** what would
311.40 **if** whether
312.10–11 **so vain a disguise of rose-colour** pink
312.19 **that** which
312.19 **but that,** but,
312.22 **it looked the very temple of authorised love.** it looked very pretty.
312.23 **gazed a moment** stood a moment, gazing
312.25 **the other maiden** the young lady in pink
312.26–27 **far side** other side
312.27 **For a little** For a moment
312.28 **a second glance** a glance
312.29 **she** that she
312.29 **he then** then he
312.30 **a supreme hesitation** a moment's supreme hesitation
312.30 **if** whether
313.1 **very bad.** bad.
313.8 **a little** a moment.
313.12 **And Pansy raised** asked Pansy, raising
313.17 **that."** that," she said.
313.37 **toward** towards
313.38 **would** she would
313.45 **say** say that
314.3 *you!* you!
314.4 **whereupon** while
314.29–30 **each of his tones** his tones
314.41 **to talk** and talk
315.1 **he's a nuisance—** he's enervating,
315.2 **she had a faint smile.** with a faint smile.
315.5 **'genteel'** genteel
315.10 **consider that that matters."** think that matters."
315.11 **consider** think
315.12 **thought of** thought about
315.14 **told you** told you that
315.18–19 **familiarly—his long, fine forefinger and thumb could make a ring for it—and** familiarly, and
315.27 **Keep him yourself."** Do it yourself."
315.31–32 **A long drop** A long pause
315.32 **had ended** was broken again,
315.34 **The girl** Pansy
315.36 **Madame Merle went on** Madame Merle said, simply,
316.2 **the young creature gently said.** said the young girl, gently.
316.15 **toward** towards
316.17 **Italian,** an Italian,
316.17 **took for granted** took for granted that

316.21 **Isabel met his hesitation. "When I know what?"** He hesitated a little.¶"When I know what?" Isabel asked, gently.

316.36–37 **without ceremony;** without saying anything;

316.44 **searched** looked about

317.2 **he spoke once more to Isabel;** he spoke to Isabel again;

317.5 **referred to** spoke of

317.6 **began.** said.

317.12 **could, just a little, I'd** could—just a little," said Rosier, "I would

317.22 **till** until

317.30 **on** upon

317.40–41 **that it might** which it would

318.4 **to measure the possibility?"** to measure that?"

318.10 **awaited** waited for

318.11 **Palazzo** the Palazzo

318.12 **though** although

318.17 **eyes.** eye.

318.24–25 **And he flattered himself** Rosier flattered himself that

318.33 **fire a moment.** fire for a moment.

318.40 **pretend she'd** pretend that she would

318.44 **—and Osmond looked up** Osmond said, looking up

319.1 **now bending** bending

319.7 **all undisturbed:** very quickly—

319.10 **the master of the house** Osmond

319.11 **to reply** to rejoin

319.14 **his host.** the master of the house.

319.15 **had a handsome face and** was a handsome man, with

319.15 **beard and was** beard—

319.22 **his hostess** this gracious lady

319.25 **he** that he

319.30 **with his sense** feeling

319.32 **nothing; then,** nothing. Then—

319.33 **eyes** eye

319.35 **"Pardon** "Excuse

319.37 **his friend,** the young girl,

319.40 **she** that she

319.42 **tone and** tone,

320.2 **toward** towards

320.3 **judged** thought

320.4 **a little** was a little

320.5 **her husband,** Osmond,

320.13 **Isabel in fact, to do him justice,** To do him justice, Isabel

320.14–15 **if she felt a pleasure or a pain.** whether she were glad or not.

320.16–18 **quite sure of his own sense of the matter; though his grey eyes had still their fine original property of keeping recognition and attestation strictly sincere.** very well pleased; his frank grey eye expressed a deep, if still somewhat shy, satisfaction.

320.18 **"heavier"** larger, stouter

320.19 **and looked** and he looked

320.21 **"I've but just** "I have only

320.26 **remarked to his wife.** remarked, smiling, to his wife.

320.31 **the same at which** the same one where

320.32 **four years since.** four years ago.

320.34 **good-bye?" his lorship asked of his hostess.** good-bye?

320.38 **I remember you there.** I remember that you were there.

320.39 **almost a dismal memory,** a melancholy sort of memory,

320.41 **her old friend went on to Isabel,** (Omitted.)

320.42–44 **he added with a look, round him, at her established home, in which she might have caught the dim ghost of his old ruefulness.** said Lord Warburton, brightly, looking about him.

320.46 **observed** remarked

321.2 **over."** were over."

321.2–5 **who had already, with her rare capacity for such inward feats, taken the measure of what meeting him again meant for her.** who had now completely recovered her self-possession.

321.6–7 **a remarkably complete blank."** a blank."

321.9 **now** had now

321.10 **so conscientiously.** very conscientiously.

321.17–18 **Lord Warburton called after him, as he moved away,** said Lord Warburton,

321.19 **his** Osmond's

321.19–20 **Then the visitor turned on Isabel the deeper, the deepest, consciousness of his look, which He** stood a moment, looking at Isabel with an eye that

321.24 **She just hesitated.** Isabel hesitated a moment.

321.27–28 **you," she bravely returned.** you," said Isabel, smiling.

321.29 **a pity** a pity that

321.30 **she** Isabel

321.34 **would press with less of his whole weight** would prove a more comfortable companion

321.35–36 **without chilling it, given it a relieved sense of having taken the air.** without chilling this organ, had freely ventilated it.

321.37 **Her friend's** Lord Warburton's

321.38–39 **one who would rather like people, or like her at least, to know him for such.** who would rather like one to know it.

321.40 **resumed.** said.

321.44 **to see** and see

321.44 **she immediately said.** said Isabel, quickly.

321.45 **you** that you

322.2 **Briton."** Englishman."

322.8–9 **to remain** remain

322.11 **thoroughly** extremely

322.20 **could make** and make

322.25 **Ralph's** Touchett's

322.29–30 **I wanted him to take with him some clever fellow—I mean some sharp young doctor; but he wouldn't hear of it.** (Omitted.)

321.32 **decide on** choose for

322.34 **and lets** and she lets

322.37 *is* is

322.38 Isabel sprang up. Isabel started up.
322.38 then now." now!"
322.40 don't mean don't mean that
322.43 he that he
323.1 decide to think of it
323.2 we had separated. we separated.
323.2 remembered remembered that
323.2 told me told me that
323.4 tell you he's here, tell you that he was here,
323.4 know know that
323.9 gallantly added. added, gallantly.
323.20 wild bold
323.21 wild; bold;
323.23 Tories, tories,
323.24–25 he calls me the King of the Goths—says I have, down to the details of my personal appearance, every sign of the brute. he calls me the head of the Communists.
323.30 he had a conception that he had a consciousness
323.36 see see that
323.37 understand understand that
323.39 of his wishing that he wished
323.41 believe believe that
323.42 knowing knowing that
324.6 implications; implication;
324.7 told her told her that
324.8 and that —that
324.11–12 at the time of that passage in her history, when she married,
324.12 this. that.
324.16–17 a person amused, at a provincial entertainment, by some innocent game of guesses— a man to whom everything suggested a cheerful interpretation—
324.25 an awfully good a very good
324.28 mean he mean that he
324.36 mean you mean that you
324.38 propose to propose
324.42 prefer like
325.6 saying you saying that you
325.8 it it's
325.9 mild gaiety. gaiety.
325.13 I do want I want
325.15–16 —after which she reflected, with a pang perhaps too visible, and then blushing a little at the thought
325.17–18 divined the pang noticed her blush
325.18–19 to her not having contributed then to the facility. to the incongruity.
325.20 had meanwhile meanwhile had
325.28 so loud—every one will hear," so loud, or every one will hear us,"
325.29 hear hear us
325.31–31 —and she sighed with the weight of her responsibility. the young girl exclaimed with a little sigh.
325.36 you." you."
325.37 told me told me that
325.40 the very same?" the same?"
325.41 not the very same. Papa has been terribly severe." it's not just the same. Papa has been very severe."

326.4 She Pansy
326.11 She Pansy
326.11 a little; a moment;
326.24 hesitated again. hesitated a moment.
326.36 as when
326.38 introduced. presented.
326.40 It will probably not surprise It probably will not be surprising to
326.44 after this had after this he had
327.3 difference he difference that he
327.21 such a burden as to make a burden that would make
327.22 So dismal had been Such had been,
327.23 Ralph's prevision Ralph's rather dismal prevision
327.24 remember remember that
327.29 thought thoughts
327.32–33 be best embodied in best be preserved by
327.41 had written sent
328.2 had taken place took place
328.3 had effected effected
328.4 had indulged— indulged
328.5–6 had protested protested
328.7 put a barrier erected a barrier
328.9 had deemed deemed
328.12 not apparently to have been made in vain; not made in vain;
328.16 had appeared appeared
328.18 had proved the most acceptable proved to be the most picturesque
328.19 there had been there was
328.21 Isabel had been Isabel was
328.21–22 not seeing his way simply to take the poor girl for funny. not having been able to judge the poor girl more humorously.
328.23 if whether
328.23–24 his sense of fun, or of the funny—which would be his sense of humour, wouldn't it?— his sense of humour
328.27 had thought thought
328.29 had also also
328.31 had appealed protested
328.31 that had made which made
328.36 had answered answered
328.38 had seen saw
328.39 had followed followed
328.40 had spent spent
328.41 had been was
328.42 had gone went
328.45 had occupied occupied
329.1 had come came
329.3 was then of was of
329.5 nothing he nothing that he
329.12 had been was
329.12 had given gave
329.17 talked of talked about
329.19 talked of talked about
329.26 and showing no symptom without a symptom
329.30 saw, saw that
329.31 and Osmond not eager and that Osmond was not eager
329.32 had been were
329.41 had, after this, chosen after this, chose

329.46 while engaged while he was engaged
330.1 had yet felt felt
330.5 union, marriage,
330.9 At present, however, But now
330.12 on upon
330.13–14 it was a representation, it was even an advertisement. it was a representation.
330.18 appeared seemed
330.29 studied impressions calculated impressions
330.30 long rides, long drives,
330.32 people who people that
330.36 had been used used
330.39 moved faster, breathed faster, moved faster,
331.4 yet but
331.4 an amplitude and a brilliancy a kind of amplitude and brilliancy
331.5 that which
331.10 What did Isabel represent? "What did Isabel represent?"
331.12–13 he then woefully exclaimed. he exclaimed.
331.18 deeply calculated. elaborately studied.
331.25 "it's "but it's
331.34 subtly considered deeply calculated
331.36 consideration. calculation.
331.38 the conscious attitude of years. a *pose* of years.
331.43–44 had made him feel great, ever, made him feel great
332.1 Miss Archer; Isabel Archer;
332.6 they may at the time have been worth. they are worth.
332.8–9 the husband of the woman he loved Gilbert Osmond
332.11 Gilbert Osmond Mr. Osmond
332.16 were was
332.20–21 Ralph had had toward the end, a sharp inward vision of Osmond's making it of small ease to his wife Ralph had, towards the end, an inward conviction that Osmond had made it uncomfortable for his wife
332.22 Mr. Touchett. her cousin.
332.25–26 so when when
332.26 had taken took
332.27 had deprived deprived
332.28–29 was keeping him kept him
332.29 had decided decided
332.30 had been was
332.32 would serve, would do,
332.37–38 the person in the world in whom he was most interested: his cousin;
332.40 wanted wished
332.41 her husband he
332.43 had held held
332.43 had kept kept
332.45 had given gave
333.6 mounted ascended
333.9–10 their sending their carriage Isabel sending a carriage
333.10 Palazzo the Palazzo
333.19 all shamelessly. in a tone of jocosity.

333.20 mean you'll mean that you will
333.22 you. Rome's you; it's
333.23 to do. I'll to do; I will
333.24–25 puffing a cigar and as if trying to see it. puffing his cigar, as if he were trying to see it.
333.28 Ralph. "I've done trying. Ralph;
333.36–37 I'll stay. I haven't a single cousin in Sicily—much less a married one." I'll stay; I haven't got any cousins in Sicily."
334.2 insist on Sicily. go to Sicily.
334.10 a very good Christian. You're a very kind man." a very good fellow. You are very kind."
334.24 desiring wanting
334.31 These two were gentlemen These two gentlemen were children
334.34 subject they subject that they
334.42 What then What
334.42 Ralph's friend demanded. (Omitted.)
335.3 to mind his likings. They're to mind it. It's
335.12 disappear. go away.
335.17 observed instead. said.
335.19 returned remarked
335.32 she that she
335.36 "Complained? Complain?
335.36–37 She has done it—what she *has* done— She has done it,
336.1 looking at it hard. blushing a little.
336.11–12 how cheered-up old Osmond will be!" how tickled Gilbert Osmond will be!"
336.13–14 shouldn't propose for his daughter shan't marry his daughter
336.14 him." him."
336.21 scarcely in the mood scarcely to be in the mood
336.22 judge think
336.28 Pansy." the girl."
336.30 Pansy the girl
336.31–32 and rather a clouded brow. with a rather sombre eye.
336.36 being—a—so being a—so
337.9 much wonder a kind of wonder
337.10 That personage Madame Merle
337.11 character person
337.19 gallant brilliant
337.21 trick trick that
337.22 disgusts; disgust;
337.24 sharpness peremptoriness
337.26 some new adventure. a new attempt.
337.27 younger person she had been used young girl, she used
337.30 by reason and by wisdom. by reason, by wisdom.
337.32 her brilliant friend Madame Merle
337.37–38 the personage in question made again Madame Merle made
338.4 her friend— Madame Merle—
338.9–10 her old ally was different, was almost detached—pushing to the extreme Madame Merle was changed —that she pushed to the extreme
338.18 our young woman our heroine

338.18 **overdid a little.** overdid it a little.

338.22–23 **was not after all of the inner circle.** was after all not one of them.

338.28 *must* must

338.40 **say** say that

338.41 **Certainly** Of course

339.9 **providence, fortune,** of providence, of fortune,

339.10 **true** true that

339.12 **strange event** marriage

339.14 **producing cause** cause

339.15 **important friendship** fertile friendship

339.15 **This had** That

339.16–19 **her aunt and at a time when she was still capable of that large inward reference, the tone almost of the philosophic historian, to her scant young annals.** her aunt.

339.19 **her change of state** the event,

339.22 **their union** her marriage

339.23 **convenient view** comfortable view

339.24–25 **consented to finger, in talk, this roundest and smoothest bead of their social rosary.** spoke of Madame Merle, and when his wife alluded to her he usually let the allusion drop.

339.26 **Madame Merle?"** her?"

339.30 **almost unnaturally good!** good!

339.31 **it makes for relaxation—for a sort of moral *détente*.** it's a sort of rest.

339.36 **sensibly different,** somewhat changed,

339.37 **not quite the same.** altered.

339.39 **may miss,** lacks,

339.41 **Madame Merle's having** Madame Merle having

339.42–43 **it might have been written,** it seemed,

340.1–2 **That reflection indeed** This reflection, however,

340.2–3 **she knew an immediate horror** Isabel felt a sort of horror

340.11 **her friend,** her brilliant friend,

340.13–14 **She was herself moreover so unable** Moreover, she herself was so unable

340.15 **wished** wished that

340.16–17 **it would have made in a manner for refreshment.** it would be a kind of refreshment.

340.17 **Wasn't it in a manner** Jealousy, after all, was in a sense

340.17 **happiness?** happiness.

340.18–19 **was wise, so wise that she might have been pretending to know** was wise; it would seem that she knew

340.25 **Her poor winged spirit** The poor girl

340.26 **its best,** her best,

340.26 **It had** she had

340.27 **It wished,** She wished,

340.28 **itself** herself

340.29 **its** her

340.30 **to be derived from that** she might derive from it

340.37–38 **one way to repair it—just immensely (oh, with the highest grandeur!) to accept it.** one way to repair it—to accept it.

341.1 **for Pansy—it was also** for Pansy. It was

341.3–4 **nothing else in her life that had the rightness of the young creature's attachment or the sweetness of her own clearness about it.** nothing in her life so much as it should be as the young girl's attachment and the pleasantness of feeling it.

341.6–7 **ardent coercive faith.** faith.

341.7 **the girl's** Pansy's

341.8 **as a definite reason** as a command, as a definite reason

341.11 **a direct admonition;** a kind of admonition;

341.12–13 **an opportunity, not eminent perhaps, but unmistakeable. Yet an opportunity** an opportunity. An opportunity

341.18 **believe** believe that

341.20 **and now she** and she

341.32 **luxuriously mild.** elaborately soft.

341.32–33 **how Pansy liked to be with her and how she studied** that Pansy liked immensely to be with her and studied

341.36 **could have had no reference** could not have had any reference

341.39–40 **she could have thought** she thought

341.45 **Palazzo** the Palazzo

342.3–4 **knew her little companion** knew that Pansy

342.9 **her stepmother,** Isabel,

342.9 **small** little

342.17–18 **had a swift length of step, though not so swift a one as on her first coming to Europe.** stepped quickly, though not so quickly as when she first came to Europe.

342.21 **father's wife,** stepmother,

342.22 **her** Pansy's

342.23 **She** Pansy

342.25 **Palazzo** the Palazzo

342.35 **was there** sat there

342.36 **unaware** unaware that

342.38 **colloquy** dialogue

342.43 **on** upon

343.4 **nothing to shock** nothing shocking

343.6 **positions,** position,

343.9 **her husband,** Gilbert Osmond,

343.11 **their visitor** Madame Merle

343.15 **Isabel asked with a smile.** Asked Isabel, smiling.

343.22 **you;** you;

343.26 **you didn't believe it,"** you didn't believe me,"

343.39 **I know very well.** I know that.

344.1 **hesitated.** hesitated a moment.

344.6 **the sort** a sort

344.16 **he** he

344.29 **"The dearest** "She is the dearest

344.29 **—but very limited."** but she is very limited."

344.33 **with lace borders."** with lace."

345.8 After which again Then
345.12 the latter Isabel
345.18 so much as much
345.33 while she stood as she stood
345.34 and pushed into pushing into
345.36 saying there's saying that there is
345.39 returned rejoined
346.3 "Pardon me; I forgot "Excuse me; I forgot that
346.14 Isabel's eyes rested on her. Isabel smiled a little.
346.19 then said then she said,
346.37 Isabel cried cried Isabel,
346.45 shan't shall not
347.1 want wish
347.11 never told you anything of the sort." never told you that."
347.12 *might* might
347.12 done so—so far as opportunity went—when done so when
347.15 and sometimes sometimes
347.16–17 because she wished not to she did not wish to
347.18 returned. said.
347.19 know know that
347.24 that which
347.30 triumphantly withdrew. took her departure.
347.41 her stepdaughter. the young girl.
347.42 if whether
348.5 positive exertion. exertion.
348.6 sense conviction
348.7 disease—of suffering as opposed to doing. To "do"— disease; it was suffering as opposed to action. To act, to do something—
348.11–12 visions of his wife's limpness under appeal. images of a flat want of zeal.
348.14 so sound a character. such a fine fellow.
348.16–17 to believe sincerely, and with proof of it, to believe, sincerely,
348.22 charming girl. young girl.
348.22 "weird" odd that
348.27 he Lord Warburton
348.28 ever were looking for? looked for?
348.32 odd he should care odd that he cared
348.33 had supposed. supposed.
348.35 think think that
348.45 tiresome she tiresome that she
349.5 so light a weight. so very flimsy.
349.9 a perfect little pearl of a peeress. a very picturesque little peeress.
349.10–11 Mrs. Osmond had grown of a sudden Isabel had suddenly grown
349.12 An impediment Somehow, an impediment
349.13 not anyhow not
349.17–19 to see her as rather letting go, under suggestion, than as clutching under deprecation—since she had certainly the faculty to think the young girl would not be tenacious, for she had the faculty
349.20 protest. resistance.

349.22–23 like him; she like him. She
349.24 had said said
349.26 rightest and easiest— happiest;
349.28–31 as if she understood his subjects with that sufficiency with which she followed those of the fashionable operas. This went far enough for attention to the music and the barytone. as if she could understand everything.
349.32–33 to another fluttered young chit to Isabel herself
349.38 Osmond had been. Osmond.
350.1 submissive attentive
350.7 to Palazzo Roccanera. to the Piazza [sic] Roccanera.
350.15 fell short of the point did not succeed in coming to the point
350.16 couldn't rise to it; couldn't;
350.17 made this made it
350.18 or insidious; insidious;
350.19–21 Isabel was instinctively much more true than false to the common genius of her sex. There was Isabel had all the qualities of her sex. It was
350.25 she wondered if Isabel asked herself whether
350.27 pronounced— exclaimed—
350.27–28 when their distinguished visitor should wish when Lord Warburton wished
350.30 studiously said nothing, said nothing,
350.36 not to be seen through. rather opaque.
350.37 She Isabel
350.39 sat down; he looked sat down, looking
350.39 she Isabel
350.41 kept his silence. sat silent.
351.7–8 slightly stouter a little stouter
351.8–9 might strike one as very looked very
351.11 stayed half an hour." stayed for half-an-hour."
351.22 of that." in that."
351.35 tapestry tapestry that
351.42 afraid afraid that
352.3 and that and
352.18–19 sit perfectly quiet sit still
352.29 nothing in life nothing
352.31 and that that
352.31 with which moreover and
352.38 and although though
352.41 an humiliation. a humiliation.
352.42 her— her—
353.4 It's very odd It is very singular that
353.12 perfectly still. still.
353.12–13 perfectly still. still;
353.22 she went on. Isabel said.
353.25 told me it told me that it
353.28 sharply. quickly;
353.37 might should
353.38 might should
353.39 might should
353.43 you." you."
353.45 she returned. she said simply.
354.1 fingered the pages while she sat si-

lent and occupied turned over the
pages, while Isabel sat silent, occupying
354.5 offensive disagreeable
354.5–6 she felt the great naturalness of
his saying it, Isabel felt it to be natural that her husband should say it,
354.6 extremely like what she had
said something very much of the
same sort that she had said
354.11 she replied. Isabel answered,
gently.
354.13 "Well, I "Well," he said, "I
354.15 remember how much I count
on remember that I count upon
354.19 had answered answered
354.21–22 made vibrations deep, so that
she had been opened the door to agitation, so that she was
354.22 he Osmond
354.24 still drawing-room silent drawing-room,
354.29 a definite influence a peculiar
influence
354.29 Warburton—this had Warburton
had
354.37 had first come first came
354.38 the link that that the link which
354.38 to be completely had completely
354.39 it had yet it still had
354.42 thought of him she always
thought; thought of Lord Warburton
she still thought;
354.43 this feeling that feeling
354.43 it seemed to her in fact on the
contrary, it seemed to her
355.3 knew knew that
355.11 knowing he knowing that he
355.12 small creature's own— young
girl's—
355.14 she Isabel
355.14 moment she moment that she
355.15 her old friend Lord Warburton
355.18–19 another satisfaction and what
might be called other chances. another satisfaction.
355.21 believe him in perfect good
faith. believe that he was in good
faith.
355.22 were was
355.23–24 had completely lost completely lost
355.29 till until
355.37–38 her husband's being in more
direct communication with Madame
Merle her husband and Madame
Merle being in more direct communication
355.38 That This
355.39 wondered wondered that
355.40–41 half an hour ago half-an-
hour before,
356.3 was now was
356.18 and where it served and served
356.25 herself herself, however,
356.26 herself, however, herself—
356.28 thought thought that
356.29 first year of their life together, so
admirably intimate at first, first year
of her marriage

356.30 had taken took
356.30–31 had begun began
356.34 deepened, increased,
356.34 now and again here and there
356.35 prospect life
356.38–39 They were a part, they were
a kind of creation and consequence,
They were a part
356.40–41 that is but of one thing, that
is, of but one thing,
356.41 *not* not
356.41 wrong he wrong that he
356.42 believed believed that
357.4–5 wearing a mask or a dress,
playing a part,
357.5 and had and he had
357.6 apprehension he apprehension
that he
357.24 she had been immensely she had
him immensely
357.28 he had succeeded. He had
succeeded that he succeeded. He succeeded
357.29 had been sincere; was sincere;
357.29 now to deny to deny
357.33 had a more wondrous vision had
a vision
357.34 him, fed through charmed senses
and oh such a stirred fancy!—she him
—she
357.36 figures. portraits.
357.38 had interested interested
357.39 There had been There was
357.44–45 she had found that she
found
358.2–3 had loved him, she had so anxiously and yet so ardently given
herself— loved him—
358.4 brought him and what might enrich
the gift. brought him.
358.5 full weeks weeks
358.7 charged hands. full hands.
358.8 would never wouldn't
358.10–11 the fantastic fact. a fact.
358.13 conscience, to some more prepared receptacle. conscience.
358.15 with the best taste who had the
best taste
358.16 should have given should give
358.16 would have been was
358.18 had been was
358.20 attaching which attached
358.29 cheek burned cheek tingled
358.32 ardour feeling
358.37–40 The finest—in the sense of
being the subtlest—manly organism she
had ever known had become her property, and the recognition of her having
but to put out her hands and take it
had been originally a sort of act of
devotion. The finest individual she
had ever known was hers; the simple
knowledge was a sort of act of devotion.
358.42 *in* in
358.44 to seize her; to do it;
358.45 pliant, subtle,
359.2 she that she
359.10 had come came

359.11 have noticed it, notice it,
359.11 had been were
359.13 had looked looked
359.13 had then appeared appeared
359.13–14 had really really
359.15 had known knew
359.16 had supposed, supposed,
359.17 had asked asked
359.18 had liked liked
359.22 It had not been this, It was not that,
359.23 this had been nothing. that was nothing.
359.25 What he had meant had been What he meant was
359.28 had found found
359.32–33 had been was
359.40 find to find
359.41 had told her told her that
359.43 that of the love the love
359.43–44 and of all and all
360.1 had elapsed, she had followed elapsed, she followed
360.1 had led led
360.2 then, *then* then, then
360.10–11 had not been was not
360.18 had known knew
360.39 grand noble
360.41 herself, avowedly, herself,
360.43 been was
361.10 he Osmond
361.19 the transmitted; and transmitted;
361.25 from what source he had derived where he had got
361.27 and after after
361.37 she Isabel
361.37 close about closing about
361.39 seemed seemed to be
362.2 things things that
362.3 see see that
362.7 or a or of a
362.20 no great insolence no very unwarrantable demand
362.20–21 a man so accomplished and a husband originally at least so tender. a husband.
362.24–25 such a thing as chastity and even as decency. such a thing as purity.
362.25–26 was far from doing anything of the sort; didn't;
362.33 that which
362.35 traditions—it was enough traditions,
362.36–37 it was this that —it was that that
262.41 it; that;
362.42 had scorched on his discovering scorched when he discovered that
363.1 his Osmond's
363.2 the a
363.2 that she could after all that, after all, she could
363.5 him? him?
363.8 certitude she conviction that she
363.11 she she
363.17 a horrible life. an awful life.
363.21 it that it
363.24–25 having had to contain himself

had only deepened his having to contain himself only deepened Osmond's
363.28 room— bedroom—
363.28 was what he wanted he wanted
363.35 on upon
363.36 on upon
363.37–38 her ache for herself became somehow her ache for *him*. her spirit rose.
364.6 she was perpetually, in their talk, in their talk she was perpetually
364.9 had warned warned
364.30 saloon drawing-room
364.42 burned had burned
364.45 Madame Merle unconsciously and familiarly associated. Madame Merle, grouped unconsciously and familiarly.
365.4 and had and she had
365.4 she that she
365.7 this unlikely; that this was not likely;
365.16 rendered her rendered
365.17–18 aware of the near presence of Edward Rosier. He stood before her; he had lost aware that Edward Rosier was standing before her. He had lost
365.20–21 felt his case to be at bottom a hard one: felt that at bottom his case was a hard one;
365.23 notify her notify her that
365.23 and then and then he
366.2 know know that
366.4 Isabel patiently answered. Isabel answered, smiling.
366.7 refused you on the spot." refused you."
366.8–9 you think me a mere Parisian trifler!" you think I'm a trifler!"
366.13 I see. You pity me— I see; you pity me,
366.16 the deficiency the movement
366.24 finally asked said
366.25 that which
366.27 her her
366.29 Mr. Rosier effectively said. Rosier exclaimed.
366.39 he that he
366.41 looking and looked
366.43 saw saw that
367.3–4 she had discovered her lover to have that she perceived that her lover had
367.13 he had formed he formed
367.21 the little maid." my little maid."
367.29 his mettle his importance
367.33 should shall
367.40 danced dance
368.2 it's really a recreation. that is a recreation.
368.4 Will you absolutely not dance?" Won't you really dance?"
368.6 a little. a moment.
368.10 is charmed with cares for
368.17 She Isabel
368.17 did as much; smiled;
368.23–24 pleasanter even than the sum of his merits warranted; delightful;
368.24 that which
368.29 didn't suit did not please

368.32 it might be it was
368.37 little maids. young girls.
368.41–42 immediate and active; most active;
368.44 might be was
369.2 unwitting; unconscious;
369.4 none [sic] less impossible. none the less unacceptable.
369.4–5 he should get back into right relations with things Lord Warburton should come to self-consciousness
369.13 knew knew that
369.16 knew Pansy to be knew that Pansy was
369.16 The girl The young girl
369.17 flush, look,
369.24 alternations alternations
369.26 think think that
369.28 she Isabel
370.2 with her own raised: "Please let looking up— "Please to let
370.5 you'd you should
370.12 that." that.''
370.25 do it dance
370.25 do nothing." dance nothing.''
370.43 knew knew that
371.5 her!" her!''
371.14 Pansy." Pansy,'' said Isabel
371.28 My husband, however, has But my husband has
371.44 suddenly turned turned, suddenly,
371.2 "I like you, however that may be, "All the same, I like you
372.5 you're that you are
372.6–7 I like you as somebody to laugh at." I like you, too.''
372.15 waited hesitated
372.17 told you told you that
372.18 quick blush sprang to his brow. sudden blush sprung to his face.
372.18 told me she told me that she
372.20 suggested he added—
372.21 through his blush. suggestively, through his blush.
372.22 told you she has told you that she had
372.26 continued empty; continued to be empty;
372.41 any one anything
372.42 loveable charming
372.43 "No one, "Nothing,
373.5 forty-two years old. forty years old.
373.6 pretend pretend that
373.10 friend. companion.
373.11 eyes, eye,
373.13 expression eye
373.14 in fear. frightened.
373.15 showed expressed
373.16 wanted wished
373.16–17 suspect her of detecting in his proposal of marrying suspect that she detected in his wish to marry
373.18–19 or of thinking it, on such a betrayal, ominous. or that if she did detect it, she thought it alarming or compromising.
373.22–23 so far as as far as
373.25–27 where, within her compan-

ion's view, she was immediately addressed by a pair of gentlemen, high personages in the Roman world, who met her as if they had been looking for her. where she encountered several acquaintances.
373.28 regretting regretting that
373.35 softly wailed, murmured,
373.41 doorways!" the doorways!''
374.19 place city
374.22 an habitation a habitation
374.23 to visit that city; to go there;
374.30 that which
374.36–37 that one had heard of. one had heard of.
374.38 sure sure that
374.41 to the monuments and museums, the to the
375.5 Palazzo the Palazzo
375.9–10 It was her husband who But her husband
375.17–18 she had somewhere a patch of common ground that she had a patch of common ground somewhere, which
375.20 should would
375.20 had really touched touched
375.23 on upon
375.24–25 begin, like fire-works, or Lent, or the opera season; begin;
375.33 bright rare shell, bright shell,
375.33–34 a polished surface and a remarkably pink lip, a polished surface,
375.43 frosted wedding-cake. wedding-cake.
376.2 Palazzo the Palazzo
376.27 encountered— encountered.
376.32 if whether
376.36 contemporary; modern;
376.39 had been used used
376.39–41 shoulders timorously bared of their tight black velvet (oh the old clothes!) bare shoulders,
376.42 had spoken spoke
376.42–43 the accent of her "Creole" ancestors, as she always confessed; a kind of Southern accent;
376.46 her manner and her manner
377.1–3 It was as impossible to imagine her vaguely sighing as to imagine a letter posted without its address. (Omitted.)
377.4 more in the movement more efficient
377.5 She ¶Henrietta
377.5 had called on had come to see
377.10 put herself out for her, since gone to see her, for
377.12–13 graciously asked. asked, smiling graciously.
377.20–21 known it at the time," known it.''
377.35 scandal disgrace
377.38 bland soft
377.39 come to see come and see
378.17–18 She gave no reason." (Omitted.)
378.29–30 "The reason's Osmond," she pregnantly remarked. "That's Osmond,'' she remarked pregnantly.

378.21 make a stand," resist,"
378.24 ingenuously added. added, ingenuously.
379.4 *had* had
379.10 brilliant. smart.
379.12 brilliant?" smart?"
379.29 and and she
379.33 enquired with unprecedented distinctness. inquired, softly.
379.35 certain certain that
379.39—guilty—?" —is guilty—"
379.42–43 as I hear, is is, as I hear,
379.44 just anxious," very anxious,"
380.2 I'll tell I tell
380.3 I engage I will engage
380.5 her gaze. her eyes.
380.6 idea idea that
380.11–12 begun a little to bore her. begun to bore her a little.
380.17 amusing himself—in his own old way— enjoying himself
380.28 *him* him
380.30 believed believed that
380.33–34 than she had imagined, though with a capacity for coarseness even there. than she had imagined.
380.35 said for edification. said, gravely.
380.37 aggravates increases
380.41 be be that
380.41 Miss Stackpole pursued, said Miss Stackpole.
381.1–3 with small bright eyes and an eager-looking nose; with cheeks into each of which a flush had come. with her small bright eyes and her eager-looking nose; a flush had come into each of her cheeks.
381.3 *gentil! Isn't it gentil!"* she said. "Isn't that
381.10 No one, man or woman, No one
381.19 give no not give a
381.21 her the Countess
381.21 the way her way
381.22 inns hotels
381.39 handed him handed to him
381.40 pursued her course took her course
382.4 but is but
382.10–11 had a special devotion had taken a great fancy
382.13–14 and yet reminded but she had reminded
382.32 stated; said;
382.33 but not but he was not
382.36 none the less, however,
383.1 she that she
383.11 loudly. loud.
383.14 went on said
383.15 patience. own reasonableness.
383.24 continued went on
383.27 think sometimes think sometimes that
383.27 knew knew that
383.28 I'd *take* I would take
383.33 he answered Goodwood exclaimed,
383.37 so far as as far as
383.41 demanded. inquired.
383.43 her her

383.44 some harm? harm?
384.5 you. It's you; it's
384.8 'more' more
384.22 real issue." question."
384.28 turned off turned away
384.30 but after then, after
384.31 then resumed. said in a moment.
384.35 after thinking some minutes, after a moment's resitation,
384.38 he said. said Goodwood.
384.43 hung back; hesitated;
385.6 prosperity. progress.
385.7 wish wish that
385.20 desired wished
385.22 vise, vice,
385.28 it struck him it seemed to him
385.36 then said, then he said,
385.37 wholly without the flourish without any of the richness
385.40–41 returned imperturbable. remarked, serenely.
385.43 knew her husband to be knew that her husband was
385.45 That knowledge This knowledge
386.4 opposition. displeasure.
368.8 aversion to it, disapproval;
386.8 partook she partook
386.10 his Osmond's
386.11 appointed and inscribed master; master;
386.15 on giving when she gave
386.18 none the less, however,
386.19 something something that
386.19 bestown. given.
386.22 upon her to the end. upon her.
380.23 call upon go and see
386.27 she didn't, to be just, to be just, she didn't
386.27 *could* could
386.29 Osmond's sore, mute protest was Osmond's objections were
386.29 he Osmond
386.30–31 if he should put forth his authority, she would then she should
386.33 rupture, rupture with her husband,
386.34 wishing wishing that
387.2–3 was no conceivable substitute is no substitute
387.3–7 the measure of propriety was in the canon of taste, and there couldn't have been a better proof that morality was, so to speak, a matter of earnest appreciation. Isabel's application of that measure had been particularly free to-day, the measure of expediency resided in her moral consciousness. It had been very liberal to-day,
389.11 a question. It's a question," she said. "It's
387.12 guess your question," know it,"
387.15 "Very possibly you guess it. Please "It's very possible," said Isabel. "Please
387.17 she said; said Isabel;
387.26–27 as if his mild hilarity had been touched with mystification. "You say a moment; a shade of perplexity mingled with his mild hilarity. "You said

387.32 stared. stared a little.
387.32–33 he wants, of all things in the world he desires
387.37 now now that
387.38 waited hesitated
387.41 tiresome." She spoke, tiresome," Isabel said, speaking
388.9 on upon
388.11 abruptly and abruptly,
388.22 see him through." help him."
388.24 debated. hesitated a moment.
388.27 seem to see suspect
388.31 another person, some one else,
388.39 the merit—for Pansy—of the merit of
388.39 Pansy. her.
389.5 Gilbert— Osmond—
389.27 how he judged for her and how he knew. that he knew it.
389.28 know know it
389.29 show her show her that
389.41 scarce scarcely
389.44 saw saw that
390.15 he answered. said Ralph.
390.16 no reply; no answer;
390.16 pulled her hand shook her hand
390.17 withdrew from the room. went out of the room.
390.19 the girl's the young girl's
390.27 Palazzo the Palazzo
390.34–35 betraying this heat. betraying it to Pansy.
390.36 causing alarm. frightening her.
390.36 guessed guessed that
390.37 more or less a little
391.7 dimly vaguely
391.15 nearer, nearer to Isabel's,
391.19 returned. rejoined.
391.21 on upon
391.32 the child Pansy
391.38 want?" desire?"
391.40 wanted wished
391.41 told him told him that
391.44 Isabel pronounced. said Isabel.
392.4 sighing at this, sighing then,
392.4 that this
392.6 who think that think
392.7 know know that
392.10 knows knows that I
392.10 him." him."
392.20 hypocritically cried. cried, hypocritically.
392.22 evidently much puzzled; she was evidently deeply puzzled;
392.23 wretched miserable
392.32–34 failed to lead did not lead
392.33 toward towards
392.39 not at all large." not very large."
392.41 have myself so little have very little
392.42–43 With which Isabel Isabel
392.44 It was what she was doing She was doing this
393.1 it was this was
393.3 think she think that she
393.4–5 her companion softly demanded. said Pansy, softly.
393.6–7 Isabel took refuge in timorous

vagueness. Isabel pusillanimously took refuge in a generalization.
393.13 The child's Pansy's
393.16 quavered out: she said, with a timorous sigh—
393.21 sure sure that
393.25 resumed; said;
393.30 he'll propose for me he will ask me to marry him.
393.33 propose ask me
393.42 conduced to Isabel's awkwardness. made Isabel feel very awkward.
394.7 sure of his knowing sure that he knows
394.19 unreservedly answered. answered.
394.24 the child Pansy
394.25–26 her companion Isabel
394.26 this friend her
395.12 Isabel was reduced to replying. said Isabel.
395.16 She Isabel
395.21 She just faltered. Isabel hesitated a moment.
395.26 she demanded. Isabel asked.
395.33–34 wish hands laid on Lord Warburton you must lay them yourself." wish to capture Lord Warburton, you must do it yourself."
395.42 That effect had never been so marked as now. That was the expression of his eyes now.
395.43 she returned. she said.
395.44–45 he doesn't after all come forward he doesn't come up to the mark
396.3 she went on. said Isabel.
396.5 her, Isabel,
396.6–7 must want to make sure of him!" must wish to capture him!"
396.15 He Osmond
396.16 I want it immensely." I wish it very much."
396.17 came in to came in, as if to
396.29 he explained, said Lord Warburton,
396.30 mentioned explained
396.31–32 or the day after. or next day.
396.36–37 on their visitor's face, on Lord Warburton's face,
396.39 his her visitor's
396.39 would should
396.44 a quarter of an hour, for a quarter of an hour,
396.45–397.1 a course he a course which he
397.6 state of things for a man of his leisure and intelligence. state of things.
397.9 had had had
397.23–24 she would be an immense success there, she certainly would, she would be immensely liked in England, Miss Osmond would,
397.27–28 to a two-legged creature. to any one.
397.30 than final interviews? a final interview?
397.30 one wanted— one wanted to—

397.33–34 Such a sense was upsetting; it muddled one's wits. Such a sense was bewildering; it made one nervous.
397.42 conditions circumstances
398.4 impudence imprudence,
398.4–5 felt it out of her husband's power perceived that it was not in her husband's power
398.5–6 A complex operation, A double operation,
398.7 their visitor, Lord Warburton;
398.15 their friend Lod Warburton,
398.21 on this prize upon Lord Warburton
398.24–26 not for any profit to a person already so generally, so perfectly provided as Gilbert Osmond. not for Gilbert Osmond's.
398.35 the other's Lord Warburton's
398.41–42 the leave-taker's movements their visitor's movements
398.42 The latter Their visitor
398.45–399.1 had had had
399.25 Mrs. Osmond Isabel
399.27 wound up terminated
399.28 rather a a rather
399.35–36 her friend Lord Warburton
399.43 he returned. said Lord Warburton.
400.5 he hung fire but an instant— he hesitated a moment—
400.15 Her voice perceptibly trembled. The young girl's voice trembled a little.
400.23 And her interlocutor and Lord Warburton
400.27 she Isabel
400.40 he couldn't Osmond could not
400.45 if whether
401.3 She Isabel
401.18 she returned. said Isabel.
401.30 mean mean that
401.44 indeed however,
402.4 suddenly asked. asked, suddenly.
402.22 returned rejoined
402.25 having prevented preventing
402.36 demanded. asked.
402.41 Gilbert, Osmond,
403.1 who has tried who tried
403.1–2 has grotesquely failed." didn't succeed."
403.3–4 Isabel said. said Isabel.
403.16 a moment; then a moment, and then
403.25 stupefy bewilder
403.27 as she turned turning
403.30 she learned how she learned that
403.32 This latter fact This latter event
403.39–40 her friend—his friend Madame Merle
404.1 the charming woman her brilliant friend
404.4 to make it known to her to inform her of this fact
404.10 discordant inharmonious
404.11 had left left
404.12 the most superfluous of shocks: an unnecessary shock;
404.15 steer wide. steer skillfully.
404.18 horrid painful

404.21 on upon
404.22 grim reality. great reality.
404.22 had cried cried
404.24 had been was
404.27 had been was
404.27 the impression. that.
404.28 had been was
404.29 and in that and that
404.29–30 the same it
404.30 had lasted lasted
404.31 his final appeal had in short faded Caspar Goodwood's visit faded
404.31–32 all the first year during the first year
404.32 her Isabel's
404.32 had dropped dropped
404.34 who was sore and sombre about you who was unhappy on your account
404.35 yet do do
404.36 unreconciled state, unhappiness,
404.40 here was a sufferer who had compensations, Caspar Goodwood had great compensations,
404.41 Mr. Goodwood's his
405.7–8 meeting it in memory or in apprehension a peculiar concussion; meeting it in one's meditation always a sort of shock;
405.9–10 commonly muffling, in an overcivilized age, the sharpness of human contacts, which muffles the sharpness of human contact.
405.13 of Boston— about Boston;
405.14–15 all bounded on the east by Madison Avenue. confined within the limits of Manhattan.
405.15 had thought thought
405.16 had had had
405.20 the young man's disappointment Caspar Goodwood's disappointment
405.21–22 had believed, believed,
405.23 little but little
405.23 had come came
405.24 had never written never wrote
405.28–29 her actual union had grown her marriage became
405.30 had not had had not
405.30–31 on finding herself when she found herself
405.31 had become became
405.32 mentioned related
405.33 needed desired
405.37–38 Caspar, and she saw herself disposed or able to settle it Caspar Goodwood; it seemed to her that she would settle it
405.38–39 easier for him than ever before. easy for him.
405.39 learned learned that
405.40 felt all afraid; felt afraid;
405.41–43 to make out—since he would make it out, as over a falsified balance-sheet or something of that sort—the intimate disarray of her affairs. to learn that she was unhappy.
406.2 stress. misery.
406.7 proving proving that
406.8 so as so that

406.11 and which were still marked enough and were striking enough
406.11 loyalty friendship
406.13–14 Her remarkably open eyes, lighted like great glazed railway-stations, had put up no shutters; Her eye had lost none of its serenity,
406.14–15 her attire had lost her toilet
406.15–16 their national reference. their national flavour.
406.16–17 it struck Isabel she had grown vague. it seemed to Isabel that she had grown restless.
406.17 vague; restless;
406.18–19 through undertaking many enquiries at once, she had managed to be entire and pointed about each. though she was perpetually in motion it was impossible to be more deliberate.
406.31 her present act the actual episode
406.32 of her of one's
406.32 of her of one's
406.36 Her friend Isabel
406.37 the other's her friend's
406.38 had guessed guessed
406.44 and had yet but she had
407.1 she Isabel
407.1–2 this confidant, Henrietta,
407.2–3 not in the least at her ease. not contented.
407.5 wretched. miserable.
407.8 I'm wretched," I am miserable."
407.8 mildly. gently.
407.13 hard to please!" difficult!"
407.26 *have* have
407.27 say say that
407.28 Isabel debated. Isabel hesitated a moment.
407.29–30 I can't announce it on the housetops." I can't tell all the world."
407.31 a laugh. a rich laugh.
407.35 surprising surprising that
407.38 roof. mansion.
407.38 had said said
407.40 had answered answered
408.8 teach herself bring herself
408.11 uncanny. sinister.
408.20 Palazzo the Palazzo
408.24 to wish the lady from New York to wish that Henrietta
409.19 her friend Isabel
409.25 to take in to contemplate
409.27 had walked walked
409.31 feel it afresh to be rather feel afresh that it was rather
409.33 reached high enough. was lofty enough.
409.42 as he had been when that he was when
409.44 had been was
409.44 liked in most places, liked over there,
410.1 There were people who had thought There were some people thought
410.6–7 great school system; school system;
410.7 had been seemed

410.8 behaved appeared
410.8 too much of everything— too much—
410.9 take in a small part. take a small part.
410.10 had seemed seemed
410.21 obliged he was obliged
410.26–27 she indeed expected that she expected
410.27 biggest greatest
410.38–39 she remembered on the contrary on the contrary, she remembered
410.40 walking all round. all walking round.
411.2 about of
411.4 Palazzo the Palazzo
411.10 or take nothing. or nothing.
411.10–11 raised no questions, asked no questions,
411.13 made and made
411.27 loose and easy demonstrative,
411.27 she Isabel
411.27 believe believe that
411.30 was open to little conversation on had little conversation upon
411.33 now, in Rome,
411.34 there was in Rome there was
411.37 save as having save having
411.38 the very oldest; an old friend;
411.40 Gilbert; Osmond;
412.6 *him*. him.
412.7 flattering herself flattering herself that
412.11 on; upon;
412.18 some tall belfry a tall belfry
412.27 Gilbert Osmond
412.28 Mr. Goodwood Goodwood
412.29 Gilbert Osmond
412.30–32 as strong and of as good a style as an English portmanteau,—he had plenty of straps and buckles which would never wear out, and a capital patent lock. as strong as an English portmanteau.
413.13 Henrietta much wondering and Henrietta wondered
413.19 Mr. Bantling on the other hand proved On the other hand, Mr. Bantling was
413.25 his host Touchett,
413.26 take up. talk about.
413.31 Ralph. his host.
413.31 that unclassable personage; Ralph;
413.32–35 so pleasant for all his queerness, so beyond anything to be done. There was always something to be done, for Goodwood, and he did it in this case by repeating several times so helpless. There was help in Goodwood, when once the fountain had been tapped; and he repeated several times
413.36 had artfully disposed had disposed
413.42 depart. leave Rome.
413.43 fear fear that
413.43 there before her eyes there,

413.44 the occurrence of this event this event occuring

413.44 by her door, at her door,

413.45 he she

414.2–3 in Gardencourt; about Gardencourt;

414.9 falsehoods, little fibs,

414.9–10 the strange, the unholy legend of the number of her lovers. the strange memory of her lovers.

414.23 know know that

414.28–29 desired to know. inquired, calmly.

414.32 calmly, tranquilly,

414.41 relapsed. resumed his former posture.

415.18 seemed to him seemed to him that

415.19 wanted wished

415.30 she's *she* is

415.30 smiled Ralph. said Ralph, smiling.

416.7 to make out if to see whether

416.8 to make out," to see,"

416.15 with a harsh ring in his voice, in a strange voice,

416.25 think it right think it is right

416.31 then with an inconsiderate laugh: then gave an inconsiderate laugh.

416.34 and will and he will

417.1 your brother's he is

417.3 Warburton Lord Warburton

417.12 made Ralph made to Ralph,

417.15 this young woman Henrietta

417.16 Henrietta declared. said Henrietta.

417.23 you've so much you have got so much

417.26–27 rather grimly asked. inquired, severely.

417.30 engaged in this act for a while. contemplated her a while.

418.5 a woman's leaving a woman leaving

418.12 train train that

419.5 simply—yet simply, but

419.15 husband?" husband?" he said, jocosely.

419.16 she said, said Isabel,

419.17 then added: then she added—

419.19 laughed Ralph; said Ralph, laughing;

419.26 She Isabel

419.26 observed, she declared,

419.38 Palazzo the Palazzo

419.46 as a man like a man

420.1 have had

420.2 sorry very sorry

420.10 common. flimsy.

420.21–22 we've liked you—!" With which he hesitated we have liked you—" And Osmond hesitated

420.29 for me, my wife; for me;

420.38 you've something about you that you have something that

421.2–3 he chose to use the tone of patronage with a grossness not in his habits he chose for once to be a little vulgar,

421.8–9 perfectly-pitched voice. perfectly modulated voice.

421.16 His host Osmond

421.19 think well of him; like him;

421.22 rather a brilliant a rather brilliant

421.28–29 his triumphant rival had in his composition a streak of perversity. his successful rival had a fantastic streak in his composition.

421.31 and could and he could

421.33 had at times grimly wished he were at times, had wished Osmond were

421.35 made the younger man perfect made Goodwood quite perfect

421.42 had had had

421.43 had been was

421.44–45 prevailing at Palazzo which prevailed at the Palazzo

421.45 had been was

422.3 that had puzzled which puzzled

422.12–13 had pretty well ceased had ceased

422.28–29 the harshness the angry pain

422.30 so far as as far as

422.33 helpless, useless. he was helpless, he was superfluous.

422.34 character fact

422.42 little wanted superfluous

422.43 inperturbable, inscrutable, imperturbable,

422.45 knew knew that

423.1 that which

423.4 the man Osmond

423.4 demonic demoniac

423.6 demonic demoniac

423.8 one's gaining a straw one's self. Goodwood's gaining by it.

423.9 Ralph Touchett," Touchett,"

423.21 Caspar said dryly. said Caspar, drily.

423.25–26 occupied?" the young man mechanically asked. occupied?"

423.32 take my advice and get married. get married.

423.45 a little bleak, a little nude,

424.4 on upon

424.8 his Goodwood's

424.11 eyes eye

424.11 clear hospitable smile, sweet hospitable smile,

424.13 he opposed but a he only opposed a

424.17 Palazzo the Palazzo

424.38 wish wish that

425.1–2 herself; she had for him the same familiar grace. herself, with the same familiar grace.

425.2 to wait to be waiting

425.3 passion passion that

425.4 round around

425.5–6 through the heaving veil he felt her hover through the rustling tissue he saw Isabel hover

425.7 perceived perceived that

425.17 she brightly returned. Isabel rejoined, brightly.

425.32 ease. smile.

425.35 so smooth, so hard. so smooth.

426.5 I tell you I say that

426.34 uttered said,
426.40 I shouldn't. that I shouldn't.
427.3 she Isabel
427.6 Palazzo the Palazzo
427.14–15 had been an enquiry was an inquiry
427.20 smiled at smiled in
427.38 markedly afraid excessively afraid
427.40 occasion, since she now had occasion; for she had
427.41 ease smile
428.6 accident accident that
428.6 supposed. thought.
428.8–9 the wonderful lady Madame Merle
428.10–11 to make her view this friend to make her look at this lady
428.15 brought home brought it home
428.19–20 which had at which at
428.21 she could see Isabel now saw
428.32 consider that Warburton think his lordship
429.18 him? him?
429.26 contraction. contradiction.
429.29 despair; I feel despair," she answered; "I feel
429.39 looking at her friend, to judge the effect looking at Isabel a moment, to judge of the effect
429.39–40 then went on: then she went on—
430.4 that's one thing, and that's one thing;
430.12 her visitor Madame Merle
430.24–25 this woman's her visitor's
430.29 that lady this lady
431.14 space before space lying before
431.14–15 whence you look where you look
431.17 passed vanished
431.18 roamed wandered about
431.21 leaving the walls of Rome behind, passing out of the walls of Rome,
431.36 had had had
431.41 to be even deeply false; to be false;
431.42 had been—deeply, deeply, deeply. had been.
432.5 so much have desired have desired
432.9 particular marriage but had not marriage, but she had not
432.9–10 had therefore had a conception therefore had had an idea
432.12 imperfect. very incomplete.
432.16 had been subject to the good old man's charity. was a victim of the good old man's benevolence.
432.17 borrowing money, borrowing money from Isabel,
432.18–19 the young woman's fresh and ingenuous fortune. the young girl's fortune.
432.21 Gilbert Gilbert Osmond
432.23–24 married her, like a vulgar adventurer, married her
432.28–29 perfectly well; very well;
432.30 since he had wanted if he wanted

432.30–31 her money would now her money to-day would
432.32 would but help would help
432.34 Gilbert Osmond
432.34–35 recognition to her of the boon recognition of the fact
432.39–40 the soft exclamation: "Poor, poor, Madame Merle!" the soft exclamation—"Poor Madame Merle!"
432.41 compassion exclamation
433.8 been. been so.
433.11 he Osmond
433.16 me. me," she said.
433.16–17 if you guess whether you know
433.18 "I trouble about them no more "No more
433.21–22 looked at his companion with a cynical directness looked at his companion for a long time, with a kind of cynical directness
433.28–29 an interest. That's an interest; that's
433.30 enquired with detachment inquired, languidly
433.35 he thoughtfully murmured. Osmond murmured, thoughtfully.
433.37 smiled Madame Merle. said Madame Merle, smiling.
433.42 Osmond just hung fire. Osmond hesitated a moment.
433.44 things things that
434.3 "Pardon "Excuse
434.3 sharply drawn. sharply marked out.
434.12 He Osmond
434.23–24 I mean make me howl like a wolf. *(Omitted.)*
434.24 I've a great need, of that. of that.
434.25 she said. said Madame Merle.
434.28 deviltry devilry
434.38 very very
434.38–39 she added with gravity in her emphasis. Madame Merle added, gravely.
434.43 end?—especially as to their common crimes. end?
434.44 as bad as yourself." bad."
435.5–6 the glow of her eye turned sombre; Her eye brightened, even flashed;
435.11 gesture gesture that
435.34 want wish
435.41 you you
435.42 he Osmond
436.4 pursued: continued:
436.12 wee bit of a tiny crack," small crack,"
436.28 having a glance giving a glance
436.28 for at
436.35 she said softly, said Madame Merle, softly,
436.36 waited, hesitated a moment;
436.42 Madame Merle pursued, said Madame Merle,
436.44 relaxing to its habit of smoothness. relaxing into its usual social expression.
436.45 Her friend Osmond

437.3 she went, the first thing, Madame Merle went,
437.6 she vaguely wailed. she murmured to herself.
437.14–15 She had not the historic sense, though she had in some directions the anecdotic, and as regards herself the apologetic, She was not an antiquarian;
437.19 Palazzo the Palazzo
437.24 the Countess forbade herself every form of active research; the Countess was not very active;
437.32 her parents' guest her aunt
437.40 and disposed to sit and preferred to sit
438.2 on upon
438.2 the Arnide. [sic] Florence.
438.2–3 She so remained She remained
438.5 enclosure inclosure
438.7 that which
438.21 and that she and she
438.30 fifty thousand dollars. forty thousand dollars.
438.38 have the money have got the money
438.43 they that they
439.5 eyes eye
439.5 Isabel debated. Isabel hesitated a moment.
439.36–37 And Rosier faced the Countess, Rosier exclaimed, glancing at the Countess,
439.40–41 Isabel called as she left him. Isabel exclaimed, leaving him.
439.43 she said gently. said Isabel gently.
439.44 returned answered,
440.1 allowing allowed
440.1 saw and saw
440.6 none the less, however,
440.12 the child the young girl
440.13–14 affectionately said. said, affectionately.
440.24 tell her tell her that
440.30 awaiting her; waiting for her;
440.30 "Pardon "Excuse
440.39 her companion Isabel
440.39 tremble. trembling.
440.40 quiver tremor
440.40 everything everything that
440.41 Isabel nevertheless pressed her. Nevertheless, Isabel went on in a moment—
441.2 could scarce trust herself; and could not trust herself. And
441.5 on upon
441.10 frocks. dresses.
441.14 an effect of a sort of
441.18 sometimes." sometimes," she said.
441.23 how little she yet knew her husband. that she did not know her husband yet.
441.23 his daughter Pansy
441.40 He Osmond
441.44 if whether
442.3–4 one's daughter. One's daughter a young girl. A young girl

442.15 little sense of sequestration. little feeling.
442.21 considered contemplated
442.27 any other. the other one.
442.28 as she should take it, after all,
442.29 likes. chooses.
442.33 theoretic tricks on picturesque tricks upon
442.38 had wanted wished
442.40 and show to show
443.3 desired wanted
443.8 his wife Isabel
443.10 strained voice bright voice
443.12 but had but she had
443.17 simpaticissimo. a delightful young man.
443.24 you." you."
443.35 really dying, dying,
443.41 never leave again. She added never leave again. "I like him much better sick than when he used to be well," said Henrietta, who, it will be remembered, had taken a few years before a sceptical view of Ralph's disabilities. She added
443.42 inasmuch as for that
443.43 ailing, sick,
444.8 telegram telegram which
444.20 but he recognised his wife without looking round. but, without looking round, he recognised his wife.
444.35 he Osmond
445.18 "I should be gratified in that case if you disobeyed me." "I shall be gratified then if you disobey me."
445.19 disobeyed disobey
445.20 mildness. gentleness.
445.31 imagination imagination that
445.43 that; this;
446.14 we, we, Mrs. Osmond, is all I know. we, we, is all that I know.
446.21 he Osmond
446.30 his Osmond's
446.44 Osmond's touch. her husband's touch.
446.45 know know that
447.6 cried Isabel. Isabel cried.
447.9 He Osmond
447.11 drawing." And he walked back drawing," he said, walking back
447.13 stood studying it. stood a moment examining his work.
447.16 could see this could see that this
447.17 designed. studied.
447.23 He Osmond
447.26 She Isabel
447.31 any weakness. one's weakness.
447.39 Everything here's of a dreariness—! Everything here is so fearfully edifying.
447.44 simpatico. nice!
447.45 I'm awfully sorry I am sorry
448.9 sure then sure
448.27 Palazzo the Palazzo
448.35 the moment she thus began the moment that she began
448.44 appear seem
448.44–45 she gave herself much trouble, she took things very hard,
449.15–16 a woman should cleave to the man with whom, uttering tremendous

vows, she had stood at the altar. a
woman should abide with her husband.
449.18 hovered stood
449.19 all unperceived; noiselessly, unperceived;
**449.20–22 and her whole face had
grown in an hour a shining intimation.
She lived assuredly, it might be said,
at the window of her spirit, but now
she was leaning far out.** a still
stranger glitter in her small dark eye.
449.23 she began, she said,
449.29 a deal to say, something to say,
**449.30–32 something really human. She
made play with her glittering eyes, in
which there was an unpleasant
fascination.** something important. She
fixed her brilliant eyes upon Isabel,
who found at last a disagreeable fascination in her gaze.
449.32 she soon resumed, the Countess
went on,
449.43 that which
449.44 beat faster. beat.
449.46 she was nevertheless the Countess seemed
450.5 you've such a beastly pure mind.
you have got such a pure mind.
**450.10 while her gathered perversity grew
vivid and dreadful.** while the sharp
animation of her bright, capricious
face emitted a kind of flash.
**450.11–12 in a sort of glare of intention
and, as seemed to Isabel even then, of
ugliness; after which she said:** looking at Isabel, and then she said—
450.15 law?" law?" she murmured.
**450.16 you know at least, if one may
mention it,** you know
450.17 before! before?
**450.18 I thought it mightn't be decent or
respectful.** I didn't suppose it was
proper.
450.19–20 hardly three years but two
years
**450.20–21 wasn't till after her death
that Pansy arrived."** was after her
death that Pansy made her appearance."
450.22 contracted to a frown; gathered
itself into a frown;
450.23–24 seemed so much more
seemed to be more
**450.29 understand. Whose wife?" Isabel
asked.** understand; whose wife's?"
said Isabel.
**450.30–31 Swiss who died—how long?
—a dozen, more than fifteen, years
ago.** Swiss, who died twelve years
ago.
**450.31–33 Miss Pansy, nor, knowing
what he was about, would have anything to say to her; and** Miss Pansy,
and
**450.33–451.13 no reason why he should.
Osmond did, and that was better;
though he had to fit on afterwards the
whole rigmarole of his own wife's having died in childbirth, and of his having, in grief and horror, banished the
little girl from his sight for a long as**

possible before taking her home from
nurse. His wife had really died, you
know, of quite another matter and in
quite another place: in the Piedmontese mountains, where they had
gone, one August, because her health
appeared to require the air, but where
she was suddenly taken worse—fatally
ill. The story passed, sufficiently; it
was covered by the appearances so
long as nobody heeded, as nobody
cared to look into it. But of course *I*
knew—without researches," the Countess lucidly proceeded; "as also, you'll
understand, without a word said between us—I mean between Osmond
and me. Don't you see him looking at
me, in silence, that way, to settle it?
—that is to settle *me* if I should say
anything. I said nothing, right or left
—never a word to a creature, if you
can believe that of me: on my honour,
my dear, I speak of the thing to you
now, after all this time, as I've never,
never spoken. It was to be enough for
me, from the first, that the child was
my niece—from the moment she was
my brother's daughter. As for her veritable mother—!" But with this Pansy's
wonderful aunt dropped—as, involuntarily, from the impression of her sister-in-law's face, out of which more
eyes might have seemed to look at her
than she had ever had to meet.

She had spoken no name, yet Isabel
could but check, on her own lips, an
echo of the unspoken. She sank to her
seat no reason he should. Osmond
did, and that was better."

Isabel stayed the name which rose in
a sudden question to her lips; she sank
down on her seat
451.14 voice voice which
**451.16–28 I've been so bored with your
not knowing. I've been bored, frankly,
my dear, with not having told you;
as if, stupidly, all this time I couldn't
have managed! *Ça me dépasse*, if
you don't mind my saying so, the
things all round you, that you've
appeared to succeed in not knowing.
It's a sort of assistance—aid to innocent ignorance—that I've always been
a bad hand at rendering; and in this
connexion, that of keeping quiet for
my brother, my virtue has at any rate
finally found itself exhausted. It's not
a black lie, moreover, you know," the
Countess inimitably added. "The facts
are exactly what I tell you."**
"I had no idea," said Isabel presently; and looked up at her in a manner that doubtless matched the apparent witlessness of this confession. I
was so tired of your not knowing! I
was tired of not having told you. It
seemed to me so dull. It's not a lie,
you know; it's exactly as I say."
"I never knew," said Isabel looking
up at her, simply.
451.29 Had Has

451.30 he was for six or seven years her lover?" he has been her lover?"
451.31–37 Things have occurred to me, and perhaps that was what they all meant."
"She has been wonderfully clever, she has been magnificent, about Pansy!" the Countess, before all this view of it, cried.
"Oh, no idea, for me," Isabel went on, "ever definitely took that form." She appeared to be making out to herself what had been and what hadn't. "And Something has occurred to me. Perhaps it was that."
"She has been wonderfully clever about Pansy!" cried the Countess. "That thing has never occurred to me," said Isabel. "And

451.38–40 She spoke as one troubled and puzzled, yet the poor Countess seemed to have seen her revelation fall below its possibilities of effect. She spoke in a low, thoughtful tone, and the poor Countess was equally surprised and disappointed at the effect of her revelation.
451.40 to kindle some responsive blaze, but had to kindle a conflagration, and as yet she had
451.41–43 Isabel showed as scarce more impressed than she might have been, as a young woman of approved imagination, with some fine sinister passage of public history. Isabel seemed more awe-stricken than anything else.
451.44 recognise how perceive that
451.44 her her
451.44–452.1 —that is with M. Merle himself," her companion resumed. the Countess asked.
452.2 he M. Merle
452.4–6 The conditions happened to make it workable, under stress (I mean at so awkward a pinch), that Osmond should acknowledge On the other hand, circumstances made it convenient enough for Osmond to acknowledge
452.7–13 she had not been dead too long to put a certain accommodation of dates out of the question—from the moment, I mean, that suspicion wasn't started; which was what they had to take care of. What was more natural than that poor Mrs. Osmond, at a distance and for a world not troubling about trifles, should have left behind her, poverina, the pledge of her brief happiness that had cost her her life? she had only been dead a year, and what was more natural than that she should have left behind a pledge of their affection?
452.13–15 Osmond had been living with her at Naples at the time of their stay in the Alps, and he in due course left it for ever— he had been living at Naples, and he left it forever—
451.15–16 the whole history was success-

fully set going. the little fable was easily set going.
452.16 in who was in
452.17 her skin, her reputation,
452.19 "Ah, poor, poor woman!" cried Isabel, who herewith burst "Ah, poor creature!" cried Isabel, bursting
452.21 a high reaction a reaction
452.21 flowed gushed
452.24 she discordantly laughed. she cried, with a discordant laugh.
452.25 a way of your own—!" a pure mind!"
452.26–27 false to his wife—and so very soon!" said Isabel with a sudden check. false to his wife," said Isabel, suddenly controlling herself.
452.29–30 "I quite agree with you, however, that it was much too soon." (Omitted.)
452.31 "But to me, to me—?" "But to me—to me—"
452.31–33 as if she had not heard; as if her question—though it was sufficiently there in her eyes—were all for herself. though there was a question in her eyes.
452.34–35 Well, it depends, my dear, on what It depends upon what
452.35–37 the lover of another woman —such a lover as he had been, cara mia, between their risks and their precautions, while the thing lasted! the lover of another woman.
452.38 affairs things
452.38–40 the lady had repented; or at all events, for reasons of her own, drawn back: and she had always had, too, a worship of appearances the lady had repented; and she had a worship of appearances
452.41 had got bored with it. got tired of it.
452.41–43 was—when he couldn't patch it on conveniently to any of those he goes in for! was!
452.44 Isabel mechanically echoed, said Isabel,
453.1–2 for six or seven years, as I say, they had kept it up." for five years they were very intimate."
453.3 She was silent a little. (Omitted.)
453.6 believed thought
453.13 believing thinking
453.15 plenty of little idiotic fibs, little fibs;
453.18 wares wares that
453.19 she finally asked. she asked, at last.
453.30–33 Besides, she has never had, about him," the Countess went on, leaving Isabel to wince for it so tragically afterwards—"she had never had, what you might call any illusions of intelligence. (Omitted.)
454.2 things things that
454.10 you you
454.22 more and more wan. of deepening dreariness.

454.27 she'd dish herself!" she would stumble!"

454.28 failed so dreadfully failed so dreadfully herself

454.30 her guest the Countess

454.35–36 her deplorable origin. I myself her lamentable parentage. I

454.36 not, naturally, because not because

454.37 hers, hers—

454.39 while she flushed flushing quickly

454.42 his daughter a great little lift. Pansy a great lift.

455.3 a *dot* a dowry.

455.4 I would refuse to believe it. I shouldn't believe it.

455.5 easy and natural and nasty; wicked,

455.6 wicked, for the comfort of it, once wicked, for once

455.16 she broke off—or *he* did. she became proper.

455.23 her. her.

455.30–31 scant of breath; short of breath;

455.38 said with the penetration of her sharp bright smile: said sotfly, with her sharp, bright smile—

455.46 wailed; murmured;

456.2 far-reaching, infinite sadness. exquisite, far-reaching sadness.

456.7 only of one thing. of only one thing.

456.16–17 the place, which affronted and almost frightened her; the place, and it made her horribly sad;

456.20 pretend pretend that

456.22 make her reach out a hand. make Isabel reach out her hand to her.

456.36–37 like suddenly, and rather awfully, seeing a painted picture move. a sort of reduplication.

456.40–42 Her being there at all had the character of ugly evidence, of handwritings, of profaned relics, of grim things produced in court. Her being there at all was a kind of vivid proof.

457.9–10 she pretended not even to smile, she did not even pretend to smile,

457.12 her young friend Isabel

457.15 a distinction. She a difference; she

457.19–20 to notice to look at her,

457.27 mildly; softly;

457.32 small girl; young girl;

457.33 small girls; young girls,

457.42 frock; dress;

458.9 Mother Superior; Superior;

458.10–11 Mother Superior poor Superior

458.17 break in her voice, a lapse in her continuity, rupture in her voice,

458.24 but was it was

458.25 from the moment for the moment

458.30 proceed. go on.

458.32 in her not betraying in not betraying

458.33 She resisted this, She did not betray herself;

458.37 saw it all saw all this

458.37–38 reflected in a large clear glass. a picture on the wall.

458.41–42 the promise of a brighter day. a symptom of a brighter day.

458.42 a moment during which a moment while

458.43–44 that knowledge. her knowledge.

458.45 she Isabel

458.5–6 an applied handled hung-up tool, as senseless and convenient as mere shaped wood and iron. a dull un-reverenced tool.

458.10–11 the hideous vision dropped. the hideous vision died away.

458.15 that which

458.17 turned slow eyes, looking down turned her eyes and looked down

458.22 our young woman Isabel

458.23 "I go "I am going

459.24 "Go to "Going to

459.36 then added: then she said,

459.43 Pansy. Pansy," she said.

459.45 While And while

460.3 recognised Madame Catherine, recognised her as Madame Catherine

460.8 pleased guarded vision to pleasant, cautious little eye towards

460.29 to accommodate. to say something agreeable.

460.33 on upon

460.36–37 kneeled down kneeled down before Isabel

461.4 Pansy breathed with faintness. said Pansy, faintly.

461.12 the girl Pansy

461.15 an air of intimacy. the quality of intimacy.

461.20 may have stood almost as still may almost have stood still,

461.21 had she if she had

461.26 she presently went on. she said presently.

461.27–28 Isabel explained; "since Isabel answered; "for

461.28 I can't be called near you." I am very far away from you."

461.41 Isabel said nothing for a minute; Isabel was silent a moment;

462.12 saw saw that

462.25 then. I leave then," she said; "I leave

462.28 child's face. girl's face.

462.33 saw saw that

462.44 considered. reflected a little.

463.3 she Pansy

463.5 hesitated, then stopped. hesitated a moment; then she stopped.

463.15 Mrs. Osmond Isabel

463.20 Isabel stiffened; she Isabel gave a start, and she

463.23 friend. visitor.

463.24 grasped her arm very gently laid her hand very gently on her arm,

463.25 wise, benevolent eyes, a wise, benevolent eye,

463.25 said in French and almost familiarly: said to her, speaking French, almost familiarly—

463.28 Madame Catherine distinctly observed. said Madame Catherine, significantly.

463.29 the door the door behind Isabel,

463.34 found found that

464.2 her utterance. her question.

464.4 She just hung fire. "It's rather hard Madame Merle hesitated a moment. "It is difficult

464.12 appearing to see appeared to see

464.12 she and she

464.14 him him that

464.19 to live in to be living in

464.30–31 she quietly remarked she announced,

464.39 felt felt that

465.5 neither reflexion not reflection,

465.7 came and went alternated

465.8–9 rose and fell came and went

465.16 She That is, she

465.17–18 they had been weighted with lead. they were leaden-weighted.

465.21 much-embracing refuge. richly-constituted refuge.

465.25 sanctuary positive sanctuary

465.34–35 she recalled to herself one of those Etruscan figures couched upon the receptacle of their ashes. if her spirit was haunted with sudden pictures, it might have been the spirit disembarrassed of the flesh.

465.37 was far. seemed far away.

465.38 well, so unimaginable. so strange.

465.39 her intelligence dropped, Isabel's imagination paused,

465.42 where she had announced she was going. where she was going.

466.3–4 to get quite away, really away, further away than little grey-green England, to die;

466.8 enlivening, exhilarating,

466.9 proof she proof that she

466.10 be she be that she

466.13 seemed to her seemed to her that

466.14 if whether

466.15 even [sic] ever

466.16–17 Wasn't it Was it not

466.17 fine delicate

466.20 never escape; not escape;

466.21 last to the end. last.

466.27 She rejoiced She was so glad

466.27 had come; was there;

466.31 remembered remembered that

466.43 felt felt that

467.8 lovely lovely that

467.11 smiled in return. answered, smiling.

467.11 felt found

467.13 brave eyes, excellent eye,

467.13 They seemed to say It seemed to say that

467.14 remember remember that

467.15–16 she thought of him, extravagantly, as a beautiful blameless knight. she thought him so kind.

467.22 found so interesting. thought so interesting.

467.27 believe it was very rough," she said, think it was rather rough," said Isabel,

467.32 to Gardencourt." there."

467.33 look awfully sad? look sad?

467.33 awfully sad very sad

467.35 awfully sad. sad.

467.35–36 awfully kind," kind,"

467.36 a breadth a frankness

467.36–37 seemed to her seemed to her that

467.39 he assured and assured

467.41 know. I was know," he said. "I was

467.44 had been was

467.45 Ralph Touchett

468.1–2 "He was awfully jolly and funny "He was immensely friendly

468.2–3 awfully wretched." awfully sad."

468.7 greatly obliged very much obliged

468.12 awfully very

468.13 awfully very

468.15 On which Isabel While Isabel

468.15–16 he and Henrietta seemed after all after all he and Henrietta seemed

468.19–20 the latter was now at liberty now Isabel was at liberty

468.31 get your own. get to your own.

468.34–35 her friend Isabel

468.35 And later, Later,

468.36–37 asked those questions asked Isabel those questions

468.38 make you a scene make a scene

469.3 regarded her guest. contemplated her friend.

469.4 hellish," awful,"

469.5 hellish. awful.

469.12 Isabel waited a moment. Isabel for a moment said nothing, then—

469.12 another." another," she rejoined.

469.17–18 was a complication, but what will going back be?" was hard; but going back will be harder still."

469.22 a scene of the rest of my life." a scene that will last always."

469.23–24 sat and considered this remainder, sat gazing at this prospect;

469.27 invitation letter

469.31 who fixed her eyes fixing her eyes

469.35 grasped perceived

469.35 this sense it

469.39–40 the right excess of intensity, a gravity too pathetic to be real—

469.43–44 locate right here in London." I'm going to reside in London."

470.2 as I can that I can

470.4 isn't a riddle." is very good."
470.5–6 "No, he isn't a bad pun—or even a high flight of American humour. Henrietta said nothing; she seemed lost in reflection.
470.6 Henrietta went on. she remarked at last.
470.7–8 as clear as the style of a good prospectus. as clear as glass—there's no mystery about him.
470.13 too infatuated with mere brain-power; too intellectual;
470.14 isn't a vulgar fault. is a glorious fault.
470.21 duly diverted, deeply diverted,
470.22 had confessed herself human was human
470.24 was a disappointment to find she was rather a disappointment to find that she
470.30 Mr. Bantling himself at least. Mr. Bantling, after all,
470.38 a mastermind. very talented.
470.39–40 woman of my modern type. lady-correspondent!
470.44 understand my mixture— understand—
471.2–3 find out the mystery and the proportions of it. That's a find out. It's a
471.10 ten o'clock two o'clock,
471.18 think it awfully odd," think it's very odd,"
471.20 think it awfully odd." think it's very odd."
471.21 so awfully odd so odd
471.27 that instead that Isabel, instead
471.28 she was was
471.30 appeared appeared to be
471.31-33 and scared—as scared as if the objects about her had begun to show for conscious things, watching her trouble with grotesque grimaces. and even frightened.
471.35 with a stillness a stillness
471.39–40 everything everything that
471.41 she had stood there that she stood there.
471.41–43 She envied the security of valuable "pieces" which change by no hair's breadth, only grow in value, while their owners lose inch by inch youth, happiness, beauty; she reflected that things change but little, while people change so much,
471.44–45 the day she had come the day that she came
472.4 and she might and to-day she might
472.4 a woman more blest. a happier woman.
472.5–6 a charming and precious Bonington— a beautiful and valuable Bonington
472.6 rested a long time. rested for a long time.
472.15 if whether
472.17 on Isabel's hot cheek. as Isabel kissed her.
472.19 luncheon her lunch

472.24 remembered remembered that
472.26–27 walking everywhere," walking,"
472.27 if whether
472.32 declined the office of saying. hesitated a moment.
472.33 was the limit of her extravagance. she said.
472.43 told Isabel told Isabel that
473.1 and was and it was
473.3–4 our young woman asked as she stood before her. Isabel asked, standing before her aunt.
473.18 wrote me wrote me that
473.26 For this repast At this repast
473.27–28 saw her aunt not to be so dry saw that her aunt was not so dry
473.30 Unmistakeably she would have found It seemed to her she would find
473.31-32 to feel a defeat, a mistake, even a shame or two. to indulge a regret.
473.32–35 if she were not even missing those enrichments of consciousness and privately trying—reaching out for some aftertaste of life, dregs of the banquet; the testimony of pain or the cold recreation of remorse. whether Mrs. Touchett were not trying, whether she had not a desire for the recreation of grief.
473.36 if she should begin to know remorse at all if she began to regret,
473.37 how it had that it had
473.37–38 over her dimly over her
473.38 failed of something, missed something,
473.40 had as yet as yet had
474.1 to struggle again to converse
474.2 She none the less presently said She presently said
474.6 returned. rejoined.
474.7 saw saw that
474.12 he's engaged he was engaged
474.14 mildly gently
474.25–26 some imputed soreness, some curious emotion,
474.38–39 how extremely wan she must have looked how extremely sad she looked
475.3 meal; lunch;
475.4 she observed she said to Isabel,
475.10–11 and as her niece and Isabel
475.12 she felt herself followed by her eyes. while her aunt followed her with her eyes.
475.15 shook her head slowly, but not heavily shook her head slowly, smiling.
475.18 she declared, Isabel replied,
475.24 told him he wouldn't. told him that.
475.39 went away— he went away;
475.43 send word send word that
476.1 toward evening towards evening
476.2 How he knew was How he knew it was
476.5–6 told the nurse she told the nurse that she

476.8 helpless very helpless
476.14 and this but this
476.14 was but one was only one
476.21 three days for three days
476.22 at moments seemed at moments he seemed
476.32 and from from
476.40 rest? rest?" he asked.
476.41 last of all. last.
476.43–44 here I thought here, I thought
477.23 he must know; he might know;
478.5 he wailed. he added softly.
478.10–11 the money," my money,"
478.35 Ralph gasped. Ralph stammered.
479.3 to stay—as long to stay, as long
479.13 many things in life. You're many things in life; you are
479.17 But he And he
479.20–21 yours can hurt you yours—can hurt you
479.24–25 you've also been loved. Ah but, Isabel—*adored!*" he just audibly and lingeringly breathed. you have also been loved."
479.26 "Oh my brother!" "Ah, my brother!"
479.34 it being her belief for it was her belief
479.40 he Ralph
479.41 vague, dim,
479.41 vagueness dimness
479.44 She quitted the place She went out of her room,
480.2 Outside Ralph's door Outside of Ralph's door
480.8–9 The two nurses were The nurse was
480.18–19 as might be, as it were,
480.21 "Dear Aunt Lydia," "Poor Aunt Lydia,"
480.25 at the height in the height
480.31–32 but neither a harsh nor a heavy one; but it was not a disagreeable one;
480.43 all unknown to her, unknown to Isabel,
481.7 found found that
481.9 how little it was that it was not
481.22 what she had left her husband to do. what she left her husband for.
481.30 a penetrating chill in the image, a deadly sadness in the thought,
481.35 would he would
481.42 utility. satisfaction.
482.3 since for
482.25 you had been you were
483.3 for an hour; a little;
483.10 on upon
483.11 Mrs. Touchett Mrs. Touchett that
483.12 thesis theory,
483.24 had had a chance, would had had time, she would
483.25 saw saw that
483.33 nobleman nobleman whom
483.38 greeted her he greeted her
484.1–2 rather irrelevantly explained. explained, rather irrelevantly.
484.27 coloured blushed
484.31 five days; three days;
484.34 if whether
485.4 eyes, eye.
485.18 on in
485.22 the letter that letter
485.29 persons people
485.45 a few yards a few feet
486.4 saw saw that
486.8 which that
486.11 at present to-day
486.12 close to her—beside her on the bench and pressingly turned to her. close to her.
486.14 an instant, a moment,
486.28 had parted parted
486.32–33 something really formidable in his resolution. She something awful in his persistency. Isabel
486.35 round around
486.37 of no use; no use;
486.41 vain no use
487.10 a good man, a fine man, one of the best; a good fellow—he was a noble fellow—
487.11 the case stands for you. the case stands.
487.12 guessed my sentiments. guessed what I thought of you.
487.24 an idea, which she scented an idea. Isabel scented his idea
487.25–26 pressing her still harder, pressing her close,
487.31–32 the deadliest of fiends." a devil!"
487.41–42 have cost cost
487.42–43 Say it will"—and he flared almost into anger: "give me one word of truth! *(Omitted.)*
487.43 know such a horror as that, know that,
488.3 his queer grim point his point
488.8–9 You can't turn anywhere; you know that perfectly. *(Omitted.)*
488.9 it is therefore that it is that
488.10 me." me."
488.10 'you'?" you?"
488.15 turn. Turn straight to me. turn; turn to me!
488.17 paused with paused a moment,
488.19 you!" you!"
488.21–23 She had believed it, but this was different; this was the hot wind of the desert, at the approach of which the others dropped dead, like mere sweet airs of the garden. *(Omitted.)*
488.23–25 it lifted her off her feet, while the very taste of it, as of something potent, acrid and strange, forced open her set teeth. it lifted her off her feet.
488.28 prove he prove that he
488.29 want wish
488.30–32 only for once listen to me. It's too monstrous of you to think of sinking back into that misery, of going to open your mouth to that poisoned air. only listen to me. It's too mon-

strous to think of sinking back into that misery.

489.6 If you'll If you

489.8 big. large.

489.17 everything he everything that he

489.17 believed just then believed

489.18–19 her dying. dying.

489.20 sink and sink. sinking and sinking.

489.24 harsh and terrible, through a confusion of vaguer sounds. through a confusion of sound.

489.26 all the rest and all the rest

489.27 her own swimming head. her own head.

489.28 she panted. she said.

489.34–41 His kiss was like white lightning, a flash that spread, and spread again, and stayed; and it was extraordinarily as if, while she took it, she felt each thing in his hard manhood that had least pleased her, each aggressive fact of his face, his figure, his presence, justified of its intense identity and made one with this act of possession. So had she heard of those wrecked and under water following a train of images before they sink. But when darkness returned she was free. His kiss was like a flash of lighting; when it was dark again she was free.

489.42 darted darted away

490.9 hat bonnet

490.10 hopes hope

490.21 started—?" started—"

490.22–23 he stiffly averted himself. But he couldn't otherwise move. he turned away.

490.27–31 On which he looked up at her—but only to guess, from her face, with a revulsion, that she simply meant he was young. She stood shining at him with that cheap comfort, and it added, on the spot, thirty years to his life. She walked him away with her, however, as if she had given him now the key to patience. On which he looked up at her.

F. O. MATTHIESSEN

The Painter's Sponge and Varnish Bottle†

I

One sign of how little technical analysis James has received is the virtual neglect of his revisions. Beyond Theodora Bosanquet's sensitive remarks in 'Henry James at Work' and occasional citation to annotate the elaborations of his later manner, they have been passed by. The only detailed exception is an essay on *Roderick Hudson* wherein the writer held that James' additions had largely served to spoil the clean outlines of its style.[1] Yet James made these revisions at the plentitude of his powers, and they constituted a *reseeing* of the problems of his craft. He knew that it would be folly to try to recast the structure of any of his works. In the first preface that he wrote, that to *Roderick Hudson*, he developed an analogy for his aims in the way his fellow-craftsman on canvas went about to freshen his surfaces, to restore faded values, to bring out 'buried secrets.' He undertook, in particular, a minute verbal reconsideration of the three early novels that he chose to re-publish.

My reason for singling out *The Portrait of a Lady* is that it is a much richer book than either of the two others. *Roderick Hudson* is full of interest for James' development, since the two halves of his nature, the creator and the critic, are in a sense projected in Roderick and Rowland. Moreover, he there first tried out his device of having his narrative interpreted by the detached observer. But the book as a whole remains apprentice work. The revision of *The American*—the most extensive of all—might tell us, among other things, how James tried to repair what he had himself come to consider the falsely romantic aspects of his denouement. But *The Portrait of a Lady* is his first unquestioned masterpiece. By considering all the issues that the revisions raise, we may see it with renewed clarity.[2]

†From *Henry James: The Major Phase* edited by F.O. Matthiessen. Copyright 1944 Oxford University Press, Inc. Reprinted by permission.

1. Hélène Harvitt, 'How Henry James Revised *Roderick Hudson*: A Study in Style,' PMLA (March 1924), 203–227.
2. James had developed early the habit of touching up his texts wherever possible; and he even made a few slight alterations in the *Portrait* between its appearance in *The Atlantic Monthly* (November 1880–December 1881) and in volume form. For instance, Madame Merle's first name was changed from Geraldine to Serena. But the changes that can instruct us in the evolution of his technique are naturally those he introduced when returning to the book after more than a quarter of a century.

James' copies of both *The American* and *The Portrait of a Lady*, containing his innumerable revisions in longhand on the margins and in inserted pages of typescript, are now in the Houghton Library at Harvard.

I want to thank again the group of Harvard and Radcliffe students with whom I read through Henry James in the winter of 1943, since they did most of the spade work for this essay.

Larger changes are very few. A page of conversation between Ralph Touchett and Lord Warburton (at the very end of Chapter xxvii) was recast in a way that shows James' more mature sense of a dramatic scene. What had been two pages of psychological scrutiny of Osmond just before his proposal to Isabel (Chapter xxix) were felt by James to be otiose, and were cut to ten lines–an item of interest for the conventional view that the older James always worked the other way. But, with two important exceptions later to be looked into, we are to be concerned here with the tiniest brush strokes. What must be kept constantly in mind, therefore, is the design of the canvas as a whole. If that is done, we may have the intimate profit of watching the artist at his easel and of gaining insight into his principles of composition.

The writer's equivalent for the single flake of pigment is the individual word; and two words which James felt to be in need of consistent readjustment—'picturesque' and 'romantic'—form in themselves an index to his aims. He had begun the book in Florence and had finished it in Venice. He had been at the time still strongly under the spell of Italian art, which, as he wrote William, had first taught him 'what the picturesque is.' He had consequently used the word freely as a kind of aesthetic catch-all, too loosely as he came to feel, for he struck it out in almost every case. He had applied it to Gardencourt, to Isabel's grandmother's house in Albany, to Osmond's *objets d'art*; he changed it in the first case to 'pictorial,' in the others to 'romantic.'[3] Some of its many other occurrences must have made the later James wince, especially where he had said that Madame Merle had 'a picturesque smile.' That was altered to 'amused.' It is significant that when the word was retained, it was qualified by the speaker, by Isabel, who says that she would be a little on both sides of a revolution, that she would admire the Tories since they would have 'a chance to behave so exquisitely. I mean so picturesquely.' 'So exquisitely' was added in the revision, and it is no accident that where, in the earlier version, Lord Warburton had remarked that Isabel found the British 'picturesque,' he was later made to say ' "quaint." ' That putting into quotation marks underscores Isabel's attitude, as, indeed, do several instances where James introduced 'romantic' not merely as a substitute for 'picturesque.' Isabel's first judgment of Caspar as 'not especially good looking' becomes 'he was not romantically, rather obscurely handsome'; and her initial response to Warburton as 'one of the most delectable persons she had met' is made much firmer—she judges him, 'though quite without luridity—as a hero of romance.'

---

3. I have included all the detailed references to both editions in the version of this essay that appeared in *The American Bookman* (Winter 1944). To avoid spotting these pages with unnecessary footnotes, I refer to that periodical any reader who is interested in following out the comparison for himself.

And when we find that she doesn't tell her sister about either his or Osmond's proposal, not simply because 'it entertained her to say nothing' but because 'it was more romantic,' and she delighted in 'drinking deep, in secret, of romance,' we have the clue to what James is building up through his greatly increased use of this adjective and noun. He is bound to sharpen the reader's impression of how incorrigibly romantic Isabel's approach to life is, an important issue when we come to judge the effect of the book's conclusion.

Another word that shows the drift of James' later concern is 'vulgar.' One of James' most limiting weaknesses, characteristic of his whole phase of American culture, was dread of vulgarity, a dread that inhibited any free approach to natural human coarseness. But here the increased intrusion of the word does no great damage. When 'the public at large' becomes 'a vulgar world,' or when Henrietta Stackpole asserts that our exaggerated American stress on brain power 'isn't a vulgar fault' (she had originally pronounced it a 'glorious' one), or when Isabel adds to her accruing reflections that Osmond had married her, 'like a vulgar adventurer,' for her money, we simply see more sharply the negative pole of James' vision.

His positive values come out in a whole cluster of words affecting the inner life of his characters, words in which we may read all the chief attributes of Jamesian sensibility. Ralph's 'delights of observation' become 'joys of contemplation.' Warburton's sisters' 'want of vivacity' is sharpened to 'want of play of mind,' just as Isabel's 'fine freedom of composition' becomes 'free play of intelligence.' On the other hand, Warburton, in Ralph's description, is toned down from 'a man of imagination' to 'a man of a good deal of charming taste,' in accordance with the high demands that James came to put upon the imagination as the discerner of truth. It is equally characteristic that Isabel's 'feelings' become her 'consciousness,' and that her 'absorbing happiness' in her first impressions of England becomes 'her fine, full consciousness.' She no longer feels that she is 'being entertained' by Osmond's conversation; rather she has 'what always gave her a very private thrill, the consciousness of a new relation.' Relations, intelligence, contemplation, consciousness—we are accumulating the words that define the Jamesian drama. No wonder that James came to feel that it had been flat to say that Isabel was fond 'of psychological problems.' As he rewrote it, she became fond, as he was, 'ever, of the question of character and quality, of sounding, as who should say, the deep personal mystery.'

II

To progress from single words to questions of style, we note at once the pervasive colloquialization. The younger James had used the conventional forms, 'cannot' and 'she would'; in his revised conversation these always appear as 'can't' and 'she'd.' Of more interest is his handling of the 'he said—she said' problem, upon which the older James could well take pride for his ingenuity. Isabel 'answered, smiling' becomes Isabel 'smiled in return' or Isabel 'gaily engaged.' Osmond 'hesitated a moment' becomes that Jamesian favorite, Osmond 'just hung fire.' And for one more out of a dozen other evasions of the obvious, the Countess Gemini no longer 'cried . . . with a laugh'; her sound and manner are condensed into one word, 'piped.'

James' humor has often been lost sight of in discussion of the solemnities of his mandarin style. But he didn't lose it himself. His original thumb-nail characterization of Isabel's sister was descriptive: 'Lily knew nothing about Boston; her imagination was confined within the limits of Manhattan.' A graphic twist brings that to life with a laugh: 'her imagination was all bounded on the east by Madison Avenue.'

The later James was more concrete. He had also learned what a source of life inheres in verbal movement. 'Their multifarious colloquies' is heavily abstract, whereas 'their plunge . . . into the deeps of talk' takes us right into the action. So too with the diverse ways in which James launched his characters into motion, as when Henrietta 'was very well dressed' became 'she rustled, she shimmered'; or when the Countess, instead of entering the room 'with a great deal of expression,' did it 'with a flutter through the air.' Such movement means that James was envisaging his scenes more dramatically; and, in the passage where Isabel has just been introduced to Osmond, we can see how natural it had become for the novelist to heighten any theatrical detail. Where he had formerly written that Isabel sat listening to Osmond and Madame Merle 'as an impartial auditor of their brilliant discourse,' he now substituted 'as if she had been at the play and had paid even a large sum for her place.' And as this scene advances, instead of saying that Madame Merle 'referred everything' to Isabel, James wrote that she 'appealed to her as if she had been on the stage, but she could ignore any learnt cue without spoiling the scene.'

Operating more pervasively, here as always, upon James' imagination, were analogies with pictures rather than with the stage. When he wanted to enrich his bare statement that the Countess 'delivered herself of a hundred remarks from which I offer the reader but a brief selection,' he said that she 'began to talk very much as if, seated brush in hand before an easel, she were applying a series of considered touches to a composition of figures already sketched in.' A phrase that shows us James' very process is when Isabel, instead of 'examining the idea' (of Warburton's 'being a personage'), is made to examine 'the image so conveyed.' The growth from ideas to images is what James had been fumbling for in his earlier preoccupation with the picturesque. The word might now embarrass him, but not the secret he had learned through it. He had originally opened the first of the chapters to be laid in Osmond's villa by remarking that 'a picturesque little group' was gathered there. What he meant to imply was made much more explicit in the revision: 'a small group that might have been described by a painter as composing well.'

That concern with composition grew from the conviction which he voiced in the preface to *Roderick Hudson*, that the novelist's subject, no less than the painter's, consisted ever in 'the related state, to each other, of certain figures and things.' And characters, he came to believe, could be best put into such relations when they were realized as visually, as lambently, as possible. This belief led him into one of his most recurrent types of revision, into endowing his *dramatis personae* with characterizing images. He had concluded his initial account of Ralph's ill health by remarking, 'The truth was that he had simply accepted the situation.' In place of that James was to introduce the poignancy that is Ralph's special note: 'His serenity was but the array of wild flowers niched in his ruin.' In comparable fashion, James added to his first description of Osmond, with no parallel in the original, an image that embodies the complex nature we are to find in him: 'He suggested, fine gold coin as he was, no stamp nor emblem of the common mintage that provides for general circulation; he was the elegant complicated medal struck off for a special occasion.'

Such elaborate images, more than any other aspect of James' later style, show his delight in virtuosity. Occasionally they seem to have been added purely because his eye fell on a dull patch of canvas, and he set out to brighten it up. Warburton's dim sisters don't contribute much in the original beyond 'the kindest eyes in the world.' But, in revising, James let himself go: their eyes are now 'like the balanced basins, the circles of "ornamental water," set, in parterres, among the geraniums.' In that image any functional intention may seem lost in the rococo flourish; but such was not usually the case. Take one very typical instance in the first detailed description of Caspar Goodwood—and it is significant of James' matured intentions that he introduced characterizing images of his chief figures at such important points. We are told in the first version that Caspar had undergone the usual gentleman athlete's education at Harvard, but that 'later, he had become reconciled to culture.' In the revision James conveyed much more of Caspar's energetic drive by means of a muscular image: 'later on he had learned that the finer intelligence too could vault and pull and strain.'

The full effect that James was trying for in such images might be instanced by the chapter which introduces Henrietta. Here we might follow James in the process of enlivening his sketch by a dozen fresh touches. The most interesting of these bring out Henrietta's character by the device of interrelating her appearance with her career. He did not rest content with saying that 'she was scrupulously, fastidiously neat. From top to toe she carried not an ink-stain.' He changed this into: 'she was as crisp and new and comprehensive as a first issue before the folding. From top to toe she had probably no misprint.' In spite of the loudness of her voice (which caused James to alter Henrietta 'murmured' to Henrietta 'rang out'), Ralph was originally surprised to find that she was not 'an abundant talker.' But in the revision the detailed glance at her profession is sustained, and he finds her not 'in the large type, the type of horrid "headlines." ' Yet she still remains fairly terrifying to Ralph, and, a few pages farther on, James emphasized that by another kind of image. To point up the fact that 'she was brave,' he added, 'she went into cages, she flourished lashes, like a spangled lion-tamer.' With that as a springboard James could rise to the final sentence of this chapter. Originally Ralph had concluded, 'Henrietta, however, is fragrant—Henrietta is decidedly fragrant!' But this became a punch line: 'Henrietta, however, does smell of the Future—it almost knocks one down!'

James remarked in his preface that he had given the reader 'indubitably too much' of Henrietta—a thing that could be said of most of his *ficelles*; but in retouching he had at least done what he could to brighten every inch. In relation to her we may note another phase of his revision, his addition of epithets to characterize the world of which she is part. In Rome she is struck by the analogy between the ancient chariot ruts and 'the iron grooves which mark the course of the American horse-car.' These become more up to date: 'the overjangled iron grooves which express the intensity of American life.' Where James had written 'the nineteenth century,' he was later to call it 'the age of advertisement'; and glancing, not at America but at Europe, he named it 'an overcivilized age.' But it was Henrietta's realm he was thinking of again when, instead of having Madame Merle remark that 'it's scandalous, how little I know about the land of my birth,' he had her call it rather, in his most revelatory addition of this type: 'that splendid, dreadful, funny country—surely the greatest and drollest of them all.'

III

So far I have avoided the question that is usually raised first about James' revisions. Didn't he sometimes overwrite to no purpose as a mere occupational disease? Occasionally, without doubt, it is the older James talking instead of a character, as when Pansy, instead of saying, 'I have no voice—just a little thread,' is made to transform this into '. . . just a small sound like the squeak of a slate-pencil making flourishes.' But look at another sample where at first it would appear as though James had taken twice as many words to say the same thing, where 'Marriage meant that a woman should abide with her husband' became 'Marriage meant that a woman should cleave to the man with whom, uttering tremendous vows, she had stood at the altar.' In its context we can at least see what James was after. This passage is part of Isabel's reflections, and both its fuller rhythm and density are meant to increase its *inner* relevance. The best way, therefore, to judge the final value of James' rewriting is to relate it in each case to the character involved, an obligatory proceeding in dealing with the writer who asked, in *The Art of Fiction*: 'What is a picture or a novel that is *not* of character?'

The diverse types of revision demanded by the different characters may also remind us that we have in this book the most interestingly variegated group that James ever created. The center of attention is always Isabel, and the changes devoted to her may be read as a brief outline of the interpretation which James hoped we should give to his heroine. A few involve her looks. Whereas acquaintances of the Archer girls used to refer to her as 'the thin one,' James' tenderness for her was later to make this sound less invidious: 'the willowy one.' From his initial description of her in the house at Albany, he wanted to emphasize that she was less mistress of her fate than she fondly believed. He pointed this up by changing 'young girl' to 'creature of conditions.' He also, as a past master of what could be gained by the specific notation, changed the conditioning of her taste from 'a glimpse of contemporary aesthetics' to 'the music of Gounod, the poetry of Browning, the prose of George Eliot'—a change which recalls that these were also Minny Temple's[4] tastes.

But James' chief interest in his heroine is revealed through another type of change. Warburton's belief that she is 'a thoroughly interesting woman' is made more intimate—'a really interesting little figure.' And a few lines below, when Ralph concludes that a character like hers 'is the finest thing in nature,' he says more precisely what he means by adding, in the revision, that she is 'a real little passionate force.' James devoted many of his later brush strokes to bringing her out as exactly that. Instead of passively wanting 'to be delighted,' she now wants 'to hurl herself into the fray.' It is equally symptomatic of her conduct that she refuses Warbur-

4. See pp. 623–24 and 632–36 in this edition [*Editor*].

ton, not because such a marriage fails 'to correspond to any vision of happiness that she had hitherto entertained,' but because it fails 'to support any enlightened prejudice in favour of the free exploration of life.' The Isabel whom the later James saw with so much lucidity is a daughter of the transcendental afterglow, far less concerned about happiness than about enlightenment and freedom.

Another addition indicates that what is most required to make her respond is 'a bait to her imagination.' That is exactly why she is caught by Osmond. Mrs. Touchett originally said that Isabel was capable of marrying him 'for his opinions'; but she heightens this with more of the girl's romanticism in saying 'for the beauty of his opinions or for his autograph of Michael Angelo.' And that is how we see Isabel reacting to him. His 'things of a deep interest' become 'objects, subjects, contacts . . . of a rich association.' She reads into them also, in a favorite phrase of the later James, 'histories within histories.' When she defends him to Ralph, the revision makes her grounds much more explicit by adding to her question, 'What do you know against him?'—'What's the matter with Mr. Osmond's type, if it be one? His being so independent, so individual, is what *I* most see in him.' And again, instead of saying 'Mr. Osmond is simply a man—he is not a proprietor,' she expands this with her feeling, 'Mr. Osmond's simply a very lonely, a very cultivated and a very honest man—he's not a prodigious proprietor.'

This is the Isabel of whom James felt it no longer adequate just to say, 'she was an excitable creature, and now she was much excited.' He transformed that into an image: 'Vibration was easy to her, was in fact too constant with her, and she found herself now humming like a smitten harp.' Such vibrations are intrinsic to the rhythm of her thought. She no longer reflects merely that 'she had loved him,' but extends that reflection with 'she had so anxiously and yet so ardently given herself.' It is not padding, therefore, when, upon discovering how wrong she has been about Osmond, she does not conclude, 'There was only one way to repair it—to accept it,' but adds '. . . just immensely (oh, with the highest grandeur!) to accept it.'

The revisions affecting Osmond are of a very different sort. Far more of them relate to his appearance, to the polished, elegant and slightly ambiguous surface which James wants the reader to study more fully. His 'sharply-cut face' becomes 'extremely modelled and composed.' James' description of his eyes is far more careful. They are no longer 'luminous' and 'intelligent' expressing 'both softness and keenness,' but 'conscious, curious eyes . . . at once vague and penetrating, intelligent and hard.' This is quite in keeping with his smile, which is now his 'cool' smile, and with his voice, of which it is now said that, though fine, it 'somehow wasn't sweet.' He does not speak 'with feeling' but 'beautifully'; and his laugh, instead of being 'not ill-natured,' has now 'a finer patience.' James has done an expert job of heightening Osmond's thoroughly studied effect. He underscores the fact that Osmond's taste was his only law by saying, not that he lived 'in a serene, impersonal way,' but 'in a sorted, sifted, arranged world,' where his 'superior qualities' become 'standards and touchstones other than the vulgar.'

Osmond is entirely devoted to forms, and to accent this trait, James introduces one of his most interesting later devices: he interrelates Osmond's character with his surroundings in a way that shows again how much the novelist had learned from the plastic arts.[5] On the first occasion that Osmond entertains Isabel, James wants her to be impressed with the rare distinction of the collector's villa. Osmond's footboy is now made deliberately picturesque: instead of remaining merely 'the shabby footboy,' he becomes 'tarnished as to livery and quaint as to type,' and, with a fine added flourish, James tells us that he might 'have issued from some stray sketch of old-time manners, been "put in" by the brush of a Longhi or a Goya.' James also added in the revision that Osmond was marked for Isabel 'as by one of those signs of the highly curious that he was showing her on the underside of old plates and in the corner of sixteenth-century drawings.' As Isabel thinks over this visit afterwards, she reflects that his care for beauty 'had been the main occupation of a lifetime of which the arid places were watered with the sweet sense of a quaint, half-anxious, half-helpless fatherhood.' In the revision these thoughts rise from her impression of how she had seen him: his preoccupation with beauty made his life 'stretch beneath it in the disposed vistas and with the ranges of steps and terraces and fountains of a formal Italian garden—allowing only for arid places freshened by the natural dews,' and so on.

In building up the reasons why she took her romantic view of him, James also embarked on an extended flight:

> What continued to please this young lady was his extraordinary subtlety. There was such a fine intellectual intention in what he said, and the movement of his wit was like that of a quick-flashing blade.

> What continued to please this young woman was that while he talked so for amusement he didn't talk, as she had heard people, for 'effect.' He uttered his ideas as if, odd as they often appeared, he were used to them and had lived with them; old polished knobs and heads and handles, of precious substance, that could be fitted if necessary to new walking-sticks—not switches plucked in destitution from the common tree and then too elegantly waved about.

5. I have given further instances from his earlier works in "Henry James and the Plastic Arts," *The Kenyon Review* (Autumn 1943).

The new passage stresses, if in oblique ways and with some needless verbiage, Osmond's utter dependence on art rather than on nature. The 'old polished knobs,' like the 'complicated medal' to which he is compared, make him indisseverable from his collector's items. It is not surprising that such a deliberately shaped work of art as he is 'mystified' Isabel. (In the first version he had merely 'puzzled' her.) It is fitting too that, as she comes under his fascination, she should feel not merely 'a good deal older than she had done a year before,' but also 'as if she were "worth more" for it, like some curious piece in an antiquary's collection.' For, in ways that her inexperience cannot possibly fathom, that is precisely how Osmond proposes to treat her. She appeals to him, not for being 'as bright and soft as an April cloud,' but in one of James' most functional revisions, 'as smooth to his general need of her as handled ivory to the palm.'

The mystification is only Isabel's, the ambiguity is all in what Osmond concealed, not in any doubts that James entertained about him. The revision increases his 'lost' quality. His 'peculiarities' are called his 'perversities,' and where it was remarked that he consulted his taste alone, James now adds 'as a sick man consciously incurable consults at last only his lawyer.' The reader accepts entirely Ralph's judgment of Osmond as a sterile dilettante; but his quality is deepened when Ralph recognizes the futility of trying to persuade Isabel, not that the man is 'a humbug,' but rather that there is something 'sordid or sinister' in him. With that deepening even Osmond becomes poignant: his 'keen, expressive, emphatic' face becomes 'firm, refined, slightly ravaged'—a far more telling portrait.

The character in this book around whom ambiguity gathers most is Madame Merle, since she has to play a double rôle throughout. James' changes involving her are chiefly of two sorts. He decided, for one thing, that her surface should be less transparent to Isabel. And so it is when Isabel asks her if she has not suffered that her 'picturesque smile' is elaborated into 'the amused smile of a person seated at a game of guesses.' She is also called 'smooth' instead of 'plump.' When Madame Merle introduced her to Osmond, Isabel wondered about 'the nature of the tie that united them. She was inclined to imagine that Madame Merle's ties were peculiar.' As James looked over that, it seemed to strike too close to the actual liaison, which he didn't want Isabel to suspect for a long time yet. So he toned it up to 'the nature of the tie binding these superior spirits. She felt that Madame Merle's ties always somehow had histories.'

But in the other type of change for Madame Merle, James felt, as he did with Osmond, that he must make her character unmistakable to the reader. So he no longer endowed her with 'a certain nobleness,' but with 'a certain courage'; not with 'geniality' but with 'grace.' Even in changing the music that Isabel overhead her playing from 'something of Beethoven's' to 'something of Schubert's,' James must have felt that he was bringing it more within Madame Merle's emotional compass. When Isabel finally comes to know her secret, the girl reflects, not just that her friend was 'false,' but 'even deeply false . . . deeply, deeply, deeply.' And Madame Merle's guilt is spoken of, not in terms 'of vivid proof,' but 'of ugly evidence . . . of grim things produced in court.'

Such details—of which there are many more—are important in allaying the usual suspicion that James' ambiguity is unintentional, the obscurantism of a man who couldn't make up his own mind. When the writing becomes denser, as it frequently does in the revision, this is owing rather to James' gradual development of one of his special gifts, the ability so to handle a conversation that he keeps in the air not merely what is said, but what isn't—the passage of thoughts without words. The situation here which challenged most this skill of the later James was when Warburton turned up again after Isabel's marriage. What she had to decide was whether, despite his honorable pretensions, he was still in love with her. Their interplay is made more subtle. To judge the value of this kind of rewriting you must follow the whole chapter, but one series of slight changes may show what James was about.

As they met again, in the first version, Isabel 'hardly knew whether she were glad or not.' Warburton, however, 'was plainly very well pleased.' In the revision his feelings are not given to us so explicitly: he 'was plainly quite sure of his own sense of the matter.' Only as the conversation advances do Isabel—and the reader—gain the evidence she is after. In a moment or two, he remarks how charming a place she has to live in. In the original he said this, 'brightly, looking about him.' But this became: 'with a look, round him, at her established home, in which she might have caught the dim ghost of his old ruefulness.' That reveals to Isabel nearly all she needs, and her impression is clinched, when, instead of turning upon her 'an eye that gradually became more serious,' he gives her, in addition, 'the deeper, the deepest consciousness of his look.' From that moment Isabel knows how unwise it would be for him to marry her stepdaughter Pansy, no matter how much Osmond wants the match.

If such a situation caused James thus to weave the texture of his style more complexly, the changes that relate to Pansy and to Ralph, though equally slight, may reveal another significant quality.

In the scale of emotional vibrations James is more impressive in striking the note of tenderness than that of passion. We can observe this in the way he heightened some of his most moving passages. How utterly Pansy is at the mercy of her father's will is underlined by several details. Consider, for instance, her smile, in connection with which we can note again James' extraordinary care to bring out every revelatory phase of his characters' looks. At the moment of Pansy's first appearance in the narrative, James remarked that her 'natural and usual expression seemed to be a smile of perfect sweetness.' But the point about Pansy is that she has had so little chance to be natural or spontaneous, and so James revised this: her face was 'painted with a fixed and intensely sweet smile.' So too with the characterizing image that he created for her. Instead of saying that Pansy entertained Isabel 'like a little lady,' James wrote that she 'rose to the occasion as the small, winged fairy in the pantomime soars by the aid of the dissimulated wire.' Thus Pansy's trapped state is suggested to us from the outset, and on the occasion when Isabel tells her that she is going to marry her father, James made two additions that show how he had learned to handle irony. Originally Isabel had said, 'My good little Pansy, I shall be very kind to you.' But to that James added: 'A vague, inconsequent vision of her coming in some odd way to need it had intervened with the effect of a chill.' And when Pansy answered, 'Very well then; I have nothing to fear,' James no longer had her declare that 'lightly,' but 'with her note of prepared promptitude.' And he also added, as part of Isabel's reflection: 'What teaching she had had, it seemed to suggest—or what penalties for non-performance she dreaded!'

We can read, in these extensions, the same thing that we have observed in the major characters, James' deepening of emotional tones. The most affecting passage in the book is the death of Ralph, for there James is expressing the tenderness of pure devotion, disencumbered of any worldly aims. The characterizing image noted above was designed to increase our sense of Ralph's precarious holds on life. To increase also our sense of his devotion to Isabel, 'his cousin' was twice changed to 'the person in the world in whom he was most interested.' The scene between these two, as he lies dying, is very short, and the only significant change is in Ralph's last speech. In the original this read: ' "And remember this," he continued, "that if you have been hated, you have also been loved." ' To that James added: ' "Ah, but, Isabel—*adored!*" he just audibly and lingeringly breathed.' There it may become a debatable matter of taste whether the simpler form is not more moving; but the later James felt impelled to a more high-keyed emotional register. Both Ralph and Isabel, instead of 'murmuring' or 'adding softly' are made to 'wail.'[6] It is difficult to keep such tones from becoming sentimental, but how little James was inclined to sentimentalize can be seen in his handling of Ralph's funeral. Originally James pronounced it 'not a disagreeable one'; but he made his later statement stronger: it was 'neither a harsh nor a heavy one.'

IV

The two most extensive passages of rewriting are yet to be looked at. One relates to the Countess Gemini, and the other to Caspar Goodwood. Both can give us insight into how James conceived dramatic structure, and how he also felt that the climax of this book needed strengthening.

In comparing the two versions, it is notable that the sequence of chapters which James pronounced, in the preface, as being the best in the book—the sequence that extends from Isabel's glimpse of the two together, with Osmond seated while Madame Merle is standing, through the long vigil in which Isabel gradually pieces together her situation—that these three chapters (XL-XLII), with their important issues, were left substantially unchanged. So too with the fateful interview between Osmond and Isabel (Chapter XLVI) which shows how hopelessly far apart they have grown. But the scene with the Countess (Chapter LI), in which Isabel's suspicions are first given explicit names, was greatly recast. Some of the reasons for this are suggested by what James wrote in his notebook at the time when the novel had begun to appear in *The Atlantic* and he was trying to see his way clear to his conclusion: 'After Isabel's marriage there are five more instalments, and the success of the whole story greatly depends upon this portion being well conducted or not. Let me then make the most of it—let me imagine the best. There has been a want of action in the earlier part, and it may be made up here. The elements that remain are in themselves, I think, very interesting, and they are only to be strongly and happily combined. The weakness of the whole story is that it is too exclusively psychological—that it depends too little on incident; but the complete unfolding of the situation that is established by Isabel's marriage may nonetheless be quite sufficiently dramatic. The idea of the whole thing is that the poor girl, who has dreamed of freedom and nobleness, who has done, as she believes, a generous, natural, clearsighted thing, finds herself in reality ground in the very mill of the conventional. After a year or two of marriage the antagonism

---

6. This is also true in the other most directly emotional scene, the death of Ralph's father:
' "My father died an hour ago."
"Ah, my poor Ralph!" the girl murmured, putting out her hand to him.'

' "My dear father died an hour ago."
"Ah, my poor Ralph!" she gently wailed, putting out her two hands to him.'

between her nature and Osmond's comes out—the open opposition of a noble character and a narrow one. There is a great deal to do here in a small compass; every word, therefore, must tell—every touch must count. If the last five parts of the story appear crowded, this will be rather a good defect in consideration of the perhaps too great diffuseness of the earlier portion.'

As James went on outlining his intentions, he was still undecided whether the revelation of Pansy's parentage should come through Madame Merle herself or through the Countess: 'Better on many grounds that it should be the latter; and yet in that way I lose the "great scene" between Madame Merle and Isabel.' Twenty-five years later he was still bothered by what he had lost. In the passage of deadly quietness between Isabel and Osmond, and, subsequently, between Isabel and Madame Merle, he seems to have felt that his drama was too inward, that he needed a more emotional scene. And so he rewrote nearly all the lines in which the Countess told Isabel of the liaison.

He had already given considerable attention to making the Countess' character a more lively mixture. Ralph's first description of her was changed from 'rather wicked' to 'rather impossible'; and in her own disarming self-characterization, instead of saying, 'I am only rather light,' she pronounced herself 'only rather an idiot and a bore.' James had originally said that her expression was 'by no means disagreeable'; but here he particularized: it was made up of 'various intensities of emphasis and wonder, of horror and joy.' Also, to a quite astonishing degree, by recurring to a bird-image for her, he sustained her in a whir. For example, in her first meeting with Isabel, she delivered her remarks 'with a variety of little jerks and glances.' But the bird-motif gave these the momentum of 'little jerks and pecks, of roulades of shrillness,' with the result that James was stimulated to a further flight of his own, and added that her accent was 'as some fond recall of good English, or rather of good American, in adversity.'

This kind of a character had dramatic possibilities, and, in his revision, James exploited them to the full. He did everything he could to make her revelations to Isabel into the 'great scene' he had missed. Isabel is alone, thinking of what will happen if, in defiance of Osmond's wishes, she goes to England to see Ralph before he dies. Then, suddenly, the Countess 'stood before her.' Thus the original, but in the rewriting the Countess 'hovered before her.' And to give us an intimation that something is coming, James added that the Countess 'lived assuredly, it might be said, at the window of her spirit, but now she was leaning far out.' As Lawrence Leighton, who first drew my attention to the importance of this scene for James' structure, remarked, this is like 'an extra blast from the trumpets' to announce the herald. It occurs to Isabel for the first time that her sister-in-law might say something, not 'important,' but 'really human.'

In what follows much subtle attention was paid to the Countess' diction. James endowed her with a more characteristic colloquial patter, with such epithets as 'poverina' and 'cara mia.' Instead of saying that Madame Merle had wanted 'to save her reputation,' she says, 'to save her skin'; and, in her view, Isabel has not merely 'such a pure mind'—she calls it 'beastly pure,' as such a woman would. Her speeches are considerably increased in length, one of them by almost a page. There is hardly any addition to her ideas, but as Mr. Leighton also observed, 'James wanted a good harangue, the sort of speech an actress could get her teeth into.' Her quality is melodramatic, but it is effectively more baleful than in the first version.

James has also built up the contrast between her and Isabel. The Countess expected—and hoped—that the girl would burst out with a denunciation of Osmond. But instead she is filled with pity for Madame Merle. She thinks even of Osmond's first wife, that 'he must have been false' to her—'and so very soon!' That last phrase is an addition that emphasizes Isabel's incurable innocence, despite all the experience through which she is passing. It glances ironically also at her own situation. When she goes on to reflect that at least Osmond has been faithful to her, the Countess says it depends on what you call faithful: 'When he married you he was no longer the lover of another woman—*such* a lover as he had been, *cara mia*, between their risks and their precautions, while the thing lasted!' Everything after the dash is added, and we can hear the Countess smacking her lips over such details, while Isabel recoils into herself. Where the first version had remarked that she 'hesitated, though there was a question in her eyes,' the utter cleavage between her and her gossipy interlocutress is now brought out: she 'hesitated as if she had not heard; as if her question—though it was sufficiently there in her eyes—were all for herself.' When, a moment or two later, Isabel wondered why Madame Merle never wanted to marry Osmond, the Countess had originally contented herself with saying that Madame Merle 'had grown more ambitious.' But to that James added: ' "besides, she has never had, about him," the Countess went on, leaving Isabel to wince for it so tragically afterwards—"she *had* never had, what you might call any illusions of *intelligence*." ' The Countess is happy to get in a dig at her brother, but for Isabel and for the reader there is the irony that Isabel herself had been fooled by just such illusions. That gives the final twist to the knife.

After this scene there remain only four chapters. There is the brief final encounter with Madame Merle, who sees in an instant that Isabel now knows everything. Isabel then says good-bye to

Pansy, but promises that she won't desert her. The rest of the book is taken up with Isabel's trip to England, with her farewell to Ralph, and with Caspar's return to her. The last chapter is largely her struggle with him, and James' significant additions are led up to by the emphases that he has given to Caspar's character earlier in the book. He has introduced many details that sharpen the impression of Caspar's indomitable energy. When Isabel first compares him with Warburton, she feels that there is 'something too forcible, something oppressive and restrictive' about him. But this was made more concrete: 'a disagreeably strong push, a kind of hardness of presence.' A revelatory image was introduced to contrast Isabel's feeling about Warburton: instead of refusing to 'lend a receptive ear' to his suit, she now 'resists conquest' at his 'large quiet hands.' But Caspar is 'a kind of fate,' now, indeed, 'a kind of grim fate.' He himself gives fuller expression to the tension between them when he has first pursued her to London. Instead of saying, 'Apparently it was disagreeable to you even to write,' he makes it 'repugnant.' And he remarks bitterly, not that his insistence on his suit 'displeases' her, but that it 'disgusts.' As the best means of characterizing him, James developed a recurrent image of armor. In his first account he had merely remarked that Caspar was 'the strongest man' Isabel had ever known; but to this he added: 'she saw the different fitted parts of him as she had seen, in museums and portraits, the different fitted parts of armoured warriors—in plates of steel handsomely inlaid with gold.' Later on, his eyes, instead of wearing 'an expression of ardent remonstrance,' seemed 'to shine through the vizard of a helmet.' And when Isabel tries to measure his possible suffering, she no longer reflects that 'he had a sound consititution,' but that 'he was naturally plated and steeled, armed essentially for aggression.'

He follows her to Italy to object strenuously to her engagement to Osmond: 'Where does he come from? Where does he belong?' That second question was added in the revision, as was also Isabel's thought, 'She had never been so little pleased with the way he said "belawng." ' But, in spite of everything, Isabel cannot escape feeling Caspar's power; and in rewriting their final scene, James made an incisive analysis of his mixed repulsion and attraction for her. She is alone under the trees at Gardencourt, when Caspar suddenly appears—just as Warburton had surprised her there once before. In what follows we are made to feel her overpowering sensation of his physical presence, from the moment that James adds that he was 'beside her on the bench and pressingly turned to her.' As he insists that her husband is 'the deadliest of fiends,' and that he, Caspar, is determined to prevent her from the 'horror' of returning to him (both 'deadliest' and 'horror' were additions), Isabel realizes that 'she had never been loved before,' To that realization the original had added: 'It wrapped her about; it lifted her off her feet.' But now James wrote: 'She had believed it, but this was different; this was the hot wind of the desert, at the approach of which the others dropped dead, like mere sweet airs of the garden. It wrapped her about; it lifted her off her feet, while the very taste of it, as of some-thing potent, acrid, and strange, forced open her set teeth.'

That image takes her as far away from her surroundings and the gentlemanly devotion of a Warburton as it does from the decadent egotism of an Osmond. For a moment she is completely overpow-ered. Caspar's voice, saying, 'Be mine, as I'm yours,' comes to her, not merely 'through a confusion of sound,' but 'harsh and terrible, through a confusion of vaguer sounds.' He takes her in his arms, and, in the first version, the climax is reached with: 'His kiss was like a flash of lightning; when it was dark again she was free.' But now James felt it necessary to say far more: 'His kiss was like white lightning, a flash that spread, and spread again, and stayed; and it was extraordinarily as if, while she took it, she felt each thing in his hard manhood that had least pleased her, each agressive fact of his face, his figure, his presence, justified of its intense identity and made one with this act of possession. So had she heard of those wrecked and under water following a train of images before they sink. But when darkness returned she was free.'

That conveys James' awareness of how Isabel, in spite of her mar-riage, has remained essentially virginal, and of how her resistance and her flight from Caspar are partly fear of sexual possession. But the fierce attraction she also feels in this passage would inevitably operate likewise for a girl of her temperament, in making her do what she conceived to be her duty, and sending her back to her hus-band.

V

That brings us to the ending of the book, which has seldom been rightly interpreted. The difference between the two versions is one of the few of James' revisions that is generally known. Henrietta has told Caspar that Isabel has gone back to Rome:

'Look here, Mr. Goodwood,' she said; 'just you wait.' On which he looked up at her.

Thus the final lines in the original. But to these James added:

—but only to guess, from her face, with a revulsion, that she simply meant he was young. She stood shining at him with that cheap comfort, and it added, on the spot, thirty years to his life. She walked him away with her, however, as if she had given him now the key to patience.

Many critics have held this difference to mean that James had changed his mind, that in the original he had given Caspar more hope. But he seems rather to have made unmistakably explicit what he had always intended to imply. He had said in his notebook outline that Isabel was to be greatly moved by Caspar's 'passionate outbreak': 'she feels the full force of his devotion—to which she has never done justice; but she refuses. She starts again for Italy—and her departure is the climax and termination of the story.' James had also observed there that Henrietta was to have 'the last word,' to utter 'a characteristic characterization of Isabel.' But he must have felt in revising that he had been too brief, that he had failed to drive home to the reader that what was being expressed was no sure promise about Isabel, but rather Henrietta's optimism, which refuses to accept defeat.

The end of Isabel's career is not yet in sight. That fact raises a critical issue about James' way of rounding off his narratives. He was keenly aware of what his method involved. As he wrote in his notebook, upon concluding his detailed project: 'With strong handling it seems to me that it may all be very true, very powerful, very touching. The obvious criticism of course will be that it is not finished—that it has not seen the heroine to the end of her situation—that I have left her *en l'air*. This is both true and false. The *whole* of anything is never told; you can only take what groups together. What I have done has that unity—it groups together. It is complete in itself—and the rest may be taken up or not, later.'

This throws a great deal of light—perhaps more than any single passage of his published work—on how James conceived of structure. He recounted in the preface to the *Portrait* how Turgenieff had encouraged him in his belief that the important thing to start with was not an air-tight plot, but rather a character or group of characters who are so living that the main question becomes to 'invent and select' the complications that such characters 'would be most likely to produce and to feel.'

Years before the *Portrait*, William James had commented on the effect of such a method, as it struck him in A *Most Extraordinary Case* (1868), one of the first half dozen stories that Henry had printed. William felt that here he understood for the first time what Henry was aiming for: 'to give an impression like that we often get of people in life: Their orbits come out of space and lay themselves for a short time along of ours, and then off they whirl again into the unknown, leaving us with little more than an impression of their reality and a feeling of baffled curiosity as to the mystery of the beginning and the end of their being,' William thought such a method difficult to make succeed, but 'with a deep justification in nature.' He was to grow somewhat less sure of its efficacy, as can be read in his tone about *The Tragic Muse*: 'the final winding up is, as usual with you, rather a losing of the story in the sand, yet that is the way in which things lose themselves in real life.' Henry, on the other hand, grew steadily to have more confidence in what he was doing, until he declared, in the preface to *Roderick Hudson*: 'Really, universally, relations stop nowhere, and the exquisite problem of the artist is eternally but to draw, by a geometry of his own, the circle within which they shall happily *appear* to do so.' That gives his essential conception of the kind of wholeness that form imposes.

He had been particularly concerned in the *Portrait* with launching Isabel Archer into action, with presenting her so vividly that his narrative would compose itself around the primary question, 'Well, what will she *do*?' It has recently been assumed that James believed entirely in the rightness of his heroine's conduct, and that since our age no longer feels as he—and she—did about the strictness of the marriage vow, we can no longer respond to the book except as to a period piece. But that is to misread not merely the ending, but all of James' own 'characteristic characterization' of Isabel. He could hardly have made a more lucid summary of the weaknesses that she exposed to Europe: 'her meagre knowledge, her inflated ideals, her confidence at once innocent and dogmatic, her temper at once exacting and indulgent'—that whole passage of analysis on the evening after her arrival at Gardencourt, a passage untouched in the revision, is meant to have our closest scrutiny.

As Isabel embarks on her 'free exploration' of life, Henrietta is outspoken in declaring that she is drifting rather to 'some great mistake,' that she is not enough 'in contact with reality,' with the 'toiling, striving' world. Ralph tells her that she has 'too much conscience'—a peculiarly American complication in the romantic temperament. Although all her diverse friends are united in their disapproval of Osmond, she proceeds to do the wrong thing for the right reasons. She has a special pride in marrying him, since she feels that she is not only 'taking,' but also 'giving'; she feels too the release of transferring some of the burden of her inheritance to another's conscience—James' way of commenting on how harm was done to her by her money. But once she discerns what Osmond is really like, and how he has trapped her, she is by no means supine in his toils. She stands up to him with dignity, she even asks Pansy, 'Will you come away with me now?' Yet Isabel knows that is impossible; she knows, even as she leaves, that she will have to return to Rome for Pansy's sake.

But much more is involved than that—James' whole conception of the discipline of suffering. It is notable that his kinship here to Hawthorne becomes far more palpable in the final version. Take the instance when, at the time of Ralph's death, Isabel realizes how Mrs. Touchett has missed the essence of life by her inability to feel. It seemed to Isabel that Ralph's mother 'would find it a blessing today to be able to indulge a regret. She wondered whether Mrs. Touchett were not trying, whether she had not a desire for the recreation of grief.' James made this much fuller, particularly the latter portion. Isabel wondered if Mrs. Touchett 'were not even missing those enrichments of consciousness and privately trying—reaching out for some aftertaste of life, dregs of the banquet; the testimony of pain or the cold recreation of remorse.' The view of suffering adumbrated there, even the phrasing, recalls Hawthorne's *The Christmas Banquet*, where the most miserable fate is that of the man whose inability to feel bars him out even from the common bond of woe.

The common bond of sin, so central to Hawthorne's thought, was also accentuated through James' retouching. When Madame Merle finally foresees what is ahead, she says to Osmond in the original, 'How do bad people end? You have made me bad.' But James extended this with a new italicized emphasis, 'How do bad people end?—especially as to their *common* crimes. You have made me as bad as yourself.' Isabel's link with humanity, if not through sin— unless her willful spirit counts as such—is through her acceptance of suffering. The inevitability of her lot is made more binding in the revision. Her reflection that 'she should not escape, she should last,' becomes 'she should never escape, she should last to the end.' She takes on heightened stature when James no longer says that, while she sat with Ralph, 'her spirit rose,' but that 'her ache for herself became somehow her ache for *him*.' The pathos of her situation is also intensified in proportion to her greater knowledge of what is involved. 'She reflected that things change but little, while people change so much' is far less affecting than 'she envied the security of valuable "pieces" which change by no hair's breadth, only grow in value, while their owners lose inch by inch, youth, happiness, beauty.'

In both the original and the revision Isabel lays the most scrupulous emphasis upon the sacredness of a promise. Despite all her eagerness for culture, hers is no speculative spirit. Osmond comes to despise her for having 'the moral horizon' of a Unitarian minister —'poor Isabel, who had never been able to understand Unitarianism!' But whether she understands it or not, she is a firm granddaughter of the Puritans, not in her thought but in her moral integrity. In portraying her character and her fate, James was also writing an essay on the interplay of free will and determinism. Isabel's own view is that she was 'perfectly free,' that she married Osmond of her most deliberate choice, and that, however miserable one may be, one must accept the consequences of one's acts. James knew how little she was free, other than to follow to an impulsive extreme everything she had been made by her environment and background.

Thus he leaves her to confront her future, and is satisfied if he has endowed his characters with so much 'felt life' that the reader must weigh for himself what is likely to lie ahead in her relation with Osmond. It may be that, as Isabel herself conjectures, he may finally 'take her money and let her go.' It may be that once she has found a husband for Pansy, she will feel that she no longer has to remain in Rome. James believed that the arbitrary circle of art should stimulate such speculations beyond its confines, and thus create also the illusion of wider life. He had about Isabel a tragic sense, but he did not write a tragedy, as he was to do in *The Wings of the Dove*, since this earlier drama was lacking in the finality of purgation and judgment. But his view of his material was not at all ambiguous. He knew how romantic Isabel was, how little experienced she was in mature social behavior. He had shown that she was completely mistaken in believing that 'the world lay before her—she could do whatever she chose.' But James also knew the meaning and the value of renunciation. The American life of his day, in its reckless plunge to outer expansiveness and inner defeat, had taught him that as his leading spiritual theme. Through Isabel Archer he gave one of his fullest and freshest expressions of inner reliance in the face of adversity. It is no wonder that, after enumerating her weaknesses, he had concluded: 'she would be an easy victim of scientific criticism if she were not intended to awaken on the reader's part an impulse more tender . . .'

ANTHONY J. MAZZELLA

The New Isabel†

A careful analysis of the revision of *The Portrait of a Lady* will reveal that there are two *Portraits*, not one, and that each is a different literary experience. The Isabel Archer who faces her destiny is not the same girl in both versions, nor is the quality of her destiny the same. She may travel the same road in each case, and meet people with the same names; but the road has different landmarks and the people are different travelers—more keenly felt, more sharply there, more fully realized—and other than what they were. The sense of her destiny is transmuted by a deeper range of images, while the destiny itself is peopled with characters who have lived

†Reprinted by permission of the author.

other lives and gone different ways. The road she now follows has sudden drops and altered vistas and intriguing byways. And overriding all, perhaps, is the fuller identity of her creator.

James had completed arrangements with Charles Scribner's Sons for publication of the New York Edition toward the end of 1905.[1] By mid-May, 1906, he had revised enough of the *Portrait* to write James B. Pinker, his literary agent, that he estimated the typed revisions, "the most intricate" pages, represented "about half the whole" of his output.[2] Several times in 1906, during the demanding process of revising the first three works for the New York Edition (*Roderick Hudson, The American,* and *The Portrait of a Lady*), James communicated his progress to Pinker, declaring on one occasion that "when the difficult business of working over those 3 first novels will be ended, the rest of the business will go infinitely faster."[3]

By mid-June, 1906, he had revised some 350 pages of the *Portrait.* By the end of July, he had completed his revisions, or certainly the first stages (more was to be altered before the final version appeared in the New York Edition), for he had advised Pinker to deliver his marked copy of the 1881 American Edition to H. O. Houghton and Company, Cambridge, Massachusetts, the printers who were to supply his proof sheets.[4] The new *Portrait of a Lady* published in 1908 was now a changed *Portrait.*

Of the thousands of changes, the most significant concern characterization, and of the characters, the most significant is Isabel. Whenever James introduced an important character for the first time, his revisions multiplied. Any examination of such introductions will easily verify this; that of Mrs. Touchett, for example, in Chapter 3, or of Madame Merle in Chapter 18. But no one received more continuous attention than Isabel, either as the subject of revision herself or as one responsible for alteration in James's conception of other characters. The point is that the original characters exist differently in the revision. And we are responding in a new way to new characters in a new work.

A major element in the refinement of Isabel into another character is an emphasis on her freedom and vulnerability. Her destiny, in the revision, becomes one that is at once unlimited and fraught with peril. The primary literary means James uses to effect this emphasis on freedom is imagistic: a use of the conventional free bird and an introduction of the image of a greyhound. James increases the effectiveness of this latter image by incorporating it in a miniature drama in which Isabel's plain sister Lilian yearns for other possibilities:

1. Sydney J. Krause, *Henry James's Revisions of The Portrait of a Lady* (Ph.D. dissertation, Columbia University, 1956), p. 21.

2. Quoted in Krause, p. 20.
3. *Ibid.,* p. 21.
4. *Ibid.*

"I have never felt like Isabel's sister, and I am sure I never shall," she had said to an intimate friend; a declaration which made it all the more creditable that she had been prolific in sisterly offices. / "I've never kept up with Isabel—it would have taken *all* my time," she had often remarked; in spite of which, however, she held her rather wistfully in sight; watching her as a motherly spaniel might watch a free greyhound. (24/III, 39)[5]

In addition to the greyhound image there is a bird image amplified initially in the revised version to include an aspect of freedom and later introduced in this new fullness in another revised passage. Isabel, in the first instance, had recently arrived at Pratt's Hotel for her stay in London when, one evening, she was startled by a visit from Caspar Goodwood. It is in his revised response to her peroration on independence that a somewhat Victorian bird becomes free: "To his mind she had always had wings, and this was but the flutter of those stainless pinions."/ "He had never supposed she hadn't wings and the need of beautiful free movements . . ." (139/III, 228). Later, when Mrs. Touchett began her journey from Paris to Italy, she made it clear to her niece that it was Isabel's decision to come along:

"Now, of course, you are completely your own mistress," she said. / "Now, of course, you're completely your own mistress and are as free as the bird on the bough. . . ." (191–92/III, 315)

This new emphasis on freedom is struck early in the novel when in Chapter 3 James revises the account of Isabel's youth. Of her primary school in the earlier version, Isabel "had expressed great disgust with the place. . . ." But in the later version, she "had protested against its laws . . ." (18/III, 29). She had earlier elected to meet Mrs. Touchett in 'the office,' "the most joyless chamber" in the house at Albany. Later, this meeting-place is called "the most depressed of its scenes" (19/III, 31), a revision which suggests, in effect, limited as well as melancholy vistas.

The element of freedom is also emphasized negatively as a limitation. In one instance, in a possible echo of the earlier greyhound image but more likely as a result of a more immediate revision—Isabel's sister, once "popular," is now "fetching" (27/III, 44)—this negative aspect of freedom is expressed in a canine image:

Isabel could have no illusions . . . as to the moderate character of her own triumphs. / Isabel could have no illusions . . . as to the limits of her own power to frisk and jump and shriek—above all with rightness of effect. (27/III, 44)

5. Throughout, page references are given first for the 1881 version and then, separated by a slash, from the New York Edition, for which the volume number is also included.

In this revision, Isabel becomes also a character who is more conscious of the effect of her actions.

In another instance, after Isabel has refused Lord Warburton's proposal of marriage, the revision of her reflection becomes more precise, less conventional, and indicative of her dislike of limitation:

> the idea [of marriage to Lord Warburton] failed to correspond to any vision of happiness . . . / the idea failed to support any enlightened prejudice in favour of the free exploration of life. . . . (94/III, 155)

And just a little later, she fears that a limitation of her freedom might mean almost a literal paralysis:

> the situation might . . . contain elements that would displease her . . . / might . . . contain oppressive, might contain narrowing elements, might prove really but a stupefying anodyne. . . . (95, III, 155–6)

Related to her fear of limitation are her altered response to Madame Merle and James's slightly different conception of minor characters. In both instances, the change stresses various aspects of freedom. When, in Chapter 28, Isabel first meets Madame Merle and notices her face, she responds to a new suggestiveness which reinforces the rightness of her attraction to this woman because it is related to her sense of freedom: "It was a face that told of a rich nature and of quick and liberal impulses . . . " / "It was a face that told of an amplitude of nature and of quick and free motions. . . ." (152/III, 249).

Early in the novel, when we meet Daniel Touchett, the reference to his money is altered to stress the value money will come to have for Isabel—the freedom that money can bring. Lord Warburton and Daniel Touchett are engaged in lively banter about wealth when Warburton remarks that Touchett should not chide him for being rich because, in the first version, " 'you are so ridiculously wealthy,' " and in the revision, because " 'you have—haven't you? —such unlimited means' " (7/III, 10).

Also early in the novel, when Isabel and her uncle are discussing the reality of fictional heroines, Daniel Touchett criticizes a lady-novelist friend of Ralph's first for being unreliable and for having " 'Too much imagination . . .' " and then for having " 'Too free a fancy . . .' " (47/III, 77). This minor change repeats the stress on freedom and comments subtly on Isabel's conception of freedom as having its roots not in life but in fiction.

And finally, the refinement of Isabel's freedom is strengthened by having another character respond to this element in her nature. The rejected Lord Warburton is walking with Isabel in the gallery of Gardencourt in Chapter 14 when she stops to examine a picture. In the first version, "there was something young and flexible in her movement, which her companion noticed." But in the revision, "there was something so young and free in her movement that her very pliancy seemed to mock at him" (113/III, 185).

Besides this emphasis on Isabel's freedom, there is in the revision a heightened sense of the danger she faces in the future. This sense of danger in Isabel's destiny begins with cosmic overtones, is visible at times in subtle ways, and eventually comes to include Pansy's fate as well. It is related to her ideas on marriage, to the conventional proposals of marriage she receives from her three suitors, and to the fatality of money. But as events in both novels move toward the area of basic sexual responses, this sense of danger in the revised version becomes a fear of a special kind of annihilation: that of the mind by the erotic. And it is this fear, as we shall see, that ultimately influences the new Isabel's major decisions.

Sitting alone in her grandmother's house in Albany on a rainy afternoon, Isabel in the first version responds with neutrality to the coming of spring: "the spring-time presented itself as a questionable improvement. Isabel, however, gave as little attention as possible to the incongruities of the season . . . ." But in the revision there is an awareness of danger and ugliness on a cosmic scale: "the spring-time was indeed an appeal—and it seemed a cynical, insincere appeal—to patience. Isabel, however, gave as little heed as possible to cosmic treacheries" (19/III, 31).

Much later, in Chapter 21, Isabel considers, with a new emphasis which subtly links her fate with bruises, a person's relationship with Mrs. Touchett: "you knew exactly where to find her, and were never liable to chance encounters with her."/" you knew exactly where to find her and were never liable to chance encounters and concussions" (192/III, 316). Also in this chapter, she considers with a slight shift in emphasis achieved through the introduction of martial imagery, the fateful implications of her Italian sojourn:

> She was glad to pause, however, on the edge of this larger knowledge; the stillness of these soft weeks seemed good to her. They were a peaceful interlude in a career which she had little warrant as yet for regarding as agitated . . . / She was glad to pause, however, on the edge of this larger adventure; there was such a thrill even in the preliminary hovering. It affected her moreover as a peaceful interlude, as a hush of the drum and fife in a career which she had little warrant as yet for regarding as agitated . . . (195/III, 321)

Later, in Chapter 29, after she has met Osmond, she comes to link her visit to Rome with time past, using an image that contains a disturbing mixture of pleasant joy and ominous suffocation and protection:

the pleasantest incident of her life—so it pleased her to qualify her little visit to Rome—was coming to an end. / . . . so it pleased her to qualify these too few days in Rome, which she might musingly have likened to the figure of some small princess of one of the ages of dress overmuffled in a mantle of state and dragging a train that it took pages or historians to hold up—that this felicity was coming to an end. (270/IV, 16)

Also in this chapter, she responds differently to Osmond's proposal, this time charging it with the ambiguous tug of fate:

The tears came into Isabel's eyes—they were caused by an intenser throb of that pleasant pain I spoke of a moment ago. / The tears came into her eyes: this time they obeyed the sharpness of the pang that suggested to her somehow the slipping of a fine bolt—backward, forward, she couldn't have said which. (271/IV, 18)

The image of the bolt as conceived by the later Isabel is ambiguously a freeing and an enslaving mechanism—a sense of unknown fate.

Before her marriage, she comes to sense danger even in Pansy's future. In the early version hers is a "moral" appreciation of Pansy's innocence, but in the revision it is "anxiously moral" (309/IV, 84). And at their meeting just before her marriage, Isabel comes to have an unsettling vision of Pansy's destiny:

"My good little Pansy," said Isabel, gently, "I shall be very kind to you." / . . . "I shall be ever so kind to you." A vague, inconsequent vision of her coming in some odd way to need it had intervened with the effect of a chill. (311/IV, 86)

This sense of an ominous future and a dangerous destiny is partly induced by the inclination of the revised Isabel to view marriage as a destructive element and as perilous. Early in the novel, in Chapter 6, the 1908 Isabel felt that few men she knew were worth "a ruinous expenditure." The 1881 Isabel objected merely to "an expenditure of imagination" (44/III, 71). Furthermore, the earlier Isabel's thoughts on marriage usually "ended by frightening her." For the later Isabel, the process ended slightly more ominously, "in alarms" (44/III, 72).

When she encounters Caspar Goodwood at Pratt's Hotel in London and he insists that she will marry, the 1881 Isabel impatiently rejoins: " 'Very well, I will then.' " The 1908 Isabel redefines the situation as threatening: ' "Very well then. We'll put it that I'm not safe' " (136/III, 223). Goodwood's response to her attitude also heightens the sense of danger: he sees her in the earlier version as acting as if she were " 'going to commit a crime' ";

but in the later version, the crime becomes " 'some atrocity' " (141/III, 229).

The later Isabel's sense of the danger surrounding marriage is reinforced by two additional revisions. In the first, her protestations to Madame Merle of ease in the presence of men is belied by the brutality of the image she uses: " 'I am not afraid of them' "/ " 'Why, I'm not afraid of them—I'm as used to them as the cook to the butcher-boys' " (214/III, 353). And in the second, she is discussing with Ralph the possibility of falling in love with Osmond: [She:] " 'The more information one has about a person the better.' " [He:] " 'I don't agree to that.' "/" 'The more information one has about one's dangers the better.' 'I don't agree to that—it may make them dangers' " (218/III, 359).

The ominous note is detailed, further, in the later Isabel's relationship with each of her suitors. Before Lord Warburton's influence becomes strong, the early Isabel is encouraged to explore English society and promises "to be delighted." The later Isabel views the prospect more violently, for she promises "to hurl herself into the fray" (54/III, 89).

When Warburton proposes, the later Isabel, unlike the earlier one, has a sense of being trapped: "though she was lost in admiration of her opportunity she managed to move back into the deepest shade of it, even as some wild, caught creature in a vast cage" (93/III, 152-3). And when she considers confiding Warburton's proposal to her cousin, she, unlike the early Isabel, conceives eliminating the possibility in highly negative terms: "she would have had to do herself violence to air this special secret to Ralph" (111/III, 158). In addition, the later Isabel's rejection of Warburton becomes sullied through her particular cast of mind:

. . . she had just given a sort of personal accent to her independence by making up her mind to refuse Lord Warburton. / . . . she had just given a sort of personal accent to her independence by looking so straight at Lord Warburton's big bribe and yet turning away from it. (98/III, 162)

For both the Warburton and the Isabel of the revision, "unhappiness" becomes ominously "a life of misery" (114/III, 187). Finally, her recollection for Ralph at Pratt's Hotel of her rejection of Warburton's suit becomes imagistically compelling in its chilling note of finality:

. . . she took no pleasure in recalling Lord Warburton's magnanimous disappointment. / . . . when she felt again in her face, as from a recurrent wave, the cold breath of her last suitor's surprise, she could only muffle her head till the air cleared. (122/III, 199-200)

The later Caspar Goodwood received similar treatment. When he is first introduced, in Chapter 4, Isabel has just been reviewing her life after her aunt's visit in Albany and has no desire to see him. The early Isabel delays seeing him and paces "the room with a certain feeling of embarrassment." The later Isabel is not embarrassed but distressed: "she moved about the room with a new sense of complications" (29/III, 47).

In Chapter 13, after telling her uncle of her rejection of Warburton, the early Isabel finds herself thinking of Goodwood's influence on her freedom and is "haunted at moments by the image of his disapproval" of what she has done. But the later Isabel, ominously placed, is haunted "by the image, by the danger, of his disapproval" (98/III, 162). And in the same chapter, his having followed her to Europe makes him for the early Isabel "a kind of fate"; for the later Isabel, "a kind of grim fate" (99/III, 163).

In Chapter 16, when Goodwood surprises her at Pratt's Hotel and declares his love, the 1881 Isabel merely "felt the force of it." The 1908 Isabel felt more, felt a trap, "felt it thrown off, into the vast of truth and poetry, as practically a bait to her imagination" (135/III, 220). And when Goodwood leaves her trembling at the beginning of Chapter 17, the early Isabel is excited; the later Isabel wants to withdraw to refuge and to safety:

> She was an excitable creature, and now she was much excited; but she wished to resist excitement, and the attitude of prayer . . . seemed to help her to be still. / Vibration was easy to her, was in fact too constant with her, and she found herself now humming like a smitten harp. She only asked, however, to put on the cover, to case herself again in brown holland, but she wished to resist excitement, and the attitude of devotion . . . seemed to help her to be still. (142/III, 232)

A sense of being trapped is also present more emphatically for the later Isabel when she first meets Gilbert Osmond at his hillside villa outside Florence:

> There was something rather severe about the place; it looked somehow as if, once you were in, it would not be easy to get out. / There was something grave and strong in the place; it looked somehow as if, once you were in, you would need an act of an energy to get out. (221/III, 364)

And the concern of the later Isabel not to commit an esthetic error in his presence is presented as a state of helplessness which does not occur to the early Isabel:

> It would have annoyed her . . . to pass by something at which the truly initiated mind would arrest itself. She was very careful . . . / It would have annoyed her . . . to pass by something at which the

truly initiated mind would arrest itself. She had no wish to fall into that grotesqueness—in which she had seen women (and it was a warning) serenely, yet ignobly, flounder. She was very careful . . . (230/III, 379)

Finally, the response of the later Isabel to her inheritance completes the sense of danger which she, but not the early Isabel, conceives as an integral part of "affronting her destiny." When, in Chapter 20, the early Isabel learns of her fortune, the narrator elects not "to enter into her meditations or to explain why it was that some of them were of a rather pessimistic cast." But the narrator who tells the later Isabel's story declines "to explain exactly why her new consciousness was at first oppressive" (183/III, 300–301). And when, in the same chapter, she meets Henrietta Stackpole in Paris and they discuss the possibilities of her wealth, the early Isabel gazes "upon this vivid but dusky picture of her future," while the later Isabel is confronted by a "lurid scene" (189/III, 311). Even the later Henrietta sees Isabel's future life not as "reality" as does the early Henrietta, but as "grim reality" (189/III, 310).

One aspect of personal reality not recognized by the early Isabel caps what is perhaps the single most important area of response in the later Isabel and is crucial as a preliminary factor in understanding her conduct and her sense of a dangerous destiny. This aspect of her being, almost mutely recognized only by the later Isabel, is a fear of sexual possession. The later Isabel is shown as being afraid of the erotic and, at the end of the revised Chapter 12, this fear is made virtually explicit. The early Isabel is going to reject Warburton and wonders only "whether she were not a cold, hard girl." But the later Isabel senses more; she wonders "whether she were not a cold, hard, priggish person" (95/III,157). This priggishness is obliquely echoed later, in the next chapter, in her letter of rejection to Warburton. While the first Isabel in refusing Warburton could see him in the implied erotic terms of a husband, the later Isabel could not:

". . . I do not find myself able to regard you in the light of a husband . . ."/". . . I am not, I am really and truly not, able to regard you in the light of a companion for life . . ." (101/III, 166)

Although this fear of the erotic rests primarily in Isabel, there is a disturbing erotic ambience which pervades the revised novel and communicates itself to the reader of that version. In this area of the erotic, James extensively revised his treatment of minor objects and secondary characters, and especially Isabel's relationship to Warburton and Goodwood. In the former relationship there is both an increase and a decrease of sexual connotation and awareness, and in the latter there is a vivid expression of male physicality.

A small cluster of changes early in the work begins the new emphasis on the erotic. It is significant that the later Isabel will recall a childhood neighbor though a bedroom reference while the early Isabel does not, and that a bedroom reference present in the early version but not related to Isabel will be removed from the later version:

> . . . the Dutch house . . . was occupied by a primary school for children . . . kept in an amateurish manner by a demonstrative lady, of whom Isabel's chief recollection was that her hair was puffed out very much at the temples . . . / . . . Isabel's chief recollection of her was that her hair was fastened with strange bedroomy combs at the temples . . . (18/III, 29)

> . . . her sister's words must have prompted a remark that she made to her husband in the conjugal chamber as the two were getting ready to go to the hotel. / . . . her sister's words had doubtless prompted a word spoken to her husband as the two were making ready for their visit. (24/III, 39)

The third of these early revisions which contribute to the sexual ambience of the 1908 version is the most powerful, for it occurs as part of the texture of the novel and is unrelated to Isabel. Isabel's sister Lilian, in the first version, is the mistress of a sedate establishment, "a house which presented a narrowness of new brown stone to Fifty-third Street . . ." But the change in the revision is staggering for its unexpectedness: this house is now "a wedge of brown stone violently driven into Fifty-third Street . . ." (24/III, 38). The sexual connotation, very evident here, is reinforced through countless other revisions in the novel's presentation of objects, characters, actions, and responses:

> [the boys Isabel knew]: local youth / suspicious swains (28/III, 46)

> [Ralph observing her]: bending his eyes . . . on her figure / . . . on her presence (88/III, 61)

> [her egotism]: she was often reminded that there were other gardens in the world than those of her virginal soul . . . / . . . of her remarkable soul . . . (44/III, 72)

> [Ralph speaking to Isabel of Warburton's health]: ". . . he's detestably robust." / ". . . he's detestably sound." (60/III, 98)

> [Warburton under the penetrating gaze of Henrietta Stackpole]: . . . there was something in Miss Stackpole's gaze that made him . . . feel vaguely embarrassed and uncomfortable. / . . . there was something . . . that made him . . . feel vaguely embarrassed—

less inviolate, more dishonoured, than he liked. (71/III, 117–18)

[Ralph and Isabel discussing Henrietta]: . . . "I did think she was trying to attract me. Excuse my superficiality." / ". . . Forgive my depravity." (78/III, 129)

[Henrietta relative to Ralph]: . . . her relations with him / . . . her renewed contact with him (80/III, 132)

[Isabel's opinion of Goodwood's arrival]: The feeling was oppressive / The feeling pressed upon her (84/III, 139)

[Goodwood's letter about England]: "If I like this country at present, it is only because you are here." / ". . . only because it holds you." (86/III, 141)

[Henrietta and Mr. Bantling]: harmless confederates / groping celibates (190/III, 312)

[Ned Rosier gazing into a room at the Palazzo Roccanera]: . . . through the open door it looked very pretty. / . . . through the open door it looked the very temple of authorised love. (324/IV, 109)

It is the largely negative aspects of physical love that are visible in the above examples. The boys Isabel knew are no longer sexually neutral but erotically dangerous; Ralph, conversely, looks upon not a physical Isabel (figure), but an almost metaphysical Isabel (presence); her soul is intellectually rendered rather than physically described (remarkable, not virginal); Warburton loses some of his physicality in the revision (sound instead of robust), but squirms in mutely sexual terms under Henrietta's gaze (no longer uncomfortable, but now less inviolate and more dishonoured); Ralph considers it depraved and not superficial that he should have felt Henrietta was trying to attract him; Isabel is no longer oppressed by Goodwood's visit, but pressed upon; Goodwood's preference for England is expressed not in neutral but in tactile terms (you are here/it holds you); Henrietta and Bantling are portrayed as amusingly pathetic sexual adventurers (groping celibates); and Rosier's vision becomes an erotic one as a pretty room becomes a temple of love.

If these elements suggest that James was increasingly concerned with the erotic in his conception of the new Isabel, his revision of her relationships, first with Warburton and then with Goodwood, confirm it.

Warburton, at the outset, is made to consider himself anew in physical terms. As the early Warburton speaks to Isabel at Gardencourt in Chapter 12, he asserts: " 'I am a very judicious fellow.' " The later Warburton is more earthy: " 'I am a very judicious animal' " (90/III, 147). James has Isabel notice the change: the early Isabel saw him "looking at her with eyes that shone with the light of . . . passion." The later Isabel sees "eyes charged with the light of . . . passion" (90/III, 148).

The later Isabel then becomes aware of a physical Warburton that never existed for her 1881 predecessor. He offers her the world:

> These words were uttered with a tender eagerness which went to Isabel's heart . . . / These words were uttered with a breadth of candour that was like the embrace of strong arms—that was like the fragrance straight in her face, and by his clean, breathing lips, of she knew not what strange gardens, what charged airs. (93/III, 152)

And when he kisses her hand he bends not "his head" but, in a hint of nakedness, "his handsome bared head" (94/III, 155).

When the early Isabel resists him, she does not feel "warranted in lending a receptive ear to her English suitor," a view that suggests little physicality and no anxiety. But when the later Isabel resists, there is a suggestion of a delicate rape avoided: she "resisted conquest at her English suitor's large quiet hands" (98/III, 161).

After her rejection of him, there are revisions which more accurately describe the situation between Isabel and Lord Warburton as one in which she is largely afraid of his masculinity. Toward the end of Chapter 21, as Isabel walks along the Mediterranean shore, she thinks again of Warburton. The earlier Isabel refers to him as a lover; the later Isabel is more careful:

> She had so definitely undertaken to forget him, as a lover, that a corresponding effort on his own part would be eminently proper. / She had so definitely undertaken to preserve no record of what had passed between them that a corresponding effort on his own part would be eminently just. (196/III, 323).

On the other hand, he continues to be present in physical terms to other characters. In Chapter 26, for example, the 1881 Mrs. Touchett thinks of Isabel as "a young lady for whom Lord Warburton had not been up to the mark." For the later Mrs. Touchett, however, she is someone "with whom Lord Warburton had not successfully wrestled" (239/III, 394).

In Chapter 27 Isabel and Warburton meet unexpectedly at the Roman Forum. While the early Isabel merely looks at a bashful figure, the later Isabel experiences at once a sense of fear and near nakedness:

> . . . he stood there, smiling a little, blushing a good deal, and raising his hat. / . . . he stood there baring his head to her perceptibly pale surprise. (252/III, 415–16)

When Isabel objects to Warburton's advances in 1881, he vows to remain silent. But the later Warburton makes a comment which for erotic innuendo in context rivals those of *Watch and Ward*: "'I'll keep it down. I'll keep it down always'" (255/III, 421). (In addition, the next substantive reference is appropriately to an excavation.)

The revised Warburton's newly physical and erotic presence is minor, however, when compared with that of the revised Caspar Goodwood; his erotic presence is detailed and explicit. And the later Isabel's final decision in the novel has as a principal motivation a deep fear of Goodwood's eroticism. For her, Goodwood achieves compelling existence solely in phallic terms, a factor embodied in his very name from the beginning.

After informing her uncle, in Chapter 13, of her refusal of Warburton, she muses on the presence of Caspar Goodwood. He represents a threat to her sense of freedom. For the early Isabel, this threat is merely oppressive and restrictive. The later Isabel thinks similarly, but her words reveal a far deeper anxiety:

> There was something too forcible, something oppressive and restrictive, in the manner in which he presented himself. / There was a disagreeably strong push, a kind of hardness of presence, in his way of rising before her. (98/III, 162)

As each continues to muse, this division in their concern is reinforced. The early Isabel objects to him because "there was something very strong about him"; the later, because "he insisted, ever, with his whole weight and force" (98/III, 162).

Each continues to register objections and each continues to reveal the hidden basis of her concern: for the early Isabel it is a dislike of personal aggression; for the later Isabel it is a fear that her freedom will be lost through erotic possession. The later Isabel fears a limitation of her freedom in yielding to Goodwood because, as the revisions reveal, she feels that she would yield to him fully as she would to no one else. When the early Isabel objects to Goodwood's showing his "seriousness too simply," the later Isabel tellingly objects on a sensual level to the manifestation of his "appetites and designs" (100/III, 165).

Even after the experience of marriage to Osmond and childbirth and the revelations of Countess Gemini, the later Isabel will continue to look at Goodwood as an erotic threat to freedom, and more so when she is apparently least free.

In the final chapter, Goodwood returns to unsettle and ultimately to galvanize Isabel who rises from a bench at Gardencourt where Warburton had surprised her six years before. The scene, in the revision, becomes a stark metaphor for all the fearful erotic ambience pervading the revised novel, and eroticism which at last becomes almost a tangible fear.

Goodwood arrives in silence and forces her to sit again. To the early Isabel, "He said nothing at first; she only felt him close to her." The later Isabel felt more: he was "beside her on the bench and pressingly turned to her" (515/IV, 430). While he argues that she has no good reason to return to Rome, the 1908 Isabel is struggling to control the disturbing impact of his erotic presence; and her subsequent words may best be viewed as the visible product of this inner anxiety. Each Isabel, continuing to confront Goodwood, says that she is going back to get away from him. But what the 1881 Isabel means, she acknowledges, is that "she had never been loved before. It wrapped her about; it lifted her off her feet." This response is almost uneventful in its brevity. The response of the later Isabel, however, reveals a desperate struggle to resist violation, physical and total:

> . . . she had never been loved before. She had believed it, but this was different; this was the hot wind of the desert, at the approach of which the others dropped dead, like mere sweet airs of the garden. It wrapped her about; it lifted her off her feet, while the very taste of it, as of something potent, acrid and strange, forced open her set teeth. (517/IV, 433–34)

When the early Isabel beseeched Goodwood to go away, she merely said it. The later, more distressed, more anguished Isabel "panted" (519/IV, 436).

And finally, fear and eroticism become a visible force in the famous kiss. The kiss is a sudden explosion for the early Isabel, nothing more: "His kiss was like a flash of lightning; when it was dark again she was free." But the kiss is so much more for the later Isabel, for in the revised version we finally begin to see *why* Isabel is afraid of the erotic:

> His kiss was like white lightning, a flash that spread, and spread again, and stayed; and it was extraordinarily as if, while she took it, she felt each thing in his hard manhood that had least pleased her, each aggressive fact of his face, his figure, his presence, justified of its intense identity and made one with this act of possession. So had she heard of those wrecked and under water following a train of images before they sink. But when darkness returned she was free. (519/IV, 436)

We have seen, through an analysis of the revisions concerning the erotic, that Isabel fears sexual possession as it affects freedom, but James had not made clear why Isabel was thus afraid. In this passage (but more so in the next sequence of revisions discussed below) he does. James suggests that, at heart, what Isabel fears is a loss through the erotic of a special freedom—the freedom of the mind to function unimpeded. And he suggests that it is essentially for this reason that she must return to Rome. She is not afraid merely of the erotic experience itself but rather its tendency to diminish the life of the mind. Goodwood threatens not so much her body as that annihilation of consciousness which comes with the intensely erotic; which would mean her "death," because for Isabel consciousness is the real center of her being. She exists supremely on the level of pure mind, and the erotic would destroy that existence.

The most extraordinary thing about the revised kiss is not the new inclusion of erotic detail but the fact that the later Isabel is operating at optimum consciousness throughout, struggling to maintain the mind's control in the midst of, for her, destructive emotion. The kiss catches up the phallic motif that surrounded Goodwood, makes it almost concrete, and then dissipates it through Isabel's control of consciousness. The fearful white lightning that threatened annihilation is itself annihilated by a conscious awareness of death. The kiss means possession, and by a mental fiat Isabel induces a scene of archetypal drowning. It is through this induced death of eroticism that Isabel secures her release and makes her decision to return to Rome.

Because the kiss meant none of this to the early Isabel, her decision to return to Rome seemed to some incomprehensible. For the later Isabel, the kiss crystallized her fears and made imminent the annihilation of the mind by the erotic. The decision to return to Rome, absurd to some for the early Isabel, is inevitable for the later Isabel, coming as it does from fear of control by the erotic of the mind's power to operate. Considered from this perspective Isabel's return to Rome in the New York Edition becomes almost positive and challenging, for in that constricting environment only the mind has intense and wide freedom of movement, and Isabel, it seems, is to be engaged in a difficult struggle with Osmond to counter his intransigence and relieve Pansy's plight. Thoreau's comments in "Civil Disobedience," as he wryly observed his captors, may be instructive here: "I could not but smile to see how industriously they locked the door on my meditations, which followed them out again without let or hindrance, and *they* were really all that was dangerous."

The danger for Isabel then, as the later James conceived it, was not what sex might do to her body but what it might do to her mind, for James went to great lengths to have the 1908 Isabel exist primarily on the level of consciousness at the same time that he was emphasizing her freedom (i.e., freedom of the mind to act fully), linking it to the "felt life," and developing the erotic as a threat to the mind's activity through displacing, diminishing, or weakening it.

In Jamesian terms, therefore, the single most important attribute distinguishing the second Isabel from the first is that the new Isabel experiences life through a significantly expanded consciousness. For her, life becomes preeminently a life of the mind. Of the revisions that demonstrate this emphasis on the mind's centrality, some are obvious, other are subtle, but all are immeasureably illuminating.

For example, whereas the first Isabel looks with "quick perception," the second Isabel sees with "clear perception" (12/III, 18), an emphasis not on speed but on the mind's lucidity. While the first "narrowly scrutinized her companions" at Gardencourt, the second, engaged in a survey of the grounds, "had also made room in it for her companions" (13/III, 21), a suggestion of mind expansiveness. And if the first looked at Lord Warburton with "startled eyes," the second "rested her wider eyes on him" (15/III, 23), an indication not only of greater control and less the fluttered girl, but also of deeper probing and absorption.

The most significant revision, however, implies an equation of the very act of living with consciousness. Early in Chapter 12, the narrator, describing his first heroine, speaks of her "vision of a completed life" and talks of her "soul." But when he describes his second heroine, he notes her "visions of a completed consciousness" and refers to her "sublime soul" (87/III, 143). In the revision, then, life becomes consciousness and Isabel grows sublime because more conscious. Earlier in the novel occurs another revision which reinforces this idea. Isabel is swept up by the beauty of Gardencourt when she suddenly thinks of those less fortunate than herself, and this momentary thought makes the first Isabel's "absorbing happiness appear to her a kind of immodesty." The second Isabel has a similar thought but it made 'her fine, full consciousness appear a kind of immodesty" (45/III, 72). Thus, happiness too, by implication, is equated with consciousness, and the entire spectrum of the second Isabel's experience reaches apotheosis in and through her consciousness. And finally, later in the novel, after she has met Gilbert Osmond, she responds to him in a way that makes human relations a matter of the mind's life:

> . . . she felt that she was being entertained. / . . . she had what always gave her a very private thrill, the consciousness of a new relation. (227/III, 374)

A further refinement of the new Isabel's consciousness appears through the introduction of a uniquely Jamesian word—"fine." Lord Warburton impresses both Isabels, but with an essential difference: he made a vivid impression on the "mind" of the first; but he sharply registered himself on the "fine sense" of the second (54/III, 89)—a revision that implies James's high estimate of the mind. This revision occurs in Chapter 7. Very late in the novel, in

Chapter 53, Isabel asks a question about the fate of a woman of sensitivity. But the phrasing of each question is significant. The first Isabel asks, "Was it not much more probable that if one were delicate one would suffer?" The second Isabel wonders whether "if one were fine one would suffer" (492/IV, 392–93), a phrase carrying with it the suggestiveness that to be fine is to be the best that one can be.

An adjunct to the expanded consciousness of the new Isabel is a clarification of her way of looking at the world: she sees it through the pages of a book. In Chapter 7, the Isabels have spent an evening with Lord Warburton. The first "thought him quite one of the most delectable persons she had met," a response whose frame of reference is everyday life. The second, however, "scarce fell short of seeing him—though quite without luridity—as a hero of romance" (55/III,91). Here the frame of reference is the imagination. This frame of reference is echoed in Chapter 31 when Isabel tells her sister Lily absolutely nothing about the offers from Warburton and Osmond. The difference in the two versions is the difference between a person engaged chiefly in a general and public reality and a consciousness absorbed in a private world of romance:

> It entertained her more to say nothing, and she had no idea of asking poor Lily's advice. / It was more romantic to say nothing, and, drinking deep, in secret, of romance, she was as little disposed to ask poor Lily's advice as she would have been to close that rare volume forever. (281/IV, 34)

The Isabel of the romance consciousness has also a consciousness that expands in other, less noticeable ways: she is aware of nuances, she responds more fully, her mind is more striking, her range of interest more broad. When strolling through Gardencourt with Ralph in Chapter 5, the first Isabel prefers "not to talk about herself," while the second, suggesting there is more to say, would rather not "dilate just yet on herself" (38/III, 62). The second also changes her locus of attention in Lord Warburton from person to mind. While she walks with him at Gardencourt in Chapter 12, she deems him incapable of being not "a frivolous person" but "a loose thinker" (89/III, 147). He, in turn, is more alert to her mental activity: the first Warburton is afraid of her "mind"; the second, of her "remarkable mind" (94/III, 154). And when she rejects his proposal at the end of Chapter 12, she does so for logical and not amorous reasons:

> If it were pride that interfered with her accepting Lord Warburton, it was singularly misplaced; and she was so conscious of liking him that she ventured to assure herself it was not. She liked him too much to marry him, that was the point; something

told her that she should not be satisfied . . . / If it had been
pride that interfered with her accepting Lord Warburton such a
bêtise was singularly misplaced; and she was so conscious of liking
him that she ventured to assure herself it was the very softness,
and the fine intelligence, of sympathy. She liked him too much
to marry him, that was the truth; something assured her there
was a fallacy somewhere in the glowing logic of the proposition
—as *he* saw it—even though she mightn't put her very finest
finger-point on it . . . (95/III, 156)

The details of this revision—the words "intelligence," "truth," and
"logic"; the foreign phrase; the delicate image of her fingertip—all
transform the response of the girl to the sphere of the cerebral.

The second Isabel responds to London in a somewhat similar
manner, so that the emphasis is slightly more on the mind than on
the senses: whereas the first was "constantly interested and often
excited," the second was "full of premises, conclusions, emotions"
(120/III, 198).

The response of the second Isabel to Madame Merle is also more
finely intellectual: when Madame Merle discussed Mrs. Touchett,
the first Isabel "agreed with her." The second, however, more alert
to nuances, "rose eagerly to the sense of her shades" (170/III,
278).

Her response to money, on the other hand, becomes strangely
sensuous. In Chapter 20, the first Isabel, in responding to her inheritance, finds she has the "leisure to contemplate the windfall"; but
her counterpart discovers she has the "leisure to measure and weigh
and otherwise handle" the legacy (183/III, 300).

Gilbert Osmond, quite understandably, sets more chords of consciousness vibrating in the second Isabel than in the first:

. . . [his] personal points struck our observant young lady as the
signs of unusual sensibility. / . . . [his] personal points struck our
sensitive young woman as signs of quality, of intensity, somehow
as promises of interest. (228/III, 376)

And while the first could marry him "for his opinions," the second
was looking for more: "the beauty of his opinions or . . . his autograph of Michael Angelo" (240/III, 396).

At the end of the novel, during her long journey from Rome to
Gardencourt, she muses on the question of Madame Merle. The
revision offers a subtle shift from creative contemplation (imagination) to pure mind (intelligence):

The only thing to regret was that Madame Merle had been so—
so strange. Just here Isabel's imagination paused, from literal inability to say what it was Madame Merle had been. / The only
thing to regret was that Madame Merle had been so—well, so

unimaginable. Just here her intelligence dropped, from literal inability to say what it was that Madame Merle had been. (492/IV,
392)

Even more subtle is the refinement in the revised version of the
technique of one character getting inside the mind of another, so
that the reader grows aware of a greater consciousness at play. This
unique ability for cerebral penetration centers, not surprisingly, in
Isabel, and highlights what had grown to become a striking focal
point in the later James: intense personal closeness occurs not on
the level of the emotions and physical intercourse but on the level
of consciousness and the interpenetration of minds.

An extraordinary example of this penetration occurs near the very
end of the novel, in Chapter 54. When Mrs. Touchett speaks to
the 1881 Isabel, we see her and we see Isabel; but when she speaks
to the 1908 Isabel, we get inside Isabel in order to become conscious of her aunt:

> Mrs. Touchett had pushed back her chair, and Isabel left the
> table and walked, rather consciously, to one of the deep windows,
> while her aunt followed her with her eyes. / Mrs. Touchett had
> pushed back her chair, and as her niece left the table and walked,
> rather consciously, to one of the deep windows, she felt herself
> followed by her eyes. (502–3/IV, 409)

Indeed, the whole of Chapter 54 exhibits a cluster of such pene-
trations. When Isabel arrives at Gardencourt and is kept waiting,
the first becomes "nervous and even frightened." But the fears of
the second take on palpable shape as she begins to penetrate the
objects around her:

> . . . she grew nervous and scared—as scared as if the objects
> about her had begun to show for conscious things, watching her
> trouble with grotesque grimaces. (499/IV, 403)

Her acute awareness, unlike that of her counterpart, begins to
probe incisively the quality of human life:

> She reflected that things change but little, while people change so
> much . . . / She envied the security of valuable "pieces" which
> change by no hair's breadth, only grow in value, while their
> owners lose inch by inch youth, happiness, beauty . . . (499/IV,
> 403)

When her aunt finally arrives, she is kissed by Isabel, who senses
her lips. In the revision, her aunt kisses her and we sense Isabel:

> Her lips felt very thin indeed as Isabel kissed her. / Her lips felt
> very thin indeed on Isabel's hot cheek. (499/IV, 404)

And later the second Isabel speculates on the nature of her aunt's grief in a revision which, unlike the former version, demonstrates an act of consciousness rather than an expression of sentimentality:

> She wondered whether Mrs. Touchett were not trying [to indulge regret], whether she had not a desire for the recreation of grief. / She wondered if she were not even missing those enrichments of consciousness and privately trying—reaching out for some after-taste of life, dregs of the banquet; the testimony of pain or the cold recreation of remorse. (501/IV, 406–7)

Also noteworthy are the increased degrees of consciousness else-where in the novel, which, in the revision, achieves fullness and becomes highly meaningful as a remarkable adventure of the mind —with its attendant tragedy for the person possessing that mind. The Isabel in the first version seems capricious; the Isabel in the second is possessed of a unique, ultimately fascinating—and, more important, comprehensible—consciousness.

When, at the start of Chapter 27, she is impressed by Rome, it is her consciousness that operates and not her feelings:

> The sense of the mighty human past was heavy upon her, but it was interfused in the strangest, suddenest, most capricious way, with the fresh, cool breath of the future. Her feelings were so mingled that she scarcely knew whither any of them would lead her . . . / The sense of the terrible human past was heavy to her, but that of something altogether contemporary would suddenly give it wings that it could wave in the blue. Her consciousness was so mixed that she scarcely knew where the different parts of it would lead her . . . (250/III, 413)

And when Warburton surprises her at the Forum, we get her mental activity instead of merely a view of him:

> . . . he stood there, smiling a little, blushing a good deal, and rais-ing his hat. / . . . he stood there baring his head to her percepti-bly pale surprise. (252/III, 415–6)

The silence that follows their talk moves from the plane of the trite communication to the level of the mute exchange of minds. At his silence, the first Isabel "knew what he was thinking of. His eyes were fixed on the ground; but at last he raised them and said grave-ly—'I have written to you several times.' " But his silence for the second Isabel "said so much more than either had said that it scarce needed his final words. 'I've written you several times' " (253/III, 418).

This exchange of minds continues in the revision when she asks pointedly if he plans to stay in Rome as long as she does:

> Lord Warburton looked at her a moment, with an uncomfortable smile. / His flushed smile, for a little, seemed to sound her. (255/III, 421)

A more remarkable communication of minds, or, more accurately, Isabel's expectation of such a communication, occurs in Chapter 30 when she longs to ask Pansy for information about her father but checks herself for this intrusion. The first Isabel is concerned that her curiosity might be discovered; the second, in a more completely rendered image, fears that Osmond's sensibility may become aware of her interest:

> . . . her imagination was hushed with the horror at the idea of taking advantage of the little girl—it was of this she would have accused herself—and of leaving an audible trace of her emotion behind. / . . . her imagination was hushed with the horror of taking advantage of the little girl—it was of this she would have accused herself—and of exhaling into the air where he might still have a subtle sense for it any breath of her charmed state. (278/IV, 29)

The revision of Isabel's love for Osmomd is particularly revealing. While the first Isabel is made to "feel that there was after all something very invidious in being in love; much as the sentiment was theoretically approved of," the second Isabel, more pointedly, is made "conscious, almost with awe, of the invidious and remorseless tide of the charmed and possessed condition, great as was the traditional honour and imputed virtue of being in love" (306/IV, 78). Thus, entering into the second Isabel's consciousness is the awareness of being helpless when possessed by another and of losing one's freedom of mind when "charmed" or bewitched. But Isabel does marry Osmond, and one may ask how she reconciles this marriage with the retention of an untrammeled life of the mind. She does so, James seems to suggest in a later revision, by viewing life with Osmond as life for consciousness:

> Osmond had the attachment of old acquaintance, and Isabel the stimulus of new, which seemed to assure her a future of beautiful hours. / Osmond had the attachment of old acquaintance and Isabel the stimulus of new, which seemed to assure her a future at a high level of consciousness of the beautiful. (308/IV, 82)

In Chapter 38, when Warburton visits Isabel at her palazzo, an exchange of minds again becomes apparent in the revision. In the first version, we view him; in the second, we accompany Isabel as *she* penetratingly views him. He has just observed, "brightly, looking about him," that her place is charming. In the revision he states that her place is charming, "with a look, round him, at her established home, in which she might have caught the dim ghost of his old ruefulness" (333/IV, 125).

The first Isabel makes an ordinary recovery from the jolt of seeing him again; for the second the recovery is remarkable and made interiorly:

"I have heard of you from time to time," said Isabel, who had now completely recovered her self-possession. / "I've heard of you from time to time," said Isabel, who had already, with her rare capacity for such inward feats, taken the measure of what meeting him again meant for her. (333/IV, 125)

The second Warburton reacts in kind. When Osmond leaves them alone together, the first Warburton merely stands there; the second mentally penetrates:

He stood a moment, looking at Isabel with an eye that gradually became more serious. "I am really very glad to see you." / Then the visitor turned on Isabel the deeper, the deepest, consciousness of his look, which gradually became more serious. "I'm really very glad to see you." (334/IV, 125–6)

When, in Chapter 41, she considers having failed Osmond, the second Isabel places herself inside his mind; the first does not; the first "was determined not to be haunted by images of a flat want of zeal." Her counterpart, with the slightest but most significantly rendered difference, "was determined not to be haunted by visions of his wife's limpness under appeal" (363/IV, 174).

Continuing, in the next chapter, her fireside musings on the value of her relationship with Gilbert Osmond, the second Isabel demonstrates, unlike her predecessor, a quality of mind that is noteworthy in its presentation of the paradox of her spiritual materialism and her intellectual eroticism. The first Isabel believes simply that the "finest individual she had ever known was hers; the simple knowledge was a sort of act of devotion." But the second considers with complexity: "The finest—in the sense of being the subtlest—manly organism she had ever known had become her property, and the recognition of her having but to put out her hands and take it had been originally a sort of act of devotion" (374/IV, 194).

Finally, in her relations with the Countess Gemini, the second Isabel is made to demonstrate two further examples of her mind's awareness—this time in the realm of memory. In the first instance, the Countess delivers one of her revelations. The early Isabel takes it passively; but the second responds, and her response reveals that the event has long remained with her:

. . . the Countess rose also, while the sharp animation of her bright, capricious face emitted a kind of flash. She stood a moment looking at Isabel, and then said—"My first sister-in-law had no children!" / . . . the Countess rose also, while her gathered perversity grew vivid and dreadful. She stood a moment in a sort of glare of intention and, as seemed to Isabel even then, of ugliness; after which she said: "My first sister-in-law had no children!" (476/IV, 363)

In the second instance, the two are discussing Madame Merle, and again the idea that Isabel will remember painfully is made clear. Madame Merle, according to the first Countess, did not care to marry Osmond merely because "she had grown more ambitious." The second Countess goes further:

". . . she had grown more ambitious. Besides, she has never had, about him," the Countess went on, leaving Isabel to wince for it so tragically afterwards—" she *had* never had, what you might call any illusions of *intelligence*. . . ." (478/IV, 369)

A revision, earlier in the novel, serves easily as a means of establishing the essential difference between the two Isabels: the first exists without much complexity; the second embraces multiple levels of existence. It is in Chapter 46 that Warburton comes to announce his departure for England, thereby dooming irrevocably Osmond's plans for his daughter and precipitating the rupture between Isabel and Osmond. But before these events can occur, Isabel is sitting seemingly between the two men and probing the minds of each. For the first Isabel, this activity is "a double operation"; for the second Isabel, the Isabel of the mind, it is "a complex operation" (417/IV, 267); and the difference between "double" and "complex" partly expresses the difference between the Isabel of 1881 and the Isabel of 1908.

Not merely a matter of heightened consciousness, however, separates the two Isabels. They are disunited by the degree of freedom and vulnerability possessed by the later Isabel who, in addition, tends to view her vulnerability more clearly as an adjunct of marriage but who is only dimly aware—unlike the first Isabel who is not aware at all—that the basis of her anxiety is a fear that the freedom constituted by the clear conduct of her consciousness may be annihilated by sexual possession. We have, then, in the later Isabel a presence of fears which emanate from, and return to, her remarkable consciousness, thus making the act of "affronting her destiny" a study—sometimes tragic and ironic—of the life of the mind for the later Isabel whereas it was frequently an uneven portrait of a girl's caprice for her predecessor. Because she exists on a compelling level of mind, the later Isabel does what she does. But her distant predecessor does what she does for reasons perhaps best ascribed to the folly of her youth and the esthetics of her incompleteness.

Henry James and the Novel

The Portrait of a Lady was a success at the time it was published, and since then reviewers, critics, and scholars have been speculating about its sources and attempting to penetrate the dim uncertainties of its genesis. Scholars have sought prototypes for its characters among James's family and friends; critics have looked for literary influences among such novelists as George Eliot, Ivan Turgenev, and Nathaniel Hawthorne (James wrote brilliantly about all three); other readers, wishing to trace common patterns of theme and technique in James's work as a whole, have examined his earlier stories and novels, his reviews and travel sketches, his notebooks and correspondence. Most recently, biographical critics have been inferring how James's artistic creation of characters reflects the whole of his personality and experience, both conscious and unconscious.

Although Isabel, the young American lady, is in the great tradition of English fictional heroines from Richardson's Clarissa Harlowe to Virginia Woolf's Clarissa Dalloway, it has been assumed that she resembles James's beloved Minny Temple,[1] just as the outlines of Gilbert Osmond are commonly supposed to have been modeled on an American friend, Francis Boott, who lived in Florence with his daughter. Seeking fictional or even live prototypes for artistic creations, however, has its disadvantages, since in the recesses of the artist's imagination the memories of live friends (or dead ones) and imaginary fictional acquaintances may mix indissolubly with aspects of his own personality. Even the early reviewers sensed how much of James there was in Isabel,[2] and at least one remained unconvinced that a woman of Isabel's "intellectual force," as he put it, could be taken in by "so transparent a cheat" as Gilbert Osmond. "If popular opinion be not at fault," he concluded wryly, "Osmond is the sort of man to attract a female James."[3]

There are, of course, undeniable similarities between James's cousin Minny, who died at twenty-four—"radiant and rare, extinguished in her first youth," James later lamented—and his first great fictional heroine.[4] We can assume that James was not simply painting Minny's portrait, but there is real literary interest in the extent to which James was invoking a deep inner image of Minny in his heroines from Daisy Miller to Milly Theale.[5] To better understand this process, contemporary critics (with an increasingly refined psychological vocabulary) tend to assume that the

1. Leon Edel, *Henry James*, Vol. 1, *The Untried Years: 1843–1870* (Philadelphia, 1953), pp. 226–238; Robert C. LeClair, "Henry James and Minny Temple," *American Literature*, 21 (March, 1949), 35–48.
2. James Herbert Morse, "The Native Element in American Fiction," *The Century Magazine*, 26 (July, 1883), 373; Leon Edel, *Henry James*, Vol. 2, *The Conquest of London: 1870–1881* (Philadelphia, 1962), p. 429.
3. H. A. Huntington, "A Pair of American Novelists," *The Dial*, 2 (January, 1882), 214–15.
4. Also see F. W. Dupee, *Henry James* (New York, 1956), pp. 36–39, 96; Edmund L. Volpe, "The Childhood of James's American Innocents," *Modern Language Notes* 71 (May, 1956), 345–47.

5. Oscar Cargill, *The Novels of Henry James* (New York, 1961), pp. 78–119; Leon Edel, *Henry James*, Vol. 5, *The Master: 1901–1916* (Philadelphia, 1972), pp. 112–16; Graham Greene, *The Lost Childhood and Other Essays*, (New York, 1951), pp. 40–45; Ford Madox Hueffer, *Portraits from Life* (New York, 1937), p. 18; Philip Rahv, "The Heiress of All the Ages," *Partisan Review*, 10 (May-June, 1943), 227–47; Ernest Sandeen, "*The Wings of the Dove* and *The Portrait of a Lady*: A Study of Henry James's Later Phase," *PMLA*, 69 (December, 1954), 1060–75; Lotus Snow, "The Disconcerting Poetry of Mary Temple: A Comparison of the Imagery of *The Portrait of a Lady* and *The Wings of the Dove*," *New England Quarterly*, 31 (September, 1958), 312–39.

author identified himself with the girl whose death had shocked him so profoundly when he himself was barely twenty-seven, a moment which he and his biographer characterize as the end of his youth. And James, the American transplanted to Europe, saw this girl as "a plant of pure American growth," whose life seemed to have ended as his was just beginning.[6]

If James identified himself with Minny, he seems also to have "projected" part of himself on to Osmond and used his old and valued friend, Frank Boott, as the model for the life and ways of an expatriated American like himself. Years later, in an autobiographical memoir, James conceded that creatively he probably couldn't have captured Osmond without the "form" of Francis Boott. James was visiting Boott, and his daughter Elizabeth, in Florence just as he was completing the first installments of *The Portrait of a Lady* in 1880, and three years earlier he had described their Florentine villa in a travel sketch which foreshadowed the setting he was to use for Osmond's villa.[7] When, in later years, James concerned himself with the question of "putting of people into books" he described in retrospect his friends' effect on his own artistic needs:

> An Italianate bereft American with a little moulded daughter in the setting of a massive old Tuscan residence was . . . what was required by a situation of my own—conceived in the light of the Novel; and I *had* it there, in the authenticated way, with its essential fund of truth, at once all the more because my admirable old friend had given it to me and none the less because he had no single note of character or temper, not a grain of the non-essential, in common with my Gilbert Osmond.[8]

That James's fictional Osmond was drawn from certain elements in his own character has led F. W. Dupee to say that the "terrible Osmond represented the kind of husband [James] fearfully fancied he might have made had he actually married Minny."[9] Leon Edel, in his exhaustive and psychologically sophisticated biography, assumes that Osmond represents the "hidden side" of James, whom he takes to be an "intensely autobiographical" writer.[10] For Edel, in this novel of "power" and "egotism" Osmond's ambition leads to dilettantism, just as, for James, this same drive led to "unbounded creativity."[11] Isabel, too, has certain biographical similarities to her author (one obvious instance are the scenes in Albany, which are similar to James's own childhood) and she is shown to be dangerously "free" to pursue her own egotistical aims. Despite their differences, Edel concludes that "Isabel and Osmond are two sides of the

6. Edel, *The Untried Years*, p. 326, 336.
7. Henry James, "Italy Revisited" (1877; reprinted in *Italian Hours* [New York, 1959]), pp. 123–25, 146–47, 162–63, 213. Also see Van Wyck Brooks, *The Dream of Arcadia: American Writers and Artists in Italy, 1760–1915* (New York, 1958); Edel, *The Conquest of London*, p. 295.
8. Henry James, "Notes of a Son and Brother" (1914, reprinted in *Henry James: Autobiography* [New York,

1956]), p. 522; Nathalia Wright, "Henry James and the Greenough Data," *American Quarterly*, 10 (Fall, 1958), pp. 338–43.
9. Dupee, *Henry James*, p. 98.
10. Leon Edel, *Henry James*, Vol. 3, *The Middle Years: 1882–1895* (Philadelphia, 1962), p. 18. Also see Quentin Anderson, *The American Henry James* (New Brunswick, N.J., 1957).
11. Edel, *The Conquest of London*, p. 426.

The Notebooks · 625

same coin, two studies in egotism—and a kind of egotism which belonged to their author."[12]

Further refinements in the examination of characters are made possible by the use of psycho-biographical methods. Edel discovered that James, who had been thought to avoid all romantic attachments, established an extended relationship with Constance Fenimore Woolson, a writer, in Florence in 1880, just as he re-embarked on writing the novel ("one of the strangest friendships in American literary history and one of the most secretive"). One might speculate that this *liaison* with an "intellectual Daisy Miller," as Edel terms her, may have led to personal anxieties which were reflected in the very characterization of Osmond. One might even have to examine whether James's choices in his personal life were merely helpful appendages to his literary creativity.

By examining an author's whole life and work we can avoid the dangers of abstracting any single work from his total output, but in James's case his great sense of privacy and his formidable output of twenty-two novels, 112 stories,[13] and innumerable travel sketches, reviews, dramas, memoirs, biographies, letters and occasional pieces make a broad-based study extremely difficult. The following excerpts from James's own writings provide a different perspective from which to view *The Portrait of a Lady*.

From *The Notebooks*†

Names. Osmond—Rosier—Mr. and Mrs. Match—Name for husband in *P. of L.*: Gilbert Osmond—Raymond Gyves—Mrs. Gift—Name in *Times*: Lucky Da Costa—Name in Knightsbridge: Tagus Shout—Other names: Couch—Bonnycastle—Theory—Cridge—Arrant—Mrs. Tippet—Noad.

P. of a L. After Isabel's marriage there are *five* more instalments, and the success of the whole story greatly depends upon this portion being well conducted or not. Let me then make the most of it—let me imagine the best. There has been a want of action in the earlier part, and it may be made up here. The elements that remain are in themselves, I think, very interesting, and they only need to be strongly and happily combined. The weakness of the whole story is that it is too exclusively psychological—that it depends to⟨o⟩ little on incident; but the complete unfolding of the situation that is established by Isabel's marriage may nonetheless be quite sufficiently dramatic. The idea of the whole thing is that the poor girl, who has dreamed of freedom and nobleness, who has done, as she believes, a generous, natural, clear-sighted thing, finds herself in

---

12. Ibid., p. 426.
13. S. Gorley Putt, *Henry James: A Reader's Guide* (Ithaca, N.Y. 1966), is the only effort to date to treat all the novels and stories.

†From *The Notebooks of Henry James*, edited by F. O. Matthiessen and Kenneth Murdock. Copyright 1947 by Oxford University Press, Inc. Reprinted by permission.

reality ground in the very mill of the conventional. After a year or two of marriage the antagonism between her nature and Osmond's comes out—the open opposition of a noble character and a narrow one. There is a great deal to do here in a small compass; every word, therefore, must tell—every touch must count. If the last five parts of the story appear crowded, this will be rather a good defect in consideration of the perhaps too great diffuseness of the earlier portion. Isabel awakes from her sweet delusion—oh, the art required for making this delusion natural!—and find herself face to face with a husband who has ended by conceiving a hatred for her own larger qualities. These facts, however, are not in themselves sufficient; the situation must be marked by important events. Such an event is the discovery of the relation that has existed between Osmond and Madame Merle, the discovery that she has married Madame Merle's lover. Madame Merle, in a word, is the mother of Pansy. Edward Rosier comes to Rome, falls in love with Pansy and wants to marry her; but Osmond opposes the marriage, on the ground of Rosier's insufficient means. Isabel favours Pansy—she sees that Rosier would make her an excellent husband, be tenderly devoted and kind to her —but Osmond absolutely forbids the idea. Lord Warburton comes to Rome, sees Isabel again and declares to her that he is resigned, that he has succeeded in accepting the fact of her marriage and that he is now disposed, himself, to marry. He makes the acquaintance of Pansy, is charmed with her, and at last tells Isabel that he should like to make her his wife. Isabel is almost shocked, for she distrusts this sentiment of Lord Warburton's; and the reader must feel that she mistrusts it justly. This same sentiment is a very ticklish business. It is honest up to a certain point; but at bottom, without knowing it, Lord W.'s real motive is the desire to be near Isabel whom he sees, now, to be a disappointed, and unhappy woman. This is what Isabel has perceived; she feels that it would ⟨be⟩ cruel to Pansy, dangerous to herself, to allow such a marriage—for which, however, there are such great material inducements that she cannot well oppose it. Her position is a most difficult one, for by begging Lord Warburton to desist she only betrays her apprehension of him—which is precisely what she wishes not to do. Besides, she is afraid of doing a wrong to Pansy. Madame Merle, meanwhile, has caught a glimpse of Warburton's state of mind and eagerly takes up the idea of his marrying the girl. Pansy is very much in love with Rosier—she has no wish to marry Lord W. Isabel is ⟨so⟩ convinced at last of this that she feels absolved from considering her prospects with Lord W. and treats the latter with such coldness that he feels the vanity of hope and withdraws from the field, having indeed not paid any direct attention to Pansy, whom he cannot in the least be accused of jilting. Madame Merle, very angry at his withdrawal, accuses Isabel of having dissuaded him, out of jealousy, because of his having been an old lover of hers and her wishing to keep him for herself; and she still opposes the marriage with Rosier, because she has been made to believe by Lord Warburton's attentions that Pansy may do something much more brilliant. Isabel resents Madame Merle's interference, demands of her what she has to do with Pansy. Whereupon Madame Merle, in whose breast the suppressed feeling of maternity has long been rankling, and who is passionately jealous of Isabel's influence over Pansy, breaks out with the cry that she alone has a right—that Pansy is her daughter. (To be settled later whether this revelation is to be made by Mme Merle herself, or by the Countess Gemini. Better on many grounds that it should be the latter; and yet in that way I lose the 'great scene' between Madame Merle and Isabel.) In any event this whole matter of Mme Merle is (like Lord W.'s state of mind about Pansy) a very ticklish one—very delicate and difficult to handle. To make it natural that she should have brought about Isabel's marriage to her old lover—this is in itself a supreme difficulty. It is not, however, an impossibility, for I honestly believe it rests upon nature. Her old interest in Osmond remains in a modified form; she wishes to do something for him, and she does it through another rather than by herself. That, I think, is perfectly natural. As regards Pansy the strangeness of her conduct is greater; but we must remember that we see only its surface—we don't see her reasoning. Isabel has money, and Mme Merle has great confidence in her benevolence, in her generosity; she has no fear that she will be a harsh stepmother, and she believes she will push the fortunes of the child she herself is unable to avow and afraid openly to patronize. In all this Osmond sinks a little into the background—but one must get the sense of Isabel's exquisitely miserable revulsion. Three years have passed—time enough for it to have taken place. His worldliness, his deep snobbishness, his want of generosity, etc.; his hatred of her when he finds that she judges him, that she morally protests at so much that surrounds her. The uncleanness of the air; the Countess Gemini's lovers, etc. Caspar Goodwood of course must reappear, and Ralph, and Henrietta; Mrs. Touchett, too, for a moment. Ralph's helpless observation of Isabel's deep misery; her determination to show him nothing, and his inability to help her. This to be a strong feature in the situation. Pansy is sent back to the convent, to be kept from Rosier. Caspar Goodwood comes to Rome, because he has heard from Henrietta that Isabel is unhappy, and Isabel sends him away. She hears from Ralph at Gardencourt, that he is ill there (Ralph, himself), that indeed he is dying. (The letter to come from Mrs. Touchett who is with him; or even it would be well that it should be a telegram; it expresses Ralph's wish to see her.) Isabel tells Osmond she wishes to go; Osmond, jealously and nastily, forbids it; and Isabel, deeply distressed and embarrassed, hesitates. Then Madame Merle, who wishes her to make a *coup de tête*, to leave Osmond, so that she may be away from Pansy, reveals to her her belief that it was Ralph who induced her father to leave her the £70,000. Isabel, then, violently affected and overcome, starts directly for England. She reaches Ralph at Gardencourt, and finds Caspar Goodwood and Henrietta also there: i.e., in London. Ralph's death—Isabel's return to London, and interview with Caspar G.—His passionate outbreak; he beseeches her to return with him to America. She is greatly moved, she feels the full force of his devotion—to which she has never done justice; but she refuses. She starts again for Italy—and her departure is the climax and termination of the story.

* * *

With strong handling it seems to me that it may all be very true, very powerful, very touching. The obvious criticism of course will be that it is not finished—that I have not seen the heroine to the end of her situation—that I have left her *en l'air*.—This is both true and false. The *whole* of anything is never told; you can only take what groups together. What I have done has that unity—it groups together. It is complete in itself—and the rest may be taken up or not, later.

—I am not sure that it would not be best that the exposure of Mme Merle should never be complete, and above all that she should not denounce herself. This would injure very much the impression I have wished to give of her profundity, her self-control, her regard for appearances. It may be enough that Isabel should believe the fact in question—in consequence of what the Countess Gemini has told her. Then, when Madame Merle tells her of what Ralph has done for her of old—tells it with the view I have mentioned of precipitating her defiance of Osmond—Isabel may charge her with the Countess G.'s secret. This Madame Merle will deny—but deny in such a way that Isabel knows she lies; and *then* Isabel may depart.—The last (October) instalment to take place wholly in England. At the very last Caspar Goodwood goes to Pratt's hotel, and is told that Mrs. Osmond has left it the night before. Later in the day he sees Henrietta who has the last word—utters the last line of the story: a characteristic characterization of Isabel.

[* * * His remarks about leaving his heroine's situation in a sense 'unfinished' are revelatory of his conception of structure, and correspond to what he was to say in the preface to *Roderick Hudson*:

'Really, universally, relations stop nowhere, and the exquisite problem of the artist is eternally but to draw, by a geometry of his own,
the circle within which they shall happily *appear* to do so.' In the
preface to the *Portrait* he discussed the problem caused for the novelist by starting with a character instead of with a story. But by
then he was no longer worried that this novel had been 'too exclusively psychological.' He asserted that his source of interest lay not
in the events but in Isabel's sense of them. He took pride that he
had produced in her a center of consciousness comparable in intensity to what he later created in Lambert Strether. He singled out as
'obviously the best thing in the book' a chapter which he hardly
reckons with in his outline, the chapter of entirely inward drama in
which Isabel, sitting alone by the dying fire, begins to realize the
relationship between Osmond and Madame Merle.

When he undertook the revision of the *Portrait* for his collected
edition, James was still thinking of the 'great scene' he had passed
up by not making the revelation of Pansy's parentage come through
Madame Merle; and he therefore devoted his most extensive rewriting to building up the scene between Isabel and the Countess
Gemini. Another detail of considerable importance in interpreting
the ending of the novel is provided by James' remark at the end of
the entry above, that the final speech by Henrietta Stackpole
('Look here, Mr. Goodwood, just you wait') is to be 'characteristic'
of her rather than of Isabel. James' note thus makes it clear that he
intended from the time of his first draft to have this speech be
indicative of Henrietta's unquenchable optimism rather than what
it has sometimes been interpreted to be, a sure forecast of Isabel's
future action.][1]

* * * The following year, 1879, I went abroad again—but only
to Paris. I stayed in London during all August, writing my little
book on Hawthorne, and on September 1st crossed over to Paris
and remained there till within a few days of Xmas. * * * In the
spring I went to Italy—partly to escape the 'season,' which had
become a terror to me. I couldn't keep out of it—(I had become a
highly-developed diner-out, etc.) and its interruptions, its repetitions, its fatigues, were horribly wearisome, and made work
extremely difficult. I went to Florence and spent a couple of
months, during which I took a short run down to Rome and to
Naples, where I had not been since my first visit to Italy, in 1869. I
spent three days with Paul Joukowsky at Posilipo, and a couple of
days alone at Sorrento. Florence was divine, as usual, and I was a
great deal with the Bootts. At that exquisite Bellosguardo at the
Hotel de l'Arno, in a room in that deep recess, in the front, I

1. This bracketed commentary is by the   *James [Editor]*.
editors of *The Notebooks of Henry*

began the *Portrait of a Lady*—that is, I took up, and worked over, an old beginning, made long before. I returned to London to meet William, who came out in the early part of June, and spent a month with me in Bolton St., before going to the continent. That summer and autumn I worked, *tant bien que mal*, at my novel which began to appear in *Macmillan* in October (1880). * * *

From A *Small Boy and Others*†

* * * I lose myself in wonder at the loose ways, the strange process of waste, through which nature and fortune may deal on occasion with those whose faculty for application is all and only in their imagination and their sensibility. There may be during those bewildered and brooding years so little for them to "show" that I liken the individual dunce—as he so often must appear—to some commercial traveler who has lost the key to his packed case of samples and can but pass for a fool while other exhibitions go forward.

I achieve withal a dim remembrance of my final submission, though it is the faintest ghost of an impression and consists but of the bright blur of a dame's schoolroom, a mere medium for small piping shuffling sound and suffered heart, as well as for the wistfulness produced by "glimmering squares" that were fitfully screened, though not to any revival of cheer, by a huge swaying, yet dominant object. This dominant object, the shepherdess of the flock, was Miss Bayou or Bayhoo—I recover but the alien sound of her name, which memory caresses only because she may have been of like race with her temple of learning, which faced my grandmother's house in North Pearl Street and really justified its exotic claim by its yellow archaic gable-end: I think of the same as of brick baked in the land of dykes and making a series of small steps from the base of the gable to the point. These images are subject, I confess, to a soft confusion—which is somehow consecrated, none the less, and out of which, with its shade of contributory truth, some sort of scene insists on glancing. The very flush of the uneven bricks of the pavement lives in it, the very smell of the street cobbles, the imputed grace of the arching umbrage—I see it all as from under trees; the form of Steuben Street, which crossed our view, as steep even to the very essence of adventure, with a summit, and still more with a nethermost and riskiest incline, very far away. There lives in it the aspect of the other house—the other and much smaller than my grandmother's, conveniently near it and within sight; which was pinkish-red picked out with white, whereas my grandmother's was

† From *Autobiography* by Henry James, edited by Frederick W. Dupee (New York, 1956), pp. 8–10. Copyright 1913 by Charles Scribner's Sons; renewed 1941 by Henry James. Reprinted by permission of Charles Scribner's Sons and Alexander R. James, Literary Executor.

greyish-brown and very grave, and which must have stood back a little from the street, as I seem even now to swing, or at least to perch, on a relaxed gate of approach that was conceived to work by an iron chain weighted with a big ball; all under a spreading tree again and with the high, oh so high white stone steps (mustn't they have been marble?) and fan-lighted door of the pinkish-red front behind me. I lose myself in ravishment before the marble and the pink. There were other houses too—one of them the occasion of the first "paid" visit that struggles with my twilight of social consciousness; a call with my father, conveying me presumably for fond exhibition (since if my powers were not exhibitional my appearance and my long fair curls, of which I distinctly remember the lachrymose sacrifice, suppositiously were), on one of our aunts, the youngest of his three sisters, lately married and who, predestined to an early death, hovers there for me, softly spectral, in long light "front" ringlets, the fashion of the time and the capital sign of all our paternal aunts seemingly; with the remembered enhancement of her living in Elk Street, the name itself vaguely portentous, as through beasts of the forest not yet wholly exorcised, and more or less under the high brow of that Capitol which, as aloft somewhere and beneath the thickest shades of all, loomed, familiar yet impressive, at the end of almost any Albany vista of reference. I have seen other capitols since, but the whole majesty of the matter must have been then distilled into my mind—even though the connection was indirect and the concrete image, that of the primitive structure, long since pretentiously and insecurely superseded—so that, later on, the impression was to find itself, as the phrase is, discounted. Had it not moreover been reinforced at the time, for that particular Capitoline hour, by the fact that our uncle, our aunt's husband, was a son of Mr. Martin Van Buren, and that *he* was the President? This at least led the imagination on—or leads in any case my present imagination of that one; ministering to what I have called the soft confusion.

The confusion clears, however, though the softness remains, when, ceasing to press too far backward, I meet the ampler light of conscious and educated little returns to the place; for the education of New York, enjoyed up to my twelfth year, failed to blight is romantic appeal. The images I really distinguish flush through the maturer medium, but with the sense of them only the more wondrous. The other house, the house of my parents' limited early sojourn, becomes that of those of our cousins, numerous at that time, who pre-eminently figured for us; the various brood presided over by my father's second sister, Catherine James, who had married at a very early age Captain Robert Temple, U.S.A. Both these parents were to die young, and their children, six in number, the two eldest boys, were very markedly to people our preliminary scene; this being true in particular of three of them, the sharply differing brothers and the second sister, Mary Temple, radiant and rare, extinguished in her first youth, but after having made an impression on many persons, and on ourselves not least, which was to become in the harmonious circle, for all time, matter of sacred legend and reference, of associated piety. Those and others with them were the numerous dawnings on which in many cases the deepening and final darknesses were so soon to follow: our father's family was to offer such a chronicle of early deaths, arrested careers, broken promises, orphaned children. It sounds cold-blooded, but part of the charm of our grandmother's house for us—or I should perhaps but speak for myself—was in its being so much and so sociably a nurseried and playroomed orphanage. The children of her lost daughters and daughters-in-law overflowed there, mainly as girls; on whom the surviving sons-in-law and sons occasionally and most trustingly looked in. Parentally bereft cousins were somehow more thrilling than parentally provided ones; and most thrilling when, in the odd fashion of that time, they were sent to school in New York as a preliminary to their being sent to school in Europe.

* * *

From *Notes of a Son and Brother*†

Immediately, at any rate, the Albany cousins, or a particular group of them, began again to be intensely in question for us; coloured in due course with reflections of the War as their lives, not less than our own, were to become—and coloured as well too, for all sorts of notation and appreciation, from irrepressible private founts. Mrs. Edmund Tweedy, bereft of her own young children, had at the time I speak of opened her existence, with the amplest hospitality, to her four orphaned nieces, who were also our father's and among whom the second in age, Mary Temple the younger, about in her seventeenth year when she thus renewed her appearance to our view, shone with vividest lustre, an essence that preserves her still, more than half a century from the date of her death,[1] in a memory or two where many a relic once sacred has comparatively yielded to time. Most of those who knew and loved, I was going to say adored, her have also yielded—which is a reason the more why thus much of her, faint echo from too far off though it prove, should be tenderly saved. If I have spoken of the elements and presences round about us that "counted," Mary Temple was to count, and in more

† From *Autobiography* by Henry James, edited by Frederick W. Dupee (New York, 1956), pp. 282–84, 518–22. Copyright 1914 by Charles Scribner's Sons; renewed 1942 by Henry James. Reprinted by permission of Charles Scribner's Sons and Alexander R. James, Literary Executor.
1. Mary Temple was born in 1845 and died in 1870 [*Editor*].

lives than can now be named, to an extraordinary degree; count as a young and shining apparition, a creature who owed to the charm of her every aspect (her aspects were so many!) and the originality, vivacity, audacity, generosity, of her spirit, an indescribable grace and weight—if one might impute weight to a being so imponderable in common scales. Whatever other values on our scene might, as I have hinted, appear to fail, she was one of the first order, in the sense of the immediacy of the impression she produced, and produced altogether as by the play of her own light spontaneity and curiosity—not, that is, as through a sense of such a pressure and such a motive, or through a care for them, in others. "Natural" to an effect of perfect felicity that we were never to see surpassed is what I have already praised all the Albany *cousinage* of those years for being; but in none of the company was the note so clear as in this rarest, though at the same time symptomatically or ominously palest, flower of the stem; who was natural at more points and about more things, with a greater range of freedom and ease and reach of horizon than any of the others dreamed of. They had that way, delightfully, with the small, after all, and the common matters —while she had it with those too, but with the great and rare ones over and above; so that she was to remain for us the very figure and image of a felt interest in life, an interest as magnanimously far-spread, or as familiarly and exquisitely fixed, as her splendid shifting sensibility, moral, personal, nervous, and having at once such noble flights and such touchingly discouraged drops, such graces of indifference and inconsequence, might at any moment determine. She was really to remain, for our appreciation, the supreme case of a taste for life as life, as personal living; of an endlessly active and yet somehow a careless, an illusionless, a sublimely forewarned curiosity about it: something that made her, slim and fair and quick, all straightness and charming tossed head, with long light and yet almost sliding steps and a large light postponing, renouncing laugh, the very muse or amateur priestess of rash speculation. To express her in the mere terms of her restless young mind, one felt from the first, was to place her, by a perversion of the truth, under the shadow of female "earnestness"—for which she was much too unliteral and too ironic; so that, superlatively personal and yet as independent, as "off" into higher spaces, at a touch, as all the breadth of her sympathy and her courage could send her, she made it impossible to say whether she was just the most moving of maidens or a disengaged and dancing flame of thought. No one to come after her could easily seem to show either a quick inward life or a brave, or even a bright, outward, either a consistent contempt for social squalors or a very marked genius for moral reactions. She had in her brief passage the enthusiasm of humanity—more, assuredly, than any charming girl who ever circled, and would fain have continued to circle, round a ballroom. This kept her indeed for a time more interested in the individual, the immediate human, than in the race or the social order at large; but that, on the other hand, made her ever so restlessly, or quite inappeasably, "psychologic." The psychology of others, in her shadow—I mean their general resort to it—could only for a long time seem weak and flat and dim, above all not at all amusing. She burned herself out; she died at twenty-four.

* * *

* * * But her[2] letter goes on after a couple of days—she had apparently not sent the previous part, and it brings her back, we can rejoicingly note, to George Eliot, whose poem, alluded to, must have been The Spanish Gipsy. This work may indeed much less have counted for her than the all-engulfing Mill on the Floss, incomparably privileged production, which shone for young persons of that contemporaneity with a nobleness that nothing under our actual star begins in like case to match. These are great recognitions, but how can I slight for them a mention that has again and again all but broken through in my pages?—that of Francis Boott and his daughter (she to become later on Mrs. Frank Duveneck and to yield to the same dismal decree of death before her time that rested on so many of the friends of our youth). When I turn in thought to the happiness that our kinswoman was still to have known in her short life, for all her disaster, Elizabeth Boott, delightful, devoted and infinitely under the charm, at once hovers for me; this all the more, I hasten to add, that we too on our side, and not least Mary Temple herself, were under the charm, and that *that* charm, if less immediately pointed, affected all our young collective sensibility as a wondrous composite thing. There was the charm for us—if I must not again speak in assurance but for myself—that "Europe," the irrepressible even as the *ewig Weibliche* of literary allusion was irrepressible, had more than anything else to do with; and then there was the other that, strange to say (strange as I, once more, found myself feeling it) owed nothing of its authority to anything so markedly out of the picture. The spell to which I in any case most piously sacrificed, most cultivated the sense of, was ever of this second cast —and for the simple reason that the other, serene in its virtue, fairly insolent in its pride, needed no rites and no care. It must be allowed that there was nothing composite in any spell proceeding, whether directly or indirectly, from the great Albany connection: this form of the agreeable, through whatever appeals, could certainly not have been more of a piece, as we say—more of a single superfused complexion, an element or principle that we could in the usual case ever so easily and pleasantly account for. The case of that one in the large number of my cousins whom we have seen to be so imcomparably the most interesting was of course anything but the

2. Minnie Temple's.

usual; yet the Albany origin, the woodnote wild, sounded out even amid her various voices and kept her true, in her way, to something we could only have called local, or perhaps family, type. Essentially, however, she had been a free incalculable product, a vivid exception to rules and precedents; so far as she had at all the value of the "composite" it was on her own lines altogether—the composition was of things that had lain nearest to hand. It mattered enormously for such a pair as the Bootts, intimately associated father and daughter, that what had lain nearest *their* hand, or at least that of conspiring nature and fortune in preparing them for our consumption, had been the things of old Italy, of the inconceivable Tuscany, that of the but lately expropriated Grand Dukes in particular, and that when originally alighting among us *en plein* Newport they had seemed fairly to reek with a saturation, esthetic, historic, romantic, that everything roundabout made precious. I was to apprehend in due course, and not without dismay, that what they really most reeked with was the delight of finding us ourselves exactly as we were; they fell so into the wondrous class of inverted romantics, several other odd flowers of which I was later on to have anxiously to deal with: we and our large crude scene of barbaric plenty, as it might have been called, beguiled them to appreciations such as made our tribute to themselves excite at moments their impatience and strike them as almost silly. It was *our* conditions that were picturesque, and I had to make the best of a time when they themselves appeared to consent to remain so but by the beautiful gaiety of their preference. This, I remember well, I found disconcerting, so that my main affectionate business with them became, under amusement by the way, that of keeping them true to type. What above all contributed was that they really couldn't help their case, try as they would to shake off the old infection; they were of "old world" production through steps it was too late to retrace; and they were in the practical way and in the course of the very next years to plead as guilty to this as the highest proper standard for them could have prescribed. They "went back," and again and again, with a charming, smiling, pleading inconsequence—any pretext but the real one, the fact that the prime poison was in their veins, serving them at need; so that, as the case turned, all my own earlier sense, on the spot, of Florence and Rome was to mix itself with their delightfully rueful presence there. I could then perfectly put up with that flame of passion for Boston and Newport in them which still left so perfect their adaptability to Italian installations that would have been impossible save for subtle Italian reasons.

I speak of course but of the whole original view: time brings strange revenges and contradictions, and all the later history was to be a chapter by itself and of the fullest. We had been all alike accessible in the first instance to the call of those references which played through their walk and conversation with an effect that their qualifying ironies and amusing reactions, where such memories were concerned, couldn't in the least abate; for nothing in fact lent them a happier colour than just this ability to afford so carelessly to cheapen the certain treasure of their past. They had enough of that treasure to give it perpetually away—in our subsequently to be more determined, our present, sense; in short we had the fondest use for their leavings even when they themselves hadn't. Mary Temple, with her own fine quality so far from composite, rejoiced in the perception, however unassisted by any sort of experience of what their background had "meant"; she would have liked to be able to know just that for herself, as I have already hinted, and I actually find her image most touching perhaps by its so speaking of what she with a peculiar naturalness dreamed of and missed. Of clear old English stock on her father's side, her sense for what was English in life—so we used to simplify—was an intimate part of her, little chance as it enjoyed for happy verifications. In the Bootts, despite their still ampler amd more recently attested share in that racial strain, the foreign tradition had exceedingly damped the English, which didn't however in the least prevent her being caught up by it as it had stamped itself upon the admirable, the infinitely civilised and sympathetic, the markedly *produced* Lizzie. This delightful girl, educated, cultivated, accomplished, toned above all, as from steeping in a rich old medium, to a degree of the rarest among her coevals "on our side," had the further, the supreme grace that she melted into American opportunities of friendship—and small blame to her, given such as she then met—with the glee of a sudden scarce believing discoverer. Tuscany could only swoon away under comparison of its starved sociabilities and complacent puerilities, the stress of which her previous years had so known, with the multiplied welcomes and freedoms, the exquisite and easy fellowships that glorified to her the home scene. Into not the least of these quick affinities had not prompt acquaintance with Mary Temple confidently ripened; and with no one in the aftertime, so long as that too escaped the waiting shears, was I to find it more a blest and sacred rite, guarded by no stiff approaches, to celebrate my cousin's memory. That really is my apology for this evocation—which might under straighter connections have let me in still deeper; since if I have glanced on another page of the present miscellany at the traps too often successfully set for my wandering feet my reader will doubtless here recognise a perfect illustration of our danger and will accuse me of treating an inch of canvas to an acre of embroidery. Let the poor canvas figure time and the embroidery figure consciousness—the proportion will perhaps then not strike us as so wrong. Consciousness accordingly still grips me to the point of a felt pressure of interest in such a matter as the recoverable history

—history in the esthetic connection at least—of its insistent deal-ings with a given case. How in the course of time for instance was it not insistently to deal, for a purpose of application, with the fine prime image deposited all unwittingly by the "picturesque" (as I absolutely required to feel it) Boott situation or Boott *data?* The direct or vital value of these last, in so many ways, was experiential, a stored and assimilated thing; but the seed of suggestion proved after long years to have kept itself apart in order that it should develop under a particular breath. A not other than lonely and bereft American, addicted to the arts and endowed for them, housed to an effect of long expatriation in a massive old Florentine villa with a treasured and tended little daughter by his side, *that* was the germ which for reasons beyond my sounding the case of Frank Boott had been appointed to plant deep down in my vision of things. So lodged it waited, but the special instance, as I say, had lodged it, and it lost no vitality—on the contrary it acquired every patience—by the fact that little by little each of its connections above ground, so to speak, was successively cut. Then at last after years it raised its own head into the air and found its full use for the imagination. An Italianate bereft American with a little moulded daughter in the setting of a massive old Tuscan residence was at the end of years exactly what was required by a situation of my own—conceived in the light of the Novel; and I *had* it there, in the authenticated way, with its essential fund of truth, at once all the more because my admirable old friend had given it to me and none the less because he had no single note of character or temper, not a grain of the non-essential, in common with my Gilbert Osmond. This combination of facts has its shy interest, I think, in the general imaginative or reproductive connection—testifying as it so happens to do on that whole question of the "putting of people into books" as to which any ineptitude of judgment appears always in order. I probably shouldn't have had the Gilbert Osmonds at all without the early "form" of the Frank Bootts, but I still more cer-tainly shouldn't have had them with the *sense* of my old inspirers. The form had to be disembarrassed of that sense and to take in a thoroughly other; thanks to which account of the matter I am left feeling that I scarce know whether most to admire, for support of one's beautiful business of the picture of life, the relation of "people" to art or the relation of art to people. * * *

From *Italy Revisited*†

* * * The river-front of Florence is in short a delightful composi-tion. Part of its charm comes of course from the generous aspect of those high-based Tuscan palaces which a renewal of acquaintance

† From Henry James, "Italy Revisited"   York, 1959], pp. 122–23, and 124–25).
(1877; reprinted in *Italian Hours* [New

with them has again commended to me as the most dignified dwell-ings in the world. Nothing can be finer than that look of giving up the whole immense ground-floor to simple purposes of vestibule and staircase, of court and high-arched entrance; as if this were all but a massive pedestal for the real habitation and people weren't properly housed unless, to begin with, they should be lifted fifty feet above the pavement. The great blocks of the basement; the great intervals, horizontally and vertically, from window to window (telling of the height and breadth of the rooms within); the armorial shield hung forward at one of the angles; the wide-brimmed roof, overshadowing the narrow street; the rich old browns and yellows of the walls: these definite elements put themselves together with admirable art.

Take a Tuscan pile of this type out of its oblique situation in the town; call it no longer a palace, but a villa; set it down by a terrace on one of the hills that encircle Florence, place a row of high-waisted cypresses beside it, give it a grassy courtyard and a view of the Florentine towers and the valley of the Arno, and you will think it perhaps even more worthy of your esteem. It was a Sunday noon, and brilliantly warm, when I again arrived; and after I had looked from my windows awhile at that quietly-basking river-front I have spoken of I took my way across one of the bridges and then out of one of the gates—that immensely tall Roman Gate in which the space from the top of the arch to the cornice (except that there is scarcely a cornice, it is all a plain massive piece of wall) is as great, or seems to be, as that from the ground to the former point. Then I climbed a steep and winding way—much of it a little dull if one likes, being bounded by mottled, mossy garden-walls—to a villa on a hill-top, where I found various things that touched me with almost too fine a point. Seeing them again, often, for a week, both by sun-light and moonshine, I never quite learned not to covet them; not to feel that not being a part of them was somehow to miss an exquisite chance. What a tranquil, contented life it seemed, with romantic beauty as a part of its daily texture!—the sunny terrace, with its tangled *podere* beneath it; the bright grey olives against the bright blue sky; the long, serene, horizontal lines of other villas, flanked by their upward cypresses, disposed upon the neighbouring hills. * * *

It is true indeed that I might after a certain time grow weary of a regular afternoon stroll among the Florentine lanes; of sitting on low parapets, in intervals of flower-topped wall, and looking across at Fiesole or down the rich-hued valley of the Arno; of pausing at the open gates of villas and wondering at the height of cypresses and the depth of loggias; of walking home in the fading light and noting on a dozen westward-looking surfaces the glow of the opposite sunset. But for a week or so all this was delightful. The villas are innumerable, and if you're an aching alien half the talk is about villas. This one has a story; that one has another; they all look as if they had stories—none in truth predominantly gay. Most of them are offered to rent (many of them for sale) at prices unnaturally low; you may have a tower and a garden, a chapel and an expanse of thirty windows, for five hundred dollars a year. In imagination you hire three or four; you take possession and settle and stay. Your sense of the fineness of the finest is of something very grave and stately; your sense of the bravery of two or three of the best something quite tragic and sinister. From what does this latter impression come? You gather it as you stand there in the early dusk, with your eyes on the long, pale-brown façade, the enormous windows, the iron cages fastened to the lower ones. Part of the brooding expression of these great houses comes, even when they have not fallen into decay, from their look of having outlived their original use. Their extraordinary largeness and massiveness are a satire on their present fate. They weren't built with such a thickness of wall and depth of embrasure, such a solidity of staircase and superfluity of stone, simply to afford an economical winter residence to English and American families. I don't know whether it was the appearance of these stony old villas, which seemed so dumbly conscious of a change of manners, that threw a tinge of melancholy over the general prospect; certain it is that, having always found this note as of a myriad old sadnesses in solution in the view of Florence, it seemed to me now particularly strong. "Lovely, lovely, but it makes me 'blue,' " the sensitive stranger couldn't but murmur to himself as, in the late afternoon, he looked at the landscape from over one of the low parapets, and then, with his hands in his pockets, turned away indoors to candles and dinner.

From *A Roman Holiday*†

If you stop, however, to observe everything worthy of your water-colors you will never reach Lateran. My business was much less with the interior of St. John Lateran, which I have never found peculiarly interesting, than with certain charming features of its surroundng precinct—the crooked old court beside it, which admits you to the Baptistery and to a delightful rear-view of the queer architectural odds and ends which in Rome may compose a florid ecclesiastical façade. There are more of these, a stranger jumble of chance detail, of lurking recesses and wanton projections and inexplicable windows, than I have memory or phrase for; but the gem of

† From Henry James, "A Roman Holi-   (Boston, 1875), pp. 122–24.
day" (1873), in *Transatlantic Sketches*

the collection is the oddly perched peaked turret, with its yellow travertine welded upon the rusty brickwork, which was not meant to be suspected, and the brickwork retreating beneath and leaving it in the odd position of a tower *under* which you may see the sky. As to the great front of the church overlooking the Porta San Giovanni, you are not admitted behind the scenes; the phrase is quite in keeping, for the architecture has a vastly theatrical air. It is extremely imposing—that of St. Peter's alone is more so; and when from far off on the Campagna you see the colossal images of the mitred saints along the top standing distinct against the sky, you forget their coarse construction and their breezy draperies. The view from the great space which stretches from the church steps to the city wall is the very prince of views. Just beside you, beyond the great alcove of mosaic, is the Scala Santa, the marble staircase which (says the legend) Christ descended under the weight of Pilate's judgment, and which all Christians must forever ascend on their knees; before you is the city gate which opens upon the Via Appia Nuova, the long gaunt file of arches of the Claudian aqueduct, their jagged ridge stretching away like the vertebral column of some monstrous mouldering skeleton, and upon the blooming brown and purple flats and dells of the Campagna and the glowing blue of the Alban Mountains, spotted with their white, high-nestling towns; and to your left is the great grassy space, lined with dwarfish mulberry-trees, which stretches across to the damp little sister-basilica of Santa Croce in Gerusalemme. During a former visit to Rome I lost my heart to this idle tract, and wasted much time in sitting on the steps of the church and watching certain white-cowled friars who were sure to be passing there for the delight of my eyes. There are fewer friars now, and there are a great many of the king's recruits, who inhabit the ex-conventual barracks adjoining Santa Croce and are led forward to practise their goose-step on the sunny turf. Here, too, the poor old cardinals who are no longer to be seen on the Pincio descend from their mourning-coaches and relax their venerable knees. These members alone still testify to the traditional splendour of the princes of the Church; for as they advance the lifted black petticoat reveals a flash of scarlet stockings and makes you groan at the victory of civilisation over colour.

From *Roman Rides*†

The Campagna differs greatly on the two sides of the Tiber; and it is hard to say which, for the rider, has the greater charm. The half-dozen rides you may take from the Porta San Giovanni possess

† From Henry James, "Roman Rides" (1873), *Transatlantic Sketches* (Boston, 1875), p. 146.

the perfection of traditional Roman interest and lead you through a far-strewn wilderness of ruins—a scattered maze of tombs and towers and nameless fragments of antique masonry. The landscape here has two great features; close before you on one side is the long, gentle swell of the Alban Mountains, deeply, fantastically blue in most weathers, and marbled with the vague white masses of their scattered towns and villas. It is hard to fancy a softer curve than that with which the mountain sweeps down from Albano to the plain; it is a perfect example of the classic beauty of line in the Italian landscape—that beauty which, when it fills the background of a picture, makes us look in the foreground for a broken column couched upon flowers and a shepherd piping to dancing nymphs. At your side, constantly, you have the broken line of the Claudian Aqueduct, carrying its broad arches far away into the plain. The meadows along which it lies are not the smoothest in the world for a gallop, but there is no pleasure greater than to wander over it. It stands knee-deep in the flower-strewn grass, and its rugged piers are hung with ivy as the columns of a church are draped for a festa. Every archway is a picture, massively framed, of the distance beyond—of the snow-tipped Sabines and lonely Soracte. As the spring advances, the whole Campagna smiles and waves with flowers; but I think they are nowhere more rank and lovely than in the shifting shadow of the aqueducts, where they muffle the feet of the columns and smother the half-dozen brooks which wander in and out like silver meshes between the legs of a file of giants. They make a niche for themselves too in every crevice and tremble on the vault of the empy conduits. The ivy hereabouts in the springtime is peculiarly brilliant and delicate; and though it cloaks and muffles these Roman fragments far less closely than the castles and abbeys of England it hangs with the light elegance of all Italian vegetation.
* * *

Reviews and Criticism

Various reviewers greeted *The Portrait of a Lady* as James's most important novel to date, some even hailing it as a "masterpiece." Partly because of William Dean Howell's high praise of James, early reviewers treated the novel respectfully, analyzed it, and compared it to the novels of Eliot, of Turgenev, of Hawthorne,[1] or to earlier stories like "Daisy Miller."[2] Other reviewers speculated about prototypes[3] or noted, biographically, an "infusion of the author's own personality" in his characters.[4] If all the reviews were not favorable, all did take the novel seriously, and most of the guidelines for future "source" and influence studies were laid there and then.[5]

James's interest in George Eliot was known by virtue of his numerous published essays and reviews, and ever since Margaret Oliphant's comparison of *Daniel Deronda* and *The Portrait of a Lady* in a review for *Blackwood's* (1882) critics have been pursuing the relationship between the two novels.[6] However, claims for a comparison with *Middlemarch* also date back to W. C. Brownell's review for *The Nation* (1882) and have continued as a fertile basis for understanding both novels.[7] The general influence of George Eliot on the novel is relatively unquestioned, as is the lesser influence of James's friend Ivan Turgenev; and claims have been set forth for Hawthorne, Hardy, George Sand, Balzac, and many others, including Victor Cherbuliez, whose fiction James held in contempt.[8] Among James's earlier works of fiction, four are still frequently invoked as bearing strong similarities to *The Portrait of a Lady*. They are: "Poor Richard" (1867), the novel-length *Watch and Ward* (1871), "Longstaff's Marriage" (1878), and "Daisy Miller" (1878),[9] whose heroine some see as the type of all

1. William Dean Howells, "Henry James, Jr.," *The Century Magazine*, 3 (November, 1882), pp. 25–29; William C. Brownell, "James's *Portrait of a Lady*," *The Nation*, 2 February 1882, pp. 102–103; Margaret Oliphant, "Recent Novels," *Blackwood's*, 81 (March, 1882), pp. 375–383. [The latter two reviews are reprinted in this edition.]
2. "American Novels," *Quarterly Review*, 155 (January, 1883), pp. 212–217.
3. Oliphant, p. 380.
4. James Herbert Morse, "The Native Element in American Fiction," *Century Magazine*, 26 (July, 1883), p. 373.
5. For further lists of reviews, see Donald M. Murray, "Henry James and the English Reviewers, 1882–1890," *American Literature*, 24 (March, 1952), pp. 1–20; also his "A Survey of Early Reviews—English," in *Perspectives on James's "The Portrait of a Lady*," ed. William T. Stafford (New York, 1967), pp. 35–38; Richard W. Foley, *Criticism in American Periodicals of the Works of Henry James from 1866 to 1916* (Washington, D.C., 1944), pp. 26–33.
6. Oliphant, p. 380; Joseph Warren Beach, *The Method of Henry James* (London, 1918), pp. 205–211; Cornelia Pulsifer Kelley, *The Early Development of Henry James*, University of Illinois Studies in Language and Literature, No. 15 (Urbana, 1930), pp. 291–300; F. R.

Leavis, *The Great Tradition* (New York, 1949), pp. 155–187; George Levine, "Isabel, Gwendolen, and Dorothea," *ELH*, 30 (September, 1963), pp. 244–257.
7. Brownell, p. 103; Oscar Cargill, *The Novels of Henry James* (New York, 1961), pp. 78–83; Leon Edel, *Henry James: The Conquest of London, 1870–1881* (Philadelphia, 1962), pp. 369–371.
8. Daniel Lerner, "The Influences of Turgenev on Henry James," *Slavonic and East European Review*, 20 (1941), pp. 28–54; Sylvia E. Bowman, "Les Héroïnes d'Henry James dans *The Portrait of a Lady* et d'Yvan Tourgueniev dans *A La Vielle*," *Etudes Anglaises*, 11 (1958), pp. 136–149; on Hawthorne, see Laurence B. Holland, *The Expense of Vision: Essays on the Craft of Henry James* (Princeton, 1964), pp. 20–21; R W. Stallman, "Some Rooms from 'The Houses that James Built,' " *Texas Quarterly*, 1 (Winter, 1958), pp. 181–192; for Hardy, see Oscar Cargill, "*The Portrait of a Lady*: A Critical Reappraisal," *Modern Fiction Studies*, 3 (Spring, 1957), pp. 11–32; and many more.
9. For "Poor Richard," see: Leon Edel, *Henry James: The Untried Years: 1843–1870* (Philadelphia, 1953), pp. 236–238; Peter Buitenhuis, "Introduction" to *Twentieth Century Interpretations of "The Portrait of a Lady"* (Englewood Cliffs, N.J., 1968), p. 3; for

of James's transatlantic heroines and whose portrait may have been influenced by James's cousin, Mary "Minny" Temple.

Watch and Ward, see Cargill, *Novels of Henry James*, p. 91; Edel, *Conquest of London*, pp. 45, 423; J. A. Ward, *The Search for Form: Studies in The Structure of James's Fiction* (Chapel Hill, 1967), pp. 69–71; for "Longstaff's Marriage," see Cargill, "Critical Reappraisal," p. 16; S. Gorley Putt, *A Reader's Guide to Henry James* (Ithaca, N.Y., 1966), p. 268. Holland (pp. 20–21) argues that James's study of Hawthorne discloses "the very matrix" of the fabrication of *The Portrait of a Lady*. For further critical articles, see Stafford and Buitenhuis.

Contemporary Reviews (1882)

American

W. C. BROWNELL

From *The Nation*†

Mr. James's novel, which caused each number of the *Atlantic Monthly* to be awaited with impatience last year, gains in its complete presentation, and, like most novels of any pretensions, is most readable when read consecutively. Unlike most novels, however, whose fate (and the fortune of whose authors) it is to appear serially, the reason for this does not consist in the condensation which the reader is thus enabled to make in spite of the author, but in the fact that it is a work of art of which the whole is equal to no fewer than all of its parts, and of which there is a certain "tendency," to lose which is to miss one of the main features of the book. In other words, 'The Portrait of a Lady' is an important work, the most important Mr. James has thus far written, and worthy of far more than mere perusal—worthy of study, one is inclined to say. It is in fact a little too important—to express by a paradox the chief criticism to be made upon it—or, at all events, the only impression left by it which is not altogether agreeable. For the first two or three hundred pages one is beguiled by a kind of entertainment always of a high order—the dissection of an interesting character by a clever and scrupulous demonstrator. After that, though it would be misleading to say that the interest flags—the interest being throughout the book remarkable for its evenness—the feeling supervenes that to be still entertained argues a happy aptitude for most serious and "intellectual" delectation. Most persons will recall some experience of the same sensation in first becoming acquainted with undisguisedly philosophical writings—such as the writings of Emerson or Burke. To others it may be indicated by saying that it is just the sensation Carlyle missed in finding the works of George Eliot

† From *The Nation*, xxxiv, 866 (February 2, 1882), 102–103.

"dool—just dool." In America, it is well known, we do not find George Eliot dull, and it is upon our appetite for this sort of provender that Mr. James doubtless relies, and undoubtedly does well to rely. Nevertheless, it is possible to feel what Carlyle meant without agreeing with it; and though maintaining firmly the absorbing interest of 'The Portrait of a Lady,' we are ready to admit that once or twice we have laid aside the book for a season, with the exhilaration which Mr. Howells has somewhere observed to be coincident with giving up a difficult task. One of the happiest of the many happy remarks made in 'The Portrait of a Lady' is in Miss Stackpole's characterization of her *fiancé:* "He's as clear as glass; there's no mystery about him. He is not intellectual, but he appreciates intellect. On the other hand, he doesn't exaggerate its claim. *I sometimes think we do in the United States.*" The person of whom this is said naturally cuts a smaller figure in the novel than the more complex organizations, in dealing with which Mr. James is most at home; and it is the inference from this circumstance that we have in mind. For not only are the simpler though perennial elements of human nature in general eschewed by Mr. James, but his true distinction—that is to say, his strength and weakness also—consists in his attempt to dispense with all the ordinary machinery of the novelist except the study of subtle shades of character. In other words, his masterpiece, as 'The Portrait of a Lady' must be called, is not only outside of the category of the old romance of which 'Tom Jones,' for example, may stand as the type, but also dispenses with the dramatic movement and passionate interest upon which the later novelists, from Thackeray to Thomas Hardy, have relied. In a sense, and to a certain extent, Turgeneff may be said to be Mr. James's master, but even a sketch or a study by Turgeneff is turbulence itself beside the elaborate placidity of these 519 pages. This involves the necessity of the utmost care in presenting the material, and accordingly we have that squaring of the elbows and minute painstaking which not only result inevitably in occasional lumbering movement, but which lend the work an air of seeming more important than any book whatever could possibly be; so that it is perhaps fortunate for its popularity (which, by the way, we believe is extraordinary) that we exaggerate the claims of intellect occasionally in the United States.

Even this measure of fault-finding, however, seems a little ungracious, not to say hypercritical, in view of the distinguished success of Mr. James's experiment in applying the development theory to novel-writing, so to speak. We have ourselves followed the succession of his stories since 'Roderick Hudson' appeared with mingled interest and regret, because he has seemed to be getting further and further away from very safe ground, where he was very strong, and into the uncertainties of an unfamiliar region of which it was impossible to tell whether its novelty or its real merit gave it its interest. The elemental characters and dramatic situations of the novel just mentioned were strongly handled, and the work being, comparatively speaking, a youthful one, its promise seemed even greater than its actual qualities. But, almost as if he had been an amateur dipping into another branch of effort after having demonstrated his ability in one, Mr. James immediately abandoned the field of imaginative romance as it is generally understood. He at once made clear his faculty for his new choice, and the field he entered on with 'The American,' and continued with the shorter stories illustrative of American types, became immediately popular. 'Daisy Miller' may almost be said to mark an era in the mental progress of many persons who exaggerate the claims of intellect occasionally; it is wearisome to recall the "discussions" it occasioned in drawing-rooms and in print. There was, to be sure, a Chauvinist view, so to speak, taken of this and its associated sketches, by persons who omitted to perceive that Mr. James had not only made the current mechanical speculations about "the coming American novel" an anachronism, but had also displayed his patriotism and the national genius by inventing a new variety of literature. But naturally Mr. James might be expected to heed rather those of his readers who appreciated and enjoyed his motives and rejoiced in his discovery of romantic sociology. And this seemed his real danger; for though to these readers this reading conveyed a peculiarly refined pleasure, on account both of its novelty and the cleverness of its execution, there was no certainty that this pleasure was not a rather temporary mood, and likely to pass away after the novelty had worn off. Instead, however, of avoiding this danger by a return to the perennially interesting material with which he first dealt, Mr. James has conquered it, *vi et armis*, by a persistence that at one time seemed a little wilful. No one can now pretend, whatever his own literary likes and dislikes may be, that romantic sociology, exploited as Mr. James has shown it capable of being, is not a thoroughly serious field of literature, whose interest is permanent and dignified.

'The Portrait of a Lady' is a modest title, though an apt one. The portrait of the lady in question is indeed the theme of the book, and it is elaborated with a minuteness so great that when finally one begins to find it confusing it becomes evident that the ordinary point of view must be changed, and the last detail awaited—as in a professedly scientific work—before the whole can appear. Miss Isabel Archer is an orphan to whom her aunt gives an opportunity of seeing the world, and to whom her aunt's husband leaves a large fortune, at the instance of his son, who is unselfishly and romantically interested to see what his cousin will make of her life when nothing prevents her from doing as she wishes. The reader at once assumes the position of this young man, and with more or less (less in our own case, we confess) sympathy, watches the progress of the drama which he has set going. At the climax the heroine discovers that she has wrecked her life most miserably. The spiritual transistion from the Isabel Archer of Albany to the Mrs. Osmond of Rome is of course accomplished in part by natural disposition and in part by the influence of the numerous characters which surround her. The way in which this influence is exhibited is a marked feature of the book. If George Eliot was the first to make of this important moral phenomenon a distinct study, Mr. James has here, in our opinion, quite surpassed her. Any one can judge by comparing the reciprocal effect upon the development of each other's characters of the Lydgates in 'Middlemarch' with that of the Osmonds here. The other characters are treated with a microscopy hardly inferior. Osmond himself is one of the most palpable of those figures in fiction which are to be called subtle. Madame Merle, his former mistress, mother of his child, who makes the marriage between him and his poverty and Isabel and her wealth, and who, up to the climax of the book, is Isabel's ideal, is, if anything, even better done. There is something almost uncanny in the perfection with which these secretive natures are turned inside out for the reader's inspection. As for the heroine, the American girl *par excellence*, it seems as if, scientifically speaking, Mr. James had said the last word on this subject; at any rate till the model herself is still further developed. For example (p. 344): "She never looked so charming as when, in the genial heat of discussion, she received a crushing blow full in the face and brushed it away as a feather." There are pages as good.

It has long been evident that Mr. James's powers of observation are not only remarkably keen, but sleepless as well. But 'The Portrait of a Lady' would not be what it is if it did not possess a *fonds* of moral seriousness, in addition to and underlying its extraordinary interest of purely intellectual curiosity. There is a specific lesson for the American girl in the first place; there are others, more general, which accompany every imaginative work of large importance. That these are nowhere distinctly stated is now nothing new in fiction even of a distinctly moral purpose. But Mr. James has carried suggestiveness in this regard further than any rival novelist, and though, unless one has ears to hear, it is entirely possible to miss the undertone of his book, to an appreciative sense there is something exquisite in the refinement with which it is conveyed. Refinement in this respect cannot be carried too far. In strictly literary matters Mr. James's fastidiousness may be objected to, perhaps, if one chooses; he has carried the method of the essayist into the domain of romance: its light touch, its reliance on suggestiveness, its weakness for indirect statement, its flattering presupposition of the reader's perceptiveness, its low tones, its polish. Upon occasion, where the circumstances really seem to warrant a little fervor, you only get from the author of 'The Portrait of a Lady' irreproachability. Objection to this may easily be carried too far, however; and those who do thus carry it too far, and argue that no people ever spoke and acted with the elegance and precision of the personages here portrayed, must of necessity pay the penalty of ultra-literalness and miss the secret of Mr. James's success. To characterize this secret with adequate fulness would require far more than the space at our disposal; but it may be sufficiently indicated by calling it the imaginative treatment of reality. In this unquestionably lies Mr. James's truly original excellence. 'The Portrait of a Lady' is the most eminent example we have thus far had of realistic art in fiction *à outrance*, because its substance is thoroughly, and at times profoundly, real, and at the same time its presentation is imaginative. On the one hand, wilfulness and fantasticality are avoided, and on the other, prose and flatness. One may even go further, and say that the book succeeds in the difficult problem of combining a scientific value with romantic interest and artistic merit.

HORACE E. SCUDDER

From *The Atlantic Monthly*†

The artist gives us this advantage, that all the elaboration of his work looks distinctly to the perfection of the central figure. One can repeat almost in a single breath the incidental story of the book. That is dissolved immediately, if the incidents deposited are the critical ones of Isabel's meeting with her aunt, her rejection successively of Goodwood and Lord Warburton, her accession to wealth, her marriage with Osmond, her temporary separation, and her final return. A person hearing the narrative might be pardoned if he failed to see the making of a great novel in it, but only when one has recited it does he become aware how each step in the fatal series is a movement in the direction of destiny. By a fine concentration of attention upon the heroine, Mr. James impresses us with her importance, and the other characters, involved as they are with her life, fall back into secondary positions. It is much to have seized and held firmly so elusive a conception, and our admiration is in-

† From *The Atlantic Monthly*, xlix (January, 1882), 127–28.

creased when reflection shows that, individual as Isabel is in the painting, one may fairly take her as representative of womanly life today. The fine purpose of her freedom, the resolution with which she seeks to be the maker of her destiny, the subtle weakness into which all this betrays her, the apparent helplessness of her ultimate position, and the conjectured escape only through patient forbearance,—what are all these, if not attributes of womanly life expended under current conditions?

The consistency of the work is observable under another aspect. Mr. James's method is sufficiently well known, and since he has made it his own the critic may better accept it amd measure it than complain of it. What renders it distinct from, say, Thackeray's method, with which it has been compared, or from George Eliot's, is the limitation of the favorite generalizations and analyses. If the reader will attend, he will see that these take place quite exclusively within the boundaries of the story and characters. That is to say, when the people in the book stop acting or speaking, it is to give to the novelist an opportunity, not to indulge in general reflections, having application to all sorts and conditions of men, of whom his *dramatis personæ* are but a part,—he has no desire to share humanity with them,—but to make acute reflections upon these particular people, and to explain more thoroughly than their words and acts can the motives which lie behind. We may, on general grounds, doubt the self-confidence or power of a novelist who feels this part of his performance to be essential, but there can be no doubt that Mr. James's method is a part of that concentration of mind which results in a singular consistency.

Yet all this carries an intimation of what is curiously noticeable in his work. It is consistent, but the consistency is with itself. Within the boundaries of the novel the logic of character and events is close and firm. We say this after due reflection upon the latest pages. There can be little doubt that the novelist suffers more in the reader's judgment from a false or ineffective scene at the close of his story than he gains from many felicitous strokes in the earlier development of plot or character. The impatient, undiscriminating objection, It does not end well, although it may incense the writer, is an ill-formulated expression of the feeling that the creation lacks the final, triumphant touch which gives life; the sixth swan in the story got a stitch-weed shirt, like the rest, but in the hurry of the last moment it lacked a few stitches, and so in the transformation the youngest brother was forced to put up with one arm and to show a wing for the other. Isabel Archer, with her fine horoscope, is an impressive figure, and one follows her in her free flight with so much admiration for her resolution and strong pinions that when she is caught in the meshes of Osmond's net one's indignation is moved, and a noble pity takes the place of frank admiration. But pity can live only in full communion with faith, and we can understand the hesitation which a reader might feel before the somewhat ambiguous passage of Isabel's last interview with Goodwood. The passage, however, admits of a generous construction, and we prefer to take it, and to see in the scene the author's intention of giving a final touch to his delineation of Goodwood's iron but untempered will, Isabel's vanishing dream of happiness, and her acceptance of the destiny which she had unwittingly chosen. We suspect that something of the reader's dissatisfaction at this juncture comes from his dislike of Goodwood, the jack-in-the-box of the story, whose unyielding nature seems somehow outside of all the events.,

To return to our point. This self-consistency is a separate thing from any consistency with the world of reality. The characters, the situations, the incidents, are all true to the law of their own being, but that law runs parallel with the law which governs life, instead of being identical with it. In Andersen's quaint story of the Emperor's New Clothes, a little child discovers the unreality of the gossamer dress, and his voice breaks in upon the illusion from the outer world. Something of the same separation from the story, of the same unconscious naturalness of feeling, prompts the criticism that, though these people walk, and sit, and talk, and behave, they are yet in an illusionary world of their own. Only when one is within the charmed circle of the story is he under its spell, and so complete is the isolation of the book that the characters acquire a strange access of reality when they talk about each other. Not only so, but the introversion which now and then takes place deepens the sense of personality. In that masterly passage which occupies the forty-second section, where Isabel enters upon a disclosure of her changed life, the reader seems to be going down as in a diving-bell into the very secrets of her nature.

What is all this but saying that in the process of Mr. James's art the suggestion always seems to come from within, and to work outward? We recognize the people to whom he introduces us, not by any external signs, but by the private information which we have regarding their souls. The smiles which they wear—and one might make an ingenious collection of their variety—do not tell what is beneath the surface, but we know what they mean, because we already have an esoteric knowledge. Mr. James is at great pains to illustrate his characters by their attitudes, their movements, their by-play, yet we carry away but a slight impression of their external appearance; these are not bodily shapes, for the most part, but embodied spirits, who enjoy their materialization for a time, and contribute to a play which goes on upon a stage just a little apart form that great stage where the world's play, with men and women for actors, is carried forward.

ANONYMOUS

From *Harper's*†

The Portrait of a Lady, by Henry James, Jun., fulfills all the technical conditions that are essential for the production of a perfect portrait in oil, save those that are mechanical or manual, and manifests clearly enough how successfully the pen may compete with the pencil in the sphere of pictorial art. Undoubtedly, in dealing with form and color, the pencil has the advantage of appealing directly to and delighting the eye, and the impressions it is thus able to make upon us are instantaneous and permanent; but it is subject to limitations which do not circumscribe the range or hamper the freedom of the pen. For however admirable a portrait in colors may be, it can present its subject in one only of his attitudes, it must drape him in an unvarying garb, it must environ him with accessories that become monotonous under their unchanging fixedness, and it can only reproduce the expression that he wore at a single moment of his life. In his contention with the limitations of his art, the painter, among other devices of technical detail that we need not specify, has been obliged to resort to the expedient of repeated sittings, so that his work shall not reflect a single fleeting or momentary play of expression, but shall combine those regnant and characteristic expressions which reflect the man when at his best, and which may be caught by studying him in different moods and fluctuations of feeling and tempérament. An artist with the pen has no need to resort to this expedient, as Mr. James demonstrates in his continuous and sustained portraiture of the heroine of his long and fragmentary but profoundly interesting tale. Instead of her repeated sittings being condensed into one final touch, which necessarily sacrifices far more than it preserves, each contributes to the completeness of the picture without detracting from its unity. And the result is a vivid and life-like portrait of a woman at different stages of her life from girlhood to womanhood, as she is insensibly influenced by varying local, personal, and social environments, or by the teachings of sweet or bitter experience, but yet ever remaining intrinsically the same, and notwithstanding the shipwreck of some of her ideals, throughout preserving her cherished illusions and her distinctive and winsome individuality. Besides this elaborate portrait, several

† From *Harper's*, lxiv (February, 1882), 474.

other subsidiary and contrasted portraits are introduced of men and women who came into the life of the heroine, and alternately checkered it with cloud or sunshine, which, like the principal figure, are painted in rich but delicate colors, and are noteworthy for the clearness and definiteness of their outlines, and for their display of emphatic but not violent contrasts.

British

MARGARET OLIPHANT

From *Blackwood's*†

We must pause * * * before we can come down contentedly to the ordinary ground of fiction, even when represented by a writer so little ordinary as Mr. Henry James. This gentleman's work in the world seems to be a peculiar one. It is to record and set fully before us the predominance of the great American race, and the manner in which it has overrun and conquered the Old World. All, or almost all, of his social studies have their scene laid on the Continent, or in this island. It is true there are occasional interludes of America, but it is not in these that he seems most at home. The manner in which the heir of time—in the shape of the cultivated and accomplished son, or, still more, daughter of the West—dominates the old-fashioned scenery of countries which were, as old people say, great and powerful before America was ever heard of, is both amusing and impressive. Italy and France and Old England have lived their lives and had their reverses, and built their old castles and towns, and even arranged their landscapes —for him. The chief use of their old families is to furnish victims, in the shape of elder sons, for those delicate beauties who come conquering and to conquer from the fashionable circles of New York or the exotic plains of California. They inspect our antiquities as Germans criticise Hamlet, with the view of showing that we ourselves are unable to appreciate, and take comparatively little interest in, either the Tower or the Poet; and they patronise our institutions, most frequently from the high aristocratic side of the question, and object to our reforms, as the Solomons of the earth—who have tried all that man can do in that direction and found it naught —have perhaps some right to do. In short, they overshadow alto-

† From *Blackwood's Edinburgh Magazine*, cxxxi (March, 1882), 374–383.

gether the background against which they pose, and make London
and Paris and Rome into Western settlements, with the most easy
consciousness that they are lords of all. In some of M. Tourgenieff's
books the same position is tacitly claimed, more or less, for the Russian; but then it is only world-playgrounds (which, if we remember
rightly, is the dignified title by which some philosophers on our own
side honour Switzerland) which are represented as in the possession
of the Muscovite. English performances of the same kind are of a
more modest description. We do indeed plant our little colonies of
pleasure all about, yet we give them, when we can, some relation to
the "natives," and love to show our respect for that society into
which, we are humbly aware, we are but sparely admitted. But Mr.
James shows us his countrymen in the attitude of conquerors, domi-
nating, not intruding, upon the foreign world about them. * * *

The political opinions of this type of American occupiers of the
soil are easily divined. It is not from any sympathy with republican
institutions that they chose France for their headquarters; indeed
they are to be found in Italy in as great luxuriance as in France,
regretting everything that has passed away—the Pope's supremacy
and the French occupation, as well as that bland Tuscan Court
where all was so amiable, and the days when Rome wished for nothing more than a good season, and Italy continued to be medieval
for the gratification of its visitors. Here are Mr. Luce's views upon
the subject in France:

> Like many of his fellow-colonists, Mr. Luce was a high—or
> rather a deep—Conservative, and gave no countenance to the
> Government recently established in France. He had no faith in
> its duration, and would assure you from year to year that its end
> was close at hand. "They want to be kept down, sir—they want
> to be kept down: nothing but the strong hand, the iron hand,
> will do for them," he would frequently say of the French people:
> and his ideal of a fine government was that of the lately abol-
> ished Empire. "Paris is much less attractive than in the days of
> the Emperor—he knew how to make a city pleasant," Mr. Luce
> had often remarked to Mrs. Touchett, who was quite of his own
> way of thinking, and wished to know what one had crossed that
> odious Atlantic for, but to get away from republics. "Why,
> madam, sitting in the Champs Elysées, opposite to the Palace of
> Industry, I have seen the Court carriages from the Tuileries pass
> up and down, as many as seven times a-day. I remember one
> occasion when they went as high as nine times. What do you see
> now? It's no use talking—the style is all gone. Napoleon knew
> what the French people want, and there'll be a cloud over Paris
> till they get the Empire back again."

We linger upon these sketches of the dominant race, of which all
readers have come to appreciate the importance through Mr.

James's very popular works, because it is more easy to enjoy studies so fine and so keen, cut with the precision of an old gem, than to find our way, as we should like, through the maze of delicate analysis and psychological study, tempered with a number of brilliant social sketches, which makes up in three very large volumes 'The Portrait of a Lady.' The one thing which the book is not, is what it calls itself. There are several portraits of subordinate ladies—of Mrs. Touchett and Miss Stackpole, for example, both of which are admirable pictures; but of the heroine, upon whom the greatest pains have been expended, and to whom endless space is afforded for the setting forth of her characteristics, we have no portrait, nor, even with the enormous amount of material supplied by Mr. James, do we find it easy to put together anything which will serve to supply the defect. We doubt much whether, in all the historical records that exist, we have as much material for the construction, let us say, of a recognisable portrait of Queen Elizabeth—no insignificant figure —as we have for that of Isabel Archer, the young lady who suddenly appears in the doorway of an old English country-house, inhabited like most other desirable places by American tenants—in this case her uncle and her cousin—fresh from her native country, prepared to take instant possession of her birthright as the explorer, discoverer, and conqueror of the old country,—and, in fact, reducing the gentlemen who meet her into instant subjection in the course of half an hour. How she does so, except by being very pretty, as we are told she is, we do not know; though the gentlemen in question are too experienced and clever in their own persons to be immediately subjugated by simple beauty. "Her head was erect, her eye brilliant, her flexible figure turned itself lightly this way and that, in sympathy with the alertness with which she evidently caught impressions. Her impressions were numerous, and they were all reflected in a clear, still smile," is Mr. James's description of his heroine; and it is about the clearest view we get of the young lady. For once in a way he is outside of her: but as he goes on he gets more and more within the circle of this irresistible young woman's personality; and we have to receive both herself and her immediate surroundings, not so much as they actually are, but as they are seen through her eyes. This is always confusing; for self-knowledge at its closest has many limitations, and the most impartial student of his own mind will probably get more light upon it by overhearing one sharp characterisation from outside than by weeks of self-examination. Isabel's aspect from outside is conveyed to us only in the raptures of her adorers; for all the men she encounters fall in love with her: first, her cousin Ralph Touchett, then Lord Warburton, then Osmond, whom she marries: besides a persistent Boston man, who makes nothing of crossing the Atlantic to get a glimpse of her, and turns up again and again with a sort of dogged inappropriateness at every new stage of her career.

There is but little vicissitude, however, in her career; she comes to "Europe" with something of the intention which Mr. James illustrated with, we think, a great deal more power, though less of the extremely refined and cultivated skill of which he is now master, in 'The Americans,' the first work by which he was known in England; that is, to get everything she can out of her life and its opportunities,—all the sensation, the information, the variety of experience which it is possible it can convey. There is this difference between the young and visionary girl and the mature man, that whereas Mr. James's first hero wanted practical satisfaction for his desires, and to get possession of all that was best, including, as the most indispensable article of all, the fairest and most costly flower of womanhood which was to be found or purchased anyhow,—Isabel prefers not to have anything but the sense of having—the wealth of spiritual possession. For this reason she likes to retain a hold upon the lovers whom she will not marry. The English lord with all his fine qualities—and it cannot be said that our American author and heroine do not do full justice to these qualities with a refined sense of the admirableness of the position, and the importance which attaches to so curious and desirable a specimen of humanity—gives her the most agreeable consciousness of power, though all his advantages do not tempt her to marry him, and she is sorry for vexing him—almost as sorry as she is agreeably excited by the incident altogether. Indeed it would appear that this accompaniment of homage is natural to the young American woman, and that she would feel herself to be treated unfairly if at least one English lord, besides innumerable other candidates of different descriptions, did not attest her power. This is very different from the more vulgar development of the American young woman, who is bent on securing a title for herself. Mr. James's young ladies never do this. They are totally different from the Irene Macgillicuddys. Their curiosity about the English aristocrat is fresh and eager. They contemplate him attentively as the greatest novelty within their reach, and like and admire him as one of the wonders of the world; but they do not care to go any further. Isabel Archer passes through this phase very serenely, liking the new interest it puts into her life. But as a matter of fact she does not care for anything much except new interests. The adventures, or rather encounters, through which we are permitted to accompany her, are in reality but a small part of her career. There are gaps in which she travels far and wide—rapidly, eagerly, arduously. "She was like a thirsty person draining cup after cup," but always coming back again to the old investigation—the earnest study of all new phenomena—the consideration of how everything affected herself. Her desire for new experiences never fails, even when she gets into the dead block in which, as is natural, her perpetually increasing circle of moral enlightenment and sensation ends. * * *

It was inevitable that such a heroine should end unhappily—even if it were not inevitable that all Mr. James's books should break off with a sharp cut of arbitrary conclusion, leaving all the questions they so skilfully raise unsolved. Isabel, through the means of a wonderful woman whom she meets in her aunt's house, and who is a sort of symbol of unusual experience, as the younger woman is of the craving for it, falls under the fascinations of a certain aesthetic and beauty-loving American, Gilbert Osmond by name, who lives on one of the heights which surround Florence, a poor yet elegant *dilettante* life, "picking up" rarities of all kinds, making amateur drawings, surrounded by the faded silks and crafty embellishments of a collector, with a pretty little Dresden shepherdess of a daughter, newly returned from the convent, whose perfect conventional simplicity, freshness, and submission, afford Mr. James the means of making one of his most finished and perfect sketches. We confess to being quite unable to understand how it is that Isabel falls into Osmond's toils, unless it is because so elaborate and self-conscious a personality recoils instinctively, even though full of an abstract admiration for truth, from the downright and veracious, and finds in the complications of an elaborately conventional mind something that has the air of being larger and richer than the true. The reader is never for a moment taken in by the superiority of this most carefully dressed and posed figure, whose being altogether is mysterious, and of whom, notwithstanding the author's elaborate descriptions, we never penetrate the *fin mot*.

"Success," says Mr. James, "for Gilbert Osmond, would be to make himself felt; that was the only success to which he could now pretend. It is not a kind of distinction that is officially recognised, unless, indeed, the operation be performed upon multitudes of men. Osmond's life would be to impress himself not largely but deeply— a distinction of the most private sort: a single character might offer the whole measure of it. The clear and sensitive nature of a generous girl would makes space for the record."

It is to be supposed, therefore, that this refined and philosophical *dilettante*, secluding himself among his faded silks and æsthetic ornaments, in his villa on Bellosguardo, is like a spider in his web awaiting the arrival of the fly which it shall be worth his while to capture. But, after all, these elaborate preparations were scarcely necessary for the capture of a young lady who was only Miss Archer, with a fortune of sixty thousand pounds. Had a Grand Duchess been his aim, it would have been comprehensible. There is far too great

an effort for an insufficient result; and the almost immediate failure
of their after relations is confusing and unaccountable. Something
of the same curious failure we remember to have found in "Daniel
Deronda," where Gwendolen and her husband, after their elaborate
drawing together, fly asunder the moment they are married, with a
suddenness and bitterness—brutality on the man's part, and misery
on the woman's—for which we find no adequate motive, since there
was neither passion between them to die out, nor motive enough
beforehand to force a union which was to end so abruptly. That
Isabel should discover her husband to be, as he describes himself,
not only conventional, but convention itself, when she believed him
to be nobly superior to the world, is one thing; but that she should
discover him to hate her is quite another; and his jealousy and tyr-
anny in the one development seem out of character with his easy
gracefulness and gentlemanliness in the other.

The last volume is full of the complete and utter failure to which
the heroine's hopes and high desires have come; but it cannot be
said that she acquits herself with the dignity that might have been
expected of her under the disappointment. Not only does she allow
her wretchedness to be taken for granted by all her friends, but it
would almost seem as if, in the utter collapse of the world about
her, this most abstract and intellectual of heroines is driven at last
to the conclusion that the only good in life is to make a snatch at
happiness anyhow—to take what is offered her at last in utter relin-
quishment of any better hope. She has left her husband to watch at
the deathbed of the devoted cousin Ralph, who has loved her all
through, and has been her best and most faithful friend; and when
all is over, is suddenly brought face to face with the true American,
the violent lover, with all the ardour and practical force of the New
World, of whom, among the rest of her sensations, she has always
been a little afraid. No trace of love for Caspar has ever appeared in
her before; but he comes upon her suddenly, when she is weak with
grief for Ralph, and contemplating with horror her return to the
bitter round of her duties with Osmond. The American not only
pours forth his passion, but proposes to her to fly with him from the
wretchedness of her fate. "Why shouldn't we be happy?" he says;
"the world is all before us, and the world is large," as—we are
obliged to remind Mr. James—a great many gentlemen in Mr.
Caspar Goodwood's position have said to a great many unhappy
wives in the pages of fiction before.

> Isabel gave a long murmur like a creature in pain: it was as if
> he were pressing something that hurt her. "The world is very
> small," she said at random; she had an immense desire to appear
> to resist. She said it at random to hear herself say something; but
> it was not what she meant. The world in truth had never seemed

so large; it seemed to open out all around her, to take the form of a mighty sea, where she floated in fathomless waters. She had wanted help, and here was help; it had come in a rushing torrent. I know not whether she believed anything that he said; but she believed that to let him take her in his arms would be the next best thing to dying. This belief for the moment was a kind of rapture in which she felt herself sinking and sinking. In the movement she seemed to beat with her feet, in order to catch herself, to feel something to rest upon.

She does not yield, it is needless to say: our author could not have so far forgotten himself. But when this impetuous lover, by no means despairing of success, finds that she has returned to her home, he is consoled by her friend Miss Stackpole, with the significant words—the last in the book—"Look here, Mr. Goodwood," she said; "just you wait!"

It is not very long since a respectable and gifted writer in another work of fiction permitted a young man of the highest virtue and honour to propose to a pure and honourable girl, utterly unprotected, that she should go away with him and be happy in a world which was large enough to conceal them, in much the same way; prefacing his proposal by the compliment that he knew she was not one of the prejudiced people who would be shocked by such a proposal: and so far was that spotless maiden from being shocked, that she took herself severely to task for her cruelty in refusing to make to her lover—poor fellow—the little sacrifice he asked. What do these gentlemen mean, we wonder? Isabel, so far as she has any body at all, is as free from fleshly stain as the purest imagination could desire. Is it only that in her search after experience her author felt it necessary that she should taste also the excitement of an unlawful passion? or is it his mind to preach that the world being so hollow and miserable, and devoid of hope, the best thing we can do is to eat and drink, for to-morrow we die? Anyhow, it is a most equivocal if not debasing conclusion, and brings us up sharp with a discord instead of the symphony of harmonising chords with which it has been the habit of art to accompany the end of every story. As a rule Mr. James rejects symphonies, and attempts no harmonising conclusions. He leaves us usually tantalised, half angry with an end which is left to our imagination. But this is not a way of leaving matters to the imagination which we can at all consent to take from his hand. Abstract as is his heroine, a congeries of thoughts and questions rather than a woman, we cannot endure the possibility, even, of a future stain for her. It is a sort of insult to his own art, which is altogether out of accord with any such harsh effects. Let smaller workmen avail themselves of these easy means of startling the reader; from him we have a right to expect better things.

In following out the chief thread of this elaborate work, we have in reality neglected the best of it, which is to be found in the characters which are secondary. Mrs. Touchett the aunt, who introduces Isabel to all the dangers of Europe,—the little dry independent woman, whose correspondence with her family is by curt telegrams —who consults her own independent fancy in all she does, asks little, and gives little in the way of affection, yet is by no means destitute of kindness,—is a curiously individual figure, so real and so odd that she must, we suspect, come from the life—that shelter of all eccentricities. Her son Ralph Touchett is by far the most lovable character in the book. The easy spectator position which his bad health and his temperament alike made natural; the smiling renunciation of life and all individual hopes which he has made without a word, without the sympathy or support of any consoler; his shuffle of easy contemplative indolence; the mild half-pathetic fun which he gets out of every incident,—go to our heart from the first appearance he makes on the scene. His love and care for his father; his profound tenderness and half-amused watch over his cousin, changing towards the end into a melancholy sense that his own act in securing her possession of a fortune has been her ruin; his unfailing courage and sweetness of temper,—make his appearance always delightful. If he did not smile in the face of fate, and turn off his worst pangs with a jest, we know and he knows that there would be in the world no more melancholy spectacle than this gradual going down of youth and hope and intelligence into the grave, imbittered by the sense that his weakness makes him powerless to help the being he loves best, and that his death will leave her to fight alone with a thousand troubles. He is conscious of all this, yet is amused with the vagaries of existence to the last, and keeps sorrow at arm's-length—keenly though he is aware of its presence. Miss Stackpole, too, is delightful in her genial Americanisms. We feel, indeed, that this lady—the correspondent of the 'Interviewer,' who comes to Europe half with the intention of watching over her friend, and more than half with the determination to fathom the inner life of England, especially in the homes of the great—is a concession on Mr. James's part to the British public,—a somewhat defiant proof that he is not afraid to take up even the conventional American of commonplace satire and make her captivate and charm the unbelieving. Her perfect boldness, combined with a modesty and purity so complete, that we are ashamed even of the thought that it is necessary to give her credit for qualities so innate and self-evident, are made delightfully comical by Henrietta's own unconsciousness of anything odd in her perfectly dauntless proceedings—her roamings about the world with Mr. Bantling in attendance—her free movements and still more free speech. Her speech, however, is free only in the way of interrogation and advice, in which her self-confidence is absolute—as is also, whenever there is any call for it, her kindness and devotion. Mr. James is not so successful with the personages who are not American. Lord Warburton is a very careful study of a fair big Englishman of rank and every heroic quality—but the author has too much the air of walking round and round the typical figure he admires so much, and pointing out his proportion—the size and nobility, the unconscious and easy grace of the aristocrat who puts his aristocracy so little forward, and is so modest and genial. And perhaps his contrast of the inanimate and submissive young ladies, who are Lord Warburton's sisters, as of the perfect little Pansy—the convent child of French and Italian breeding,— with his all-fascinating and all-intelligent American young woman, is not a very fair proceeding. This, however, we leave to his own conscience.

The book altogether is one of the most remarkable specimens of literary skill which the critic could lay his hand upon. It is far too long, infinitely ponderous, and pulled out of all proportion by the elaboration of every detail; but there is scarcely a page in it that is not worked out with the utmost skill and refinement, or which the reader will pass over without leaving something to regret—that is, if he has leisure for the kind of reading which is delightful for its own sake in complete independence of its subject. The conversation in it is an art by itself. To give an appearance of actualness and spontaneity to an artificial production so careful, refined, and elaborate, must have required a prodigious effort. We have heard it characterised very cleverly as resembling one of those games in which one of the party has to go out while the others task their ingenuity in devising how to puzzle him. When he returns with his mind on the full strain, the ingenious succession of questions and answers which are struck out by a party accustomed to the art may approach, if it is very well done, the perfection of the endless pages in which Mr. James carries on his word-fence with the most curious *vraisemblance* and air of being real. But nothing so elaborate ever could be real, and the dazzle sometimes fatigues, though the effect is one which cannot be contemplated without admiration.

Essays in Criticism

GRAHAM GREENE

The Portrait of a Lady†

'The conception of a certain young lady affronting her destiny'—
that is how Henry James described the subject of this book, for
which he felt, next to *The Ambassadors,* the greatest personal tenderness. In his wonderful preface (for no other book in the collected edition of his works did he write a preface so rich in revelations and memories) he compares *The Portrait of a Lady* several
times to a building, and it is as a great, leisurely built cathedral that
one thinks of it, with immense smooth pillars, side-chapels, and
aisles, and a dark crypt where Ralph Touchett lies in marble like a
crusader with his feet crossed to show that he has seen the Holy
Land; sometimes, indeed, it may seem to us too ample a shrine for
one portrait until we remember that this master-craftsman always
has his reasons: those huge pillars are required to bear the weight of
Time (that dark backward and abysm that is the novelist's abiding
problem): the succession of side-chapels are all designed to cast
their particular light upon the high altar: no vista is without its
ambiguous purpose. The whole building, indeed, is a triumph of
architectural planning: the prentice hand which had already produced some works—*Roderick Hudson* and *The American*—impressive if clumsy, and others—*The Europeans* and *Washington Square*
—graceful if slight, had at last learnt the whole secret of planning
for permanence. And the subject? 'A certain young woman affronting her destiny.' Does it perhaps still, at first thought, seem a little
inadequate?

The answer, of course, is that it all depends on the destiny, and
about the destiny Henry James has in his preface nothing to tell us.
He is always something of a conjurer in these prefaces:he seems
ready to disclose everything—the source of his story: the technique
of its writing: even the room in which he settles down to work and
the noises of the street outside. Sometimes he blinds the reader
with a bold sleight of hand, calling, for example, *The Turn of the
Screw* 'a fairy-tale pure and simple'. We must always remain on our
guard while reading these prefaces, for at a certain level no writer
has really disclosed less.

The plot in the case of this novel is far from being an original
one: it is as if James, looking round for the events which were to
bring his young woman, Isabel Archer, into play, had taken the first
to hand: a fortune-hunter, the fortune-hunter's unscrupulous mis-

† From *Collected Essays* by Graham
Greene. Copyright 1951 by Graham
Greene. Reprinted by permission of The
Viking Press, Inc., and Laurence Pollin-
ger Limited.

tress, and a young American heiress caught in the meshes of a love-less marriage. (He was to use almost identically the same plot but with deeper implications and more elaborate undertones in *The Wings of the Dove*.) We can almost see the young James laying down some popular three-decker of the period in his Roman or Venetian lodgings and wondering. 'What could I do with even that story?' For a plot after all is only the machinery—the machinery which will show the young woman (what young woman?) affront-ing her destiny (but what destiny?). In his preface, apparently so revealing, James has no answer to these questions. Nor is there any-thing there which will help us to guess what element it was in the melodramatic plot that attracted the young writer at this moment when he came first into his full powers as a novelist, and again years later when as an old man he set to work to crown his career with the three poetic masterpieces, *The Wings of the Dove*, *The Ambas-sadors*, and *The Golden Bowl*.

The first question is the least important and we have the answer in Isabel Archer's relationship to Milly Theale in *The Wings of the Doves*: it is not only their predicament which is the same, or nearly so (Milly's fortune-hunter, Merton Densher, was enriched by the later James with a conscience, a depth of character, a dignity in his corruption that Gilbert Osmond lacks: indeed in the later book it is the fortune-hunter who steals the tragedy, for Milly dies and it is the living whom we pity): the two women are identical. Milly Theale, if it had not been for her fatal sickness, would have affronted the same destiny and met the same fate as Isabel Archer: the courage, the generosity, the confidence, and inexperience belong to the same character, and James has disclosed to us the source of the later portrait—his young and much-loved cousin Mary Temple who died of tuberculosis at twenty-four. This girl of infinite poten-tiality, whose gay sad troubled letters can be read in *Notes of a Son and Brother*, haunted his memory like a legend; it was as if her image stood for everything that had been graceful, charming, happy in youth—'the whole world of the old New York, that of the earlier dancing years'—everything that was to be betrayed by life. We have only to compare these pages of his autobiography, full of air and space and light, in which the figures of the son and brother, the Albany uncles, the beloved cousin, move like the pastoral figures in a Poussin landscape, with his description of America when he revis-ited the States in his middle age, to see how far he had travelled, how life had closed in. In his fiction he travelled even farther. In his magnificent last short story, *The Jolly Corner*, Brydon, the returned expatriate, finds his old New York house haunted by the ghost of himself, the self he would have become if he had remained in America. The vision is pursued by the unwitting Brydon from room to room until finally it is brought to bay under the fanlight in the hall and presents a face 'evil, odious, blatant, vulgar'. At that moment one remembers what James also remembered: 'the spring-time of '65 as it breathed through Denton streets', the summer twilight sailing back from Newport, Mary Temple.

In none of the company was the note so clear as in this rarest, though at the same time symptomatically or ominously palest, flower of the stem; who was natural at more points and about more things, with a greater sense of freedom and ease and reach of horizon than any of the others dreamed of. They had that way, delightfully, with the small, after all, and the common matters—while she had it with those too, but with the great and rare ones over and above; so that she was to remain for us the very figure and image of a felt interest in life, an interest as magnanimously farspread, or as familiarly and exquisitely fixed, as her splendid shifting sensibility, moral, personal, nervous, and having at once such noble flights and such touchingly discouraged drops, such graces of indifference and inconsequence, might at any moment determine. She was really to remain, for our appreciation, the supreme case of a taste for life as life, as personal living; of an endlessly active and yet somehow a careless, an illusionless, a sublimely forewarned curiosity about it: something that made her, slim and fair and quick, all straightness and charming tossed head, with long light and yet almost sliding steps and a large light postponing, renouncing laugh, the very muse or amateur priestess of rash speculation.

Even if we had not James's own word for it, we could never doubt that here is the source: the fork of his imagination was struck and went on sounding. Mary Temple, of course, never affronted her destiny: she was betrayed quite simply by her body, and James uses words of her that he could as well have used of Milly Theale dying in her Venetian palace—'death at the last was dreadful to her; she would have given anything to live', but isn't it significant that whenever an imaginary future is conceived for this brave spontaneous young woman it always ends in betrayal? Milly Theale escapes from her betrayal simply by dying; Isabel Archer, tied for life to Gilbert Osmond—that precious vulgarian, cold as a fishmonger's slab—is deserted even by her creator. For how are we to understand the ambiguity of the closing pages when Isabel's friend, Henrietta Stackpole, tries to comfort the faithful and despairing 'follower' (this word surely best describes Caspar Goodwood's relationship to Isabel)?

'Look here, Mr. Goodwood,' she said, 'just you wait!'
On which he looked up at her—but only to guess, from her face, with a revulsion, that she simply meant he was young. She stood shining at him with that cheap comfort, and it added, on the spot, thirty years to his life. She walked him away with her, however, as if she had given him now the key to patience.

It is as if James, too, were handing his more casual readers the key to patience, while at the same time asserting between the lines that there is no way out of the inevitable betrayal except the way that Milly Theale and Mary Temple took involuntarily. There is no possibility of a happy ending: this is surely what James always tells us, not with the despairing larger-than-life gestures of a romantic novelist but with a kind of bitter precision. He presents us with a theorem, but it is we who have to work out the meaning of x and discover that x equals no-way-out. It is part of the permanent fascination of his style that he never does all the work for us, and there will be careless mathematicians prepared to argue the meaning of that other ambiguous ending, when Merton Densher, having gained a fortune with Milly Theale's death, is left alone with his mistress, Kate Croy, who had planned it all, just as Mme Merle had planned Isabel's betrayal.

> He heard her out in stillness, watching her face but not moving. Then he only said: 'I'll marry you, mind you, in an hour.'
> 'As we were?'
> 'As we were.'
> But she turned to the door, and her headshake was now the end. 'We shall never be again as we were!'

Some of James's critics have preferred to ignore the real destiny of his characters, and they can produce many of his false revealing statements to support them; he has been multitudinously discussed as a social novelist primarily concerned with the international scene, with the impact of the Old World on the New. It is true the innocent figure is nearly always American (Roderick Hudson, Newman, Isabel and Milly, Maggie Verver and her father), but the corrupted characters—the vehicles for a sense of evil unsurpassed by the theological novelists of our day, M. Mauriac or M. Bernanos—are also American: Mme Merle, Gilbert Osmond, Kate Croy, Merton Densher, Charlotte Stant. His characters are mainly American, simply because James himself was American.

No, it was only on the superficial level of plot, one feels, that James was interested in the American visitor; what deeply interested him, what was indeed his ruling passion, was the idea of treachery, the 'Judas complex'. In a very early novel which he never reprinted, *Watch and Ward*, James dealt with the blackmailer, the man enabled to betray because of his intimate knowledge. As he proceeded in his career he shed the more obvious melodramatic trappings of betrayal, and in *The Portrait of a Lady*, melodrama is at the point of vanishing. What was to follow was only to be the turning of the screw. Isabel Archer was betrayed by little more than an acquaintance; Milly Theale by her dearest friend; until we reach the complicated culmination of treacheries in *The Golden Bowl*.

But how many turns and twists of betrayal we could follow, had we space and time, between *Watch and Ward* and that grand climax!

This then is the destiny that not only the young women affront —you must betray or, more fortunately perhaps, you must be betrayed. A few—James himself, Ralph Touchett in this novel, Mrs. Assingham in *The Golden Bowl*—will simply sadly watch. We shall never know what it was at the very start of life that so deeply impressed on the young James's mind this sense of treachery; but when we remember how patiently and faithfully throughout his life he drew the portrait of one young woman who died, one wonders whether it was just simply a death that opened his eyes to the inherent dissappointment of existence, the betrayal of hope. The eyes once open, the material need never fail him. He could sit there, an ageing honoured man in Lamb House, Rye, and hear the footsteps of the traitors and their victims going endlessly by on the pavement. It is of James himself that we think when we read in *The Portrait of a Lady* of Ralph Touchett's melancholy vigil in the big house in Winchester Square:

> The square was still, the house was still; when he raised one of the windows of the dining-room to let in the air he heard the slow creak of the boots of a lone constable. His own step, in the empty place, seemed loud and sonorous; some of the carpets had been raised, and whenever he moved he roused a melancholy echo. He sat down in one of the armchairs; the big dark dining table twinkled here and there in the small candle-light; the pictures on the wall, all of them very brown, looked vague and incoherent. There was a ghostly presence as of dinners long since digested, of table-talk that had lost its actuality. This hint of the supernatural perhaps had something to do with the fact that his imagination took a flight and that he remained in his chair a long time beyond the hour at which he should have been in bed; doing nothing not even reading the evening paper. I say he did nothing, and I maintain the phrase in the face of the fact that he thought at these moments of Isabel.

ARNOLD KETTLE

Henry James: *The Portrait of a Lady* †

Compared with this the English novels which precede it, except perhaps those of Jane Austen, all seem a trifle crude. There is a habit of perfection here, a certainty and a poise, which is quite different from the merits and power of *Oliver Twist* or *Wuthering*

† From *An Introduction to the English Novel* (London: Hutchinson's University Library, 1953) II, 13–34. Reprinted by permission of Harper & Row, Publishers, and Hutchinson Publishing Group.

Heights or even *Middlemarch*. The quality has something to do with the full consciousness of Henry James's art. Nothing in *The Portrait of a Lady* is unconscious, nothing there by chance, no ungathered wayward strands, no clumsiness. No novelist is so absorbed as James in what he himself might call his 'game.' But it is not an empty or superficial concern with 'form' that gives *The Portrait of a Lady* its quality. James's manner, his obsession with style, his intricate and passionate concern with presentation, do not spring from a narrow 'aesthetic' attitude to his art.

"James had in his style and perhaps in the life which it reflected an idiosyncrasy so powerful, so overweening, that to many it seemed a stultifying vice, or at least an inexcusable heresy . . . He enjoyed an excess of intelligence and he suffered, both in life and art, from an excessive effort to communicate it, to represent it in all its fullness. His style grew elaborate in the degree that he rendered shades and refinements of meaning and feeling not usually rendered at all. . . . His attention and all his labour was to represent dramatically intelligence at its most difficult, its most lucid, its most beautiful point. This is the sum of his idiosyncrasy."[1]

The Portrait of a Lady is not one of James's 'difficult' novels; but Mr. Blackmur's remarks usefully remind us of the inadequacy of a merely formal approach to James's work. The extraordinary richness of texture of his novels makes such an approach tempting; but it will take us neither to James's triumphs nor to his failures.

The beauty of texture derives immediately from two qualities, which are ultimately inseparable. One is James's ability to make us know his characters more richly, though not necessarily more vividly, than we know the characters of other novelists; the other is the subtlety of his own standpoint. Without the latter quality the former would not, of course, be possible. You cannot control the responses of your reader unless you are in complete control of your material.

In *The Portrait of a Lady* there are—looking at the question from an analytical point of view—two kinds of characters: those whom we know from straightforward, though not unsubtle, description by the author and those who reveal themselves in the course of the book. The latter are, obviously, the important ones. The former —Mrs. Touchett, Henrietta Stackpole, the Countess Gemini, Pansy Osmond—are interesting primarily in their relationship to the chief characters, in their part in the pattern; we do not follow their existence out of their function in the book. But they are nevertheless not 'flat' characters. They come alive not as 'characters,' not as personified 'humours,' but as complete people (Pansy, perhaps, is the

1. Henry James, *The Art of the Novel*, ed. R. P. Blackmur (New York, 1934), p. xii.

exception, but then is not the intention that we should see her as scarcely an independent being at all?) and if we do not follow them out of the part of the plot which concerns them it is because our interests are more involved elsewhere, not because they do not have a full existence of their own.

The way Henry James introduces his characters to us depends entirely on the kind of function they are to have in his story. The main characters are never described as they *are* (i.e. as the author knows them to be) but—by and large—as Isabel Archer sees them. We know them at first only by the first impression that they make. We get to know better what they are like in the way that, in life, we get to know people better through acquaintance. And just as in life we are seldom, if ever, quite certain what another person is like, so in a Henry James novel we are often pretty much at sea about particular characters for considerable portions of the book. In *The Portrait of a Lady* the person whom at first we inevitably know least about is Madame Merle. Henry James lets us know right from the start that there is something sinister about her; we are made quickly to feel that Isabel's reaction to her is less than adequate, but the precise nature of her character is not revealed until fairly far into the book.

It is not quite true to say that everything in *The Portrait of a Lady* is revealed through Isabel's consciousness. We know, from the start, certain things that Isabel does not know. We know, for instance—and twice Henry James explicitly reminds us of it—more about Ralph Touchett's feeling for Isabel than she herself perceives.

Indeed, there is a sense in which the novel is revealed to us through Ralph's consciousness, for his is the 'finest,' the fullest intelligence in the book and therefore he sees things—about Madame Merle, about Osmond, about Isabel herself—which Isabel does not see and inevitably such perceptions are transmitted to the reader. Again, we are offered important scenes—between Madame Merle and Osmond, between the Countess and Madame Merle—which reveal to us not the whole truth but enough of the truth about Madame Merle's stratagems to put us at an advantage over Isabel.

The truth is that Henry James's purpose in this novel is not to put Isabel betweeen the reader and the situation (in the way that Strether's consciousness is used in *The Ambassadors*) but to reveal to the reader the full implications of Isabel's consciousness. For this to happen we must see Isabel not merely from the inside (i.e. know how she feels) but from the outside too. The method is, in fact, precisely the method of *Emma*, except that Jane Austen is rather more scrupulously consistent than Henry James. The scenes 'outside' Emma herself (like Jane Fairfax's visits to the post office) are brought to our knowledge by being related by a third party in the presence of Emma herself. Our only 'advantage' over Emma herself is provided by the words which Jane Austen uses to describe her. Henry James, as we have seen, takes greater liberties. Yet it is worth observing that the great scene at the centre of *The Portrait of a Lady* (Chapter XIII), in which Isabel takes stock of her situation, is of precisely the same *kind* as the scene in which (Vol. I, Chapter XVI) Emma takes stock of her dealings with Harriet.

Since James's purpose is to render the full implications of Isabel's situation it is necessary that we should know more than Isabel, should see her, that is to say, from the outside. The question remains: how *much* more should we know? And James's anwer is: just as much as is necessary for a fully sympathetic understanding. Thus we are to know that Madame Merle has drawn Isabel into a trap, but we are not to know why. The full story is kept back, not because Henry James is interested in suspense in the melodramatic sense, but because if we were in on the secret the nature of Isabel's discovery of her situation could not be so effectively revealed. It is necessary to the novel that we should *share* Isabel's suspicions and her awakening. In order to give the precise weight (not just the logical weight but the intricate weight of feelings, standards, loyalties) to the issues involved in her final dilemma we must know not just what has happened to Isabel but the way it has happened.

It is from such a consideration that there will emerge one of Henry James's cardinal contributions to the art of the novel. With James the question "What happened?" carries the most subtle, the most exciting ramifications. To no previous novelist had the answer to such a question seemed so difficult, its implications so interminable. To a George Eliot the question is complicated enough: to understand what happened to Lydgate we must be made aware of innumerable issues, facets of character, moral choices, social pressures. And yet deep in George Eliot's novel is implicit the idea that if the reader only knows enough facts about the situation he will know the situation. It is the aim of Henry James to avoid the 'about' or, at least, to alter its status, to transform quantity into quality. His is the poet's ambition: to create an object about which we say not "It means. . . ." but "It is. . . ." (in this he is with Emily Brontë.) We cannot *understand* Isabel Archer, he implies, unless we feel as she feels. And it is, indeed, because he succeeds in this attempt that *The Portrait of a Lady* though not a greater novel than *Middlemarch* is a more moving one.

As a rule when Henry James describes a character (as opposed to allowing the person to be revealed in action) the description is of the kind we have noticed in *Emma* or *Middlemarch*.

"Mrs. Touchett was certainly a person of many oddities, of which her behaviour on returning to her husband's house after many months was a noticeable specimen. She had her own way of doing all that she did, and this is the simplest description of a character which, although by no means without liberal motions, rarely succeeded in giving an impression of suavity. Mrs. Touchett might do a great deal of good, but she never pleased. This way of her own, of which she was so fond, was not intrinsically offensive—it was just unmistakeably distinguished from the way of others. The edges of her conduct were so very clear-cut that for susceptible persons it sometimes had a knife-like effect. That hard fineness came out in her deportment during the first hours of her return from America, under circumstances in which it might have seemed that her first act would have been to exchange greetings with her husband and son. Mrs. Touchett, for reasons which she deemed excellent, always retired on such occasions into impenetrable seclusion, postponing the more sentimental ceremony until she had repaired the disorder of dress with a completeness which had the less reason to be of high importance as neither beauty nor vanity were concerned in it. She was a plain-faced old woman, without graces and without any great elegance, but with an extreme respect for her own motives. She was usually prepared to explain these—when the explanation was asked as a favour; and in such a case they proved totally different from those that had been attributed to her. She was virtually separated from her husband, but she appeared to perceive nothing irregular in the situation. It had become clear, at an early stage of their community, that they should never desire the same thing at the same moment, and this appearance had prompted her to rescue disagreement from the vulgar realm of accident. She did what she could to erect it into a law—a much more edifying aspect of it—by going to live in Florence, where she bought a house and established herself; and by leaving her husband to take care of the English branch of his bank. This arrangement greatly pleased her; it was so felicitously definite. It struck her husband in the same light, in a foggy square in London, where it was at times the most definite fact he discerned; but he would have preferred that such unnatural things should have a greater vagueness. To agree to disagree had cost him an effort; he was ready to agree to almost anything but that, and saw no reason why either assent or dissent should be so terribly consistent.

Mrs. Touchett indulged in no regrets nor speculations, and usually came once a year to spend a month with her husband, a period during which she apparently took pains to convince him that she had adopted the right system. She was not fond of the English style of life, and had three or four reasons for it to which she currently alluded; they bore upon minor points of that ancient order, but for Mrs. Touchett they amply justified non-residence. She detested bread-sauce, which, as she said, looked like a poultice and tasted like soap; she objected to the consumption of

beer by her maid-servants; and she affirmed that the British laundress (Mrs. Touchett was very particular about the appearance of
her linen) was not a mistress of her art." [Chap. III]

Here the description depends for its effect entirely on the quality
of the author's wit, his organized intellectual comment, and the wit
is of the sort (a penetrating delicacy of observation within an
accepted social group) achieved by Jane Austen or George Eliot.

But some of the described characters in *The Portrait of a Lady*
come poetically to life. This is the description of Isabel's first meeting with the Countess Gemini.

"The Countess Gemini simply nodded without getting up;
Isabel could see she was a woman of high fashion. She was thin
and dark and not at all pretty, having features that suggested
some tropical bird—a long beak-like nose, small, quickly-moving
eyes and a mouth and chin that receded extremely. Her expression, however, thanks to various intensities of emphasis and
wonder, of horror and joy, was not inhuman, and, as regards her
appearance, it was plain she understood herself and made the
most of her points. Her attire, voluminous and delicate, bristling
with elegance, had the look of shimmering plumage, and her attitudes were as light and sudden as those of a creature who
perched upon twigs. She had a great deal of manner; Isabel, who
had never known anyone with so much manner, immediately
classed her as the most affected of women. She remembered that
Ralph had not recommended her as an acquaintance; but she was
ready to acknowledge that to a casual view the Countess Gemini
revealed no depths. Her demonstrations suggested the violent
waving of some flag of general truce—white silk with fluttering
streamers." [Chap. XXIV]

We are never to get to know the Countess very well, but already
we see her with a peculiar vividness, the vividness evoked by poetic
imagery. The bird image was a visual force so intense that it goes
beyond surface illumination—"bristling with elegance" in its context contains a world of comment as well as vividness. So does the
image of the flag of truce.

Henry James predominant interest is, however, by no means in
character. *The Portrait of a Lady*, he tells us in his Preface, has as
its corner-stone "the conception of a certain young woman affronting her destiny." The interest, it is already indicated, is not primarily a psychological one, not a matter of mere personal analysis. And
The Portrait of a Lady is indeed a novel of the widest scope and relevance. Though it is in the line of Jane Austen it has a quality
which it is not misleading to call symbolic (already we have hinted
at a link with what would appear at first to be a wholly different
novel, *Wuthering Heights*). *The Portrait of a Lady* is a novel about
destiny. Or, to use a concept rather more in tone with the language

of the book itself, it is a novel about freedom. It would not be out-
rageous, though it might be misleading, to call it a nineteenth-century *Paradise Lost.*

Henry James is, of course, far too sophisticated an artist to offer us
the 'subject' of his book on a platter. In his moral interest he avoids
like the plague anything approaching the abstract.

> "I might envy," he writes in his Preface, "though I couldn't
> emulate, the imaginative writer so constituted as to see his fable
> first and to make out its agents afterwards: I could think so little
> of any fable that didn't need its agents positively to launch it; I
> could think so little of any situation that didn't depend for its
> interest on the nature of the persons situated, and thereby on
> their way of taking it."

And again, a little later:

> "There is, I think, no more nutritive or suggestive truth in this
> connexion than that of the perfect dependence of the 'moral'
> sense of a work of art on the amount of felt life concerned in
> producing it."[2]

James's novel is not a moral fable; but its moral interest is nevertheless central. Only the business of "launching," of presenting
with all the necessary depth of "felt life," that "ado" which is the
story of Isabel Archer, all this may easily distract our attention from
the central theme. Indeed there was a time when James's novels
apparently were regarded as "comedies of manners" (cf. Trollope)
and even so superbly intelligent a reader as E. M. Forster seems to
have missed the point of them almost completely.

The launching of *The Portrait of a Lady* is beautifully done. Gardencourt, the house in Albany, upper-class London: they are called
up with magnificent certainty and solidity. So too are the people of
the book: the Touchetts, Caspar Goodwood, Henrietta Stackpole,
Lord Warburton, Isabel herself. If these characters are to contribute
to a central pattern it will not be, it is clear, in the manner of anything approaching allegory. They are all too "round,' too 'free' to be
felt, for even a moment, simply to be 'standing for' anything. It is
one of Henry James's achievements that he can convince us that his
characters have a life outside the pages of his novel without ever
leading us into the temptation of following them beyond his purpose. It is because everything in these early chapters of *The Portrait
of a Lady* is realized with such fullness, such apparent lack of
pointed emphasis, that we are slow to recognize the basic pattern of

2. I quote with some uneasiness from
James's Preface (written, it will be recalled, some quarter of a century after
the novel), not because I doubt the relevance or interest of his observations but
because I am conscious of the difficulty
of assimilating out of context sentences
written in his most idiosyncratic, complex style.

the novel, but it also on this account that our imagination is so firmly engaged.

Before the end of the first chapter, however, a subsidiary theme has already been fairly fully stated and three of the main themes announced or, at any rate, indicated. The subsidiary theme is that generally referred to in Henry James's novels as the international situation—the relation of America to Europe. Graham Greene in a recent introduction to *The Portrait of a Lady* has tried to play down the importance of this theme. "It is true the innocent figure is nearly always American (Roderick Hudson, Newman, Isabel and Milly, Maggie Verver and her father), but the corrupted characters . . . are also American: Mme. Merle, Gilbert Osmond, Kate Croy, Merton Densher, Charlotte Stant. His characters are mainly American, simply because James himself was American."[3] In fact, of course, neither Kate Croy nor Densher is an American and one of the points about the other "corrupted" characters is that they are all expatriates, europeanized Americans, whom it is at least possible to see as corrupted by Europe.[4] The theme of the impact of European civilization on Americans—innocent or not—is not a main theme of *The Portrait of a Lady* but it is nevertheless there and we shall return to it later. And it is broached in the very first pages of the novel in the description of the Touchett *ménage* and in such details as the failure of Mr. Touchett to understand (or rather, his pretence at not understanding) Lord Warburton's jokes.

The main themes indicated in the first chapters are the importance of wealth, the difficulty of marriage and—fundamental to the other two—the problem of freedom or independence. In each case the theme appears to be merely a casual subject of conversation but in fact there is nothing casual there. The vital theme of freedom is introduced in the form of a joke—one of Mrs. Touchett's eccentric telegrams: " 'Changed hotel, very bad, impudent clerk, address here. Taken sister's girl, died last year, go to Europe, two sisters, quite independent'." The telegram is discussed by Mr. Touchett and Ralph.

" 'There's one thing very clear in it,' said the old man; 'she has given the hotel-clerk a dressing.'

'I'm not sure even of that, since he has driven her from the field. We thought at first that the sister mentioned might be the sister of the clerk; but the subsequent mention of a niece seems to prove that the allusion is to one of my aunts. Then there was a question as to whose the two other sisters were; they are probably two of my late aunt's daughters. But who's "quite independent," and in what sense is the term used?—that point's not yet set-

3. See p. 670 in this edition [*Editor*].
4. For a fuller discussion of this problem see *Henry James, the Major Phase* by F. O. Matthiessen and *Maule's Curse* by Yvor Winters.

tled. Does the expression apply more particularly to the young lady my mother has adopted, or does it characterize her sisters equally?—and is it used in a moral or in a financial sense? Does it mean that they've been left well off, or that they wish to be under no obligations?—or does it simply mean that they're fond of their own way?" [Chap. I]

Ralph's frivolous speculations do in fact state the basic problem to be dealt with in the novel. The point is indeed not yet settled: it will take the whole book to settle it. And even then, 'settle' is not the right word. One does not, Henry James would be quick to remind us, settle life.

The independence of Isabel is the quality about her most often emphasized. Mrs. Touchett has taken her up, but she is not, she assures Ralph "a candidate for adoption." " 'I'm very fond of my liberty'," she adds.[Chap. II] From the very first the ambiguous quality of this independence is stressed. Isabel is attractive, interesting, 'fine' ("she carried within her a great fund of life, and her deepest enjoyment was to feel the continuity between the movements of her own soul and the agitations of the world"[Chap. IV]); but she is also in many respects inexperienced, naïve. " 'It occurred to me,' Mrs. Touchett says, 'that it would be a kindness to take her about and introduce her to the world. She thinks she knows a great deal of it—like most American girls; but like most American girls she's ridiculously mistaken'."[Chap. V] Henry James does not allow us, charming creature as she is, to idealize Isabel:

> "Altogether, with her meagre knowledge, her inflated ideals, her confidence at once innocent and dogmatic, her temper at once exacting and indulgent, her mixture of curiosity and fastidiousness, of vivacity and indifference, her desire to look very well and to be if possible even better, her determination to see, to try, to know, her combination of the delicate desultory flame-like spirit and the eager and personal creature of conditions: she would be an easy victim of scientific criticism if she were not intended to awaken on the reader's part an impulse more tender and more purely expectant." [Chap. VI]

The Portrait of a Lady is the revelation of the inadequacy of Isabel's view of freedom.

The revelation is so full, so concrete, that to abstract from it the main, insistent theme must inevitably weaken the impression of the book. But analysis involves such abstraction and we shall not respond fully to James's novel unless we are conscious of its theme. The theme in its earlier stages is fully expressed in the scene in which Caspar Goodwood for the second time asks Isabel to marry him (she has just refused Lord Warburton).

" 'I don't know,' she answered rather grandly. 'The world—with all these places so arranged and so touching each other—comes to strike one as rather small.'

'It's a sight too big for *me!*' Caspar exclaimed with a simplicity our young lady might have found touching if her face had not been set against concessions.

This attitude was part of a system, a theory, that she had lately embraced, and to be thorough she said after a moment: 'Don't think me unkind if I say it's just *that*—being out of your sight—that I like. If you were in the same place I should feel you were watching me, and I don't like that—I like my liberty too much. If there's a thing in the world I'm fond of,' she went on with a slight recurrence of grandeur, 'it's my personal independence.'

But whatever there might be of the too superior in this speech moved Caspar Goodwood's admiration; there was nothing he winced at in the large air of it. He had never supposed she hadn't wings and the need of beautiful free movements—he wasn't, with his own long arms and strides, afraid of any force in her. Isabel's words, if they had been meant to shock him, failed of the mark and only made him smile with the sense that here was common ground. 'Who would wish less to curtail your liberty than I? What can give me greater pleasure than to see you perfectly independent—doing whatever you like? It's to make you independent that I want to marry you.'

'That's a beautiful sophism,' said the girl with a smile more beautiful still.

'An unmarried woman—a girl of your age—isn't independent. There are all sorts of things she can't do. She's hampered at every step.'

'That's as she looks at the question,' Isabel answered with much spirit. 'I'm not in my first youth—I can do what I choose—I belong quite to the independent class. I've neither father nor mother; I'm poor and of a serious disposition; I'm not pretty. I therefore am not bound to be timid and conventional; indeed I can't afford such luxuries. Besides, I try to judge things for myself; to judge wrong, I think, is more honourable than not to judge at all. I don't wish to be a mere sheep in the flock; I wish to choose my fate and know something of human affairs beyond what other people think it compatible with propriety to tell me.' She paused a moment, but not long enough for her companion to reply. He was apparently on the point of doing so when she went on: 'Let me say this to you, Mr. Goodwood. You're so kind as to speak of being afraid of my marrying. If you should hear a rumour that I'm on the point of doing so—girls are liable to have such things said about them—remember what I have told you about my love of liberty and venture to doubt it'." [Chap. XVI]

The Portrait of a Lady is far from allegory yet one is permitted to feel, in the symbolic quality of the novel, that the characters, though unmistakably individuals, are more than individuals. Thus, in her rejection of Caspar Goodwood, Isabel is rejecting America, or at least that part of America that Goodwood represents, young, strong, go-ahead, uninhibited, hard. For Goodwood (as for Henrietta, who essentially shares his quality) the problem of freedom is simple and might be expressed in the words of Mr. Archibald Macleish's American Dream:

> "America is promises
> For those that take them."

Goodwood—and it would be wrong to see him as a wholly unsympathetic character—is prepared to take them with all that taking implies. To him and Henrietta (and they are, on one level, the most sensible, positive people in the book) Isabel's problem is not a problem at all. Freedom for them has the simple quality it possessed for the nineteenth-century liberal.

The rejection of Lord Warburton has, similarly, a symbolic quality—though, again, one must insist that this is not an allegory. Warburton is a liberal aristocrat. He embodies the aristocratic culture of Europe (that has so attracted Isabel at Gardencourt) and adds his own reforming ideas—a combination which Henry James, had he been the kind of aesthetic snob he is often held to be, might have found irresistible. Ralph Touchett sums up Warburton's social position magnificently:

" '. . . He says I don't understand my time, I understand it certainly better than he, who can neither abolish himself as a nuisance nor maintain himself as an institution'." [Chap. VIII]

Isabel's rejection of Lord Warburton is not a light one. She feels very deeply the attraction of the aristocratic standards. But she feels also the limitations of Warburton and his sisters, the Misses Molyneux (it is worth comparing them with another 'county' family—the Marchants—in the wonderful *Princess Casamassima*; Henry James's attitude to the British aristocracy is by no means uncritical).

" '. . . So long as I look at the Misses Molyneux they seem to me to answer a kind of ideal. Then Henrietta presents herself, and I'm straightway convinced by *her*; not so much in respect to herself as in respect to what masses behind her'." [Chap. X]

Ralph, too, (though he does not undervalue her) disposes of Henrietta:

" 'Henrietta . . . does smell of the Future—it almost knocks one down!' " [Chap. X]

Goodwood and Warburton rejected (almost like two temptations), Isabel is now 'free' to affront her destiny. But she is not free because she is poor. She has never, we are told early on, known anything about money, and it is typical of this novel that this fine, romantic indifference to wealth should be one of the basic factors in Isabel's tragedy.

Henry James's characters always have to be rich and the reason is not the obvious one. "I call people rich," says Ralph Touchett, "when they're able to meet the requirements of their imagination." [Chap. XVIII] It is for this reason that he persuades his father to leave Isabel a fortune. She must be rich in order to be free of the material world. She must be free in order to 'live.'

It is Ralph's one supreme mistake in intelligence and it is the mistake that ruins Isabel. For it is her wealth that arouses Madame Merle's realization that she can use her and leads directly to the disastrous, tragic marriage with Osmond. And in the superb scene in which, sitting in the candlelight in the elegant, spiritually empty house in Rome, Isabel takes stock of her tragedy, she painfully reveals to herself the conclusion:

> "But for her money, as she saw to-day, she would never have done it. And then her mind wandered off to poor Mr. Touchett, sleeping under English turf, the beneficent author of infinite woe! For this was the fantastic fact. At bottom her money had been a burden, had been on her mind, which was filled with the desire to transfer the weight of it to some other conscience, to some more prepared receptacle. What would lighten her own conscience more effectually than to make it over to the man with the best taste in the world? Unless she should have given it to a hospital there would have been nothing better she could do with it; and there was no charitable insitution in which she had been as much interested as in Gilbert Osmond. He would use her fortune in a way that would make her think better of it and rub off a certain grossness attaching to the good luck of an unexpected inheritance. There had been nothing very delicate in inheriting seventy thousand pounds; the delicacy had been all in Mr. Touchett's leaving them to her. But to marry Gilbert Osmond and bring him such a portion—in that there would be delicacy for her as well. There would be less for him—that was true; but that was his affair, and if he loved her he wouldn't object to her being rich. Had he not had the courage to say he was glad she was rich?" [Chap. XLII]

It is at the moment when Ralph is dying that the theme is finally stated in the form at once the most affecting and most morally profound.

> "She raised her head and her clasped hands; she seemed for a moment to pray to him. 'Is it true—is it true?' she asked.
> 'True that you've been stupid? Oh no,' said Ralph with a sensible intention of wit.
> 'That you made me rich—that all I have is yours?'

He turned away his head, and for some time said nothing. Then at last: 'Ah, don't speak of that—that was not happy.' Slowly he moved his face toward her again, and they once more saw each other.

'But for that—but for that—!' And he paused. 'I believe I ruined you,' he wailed.

She was full of the sense that he was beyond the reach of pain; he seemed already so little of this world. But even if she had not had it she would still have spoken, for nothing mattered now but the only knowledge that was not pure anguish—the knowledge that they were looking at the truth together. 'He married me for the money,' she said. She wished to say everything; she was afraid he might die before she had done so.

He gazed at her a little, and for the first time his fixed eyes lowered their lids. But he raised them in a moment, and then, 'He was greatly in love with you,' he answered.

'Yes, he was in love with me. But he wouldn't have married me if I had been poor. I don't hurt you in saying that. How can I? I only want you to understand. I always tried to keep you from understanding; but that's all over.'

'I always understood,' said Ralph.

'I thought you did, and I didn't like it. But now I like it.'

'You don't hurt me—you make me very happy.' And as Ralph said this there was an extraordinary gladness in his voice. She bent her head again, and pressed her lips to the back of his hand. 'I always understood,' he continued, 'though it was so strange—so pitiful. You wanted to look at life for yourself—but you were not allowed; you were punished for your wish. You were ground in the very mill of the conventional!'

'Oh yes, I've been punished,' Isabel sobbed." [Chap. LIV]

The necessity here of stating in its dreadful simplicity the agonizing truth so that the relationship of the two may be purified and deepened shows an intuition the very opposite of sentimental.

Isabel, then, imagining herself free, has in fact delivered herself into bondage. And the bondage has come about not casually but out of the very force and fortune of her own aspirations to freedom. She has sought life and because she has sought it in this way she has found death.

Freedom, to Isabel and to Ralph (for he has been as much concerned in the issue as she), has been an idealized freedom. They have sought to be free not through a recognition of, but by an escape from, necessity. And in so doing they have delivered Isabel over to an exploitation as crude and more corrupting than the exploitation that would have been her fate if Mrs. Touchett had never visited Albany.

" 'Do you still like Serena Merle?' " is Mrs. Touchett's last question of Isabel.

" 'Not as I once did. But it doesn't matter, for she's going to
America.'

'To America? She must have done something very bad.'

'Yes—very bad.'

'May I ask what it is?"

'She made a comvenience of me.'

'Ah,' cried Mrs. Touchett, 'so she did of me! She does of
everyone.' " [Chap. LIV]

The Portrait of a Lady is one of the most profound expressions in literature of the illusion that freedom is an abstract quality inherent in
the individual soul.

It is interesting to compare James's book with another great novel
written not very long before, *Madame Bovary*, the story of another
woman "ground in the very mill of the conventional." It is true
that Emma Bovary is, unlike Isabel Archer, not in the least 'fine,'
that she fails to escape her petty–bourgeois social *milieu* and
that she is quite incapable of the exalted moral discipline to which
Isabel is dedicated, yet we will learn something of James's novel, I
think, from a glance at Flaubert's. What is shocking in *Madame
Bovary* is the appalling passivity of Flaubert's characters, their inability to fight in any effective way the bourgeois world which Flaubert detests and which relentlessly warps and destroys all fineness in
them. The strength of the novel lies in the very ruthlessness of its
exposure of romantic attitudes; but therein also lies its weakness,
the sense we get of something less than the human capacity for heroism, the uneasy suspicions of a *roman á thèse*. *The Portrait of a
Lady* gives, as a matter of fact, no more positive response to its revelation of bourgeois values than *Madame Bovary*, yet we do experience a sense of human resilience and dignity. The interesting question is how far this sense—embodied in the 'fineness' of Isabel herself—is merely romantic and illusory.

The issue can perhaps be put in this way: is not the accumulated
effect of the novel to present human destiny as inexorably one of
suffering and despair? There are a number of tendencies making for
this effect. In the first place there is the insistent use of dramatic
irony in the construction of the book. Chapter after chapter in the
early reaches of the novel is designed to emphasize the fatality
facing Isabel's aspirations. The fifth chapter tells us she has come to
Europe to find happiness; the sixth that she likes unexpectedness
("I shall not have success (in Europe) if they're too stupidly conventional. I'm not in the least stupidly conventional"). The seventh
chapter ends with the following exchange:

" 'I always want to know the things one shouldn't do.'

'So as to do them?' asked her aunt.

'So as to choose,' said Isabel."

The eighth draws to a close with

" 'I shall never make anyone a martyr.'

'You'll never be one, I hope.'

'I hope not. . . .' "

This is all, it may be argued, simply Henry James at work, extracting from every situation its maximum of point. But the art, it seems to me, is in a subtle sense self–betraying. What is achieved is a kind of inevitability, a sense of Isabel's never standing a chance, which amounts not to objective irony but to the creation of something like an external destiny. Is not martyrdom becoming, in a sense at once insidious and—with all the associations and overtones one may care to give the word—romantic? Is there not to be here a breath—a very sophisticated and infinitely worldly breath—of the emotional and moral inadequacy involved in George Eliot's vision of those latter–day Saint Theresas?

Our final judgement must depend on the climax—the famous ending—of the book. It is from this ultimate impression that we shall have to decide whether James indeed plays fair with Isabel and us, whether he reveals in full profundity and (in the least cold sense of the word) objectivity a tragic situation or whether there is a certain sleight of hand, the putting across not of life but of something which merely for the moment passes for life. But before we consider this final climax it is worth noting what would seem an odd weakness in the novel. Is it not a little strange that of all the essential parts of Isabel's story which revealed to us the section of her life most pointedly avoided is that immediately before her decision to marry Osmond? She has met him, got to know him somewhat; she then goes away for a year, travelling in Europe and the Middle East with Madame Merle. When she comes back to Florence she has decided to marry Osmond. This is, from the novelist's point of view, the most difficult moment in the book. How to convince us that a young woman like Isabel would in fact marry a man like Osmond? And it is a moment which, despite the revealing conversation with Ralph (which does indeed tell us something) is, I suggest, not satisfactorily got over. And the point is that if Isabel's marriage to Osmond is in any sense a fraud perpetrated upon us for his own ends by the author, the book is greatly weakened.

At the end of the novel Isabel, after Ralph's death and another encounter with Caspar Goodwood, returns to Rome. Is her return to Osmond irrevocable, an acceptance now and for ever of her 'destiny,' or is it tentative, no ending, the situation unresolved? Mr. F. O. Matthiessen, arguing in the latter sense, has a most interesting observation:

"The end of Isabel's career is not yet in sight. That fact raises a critical issue about James's way of rounding off his narratives.

He was keenly aware of what he method involved. As he wrote in his notebook, upon concluding his detailed project: 'With strong handling it seems to me that it may all be very true, very powerful, very touching. The obvious criticism of course will be that it is not finished—that it has not seen the heroine to the end of her situation—that I have left her *en l'air*. This is both true and false. The *whole* of anything is never told; you can only take what groups together. What I have done has that unity—it groups together. It is complete in itself—and the rest may be taken up or not, later'."[5]

James's own evidence is of course conclusive as to his intention, but it is not necessarily relevant as to what is in fact achieved; and it seems to me that, although the ending of *The Portrait of a Lady* does not completely and irrevocably round off the story—the possibility of Isabel's later reconsidering her decision is not excluded—yet the dominant impression is undoubtedly that of the deliberate rejection of 'life' (as offered by Caspar Goodwood) in favour of death, as represented by the situation in Rome. The scene with Goodwood is indeed very remarkable with its candid, if tortured, facing of a sexual implication which James is apt to sheer off. On the whole the effect of this scene, though one understands completely the quality of Isabel's reaction, is further to weight the scales against a return to Rome. Even if Goodwood himself is impossible, the vitality that he conveys is a force to be reckoned with and Isabel's rejection of this vitality involves more clearly than ever the sense that she is turning her face to the wall.

Isabel's return to Rome is certainly not a mere surrender to the conventional force of the marriage vow. The issue as to whether or not she should leave her husband is twice quite frankly broached by Henrietta, as well as by Goodwood. Isabel's first reply to Henrietta is significant:

> " 'I don't know what great unhappiness might bring me to; but it seems to me I shall always be ashamed. One must accept one's deeds. I married him before all the world; I was perfectly free; it was impossible to do anything more deliberate. One can't change that way,' Isabel repeated." [Chap. XLVII]

Later, when she discovers how little free she had in fact been, it is her obligation towards Pansy that becomes the most important factor. But always there is the sense of some deep inward consideration that makes the particular issues—the character of Osmond, her own mistakes, the needs of Pansy, the importunity of Goodwood—irrelevant. The recurring image in the last pages is of a sea or torrent in which Isabel is immersed. Goodwood becomes identified with the torrent. Her temptation is to give herself up to it.[6] When she breaks loose from him and the image she is once more 'free,' free and in darkness. The lights now are the lights of Gardencourt and now she knows where to turn. "There was a very straight path." [Chap. LV]

It seems to me inescapable that what Isabel finally chooses is something represented by a high cold word like duty or resignation, the duty of an empty vow, the resignation of the defeated, and that in making her choice she is paying a final sacrificial tribute to her own ruined conception of freedom. For Henry James, though he sees the tragedy implicit in the Victorian ruling–class view of freedom, is himself so deeply involved in that illusion that he cannot escape from it. His books are tragedies precisely because their subject is the smashing of the bourgeois illusion of freedom in the consciousness of characters who are unable to conceive of freedom in any other way. His 'innocent' persons have therefore always the characters of victims; they are at the mercy of the vulgar and the corrupt, and the more finely conscious they become of their situation the more unable are they to cope with it in positive terms. Hence the contradiction of a Fleda Vetch[7] whose superior consciousness (and conscience) leads her in effect to reject life in favour of death. This is a favourite, almost an archetypal situation, in James's novels. It achieves its most striking expression in *The Portrait of a Lady* and *The Wings of the Dove* in which another rich American girl meets, even more powerfully and more exquisitely, the fate of Isabel Archer.

For James in his supreme concern for 'living' (Milly Theale in *The Wings of the Dove*, Strether in *The Ambassadors* have, like Isabel, this immense, magnificent desire to 'live') ultimately, in effect, turns his back on life. This is not unconnected, I think, with the fact that his characters never do anything like work. This description of Madame Merle is not untypical of a day in the life of a Henry James figure:

"When Madame Merle was neither writing, nor painting, nor touching the piano, she was usually employed upon wonderful tasks of rich embroidery, cushions, curtains, decorations for the chimney-piece; an art in which her bold, free invention was as noted as the agility of her needle. She was never idle, for when engaged in none of the ways I have mentioned she was either reading (she appeared to Isabel to read 'everything important'), or walking out, or playing patience with the cards, or talking with her fellow inmates." [Chap. XIX]

6. It is at such a moment that one sees the force of Stephen Spender's linking of James with Conrad's "in the destructive element immerse" in an otherwise not very helpful book (*The Destructive Element*, 1937).
7. In *The Spoils of Poynton*.

The contemplation of such a way of life is likely, after all, to lead to idealism, for the necessities behind such an existence are by no means obvious. It is a superficial criticism to accuse James of snobbery or even of being limited by his social environment (what artist is not?). But there can be no doubt that what the bourgeois world did for James was to turn him into a moral idealist chasing a chimera of ideal conduct divorced from social reality.

It is not that his sense of social reality is in any way weak. On the contrary his picture of his world has, it has already been emphasized, a magnificent solidity, a concrete richness of the subtlest power. Nor is he in any easy, obvious sense taken in by that world (note his attitude to Warburton, his description of American–French society in Chapter XX and his total contempt for Osmond and his values); his picture of European bourgeois life is in its objective aspect as realistic as that of Balzac or Flaubert or Proust. No, if we are to isolate in James's novels the quality that is ultimately their limitation, it is to the core of his point of view, his philosophy, that we are led. The limiting factor in *The Portrait of a Lady* is the failure of James in the last analysis to dissociate from Isabel's errors of understanding.

One of the central recurring themes of James's novels is the desire to 'live,' to achieve a fullness of consciousness which permits the richest yet most exquisite response to the vibrations of life. And yet with this need to live is associated almost invariably the sense of death. Living, he seems to be saying again and again, involves martyrdom. The pleasure he finds in the contemplation and description of living at its most beautiful, most exalted point is subtly increased if the living creature is faced with death. Ralph Touchett is not alone among the dying swans of James's books: he is one of a line culminating in Strether (who discovers how to live too late) and in the fabulous Milly Theale. The attraction of this subject to James seems to me most significant. "Very true . . . very powerful . . . very touching . . ." one can almost hear him breathing out the words. It is a kind of apotheosis of his vision of life. And it is intimately, inextricably, linked up with his philosophic idealism. His 'good' characters, in their unswerving effort to live finely, turn out to be, in the full implication of the phrase, too good for this world. Their sensibility becomes an end in itself, not a response to the actual issues of life. The freedom they seek turns out to be an idealized freedom; it ends, therefore, can only end, in a desire not merely to be free *in* this world but to be free *of* this world.

The popularity of James's novels among our intelligentsia today is significant too. It includes, I feel certain, not merely a genuine admiration for his extraordinary qualities, but also a powerful element of self–indulgence. It is not only pleasanter but easier to involve oneself in an idealized sensibility, a conscience[8] removed into realms outside the common and often crude basis of actual living. Many besides Isabel Archer imagine tht they can buy themselves out of the crudities through the means of a high–grade consciousness and a few thousand pounds. And Henry James, albeit unconsciously, offers a subtle encouragement. He expresses the fate of Isabel Archer but expresses it in a way that suggests that it has, if not inevitability, at least a kind of glory to it. So that when Isabel takes her decision to return to Rome the dominant sense is not of the waste and degradation of a splendid spirit, but of a kind of inverted triumph. Better death than a surrender of the illusion which the novel has so richly and magnificently and tragically illuminated.

DOROTHY VAN GHENT

On *The Portrait of a Lady*†

To go from Hardy's *Tess* to James's *The Portrait of a Lady* is to go from Stonehenge to St. Peter's and from a frozen northern turnip field, eyed hungrily by polar birds, to the Cascine gardens where nightingales sing. Though both books concern the "campaign" of a young woman—a campaign that, expressed most simply, is a campaign *to live*—a greater difference of atmosphere could scarcely be imagined nor of articulation of what it means *to live*. The gaunt arctic birds in Tess have witnessed, with their "tragical eyes," cataclysms that no human eye might see, but of which they retain no memory. The birds offer a symbol of Tess's world: a world inimical to consciousness, where one should have no memory (Tess's fatal error is to remember her own past), where the eye of the mind should remain blank, where aesthetic and moral perceptivity is traumatic. The nightingales that sing to Isabel Archer and her lover in the "grey Italian shade" also offer a symbol of a world: they are the very voice of memory, of an imperishable consciousness at once recreating and transcending its ancient, all-human knowledge. It is to the tutelage of the European memory that Isabel Archer passionately surrenders herself in her campaign *to live*, that is, to become conscious; for, in James's world, the highest affirmation of life is the development of the subtlest and most various consciousness. In doing so, she must—like the girl in the barbarous legend of

---

8. It is interesting to speculate whether Conrad, when he referred to James as "the historian of fine consciences" was using the word in its English sense or with the French implication of 'consciousness.'

† From *The English Novel: Form and Function.* Copyright 1953 by Dorothy Van Ghent. Reprinted by permission of Holt, Rinehart & Winston, Inc.

the nightingale, who, likewise in a foreign land, read an obscene crime in the weaving of a tapestry—come into knowledge of an evil which, in its own civilized kind, is as corrupting and implacable as that in the old tale. But consciousness here, as an activity nourished by knowledge, transcends the knowledge which is its content: and this too is in analogy with the ancient symbolic tale, where knowledge of evil is transcended, in the very doom of its reiteration, by the bird's immortal song.

The Portrait is not, like *Tess*, a tragedy, but it is as deeply informed with the tragic view of life: that tragic view whose essence is contained in the words, "He who loses his life shall find it," and "Except a corn of wheat fall into the ground and die, it abideth alone: but if it die, it bringeth forth much fruit." We associate tragic seriousness of import in a character's destiny with tension between the power of willing (which is "free") and the power of circumstances ("necessity") binding and limiting the will; and if either term of the tension seems lacking, seriousness of import fails. Apparently, no two authors could be at further antipodes than James and Hardy in the respective emphases they place on these terms. In Hardy, the protagonist's volition founders at every move on a universally mechanical, mysteriously hostile necessity; it is only in Tess's last acts, of blood sacrifice and renunciation of life, that her will appallingly asserts its freedom and that she gains her tragic greatness. In James's *Portrait*, and in his other novels as well, the protagonist appears to have an extraordinarily unhampered play of violition. This appearance of extraordinary freedom from the pressure of circumstances is largely due to the "immense deal of money" (the phrase is taken from an early page of *The Portrait*) with which James endows his world—for, in an acquisitive culture, money is the chief symbol of freedom. The vague rich gleams of money are on every cornice and sift through every vista of the world of *The Portrait*, like the muted gold backgrounds of old Persian illuminations; and the human correlative of the money is a type of character fully privileged with easy mobility upon the face of the earth and with magnificent opportunities for the cultivation of aesthetic and intellectual refinements. It is by visualizing with the greatest clarity the lustrously moneyed tones of the James universe that we make ourselves able to see the more clearly what grave, somber shapes of illusion and guilt he organizes in this novel. The tension between circumstances and volition, "necessity" and "freedom," is demonstrated at the uppermost levels of material opportunity where, presumably, there is most freedom and where therefore freedom becomes most threatening—and where necessity wears its most insidious disguise, the disguise of freedom.

In following the previous studies, the reader will perhaps have been impressed with the fact that the novel as a genre has shown, from *Don Quixote* on, a constant concern with the institutions created by the circulation of money and with the fantasies arising from the having of it, or, more especially, the not having it; a concern not always so direct as that of *Moll Flanders* and *Vanity Fair*, but almost inevitably implicit at least, expressed in indirect forms of aspiration and encitement to passion. As the definitively middle-class literary genre, the novel purchased its roots in a money-conscious social imagination. The wealth shining on the James world is a kind of apogee of the novel's historical concern with money, showing itself, in *The Portrait*, as a grandly sweeping postulate of possession: as if to say, "Here, now, is all the beautiful money, in the most liberating quantities: what ambition, what temptation, what errors of the will, what evil, what suffering, what salvation still denote the proclivities of the human even in a world so bountifully endowed?"

The "international myth"[1] that operates broadly in James's work, and that appears, in this novel, in the typical confrontation of American innocence and moral rigor with the tortuosities of an older civilization, gives its own and special dimension to the moneyed prospect. James came to maturity in a post-Civil War America euphoric with material achievement. In terms of the Jamesian "myth," American wealth is now able to buy up the whole museum of Europe, all its visible "point" of art objects and culture prestige, to take back home and set up in the front yard (we need look no further, for historical objectification of this aspect of the "myth," than to William Randolph Hearst's epic importation of various priceless chunks of Europe to California). If the shadows of the physically dispossessed—the sweat and the bone-weariness and the manifold anonymous deprivation in which this culture-buying power had its source—are excluded from James's money-gilded canvas, the shadow of spiritual dispossession is the somber shape under the money outline. We are not allowed to forget the aesthetic and moral impoverishment that spread its gross vacuum at the core of the American acquisitive dream—the greed, the obtuse or rapacious presumption, the disvaluation of values that kept pace to pace with material expansion. James's characteristic thematic contrasts, here as in other novels, are those of surface against depth, inspection against experience, buying power against living power, the American tourist's cultural balcony against the European abyss of history and memory and involved motive where he perilously or callously teeters. In *The Portrait*, the American heroine's pilgrimage in

1. Discussion of James's "international myth" will be found in *The Question of Henry James*, edited by F. W. Dupee (New York: Henry Holt & Company, Inc., 1945), and Philip Rahv's *Image and Idea* (New York: New Directions, 1949).

Europe becomes a fatally serious spiritual investment, an investment of the "free" self in and with the circumstantial and binding
past, a discovery of the relations of the self with history, and a
moral renovation of history in the freedom of the individual conscience. It is a growing of more delicate and deeper-reaching roots
and a nourishment of a more complex, more troubled, more creative
personal humanity. It is, in short, what is ideally meant by "civilization," as that word refers to a process that can take place in an individual.

The postulate of wealth and privilege is, in revised terms, that of
the second chapter of Genesis (the story of Adam in the garden)
—that of the optimum conditions which will leave the innocent
soul at liberty to develop its potentialities—and, as in the archetype
of the Fall of Man, the postulate is significant not as excluding
knowledge of good and evil, but as presenting a rare opportunity
for such knowledge. It is the bounty poured on Isabel Archer
(significantly, the man who gives her the symbolical investiture of
money is a man who is fatally ill; significantly, also, she is under an
illusion as to the giver) that makes her "free" to determine her
choice of action, and thus morally most responsible for her choice;
but it is the very bounty of her fortune, also, that activates at once,
as if chemically, the proclivity to evil in the world of privilege that
her wealth allows her to enter—it is her money that draws Madame
Merle and Osmond to her; so that her "freedom" is actualized as
imprisonment, in a peculiarly ashen and claustral, because peculiarly
refined, suburb of hell. Isabel's quest had, at the earliest, been a
quest for happiness—the naïvely egoistic American quest; it con-
verts into a problem of spiritual salvation, that is, into a quest of
"life"; and again the Biblical archetype shadows forth the problem.
After eating of the fruit of the tree of knowledge of good and evil,
how is one to regain access to the tree of life?

The great fairy tales and saints' legends have identified life with
knowledge. For the fairy–tale hero, the fruit of the tree of life that
is the guerdon of kingdom is the golden fleece or the golden apples
that his wicked stepmother or usurping uncle have sent him in
quest of; and to achieve the guerdon he must go through all tor-
menting knowledge—of serpents, floods, fire, ogres, enchantment,
and even of his own lusts and murderous capacities. The ordeal of
the heroes of saints' legends is also an ordeal of knowledge of evil,
and the guerdon is life. As do these ancient tales, *The Portrait* identifies life with the most probing, dangerous, responsible awareness—identifies, as it were, the two "trees," the tree of the Fall and
the tree of the Resurrection. The heroine's voluntary search for
fuller consciousness leads her, in an illusion of perfect freedom to
choose only "the best" in experience, to choose an evil; but it is this

that, by providing insight through suffering and guilt, provides also access to life—to the fructification of consciousness that is a knowledge of human bondedness. At the very end of the book, Caspar Goodwood gives passionate voice to the illusion of special privileges of choice and of a good to be had by exclusion and separateness: he says to Isabel,

> "It would be an insult to you to assume that you care for . . . the bottomless idiocy of the world. We've nothing to do with all that; we're quite out of it . . . We can do absolutely as we please; to whom under the sun do we owe anything? What is it that holds us, what is it that has the smallest right to interfere . . . ? The world's all before us—and the world's very big." [Chap. LV]

Isabel answers at random, "The world's very small." What attitude of mind takes her back to Rome, back to old evil and old servitude, is not described; we know only that she does go back. But it is evident that she does so because the "small" necessitous world has received an extension, not in the horizontal direction of imperial mobility that Caspar Goodwood suggests, but an invisible extension in depth, within her own mind—an extension into the freedom of personal renunciation and inexhaustible responsibility. The knowledge she has acquired has been tragic knowledge, but her story does not stop here, as it would if it were a tragedy—it goes on out of the pages of the book, to Rome, where we cannot follow it; for the knowledge has been the means to "life," and having learned to live, she must "live long," as she says. It is only the process of the learning that the portrait frame itself holds.

The title, *The Portrait*, asks the eye to see. And the handling of the book is in terms of seeing. The informing and strengthening of the eye of the mind is the theme—the ultimate knowledge, the thing finally "seen," having only the contingent importance of stimulating a more subtle and various activity of perception. The dramatization is deliberately "scenic," moving in a series of recognition scenes that are slight and low-keyed at first, or blurred and erroneous, in proportion both to the innocence of the heroine and others' skill in refined disguises and obliquities; then, toward the end, proceeding in swift and livid flashes. For in adopting as his compositional center the growth of a consciousness, James was able to use the bafflements and illusions of ignorance for his "complications," as he was able to use, more consistently than any other novelist, "recognitions" for his crises. Further, this action, moving through errors and illuminations of the inward eye, is set in a symbolic construct of things to be seen by the physical eye—paintings and sculptures, old coins and porcelain and lace and tapestries, most of all buildings: the aesthetic riches of Europe, pregnant with memory, with "histories within histories" of skills and motivations, temptations and suffering. The context of particulars offered to physical sight (and these may be settings, like English country houses or Roman ruins, or objects in the setting, like a porcelain cup or a piece of old lace draped on a mantel, or a person's face or a group of people—and the emphasis on the visual is most constant and notable not in these particulars, extensive as they are, but in the figurative language of the book, in metaphors using visual images as their vehicle) intensifies the meaning of "recognition" in those scenes where *sight* is *insight*, and provides a concrete embodiement of the ambiguities of "seeing."

In James's handling of the richly qualitative setting, it is characteristically significant that he suggests visual or scenic traits almost always in such a way that the emphasis in on *modulations of perception in the observer*. The "look" of things is a response of consciousness and varies with the observer; the "look" of things has thus the double duty of representing external stimuli, by indirection in their passage through consciousness, and of representing the observer himself. For instance, when Ralph takes Isabel through the picture gallery in the Touchett home, the "imperfect" but "genial" light of the bracketed lamps shows the pictures as "vague squares of rich colour," and the look of the pictures is Isabel's state at the moment—her eager and innately gifted sensibility and her almost complete ignorance, her conscious orientation toward an unknown "rich" mode of being that is beautiful but indeterminate. Let us take another example from late in the book. Directly after that conversation with Madame Merle when Isabel learns, with the full force of evil revelation, Madame Merle's part in her marriage, she goes out for a drive alone.

> She had long before this taken old Rome into her confidence, for in a world of ruins the ruin of her happiness seemed a less unnatural catastrophe. She rested her weariness upon things that had crumbled for centuries and yet still were upright; she dropped her secret sadness into the silence of lonely places, where its very modern quality detached itself and grew objective, so that as she sat in a sun-warmed angle on a winter's day, or stood in a mouldy church to which no one came, she could almost smile at it and think of its smallness. Small it was, in the large Roman record, and her haunting sense of the continuity of the human lot easily carried her from the less to the greater. She had become deeply, tenderly acquainted with Rome: it interfused and moderated her passion. But she had grown to think of it chiefly as the place where people had suffered. This was what came to her in the starved churches, where the marble columns, transferred from pagan ruins, seemed to offer her a companionship in endurance and the musty incense to be a compound of long-unanswered prayers. [Chap. XLIX]

Here the definition of visible setting—churches and marble columns and ruins, and comprehending all these, Rome—though it is full, is vague and diffuse, in the external sense of the "seen"; but in the sense that it is a setting evoked by Isabel's own deepened consciousness, it is exactly and clearly focused. It is Rome *felt*, felt as an immensity of human time, as a great human continuum of sadness and loneliness and passion and aspiration and patience; and it has this definition by virtue of Isabel's personal ordeal and her perception of its meaning. The "vague squares of rich colour" have become determinate.

The theme of "seeing" (the theme of the developing consciousness) is fertile with ironies and ambiguities that arise from the natural symbolism of the act of seeing, upon which so vastly many of human responses and decisions are dependent. The eye, as it registers surfaces, is an organ of aesthetic experience, in the etymological sense of the word "aesthetic," which is a word deriving from a Greek verb meaning "to perceive"—to perceive through the senses. James provides his world with innumerable fine surfaces for this kind of perception; it is a world endowed with the finest selective opportunities for the act of "seeing," for aesthetic cultivation. But our biological dependence upon the eye has made it a symbol of intellectual and moral and spiritual perception, forms of perception which are—by the makers of dictionaries—discriminated radically from aesthetic perception. Much of James's work is an exploration of the profound identity of the aesthetic and the moral. (In this he is at variance with the makers of dictionaries, but he has the companionship of Socrates' teacher Diotima, as her teaching is represented by Plato in the *Symposium*. Diotima taught that the way to spiritual good lay through the hierarchies of the "beautiful," that is, through graduations from one form of aesthetic experience to another.) Aesthetic experience proper, since it is acquired through the senses, is an experience of *feeling*. But so also moral experience, when it is not sheerly nominal and ritualistic, is an experience of *feeling*. Neither one has reality—has psychological depth—unless it is "felt" (hence James's so frequent use of phrases such as "felt life" and "the very *taste* of life," phrases that insist on the feeling-base of complete and integrated living). Furthermore, both aesthetic and moral experience are nonutilitarian. The first distinction that aestheticians usually make, in defining the aesthetic, is its distinction from the useful; when the aesthetic is converted to utility, it becomes something else, its value designation is different—as when a beautiful bowl becomes valuable not for its beauty but for its capacity to hold soup. So also the moral, when it is converted to utility, becomes something else than the moral—becomes even immoral, a parody of or a blasphemy against the moral life (in our richest cultural heritage, both Hellenic and Christian, the moral life is symbolically associated with utter loss of utility goods and even with loss of physical life—as in the Gospel passage, "Leave all that thou hast and follow me," or as in the career of Socrates, or as in Sophocles' *Antigone*). Moral and aesthetic experience have then in common their foundation in feeling and their distinction from the useful. The identity that James explores is their identity in the most capacious and most integrated—the most "civilized"—consciousness, whose sense relationships (aesthetic relationships) with the external world of scenes and objects have the same quality and the same spiritual determination as its relationships with people (moral relationships). But his exploration of that ideal identity involves cognizance of failed integration, cognizance of the many varieties of one-sidedness or one-eyedness or blindness that go by the name of the moral or the aesthetic, and of the destructive potentialities of the human consciousness when it is one-sided either way. His ironies revolve on the ideal concept of a spacious integrity of feeling: feeling, ideally is *one*—and there is ironic situation when feeling is split into the "moral" and the "aesthetic," each denying the other and each posing as *all*.

There is comic irony in Henrietta Stackpole's moral busybodyness as she flutters and sputters through Europe obtaining feature materials for her home-town newspaper, "featuring" largely the morally culpable un-Americanism of Europeans to serve her readers as a flattering warning against indulgence in the aesthetic. Henrietta is a stock James comedy character, and she is essential. Without Henrietta's relative incapacity to "see" more than literal surfaces, the significant contrast between surface and depth, between outward and inward "seeing," between undeveloped and developed consciousness, would lose a needed demonstration. (But let us say for Henrietta that, like Horatio in *Hamlet*, she is employed by the dramatist for as many sorts of purposes as his scenes happen to demand; when a foil of obtuseness is wanted, Henrietta is there, and when a foil of good interpretive intelligence or plain charitable generosity is wanted, Henrietta is also there. She is the type of what James technically called the *ficelle*, a wholly subordinate character immensely useful to take in confidences from the principals and to serve other functions of "relief"—"relief" in that sense in which the lower level of a relievo provides perspective for the carved projections.) In Mrs. Touchett, what appears at first as the comic irony of absolute aesthetic insensitivity accompanied by a rugged moral dogmatism ("she had a little moral account-book—with columns unerringly ruled and a sharp steel clasp—which she kept with exemplary neatness") becomes at the end of the book, with her son's death, the tragic irony of that kind of ambiguous misery which is an inability to acknowledge or realize one's own suffering, when suffering is real but the channels of feeling have become nearly atrophied by lack of use. At the midday meal, when Isabel and Mrs. Touchett come together after the night of Ralph's death,

> Isabel saw her aunt not to be so dry as she appeared, and her old pity for the poor woman's inexpressiveness, her want to regret, of disappointment, came back to her. Unmistakably she would have found it a blessing to-day to be able to feel a defeat, a mistake, even a shame or two. [Isabel] wondered if [her aunt] were not even missing those enrichments of consciousness and privately trying—reaching out for some aftertaste of life, dregs of the banquet; the testimony of pain or the cold recreation of remorse. On the other hand perhaps she was afraid; if she should begin to know remorse at all it might take her too far. Isabel could perceive, however, how it had come over her dimly that she had failed of something, that she saw herself in the future as an old woman without memories. Her little sharp face looked tragical. [Chap. LIV]

Mrs. Touchett's habitual moralistic denial of feeling as an aesthetic indulgence has left her deserted even by herself, even by her love of her son, even by memory, even by suffering. She is stranded in a morality that is tragically without meaning.

In Madame Merle and Osmond the ironies intrinsic to James's theme receive another turn. Madame Merle first appeals to Isabel's admiration by her capacity for "feeling"—for that kind of feeling to which the term "aesthetic" has been specially adapted in common modern use: feeling for the arts, the sensuous perceptivity underlying the arts, and, by extension, feeling for the finer conventions of manners as "arts of living." (Madame Merle "knew how to feel . . . This was indeed Madame Merle's great talent, her most perfect gift.") At Gardencourt, when she is not engaged in writing letters, she paints (she "made no more of brushing in a sketch than of pulling off her gloves") or she plays the piano (she "was a brave musician") or she is "employed upon wonderful tasks of rich embroidery." (The presentation is just a bit insidious, not only because of Madame Merle's so very great plasticity in going from one art to another, but also in the style of the phrases: the suggestion of conventional fluidity in the comparison of her ease in painting with the ease of "pulling off her gloves," the word "brave"—an honorific word in certain places, but carrying here the faintest note of bravado—and the word "employed," suggesting, as it reverberates, Madame Merle's not disinterested professional aestheticism.) Her senses are active and acute: walking in the English rain, she says,

> "It never wets you and it always smells good." She declared that in England the pleasures of smell were great . . . and she

used to lift the sleeve of her British overcoat and bury her nose in it, inhaling the clear, fine scent of the wool. [Chap. XIX]

Just how acute her perceptions are is shown never more clearly than in that scene in which she learns of the distribution of property after Mr. Touchett's death, occurring in Chapter XX of Volume I. Mrs. Touchett has just told her that Ralph, because of the state of his health, had hurried away from England before the reading of the will, in which Isabel had been left half of the fortune accruing to him. With this news, Madame Merle "remained thoughtful a moment, her eyes bent on the floor," and when Isabel enters the room, Madame Merle kisses her—this being "the only allusion the visitor, in her great good taste, made . . . to her young friend's inheritance." There are no other signs than these (and the episode is typical of James's minor "recognition scenes") of just how quickly and acutely Madame Merle's senses—her perception, her intuition—have functioned in apprising her of the possibilities of exploitation now opened, and in apprising her also of the fact that Ralph is the real donor of Isabel's fortune, a fact of which Isabel herself remains ignorant until Madame Merle viciously informs her. Madame Merle's feeling for situation is so subtly educated that she needs but the slightest of tokens in order to respond. And yet, with a sensitivity educated so exquisitely and working at such high tension she is morally insensible—or almost so; not quite—for, unlike Osmond, whose damnation is in ice where the moral faculty is quite frozen, she still has the spiritual capacity of those whose damnation is in fire, the capacity to know that she is damned.

Madame Merle and Osmond use their cultivated aestheticism for utility purposes—Madame Merle, to further her ambition for place and power; Osmond, to make himself separate and envied. Their debasement of the meaning of the aesthetic becomes symbolically vicious when it shows itself in their relationships with people—with Isabel, for instance, who is for them an object of virtu that differs from other objects of virtu in that it bestows money rather than costs it. This is the evil referred to by Kant in his second Categorical Imperative: the use of persons as means—an evil to which perhaps all evil human relationships reduces. In the case of Madame Merle and Osmond, it has a peculiar and blasphemous ugliness, inasmuch as the atmosphere of beauty in which they live—beauty of surroundings and of manners—represents the finest, freest product of civilization and is such, ideally, as to induce the most reverential feeling for people as well as for things. Isabel first appeals to Osmond as being "as smooth to his general need of her as handled ivory to the palm": it is an "aesthetic" image suggesting his fastidiousness but, ironically, suggesting at the same time his coarseness—for while ivory, like pearls, may be the more beautiful for handling, "handled ivory" might also be the head of a walking stick, and it is in some sort as a walking stick that he uses Isabel. An extension at the same figure, without the aesthetic and with only the utilitarian connotation, indicates Osmond's real degeneracy: Isabel finally realizes that she has been for him "an applied handled hung-up tool, as senseless and convenient as mere wood and iron." But the evil is not one that can be isolated or confined; it is automatically proliferative. Morally dead himself, incapable of reverence for the human quality in others, Osmond necessarily tries to duplicate his death in them, for it is by killing their volition that he can make them useful; dead, they are alone "beautiful." He urges upon Isabel the obscene suggestion that she, in turn, "use" Lord Warburton by exploiting Warburton's old love for herself in order to get him to marry Pansy; and Osmond can find no excuse for her refusal except that she has her private designs for "using" the Englishman. But it is in Osmond's use of Pansy, his daughter, that he is most subtly and horribly effective. He has made her into a work of art, the modeling materials being the least artful of childish qualities—her innocence and gentleness; and he has almost succeeded in reducing her will to an echo of his own. The quaint figure of Pansy, always only on the edge of scenes, is of great structural importance in the latter half of the book; for she shows the full measure of the abuse that Isabel resists, and it is to nourish in her whatever small germ of creative volition may remain—to salvage, really, a life—that Isabel returns to Rome and to Osmond's paralyzing ambiance.

The moral question that is raised by every character in the book is a question of the "amount of felt life" that each is able to experience, a question of how many and how various are the relationships each can, with integrity, enter into. Or, to put the matter in its basic metaphor, it is a question of how much each person is able to "see," and not only to see but to compose into creative order. The moral question, since it involves vision, feeling, and composition, is an aesthetic one as well. Madame Merle and Osmond are blind to certain relations: "I don't pretend to know what people are meant for," Madame Merle says, ". . . I only know what I can do with them." Mrs. Touchett is blind to certain others. Let us stop for a moment with Henrietta Stackpole's comic crudity of vision, for the "eye" is all–important, and the ranges of vision really begin with an eye like that of Henrietta. It is "a peculiarly open, surprised-looking eye." "The most striking point in her appearance was the remarkable fixedness of this organ."

She fixed her eyes on [Ralph], and there was something in their character that reminded him of large polished buttons—buttons that might have fixed the elastic loops of some tense receptacle: he seemed to see the reflection of surrounding objects on the pupil. The expression of a button is not usually deemed human, but there was something in Miss Stackpole's gaze that made him, a very modest man, feel vaguely embarrassed—less inviolate, more dishonoured, than he liked. [Chap. X]

Henrietta, with her gregariously refractive button-sight, has also "clear–cut views on most subjects . . . she knew perfectly in advance what her opinions would be." Henrietta's is the made-up consciousness, the pseudo consciousness, that is not a process but a content hopelessly once and for all given, able to refract light but not to take it in. (We can understand Henrietta's importance, caricatural as she is, by the fact that she is the primitive form of the pseudo consciousness which Madame Merle and Osmond, in their so much more sophisticated was, exhibit: theirs too is the made-up consciousness, a rigidified content, impervious and uncreative.) The Misses Molyneux, Lord Warburton's sisters, have "eyes like the balanced basins, the circles of 'ornamental water,' set, in parterres, among the geraniums." Let us note that the figure is drawn from an "aesthetic" arrangement, that of formal gardens—and in this sense has directly opposite associations to those of Henrietta's buttons (presumably very American, very *useful* buttons). The Misses Molyneux's eyes, like Henrietta's, also merely reflect surrounding objects, and reflect more limitedly, far less mobily; but the image is significant of certain kinds of feeling, of "seeing," that Henrietta is incapable of, and that have derived from ancient disciplines in human relationships—contemplative feeling, reverence, feeling for privacy and for grace. Extremely minor figures such as these, of the bottoms and the basins, are pregnant with the extraordinarily rich, extraordinarily subtle potentialities of the theme of "seeing" as an infinitely graduated cognizance of relations between self and world.

In this book, the great range of structural significance through figurative language is due to the fact that whatever image vehicle a figure may have—even when the image is not itself a visual one—the general context is so deeply and consistently characterized by acts of "seeing" that every metaphor has this other implied extension of meaning. For example, a very intricate and extensive symbolic construct is built on a metaphor of opening doors. Henrietta, Ralph says, "walks in without knocking at the door." "She's too personal," he adds. As her eyes indiscriminately take in everything that is literally to be seen, so she walks in without knocking at the door of personality: "she thinks one's door should stand ajar." The correspondence of eyes and doors lies in the publicity Henrietta assumes (she is a journalist): her eye is public like a button, and responds as if everything else were public, as if there were no doors, as if there were nothing to be seen but what the public (the Ameri-

can newspaper public) might see without effort and without discomfort. In James's thematic system of surfaces and depths, "sight"
is something achieved and not given, achieved in the loneliness of
the individual soul and in the lucidity of darkness suffered; privacy
is its necessary stamp, and it cannot be loaned or broadcast any
more than can the loneliness or the suffering. "I keep a band of
music in my ante-room," Ralph tells Isabel.

> "It has orders to play without stopping; it renders me two ex-
> cellant services. It keeps the sounds of the world from reaching
> the private apartments, and it makes the world think that danc-
> ing's going on within."

The notation has its pathos through Ralph's illness. Isabel "would
have liked to pass through the ante-room . . . and enter the private
apartments." It is only at the end, through her own revelations of
remorse and loss, that those doors open to her.

The ironic force of the mataphor of doors, as it combines with
the metaphor of "seeing," has a different direction in the crucial
scene in Chapter LI of the second volume—one of the major "recognition scenes" in the book, where Isabel sees Osmond's full
malignancy, a malignancy the more blighting as it takes, and sincerely takes, the form of honor, and where Osmond sees unequivo-
cally the vivid, mysterious resistance of a life that he has not been
able to convert into a tool. Isabel comes to tell him that Ralph is
dying and that she must go to England. She opens the door of her
husband's study without knocking.

> "Excuse me for disturbing you," she said.
> "When I come to your room I always knock," he answered
> going on with his work.
> "I forgot; I had something else to think of. My cousin's
> dying."
> "Ah, I don't believe that," said Osmond, looking at his draw-
> ing through a magnifying glass. "He was dying when we married;
> he'll outlive us all."

Osmond is here engaged in an activity representative of a man of
taste and a "collector"—he is making traced copies of ancient coins
(the fact that it is an act of tracing, of copying, has its own significance, as has the object of his attention: coins). What he "sees" in
the situation that Isabel describes to him is quite exactly what he
sees in the fact that she has opened the door without knocking; a
transgression of convention; and what he does not see is the right of
another human being to feel, to love, to will individually. Further,
what he appallingly does not see is his dependence, for the fortune
Isabel has brought him, on the selfless imagination of the dying
man, Ralph; or, even more appallingly (for one can scarcely suppose

that Madame Merle had left him ignorant of the source of Isabel's
wealth), what he does not see is any reason for the moral responsibility implied by "gratitude," a defect of vision that gives a special
and hideous bleakness to his use of the word "grateful," when he
tells Isabel that she has not been "grateful" for his tolerance of her
esteem for Ralph. The metaphor of the "doors" thus goes through
its changes, each associated with a depth or shallowness, a straightness or obliquity of vision, from Henrietta's aggressive myopia, to
Ralph's reticence and insight, to Osmond's refined conventionalism
and moral astigmatism.

Let us consider in certain other examples this reciprocity between
theme and metaphor, insight and sight, image and eye. Isabel's
native choice is creativity, a "free exploration of life," but exploration is conducted constantly—vision is amplified constantly—at the
cost of renunciations. It is in the "grey depths" of the eyes of the
elder Miss Molyneux, those eyes like the balanced basins of water
set in parterres, that Isabel recognizes what she has had to reject in
rejecting Lord Warburton: "the peace, the kindness, the honour,
the possessions, a deep security and a great exclusion." Caspar
Goodwood has eyes that "seemed to shine through the vizard of a
helmet." He appears always as an armor-man: "she saw the different fitted parts of him as she had seen, in museums and portraits,
the different fitted parts of armoured warriors—in plates of steel
handsomely inlaid with gold." "He might have ridden, on a
plunging steed, the whirlwind of a great war." The image is one of
virility, but of passion without relation, aggressive energy without
responsibility. The exclusions implied by Caspar's steel-plated
embrace are as great as those implied by the honor and the peace
that Lord Warburton offers; and yet Isabel's final refusal of Caspar
and of sexual possession is tragic, for it is to a sterile marriage that
she returns.

Architectural images, and metaphors whose vehicle (like doors
and windows) is associated with architecture, subtend the most various and complex of the book's meanings; and the reason for their
particular richness of significance seems to be that, of all forms that
are offered to sight and interpretation, builders are the most natural
symbols of civilized life, the most diverse also as to what their
fronts and interiors can imply of man's relations with himself and
with the outer world. Osmond's house in Florence has an "imposing front" of a "somewhat incommunicative character."

> It was the mask, not the face of the house. It had heavy lids, but
> no eyes; the house in reality looked another way—looked off
> behind. . . . The windows of the ground-floor, as you saw them
> from the piazza, were, in their noble proportions, extremely archi-

tectural; but their function seemed less to offer communication with the world than to defy the world to look in. [Chap. XXII]

(One notes again here the characteristic insistence on *eyes* and *looking.*) The description, perfectly fitting an old and noble Florentine villa, exactly equates with Osmond himself, and not only Isabel's first illusional impression of him—when it is his renunciatory reserve that attracts her, an appearance suggesting those "deeper rhythms of life" that she seeks—but also her later painful knowledge of the face behind the mask, which, like the house, is affected with an obliquity of vision, "looked another way—looked off behind." The interior is full of artful images; the group of people gathered there "might have been described by a painter as composing well"; even the footboy "might, tarnished as to livery and quaint as to type, have issued from some stray sketch of old-time manners, been 'put in' by the brush of a Longhi or a Goya"; the face of little Pansy is "painted" with a "fixed and intensely sweet smile." Osmond's world, contained within his eyeless house, is "sorted, sifted, arranged" for the eye; even his daughter is one of his arrangements. It is a world bred of ancient disciplines modulating through time, selection and composition, to the purest aesthetic form.

> [Isabel] carried away an image from her visit to his hill-top . . . which put on for her a particular harmony with other supposed and divined things, histories within histories . . . It spoke of the kind of personal issue that touched her most nearly; of the choice between objects, subjects, contacts—what might she call them? —of a thin and those of a rich association . . . of a care for beauty and perfection so natural and so cultivated together that the career appeared to stretch beneath it in the disposed vistas and with the ranges of steps and terraces and fountains of a formal Italian garden . . . [Chap. XXVI]

The illusion is one of a depth and spaciousness and delicacy of relationships, an illusion of the civilized consciousness.

But while Osmond's world suggests depth, it is, ironically, a world of surfaces only, for Osmond has merely borrowed it. The architectural metaphor shifts significantly in the passage (Chapter XLII) in which Isabel takes the full measure of her dwelling. "It was the house of darkness, the house of dumbness, the house of suffocation."

> She had taken all the first steps in the purest confidence, and then she had suddenly found the infinite vista of a multiplied life to be a dark, narrow alley with a dead wall at the end. Instead of leading to the high places of happiness . . . it led rather down-

ward and earthward, into realms of restriction and depression where the sound of other lives, easier and freer, was heard as from above . . .

"When she saw this rigid system close about her, draped though it was in pictured tapestries . . . she seemed shut up with an odour of mould and decay." Again the architectural image changes its shape in that passage (quoted earlier in this essay) where Isabel takes her knowledge and her sorrow into Rome, a Rome of architectural ruins. Here also are depth of human time, "histories within histories," aesthetic form, but not "arranged," not borrowable, not to be "collected"—only to be *lived* in the creative recognitions brought to them by a soul itself alive. The image that accompanies Ralph through the book—"his serenity was but the array of wild flowers niched in his ruin"—gains meaning from the architectural images so frequent in the Roman scenes (as, for instance, from this:

> [Isabel] had often ascended to those desolate ledges from which the Roman crowd used to bellow applause and where now the wild flowers . . . bloom in the deep crevices).

Whereas Osmond's forced "arrangements" of history and art and people are without racination, blighting and lifeless, Ralph's "array of wild flowers" is rooted, even if precariously rooted in a ruin; it is a life *grown*, grown in history, fertilized in the crevices of a difficult experience. The metaphor is another version of St. John's "Except a corn of wheat fall into the ground and die, it abideth alone; but if it die, it bringeth forth much fruit." Isabel, still seeking that freedom which is growth, goes back to Osmond's claustral house, for it is there, in the ruin where Pansy has been left, that she has placed roots, found a crevice in which to grow straightly and freshly, found a fertilizing, civilizing relationship between consciousness and circumstances.

WILLIAM H. GASS

The High Brutality of Good Intentions†

"Art," Yeats wrote in his essay on "The Thinking of the Body," "bids us touch and taste and hear and see the world, and shrinks from what Blake calls mathematic form, from every abstract thing, from all that is of the brain only, from all that is not a fountain jetting from the entire hopes, memories, and sensations of the body." Yet the world that we are permitted to touch and taste and hear

† From *Accent*, XVIII (Winter, 1958), 62–71. © 1958 by *Accent*. Reprinted by permission of *Accent* and the author.

and see in art, in Yeats's art as much as in any other, is not a world of pure Becoming, with the abstractions removed to a place safe only for philosophers; it is a world invested out of the ordinary with formal natures, with types and typicals, by abstractions and purest principles; invested to a degree which, in comparison with the real, renders it at times grotesque and always abnormal. It is charged with Being. Touching it provides a shock.

The advantage the creator of fiction has over the moral philosopher is that the writer is concerned with the exhibition of objects, thoughts, feelings and actions where they are free from the puzzling disorders of the real and the need to come to conclusions about them. He is subject only to those calculated disorders which are the result of his refusal, in the fact of the actual complexities of any well-chosen "case," to take a stand. The moral philosopher is expected to take a stand. He is expected to pronounce upon the principles of value. The writer of fiction, in so far as he is interested in morals, rather than, for instance, metaphysics, can satisfy himself and the requirements of his art by the exposure of moral principle in the act, an exposure more telling than life because it is, although concrete, concrete in no real way—stripped of the irrelevant, the accidental, the imcomplete—every bit of paste and hair and string part of the intrinsic nature of the article. However the moral philosopher comes by his conclusions, he does not generally suppose (unless he is also a theologian) that the world is ordered by them or that the coming together of feelings and intents or the issuance of acts or the flow of consequences, which constitute the moral facts, was designed simply in order to display them.

It is the particular achievement of Henry James that he was able to transform the moral color of his personal vision into the hues of his famous figure in the carpet; that he found a form for his awareness of moral issues, an awareness that was so pervasive it invaded furniture and walls and ornamental gardens and perched upon the shoulders of his people a dove for spirit, beating its wings with the violence of all Protestant history; so that of this feeling, of the moving wing itself, he could make a *style*. This endeavor was both aided and hindered by the fact that, for James, art and morality were so closely twined, and by the fact that no theory of either art or morality had footing unless, previous to it, the terrible difficulties of vision and knowledge, of personal construction and actual fact, of, in short, the relation of reality to appearance had been thoroughly overcome. James's style is a result of his effort to master, at the level of his craft, these difficulties, and his effort, quite apart from any measure of its actual success with these things, brought to the form of the novel in English an order of art never even, before him, envisioned by it.

Both Henry James and his brother were consumed by a form of The Moral Passion. Both struggled to find in the plural world of practice a vantage for spirit. But William was fatally enmeshed in the commercial. How well he speaks for the best in his age. He pursues the saint; he probes the spiritual disorders of the soul; he commiserates with the world–weary and encourages the strong; he investigates the nature of God, His relation to the world, His code; he defends the possible immortality of the soul and the right to believe: and does all so skillfully, with a nature so sensitive, temperate and generous, that it is deeply disappointing to discover, as one soon must, that the lenses of his mind are monetary, his open hand is open for the coin, and that the more he struggles to understand, appreciate, and rise, the more instead he misses, debases, and destroys.

> In the religion of the once-born the world is a sort of rectilinear or one-storied affair, whose accounts are kept in one denomination, whose parts have just the values which naturally they appear to have, and of which a simple algebraic sum of pluses and minuses will give the total worth. Happiness and religious peace consist in living on the plus side of the account. In the religion of the twice-born, on the other hand, the world is a double-storied mystery. Peace cannot be reached by the simple addition of pluses and elimination of minuses from life. Natural good is not simply insufficient in amount and transient, there lurks a falsity in its very being. Cancelled as it all is by death if not by earlier enemies, it gives no final balance, and can never be the thing intended for our lasting worship.[1]

Even when William, in a passage not obviously composed with the bookkeeper's pen, makes a literary allusion, as here:

> Like the single drops which sparkle in the sun as they are flung far ahead of the advancing edge of a wave-crest or of a flood, they show the way and are forerunners. The world is not yet with them, so they often seem in the midst of the world's affairs to be preposterous . . .[2]

it turns out to be a covert reference to "getting and spending."

Henry James was certainly aware that one is always on the market, but as he grew as an artist he grew as a moralist and his use of the commercial matrix of analogy[3] became markedly satirical or

1. William James, *The Varieties of Religious Experience*, Modern Library, New York, p. 163. God does a wholesale not a retail business, p. 484. The world is a banking house, p. 120. Catholic confession is a method of periodically auditing and squaring accounts, p. 126. Examples could be multiplied endlessly, not only in *The Varieties* but in all his work. In *The Varieties* alone consult pages: 28, 38, 39, 133, 134, 135, 138, 330, 331, 333, 340, 347, 429fn, 481, 842.

2. *Ibid.*, p. 450.

3. Mark Schorer's expression, "Fiction and the Matrix of Analogy," *The Kenyon Review*, XI, No. 4 (1949). The commercial metaphor pervades James's work and has been remarked so frequently that it scarcely requires documentation.

ironic and his investigation of the human trade more self–conscious and profound until in nearly all the works of his maturity his theme is the evil of human manipulation, a theme best summarized by the second formulation of Kant's categorical imperative:

> So act as to treat humanity, whether in thine own person or in that of any other, in every case as an end withal, never as a means only.

Nothing further from pragmatism can be imagined, and if we first entertain the aphorism that though William was the superior thinker, Henry had the superior thought, we may be led to consider the final effect of their rivalry,[4] for the novels and stories of Henry James constitute the most searching criticism available of the pragmatic ideal of the proper treatment and ultimate worth of man. That this criticism was embodied in Henry James's style, William James was one of the first to recognize. "Your methods and my ideals seem the reverse, the one of the other," he wrote to Henry in a letter complaining about the "interminable elaboration" of *The Golden Bowl*. Couldn't we have, he asks, a "book with no twilight or mustiness in the plot, with great vigour and decisiveness in the action, no fencing in the dialogue, no psychological commentaries, and absolute straightness in the style?"[5] Henry would rather have gone, he replies, to a dishonored grave.

The Portrait of a Lady is James's first fully exposed case of human manipulation; his first full-dress investigation, at the level of what Plato called "right opinion," of what it means to be a consumer of persons, and of what it means to be a person consumed. The population of James's fictional society is composed, as populations commonly are, of purchasers and their purchases, of the handlers and the handled, of the users and the used. Sometimes actual objects, like Mrs. Gereth's spoils, are involved in the transaction, but their involvement is symbolic of a buying and a being sold which is on the level of human worth (where the quality of the product is measured in terms of its responsiveness to the purchaser's "finest feelings," and its ability to sound the buyer's taste discreetly aloud), and it is for this reason that James never chooses to center his interest upon objects which can, by use, be visibly consumed. In nearly all of the later novels and stories, it is a human being, not an object, it is first Isabel Archer, then Pansy, who is the spoil, and it is by no means true that only the "villains" fall upon her and try to carry her off; nor is it easy to discover just who the villains really are.

Kant's imperative governs by its absence—as the hollow center. It

4. Leon Edel develops this theme in the first volume of his biography, *Henry James: The Untried Years, 1834–1870*.

5. Quoted by R. B. Perry, *The Thought and Character of William James*, 2 vols., Boston (1935), Vol. I, p. 424.

is not that some characters, the "good" people, are busy being the moral legislators of mankind and that the others, the "bad" people, are committed to a crass and shallow pragmatism or a trifling estheticism; for were that the case *The Portrait* would be jsut another skillful novel of manners and James would be distinctly visible, outside the work, nodding or shaking his head at the behavior of the animals in his moral fable. He would have managed no advance in the art of English fiction. James's examination of the methods of human consumption goes too deep. He is concerned with all of the ways in which men may be reduced to the status of objects and because James pursues his subject so diligently, satisfying himself only when he has unravelled every thread, and because he is so intent on avoiding in himself what he has revealed as evil in his characters and exemplifying rather what he praises in Hawthorne who, he says, "never intermeddled,"[6] the moral problem of *The Portrait* becomes an esthetic problem, a problem of form, the scope and course of the action, the nature of the characters, the content of dialogue, the shape and dress of setting, the points-of-view, the figures of speech, the very turn and tumble of the sentences themselves directed by the problem's looked-for solution, and there is consequently no suggestion that one should choose up sides or take to heart his criticism of a certain society nor any invitation to discuss the moral motivations of his characters *as if* they were surrogates for the real.

The moral problem, moreover, merges with the esthetic. It is possible to be an artist, James sees, in more than paint and language, and in *The Portrait*, as it is so often in his other work, Isabel Archer becomes the unworked medium through which, like benevolent Svengali, the shapes and admirers of beautifully brought out persons express their artistry and themselves. The result is very often lovely, but it is invariably sad. James has the feeling, furthemore, and it is a distinctly magical feeling, that the novelist takes possession of his subject through his words; that the artist is a puppeteer; his works are the works of a god. He constantly endeavors to shift the obligation and the blame, if there be any, to another: his reflector, his reverberator, his sensitive gong. In *The Portrait* James begins his movement toward the theory of the point-of-view. The phrase itself occurs incessantly. Its acceptance as a canon of method means the loss of a single, universally objective reality. He is committed, henceforth, to a standpoint philosophy, and it would seem, then, that the best world would be that observed from the most sensitive, catholic, yet discriminating standpoint. In this way, the esthetic problem reaches out to the metaphysical. This marvelous

6. *The American Essays of Henry James,* (1956), "Nathaniel Hawthorne," p. 23. ed. by Leon Edel, Vintage, New York

observer: what is it he observes? Does he see the world as it really is, palpitating with delicious signs of the internal, or does he merely fling out the self-capturing net? James struggles with this question most obviously in *The Sacred Fount* but it is always before him. So many of his characters are "perceptive." They understand the value of the unmolded clay. They feel they know, as artists, what will be best for their human medium. They will *take up* the young lady (for so it usually is). They will *bring* her *out*. They will do for her; *make something* of her. She will be *beautiful* and *fine*, in short, she will inspire *interest, amusement,* and *wonder*. And their pursuit of the ideally refractive medium parallels perfectly Henry James's own, except he is aware that his selected lens dare not be perfect else he will have embodied a god again, and far more obnoxious must this god seem in the body of a character than he did in the nib of the author's pen; but more than this, James knows, as his creations so often do not, that this manipulation is the essence, the ultimate germ, of the evil the whole of his work condemns, and it is nowhere more brutal than when fronted by the kindest regard and backed by a benevolent will.

The Portrait of a Lady, for one who is familiar with James, opens on rich sounds. None of his major motifs is missing. The talk at tea provides us with five, the composition of the company constitutes a sixth, and his treatment of the setting satisfies the full and holy seven. The talk moves in a desultory fashion ("desultory" is the repetitive word) and in joking tones ("That's a sort of joke" is the repetitive phrase) from health and illness, and the ambiguity of its value, to boredom, considered as a kind of sickness, and the ambiguity of its production.[7] Wealth is suggested as a cause of boredom, then marriage is proposed as a cure. The elder Touchett warns Lord Warburton not to fall in love with his niece, a young lady recently captured by his wife to be exhibited abroad. The questions about her are: has she money? is she interesting? The jokes are: is she marriageable? is she engaged? Isabel is the fifth thing, then—the young, spirited material. Lord Warburton is English, of course, while the Touchetts are Americans. Isabel's coming will sharpen the contrast, dramatize the confrontation. Lastly, James dwells lovingly on the ancient red brick house, emphasizing its esthetic appeal, its traditions, its status as a work of art. In describing the grounds he indicates, too, what an American man of money may do: fall in love with a history not his own and allow it, slowly, to civilize him, draw him into Europe. Lord Warburton is said to be bored. It is suggested that he is trying to fall in love. Ralph is described as cynical, without belief, a condition ascribed to his illness by his father.

7. Illness, in James's novels, either signifies the beautiful thing (the Minny Temple theme) or it provides the excuse for spectatorship and withdrawal, the opportunity to develop the esthetic sense (the Henry James theme).

"He seems to feel as if he had never had a chance." But the best of the ladies will save us, the elder Touchett says, a remark made improbable by his own lack of success.

The structure of the talk of this astonishing first chapter foreshadows everything. All jests turn earnest, and in them, as in the aimless pattern of the jesters' leisure, lies plain the essential evil, for the evil cannot be blinked even though it may not be so immediately irritating to the eye as the evil of Madame Merle or Gilbert Osmond. There is in Isabel herself a certain willingness to be employed, a desire to be taken up and fancied, if only because that very enslavement, on other terms, makes her more free. She refuses Warburton, not because he seeks his own salvation in her, his cure by "interest," but rather because marriage to him would not satisfy her greed for experience, her freedom to see and feel and do. Neither Warburton nor Goodwood appeals as a person to Isabel's vanity. She is a great subject. She will make a great portrait. She knows it. Nevertheless Isabel's ambitions are at first naive and inarticulate. It is Ralph who sees the chance, in her, for the really fine thing; who sees in her his own chance, too, the chance at life denied him. It is Ralph, finally, who empowers her flight and in doing so draws the attention of the hunters.

Ralph and Osmond represent two types of the artist. Osmond regards Isabel as an opportunity to create a work which will flatter himself and be the best testimony to his taste. Her intelligence is a silver plate he will heap with fruits to decorate his table. Her talk will be for him "a sort of served dessert." He will rap her with his knuckle. She will ring. As Osmond's wife, Isabel recognizes that she is a piece of property; her mind is attached to his like a small garden–plot to a deer park. But Ralph obeys the strictures *The Art of Fiction* was later to lay down. He works rather with the medium itself and respects the given. His desire is to exhibit it, make it whole, refulgent, round. He wants, in short, to make an image or to see one made—a portrait. He demands of the work only that it be "interesting." He effaces himself. The "case" is his concern. *The Portrait's* crucial scene, in this regard, is that between Ralph and his dying father. Ralph cannot love Isabel. His illness prevents him. He feels it would be wrong. Nevertheless, he takes, he says, "a great interest" in his cousin although he has no real influence over her.

> "But I should like to do something for her . . . I should like to put a little wind in her sails . . . I should like to put it into her power to do some of the things she wants. She wants to see the world for instance. I should like to put money in her purse."

The language is unmistakable. It is the language of Iago. Ralph wants her rich.

"I call people rich when they're able to meet the requirements of their imagination. Isabel has a great deal of imagination."

With money she will not have to marry for it. Money will make her free. It is a curious faith. Mr. Touchett says, "You speak as if it were for your mere amusement," and Ralph replies, "So it is, a good deal." Mr. Touchett's objections are serenely met. Isabel will be extravagant but she will come to her senses in time. And, Ralph says,

". . . it would be very painful to me to think of her coming to the consciousness of a lot of wants she should be unable to satisfy. . . ."

"Well, I don't know . . . I don't think I enter into your spirit. It seems to me immoral."

"Immoral, dear daddy?"

"Well, I don't know that it's right to make everything so easy for a person."[8]

"It surely depends upon the person. When the person's good, your making things easy is all to the credit of virtue. To facilitate the execution of good impulses, what can be a nobler act? . . ."

"Isabel's a sweet young thing; but do you think she's so good as that?"

"She's as good as her best opportunities . . ."

"Doesn't it occur to you that a young lady with sixty thousand pounds may fall a victim to the fortune-hunters?"

"She'll hardly fall a victim to more than one."

"Well, one's too many."

"Decidedly. That's a risk, and it has entered into my calculation. I think it's appreciable, but I think it's small, and I'm prepared to take it . . ."

"But I don't see what good you're to get of it. . . ."

"I shall get just the good I said a few moments ago I wished to put into Isabel's reach—that of having met the requirements of my imagination. . . ."

The differences between Gilbert Osmond and Ralph Touchett are vast, but they are also thin.

Isabel Archer is thus free to try her wings. She is thrown upon the world. She becomes the friend of Madame Merle, "the great round world herself": polished, perfect, beautiful without a fault, mysterious, exciting, treacherous, repellent, and at bottom, like Isabel, identically betrayed; like Isabel again, seeking out of her own ruin to protect Pansy, the new subject, "the blank page," from that same round world that is herself. It is irony of the profoundest sort

8. A remark characteristic of the self-made man. In the first chapter, Mr. Touchett attributes Warburton's "boredom" to idleness. "You wouldn't be bored if you had something to do; but all you young men are too idle. You think too much of your pleasure. You're too fastidious, and too indolent, and too rich." Caspar Goodwood is the industrious suitor.

712 · *William H. Gass*

that "good" and "evil" in their paths should pass so closely. The dark ambitions of Serena Merle are lightened by a pathetic bulb, and it is only those whose eyes are fascinated and convinced by surface who can put their confident finger on the "really good." Ralph Touchett, and we are not meant to miss the appropriateness of his name, has not only failed to respect Isabel Archer as an end, he has failed to calculate correctly the qualities of his object. Isabel is a sweet, young thing. She is not yet, at any rate, as good as her best opportunities. The sensitive eye was at the acute point blind. Ralph has unwittingly put his bird in a cage. In a later interview, Isabel tells him she has given up all desire for a general view of life. Now she prefers corners. It is a corner she's been driven to. Time after time the "better" people curse the future they wish to save with their bequests. Longdon of *The Awkward Age* and Milly Theale of *The Wings of the Dove* come immediately to mind. Time after time the better artists fail because their point-of-view is ultimately only *theirs*, and because they have brought the esthetic relation too grandly, too completely into life.

In the portrait of Fleda Vetch of *The Spoils of Poynton* James has rendered an ideally considerate soul. Fleda, a person of modest means and background, possesses nevertheless the true sense of beauty. She is drawn by her friend Mrs. Gereth into the full exercise of that sense and to an appreciation of the ripe contemplative life which otherwise might have been denied her. Yet Fleda so little awards the palm to mere cleverness or sensibility that she falls in love with the slow, confused, and indecisive Owen Gereth. Fleda furthermore separates her moral and her esthetic ideals. Not only does she refuse to manipulate others, she refuses, herself, to be manipulated. The moral lines she feels are delicate. She takes all into her hands. Everyone has absolute worth. Scruples beset and surround her and not even Mrs. Gereth's righteousness, the warmth of her remembered wrongs, can melt them through. The impatience which James generates in the reader and expresses through Mrs. Gereth is the impatience, precisely, of his brother: for Fleda to act, to break from the net of scruple and seize the chance. It would be for the good of the good. It would save the spoils, save Owen, save Mrs. Gereth, save love for herself; but Fleda Vetch understands, as few people in Henry James ever do, the high brutality of such good intentions. She cannot accept happiness on the condition of moral compromise, for that would be to betray the ground on which, ideally, happiness ought to rest. Indeed it would betray happiness itself, and love, and the people and their possessions that have precipitated the problem and suggested the attractive and fatal price.

It is not simply in the organization of character, dialogue, and action that Henry James reveals The Moral Passion, nor is it reflected further only in his treatment of surroundings[9] but it represents itself and its ideal in the increasing scrupulosity of the style: precision of definition, respect for nuance, tone, the multiplying presence of enveloping metaphors, the winding around the tender center of ritual lines, like the approach of the devout and worshipful to the altar, these circumlocutions at once protecting the subject and slowing the advance so that the mere utility of the core is despaired of and it is valued solely in the contemplative sight. The value of life lies ultimately in the experienced quality of it, in the integrity of the given not in the usefulness of the taken. Henry James does not peer through experience to the future, through this future to the future futures, endlessly down the infinite tube. He does not find in today only what is needful for tomorrow. His aim is rather to appreciate and to respect the things of his experience and to set them, finally, free.

DOROTHEA KROOK

The Portrait of a Lady †

Reviewing the genesis of *The Portrait of a Lady* in his Preface to the New York edition, James recalls that it was produced in those early years of his life in London when to his dazzled sense the 'international light' lay especially 'thick and rich upon the scene'. Written when James was at the height of his powers in his early, 'direct' mode, *The Portrait of a Lady* may indeed be taken as his grand definitive statement of the international theme in that mode, which he was to surpass only in the great works of his later period, *The Ambassadors*, *The Wings of the Dove* and *The Golden Bowl*; and since in *The Portrait* (James tells us) it is 'the light in which so much of the picture hung', it is virtually as important as the picture and will be treated accordingly.

In the picture itself, however, the richest element is the 'engaging young woman', Isabel Archer; and in the same Preface James firmly directs our attention to her as the centre of interest in his story. She was the 'seed' from which the story sprang, the seminal 'idea entertained' which carries its own 'lurking forces of expansion', its own 'necessities of upspringing' and 'beautiful determinations . . . to

9. When, for instance, in *The Portrait* Gilbert Osmond proposed to Isabel, the furnishings of the room in which their talk takes place seem to Osmond himself "ugly to distress" and "the false colours, the sham splendour . . . like vulgar, bragging, lying talk"—an obvious commentary by the setting on the action.
† From *The Ordeal of Consciousness in Henry James* (New York: Cambridge University Press, 1962), pp. 26–27; 39–60. Reprinted by permission of the author and the publisher.

grow as tall as possible, to push into the light and air and thickly flower there'. For the novelist—for a James as for a Turgenev—she was one of those persons 'who hovered before him, soliciting him, . . . interesting him, and appealing to him just as they were and by what they were'; and once thus ensnared, the novelist was left but with one task, namely, 'to find for them the right relations, those that will most bring them out; to imagine, to invent and select and piece together the situations most useful and favourable to the sense of the creatures themselves, the complications they would be most likely to produce and to feel'. Isabel Archer accordingly is brought out in three principal relations: first, her relation with Lord Warburton, her very upperclass English suitor; next with Caspar Goodwood, her very provincial American suitor; and, last, with Gilbert Osmond, the cosmopolitan American whom she finally marries. Of these the last is the most important for the main tragic theme of the story, and is the most profoundly explored and most fully exhibited. But all three are equally important for James's international theme; and each on its own scale is a masterpiece of the novelist's art.

* * *

Osmond is * * * an American by birth, who having lived in Europe since childhood is completely Europeanised; like Charlotte Stant in *The Golden Bowl*, he is a classic case of the Jamesian expatriate, deracinate American. He lives now with his young daughter Pansy in a charming villa on a hill just outside Florence. The villa is exquisitely appointed, and filled with *objets d'art* of a quality which cannot fail to proclaim Gilbert Osmond to be a man of unusually cultivated taste even in a community in which taste is not as rare as elsewhere. For Isabel Archer, however, he is more than merely a man of cultivated taste. He is poor; he is solitary; he is handsome, in the finest, least obtrusive way. He is grave and somewhat sombre, yet with an effect not at all depressing but only intriguing. He has evidently suffered, and this has left scars, but the scars are not disfiguring. And, above everything, he has personal distinction of a kind and in a degree overwhelming to her.

This is evident in every detail of his bearing, his manners, his conversation, his conduct; and it is this, more than anything, that makes him for Isabel the first really *interesting* man she has known. It is not until she meets Gilbert Osmond that she perceives how fundamentally uninteresting were the other men she had known— Lord Warburton, Cousin Ralph, Caspar Goodwood. For Osmond is not merely clever, witty and good-natured like Cousin Ralph Touchett. He is not merely well-bred, decent and kind like Lord Warburton; and he is not, like Caspar Goodwood, 'too serious'—serious, that is, in a way incompatible with being also 'a delightful person'. He does not, like poor Caspar Goodwood, 'show his appetites and designs too simply and artlessly': on the contrary (Isabel notes, we may imagine, with inexpressible pleasure and relief), he shows them either not at all, or with the utmost restraint—with the finest delicacy of consideration (as Isabel sees it) for the feelings of other people. He is all too evidently a man who is easily bored; but he appears not to find Isabel Archer boring. On the contrary, he finds her 'interesting': not, in the first instance, we are meant to note, enchanting or adorable or irresistible, but interesting; and he expresses this interest from the start in a way that entirely meets her conception of the way in which a man of cultivated mind and developed sensibility should express his interest in a woman. So here, at last, in the person of Gilbert Osmond, is a man who—to adopt Ralph Touchett's formula—satisfies the requirements of Isabel Archer's imagination.

There are numerous passages in this part of the book, all too long to quote, in which James renders for us the exact quality of Osmond's enchantment for Isabel. The following short passage, however, shows it admirably enough, with the aesthetic aspect of Isabel's view of Osmond properly emphasised:

> Isabel though him interesting—she came back to that; she liked so to think of him. She had carried away an image from her visit to his hill-top which her subsequent knowledge of him did nothing to efface and which put on for her a particular harmony with other supposed and divined things, histories within histories: the image of a quiet, clever, sensitive, distinguished man, strolling on a moss-grown terrace above the sweet Val d'Arno and holding by the hand a little girl whose bell-like clearness gave a new grace to childhood. The picture had no flourishes, but she liked its lowness of tone and the atmosphere of summer twilight that pervaded it. [Chap. XXVI]

Their friendship develops and Osmond confides in her little by little the story of his life. He tells her of the death of his wife, of whom he says little—which Isabel takes as a mark of his habitual restraint about matters that have affected him deeply. He speaks of his devotion to Pansy, his young daughter; speaks little of his poverty, though it is evident to Isabel that he finds it oppressive; and speaks much of Italy and art and literature in a way that Isabel of course finds enchanting but also peculiarly touching: what touches her is his noble contentment, as she sees it, in the pursuit of his cultivated tastes—in spite of the poverty that forces him to pursue them on a scale so gallingly modest.

And so Isabel Archer (like Desdemona) comes more and more to love him for for the dangers he has passed, and he in his own way comes to love her that she does pity them. Their courtship proceeds; and against the wishes of her family and friends—chiefly, those of her Aunt Touchett, who expresses her dislike of Osmond with characteristic emphasis, but also against the advice of her cousin Ralph and her friend Henrietta, who both come to Rome for the express purpose of dissuading her from the marriage—Isabel becomes engaged to Gilbert Osmond, and in due course they marry.

At this point it may be useful to set out explicitly Isabel Archer's principal reasons for choosing to marry Gilbert Osmond. For in view of what happens to the marriage, it is important that these reasons should be 'good' or 'creditable' enough to save Isabel from being condemned as a mere simpleton who deserves what she gets for being such a fool as to marry a man like Osmond. Nor is it merely gratuitous to urge that these reasons *are* sufficiently good or creditable, since this very point has been disputed by some modern critics of *The Portrait of a Lady*: who have seen in Isabel Archer nothing but a half-educated American girl with a head stuffed full of sentimental nonsense about life and art and Europe and gracious living—the sort of 'sentimental idealism' which, as everyone knows, is the weaker side of the American national character, and therefore needs to be exposed rather than condoned as (according to these critics) James condones it in *The Portrait of a Lady*.

To take this view is, of course, to drain the whole central relationship of the book of its tragic meaning, and *a fortiori* to diminish almost out of existence Isabel Archer's stature as a tragic heroine. It is accordingly important for those who believe that this central relationship *is* tragic in the fullest sense of the word to establish the moral sufficiency of the reasons that led Isabel Archer to enter into her tragically disastrous marriage.

It has already been noted that what pre-eminently draws Isabel to Osmond is his sovereign personal distinction—the single quality that for her subsumes all his other qualities. But to this power of his to satisfy the requirements of her imagination must be added two vital elements of her own nature. The first is her ardent desire to develop her mind and her sensibilities: her need, that is, to give direction and form to her vague aspiration after knowledge and virtue—'experience' in the largest, noblest sense of the word. This, James desires us to understand, is one of the most engaging characteristics of his engaging young woman Isabel Archer; and for the reason chiefly that it argues the presence of that intellectual energy and moral spontaneity, so lamentably lacking in the English and Europeans, which James had already remarked as one of the most inspiring features of the American national character.

To take this view of Isabel Archer's American 'idealism' help us to understand, among other things, what James is referring to in a frequently misunderstood passage in the Preface in which he speaks of Isabel's *presumption*. The word is used, I believe, with an irony

at once comic and tragic, and in both aspects with a mitigating tenderness. The comic emphasis lies nearest the surface. It is to be
detected in the many references to the vanity, self-centredness, even
arrogance of his engaging young woman, which James exposes with
so much pleasant wit in the earlier portions of the book. Even here,
however, the irony is not directed so much against the vanity, self-
centredness, arrogance as such, but is intended rather to diect our
amused attention to the perpetual struggle in Isabel between these
frailties of her all too feminine nature and the high moral principles
to which she is, both by temperament and training, wholeheartedly
committed. The struggle is genuine and equal because both sides
are equally real and powerful: in Henry James's view of man's nature
we will not find a trace of the shallow realism which proceeds on
the axiom that the baser elements in a human soul are always more
real because more base; and its interest and amusement for us is
precisely in the fact that it is exhibited as so thoroughly equal.

In its more serious aspect, Isabel Archer's 'presumption' may be
seen as the natural concomitant of her passionate desire to grow in
knowledge and virtue in a society which holds both in small esteem.
It appears presumptuous to those around her (that is what *they*
would call it, James is saying) because they are themselves so little
moved by any passion of this kind, and can therefore barely recognise it for what it is; and the tenderness of James's irony is accordingly for all that is beautiful and noble in his heroine's spirit, and
the irony itself for what she will have to suffer for being what she is
in the society in which she find herself.

But besides this, the irony has still another, deeper meaning. It
suggests, first, that this kind of 'presumption' belongs inescapably to
every genuinely adventurous, enquiring, questing mind—is in fact
almost only another name for these admirable qualities; and,
second, that it is the more dangerous for being a part of something
essentially good and noble. Knowledge puffeth up, warned St. Paul,
meaning that knowledge need not but, alas, too often does make a
man proud, vainglorious, 'presumptuous'; and for a young person
especially (James, particularising Paul's wisdom, tells us) it is
difficult not to feel the kind of pride or 'vainglory' in her growing
knowledge which is, or may be, inimical to the soul's health. So
Isabel Archer's love of appearances struggles with her love of truth
and reality, and her disinterested passion for knowledge with her
sense of personal power in the acquisition of it; and all this too is
exhibited in those opening portions of the book with an irony
equally penetrating and tender.

This is a theme that James is to return to, sometimes again with
the comic emphasis, more often after *The Portrait of a Lady* with
the tragic—this profound spiritual dilemma, shared by some of his
most highly developed vessels of consciousness, arising from the co-

presence in them of the creative passion for knowledge, which makes them the beloved of the gods, and the destructive pride this same passion generates, which is likely to put them if they are not very careful straight into the hands of the devil. *The Aspern Papers*, *The Sacred Fount* and *The Turn of the Screw* are among the works in which this theme is most prominent; indeed, in the last two it is the very heart of the moral fable. But it is present also, though not so prominently, in the story of Hyacinth Robinson in *The Princess Casamassima*, of Fleda Vetch in *The Spoils of Poynton*, Nanda Brookenham in *The Awkward Age*, Milly Theale in *The Wings of the Dove*. And in all these stories, as in *The Portrait of a Lady*, the destructive element is always and insistently shown as the obverse side of a nature essentially good—essentially generous, passionate and disinterested. 'I don't believe that such a generous mistake as yours can hurt you for more than a little', says Ralph Touchett almost with his last breath to his weeping cousin Isabel as she kneels by his bedside at Gardencourt a few hours before his death. [Chap. LIV] This may be taken as an epigraph for most of James's stories about the 'presumption' of his finest vessels of consciousness, from Isabel Archer and the governess in *The Turn of the Screw* to Milly Theale and Maggie Verver. It is the generosity of the mistake that in each instance redeems it, always gloriously, even when its visible consequences are deprivation or death.

Returning to Isabel's reasons for marrying Gilbert Osmond; the first, as we saw, is her ardent desire to enlarge and enrich her experience of life, to grow in wisdom and virtue under the guidance of this most superior of men. The second is her desire, equally ardent, to serve. More specifically, it is the desire to do something with her money that will be at once useful and imaginative; most specifically, to use her money in the service of someone she loves. These are the two fundamental needs of her nature; and in Gilbert Osmond she believes she has found someone who will satisfy both. Osmond, she believes, is a man to whom her fortune will be of real service, whose enjoyment of it she can intimately share. At the same time (she also believes) he is a man who in his turn will share her desire for self-development, and by virtue of his superior gifts and accomplishments will contribute everything in the world to the enlargement of her mind, the refinement of her sensibilities, indeed to the extension—the most splendid extension imaginable—of her life's experience. Thus by adding to the attraction of Osmond's great personal distinction these two conditions of her own nature, her desire for self-development and her desire to serve, and to these again her certainty that Osmond, supremely, will meet these needs of her nature, we arrive at a reasonably complete view of Isabel Archer's motives for marrying Gilbert Osmond. And if these can be seen as 'creditable', that is, as motives that could prevail only with an essentially noble nature, the tragic impact of the catastrophe that follows is ensured.

We do not meet Isabel and Osmond again until three years later; and this second part of the story opens with a memorable scene in the Osmonds' grand house in Rome, at one of Mrs. Osmond's Thursday evening receptions. A young American named Rosier, who is in love with Pansy Osmond, now aged nineteen, and wishes to marry her, has learnt from Madame Merle that her father will not hear of the suit. Determined to seek Mrs. Osmond's assistance, young Rosier goes to the Osmonds' house, and on entering the first *salon*, which is already full of people, sees Pansy's father standing by the fire and goes up to him to pay his respects.

This is our first view of Osmond since the time, three years back, when he and Isabel were wandering the streets of Rome full to the brim with their happiness in each other: when Gilbert Osmond saw Isabel as the most charming and graceful woman he had ever known, and Isabel felt that 'she had never known a person of so fine a grain' as Gilbert Osmond. It is this same Osmond whom young Rosier now approaches; and in the brief colloquy that follows, we have vividly suggested to us the appalling difference between the man Isabel had fallen in love with and the man she is now married to.

Osmond stood before the chimney, leaning back with his hands behind him; he had one foot up and was warming the sole. Half a dozen persons, scattered near him, were talking together; but he was not in the conversation; his eyes had an expression, frequent with him, that seemed to represent them as engaged with objects more worth their while than the appearances actually thrust upon them. . . .

Rosier goes up to him:

Osmond put out his left hand, without changing his attitude. 'How d'ye do? My wife's somewhere about.'

'Never fear; I shall find her', said Rosier cheerfully.

Osmond, however, took him in; he had never in his life felt himself so efficiently looked at. 'Madame Merle has told him, and he doesn't like it', he privately reasoned. . . . He had never especially delighted in Gilbert Osmond, having a fancy he gave himself airs. But Rosier was not quickly resentful, and where politeness was concerned had ever a strong need of being quite in the right. He looked round him and smiled, all without help, and then in a moment, 'I saw a jolly good piece of Capo di Monte to-day', he said.

Osmond answered nothing at first; but presently while he warmed his boot-sole, 'I don't care a fig for Capo di Monte!' he returned.

'I hope you're not losing your interest?'

'In old pots and plates? Yes, I'm losing my interest.'

Rosier for an instant forgot the delicacy of his position.

'You're not thinking of parting with a—a piece or two?'

'No, I'm not thinking of parting with anything at all, Mr. Rosier', said Osmond, with his eyes still on the eyes of his visitor.

'Ah, you want to keep, but not to add', Rosier remarked brightly.

'Exactly. I've nothing I wish to match.'

Poor Rosier was aware he had blushed; he was distressed at his want of assurance. 'Ah, well, *I* have', was all he could murmur; and he knew his murmur was partly lost as he turned away. [Chap. XXXVII]

This is how James gives us Gilbert Osmond in his new character; and it is not often that a novelist succeeds in suggesting so much by means so simple and economical. All the strokes in this short scene are characteristically light and unemphatic; but they are brilliantly sufficient to administer a shock of apprehension and foreboding. There is something in the posture of the man, standing before the chimney with one foot up warming the sole of his boot, in the gesture with which extends his left hand to the young man, in the 'dry impertinence' (as the young man is afterwards to name it to himself) of his remarks and rejoinders—something which shows us Gilbert Osmond in a light disconcertingly different from that in which we last saw him. What we receive from this new glimpse of Osmond is a clear intimation of some portentous, calamitous alteration in the relationship upon which our attention is focused. Osmond, astonishingly, now gives the impression of being coarse; and brutal, or at least brutalised; and cold and ruthless: in every way, in short, not 'a delightful person'. And if he is all this, he is appallingly unlike the man Isabel Archer had thought she was marrying; and if he is not what Isabel thought he was, what is he; and what has happened—to him, to her, to the marriage?

This is the effect upon the reader of that brief, brilliant opening scene between Osmond and young Rosier. From this point, we are launched into the second half of the story, which discloses to us exactly what has happened and how it happened, and culminates (though it does not end there) in Isabel's great midnight meditation when she sits before the dying fire of her sitting-room and reviews her whole relationship with her husband. In this meditative vigil [Chap. XLII] which is in effect a long and intense interior monologue, Isabel discloses the reasons for the failure of her marriage, and this accordingly calls for the closest attention if we are to understand fully the principal tragic relationship of the book.[1]

1. It is worth noting that James himself thought this interior monologue 'ob- viously the best thing in the book' (*The Portrait of a Lady*, Preface).

What first emerges from Isabel's analysis of the failure of her marriage is the real character of Gilbert Osmond. He has indeed turned out to be a man very different from Isabel's first conception of him. He has indeed turned out to be a brute: morally coarse, to the last fibre; cold-hearted; appallingly egotistical; and capable of acts of calculated violence—'mental cruelty', as it is now technically called—that have a power to terrify far exceeding that of mere physical acts of violence. This is the man in whom Isabel Archer had believed herself to see the perfection of delicate feeling and moral refinement; and what makes the disclosure of his real character so terrible is, of course, the betrayal it implies of Isabel's trust and love: of her trust in his goodness upon which her love had been founded; and of all her dearest hopes of self-fulfilment through love and service of the man who had thus betrayed her.

The knowledge of how completely and cruelly she has been deceived induces in her condition of utter wretchedness—a dry-eyed misery of despair (we are told)—which is most poignantly conveyed in certain passages of the midnight meditation. Before their marriage, she recalls,

> He had told her he loved the conventional; but there was a sense in which this seemed a noble declaration. In that sense, that of the love of harmony and order and decency and of all the stately offices of life, she went with him freely, and his warning had contained nothing ominous. But when, as the months had elapsed, she had followed him further and he had led her into the mansion of his own habitation, then, *then* she had seen where she really was.
>
> She could live it over again, the incredulous terror with which she had taken the measure of her dwelling. Between those four walls she had lived ever since; they were to surround her for the rest of her life. It was the house of darkness, the house of dumbness, the house of suffocation. Osmond's beautiful mind gave it neither light nor air; Osmond's beautiful mind indeed seemed to peep down from a small high window and mock at her. Of course it had not been physical suffering; for physical suffering there might have been a remedy. She could come and go; she had her liberty; her husband was perfectly polite. He took himself so seriously; it was something appalling. Under all his culture, his cleverness, his amenity, under his good-nature, his facility, his knowledge of life, his egotism lay hidden like a serpent in a bank of flowers. [Chap. XLII]

Again:

> She knew of no wrong he had done; he was not violent, he was not cruel: she simply believed he hated her. That was all she accused him of, and the miserable part of it was precisely that it was not a crime, for against a crime she might have found

redress. He had discovered that she was so different, that she was not what he had believed she would prove to be. [Chap. XLII]

Then, recalling that he had told her she had 'too many ideas' she begins to see what it was in her that he found so repellent:

> It had not been this, however, his objecting to her opinions; this had been nothing. She had no opinions—none that she would not have been eager to sacrifice in the satisfaction of feeling herself loved for it. What he had meant had been the whole thing —her character, the way she felt, the way she judged. . . . She had a certain way of looking at life which he took as a personal offence. [Chap. XLII]

Finally, she sees also the nature of her offence:

> The real offence, as she ultimately perceived, was her having a mind of her own at all. Her mind was to be his—attached to his own like a small garden-plot to a deer-park. He would rake the soil gently and water the flowers; he would weed the beds and gather an occasional nosegay. It would be a pretty piece of property for a proprietor already far-reaching. He didn't wish her to be stupid. On the contrary, it was because she was clever that she had pleased him. But he expected her intelligence to operate altogether in his favour, and so far from desiring her mind to be a blank he had flattered himself that it would be richly receptive. [Chap. XLII]

James, speaking throughout this interior monologue through Isabel's consciousness, accommodates the analysis to her capacities, allowing her with his customary dramatic propriety all the pain, bewilderment and confusion that is bound to limit her insight into the ultimate grounds of Osmond's hatred of her. But within those dramatic limits, the analysis of Osmond's vicious aestheticism is made with precision, and the judgement upon it pronounced with clarity and firmness. Gilbert Osmond's fine aestheticism is a sham and a delusion, its real name being vulgar vanity and egotism. In his relations with his wife it expresses itself as a common desire to dominate her; and in his relation to the world, to 'society', it expresses itself in a curiously ambiguous attitude to the values and standards of that society. A sophisticated conventionality, one might call it, which is not the less but the more shabby and shoddy for being sophisticated, which affects to despise the world but in fact submits itself and conforms itself wholly to the standards of the world: this, we are meant to see, is the last refinement of Osmond's vulgar vanity and egotism. It implied, Isabel discovers,

> a sovereign contempt for every one but some three or four very exalted people whom he envied, and for everything in the world but half a dozen ideas of his own. That was very well; she would

have gone with him even there a long distance; for he pointed out to her so much of the baseness and shabbiness of life, opened her eyes so wide to the stupidity, the depravity, the ignorance of mankind, that she had been properly impressed with the infinite vulgarity of things and of the virtue of keeping one's self unspotted by it. But this base, ignoble world, it appeared, was after all what one was to live for; one was to keep it for ever in one's eye, in order not to enlighten or convert or redeem it, but to extract from it some recognition of one's own superiority. On the one hand it was despicable, but on the other it afforded a standard. [Chap. XLII]

So it is the discovery of Osmond's base worldliness and the corrupt values springing from it that first undermines and finally destroys the loving trust in his essential goodness with which Isabel entered into the marriage; and it is this, along with Osmond's egotism, coldness and brutality, that constitutes the betrayal which is the heart of the tragedy. Nevertheless, if this were in fact the whole tragedy of *The Portrait of a Lady* there would be, paradoxically, no tragedy in the proper sense of the word. The heroine, Isabel Archer, would be the totally innocent and helpless victim of a cruel combination of circumstances which she had been powerless to avert; and she would then bear no responsibility for the disaster following from them. The story of *The Portrait of a Lady* would in that case be a story pitiful and heart-breaking indeed, as a story of human suffering always is; but it would not be a tragedy, for a mere victim cannot be a tragic hero or heroine: the tragic effect in drama depends upon our recognising that the hero shall be in some sense and in some degree responsible for the fate that overtakes him.

Now Isabel Archer, we discover, is not in fact a mere victim. On the contrary, she carries a proper share of the moral responsibility for the disaster that overtakes her. Nor is Osmond, on his side, merely a vicious brute. He too (we discover) has been deceived, in a subtly interesting way; he too has been misled into a fatal error of judgement which has helped to precipitate the castastrophe; and it is in James's dramatic exposé of this joint responsibility for the tragic catastrophe that his gift of moral analysis is perhaps at its most brilliant.

What we discover first is that Osmond's original motives for wishing to marry Isabel had not been as base as might be supposed. He had certainly not been a mere adventurer who was marrying her for her money—like another Morris Townsend in *Washington Square* who was only less crude in his tactics. If Isabel, we are made to understand, had been in the least (for instance) like her impossible friend Henrietta Stackpole, he would not have married her were she ten times the heiress she was. Nor had he been merely the aesthetic dilettante (as some critics have thought him), who merely desired to possess Isabel Archer as the finest piece in his collection of 'fine things'. The money-motive had indeed not been absent, and the aesthetic motive had certainly been present; but his main reason for wanting to marry her was, simply, that he liked her: that he found her really charming and graceful (as he tells Madame Merle); that he was in fact, to his capacity, in love with Isabel—genuinely, even ardently, in love.

This genuineness of his feeling for Isabel comes out most clearly in his several 'speeches' during the period of the courtship; and since they are generally overlooked by those readers who see Osmond as nothing but an aesthetic dilettante or vulgar adventurer or both (and consequently miss the finer points of James's conception and execution of Gilbert Osmond), it is perhaps worth quoting two of them. In the first passage Osmond is commenting on her relations' disapproval of their engagement:

'Of course [he says] when a poor man marries a rich girl he must be prepared for imputations. I don't mind them; I only care for one thing—for your not having the shadow of a doubt. I don't care what people of whom I ask nothing think—I'm not even capable perhaps of wanting to know. I've never so concerned myself, God forgive me, and why should I begin to-day, when I have taken to myself a compensation for everything? I won't pretend I'm sorry you're rich; I'm delighted. I delight in everything that's yours—whether it be money or virtue. Money's a horrid thing to follow, but a charming thing to meet. It seems to me, however, that I've sufficiently proved the limits of my itch for it: I never in my life tried to earn a penny, and I ought to be less subject to suspicion than most of the people one sees grubbing and grabbing. I suppose it's their business to suspect—that of your family; it's proper on the whole they should. They'll like me better some day; so will you, for that matter. Meanwhile my business is not to make myself bad blood, but simply to be thankful for life and love.' [Chap. XXXV]

Then, on another occasion:

'It has made me better, loving you; . . . it has made me wiser and easier and—I won't pretend to deny—brighter and nicer and even stronger. I used to want a great many things before and to be angry I didn't have them. Theoretically I was satisfied, as I once told you. I flattered myself I had limited my wants. But I was subject to irritation; I used to have morbid, sterile, hateful fits of hunger, of desire. Now I'm really satisfied, because I can't think of anything better. It's just as when one has been trying to spell out a book in the twilight and suddenly the lamp comes in. I had been putting out my eyes over the book of life and finding nothing to reward me for my pains; but now that I can read it properly I see it's a delightful story. My dear girl, I can't tell you how life seems to stretch there before us—what a long summer afternoon awaits us. It's the latter half of an Italian day—with a golden haze, and the shadows just lengthening, and that divine delicacy in the light, the air, the landscape, which I have loved all my life and which you love to-day. Upon my honour, I don't see why we shouldn't get on. We've got what we like—to say nothing of having each other. We've the faculty of admiration and several capital convictions. We're not stupid, we're not mean, we're not under bonds to any kind of ignorance or dreariness. You're remarkably fresh, and I'm remarkably well-seasoned. We've my poor child to amuse us; we'll try and make up some little life for her. It's all soft and mellow—it has the Italian colouring.' [Chap. XXXV]

It is typical of James's high conscience as an artist that he should have insisted at this point on presenting Osmond so directly. The technical difficulty of getting the speeches just 'right' must have been enormous—to show Osmond's feeling as genuine and attractive enough to make psychological and dramatic sense of his irresistible charm for Isabel at this critical stage of their relationship, yet at the same time to make it only the kind and degree of genuineness and attractiveness that would be consistent with the character he is to disclose after the marriage. James, one could argue, need not have made things so difficult for himself; he might have evaded altogether this difficult and delicate task and given us Osmond entirely by description—and probably no one would have noticed the difference. But he has done it the difficult way; he has done it with brilliant success; and it does make—or ought to make—a great difference for our understanding of Osmond's side of the affair. For though in such passages as those quoted above the sincerity, exhilaration and ardour are of course tainted with sophistication, and though the aesthetic emphasis is of course dangerously present ('It's all soft and mellow—it has the Italian colouring'), yet the feeling is genuine and strong. Osmond really does 'like' Isabel; he really does look forward to finding in his marriage with her the perfection of personal happiness; he really does have the highest expectations of their life together—expectations, in their way, quite as high as Isabel's own. Consequently (James means us to see) *his* disappointment of *his* expectations, though not morally justifiable and never justified, is yet as genuine as Isabel's, his sense of betrayal as strong; and this—which, as we shall see, Isabel herself comes to recognise —is an important aspect of the tragedy which may be ignored only on pain of losing half its truth, power and subtlety.

So (to return) the interest that Isabel Archer has for Osmond is genuine, and his 'liking' for her is genuine. There is, however, one thing that Gilbert Osmond does not like in Isabel Archer; and upon this, we already know, hangs the greater part of the tragedy.

It happens to be the very same thing that had filled Lord Warburton with nervous apprehension. Lord Warburton had called it her mind, her 'remarkable mind'; Osmond calls it her ideas. It is her ideas that Osmond does not like, and in particular (we soon come to realise) the moral emphasis of her ideas. These he sees as the regrettable product of her provincial upbringing in her native town of Albany; and to a man of developed aesthetic sensibility there is nothing more distasteful than moral ideas in a charming woman, especially when she happens to take them really seriously. He is confident, however, that he can cope with this flaw—serious indeed but not (he believes) irremediable—in an otherwise delightful nature; and to cope with it means of course, for Gilbert Osmond, not to accept it or accommodate himself to it but to master it: to suppress it if necessary; or, if it proves stubborn, to eradicate it—destroy it root and branch. He intimates this intention to Madame Merle early on in the story, in a brief exchange with her:

> 'She's really very charming. I've scarcely known anyone more graceful.'
> 'It does me good to hear you say that' [she replies]. 'The better you like her the better for me.'
> 'I like her very much. She's all you described her, and into the bargain capable, I feel, of great devotion. She has only one fault.'
> 'What's that?'
> 'Too many ideas.'
> 'I warned you she was clever.'
> 'Fortunately they're very bad ones', said Osmond.
> "Why is that fortunate?"
> '*Dame*, if they must be sacrificed!' [Chap. XXVI]

From this it is clear just how intensely Gilbert Osmond dislikes Isabel Archer's 'ideas', how ruthlessly determined he is to get rid of them, and how assured of his competence to accomplish this desirable end without undue inconvenience to himself.

But in this last supposition he is fatally mistaken. Isabel's ideas, it turns out, are not so easily suppressed. Though she desires above everything to be a loyal and loving wife to Gilbert Osmond ('She had no opinions—none that she would not have been eager to sacrifice in the satisfaction of feeling herself loved for it' [Chap. XLII]), it is impossible for her, being what she is, not to voice her ideas—her moral ideas—about many things in the life of her husband and the life of the society into which she has been drawn by her marriage. In particular (we learn) it is impossible for her not to express her opinions about the degenerate morals of the fashionable Roman society in which her husband chooses to live; and since he identifies himself with the values of that society, it is unavoidable that her criticisms should by implication be directed also against him personally. And this is what Gilbert Osmond cannot bear: that her criticisms should be directed against *him*—against his standards, his attitudes, his 'assumptions'. This is an assault upon his vanity and egotism for which nothing can compensate; and it is perhaps not surprising that it should lead him in the end to hate his wife with a cold, implacable hatred. This is how Isabel herself comes to see it:

> It was her scorn of his assumptions, it was this that made him draw himself up. He had plenty of contempt, and it was proper his wife should be as well furnished; but that she should turn the hot light of her disdain upon his own conception of things—this was a danger he had not allowed for. He believed he should have regulated her emotions before she came to it; and Isabel could easily imagine how his ears had scorched on his discovering he had been too confident. When one had a wife who gave one that sensation there was nothing left but to hate her. [Chap. XLII]

This expresses the final tragic horror of Isabel Archer's situation: that she should be hated not for what is worst but for what is best in her—for her free enquiring mind, for her moral purity, for her desire to uphold, to her capacity, what she believes to be right and good. And this, we are meant to see, is indeed one of the profoundest of the tragic ironies of life: to be rejected and despised—hated, as Osmond comes to hate Isabel—for what is best in one, and by those in whom one had placed one's most loving trust.

Yet Isabel herself, it has already been suggested, bears her share of responsibility for the tragedy. The nature of that responsibility, or part of it at least, emerges very clearly in certain passages of her interior monologue, in which she recognises that she herself had encouraged Osmond before their marriage to suppose that her free enquiring mind and her moral ideas were not a serious matter, and had to this extent positively deceived him, or at any rate helped him in his self-deception. 'Scanning the future with dry, fixed eyes,' Isabel in her midnight meditation feels, strangely, that 'there were times when she almost pitied him':

> For if she had not deceived him in intention she understood how completely she must have done so in fact. She had effaced herself when he first knew her; she had made herself small, pretending there was less of her than there really was. It was because she had been under the extraordinary charm that he, on his side, had taken pains to put forth. [Chap. XLII]

And again:

> She lost herself in infinite dismay when she thought of the magnitude of *his* deception. It was a wonder perhaps, in view of this, that he didn't hate her more. . . . She had known she had too

many ideas; she had more even .than he had supposed, many more than she had expressed to him when he had asked her to marry him. Yes, she *had* been hypocritical; she had liked him so much. [Chap. XLII]

'She had been under the extraordinary charm that he . . . had taken pains to put forth'; 'she had liked him so much'. Of course there is every excuse, one is tempted to say. If she deceived him, if she was 'hypocritical', it was out of love and for the sake of love; and who, remembering Osmond's sovereign personal power over her, could hold her morally culpable for thus deceiving him?

All this is true; and the punishment, as always in tragedy, is or seems to be far in excess of the crime. Yet (James answers us—or, rather, his fable answers us) a deception is a deception; a lapse from truth carries its own punishment; the wages of sin, as religious people say, is death—in this instance, spiritual death. Isabel has to suffer because she had not the courage to *be herself*, completely and uncompromisingly, against all temptations. Because for the sake of love she lapsed from truth, the love for which she lapsed failed her; and this is one truth about the human condition that the central story of *The Portrait of a Lady* presses upon our attention.

But there is a further and deeper aspect of Isabel's culpability to take account of. This is to be discovered in the fatal aestheticism that she herself is tainted with; and it is this, we are meant to see, that was from the beginning the real common ground, and to the end remains the deepest bond, between herself and Osmond. In her it is never, of course, as vicious as it is in Osmond; compared with his indeed it is innocent. And yet not so innocent as not to be culpable, and therefore doomed to earn its own retribution.

The evidences for Isabel's aestheticism are scattered throughout the book, and cannot all be cited in detail. We have already noted James's early ironic references, with all the necessary mitigations, to her vanity, her self-centredness, her tendency to self-dramatisation —all functions, as we saw, of her desire to appear good as well as be good, and therefore also the first signs of her growing commitment to the aesthetic view of things. The next important sign is her tremendous enthusiasm for Madame Merle as a personage 'rare, superior, pre-eminent', possessed of a 'greatness' that Isabel finds peculiarly (and dangerously) fascinating. ('To be so cultivated and civilised, so wise and so easy, and still make so light of it—that was really to be a great lady, especially when one so carried and presented one's self. It was as if somehow she had all society under contribution, and all the arts and graces it practised.') [Chap. XIX] It reaches a peak in her receptiveness to Osmond's charm, expressed in her many private reflections upon his 'fineness'. [Chaps. XXIII, XXIV, XXVI] It is to be discerned in the very midnight vigil in which she is seeking to understand the reasons for the disastrous failure of her marriage: we remember that 'when he pointed out to her so much of the baseness and shabbiness of life, opened her eyes so wide to the stupidity, the depravity, the ignorance of mankind . . . she had been properly impressed with the infinite vulgarity of things, and of the virtue of keeping one's self unspotted by it;' and it is significant that when she decides to support her husband in encouraging Warburton's suit with Pansy, the *amusement* she will derive from it has a place in her calculations. ('It would occupy her, and she desired occupation. It would even amuse her, and if she could really amuse herself she perhaps might be saved'. [Chap. XLI]) Isabel herself never becomes fully conscious of this taint in herself; she does not to the end see it face to face, she knows it only by its effects. But the reader is expected to see it, and to give it the weight that is due to it. The sense of beauty is one thing, aestheticism, the 'touchstone of taste' (as James is to call it in a later work), is quite another thing. For aestheticism seeks always to substitute the appearnce for the reality, the surface for the substance, the touchstone of taste for the touchstone of truth: that truth which in the life of man (Henry James comes more and more to insist) is in the first instance moral and only secondarily and derivatively aesthetic. Isabel Archer is too susceptible—just that shade too susceptible—to fine appearances, to a brilliant surface, to the appeal, in short, of the merely aesthetic, to be morally altogether sound. And this perhaps is what old Mr. Touchett dimly recognised when he asked Ralph whether he really thought his cousin Isabel was 'so good as that'; and for this Isabel has to suffer, and through her suffering learn that the aesthetic is not coextensive with the moral, and that the touchstone of taste is not the touchstone by which a good life can be lived.

This conflict of the aesthetic and the moral in a highly civilised society is to emerge in James's later novels as one of his great themes, perhaps his very greatest. In *The Portrait of a Lady* it receives only its first and more or less tentative statement. We may judge the tentativeness, even the inconclusiveness, from the course of the fable itself. Nothing 'happens' as a result of this discovery; neither Isabel herself nor Osmond is significantly affected by it: neither is altered by it as (for instance) the Prince in *The Golden Bowl* is profoundly and irrevocably altered when he discovers that 'his touchstone of taste is all at sea'. The theme is further developed in several of the works that follow *The Portrait of a Lady*—in *The Princess Casamassima, The Awkward Age* and, most particularly, in *The Ambassadors*. But for its definitive rendering we have to wait until *The Golden Bowl*, where we will find the whole fable directed to the single end of exhibiting the triumphant supersession of the aesthetic by the moral.

* * *

LAURENCE B. HOLLAND

The Marriage†

The first of the important characters to be engaged by the plot and implicated in its moral consequences are those who initiate it and display the main outline of its significance, the interconnection of marital and familial, monetary, and aesthetic concerns: the older Touchetts, Daniel and Lydia, still linked but no longer intimate in their "experiment in matrimony." They find awakened interest, and Mrs. Touchett finds convenience as a hostess, in the niece they have taken up and are supporting while diverting her from the dry sands of German philosophy to a more direct exposure to Europe and the past. It is Mrs. Touchett's telegram (she has mastered " 'the art of condensation' ") that announces in Chapter One that she has " 'Taken sister's girl' " and that Isabel is soon to arrive at Gardencourt. Touchett himself, with his earned and banked resources, long ago bought a house, which imaged all English history since Edward VI, for the simple reason that it was "a great bargain." But as a consequence of this purchase he now has it in his "careful keeping" and has acquired "a real aesthetic passion" for his Gardencourt. He stands firm against the aimless boredom, the jocular detachment, of his son and his son's friend, Lord Warburton, and has suggested that Warburton " ' "take hold" of something' "—indeed marry an interesting woman so that his " 'life will be more interesting,' " though he jokingly excludes the niece of whose impending arrival he has just heard. Later, in his bequest to Isabel, he deliberately consents to play along with his son's plan to make Isabel rich although he fears it is risky to the point of being irresponsible, even " 'immoral.' " [Chaps. I, III, XVII]

That plan, if immoral, is also creative. Ralph Touchett's plan is founded on renouncing prospects of marriage with Isabel and on translating his affection into something paternal and fraternal instead. And it is founded on actions in which *both* the renunciation and the use of his inherited wealth are fused. If he is, as one character claims, " 'Prospero enough to make [Isabel] what she has become,' " he is nonetheless like the plotter Iago in wanting to " 'put money in her purse.' " He want to put money in her purse so that he might, and she might, "meet the requirements of their imagination." With his permissive and playful imagination, he has, as he remarks, " 'amused myself with planning out a high destiny for you' " and after her disastrous marriage to Osmond he spends

† From *The Expense of Vision: Essays on the Craft of Henry James* (Princeton: Princeton University Press, 1964), pp. 28–42. Reprinted by permission of the publisher.

what time he can watching her, entertained in trying to see through the mask of tranquil satisfaction she has assumed. He presses the limits of their "tacit convention" not to discuss Osmond's conduct openly, for he is so involved in her predicament that he feels "an almost savage desire to hear her complain of her husband," longing "for his own satisfaction more than for hers" to show that he understood her situation, trying again and again "to make her betray Osmond" though "he felt cold-blooded, cruel, dishonourable almost, in doing so." He is turning about in pained fascination the figure detained in the imagination's shop. It is an anguished entertainment, founded on money and imagination, love and sacrifice, and when Isabel later disobeys her husband to rush to Ralph's deathbed, his affection for his cousin becomes adoration in his final declaration. [Chaps. XIII, XVIII, XXXIV, XLV, LIV]

Unlike Ralph, who has renounced the prospect of marriage, his friend Lord Warburton, young Ned Rosier, and Caspar Goodwood find their place as suitors in the novel's action. Warburton exerts a definite but ambivalent charm throughout the novel. He pursues an active career in Parliament and is a "nobleman of the newest pattern" for he combines the security of his wealth and station with the programs of the " 'radicals of the upperclass' " who, in Daniel Touchett's view, indulge in their theories as a luxuriously safe " 'amusement' " without profound commitment. Isabel continues to like Warburton's manliness and all "his merits—properties these partaking of the essence of great decent houses, as one might put it." When he proposes to her she feels "that a territorial, a political, a social magnate had conceived the design of drawing her into" his "system," though she recognized that in his genuine tact and decency he was "looking at her with eyes charged with the light of a passion that had sifted itself clear of the baser parts of emotion— the heat, the violence, the unreason. . . ." Though he insists that he simply offers her " 'the chance of taking the common lot in a comfortable way' " she declines his "big bribe" on the grounds that she cannot detach herself from " 'the common lot,' "—from the " 'usual chances and dangers, from what most people know and suffer,' "—that, as she says, " 'I can't escape my fate.' " [Chaps. VIII, XII, XIII, XIV, XXVII]

His presence becomes more disturbing in the later part of the novel; at the age of 42 he has become Pansy's suitor, and Madame Merle and Osmond find him the answer to their ambitions for Pansy, and Osmond demands that Isabel encourage the match. Though Isabel finds Warburton's friendship a comfort—"it was like having a large balance at the bank"—it becomes problematical because there are definite grounds for the suspicion Ralph and the Countess Gemini share: that a large part of Warburton's interest in

Pansy is the desire to be near her stepmother. There is a complicated emotional involvement beneath the oddity, as Osmond puts it to Isabel, that " 'Pansy's admirers should all be your old friends.' " Isabel displays more interest in Warburton's robust masculinity than she did earlier, noticing now how Pansy gives "quiet oblique glances at his person, his hands, his feet, his clothes," how Pansy's "eyes, as usual, wandered up and down his robust person as if he had offered it to her for exhibition." These are the observations of a vicarious participant. [Chaps. XXXIX, XLI, XLIII, XLVIII]

Warburton and Isabel tacitly recognize this involvement on one occasion when Isabel "met his eyes, and for a moment they looked straight at each other," and this recognition simply tightens her dilemma, for the plot has created a situation which complicates the relation between her roles as wife and parent and her relation with her former suitor: to obey her husband's demand by encouraging Warburton's courtship of Pansy would prove that she did not fear Warburton's presence but risk making her relation to him more intimate; to disobey her husband out of concern for Pansy's feelings by encouraging Pansy's favorite, Ned Rosier, would safeguard her conduct from emotional complications with Warburton but virtually acknowledge that she fears Warburton's proximity and envies Pansy his affection. She assures Warburton he may court Pansy if he pleases, but instantly afterward promises Ned to " 'do what I can' " to favor his suit; yet even after Pansy confesses her love for the younger man, Isabel does not speak in his favor but speaks, albeit without force, of Pansy's obligation to respect her father's desire and of the importance of Warburton's title and fortune. [Chaps. XLIII, XLV]

The crisis is not resolved by Isabel but by a decision of Warburton which is in keeping with the basic design of the plot. He withdraws without making a proposal, understanding Isabel's predicament and recognizing that the younger girl is not in love with him. Later when Isabel learns that Warburton, after a courtship of three weeks, has married " 'A member of the aristocracy; Lady Flora, Lady Felicia—something of that sort,' " she reflects that Warburton "was dead for poor Pansy; by Pansy he might have lived." But instead of becoming the perfect little pearl of a peeress, Pansy will wait in hopes of marrying Ned who looks to her so like a "nobleman." [Chaps. XLV, LIV]

Before Pansy's prospects and Isabel's concern turn from Warburton to the young man, Ned Rosier's place in the action seems inconsequential, for there is justice in Isabel's feeling that Ned is "really so light a weight. He was much more of the type of the useless fine gentleman than the English nobleman," and Warburton is probably not envious in remarking that Ned still " 'doesn't look much more than twelve today.' " He is an American expatriate and dilettante (" 'There's nothing for a gentleman in America' "). And he lacks not only Warburton's title but a career (" "American diplomacy—that's not for gentlemen either' "), and instead of Warburton's radical views he has the "grim politics," reactionary and Napoleonic, which he parrots (prophetic soul) from one Mr. Luce. Yet for all the novel's frivolous attention to the decorations of his mantelpiece, his prominent position in the plot suggests his importance, for he is carefully introduced just after Madame Merle learns that Isabel has inherited a fortune, and his arrival in Rome is the first narrated incident to follow Isabel's marriage. With his "cultivated tastes" and collection of bibelots, he all but lives at the auctioneer's, yet he could not possibly have a career as shopkeeper because, as he says, " 'I can buy very well, but I can't sell.' " In the course of the novel, however, he has found temporarily a place in the world of affairs. He has been drawn into the final crisis by paying court to Pansy and rendering himself eligible by the commercial transaction which he announces to Isabel when he finds her seated in the "despoiled arena" of the Coliseum: he has sold his *objets d'art* (all but his enamels) for $50,000 cash. [Chaps. XX, XLI, XLIII, L]

Ned's relation with Isabel spans the years from their childhood to a point which lies beyond the range of her personal desire, but the relation of Caspar Goodwood is at once more confined and more intimate. The first suitor to propose to Isabel (in Albany), he is the last to confront her in the novel, when he tries to persuade her to leave her husband. With his square jaw and the "hardness of presence, in his way of rising before her" that Isabel finds disagreeable, his manner presents a distinct combination of masculine vigor and the awkward and genuine assertiveness of the American businessman. Isabel is critical of the sameness of his apparel, the simplicity of his manner, and later his literalness, and she early compares the prospect of "conquest at her English suitor's [Warburton's] large quiet hands" to the more unsettling prospect of letting Caspar "take positive possession of her." He manages a large cotton mill in Massachusetts and is the son of its founder; his business acumen, energy, and career distinguish him from both Warburton and Rosier. So complete is his association with the realm of business that in a later scene with Isabel, when restating his love for her and trying to understand her distance from him, his very idiom makes the world of business the dividing line between himself and the intimacy of Isabel's feelings: the phrase "none of my business" becomes a virtual refrain as he concedes, time and again, that " 'It's none of my business—very true. But I love you.' " [Chaps. XIII, XLVII, XLVIII]

Yet within the novel's perspective her feelings are related, curiously, to his business, for his business capacity includes the "sharp eye" that has already led him to one patented invention and it includes "the art," as James said, "of managing men." Two statements which James added in revision enforce Goodwood's connection with the plot and the artistry of making it: in his "clear–burning eyes" sits "some watcher at a window," and he is expected someday to "write himself in bigger letters."[1] It is he, Isabel expects, who will see through her mask if anyone can and "make . . . out, as over a falsified balance-sheet . . . the intimate disarray of her affairs." He had "invested his all in her happiness, while the others had invested only a part." The plot renders these scattered metaphors central, rather than peripheral or incidental, to the novel's design. By the final chapter, when Caspar's strong desire is buttressed by Ralph's last request to " 'Do everything you can for her; do everything she'll let you,' " Caspar's "aimless, fruitless passion" has become profound and possessive, and the plot has made of him an image of a grasping and possessive imagination. [Chaps. XIII, XLVII, LV]

The plot's chief instruments and artificers, however, are those who give the confluence of events its distinct shape: Madame Merle and her former lover, Gilbert Osmond. With one marriage a failure, others are seemingly out of the question for Serena Merle, and she finds it impossible to acknowledge Pansy Osmond as her daughter. She conceives the simultaneous arrangement of Isabel's marriage and the provision eventually for Pansy's, hoping to " 'amuse' " her former lover and urging him to " 'profit, ' " by her deep familiarity with social arrangements. She is an expatriate, so steeped now in " 'the old, old world' " as to be " 'the great round world itself. ' " Madame Merle seems to be deeply conventional in a world where the conventional touches upon everything, including, as Isabel recognizes, language itself. Not only does Madame Merle practice the arts of conversation and the needle, to say nothing of music, but she paints: she "made no more of brushing in a sketch than of pulling off her gloves." Isabel's partial awakening to the facts of her betrayal include the recognition (which the preface was to echo later) that Madame Merle had been a powerful "agent" in her "destiny." [Chaps. XIX, XXII, XXIII, XLIX]

Indeed, she has done for James what the Countess Gemini finally divulges that she has done for Osmond: " 'She has worked for him, plotted for him, suffered for him; she has even more than once found money for him.' " Her plotting, once it is revealed, not only calls forth Isabel's scorn but her compassion when she recognizes that Madame Merle has, as the Countess says, " 'failed so dread-

1. Cf. p. 99 of the first edition, Boston, 1881.

fully that she's determined her daughter shall make it up.' " Her own ambitions and desires, like Isabel's, are channeled, by the plot she does so much to instigate, into the prospects for Pansy's marriage. Her final failure is to be excluded even as a silent partner from the arrangements she had wanted so much to be " '*my* work' " by Osmond who abandons her. [Chaps. XLIX, LI]

It is Osmond who is stirred to a renewed interest in life by collaboration in his colleague's plot. An "odd mixture of the detached and involved," living by himself in a "sifted, arranged world" in Italy, "thinking about art and beauty and history," this proud " 'provincial' " is an American expatriate artist and dilettante. He longs nostalgically for the authority of a pope and suggests occasionally in his demeanor a "prince in exile," a " 'prince who has abdicated in a fit of fastidiousness and has been in a state of disgust ever since.' " He is the incarnation of taste and, as he himself puts it, " 'convention itself.' " He had once had the decency to acknowledge his own daughter Pansy and, unlike Madame Merle's husband who rejected the child utterly, to make himself responsible for her care; during his engagement to Isabel he suggests that together they will "make up some little life" for Pansy, as if they were to invent it; late in the novel, "playing theoretic tricks on the delicate organism of his daughter," and wanting to "show that if he regarded his daughter as a precious work of art it was natural he should be more careful about the finishing touches," he sends her back to the Roman convent to insure her complete subservience to his will. [Chaps. XXIII, XXIV, XXVII, XXIX, XXXV, L]

He is imaged as a commemorative "gold coin" and is discovered late in the novel devoting his art to copying an illustration of an "antique coin," scorning money but using and seeking it. His old villa in Florence—"a blank-looking structure," broken by only "a few windows," its front façade the "mask" rather than the "face of the house"—harbors inside a large "writing–table of which the ingenious perfection bore the stamp" not of Renaissance Florence but of "London and the nineteenth century." There lives the man "with eyes at once vague and penetrating . . . , expressive of the observer as well as of the dreamer," to whose "deep art" Isabel eventually succumbs. If he discreetly seeks public approval, looking "out of his window even when he appeared to be most detached from it" so as to gain its recognition rather than to "enlighten or convert or redeem it," he is also the watcher inside their common dwelling whom Isabel recognizes in her long night of meditation— the watcher who "seemed to peep down from a small high window and mock at her." "Her mind," she comes to understand, "was to be his. . . . He would rake the soil gently and water the flowers. . . . It would be a pretty piece of property for a proprietor already far-reaching." He is the figure—the watcher inside the House of Fiction—in whom Caspar recognizes much later a "demonic imagination." [Chaps. XXII, XXXIII, XLII, XLVIII, LI]

So intimately is James implicated in the action of his novel that letters he was writing while working on the *Portrait* are echoed in the passages where Osmond's mind and feelings are stirred by the workings of the plot and he proposes marriage to Isabel. James wrote that he was "much more interested in my current work than anything else," that he was "working with great ease, relish, and success," that his work would bring $6,000 from serialization alone, that it would "rend the veil" which covered his "ferocious ambition," that it would be from the finished *Portrait*, his most ambitious early effort, "that I myself shall pretend to date."[2] It is Ralph who notices that the costumed "fine lady" which the once "free, keen" Isabel has become "represented Gilbert Osmond," who now "was in his element; at last he had material to work with." His calculated effects "were produced by no vulgar means, but the motive was as vulgar as the art was great. . . . 'He works with superior material,' Ralph said to himself; 'it's rich abundance compared with his former resources.'" It is the excitement of such opportunities that earlier had awakened Osmond. Just before his proposal Osmond finds himself pleased with his newly aroused "sense of success," feeling that his earlier successes had rested "on vague laurels," and that his present success was "easy . . . only because he had made an altogether exceptional effort." While the "desire to have something or other to show for his 'parts' . . . had been the dream of his youth," now it was to materialize with Isabel's help and at her expense: "If an anonymous drawing on a museum wall had been conscious and watchful it might have known this peculiar pleasure of being at last . . . identified—as from the hand of a great master—by the so high and so unnoticed fact of style. His 'style' is what the girl had discovered with a little help; and now, beside herself enjoying it, she should publish it to the world without his having any of the trouble. She would do the thing for him and he would not have waited in vain." In this view of Osmond are joined both the finished work of art—the drawing with which Osmond is associated so intimately—and the master whose style was displayed in making it.[3] [Chaps. XXIX, XXXIX]

2. Quoted by Leon Edel in his "Introduction" to *The Portrait of a Lady* (Boston: Riverside Edition, 1956), pp. vi, viii.

3. The passage about the anonymous drawing was added in revision. It reinforces the association in the original edition between Osmond's courtship of Isabel and the aims of art. The earlier version included the reference to his London writing desk, described him as a "watcher," and associated Osmond's marriage to Isabel with the desire to make himself felt "deeply" rather than on vast "multitudes." In 1881, Osmond had been inspired by Isabel to write a sonnet. See pp. 198, 263, 267, 375–376, of the 1881 edition.

The useful girl is Isabel with her combination of caution and curiosity, inexperience and alertness, and the strength of will which leads her to confront life's options " 'So as to choose.' " Her suspicion of the poisoned cup of experience and her fear of suffering are countered by her desire to join in what ordinary " 'people know and suffer.' " Her desire "to leave the past behind her" and encounter always fresh beginnings is balanced by her deepening response to the appeal of the past and tradition. Her acknowledged ignorance "about bills" or " 'anything about money' " is countered by the definiteness of her aversion " 'to being under pecuniary obligations' " and the assurance of her delusion that in going to Europe she is literally " 'travelling at her own expense.' " The "something cold and dry in her temperament" which an "unappreciated suitor" would notice is countered by the boldness of her "ridiculously active" imagination which renders her vulnerable to delusions, being so "wide-eyed" as to suffer from "seeing too many things at once" and incurring the "penalty of having given undue encouragement to the faculty of seeing without judging." Her mind in sum is a "tangle of vague outlines at the start," but the interaction of her capacity for experience with the plot which forms that experience joins her conscience and her imagination and fills in the outlines of both Isabel's and the *Portrait's* vision. [Chaps. III, IV, V, VI, VII,

In the course of experiencing the lures and pressures that shape her destiny in the novel, the action brings her maternal instincts into the foreground. Mrs. Touchett's taunting fear that Isabel may decide that her " 'mission in life's to prove that a stepmother may sacrifice herself—and that, to prove it, she must first become one' " is confirmed by Isabel's feeling toward Pansy and by her eventual actions, and it is given another dimension by Isabel's late recognition that her feeling for Osmond himself contained "a maternal strain—the happiness of a woman who felt that she was a contributor, that she came with charged hands." [Chaps. XXVI, XLII]

Moreover, the plotted action which involves her with Osmond and Pansy dissociates both Isabel and finally Pansy from the securities and settled conventions of the strictly aristocratic tradition, embodied in Lord Warburton, and involves each instead in something more problematical and hazardous. For Pansy it is the prospect of a marriage founded on no more than sheer mutual affection and a great sufficiency of cash; Pansy herself, whom Isabel feels to be a blank page she hopes will be filled with "an edifying text," displays nothing but her fragile charm and the genuineness of her devotion; Ned Rosier has neither settled status nor job and office, his mind and tastes are not exceptional, and his only recommendation is the genuine commitment defined by his courtship and the sale of his prized treasures. [Chaps. XXVI, XLI]

Isabel's involvement is with the actual form of her strange marriage with Osmond. Within that form Isabel's and Osmond's child is born (he dies at the age of six months) and Isabel acquires her stepdaughter. Within a few years, however, it is clear that intimacy between Isabel and Osmond has ceased, and by the end his attitude is one of contempt; as Isabel finally tells him, " 'It's malignant.' " Yet the form, as a sheer institutional form, still holds and within it takes place a striking confrontation when Isabel distinguishes between her own and her husband's conceptions of aristocracy and tradition. It is not only striking but significant because their different attitudes together reveal conflicting tendencies that are widespread in American culture but which are particularly pressing in the Genteel Tradition, and these tendencies are embodied in the marriage which the plot has figured for them. [Chap. LI]

Isabel's view of aristocracy is distinguished by being ethical and experiential and envisions the reconciliation of duty with enjoyment: the "union of great knowledge with great liberty; the knowledge would give one a sense of duty and the liberty a sense of enjoyment." Osmond's is at once more formal and more active; it is "altogether a thing of forms, a conscious, calculated attitude." And while both characters respect tradition, the "old, the consecrated, the transmitted," and both speak as if dissociated from it and encountering it from some distance, Isabel's attitude is eclectic and based on her determination "to do what she chose with it." Osmond's view is at once more conservative in its deference to older social patterns, more desperate in his sense of alienation from them, and more radical in his means to attain them, as befits the prince in exile from America and would-be pope who longs for the deference paid an aristocrat but has not inherited the traditional aristocratic forms. He has a "large collection" of traditions and feels that the "great thing was to act in accordance with them" rather than to choose among them; and his proprietorship, like his manner, is founded on the realization that distinguishes him from the European who could simply find or tranquilly inherit his traditions: Osmond, the American expatriate, knows that "if one was so fortunate as not to have [tradition] one must immediately proceed to make it." [Chap. XLII]

Isabel's determination to "choose," and Osmond's to construct or "make," are sharply delineated by the mutual antagonism of the two characters, but they are joined in perilous proximity by the bond of their marriage and both are related to other social realities which are part of their American background. These are the money economy and obsessive attitudes toward money, which characterize the culture of American capitalism, and characteristic American attitudes (one utilitarian, the other guilt–ridden) toward inherited wealth.

Osmond, the son of a "rich and wild" father and a mother who combined a practical "administrative" view with a talent for poor poetry, has made in his expatriation a " 'wilfull renunciation' " which is nonetheless a social construct; it is founded on the habitual intent to utilize economic resources without creating them and is centered on his immediate family. Determined " 'not to strive nor struggle' " in the business world, yet content with the independent income derived therefrom (though he thinks it " 'little' "), he carefully harbors and manages his economic resources, buys and builds his collection and refines his tastes, buys and constructs his walled substitute for a world of forms which he might prefer to have inherited. Making his " 'life an art' " as he advised Isabel to do, he attempts to mold Pansy, with his "artistic" or "plastic view" of her capacities, in accordance with his desire for dominance. He is the genteel embodiment of "convention" in a strikingly modern version recognizable since 1789: convention become conscious and deliberate, the result less of habit and tacit agreement than of calculated control, deliberate formulation, and the determination not simply to order life as it is but to shape it more firmly and actually change it. When the opportunity to gain Isabel and her fortune presents itself, he is happy for the opportunity to put it and her to use. [Chaps. XXIV, XXVI, XXXV]

Isabel and her fortune come to be as closely associated in her own mind as they are in Osmond's and as they are throughout the novel. In Chapter I Daniel Touchett, after reading the reference in his wife's telegram to Isabel's being " 'independent,' " asks this question: is the word " 'used in a moral or in a financial sense?' " His question proves to have point. After Isabel has accustomed herself to the fact that she is rich, she is enchanted by a "maze of visions" of what a generous, independent, responsible girl could do with such resources, and her fortune "became to her mind a part of her better self; it gave her importance, gave her even, to her own imagination, a certain ideal beauty." Her attitude has less conscious origins in her temperament and in her environment, the attitudes toward experience and money being so intimate that the novel renders the one the image of the other. When Osmond proposes, Isabel is checked by a sense of dread, her hesitancy being founded on "the force which . . . ought to have banished all dread—the sense of something within herself, deep down, that she supposed to be inspired and trustful passion." Yet that fount of passion is one which Isabel inclines to save as against the alternative she anticipates, that of spending it entirely: "It was there like a large sum stored in a bank—which there was a terror in having to begin to spend. If she touched it, it would all come out." (This analogy between a bank and Isabel's capacity for passion was added in revision.) By the time she is engaged, her consent is taking the form of an act of absolution and benefaction but also of proprietorship. [Chaps. I, XXI, XXIX]

She is gratified by Pansy's affection, for "Pansy already so represented part of the service she should render," and if she feels "humility" in surrendering to Osmond, she feels also "a kind of pride" in the knowledge that "she should be able to be of use to him" and that "she was not only taking, she was giving." When Isabel looks back on her decision later, she recognizes that she never would have married him "but for her money." Her money had been the contribution to the marriage that appealed to her "maternal strain," yet the indelicacy of having merely inherited it was also a "burden" on her conscience which she longed to transfer to someone else. "What would lighten her own conscience more effectually than to make it over to the man with the best taste in the world" when she could think of no charitable institution as interesting as he? "He would use her fortune in a way that would make her think better of it and rub off a certain grossness attaching to the good luck of an unexpected inheritance." Moreover, she had felt that the "subtlest . . . manly organism she had ever known had become her property, and the recognition of having but to put out her hands and take it had been originally a sort of act of devotion." [Chaps. XXXV, XLII]

These divergent views—of proprietorship, the propriety of money, domestic economy, parental care, tradition, and aristocratic forms and values—are held juxtaposed within the bond of Isabel's and Osmond's marriage. Their variety, their tension, and their proximity are an indication that not only the separate views themselves but their interconnections are being examined, and that the form which joins them, the marriage, is being subjected to a test under the pressures shaped by the plot. Indeed, the marriage institution as displayed is not a settled institutional mold but is a form in the process of being shaped. The terms "experiment" for the Touchetts' marriage and "undertaking" for matrimony in general are decidedly apt in the context of the *Portrait*—and with them the term "form," which is used by Caspar when condemning the " 'ghastly form' " which Isabel's marriage has become and is used also when Osmond, urging Isabel not to leave, is said to speak "in the name of something sacred and precious—the observance of a magnificent form." [Chaps. I, LI, LV]

For the *Portrait* reveals in the institution the principal functions of a form: the capacity to sustain a fully developed relationship; but also the capacity to precede the full development of a process or experience while yet prefiguring it, and thus to shape the plans and aspirations for personal and social experience, to embody emerging possibilities as well as actual achievements; and the capacity to survive the process or experience itself, remaining a skeletal but nonetheless real image of possibilities no longer (or not yet again) actual. Within the context of the *Portrait*, the marriages of the Countess and much later of Warburton image the institution reduced to its most factitiously conventional status, while Daniel Touchett's hopes for Ralph's and Isabel's marriage, and earlier for Warburton's, and Isabel's hopes for Pansy's, view the institution as a form of aspiration and commitment, with the Touchetts' marriage (and Henrietta Stackpole's) falling in between.

Indeed, the *Portrait* gives body to ambivalent remarks James made in letters to his brother and Grace Norton, in 1878 and 1881, on the subject of marriage, confirming his intention not to marry but insisting on the importance of the institution, associating the form of marriage with commitments of the profoundest sort, and displaying a firm regard for the institution despite his own decision. He wrote that "I believe almost as much in matrimony for most other people as I believe in it little for myself," and that "one's attitude toward marriage is . . . the most characteristic part doubtless of one's general attitude toward life. . . . If I were to marry I should be guilty in my own eyes of inconsistency—I should pretend to think quite a bit better of life than I really do." These letters make the form of marriage an image of commitments to life itself, whether within or beyond the range of one's actual conduct. These are commitments which James's imagination entertained and made in his fiction, if nowhere else, and they are at issue in the *Portrait*.[4]

There the plot—like the world it represents endowing and then drawing on Isabel's banked resources of temperament and inheritance—focuses first on the prospective form of her marriage; then as that becomes a hollow shell it widens its focus to include the prospects for Pansy's. In the process, Isabel's acts of confronting and imagining experience become acts of paying and suffering and responsible commitment as she is led by her husband "into the mansion of his own habitation" and made a victim of her world (including her own temperament and illusions) and of the *Portrait* which creates and paints her. [Chap. XLII]

CHARLES FEIDELSON

The Moment of *The Portrait of a Lady*†

It was in Florence, in the spring of 1880, as James later recorded in his notebook, that he began *The Portrait of a Lady*—"that is, . . . took up, and worked over, an old beginning, made long before." One would like to know more about that *Ur-Portrait*, why it had

---

4. Quoted by F. O. Matthiessen, *The James Family* (New York, 1947), pp. 294–295.

† Charles Feidelson, "The Moment of *The Portrait of a Lady*," *Ventures*, 8, II (1968), pp. 47–55.

been put aside, and why it caught his attention again just at this moment. But it is clear that James felt himself to be at a turning point of his career, in some sense at a *new* beginning. He was 37 years old; in the past five years he had published some twelve volumes, including two full-length novels of which he later approved enough to admit them to his New York Edition; and he had another volume in preparation. Yet, a little over a year before, commenting on his most recent work in a letter to William James, he was inclined to treat all his writings up to this time as merely a series of "experiments of form." They were only the first stage of a "step-by-step evolution" that he anticipated. If up to now, he said, he had not wished to "run the risk of wasting or gratuitously using big situations," it was precisely because he held strongly to "the importance of subject" in fiction; and "big situations" were in the offing—"to these I am coming now." Some months later, planning *The Portrait of a Lady*, he wrote that he now intended to test whether he could attain *"form"* in *"big subjects"*; he was "determined that [this] novel . . . [should] be 'big.' "[1]

With remarkable obliquity, however, he had chosen a subject which, on the face of it, was as far removed from "bigness" as possible. In his preface, written some twenty-five years later, James says nothing about the "old beginning" that he took up and reworked in *the Portrait*; but he makes a great deal of the long gestation of the book, and he ascribes this to the slightness of the single character that gave him his start. Isabel Archer, who was to become the central figure, hovered before him as a person almost devoid of characteristics: "all the usual elements of a 'subject,' certainly of a setting, . . . need [ed] to be super-added." She was "the mere slim shade of an intelligent but presumptuous girl." How could so fleeting an image of so slight a being be "endowed with the high attributes of a Subject"? This problem, according to the preface, was what most engaged his attention and spurred him on. For he reflected that unimportant young girls *do* somehow "insist on mattering" in human experience. And his heroine's very lack of external definition made her somehow "vivid," gave her an implication of "possibilities." She insisted on her intrinsic "destiny" in spite of "being still at large, not confined by the conditions, not engaged in the tangle, to which we look for much of the impress that constitutes an identity." Moreover, her indeterminacy as a person answered to a distinctive "habit of . . . [his] own imagination," his inclination to take images of human character as "seeds" out of which the structures of his stories—their "situations" or "subjects" in the fullest

---

1. *The Notebooks of Henry James*, ed. F. O. Matthiessen and K. B. Murdock, New York, 1947, 29. *The Letters of* Henry James, ed. Percy Lubbock, New York, 1920, I, 66. *The James Family*, ed. F. O. Matthiessen, New York, 1947, 325.

sense—would organically "flower" instead of being imposed *ab extra*.[2]

Essentially, then, James at the time of the *Portrait* was intent upon something more complex than advancing from "experiments of form" to a concern with "subject." That was a rough-and-ready way of stating the case, suitable to William's understanding. More fundamentally, he was preoccupied with the meaning of "form" and "subject," the kind of form which would make a small subject big and the kind of subject that would stimulate significant "experiments of form." Why and in what sense? Even at the end of his career James was still studying the "veiled face of his Muse," pursuing an "art of representation" which "bristle[d] with questions the very terms of which [were] difficult to apply and to appreciate"; and a year before the momentous spring of 1880 he was already adopting a radically problematic attitude: "Nothing is my *last word* about anything."[3] Thus it is useless to try to define his "position" at any time, but one can look for the basic question behind the questions he explicitly asked at particular points. On occasion, the perennial issues of his art showed through in especially decisive terms.

Though the preface to the *Portrait* is extremely devious and elliptical, one gathers that there were two ways to treat Isabel Archer—two novelistic forms and two versions of the subject that suggested themselves—as well as two correlative roles available to James himself in relation to his story. One way—the "easy" way—was almost literally to "super-add" a subject to the central figure by surrounding her with other characters and emphasizing their view of her. In other words, James could build up a social novel around her, confer importance on her by adducing a context of people and events in which she would gain a factitious significance. Though he refers to this device with some scorn, he also virtually confesses that to some extent he did just that, constructing "a square and spacious house . . . while she stood there in perfect isolation." For he had certain obligations to his reader, a social contract with his audience. He must write as a public man, a literary "architect" working with recognizable materials of the social scene. Yet all the while another maneuver, technically more difficult but proportionately more meaningful, was closer to his heart. He proposed to make the most of Isabel's odd claim to intrinsic importance, thereby demonstrating his faith in the "germinal" potentialities of an isolated character. Isabel's claim to some sort of "destiny," from this standpoint, consisted in her claim to a personal "consciousness"; if she had

2. "Preface to 'The Portrait of a Lady,'" *The Art of the Novel: Critical Prefaces by Henry James*, ed. R. P. Blackmur, New York and London, 1953, 40–58.

3. *The Art of the Novel*, 3. *The Selected Letters of Henry James*, ed. Leon Edel, New York, 1955, 76.

remained indeterminate for so long as an image in his mind, it was because her "character" was so purely an instance of human consciousness *per se*, abstracted from all external determinants. Therefore he undertook to "place the centre of the subject in the young woman's own consciousness." Instead of simply devising a world to define her, he would discover the world entailed by her way of seeing, her view of herself and others; instead of his "endowing" her, he would let her endow the book, with "the high attributes of a Subject." If he could "translate her into the highest terms of that formula"—the formula of "consciousness"—he would be as faithful as possible both to the quality he had initially felt in her and to the way he had originally entertained her image, *his* unconditioned process of imagination.

It is tempting to suppose that in pointing out these two different approaches to Isabel James is alluding on the one hand to residues of the *Ur-Portrait* and on the other to the new start that he made in 1880. (He was certainly not above telescoping and suppressing facts in his autobiographical writings, "for worry-saving," as he said.)[4] However that may be, the two faces of the *Portrait* indicated in the preface correspond to what we might call recessive and dominant strains in James's notion of himself and his art, which correspond in turn to two obvious factors in the development of the traditional into the "modern" novel. James was predisposed to the idea that the bigness of "big subjects" lay in the significance of characters as social types and of action as social paradigm. For him, Balzac was always the exemplary Novelist insofar as he granted that title to anyone, and in the mid-eighties, well after the *Portrait*, he embarked on two major social novels, *The Bostonians* and *The Princess Casamassima*. Though of course there was nothing to prevent the social novelist from dealing with the inside of his characters, an effect of solid actuality was far more certain when personal "identity" was defined, in exactly the opposite way from Isabel's, by the external "impress" of social "conditions." A fear of thinness in his subject-matter, such as James showed in his letters of the period of the *Portrait*, was recurrent with him, as in a notebook entry of 1893: "The great question of *subject* surges in grey dimness about me. It is everything—it is everything."[5] But if "the question of subject" was a recurrent matter of concern to him, it was because he persistently raised it through his compulsion to turn the strictly social novel upside down. Wishing to draw upon the substance of social history, he nevertheless felt a need to invest social history with meaning, to make it "big" in another way, by "plac[ing] the centre of the subject" in someone's "consciousness." By the time

4. Virginia Harlow, *Thomas Sergeant Perry: a Biography*, Durham, North Carolina, 1950, 344.

5. *Notebooks*, 135.

James was in a position to look back on his career from the vantage point of his New York Edition (1907–9), he had come to see this inversion of emphasis as his deepest "instinctive disposition."[6] Taking his own later works as the secret goal of his development, he found the novel of consciousness emerging as far back as *Roderick Hudson* (1876) and coming to fruition in his most recent books, *The Ambassadors*, *The Wings of the Dove*, and *The Golden Bowl*.

Though this view of his career is broached in the two preceding prefaces (to *Roderick Hudson* and *The American*), the preface to the *Portrait* is the first to intimate that James actually wrote his book in full awareness of the direction in which he was headed and the problems involved. And in the *Portrait* (to come to the book itself) it is as if the matters at issue for the author were being marked out, contemplated, and set in order in the course of the narrative. On the one hand, in large-scale effect, as James insists in the preface, the *Portrait* is a novel of "consciousness." The prime locus of reality has been shifted to the "inward life" of the heroine, and the effort of the novelist to a "representation . . . of . . . *seeing*." Isabel's famous reverie (Chapter XLII), which James cites as an example of the human substance attained by these indirect means, is not only "the best thing in the book" but also, as he says, "a supreme illustration of the general plan." On the other hand, Isabel is still far removed from the full-fledged "center of consciousness" of James's later fiction: for the most part, the narrator does not see directly through her eyes, and he sees many things that she does not. What is more, when we open the *Portrait*, we find ourselves in an intensely external milieu, which could scarcely be more distant from the world projected through Isabel's midnight meditations:

> Under certain circumstances there are few hours in life more agreeable than the hour dedicated to the ceremony known as afternoon tea. There are circumstances in which, whether you partake of the tea or not—some people of course never do,—the situation is in itself delightful. Those that I have in mind in beginning to unfold this simple history offered an admirable setting to an innocent pastime.[7]

The emphasis is wholly on containing "circumstances," an environing "situation" celebrated by a tea ceremony; "inward life" is reduced to the experience of the "agreeable." And the narrator, with whatever irony, speaks as the very voice of the "admirable setting" that he conjures up, the ceremonious painter of an all-encompassing social order.

6. *The Art of the Novel*, 70.
7. *The Portrait of a Lady*, Chapter I (*The Novels and Tales of Henry James. The New York Edition*, III, 1). In this passage and in others cited below, there are no important differences between the wording of the New York Edition and the version published in 1881.

As applied to Isabel herself, this narrative stance leads directly into a broad vein of social comedy. The elaborate "circumstances" —"those that I have in mind in beginning to unfold this simple history"—implicitly back up the speaker in succeeding chapters where Isabel is subjected to long passages of censorious analysis tempered by amused indulgence. Far into the book, we are asked to adopt an appreciative, sympathetic, but essentially moralistic attitude toward the heroine, grounded in a conservative social wisdom. Isabel is rendered as a pleasing but foolish girl—full of a commendable energy and idealistic aspirations; intellectually curious, spontaneous, and affectionate; but at best an exemplary figure in a cautionary tale, one who will become "consistently wise only at the cost of an amount of folly which will constitute almost a direct appeal to charity."[8] Though the narrator deprecates the "scientific criticism"[9] of more rigid moralists, he himself conventionalizes Isabel by the terms in which he describes her; and his lofty amusement follows from his conviction that her departures from the social norm will only bring her back again in the long run.

Yet there is good reason to suspect the intentions of a would-be "historian" who sees fit to begin his tale in "the perfect middle of a splendid summer afternoon . . . a little eternity . . . an eternity of pleasure." He soon reveals that the immemorial order he admires is incapable of supporting anything but a tea party. Far from providing a secure framework for a comedy of youthful folly and adult wisdom, the social world of the *Portrait* is populated by ailing people. Their deep-seated malaise is summarized by the invalid Ralph Touchett: "There's something the matter with us all."[1] All of them are in quest of value, meaning, a ground for life. They do not profoundly question the social scheme in which they find themselves, but neither do they have any profound loyalty to it. Instead, they more or less ineptly work out individual values through the "circumstances" given to them. The ground that they either avowedly miss or too stridently claim can be described in various ways—as knowledge, or love, or freedom. They want to believe that they are in touch with truth, with each other, and with human possibility. But it is freedom that most preoccupies them. All have this aim in common—Lord Warburton, the aristocratic radical; Caspar Goodwood, the free enterprise industrialist; Ralph Touchett, the libertine of fancy; Henrietta Stackpole, the enfranchised woman; Mrs. Touchett, the crotchety lady of independent means; and old Mr. Touchett, the Franklinesque Yankee. At the same time, the circumstances in which they are enmeshed distort or wholly destroy the value they seek. The free will of Goodwood is ironically

8. *Portrait*, Chapter XII (III, 145).   1. *Portrait*, Chapter XIV (III, 191).
9. *Portrait*, Chapter VI (III, 69).

inverted into a rigid, mechanical personal manner and the service of his industrial machine; the "independent" Mrs. Touchett is reduced to social superstitions and ritual observances; Warburton vacillates absurdly between his political libertarianism and the inbred habits of a great landowner; in Henrietta the breath of the prairies is transformed into journalistic clichés; Ralph Touchett feels free to claim nothing but the freedom of irony itself. In short, we are in a late-nineteenth-century milieu, where life still defines itself primarily in social terms and yet society, as such, is no longer serving as an effectual medium of value. Only old Mr. Touchett, despite his unhappy marriage, has moral stability, and he himself points out that he is the relic of another age.

Isabel Archer irrupts onto this scene as a harbinger of meaning in life. If freedom is what her acquaintances most distinctly yearn for, it is what her own life of "consciousness" or "imagination" most distinctly gives her—what James elsewhere called "a strong and special implication of liberty."[2] Even while the narrator is still apparently aiming at a comedy of acculturation, he begins to transpose his story into another key. Like the circle of people around Isabel, he is fascinated by her conviction of inner possibilities, the birthright of "consciousness"; and he has access to something more than the others—the very process of her self-awareness, her unfolding image of her own imaginative life. In this light, her whimsical twists and turns of behavior and opinion are no longer reducible to the vagaries of an inexperienced girl. They manifest "her visions of a completed consciousness," her tentative, shifting perspectives on her destiny as an imaginative being.[3] Concurrently, there is a decisive change of direction in the plot of the *Portrait*. While the narrator broods over Isabel—"translating" the "little concerns" of a social non-entity into James's "highest terms"—Ralph Touchett follows suit and presents her with a fortune in order (as he says) to enable her "to meet the requirements of [her] imagination" and thereby to meet *his*.[4] By putting monetary power, the foundation of the social order, at her imaginative disposal, he "place[s] the centre of the subject"—not only for the narrator but for all beholders—squarely "in the young woman's own consciousness." She, rather than Gardencourt or London or Paris or Florence or Rome, becomes the true scene of the story, and the uppermost question is what shape her imaginative consciousness will impose upon a social world which she is free to establish around herself.

The result, however, is disastrous, and on a scale far beyond the mere penalties of "folly" that we have been led to expect on another plane. Beginning as social comedy and modulating into a

2. *The Art of the Novel*, 292.
3. *Portrait*, Chapter XII (III, 143).
4. *Portrait*, Chapter XVIII (III, 261, 265).

sort of comedy of triumphant consciousness, the *Portrait* soon reveals a further logic. The comedy of consciousness gives way to a tale of an evil fate. Both the effete world of social "circumstances" and the range of Isabel's imagination are being redefined even as they are presented to us. Two new characters—Madame Merle and Gilbert Osmond—give a very different coloration to the social milieu. Like the restive people whom we meet at the beginning of the book, these two are products of a declining social order; but they batten on the decay—in them, the prevalent malaise has been resolved by a cynical accommodation to conventional values and the mechanics of power. Meanwhile, Isabel's "implication of liberty" is being heavily qualified. Instead of the redemptive imagination that Ralph attributes to her, capable of converting the world into the medium of its own freedom, the narrator can credit her only with a much more limited faculty, self-absorbed, fearful of others, and afflicted with a positive "capacity for ignorance."[5] Measured by her response to Madame Merle and Osmond, Isabel stands convicted of the "romantic" vice which is implicit in her imaginative virtue: she is lost in "the beautiful circuit and subterfuge of . . . thought and . . . desire," free only in the sense that her consciousness of "real" conditions, the *"related, . . . measurable state"* of ordinary human experience, is minimal.[6] In the preface to the *Portrait*, there are hints of this development, suggestions that the "destiny" claimed by Isabel as a free consciousness is but the obverse of her "fate." But the preface goes no further. As spelled out in the book, and finally sealed by her marriage to Osmond, the specific fate of Isabel is to be a consciousness which is a good deal less than total in an exploitative world which is far more rigidly determined and determinative than anything she has earlier rejected in Warburton and Goodwood. The subject of the book is more than ever centered in her, but now the subject, pondered by Ralph at a distance and by the narrator from close at hand, is the pathos of one who has been called to a task out of all proportion to her gifts. Once resistant to all social definition, James's heroine of consciousness is doomed to betray herself and to be betrayed—not merely to fail in her quest for freedom but to be "ground in the very mill of the conventional."[7]

With many variations, this is a direction which the later Jamesian novel of consciousness was often to take. There is much of the pathetic fate of Isabel Archer in the doom of such figures as Fleda Vetch of *The Spoils of Poynton*, Lambert Strether of *The Ambassadors*, or Milly Theale of *The Wings of the Dove*. But James would hardly have seen the makings of a *"big* subject" in the char-

5. *Portrait*, Chapter XIX (III, 284).
6. For James's distinction between the "romantic" and the "real," see *The Art*
of the Novel, 31–33.
7. *Portrait*, Chapter LIV (IV, 415). Cf. *Notebooks*, 15.

acter of Isabel if the ultimate meaning he could find in her had been no more than the pathos of a defeated consciousness in a decadent society. From beneath both the comedy and the pathos of the book there gradually emerges a theme that is hard and grim, yet grimly affirmative—the outline of a *tragedy* of consciousness. Unfamiliar and disconcerting, this tragic theme almost forcibly intrudes itself upon the narrator, as in the following passage, just after Gilbert Osmond has made his first declaration of love to Isabel:

> What had happened was something that for a week past her imagination had been going forward to meet; but here, when it came, she stopped—that sublime principle somehow broke down. The working of this young lady's spirit was strange, and I can only give it to you as I see it, not hoping to make it seem altogether natural. Her imagination, as I say, now hung back: there was a last vague space it couldn't cross—a dusky, uncertain tract which looked ambiguous and even slightly treacherous, like a moorland seen in the winter twilight. But she was to cross it yet.[8]

Here the majestic self-assurance of the speaker in the early chapters of the *Portrait* has receded as far into the past as the rich estate of Gardencourt where Isabel made her first appearance at "the perfect middle of a . . . summer afternoon." His old coordinates have gone; he cannot hope "to make it seem altogether natural." And the Lady he portrays—neither a consciousness fatally enmeshed in a social order nor a triumphant consciousness freely reshaping the world around her—is confronted with the strangeness of her own nature. She is more than ever a world unto herself, for the very "happening" she rejects (Osmond's declaration) is what she herself has conceived and invited. The "working of . . . [her] spirit" has become the proving ground for whatever values can arise in the world of the book; her imagination is the sole measure of reality. But her imagination now opens out upon a tragic landscape where all choices are suspect. She finds herself conceiving (and desperately rejecting) an inner world of inverted liberty—a barren moorland without landmarks, a twilight realm of conflicting purposes, the "dusky, uncertain tract" of an imagination that founders on itself.

Eventually, as the narrator foretells, she will not only glimpse it but "cross" it in the sense of accepting it and locating herself in it, thereby attaining a stature in the winter twilight of consciousness that she never had on summer afternoons at Gardencourt. To "cross" the dusky tract is not to pass beyond it, as she attempts in her marriage to Osmond, which only postpones it by "brush[ing] away numberless questions."[9] But to take her stand at the treacherous center of her consciousness, as she does in defying Osmond, is

8. *Portrait*, Chapter XXIX (IV, 22f.).   9. *Portrait*, Chapter XXXV (IV, 82).

at least to escape from his "house of darkness," the mill of the conventional, where all values go dead.[1] What saves her from him, and will presumably sustain her after she returns to him at the end, is the posture she adopts in the dim world of her midnight meditation, "the best thing in the book." It is the posture of a mind whose every movement brings the very grounds of its movement into question, but which nevertheless moves, exploring the desert of its own uncertainty. Unlike James's later protagonists—notably Maggie Verver of *The Golden Bowl*—Isabel arrives at this standpoint slowly and unwillingly. Only at the last instant does she completely turn away from "the infinite vista of a multiplied life"—the "romantic" imagination which has exposed her to the doom of the romantic[2]—and embrace the perilous freedom of an embattled consciousness. Nevertheless, the great discovery of the *Portrait*, the discovery fundamental to James's later fiction, was that "plac[ing] the centre of the subject in . . . [her] consciousness" meant most when it meant *that*.

As time went on, James had a greater and greater need for this shift of center and for giving it as much significance as he could. Exactly in the degree that he was enamoured of social phenomena —"the color, the relief, the expression, the surface, the substance of the human spectacle"[3]—and precisely because he believed that such things were the proper language of fiction, his awareness of the deterioration of public values in the modern world was acute. Simply by using this social language faithfully, he repeatedly disclosed the spiritual impoverishment of the society around him. The novel of consciousness was his response. By inventing "supersubtle" creatures, as he pointed out, he was not merely indulging his own "romantic" tendency, not even when these figures themselves were haplessly "romantic" in their cast of mind and their fate. In a world that was too senselessly immersed in the "real" even to produce salient victims, his projections of "consciousness" had a very "real" function. They were an exercise of "operative irony," an "aid given to true meanings to be born," a "high and helpful public and, as it were, civic use of the imagination."[4] A profounder way to meet the bankruptcy of public meanings, however, was to take the inner world as its tragic counterpart rather than its ironic opposite. Beginning with Isabel Archer, James had in view a protagonist whose "inward life" would be the *other side* of that social tapestry in which the threads were rotting away. And on this side of the fabric he postulated a struggle to *make* a sense which could no longer be read in the social signs. "Consciousness," deprived of

1. *Portrait*, Chapter XLII (IV, 196).
2. *Portrait*, Chapter XLII (IV, 189).
3. "The Art of Fiction," *Partial Portraits* (1888), reprinted in *The Future of the Novel*, ed. Leon Edel, New York, 1956, 14.
4. *The Art of the Novel*, 222, 223, 224.

every reference-point except its own intrinsic freedom, could only be fatally inconclusive, but it might also be tragically heroic. Something of that sort was what he was ultimately proposing when he undertook to make a Lady out of the "mere slim shade of [a] . . . presumptuous girl."

Selected Bibliography

Articles reprinted in this edition are not included in this bibliography.

CHECKLISTS

Beebe, Maurice and William T. Stafford. "Criticism of Henry James: A Selected Checklist," *Modern Fiction Studies*, XII (Spring, 1966), 117–77. See also *Modern Fiction Studies*, III (Spring, 1957), 73–94.

Edel, Leon, and Dan H. Laurence. *A Bibliography of Henry James*. London, 1961. Pp. 52–54.

Foley, Richard N. *Criticism in American Periodicals of the Works of Henry James from 1866 to 1916*. Washington, D.C., 1944. Pp. 26–30.

Gard, Roger, ed. *Henry James: The Critical Heritage*. London, 1968. Pp. 93–138.

Murray, Donald M. "Henry James and the English Reviewers, 1882–1890," *American Literature*, XXIV (March, 1952), 1–20.

GENERAL STUDIES

Abel, Darrel. *American Literature*. New York, 1963. Pp. 256–69.

Allen, Walter. *The English Novel: A Short Critical History*. London, 1954. Pp. 253–56.

Anderson, Quentin. *The American Henry James*. New Brunswick, N.J., 1957. Pp. 183–98.

Beach, Joseph Warren. *The Method of Henry James*. New Haven, 1918. Pp. 205–11.

Bethurum, Dorothy. "Morality and Henry James," *Sewanee Review*, XXXI (July, 1923), 324–30.

Blackmur, Richard P. "Introduction" to *The Art of the Novel: Critical Prefaces*, by Henry James. New York, 1934. Pp. vii–xxxix.

Bosanquet, Theodora. *Henry James at Work*. London, 1924. P. 23.

——. "The Revised Version," *The Little Review*, V (August, 1918), 56–62.

Bowden, Edwin T. *The Dungeon of the Heart*. New York, 1961. Pp. 89–102.

——. *The Themes of Henry James*. New Haven, 1956. Pp. 54–60.

Bridgman, Richard. *The Colloquial Style in America*. New York, 1966.

Brooks, Van Wyck. "Henry James: An International Episode," *Dial*, LXXV (July, 1923), 225–38.

——. *The Pilgrimage of Henry James*. New York, 1925.

Brown, E. K. "Two Formulas for Fiction: Henry James and H. G. Wells," *College English*, VIII (October, 1946), 7–17.

Brownell, W. C. *American Prose Masters*. New York, 1909.

Buitenhuis, Peter. *The Grasping Imagination: The American Writings of Henry James*. Toronto, 1970. Pp. 105–12.

Canby, Henry Seidel. *Turn West, Turn East: Mark Twain and Henry James*. Boston, 1951. Pp. 153–60.

Cargill, Oscar. *The Novels of Henry James*. New York, 1961. Pp. 78–119.

Chase, Richard. *The American Novel and Its Tradition*. Garden City, 1957. Pp. 117–37.

Cowley, Malcolm. "The Two Jameses," *New Republic*, February 5, 1945, 177–80.

Crews, Frederick C. *The Tragedy of Manners: Moral Drama in the Later Novels of Henry James*. New Haven, Conn., 1957. Pp. 13–19.

Drew, Elizabeth. "The Game of Art." In *The Novel*, Pp. 224–44. New York, 1963.

Dupee, F. W. *Henry James*. Garden City, N.Y., 1956. Pp. 97–106.

Edel, Leon. *Henry James*, Vol. 2, *The Conquest of London: 1870–1881*. Philadelphia, 1962. Pp. 417–36. (See also the other four volumes of Edel's definitive biography of James.)

Edgar, Pelham. *Henry James: Man and Author.* London, 1927. Pp. 245–55.
Gale, Robert L. "Henry James and Italy," *Nineteenth Century Fiction,* XIV (September, 1959), 157–170.
————. *The Caught Image: Figurative Language in the Fiction of Henry James.* Chapel Hill, N.C., 1964.
Geismar, Maxwell. *Henry James and the Jacobites.* Boston, 1962. Pp. 39–47.
Grattan, C. Hartley. *The Three Jameses: A Family of Minds.* New York, 1932. Pp. 208–357.
Hafley, James. "*Malice in Wonderland,*" *Arizona Quarterly,* XV (Spring, 1959), 5–12.
Harvey, W. J. *Character and the Novel.* London, 1965.
Holder-Barell, Alexander. *The Development of Imagery and Its Functional Significance in Henry James's Novels.* Bern, 1959.
Howells, William Dean. "Henry James, Jr.," *Century,* XXV (November, 1882), 24–29.
Hueffer, Ford Madox. *Henry James: A Critical Study.* New York, 1916.
Jefferson, D. W. *Henry James.* New York, 1961. Pp. 36–43.
Kelley, Cornelia P. *The Early Development of Henry James.* Urbana, Ill., 1930. Pp. 284–300.
Leavis, F. R. *The Great Tradition.* Garden City, N.Y., 1954. Pp. 155–87.
Leavis, Q. D. "A Note of Literary Indebtedness: Dickens, George Eliot, Henry James," *Hudson Review,* VIII (Autumn, 1955), 423–28.
Lebowitz, Naomi. *The Imagination of Loving: Henry James's Legacy to the Novel.* Detroit, 1965. Pp. 64–86.
Lerner, Daniel. "The Influence of Turgenev on Henry James," *Slavonic Yearbook,* XX (December, 1941), 28–54.
Levine, George. "Isabel, Gwendolen, and Dorothea," *ELH,* XXX (September, 1963), 244–57.
Levy, Leo B. *Versions of Melodrama: A Study of the Fiction and Drama of Henry James, 1865–1897.* Berkeley, Calif., 1957. Pp. 40–52.
Leyburn, Ellen D. *Strange Alloy: The Relation of Comedy to Tragedy in the Fiction of Henry James.* Raleigh, N.C., 1968.
Liljegren, Sten Bodvar. *American and European in the Works of Henry James.* London, 1920. Pp. 17–35.
Lubbock, Percy. "Henry James," *Living Age,* CCXC (September 16, 1916), 733–41.
Lucas, John. "Manliest of Cities: The Image of Rome in Henry James," *Studii Americani* (Rome), XI (1965), 117–136.
Mackenzie, Manfred. "Ironic Melodrama in *The Portrait of a Lady,*" *Modern Fiction Studies,* XII (Spring, 1966), 7–23.
Markov-Totevy, Georges. *Henry James.* Translated by John Cumming. New York, 1969. Pp. 81–94.
Matthiessen, F. O. *The James Family.* New York, 1947.
————. *Henry James: The Major Phase.* New York, 1944. Pp. 152–86.
McElderry, Bruce R., Jr. *Henry James.* New York, 1965. Pp. 58–63.
McIntyre, Clara. "The Later Manner of Henry James," *PMLA,* XXVII (1912), 361–64.
Nowell-Smith, S., ed. *The Legend of the Master.* New York, 1948.
Poirier, Richard. *The Comic Sense of Henry James: A Study of the Early Novels.* New York, 1960. Pp. 183–246.
Pound, Ezra. "Henry James," *Little Review,* V (August, 1918), 5–41.
Putt, S. Gorley. *Henry James: A Reader's Guide.* Ithaca, 1966. Pp. 135–60.
Rahv, Philip. "The Heiress of All the Ages," *Image and Idea: Fourteen Essays on Literary Themes.* New York, 1957. Pp. 51–76.
Reid, Stephen. "Moral Passion in *The Portrait of a Lady* and *The Spoils of Poynton,*" *Modern Fiction Studies,* XII (Spring, 1966), 24–43.
Roberts, Morris. *Henry James's Criticism* (Cambridge, Mass., 1929).
Rourke, Constance. "The American." In *American Humor: A Study of National Character,* pp. 235–65. New York, 1931.
Sackville-West, Edward. "The Code of Ladyhood," *New Statesman and Nation,* XXV (1943), 259.
Scott, Dixon. "Henry James." In *Men of Letters,* pp. 78–110. New York, 1923.
Sears, Sallie. *The Negative Imagination: Form and Perspective in the Novels of Henry James.* Ithaca, N.Y., 1968.
Sharp, Sister M. Corona. *The Confidante in Henry James: Evolution and Moral Value of a Fictive Character.* South Bend, Ind., 1963. Pp. 67–96.
Stewart, J. I. M. *Eight Modern Writers.* New York, 1963. Pp. 87–92.
Tanner, Tony. "The Fearful Self: Henry James's *The Portrait of a Lady,*" *Critical Quarterly,* VII (Autumn, 1965), 205–19.
Tilley, Arthur. "The New School of Fiction," *National Review,* I (April, 1883), 257–68.

Traschen, I. "Henry James and the Art of Revision," *Philological Quarterly*, XXXV (1956), 39–47.

Ward, Joseph A. *The Imagination of Disaster: Evil in the Fiction of Henry James*. Lincoln, Neb., 1961. Pp. 44–55.

———. *The Search for Form: Studies in the Structure of James's Fiction*. Chapel Hill, N.C., 1967.

Wegelin, Christof. *The Image of Europe in the Fiction of Henry James*. Dallas, Tex., 1958. Pp. 63–78.

Weinstein, Philip M. *Henry James and the Requirements of the Imagination*. Cambridge, Mass., 1971. Pp. 31–71.

West, Rebecca. *Henry James*. New York, 1916. Pp. 67–70.

Wilson, Edmund. "The Exploration of James," *New Republic*, L (March 16, 1927), 112–13.

Winner, Viola Hopkins. *Henry James and the Visual Arts*. Charlottesville, Va., 1970.

Wright, Nathalia. *American Novelists in Italy*. Philadelphia, 1965. Pp. 198–248.

———. "Henry James and the Greenough Data," *American Quarterly*, X (1958), 338–43.

SPECIFIC PROBLEMS

Anderson, Charles R. "Person, Place, and Thing in James's *The Portrait of a Lady*." In *Essays on American Literature in Honor of J. B. Hubbell*, ed. Clarence Gohdes, pp. 164–82. Durham, N.C., 1967.

Anderson, Quentin. "Introduction" to *The Portrait of a Lady*. New York, 1963. Pp. v–xiii.

Bazzanella, Dominic J. "The Conclusion to *The Portrait of a Lady* Re-examined," *American Literature*, XLI (1969), 55–63.

Blackmur, R. P. "Introduction" to *The Portrait of a Lady*. New York, 1961. Pp. 5–12.

Blehl, Vincent F., S. J. "Freedom and Commitment in James's *The Portrait of a Lady*," *Personalist*, XLII (Summer, 1961), 368–81.

Burrell, John Sugus. "Henry James: A Rhapsody of Youth," *Dial*, LXIII (September 27, 1917), 260–62.

Buitenhuis, Peter. "Introduction" to *Twentieth Century Interpretations of "The Portrait of A Lady."* Englewood Cliffs, N.J., 1968. Pp. 1–13.

Cargill, Oscar. "Afterword" to *The Portrait of a Lady*. New York, 1964. Pp. 547–56. (This Signet edition is the only available reprint of the 1881 edition.)

Dove, John Roland. "Tragic Consciousness in Isabel Archer." In *Studies in American Literature* (Louisiana State University Studies, Humanities Series, No. 8), ed. Waldo McNeir and Leo B. Levy, pp. 78–94. Baton Rouge, 1960.

Edel, Leon. "Introduction" to *The Portrait of a Lady*. Boston, 1963. Pp. v–xx.

———. "Who *Was* Gilbert Osmond?" *Modern Fiction Studies*, VI (Summer, 1960), 164.

Friend, Joseph H. "The Structure of *The Portrait of a Lady*," *Nineteenth-Century Fiction*, XX (June, 1965), 85–95.

Gale, Robert L. "A Possible Source for Elements in *The Portrait of a Lady*," *Studii Americani* (Rome), II (1965), 137–41.

Galloway, David. *Henry James: The Portrait of a Lady*. London, 1967.

Grenander, M. E., Beverly J. Rahn, and Francine Valvo. "The Time-Scheme in *The Portrait of a Lady*," *American Literature*, XXXII (May, 1960), 127–35.

Kenney, Blair Gates. "The Two Isabels: A Study in Distortion," *Victorian Newsletter*, XXV (Spring, 1964), 15–17.

Kleinberg, Seymour. "Ambiguity and Ambivalence: The Psychology of Sexuality in Henry James' *The Portrait of a Lady*," *Markham Review*, V (May, 1969), 2–7.

Krause, Sydney J. "James's Revisions of the Style of *The Portrait of a Lady*," *American Literature*, XXX (March, 1958), 76–88.

Leavis, F. R. "*The Portrait of a Lady* Reprinted," *Scrutiny*, XV (Summer, 1948), 235–41.

Marcell, David W. "High Ideals and Catchpenny Realities in Henry James's *The Portrait of a Lady*." In *Essays in Modern American Literature*, ed. Richard E. Langford, pp. 26–34. Deland, Fla., 1963.

Mazzella, Anthony J. "James' *The Portrait of a Lady*" *The Explicator*, XXX (January, 1972), Item 37.

Millett, Fred B. "Introduction" to *The Portrait of a Lady*. New York, 1951. Pp. v–xxxv.

Mills, A. R. "*The Portrait of a Lady* and Dr. Leavis," *Essays in Criticism*, XIV (October, 1964), 380–87.

Monteiro, George. "John Hay's Review of *The Portrait of a Lady*," *Books at Brown*, XIX (1963), 95–104. Reprinted in *Henry James and John Hay: The Record of a Friendship*, Providence, R.I., 1965, pp. 65–76.

Montgomery, Marion. "The Flaw in the Portrait: Henry James vs. Isabel Archer," *University of Kansas City Review*, XXVI (March, 1960), 215–20.

Moody, A. D. "Henry James's Portrait of an Ideal," *Melbourne Critical Review*, IV (1961), 77–92.

Offen, Susan. "Isabel Archer: An Analysis of Her Fate," *Hunter College Studies*, II (1964), 41–50.

Patterson, Rebecca. "Two Portraits of a Lady," *Midwest Quarterly*, I (Summer, 1960), 343–61.

Poirier, Richard. "*The Portrait of a Lady.*" In *The American Novel*, ed. Wallace Stegner, pp. 47–60. New York, 1965.

Powers, Lyall H. "*The Portrait of a Lady*: The Eternal Mystery of Things," *Nineteenth-Century Fiction*, XIV (September, 1959), 143–55.

Rodenbeck, John. "The Bolted Door in James's *The Portrait of a Lady*," *Modern Fiction Studies*, X (Winter, 1964–65), 330–40.

Sandeen, Ernest. "*The Wings of the Dove* and *The Portrait of a Lady*: A Study of Henry James's Later Phase," *PMLA*, LXIX (December, 1954), 1060–75.

Smith, Thomas F. "Balance in Henry James's *The Portrait of a Lady*," *Four Quarters*, XIII (May, 1964), 11–16.

Snow, Lotus. "The Disconcerting Poetry of Mary Temple: A Comparison of the Imagery of *The Portrait of a Lady* and *The Wings of the Dove*," *New England Quarterly*, XXXI (September, 1958), 312–39.

Stafford, William T. "Introduction" to *Perspectives on James's "The Portrait of a Lady.*" New York, 1967. Pp. ix–xix.

Stallman, R. W. "The Houses That James Built—*The Portrait of a Lady.*" In *The Houses That James Built and Other Literary Studies*, pp. 1–33. East Lansing, Mich., 1961.

———. "Who Was Gilbert Osmond?" *Modern Fiction Studies*, IV (Summer, 1958), 127–35.

Stein, William Bysshe. "*The Portrait of a Lady*: *Vis Inertiae*," *Western Humanities Review*, XIII (Spring, 1959), 177–90.

Strandberg, Victor H. "Isabel Archer's Identity Crisis: The Two Portraits of a Lady," *University Review*, XXXIV (1968), 283–90.

Thorberg, Raymond. "'Flavien,' 'Tenants,' and *The Portrait of a Lady*," *South Atlantic Bulletin*, XXXIV (1969), 10–13.

Tribble, Joseph L. "Cherbuliez's *Le Roman d'une Honête Femme*: Another Source of James's *The Portrait of a Lady*," *American Literature*, XL (1968), 279–93.

Wilding, Michael. "*The Portrait of a Lady* and the World and Choice." *Balcony*, I (1965), 28–35.

NORTON CRITICAL EDITIONS